THE MYSTERIES OF LONDON

VALANCOURT CLASSICS

THE

MYSTERIES OF LONDON

BY

GEORGE W. M. REYNOLDS

With a Foreword by Louis James and
Annotations by Dick Collins

VOL. I.

Kansas City:
VALANCOURT BOOKS
2013

The Mysteries of London, vol. I, by George W. M. Reynolds
Originally published in weekly parts commencing in 1844
First one-volume edition, London: Geo. Vickers, 1845
First Valancourt Books edition 2013

ISBN 978-1-939140-02-9 (*trade paper*)

All Valancourt Books publications are printed on acid free paper that meets all ANSI standards for archival quality paper.

Design and typography by James D. Jenkins
Set in Dante MT

Published by Valancourt Books
Kansas City, Missouri
http://www.valancourtbooks.com

10 9 8 7 6 5 4 3 2 1

FOREWORD

One mystery of Reynolds's seminal and hugely popular masterwork for the modern reader is this—how could it have remained unknown to Victorian scholars for so long? It was almost certainly the most widely read single work of fiction in mid-nineteenth century Britain, and attracted more readers than did the novels of Dickens, Bulwer-Lytton or Trollope. Together with its continuation, *The Mysteries of the Court of London*, it contained twelve volumes of four and half million words, making it also the longest continuous prose fiction of its time. It influenced the 'respectable' English novel, setting the scene (literally) for Thackeray's *Vanity Fair* (1847-8), and Dickens's *Bleak House* (1852-3), while its intricate plots prepared the way for the 'sensation novels' of the sixties. It was read and imitated on the Continent, particularly in France. Overseas, readers in the colonies waited eagerly for the latest instalment of the work. In India Reynolds had a 'classic' status, valued as a teacher and reformer above Dickens.[1] Yet a recent standard study of literature in the period, Philip Davis's volume on *The Victorians* (2002) in *The Oxford English Literary History*, gives Reynolds's *Mysteries* nothing more than a six-line passing reference.

Before asking why the work has been largely airbrushed out of literary history, one must consider the reasons for its success. It was very much the product of its time. *The Mysteries of London* appeared when England was rapidly changing from a rural nation, with traditional beliefs and ways, into a predominantly urban one, in which town-dwellers outnumbered those in the country. The city of London had emerged as an international phenomenon, by far the largest city in the western world, the home of a third of England's town-dwellers. The first impact of urbanisation had been numbing, but as legislation began to redress the appalling living conditions in the new sprawling towns, writers began to assess its seismic impact on everything from social relationships to public health to literature and religious belief. The social novels of Disraeli and Mrs. Gaskell aroused awareness on

1 See Anne Humpherys and Louis James, eds., *G. W. M. Reynolds: Nineteenth Century Fiction, Politics, and the Press* (Aldershot: Ashgate, 2008).

the 'two nations' in the north and south of Britain, while Dickens evoked the infinite variety of the London streets. While most middle class novelists were aware of the social inequalities in this new era, the emphasis in their fiction was on understanding and reconciliation.

Reynolds had a different perspective. Rebelling against his upper middle class family from the age of sixteen, and having lived a formative stage of his life in the radical world of Paris, his fiction and journalism stormed against the wrongs of privilege and wealth inflicted on the exploited poor. Briefly, he took a lead in the Chartist movement. In an age of revolutions taking place just across the channel, nervous Victorian middle class readers accused Reynolds of being a rabble-raiser, the 'can on the mad dog's tail', a traitor to his class. According to one Home Office correspondent of 1848, he was 'the most wicked and dangerous man in London.'[1] But radical working class leaders also had their reservations about Reynolds. Reynolds had no illusions about the dangers of untutored mob power, and declared in print that to give the people democracy without political education was as dangerous as offering a child an open razor. Ostracised by the 'respectable' Victorians as a dangerous radical on one hand, suspected by working class leaders as having middle class sympathies on the other, he scandalised both groups by writing sensational fiction that dramatised social and sexual conflicts in terms of high melodrama. Reynolds became studiously ignored by the public eminences that recorded the mid-Victorian period for modern historians. Even those who noted Reynolds's popularity did him a disservice, as when Mayhew noted the delight with which costermongers read his works. Yet, to paraphrase Hilaire Belloc's mock obituary, 'if his views were scarlet, his books were read.' Reynolds's audience was very much wider than the semi-literate cited in Mayhew's example. It embraced the great mass of lower middle classes and artisans, most of them intelligent, hard-working men and women, who, while they enjoyed their literature as entertainment, liked it to reflect matters of public interest, and shared Reynolds's suspicions of power, authority and the moral hypocrisy. This was what Wilkie Collins was to call the great 'unknown public' of general readers, the 'invisible' common people on whom rested much of the true strength of the Victorian age.

1 E. Weston to Grey, H.O. 45, OS 2410, p. 334.

Many of Reynolds's views had in fact been prefigured in a signally non-political work, Pierce Egan's *Life in London* (1820-1). Egan's work proclaimed that the new focus on the life of the city created a new subject for literature. The ascendancy of the natural world over the town was now overturned. '[The painter] Poussin never had a more luxuriant, variegated, and interesting subject for landscape', wrote Egan. 'There is not a *street* in London but what may be compared to a large or small volume of intelligence, abounding with anecdote, incident and peculiarities. . . . even the *poorest cellar* contains some *trait* or other. . .'[1] Egan showed London made up of many separate locales, communities each distinguished by different histories, class, dress, occupations, and ways of speech. Social hierarchies disappeared, for each individual had human secrets, tragedies and triumphs. This multifarious city was both fragmented and a quivering organism, a web of contrasts—'the Extremes, in every point of view, are daily to be met with in the Metropolis', wrote Egan. Piety and crime stood in sharp contrast: 'the highest veneration for and practice of religion distinguish the Metropolis, contrasted with the most horrid commission of crimes: and the *experience* of the oldest inhabitant scarcely renders him safe against the specious plans and artifices continually laid to entrap the vigilant.' Although Egan did not use the word, he showed city life as a world of *mysteries*, for 'the next-door neighbour of a man in London is as great a stranger to him as if he lived at the distance of York.'

Egan's work took a new form, part exposé journalism, part London guidebook, part human drama in which Jerry from the country was introduced to city life by 'man about town' Corinthian Tom. It took England by storm. Egan himself recorded over a hundred imitations and derivative works; dramatic versions dominated the London stage in the eighteen-twenties.

The plot provided a template for 'discoveries' of other cities, and it was intermittently reprinted till towards the end of the century. Egan's organising principle was to show the city as a pattern of contrasting 'light' and 'shade', a principle his successors were to develop as they looked for new forms with which to entertain a rapidly expanding mass market of readers. The materialism of city life

1 Pierce Egan, Sr., *Life in London* (1820-21) (London: Sherwood, Neely, and Jones), pp. 17, 22-24.

rejected superstition and the occult world of the traditional gothic story, and as the dark castles and Italianate landscape of Mrs. Radcliffe and Monk Lewis lost their power to thrill, writers turned to the mysteries that lay all around them, hidden down darkened alleys, in the cellars and shuttered buildings of the city streets. Demonic monks were exchanged for thieves and footpads; the intrigues of the Inquisition were replaced by the dark secret forces, organised by both rich and poor, behind the web of city life.

Post-Egan, many novelists dramatised the city as a locale for crime. W. H. Ainsworth meticulously reconstructed life in the streets of eighteenth-century London for his novel of the thief and notorious escapee *Jack Sheppard* (1839). At the other end of the social spectrum, the 'silver fork novel' pioneered by Bulwer-Lytton in *Pelham* (1828) evoked exotic scenes of the voluptuous lives of the London rich inhabiting the spacious squares around Mayfair and the West End. From the 1840s the most significant urban writer was Dickens, revealing the romantic side of everyday London life in *Sketches by Boz* (1835-6), and shaping a new direction for urban fiction with *Oliver Twist* (1837-8). On one hand this novel startled its readers with its revelations of the London underworld, drawn with all the topographical detail popularised by Egan. But it is also seen through the eyes of Oliver, a terrified child, which gives the narrative a passionate, subjective, perspective. Dickens added yet another dimension. Drawing on the vision of Bunyan's ever-popular *Pilgrim's Progress*, Dickens made London the setting for a melodramatic conflict between spiritual good and evil, with Oliver as 'the Principle of Good', while Fagin, called 'the Old 'Un', (a soubriquet for Satan), acquired a demonic caste. The link with Bunyan is there in the book's subtitle—'the Parish Boy's Progress'.

Reynolds's *Mysteries* bear many traces of *Oliver Twist*—the alternating detailed objectivity and passionate subjectivity, the closely juxtaposed worlds of wealth and poverty, and the pulsating moments of high melodrama. Like Dickens, too, Reynolds intimated city life was a moral pilgrimage, and through the first two volumes of *The Mysteries* he traced the contrasting moral paths of the two Markham brothers—the 'good' Richard, and the 'bad' Eugene. There are, of course, great differences from Bunyan's fable. The struggle is one worked out, finally, not in the Celestial City, but in the here and now of the

London streets, and Reynolds sets his heaven and hell in the modern London that was beginning to be investigated by the new science of sociology, a metropolis controlled by social evolution and the laws of economics. Nevertheless he draws the city on an epic scale, and set within aeons of world history. Reynolds looks to the emergence of Civilization in Europe from the Dark Ages that took place between the tenth and thirteenth centuries, before his gaze comes to rest on London at a precise date, July 1831. London has become, not only the largest in Europe, but, through colonisation and Empire, the centre of the whole globe. Yet it is a city 'in which contrasts of a strange nature abound', for 'the most unbounded wealth is the neighbour of the most hideous poverty.'

Reynolds was often accused of insincerity and mass exploitation. Although in fact he remained remarkably true to his Radical convictions, anyone expecting *The Mysteries of London* to be a conventional political 'novel of ideas' will be disappointed. Reynolds saw his twelve volumes 'one vast whole, which may be termed an Encyclopædia of tales.' Like a newspaper, particularly that in the French form of the *feuilleton*, one that combined news with serialised fiction, *The Mysteries* contains a great variety of material and kinds of writing. There is documentary description as sharp as anything in Dickens or Mayhew; digressions on economics, criminal biography in the style of the 'Newgate Calendar', melodramatic horror, and scenes of luxury as voluptuous as any in a fashionable 'silver fork novel'. Some scenes, like the horrific room where the public executioner educates his son to his trade, have a touch of surrealism; strands such as the preternatural hate of Tidkins, the hideous 'resurrection man', for the noble Markham, become psychological melodramas of good versus evil.

Readers might expect Reynolds as a Radical to show members of the deserving poor pitted against the evil rich. But the villains come equally from wealth and poverty—although the poor may have been driven to crime by their social betters—and in the end, the happiness of the good is equated, not with the simple life, but with acquiring comfortable wealth. In Dickens's fiction, ultimate 'Good' is represented by the innocent child. But there are few children in Reynolds's fiction, and these are often unhappy victims. Although he himself was a devoted family man, Reynolds gives little space in his fiction to the Victorian ideal of love and harmony, the family circle. For Reynolds's detractors, his writing lacked a moral basis. However this is to misunderstand the nature of Reynolds's fiction. This inhabits the symbolic universe of the imagination, and was written not for an audience looking for the domestic realism of the middle class novel, but a readership tuned by the conventions of popular culture to accept a range of fictional perspectives. Here the dimensions of reality varied in *kind*, from the documentary realism of newspaper reports, to the moral fantasy of folk tales, or to the ritualised conflict between good and evil of contemporary melodrama. For Reynolds's readers, fictional characters take the form of moral synecdoche, a part representing the whole. Greenwood embodies the evils of a whole class of unscrupulous lawyers and financiers; the loathsome Reverend Tracy, the hypocrisy of typical establishment religion. 'Good' characters like Richard Markham or Ellen Monroe are, like Dickens's Oliver Twist, in effect classless, the representation of courageous humanity with whom readers of any background could empathise.

The final happiness of the 'good' characters in Reynolds's fiction may appear a convention. But in Reynolds's work it also reflects a wider optimism about the human struggle. Controversially, Reynolds sees destiny as directed not by a benevolent divine Providence, but by courageous human endeavour. Ellen Monroe loses her virtue, and bears her seducer an illegitimate child. By the conventions of the middle class novel she would have been ruined, and died in poverty. But Reynolds shows her rebelling against fate, gathering her energies, and turning her persecutors' wiles against them as she assumes a disguise to humiliate one seducer, and then blackmails the other into a marriage to legitimise her child. 'Respectable' Victorian middle class readers, if they knew of his writing, would have rejected such accounts of feminine spirit as 'disgusting', and whitewashed Reynolds out of the literary scene. But if he was more direct in his portrayal of violence and sexual passion than contemporary mores allowed, Reynolds never allowed an indecent word on his pages, and he had too great a respect for women to exploit their physicality in explicit pornography. For that, the reader has to turn to upper class journals like *The Pearl*. Reynolds was frequently accused of debauching his readership. But in fact he provided his mass readership with a world of excitement, controversy, and, however this was spiced with sensation and melodrama, information—for as we have noted, Reynolds believed passionately that any social advance must be based on education.

In the twentieth century Reynolds found an unexpected advocate in the champion of moral values in literature, Q. D. Leavis. Contrasting his writing favourably against modern standards of popular literature, she wrote of the 'considerable achievement' of his 'constant appeal to open-mindedness in politics and non-material standards of living without any appeals to religious sentiment or anything cheap in the radicalism for which [he] stood.'[1] Others have begun to bring Reynolds back into the limelight. In 1996 Trefor Thomas's abridged reprint of *The Mysteries of London* pioneered a growing industry in reprinting Reynolds's work of which this Valancourt Books edition is the latest and most valuable example. Reynolds's *Mysteries* now begins to emerge out of the shadows for a new generation of readers.

LOUIS JAMES

1 Q. D. Leavis, *Fiction and the Reading Public* (1932, Harmondsworth: Penguin Books, 1979), p. 145.

NOTE ON THE TEXT

The Mysteries of London was published serially in fifty-two weekly parts beginning in 1844. Each part was eight pages and featured one large woodcut illustration and sold for one penny. When the story had concluded, the fifty-two weekly parts were bound together in volume form with a title page and table of contents and sold as a book. The first edition published in book form was issued by George Vickers of London in 1845. This edition follows that text verbatim with the exception of obvious printer's errors, such as transposed or upside-down characters, or other plain errors, such as one instance of the word "ladyship" when "lordship" was clearly intended. Such errors have been silently corrected, but otherwise the text here presented is identical to the original. Obsolete spellings such as "sate" for "sat" and inconsistent spellings and punctuation have been retained as in the original.

After a falling-out with Vickers, Reynolds switched printers, and later copies of *The Mysteries of London* were sold under the imprint of John Dicks of London. The Dicks printings were paginated identically to the earlier editions and were virtually identical to the Vickers printings in all respects, aside from minor spelling and punctuation variations not affecting the story. The illustrations reprinted in this volume are from a copy of the Dicks edition in the collection of the present publisher, and all the original illustrations are included here.

Following the success of the first series of *Mysteries*, which is reprinted in its entirety in this volume, Reynolds went on to pen a second series of equal length, which was published as Vol. 2; two additional volumes later followed, written by other authors. Reynolds later published a new series comprising eight volumes under the title *The Mysteries of the Court of London* from 1848-1856.

THE MYSTERIES OF LONDON.

PROLOGUE.

Between the 10th and 13th centuries Civilisation withdrew from Egypt and Syria, rested for a little space at Constantinople, and then passed away to the western climes of Europe.

From that period these climes have been the grand laboratory in which Civilisation has wrought out refinement in every art and every science, and whence it has diffused its benefits over the earth. It has taught commerce to plough the waves of every sea with the adventurous keel; it has enabled handfuls of disciplined warriors to subdue the mighty armaments of oriental princes; and its daring sons have planted its banners amidst the eternal ice of the poles. It has cut down the primitive forests of America; carried trade into the interior of Africa; annihilated time and distance by the aid of steam; and now contemplates how to force a passage through Suez and Panama.

The bounties of Civilisation are at present almost everywhere recognised.

Nevertheless, for centuries has Civilisation established, and for centuries will it maintain, its headquarters in the great cities of Western Europe: and with Civilisation does Vice go hand-in-hand.

Amongst these cities there is one in which contrasts of a strange nature exist. The most unbounded wealth is the neighbour of the most hideous poverty; the most gorgeous pomp is placed in strong relief by the most deplorable squalor; the most seducing luxury is only separated by a narrow wall from the most appalling misery.

The crumbs which fall from the tables of the rich would appear delicious viands to starving millions; and yet those millions obtain them not!

In that city there are in all districts five prominent buildings: the church, in which the pious pray; the gin-palace, to which the wretched poor resort to drown their sorrows; the pawn-broker's, where miserable creatures pledge their raiment, and their children's raiment, even unto the last rag, to obtain the means of purchasing food, and—alas! too often—intoxicating drink; the prison, where the victims of a vitiated condition of society expiate the crimes to which they have been driven by starvation and despair; and the workhouse, to which the destitute, the aged, and the friendless hasten to lay down their aching heads—and die!

And, congregated together in one district of that city, is an assemblage of palaces, whence emanate by night the delicious sounds of music; within whose walls the foot treads upon rich carpets; whose sideboards are covered with plate; whose cellars contain the choicest nectar of the temperate and torrid zones; and whose inmates recline beneath velvet canopies, feast at each meal upon the collated produce of four worlds, and scarcely have to breath a wish before they find it gratified.

Alas! how appalling are these contrasts!

And, as if to hide its infamy from the face of heaven, this city wears upon its brow an everlasting cloud, which even the fresh fan of the morning fails to disperse for a single hour each day!

And in one delicious spot of that mighty city—whose thousand towers point upwards, from horizon to horizon, as an index of its boundless magnitude—stands the dwelling of one before whom all knees bow, and towards whose royal footstool none dares approach save with downcast eyes and subdued voice. The entire world showers its bounties upon the head of that favoured mortal; a nation of millions does homage to the throne whereon that being is exalted. The dominion of this personage so supremely blest extends over an empire on which the sun never sets—an empire greater than Jenghiz Khan achieved or Mohammed conquered.

This is the parent of a mighty nation; and yet around that parent's seat the children crave for bread!

Women press their little ones to their dried-up breasts in the agonies of despair; young delicate creatures waste their energies in toil from the dawn of day till long past the hour of midnight, perpetuating their unavailing labour from the hour of the brilliant sun to that when the dim candle sheds its light around the attic's naked walls; and even the very pavement groans beneath the weight of grief which the poor are doomed to drag over the rough places of this city of sad contrasts.

For in this city the daughter of the peer is nursed in enjoyments, and passes through an uninterrupted avenue of felicity from the cradle to the tomb; while the daughter of poverty opens her eyes at her birth upon destitution in all its most appalling shapes, and at length sells her virtue for a loaf of bread.

There are but two words known in the moral alphabet of this great city; for all virtues are summed up in the one, and all vices in the other: and those words are

WEALTH. | POVERTY.

Crime is abundant in this city; the lazar-house, the prison, the brothel, and the dark alley, are rife with all kinds of enormity; in the same way as the palace, the mansion, the club-house, the parliament, and the parsonage, are each and all characterised by their different degrees and shades of vice. But wherefore specify crime and vice by their real names, since in this city of which we speak they are absorbed in the multi-significant words—WEALTH and POVERTY?

Crimes borrow their comparative shade of enormity from the people who perpetrate them: thus it is that the wealthy may commit all social offences with impunity; while the poor are cast into dungeons and coerced with chains, for only following at a humble distance in the pathway of their lordly precedents.

From this city of strange contrasts branch off two roads, leading to two points totally distinct the one from the other.

One winds its tortuous way through all the noisome dens of crime, chicanery, dissipation, and voluptuousness: the other meanders amidst rugged rocks and wearisome acclivities, it is true, but on the wayside are the resting-places of rectitude and virtue.

Along those roads two youths are journeying.

They have started from the same point; but one pursues the former path, and the other the latter.

Both come from the city of fearful contrasts; and both follow the wheels of fortune in different directions.

Where is that city of fearful contrasts?

Who are those youths that have thus entered upon paths so opposite the one to the other?

And to what destinies do those separate roads conduct them?

CHAPTER I.

THE OLD HOUSE IN SMITHFIELD.

Our narrative opens at the commencement of July, 1831.

The night was dark and stormy. The sun had set behind huge piles of dingy purple clouds, which, after losing the golden hue with which they were for awhile tinged, became sombre and menacing. The blue portions of the sky that here and there had appeared before the sunset, were now rapidly covered over with those murky clouds which are the hiding-places of the storm, and which seemed to roll themselves together in dense and compact masses, ere they commenced the elemental war.

In the same manner do the earthly squadrons of cavalry and mighty columns of infantry form themselves into one collected armament, that the power of their onslaught may be the more terrific and irresistible.

That canopy of dark and threatening clouds was formed over London; and a stifling heat, which there was not a breath of wind to allay or mitigate, pervaded the streets of the great metropolis.

Everything portended an awful storm.

In the palace of the peer and the hovel of the artisan the windows were thrown up; and at many, both men and women stood to contemplate the scene—timid children crowding behind them.

The heat became more and more oppressive.

At length large drops of rain fell, at intervals of two or three inches apart, upon the pavement.

And then a flash of lightning, like the forked tongue of one of those fiery serpents of which we read in oriental tales of magic and enchantment, darted forth from the black clouds overhead.

At an interval of a few seconds the roar of the thunder, reverberating through the arches of heaven—now sinking, now exalting its fearful tone, like the iron wheels of a chariot rolled over a road with patches of uneven pavement here and there—stunned every ear, and struck terror into many a heart—the innocent as well as the guilty.

It died away, like the chariot, in the distance; and then all was solemnly still.

The interval of silence which succeeds the protracted thunder-clap is appalling in the extreme.

A little while—and again the lightning illuminated the entire vault above: and again the thunder, in unequal tones,—amongst which was one resembling the rattling of many vast iron bars together,—awoke every echo of the metropolis from north to south, and from east to west.

This time the dread interval of silence was suddenly interrupted by the torrents of rain that now deluged the streets.

There was not a breath of air; and the rain fell as perpendicularly straight as a line. But with it came a sense of freshness and of a pure atmosphere, which formed an agreeable and cheering contrast to the previously suffocating heat. It was like the spring of the oasis to the wanderer in the burning desert.

But still the lightning played, and the thunder rolled, above.

At the first explosion of the storm, amidst the thousands of men and women and children, who were seen hastening hither and thither, in all directions, as if they were flying from the plague, was one person on whose exterior none could gaze without being inspired with a mingled sentiment of admiration and interest.

He was a youth, apparently not more than sixteen years of age, although taller than boys usually are at that period of life. But the tenderness of his years was divined by the extreme effeminacy and juvenile loveliness of his countenance, which was as fair and delicate as that of a young girl. His long luxuriant hair, of a beautiful light chestnut colour, and here and there borrowing dark shades from the frequent undulations in which it rolled, flowed not only over the collar of his closely-buttoned blue frock coat, but also upon his shoulders. Its extreme profusion, and the singular manner in which he wore it, were, however, partially concealed by the breadth of the brim of his hat, that was placed as it were entirely upon the back of his head, and, being thus thrown off his countenance, revealed the high, intelligent, and polished forehead above which that rich hair was carefully parted.

His frock coat, which was single-breasted, and buttoned up to the throat, set off his symmetrical and elegant figure to the greatest advantage. His shoulders were broad, but were characterised by that fine fall or slope which is so much admired in the opposite sex. He wore spurs upon the heels of his diminutive polished boots;

and in his hand he carried a light riding-whip. But he was upon foot and alone; and, when the first flash of lightning dazzled his expressive hazel eyes, he was hastily traversing the foul and filthy arena of Smithfield-market.[1]

An imagination poetically inspired would suppose a similitude of a beautiful flower upon a fetid manure heap.

He cast a glance, which may almost be termed one of affright, around; and his cheek became flushed. He had evidently lost his way,

1 The main meat-market supplying London, where slaughtering also took place. It was notorious for its filth and stench. Much of the industry of the East End was bound to Smithfield and the meat-trade, from butchery through the making of leather goods to making straw hats, using the straw salvaged from the cattle-yards.

and was uncertain where to obtain an asylum against the coming storm.

The thunder burst above his head; and a momentary shudder passed over his frame. He accosted a man to inquire his way; but the answer he received was rude, and associated with a ribald joke.

He had not courage to demand a second time the information he sought; but, with a species of haughty disdain at the threatening storm, and a proud reliance upon himself, proceeded onwards at random.

He even slackened his pace; a contemptuous smile curled his lips, and the glittering white teeth appeared as it were between two rose-leaves.

His chest, which was very prominent, rose up and down almost convulsively; for it was evident that he endeavoured to master conflicting feelings of vexation, alarm, and disgust—all produced by the position in which he found himself.

To one so young, so delicate, and so frank in appearance, the mere fact of losing his way by night in a disgusting neighbourhood, during an impending storm, and insulted by a low-life ruffian, was not the mere trifle which it would have been considered by the hardy and experienced man of the world.

Not a public conveyance was to be seen; and the doors of all the houses around appeared inhospitably closed: and every moment it seemed to grow darker.

Accident conducted the interesting young stranger into that labyrinth of narrow and dirty streets which lies in the immediate vicinity of the north-western angle of Smithfield-market.

It was in this horrible neighbourhood that the youth was now wandering. He was evidently shocked at the idea that human beings could dwell in such fetid and unwholesome dens; for he gazed with wonder, disgust, and alarm upon the houses on either side. It seemed as if he had never beheld till now a labyrinth of dwellings whose very aspect appeared to speak of hideous poverty and fearful crime.

Meantime the lightning flashed, and the thunder rolled; and at length the rain poured down in torrents. Obeying a mechanical impulse, the youth rushed up the steps of a house at the end of one of those dark, narrow, and dirty streets the ominous appearance of which was every now and then revealed to him by a light streaming from a narrow window, or the glare of the lightning. The framework of the door projected somewhat, and appeared to offer a partial protection from the rain. The youth drew as closely up to it as possible; but to his surprise it yielded behind him, and burst open. With difficulty he saved himself from falling backwards into the passage with which the door communicated.

Having recovered from the sudden alarm with which this incident had inspired him, his next sentiment was one of pleasure to think that he had thus found a more secure asylum against the tempest. He, however, felt wearied—desperately wearied; and his was not a frame calculated to bear up against the oppressive and crushing feeling of fatigue. He determined to penetrate, amidst the profound darkness by which he was surrounded, into the dwelling; thinking that if there were any inmates they would not refuse him the accommodation of a chair; and if there were none, he might find a seat upon the staircase.

He advanced along the passage, and groped about. His hand encountered the lock of a door: he opened it, and entered a room. All was dark as pitch. At that moment a flash of lightning, more than usually vivid and prolonged, illuminated the entire scene. The glance which he cast around was as rapid as the glare which made objects visible to him for a few moments. He was in a room entirely empty; but in the middle of the floor—only three feet from the spot where he stood—there was a large square of jet blackness.

The lightning passed away: utter darkness again surrounded him; and he was unable to ascertain what that black square, so well defined and apparent upon the dirty floor, could be.

An indescribable sensation of fear crept over him; and the perspiration broke out upon his forehead in large drops. His knees bent beneath him; and, retreating a few steps, he leaned against the doorposts for support.

He was alone—in an uninhabited house, in the midst of a horrible neighbourhood; and all the fearful tales of midnight murders which he had ever heard or read, rushed to his memory; then, by a strange but natural freak of the fancy, those appalling deeds of blood and crime were suddenly associated with that incomprehensible but ominous black square upon the floor.

He was in the midst of this terrible waking-dream—this more than ideal nightmare—when hasty steps approached the front door from the street; and, without stopping, entered the passage. The youth crept silently towards the farther end, the perspiration oozing from every pore. He felt the staircase with his hands; the footsteps advanced; and, light as the fawn, he hurried up the stairs. So noiseless were his motions, that his presence was not noticed by the new comers, who in their turns also ascended the staircase.

The youth reached a landing, and hastily felt for the doors of the rooms with which it communicated. In another moment he was in a chamber, at the back part of the house. He closed the door, and placed himself against it with all his strength—forgetful, poor youth! that his fragile form was unavailing, with all its power, against even the single arm of a man of only ordinary strength.

Meantime the new-comers ascended the stairs.

CHAPTER II.

THE MYSTERIES OF THE OLD HOUSE.

FORTUNATELY for the interesting young stranger, the individuals who had just entered the house did not attempt the door of the room in which he had taken refuge. They proceeded straight—and with a steadiness which seemed to indicate that they knew the locality well—to the front chamber upon the same floor.

In a few moments there was a sharp grating noise along the wall; and then a light suddenly shone into the room where the young stranger was concealed. He cast a terrified glance around, and beheld a small square window in the wall, which separated the two apartments. It was about five feet from the floor—a height which permitted the youth to avail himself of it, in order to reconnoitre the proceedings in the next room.

By means of a candle which had been lighted by the aid of a lucifer-match, and which stood upon a dirty deal table, the young stranger beheld two men, whose outward appearance did not serve to banish his alarm. They were dressed like operatives of the most humble class. One wore a gabardine and coarse leather gaiters, with laced-up boots; the other had on a fustian shooting-jacket and long corduroy trousers. They were both dirty and unshaven. The one with the shooting-jacket had a profusion of hair about his face, but which was evidently not well acquainted with a comb: the other wore no whiskers, but his beard was of three or four days' growth. Both were powerful, thick-set, and muscular men; and the expression of their countenances was dogged, determined, and ferocious.

The room to which they had betaken themselves was cold, gloomy, and dilapidated. It was furnished with the deal table before mentioned, and three old crazy chairs, upon two of which the men now seated themselves. But they were so placed that they commanded, their door being open, a full view of the landing-place; and thus the youthful stranger deemed it impolitic to attempt to take his departure for the moment.

"Now, Bill, out with the bingo," said the man in the gabardine to his companion.

"Oh! you're always for the lush, you are, Dick," answered the latter in a surly tone, producing at the same time a bottle of liquor from the capacious pocket of his fustian coat. "But I wonder how the devil it is that Crankey Jem ain't come yet. Who the deuce could have left that infernal door open?"

"Jem or some of the other blades must have been here and left it so. It don't matter; it lulls suspicion."

"Well, let's make the reglars all square," resumed the man called Bill, after a moment's pause; "we'll then booze a bit, and talk over this here new job of our'n."

"Look alive, then," said Dick; and he forthwith took from beneath his gabardine several small parcels done up in brown paper.

The other man likewise divested the pockets of his fustian coat of divers packages; and all these were piled upon the table.

A strange and mysterious proceeding then took place.

The person in the fustian coat approached the chimney, and applied a small turnscrew, which he took from his pocket, to a screw in the iron frame-work of the rusty grate. In a few moments he was enabled to remove the entire grate with his hands; a square aperture of considerable dimensions was then revealed. Into this place the two men thrust the parcels which they had taken from their pockets: the grate was replaced, the screws were fastened once more, and the work of concealment was complete.

The one in the gabardine then advanced towards that portion of the wall which was between the two windows; and the youth in the adjoining room now observed for the first time that the shutters of those windows were closed, and that coarse brown paper had been pasted all over the chinks and joints. Dick applied his hand in a peculiar manner to the part of the wall just alluded to, and a sliding panel immediately revealed a capacious cupboard. Thence the two men took food of by no means a coarse description, glasses, pipes, and tobacco; and, having hermetically closed the recess once more, seated themselves at the table to partake of the good cheer thus mysteriously supplied.

The alarm of the poor youth in the next chamber, as he contemplated these extraordinary proceedings, may be better conceived than depicted. His common sense told him that he was in the den of lawless thieves—perhaps murderers; in a house abounding with the secret means of concealing every kind of infamy. His eyes wandered away from the little window that had enabled him to observe the above-described proceedings, and glanced fearfully around the room in which he was concealed. He almost expected to see the very floor open beneath his feet. He looked down mechanically as this idea flitted through his imagination; and to his horror and dismay he beheld a trap-door in the floor. There was no mistaking it: there it was—about three feet long and two broad, and a little sunken beneath the level of its frame-work.

Near the edge of the trap-door lay an object which also attracted the youth's attention and added to his fears. It was a knife with a long blade pointed like a dagger. About three inches of this blade was covered with a peculiar rust: the youth shuddered; could it be human blood that had stained that instrument of death?

Every circumstance, however trivial, aided, in such a place as that, to arouse or confirm the worst fears, the most horrible suspicions.[1]

The voices of the two men in the next room fell upon the youth's

---

1 The Fleet River rose near Kentish Town, now in North London, and ran down into the Thames. On its way it passed Coldbath Prison, Saffron Hill, and Chick Street/West Street. By this time it was an open sewer, in which, infamously, the bodies of those who had fallen in drunk—or murdered—were often found. Many houses had a trap-door opening above it, for use as a latrine or rubbish chute. The Fleet became a symbol of the 'undercurrent of crime' threatening the City. Curiously, this fear grew after it was bricked over: the new London sewerage system was widely distrusted, not only because it was thought everyone's sewage would now flow through your home, but because it was believed thieves, murderers *and worse* would have a direct access to your bathroom. Absurd as this seems to us, serials like *The Wild Boys of London* played to this fear, and even into the 1960s the 'trap-door over the river' motif was common in films: especially those which played to the fear of immigrants, like Sax Rohmer's *Fu Manchu* series.

ear; and, perceiving that escape was still impracticable, he determined to gratify that curiosity which was commingled with his fears.

"Well, now, about this t'other job, Dick?" said Bill.

"It's Jem as started it," was the reply. "But he told me all about it, and so we may as well talk it over. It's up Islington way—up there between Kentish Town and Lower Holloway."

"Who's crib is it?"

"A swell of the name of Markham. He is an old fellow, and has two sons. One, the eldest, is with his regiment; t'other, the youngest, is only about fifteen, or so—a mere kid."

"Well, there's no danger to be expected from him. But what about the flunkies?"

"Only two man-servants and three wimen. One of the man-servants is the old butler, too fat to do any good; and t'other is a young tiger."[1]

"And that's all?"

"That's all. Now you, and I, and Jem is quite enough to crack that there crib. When is it to be done?"

"Let's say to-morrow night; there is no moon now to speak on, and business in other quarters is slack."

"So be it. Here goes, then, to the success of our new job at old Markham's;" and as the burglar uttered these words he tossed off a bumper of brandy.

This example was followed by his worthy companion; and their conversation then turned upon other topics.

"I say, Bill, this old house has seen some jolly games, han't it?"

"I should think it had too. It was Jonathan Wild's favourite crib; and he was no fool at keeping things dark."[2]

---

1 tiger: footman, junior servant.

2 Jonathan Wild: born Wolverhampton, c. 1682, executed at Tyburn 24 May 1725. One of the worst villains England ever produced, Wild was a thief, murderer and receiver of stolen goods, who also held the post of Thief-Taker General under Sir Robert Walpole. For many years he ran a 'retrieval' service, whereby he would sell stolen goods back to the owners for a high price. He ran a huge stable of criminals, and if any got out of hand, or disobeyed orders, he would hand them over to be hanged. The famous Jack Sheppard was one such. Wild had several houses in London where he stored goods and hid criminals: one was right next to the Old Bailey. Another was no. 3, West Street, otherwise known as Chick Lane, which is where the present action was set. The house was demolished in the 1840s, and the many discoveries made in it fascinated writers like Reynolds and Thomas Prest, who wrote a serial, *The Old House of West Street.*

"No, surely. I dare say the well-staircase in the next room there, that's covered over with the trap-door, has had many a dead body flung down it into the Fleet."

"Ah!—and without telling no tales too. But the trap-door has been nailed over for some years now."

The unfortunate youth in the adjacent chamber was riveted in silent horror to the spot, as these fearful details fell upon his ears.

"Why was the trap-door nailed down?"

"Cos there's no use for *that* now, since the house is uninhabited, and no more travellers come to lodge here. Besides, if we wanted to make use of such a conwenience, there's another——"

A loud clap of thunder prevented the remainder of this sentence from reaching the youth's ears.

"I've heard it said that the City is going to make great alterations in this quarter," observed Dick, after a pause. "If so be they comes near us, we must shift our quarters."

"Well, and don't we know other cribs as good as this—and just under the very nose of the authorities too? The nearer you gets to them the safer you finds yourself. Who'd think now that here, and in Peter-street, and on Saffron-hill[1] too, there was such cribs as this? Lord, how such coves as you and me does laugh when them chaps in the Common Council and the House of Commons gets on their legs and praises the blue-bottles up to the skies as the most acutest police in the world, while they wotes away the people's money to maintain 'em!"

"Oh! as for alterations, I don't suppose there'll be any for the next twenty years to come. They always talks of improvements long afore they begins 'em."

"But when they *do* commence, they won't spare this lovely old crib! It 'ud go to my heart to see them pull it about. I'd much sooner take and shove a dozen stiff uns myself down the trap than see a single rafter of the place ill-treated—that I would."

"Ah! if so be as the masons does come to pull its old carcass about, there'll be some fine things made known to the world. Them cellars down stairs, in which a man might hide for fifty years and never be

1 Peter Street and Saffron Hill: both streets still exist, but their character has changed enormously. Now a rather dull, respectable thoroughfare near Farringdon tube-station, Saffron Hill in 1844 was one of the 'worst streets in London:' Peter Street in Soho had much the same reputation.

smelt out by the police, will turn up a bone or two, I rather suspect; and not of a sheep, nor a pig, nor a bull neither."

"Why—half the silly folks in this neighbourhood are afeerd to come here even in the daytime, because they say it's haunted," observed Bill, after a brief pause. "But, for my part, I shouldn't be frightened to come here at all hours of the night, and sit here alone too, even if every feller as was scragged at Tyburn or Newgate,[1] and every one wot has been tumbled down these holes into the Fleet, was to start up, and——"

The man stopped short, turned ghastly pale, and fell back stupified and speechless in his chair. His pipe dropped from between his fingers, and broke to pieces upon the floor.

"What the devil's the matter now?" demanded his companion, casting an anxious glance around.

"There! there! don't you see ——," gasped the terrified ruffian, pointing towards the little window looking into the next room.

"It's only some d——d gammon of Crankey Jim," ejaculated Dick, who was more courageous in such matters than his companion. "I'll deuced soon put that to rights!"

Seizing the candle, he was hurrying towards the door, when his comrade rushed after him, crying, "No—I won't be left in the dark! I can't bear it! Damme, if you go, I'll go with you!"

The two villains accordingly proceeded together into the next room.

CHAPTER III.

THE TRAP-DOOR.

THE youthful stranger had listened with ineffable surprise and horror to the conversation of the two ruffians. His nerves had been worked up by all the circumstances of the evening to a tone bordering upon madness—to that pitch, indeed, when it appeared as if there were no alternative left save to fall upon the floor and yield to the *delirium tremens* of violent emotions.

He had restrained his feelings while he heard the burglary at Mr.

1 Scragged: hanged. Tyburn was the main place of execution for criminals until the 1780s, and stood roughly where Marble Arch stands today. Newgate was the main prison of London, and stands roughly where the Old Bailey does today.

Markham's dwelling coolly planned and settled; but when the discourse of those two monsters in human shape developed to his imagination all the horrors of the fearful place in which he had sought an asylum,—when he heard that he was actually standing upon the very verge of that staircase down which innumerable victims had been hurled to the depths of the slimy ditch beneath,—and when he thought how probable it was that his bones were doomed to whiten in the dark and hidden caverns below, along with the remains of other human beings who had been barbarously murdered in cold blood,—reason appeared to forsake him. A cold sweat broke forth all over him; and he seemed about to faint under the oppression of a hideous nightmare.

He threw his hat upon the floor—for he felt the want of air. That proud forehead, that beautiful countenance were distorted with indescribable horror; and an ashy pallor spread itself over his features.

Death, in all its most hideous forms, appeared to follow—to surround—to hem him in. There was no escape—a trap-door here—a well, communicating with the ditch, there—or else the dagger;—no matter in what shape—still Death was before him—behind him—above him—below him—on every side of him.

It was horrible—most horrible!

Then was it that a sudden thought flashed across his brain: he resolved to attempt a desperate effort to escape. He summoned all his courage to his aid, and opened the door so cautiously that, though the hinges were old and rusted, they did not creak.

The crisis was now at hand. If he could clear the landing unperceived, he was safe. It was true that, seen or unseen, he might succeed in escaping from the house by means of his superior agility and nimbleness; but he reflected that these men would capture him again, in a few minutes, in the midst of a labyrinth of streets with which he was utterly unacquainted, but which they knew so well. He remembered that he had overheard their secrets and witnessed their mysterious modes of concealment; and that, should he fall into their power, death must inevitably await him.

These ideas crossed his brain in a moment, and convinced him of the necessity of prudence and extreme caution. He must leave the house unperceived, and dare the pitiless storm and pelting rain; for the tempest still raged without.

He once more approached the window to ascertain if there were any chance of stealing across the landing-place unseen. Unfortunately he drew too near the window: the light of the candle fell full upon his countenance, which horror and alarm had rendered deadly pale and fearfully convulsed.

It was at this moment that the ruffian, in the midst of his unholy vaunts, had caught sight of that human face—white as a sheet—and with eyes fixed upon him with a glare which his imagination rendered stony and unearthly.

The youth saw that he was discovered; and a full sense of the desperate peril which hung over him, rushed to his mind. He turned, and endeavoured to fly away from the fatal spot; but, as imagination frequently fetters the limbs in a nightmare, and involves the sleeper in danger from which he vainly attempts to run, so did his legs now refuse to perform their office.

His brain whirled—his eyes grew dim: he grasped at the wall to save himself from falling—but his senses were deserting him—and he sank fainting upon the floor.

He awoke from the trance into which he had fallen, and became aware that he was being moved along. Almost at the same instant his eyes fell upon the sinister countenance of Dick, who was carrying him by the feet. The other ruffian was supporting his head.

They were lifting him down the staircase, upon the top step of which the candle was standing.

All the incidents of the evening immediately returned to the memory of the wretched boy, who now only too well comprehended the desperate perils that surrounded him.

The bottom of the staircase was reached: the villains deposited their burden for a moment in the passage, while Dick retraced his steps to fetch down the candle.

And then a horrible conflict of feelings and inclinations took place in the bosom of the unhappy youth. He shut his eyes; and for an instant debated within himself whether he should remain silent or cry out. He dreamt of immediate—instantaneous death; and yet he thought that he was young to die—oh! so young—and that men could not be such barbarians——

But when the two ruffians stooped down to take him up again, fear surmounted all other sentiments, feelings, and inclinations; and his deep—his profound—his heartfelt agony was expressed in one long, loud, and piercing shriek!

And then a fearful scene took place.

The two villains carried the youth into the front room upon the ground-floor, and laid him down for a moment.

It was the same room to which he had first found his way upon entering that house.

It was the room in which, by the glare of the evanescent lightning, he had seen that black square upon the dirty floor.

For a few instants all was dark. At length the candle was brought by the man in the fustian coat.

The youth glanced wildly around him, and speedily recognised that room.

He remembered how deep a sensation of horror seized him when that black square upon the floor first caught his eyes.

He raised himself upon his left arm, and once more looked around.

Great God! was it possible?

That ominous blackness—that sinister square was the mouth of a yawning gulf, the trap-door of which was raised.

A fetid smell rose from the depths below, and the gurgling of a current was faintly heard.

The dread truth was in a moment made apparent to that unhappy boy—much more quickly than it occupies to relate or read. He started from his supine posture, and fell upon his knees at the feet of those merciless villains who had borne him thither.

"Mercy, mercy! I implore you! Oh! do not devote me to so horrible a death! Do not—*do not murder me!*"

"Hold your noisy tongue, you fool," ejaculated Bill, brutally. "You have heard and seen too much for our safety; we can't do otherwise."

"No, certainly not," added Dick. "You are now as fly to the fakement as any one of us."

"Spare me, spare me, and I will never betray you! Oh! do not send me out of this world, so young—so very young! I have money, I have wealth, I am rich, and I will give you all I possess!" ejaculated the agonized youth; his countenance wearing an expression of horrible despair.

"Come; here's enough. Bill, lend a hand!" and Dick seized the boy by one arm, while his companion took a firm hold of the other.

"Mercy, mercy!" shrieked the youth, struggling violently; but struggling vainly. "You will repent when you know—I am not what I——"

He said no more: his last words were uttered over the mouth of the chasm ere the ruffians loosened their hold;—and then he fell.

The trap-door was closed violently over the aperture, and drowned the scream of agony which burst from his lips.

The two murderers then retraced their steps to the apartment on the first floor.

* * * * *

On the following day, about one o'clock, Mr. Markham, a gentleman of fortune residing in the northern environs of London, received the following letter:—

"The inscrutable decrees of Providence have enabled the undersigned to warn you, that this night a burglarious attempt will be made upon your dwelling. The wretches who contemplate this infamy are capable of a crime of much blacker die. Beware!

"An Unknown Friend."

This letter was written in a beautiful feminine hand. Due precaution was adopted at Mr. Markham's mansion; but the attempt alluded to in the warning epistle was, for some reason or another, not made.

CHAPTER IV.

THE TWO TREES.

It was between eight and nine o'clock, on a delicious evening, about a week after the events related in the preceding chapters, that two youths issued from Mr. Markham's handsome, but somewhat secluded dwelling, in the northern part of the environs of London, and slowly ascended the adjacent hill. There was an interval of four years between the ages of these youths, the elder being upwards of nineteen, and the younger about fifteen; but it was easy to perceive by the resemblance which existed between them that they were brothers. They walked at a short distance from each other, and exchanged not a word as they ascended the somewhat steep path which conducted them to the summit of the eminence that overlooked the mansion they had just left. The elder proceeded first; and from time to time he clenched his fists, and knit his brows, and gave other silent but expressive indications of the angry passions which were concentrated in his breast. His brother followed him with downcast eyes, and with a countenance denoting the deep anguish that oppressed him. In this manner they arrived at the top of the hill, where they seated themselves upon a bench, which stood between two young ash saplings.

For a long time the brothers remained silent; but at length the younger of the two suddenly burst into tears, and exclaimed, "Oh! why, dearest Eugene, did we choose this spot to say farewell—perhaps for ever?"

"We could not select a more appropriate one, Richard," returned the elder brother. "Four years ago those trees were planted by our hands; and we have ever since called them by our own names. When we were wont to separate, to repair to our respective schools, we came hither to talk over our plans, to arrange the periods of our correspondence, and to anticipate the pursuits that should engage us during the vacations. And when we returned from our seminaries, we hastened hither, hand-in-hand, to see how our trees flourished; and he was most joyous and proud whose sapling appeared to expand the more luxuriantly. If ever we quarrelled, Richard, it was here that we made our peace again; and, seated upon this bench, we have concocted plans for the future; which, haply, will never now be realised!"

"You are right, my dear brother," said Richard, after a pause, during which he appeared to reflect profoundly upon Eugene's words; "we could not have selected a better spot. Still it is all those happy days to which you allude that now render this moment the more bitter. Tell me, must you depart? Is there no alternative? Can I not intercede with our father? Surely, surely, he will not discard one so young as you, and whom he has loved—must still love—so tenderly?"

"Intercede with my father!" repeated Eugene, with an irony which seemed extraordinary in one of his tender age; "no, never! He has signified his desire, he has commanded me no longer *to pollute his dwelling*—those were his very words, and he shall be obeyed."

"Our father was incensed, deeply incensed, when he spoke," urged Richard, whose voice was rendered almost inaudible by his sobs; "and to-morrow he will repent of his harshness towards you."

"Our father had no right to blame me," said Eugene violently; "all that has occurred originated in his own conduct towards me. The behaviour of a parent to his son is the element of that son's ruin or success in after life."

"I know not how you can reproach our father, Eugene," said Richard, somewhat reproachfully, "for he has ever conducted himself with tenderness towards us; and since the death of our dear mother——"

"You are yet too young, Richard," interrupted Eugene impatiently, "to comprehend the nature of the accusation which I bring against my father. I will, however, attempt to enable you to understand my meaning, so that you may not imagine that I am acting with duplicity when I endeavour to find a means of extenuation, if not of justification, for my own conduct. My father lavished his gold upon my education, as he also did upon yours; and he taught us from childhood to consider ourselves the sons of wealthy parents who would enable their children to move with *éclat* in an elevated sphere of life. It was just this day year that I joined my regiment at Knightsbridge. I suddenly found myself thrown amongst gay, dissipated, and wealthy young men—my brother officers. Many of them were old acquaintances, and had been my companions at the Royal Military College at Sandhurst. They speedily enlisted me in all their pleasures and debaucheries, and my expenditure soon exceeded my pay and my allowance. I became involved in debts, and was compelled to apply to my father to relieve me from my embarrassments. I wrote a humble and submissive letter, expressing contrition for my faults, and promising to avoid similar pursuits in future. Indeed, I was wearied of the dissipation into which I had plunged, and should have profited well by the experience my short career of pleasure and folly had enabled me to acquire. I trembled upon that verge when my father could either ruin or save me. He did not reply to my letter, and I had not courage to seek an interview with him. Again did I write to him: no answer. I had lost money at private play, and had contracted debts in the same manner. Those, Richard, are called *debts of honour*, and must be paid in full to your creditor, however wealthy he may be, even though your servants and tradesmen should be cheated out of their hard-earned and perhaps much-needed money altogether. I wrote a third time to our father, and still no notice was taken of my appeal. The officers to whom I owed the money lost at play began to look coldly upon me, and I was reduced to a state of desperation. Still I waited for a few days, and for a fourth time wrote to my father. It appears that he was resolved to make me feel the inconvenience of the position in which I had placed myself by my follies; and he sent me no answer. I then called at the house, and he refused to see me. This you know, Richard. What could I do? Driven mad by constant demands for money which I could not pay, and smarting under the chilling glances and taunting allusions of my brother officers, I sold my commission. You are acquainted with the rest. I came home, threw myself at my father's feet, and he spurned me away from him! Richard, was my crime so very great? and has not the unjust, the extreme severity of my father been the cause of all my afflictions?"

"I dare not judge between you," said Richard mildly.

"But what does common sense suggest?" demanded Eugene.

"Doubtless our father knows best," returned the younger brother.

"Old men are often wrong, in spite of their experience—in spite of their years," persisted Eugene.

"My dear brother," said Richard, "I am afraid to exercise my judgment in a case where I stand a chance of rebelling against my father, or questioning his wisdom; and, at the same time, I am anxious to believe everything in your justification."

"I knew that you would not comprehend me," exclaimed Eugene, impatiently. "It is ridiculous not to dare to have an opinion of one's own! My dear brother," he added, turning suddenly round, "you have been to Eton to little purpose: I thought that nearly as much of the world was to be seen there as at Sandhurst. I find that I was mistaken."

And Eugene felt and looked annoyed at the turn which the conversation had taken.

Richard was unhappy, and remained silent.

In the meantime the sun had set; and the darkness was gradually becoming more intense.

Suddenly Eugene grasped his brother's hand, and exclaimed, "Richard, I shall now depart!"

"Impossible!" cried the warm-hearted youth: "you will not leave me thus—you will not abandon your father also, for a hasty word that he has spoken, and which he will gladly recal to-morrow? Oh! no—Eugene, you will not leave the dwelling in which you were born, and where you have passed so many happy hours! What will become of you? What do you purpose? What plan have you in view?"

"I have a few guineas in my pocket," returned Eugene; "and many a princely fortune has been based upon a more slender foundation."

"Yes," said Richard hastily; "you read of fortunes being easily acquired in novels and romances; and in past times persons may have enriched themselves suddenly; but in the great world of the present day, Eugene, I am afraid that such occurrences are rare and seldom seen."

"You know nothing of the world, Richard," said Eugene, almost contemptuously. "There are thousands of persons in London who live well, and keep up splendid establishments, without any apparent resources; and I am man of the world enough to be well aware that those always thrive the best in the long run who have the least to lose at starting. At all events I shall try *my* fortune. I will not, cannot succumb to a parent who has caused my ruin at my very first entrance into life."

"May God prosper your pursuits, and send you the fortune which you appear to aim at!" ejaculated Richard fervently. "But once again—and for the last time, let me implore you—let me entreat you not to push this rash and hasty resolve into execution. Do stay—do not leave me, my dearest, dearest brother!"

"Richard, not all the powers of human persuasion shall induce me to abandon my present determination," cried Eugene emphatically, and rising from the bench as he spoke. "It is growing late, and I must depart. Now listen, my dear boy, to what I have to say to you."

"Speak, speak!" murmured Richard, sobbing as if his heart would break.

"All will be yet well," said Eugene, slightly touched by his brother's profound affliction. "I am resolved not to set foot in my father's house again; you must return thither and pack me up my papers and my necessaries."

"And you will not leave this spot until my return?" said Richard.

"Solemnly I promise *that*," answered Eugene. "But stay; on your part you must faithfully pledge yourself not to seek my father, nor in any way interfere between him and me. Nay, do not remonstrate; you must promise."

"I promise you all—anything you require," said Richard mournfully; and, after affectionately embracing his brother, he hurried down the hill towards the mansion, turning back from time to time to catch a glimpse of Eugene's figure through the increasing gloom, to satisfy himself that he was still there between the two saplings.

Richard entered the house, and stole softly up to the bed-room which his brother usually occupied when at home. He began his mournful task of putting together the few things which Eugene had desired him to select; and while he was thus employed the tears rolled down his cheeks in torrents. At one moment he was inclined to hurry to his father, and implore him to interfere in time to prevent Eugene's departure; but he remembered his solemn promise, and he would not break it. Assuredly this was a sense of honour so extreme, that it might be denominated *false*; but it was, nevertheless, the sentiment which controlled all the actions of him who cherished it. Tenderly, dearly as he loved his brother—bitterly as he deplored his intended departure, he still would not forfeit his word and take the simple step which would probably have averted the much-dreaded evil. Richard's sense of honour and inflexible integrity triumphed, on all occasions, over every other consideration, feeling, and desire; and of this characteristic of his brother's nature Eugene was well aware.

Richard had made a small package of the articles which he had selected, and was about to leave the room to return to his brother, when the sound of a footstep in the passage communicating with the chamber, suddenly fell upon his ear.

Scarcely had he time to recover from the alarm into which this circumstance had thrown him, when the door slowly opened, and the butler entered the apartment.

He was a man of about fifty years of age, with a jolly red face, a somewhat bulbous nose, small laughing eyes, short grey hair standing upright in front, whiskers terminating an inch above his white cravat, and in person considerably inclined to corpulency. In height he was about five feet seven inches, and had a peculiar shuffling rapid walk, which he had learnt by some twenty-five years' practice in little journeys from the side-board in the dining-room to his own pantry, and back again. He was possessed of an excellent heart, and was a good-humoured companion; but pompous, and swelling with importance in the presence of those whom he considered his inferiors. He was particularly addicted to hard words; and as, to use his own expression, he was "self-taught," it is not to be wondered if he occasionally gave those aforesaid hard words a pronunciation and a meaning which militated a little against received rules. In attire, he was unequalled for the whiteness of his cravat, the exuberance of his shirt-frill, the elegance of his waistcoat, the set of his kerseymere tights, and the punctilious neatness of his black silk stockings, and his well-polished shoes.

"Well, Master Richard," said the butler, as he shuffled into the room, with a white napkin under his left arm, "what in the name of everythink indiwisible is the matter now?"

"Nothing, nothing, Whittingham," replied the youth. "You had better go down stairs—my father may want you."

"If so be your father wants anythink, Tom will despond to the summins as usual," said the butler, leisurely seating himself upon a chair close by the table whereon Richard had placed his package. "But might I be so formiliar as to inquire into the insignification of that bundle of shirts and ankerchers?"

"Whittingham, I implore you to ask me no questions: I am in a hurry—and——"

"Master Richard, Master Richard," cried the butler, shaking his head gravely, "I'm very much afeerd that somethink preposterious is going to incur. I could not remain a entire stranger to all that has transpirated this day; and now I know what it is," he added, slapping his right hand smartly upon his thigh; "your brother's a-going to amputate it!"

"To what?"

"To cut it, then, if you reprehend that better. But it shan't be done, Master Richard—it shan't be done!"

"Whittingham——"

"That's my nomenklitter, Master Richard," said the old man, doggedly; "and it was one of the fust you ever learned to pernounce. Behold ye, Master Richard, I have a right to speak—for I have knowed you both from your cradles—and loved you too! Who was it, when you come into this subluminary spear—who was it as nussed you—and——"

"Good Whittingham, I know all that, and——"

"I have no overdue curiosity to satisfy, Master Richard," observed the butler; "but my soul's inflicted to think that you and Master

Eugene couldn't make a friend of old Whittingham. I feel it here, Master Richard—here, on my buzzim!"—and the worthy old domestic dealt himself a tremendous blow upon the chest as he uttered these words.

"I must leave you now, Whittingham, and I desire you to remain here until my return," said Richard. "Do you hear, Whittingham?"

"Yes, Master Richard; but I don't choose to do as you would wish in this here instance. I shall foller you."

"What, Whittingham?"

"I shall foller you, sir."

"Well—you can do that," said Richard, suddenly remembering that his brother had in no wise cautioned him against such an intervention as this; "and pray God it may lead to some good."

"Ah! now I see that I am raly wanted," said the butler, a smile of satisfaction playing upon his rubicund countenance.

Richard now led the way from the apartment, the butler following him in a stately manner. They descended the stairs, crossed the garden, and entered the path which led to the top of the hill.

"Two trees, I suppose?" said the old domestic inquiringly.

"Yes—he is there!" answered Richard; "but the reminiscence of the times when we planted those saplings has failed to induce him to abandon a desperate resolution."

"Ah! he ain't got Master Richard's heart—I always knowed that," mused the old man half audibly as he trudged along. "There are them two lads—fine tall youths—both black hair, and intelligible black eyes—admirably formed—straight as arrows—and yet so diversified in disposition!"

Richard and the butler now reached the top of the hill. Eugene was seated upon the bench in a deep reverie; and it was not until his brother and the faithful old domestic stood before him, that he awoke from that fit of abstraction.

"What! is that you, Whittingham?" he exclaimed, the moment he recognised the butler. "Richard, I did not think you would have done this."

"It wasn't Master Richard's fault, sir," said Whittingham; "I was rayther too wide awake not to smell what was a-going on by virtue of my factory nerves; and so——"

"My dear Whittingham," hastily interrupted Eugene, "I know

that you are a faithful servant to my father, and very much attached to us: on that very account, pray do not interfere!"

"Interfere!" ejaculated Whittingham, thoroughly amazed at being thus addressed, while a tear started into his eye: "not interfere, Master Eugene? Well, I'm—I'm—I'm—regularly flabbergasted!"

"My mind is made up," said Eugene, "and no persuasion shall alter its decision. I am my own master—my father's conduct has emancipated me from all deference to parental authority. Richard, you have brought my things? We must now say adieu."

"My dearest brother——"

"Master Eugene——"

"Whither are you going?"

"I am on the road to fame and fortune!"

"Alas!" said Richard mournfully, "you may perhaps find that this world is not so fruitful in resources as you now imagine."

"All remonstrances—all objections are vain," interrupted Eugene impatiently. "We must say adieu! But one word more," he added, after an instant's pause, as a sudden thought seemed to strike him; "*you* doubt the possibility of my success in life, and *I* feel confident of it. Do *you* pursue your career under the auspices of that parent in whose wisdom you so blindly repose: I will follow *mine*, dependent only on mine own resources. This is the 10th of July, 1831; twelve years hence, on the 10th of July, 1843, we will meet again upon this very spot, between the two trees, if they be still standing. Remember the appointment: we will *then* compare notes relative to our success in life!"

The moment he had uttered these words, Eugene hastily embraced his brother, who struggled in vain to retain him; and, having wrung the hand of the old butler, who was now sobbing like a child, the discarded son threw his little bundle over his shoulder, and hurried away from the spot.

So precipitately did he descend the hill in the direction leading away from the mansion, and towards the multitudinous metropolis at a little distance, that he was out of sight before his brother or Whittingham even thought of pursuing him.

They lingered for some time upon the summit of the hill, without exchanging a word; and then, maintaining the same silence, slowly retraced their steps towards the mansion.

CHAPTER V.

ELIGIBLE ACQUAINTANCES.

Four years passed away.

During that interval no tidings of the discarded son reached the disconsolate father and unhappy brother; and all the exertions of the former to discover some trace of the fugitive were fruitless. Vainly did he lavish considerable sums upon that object: uselessly did he despatch emissaries to all the great manufacturing towns of England, as well as to the principal capitals of Europe, to endeavour to procure some information of him whom he would have received as the prodigal son, and to welcome whose return he would have "killed the fatted calf:"—all his measures to discover his son's retreat were unavailing.

At length, after a lapse of four years, he sank into the tomb—the victim of a broken heart!

A few days previous to his death, he made a will in favour of his remaining son, the guardianship of whom he intrusted to a Mr. Monroe, who was an opulent City merchant, and an old and sincere friend.

Thus, at the age of nineteen, Richard found himself his own master, with a handsome allowance to meet his present wants, and with a large fortune in the perspective of two years more. Mr. Monroe, feeling the utmost confidence in the young man's discretion and steadiness, permitted him to reside in the old family mansion, and interfered with him and his pursuits as little as possible.

The ancient abode of the family of Markham was a spacious and commodious building, but of heavy and sombre appearance. This gloomy aspect of the architecture was increased by the venerable trees that formed a dense rampart of verdure around the edifice. The grounds belonging to the house were not extensive, but were tastefully laid out; and within the enclosure over which the dominion of Richard Markham extended, was the green hill surmounted by the two ash trees. From the summit of that eminence the mighty metropolis might be seen in all its vastitude—that metropolis whose one single heart was agitated with so many myriads of conflicting passions, warring interests, and opposite feelings.

Perhaps a dozen pages of laboured description will not afford the reader a better idea of the characters and dispositions of the two brothers than that which has already been conveyed by their conversation and conduct detailed in the preceding chapter. Eugene was all selfishness and egotism, Richard all generosity and frankness: the former deceitful, astute, and crafty, the latter honourable even to a fault.

With Eugene, for the present, we have little to do; the course of our narrative follows the fortunes of Richard Markham.

The disposition of this young man was somewhat reserved, although by no means misanthropical nor melancholy. That characteristic resulted only from the domesticated nature of his habits. He was attached to literary pursuits, and frequently passed entire hours together in his study, poring over works of a scientific and instructive nature. When he stirred abroad for the purpose of air and exercise, he preferred a long ramble upon foot, amongst the fields in the vicinity of his dwelling, to a parade of himself and his fine horse amid the busy haunts of wealth and fashion at the West End of London.

It was, nevertheless, upon a beautiful afternoon in the month of August, 1835, that Richard appeared amongst the loungers in Hyde Park.[1] He was on foot, and attired in deep mourning; but his handsome countenance, symmetrical form, and thoroughly genteel and unassuming air attracted attention.

Parliament had been prorogued a fortnight before; and all London was said to be "out of town." Albeit, it was evident that a considerable portion of London was "in town," for there were many gorgeous equipages rolling along "the drive," and the enclosure was pretty well sprinkled with well-dressed groups and dotted with solitary fashionable gentlemen upon foot.

From the carriages that rolled past many bright eyes were for a moment turned upon Richard; and in these equipages there were not wanting young female bosoms which heaved at the contrast afforded by that tall and elegant youth, so full of vigour and health, and whose

1 Hyde Park: a large open space in Westminster, just to the west of Mayfair, and in the 1840s very much 'the place to be seen.' As well as Rotten Row, a fashionable place to ride horses, the Park has a circle of roads inside its perimeter, known as the Carriage Drives: referred to below as 'the drive.'

countenance beamed with intelligence, and the old, emaciated, and semi-childish husbands seated by their sides, and whose wealth had purchased their hands, but never succeeded in obtaining their hearts.

Richard, wearied with his walk, seated himself upon a bench, and contemplated with some interest the moving pageantry before him. He was thus occupied when he was suddenly accosted by a stranger, who seated himself by his side in an easy manner, and addressed some common-place observation to him.

This individual was a man of about two-and-thirty, elegantly attired, agreeable in his manners, and prepossessing in appearance. Under this superficial tegument of gentility a quicker eye than Richard Markham's would have detected a certain swagger in his gait and a kind of dashing recklessness about him which produced an admirable effect upon the vulgar or the inexperienced, but which were not calculated to inspire immediate confidence in the thorough man of the world. Richard was, however, all frankness and honour himself, and he did not scruple to return such an answer to the stranger's remark as was calculated to encourage farther conversation.

"I see the count is abroad again," observed the stranger, following with his eyes one of the horsemen in "the drive." "Poor fellow! he has been playing at hide-and-seek for a long time."

"Indeed! and wherefore?" exclaimed Richard.

"What! are you a stranger in London, sir?" cried the well-dressed gentleman, transferring his eyes from the horseman to Markham's countenance, on which they were fixed with an expression of surprise and interest.

"Very nearly so, although a resident in its immediate vicinity all my life;" and, with the natural ingenuousness of youth, Richard immediately communicated his entire history, from beginning to end, to his new acquaintance. Of a surety there was not much to relate; but the stranger succeeded in finding out who the young man was, under what circumstances he was now living, and the amount of his present and future resources.

"Of course you mean to see life?" said the stranger.

"Certainly. I have already studied the great world by the means of books."

"But of course you know that there is nothing like experience."

"I can understand how experience is necessary to a man who is anxious to make a fortune, but not to him who has already got one."

"Oh, decidedly! It is frequently more difficult to keep a fortune than it was to obtain one."

"How—if I do not speculate?"

"No; but others will speculate upon you."

"I really cannot comprehend you. As I do not wish to increase my means, having enough, I shall neither speculate with my own nor allow people to speculate with it for me; and thus I can run no risk of losing what I possess."

The stranger gazed half incredulously upon Markham for a minute; and then his countenance expressed a species of sneer.

"You have never played?"

"Played! at——?"

"At cards; for money, I mean."

"Oh! never!"

"So much the better: never do. Unless," added the stranger, "it is entirely amongst friends and men of honour. But will you avail yourself of my humble vehicle, and take one turn round 'the Drive?'"

The stranger pointed as he spoke to a very handsome phaeton and pair at a little distance, and attended by a dapper-looking servant in light blue livery with silver lace.

"Might I have the honour of being acquainted with the name of a gentleman who exhibits so much kindness——"

"My dear sir, I must really apologise for my sin of omission. You confided your own circumstances so frankly to me that I cannot do otherwise than show you equal confidence in return. Besides, *amongst men of honour*," he continued, laying particular stress upon a word which is only so frequently used to be abused, "such communications, you know, are necessary. I do not like that system of familiarity based upon no tenable grounds, which is now becoming so prevalent in London. For instance, nothing is more common than for one gentleman to meet another in Bond-street, or the Park, or in Burlington Arcade, for example's sake, and for the one to say to the other—*'My dear friend, how are you?'*—*'Quite well, old fellow, thank you; but, by-the-by, I really forget your name!'* However," added the fashionable gentleman with a smile, "here is my card. My town-quarters are Long's Hotel, my country seat is in Berkshire, and my shooting-box is in Scotland, at all of which I shall be most happy to see you."

Richard, who was not only highly satisfied with the candour and openness of his new friend, but also very much pleased and amused with him, returned suitable acknowledgments for this kind invitation; and, glancing his eyes over the card which had been placed in his hands, perceived that he was conversing with the HONOURABLE[1] ARTHUR CHICHESTER.

As they were moving towards the phaeton, a gentleman, elegantly attired, of about the middle age, and particularly fascinating in his manners, accosted Mr. Chichester.

"Ah! who would have thought of meeting you here—when London is actually empty, and I am ashamed of being yet left in it? Our mutual friend the duke assured me that you were gone to Italy!"

"The duke always has some joke at my expense," returned Mr. Chichester. "He was once the cause of a very lovely girl committing suicide. She was the only one I ever loved; and he one day declared in her presence that I had just embarked for America. Poor thing! she went straight up to her room, and——"

"And!" echoed Richard.

"Took poison!" added Mr. Chichester, turning away his head for a moment, and drawing an elegant cambric handkerchief across his eyes.

"Good heavens!" ejaculated Markham.

"Let me not trouble you with my private afflictions. Sir Rupert, allow me to introduce my friend Mr. Markham:—Mr. Markham, Sir Rupert Harborough."

The two gentlemen bowed, and the introduction was effected.

"Whither are you bound?" inquired Sir Rupert.

"We were thinking of an hour's drive," leisurely replied Mr. Chichester; "and it was then my intention to have asked my friend Mr. Markham to dine with me at Long's. Will you join us, Sir Rupert?"

"Upon my honour, nothing would give me greater pleasure; but I am engaged to meet the duke at Tattersall's; and I am then under a solemn promise to dine and pass the evening with Diana."

"Always gallant—always attentive to the ladies!" exclaimed Mr. Chichester.

"You know, my dear fellow, that Diana is so amiable, so talented,

1 Members of titled families, not themselves bearing a specific title, affix 'the Honourable' (the Hon.) to their names.

so fascinating, so accomplished, and so bewitching, that I can refuse her nothing. It is true her wants and whims are somewhat expensive at times; but——"

"Harborough, I am surprised at you! What! complain of the fantasies of the most beautiful woman in London—if not in England—you a man of seven thousand a year, and who at the death of an uncle——"

"Upon my honour I begrudge her nothing!" interrupted Sir Rupert, complacently stroking his chin with his elegantly-gloved hand. "But, by the way, if you will honour me and Diana with your company this evening—and if Mr. Markham will also condescend——"

"With much pleasure," said Mr. Chichester; "and I am sure that my friend Mr. Markham will avail himself of this opportunity of forming the acquaintance of the most beautiful and fascinating woman in England."

Richard bowed: he dared not attempt an excuse. He had heard himself dubbed the friend of the Honourable Mr. Arthur Chichester; his ears had caught an intimation of a dinner at Long's, which he knew by report to be the headquarters of that section of the fashionable world that consists of single young gentlemen; and he now found himself suddenly engaged to pass the evening with Sir Rupert Harborough and a lady of whom all he knew was that her name was Diana, and that she was the most beautiful and fascinating creature in England.

Truly, all this was enough to dazzle him; and he accordingly resigned himself to Mr. Arthur Chichester's good will and pleasure.

Sir Rupert Harborough now remembered "that he must not keep the duke waiting;" and having kissed the tip of his lemon-coloured glove to Mr. Chichester, and made a semi-ceremonious, semi-gracious bow to Markham—that kind of bow whose formality is attempered by the blandness of the smile accompanying it—he hastened away.

It may be, however, mentioned as a singular circumstance, and as a proof of how little he cared about keeping "the duke" waiting, that, instead of proceeding towards Tattersall's, he departed in the direction of Oxford-street.

This little incident was, however, unnoticed by Richard—for the simple reason, that at this epoch of his life he did not know where Tattersall's was.[1]

"What do you think of my friend the baronet?"[2] inquired Mr. Chichester, as they rolled leisurely along "the Drive" in the elegant phaeton.

"I am quite delighted with him," answered Richard; "and if her ladyship be only as agreeable as her husband——"

"Excuse me, but you must not call her '*her ladyship*.' Address her and speak of her simply as Mrs. Arlington."

"I am really at a loss to comprehend——"

"My dear friend," said Chichester, sinking his voice, although there was no danger of being overheard, "Diana is not the wife of Sir Rupert Harborough. The baronet is unmarried; and this lady——"

"Is his mistress," added Markham hastily. "In that case I most certainly shall not accept the kind invitation I received for this evening."

"Nonsense, my dear friend! You must adapt your behaviour to the customs of the sphere in which you move. You belong to the aristocracy—like *me*—and like *the baronet!* In the upper class, even supposing you have a wife, she is only an encumbrance. Nothing is so characteristic of want of gentility as to marry early; and as for children, pah! they are the very essence of vulgarity! Then, of course, every man of fashion in London has his mistress, even though he only keeps her for the sake of his friends. This is quite allowable amongst the aristocracy. Remember, I am not advocating the cause of immorality: I would not have every butcher, and tea-dealer, and linen-draper do the same. God forbid! *Then* it would, indeed, be the height of depravity!"

"Since it is the fashion, and you assure me that there is nothing wrong in this connexion between the baronet and Mrs. Arlington—at least, that the usages of high life admit it—I will not advance any farther scruples," said Richard; although he had a slight suspicion,

---

1 Tattersall's: Richard Tattersall's Highflyer Club, 'the established head-quarters of the patrons of "the Turf,"' in Grosvenor Place. It was also known as 'The Corner,' and was reached via a low arch. Markham and his new friends are in Hyde Park; Oxford Street joins Marble Arch at the north-east corner of the Park. Grosvenor Place comes off Hyde Park Corner, at the south-east corner, and runs parallel with the grounds of Buckingham Palace; so that Harborough is going in exactly the wrong direction for his story about the duke.

2 Baronet: the lowest order of knighthood. Established by James VI and I (1603-1625), the title was often sold to the highest bidder.

like the ringing of far-distant bells in the ears, that the doctrine which his companion had just propounded was not based upon the most tenable grounds.

It was now half-past six o'clock in the evening; and, one after the other, the splendid equipages and gay horsemen withdrew in somewhat rapid succession. The weather was nevertheless still exquisitely fine; indeed, it was the most enchanting portion of the entire day. The sky was of a soft and serene azure, upon which appeared here and there thin vapours of snowy white, motionless and still; for not a breath of wind stirred the leaf upon the tree. Never did Naples, nor Albano, nor Sorrentum, boast a more beautiful horizon; and as the sun sank towards the western verge, he bathed all that the eye could embrace—earth and sky, dwelling and grove, garden and field—in a glorious flood of golden light.

At seven o'clock Mr. Chichester and his new acquaintance sat down to dinner in the coffee-room at Long's Hotel. The turtle was unexceptionable; the iced punch faultless. Then came the succulent neck of venison, and the prime Madeira. The dinner passed off pleasantly enough; and Richard was more and more captivated with his friend. He was, however, somewhat astonished at the vast quantities of wine which the Honourable Mr. Chichester swallowed, apparently without the slightest inconvenience to himself.

Mr. Chichester diverted him with amusing anecdotes, lively sallies, and extraordinary narratives; and Richard found that his new friend had not only travelled all over Europe, but was actually the bosom friend of some of the most powerful of its sovereigns. These statements, moreover, rather appeared to slip forth in the course of conversation, than to be made purposely; and thus they were stamped with an additional air of truth and importance.

At about half-past nine the Honourable Mr. Chichester proposed to adjourn to the lodgings of Mrs. Arlington. Richard, who had been induced by the example of his friend and by the excitement of an interesting conversation, to imbibe more wine than he was accustomed to take, was now delighted with the prospect of passing an agreeable evening; and he readily acceded to Mr. Chichester's proposal.

Mrs. Arlington occupied splendidly furnished apartments on the first and second floors over a music-shop in Bond-street: thither, therefore, did the two gentlemen repair on foot; and in a short time they were introduced into the drawing-room where the baronet and his fair companion were seated.

CHAPTER VI.

MRS. ARLINGTON.

THE Honourable Mr. Arthur Chichester had not exaggerated his description of the beauty of the Enchantress—for so she was called by the male portion of her admirers. Indeed, she was of exquisite loveliness. Her dark-brown hair was arranged *en bandeaux*, and parted over a forehead polished as marble. Her eyes were large, and of that soft dark melting blue which seems to form a heaven of promises and bliss to gladden the beholder.

She was not above the middle height of woman; but her form was modelled to the most exquisite and voluptuous symmetry. Her figure reminded the spectator of the body of the wasp, so taper was the waist, and so exuberant was the swell of the bust.

Her mouth was small and pouting; but, when she smiled, the parting roses of the lips displayed a set of teeth white as the pearls of the East.

Her hand would have made the envy of a queen. And yet, above all these charms, a certain something which could not be exactly denominated boldness nor effrontery, but which was the very reverse of extreme reserve, immediately struck Richard Markham.

He could not define the fault he had to find with this beautiful woman; and still there was something in her manners which seemed to proclaim that she did not possess the tranquillity and ease of a wife. She appeared to be constantly aiming at the display of the accomplishments of her mind, or the graces of her attitudes. She seemed to court admiration by every word and every motion; and to keep alive in the mind of the baronet the passion with which she had inspired him. She possessed not that confidence and contented reliance upon the idea of unalienable affections which characterise the wife. She seemed to be well aware that no legal nor religious ties connected the baronet to her; and she, therefore, kept her imagination perpetually upon the rack to weave new artificial bonds to cast around him. And, as if each action or each word of the baronet severed those bonds of silk and wreathed flowers, she found, Penelope-like, that at short intervals her labours were to be achieved over again.

This constant state of mental anxiety and excitement imparted a corresponding restlessness to her body; and those frequent changes of attitude, which were originally intended to develop the graces of her person, or allow her lover's eye to catch short glimpses of her heaving bosom of snow, became now a settled habit.

Nevertheless, she was a lovely and fascinating woman, and one for whom a young heart would undertake a thousand sacrifices.

By accident Richard was seated next to Mrs. Arlington upon the sofa. He soon perceived that she was, indeed, as accomplished as the baronet had represented her to be; and her critical opinions upon the current literature, dramatic novelties, and new music of the day were delivered with judgment and good taste.

Richard could not help glancing from time to time in admiration at her beautiful countenance, animated as it now was with the excitement of the topics of discourse; and whenever her large blue eyes met his, a deep blush suffused his countenance, and he knew not what he said or did.

"Well, what shall we do to amuse ourselves?" said Chichester, at the expiration of about an hour, during which coffee had been handed round.

"Upon my honour," exclaimed the baronet, "I am perfectly indifferent. What say you to a game of whist or *écarté*?"

"Just as you choose," said Chichester carelessly.

At this moment the door opened, and a roguish-looking little tiger—a lad of about fourteen, in a chocolate-coloured livery, with three rows of bright-crested buttons down his Prussian jacket—entered to announce another guest.

A short, stout, vulgar-looking man, about forty years of age, with a blue coat and brass buttons, buff waistcoat, and grey trousers, entered the room.

"Holloa, old chap, how are you?" he exclaimed in a tone of most ineffable vulgarity. "Harborough, how are you? Chichester, my tulip, how goes it?"

The baronet hastened to receive this extraordinary visitor, and, as he shook hands with him, whispered something in his ear. The stranger immediately turned towards Richard, to whom he was introduced by the name of Mr. Augustus Talbot.

This gentleman and the baronet then conversed together for a few moments; and Chichester, drawing near Markham, seized the opportunity of observing, "Talbot is an excellent fellow—a regular John Bull—not over polished, but enormously rich and well connected. You will see that he is not more cultivated in mind than in manners; but he would go to the devil to do any one a service; and, somehow or another, you can't help liking the fellow when once you know him."

"Any friend of yours or of the baronet's will be agreeable to me," said Richard; "and, provided he is a man of honour, a little roughness of manner should be readily overlooked."

"You speak like a man of the world, and as a man of honour yourself," said Mr. Chichester.

Meantime the baronet and Mr. Talbot had seated themselves, and the Honourable Mr. Chichester returned to his own chair.

The conversation then became general.

"I didn't know that you were in town, Talbot," said Mr. Chichester.

"And I forgot to mention it," observed the baronet.

"Or rather," said the lady, "you meditated a little surprise for your friend Mr. Chichester."

"I hope you've been well, ma'am, since I saw you last—that is the day before yesterday," said Mr. Talbot. "You was complaining then of a slight cold, and I recommended a treacle-posset and a stocking tied round the throat."

"My dear Talbot, take some liqueur," cried the baronet, rising hastily, and purposely knocking down his chair to drown the remainder of Mr. Talbot's observation.

"But I dare say you didn't follow my advice, ma'am," pursued Mr. Talbot, with the most imperturbable gravity. "For my part I am suffering dreadful with a bad foot. I'll tell you how it were, ma'am. I've got a nasty soft corn on my little toe; and so what must I do, but yesterday morning I takes my razor, sharpens it upon the paytent strap, and goes for to cut off master corn. But instead of cutting the corn, I nearly sliced my toe off; and——"

"By the way, Diana, has the young gentleman called yet, whom we met the other evening at the Opera?" said the baronet, abruptly interrupting this vulgar tirade.

"Do you mean the effeminate youth whom we dubbed the *Handsome Unknown?*" said the Enchantress.

"Yes: he who was so very mysterious, but who seemed so excessively anxious to form our acquaintance."

"He promised to call some evening this week," answered Diana, "and play a game of *écarté*. He told me that he was invincible at *écarté*."

"Talking of *écarté*, let us play a game," ejaculated Mr. Chichester, who was sitting upon thorns lest Mr. Talbot should commence his vulgarities again.

"Well, I'll take a hand with pleasure," said this individual: then turning towards Diana, he added, "I will tell you the rest of the adventure about the soft corn another time, ma'am."

"What a nuisance this is!" whispered Chichester to the baronet. "The young fellow does stare so."

"You must give him some explanation or another," hastily replied the baronet; "or I'll tell Diana to say something presently that will smooth down matters."

The cards were produced, and Mr. Talbot and the Honourable Mr. Chichester sat down to play.

Sir Rupert backed the former, and considerable sums in gold and notes were placed upon the table. Presently the lady turned towards Richard, and said with a smile, "Are you fond of *écarté*? I must venture a guinea upon Mr. Chichester. Sir Rupert is betting against him; and I love to oppose Sir Rupert at cards. You will see how I shall tease him presently."

With these words the Enchantress rose and seated herself near Mr. Chichester. Of course Markham did the same; and in a very short time he was induced by the lady to follow her and back the same side which she supported.

Mr. Chichester, however, had a continued run of ill luck, and lost every rubber. Richard was thus the loser of about thirty sovereigns; but he was somewhat consoled by having so fair a companion in his bad fortune. He would have suffered himself to be persuaded by her to persist in backing Mr. Chichester, as she positively assured him that the luck must change, had not that gentleman himself suddenly risen, thrown down the cards, and declared that he would play no more.

"Would you, ma'am, like to take Mr. Chichester's place?" said Mr. Talbot.

Mr. Chichester shook his head to the baronet, and the baronet did the same to Diana, and Diana accordingly declined. The card-table was therefore abandoned; and Mrs. Arlington, at the request of Sir Rupert, seated herself at the piano. Without any affectation she sang and accompanied herself upon the instrument in a manner that quite ravished the heart of Richard Markham.

Suddenly the entire house echoed with the din of the front-door knocker, and almost simultaneously the bell was rung with violence.

In a few moments the young tiger announced Mr. Walter Sydney.

He was a youth apparently not more than nineteen or twenty, of middle height, and very slim. He wore a tight blue military frock coat buttoned up to the throat; ample black kerseymere trousers, which did not, however, conceal the fact that he was the least thing knock-kneed, and a hat with tolerably broad brims. His feet and hands were small to a fault. His long light chestnut hair flowed in luxuriant undulations over the collar of his coat, even upon his shoulders, and gave him a peculiarly feminine appearance. His delicate complexion, upon the pure red and white of which the dark dyes of no beard had yet infringed, wore a deep blush as he entered the room.

"Mr. Sydney, you are welcome," said Mrs. Arlington, in a manner calculated to reassure the bashful youth. "It was but an hour ago that we were talking of you, and wondering why we had not received the pleasure of a visit."

"Madam, you are too kind," replied Mr. Sydney, in a tone which sounded upon the ear like a silver bell—so soft and beautiful was its cadence. "I am afraid that I am intruding: I had hoped to find you alone—I mean yourself and Sir Rupert Harborough—and I perceive that you have company——"

He stammered—became confounded with excuses—and then glanced at his attire, as much as to intimate that he was in a walking dress.

Both the baronet and Diana hastened to welcome him in such a manner as to speedily place him upon comfortable terms with himself once more; and he was then introduced to Mr. Chichester, Mr. Talbot, and Mr. Markham.

The moment the name of Markham was mentioned, the youthful visitor started perceptibly, and then fixed his intelligent hazel eyes upon the countenance of Richard with an expression of the most profound interest mingled with surprise.

Mr. Chichester made an observation at the same moment, and Sydney immediately afterwards entered with ease and apparent pleasure into a conversation which turned upon the most popular topics of the day. Richard was astonished at the extreme modesty, propriety, and good sense with which that effeminate and bashful youth expressed himself; and even the baronet, who was in reality well informed, listened to his interesting visitor with attention and admiration. Still there was a species of extreme delicacy in his tastes, as evidenced by his remarks, which bordered at times upon a fastidiousness, if not an inexperience actually puerile or feminine.

At half-past eleven supper was served up, and the party sat down to that most welcome and sociable of all meals.

It was truly diverting to behold the manner in which Mr. Talbot fell, tooth and nail, upon the delicacies which he heaped upon his plate; and his applications to the wine-bottle were to correspond. At one time he expressed his regret that it was too vulgar to drink half-and-half; and on another he vented his national prejudices against those who maintained that Perigord pies were preferable to rump steaks, or that claret was more exquisite than port or sherry. Once, when, it would appear, Mr. Chichester kicked him under the table, he roared out a request that his soft corn might be remembered; and as his friends were by no means anxious for a second edition of that interesting narrative—especially before Mr. Walter Sydney—they adopted the prudent alternative of conveying their remonstrances to him by means of winks instead of kicks.

After supper Mr. Talbot insisted upon making a huge bowl of punch in his own fashion; but he found that Mr. Chichester would alone aid him in disposing of it. As for Mr. Walter Sydney, he never appeared to do more than touch the brim of the wine-glass with his lips.

In a short time Mr. Talbot insisted upon practising his vocal powers by singing a hunting song, and was deeply indignant with his friends because they would not join in the very impressive but somewhat common chorus of *"Fal de lal lal, fal de lal la."* It is impossible to say what Mr. Talbot would have done next; but, much to the horror of the baronet, Mr. Chichester, and Diana—and equally to the surprise of Richard Markham and Walter Sydney—he suddenly lost his balance, and fell heavily upon the floor and into a sound sleep simultaneously.

"What a pity," said Mr. Chichester, shaking his head mournfully, and glancing down upon the prostrate gentleman, as if he were pronouncing a funeral oration over his remains; "this is his only fault—and, as it happens every night, it begins materially to disfigure his character. Otherwise, he is an excellent fellow, and immensely rich!"

At this moment the eyes of Richard caught those of Walter Sydney. An ill-concealed expression of superlative contempt and ineffable disgust was visible upon the handsome countenance of the latter; and the proud curl of his lip manifested his opinion of the scene he had just witnessed. In a few moments he rose to depart. To Diana he was only coldly polite; to the baronet and Chichester superbly distant and constrained; but towards Markham, as he took leave of him, there was a cordiality in his manner, and a sincerity in the desire which he expressed "that they should meet again," which formed a remarkable contrast with his behaviour towards the others.

That night slumber seemed to evade the eyes of Richard Markham. The image of Mrs. Arlington, and all that she had said, and the various graceful and voluptuous attitudes into which she had thrown herself, occupied his imagination. At times, however, his thoughts wandered to that charming youth—that mere boy—who seemed to court his friendship, and who was so delicate and so fragile to encounter the storms and vicissitudes of that world in whose dizzy vortex he was already found. Nor less did Richard ever and anon experience a sentiment of profound surprise that the elegant and wealthy Sir Rupert Harborough, the accomplished and lovely Diana, and the fastidious Mr. Arthur Chichester, should tolerate the society of such an unmitigated vulgarian as Mr. Talbot.

CHAPTER VII.

THE BOUDOIR.

It was the morning after the events related in the last chapter.

The scene changes to a beautiful little villa in the environs of Upper Clapton.

This charming retreat, which consisted of a main building two stories high, and wings each containing only one apartment, was constructed of yellow bricks that had retained their primitive colour, the dwelling being too far from the metropolis to be affected by its smoky exhalations.

The villa stood in the midst of a small garden, beautifully laid out in the French style of Louis XV.; and around it—interrupted only by the avenue leading to the front door of the dwelling—was a grove of evergreens. This grove formed a complete circle, and bounded the garden; and the entire enclosure was protected by a regular paling, painted white.

This miniature domain, consisting of about four acres, was one of the most beautiful spots in the neighbourhood of London; and behind it—far as the eye could reach—stretched the green fields, smiling and cultivated like those of Tuscany.

In front of the villa was a small grass plot, in the centre of which was a basin of clear and pellucid water, upon whose surface floated two noble swans, and other aquatic birds of a curious species.

Every now and then the silence of the morning was broken by the bay of several sporting-dogs, which occupied, in the rear of the building, kennels more cleanly and more carefully attended upon than the dwellings of many millions of Christians.

And yet the owner of that villa wanted not charity: witness the poor woman and two children who have just emerged from the servants' offices laden with cold provisions, and with a well-filled bundle of other necessaries.

At the door of a stable a groom was seen dismounting from the back of a thorough-bred chestnut mare, which had just returned from an airing, and upon which he cast a glance of mingled pride and affection.

The windows of the villa were embellished with flowers in pots and vases of curious workmanship; and outside the casements of the chambers upon the first floor were suspended cages containing beautiful singing birds.

To the interior of one of those rooms must we direct the attention of the reader. It was an elegant *boudoir:* and yet it could scarcely justify the name; for by a *boudoir* we understand something completely feminine, whereas this contained articles of male and female use and attire strangely commingled—pell-mell—together.

Upon a toilet-table were all the implements necessary for the decoration and embellishment of female beauty; and carelessly thrown over a chair were a coat, waistcoat, and trousers. A diminutive pair of patent-leather Wellington boots kept company with delicate morocco shoes, to which sandals were affixed. A huge press, half-open, disclosed an array of beautiful dresses—silk, satin, and precious stuffs of all kinds; and on a row of pegs were hung a scarlet hunting coat, a shooting-jacket, a jockey-cap, and other articles of attire connected with field sports and masculine recreations. Parasols, foils, singlesticks, dandy-canes, and hunting-whips, were huddled together in one corner of that bureau. And yet all the confusion of these various and discrepant objects was so regular in appearance—if the phrase can be understood—that it seemed as if some cunning hand had purposely arranged them all so as to strike the eye in a manner calculated to encourage the impression that this elegant boudoir was inhabited by a man of strange feminine tastes, or a woman of extraordinary masculine ones.

There was no pompous nor gorgeous display of wealth in this boudoir: its interior, like that of the whole villa throughout, denoted competence and ease—elegance and taste, but no useless luxury nor profuse expenditure.

The window of the boudoir was half open. A bowl of chrystal water, containing gold and silver fish, stood upon a table in the recess of the casement. The chirrup of the birds echoed through the room, which was perfumed with the odour of sweet flowers.

By the wall facing the window stood a French bed, on the head and foot of which fell pink satin curtains, flowing from a gilt-headed arrow fixed near the ceiling.

It was now nine o'clock, and the sun shed a flood of golden light through the half-open casement upon that couch which was so voluptuous and so downy.

A female of great beauty, and apparently about five-and-twenty years of age, was reading in that bed. Her head reposed upon her hand, and her elbow upon the pillow: and that hand was buried in a mass of luxuriant light chestnut hair, which flowed down upon her back, her shoulders, and her bosom; but not so as altogether to conceal the polished ivory whiteness of the plump fair flesh.

The admirable slope of the shoulders, the swan-like neck, and the exquisite symmetry of the bust, were descried even amidst those masses of luxuriant and shining hair.

A high and ample forehead, hazel eyes, a nose perfectly straight, small but pouting lips, brilliant teeth, and a well rounded chin, were additional charms to augment the attractions of that delightful picture.

The whole scene was one of soft voluptuousness—the birds, the flowers, the vase of gold and silver fish, the tasteful arrangements of the boudoir, the French bed, and the beautiful creature who reclined in that couch, her head supported upon the well-turned and polished arm, the dazzling whiteness of which no envious sleeve concealed!

From time to time the eyes of that sweet creature were raised from the book, and thrown around the room in a manner that denoted, if not mental anxiety, at least a state of mind not completely at ease. Now and then, too, a cloud passed over that brow which seemed the

very throne of innocence and candour; and a sigh agitated the breast which the sunbeams covered as it were with kisses.

Presently the door was opened softly, and an elderly female, well but simply dressed, and of placid and reserved aspect, entered the room.

"Mr. Stephens is below," said the servant; "I told him you had not risen yet, and he says he will await your convenience."

"I know not how it is," exclaimed the lady impatiently, "but I never felt less disposed for the visit of him whom I regard as my benefactor. Ah! Louisa," she added, a cloud overspreading her entire countenance, "I feel as if one of those dreadful attacks of despondency—one of those fearful fits of alarm and foreboding—of presentiment of evil, were coming on; and——"

"Pray calm yourself," interrupted the servant, speaking in a kind and imploring tone. "Remember that the very walls have ears; that a word spoken in too high a tone may betray your secret; and heaven alone knows what would be the result of such an appalling discovery!"

"Yes—it is that horrible mystery," ejaculated the lady, "which fills me with the most acute apprehensions. Compelled to sustain a constant cheat—to feel that I am a living, a breathing, a moving falsehood, a walking lie;—forced to crush all the natural amenities—ay, and even the amiable weaknesses of my sex; governed by an imperious necessity against which it is now impossible to rebel,—how can I do otherwise than experience moments of unutterable anguish!"

"You must still have patience—patience only for a few months—three short months,—and the result of all this suspense—the end of all this anxiety, will be no doubt as advantageous—as immensely important and beneficial—as we are led to believe."

"True: we are bound to believe a man who seems so serious in all his actions with regard to me," said the lady, after a short pause, during which she seemed to be wrapped up in a deep reverie. "But why does he keep me in the dark with regard to the true nature of that grand result? Why does he not trust me, who have placed such unbounded, such implicit confidence in him?"

"He is afraid lest an unguarded moment on your part should betray what he assures us to be of the most vital—the last importance," answered the domestic, in a kindly remonstrative tone. "And really, my dearest girl," she added, affectionately,—"pardon me for calling you so——"

"Ah! Louisa, you are my dearest friend!" said the lady energetically. "You, and you alone, have supported my courage during the four years and a half that this horrible deceit has already lasted; your kindness——"

"I have only done my duty, and acted as my heart dictated," mildly replied the female dependant. "But as I was observing, you are so very imprudent, as it is; and can you expect that Mr. Stephens will reveal to you the minute details of a scheme, which——"

"Imprudent!" hastily exclaimed the lady: "how am I imprudent? Do I not follow all *his* directions—all *your* advice? Have I not even learned to talk to the very groom in his own language about the horses and the dogs? and do I not scamper across the country, upon my chestnut mare, with him following upon the bay horse at my heels, as if we were both mad? And then you say that I am imprudent, when I have done all I can to sustain the character which I have assumed? And with the exception of these rides, how seldom do I go abroad? Half-a-dozen names include all my acquaintances: and no one—no one ever comes here! This is, indeed, a hermit's dwelling! How can you say that I am imprudent?"

"Without going out of this very room," began Louisa, with a smile, "I could——"

"Ah! the eternal remonstrances against these habiliments of my sex!" exclaimed the lady, drawing back the satin curtain at the head of the bed with her snow-white arm, and glancing towards the bureau which contained the female dresses: "ever those remonstrances! Alas! I should die—I could not support this appalling deceit—were I not to gratify my woman's feelings from time to time! Do you think that I can altogether rebel against nature, and not experience the effects? And, in occasionally soothing my mind with the occupations natural to my sex, have I ever been imprudent? When I have dressed my hair as it should ever be dressed—when I have put on one of those silk or muslin robes, merely to see myself reflected in my mirror—and, oh! what a pardonable vanity under such circumstances!—have I ever been imprudent enough to set foot outside this retreat—this boudoir, to which you alone are ever admitted? Do I ever dress with the blinds of the windows raised? No: I have done all that human being can do to support my spirits during this sad trial, and sustain the character I have assumed. But if it be desired that I should altogether forget my sex—and cling to the garb of a man; if I may never—not even for an hour in the evening—follow my fantasy, and relieve my mind by resuming the garb which is natural to me—within these four walls—unseen by a soul save you——"

"Yes, yes, you shall have your way," interrupted Louisa soothingly. "But Mr. Stephens waits: will you not rise and see him?"

"It is my duty," said the lady resignedly. "He has surrounded me with every comfort and every luxury which appetite can desire or money procure; and, however he may ultimately benefit by this proceeding, in the meantime my gratitude is due to him."

"The delicacy of his conduct towards you equals his liberality," observed Louisa pointedly.

"Yes; notwithstanding the peculiarity of our relative position, not a word, not a look disrespectful towards me from the first moment of our acquaintance! He faithfully adheres to his portion of the contract, and I will as religiously observe mine."

"You speak wisely and consistently," said Louisa; "and the result of your honourable conduct towards Mr. Stephens will no doubt be a recompense which will establish your fortunes for life."

"That hope sustains me. Oh! how happy, thrice happy shall I be, when, the period of my emancipation being arrived, I may escape to some distant part of my own native country, or to some foreign clime, resume the garb belonging to my sex, and live in a way consistent with nature, and suitable to my taste. It is in anticipation of those golden moments that I from time to time retire into the impenetrable mystery of this boudoir, and dress myself in the garb which I love, and which is my own. And when that elysian age shall come, oh! how shall I divert my mind with a retrospection upon these long weary weeks and months, during which I have been compelled to study habits opposed to my taste and feeling—to affect a love of horses and dogs, that a manly predilection may avert attention from a feminine countenance,—and to measure each word that falls from my lips, to study each attitude which my form assumes, and to relinquish pursuits and occupations which my mind adores."

The lady threw herself back upon her pillow and gave way to a delicious reverie. Louisa did not attempt to disturb her for some minutes. At length she murmured something about "keeping Mr. Stephens waiting rather longer than usual;" and her mistress, acting by a sudden impulse, rose from her couch.

Then followed the mysterious toilet.

Stays, curiously contrived, gave to that exquisitely modelled form as much as possible the appearance of the figure of a man. The swell of the bosom, slightly compressed, was rendered scarcely apparent by padding skilfully placed, so as to fill up and flatten the undulating bust. The position of the waist was lowered; and all this was effected without causing the subject of so strange a transformation any pain or uneasiness.

The semi-military blue frock coat, buttoned up to the throat, completed the disguise; and as this species of garment is invariably somewhat prominent about the chest, the very fashion of its make materially aided an effectual concealment, by averting surprise at the gentle protuberance of the breast, in the present instance.

Louisa arranged the luxuriant and flowing hair with particular attention, bestowing as much as possible a masculine appearance upon that which would have been a covering worthy of a queen.

The toilet being thus completed, this strange being to whom we have introduced our readers, descended to a parlour on the ground floor.

When Louisa left the boudoir she carefully locked the door and consigned the key to her pocket.

CHAPTER VIII.

THE CONVERSATION.

THE parlour which that lovely and mysterious creature—who now seemed a youth of about twenty—entered upon the ground floor, was furnished with taste and elegance. Everything was light, airy, and graceful. The windows were crowded with flowers that imparted a delicious perfume to the atmosphere, and afforded a picture upon which the eye rested with pleasure.

A recess was fitted up with book-shelves, which were supplied with the productions of the best poets and novelists of England and France.

Around the walls were suspended several paintings—chiefly consisting of sporting subjects. Over the mantel, however, were two miniatures, executed in water-colours in the first style of the art, and representing the one a lovely youth of sixteen, the other a beautiful girl of twenty.

And never was resemblance more striking. The same soft and intelligent hazel eyes—the same light hair, luxuriant, silky, and shining—the same straight nose—the same vermilion lips, and well-turned chin. At a glance it was easy to perceive that they were brother and sister; and as the countenance of the former was remarkably feminine and delicate, the likeness between them was the more striking.

Beneath the miniature of the brother, in small gilt letters upon the enamelled frame, was the word WALTER: under the portrait of the sister was the name of ELIZA.

Attired as she now was, the mysterious being whom we have introduced to our readers, perfectly resembled the portrait of *Walter:*

attired as she ought to have been, consistently with her sex, she would have been the living original of the portrait of *Eliza*.

Upon a sofa in the parlour, some of the leading features of which we have just described, a man, dressed with great neatness, but no ostentatious display, was lounging.

He was in reality not more than three or four and thirty years of age; although a seriousness of countenance—either admirably studied, or else occasioned by habits of business and mental combination—made him appear ten years older. He was handsome, well-formed, and excessively courteous and fascinating in his manners: but, when he was alone, or not engaged in conversation, he seemed plunged in deep thought, as if his brain were working upon numerous plans and schemes of mighty and vital import.

The moment the heroine of the boudoir entered the parlour, Mr. Stephens—for he was the individual whom we have just described—rose and accosted her in a manner expressive of kindness, respect, and patronage.

"My dear Walter," he exclaimed, "it is really an age since I have seen you. Six weeks have elapsed, and I have not been near you. But you received my letter, stating that I was compelled to proceed to Paris upon most particular business?"

"Yes, my dear sir," answered the lady,—or in order that some name may in future characterise her, we will call her Walter, or Mr. Walter Sydney, for that was indeed the appellation by which she was known,—"yes, my dear sir, I received your letter, and the handsome presents and remittances accompanying it. For each and all I return you my sincere thanks: but really, with regard to money, you are far too lavish towards me. Remember that I scarcely have any opportunity of being extravagant," added Walter, with a smile: "for I scarcely ever stir abroad, save to take my daily rides; and you know that I never receive company, that my acquaintances are limited, so limited——"

"I know, my dear Walter, that you follow my advice as closely as can be expected," said Mr. Stephens. "Three short months more and my object will be achieved. We shall then be both of us above the reach of Fortune's caprices and vicissitudes. Oh! how glorious—how grand will be this achievement! how well worth all the sacrifices that I have required you to make."

"Ah! my dear sir," observed Walter, somewhat reproachfully, "you must remember that you are now talking enigmas to me; that I am at present only a blind instrument in your hands—a mere machine—an automaton——"

"Do not press me upon this head, Walter," interrupted Mr. Stephens, hastily. "You must not as yet be led to comprehend the magnitude of my views: you must have patience. Surely I have given you ample proofs of my good feeling and my honourable views towards yourself. Only conceive what would be your present position without me; not a relation, not a friend in the wide world to aid or protect you! I do not say this to vaunt my own conduct: I am merely advancing arguments to prove how confident I am in the success of my plans, and how sincere I am in my friendship towards you. For, remember, Walter—I always forget your sex: I only look upon you as a mere boy—a nephew, or a son, whom I love. Such is my feeling: I am more than a friend; for, I repeat, I feel a paternal attachment towards you!"

"And I entertain feelings of deep—yes, of the deepest gratitude towards you," said Walter. "But the motive of my constant intercession to be admitted more into your confidence, is to be convinced—by my own knowledge—that my present conduct tends to facilitate no dishonest, no dangerous views. Oh! you will pardon me when I say this; for there are times when I am a prey to the most horrible alarms—when fears of an indescribable nature haunt me for hours together—and when I seem to be walking blindfold upon the brink of an abyss!"

"Walter, I am surprised that you should thus give way to suspicions most injurious to my honour," said Mr. Stephens, whose countenance remained perfectly collected and unchanged; "for the hundredth time do I assure you that you have nothing to fear."

"Then wherefore this disguise? why this constant cheat relative to my sex? why this permanent deception?" demanded Walter, in an impassioned tone.

"Cannot the most rigorous honesty be connected with the most profound prudence—the most delicate caution?" said Mr. Stephens, adopting an attitude and manner of persuasion. "Do not judge of motives by their mere superficial aspect: strange devices—but not the less honourable for being singular—are frequently required in the world to defeat designs of infamy and baseness."

"Pardon my scepticism," said Walter, apparently convinced by this reasoning; "I was wrong, very wrong to suspect you. I will not again urge my anxiety to penetrate your secrets. I feel persuaded that you conceal the means by which our mutual prosperity is to be effected, simply for my good."

"Now you speak rationally, my dear, my faithful and confiding Walter," exclaimed Mr. Stephens. "It was just in this vein that I was anxious to find you; for I have an important communication to make this morning."

"Speak: I am ready to follow your instructions or advice."

"I must inform you, Walter, that in order effectually to work out my plans—in order that there should not exist the slightest chance of failure—a third person is required. It will be necessary that he should be conversant with our secret: he must know all; and, of course, he must be taken care of hereafter. To be brief, I have already fallen in with the very individual who will suit me; and I have acquainted him with the entire matter. You will not object to receive him occasionally as a guest?"

"My dear sir, how can I object? Is not this your house? and am not I in your hands? You now that you can command me in all respects."

"I thought that you would meet my views with this readiness and good will," said Mr. Stephens. "To tell you the real truth, then—I have taken the liberty of inviting him to dine with us here this day."

"To-day!"

"Yes. Are you annoyed?"

"Oh! not at all: only, the preparations——"

"Do not alarm yourself. While you were occupied with your toilet, I gave the necessary instructions to the cook. The old woman is almost blind and deaf, still she knows full well how to serve up a tempting repast; and as I am believed by your three servants to be your guardian, my interference in this respect will not have appeared strange."

"How could they think otherwise?" ejaculated Walter. "Did not you provide those dependants who surround me? Do they not look upon you as their master as well as myself? Are they not aware that the villa is your own property? And have they not been led to believe—with the exception of Louisa, who alone of the three knows the secret—that the state of my health compelled you to place me here for the benefit of a purer air than that which your residence in the city affords?"

"Well, since my arrangements meet with your satisfaction," said Mr. Stephens, smiling, "I am satisfied. But I should tell you that I invited my friend hither not only to dine, but also to pass the day, that we might have an opportunity of conversing together at our leisure. Indeed," added Mr. Stephens, looking at his watch, "I expect him here every moment."

Scarcely were the words uttered when a loud knock at the front door echoed through the house.

In a few minutes Louisa appeared, and introduced "Mr. Montague."

CHAPTER IX.

A CITY MAN.—SMITHFIELD SCENES.

George Montague was a tall, good-looking young man of about three or four-and-twenty. His hair and eyes were black, his complexion rather dark, and his features perfectly regular.

His manners were certainly polished and agreeable; but there was, nevertheless, a something reserved and mysterious about him—an anxiety to avert the conversation from any topic connected with himself—a studied desire to flatter and gain the good opinions of those about him, by means of compliments at times servile—and an occasional betrayal of a belief in a code of morals not altogether consistent with the well-being of society, which constituted features in his character by no means calculated to render him a favourite with all classes of persons. He was, however, well-informed upon most topics, ambitious of creating a sensation in the world, no matter by what means; resolute in his pursuit after wealth, and careless whether the paths leading to the objects which he sought were tortuous or straightforward. He was addicted to pleasure, but never permitted it to interfere with his business or mar his schemes. *Love* with him was merely the blandishment of beauty; and *friendship* was simply that bond which connected him with those individuals who were necessary to him. He was utterly and completely selfish; but he was somehow or another possessed of sufficient tact to conceal most of his faults—of the existence of which he was well aware. The consequence was that he was usually welcomed as an agreeable companion; some even went so far as to assert that he was a "devilish good fellow;" and all admitted that he was a thorough man of the world. He must have commenced his initiation early, thus to have acquired such a character ere he had completed his four-and-twentieth year!

London abounds with such precocious specimens of thorough heartlessness and worldly-mindedness. The universities and great public schools let loose upon society every half-year a cloud of young men, who think only how soon they can spend their own property in order to prey upon that of others. These are your "young men *about* town:" as they grow older they become "men *upon* the town." In their former capacity they graduate in all the degrees of vice, dissipation, extravagance, and debauchery; and in the latter they become the tutors of the novices who are entering in their turn upon the road to ruin. The transition from the young man about town to the man upon the town is as natural as that of a chrysalis to a butterfly. These men *upon* the town constitute as pestilential a section of male society as the women *of* the town do of the female portion of the community. They are alike the reptiles produced by the great moral dung-heap.

We cannot, however, exactly class Mr. George Montague with the men upon the town in the true meaning of the phrase, inasmuch as he devoted his attention to commercial speculations of all kinds and under all shapes, and his sphere was chiefly the City; whereas men upon the town seldom entertain an idea half "so vulgar" as mercantile pursuits, and never visit the domains of the Lord Mayor save when they want to get a bill discounted, or to obtain cash for a check of too large an amount to be entrusted to any of their high-born and aristocratic companions.

Mr. George Montague was, therefore, one of that multitudinous class called "City men," who possess no regular offices, but have their letters addressed to the Auction Mart or Garraway's, and who make their appointments at such places as "the front of the Bank," "the Custom-house Wharf," and "under the clock at the Docks."

City men are very extraordinary characters. They all know "a certain speculation that would make a sure fortune, if one had but the capital to work upon;" they never fail to observe, while making this assertion, that they *could* apply to a friend if they chose, but that they do not choose to lay themselves under the obligation; and they invariably affirm that nothing is more easy than to make a fortune in the City, although the greater portion of them remain without that happy consummation until the day of their deaths. Now and then, however, one of these City men *does* succeed in "making a hit" by some means or other; and then his old friends, the very men who are constantly enunciating the opinion relative to the facility with which fortunes are obtained in the City, look knowing, wink at each other, and declare "that it never could have been done unless he'd had somebody with plenty of money to back him."

Now Mr. Montague was one of those who adopted a better system of logic than the vulgar reasoning. He knew that there was but little merit in producing bread from flour, for instance: but he perceived that there was immense credit due to those who could produce their bread without any flour at all. Upon this principle he acted, and his plan was not unattended with success. He scorned the idea "that money was necessary to beget money;" he began his "City career," as he sometimes observed, without a farthing; and he was seldom without gold in his pocket.

No one knew where he lived. He was sometimes seen getting into a Hackney omnibus at the Flower Pot, a Camberwell one at the Cross Keys; or running furiously after a Hammersmith one along Cheapside; but as these directions were very opposite, it was difficult to deduce from them any idea of his domiciliary whereabouts.

He was young to be a City man; the class does not often include members under thirty; but of course there are exceptions to all rules; and Mr. George Montague was one.

He was then a City man: but if the reader be anxious to know what sort of *business* he transacted to obtain his living; whether he dabbled in the funds, sold wines upon commission, effected loans and discounts, speculated in shares, got up joint-stock companies, shipped goods to the colonies, purchased land in Australia at eighteenpence an acre and sold it again at one-and-nine,[1] conducted compromises for insolvent tradesmen, made out the accounts of bankrupts, arbitrated between partners who disagreed, or bought in things in a friendly way at public sales; whether he followed any of these pursuits, or meddled a little with them all, we can no more satisfy our readers than if we attempted the biography of the Man in the Moon,—all we

1 one-and-nine: one shilling and nine pence, or twenty-one pence, old style.

can say is, that he was invariably in the City from eleven to four; that he usually had "an excellent thing in hand just at that moment;" and, in a word, that he belonged to the class denominated *City Men!*

We have taken some pains to describe this gentleman; for reasons which will appear hereafter.

Having been duly introduced to Walter Sydney by Mr. Stephens, and after a few observations of a general nature, Mr. Montague glided almost imperceptibly into topics upon which he conversed with ease and fluency.

Presently a pause ensued; and Mr. Stephens enquired "if there were anything new in the City?"

"Nothing particular," answered Montague. "I have not of course been in town this morning; but I was not away till late last night. I had a splendid thing in hand, which I succeeded in bringing to a favourable termination. By-the-by there was a rumour on 'Change yesterday afternoon, just before the close, that Alderman Dumkins is all wrong."

"Indeed," said Stephens; "I thought he was wealthy."

"Oh! no; *I* knew the contrary eighteen months ago! It appears he has been starting a joint-stock company to work the Ercalat tin-mines in Cornwall——"

"And I suppose the mines do not really exist?"

"Oh! yes; they do—upon his maps! However, he has been exhibiting certain specimens of tin; which he has passed off as Ercalat produce; and it is now pretty generally known that the article was supplied him by a house in Aldgate."

"Then he will be compelled to resign his gown?"

"Not he! On the contrary, he stands next in rotation for the honours of the civic chair; and he intends to go boldly forward as if nothing had happened. You must remember that the aldermen of the City of London have degenerated considerably in respectability during late years, and that none of the really influential and wealthy men in the City will have anything to do with the corporation affairs. You do not see any great banker nor merchant wearing the aldermanic gown. The only alderman who really possessed what may be called a large fortune, and whose pecuniary position was above all doubt, resigned his gown the other day in disgust at the treatment which he received from his brother authorities, in consequence of his connexion with the *Weekly Courier*—the only newspaper that boldly, fearlessly, and effectually advocates the people's cause."[1]

"And Dumkins will not resign, you think?"

"Oh! decidedly not. But for my part," added Montague, "I feel convinced that the sooner some change is made in the city administration the better. Only conceive the immense sums which the corporation receives from various sources, and the uses to which they are applied. Look at the beastly guzzling at Guildhall, while there are in the very heart of the city Augean stables of filth, crime, and debauchery to be cleansed—witness Petticoat-lane, Smithfield——"

A species of groan or stifled exclamation of horror issued from the lips of Walter as Montague uttered these words: her countenance grew deadly pale, and her entire frame appeared to writhe under a most painful reminiscence or emotion.

"Compose yourself, compose yourself," said Stephens, hastily. "Shall I ring for a glass of water, or wine, or anything——"

"No, it is past," interrupted Walter Sydney; "but I never think of that horrible—that appalling adventure without feeling my blood curdle in my veins. The mere mention of the word Smithfield——"

"Could I have been indiscreet enough to give utterance to anything calculated to annoy?" said Montague, who was surprised at this scene.

"You were not aware of the reminiscence you awoke in my mind by your remark," answered Walter, smiling; "but were you acquainted with the particulars of that fearful night, you would readily excuse my weakness."

"You have excited Mr. Montague's curiosity," observed Stephens, "and you have now nothing to do but to gratify it."

"It is an adventure of a most romantic kind—an adventure which you will scarcely believe—and yet one that will make your hair stand on end."

"I am now most anxious to learn the details of this mysterious occurrence," said Montague, scarcely knowing whether these remarks were made in jest or earnest.

Walter Sydney appeared to reflect for a few moments; and then commenced the narrative in the following manner:—

"It is now a little more than four years ago—very shortly after

1 A Chartist newspaper, to which Reynolds was a contributor.

I first arrived at this house—that I rode into town, attended by the same groom who is in my service now. I knew little or nothing of the City, and felt my curiosity awakened to view the emporium of the world's commerce. I accordingly determined to indulge in a ramble by myself amidst the streets and thoroughfares of a place of which such marvellous accounts reach those who pass their youth in the country. I left the groom with the horses at a livery-stable in Bishopsgate-street, with a promise to return in the course of two or three hours. I then roved about to my heart's content, and never gave the lapse of time a thought. Evening came, and the weather grew threatening. Then commenced my perplexities. I had forgotten the address of the stables where the groom awaited my return; and I discovered the pleasing fact that I had lost my way just at the moment when an awful storm seemed ready to break over the metropolis. When I solicited information concerning the right path which I should pursue, I was insulted by the low churls to whom I applied. To be brief, I was overtaken by darkness and by the storm, in a place which I have since ascertained to be Smithfield market. I could not have conceived that so filthy and horrible a nuisance could have been allowed to exist in the midst of a city of so much wealth. But, oh! the revolting streets which branch off from that Smithfield. It seemed to me that I was wandering amongst all the haunts of crime and appalling penury of which I had read in romances, but which I never could have believed to exist in the very heart of the metropolis of the world. Civilisation appeared to me to have chosen particular places which it condescended to visit, and to have passed others by without even leaving a foot-print to denote its presence."

"But this horrible adventure?" said Montague.

"Oh! forgive my digression. Surrounded by darkness, exposed to the rage of the storm, and actually sinking with fatigue, I took refuge in an old house, which I am sure I could never find again; but which was situated nearly at the end, and on the right-hand side of the way, of one of those vile narrow streets branching off from Smithfield. That house was the den of wild beasts in human shape! I was compelled to hear a conversation of a most appalling nature between two ruffians, who made that place the depôt for their plunder. They planned, amongst other atrocious topics, the robbery of a country-seat, somewhere to the north of Islington, and inhabited by a family of the name of Markham."

"Indeed! What—how strange!" ejaculated Montague: then immediately afterwards, he added, "How singular that you should have overheard so vile a scheme!"

"Oh! those villains," continued Walter, "were capable of crimes of a far deeper dye! They discussed horror upon horror, till I thought that I was going raving mad. I made a desperate attempt to escape, and was perceived. What then immediately followed I know not, for I became insensible: in a word, Mr. Montague, I fainted!"

A deep blush suffused her countenance, as she made this avowal—for it seemed to have a direct relation to her sex; and she was well aware that the secret connected therewith had been revealed by her benefactor to George Montague. On his part, he gazed upon her with mingled interest and admiration.

"I awoke to encounter a scene of horror," she continued, after a short pause, "which you must fancy; but the full extent of which I cannot depict. I can only *feel* it even now. Those wretches were conveying me to a room upon the ground-floor—a room to which the cells of the Bastille or the Inquisition could have produced no equal. It had a trap-door communicating with the Fleet Ditch! I begged for mercy—I promised wealth—for I knew that my kind benefactor," she added, glancing towards Mr. Stephens, "would have enabled me to fulfil my pledge to them; but all was in vain. The murderers hurled me down the dark and pestiferous hole!"

"Merciful heavens!" ejaculated Montague.

"It would appear that the house in question," proceeded Walter, "stood upon the side of, and not over the Ditch. There can be, however, no doubt that the trap-door was contrived for the horrible purpose of disposing of those victims who fell into the merciless hands of the occupants of the dwelling; for when I had fallen some distance, instead of being immersed in black and filthy mud, I was caught upon a sloping plank which shelved towards a large aperture in the wall of the Ditch. I instinctively clung to this plank, and lay stretched upon it for some moments until I had partially recovered my presence of mind. The circumstance of having thus escaped a dreadful death gave me an amount of courage at which I myself was astonished. At length I began to reason whether it would be better to remain there until morning, and then endeavour to reach the trap-door above my head, or to devise some means of immediate escape. I decided upon the latter proceeding; for I reflected that the morning would not afford light to that subterranean hole to enable me to act with certainty; and I, moreover, dreaded the extreme vengeance of those ruffians who had already given me a sample of their brutality, should I happen to encounter them on emerging from the trap-door. Lastly, I considered that it was also probable that I might not succeed in raising the trap-door at all."

"What a fearful situation!" observed Montague.

"Horrible even to think of," added Stephens, who listened with the deepest attention to this narrative, although he had heard it related on former occasions.

"With my hands and legs I groped about," continued Walter, "and I speedily ascertained my exact position with regard to the locality. My feet were close to a large square aperture in the perpendicular wall overhanging the Ditch; and the floor of the cellar was only a couple of feet below the aperture. I accordingly got cautiously off the board, and stood upon the damp ground. After the lapse of several minutes, during which I nerved myself to adopt the idea that had struck me, I passed my head through the aperture, and looked out over the Ditch. The stream appeared rapid, to judge by its gurgling sound; and the stench that exhaled from it was pestiferous in the extreme. Turning my head to the left I saw hundreds of lights twinkling in the small narrow windows of two lines of houses that overhung the Ditch. The storm had now completely passed away—the rain had ceased—and the night was clear and beautiful. In a few minutes I was perfectly acquainted with the entire geography of the place. The means of escape were within my reach. About three feet above the aperture through which I was now looking, a plank crossed the Ditch; and on the opposite side—for the Ditch in that part was not above two yards wide from wall to wall—was a narrow ledge running along the side of the house facing the one in which I was, and evidently communicating with some lane or street close by. I can scarcely tell you how I contrived to creep through the aperture and reach the plank overhead. Nevertheless, I attempted the dangerous feat, and I accomplished it. I crossed the plank, and reached the ledge of which I have spoken: it terminated in the very street where stood the terrible den from which I had just so miraculously escaped. Indeed, I emerged upon that street only at a distance of a few yards from the door of that detestable place. To hurry away in a contrary direction was my first and most natural impulse; but I had not proceeded far when the door of a house was suddenly thrown violently open, and out poured a crowd of men and women, among whom I was, as it were, immediately hemmed in."

"What! another adventure?" exclaimed Montague.

"One calculated to inspire feelings of deep disgust, if not of alarm," answered Walter. "It appeared that two women had been quarrelling and had turned out to fight. They fell upon each other like wild cats, or as you would fancy that tigers would fight. A clear and lovely moon lighted this revolting scene. A circle was formed round the termagants, and for ten minutes did they lacerate themselves with fists and nails in a fearful manner. Their clothes were torn into ribands—their countenances were horribly disfigured with scratches—the blood poured from their noses—and their hair, hanging all dishevelled over their naked shoulders, gave them a wild, ferocious, and savage appearance, such as I never could have expected to encounter in the metropolis of the civilised world."

"And in the very heart of the City," added Mr. Montague.

"Suddenly a cry of '*The Bluebottles!*' was raised, and the crowd, belligerents and all, rushed pell-mell back again into the house. In spite of all my endeavours to escape I was hurried in with that hideous mob of ferocious-looking men and brazen-faced women. In a few moments I found myself in a large room, in which there were at least thirty wretched beds huddled close together, and so revoltingly dirty that the cold pavement or a hedge-side would have seemed a more preferable couch. And, oh! how can I describe the inmates of that den, many of whom were crowding round a fire cooking provender, which filled the place with a sickening and most fetid odour. There were young girls almost naked, without shoes or stockings, and whose sunken cheeks, dimmed eyes, and miserable attire contrasted strangely with their boisterous mirth. Some of these unfortunate creatures, nevertheless, retained traces of original beauty prematurely faded. The men were hatless and shoeless; indeed the entire assembly consisted of males and females evidently of the most wretched description. Scarcely had I time to cast a glance around me when I was questioned as to how I came there? what I wanted? and whether I meant to stand anything? 'I tell you what it is,' said one to his companions, 'he's a swell who is come to have a look at these kind of cribs, and he must pay his footing.' I immediately comprehended the nature of the impression which my presence had created, and presented the individual who had spoken with a couple of half-crowns. The sight of the money produced an immense feeling in my favour. Heaven only knows how many gallons of beer were fetched from a neighbouring public-house; and when the inmates of that lazar-house—for I can scarcely call it anything else—had all partaken of the liquor, I was overwhelmed with offers of service. One declared, that if I merely came to see the neighbourhood he would take me round to every place in the street; another assured me, that if I had committed a forgery or any other 'genteel crime,' he would either help me to lie secure until the matter had blown over, or to escape from the country; and so on. I suffered the wretches to retain the impression that curiosity had alone led me thither; and as soon as I had made this announcement the mistress of the house was summoned to do the honours of the establishment. A blear-eyed old crone made her appearance, and insisted upon showing me over the house. 'These rooms,' said she, meaning the two upon the ground floor, 'are for those who can afford to pay threepence for their bed and who have supper to cook.' We then ascended to the first floor. 'These are the fourpenny beds,' said the old woman, pointing with pride and satisfaction to some thirty or forty couches, a shade cleaner, and the least thing further off from each other than those down stairs. The rooms on the first floor were also filled with lodgers; and another demand was made upon my purse. On the third floor and in the attics were the most horrible scenes of wretchedness which I had yet beheld. Those dens were filled with straw beds, separated from each other only by pieces of plank about eight or ten inches in height. Men, women, and children were all crowded together—sleeping pell-mell. Oh! it was a horrible, horrible spectacle. To be brief, I escaped from that moral plague-house; and in a few moments was traversing Smithfield once more. Even the tainted air of that filthy enclosure was refreshing after the foul atmosphere from which I had just emerged.

Louisa entered the room at this moment to announce that luncheon was prepared in another apartment.

"And you never took any steps to root out that nest of villains in the Old House whence you escaped alive so miraculously?" said Montague, sipping a glass of exquisite wine after his luncheon.

"I wrote two anonymous letters the very next morning," answered Walter: "one to Mr. Markham, warning him of the contemplated burglary at his house; and another to the Lord Mayor of London. It did not altogether suit Mr. Stephens's plans——"

"No—not to make a fuss about an affair which would have been sure to bring your name into notoriety," added this gentleman hastily.

"That adventure has no doubt given you a distaste for late rambles," said Montague.

"In the City—decidedly so," was the reply. "I seldom go into London, early or late—I have so few inducements—so few acquaintances! By the way, a few evenings ago I treated myself to a visit to the Opera, and there accident threw me into conversation with a gentleman and lady who sat in the same box as myself. The result was an invitation to the abode of the lady—a Mrs. Arlington——"

"Mrs. Arlington," ejaculated Montague, a light flush animating his countenance.

"The same. She is *the friend* of Sir Rupert Harborough. I am anxious to see something of the world now and then—and to avail myself of my present garb for that purpose. I accordingly called upon Mrs. Arlington last evening, and learnt 'a lesson of life.' I saw an elegant woman, a baronet, a fashionable gentleman, and a very interesting young man, associating with a vulgar wretch of the name, I believe, of Talbot, whose manners would have disgraced a groom. I must, however, observe that the interesting young gentleman to whom I allude did not seem to be more pleased with the conversation and conduct of this vulgarian than myself. One coincidence somewhat extraordinary occurred—that same interesting young man was no other than Mr. Richard Markham, one of the sons of——"

"Ah! indeed—how singular!" exclaimed George Montague, not waiting till Walter finished his sentence; "very singular!" he added; then, having tossed off a bumper of Madeira, he walked up to the window, where he affected to inhale with delight the exquisite fragrance of the flowers that adorned the casement.

CHAPTER X.

THE FRAIL ONE'S[1] NARRATIVE.

WE must now return to Richard Markham.

Sir Rupert Harborough and the Honourable Arthur Chichester apparently took a very great fancy to him, for they were constantly making appointments to meet him in town, and hastening to his own house to ferret him out when he did not appear at their usual places of rendezvous. He dined at least three times a week at Mrs. Arlington's, and, to confess the truth, his morning calls were repeated at intervals which gradually grew shorter and shorter.

Richard thus frequently passed hours together alone with Diana. In spite of himself he now and then suffered his eyes to rest tenderly upon her countenance; and by degrees her glances encountered his and were not immediately withdrawn. Those glances were so languishing, and withal so melancholy, that they inspired Richard with a passion amounting almost to a delirium; and he felt at times as if he could have caught that beauteous creature in his arms and clasped her rapturously to his bosom.

One morning, as he took leave of her, he fancied that her hand gently pressed his own. The idea filled him with a joy till then unknown, and which he could not describe even to himself.

On the following morning he called a little earlier than usual. Diana was in a delicious *déshabillé*, which set off her voluptuous person to its very greatest advantage. Richard was more tender than usual—the Enchantress more enchanting.

They were seated upon the sofa together, and a pause in their conversation ensued. Richard heaved a deep sigh, and suddenly exclaimed, "I am always thinking of the period when I must bid adieu to your charming society."

"Bid adieu!" cried Diana; "and wherefore?"

"It must happen, sooner or later, that our ways in the world will be different."

"Then you are not your own master?" asked Diana, inquiringly.

1 Frail: a common euphemism for a prostitute or fallen woman.

"Certainly I am. But all friends must part some time or another."

"True," said Diana; then, in a subdued tone, she added, "There are certain persons who are attracted towards each other by kindred feelings and emotions, and it is painful—very painful, for them to part!"

"Heavens, Diana!" ejaculated Richard; "you feel as I do!"

She turned her face towards him: her cheeks were suffused in blushes, and her eyes were filled with tears. But through those tears she cast upon him a glance which ravished his inmost soul. It seemed fraught with love and tenderness, and inspired him with emotions which he had never known before. The words "You feel as I do," contained the ingenuous and unsophisticated avowal of a new passion on the part of a mind that was as yet as unskilled in the ways of this world as the unfledged bird in the nest of its mother is ignorant of the green woods. But those tears which stood in the lady's eyes, and the blushes which dyed her cheeks, and the glance which, like a sunbeam in the midst of an April shower, she darted upon the youth at her side, inspired him with courage, awakened undefined hopes, and filled him with an ecstacy of joy.

"Why do you weep, Diana? why do you weep?"

"You love me, Richard," she replied, turning her melting blue eyes fully upon him, and retaining them for some moments fixed upon his countenance: "you love me; and I feel—I know that I am not worthy of your affection!"

Richard started as if he were suddenly aroused from a dream—as if he had abruptly awoke to a stern truth from a pleasing vision. He suffered her hand, which he had taken in his, to fall from his grasp; and for some moments he remained buried in a profound reverie.

"Ah! I knew that I should remind you of your duty towards yourself," said Diana, bitterly. "No—I am not worthy of you. But that you may hereafter give me credit for frankness and candour,—that you may be actually warned by myself *against* myself,—that you may learn to esteem me as a friend, if you will, I shall in a few words relate to you the incidents that made me what I am!"

"Proceed," said Richard, "proceed! Believe me I shall listen with attention,—with the greatest attention!"

"My father was a retired tradesman," began Mrs. Arlington; "and as I was his only child and he enjoyed a competency, he gave me the best education that money could procure. Probably the good old man made up his mind that I should one day espouse a nobleman; and, as my mother had died when I was very young, there was no one near me to correct the vanity with which my father's adulation and ambitious pretensions inspired me. About three years ago I met at the theatre—whither I went with some friends—a young gentleman—tall, handsome, and fascinating like yourself. He contrived to obtain a formal introduction to my father, and was invited to our house, at which he speedily became a constant visitor. He had a happy tact in suiting his humours or tastes to those with whom he came in contact; and he quite won my father's heart by playing chess with him, telling him the news of the City, and reading the evening paper to him. George Montague soon became an established favourite; and my father could do nothing without him. At length Montague proposed to him certain speculations in the funds: my father was allured by the prospect of quadrupling his capital, and consented. I must confess that the young man's handsome person had produced a certain effect upon me—a giddy young girl as I was at that time; and I rather encouraged my father in these schemes than otherwise. At first the speculations were eminently successful; but in a short time they took a turn. Day after day did Montague come to the house to announce fresh losses and the necessity of farther advances. He declared that he should now speculate for a grand stake, which could not fail shortly to turn to his advantage. A species of infatuation seized upon my father; and I was not aware of the ruinous course he was pursuing until it was too late. At length my father was totally ruined; and George come to announce to us the failure of our last chance. My father now repented when it was too late. Eight short months had sufficed to dissipate his whole fortune; he had not even enough left to pay the few debts which he had contracted, and which he had neglected to liquidate, trusting each day to the arrival of the lucky moment when he should find himself the master of millions!"

"Oh! the absurd hope!" exclaimed Richard, deeply interested in this narrative.

"Alas! this event was a fatal blow to my father's health, at the same time that it wrecked his happiness," continued Diana. "He implored Montague not to desert 'his darling child'—for so he called me—in case anything should happen to himself; and that same day—the day on which he saw all his prospects and hopes in this life blasted—he put a period to his existence by means of poison!"

"This was horrible!" cried Markham. "Oh! that villain Montague!"

"My father's creditors came to seize the few effects which remained," said Diana, after a pause: "and I was about to be turned houseless and unprotected into the streets, when Montague arrived. He took gold from his pocket, and satisfied the demands of the creditors. He moreover supplied me with money for my immediate wants. I was totally dependent upon him;—I had no relations—no friends to whom I could apply for succour or comfort. He seemed to commiserate my position——"

"Perhaps," observed Richard, "he was not so very guilty, after all, relative to the loss of your father's property?"

"Judge by the sequel," answered Diana bitterly. "He was as base as he was in reality unfeeling. The transition from that state of dependence upon a young man to a more degraded one still, was to be expected. He no longer talked to me of marriage, as he once had done; but he took advantage of my forlorn situation. I became his mistress."

"Ah! it was base—it was ungenerous—it was unmanly!" ejaculated Richard.

"He seemed to be possessed of ample resources; but he accounted for this circumstance by assuring me that he had found another friend who was backing him in the same speculations in which my poor father had failed. We lived together for four months; and he then coolly informed me that we must part. I found that I had never really entertained any very sincere affection for him; and the little love which I experienced at first, had been quenched in my bosom by his cold cruelty. He seemed unfeeling to a degree. Observations, calculated to wound most acutely, fell from his lips upon all occasions——"

"The dastard!" exclaimed Richard, profoundly touched by this recital.

"If I wept at this cruelty, he treated me with increased brutality. You may, therefore, suppose that I was not deeply distressed to part with him. He gave me twenty guineas, and bade me a chilling farewell. From that moment I have neither seen nor heard of him. A few weeks after our separation my money was exhausted. I resolved to lead a virtuous and honourable life, and atone for my first fault. O God! I did not then know that society will not receive the penitent frail one;—that society excludes poor deceived woman from all hopes of reparation, all chances of repentance! I endeavoured to obtain a situation as a governess;—I might as well have attempted to make myself queen of England. Character—references! I had neither. Vainly did I implore one lady to whom I applied to give me a month's trial. She insulted me grossly. To another I candidly confessed my entire history: she patiently heard me to the end, and then ordered her lacquey to turn me out of the house. Oh! society does more than punish: it pursues the unfortunate female who has made one false step, with the most avenging and malignant cruelty;—it hunts her to suicide or to new ways of crime. These are the dread alternatives. At that moment, had some friendly hand been stretched out to aid me,—had I met with one kind heart that would have believed in the possibility of repentance,—had I only been blest with the chance of entering upon a career of virtue, I should have been saved! Yes—I should have redeemed my first fault, as far as redemption was possible;—and to accomplish that aim, I would have worked my nails down to the very quick,—I would have accepted any position, however menial,—I would have made any sacrifice, enjoyed any lot, so long as I was assured of earning my bread in a manner which need not make me blush. But society treated me with contempt. Why, in this Christian country, do they preach the Christian maxim, that '*there is more joy over one sinner who repenteth, than over ninety-and-nine just persons who need no repentance?*' Why is this maxim preached, when the entire conduct of society expresses in terms which cannot be misunderstood, a bold denial of its truth?"

"Merciful heavens," ejaculated Richard, "can this be true? are you drawing a correct picture, Diana, or inventing a hideous fiction?"

"God knows how true is all I say!" returned Mrs. Arlington, with profound sincerity of tone and manner. "Want soon stared me in the face: what could I do? Chance threw me in the way of Sir Rupert Harborough:—compelled by an imperious necessity, I became his mistress. This is my history."

"And the baronet treats you kindly?" said Richard, inquiringly.

"The terms upon which our connexion is based do not permit him an opportunity of being either very kind or very cruel."

"I must now say farewell for the present," exclaimed Markham, afraid of trusting himself longer with the Syren who had fascinated him with her misfortunes as well as by her charms. "In a day or two I will see you again. Oh! I cannot blame you for what you have done:—I commiserate—I pity you! Could any sacrifice that I am capable of making, restore you to happiness and—and—"

"Honour, you would say," exclaimed Diana, firmly.

"I would gladly make that sacrifice," added Richard. "From this moment we will be friends—very sincere friends. I will be your brother,—dearest Diana—and you shall be my sister!"

The young man rose from the sofa, as he uttered these disjointed sentences in a singularly wild and rapid manner; and Diana, without making any reply, but apparently deeply touched, pressed his hand for some moments between both her own.

Richard then hastily escaped from the presence of that charming and fascinating creature.

CHAPTER XI.

"THE SERVANTS' ARMS."

UPON the same day that this event took place, Mr. Whittingham, the butler of Richard Markham, had solicited and obtained permission to pass the evening with a certain Mr. Thomas Suggett, who occupied the distinguished post of *valet de chambre* about the person of the Honourable Arthur Chichester. Whittingham was determined to enjoy himself:—he seemed suddenly to have cast off twenty years from his back, and to walk the more upright for having rid himself of the burthen;—his hat was slightly cocked on one side; and, as he walked along, with Mr. Thomas Suggett tucked under his arm, he struck his silver-headed bamboo, which he always carried with him when he went abroad on Sundays and holidays, very forcibly upon the pavement. Mr. Suggett declared "that, for his part, he was very well disposed for a spree;" and he threw into his gait a most awful swagger, which certainly excited considerable attention, because all the small boys in the streets laughed at him as he wended on his way.

"I wonder what them urchins are garping at so," said Whittingham. "It mystificates me in no inconsiderable degree. Raly the lower orders of English is exceedingly imperlite. I feel the most inwigorated disgust and the most unboundless contempt for their manners."

"That's jist like me," observed Suggett: "I can't a-bear the lower orders. I hate everythink wulgar.—But, by the bye, Mr. Whittingham, do you smoke?"

"I can't say but what I like a full-flavoured Havannah—a threepenny, mind," added the butler, pompously.

"Just my taste, Mr. Whittingham. If I can't afford threepennies, I won't smoke at all."

Mr. Suggett entered a cigar shop, purchased half-a-dozen *real Havannahs*, (manufactured in St. John-street, Clerkenwell), joked with the young lady who served him, and then presented the one which he considered the best to his companion. The two gentlemen's gentlemen accordingly lighted their cigars, and then continued their walk along the New Road, in the vicinity of which Mr. Whittingham had met Mr. Suggett by appointment upon this memorable afternoon.

In a short time Mr. Suggett stopped suddenly at the door of a large white public-house, not a hundred miles distant from the new church, St. Pancras.

"This is a nice crib," said he. "Excellent company; and to-night there is a supper at eleven."

"The very identified thing," acquiesced Mr. Whittingham; and into the public-house they walked.

Nothing could be more neat and cleanly than the bar of the *Servants' Arms*—no one more obliging nor bustling than the "young lady" behind the bar. The *Servants' Arms* was reported to draw the best liquor in all the neighbourhood; and its landlord prided himself upon the superiority of his establishment over those which sold beer "at three-pence a-pot in your own jugs." And then what a rapid draught the landlord had for all his good things; and how crowded was the space before the bar with customers.

"Glass of ale—mild, Miss, if you please," said one.

"A quartern of gin and three outs, Caroline," cried a second, who was more familiar.

"Pint of half-and-half, here," exclaimed a third.

"Six of brandy, warm, Miss—four of gin, cold, and a pint of ale with the chill off—parlour!" ejaculated the waiter, who now made his appearance at the bar.

"Pot of porter; and master's compliments, and can you lend him yesterday's *Advertiser* for half an hour or so?" said a pretty little servant girl, placing a large yellow jug on the bright lead surface of the bar.

"Pot of ale, and a screw, Miss."

"Pint of gin, for mixing, please."

"Bottle of Cape wine, at eighteen, landlord."

"Four-penn'orth of rum, cold without."

"Half pint of porter, and a pipe, Caroline."

Such were the orders, issued from all quarters at the same moment, and to which Caroline responded with incredible alacrity; finding time to crack a joke with the known frequenters of the house, and to make a pleasant observation upon the weather to those whose faces were strange to her;—while the landlord contented himself with looking on, or every now and then drawing a pot of beer, apparently as a great favour and in a lazy independant manner. Nevertheless, he was a good, civil kind of a man: only somewhat independent, because he was growing rich. He was never afraid at the end of the month to see Truman and Hanbury's collector, and Nicholson's man, alight from their gigs at his door. They were always sure to find the money ready for them, when they sate down to write their receipts in the little narrow slip of a parlour behind the bar. In fact, the landlord of the *Servants' Arms*, was reported to be doing "a very snug business:"—and so he was.

Messrs. Whittingham and Suggett sauntered leisurely into the parlour of the *Servants' Arms*, and took their seats at the only table which remained unoccupied.

"Good evening, Sir," said the waiter, addressing Mr. Suggett with a sort of semi-familiarity, which showed that the latter gentleman was in the habit of "using the house."

"How are you, William?" cried Mr. Suggett, in a patronising manner. "George been here lately?"

"Not very: I think he's down in the country."

"Oh! Well, what shall we have, Mr. Whittingham—brandy and water?"

"That's my inwariable beverage, Mr. Suggett."

"Two sixes, gentlemen?" said the waiter.

"No," answered Mr. Whittingham, solemnly; "two shillings' worth, to begin with."

The liquor was supplied, and when the two gentlemen had tasted it, and found it to their liking, they glanced around the room to survey the company. It soon appeared that Mr. Suggett was well known to many of the gentlemen present; for, upon making his survey, he acknowledged, with a nod or a short phrase, the bows or salutations of those with whom he was acquainted.

"Ah! Mr. Guffins, always up in the same corner, eh?" said he, addressing a middle-aged man in seedy black: "got a new work in the press, 'spose? You literary men contrive to enjoy yourselves, I know. How do you do, Mr. Mac Chizzle?" looking towards a short, pock-marked man, with a quick grey eye, and black hair combed upright off his forehead: "how get on the clients? Plenty of business, eh? Ah! you lawyers always contrive to do well. Mr. Drummer, your servant, sir. Got a good congregation still, sir?"

"The chapel thriveth well, I thank you—as well as can be expected in these times of heathen abominations," answered a demure-looking middle-aged gentleman, who was clad in deep black and wore a white neck-cloth, which seemed (together with the condition of his shirt and stockings) to denote that although he had gained the confidence of his flock, he had certainly lost that of his washer-woman. After having taken a long draught of a pint of half-and-half which stood before him, he added, "There is a many savoury vessels in my congregation—reputable, pious, and prayer-full people, which pays regular for their sittings and fears the Lord."

"Well, I am glad of that," ejaculated Mr. Suggett. "But, ah!" he cried, observing a thin white-haired old gentleman, with huge silver spectacles hanging half-way down his nose,—"I'm glad to see Mr. Cobbington here. How gets on the circulating library, eh—sir?"

"Pretty well—pretty well, thank'ee," returned the bookseller: "pretty well—considering."

A great many people qualify their observations and answers by the addition of the word "*considering*;" but they seldom vouchsafe an explanation of *what is to be considered*. Sometimes they use the phrase "considering all things;" and then the mind has so much to consider, that it cannot consider any one thing definitively. It would be much more straightforward and satisfactory if persons would relieve their friends of all suspense, and say boldly at once, as the case may be, "*considering* the execution I have got in my house;"[1] or "*considering* the writ that's out against me;" or even "*considering* the trifling annoyance of not having a shilling in my pocket, and not knowing where to look for one." But, somehow or another, people never will be candid now-a-days; and Talleyrand was right when he said that "language was given to man to enable him to conceal his thoughts."

But to continue.

Mr. Suggett glanced a little further around the room, and recognized another old acquaintance.

"Ah! Snoggles, how are you?"

"Very well, thank'ee—how be you?"

"Blooming; but how come you here?"

"I dropped in quite permiscuously," answered Snoggles, "and finding good company, stayed. But it is up'ards o' three years since I see you, Mr. Suggett."

---

1 execution: in this sense, the execution of a writ for distraint of goods; or, in short, having the bailiffs in. This sense is still current in Ireland.

"About. What grade do you now fill in the profession? Any promotion?"

"I'm sorry to say not," replied Mr. Snoggles, shaking his head mournfully. "I've tumbled off the box down to a level with the osses;" which, being interpreted, means that Mr. Snoggles had fallen from the high estate of coachman to the less elevated rank of ostler. "But what rank do you *now* hold?"

"I left off the uniform of *tiger* last month," answered Mr. Suggett, "and received the brevet of walley-de-chambre."

"That gentleman one of the profession?" demanded Snoggles, alluding to Mr. Whittingham.

"Mr. Markham's butler, sir, at your service," said Whittingham, bowing with awe-inspiring stiffness: "and I may say, without exaggerating, sir, and in no wise compromising my indefatigable character for weracity, that I'm also Mr. Markham's confidential friend. And what's more, gen'leman," added the butler, glancing proudly around the room. "Mr. Richard Markham is the finest young man about this stupendous city of the whole universe—and that's as true as that this is a hand."

As Mr. Whittingham concluded this sentence, he extended his arm to display the hand relative to which he expressed such confidence; and while he flourished the arm to give weight to his language, the aforesaid hand encountered the right eye of the dissenting parson.

"A case of assault and battery," instantly exclaimed Mr. Mac Chizzle, the lawyer; "and here are upwards of a dozen witnesses for the plaintiff."

"I really beg the gentleman's pardon," said Whittingham.

"Special jury—sittings after term—damages five hundred pounds," exclaimed Mac Chizzle.

"No harm was intended," observed Suggett.

"Not a bit," added Snoggles.

"Verdict for Plaintiff—enter up judgment—issue execution—*ca. sa.*[1] in no time," said Mac Chizzle doggedly.

"I am used to flagellations and persecutions at the hands of the ungodly," said the Reverend Mr. Drummer, rubbing his eye with his fist, and thereby succeeding in inflaming it.

---

1 Abbreviation of *capias ad satisfaciendum*, a writ issued upon a judgment in a personal action for the recovery of money.

"Perhaps the reverend gentleman wouldn't take it amiss if I was to offer him my apologies in a extra powerful glass of brandy and water?" exclaimed Whittingham.

"Bribery," murmured Mac Chizzle.

"No, let us have a bowl of punch at once," exclaimed Suggett.

"And corruption," added the lawyer.

The bowl of punch was ordered, and the company was invited to partake of it. Even Mr. Mac Chizzle did not hesitate; and the dissenting minister, in order to convince Mr. Whittingham that he entirely forgave him, consented to partake of the punch so often that he at length began slapping Mr. Whittingham upon the back, and declaring that he was the best fellow in the world.

The conversation became general; and some of it is worth recording.

"I hope to have your patronage, sir, for my circulating library," said Mr. Cobbington to the butler.

"Depends, sir, upon the specified nature of the books it contains," was the reply.

"I have nothing but moral romances in which vice is always punished and virtue rewarded."

"That conduct of yours is highly credulous to you."

"All books is trash, except one," observed Mr. Drummer, winking his eyes in an extraordinary manner. "They teaches naught but swearing, lewd conversation, ungodliness, and that worst of all vices—intemperance."

"I beg you to understand, sir," exclaimed Mr. Guffins, who had hitherto remained a silent spectator of the proceedings, although a persevering partaker of the punch; "I beg you to understand, Mr. Drummer, *my* works, sir, are not the trash you seem to allude to."

"I won't understand nothing nor nobody," answered the reverend gentleman, swaying backwards and forwards in his chair. "Leave me to commune with myself upon the vanities of this wicked world, and—and—drink my punch in quiet."

"Humbug!" exclaimed the literary man, swallowing his resentment and the remainder of his punch simultaneously.

"Ah!" said the bookseller, after a pause; "nothing now succeeds unless it's in the comic line. We have comic Latin grammars, and comic Greek grammars; indeed, I don't know but what English grammar, too, is a comedy altogether. All our tragedies are made into comedies by the way they are performed; and no work sells without comic illustrations to it. I have brought out several new comic works, which have been very successful. For instance, '*The Comic Wealth of Nations;*' '*The Comic Parliamentary Speeches;*' '*The Comic Report of the Poor-Law Commissioners,*' with an Appendix containing the '*Comic Dietary Scale;*' and the '*Comic Distresses of the Industrious Population.*' I even propose to bring out a '*Comic Whole Duty of Man.*' All these books sell well: they do admirably for the nurseries of the children of the aristocracy. In fact they are as good as manuals and text-books."

"This rage for the comic is most unexpressedly remarkable," observed the butler.

"It is indeed!" ejaculated Snoggles; and, in order to illustrate the truth of the statement, he jerked a piece of lemon-peel very cleverly into the dissenting parson's left eye.

"That's right—stone me to death!" murmured the reverend gentleman. "My name is Stephen—and it is all for righteousness' sake! I know I'm a chosen vessel, and may become a martyr. My name is Stephen, I tell you—Stephen Drum—um—ummer!"

He then began an eulogium upon meekness and resignation under injuries, and reiterated his conviction that he was a chosen vessel; but, becoming suddenly excited by a horse-laugh which fell upon his ear, he forgot all about the chosen vessel, and lifted another very savagely from the table. In a word, he seized a pewter pot in his hand, and would have hurled it at Mr. Snoggles' head, had not Mr. Whittingham stopped the dangerous missile in time, and pacified the reverend gentleman by calling for more punch.

"We must certainly have those two men bound over to keep the peace," said Mac Chizzle; "two sureties in fifty, and themselves in a hundred, each."

"I shall dress the whole scene up for one of the *Monthlies,*" observed Mr. Guffins.

"If you do, you'll be indictable for libel," said Mac Chizzle. "The greater the truth, the greater the libel."

In the meanwhile Suggett and his friend Snoggles drew close to each other, and entered into conversation.

"It must be about three years since I saw you last," said the latter.

"Three year, come January," observed Suggett.

"Ah! I've seed some strange wicissitudes in the interval," continued Snoggles. "I went abroad as coachman, with a dashing young chap of the name of Winchester—"

"The devil you did! how singular! why my present guvner's name is Chichester."

"Well, I des say they're cousins then," said the ostler; "but I hope your'n won't treat you as mine did me. He seemed to have no end of tin for some months, and lived—my eye, how he lived! King's Bench dinners ain't nothin' to what his'n was; and yet I've heard say that the prisoners live there better than their creditors outside. Howsomever—things didn't always go on swimmingly. We went to Baden—called so cos of the baths; and there my guvner got involved in some gambling transactions, as forced him to make his name *Walker*. Well, he bolted, leaving all his traps behind, and me amongst them, and not a skurrick to pay the hotel bill and find my way back agin to England. The landlord he seized the traps, and I was forced to walk all the way to— I forget the name of the place—"

"Constantinople, perhaps," said Suggett, kindly endeavouring to assist his friend in his little geographical embarrassments.

"No; that ain't it," returned Snuggles. "Howsomever, I had every kind of difficulty to fight up against; and I never see my guvner from that day to this. He owed me eight pound, nineteen, and sixpence for wages; and he was bound by contract to bring me back to England."

"Disgraceful raskel, that he was!' ejaculated Mr. Suggett. "I raly think that we gentlemen ought to establish a society for our protection. The Licensed Witlers have *their* Association; why shouldn't we have the Gentlemen's Gentlemen organized into a society?"

"Why not?" said Snoggles.

The waiter now acquainted the company that supper was ready in an upstairs room for those who liked to partake of it. All the gentlemen whose names have been introduced to the reader in connection with the parlour of the *Servants' Arms*, removed to the banqueting saloon, where the table was spread with a snow-white cloth and black handled knives and forks. At intervals stood salt-cellars and pepper boxes, the latter resembling in shape the three little domes upon the present National Gallery in Trafalgar Square. A huge round of boiled beef tripe both boiled and fried, and rump steaks, formed the supper. The methodist parson insisted upon being allowed to say grace—or, as he expressed it, "ask a blessing," for which purpose the same neighbours who had kindly helped him up the stairs, now sustained him upon his legs. Dread was the havoc then made upon the various dainties on the table, Mr. Guffins being especially characterised by a good appetite upon this occasion.

The Reverend Mr. Drummer was also far from being behind-hand in this onslaught upon the luxuries supplied by the *Servants' Arms*; and while he bolted huge mouthfuls of boiled beef, he favoured the company with an excellent moral dissertation upon abstemiousness and self-mortification. Mr. Drummer was, however, one of those who content themselves with inculcating morality, and do not consider it necessary to set an example in their own persons; for, after having clearly demonstrated that gluttony and drunkenness lead to blasphemy, ungodliness, and profane swearing, he abruptly turned to the landlord, who presided at the supper-table, and, holding his plate to be filled for the fourth time, exclaimed, "D—n your eyes, don't cut it so infernally thick!"

After supper, "glasses round" of hot brandy and water were introduced, and the conversation was carried on with considerable spirit. It was midnight before the party thought of breaking up, although several of the gentlemen present had already begun to see three or four Dutch clocks staring them in the face besides the one which graced the wall. As for the Reverend Mr. Drummer, he declared that he was so affected by the ungodly proceedings of those present that he should forthwith endeavour to wash away their guilt with his tears; and it is distressing to be compelled to observe that all the reward this truly pious and deserving man experienced at the hands of the ungrateful company, was the cruel accusation that he was "crying drunk." This disgraceful behaviour produced such an effect upon his naturally nervous temperament, that he fell flat upon the floor, and was compelled to be taken in a wheelbarrow to his own house close by.

We may also add here that on the following day this proceeding was rumoured abroad, so that the much injured minister was necessitated to justify his conduct from the pulpit on the ensuing sabbath. This he did so effectually, that two old ladies, who carried small flasks of brandy in their pockets, were conveyed out of the chapel in a peculiar state—no doubt overpowered by the minister's eloquence. They however recovered at the expiration of some hours, and immediately opened a subscription to present a piece of plate to the Reverend Stephen Drummer, together with a vote of thanks and confidence on the part of the congregation. The vote was respectfully, but gratefully declined by this holy man; but, after some little entreaty, he was prevailed upon to accept the plate. From that time to the present day his congregation has been rapidly increasing; and, although envy and jealousy have declared that he himself helped to augment its numbers in the shape of three innocent little children by different servant-girls, he very properly disdained to contradict the report, and is considered by his flock to be a chosen and savoury vessel of the Lord.

CHAPTER XII.

THE BANK-NOTES.

When Richard left the presence of Diana, after the full confession of her frailty, he hurried home on horseback at a rate which kept pace with his thoughts.

Upon reaching his dwelling, he retired to his apartment, and sate himself down seriously to consider all that had taken place.

His eyes were now open to two facts:—in the first instance he saw that he had been giving way to a passion which was dishonourable in respect to the relations existing between its object and another individual—the baronet; and, secondly, he perceived that even if that barrier were removed, Diana was not the being whom he ought to make the partner of his fortunes. He was endowed with feelings and notions of the most scrupulous honour; and he deeply regretted that he should ever have been induced to utter a word or manifest a sentiment towards Diana, which he would have been ashamed for the baronet to become acquainted with. To such an extent did he carry his notions of honour, that if, for instance, he had pledged himself to keep a secret, he would sooner have suffered himself to be put to death than have forfeited his word. Even were a crime communicated to him in confidence, he would not have benefitted society by handing the perpetrator over to justice. He thus fell into an extreme almost as dangerous and fatal as the total absence of moral rectitude.

If the reader should marvel how a young man possessing such

punctilious sentiments, could have so far forgotten himself as to declare his affection to one who stood in the light of a friend's wife,—let it be remembered that he was surprised into a partial avowal of that passion: and that a certain impulse, favoured by a rapid succession of visits, parties, and *téte-â-téte* interviews, in which the object thereof was always present, had hurried him onward up to that point when a word was to decide his fate.

Love is a stream so rapid that he who embarks upon it does not observe that his rude boat crushes the beauteous flowers upon the banks between which it passes:—it is a river whose waters are those of oblivion, in which all other passions, sentiments, and ideas are swallowed up.

O woman, what power hast thou over the heart of man! Thou wast born a creature of grace and fascination: to whatever clime thou dost belong, neither habit nor costume can deface in thee that natural charm of witchery and love which characterises thee in all the relations of life.

Richard had not been long alone, when a knock at his door aroused him from the reverie in which he had been plunged; and Mr. Chichester entered the room.

"My dear Markham," said he, "you must excuse the liberty which I take in thus intruding upon your privacy; but what is the meaning of this? You were to lunch with Harborough to-day, and we were all to dine together in the evening. You called at Diana's; and from what you said upon leaving, she fancied you were coming straight home. So I have galloped all this way after you. You shut yourself up from your friends as if you had a design upon your life."

"I am not well—I am anxious to be alone."

"But I shall not allow you to remain alone," said Chichester. "If you should feel melancholy, what guarantee have I that you will not commit suicide, or do what is nearly as bad—sit down and write sentimental poetry?"

"I am not very likely to do either."

"You must come and join us: the baronet ——"

"I would rather ——"

"I can take no excuse. Order round your chestnut, and let us be off."

"Well—at all events I must go straight into the City first," said Markham. "I have occasion to call at my guardian's banker."

"Will you join me at seven precisely this evening, at Harborough's own lodgings in Conduit-street? We shall expect you."

"You may rely upon me," answered Markham, who now suddenly experienced an anxiety for society and bustle. "But who will be there?"

"Only the baronet, you, I, and Talbot—a *partie quarre*. Talbot is really a good fellow at heart, and has taken a great liking to you. Besides, he is the most liberal and generous fellow in existence. He sent a hundred pounds to every hospital in London yesterday morning—his annual donations; and he thinks that no one knows anything about it. He always puts himself down as X. Y. Z. in the lists of charitable subscriptions: he is so unostentatious!"

"Those are admirable traits in his character."

"They are, indeed. Just now, for instance, he heard of a horrid case of distress. Only conceive a poor man, with nine small children and a wife just ready to present him with a tenth, dragged to Whitecross Street Prison,[1] for a paltry hundred pounds! Talbot instantly called me aside, and said, '*Chichester, my dear fellow, I have not time to attend to any business to-day. There is a five hundred pound note; have the kindness to get it changed for me, and devote a hundred pounds to save the unhappy family.*' Those were Talbot's own words," added Mr. Chichester, surveying Richard in a peculiar manner from under his eyebrows.

"How liberal! how grand! how noble!" exclaimed Richard, forgetting all Mr. Talbot's vulgarity and coarseness, as he listened to these admirable traits of philanthropy. "To be candid with you, I am myself going to the banker's to draw some money; and when I see you this evening, I shall be happy to place twenty pounds in your hands for the use of that poor family."

"No, my dear fellow, keep your money: the baronet and I shall take care of those poor people."

"Nay—I insist—"

"Well—I am sorry now that I told you of the circumstance."

"And I am very glad."

"There—you shall have your own way then. But, by the by," added Chichester, a sudden thought appearing to strike him, "you are going into the City, and to your banker's?"

1 Whitecross Street Prison: an old prison for debtors, pulled down in 1877. Whitecross Street ran between Fore Street and Old Street, in Moorfields; the prison stood on the corner of Fore Street.

"Yes. And you?"

"I am anxious to get back to the West End as hastily as possible," answered Chichester. "You could do me a service, if you would?"

"Name it," said Richard.

"Get this note changed for me in the City," returned Chichester: and as he spoke he drew a Bank of England note for five hundred pounds from his pocket.

"Oh! certainly," cried Markham; and he took charge of the note accordingly.

He and Mr. Chichester then separated. Richard mounted his horse and rode towards the City, while his friend proceeded to the West End.

At seven o'clock Richard was ushered into Sir Rupert Harborough's drawing-room in Conduit-street, Hanover Square.

"There!" exclaimed Chichester, who was lounging upon the sofa; "I knew that my melancholy young gentleman would be punctual."

"Delighted to see you, Markham," said the baronet, pressing his hand with more than usual fervour.

"How are you, my tulip?" shouted Talbot. "Why, Chichester said you had the blue devils!"

"I really felt unequal to society to-day," returned Richard; "and I fancied that a little rest——"

"A little humbug!" ejaculated Mr. Talbot. "That's all my eye and my elbow, Markham. A d—d good bottle of champagne will soon put you to rights. But when I'm ill, what do you think I always take?"

"I really can't guess."

"Why, going to bed I always take a pint of dog's nose. There's nothing like dog's-nose for getting into the system. You must have it in the pewter, you know—and nice and hot: you will then sweat a bucket-full in the course of the night, and get up in the morning as right as a trivet. I can assure you there's nothing like dog's-nose."

"And pray what is dog's-nose?" enquired Richard.

"Well, may I be hanged! you are jolly green not to know what dog's-nose is! You take half a pint of the best half-and-half—or you may have ale all alone, if you like—a quartern of blue ruin——"

"It is a mixture of gin, beer, and sugar," said Mr. Chichester, impatiently.

"Well, and why couldn't you let me tell the gentleman how

to make dog's-nose in my own manner?" asked Talbot, somewhat sulkily. "However, there's nothing better than dog's-nose for the gripes, or wind on the stomach, or the rheumatics. For my part——"

"D—n your part!" cried the Honourable Arthur Chichester, now absolutely losing all patience.

Fortunately for all parties, the door was at that moment thrown open, and a valet announced that dinner was served up. Richard took advantage of the haste with which Mr. Talbot rushed down stairs to the dining-room, to slip a bundle of Bank of England notes and a quantity of gold into Chichester's hand, whispering at the same time, "There is your change, together with my twenty pounds for the poor family."

"Thank you, my boy," said Chichester; and over Markham's shoulder, he exchanged with the baronet a significant glance of satisfaction amounting almost to joy.

Meantime Mr. Talbot had rushed to his place at the dinner-table, declaring that "he was uncommonly peckish," and began sharpening his two knives one against the other. The baronet took his seat at the top of the table; Mr. Chichester at the bottom; and Markham sate opposite to Talbot.

"This soup is unexceptionable," observed Chichester: "I never tasted better save once—and that was at the King of Prussia's table."

"Ah! I once had d—d good pea-soup, I remember, at the Duke of Lambeth's table," ejaculated Mr. Talbot. "But, I say, who the devil's that kicking my unfortunate soft corn?"

"A glass of wine, Markham?" said Chichester.

"I suppose we'd all better join in," suggested Talbot.

"*I* shall be happy to drink wine with *you*, Mr. Talbot," said the baronet, with a reproving emphasis upon the pronouns.

"Just as you please," returned the man of charity, who certainly required some virtue or another to cover such a multitude of sins of vulgarity. "I wonder what's coming next. I say, Harborough, you haven't ordered any tripe, have you? I am so fond of tripe. There's nothing like tripe and onions for supper."

The dinner passed away; and the bottle was circulated pretty freely. Richard regained his good spirits, and offered no objection when Chichester proposed a stroll up Regent's-street with a cigar.

The baronet and Talbot went together first; and Markham was about to follow, when Chichester drew him back into the dining-room, and said, "Excuse me: but you went to your banker's to-day. If you have much money about you, it is not safe to carry it about the streets of London at night-time."

"I have fifty-five pounds in gold and fifty pounds in notes," answered Markham.

"Notes are safe enough," returned Chichester; "but gold is dangerous. Some one would be sure to *frisk* your purse. Here—I tell you how we can manage it—give me fifty sovereigns, and I will give you a fifty pound note in exchange. I can then lock up the gold in the baronet's writing-desk, the key of which, I see, he has fortunately left in the lock."

Chichester glanced, as he spoke, to the writing-desk, which stood upon a little table between the windows.

"I am much obliged to you for the thought," said Richard: "it is very considerate of you."

He accordingly handed over his purse of gold to his kind friend, and received in exchange a fifty pound note, which Mr. Chichester selected from a huge roll that he took from his pocket.

The two gentlemen then hastened to rejoin the baronet and Talbot, whom they overtook in Regent-street.

They all walked leisurely along towards the Quadrant;[1] and while Talbot engaged Markham in conversation upon some trivial topic or another, Chichester related in a few words to the baronet the particulars of the little pecuniary arrangement which had just taken place.

CHAPTER XIII.

THE HELL.

AFTER having taken a few turns in Regent-street, the baronet observed "that it was devilish slow work;" Mr. Talbot suggested the propriety of "a spree;" and Mr. Chichester declared "that as his friend Markham was anxious to see *life*, the best thing they could all do was to drop in for an hour at No. —, Quadrant."

1 The Quadrant: now the southern end of Regent Street, between Piccadilly Circus and the junction of Glasshouse Street and Vigo Street.

"What place is that?" demanded Markham.

"Oh; only an establishment for cards and dice, and other innocent diversions," carelessly answered Chichester.

The Quadrant of an evening is crowded with loungers of both sexes. Beneath those arcades walk the daughters of crime, by ones and twos—dressed in the flaunting garb that tells so forcibly the tale of broken hearts, and blighted promise, and crushed affections,—to lose an hour amidst the haunts of pleasure and of vice, and to court the crime by which alone they live. The young men that saunter arm-in-arm up and down, and the hoary old sinners, whose licentious glances seem to plunge down into the depths of the boddices of those frail but beauteous girls, little think of the amount of mental suffering which is contained beneath those gay satins and rustling silks. They mark the heaving of the voluptuous bosom, but dream not of the worm that gnaws eternally within:—they behold smiles upon the red lips, and are far from suspecting that the hearts of those who laugh so joyfully are all but broken!

Thus is it that in the evening the Quadrant has a characteristic set of loungers of its own:—or, at least, it is frequented after dusk by a population whose characters are easily to be defined.

A bright lamp burnt in the fan-light over the door of No. —. Mr. Chichester gave a loud and commanding knock; and a policeman standing by, who doubtless had several golden reasons for not noticing anything connected with that establishment, instantly ran across the road after a small boy whom he suspected to be a thief, because the poor wretch wore an uncommonly shabby hat. The summons given by Mr. Chichester was not immediately answered. Five minutes elapsed ere any attention was paid to it; and then the door was only opened to the small extent allowed by a chain inside. A somewhat repulsive looking countenance was at the same time protruded from behind the door.

"Well?" said the man to whom the countenance belonged.

"All right," returned Chichester.

The chain was withdrawn, and the door was opened to its full extent. The party was thereupon admitted, with some manifestations of impatience on the part of the porter, who no doubt thought that the door was kept open too long, into a passage at the end of which was a staircase covered with a handsome carpet.

Chichester led the way, and his companions followed, up to a suite of rooms on the first floor. These were well furnished, and brilliantly lighted; and red moreen curtains, with heavy and rich fringes, were carefully drawn over the windows. Splendid mirrors stood above the mantels, which were also adorned with French timepieces in *or molu*, and candelabra of the same material. On one side of the front room stood a bouffet covered with wines and liquors of various descriptions.

In the middle of that same front apartment was the *rouge et noir* table. On each side sate a *Croupier*, with a long rake in his hand, and a green shade over his eyes. Before one of them was placed a tin case: this was the *Bank*;—and on each side of that cynosure of all attention, stood little piles of markers, or counters.

Two or three men—well but flashily dressed, and exhibiting a monstrous profusion of Birmingham jewellery about their persons—sate at the table. These were the *Bonnets*—individuals in reality in the pay of the proprietor of the establishment, and whose duties consist in enticing strangers and visitors to play, or in maintaining an appearance of playing deeply when such strangers and visitors first enter the room.

The countenances of the croupiers were cold, passionless, and totally devoid of any animation. They called the game, raked up the winnings, or paid the losings, without changing a muscle of their features. For all that regarded animation or excitement, they might have been easily passed off as automatons.

Not so was it with the Bonnets. These gentlemen were compelled to affect exuberant joy when they won, and profound grief or rage when they lost. From time to time they paid a visit to the sideboard, and helped themselves to wine or spirits, or regaled themselves with cigars. These refreshments were supplied gratuitously to all comers by the proprietor: this apparent liberality was upon the principle of throwing out a sprat to catch a whale.

When none save the Croupiers and Bonnets are present, they throw aside their assumed characters, and laugh, and joke, and chatter, and smoke, and drink; but the moment steps are heard upon the staircase, they all relapse with mechanical exactitude into their business aspect. The Croupiers put on their imperturbable countenances as easily as if they were masks; and the Bonnets appear to be as intent upon the game, as if its results were to them perspective life or death.

The Croupiers are usually trustworthy persons well known to the proprietor, or else shareholders themselves in the establishment. The Bonnets are young men of education and manners, who have probably lost the ample fortunes wherewith they commenced life, in the very whirlpool to which for a weekly stipend, they are employed to entice others.

In one of the inner rooms there was a roulette-table; but this was seldom used. A young lad held the almost sinecure office of attending upon it.

The front room was tolerably crowded on the evening when Chichester, Markham, the baronet, and Talbot, honoured the establishment with a visit.

The moment they entered the apartment, Richard instinctively drew back, and, catching hold of Chichester's arm, whispered to him in a hurried and anxious manner, "Tell me, is this a Gambling-House? is it what I have heard called a Hell?"

"It is a Gambling-House, if you will, my dear fellow," was the reply; "but a most respectable one. Besides—you must see life, you know!"

With these words he took Markham's arm, and conducted him up to the *rouge et noir* table.

A young officer, whose age could not have exceeded twenty, was seated at the further end of the green-baize covered board. A huge pile of notes and gold lay before him; but at rapid intervals one of the Croupiers raked away the stakes which he deposited; and thus his heap of money was gradually growing smaller.

"Well, this is extraordinary!" ejaculated the young officer: "I never saw the luck set so completely in against me. However—I can afford to lose a little; for I broke your bank for you last night, my boys?"

"What does that mean?" demanded Richard in a whisper.

"He won all the money which the proprietor deposited in that tin case, he means," replied Chichester.

"And how much do you suppose that might be?"

"About fifteen hundred to two thousand pounds."

"Here—waiter!" exclaimed the young officer, who had just lost another stake,—"a glass of claret."

The waiter handed him a glass of the wine so demanded. The young officer did not notice him for a moment, but waited to see the result of the next chance.

He lost again.

He turned round to seize the glass of wine; but when his eyes caught sight of it, his countenance became almost livid with rage.

"Fool! idiot!" he ejaculated, starting from his seat; "bring me a tumbler—a large tumbler full of claret; my mouth is as parched as h—l, and my stomach is like a lime-kiln."

The waiter hastened to comply with the wishes of the young gambler. The tumbler of claret was supplied; and the game continued.

Still the officer lost.

"A cigar!" he shouted, in a fearful state of excitement—"bring me a cigar!"

The waiter handed him a box of choice Havannahs, that he might make his selection.

"Why the devil don't you bring a light at the same time, you d—d infernal rascal?" cried the gamester; and while the domestic hastened to supply this demand also, he poured a volley of most horrible oaths at the bewildered wretch's head.

Again the play proceeded.

And again the young officer lost.

His pile of gold was gone: the Croupier who kept the bank changed one of his remaining notes.

"That makes three thousand that I have lost already, by G—d!" ejaculated the young officer.

"Including the amount you won last night, I believe," said one of the Bonnets.

"Well, sir, and suppose it is—what the deuce is that to you?" demanded the officer fiercely. "Have I not been here night after night for those six weeks? and have I not lost thousands—thousands? When did I ever get a vein of good luck until last night? But never mind—I'll play on—I'll play till the end: I will either win all back, or lose everything together. And then—in the latter case—"

He stopped: he had just lost again. His countenance grew ghastly pale, and he bit his lips convulsively.

"Claret—more claret!" he exclaimed, throwing away the Havannah, "that cigar only makes me the more thirsty."

And again the play proceeded.

"I am really afraid to contemplate that young man's countenance," whispered Markham to Chichester.

"Why so?"

"I have an idea that if he should prove unsuccessful he will commit suicide. I have a great mind just to mention my fears to those men in the green shades, who seem to be winning all his money."

"Pray be quiet. They will only laugh at you."

"But the life of a fellow-creature?"

"What do they care?"

"Do you mean to say they are such wretches——"

"I mean that they do not care one fig what may happen so long as they get the money."

Markham was struck speechless with horror as he heard this cold-blooded announcement. Chichester had however stated nothing but the truth.

The proceedings were now fearfully interesting. The young officer was worked up to a most horrible state of excitement: his losses continued to be unvaried by a single gleam of good fortune. Still he persisted in his ruinous career: note after note was changed. At length his last was melted into gold. He now became absolutely desperate: his countenance was appalling;—the frenzy of gambling and the inflammatory effects of the liquors he had been drinking, rendered his really handsome features positively hideous.

Markham had never beheld such a scene before, and felt afraid. His companions surveyed it with remarkable coolness.

The play proceeded; and in a few moments the officer's last stake was swept away.

Then the croupiers paused, as it were, by common consent; and all eyes were directed towards the object of universal interest.

"Well—I said I would play until I won all or lost all," he said; "and I have done so. Waiter, give me another tumbler of claret: it will compose me."

He laughed bitterly as he uttered these words.

The claret was brought: he drained the tumbler, and threw it upon the table where it broke into a dozen pieces.

"Clear this away, Thomas," said one of the Croupiers, completely unmoved.

"Yes, sir;" and the fragments of the tumbler disappeared forthwith.

The Bonnets, perceiving the presence of other strangers, were now compelled to withdraw their attention from the ruined gambler, and commence playing.

And so the play again proceeded.

"Where is my hat, waiter?" demanded the young officer, after a pause, during which he had gazed vacantly upon the game.

"In the passage, sir—I believe."

"No—I remember, it is in the inner room. But do not trouble yourself—I will fetch it myself."

"Very good, sir;" and the waiter did not move.

The young officer sauntered, in a seeming leisurely manner, into the innermost room of the suite.

"What a shocking scene!" whispered Markham to Chichester. "I am glad I came hither this once: it will be a lesson for me which I can never forget."

At this instant the report of a pistol echoed sharply through the rooms.

There was a simultaneous rush to the inner apartment:—Markham's presentiments were fulfilled—the young officer had committed suicide.

His brains were literally blown out, and he lay upon the carpet weltering in his blood.

A cry of horror burst from the strangers present; and then, with one accord, they hastened to the door. The baronet, Chichester, and Talbot, were amongst the foremost who made this movement, and were thereby enabled to effect their escape.

Markham stood rivetted to the spot, unaware that his companions had left him, and contemplating with feelings of supreme horror the appalling spectacle before him.

Suddenly the cry of "The police" fell upon his ears; and heavy steps were heard hurrying up the staircase.

"The Bank!" ejaculated one of the Croupiers.

"All right!" cried the other; and in a moment the lights were extinguished, as by magic, throughout the entire suite of rooms.

Obeying a natural impulse, Markham hastened towards the door; but his progress was stopped by a powerful hand, and in an instant the bull's-eye of a lantern glared upon his countenance.

He was in the grasp of a police officer.

CHAPTER XIV.

THE STATION-HOUSE.

Of all the persons who were in the gambling-house at the moment when the police, alarmed by the report of the pistol, broke in, Richard Markham was alone captured. The others, aware of the means of egress in emergencies of this kind, had rushed up stairs, entered upon the leads, and thus obtained admittance into the adjacent dwelling, from whose friendly doors they subsequently issued one by one when all was once more quiet in the street.

The police-officer conducted Markham to the nearest station-house. They entered a low dark gloomy apartment, which was divided into two parts by means of a thick wooden bar running across the room, about two feet and a half from the ground. There was a small dull fire in the grate; and in a comfortable arm-chair near it, was seated the inspector—a short, stout, red-faced, consequential-looking man, with a pen stuck behind his left ear. A policeman in uniform was standing at a high desk, turning over the leaves of a large book; and another officer in plain clothes (and very plain and shabby they were too) was lounging before the fire, switching the dust out of his trousers with a thin cane.

"Well, what now?" said the inspector, gruffly, as Markham was conducted into the office, and led behind the bar, towards the fire.

"Me, and Jones, and Jenkins, broke into No. —, in the Quadrant, as we heard a pistol—or else we should ha' known ourselves better; and this young feller is all we caught. Jones and Jenkins is staying in the house along with the dead body of the man as killed his self."

The inspector indulged in a good long stare at Markham; and, when his curiosity was completely gratified, he said, "Now, Crisp, we'll enter that charge, if you please."

The policeman standing at the desk turned to the proper leaf in the large book before him, and then took down the deposition of the officer who had apprehended Markham.

When this was done, the inspector proceeded, in a very pompous and magisterial manner, to question the prisoner.

"What is your name, young man?"

"Richard Markham."

"Oh! Richard Markham. Put that down, Crisp. Where do you live?"

"At Markham Place, near Holloway."

"Put that down, Crisp. Now, do you want to let any of your friends know that you are in trouble?"

"First tell me of what I am accused, and why I am detained."

"You are accused of being in an unlawful house for an unlawful purpose—namely, gambling; and a suicide has been committed there, they say. You will be wanted afore the coroner as well as the magistrate."

"Can I be released until to-morrow by giving security for my appearance?"

"No—I can't part with you. It is said that it is suicide—and I believe it: still it might be murder. But you seem a respectable young gentleman, and so you shan't be locked up in a cell all night. You may sit here by the fire, if you'll be quiet."

"I am at least obliged to you for this courtesy. But can you give me any idea of the extent of the penalty to which I am liable? I did not gamble myself—I merely accompanied——"

"You needn't criminate anybody, you know," interrupted the Inspector. "The Magistrate will fine you a few pounds, and that will be all."

"Then I should prefer not to acquaint my friends with my position," said Markham, "since I can release myself from my present difficulty without their assistance."

Reassured by this conviction, though still strangely excited by the appalling scene which he had witnessed, Richard seated himself by the fire, and soon fell into conversation with the policemen. These men could talk of nothing but themselves or their pursuits: they appeared to live in a world of policeism; all their ideas were circumscribed to station-houses, magistrates' offices, prisons, and criminal courts of justice. Their discourse was moreover garnished with the slang terms of thieves; they could not utter a sentence without interpolating a swell-mob phrase or a Newgate jest. They seemed to be so familiar with crime (though not criminal themselves) that they could not devote a moment to the contemplation of virtue: they only conversed about persons who were "in trouble," but never condescended to lavish a thought to those who were out of it.

"Crankey Jem has done it brown at last, hasn't he?" said Crisp.

"He has indeed," replied the inspector. "But what could he have done with all the swag?"[1]

"Oh! he's fadded[2] that safe enough," observed the officer in plain clothes. "My eye! What a slap-up lily benjamin[3] he had on when he was nabbed."

"Yes—and sich a swell bandanna fogle[4] in the gropus."[5]

1 Booty, plunder. [Reynolds's note.]

2 Secured. [Reynolds's note.]

3 White Upper Coat: synonymous with "White Poodle." [Reynolds's note.]

4 Handkerchief. [Reynolds's note.]

5 Pocket. [Reynolds's note.]

"He hadn't any ready tin though; for he wanted to peel,[1] and put the white-poodle up the spout[2] for a drop of max."[3]

"And because you wouldn't let him he doubled you up with a wallop in your dumpling-depot;[4] didn't he?"

"Yes—but I bruised his canister[5] for him though."

"This'll be the third time he's been up afore the beaks[6] at the Old Bailey."

"Consequently he's sartain sure to be lagged."[7]

"Ah! it must be a clever nob in the fur trade[8] who'll get him off."

"Well—talking makes me thirsty," said Crisp. "I wish I'd someot to sluice my ivories[9] with."

Markham entertained a faint idea that Mr. Crisp was athirst; he accordingly offered to pay for anything which he and his brother policemen chose to drink.

The officer in plain clothes was commissioned to procure some "heavy-wet"—*alias* porter; and even the pompous and magisterial inspector condescended to take what he called "a drain," but which in reality appeared to be something more than a pint.

The harmony was disturbed by the entrance of a constable dragging in a poor ragged, half-starved, and emaciated lad, without shoes and stockings.

"What's the charge?" demanded the inspector.

"A rogue and vagabond," answered the constable.

"Oh! very well: put that down, Crisp. How do you know?"

"Because he's wandering about and hasn't nowhere to go to, and no friends to refer to; and I saw him begging."

"Very good; put that down, Crisp. And I suppose he's without food and hungry?"

"I have not tasted food—" began the poor wretch, who stood shivering at the bar.

"Come, no lies," ejaculated the inspector.

1 Strip. [Reynolds's note.]
2 Pawn the coat. [Reynolds's note.]
3 Gin. [Reynolds's note.]
4 Stomach. [Reynolds's note.]
5 Head. [Reynolds's note.]
6 Judges. [Reynolds's note.]
7 Transported. [Reynolds's note.]
8 Barrister. [Reynolds's note.]
9 Teeth. [Reynolds's note.]

"No lies!" echoed the constable, giving the poor wretch a tremendous shake.

"Have you put it all down, Crisp?"

"Yes, sir."

"Well, let him have a bit of bread, and lock him up. He'll get three months of it on the stepper to-morrow."

The poor creature was supplied with a cubic inch of stale bread, and then thrust into a filthy cell.

"What do you think that unfortunate creature will be done to?" enquired Markham.

"Three months on the stepper—the treadmill, to be sure."

"But what for?"

"Why, for a rogue and vagabond."

"A vagabond he may be," said Markham, "because he has no home to go to; but how do you know he is a rogue?"

"Why—he was found begging, wasn't he?"

"And does that make a man a rogue?"

"Certainly it do—in the eye of the law."

"Ah! and that eye can see without spectacles too," added Mr. Crisp with a laugh.

Markham was reflecting profoundly upon the law's definitions of *rogue* and *vagabond*, when another constable entered, leading in an elderly man, belonging to the humbler class, but very cleanly in appearance.

"Well, what's the charge?" demanded the inspector.

"This fellow will come upon my beat with his apple-cart, and I can't keep him off. So I've sent his cart to the Green Yard, and brought him here."

"Please, sir," said the poor fellow, wiping away a tear from his eye, "I endeavour to earn an honest living by selling a little fruit in the streets. I have a wife and seven children to support, and I only stayed out so long to-night because I had had a bad day of it, and the money is so much wanted at home—it is indeed, sir! I do hope you'll let me go, sir: my poor wife will be ready to break her heart when she finds that I don't come home; and my eldest boy always sits up for me. Poor little fellow! he will cry so if he don't kiss *Father* before he goes to bed."

There was something profoundly touching in this poor man's

manner and language; and Markham felt inclined to interfere in his behalf. He, however, remembered that he was only allowed to sit in that room by sufferance, and that he was at the mercy of the caprice of ignorant, tyrannical, and hard-hearted men: he accordingly held his tongue.

"Come, Crisp—have you got that down?" said the inspector.

"Yes, sir."

"Well, let the man be locked up: the magistrate must decide in the morning."

And the poor fellow, in spite of his remonstrances, was removed to a cell.

"I could not exactly understand what this new prisoner has done," said Markham.

"Obstructed the way and created a nuisance," replied the inspector pompously.

"But he is endeavouring to earn his bread honestly, I think; and the road is open to every one."

"Oh! no such thing. Those little carts frighten the horses in the great folks' carriages, and can't be allowed. He must have a month of it—he's been warned several times, and is incorrigible. I'll tell the magistrate so."

"And what will become of his family?"

"Family! why, go to the workhouse, to be sure!" Presently a third constable made his appearance, accompanied by a poor miserable-looking woman and three small children—all wretchedly clad and careworn.

"What's the charge now?"

"Charge from the workus. This here o'oman was admitted to-night to the Union with them three children; and cos the master ordered her to be separated from her children, she kicked up hell's delight. So the master turned 'em all out together, called me up, and give 'em in charge."

"Put that down, Crisp."

"Yes—and it is true too," sobbed the poor woman. "I am not ashamed to own that I love my children; and up to this blessed hour they have never been separated from me. It would break their poor little hearts to be torn away from me—that it would, God bless them! I love them all, poor—miserable as I am!"

A flood of tears drowned the voice of this wretched mother.

"Inspector," said Markham, touched to the quick by this affecting scene, "you will allow me ——"

"Silence, young man. It's a charge from the workus, and the workus is paramount."

"So it appears, indeed!" cried Richard bitterly.

"Silence, I say. Don't interfere, there's a good lad. Crisp, have you got it all down?"

"Yes, sir."

"Lock em up, then."

"At least we shall be together!" exclaimed the unfortunate mother, to whom the three little children clung with all the tenacity of sincere affection.

An hour elapsed, when another policeman entered, bringing in a man dressed as a hostler, and whose face was all covered with blood.

"Well—what now?"

"Fighting in the *Blue Dragon*: the landlord turned him out, and so I took him up."

"Put that down, Crisp. What's your name, my fine fellow?"

"John Snoggles."

"Put that down, Crisp. He's a nice bird, isn't he, Mr. Markham?" added the inspector.

"Markham!" ejaculated the new prisoner.

"Yes—that is my name," said Richard: "do you know me?"

"Not that I am aweer of sir. Only the name reminded me that I have been this evening in the company of a gentleman as is in the service of a Mr. Markham. I left the *Servant's Arms* at twelve precisely, and walked straight down to this here wicinity—I ain't been more than half an hour coming—when I gets into a row——"

"Well, well," said Richard, somewhat impatiently, "and what is the name of the person with whom you have passed the evening?"

"With several gentlemen—but the one I named was Vittingham."

"Whittingham! he is my butler. Poor fellow! how anxious he will be about me."

"He's too drunk to be anxious," said Snoggles drily: "I was the on'y one as come away sober."

"I tell you what he could do, if you like," observed the inspector, who now began to entertain an idea of Markham's standing in society by the mention of the word *butler*: "there is no one here to make any charge against the fellow—the constable will withdraw it, and he can take a note home for you."

"A thousand thanks!" ejaculated Markham. "But you intimated that he was tipsy?"

"He is certainly elevated," answered Snoggles.

"Well, can you be at my house to-morrow morning by six or seven o'clock?"

"Of course I can, sir."

"I need not write: you can say that you have seen me, and that I shall be home in the course of the day. Do not mention where I am: I would not have him coming here to seek me."

Markham slipped half a sovereign into the hands of Snoggles, who took his departure with a faithful promise to execute the commission entrusted to him, and not a little pleased at having so pleasantly escaped a night in the station-house.

It was now past one o'clock; and Markham, feeling rather drowsy, lay down to slumber for a few hours upon a bench, wrapped up in Mr. Crisp's police-coat.

CHAPTER XV.

THE POLICE-OFFICE.

THE morning was rainy, cold, and lowering.

Markham awoke unrefreshed by his sleep, which had been haunted by the ghost of the young officer who had committed suicide at the Hell. He shivered and felt nervous; as if under the impulse of some impending danger whose nature he could not altogether define. By the good offices of Crisp he obtained the means of washing himself and arranging his toilette previous to an appearance at the police-court; and the same intervention procured him a good breakfast. As he, however, could not eat a morsel, Mr. Crisp very kindly and considerately devoured it all for him.

At about half-past nine o'clock the various constables connected with the charges entered in the police-sheet, arrived at the station-house for the purpose of conducting their prisoners to the Police-court. All those persons who were charged with felony were handcuffed; but of this class the most knowing contrived to bring their hands beneath their garments in some way or other, and thus conceal the symbol of ignominy as they passed through the streets.

Richard was astonished at the number of women who were charged with intoxication and disorderly conduct; and the chivalrous admiration of the whole sex which he felt, and which is so natural to youth, was considerably diminished by the hardened appearance and revolting language of these females.

Markham and the constable who had arrested him proceeded in a cab together to the police-office in Marlborough Street. Upon reaching that establishment, the officer said, "The Magistrate will hear the *drunk* and *assault* charges first; so it may be an hour or more before your business will come on. I ought by rights to lock you up; but if you like, we can stay together in the public-house there; and one of my partners will let us know when the case is coming on."

This arrangement was very acceptable to Richard; and to the nearest public-house did he and the constable accordingly adjourn. For this handsome accommodation all that he had to pay was half-a-guinea to the officer, besides liquidating the score for as much liquor as the said officer and every one of his "partners" who happened to drop in, could consume.

For the present we must request the reader to accompany us to the interior of the police-office.

In a small, low, badly-lighted room, sate an elderly gentleman at a desk. This was the Magistrate. Near him was the clerk, whom the worthy functionary consulted so often that it almost seemed as if this clerk were a peripatetic law-manual or text-book. In front of the desk were the bar and the dock; and the space between them and the door was filled with policemen and the friends of those "who had got into trouble."

The first charge was called. A man dressed in the garb of a common labourer was accused of being drunk and incapable of taking care of himself. The Magistrate put on a most awfully severe and frowning countenance, and said in a gruff tone, "Well, my man, what do you say to this charge?"

"Please your worship," observed the prisoner, scratching his head, "I am out of work, and my wife has pawned all our little bits of things for food for the children, and yesterday morning I was forced to go out to look for work without any breakfast. There was but a little bread left, and that I would not touch for all the world. Well, your worship, I was fortunate enough to get the promise of some work for Monday; and meeting a friend, he asked me to have a glass. Now beer upon an empty stomach, your worship——"

The Magistrate, who had been reading a newspaper during this defence, now lifted up his head, and exclaimed, "Well, you don't deny the charge: you are fined five shillings. Call the next case."

"But your worship——"

"Call the next case."

The poor fellow was dragged away from the bar by two huge policemen; and an elegantly dressed person of about twenty-six years of age was introduced to the notice of the magistrate.

"What is your name?" enquired the clerk.

"Name! Oh—John Jenkins," was the reply, delivered in a flippant and free-and-easy manner.

The Clerk and the Magistrate whispered together.

A constable then stood forward, and stated the charge. The prisoner at the bar had turned out of a flash tavern in the Haymarket at one in the morning, and commenced crowing like a cock, and ringing at front-door bells, and playing all imaginable kinds of antics. When the constable interfered, the gentleman knocked him down; and had not another policeman come up to the spot at the moment, the said gentleman never would have been taken into custody.

The Magistrate cross-questioned the policeman who gave evidence in this case, with great severity; and then, turning with a bland smile to the prisoner, who was surveying the clerk through his eye glass in as independent a manner as if he were lounging over the front of his box at the opera, the worthy functionary said in a tone of gentle entreaty, "Now really we have reason to suspect that John Jenkins is *not* your name. In fact, my lord, we know you."

"Well, then," exclaimed the prisoner, turning his eye-glass from the clerk upon the magistrate, "chalk me up as Lord Plymouth, since you are down upon me in this way."

"My lord—my lord," said the Magistrate, with parental urbanity of manner, "these little freaks of yours are really not creditable: upon my honour they are not. I sit here to administer justice to the rich as well as to the poor——"

"Oh! you do, do you?" cried the nobleman. "Now I tell you what it is—if you dare talk any of your nonsense about prisons and houses of correction to me, I'll not stand it. You know as well as I do that whenever a barrister is to be appointed magistrate, the Home Secretary sends for him and tells him to mind his P's and Q's towards the aristocracy. So none of your nonsense; but be quick and let me off with the usual fine."

"My lord," ejaculated the Magistrate, glancing with consternation from the prisoner to the clerk, and from the clerk to the prisoner; "did I not say that I sate here to administer equal justice to the rich and the poor? The fine for drunkenness is five shillings, my lord—and in that sum I fine you. As for the assault upon the policeman, I give you leave to speak to him outside."

The nobleman demanded change for a ten pound note, and threw the five shillings in a contemptuous and insolent manner towards the Clerk, who thanked his lordship as if he had just received an especial favour. The assault was easily settled *outside*; and the nobleman drove away in an elegant cab, just as the wife of the poor labourer departed in tears from her husband's cell for the purpose of pledging every remaining article of clothing that could possibly be dispensed with, to raise the five shillings wherewith to procure his liberation.

Several other cases of intoxication, disorderly conduct, and "obstruction of the police in the exercise of their duty"—which last embraced the veriest trifles as well as the most daring attempts at rescue—were then disposed of. In all instances the constables endeavoured to exaggerate the conduct of the accused, and never once attempted to palliate it; and as the Magistrate seemed to place implicit confidence in every word the police uttered (although one or two cases of gross perjury were proved against them), convictions were much more frequent than acquittals.

The cases of the poor starving emaciated beggar, the apple-cart man, and the affectionate mother, who had all three so powerfully excited Markham's attention at the station-house, were called on one after another consecutively. Fortunately the inspector was not present at the time to use his influence against the two first, and the master of the workhouse did not appear to press the charge against the last. They were all three accordingly discharged, with a severe admonition—the first against begging and being houseless—the second against earning an honest livelihood by selling fruit in the streets—and the third against clamouring in a workhouse for the mere trifle of being separated from her children.

As these three individuals emerged from the police-office, they were accosted by Mr. Crisp, who informed them that they were "wanted" by a gentleman at a public-house in the neighbourhood. Thither did the trio of unfortunates, accompanied by the poor woman's children, proceed; and great was their surprise when Mr. Crisp officiously introduced them into a private room which Markham had engaged.

Richard and the police-officer in whose charge he remained, were there; and the moment the poor creatures were shown in, they were accosted by that young man whose ingenuous countenance inspired them with confidence and hope.

"My good friends," said he, "I was in the station-house last night when you arrived; and your sad tales touched me to the quick. Now, with regard to you, my poor lad," he continued, addressing himself to the *rogue and vagabond*, "what prospect have you before you? In what way could a friend aid you?"

"My brother, sir, is well off, and would assist me," replied the poor creature, "if I could but get to him. He lives in Edinburgh, and is well to do as a wheelwright."

"Here are two guineas for you, my friend," said Richard. "They will take you home; and then may your reception be as favourable as you seem to think. There—I do not want you to thank me: go—and commence your journey at once."

The poor fellow pressed Markham's hand with the most enthusiastic gratitude, and took his departure with tears in his eyes and gladness in his heart.

"And now, my good man," said Richard to the owner of the apple-cart, "what do you propose to do?"

"To speak the truth, sir, I don't know. The police seem determined that I shan't earn an honest livelihood: and as I am equally resolved not to see my children starve before me, I have nothing left to do but to become a thief. I shan't be the first whom the police have driven to that last resource in this city."

"You speak bitterly," said Markham.

"Yes—because I tell the truth, sir. My cart is to be returned to me;

but of what use is it, or the stock that is in it, since I don't dare go about to sell fruit?"

"Could you not open a little shop?"

"Ah! sir—that requires money!"

"How much?"

"A matter of four or five pounds, sir," replied the man; "and where could a poor devil like me——"

"I will give you five pounds for the purpose;" interrupted Markham; and taking from his pocket-book a bank note, he handed it to the poor man.

We will not attempt to depict his gratitude: words would completely fail to convey an idea of the exuberant joy which filled the heart of that good and affectionate father, who would rather have become a thief than seen his children starve!

"And now, my good woman, what can I do for you?" said Markham, turning to the third object of his charity. "How in the name of heaven, came you reduced, with three children, to such a state of want and destitution?"

"My husband, sir, is in prison," answered the poor creature, bursting into tears, while her children clung the more closely around her.

"In prison! and for what crime?"

"Oh! crime, sir—it is only a crime in the eye of the law, but not in the eye of either man or heaven."

"My good woman, this is absurd. Is there any offence of which the law alone takes cognizance, and which is not reprehensible in the eye of God?"

"On the contrary, sir—God has given us for our general use and benefit the very thing which the law has forbidden us to take."

"This is trifling!" exclaimed Richard impatiently. "Can you, whom I behold so affectionate to your children, be hardened in guilt?"

"Do not think so, sir! My husband was a hard working man—never spent an hour at the public-house—never deprived his family of a farthing of his wages. He was a pattern to all married men—and his pride was to see his children well-dressed and happy. Alas, sir—we were too happy not to meet with some sad reverse! My husband in an evil hour went out shooting one afternoon, when there was a holiday at the factory where he worked; and he killed a hare upon a nobleman's grounds near Richmond. He was taken up and tried for poaching, and was sentenced to a year's imprisonment with hard labour! This term expires in six weeks; but in the meantime—O God! what have we not suffered!"

"Ah! forgive me," ejaculated Markham, deeply touched by this recital: "I spoke harshly to you, because I did not remember that the law could be guilty of a deed of such inhuman atrocity. And yet I have heard of many—many such cases ere now! Merciful heavens! is it possible that the law, which with the right hand protects the privileges of the aristocracy, can with the left plunge whole families into despair!"

"Alas! it is too true!" responded the poor woman, pointing towards her pale and shivering offspring.

"Well—cheer up—your husband will be restored to you in six weeks," said Markham. "In the meantime here is wherewith to provide for your family."

Another five-pound note was taken from the pocket-book, and transferred to the hand of the poor but tender-hearted mother. The children clung to Richard's knees, and poured forth their gratitude in tears: their parent loaded him with blessings which came from the very bottom of her heart, and called him the saviour of herself and famished little ones. Never until that day had Richard so entirely appreciated the luxury of possessing wealth!

Scarcely was this last matter disposed of, when information arrived that Markham's case would be heard in about ten minutes. To the police-court did he and the constable who had charge of him, proceed accordingly; and in due time the young man found himself standing at the bar in the presence of a magistrate.

The usual questions were put relative to name, age, and residence, to all of which Richard answered in a candid and respectful manner. The constable then stated the nature of the charge, with which the reader is already acquainted. Evidence was also gone into to show that the officer, whose death had led to the irruption into the gambling-house on the part of the police, had died by his own hand, and not in consequence of any violence. This point was sufficiently proved by a medical man.

Markham, in his defence, stated he had accompanied some friends, whose names he declined mentioning, to the gaming-house on the preceding evening; that he had not played himself, nor had he intended to play; and that he had been led into the establishment without previously being acquainted with the exact nature of the place he was about to visit.

The Magistrate remonstrated with him upon the impropriety of being seen in such houses, and inflicted a fine of five pounds, which was of course immediately paid.

As he was leaving the police-court, Markham was informed by a beadle who accosted him, that his presence would be required at the gambling-house that same afternoon, at four o'clock, to give evidence at the coroner's inquest concerning the means by which the deceased officer came by his death.

CHAPTER XVI.

THE BEGINNING OF MISFORTUNES.

At eight o'clock in the morning after the scene at the Hell, and while Richard was still in the custody of the police, Sir Rupert Harborough and the Honourable Arthur Chichester were hastening, in a handsome cabriolet, belonging to the former, to Markham Place.

The conversation of these gentlemen during the drive will tend to throw some light upon one or two preceding incidents that may have appeared a little mysterious to the reader.

"I wonder what became of him last night," said Chichester.

"Upon my honour at the moment I did not care," returned the baronet.

"Nor I either. I was only intent upon getting off myself."

"He will not be pleased at our having left him in that unceremonious manner."

"Oh! trust to me—any explanation will do. He is so exceedingly green."

"And so marvellously particular in his conduct. If it had not been for us, he would have remained quite a saint."

"I am not afraid," observed Chichester, "of being able to manage him and of turning him to immense advantage in our plans. But that vulgar beast Talbot will most certainly spoil all. Even the idea of the fellow's wealth and charities will not always induce Markham to put up with his vulgarities. Besides, the wretch has such execrable bad taste. Last evening, for instance, when I casually dropped a neat little lie about the soup at the King of Prussia's table, Talbot instantly paraded the Duke of Lambeth's pea-soup. Only fancy a Duke and pea-soup united together!"

"And then his dog's nose, and sore feet, and boiled tripe," said the baronet. "After all the drilling we gave him in the first instance, when he stipulated upon associating with us in order to see how we worked the thing, he is still incorrigible. Then, when I think of all the money I have already laid out in buying the materials—in getting the proper paper—and in keeping him in feather all the time he was at work, my blood boils to see that he hangs like a millstone round our necks, and threatens by his vulgarity to spoil all."

"But what could we do?" cried Chichester. "You told me in the first instance to find an engraver on whom we could rely; and I was compelled to enlist the fellow Pocock in our cause. He was the very man, so far as knowledge went, having been employed all his life in working for Bankers. But his atrocious vulgarity is his bane; and even his aristocratic name of Talbot which I made him assume, does not help him to pass himself off as a gentleman. It was a pity he could not listen to reason and take the sum of ready money down, which you offered him in the first instance. But, no—he must needs cry *thirds*, and insist upon going about with us to see fair play."

"And get his share," added the baronet.

"Yes. Even the very first night that he ever saw Markham," continued Chichester, "his greediness would have induced him to risk the ruin of everything by winning a few paltry pounds of the young fellow at Diana's lodgings. But I d—d soon stopped *that*. I didn't even want to take the twenty pounds yesterday, which Markham offered for the poor family concerning whom I invented so capital a story."

"No—it is not a few pounds that will do us any good, or remunerate me for my large outlay," said the baronet. "We want thousands—and this Markham is the very instrument we require. The first trial was made yesterday, and succeeded admirably. The note has actually been changed at a banker's: no one can expect a better test than that. Now if this Talbot is to ruin us with Markham—the very person we want—the most excellent medium we could require—himself being above all suspicion, and entertaining no suspicion ——"

"It would be enough to break one's heart," added Chichester.

"Besides, my creditors are so clamorous, settle with them I must," continued the baronet. "And then Diana costs me a fortune. I must get rid of her without delay; for I expect that she is getting sentimental on this youth, and will not interest herself in our affair for fear of letting him into a scrape."

"Why, it is very certain," observed Chichester, "that according to the admirable way in which we have arranged our plans, if an explosion took place, we could not possibly be implicated. However—we must make haste and work London, and then off to Paris. We might get rid of four or five thousand pounds worth amongst the money-changers in the Palais-Royal. Then off to Germany in due rotation—Italy next—touch at Spain—and home to England."

"Upon my honour, it is a noble scheme—a grand, a princely scheme!" cried the baronet, elated with the idea. "My God! if it were spoilt in its infancy by any fault of ours or our associates!"

"And Talbot is such a drunken beast, that we can scarcely rely upon him," said Chichester. "He will one day commit himself and us too: the fellow does not know how to get tipsy like a gentleman."

"We will tell him the candid truth and see what he says," pursued the baronet. "When he finds that we are determined not to tolerate him with us, and that we will quash the whole thing at once if he insists upon remaining, he must yield. There was that young Walter Sydney who seemed at first to have taken a fancy to Diana. I thought of making use of him too;—but he never called again after that drunken display of Mr. Talbot's. He was evidently disgusted with him for his conduct, and with us for associating with him."

"Well," said Chichester, "let us resolve, then, to have an explanation with Talbot in the sense you have mentioned; and you must also speak seriously to Diana and get her to make use of young Markham."

"And if she will not," added the baronet, "I shall get rid of her without delay. What is the use of having an expensive mistress, unless you can use her either as a *blind* or a *plant?*"

The delectable conversation terminated here, because those who had carried it on, were now arrived at their destination.

The baronet's tiger knocked at the front door, and Mr. Whittingham speedily made his appearance.

"Is your master at home?" demanded Chichester.

"No sir; he has not domesticated himself in his own abode since he went out shortly after you yesterday. But a person of my acquaintance—a man of perfect credibleness—has just come to ensure me that my young master will be here again in the currency of the day."

"Where did this person see your master?" enquired Chichester, struck by the absence of Markham the entire night.

"His respondencies is evasive and dissatisfactory," said Whittingham.

"This is very remarkable!" ejaculated Chichester: then, after a pause, he added, "But we will await Mr. Markham's return; and I will just see this man and interrogate him alone—*alone*, do you hear, Whittingham."

"I hear, sir, because my accoustic propensities is good. I will send this person to you into the library."

Mr. Chichester alighted from the vehicle and hastened to the library, while the baronet repaired to the stables to see that his horse (concerning which he was very particular) was properly cared for.

Mr. Chichester walked up and down the library, reflecting upon the probable causes of Richard's absence. At the moment he fancied that he might have fallen into the hands of the police; but then he thought that, had this been the case, Markham would have sent for himself or the baronet. He did not imagine that the noble nature of the young man whom he was conducting headlong to his ruin, would scorn to take any steps calculated to compromise his friends.

The door of the library opened, and a man entered.

"What? John!" ejaculated Mr. Chichester, turning very pale and manifesting much confusion.

"Mr. Winchester!" cried Snoggles—for it was he.

"Hush, my good fellow—don't say a word!" said Chichester, recovering his presence of mind. "I am really glad to see you—I have often thought of you since that unpleasant affair. I hope it put you to no inconvenience. At all events, I will make matters all right now."

"Better late than never," said Snoggles.

"Well—and you must promise me faithfully not to mention this affair to any one, and I will always stand your friend. And, remember—my name is Chichester *now*—not Winchester. Pray do not forget that."

"No—no: I'm fly enough—I'm down to trap," replied Snoggles, with a leer of insolent familiarity.

"Here is a twenty-pound note—that will cover all your losses, and recompense you into the bargain."

"That'll do."

"It would be better that you should not say that you ever knew me before."

"Just as you like."

"I prefer that course. But now to another point. Where did you see Mr. Richard Markham?"

"At the station-house, in ——— street."

"The station-house! And for what?"

"Ah! there you beat me. I can't say! All that I know is that he gave me half-a-sovereign to come and tell his old butler this morning that he should be home in the course of the day."

"And that is all you know?"

"Everything."

"Now can I rely upon you in respect to keeping the other matter secret?" demanded Chichester.

"I have already told you so," answered Snoggles.

"And you need not tell old Whittingham that his master is at the station-house."

Snoggles withdrew; and Mr. Chichester was immediately afterwards joined by the baronet.

"Markham is at the station-house in ——— street."

"The deuce he is! and for what?"

"I cannot learn. Do you not think it is odd that he did not send for either of us?"

"Yes. We will return to town this moment," said the baronet, "and send some one unknown to him to hear the case at the police-office. We shall then learn whether anything concerning the notes transpires, and what to say to him when we see him."

"Yes: there is not a moment to lose," returned Chichester.

The cabriolet was brought round to the door again in a few minutes, during which interval Chichester assured Whittingham that he had learned nothing concerning his master, and that he and the baronet were only returning to town for the purpose of looking after him.

As soon as the vehicle was out of sight, Mr. Whittingham returned in a disconsolate manner to his pantry, where Mr. Snoggles was occupied with a cold pasty and a jug of good old ale.

"Well, I've learnt someot to-day, I have," observed Snoggles, who could not keep a secret for the life of him.

"What's that?" demanded Whittingham.

"Why that Winchester is Chichester, and Chichester is Winchester."

"They are two irrelevant cities," observed the butler; "and not by no manner of means indentical."

"The cities is different, but the men is the same," said Snoggles.

"I can't apprehend your meaning."

"Well—I will speak plain. Did you hear me tell Suggett the story about my old master, last night at the *Servants' Arms?*"

"No—I was engaged in a colloquial discourse at the time."

"Then I will tell you the adventur' over agin;"—and Mr. Snoggles related the incident accordingly.

Mr. Whittingham was quite astounded; and he delivered himself of many impressive observations upon the affair, but which we shall not be cruel enough to inflict upon our readers.

It was about half-past twelve o'clock when Richard returned home. His countenance was pale and anxious; and he vainly endeavoured to smile as he encountered his faithful old dependant.

"Ah! Master Richard, I was sadly afraid that you had fallen into some trepidation!"

"A very unpleasant adventure, Whittingham—which I will relate to you another time—kept me away from home. I was with Sir Rupert Harborough and Mr. Chichester——"

"Mr. Chichester ain't no good, sir," interrupted the butler emphatically.

"What do you mean, Whittingham?"

"I mean exactly what I say, Master Richard,—and nothing more nor less. Both the baronet and Mr. Chichester have been here this morning."

Then, with a considerable amount of circumlocution and elaborate comment, the butler related the conduct of Chichester towards Snoggles, and their accidental meeting that morning.

"This is very extraordinary," said Richard, musing.

"I can't say I ever regularly admired this Mr. Chichester," observed Whittingham. "He seems too dashing, too out-and-out, and too—too—circumwenting in his discourse, to be anythink exceeding and excessive good. Now I like the baronet much better; he isn't so formiliar in his manners. Whenever he speaks to me he always says '*Mr. Whittingham;*' but Mr. Chichester calls me plain '*Whittingham.*' As for that wulgar fellow Talbot, who has called here once or twice, he slaps me on the shoulder, and bawls out, '*Well, Whittingham, my tulip, how are you?*' Now, you know, Master Richard, it's not conformant to perceived notions to call a butler a tulip."

"I have been deceived in my acquaintances—no doubt I have been deceived," said Richard, musing audibly, and pacing the library with agitated steps. "There is something suspicious in the connexion of that man Talbot—however rich he may be—with so elegant a gentleman as the baronet;—then this conduct of Chichester's towards his servant—their taking me to a common gambling-house—their deserting me in the moment of need,—yes, I have been deceived! And then, Diana—I ought never more to see her: her influence, her fascination are too dangerous!"

"A gambling-house!" ejaculated Whittingham, whose ears caught fragments of these reflections.

"My old friend," said Richard, turning suddenly towards the butler, "I am afraid I have been enticed—inveigled into society which is not creditable to me or my position. I will repair my fault. Mr. Monroe, my guardian, advised me some weeks ago to indulge in a tour upon the continent: I will avail myself of this permission. At four o'clock I have an appointment—a pressing appointment to keep in town: by seven at latest I shall return. Have a post-chaise at the door and all things in readiness: we will proceed to Dover to-night. You alone shall accompany me."

"Let's do it, sir—let's do it," exclaimed the faithful old dependant: "it will separate you from them flash fellows which lead young men into scrapes, and from them wulgar persons which call butlers tulips."

Whittingham retired to make the preparations for the contemplated journey, and Richard seated himself at the table to write a couple of letters.

The first was to Mrs. Arlington, and ran thus:—

"Circumstances of a very peculiar nature, and which I cannot at present explain to you, compel me to quit London thus abruptly. I hope you will not imagine that I leave your agreeable society without many regrets. We shall probably meet again, when I may perhaps confide to you the motives of this sudden departure; and you will then understand that I could not have remained in London another minute with safety to myself. I scarcely know what I write—I am so agitated and uneasy. Pray excuse this scrawl.

"RICHARD MARKHAM."

The second letter was to Mr. Monroe, and was couched in the following terms:—

"You will be surprised, my dear sir, to find that I am immediately about to avail myself of your kind recommendation and permission to visit the continent. I conceive it to be my duty—in consequence of rumours or reports which may shortly reach your ears concerning me—to inform you that I have this moment only awoke to the fearful perils of the career in which I have for some weeks past been blindly hurrying along, till at length yesterday——: but I dare not write any more. I am penitent—deeply penitent: let this statement induce you to defend and protect my reputation,

"Ever your sincerely obliged,

"R. MARKHAM."

Having hastily folded, addressed, and sealed these letters, Markham hurried up to his bed-room to select certain articles of clothing and other necessaries which he should require upon his journey.

He was interrupted in the middle of this occupation, by the entrance of Whittingham, who came to announce that two persons of somewhat strange and suspicious appearance desired an immediate interview with him.

Scarcely was this message delivered, when the two men, who had followed Whittingham up-stairs, walked very unceremoniously into the bed-room.

"This is Richard Markham, 'spose?" said one, advancing towards the young man.

"Yes—my name is Markham: but what means this insolent and unpardonable intrusion?"

"Intrusion indeed!" repeated the foremost of the ill-looking strangers. "However, not to keep you waiting, my young friend, I must inform you that me and this man here are officers; and we've a warrant to take you."

"A warrant!" ejaculated both Richard and Whittingham at the same moment.

"Come, come, now—I des say you haven't been without your misgivings since yesterday;—but if young gen'lemen will play such pranks, why, they must expect some time or another to be wanted—that's all!"

"But what have I done?" demanded Richard. "There must be some mistake. I cannot be the person whom you require."

"Did you not call at a certain bankers' in the City yesterday?" demanded the officer.

"Certainly—I had some money to receive, which Mr. Monroe my guardian had paid into their hands for my use."

"And you changed a five hundred pound note? The clerk did it for your accommodation."

"I do not deny it: I required change. But how is all this connected with your visit?"

"That five hundred pound note was a forgery!"

"A forgery! Impossible!" cried Richard.

"A forgery!" said Whittingham: "this is really impudence of too consummating a nature!"

"Come, there's no mistake, and all this gammon won't do. Me and my partner came in a hackney-coach, which stands at the corner of the lane; so if you're ready, we'll be off to Bow Street at once."

"I am prepared to accompany you," said Richard, "because I am well aware that I shall not be detained many minutes at the magistrate's office."

"That's no business of mine," returned the principal officer: then, addressing his companion, he said "Jem, you'll stay here and take a survey of the premises; while I get off with the prisoner. You can follow as soon as you've satisfied yourself whether there's any evidence upon the premises."

It was with great difficulty that Richard overruled the desire of Whittingham to accompany him, but at length the faithful old man was induced to comprehend the necessity of staying behind, as an officer was about to exercise a strict search throughout the house, and Markham did not choose to leave his property to the mercy of a stranger.

This point having been settled, Richard took his departure with the officer in whose custody he found himself. They entered the hackney-coach, which was waiting at a little distance, and immediately proceeded by the shortest cuts towards the chief office in Bow street.

Upon their arrival at that ominous establishment, Richard's pocket-book and purse were taken away from him; and he himself was thrust into a cell until the charge at that moment before the magistrate was disposed of.

Here must we leave him for the present; as during the night which followed his arrest, scenes of a terrible nature passed elsewhere.

CHAPTER XVII.

A DEN OF HORRORS.

However filthy, unhealthy, and repulsive the entire neighbourhood of West Street (Smithfield), Field Lane,[1] and Saffron Hill, may appear at the present day, it was far worse some years ago. There were then but few cesspools; and scarcely any of those which did exist, possessed any drains. The knackers' yards of Cow Cross, and the establishments in Castle Street where horses' flesh is boiled down to supply food for the dogs and cats of the metropolis, send forth now, as they did then, a fœtid and sickening odour which could not possibly be borne by a delicate stomach. At the windows of those establishments the bones of the animals are hung to bleach, and offend the eye as much as the horrible stench of the flesh acts repugnantly to the nerves. Upwards of sixty horses a day are frequently slaughtered in each yard; and many of them are in the last stage of disease when sent to their "long home." Should there not be a rapid demand for the "meat" on the part of the itinerant purveyors of that article for canine and feline favourites, it speedily becomes putrid; and a smell, which would alone appear sufficient to create a pestilence, pervades the neighbourhood.

1 Field Lane: no longer there, Field Lane previously connected Saffron Hill with Holborn Hill. It is now the southern portion of Saffron Hill between Greville Street and Charterhouse Street.

As if nothing should be wanting to render that district as filthy and unhealthy as possible, water is scarce. There is in this absence of a plentiful supply of that wholesome article, an actual apology for dirt. Some of the houses have small back yards, in which the inhabitants keep pigs. A short time ago, an infant belonging to a poor widow, who occupied a back room on the ground-floor of one of these hovels, died, and was laid upon the sacking of the bed while the mother went out to make arrangements for its interment. During her absence a pig entered the room from the yard, and feasted upon the dead child's face!

In that densely populated neighbourhood that we are describing hundreds of families each live and sleep in one room. When a member of one of these families happens to die, the corpse is kept in the close room where the rest still continue to live and sleep. Poverty frequently compels the unhappy relatives to keep the body for days—aye, and weeks. Rapid decomposition takes place;—animal life generates quickly; and in four-and-twenty hours myriads of loathsome animalculæ are seen crawling about. The very undertakers' men fall sick at these disgusting—these revolting spectacles.

The wealthy classes of society are far too ready to reproach the miserable poor for things which are really misfortunes and not faults. The habit of whole families sleeping together in one room destroys all sense of shame in the daughters: and what guardian then remains for their virtue? But, alas! a horrible—an odious crime often results from that poverty which thus huddles brothers and sisters, aunts and nephews, all together in one narrow room—the crime of incest!

When a disease—such as the small-pox or scarlatina—breaks out in one of those crowded houses, and in a densely populated neighbourhood, the consequences are frightful: the mortality is as rapid as that which follows the footsteps of the plague!

These are the fearful mysteries of that hideous district which exists in the very heart of this great metropolis. From John Street to Saffron Hill—from West Street to Clerkenwell Green, is a maze of narrow lanes, choked up with dirt, pestiferous with nauseous odours, and swarming with a population that is born, lives, and dies, amidst squalor, penury, wretchedness, and crime.

Leading out of Holborn, between Field Lane and Ely Place, is Upper Union Court—a narrow lane forming a thoroughfare for only foot passengers. The houses in this court are dingy and gloomy: the sunbeams never linger long there; and should an Italian-boy pass through the place, he does not stop to waste his music upon the inhabitants. The dwellings are chiefly let out in lodgings; and through the open windows upon the ground-floor may occasionally be seen the half-starved families of mechanics crowding round the scantily-supplied table. A few of the lower casements are filled with children's books, pictures of actors and highwaymen glaringly coloured, and lucifer-matches, twine, sweet-stuff, cotton, &c. At one door there stands an oyster-stall, when the comestible itself is in season: over another hangs a small board with a mangle painted upon it. Most of the windows on the ground-floors announce rooms to let, or lodgings for single men; and perhaps a notice may be seen better written than the rest, that artificial-flower makers are required at that address.

It was about nine o'clock in the evening when two little children—a boy of seven and a girl of five—walked slowly up this court, hand in hand, and crying bitterly. They were both clothed in rags, and had neither shoes nor stockings upon their feet. Every now and then they stopped, and the boy turned towards his little sister, and endeavoured to console her with kind words and kisses.

"Don't cry so, dear," he said: "I'll tell mother that it was all my fault that we couldn't bring home any more money; and so she'll beat me worst. Don't cry—there's a good girl—pray don't!"

And the poor little fellow endeavoured to calm his own grief in order to appease the fears of his sister.

Those children had now reached the door of the house in which their mother occupied an attic; but they paused upon the step, evincing a mortal repugnance to proceed any farther. At length the little boy contrived by promises and caresses to hush the violence of his sister's grief; and they entered the house, the door of which stood open for the accommodation of the lodgers.

Hand in hand these poor children ascended the dark and steep staircase, the boy whispering consolation in the girl's ears. At length they reached the door of the attic: and there they stood for a few moments.

"Now, Fanny dear, don't cry, there's a good girl; pray don't now—and I'll buy you some nice pears to-morrow with the first halfpenny I get, even if I shouldn't get another, and if mother beats me till I'm dead when we come home."

The boy kissed his sister once more, and then opened the attic-door.

A man in a shabby black coat, and with an immense profusion of hair about his hang-dog countenance, was sitting on one side of a good fire, smoking a pipe. A thin, emaciated, but vixenish looking woman was arranging some food upon the table for supper. The entire furniture of the room consisted of that table, three broken chairs, and a filthy mattress in one corner.

As soon as the boy opened the door, he seemed for a moment quite surprised to behold that man at the fireside: then, in another instant, he clapped his little hands joyously together, and exclaimed, "Oh! how glad I am: here's father come home again!"

"Father's come home again!" echoed the girl; and the two children rushed up to their parent with the most pure—the most unfeigned delight.

"Curse your stupidity, you fools," cried the man, brutally repulsing his children; "you've nearly broke my pipe."

The boy fell back, abashed and dismayed: the little girl burst into tears.

"Come, none of this humbug," resumed the man; "let's know what luck you've had to-day, since your mother says that she's been obliged to send you out on the tramp since I've been laid up for this last six months in the jug."

"Yes, and speak out pretty plain, too, Master Harry," said the mother in a shrill menacing tone; "and none of your excuses, or you'll know what you have got to expect."

"Please, mother," said the boy, slowly taking some halfpence from his pocket, "poor little Fanny got all this. I was so cold and hungry I couldn't ask a soul; so if it ain't enough, mother, you must beat me—and not poor little Fanny."

As the boy uttered these words in a tremulous tone, and with tears trickling down his face, he got before his sister, in order to shield her, as it were, from his mother's wrath.

"Give it here, you fool!" cried the woman, darting forward, and seizing hold of the boy's hand containing the halfpence: then, having hastily glanced over the amount, she exclaimed, "You vile young dog! I'll teach you to come home here with your excuses! I'll cut your liver out of ye, I will!"

"How much has he brought?" demanded the man.

"How much! Why not more than enough to pay for the beer," answered the woman indignantly. "Eightpence-halfpenny—and that's every farthing! But won't I take it out in his hide, that's all?"

The woman caught hold of the boy, and dealt him a tremendous blow upon the back with her thin bony fist. He fell upon his knees, and begged for mercy. His unnatural parent levelled a volley of abuse at him, mingled with oaths and filthy expressions, and then beat him—dashed him upon the floor—kicked him—all but stamped upon his poor body as he writhed at her feet.

His screams were appalling.

Then came the turn of the girl. The difference in the years of the children did not cause any with regard to their chastisement; but while the unnatural mother dealt her heavy blows upon the head, neck, breast, and back of the poor little creature, the boy clasped his hands together, exclaiming, "O Mother! it was all my fault—pray don't beat little Fanny—pray don't!" Then forgetting his own pain, he threw himself before his sister to protect her—a noble act of self-devotion in so young a boy, and for which he only received additional punishment.

At length the mother sate down exhausted; and the poor lad drew his little sister into a corner, and endeavoured to soothe her.

The husband of that vile woman had remained unmoved in his seat, quietly smoking his pipe, while this horrible scene took place; and if he did not actually enjoy it, he was very far from disapproving of it.

"There," said the woman, gasping for breath, "that'll teach them to mind how they come home another time with less than eightpence in their pockets. One would actually think it was the people's fault, and not the children's: but it ain't—for people grows more charitable every day. The more humbug, the more charity."

"Right enough there," growled the man. "A reg'lar knowing beggar can make his five bob a day. He can walk through a matter of sixty streets; and in each street he can get a penny. He's sure o' that. Well, there's his five bob."

"To be sure," cried the woman: "and therefore such nice-looking little children as our'n couldn't help getting eighteen-pence if they was to try, the lazy vagabonds! What would ha' become of me all the time that you was in the Jug this last bout, if they hadn't have worked better than they do now? As it is, every thing's up the spout—all made away with——"

"Well, we'll devilish soon have 'em all down again," interrupted the man. "Dick will be here presently; and he and I shall soon settle some job or another. But hadn't you better give them kids their supper, and make 'em leave off snivellin' afore Dick comes?"

"So I will, Bill," answered the woman; and throwing the children each a piece of bread, she added, in a cross tone, "And now tumble into bed, and make haste about it; and if you don't hold that blubbering row I'll take the poker to you this time."

The little boy gave the larger piece of bread to his sister; and, having divested her of her rags, he made her as comfortable as he could on the filthy mattress, covering her over not only with *her* clothes but also with *his own*. He kissed her affectionately, but without making any noise with his lips, for fear that *that* should irritate his mother; and then lay down beside her.

Clasped in each other's arms, those two children of poverty—the victims of horrible and daily cruelties—repulsed by a father whose neck they had longed to encircle with their little arms, and whose hand they had vainly sought to cover with kisses; trembling even at the looks of a mother whom they loved in spite of all her harshness towards them, and from whose lips one word—one single word of kindness would have gladdened their poor hearts;—under such circumstances, we say, did these persecuted but affectionate infants, still smarting with the pain of cruel blows, and with tears upon their cheeks, thus did they sink into slumber in each other's arms!

Merciful God! it makes the blood boil to think that this is no overdrawn picture—that there is no exaggeration in these details; but that there really exist monsters in a human form—wearing often, too, the female shape—who make the infancy and early youth of their offspring one continued hell—one perpetual scene of blows, curses, and cruelties! Oh! for how many of our fellow-creatures have we to blush:—how many demons are there who have assumed our mortal appearance, who dwell amongst us, and who set us examples the most hideous—the most appalling!

As soon as the children were in bed, the woman went out, and returned in a few minutes with two pots of strong beer—purchased with the alms that day bestowed by the charitable upon her suffering offspring.

She and her husband then partook of some cold meat, of which there was a plentiful provision—enough to have allowed the boy and the girl each a good slice of bread.

And the bread which this man and this woman ate was new and good; but the morsels thrown to the children were stale and mouldy.

"I tell you what," said the woman, whispering in a mysterious tone to her husband, "I have thought of an excellent plan to make Fanny useful."

"Well, Polly, and what's that?" demanded the man.

"Why," resumed his wife, her countenance wearing an expression of demoniac cruelty and cunning, "I've been thinking that Harry will soon be of use to you in your line. He'll be so handy to shove through a window, or to sneak down a area and hide himself all day in a cellar to open the door at night,—or a thousand things."

"In course he will," said Bill, with an approving nod.

"Well, but then there's Fanny. What good can she do for us for years and years to come? She won't beg—I know she won't. It's all that boy's lies when he says she does: he is very fond of her, and only tells us that to screen her. Now I've a very great mind to do someot that will make her beg—aye, and be glad to beg—and beg too in spite of herself."

"What the hell do you mean?"

"Why, doing *that* to her which will put her entirely at our mercy, and at the same time render her an object of such interest that the people *must* give her money. I'd wager that with my plan she'd get her five bob a day; and what a blessin' that would be."

"But how?" said Bill impatiently.

"And then," continued the woman, without heeding this question, "she wouldn't want Henry with her; and you might begin to make him useful some how or another. All we should have to do would be to take Fanny every day to some good thoroughfare, put her down there of a mornin', and go and fetch her agen at night; and I'll warrant she'd keep us in beer—aye, and in brandy too."

"What the devil are you driving at?" demanded the man.

"Can't you guess?"

"No—blow me if I can."

"Do you fancy the scheme?"

"Am I a fool? Why, of course I do: but how the deuce is all this to be done? You never could learn Fanny to be so fly as that?"

"I don't want to learn her anything at all. What I propose is to force it on her."

"And how is that?" asked the man.

"By putting her eyes out," returned the woman.

Her husband was a robber—yes, and a murderer: but he started when this proposal met his ear.

"There's nothin' like a blind child to excite compassion," added the woman coolly. "I know it for a fact," she continued, after a pause, seeing that her husband did not answer her. "There's old Kate Betts, who got all her money by travelling about the country with two blind girls; and she made 'em blind herself too—she's often told me how she did it; and that has put the idea into my head."

"And how did she do it?" asked the man, lighting his pipe, but not glancing towards his wife; for although her words had made a deep impression upon him, he was yet struggling with the remnant of a parental feeling, which remained in his heart in spite of himself.

"She covered the eyes over with cockle shells, the eye-lids, recollect, being wide open; and in each shell there was a large black beetle. A bandage tied tight round the head, kept the shells in their place; and the shells kept the eyelids open. In a few days the eyes got quite blind, and the pupils had a dull white appearance."

"And you're serious, are you?" demanded the man.

"Quite," returned the woman, boldly: "why not?"

"Why not indeed?" echoed Bill, who approved of the horrible scheme, but shuddered at the cruelty of it, villain as he was.

"Ah! why not?" pursued the female: "one must make one's children useful somehow or another. So, if you don't mind,—I'll send Harry out alone to-morrow morning and keep Fanny at home. The moment the boy's out of the way, I'll try my hand at Kate Betts's plan."

The conversation was interrupted by a low knock at the attic-door.

CHAPTER XVIII.

THE BOOZING-KEN.

"Come in," exclaimed Bill: "I des say it's Dick Flairer."

"Well, Bill Bolter, old fellow—here you are at last," cried the new comer. "I s'pose you knowed I should come here this evenin'. If you hadn't sent me that message t'other day by the young area-sneak[1] what got his discharge out o' Coldbath Jug,[2] I should ha' come all the same. I remembered very well that you was sentenced to six months on it; and I'd calkilated days and weeks right enough."

"Sit down, Dick, and blow a cloud. Wot news since I see you last?"

"None. You know that Crankey Jem is nabbed. He and the Resurrection Man did a pannie[3] together somewhere up Soho way. They got off safe with the swag; and the Resurrection Man went on to the Mint.[4] Jem took to the Old House in Chick Lane,[5] and let me in for my reglars.[6] But after a week or ten days the Resurrection Man nosed[7] upon him, and will turn King's Evidence[8] afore the beaks. So Jem was handed over to the dubsman;[9] and this time he'll get lagged for life."

"In course he will. He has been twice to the floating academy.[10] There ain't no chance this time."

---

1 A thief who sneaks down areas to see what he can steal in kitchens. [Reynolds's note.]

2 Prison. [Reynolds's note.] Coldbath Prison, Clerkenwell, stood where Mount Pleasant Sorting Office stands today.

3 Burglary. [Reynolds's note.]

4 The Mint: not the Royal Mint, at the Tower of London, but the notorious Liberty, or no-go area for the Law, in Southwark.

5 West-street, Smithfield. [Reynolds's note.]

6 Gave him a share. [Reynolds's note.]

7 Informed. [Reynolds's note.]

8 When Reynolds was writing, the science of policing barely existed. The best hope for convicting a felon was for one of his companions to 'turn King's Evidence'—that is, to inform on him in court, in return for immunity from prosecution. The system was naturally hated by the criminal fraternity, but it was open to many abuses, and cases were known of criminals informing against the wrong man, or against the choice of the police, in return for their freedom.

9 Turnkey. [Reynolds's note.]

10 The Hulks. [Reynolds's note.]

"But as for business," said Dick Flairer, after a pause, during which he lighted his pipe and paid his respects to the beer, "my gropus is as empty as a barrister's bag the day after sessions. I have but one bob left in my cly[1] and that we'll spend in brandy presently. My mawleys[2] is reg'larly itching for a job."

"Someot must be done—and that soon too," returned Bill Bolter. "By-the-bye, s'pose we try that crib which we meant to crack four year or so ago, when you got nabbed the very next mornin' for faking a blowen's flag from her nutty arm."[3]

"What—you mean Markham's up between Kentish Town and Lower Holloway?" said Dick.

"The same. Don't you recollect—we settled it all the wery night as we threw that young fellow down the trap in Chick Lane? But, by goles—Dick—what the deuce is the matter with you?"

Dick Flairer had turned deadly pale at the mention of this circumstance: his knees shook; and he cast an uneasy and rapid glance around him.

"Come, Dick—don't be a fool," said the woman: "you don't think there is any ghosts here, do you?"

"Ghosts!" he exclaimed, with a convulsive start; then, after a moment's silence, during which his two companions surveyed him with curiosity and fear, he added in a low and subdued tone, "Bill, you know there wasn't a man in all the neighbourhood bolder than me up to the time when you got into trouble: you know that I didn't care for ghosts or churchyards, or dark rooms, or anything of that kind. Now it's quite altered. If ever a man seed speret of a person, that man was me about two months ago!"

"What the devil does this mean?" cried Bolter, looking uneasily around him in his turn.

"Two months ago," continued Dick Flairer, "I was up Hackney way, expecting to do a little business with Tom the Cracksman,[4] which didn't come off; for Tom had been at the boozing-ken[5] all the night before, and had blowed his hand up in a lark with some davy's-dust.[6]

---

1 Waistcoat-pocket. [Reynolds's note.]

2 Hands. [Reynolds's note.]

3 Stealing a lady's reticule from her pretty arm. [Reynolds's note.]

4 The Burglar. [Reynolds's note.]

5 Public-house. [Reynolds's note.]

6 Gunpowder. [Reynolds's note.]

Well, I was coming home again, infernal sulky at the affair's breaking down, when just as I got to Cambridge-Heath-gate I heerd the gallopin' of horses. I looks round, nat'rally enough;—but who should I see upon a lovely chestnut mare——"

"Who?" said Bill anxiously.

"The speret of that wery same young feller as you and I threw down the trap at the old house in Chick Lane four year and some months ago!"

"Mightn't it have been a mistake, Dick?" demanded Bill.

"Why, of course it was," exclaimed the woman.

"No, it warn't," said Dick very seriously. "I never tell a lie to a pal,[1] Bill—and that you knows well enough. I seed that young man as plain as I can now see you, Bill—as plain as I see you, Polly Bolter. I thought I should have dropped: I fell right against a post in the foot path; but I took another good long look. There he was—the same face—the same hair—the same dress—everything the same! I couldn't be mistaken: I'd swear to it."

"And would you tell this story to the parish-prig,[2] if so be as you was going to Tuck-up Fair[3] to-morrow morning?" demanded Bill.

"I would, by G—d!" cried Dick solemnly, striking his hand upon the table at the same time.

There was a long pause. Even the woman, who was perhaps more hardened in vice and more inaccessible to anything in the shape of sentiment than her male companions, seemed impressed by the positive manner in which the man told his story.

"Well—come, this won't do!" ejaculated Dick, after the lapse of some minutes. "Ghost or no ghost, we can't afford to be honest."

"No—we must be up to someot," returned Bill;—"if we went and offered ourselves to the parish prig he wouldn't take us as his clerk and sexton; so if he won't give us a lift, who the devil will? But, about that Markham's place?"

"The old fellow died a few months ago, I heard," said Dick; "the eldest son run away; and that brought about the father's death. As for the young 'un, he was grabbed this arternoon for smashing queer screens."[4]

---

1 A companion. [Reynolds's note.]

2 Chaplain. [Reynolds's note.]

3 The Gallows. [Reynolds's note.]

4 Passing forged notes. [Reynolds's note.]

"The devil he was! Well, there ain't no good to be done in that quarter, then? Do you know any other spekilation?"

"Tom the Cracksman and me was going to do a pannie in a neat little crib up by Clapton, that time when he blowed his hand nearly off, larking with his ben-culls.[1] I don't see why it shouldn't be done now. Tom told me about it. A young swell, fond of horses and dogs—lives exceeding quiet—never no company scarcely—but plenty of tin."

"Servants?" said Bill, interrogatively.

"One man—an old groom; and two women—three in all," replied Dick.

"That'll do," observed the woman, approvingly.

"Must we speak to the Cracksman first?" demanded Bill.

"Yes—fair play's a jewel. I don't believe the Resurrection Man would ever have chirped[2] if he had been treated properly. But if this thing is to be done, let it be done to-morrow night; and now let us go to the boozing-ken and speak to the Cracksman."

"I'm your man," said Bill; and the two thieves left the room together.

At the top of Union Court is Bleeding Hart Yard, leading to Kirby Street, at right angles to which is a narrow alley terminating on Great Saffron Hill. This was the road the burglars took.

It was now eleven o'clock, and a thick fog—so dense that it seemed as if it could be cut with a knife—prevailed. The men kept close together, for they could not see a yard before them. Here and there lights glimmered in the miserable casements; and the fog, thus faintly illuminated at intervals, appeared of a dingy copper colour.

The burglars proceeded along Saffron Hill.

The streets were nearly empty; but now and then the pale, squalid, and nameless forms of vice were heard at the door-ways of a few houses, endeavouring to lure the passers-by into their noisome abodes. A great portion of the unwholesome life of that district had sought relief from the pangs of misery and the remorse of crime, in sleep. Alas! the slumbers of the poor and of the guilty are haunted by the lean, lank, and gaunt visages of penury, and all the fearful escort of turpitude!

1 Friends. [Reynolds's note.]
2 Informed. [Reynolds's note.]

Through the broken shutters of several windows came the sounds of horrible revelry—ribald and revolting; and from others issued cries, shrieks, oaths and the sounds of heavy blows—a sad evidence of the brutality of drunken quarrels. Numerous Irish families are crowded together in the small back rooms of the houses on Saffron Hill; and the husbands and fathers gorge themselves, at the expense of broken-hearted wives and famishing children, with the horrible compound of spirit and vitriol, sold at the low gin-shops in the neighbourhood. Hosts of "Italian masters" also congregate in that locality; and the screams of the unfortunate boys, who writhe beneath the lash of their furious employers on their return home after an unsuccessful day with their organs, monkies, white mice, or chalk images, mingle with the other appalling or disgusting sounds, which make night in that district truly hideous.[1]

Even at the late hour at which the two burglars were wending their way over Saffron Hill, boys of ages ranging from seven to fifteen, were lurking in the courts and alleys, watching for any decently dressed persons, who might happen to pass that way. Those boys had for the most part been seduced from the control of their parents by the receivers of stolen goods in Field Lane, or else had been sent into the streets to thieve by those vile parents themselves.

Thus, as the hulks, the convict-ships, the penitentiaries, and the gallows, relieve society of one generation of villains, another is springing up to occupy the vacancy.

And this will always be the case so long as laws tend only to punish—and aim not to reform.

Dick Flairer and Bill Bolter proceeded, without exchanging many words together, through the dense fog, until they reached a low public-house, which they entered.

Nothing could be more filthy nor revolting than the interior of this "boozing-ken." Sweeps, costermongers, Jews, Irish bricklayers, and women of the town were crowding round the bar, drinking various malt and spirituous liquors fearfully adulterated. The beer,

---

1 The reference to white mice recalls the case of Bishop, Williams, and May, three resurrection-men convicted of the murder of the so-called 'Italian Boy' in 1831. Witnesses identified the victim as a beggar who exhibited white mice in a cage. The three men lived in Bethnal Green, a half-mile or so from 11, Suffolk Place, where Reynolds lived in the 1840s. Suffolk Place was on the corner of Hackney Road and Cambridge Heath Road, where much of this action is set.

having been originally deluged with water to increase the quantity, had been strengthened by drugs of most deleterious qualities—such as tobacco-juice and *cocculus-indicus*. The former is a poison as subtle as that of a viper: the latter is a berry of such venomous properties, that if thrown into a pond, it will speedily send the fish up to the surface to gasp and die.[1] The gin was mixed with vitriol, as hinted above; and the whiskey, called "Paddy's Eye-Water," with spirits of turpentine. The pots and glasses in which the various beverages were served up, were all stood upon double trays, with a cavity between, and numerous holes in the upper surface. The overflowings and drainings were thus caught and saved; and the landlord dispensed the precious compound, which bore the name of "all sorts," at a half-penny a glass.

The two burglars nodded familiarly to the landlord and his wife, as they passed the bar, and entered a little, low, smoky room, denominated "the parlour." A tremendous fire burnt in the grate, at which a short, thin, dark man, with a most forbidding countenance, was sitting, agreeably occupied in toasting a sausage. The right hand of this man had lost the two middle fingers, the stumps of which were still covered with plaister, as if the injury had been recent. He was dressed in a complete suit of corduroy: the sleeves of his jacket, the lower part of his waistcoat, and the front of his trowsers, were covered with grease. On the table near him stood a huge piece of bread and a pot of beer.

This individual was Tom the Cracksman—the most adroit and noted burglar in the metropolis. He kept a complete list of all the gentlemen's houses in the environs of London, with the numbers of servants and male inhabitants in each. He never attempted any dwelling within a circuit of three miles of the General Post Office; his avocation was invariably exercised in the suburbs of London, where the interference of the police was less probable.

At the moment when we introduce him to our readers, he was somewhat "down in his luck," as he himself expressed it, the accident which had happened to his hand, through playing with gunpowder, having completely disabled him for the preceding two months, and the landlord of the "boozing-ken" having made it an invariable rule

1 *Cocculus indicus* is the dried fruit of the *anamirta cocculus*, a climbing plant native to India. In small quantities it acts as a narcotic; in larger, it is fatal.

never to give credit. Thus, though the Cracksman had spent hundreds of pounds in that house, he could not obtain so much as a glass of "all sorts" without the money.

The Cracksman was alone in the parlour when Dick Flairer and Bill Bolter entered. Having toasted his sausage, the renowned burglar placed it upon the bread, and began eating his supper by means of a formidable clasp-knife, without deigning to cast a glance around.

At length Bill Bolter burst out into a loud laugh, and exclaimed, "Why, Tom, you're getting proud all on a sudden: you won't speak to your friends."

"Halloo, Bill, is that you?" ejaculated the burglar. "When did they turn you out of the jug?"

"This mornin' at twelve; and with never a brown in my pocket. Luckily the old woman had turned the children to some use during the time I was at the stepper, or else I don't know what would have become on us."

"And I'm as completely stitched up as a man could be if he'd just come out o' the workus," said Tom. "I just now spent my last tanner[1] for this here grub. Ah! it's a d——d hard thing for a man like me to be brought down to cag-mag,"[2] he added, glancing sulkily at the sausage, which he was eating half raw.

"We all sees ups and downs," observed Dick Flairer. "My opinion is that we are too free when we have the blunt."

"And there's them as is too close when we haven't it," returned the Cracksman bitterly. "There's the landlord of this crib, won't give a gen'leman like me tick not for one blessed farden. But things can't go on so: I'm blowed if I won't do a crack that shall be worth while; and then I'll open a ken in opposition to this. You'd see whether I'd refuse a pal tick in the hour of need."

"Well, you don't suppose that we are here just to amuse ourselves," said Dick: "we come to see you."

"Is anythink to be done?" demanded the Cracksman.

"First answer me this," cried Dick: "has that crib at Upper Clapton been cracked yet?"

"What where there's a young swell——"

"I don't know nothing more about it than wot you told me,"

1 Sixpence. [Reynolds's note.]
2 Bad Meat. [Reynolds's note.]

interrupted Dick. "Me and you was to have done it; and then you went larking with the davy's-dust——"

"I know the crib you mean," said the Cracksman hastily: "that job is yet to be done. Are you the chaps to have a hand in it."

"That's the very business that we're come for," answered Bill.

"Well," resumed the Cracksman, "it seems we're all stumped up, and can't hold out no longer. We won't put this thing off—it shall be done to-morrow night. Eleven's the hour. I will go Dalston way—you two can arrange about the roads you'll take, so long as you don't go together; and we'll all three meet at the gate of Ben Price's field at eleven o'clock."

"So far, so good," said Dick Flairer. "I've got a darkey[1] but we want the kifers[2] and tools."

"And a sack," added Bill.

"We must get all these things of old Moses Hart, the fence;[3] and give him a share of the swag," exclaimed the Cracksman. "Don't bother yourselves about *that*; I'll make it all right."

"Well, now that's settled," said Dick. "I've got a bob in my pocket, and we'll have a rinse of the bingo."

The burglar went out to the bar, and returned with some brandy, which he and his companions drank pure.

"So Crankey Jem's in quod?" observed the Cracksman, after a pause.

"Yes—and the Resurrection Man too: but he has chirped, and will be let out after sessions."

"You have heard of his freak over in the Borough I s'pose," said the Cracksman.

"No I haven't," answered Bill. "What was it?"

"Oh! a capital joke. The story's rather long; but it will bear telling. There's a young fellow of the name of Sam Chisney; and his father died about two year ago leaving two thousand pounds in the funds. The widder was to enjoy the interest during *her* life; and then it was to come, principal and interest both, to Sam. Well, the old woman gets into debt, and is arrested. She goes over to the Bench, takes the Rules,[4] and hires a nice lodging on the ground floor in Belvidere

1 Dark lanthorn. [Reynolds's note.]

2 Implements used by burglars. [Reynolds's note.]

3 Receiver of Stolen Goods. [Reynolds's note.]

4 That is, she declares herself insolvent to avoid legal process.

Place. The young feller wants his money very bad, and doesn't seem at all disposed to wait for the old lady's death, particklar as she might live another ten years. Well, he comes across the Resurrection Man, and tells him just how he's sitivated. The Resurrection Man thinks over the matter; and, being a bit of a scholar, understands the business. Off they goes and consults a lawyer named Mac Chizzle, who lives up in the New Road, somewhere near the *Servants' Arms* there."

"I know that crib well," observed Bill. "It's a wery tidy and respectable one."

"So Mac Chizzle, Sam Chisney, and the Resurrection Man lay their heads together, and settle the whole business. The young chap then goes over to the old woman, and tells her what is to be done. She consents: and all's right. Well, that very day the old lady is taken so bad—so very bad, she thinks she's a goin' to die. She won't have no doctor; but she sends for a nurse as she knows—an old creatur' up'ards of seventy and nearly in her dotage. Then Sam comes; and he's so sorry to see his poor dear mother so ill; and she begins to talk very pious, and to bless him, and tell him as how she feels that she can't live four-and-twenty hours. Sam cries dreadful, and swears he won't leave his poor dear mother—no, not for all the world. He sits up with her all night, and is so exceedin' kind; and he goes out and gets a bottle of medicine—which arter all worn't nothink but gin and peppermint. The old nurse is quite pleased to think that the old woman has got such a attentive son; and he sends out to get a little rum; and the old nurse goes to bed blind drunk."

"What the devil was all that for?" demanded Dick.

"You'll see in a moment," resumed the Cracksman. "Next night at about ten o'clock the young fellow says to the nurse—'Nurse, my poor dear mother is wasting away: she can't last out the night. I do feel so miserable; and I fancy a drop of the rum that they sell at a partickler public, close up by Westminster Bridge.' 'Well, my dear,' says the nurse, 'I'll go and get a bottle there; for I feel that we shall both want someot to cheer us through this blessed night.' So the old nurse toddles off to get the rum at the place Sam told her. He had sent her away to a good long distance on purpose. The moment she was gone, Mrs. Chisney gets up, dresses herself as quick as she can, and is all ready just as a hackney-coach drives up to the door. Sam runs down: all was as right as the mail. There was the Resurrection

Man in the coach, with the dead body of a old woman that had only been buried the day before, and that he'd had up again during the night. So Sam and the Resurrection Man they gets the stiff 'un up stairs, and Mrs. Chisney she jumps into the coach and drives away to a comfortable lodging which Mac Chizzle had got for her up in Somers Town."

"Now I begin to twig,"[1] exclaimed Dick Flairer.

"Presently the old nurse comes back; and Sam meets her on the stairs, whimpering as hard as he could; and says, 'Oh! nurse—your poor dear missus is gone: your poor dear missus is gone!' So she was; no mistake about that. Well, the nurse begins to cry; but Sam gets her up stairs, and plies her so heartily with the rum that she got blind drunk once more, without ever thinking of laying the body out; so she didn't find out it was quite cold. Next day she washed it, and laid it out properly; and as she was nearly blind, she didn't notice that the features wasn't altogether the same. The body, too, was a remarkable fresh 'un; and so everything went on as well as could be wished. Sam then stepped over to the Marshal of the Bench, and give him notice of his mother's death; and as she died in the Rules, there must be an inquest. So a jury of prisoners was called: and the old nurse was examined; and she said how exceedin' attentive the young man had been, and all that; and then Sam himself was called. Of course he told a good tale; and then the Coroner says, 'Well, gentlemen, I s'pose you'll like to look at the body.' So over they all goes to Belvidere Place, and the foreman of the Jury just pokes his nose in at the door of the room where the corpse was lying; and no one else even went more than half up the staircase. After this, the jury is quite satisfied, and return a verdict of *'Died from Natural Causes, accelerated by confinement in the Rules of the King's Bench Prison;'* and to this—as they were prisoners themselves—they added some very severe remarks upon *'the deceased's unfeeling and remorseless creditors.'* Then comes the funeral, which was very respectable; and Sam Chisney was chief mourner; and he cried a good deal. All the people who saw it said they never saw a young man so dreadful cut up. In this way they killed the old woman: the son proved her death, got the money, and sold it out every farden; and he and his mother is keeping a public-house together somewhere up Spitalfields way. The Resurrection Man and

1 Twig: catch on, understand. From Irish *tuig* (pronounced twig).

Mac Chizzle each got a hundred for their share in the business; and the thing passed off as comfortable as possible."

"Well, I'm blowed if that isn't the best lark I ever heard," ejaculated Dick, when the Cracksman had brought his tale to an end.

"So it is," added Bill.

The parlour of the "boozing-ken" now received some additional guests—all belonging to the profession of roguery, though not all following precisely the same line. Thus there were Cracksmen, Magsmen,[1] Area-sneaks, Public Patterers,[2] Buzgloaks,[3] Dummy-Hunters,[4] Compter-Prigs,[5] Smashers,[6] Flimsy-Kiddies,[7] Macers,[8] Coiners, Begging-Letter Impostors, &c. &c.

The orgies of that motley crew soon became uproarious and revolting. Those who had money lavished it with the most reckless profusion; and thus those who had none were far from being in want of liquor.

The Cracksman was evidently a great man amongst this horrible fraternity: his stories and songs invariably commanded attention.

It is not our purpose to detain the reader much longer in the parlour of the "boozing-ken." We have doubtless narrated enough in this and the preceding chapter to give him a faint idea of some of the horrors of London. We cannot, however, allow the morning scene to pass unnoticed.

CHAPTER XIX.

MORNING.

The orgie lasted throughout the night in the "boozing-ken." There

1 Swell-mobites. [Reynolds's note.]

2 Swell-mobites who affect to be dissenting ministers, and preach in the open air in order to collect crowds, upon whose pockets their confederates work. [Reynolds's note.]

3 Common thieves. [Reynolds's note.]

4 Thieves who steal pocket-handkerchiefs. [Reynolds's note.]

5 Swell-mobites who steal from the compters in shops, while their confederates make some trifling purchase. These thieves often contrive to empty the till. [Reynolds's note.]

6 Persons who pass false money. [Reynolds's note.]

7 Persons who pass forged bank-notes at races, fairs. [Reynolds's note.]

8 Common cheats. [Reynolds's note.]

were plenty of kind guests who, being flush of money, treated those that had none; and thus Tom the Cracksman, Dick Flairer, and Bill Bolter, were enabled to indulge, to their heart's content, in the adulterated liquors sold at the establishment.

The cold raw November morning was ushered in with a fine mizzling rain. The gas-lights were extinguished in the parlour; and the dawn of day fell upon countenances inflamed with debauchery, and rendered hideous by dirt and dark bristling beards.

That was a busy hour for the landlord and landlady of the "boozing-ken." The neighbours who "used the house," came in, one after another—male and female, to take their "morning." This signified their first dram.

Then was it that the "all sorts" was in great demand. Old clothesmen, sweeps, dustmen, knackers, crimps, and women of the town, crowded round the bar, imbibing the strange but potent compound. Even young boys and girls of tender age seemed as a matter of course to require the morning stimulant ere they commenced the avocations or business of the day. Matted hair, blear-eyes, grimy faces, pestiferous breaths, and hollow cheeks, combined with rags and tatters, were the characteristics of the wretches that thronged about the bar of that lowest of low drinking-dens.

Nothing is more revolting to the eye than the unwashed aspect of dissipation by the dingy light of the early dawn. The women had evidently jumped from their beds and huddled on their miserable attire without the slightest regard to decency, in order to lose no time in obtaining their morning dram. The men appeared as if they had slept in their clothes all night; and the pieces of straw in the coarse matted hair of many of them, plainly denoted of what materials their beds were made.

They all entered shivering, cold, depressed, and sullen. The dram instantly produced an extraordinary change in each. Artificial gaiety—a gaiety which developed itself in ribald jokes, profane oaths, and obscene talk—was diffused around. Those who could afford it indulged in a second and a third glass; and some tossed for pots of beer. The men lighted their pipes; and the place was impregnated with the narcotic fumes of the strongest and worst tobacco—that bastard opium of the poor.

Presently the policeman "upon that beat" lounged in, and was complimented by the landlady with a glass of her "best cordial gin." He seemed well acquainted with many of the individuals there, and laughed heartily at the jokes uttered in his presence. When he was gone, the inmates of the "boozing-ken" all declared, with one accord, "that he was the most niblike[1] blue-bottle in the entire force."

In the parlour there were several men occupied in warming beer, toasting herrings, and frying sausages. The tables were smeared over with a rag as black as a hat, by a dirty slip-shod drab of a girl; and with the same cloth she dusted the frame of wire-work which protected the dingy face of the huge Dutch clock. Totally regardless of her presence, the men continued their obscene and filthy discourse; and she proceeded with her work as coolly as if nothing offensive met her ears.

There are, thank God! thousands of British women who constitute the glory of their sex—chaste, virtuous, delicate-minded, and pure in thought and action,—beings who are but one remove from angels now, but who will be angels hereafter when they succeed to their inheritance of immortality. It must be to such as these that the eyes of the poet are turned when he eulogises, in glowing and impassioned language, the entire sex comprehended under the bewitching name of WOMAN! For, oh! how would his mind be shocked, were he to wander for a few hours amidst those haunts of vice and sinks of depravity which we have just described;—his spirit, towering on eagle-wing up into the sunny skies of poesy, would flutter back again to the earth, at the aspect of those foul and loathsome wretches, who, in the female shape, are found in the dwelling-places of poverty and crime!

But to continue.

Bill Bolter took leave of his companions at about eight o'clock in the morning, after a night of boisterous revelry; and rapidly retraced his steps homewards.

Field Lane was now swarming with life. The miserable little shops were all open; and their proprietors were busy in displaying their commodities to the best advantage. Here Jewesses were occupied in suspending innumerable silk handkerchiefs to wires and poles over their doors: there the "translators" of old shoes were employed in spreading their stock upon the shelves that filled the place where the

1 Gentlemanly—agreeable. [Reynolds's note.]

windows ought to have been. In one or two low dark shops women were engaged in arranging herrings, stock-fish, and dried haddocks: in another, coals, vegetables, and oysters were exposed for sale; and not a few were hung with "old clothes as good as new." To this, we may add that in the centre of the great metropolis of the mightiest empire in the world—in a city possessing a police which annually costs the nation thousands of pounds—and in a country whose laws are vaunted as being adapted to reach and baffle all degrees of crime—numbers of receivers of stolen goods were boldly, safely, and tranquilly exposing for sale the articles which their agents had "picked up" during the preceding night.

There was, however, nothing in the aspect of Field Lane at all new to the eyes of Bill Bolter. Indeed he merely went down that Jew's bazaar, in his way homewards, because he was anxious to purchase certain luxuries in the shape of red-herrings for his breakfast, he having borrowed a trifle of a friend at the "boozing-ken" to supply his immediate necessities.

When he arrived at his lodgings in Lower Union Court, he was assailed with a storm of reproaches, menaces, and curses, on the part of his wife, for having stayed all night at the "boozing ken." At first that cruel and remorseless man trembled—actually turned pale and trembled in the presence of the virago who thus attacked him. But at length his passion was aroused by her taunts and threats; and, after bandying some horrible abuse and foul epithets with the infuriate woman, he was provoked to blows. With one stroke of his enormous fist, he felled her to the ground, and then brutally kicked her as she lay almost senseless at his feet.

He then coolly sate down by the fire to cook his own breakfast, without paying the least attention to the two poor children, who were crying bitterly in that corner of the room where they had slept.

In a few minutes the woman rose painfully from the floor. Her features were distorted and her lips were livid with rage. She dared not, however, attempt to irritate her furious husband any farther: still her passion required a vent. She looked round, and seemed to reflect for a moment.

Then, in the next instant, all her concentrated rage burst upon the heads of her unhappy offspring.

With a horrible curse at their squalling, the woman leapt, like a tiger-cat, upon the poor little boy and girl. Harry, as usual, covered his sister with his own thin and emaciated form as well as he could; and a torrent of blows rained down upon his naked flesh. The punishment which that maddened wretch thus inflicted upon him, was horrible in the extreme.

A thousand times before that day had Polly Bolter treated her children with demoniac cruelty; and her husband had not attempted to interfere. On the present occasion, however, he took it into his head to meddle in the matter—for the simple reason that, having quarrelled with his wife, he hated her at the moment, and greedily availed himself of any opportunity to thwart or oppose her.

Starting from his chair, he exclaimed, "Come, now—I say, leave those children alone. They haven't done nothing to you."

"You mind your own business," returned the woman, desisting for an instant from her attack upon the boy, and casting a look of mingled defiance and contempt at her husband.

That woman's countenance, naturally ugly and revolting, was now absolutely frightful.

"I say, leave them children alone," cried Bill. "If you touch 'em again, I'll drop down on you."

"Oh, you coward! to hit a woman! I wish I was a man, I'd pay you off for this: and if I was, you wouldn't dare strike me."

"Mind what you say, Poll; I'm in no humour to be teased this morning. Keep your mawleys[1] off the kids, or I'm blessed if I don't do for you."

"Ugh—coward! This is the way I dare you;" and she dealt a tremendous blow upon her boy's shoulder.

The poor lad screamed piteously: the hand of his mother had fallen with the weight of a sledge hammer upon his naked flesh.

But that ferocious blow was echoed by another, at scarcely a moment's interval. The latter was dealt by the fist of Bill Bolter, and fell upon the back part of the ruthless mother's head with stunning force.

The woman fell forward, and struck her face violently against the corner of the deal table.

Her left eye came in contact with the angle of the board, and was literally crushed in its socket—an awful retribution upon her who

1 Hands. [Reynolds's note.]

only a few hours before was planning how to plunge her innocent and helpless daughter into the eternal night of blindness.

She fell upon the floor, and a low moan escaped her lips. She endeavoured to carry her right hand to her now sightless eye; but her strength failed her, and her arm fell lifeless by her side. She was dying.

The man was now alarmed, and hastened to raise her up. The children were struck dumb with unknown fears, and clasped each other in their little arms.

The woman recovered sufficient consciousness, during the two or three seconds which preceded the exhalation of her last breath, to glance with her remaining eye up into her husband's face. She could not, however, utter an articulate sound—not even another moan.

But no pen could depict, and no words describe, the deadly—the malignant—the fiendish hatred which animated her countenance as she thus met her husband's gaze.

The tigress, enveloped in the folds of the boa-constrictor, never darted such a glance of impotent but profound and concentrated rage upon the serpent that held it powerless in its fatal clasp.

She expired with her features still distorted by that horrible expression of vindictive spite.

A few moments elapsed before the man was aware that his wife was dead—that he had murdered her!

He supported her mechanically, as it were; for he was dismayed and appalled by the savage aspect which her countenance had assumed—that countenance which was rendered the more hideous by the bleeding eye-ball crushed in its socket.

At length he perceived that she was no more; and, with a terrible oath, he let her head drop upon the floor.

For a minute he stood and contemplated the corpse:—a whirlwind was in his brain.

The voices of his children aroused him from his reverie.

"Father, what's the matter with mother?" asked the boy, in a timid and subdued tone.

"Mother's hurt herself," said Fanny: "poor mother!"

"Look at mother's eye, father," added the boy: "do look at it! I'm sure something dreadful is the matter."

"Damnation!" ejaculated the murderer: and, after another minute's hesitation, he hurried to the door.

"O, father, father, don't leave us—don't go away from us!" cried the little boy, bursting into an agony of tears: "pray don't go away, father! I think mother's dead," added he with a glance of horror and apprehension towards the corpse: "so don't leave us, father—and I and Fanny will go out and beg, and do anything you like; only pray don't leave us; don't, don't, leave us!"

With profound anguish in his heart, the little fellow clung to his father's knees, and proffered his prayer in a manner the most ingenuous—the most touching.

The man paused, as if he knew not what to do.

His hesitation lasted but a moment. Disengaging himself from the arms of his child, he said in as kind a tone as he could assume—and that tone was kinder than any he had ever used before—"Don't be foolish, boy; I shall be back directly. I'm only going to fetch a doctor—I shan't be a minute."

"Oh, pray don't be long, father!" returned the boy, clasping his little hands imploringly together.

In another moment the two children were alone with the corpse of their mother; while the murderer was rapidly descending the stairs to escape from the contemplation of that scene of horror.

CHAPTER XX.

THE VILLA.

Again the scene changes. Our readers must accompany us once more to the villa in the neighbourhood of Upper Clapton.

It was the evening of the day on which was perpetrated the dreadful deed related in the preceding chapter. The curtains were drawn over the dining-room windows; a cheerful fire burned in the grate; and a lamp, placed in the middle of the table, diffused a pleasant and mellowed light around. An air of comfort, almost amounting to luxury, pervaded that apartment; and its general temperature was the better appreciated, as the wind whistled without, and the rain pattered against the windows.

At the table, on which stood a dessert of delicious fruits, conserves, cakes, and wines, sate Walter Sydney and George Montague.

They had now been acquainted nearly three months; and during that period they had met often. Montague had, however, seldom called at the villa, save when expressly invited by his friend Stephens: still, upon those occasions, he and Walter were frequently alone for some time together. Thus, while Stephens was examining into the economy of the stables, or superintending improvements in the garden, Montague and that mysterious lady in man's attire, were thrown upon their own resources to entertain each other.

The reader cannot be surprised if an attachment sprung up between them. So far as that lovely woman was concerned, we can vouch that her predilection towards George Montague was the sincere and pure sentiment of a generous and affectionate heart. How worthy of such a passion his own feelings on the subject might have been, must appear hereafter.

The masculine attire and habits which the lady had assumed, had not destroyed the fine and endearing characteristics of her woman's heart. She was at first struck by Montague's handsome person;—then his varied conversation delighted her;—and, as he soon exerted all his powers to render himself agreeable to the heroine of the villa, it was not long before he completely won her heart.

The peculiarity of her position had taught her—and necessarily so—to exercise an almost complete command over the expression of her feelings. Thus, though an explanation had taken place between herself and Montague, and a mutual avowal of affection made, Stephens remained without a suspicion upon the subject.

On the evening when we again introduce our readers to the villa, Montague was there by the express desire of Mr. Stephens; but this latter individual had been detained by particular business elsewhere. Walter—for so we must continue to call that mysterious being—and Montague had therefore dined tête-à-tête; and they were now enjoying together the two or three pleasant hours which succeed the most important meal of the day.

The plans of the lovers will be comprehended by means of the ensuing conversation, better than if drily detailed in our own narrative style:—

"Another fortnight—two short weeks only," said the lady, "and the end of this deception will have arrived."

"Yes—another fortnight," echoed Montague; "and everything will then be favourable to our wishes. The 26th of November——"

"My poor brother, were he alive, would be of age on the 25th," observed the lady, mournfully.

"Of course—precisely!" ejaculated Montague. "On the 26th, as I was saying, Stephens's plans will be realized; and you will be worth ten thousand pounds."

"Oh! it is not so much for the money that I shall welcome that day: but chiefly because it will be the last on which I shall be doomed to wear this detestable disguise."

"And shall not I be supremely happy to leave this land with you—to call you my own dear beloved wife—and to bear you away to the sunny climes of the south of Europe, where we may live in peace, happiness, and tranquillity to the end of our days?"

"What a charming—what a delicious picture!" ejaculated the lady, her bosom heaving with pleasurable emotions beneath the tight frock which confined it. "But——oh! if the plans of Mr. Stephens should fail;—and that they *might* fail, I am well assured, for he has often said to me, '*Pray be circumspect, Walter: you know not how much depends upon your discretion!*'"

"Those plans *will* not—*cannot* fail!" cried Montague emphatically. "He has told me all—and everything is so well arranged, so admirably provided for!"

"He has told you everything," said the lady, reproachfully; "and he has told me nothing."

"And I dare not enlighten you."

"Oh! I would not hear the secret from your lips. I have a confidence the most blind—the most devoted in Mr. Stephens; and I feel convinced that he must have sound reasons for keeping me thus in the dark with reference to the principal motives of the deception which I am sustaining. I know, moreover—at least, he has declared most solemnly to me, and I believe his word—that no portion of his plan militates against honour and integrity. He is compelled to meet intrigue with intrigue; but all his proceedings are justifiable. There can be no loss of character—no danger from the laws of the country. In all this I am satisfied—because a man who has done so much for me and my poor deceased mother, would not lead me astray, nor involve me either in disgrace or peril."

"You are right," said Montague. "Stephens is incapable of deceiving you."

"And more than all that I have just said," continued Walter, "I am aware that there is an immense fortune at stake; and that should the plans of Mr. Stephens fully succeed, I shall receive ten thousand pounds as a means of comfortable subsistence for the remainder of my life."

"And that sum, joined to what I possess, and to what *I shall have*," added Montague, "will enable us to live in luxury in a foreign land. Oh! how happy shall I be when the time arrives for me to clasp you in my arms—to behold you attired in the garb which suits your sex, and in which I never yet have seen you dressed—and to call you by the sacred and endearing name of WIFE! How beautiful must you appear in those garments which——"

"Hush, George—no compliments!" cried the lady, with a smile

and a blush. "Wait until you see me dressed as you desire; and, perhaps, then—*then*, you may whisper to me the soft and delicious language of love."

The time-piece upon the mantel struck eleven; and Montague rose to depart.

It was an awful night. The violence of the wind had increased during the last hour; and the rain poured in torrents against the windows.

"George, it is impossible that you can venture out in such weather as this," said the lady, in a frank and ingenuous manner: "one would not allow a dog to pass the door on such a night. Fortunately there is a spare room in my humble abode; and that chamber is at your service."

Walter rang the bell, and gave Louisa the necessary instructions.

In another half-hour Montague was conducted to the apartment provided for him, and Walter retired to the luxurious and elegant boudoir which we have before described.

The satin curtains were drawn over the casement against which the rain beat with increasing fury: a cheerful fire actually roared in the grate; and the thick carpet upon the floor, the inviting lounging-chair close by the hearth, and the downy couch with its snow-white sheets and warm clothing, completed the air of comfort which prevailed in that delicious retreat. The vases of sweet flowers were no longer there, it was true; but a fragrant odour of bergamot and lavender filled the boudoir. Nothing could be more charming than this warm, perfumed, and voluptuous chamber—worthy of the lovely and mysterious being who seemed the presiding divinity of that elysian bower.

Walter threw herself into the easy-chair, and dismissed her attendant, saying, "You may retire, Louisa,—I will undress myself without your aid to-night; for as yet I do not feel inclined to sleep. I shall sit here, before this cheerful fire, and indulge in the luxury of hopes and future prospects, ere I retire to rest."

Louisa withdrew, and Walter then plunged into a delicious reverie. The approaching emancipation from the thraldom of an assumed sex—her affection for George Montague—and the anticipated possession of an ample fortune to guard against the future, were golden visions not the less dazzling for being waking ones.

Half an hour had passed away in this manner, when a strange

noise startled Walter in the midst of her meditations. She thought that she heard a shutter close violently and a pane of glass smash to pieces almost at the same moment. Alarm was for an instant depicted upon her countenance: she then smiled, and, ashamed of the evanescent fear to which she had yielded, said to herself, "It must be one of the shutters of the dining-room or parlour down stairs, that has blown open."

Taking the lamp in her hand she issued from the boudoir, and hastily descended the stairs leading to the ground floor. In her way thither she could hear, even amidst the howling of the wind, the loud barking of the dogs in the rear of the villa.

The hall, as she crossed it, struck piercing cold, after the genial warmth of the boudoir which she had just left. She cautiously entered the parlour on the left hand of the front door: all was safe. Having satisfied herself that the shutters in that apartment were securely closed and fastened, she proceeded to the dining-room.

She opened the door and was about to cross the threshold, when—at that moment—the lamp was dashed from her hand by some one inside the room; and she herself was instantly seized by two powerful arms, and dragged into the apartment.

A piercing cry issued from her lips; and then a coarse and hard hand was pressed violently on her mouth. Further utterance was thus stopped.

"Here—Bill—Dick," said a gruff voice; "give me a knife—I must settle this feller's hash—or I'm blessed if he won't alarm the house."

"No more blood—no more blood!" returned another voice, hastily, and with an accent of horror. "I had enough of that this mornin'. Gag him, and tie him up in a heap."

"D—n him, do for him!" cried a third voice. "Don't be such a cursed coward, Bill."

"Hold your jaw, will ye—and give me a knife, Dick," said the first speaker, who was no other than Tom the Cracksman. "The fellow struggles furious—but I've got hold on him by the throat."

Scarcely had these words issued from the lips of the burglar, when the door was thrown open, and Montague entered the room.

He held a lamp in one hand, and a pistol in the other; and it was easy to perceive that he had been alarmed in the midst of his repose, for he had nothing on save his trousers and his shirt.

On the sudden appearance of an individual thus armed, Tom the Cracksman exclaimed, "At him—down with him! We must make a fight of it."

The light of the lamp, which Montague held in his hand, streamed full upon the countenance and person of Walter Sydney, who was struggling violently in the suffocating grasp of the Cracksman.

"Hell and furies!" ejaculated Dick Flairer, dropping his dark lanthorn and a bunch of skeleton keys upon the floor, while his face was suddenly distorted with an expression of indescribable horror; then, in obedience to the natural impulse of his alarm, he rushed towards the window, the shutters and casement of which had been forced open, leapt through it, and disappeared amidst the darkness of the night.

Astonished by this strange event, Bill Bolter instantly turned his eyes from Montague, whom he was at that moment about to attack, towards the Cracksman and Walter Sydney.

The colour fled from the murderer's cheeks, as if a sudden spell had fallen upon him: his teeth chattered—his knees trembled—and he leant against the table for support.

There was the identical being whom four years and five months before, they had hurled down the trap-door of the old house in Chick Lane:—and who, that had ever met that fate as yet, had survived to tell the tale?

For an instant the entire frame of the murderer was convulsed with alarm: the apparition before him—the vision of his assassinated wife—and the reminiscences of other deeds of the darkest dye, came upon him with the force of a whirlwind. For an instant, we say, was he convulsed with alarm;—in another moment he yielded to his fears, and, profiting by his companion's example, disappeared like an arrow through the window.

Amongst persons engaged in criminal pursuits, a panic-terror is very catching. The Cracksman—formidable and daring as he was—suddenly experienced an unknown and vague fear, when he perceived the horror and unassumed alarm which had taken possession of his comrades. He loosened his grasp upon his intended victim: Walter made a last desperate effort, and released himself from the burglar's power.

"Approach me, and I will blow your brains out," cried Montague, pointing his pistol at the Cracksman.

Scarcely were these words uttered, when the burglar darted forward, dashed the lamp from the hands of Montague, and effected his escape by the window.

Montague rushed to the casement, and snapped the pistol after him: the weapon only flashed in the pan.

Montague closed the window and fastened the shutters. He then called Walter by name; and, receiving no answer, groped his way in the dark towards the door.

His feet encountered an obstacle upon the carpet: he stooped down and felt with his hands;—Walter Sydney had fainted.

Scarcely two minutes had elapsed since Montague had entered the room; for the confusion and flight of the burglars had not occupied near so much time to enact as to describe. The entire scene had moreover passed without any noise calculated to disturb the household.

There were consequently no servants at hand to afford Walter the succour which he required.

For a moment Montague hesitated what course to pursue; but, after one instant's reflection, he took her in his arms, and carried her up into her own enchanting and delicious boudoir.

CHAPTER XXI.

ATROCITY.

George Montague placed his precious burden upon the bed, and for a moment contemplated her pale but beautiful countenance with mingled feelings of admiration, interest, and desire. The lips were apart, and two rows of pearl glittered beneath. The luxuriant light chesnut hair rolled over his arm, on which he still supported that head of perfect loveliness: his hand thus played with those silken, shining tresses.

Still she remained motionless—lifeless.

Gently withdrawing his arm, Montague hastened to sprinkle her countenance with water. The colour returned faintly, very faintly to her cheeks; and her lips moved gently; but she opened not her eyes.

For a moment he thought of summoning Louisa to her assistance; then, obedient to a second impulse, he hastily loosened the hooks of her semi-military frock-coat.

Scarcely had his hand thus invaded the treasures of her bosom, when she moved, and unclosed the lids of her large melting hazel-eyes.

"Where am I?" she exclaimed, instinctively closing her coat over her breast.

"Fear not, dearest," whispered Montague; "it is I—I who love you."

The scene with the burglars instantly flashed to the mind of the lady; and she cried in a tone rendered tremulous by fear—"And those horrible men—are they all three gone?"

"They are gone—and you are safe."

"Oh! you will pardon me this weakness," continued Walter, hastily moving from the bed to a chair; "but two of those villains—I recognised them but too well—were the men who threw me down the trap-door in the old house near Smithfield."

"Hence their alarm—their panic, when they saw you," exclaimed Montague: "they fancied that they beheld a spirit instead of a reality. This accounts for their sudden and precipitate flight, till this moment unaccountable to me."

"And you, George," said the lady, glancing tenderly towards the young man—"you are my saviour from a horrible death! Another moment, and it would have been too late—they were going to murder me! Oh! how can I sufficiently express my gratitude."

She tendered him her hand, which he pressed rapturously to his lips;—and she did not withdraw it.

"I heard a noise of a shutter closing violently, and of a pane of glass breaking," said Montague: "I started from my bed and listened. In a few moments afterwards I heard footsteps on the stairs——"

"Those were mine, as I descended," interrupted Walter; "for I was alarmed by the same disturbance."

"And, then, while I was hastily slipping on my clothes," added Montague, "I heard a scream. Not another moment did I wait; but——"

"You came in time, I repeat, to save my life. Never—never shall I sufficiently repay you."

Again did Montague press the fair hand of that enchanting woman to his lips; and then, as he leant over her, their eyes met, and they exchanged glances of love—her's pure and chaste, his ardent and brimful of desire. He was maddened—he was emboldened by those innocent tokens of affection upon her part; and, throwing his arms around her, he imprinted hot and burning kisses upon her lips.

With difficulty did she disengage herself from his embrace; and she cast upon him a look of reproach mingled with melancholy.

"Pardon me, dearest one," he exclaimed, seizing her hand once more and pressing it to his lips, "is it a crime to love you so tenderly—so well?"

"No, George—no: you are my saviour—you soon will be my husband—you need not ask for my forgiveness. But now leave me—retire to your own room as noiselessly as you can; and to-morrow—to-morrow," she added with a blush, "it is not necessary that Louisa should know that you were *here*."

"I understand you, dearest," returned Montague; "your wishes shall ever be my commands. Good night, beloved one!"

"Good night, dear George," said the lady;—and in another moment she was again alone in the boudoir.

Montague returned to his apartment, full of the bliss which he had derived from the caresses enjoyed in a chamber that seemed sacred to mystery and love. He paced his own room with hasty and agitated steps: his brain was on fire.

His own loose ideas of morality induced him to put but little faith in the reality of female virtue. He moreover persuaded himself that the principles of rectitude—supposing that they had ever existed—in the bosom of the enchanting creature he had just left, had been undermined or destroyed by the cheat which she was practising with regard to her sex. And, lastly, he fancied that her affections were too firmly rivetted in him to refuse him anything.

Miserable wretch! he was blinded by his own mad desires. He knew not that woman's virtue is as real, as pure, and as precious as the diamond; he remembered not that the object of his licentious passion was innocent of aught criminal in the disguise which she had assumed;—he reflected not that the caresses which she had ere now permitted him to snatch, were those which the most spotless virgin may honourably award to her lover.

He paced his room in a frenzied manner—allowing his imagination to picture scenes and enjoyments of the most voluptuous kind. By degrees his passion became ungovernable: he was no longer the cool, calculating man he hitherto had been;—a new chord appeared to have been touched in his heart.

At that moment he would have signed a bond, yielding up all hopes of eternal salvation to the Evil One, for a single hour of love in the arms of that woman whom he had left in the boudoir!

His passion had become a delirium:—he would have plunged into the crater of Vesuvius, or throw himself from the ridge of the Alpine mountain into the boiling torrent beneath, had she gone before him.

An hour thus passed away, and he attempted not to subdue his feelings: he rather encouraged their wild and wayward course by recalling to his imagination the charms of her whose beauty had thus strangely affected him,—the endearing words which she had uttered,—the thrilling effect of the delicious kiss he had received from her moist vermilion lips,—and the voluptuous contours of that snowy bosom which had been for a moment revealed to his eyes.

An hour passed: he opened the door of his chamber and listened.

A dead silence prevailed throughout the house.

He stole softly along the passage and through the anteroom which led to the boudoir.

When he reached the door of that chamber he paused for a moment. What was he about to do? He waited not to answer the question, nor to reason within himself: he only chose to remember that a thin partition was all that separated him from one of the most beauteous creatures upon whom the sun ever shone in this world.

His fingers grasped the handle of the door: he turned it gently;—the door was not locked!

He entered the boudoir as noiselessly as a spectre. The lamp was extinguished; but the fire still burnt in the grate; and its flickering light played tremulously on the various objects around, bathing in a rich red glare the downy bed whereon reposed the heroine of the villa.

The atmosphere was warm and perfumed.

The head of the sleeper was supported upon one naked arm, which was round, polished, and of exquisite whiteness. The other lay outside the clothes, upon the coverlid. Her long hair flowed in undulations upon the snowy pillows. The fire shone with Rembrandt effect upon her countenance, one side of which was completely irradiated, while the other caught not its mellow light. Thus the perfect regularity of the profile was fully revealed to him who now dared to intrude upon those sacred slumbers.

"She shall be mine! she shall be mine!" murmured Montague; and he advanced toward the bed.

At that moment—whether aroused by a dream, or startled by the almost noiseless tread of feet upon the carpet, we cannot say—the lady awoke.

She opened her large hazel eyes; and they fell upon a figure to whom her imagination, thus suddenly surprised, and the flickering light of the fire, gave a giant stature.

Her fears in one respect were, however, immediately relieved; for the voice of Montague fell upon her ears almost as soon as her eyes caught sight of him.

"Pardon—pardon, dearest one!" he said in a hurried and subdued tone.

"Ah! is it so?" quickly ejaculated the lady, who in a moment comprehended how her privacy had been outraged; and passing her arm beneath the pillow, she drew forth a long, sharp, shining dagger.

Montague started back in dismay.

"Villain, that you are—approach this bed, and, without a moment's hesitation, I will plunge this dagger into your heart!"

"Oh! forgive me—forgive me!" ejaculated the young man, cruelly embarassed. "Dazzled by your beauty—driven mad by your caresses—intoxicated, blinded with passion—I could not command myself—I had no power over my actions."

"Attempt no apology!" said the lady, with a calm and tranquil bitterness of accent that showed how profoundly she felt the outrage—the atrocity,—that he, whom she loved so tenderly, had dared to meditate against her: "attempt no apology—but leave this room without an instant's delay, and without another word. Within my reach is a bell-rope—one touch of my finger and I can call my servants to my assistance. Save me that exposure—save yourself that disgrace. To-morrow I will tell you my opinion of your conduct."

There was something so determined—so cool—so resolute in the manner and the matter of this address, that Montague felt abashed—humbled—beaten down to the very dust. Even his grovelling soul at that moment comprehended the Roman mind of the woman whom he would have disgraced: a coward when burglars menaced her life, she was suddenly endowed with lion-daring in defence of her virtue.

The crest-fallen young man again attempted to palliate his intrusion: with superb scorn she waved her hand imperiously, as a signal to leave the room.

Tears of vexation, shame, and rage, started into his eyes, as he obeyed that silent mandate which he now dared no longer to dispute.

The moment the wretch had left the boudoir, the lady sprang from the bed and double-locked the door.

She then returned to her couch, buried her head in the pillow, and burst into an agony of tears.

CHAPTER XXII.

A WOMAN'S MIND.

WHEN Louisa entered the boudoir on the morning which succeeded this eventful night, nothing in Walter's countenance denoted the painful emotions that filled her bosom. She narrated the particulars of the burglarious entry of the dwelling, and Montague's opportune arrival upon the scene of action, with a calmness which surprised her faithful attendant. The truth was, that the attempt of the robbers upon the house, and even the danger in which her own life had been placed, had dwindled, in her own estimation, into events of secondary importance, when compared with that one atrocity which had suddenly wrecked all her hopes of love and happiness for ever.

The usual mysterious toilet was speedily performed; and, with a firm step and a countenance expressive of a stern decision, she descended to the breakfast-parlour.

Montague was already there—pale, haggard, abashed, and trembling. He knew that the chance of possessing a lovely woman and ten thousand pounds was then at stake; and, in addition to the perilous predicament of his nearest and dearest hopes, his position was embarrassing and unpleasant in the extreme. Had he succeeded in his base attempt, he would have been a victor flushed with conquest, and prepared to dictate terms to a woman entirely at his mercy:—but he had been foiled, and he himself was the dejected and baffled being who would be compelled to crave for pardon.

As Louisa entered the room close upon the heels of Walter, the latter greeted George Montague with a most affable morning's welcome, and conversed with him in a manner which seemed to say that she had totally forgotten the occurrence of the night.

But the moment that Louisa had completed the arrangements of the breakfast table, and had left the room, Walter's tone and manner underwent an entire and sudden change.

"You must not think, sir," she said, while a proud smile of scorn and bitterness curled her lips, "that I have this morning tasted of the waters of oblivion. To save you, rather than myself, the shame of being exposed in the presence of my servant, I assumed that friendly and familiar air which appears to have deceived you."

"What! then you have not forgiven me?" exclaimed Montague, profoundly surprised.

"Forgive you!" repeated the lady, almost indignantly: "do you suppose that I think so little of myself, or would give you such scope to think so little of me, as to pass by in silence a crime which was atrocious in a hundred ways? I loved you sincerely—tenderly—oh! God only knows how I loved you; and you would have taken advantage of my sincere and heartfelt affection. The dream in which I had indulged is now dispelled; the vision is over; the illusion is dissipated. Never would I accompany to the altar a man whom I could not esteem; and I can no longer esteem you. Then again, I offered you the hospitality of my abode; and that sacred rite you would have infamously violated. I cannot, therefore, even retain you as a friend. In another sense, too, your conduct was odious. You saved my life—and for that I shall ever remember you with gratitude: but you nevertheless sought to avail yourself of that service as a means of robbing me of my honour. Oh! all this was abominable—detestable on your part; and what is the result? My love can never avail you now; I will crush it—extinguish it in my bosom first. My friendship cannot be awarded; my gratitude alone remains. That shall accompany you; for we must now separate—and for ever."

"Separate—and for ever!" ejaculated Montague, who had listened with deep interest and various conflicting emotions to this strange address: "no—you cannot mean it? you will not be thus relentless?"

"Mr. Montague," returned the lady, with great apparent coolness—though in reality she was inflicting excruciating tortures upon her own heart; "no power on earth can alter my resolves. We shall part—here—now—and for ever; and may happiness and prosperity attend you."

"But Mr. Stephens?" cried Montague: "what can you say to him? what will he think?"

"He shall never know the truth from *me*," answered Walter solemnly.

"This is absurd!" ejaculated Montague, in despair at the imminent ruin of all his hopes. "Will not my humblest apology—my sincerest excuses—my future conduct,—will nothing atone for one false step, committed under the influence of generous wines and of a passion which obtained a complete mastery over me? will nothing move your forgiveness?"

"Nothing," answered Walter, with unvaried coolness and determination. "Were I a young girl of sixteen or seventeen, it might be different: *then* I might be deceived by your sophistry. *Now*, it is impossible! I am five and twenty years old; and circumstances," she added, glancing over her male attire, "have also tended to augment my experience in the sinuosities of human designs and the phases of the human heart."

"Yes—you are twenty-five, it is true," cried Montague; "but that age has not robbed your charms of any of the grace and freshness of youth. Oh! then let your mind be cautious how it adopts the severe notions of riper years!"

"I thank you for the compliment which you pay me," said Walter, satirically; "and I can assure you that it does not prove a welcome preface to the argument which you would found upon it. Old or young—experienced or ignorant in the ways of the world—a woman were a fool to marry where she could not entertain respect for her husband. I may be wrong: but this is my conviction;—and upon it will I act."

"This is but an excuse to break with me," said Montague: "you no longer love me."

"No—not as I did twelve hours ago."

"You never loved me! It is impossible to divest oneself of that passion so suddenly as this."

"Love in my mind is a species of worship or adoration, and can be damaged by the evil suspicions that may suddenly be thrown upon its object."

"No—that is not love," exclaimed Montague, passionately: "true love will make a woman follow her lover or her husband through all the most hideous paths of crime—even to the scaffold."

"The woman who truly loves, will follow her husband as a duty, but not her lover to countenance him in his crimes. We are not, however, going to argue this point:—for my part, I am not acting according to the prescribed notions of romances or a false sentimentality, but strictly in accordance with my own idea of what is suitable to my happiness and proper to my condition. I repeat, I am not the heroine of a novel in her teens—I am a woman of a certain age, and can reflect calmly in order to act decidedly."

Montague made no reply, but walked towards the window. Strange and conflicting sentiments were agitating in his brain.

'Twas thus he reasoned within himself.

"If I use threats and menaces, I shall merely open her eyes to the real objects which Stephens has in view; and she will shrink from the fearful dangers she is about to encounter. Whether she changes her mind or not with regard to me, and whether I proceed farther in the business or not, the secret is in my hands; and Stephens will pay me handsomely to keep it. Perhaps I had even better stop short where I am: I am still in a position to demand hush-money, and avoid the extreme peril which must accrue to all who appear prominently in the affair on the 26th of the month."

The selfish mind of George Montague thus revolved the various phases of his present position: and in a few moments he was determined how to act.

Turning towards Walter Sydney, he exclaimed, "You are decided not to forgive me?"

"I have made known to you my resolution—that we should now part, for ever."

"How can we part for ever, when your friend and benefactor, Mr. Stephens, requires my services?"

"Mr. Stephens informed me '*that a third person was necessary to the complete success of his designs, and that he had fixed upon you.*' Consequently, another friend may fill the place which he intended you to occupy."

"You seem to have well weighed the results of your resolution to see me no more," said Montague bitterly.

"There is time for thought throughout the livelong night, when sleep is banished from the pillow," returned the lady proudly.

"I can scarcely comprehend your conduct," said Montague, after another pause. "You do not choose that your servants should know what occurred last night: is it your intention to acquaint Mr. Stephens with the real truth?"

"That depends entirely upon yourself. To speak candidly, I do *not* wish to come to any explanation with Mr. Stephens upon the subject. He will blame me for having concealed from him the attachment which has subsisted between us; and he will imagine that some levity on my part must have encouraged you to violate the sanctity of my chamber. If you, sir, are a man of honour," added the lady emphatically,—"and if you have a spark of feeling and generosity left, you will take measures with Mr. Stephens to spare me that last mortification."

"I will do as you require," returned Montague, well pleased with this arrangement. "This very day will I communicate to Mr. Stephens my desire to withdraw from any further interference in his affairs; and I will allege the pressing nature of my own concerns as an excuse."

"Act as you will," said the lady; "but let there remain behind no motive which can lead you to repeat your visits to this house. You comprehend me?"

"Perfectly," replied Montague. "But once more let me implore you—"

"Enough—enough!" exclaimed Walter. "You know not the firmness of the female mind: perhaps I have this morning taught you a lesson in that respect. We must now part, Mr. Montague, and believe me—believe me, that, although no power on earth can alter the resolution to which I came during the long and painful vigil of the past night, I still wish you well;—and, remember, my gratitude accompanies you!"

Walter hesitated for a moment, as if another observation were trembling upon her tongue: then stifling her emotions with a powerful effort, she waved her hand to the delinquent, and abruptly left the room.

"Is this a loftiness of mind of which not even the greatest of men often afford example? or is it the miserable caprice of a vacillating woman?" said Montague to himself, as he prepared to take his departure from the villa in which he had spent some happy hours. "I must candidly admit that this time I am at fault. All appears to be lost in this quarter—and that, too, through my own confounded folly. But Stephens' secret still remains to me; and that secret shall be as good as an annuity for years to come. Let me see—I must have money now to insure my silence, upon breaking off all further connexion with the business. Then I must keep an eye upon him; and should he succeed on the 26th of this month—and he *must* succeed, if this punctilious lady does not see through his designs in the meantime—then can I step forward and demand another sum under a threat of exposing the entire scheme. And then, too," he added, while his countenance wore an expression of mingled revenge and triumph,—"then, too, can I appear before this vain, this scrupulous, this haughty woman, and with one word send her on her knees before me! Then will she stoop her proud brow, and her prayers and intercessions upon that occasion shall be expressed as humbly as her reproaches and her taunts were tyrannically levelled at me to-day! Yes!—I will keep my eye upon Walter Sydney and her benefactor Stephens," he said, with an ironical chuckle: "they may obtain their princely fortune, but a due share shall find its way into my pocket!"

These or similar reflections continued to occupy the mind of George Montague, after he had left the villa, and while he was on his way to the nearest point where he could obtain a conveyance to take him into the City.

CHAPTER XXIII.

THE OLD HOUSE IN SMITHFIELD AGAIN.

THE visitor to the Polytechnic Institution or the Adelaide Gallery,[1] has doubtless seen the exhibition of the microscope. A drop of the purest water, magnified by that instrument some thousands of times, appears filled with horrible reptiles and monsters of revolting forms.

Such is London.

Fair and attractive as the mighty metropolis may appear to the superficial observer, it swarms with disgusting, loathsome, and venomous objects, wearing human shapes.

Oh! London is a city of strange contrasts!

---

1 The Adelaide Gallery, which was situated at the northern, or St. Martin's Church, end of the Lowther Arcade, was started as a science "show." Its principal attractions were Perkins's steam-gun, which discharged a shower of bullets, but was never adopted in serious warfare; and the gymnotus, or electrical eel, a creature which emitted shocks on its back being touched. Parents and persons in charge of youth were great patrons of the Adelaide Gallery, which flourished until a rival institution appeared in the shape of the Polytechnic, in Upper Regent Street, which speedily and completely took the wind out of the sails of the original establishment." Edmund Yates, *His Recollections and Experiences*, 1885 [chapter on 1847-1852]. In 1852, it became the Royal Marionette Theatre. (Footnote courtesy of Lee Jackson's Victorian London website.)

The bustle of business, and the smile of pleasure,—the peaceful citizen, and the gay soldier,—the splendid shop, and the itinerant pastry-stall,—the gorgeous equipage, and the humble market-cart,—the palaces of nobles, and the hovels of the poor,—the psalm from the chapel, and the shout of laughter from the tavern,—the dandies lounging in the west-end streets, and the paupers cleansing away the mud,—the funeral procession, and the bridal cavalcade,—the wealthy and high-born lady whose reputation is above all cavil, and the lost girl whose shame is below all notice,—the adventurer who defends his honour with a duel, and the poor tradesman whom unavoidable bankruptcy has branded as a rogue,—the elegantly-clad banker whose insolvency must soon transpire, and the ragged old miser whose wealth is not suspected,—the monuments of glory, and the hospitals of the poor,—the temples where men adore a God with affectation, and the shrines at which they lose their gold to a deity whom they adore without affectation,—in a word, grandeur and squalor, wealth and misery, virtue and vice,—honesty which has never been tried, and crime which yielded to the force of irresistible circumstances,—all the features, all the characteristics, all the morals, of a great city, must occupy the attention of him who surveys London with microscopic eye.

And what a splendid subject for the contemplation of the moralist is a mighty city which, at every succeeding hour, presents a new phase of interest to the view;—in the morning, when only the industrious and the thrifty are abroad, and while the wealthy and the great are sleeping off the night's pleasure and dissipation:—at noon, when the streets are swarming with life, as if some secret source without the walls poured at that hour myriads of animated streams into the countless avenues and thoroughfares;—in the evening, when the men of pleasure again venture forth, and music, and dancing, and revelry prevail around;—and at night,—when every lazar-house vomits forth its filth, every den lets loose its horrors, and every foul court and alley echoes to the footsteps of crime!

It was about two o'clock in the morning, (three hours after the burglarious attempt upon the villa,) that a man, drenched by the rain which continued to pour in torrents, with his hat drawn over his eyes, and his hands thrust in his pockets to protect them against the cold, crept cautiously down West Street, from Smithfield, dodged past the policeman, and entered the old house which we have described at the opening of our narrative.

Having closed and carefully bolted the front door, he hastily ascended to the room on the first floor where Walter Sydney had seen him and his companion conceal their plunder four years and four months previously.

This man—so wet, so cold, and so miserable—was Bill Bolter, the murderer.

Having groped about for a few moments, he found a match, struck it, and obtained a light. One of the secret recesses furnished a candle; and the flickering glare fell upon the haggard, unshaven, and dirty countenance of the ruffian.

Scarcely had he lighted the candle, when a peculiar whistle was heard in the street, just under the window. The features of Bolter became suddenly animated with joy; and, as he hastily descended the stairs, he muttered to himself, "Well, at all events here's one on 'em."

The individual to whom he opened the door was Dick Flairer—in no better plight, mentally and bodily, than himself.

"Is there any bingo, Bill?" demanded Dick, the moment he set foot in the up-stairs room.

"Not a drain," answered Bolter, after a close inspection of the cupboard in the wall between the windows; "and not a morsel of grub neither."

"Blow the grub," said Dick. "I ain't in no humour for eating; but I could drink a gallon. I've been thinking as I come along, and after the first shock was over, wot cursed fools you and me was to be humbugged in this here affair. Either that young feller was the brother of the one which we threw down the trap ——"

"No: I could swear that he is the same," interrupted Bill.

"Well—then he must have made his escape—and that's all," added Dick Flairer.

"That must be it," observed Bolter, after a long pause. "But it was so sudden upon us—and then without no time to think—and all that——"

"You may say what you like, Bill—but I shall never forgive myself. I was the first to bolt; and I was a coward. How shall I ever be able to look the Cracksman in the face again, or go to the parlour of the boozing-ken?"

"It's no use complaining like this, Dick. You was used to be the bold 'un—and now it seems as if it was me that must say 'Cheer up.' The fact is, someot must be done without delay. I told you and Tom what had happened at my crib; and so, lay up for some time I must. Come, now—Dick, you won't desert a pal in trouble?"

"There's my hand, Bill. On'y say wot you want done, and I'm your man."

"In the first place, do you think it's safe for me to stay here? Won't that young feller give the alarm, and say as how his house was attempted by the same cracksmen that wanted to make a stiff 'un of him between four and five years ago at this old crib; and then won't the blue-bottles come and search the place from chimley-pot down to foundation-stone?"

"Let 'em search it," ejaculated Flairer: "they'll on'y do it once; and who cares for that? You can lie as snug down stairs for a week or so as if you was a thousand miles off. Besides, who'd think for a instant that you'd hide yourself in the wery spot that the young feller could point out as one of our haunts? Mark me, Bill—if yer goes up to Rat's Castle in Saint Giles's,[1] you would find too many tongues among them cursed Irishers to ask '*Who is he?*' and '*What is he?*' If you goes over to the Mint, you'll be sure to be twigged by a lot o' them low buzgloaks and broken-down magsmen as swarms there; and they'll nose upon you for a penny. Whitechapel back-slums isn't safe; for the broom-gals, the blacks, and the ballad singers which occupies all that district, is always a quarrelling; and the blue-bottles is constantly poking their nose in every crib in consekvence. Here you are snug; and I can bring you your grub and tell you the news of an evenin' arter dark."

"But to be penned up in that infernal hole for a fortnit or three weeks, till the storm's blowed over, is horrible to think on," said Bill.

"And scragging[2] more horrible still," said Dick, significantly.

1 Saint Giles's: the infamous Rookery of St. Giles's, in Westminster. A maze of streets and alleyways, of which only Bainbridge Street and Dyott Street remain, once including Church Street, Bickeridge Street and George Street. It was known as the worst place in England, and certainly the parish of St. Giles was the poorest in England. The houses were run together, with passages and tunnels leading everywhere, so that a criminal could evade capture there for years. In effect it was a no-go area for the police. The poverty and filth were appalling, and it was pulled down in the mid-1840s to make way for New Oxford Street.

2 Hanging. [Reynolds's note.]

Bill Bolter shuddered; and a convulsive motion agitated his neck, as if he already felt the cord around it. His countenance became ashy pale; and, as he glanced fearfully around, he exclaimed, "Yes, you're right, Dick: I'll take myself to the hiding-crib, and you can give me the office[1] at any moment, if things goes wrong. To-morrow you must try and find out whether there's much of a row about the affair in the Court."

The ruffian never expressed the least anxiety relative to the fate of his children.

"To-morrow!" exclaimed Dick: "to-day you mean—for it can't be far off from three o'clock. And now talking about grub is all very easy; but getting it is quite another thing. Neither you nor me hasn't got a scurrick; and where to get a penny loaf on tick I don't know."

"By hell, I shall starve, Dick!" cried the murderer, casting a glance of alarm and horror upon his companion.

"Whatever I get shall be for you first, Bill; and to get anythink at all I must be wide awake. The grass musn't grow under my feet."

At that moment a whistle, similar to the sound by which Dick Flairer had notified his approach to Bill Bolter, emanated from the street and fell upon the ears of those worthies.

Dick hastened to respond to this summons, and in a short time introduced the Cracksman.

The moment this individual entered the room, he demanded if there were anything to eat or to drink upon the premises. He of course received a melancholy negative: but, instead of being disheartened, his countenance appeared to wear a smile of pleasure.

"Now, you see, I never desert a friend in distress," he exclaimed; and, with these words, he produced from his pocket a quantity of cold victuals and a large flask of brandy.

Without waiting to ask questions or give explanations, the three thieves fell tooth and nail upon the provender.

"I knowed you'd come to this here crib, because Bill don't dare go to the boozing-ken till the affair of the Court's blowed over," said the Cracksman, when his meal was terminated; "and so I thought I'd jine you. Arter I left the place out by Clapton——"

"And how the devil did you get away?" demanded Dick.

"Just the same as you did. It would have sarved you right if I'd

1 Inform, give warning. [Reynolds's note.]

never spoke to you agen, and blowed you at the ken into the bargain; but I thought to myself, thinks I, 'It must be someot very strange that made the Flairer and the Bolter cut their lucky and leave their pal in the lurch; so let's hear wot they has to say for themselves fust.' Then, as I come along, I found a purse in a gentleman's pocket just opposite Bethnal Green New Church; and that put me into good humour. So I looked in at the ken, got the grub and the bingo, and come on here."

"You're a reg'lar trump, Tom!" ejaculated Dick Flairer; "and I'll stick to you like bricks from this moment till I die. The fact is—me and Bill has told you about that young feller which we throwed down the trap some four or five year back."

"Yes—I remember."

"Well—we seed him to-night."

"To-night! What—at the crib up there?"

"The swell that you got a grip on in the dark was the very self-same one."

"Then he must have got clear off—that's all!" cried the Cracksman. "It was no ghost—but rale plump flesh and hot blood, I'll swear."

"So we both think now, to be sure," said Dick: "but you don't bear any ill-will, Tom?"

"Not a atom. Here's fifteen couters[1] which was in the purse of the swell which I met at Bethnal Green; and half that's yourn. But, about Bill there—wot's he a-going to do?"

Dick pointed with his finger downwards: Tom comprehended the signal, and nodded approvingly.

The brandy produced a cheering effect upon the three ruffians: and pipes and tobacco augmented their joviality. Their discourse gradually became coarsely humorous; and their mirth boisterous. At length Bill Bolter, who required every possible means of artificial stimulant and excitement to sustain his spirits in the fearful predicament in which he was placed, called upon the Cracksman for a song.

Tom was famous amongst his companions for his vocal qualifications; and he was not a little proud of the reputation he had acquired in the parlours of the various "boozing-kens" and "patter-cribs"[2] which he was in the habit of frequenting. He was not, therefore,

1 Sovereigns. [Reynolds's note.]

2 Flash houses. [Reynolds's note.]

backward in complying with his friend's request; and, in a somewhat subdued tone, (for fear of making *too much noise*—a complaint not often heard in Chick Lane), he sang the following lines:—

THE THIEVES' ALPHABET.

A was an Area-sneak leary and sly;
B was a Buzgloak, with fingers so fly;
C was a Cracksman, that forked all the plate;
D was a Dubsman, who kept the jug-gate.
For we are rollicking chaps,
All smoking, singing, boozing;
We care not for the traps,
But pass the night carousing!

E was an Efter,[1] that went to the play;
F was a Fogle he knapped on his way;
G was a Gag, which he told to the beak;
H was a Hum-box,[2] where parish-prigs speak.
CHORUS.

I was an Ikey[3] with swag all encumbered;
J was a Jug, in whose cell he was lumbered;
K was a Kye-bosh,[4] that paid for his treat;
L was a Leaf[5] that fell under his feet.
CHORUS.

M was a Magsman, frequenting Pall-Mall;
N was a Nose that turned chirp on his pal;
O was an Onion,[6] possessed by a swell;
P was a Pannie, done niblike and well.
CHORUS.

Q was a Queer-screen, that served as a blind;[7]

---

1 A thief who frequents theatres. [Reynolds's note.]
2 Pulpit. [Reynolds's note.]
3 A Jew fence: a receiver of stolen goods. [Reynolds's note.]
4 1s. 6d. [Reynolds's note.]
5 The drop. [Reynolds's note.]
6 A watch seal. [Reynolds's note.]
7 Served to deceive the unwary. [Reynolds's note.]

R was a Reader,[1] with flimsies well lined;
S was a Smasher, so nutty and spry;
T was a Ticker,[2] just faked from a cly.
CHORUS.

U was an Uptucker,[3] fly with the cord;
V was a Varnisher,[4] dressed like a lord;
Y was a Yoxter[5] that eat caper sauce;[6]
Z was a Ziff[7] who was flashed on the horse.[8]
For we are rollicking chaps
All smoking, singing, boozing:
We care not for the traps,
But pass the night carousing.[9]

In this manner did the three thieves pass the first hours of morning at the old house in Chick Lane.

At length the heavy and sonorous voice of Saint Paul's proclaimed six o'clock. It still wanted an hour to sun-rise; but they now thought it prudent to separate.

Tom the Cracksman and Dick Flairer arranged together a "little piece of business" for the ensuing night, which they hoped would prove more fortunate than their attempt on the villa at Upper Clapton; but Dick faithfully promised Bill Bolter to return to him in the evening before he set out on the new expedition.

Matters being thus agreed upon, the moment for the murderer's concealment arrived. We have before stated that the entire grate in the room which the villains frequented, could be removed; and that, when taken out of its setting, it revealed an aperture of considerable dimensions. At the bottom of this square recess was a trap-door, communicating with a narrow and spiral staircase, that led into a vault adjoining and upon the same level with the very cellar from which Walter Sydney had so miraculously escaped.

1 Pocket book. [Reynolds's note.]
2 Watch. [Reynolds's note.]
3 Jack Ketch. [Reynolds's note.]
4 Utterer of false sovereigns. [Reynolds's note.]
5 A convict returned from transportation before his time. [Reynolds's note.]
6 Hanged. [Reynolds's note.]
7 A juvenile thief. [Reynolds's note.]
8 Privately whipped in prison. [Reynolds's note.]
9 This song is entirely original. [Reynolds's note.]

The possibility of such an architectural arrangement being fully carried out, with a view to provide a perfect means of concealment, will be apparent to our readers, when we state that the side of the house farthest from the Fleet Ditch was constructed with a double brick wall, and that the spiral staircase consequently stood between those two partitions. The mode in which the huge chimneys were built, also tended to ensure the complete safety of that strange hiding-place, and to avert any suspicion that might for a moment be entertained of the existence of such a retreat in that old house.

Even in case the secret of the moveable grate should be discovered, the eye of the most acute thief-taker would scarcely detect the trap-door at the bottom of the recess, so admirably was it made to correspond with the brick-work that formed its frame.

The vault with which the spiral staircase corresponded, was about fourteen feet long by two-and-a-half wide. An iron grating of eight inches square, overlooking the Fleet Ditch, was all the means provided to supply that living tomb with fresh—we cannot say pure—air. If the atmosphere of the hiding-place were thus neither wholesome nor pleasant, it did not at least menace existence; and a residence in that vault for even weeks and weeks together was deemed preferable to the less "cribbed, cabined, and confined" sojourn of Newgate.

But connected with the security of this vault was one fearful condition. The individual who sought its dark solitude, could not emancipate himself at will. He was entirely at the mercy of those confederates who were entrusted with his secret. Should anything happen to these men,—should they be suddenly overtaken by the hand of death, then starvation must be the portion of the inmate of that horrible vault: and should they fall into the hands of justice, then the only service they could render their companion in the living tomb, would be to reveal the secret of his hiding-place.

Up to the time of which we are writing, since the formation of that strange lurking-hole in the days of the famous Jonathan Wild, three or four persons had alone availed themselves of the vault as a means of personal concealment. In the first place, the secret existed but with a very few; and secondly, it was only in cases where life and death were concerned that a refuge was sought in so fearful an abode.

When the grate was removed and the trap-door was opened, the entire frame of Bill Bolter became suddenly convulsed with horror. He dreaded to be left to the mercy of his own reflections!

"It's infernally damp," said Bill, his teeth chattering as much with fear as with the cold.

Fearful, however, of exciting the disgust and contempt of his companions at what might be termed his pusillanimous conduct, he mustered up all his courage, shook hands with the Cracksman and Flairer, and then insinuated his person through the aperture.

"You may as well take the pipes and baccy along with you, old feller," returned Dick.

"And here's a thimble-full of brandy left in the flask," added the Cracksman.

"This evenin' I'll bring you a jolly wack of the bingo," said Flairer.

Provided with the little comforts just specified, the murderer descended the spiral staircase into the vault.

The trap-door closed above his head; and the grate was replaced with more than usual care and caution.

The Cracksman and Dick Flairer then took their departure from the old house, in the foundation of which a fellow-creature was thus strangely entombed alive!

CHAPTER XXIV.

CIRCUMSTANTIAL EVIDENCE.

Let us now return to Mr. Whittingham, whom we left in serious and unfeigned tribulation at the moment when his young master was taken into custody upon the charge of passing a forged note.

The Bow Street runner whom the officer had left behind to search the house, first possessed himself of the two letters which were lying upon the table in Markham's library, and which were addressed respectively to Mrs. Arlington and Mr. Monroe. The functionary then commenced a strict investigation of the entire premises; and, at the end, appeared marvellously surprised that he had not found a complete apparatus for printing forged notes, together with a quantity of the false articles themselves. This search, nevertheless, occupied three hours; and, when it was over, he took his departure, quite sulky because he had nothing to offer as evidence save the two sealed letters, which might be valuable in that point of view, or might not.

The moment this unwelcome guest had quitted the house, the

butler, notwithstanding the lateness of the hour—for it was now dusk—ordered the market cart to be got ready; and, with the least possible delay, he proceeded into town.

Upon his arrival in Bow Street, he found the police-office closed: but upon enquiry he learnt that the investigation of Richard Markham's case had been postponed until the following morning at eleven o'clock, the prisoner having declared that he could produce a witness who would satisfactorily show his (the prisoner's) entire innocence in the transaction. In the meantime, he had been removed to Clerkenwell Prison.

Without asking another question, Whittingham mounted his cart once more, and drove away at a rattling pace to Clerkenwell Prison. There he began to thunder like a madman at the knocker of the governor's private entrance, and could hardly believe his senses when a servant-girl informed him that it was past the hours to see the prisoners. Whittingham would have remonstrated; but the girl slammed the door in his face. He accordingly had no alternative save to drive direct home again.

The very next morning at nine o'clock Mr. Whittingham entered the *Servants' Arms* Tavern; and with but little of his usual circumlocution and verbosity, enquired the address of Mr. Mac Chizzle, the lawyer, who had been one of the party at that house the evening but one before.

"Here is his card," said the landlord. "He uses my house reglar, and is a out-and-out practitioner."

Whittingham did not wait to hear any further eulogium upon the attorney. It had struck him that his young master might require a "professional adviser:" and having the supreme felicity of being totally unacquainted with the entire fraternity, he had felt himself somewhat puzzled how to supply the *desideratum*. In this dilemma, he had suddenly bethought himself of Mac Chizzle; and, without waiting to ponder upon the propriety of the step he was taking, he rushed off in the manner described to procure that individual's address.

"Well, what do you want?" cried the lawyer, who was astonished at the unceremonious manner in which Whittingham suddenly rushed into his office: "what do you want?"

"Law," was the laconic answer.

"Well, you can have plenty of that here," said Mr. Mac Chizzle. "But—I think you are the gentleman with whom I had the pleasure of passing a pleasant evening at the *Servants' Arms*, a day or two ago."

"The indentical same," returned Whittingham, flinging his hat upon the floor and himself into a chair.

"Take time to breathe, sir," said the lawyer. "If you're come for advice you couldn't have selected a better shop; but I must tell you before-hand that mine is quite a ready money business."

"Very good, sir. I'll tell you my story first and foremost; and you can then explain the most legible means of preceeding. I want law and justice."

"*Law* you can have in welcome; but whether you will obtain *justice* is another consideration."

"I'm bewildered in a labyrinth of mazes, sir," said the butler. "I always opiniated that law and justice was the same thing."

"Quite the reverse, I can assure you. Law is a human invention: justice is a divine inspiration. What is law to-day, is not law to-morrow, and yet everything is still denominated *justice*. A creditor sues for justice when he appeals to a tribunal against his debtor; and how is that justice awarded? Why—if a man can't pay five pounds, the law immediately makes his debt ten pounds; and if he can't live out of doors, the law immediately shuts him up in prison by way of helping him out of his difficulties. That is law, sir; but it is not justice."

"Right, sir—very right."

"*Law*, you see, sir," continued Mac Chizzle, who was particularly fond of hearing himself talk—"*law* is omnipotent, and beats *justice* to such an extreme, that justice would be justified in bringing an action of assault and battery against law. Law even makes religion, sir; and gives the attributes of the Deity, for no one dares assert that God possesses a quality or a characteristic, unless in conformity with the law. And as these laws are always changing, so of course does the nature of the deity, as established by the law, vary too; so that men may be said to go to heaven or to another place by the turnpike roads laid down by the law."

"I like your reasonable powers amazingly," said the butler, somewhat impatiently; "and I will now proceed to unfold the momentary object of my visit."

"Give yourself breathing time, my dear sir. As I was observing,

Law is more powerful than even *Justice* and *Religion*; and I could now show that it exercises the same predominating influence over *Morality* also. For instance, Law, and not Conscience, defines virtues and vices. If I murder you, I commit a crime; but the executioner who puts me to death for the action, does *not* commit a crime. Neither does the soldier who kills his fellow-creature in battle. Thus, murder is only a crime when it is not legalised by human statutes,—or, in plain terms, when it is not according to law."

"I comprehend, sir," said Whittingham; and, seeing that Mr. Mac Chizzle now paused at length, he narrated the particulars of his master's arrest upon an accusation of passing a forged note for five hundred pounds.

"This is an ugly case, Mr. Whittingham."

"You must go down to him at Bow-Street: his case comes on at eleven o'clock."

"Well, there is plenty of time: it is only half-past nine o'clock. I think we had better instruct counsel."

"Construct counsel!" ejaculated Whittingham; "I want you to get him liberated at once."

"Ah, I dare say you do," said the lawyer, coolly. "That is often more easily said than done. From what you have told me I should not wonder if your master was committed for trial."

"But he is innocent, sir—he is innocent—as the young lamb in the meadows which is unborn!" cried Whittingham. "Master Richard would no more pass a fictious note than I should endeavour to pass a race-horse if I was mounted on a donkey."

Mr. Mac Chizzle smiled, and summoned his clerk by the euphonious name of "Simcox." Mr. Simcox was somewhat slow in making his appearance; and when he did, a very comical one it was—for his hair was red, his eyes were green, his countenance was studded with freckles, and his eye-lashes were white.

"Simcox," said Mr. Mac Chizzle, "I am going out for a few hours. If the gentleman calls about the thousand pound bill, tell him that I can get it discounted for him, for fifty pounds in money and eight hundred in wine—which allows a hundred and fifty for discount and *my* commission. If the lady calls whose husband has run away from her, tell her that I've sent to Paris to make enquiries after him, and that if she'll leave another fifty pounds, I'll send to Vienna. By-the-bye, that bothering fellow Smith is certain to call: tell him I'm gone into the country, and shall be away for a fortnight. If Jenkins calls, tell him I shall be home at five and he must wait, as I want to see him."

"Very well, sir," said Simcox. "And if the gentleman calls about the loan."

"Why, that I shall see a party about it this evening. The first party declines; but I have another party in view."

Somehow or another, men of business have always got a particular "party" in view to accomplish a particular purpose, and they are always being disappointed by their "parties"—whom, by-the-bye, they never condescend to name. To be "deceived by a party;" or "having a party to meet;" or "being engaged so long with a particular party," are excuses which will last as long as business itself shall exist, and will continue to be received as apologies as long as any apologies are received at all. They will wear out every other lie.

Whittingham was too much occupied by the affairs of his master, to pay any attention to the orders which the solicitor gave his clerk; and he was considerably relieved when he found himself by the side of his professional adviser, rolling along the streets in a cabriolet.

At length the lawyer and the faithful domestic were set down at the Police-Office in Bow Street; and in a few moments they were admitted, in the presence of a policeman, to an interview with Markham in one of the cells attached to the establishment.

Richard's countenance was pale and care-worn: his hair was dishevelled; and his attire seemed put on slovenly. But these circumstances scarcely attracted the eyes of Whittingham:—a more appalling and monstrous spectacle engrossed all the attention of that faithful old dependant; and this was the manacle which confined his revered master's hands together.

Whittingham wept.

"Oh! Master Richard," he exclaimed in a voice broken by sobs, "what an unforeseen and perfidious adventure is this! You surely never could—no, I know you didn't!"

"Do not grieve yourself, my faithful friend," said Richard, deeply affected: "my innocence will soon be proved. I have sent for Mr. Chichester, who will be here presently: and he can shew in one moment how I became possessed of the two notes."

"Two notes!" cried Whittingham.

"Yes—I had another of fifty pounds' value in my purse, which I also received from Chichester, and which has turned out to be a spurious one. Doubtless he has been deceived himself——"

"Oh! that ere Winchester, or Kidderminster—or—whatever his name may be," interrupted the butler, a strange misgiving oppressing his mind: "I'm afeard he won't do the thing that's right. But here is a profound adwiser, Master Richard, that I've brought with me; and he'll see law done, he says—and I believe him too."

Markham and Mac Chizzle then entered into conversation together: but scarcely had the unfortunate young man commenced his account of the peculiar circumstances in which he was involved, when the jailor entered to conduct him into the presence of the magistrate.

Markham was placed in the felon's dock, and Mr. Mac Chizzle intimated to the sitting magistrate, in a simpering tone, that he appeared for the prisoner.

Now we must inform our readers that Mac Chizzle was one of those low pettifoggers, who, without being absolutely the black sheep of the profession, act upon the principle "that all are fish that come to their net," and practise indiscriminately in the civil and the criminal courts—conduct a man's insolvency, or defend him before the magistrate—discount bills and issue no end of writs—act for loan societies and tally shops—in a word, undertake anything that happens to fall in their way, so long as it brings grist to the mill.

Mr. Mac Chizzle was not, therefore, what is termed "a respectable solicitor;" and the magistrate's countenance assumed an appearance of austerity—for he had previously been possessed in Markham's favour—when that individual announced that he appeared for the prisoner. Thus poor Whittingham, in his anxiety to do his beloved master a great deal of good, actually prejudiced his case materially at its outset.

Though unhappy and care-worn, Richard was not downcast. Conscious innocence supported him. Accordingly when he beheld Mr. Chichester enter the witness-box, he bowed to him in a friendly and even grateful manner; but, to his ineffable surprise, that very fashionable gentleman affected not to notice the salutation.

It is not necessary to enter into details. The nature of the evidence against Markham was that he had called at his guardian's banker's the day but one previously, to receive a sum of money; that he requested the cashier to change a five hundred pound Bank of England note; that, although an unusual proceeding, the demand was complied with; that the prisoner wrote his name at the back of the note, and that in the course of the ensuing morning it was discovered that the said note was a forgery. The prisoner was arrested; and upon his person was found a second note, of fifty pounds' value, which was also a forgery. Two letters were also produced—one to Mrs. Arlington, and another to Mr. Monroe, which not only proved that the prisoner had intended to leave the country with strange abruptness, but the contents of which actually appeared to point at the crime now alleged against him, as the motive of his flight.

Markham was certainly astounded when he heard the stress laid upon those letters by the solicitor for the prosecution, and the manner in which their real meaning was made to tell against him.

The Magistrate called upon him for his defence; and Markham, forgetful that Mac Chizzle was there to represent him, addressed himself in an earnest tone to Mr. Chichester, exclaiming, "You can now set me right in the eyes of the magistrate, and in the opinion of even the prosecuting counsel, who seems so anxious to distort every circumstance to my disadvantage."

"I really am not aware," said Mr. Chichester, caressing his chin in a very *nonchalant* manner, "that I can throw any light upon this subject."

"All I require is the truth," ejaculated Richard, surprised at the tone and manner of his late friend. "Did you not give me that note for five hundred pounds to change for you? and did I not receive the second note from you in exchange for fifty sovereigns?"

Mr. Chichester replied in an indignant negative.

The magistrate shook his head: the prosecuting solicitor took snuff significantly;—Mac Chizzle made a memorandum;—and Whittingham murmured, "Ah! that mitigated villain Axminster."

"What do I hear!" exclaimed Richard: "Mr. Chichester, your memory must fail you sadly. I suppose you recollect the occasion upon which Mr. Talbot gave you the five hundred pound note?"

"Mr. Talbot never gave me any note at all," answered Chichester, in a measured and determined manner.

"It is false—false as hell!" cried Markham, more enraged than alarmed; and he forthwith detailed to the magistrate the manner in which he had been induced to change the one note, and had become possessed of the other.

"This is a very lame story, indeed," said the magistrate; "and you must try and see if you can get a jury to believe it. You stand committed."

Before Richard could make any reply, he was lugged out of the dock by the jailor; the next case was called on; and he was hurried back to his cell, whither Mac Chizzle and the butler were permitted to follow him.

CHAPTER XXV.

THE ENCHANTRESS.

"Oh! how can I prove my innocence now?" exclaimed Richard, wringing his hands, and walking hastily up and down the cell: "how shall I convince the world that a fearful combination of circumstances has so entangled me in this net, that never was man so wronged before? how can I communicate my dread position to Monroe? how ever again look society in the face? how live after this exposure—this disgrace?"

"Master Richard, Master Richard," cried the poor old butler, "don't take on so—don't now! Your innocence must conspire on the day of trial, and the jury will do you justice. Now, don't take on so, Master Richard—pray don't!"

As the faithful domestic uttered these words, the tears chased each other so rapidly down his cheeks that he seemed to need consolation quite as much as his master.

"Oh! that villain Chichester—the wretch—the cheat!" continued Richard; "and no doubt his vulgar companion Talbot is as bad. And the baronet—perhaps he also——"

Markham stopped short, and seated himself upon the bench. He suddenly became very faint, and turned ashy pale. Whittingham hastened to loosen his shirt-collar, and the policeman present humanely procured a glass of water.

In a few minutes he recovered: and he then endeavoured to contemplate with calmness the full extent of the perils which environed him. His opinion of Chichester and Talbot was already formed: but the baronet—could he have been a party to their scheme of villany?

After a moment's reflection, he answered the question to himself in an affirmative.

He had, then, fallen into a nest of adventurers and swindlers. But Diana—oh! no, she could not have been cognizant of the treacherous designs practised against him: she was doubtless made use of as an instrument to further the plans of the conspirators!

Such were his convictions. Should he then give her due warning in time, and afford her an opportunity of abandoning, ere it might be too late, an individual who would doubtless involve her, in the long run, in infamy and peril?

To pen a hasty note to Mrs. Arlington was now a duty which he conceived entailed upon him, and which he immediately performed. He then wrote a letter to Mr. Monroe, detailing the particulars of his unfortunate position, and beseeching him not to be prejudiced against him by the report which he might read in the newspapers the following day.

"Whittingham, my old friend," said Markham, when he had disposed of these matters; "we must now separate for the present. This letter for Mr. Monroe you will forward by post: the other, to Mrs. Arlington, you will take yourself to Bond Street, and deliver into her own hand." Then, addressing himself to Mac Chizzle, he observed, "I thank you, sir, for your attendance here to-day. Whittingham will give you the address of my guardian, Mr. Monroe; and that gentleman will consult with you upon the proper course to be pursued. He will also answer any pecuniary demands you may have occasion to make upon him."

Richard had preserved an unnatural degree of calmness as he uttered these words; and Whittingham was himself astonished at the coolness with which his young master delivered his instructions. The old butler wept bitterly when he took leave of "Master Richard;" and it cost the young man himself no inconsiderable effort to restrain his own tears.

"What is raly your inferential opinion in this matter?" demanded the butler of the lawyer, as they issued from the door of the police-office together.

"Why, that it was a capital scheme to raise the wind, and a very great pity that it did not succeed to a far greater extent," cried the professional adviser.

"Well, if you put that opinion down in your bill and charge six-and-eightpence for it," said Whittingham, with a very serious countenance, "I shall certainly dispute the item, and computate it, when I audit the accounts."

"I am really at a loss to comprehend you," said the lawyer. "Of course there are no secrets between you and me: indeed, you had much better tell me the whole truth——"

"Truth!" ejaculated Whittingham: "of course I shall tell you the truth."

"Allow me to ask a question or two, then," resumed the lawyer. "I suppose that you were in the plant, and divided the swag?"

Mr. Whittingham stared at the professional man with the most unfeigned astonishment, which, indeed, was so great that it checked all reply.

"Well," proceeded the shrewd Mr. Mac Chizzle, "it wasn't a bad dodge either. And I suppose that this Monroe is a party to the whole concern?"

"Is it possible, Mr. Mac Chizzle," exclaimed the butler, "that——"

"But the business is awkward—very awkward," added the solicitor, shaking his head. "It was however fortunate that nothing transpired to implicate you also. When one pal is at large, he can do much for another who is in lavender. It would have been worse if you had been lumbered too—far worse."

"Plant—pal—lumbered—lavender!" repeated Whittingham, with considerable emphasis on each word as he slowly uttered it. "I suppose you raly think my master is guilty of the crime computed to him?"

"Of course I do," replied Mac Chizzle: "I can see as far into a brick wall as any one."

"Well, it's of no use argufying the pint," said the butler, after a moment's pause. "Here is Mr. Monroe's address: perhaps when you have seen him, you will arrive at new inclusions."

Mr. Whittingham then took leave of the solicitor, and proceeded to Bond Street.

Within a few yards of the house in which Mrs. Arlington resided, the butler ran against an individual who, with his hat perched jauntily on his right ear, was lounging along.

"Holloa, you fellow!" ejaculated Mr. Thomas Suggett—for it was he—"what do you mean by coming bolt agin a gen'leman in that kind of way?"

"Oh! my dear sir," cried Whittingham, "is that you? I am raly perforated with delight to see you."

Mr. Suggett gave a good long stare at Mr. Whittingham, and then exclaimed, "Oh! it is you—is it? Well, I must say that your legs are in a very unfinished condition."

"How, sir,—how?" demanded the irritated butler.

"Why, they want a pair of fetters, to be sure," said Suggett; and breaking into a horse-laugh, he passed rapidly on.

Whittingham felt humiliated; and the knock that he gave at the door of Diana's lodgings was sneaking and subdued. In a few minutes, however, he was ushered into a back room on the first floor, where Mrs. Arlington received him.

"Here is a letter, ma'am, which I was to deliver only into your own indentical hand."

"Is it—is it from your master?" demanded the Enchantress.

"It is, ma'am."

"Where *is* Mr. Markham?" asked Diana, receiving the letter with a trembling hand.

"He is now in Bow-street Police-Office, ma'am: in the course of the day he will be in Newgate;"—and the old butler wiped away a tear.

"Good heavens!" exclaimed Diana; "then it is really too true!"

She immediately tore open the letter, and ran her eye over the contents, which were as follow:—

"The villany of one of the individuals with whom you are constantly associating, and in whom it has been my misfortune to place unlimited confidence, will perhaps involve you in an embarrassment similar to the one in which I am now placed. I cannot, I do not for one moment imagine that you are in any way conversant with their vile schemes:—I can read your heart; I know that you would scorn such a confederacy. Your frankness, your candour are in your favour: your countenance, which is engraven upon my memory, and which I behold at this moment as if it were really before me, forbids all suspicions injurious to your honour. Take a timely warning, then: take warning from one who wishes you well: and dissolve the connexion ere it be too late. "R. M."

"When shall you see your master again?" enquired Diana of the butler, after the perusal of this letter.

"To-morrow, ma'am—with the blessing of God."

"My compliments to him—my very best remembrances," said Mrs. Arlington; "and I feel deeply grateful for this communication."

Whittingham bowed, and rose to depart.

"And," added Diana, after a moment's pause, "if there be anything in which my humble services can be made available, pray do not hesitate to come to me. Indeed, I hope you will call—often—and let me know how this unfortunate business proceeds."

"Then you don't believe that Master Richard is capable of this obliquity, madam?" cried the butler.

"Oh! no—impossible!" said Diana emphatically.

"Thankee, ma'am, thankee," exclaimed Whittingham: "you have done my poor old heart good. God bless you, ma'am—God bless you."

And with these words the faithful dependant took his departure, not a little delighted to think that there was at least one person in the world who believed in the innocence of "Master Richard." In fact, the kindness of Diana's manner and the sincerity with which she had expressed herself on that point, effectually wiped away from the mind of the butler the reminiscences of Mac Chizzle's derogatory suspicions, and Suggett's impertinence.

After a few minutes' profound reflection, Diana returned to the drawing-room, where Sir Rupert Harborough, Mr. Chichester, and Talbot were seated.

Her fine countenance wore an expression of melancholy seriousness; and there was a nervous movement of the under lip that denoted the existence of powerful emotions in her bosom.

"Well, Di.," exclaimed the baronet; "you seem annoyed."

"You will be surprised, gentlemen, when I inform you who has been here," she said, resuming her seat upon the sofa.

"Indeed!" cried Chichester, turning pale: "who could it be?"

"Not an officer, I hope?" exclaimed the baronet.

"The chimley-sweeps, perhaps," suggested Mr. Talbot.

"A person from Mr. Markham," said Diana, seriously. "By his appearance I should conceive him to be the faithful old servant of his family, of whom I have heard him speak."

"Whittingham, I'll be bound!" ejaculated Chichester. "And what did he want?"

"He brought me a letter from his master," returned Diana. "You may read it, if you please."

And she tossed it contemptuously towards Chichester.

"Read out," cried Talbot.

Mr. Chichester read the letter aloud, as he was requested.

"And what makes the young spark write to you in that d——d impudent and familiar style?" demanded the baronet, angrily.

"You cannot but admit that his letter is couched in a most friendly manner," said the lady, somewhat bitterly.

"Friendly be hanged!" cried the baronet. "I dare say you feel a most profound and sisterly sympathy for the young gaol-bird. After all, your profuse expenditure and extravagance helped to involve me in no end of pecuniary trouble; and I was compelled to have recourse to any means to obtain money. Somebody must suffer;—better Markham than any one of us."

"You do well, sir, to reproach *me* for being the cause of your embarrassments," answered Diana, her countenance becoming almost purple with indignation. "Have I not basely lent these rooms to your purposes, and acted as an attraction to the young men whom you have inveigled here to plunder at cards? I have never forgiven myself for the weakness which prompted me thus far to enter into your schemes. But when you informed me of your plans relative to the forged notes, I protested vehemently against so atrocious a measure. Indeed, had it not been for your solemn assurance that you had abandoned the idea—at all events so far as it concerned Markham—I would have placed him upon his guard—in spite of your threats, your menaces, your remonstrances!"

Diana had warmed as she proceeded; and by the time she reached the end of her reply to the baronet's villanous speech, she had worked herself up almost into a fury of rage and indignation. Her bosom heaved convulsively—her eyes dilated; and her lips expressed ineffable scorn.

"Perdition!" exclaimed the baronet: "the world is coming to a pretty pass when one's own mistress undertakes to give lessons in morality."

"A desperate necessity, sir," retorted Diana, "made me your mistress;—but I would sooner seek an asylum at the workhouse this moment, than become a partner in villany of this stamp."

"And, as far as I care," said the baronet, "you may go to the workhouse as soon as you choose."

With these words he rose and put on his hat.

Diana was about to answer this last brutal speech; but she determined not to provoke a discussion which only exposed her to the insolence of the man who was coward enough to reproach her with a frailty which had ministered to his pleasures. She bit her lips to restrain the burst of emotions which struggled for vent; and at that moment her bearing was as haughty and her aspect as proud as the superb dignity of incensed Juno.

"Come, Chichester," said the baronet, after a pause of a few minutes; "I shall be off. Talbot—this is no longer a place for any one of us. Madam," he added, turning with mock ceremony to Diana, "I wish you a very good afternoon. This is the last time you will ever see me in these apartments."

"I wish it to be so," said Diana, still stifling her rage with difficulty.

"And I need scarcely observe," exclaimed the baronet, "that after all that has passed between us——"

"Oh! I comprehend you, sir," interrupted the Enchantress, scornfully: "you need not fear me—your secrets are safe in my possession."

The baronet bowed, and strode out of the room, followed by Chichester and Talbot.

The Enchantress was then alone.

She threw herself at full length upon the sofa, and remained for a long time buried in profound thought. A tear started into her large blue eye; but she hastily wiped it away with her snowy handkerchief. From time to time her lips were compressed with scorn; and then a prolonged sigh would escape her breast.

Had she given a free vent to her tears, she would have experienced immediate relief: she endeavoured to stifle her passion—and it nearly suffocated her.

But how beautiful was she during that painful and fierce struggle with her feelings! Her countenance was flushed; and her eyes, usually so mild and melting, seemed to burn like two stars.

"No," she exclaimed, after a long silence, "I must not revenge myself that way! Up to the present moment, I have eaten *his* bread and have been to him as a wife; and I should be guilty of a vile deed of treachery were I to denounce him and his companions. Besides—who would believe my testimony, unsupported by facts, against the indignant denial of a man of rank, family, and title? I must stifle my resentment for the present. The hour of retribution will no doubt arrive, sooner or later; and Harborough shall yet repent the cruel—the cowardly insults he has heaped on my head this day!"

She paused, and again appeared to reflect profoundly. Suddenly a gleam of satisfaction passed over her countenance, and she started up to a sitting posture upon the sofa. The ample skirts of her dress were partly raised by her attitude, and revealed an exquisitely turned leg to the middle of the swell of the calf. The delicate foot, imprisoned in the flesh-coloured stocking of finest silk, tapped upon the carpet, in an agitated manner, with the tip of the glossy leather shoe.

That gleam of satisfaction which had suddenly appeared upon her countenance, gradually expanded into a glow of delight, brilliant and beautiful.

"Perhaps he thinks that I shall endeavour to win him back again to my arms," she said, musing aloud;—"perhaps he imagines that his countenance and support are imperatively necessary to me? Oh! no—Sir Rupert Harborough," she exclaimed, with a smile of triumph; "you may vainly await self-humiliation from me! To-morrow—yes, so soon as to-morrow shall you see that I can command a position more splendid than the one in which you placed me!"

Obeying the impulse of her feelings, she hastened to unlock an elegant rosewood writing-desk, edged with silver; and from a secret drawer she took several letters—or rather notes—written upon paper of different colours. Upon the various envelopes were seals impressed with armorial bearings, some of which were surmounted by coronets.

She glanced over each in a cursory manner, which showed she was already tolerably familiar with their contents. The greater portion she tossed contemptuously into the fire;—a few she placed one upon the other, quite in a business-like way, upon the table.

When she had gone through the entire file, she again directed her attention to those which she had reserved; and as she perused them one after the other, she mused in the following manner:—

"Count de Lestranges is brilliant in his offers, and immensely rich—no doubt; but he is detestably conceited, and would think more of himself than of his mistress. His appeal must be rejected;" and she threw the French nobleman's perfumed epistle into the fire.

"This," she continued, taking up another, "is from Lord Templeton. Five thousand a-year is certainly handsome; but then he himself is so old and ugly! Away with this suitor at once." The English Peer's *billet-doux* followed that of the French Count.

"Here is a beautiful specimen of calligraphy," resumed Diana, taking up a third letter; "but all the sentiments are copied, word for word, out of the love-scenes in Anne Radcliffe's romances. Never was such gross plagiarism! He merits the punishment I thus inflict upon him;"—and her plump white hand crushed the epistle ere she threw it into the fire.

"But what have we here? Oh! the German baron's killing address—interspersed with remarks upon the philosophy of love. Ah! my lord, love was not made for philosophers—and philosophers are incapable of love; so we will have none of you."

Another offering to the fire.

"Here is the burning address of the Greek *attaché* with a hard name. It is prettily written;—but who could possibly enter upon terms with an individual of the name of Thesaurochrysonichochrysides?"

To the flames went the Greek lover's note also.

"Ah! this seems as if it were to be the successful candidate," said Diana, carefully perusing the last remaining letter. "It is written upon a plain sheet of white paper and without scent. But then the style—how manly! Yes—decidedly, the Earl of Warrington has gained the prize. He is rich—unmarried—handsome—and still in the prime of life! There is no room for hesitation."

The Enchantress immediately penned the following note:

> "I should have replied without delay to your lordship's letter of yesterday week, but have been suffering severely from cold and bad spirits. The former has been expelled by my physician: the latter can only be forced to decamp by the presence of your lordship.
>
> "DIANA ARLINGTON."

Having despatched this note to the Earl of Warrington, the Enchantress retired to her bed-room, to prepare her toilette for the arrival of the nobleman around whom she had thus suddenly decided upon throwing her magic spells.

At eight o'clock that evening, a brilliant equipage stopped at the door of the house in which Mrs. Arlington resided.

The Earl of Warrington alighted, and was forthwith conducted into the presence of the Enchantress.

And never was she more bewitching:—never had she appeared more transcendently lovely.

A dress of the richest black velvet, very low in the *corsage*, set off her voluptuous charms and displayed the pure and brilliant whiteness of the skin to the highest advantage. Her ears were adorned with pendants of diamonds; and a tiara glittering with the same precious stones, encircled her brow. There was a soft and languishing melancholy in her deep blue eyes and in the expression of her countenance, which formed an agreeable contrast to the dazzling loveliness of her person and the splendour of her attire.

She was enchanting indeed.

Need we say that the nobleman, who had already been introduced to her and admired her, was enraptured with the prize that thus surrendered itself to him?

Diana became the mistress of the Earl of Warrington, and the very next day removed to a splendid suite of apartments in Albemarle Street, while his lordship's upholsterers furnished a house for her reception.

CHAPTER XXVI.

NEWGATE.

NEWGATE! what an ominous sound has that word.

And yet the horror exists not in the name itself; for it is a very simple compound, and would not grate upon the ear nor produce a shudder throughout the frame, were it applied to any other kind of building.

It is, then, its associations and the ideas which it conjures up that render the word NEWGATE fearful and full of dark menace.

At the mere mention of this name, the mind instantaneously becomes filled with visions of vice in all its most hideous forms, and crime in all its most appalling shapes;—wards and court-yards filled with a population peculiar to themselves,—dark gloomy passages, where the gas burns all day long, and beneath the pavement of which are interred the remains of murderers and other miscreants who have expiated their crimes upon the scaffold,—shelves filled with the casts of the countenances of those wretches, taken the moment after they were cut down from the gibbet,—condemned cells,—the chapel in which funeral sermons are preached upon men yet alive to hear them, but who are doomed to die on the morrow,—the clanking of chains, the banging of huge doors, oaths, prayers, curses, and ejaculations of despair!

Oh! if it were true that the spirits of the departed are allowed to revisit the earth for certain purposes and on particular occasions,—if the belief of superstition were well founded, and night could be peopled with the ghosts and spectres of those who sleep in troubled graves,—what a place of ineffable horrors—what a scene of terrible sights, would Newgate be at midnight! The huge flag-stones of the pavement would rise, to permit the phantoms of the murderers to issue from their graves. Demons would erect a gibbet at the debtor's door; and, amidst the sinister glare of torches, an executioner from hell would hang those miscreants over again. This would be part of their posthumous punishment, and would occur in the long—long nights of winter. There would be no moon; but all the windows of Newgate looking upon the court-yards (and there are none commanding the streets) would be brilliantly lighted with red flames, coming from an unknown source. And throughout the long passages of the prison would resound the orgies of hell; and skeletons wrapped in winding sheets would shake their fetters; and Greenacre[1] and Good[2]—Courvoisier[3] and Pegsworth[4]—Blakesley[5] and Marchant,[6] with all their predecessors in the walks of murder, would come in fearful procession from the gibbet, returning by the very corridors which they traversed in their way to death on the respective mornings of their execution. Banquets would be served up to them in the condemned cells; demons would minister to them; and their food should be the flesh, and their drink the gore, of the victims whom they had assassinated upon earth!

All would be horrible—horrible!

But, heaven be thanked! such scenes are impossible; and never can it be given to the shades of the departed to revisit the haunts which they loved or hated—adored or desecrated, upon earth!

---

1 James Greenacre, executed at Newgate, 2nd of May, 1837, for murdering and mutilating Hannah Brown.

2 Daniel Good, executed in 1842 for the murder of Jane Good, alias Jane Jones. The body had been so extensively mutilated and destroyed that another count charged him with the murder of an unknown woman, it not being entirely sure that it was Jane Good/Jane Jones.

3 Francois Benjamin Courvoisier, executed 6th of July, 1840, for murdering Lord William Russell while sleeping in his house in Norfolk Street, Park Lane.

4 John Pegsworth, executed in 1837 for the murder of John Holiday Ready.

5 Robert Blakesley, executed 1841 for the murder of James Burden.

6 William John Marchant, a young footman, who was hanged for murdering a housemaid in a magistrate's drawing-room, at 21 Cadogan Place, Chelsea. The "high-society" setting of the murder made it a great favourite in the press at the time; and Marchant's claim that, as he walked around town, he thought he was followed by the ghost of the murdered Elizabeth Paynton, made it an instant classic.

Newgate!—fearful name!

And Richard Markham was now in Newgate.

He found, when the massive gates of that terrible prison closed behind him, that the consciousness of innocence will not afford entire consolation, in the dilemma in which unjust suspicions may involve the victim of circumstantial evidence. He scarcely knew in what manner to grapple with the difficulties that beset him;—he dared not contemplate the probability of a condemnation to some infamous punishment;—and he could scarcely hope for an acquittal in the face of the testimony that conspired against him.

He recalled to mind all the events of his infancy and his boyish years, and contrasted his present position with that which he once enjoyed in the society of his father and Eugene.

His brother?—aye—what had become of his brother?—that brother, who had left the paternal roof to seek his own fortunes, and who had made so strange an appointment for a distant date, upon the hill-top where the two trees were planted? Four years and four months had passed away since the day on which that appointment was made; and in seven years and eight months it was to be kept.

They were then to compare notes of their adventures and success in life, and decide who was the more prosperous of the two,—Eugene, who was dependent upon his own resources, and had to climb the ladder of fortune step by step;—or Richard, who, placed by his father's love half-way up that ladder, had only to avail himself, it would have seemed, of his advantageous position to reach the top at his leisure?

But, alas! probably Eugene was a miserable wanderer upon the face of the earth; perhaps he was mouldering beneath the sod that no parental nor fraternal tears had watered;—or haply he was languishing in some loathsome dungeon the doors of which served as barriers between him and all communion with his fellow-men!

It was strange—passing strange that Eugene had never written since his departure; and that from the fatal evening of his separation on the hill-top all traces of him should have been so suddenly lost.

Peradventure he had been frustrated in his sanguine expectations, at his very outset in life;—perchance he had terminated in disgust an existence which was blighted by disappointment?

Such were the topics of Markham's thoughts, as he walked up

and down the large paved court-yard belonging to that department of the prison to which he had been consigned;—and, of a surety, they were of no pleasurable description. Uncertainty with regard to his own fate—anxiety in respect to his brother—and the dread that his prospects in this life were irretrievably blighted—added to a feverish impatience of a confinement totally unmerited—all these oppressed his mind.

That night he had nothing but a basin of gruel and a piece of bread for his supper. He slept in the same ward with a dozen other prisoners, also awaiting their trials: his couch was hard, cold, and wretched; and he was compelled to listen to the ribald talk and vaunts of villany of several of his companions. Their conversation was only varied by such remarks as these:—

"Well," said one, "I hope I shan't get before the Common-Serjeant: he's certain to give me toko for yam."[1]

"I shall be sure to go up the first day of sessions, and most likely before the Recorder, as mine is rather a serious matter," observed a second. "He won't give me more than seven years of it, I know."

"For my part," said a third, "I'd much sooner wait till the Wednesday, when the Judges come down: they never give it so severe as them City beaks."

"I tell you what," exclaimed a fourth, "I shouldn't like to have my meat hashed at evening sittings before the Commissioner in the New Court. He's always so devilish sulky, because he has been disturbed at his wine."

"Well, you talk of the regular judges that come down on a Wednesday," cried a fifth; "I can only tell you that Baron Griffin and Justice Spikeman are on the rota for next sessions; and I'm blowed if I wouldn't sooner go before the Common-Serjeant a thousand times, than have old Griffin meddle in my case. Why—if you only look at him, he'll transport you for twenty years."

At this idea, all the prisoners who had taken part in this conversation, burst out into a loud guffaw—but not a whit the more hearty for being so boisterous.

"Is it possible," asked Markham, who had listened with some interest to the above discourse,—"is it possible that there can be any advantage to a prisoner to be tried by a particular judge?"

---

1 toko for yam: a stiff sentence.

"Why, of course there is," answered one of the prisoners. "If a swell like you gets before Justice Spikeman, he'll let you off with half or a quarter of what the Recorder or Common-Serjeant would give you: but Baron Griffin would give you just double, because you happened to be well-dressed."

"Indeed!" ejaculated Markham, whose ideas of the marvellous equality and admirable even-handedness of English justice, were a little shocked by these revelations.

"Oh! yes," continued his informant, "all the world knows these things. If I go before Spikeman, I shall plead Guilty, and whimper a bit, and he'll be very lenient indeed; but if I'm heard by Griffin, I'll let the case take its chance, because he wouldn't be softened by any show of penitence. So you see, in these matters, one must shape one's conduct according to the judge that one goes before."

"I understand," said Markham: "even justice is influenced by all kinds of circumstances."

The conversation then turned upon the respective merits of the various counsel practising at the Central Criminal Court.

"I have secured Whiffins," said one: "he's a capital fellow—for if he can't make anything out of your case, he instantly begins to bully the judge."

"Ah! but that produces a bad effect," observed a second; "and old Griffin would soon put him down. I've got Chearnley—he's such a capital fellow to make the witnesses contradict themselves."

"Well, I prefer Barkson," exclaimed a third; "his voice alone frightens a prosecutor into fits."

"Smouch and Slike are the worst," said a fourth: "the judges always read the paper or fall asleep when they address them."

"Yes—because they are such low fellows, and will take a brief from any one," exclaimed a fifth; "whereas it is totally contrary to etiquette for a barrister to receive instructions from any one but an attorney."

"The fact is that such men as Smouch and Slike do a case more harm than good, with the judges," observed a sixth. "They haven't the ear of the Court—and that's the real truth of it."

These remarks diminished still more the immense respect which Markham had hitherto entertained for English justice; and he now saw that the barrister who detailed plain and simple facts, did not stand half such a good chance of saving his client as the favoured one "who possessed the ear of the Court."

By a very natural transition, the discourse turned upon petty juries.

"I think it will go hard with me," said one, "because I am tried in the City. I wish I had been committed for the Middlesex Sessions at Clerkenwell."

"Why so!" demanded another prisoner.

"Because, you see, I'm accused of robbing my master; and as all the jurymen are substantial shop-keepers, they're sure to convict a man in my position,—even if the evidence isn't complete."

"I'm here for swindling tradesmen at the West-End of the town," said another.

"Well," exclaimed the first speaker, "the jury will let you off, if there's the slightest pretence, because they're all City tradesmen, and hate the West-End ones."

"And I'm here for what is called '*a murderous assault upon a police-constable*,'" said a third prisoner.

"Was he a Metropolitan or a City-Policeman?"

"A Metropolitan."

"Oh! well—you're safe enough; the jury are sure to believe that he assaulted you first."

"Thank God for that blessing!"

"I tell you what goes a good way with Old Bailey Juries—a good appearance. If a poor devil, clothed in rags and very ugly, appears at the bar, the Foreman of the Jury just says, '*Well, gentlemen, I think we may say* GUILTY; *for my part I never saw such a hang-dog countenance in my life.' But if a well-dressed and good-looking fellow is placed in the dock, the Foreman is most likely to say, 'Well, gentlemen, for my part I never can nor will believe that the prisoner could be guilty of such meanness; so I suppose we may say* NOT GUILTY, *gentlemen*.'"

"Can this be true?" ejaculated Markham.

"Certainly it is," was the reply. "I will tell you more, too. If a prisoner's counsel don't tip the jury plenty of soft sawder, and tell them that they are enlightened Englishmen, and that they are the main prop, not only of justice, but also of the crown itself, they will be certain to find a verdict of *Guilty*."

"What infamy!" cried Markham, perfectly astounded at these revelations.

"Ah! and what's worse still," added his informant, "is that Old Bailey juries always, as a matter of course, convict those poor devils who have no counsel."

"And this is the vaunted palladium of justice and liberty!" said Richard.

In this way did the prisoners in Markham's ward contrive to pass away an hour or two, for they were allowed no candle and no fire, and had consequently been forced to retire to their wretched couches immediately after dusk.

The night was thus painfully long and wearisome.

Markham found upon enquiry that there were two methods of living in Newgate. One was to subsist upon the gaol allowance: the other to provide for oneself. Those who received the allowance were not permitted to have beer, nor were their friends suffered to add the slightest comfort to their sorry meals; and those who paid for their own food, were unrestricted as to quantity and quality.

Such is the treatment prisoners experience *before* they are tried;—and yet there is an old saying *that every one must be deemed innocent until he be proved guilty*. The old saying is a detestable mockery!

Of course Markham determined upon paying for his own food; and when Whittingham called in the morning, he was sent to make the necessary arrangements with the coffee-house keeper in the Old Bailey who enjoyed the monopoly of supplying that compartment of the prison.

The most painful ordeal which Richard had to undergo during his captivity in Newgate, was his first interview with Mr. Monroe. This gentleman was profoundly affected at the situation of his youthful ward, though not for one moment did he doubt his innocence.

And here let us mention another revolting humiliation and unnecessary cruelty to which the *untried* prisoner is compelled to submit. In each yard is a small enclosure, or cage, of thick iron bars, covered with wire-work; and beyond this fence, at a distance of about two feet, is another row of bars similarly interwoven with wire. The visitor is compelled to stand in this cage to converse with his relative or friend, who is separated from him by the two gratings. All private discourse is consequently impossible.

What can recompense the prisoner who is acquitted, for all the mortifications, insults, indignities, and privations he has undergone in Newgate previous to that trial which triumphantly proclaims his innocence?

Relative to the interview between Markham and Monroe, all that it is necessary to state is that the young man's guardian promised to adopt all possible means to prove his innocence, and spare no expense in securing the most intelligent and influential legal assistance. Mr. Monroe moreover intimated his intention of removing the case from the hands of Mac Chizzle to those of a well-known and highly respectable solicitor. Richard declared that he left himself entirely in his guardian's hands, and expressed his deep gratitude for the interest thus demonstrated by that gentleman in his behalf.

Thus terminated the first interview in Newgate between Markham and his late father's confidential friend.

He felt somewhat relieved by this visit, and entertained strong hopes of being enabled to prove his innocence upon the day of trial.

But it then wanted a whole month to the next sessions—thirty horrible days which he would be compelled to pass in Newgate!

CHAPTER XXVII.

THE REPUBLICAN AND THE RESURRECTION MAN.

As Richard was walking up and down the yard, an hour or two after his interview with Mr. Monroe, he was attracted by the venerable appearance of an elderly gentleman who was also parading that dismal place to and fro.

This individual was attired in a complete suit of black; and his pale countenance, and long gray hair flowing over his coat-collar, were rendered the more remarkable by the mournful nature of his garb. He stooped considerably in his gait, and walked with his hands joined together behind him. His eyes were cast upon the ground; and his meditations appeared to be of a profound and soul-absorbing nature.

Markham immediately experienced a strange curiosity to become acquainted with this individual, and to ascertain the cause of his imprisonment. He did not, however, choose to interrupt that venerable man's reverie. Accident presently favoured his wishes, and placed within his reach the means of introduction to the object of his curiosity. The old gentleman changed his line of walk in the spacious yard, and tripped over a loose flagstone. His head came suddenly in contact with the ground. Richard hastened to raise him up, and conducted him to a bench. The old gentleman was very grateful for these attentions; and, when he was recovered from the effects of his fall, he surveyed Markham with the utmost interest.

"What circumstance has thrown you into this vile den?" he inquired, in a pleasant tone of voice.

Richard instantly related, from beginning to end, those particulars with which the reader is already acquainted.

The old man remained silent for some minutes, and then fixed his eyes upon Markham in a manner that seemed intended to read the secrets of his soul.

Richard did not quail beneath that eagle glance; but a deep blush suffused his countenance.

"I believe you, my boy—I believe every word you have uttered," suddenly exclaimed the stranger—"you are the victim of circumstances; and deeply do I commiserate your situation."

"I thank you sincerely—most sincerely for your good opinion," said Richard. "And now, permit me to ask you what has plunged you into a gaol? No crime, I feel convinced before you speak!"

"Never judge hastily, young man," returned the old gentleman. "My conviction of your innocence was principally established by the very circumstance which would have led others to pronounce in favour of your guilt. You blushed—deeply blushed, but it was not the glow of shame: it was the honest flush of conscious integrity unjustly suspected. Now with regard to myself, I know why you imagine me to be innocent of any crime; but, remember that a mild, peaceable and venerable exterior frequently covers a heart eaten up with every evil passion, and a soul stained with every crime. You were, however, right in your conjecture relative to myself. I am a person accused of a political offence—a libel upon the government, in a journal of considerable influence which I conduct. I shall be tried next session; my sentence will not be severe, perhaps; but it will not be the less unjust. I am the friend of my fellow-countrymen and my fellow-creatures: the upright and the enlightened denominate me a philanthropist: my enemies denounce me as a disturber of the public peace, a seditious agitator, and a visionary. You have undoubtedly heard of Thomas Armstrong?"

"I have not only heard of you, sir," said Richard, surveying the great Republican writer with profound admiration and respect, "but I have read your works and your essays with pleasure and interest."

"In certain quarters," continued Armstrong, "I am represented as a character who ought to be loathed and shunned by all virtuous and honest people,—that I am a moral pestilence,—a social plague; and that my writings are only deserving of being burnt by the hands of the common hangman. The organs of the rich and aristocratic classes, level every species of coarse invective against me. And yet, O God!" he added enthusiastically, "I only strive to arouse the grovelling spirit of the industrious millions to a sense of the wrongs under which they labour, and to prove to them that they were not sent into this world to lick the dust beneath the feet of majesty and aristocracy!"

"Do you not think," asked Richard, timidly, "that you are somewhat in advance of the age? Do you not imagine that a republic would be dangerously premature?"

"My dear youth, let us not discuss this matter in a den where all our ideas are concentrated in the focus formed by our misfortunes. Let me rather assist you with my advice upon the mode of conduct you should preserve in this prison, so that you may not become too familiar with the common herd, nor offend by being too distant."

Mr. Armstrong then proffered his counsel upon this point.

"I feel deeply indebted to you for your kindness," exclaimed Markham: "very—very grateful!"

"Grateful!" cried the old man, somewhat bitterly. "Oh! how I dislike that word! The enemies who persecute me now, are those who have received the greatest favours from me. But there is one—one whose treachery and base ingratitude I never can forget—although I can forgive him! Almost four years ago, I accidently learnt that a young man of pleasing appearance, genteel manners, and good acquirements, was in a state of the deepest distress, in an obscure lodging in Hoxton Old Town. I called upon him: the account which had reached my ears was too true. He was bordering upon starvation, and—although he assured me that he had relations and friends moving in a wealthy sphere—he declared that particular reasons, which he implored me not to dive into, compelled him to refrain from addressing them. I relieved his necessities; I gave him money and procured him clothes. I then took him as my private secretary,

and soon put the greatest confidence in him. Alas! how was I recompensed? He betrayed all my political secrets to the government: he literally sold me! At length he absconded, taking with him a considerable sum of money, which he abstracted from my desk."

"How despicable!" ejaculated Richard.

"That is not all. I met him afterwards, and forgave him!" said Armstrong.

"Ah! you possess, sir, a noble heart," cried Richard: "I hope that this misguided young man gave sincere proofs of repentance!"

"Oh! he was very grateful!" ejaculated Mr. Armstrong, with a satirical smile: "when he heard that there was a warrant issued for my apprehension upon a charge of libel on the government, he secretly instructed the officers relative to my private haunts, and thus sold me again!"

"The villain!" cried Markham, with unfeigned indignation. "Tell me his name, that I may avoid him as I would a poisonous viper!"

"His name is George Montague," returned Mr. Armstrong.

"George Montague!" cried Richard.

"Do you know him? have you heard of him before? If you happen to be aware of his present abode—"

"You would send and have him arrested for the robbery of the money in your desk?"

"No—write and assure him of my forgiveness once more," replied the noble-hearted republican. "But how came you acquainted with his name?"

"I have heard of that young man before, but not in a way to do him honour. A tale of robbery and seduction—of heartless cruelty and vile deceit—has been communicated to me relative to this George Montague. Can you forgive such a wretch as he is?"

"From the bottom of my heart," answered the republican.

Markham gazed upon that venerable gentleman with profound respect. He remembered to have seen the daily Tory newspapers denounce that same old man as "an unprincipled agitator—the enemy of his country—the foe to morality—a political ruffian—a bloody-minded votary of Robespierre and Danton:"—and he now heard the sweetest and holiest sentiment of Christian morality emanate from the lips of him who had thus been fearfully represented. And that sentiment was uttered without affectation, but with unequivocal sincerity!

For a moment, Richard forgot his own sorrows and misfortunes, as he contemplated the benign and holy countenance of him whom a certain class loved to depict as a demon incarnate!

The old man did not notice the interest which he had thus excited, for he had himself fallen into a profound reverie.

Presently the conversation was resumed; and the more that Markham saw of the Republican, the more did he respect and admire him.

In the course of the afternoon Markham was accosted by one of his fellow-prisoners, who beckoned him aside in a somewhat mysterious manner. This individual was a very short, thin, cadaverous-looking man, with coal-black hair and whiskers, and dark piercing eyes half concealed beneath shaggy brows of the deepest jet. He was apparently about five and thirty years of age. His countenance was downcast; and when he spoke, he seemed as if he could not support the glance of the person whom he addressed. He was dressed in a seedy suit of black, and wore an oil-skin cap with a large shade.

This person, who was very reserved and retired in his habits, and seldom associated with his fellow-prisoners, drew Markham aside, and said, "I've taken a liberty with your name; but I know you won't mind it. In a place like this we must help and assist each other."

"And in what way—" began Markham.

"Oh! nothing very important; only it's just as well to tell you in case the turnkey says a word about it. The fact is, I haven't half enough to eat with this infernal gruel and soup that they give those who, like me, are forced to take the gaol allowance, and my old mother—who is known by the name of the Mummy—has promised to send me in presently a jolly good quartern loaf and three or four pound of Dutch cheese."

"But I thought that those who took the gaol allowance were not permitted to receive any food from outside?" said Markham.

"That's the very thing," said the man: "so I have told the Mummy to direct the parcel to you, as I know that you grub yourself at your own cost."

"So long as it does not involve me——"

"No—not in the least, my good fellow," interrupted the other. "And, in return," he added, after a moment's pause, "if I can ever do you a service, outside or in, you may reckon upon the Resurrection Man."

"The Resurrection Man!" ejaculated Richard, appalled, in spite of himself, at this ominous title.

"Yes—that's my name and profession," said the man. "My godfathers and godmothers called me Anthony, and my parents had previously blessed me with the honourable appellation of Tidkins: so you may know me as Anthony Tidkins, the Resurrection Man."

"And are you really ——" began Richard, with a partial shudder; "are you really a ——"

"A body-snatcher?" cried Anthony; "of course I am—when there's any work to be done; and when there isn't, then I do a little in another line."

"And what may that be?" demanded Markham.

This time the Resurrection Man *did* look his interlocutor full in the face; but it was only for a moment; and he again averted his glance in a sinister manner, as he jerked his thumb towards the wall of the yard, and exclaimed, "Crankey Jem on t'other side will tell you if you ask him. They would not put us together: no—no," he added, with a species of chuckle; "they know a trick worth two of that. We shall both be tried together: fifteen years for him—freedom for me! That's the way to do it."

With these words the Resurrection Man turned upon his heels, and walked away to the farther end of the yard.

We shall now take leave of Markham for the present: when we again call the reader's attention to his case, we shall find him standing in the dock of the Central Criminal Court, to take his trial upon the grave accusation of passing forged notes.

CHAPTER XXVIII.

THE DUNGEON.

Return we now to Bill Bolter, the murderer, who had taken refuge in the subterranean hiding-place of the Old House in Chick Lane.

Heavily and wearily did the hours drag along. The inmate of that terrible dungeon was enabled to mark their lapse by the deep-mouthed bell of St. Sepulchre's Church, on Snow Hill, the sound of which boomed ominously at regular intervals upon his ear.[1]

That same bell tolls the death-note of the convict on the morning of his execution at the debtors' door of Newgate.

The murderer remembered this, and shuddered.

A faint—faint light glimmered through the little grating at the end of the dungeon; and the man kept his eyes fixed upon it so long, that at length his imagination began to conjure up phantoms

---

1 St. Sepulchre's Church was the nearest to Newgate prison, and its bell was used to time executions. In former days, when prisoners were carried to Tyburn for hanging, it was customary to stop at St. Sepulchre's and give them a drink of beer. The bell-man of St. Sepulchre's traditionally read a sermon outside the prison walls the night before an execution.

to appal him. That small square aperture became a frame in which hideous countenances appeared; and then, one gradually changed into another—horrible dissolving views that they were!

But chiefly he beheld before him the tall gaunt form of his murdered wife—with one eye smashed and bleeding in her head:—the other glared fearfully upon him.

This phantasmagoria became at length so fearful and so real in appearance, that the murderer turned his back towards the little grating through which the light struggled into the dungeon in two long, narrow, and oblique columns.

But then he imagined that there were goblins behind him; and this idea soon grew as insupportable as the first;—so he rose, and groped his way up and down that narrow vault—a vault which might become his tomb!

This horrible thought never left his memory. Even while he reflected upon other things,—amidst the perils which enveloped his career, and the reminiscences of the dread deeds of which he had been guilty,—amongst the reasons which he assembled together to convince himself that the hideous countenances at the grating did not exist in reality,—there was that one idea—unmixed—definite—standing boldly out from all the rest in his imagination,—*that he might be left to die of starvation!*

At one time the brain of this wretch was excited to such a pitch that he actually caught his head in his two hands, and pressed it with all his force—to endeavour to crush the horrible visions which haunted his imagination.

Then he endeavoured to hum a tune; but his voice seemed to choke him. He lighted a pipe, and sate and smoked; but as the thin blue vapour curled upwards, in the faint light of the grating, it assumed shapes and forms appalling to behold. Spectres, clad in long winding sheets—cold grisly corpses, dressed in shrouds, seemed to move noiselessly through the dungeon.

He laid aside the pipe; and, in a state of mind bordering almost upon frenzy, tossed off the brandy that had remained in the flask.

But so full of horrible ideas was his mind at that moment, that it appeared to him as if he had been drinking blood!

He rose from his seat once more, and groped up and down the dungeon, careless of the almost stunning blows which he gave his head, and the violent contusions which his limbs received, against the uneven walls.

Hark! suddenly voices fell upon his ears.

He listened with mingled fear and joy,—fear of being discovered, and joy at the sound of human tones in the midst of that subterranean solitude.

Those voices came from the lower window of the dwelling on the other side of the ditch.

"How silent and quiet everything has been lately in the old house opposite," said a female.

"Last night—or rather early this morning, I heard singing there," replied another voice, which was evidently that of a young woman.

Oh! never had the human tones sounded so sweet and musical upon the murderer's ears before!

"It is very seldom that any one ever goes into that old house now," said the first speaker.

"Strange rumours are abroad concerning it: I heard that there are subterranean places in which men can conceal themselves, and no power on earth could find them save those in the secret."

"How absurd! I was speaking to the policeman about that very thing a few days ago; and he laughed at the idea. He says it is impossible; and of course he knows best."

"I am not so sure of that. Who knows what fearful deeds have those old walls concealed from human eye? For my part, I can very well believe that there are secret cells and caverns. Who knows but that some poor wretch is hiding there this very moment?"

"Perhaps the man that murdered his wife up in Union Court."

"Well—who knows? But at this rate we shall never get on with our work."

The noise of a window being shut down fell upon the murderer's ears: and he heard no more.

But he had heard enough! Those girls had spoken of him:—they had mentioned him as *the man who had murdered his wife*.

The assassination, then, was already known: the dread deed was bruited abroad:—thousands and thousands of tongues had no doubt repeated the tale here and there—conveying it hither and thither—far and wide!

And throughout the vast metropolis was he already spoken of as *the man who had murdered his wife!*

And in a few hours more, would millions in all parts hear of *the man who had murdered his wife!*

And already were the officers of justice actively in search of *the man who had murdered his wife!*

Heavily—heavily passed the hours.

At length the dungeon became pitch dark; and then the murderer saw sights more appalling than when the faint gleam stole through the grating.

In due time the sonorous voice of Saint Sepulchre proclaimed the hour of nine.

Scarcely had the last stroke of that iron tongue died upon the breeze, when a noise at the head of the spiral staircase fell upon the murderer's ears. The trap-door was raised, and the well-known voice of Dick Flairer was heard.

"Well, Bill—alive or dead, eh—old fellow!" exclaimed the burglar.

"Alive—and that's all, Dick," answered Bill Bolter, ascending the staircase.

"My God! how pale you are, Bill," said Dick, the moment the light of the candle fell upon the countenance of the murderer, as he emerged from the trap-door.

"Pale, Dick!" ejaculated the wretch, a shudder passing over his entire frame; "I do not believe I can stand a night of that infernal hole."

"You must, Bill—you must," said Flairer: "all is discovered up in Union Court there, and the police are about in all directions."

"When was it found out? Tell me the particulars—speak!" said the murderer, with frenzied impatience.

"Why, it appears that the neighbours heard a devil of a noise in your room, but didn't think nothink about it, 'cos you and Polly used to spar a bit now and then. But at last the boy—Harry, I mean—went down stairs and said that his mother wouldn't move, and that his father had gone away. So up the neighbours went—and then everything was blown. The children was sent to the workus, and the coroner held his inquest this afternoon at three. Harry was had up before him; and—"

"And what?" demanded Bolter, hastily.

"And, in course," added Dick, "the Coroner got out of the boy all the particklars: so the jury returned a verdict ——"

"Of *Wilful Murder*, eh?" said Bill, sinking his voice almost to a whisper.

"*Wilful Murder against William Bolter*," answered Dick, coolly.

"That little vagabond Harry!" cried the criminal—his entire countenance distorted with rage; "I'll be the death on him!"

"There's no news at all about t'other affair up at Clapton, and no stir made in it at all," said Dick, after a moment's pause: "so that there business is all right. But here's a lot of grub and plenty of lush, Bill: that'll cheer ye, if nothink else will."

"Dick!" exclaimed the murderer, "I cannot go back into that hole—I had rather get nabbed at once. The few hours I have already been there have nearly drove me mad; and I can't—I won't attempt the night in that infernal cold damp vault. I feel as if I was in my coffin."

"Well, you know best," said Dick, coolly. "A hempen neckcloth at Tuck-up fair, and a leap from a tree with only one leaf, is what you'll get if you're perverse."

"My God—my God!" ejaculated Bolter, wringing his hands, and throwing glances of extreme terror around the room: "what am I to do? what am I to do?"

"Lie still down below for a few weeks, or go out and be scragged," said Dick Flairer. "Come, Bill, be a man; and don't take on in this here way. Besides, I'm in a hurry, and must be off. I've brought you enough grub for three days, as I shan't come here too often till the business has blowed over a little."

Bill Bolter took a long draught from a quart bottle of rum which his friend had brought with him; and he then felt his spirits revive. Horrible as the prospect of a long sojourn in the dungeon appeared, it was still preferable to the fearful doom which must inevitably follow his capture; and, accordingly, the criminal once more returned to his hiding-place.

Dick Flairer promised to return on the third evening from that time; and the trap-door again closed over the head of the murderer.

Bolter supped off a portion of the provisions which his friend had brought him, and then lay down upon the hard stone bench to sleep. A noisome stench entered the dungeon from the Ditch, and the rats ran over the person of the inmate of that subterranean hole. Repose was impossible: the miserable wretch therefore sate up, and began to smoke.

By accident he kicked his leg a little way beneath the stone bench: the heel of his boot encountered something that yielded to the touch; and a strange noise followed.

That noise was like the rattling of bones!

The pipe fell from the man's grasp; and he himself was stupefied with sudden terror.

At length, exercising immense violence over his feelings, he determined to ascertain whether the horrible suspicions which had entered his mind were well-founded or not.

He thrust his hand beneath the bench, and encountered the mouldering bones of a human skeleton.

With indescribable feelings of agony and horror he threw himself upon the bench—his hair on end, and his heart palpitating violently.

Heaven only can tell how he passed that long weary night—alone, in the darkness of the dungeon, with his own thoughts, the skeleton of some murdered victim, and the vermin that infected the subterranean hole.

He slept not a wink throughout those live-long hours, the lapse of which was proclaimed by the voice of Saint Sepulchre's solemn and deep-toned bell.

And none who heard the bell during that night experienced feelings of such intense anguish and horror as the murderer in his lurking-hole. Not even the neighbouring prison of Newgate, nor the hospital of Saint Bartholomew, nor the death-bed of a parent, knew mental suffering so terrible as that which wrung the heart of this guilty wretch.

The morning dawned; and the light returned to the dungeon.

The clock had just struck eight, and the murderer was endeavouring to force a mouthful of food down his throat, when the voice of a man in the street fell upon his ear. He drew close up to the grating, and clearly heard the following announcement:—

"Here is a full and perfect account of the horrible assassination committed by the miscreant William Bolter, upon the person of his wife; with a portrait of the murderer, and a representation of the room as it appeared when the deed was first discovered by a neighbour. Only one Penny! The fullest and most perfect account—only one Penny!"

A pause ensued, and then the voice, bawling more lustily than before, continued thus:—

"A full and perfect account of the bloody and cruel murder in Upper Union Court; shewing how the assassin first dashed out one of his victim's eyes, and then fractured her skull upon the floor. Only one Penny, together with a true portrait of the murderer, for whose apprehension a reward of One Hundred Pounds is offered! Only one Penny!"

"A reward of one hundred pounds!" cried another voice: "my eye! how I should like to find him!"

"Wouldn't I precious soon give him up!" ejaculated a third.

"I wonder whereabouts he is," said a fourth. "No doubt that he has run away—perhaps to America—perhaps to France."

"That shews how much you know about such things," said a fifth speaker. "It is a very strange fact, that murderers always linger near the scene of their crime; they are attracted towards it, seemingly, as the moth is to the candle. Now, for my part, I shouldn't at all wonder if the miscreant was within a hundred yards of us at the present moment."

"Only one Penny! The fullest and most perfect account of the horrible and bloody murder——"

The itinerant vender of pamphlets passed on, followed by the crowd which his vociferations had collected; and his voice soon ceased to break the silence of the morning.

Bolter sank down upon the stone bench, a prey to maddening feelings and fearful emotions.

A hundred pounds were offered for his reward! Such a sum might tempt even Dick Flairer or Tom the Cracksman to betray him.

Instinctively he put his fingers to his neck, to feel if the rope were there yet, and he shook his head violently to ascertain if he were hanging on a gibbet, or could still control his motions.

The words "miscreant," "horrible and bloody murder," and "portrait of the assassin," still rang in his ears—loud—sonorous—deep—and with a prolonged echo like that of a bell!

Already were men speculating upon his whereabouts, and anxious for his apprehension—some for the reward, others to gratify a morbid curiosity: already were the newspapers, the cheap press, and the pamphleteers busy with his name.

None now mentioned him save as *the miscreant William Bolter*.

Oh! if he could but escape to some foreign land,—if he could but avoid the ignominious consequences of his crime in this,—he would dedicate the remainder of his days to penitence,—he would toil from the dawn of morning till sunset to obtain the bread of honesty,—he would use every effort, exert every nerve to atone for the outrage he had committed upon the laws of society!

But—no! it was too late. The blood-hounds of the law were already upon his track.

An hour passed away; and during that interval the murderer sought to compose himself by means of his pipe and the rum-bottle: but he could not banish the horrible ideas which haunted him.

Suddenly a strange noise fell upon his ear.

The blood appeared to run cold to his very heart in a refluent tide; for the steps of many feet, and the sounds of many voices, echoed through the old house.

The truth instantly flashed to his mind: the police had entered the premises.

With hair standing on end, eye-balls glaring, and forehead bathed in perspiration, the murderer sate motionless upon the cold stone bench—afraid even to breathe. Every moment he expected to hear the trap-door at the head of the spiral staircase move: but several minutes elapsed, and his fears in this respect were not accomplished.

At length he heard a sound as of a body falling heavily; and then a voice almost close to him fell upon his ear.

The reader will remember that the vault in which he was concealed, joined the cellar from whence Walter Sydney had escaped. The officers had entered that cellar by means of the trap-door in the floor of the room immediately above it. Bolter could overhear their entire conversation.

"Well, this is a strange crib, this is," said one. "Show the bull's-eye up in that farther corner: there may be a door in one of them dark nooks."

"It will jist end as I said it would," exclaimed another: "the feller wouldn't be sich a fool as to come to a place that's knowed to the Force as one of bad repute."

"I didn't think, myself, there was much good in coming to search this old crib: but the inspector said *yes*, and so we couldn't say *no*."

"Let's be off: the cold of this infernal den strikes to my very bones. But I say—that there shelving board that we first lighted on in getting down, isn't made to help people to come here alive."

"Turn the bull's-eye more on it."

"Now can you see?"

"Yes—plain enough. It leads to a hole that looks on the ditch. But the plank is quite old and rotten; so I dare say it was put there for some purpose or another a long time ago. Pr'aps the thieves used to convey their swag through that there hole into a boat in the ditch, and——"

"No, no," interrupted the other policeman: "it wasn't swag that they tumbled down the plank into the Fleet: it was stiff 'uns."

"Very likely. But there can't be any of that kind of work ever going on now: so let's be off."

The murderer in the adjoining vault could hear the policemen climb up the plank towards the trap-door: and in a few minutes profound silence again reigned throughout the old house.

This time he had escaped detection; and yet the search was keen and penetrating.

The apparent safety of his retreat restored him to something like good spirits; and he began to calculate the chances which he imagined to exist for and against the probability of his escape from the hands of justice.

"There is but five men in the world as knows of this hiding-place," he said to himself; "and them is myself, Dick Flairer, Crankey Jem, the Resurrection Man, and Tom the Cracksman. As for me, I'm here—that's one what won't blab. Dick Flairer isn't likely to sell a pal: Tom the Cracksman I'd rely on even if he was on the rack. Crankey Jem is staunch to the backbone; besides, he's in the Jug: so is the Resurrection Man. They can't do much harm there. I think I'm tolerably safe; and as for frightening myself about ghosts and goblins——"

He was suddenly interrupted by the rattling of the bones beneath the stone-bench. He started: and a profuse perspiration instantly broke out upon his forehead.

A huge rat had disturbed those relics of mortality; but this little incident tended to hurl the murderer back again into all that appalling gloominess of thought from which he had for a moment seemed to be escaping.

Time wore on: and heavily and wearily still passed the hours. At length darkness again came down upon the earth: the light of the little grating disappeared; and the vault was once more enveloped in the deepest obscurity.

The murderer ate a mouthful, and then endeavoured to compose himself to sleep, for he was worn out mentally and bodily.

The clock of Saint Sepulchre's proclaimed the hour of seven, as he awoke from a short and feverish slumber.

He thought he heard a voice calling him in his dreams; and when he started up he listened with affright.

"Bill—are you asleep?"

It was not, then, a dream: a human voice addressed him in reality.

"Bill—why don't you answer?" said the voice. "It's only me!"

Bolter suddenly felt relieved of an immense load; it was his friend Dick who was calling him from the little trap-door. He instantly hurried up the staircase, and was surprised to find that there was no light in the room.

"My dear feller," said Dick, in a hurried tone, "I didn't mean to come back so soon again, but me and Tom is a-going to do a little business together down Southampton way—someot that he has been told of; and as we may be away a few days, I thought I'd better come this evenin' with a fresh supply. Here's plenty of grub, and rum, and bakker."

"Well, this is a treat—to hear a friendly voice again so soon," said Bill;—"but why the devil don't you light the candle?"

"I'm a-going to do it now," returned Dick; and he struck a lucifer-match as he spoke. "I thought I wouldn't show a light here sooner than was necessary; and we must not keep it burning too long; 'cos there may be chinks in them shutters, and I des say the blue-bottles is on the scent."

"They come and searched the whole place this mornin'," said Bill: "but they didn't smell me though."

"Then you're all safe now, my boy," cried Dick. "Here, look alive—take this basket, and pitch it down the stairs: it's well tied up, and chock full of cold meat and bread. Put them two bottles into your pocket: there—that's right. Now—do you want anythink else?"

"Yes—a knife. I was forced to gnaw my food like a dog for want of one."

"Here you are," said Dick; and, taking a knife from the secret cupboard between the windows, he handed it to his friend. "Now are you all right?"

"Quite—that is, as right as a feller in my sitivation can be. You won't forget to come——"

Bolter was standing within two or three steps from the top of the staircase; and the greater part of his body was consequently above the trap-door.

He stopped suddenly short in the midst of his injunction to his companion, and staggered in such a way that he nearly lost his footing.

His eye had caught sight of a human countenance peering from behind the half-open door of the room.

"Damnation!" exclaimed the murderer: "I'm sold at last!"—and, rushing up the steps, he fell upon Dick Flairer with the fury of a tiger.

At the same moment four or five officers darted into the room:—but they were too late to prevent another dreadful deed of blood.

Bolter had plunged the knife which he held in his hand, into the heart of Dick Flairer, the burglar.

The blow was given with fatal effect: the unfortunate wretch uttered a horrible cry, and fell at the feet of his assassin, stone dead.

"Villain! what have you done?" ejaculated the serjeant who headed the little detachment of police.

"I've drawn the claret of the rascal that nosed upon me," returned Bolter doggedly.

"You were never more mistaken in your life," said the serjeant.

"How—what do you mean? Wasn't it that scoundrel Dick that chirped against me?"

"No—ten thousand times *No!*" cried the officer: "it was a prisoner in Newgate who split upon this hiding place. Somehow or another he heard of the reward offered to take you; and he told the governor the whole secret of the vault. Without knowing whether we should find you here or not, we came to search it."

"Then it was the Resurrection Man who betrayed me after all!" exclaimed Bolter; and, dashing the palms of his two hands violently against his temples, he added, in a tone of intense agony, "I have murdered my best friend—monster, miscreant that I am!"

The policeman speedily fixed a pair of manacles about his wrists; and in the course of a quarter of an hour he was safely secured in one of the cells at the station-house in Smithfield.

On the following day he was committed to Newgate.

CHAPTER XXIX.

THE BLACK CHAMBER.

Once more does the scene change.

The reader who follows us through the mazes of our narrative, has yet to be introduced to many strange places—many hideous haunts of crime, abodes of poverty, dens of horror, and lurking-holes of perfidy—as well as many seats of wealthy voluptuousness and aristocratic dissipation.

It will be our task to guide those who choose to accompany us, to scenes and places whose very existence may appear to belong to the regions of romance rather than to a city in the midst of civilisation, and whose characteristic features are as yet unknown to even those that are the best acquainted with the realities of life.

About a fortnight had elapsed since the events related in the preceding chapter.

In a small, high, well-lighted room five individuals were seated at a large round oaken table. One of these persons, who appeared to be the superior, was an elderly man with a high forehead, and thin white hair falling over the collar of his black coat. He was short and rather corpulent: his countenance denoted frankness and good-nature; but his eyes, which were small, grey, and sparkling, had a lurking expression of cunning, only perceptible to the acute observer. The other three individuals were young and gentlemanly-looking men, neatly dressed, and very deferential in their manners towards their superior.

The door of this room was carefully bolted. At one end of the table was a large black tray covered with an immense quantity of bread-seals of all sizes. Perhaps the reader may recall to mind that, amongst the pursuits and amusements of his school-days, he diverted himself with moistening the crumb of bread, and kneading it with his fingers into a consistency capable of taking and retaining an accurate impression of a seal upon a letter. The seals—or rather blank bread-stamps—now upon the tray, were of this kind, only more carefully manufactured, and well consolidated with thick gum-water.

Close by this tray, in a large wooden bowl were wafers of all sizes and colours; and in a box also standing on the table, were numbers of wafer-stamps of every dimension used. A second box contained thin blades of steel, set fast in delicate ivory handles, and sharp as razors. A third box was filled with sticks of sealing-wax of all colours, and of foreign as well as British manufacture. A small glass retort fixed over a spirit-lamp, was placed near one of the young men. A tin-box containing a little cushion covered with printer's red ink in one compartment, and several stamps such as the reader may have seen used in post-offices, in another division, lay open near the other articles mentioned. Lastly, an immense pile of letters—some sealed, and others wafered—stood upon that end of the table at which the elderly gentleman was seated.

The occupations of these five individuals may be thus described in a few words.

The old gentleman took up the letters one by one, and bent them open, as it were, in such a way, that he could read a portion of their contents when they were not folded in such a manner as effectually to conceal all the writing. He also examined the addresses, and consulted a long paper of an official character which lay upon the table at his right hand. Some of the letters he threw, after as careful a scrutiny as he could devote to them without actually breaking the seals or wafers, into a large wicker basket at his feet. From time to time, however, he passed a letter to the young man who sate nearest to him.

If the letters were closed with wax, an impression of the seal was immediately taken by means of one of the bread stamps. The young man then took the letter and held it near the large fire which burnt in the grate until the sealing-wax became so softened by the heat that the letter could be easily opened without tearing the paper. The third clerk read it aloud, while the fourth took notes of its contents. It was then returned to the first young man, who re-sealed it by means of the impression taken on the bread stamp, and with wax which precisely matched that originally used in closing the letter. When this ceremony was performed, the letter was consigned to the same basket which contained those that had passed unopened through the hands of the Examiner.

If the letter were fastened with a wafer, the second clerk made the water in the little glass retort boil by means of the spirit-lamp; and when the vapour gushed forth from the tube, the young man held the letter to its mouth in such a way that the steam played full upon the identical spot where the wafer was placed. The wafer thus became moistened in a slight degree; and it was only then necessary to pass one of the thin steel blades skilfully beneath the wafer, in order to open the letter. The third young man then read this epistle, and the fourth took notes, as in the former instance. The contents being thus ascertained, the letter was easily fastened again with a very thin wafer of the same colour and size as the original; and if the job were at all clumsily done, the tin-box before noticed furnished the means of imprinting a red stamp upon the back of the letter, in such a way that a portion of the circle fell precisely over the spot beneath which the wafer was placed.

These processes were accomplished in total silence, save when the contents of the letters were read; and then, so accustomed were those five individuals to hear the revelations of the most strange secrets and singular communications, that they seldom appeared surprised or amused—shocked or horrified, at anything which those letters made known to them. Their task seemed purely of a mechanical kind: indeed, automatons could not have shewn less passion or excitement.

Oh! vile—despicable occupation,—performed, too, by men who went forth, with heads erect and confident demeanour, from their atrocious employment—after having violated those secrets which are deemed most sacred, and broken the seals which merchants, lovers, parents, relations, and friends had placed upon their thoughts!

Base and diabolical outrage—perpetrated by the commands of the Ministers of the Sovereign!

Reader, this small, high, well-lighted room, in which such infamous scenes took place with doors well secured by bolts and bars, was the *Black Chamber of the General Post-Office, Saint Martin's-le-Grand.*

And now, reader, do you ask whether all this be true;—whether, in the very heart of the metropolis of the civilized world, such a system and such a den of infamy can exist;—whether, in a word, the means of transferring thought at a cheap and rapid rate, be really made available to the purposes of government and the ends of party policy? If you ask these questions, to each and all do we confidently and boldly answer "YES."

The first letter which the Examiner caused to be opened on the occasion when we introduce our readers to the Black Chamber, was from the State of Castelcicala, in Italy, to the representative of that Grand-Duchy at the English court. Its contents, when translated, ran thus:—

City of Montoni, Castelcicala.

"I am desired by my lord the Marquis of Gerrano, his Highness's Secretary of State for Foreign Affairs, to inform your Excellency that, in consequence of a general amnesty just proclaimed by His Serene Highness, and which includes all political prisoners and emigrants, passports to return to the Grand Duchy of Castelcicala, may be accorded to his Highness Alberto Prince of Castelcicala, nephew of his Serene Highness the Reigning Grand Duke, as well as to all other natives of Castelcicala now resident in England, but who may be desirous of returning to their own country,

"I have the honour to renew to your Excellency assurances of my most perfect consideration.

"BARON RUPERTO,

"Under-Secretary of State for Foreign Affairs, &c. &c."

The second letter perused upon this occasion, by the inmates of the Black Chamber, was from a famous London Banker to his father at Manchester:—

"You will be astounded, my dear father, when your eye meets the statement I am now at length compelled to make to you. The world believes my establishment to be as firmly based as the rocks themselves: my credit is unlimited, and thousands have confided their funds to my care. Alas, my dear father, I am totally insolvent: the least drain upon the bank would plunge me into irredeemable ruin and dishonour. I have, however, an opportunity of retrieving myself, and building up my fortunes: a certain government operation is proposed to me; and if I can undertake it, my profits will be immense. Fifty thousand pounds are absolutely necessary for my purposes within six days from the present time. Consider whether you will save your son by making him this advance; or allow him to sink into infamy, disgrace and ruin, by withholding it. Whichever way you may determine breathe not a word to a soul. The authorities in the Treasury have made all possible inquiries concerning me, and believe me to be not only solvent, but immensely rich. I expect your answer by return of post.

"Your affectionate but almost heart-broken son,

"James Tomlinson."

The writer of this letter flattered himself that the government had already made "all possible enquiries:"—he little dreamt that his own epistle was to furnish the Treasury, through the medium of the Post Office, with the very information which he had so fondly deemed unknown to all save himself.

When the third letter was opened, the clerk whose duty it was to read it, looked at the signature, and, addressing himself to the Examiner, said, "From whom, sir, did you anticipate that this letter came?"

"From Lord Tremordyn. Is it not directed to Lady Tremordyn?" exclaimed the Examiner.

"It is, sir," answered the clerk. "But it is written by that lady's daughter Cecilia."

"I am very sorry for that. The Home Office," said the Examiner, "is particularly anxious to ascertain the intention of Lord Tremordyn in certain party matters; and it is known," he added, referring to the official paper beside him, "that his lordship communicates all his political sentiments to her ladyship, who is now at Bath."

"Then, sir, this letter need not be read?" cried the clerk interrogatively.

"Not read, young man!" ejaculated the Examiner, impatiently. "How often am I to tell you that every letter which is once opened is to be carefully perused? Have we not been able to afford the government and the police some very valuable information at different times, by noting the contents of letters which we have opened by mistake?"

"Certainly," added the first clerk. "There is that deeply-planned and well-laid scheme of Stephens, and his young lady disguised as a man, who lives at Upper Clapton, which we discovered by the mere accident of opening a wrong letter."

"I beg your pardon, sir," said the clerk whose duty it was to read the epistles, and whose apology to the Examiner was delivered in a most deferential manner. "I will now proceed with the letter of the Honourable Miss Cecilia Huntingfield to her mother Lady Tremordyn."

The young clerk then read as follows:—

"Oh! my dear mother, how shall I find words to convey to you the fearful tale of my disgrace and infamy of which I am the unhappy and guilty heroine? A thousand times before you left London, I was on the point of throwing myself at your feet and confessing all! But, no—I could not—I dared not. And now, my dear parent, I can conceal my shame no longer! Oh! how shall I make you comprehend me, without actually entrusting this paper with the fearful secret? My God! I am almost distracted. Surely you can understand my meaning? If not, learn the doleful tidings at once, my dearest and most affectionate parent: I AM ABOUT TO BECOME A MOTHER! Oh! do not spurn me from you—do not curse your child! It has cost me pangs of anguish ineffable, and of mental agony an idea of which I could not convey to you, to sit down and rend your heart with this avowal. But O heavens! what am I to do? Concealment is no longer possible: IN THREE MONTHS MORE I SHALL BE A MOTHER! That villain Harborough—the friend of our family, Sir Rupert Harborough,—the man in whom my dear father put every confidence,—that wretch has caused my shame! And yet there are times, my dear mother, when I feel that I love him;—for he is the father of the child which must soon publish my disgrace! And now, my fond—confiding—tender parent, you know all. Oh! come to my rescue: adopt some means to conceal my shame;—shield me from my father's wrath! I can write no more at present: but my mind feels relieved now I have thus opened my heart to my mother.

"Your afflicted and almost despairing daughter,

"CECILIA HUNTINGFIELD."

Thus was a secret involving the honour of a noble family,—a secret compromising the most sacred interests—revealed to five men at one moment, by means of the atrocious system pursued in the Black Chamber of the General Post Office.

The fourth letter was from Mr. Robert Stephens of London to his brother Mr. Frederick Stephens of Liverpool:—

"My dear Brother,

"I write you a few hasty instructions, to which I solicit your earnest attention. You are well aware that the 26th instant is my grand day—the day to which I have been so long and so anxiously looking forward. All my schemes are so well organized that detection is impossible. That fellow Montague gave me a little trouble a fortnight or so ago, by suddenly and most unexpectedly declaring that he would not act as the witness of identity; and I was actually compelled to give him five hundred pounds to silence him. What could have been his motive for shirking out of the affair, I cannot tell. Be that as it may, I have supplied his place with another and better man—a lawyer of the name of Mac Chizzle. But now for my instructions. The grand blow will be struck soon after mid-day on the 26th instant. Immediately it is done I shall give Walter (I always speak of HER as a man) the ten thousand pounds I have promised him, and then off to Liverpool in a post-chaise and four. Now, if there be a packet for America on the 27th, secure me a berth; if not, ascertain if there be a vessel sailing for Havre or Bordeaux on that day, and then secure me a berth in such ship:—but should there be none in this instance also, then obtain a list of all the ships which, according to present arrangements, are to leave Liverpool on the 27th, with their place of destination, and all other particulars.

"Burn this letter the moment you have read it: we then know that it cannot possibly have told tales.

"Your affectionate brother,

"Robert Stephens."

Poor deluded man! he believed that letters confided to the General Post Office administration could "tell no tales" during their progress from the sender to the receiver:—how miserably was he mistaken!

And here we may observe, that if the system of opening letters at the General Post Office were merely adopted for the purpose of discovering criminals and preventing crime, we should still deprecate the proceeding, although our objections would lose much of their point in consideration of the motive; but when we find—and know it to be a fact—that the secrets of correspondence are flagrantly violated for political and other purposes, we raise our voice to denounce so atrocious a system, and to excite the indignation of the country against the men who can countenance or avail themselves of it!

Numerous other letters were read upon the occasion referred to in this chapter; and their contents carefully noted down. The whole ceremony was conducted with so much regularity and method, that it proceeded with amazing despatch; and the re-fastening of the letters was managed with such skill that in few, if any instances, were the slightest traces left to excite suspicion of the process to which those epistles had been subjected.

It was horrible to see that old man forgetting the respectability of his years, and those four young ones laying aside the fine feelings which ought to have animated their bosoms,—it was horrible to see them earnestly, systematically, and skilfully devoting themselves to an avocation the most disgraceful, soul-debasing, and morally execrable!

When the ceremony of opening, reading, and resealing the letters was concluded, one of the clerks conveyed the basket containing them to that department of the establishment where they were to undergo the process of sorting and sub-sorting for despatch by the evening mails; and the Examiner then proceeded to make his reports to the various offices of the government. The notes of the despatch from Castelcicala were forwarded to the Foreign Secretary: the contents of the Banker's letter to his father were copied and sent to the Chancellor of the Exchequer: the particulars of Miss Cecilia Huntingfield's affecting epistle to her mother were entered in a private book in case they should be required at a future day;—and an exact copy of Robert Stephens' letter to his brother was forwarded to the Solicitor of the Bank of England.

CHAPTER XXX.

THE 26TH OF NOVEMBER.

As soon as the first gleam of morning penetrated through the curtains of the boudoir in the Villa near Upper Clapton, Walter leapt from her couch.

Conflicting feelings of joy and sorrow filled her bosom. The day—the happy day had at length arrived, when, according to the promise of the man on whom she looked as her benefactor, a grand event was to be accomplished, which would release her from the detestable disguise which she had now maintained for a period of nearly five years. The era had come when she was again to appear in the garb that suited alike her charms and her inclinations. This circumstance inspired her with the most heartfelt happiness.

But, on the other hand, she loved—tenderly loved one who had meditated against her an outrage of a most infamous description. Instead of hailing her approaching return to her female attire as the signal for the consummation of the fond hopes in which she had a few weeks before indulged,—hopes which pictured to her imagination delicious scenes of matrimonial bliss in the society of George Montague,—she was compelled to separate that dream of felicity from the fact of her emancipation from a thraldom repulsive to her delicacy and her tastes.

It was, therefore, with mingled feelings of happiness and melancholy, that she commenced her usual toilette—that masculine toilette which she was that day to wear for the last time.

"You ought to be in good spirits this morning, my dearest mistress," said Louisa, as she entered the room: "the period so anxiously looked forward to by you has at length arrived."

"And to-morrow—to-morrow," exclaimed Walter, her hazel eyes lighting up with a brilliant expression of joy, "you, my excellent Louisa, will assist me to adorn myself with that garb which I have neglected so of late!"

"I shall be happy both for your sake and mine," returned Louisa, who was indeed deeply attached to her mistress; "and when I see you recovering all your usual spirits, in a foreign land——"

"In Switzerland," hastily interrupted Walter; "in Switzerland—whither you will accompany me, my good and faithful Louisa; and to which delightful country we will proceed without delay! There indeed I shall be happy—and, I hope, contented!"

"Mr. Stephens is to be here at ten, is he not?" said Louisa, after a short pause.

"At ten precisely; and we then repair forthwith to the West End of the town, where certain preliminaries are requisite previously to receiving an immense sum of money which will be paid over to us at the Bank of England. This much Mr. Stephens told me yesterday. He had never communicated so much before."

"And this very afternoon it is your determination to leave London?" said Louisa.

"I am now resolved upon that step," replied the lady. "You alone shall accompany me: Mr. Stephens has promised to provide for the groom and the old cook. Therefore, while I am absent this morning about the momentous business the real nature of which, by-the-bye, has yet to be explained to me, you will make all the preparations that may be necessary for our journey."

This conversation took place while Louisa hastily lighted the fire in the boudoir. In a few minutes the grate sent up a cheering and grateful heat; and the flames roared up the chimney. The lady, with an elegant dressing-gown folded loosely around her, and her delicate white feet thrust into red morocco slippers, threw herself into her luxurious easy-chair, while Louisa hastened to serve up breakfast upon a little rose-wood table, covered with a napkin as white as snow. But the meal passed away almost untouched: the lady's heart was too full of hope and tender melancholy to allow her to experience the least appetite.

The mysterious toilette was completed: and Walter descended to the parlour, attired in masculine garments for the last time!

At ten o'clock precisely Mr. Stephens arrived. He was dressed with peculiar neatness and care; but his countenance was very pale, and his eyes vibrated in a restless manner in their sockets. He, however, assumed a bold composure; and thus the profound anxiety to which he was at that moment a prey, was unnoticed by Walter Sydney.

They seated themselves upon the sofa, and looked at each other for an instant without speaking. Those glances on either side expressed, in the ardent language of the eye, the words—"This is the day!"

"Walter," said Mr. Stephens, at length breaking the silence which had prevailed, "your conduct to-day must crown my designs with glorious success, or involve me in irretrievable ruin."

"You may rely with confidence upon my discretion and prudence," answered Walter. "Command me in all respects—consistently with honour."

"Honour!" exclaimed Stephens impatiently: "why do you for ever mention that unmeaning word? *Honour* is a conventional term,

and is often used in a manner inconsistently with common sense and sound judgment. *Honour* is all very well when it is brought in contact with *honour* only; but when it has to oppose fraud and deceit, it must succumb if it trust solely to its own force. The most honest lawyer sets chichanery and quibble to work, to counteract the chicanery and quibble of his pettifogging opponent: the politician calls the machinery of intrigue into play, in order to fight his foeman with that foeman's own weapon:—if the French employ the aid of riflemen concealed in the thicket while the fair fight takes place upon the plain, the English must do the same."

"I certainly comprehend the necessity of frequently fighting a man with his own weapons," said Walter; "but I do not see to what point in our affairs your reasoning tends."

"Suppose, Walter," resumed Stephens, speaking very earnestly, and emphatically accentuating every syllable, "suppose that you had a friend who was entitled to certain rights which were withheld from him by means of some detestable quibble and low chicanery; suppose that by stating that your friend's name was George instead of William, for instance, you could put him in possession of what is justly and legitimately his due, but which, remember, is shamefully and most dishonestly kept away from him;—in this case, should you hesitate to declare that his name was George, and not William?"

"I think that I should be inclined to make the statement, to serve the cause of justice and to render a friend a signal service," answered Sydney, after a moment's hesitation.

"I could not have expected a different reply," exclaimed Stephens, a gleam of joy animating his pale countenance: "and you would do so with less remorse when you found that you were transferring property from one individual who could well spare what he was never justly entitled to, to a person who would starve without the restoration of his legitimate rights."

"Oh! certainly," said Walter; and this time the reply was given without an instant's meditation.

"Then," continued Stephens, more and more satisfied with the influence of his sophistry, "you would in such a case eschew those maudlin and mawkish ideas of *honour*, which arbitrarily exact that a falsehood must never be told for a good purpose, and that illegitimate means must never—never be adopted to work out virtuous and profitable ends?"

"My conduct in assuming this disguise," returned Sydney, with a smile and a blush, "has proved to you, I should imagine, that I should not hesitate to make use of a deceit comparatively innocent, with a view to oppose fraud and ensure permanent benefit to my friend and myself."

"Oh! Walter, you should have been a man in person as well as in mind!" cried Stephens, enthusiastically. "Now I have no fears of the result of my plans; and before sun-set you shall be worth ten thousand pounds!"

"Ten thousand pounds!" repeated Walter, mechanically. "How much can be done with such a sum as that!"

"You expressed a wish to leave this country, and visit the south of Europe," said Stephens: "you will have ample means to gratify all your tastes, and administer to all your inclinations. Only conceive a beautiful little cottage on the shore of the lake of Brienz—that pearl of the Oberland; the fair boat-women—the daughters of Switzerland—passing in their little shallops beneath your windows, and singing their national songs, full of charming tenderness, while the soft music mingles with the murmuring waves and the sounds of the oars!"

"Oh! what an enchanting picture!" cried Walter. "And have you ever seen such as this?"

"I have; and I feel convinced that the existence I recommend is the one which will best suit you. To-day," continued Stephens, watching his compatriot's countenance with a little anxiety, "shall you recover your rights;—to-day shall you oppose the innocent deceit to the enormous fraud;—to-day shall you do for *yourself* what you ere now stated you would do for a *friend!*"

"If you have drawn my own case in putting those queries to me,—if immense advantages will be derived from my behaviour in this affair,—if I am merely wresting from the hands of base cupidity that which is justly mine own,—and if the enemy whom we oppose can well afford to restore to me the means of subsistence, and thus render me independent for the remainder of my days,—oh! how can I hesitate for a moment? how can I refuse to entrust myself wholely and solely—blindly and confidently—in your hands,—you who have done so much for me, and who have taught me to respect, honour, and obey you?"

The lady uttered these words with a species of electric enthusiasm, while her eyes brightened, and her cheeks were suffused with the purple glow of animation. The specious arguments and the glowing description of Swiss life, brought forward by Stephens with admirable dexterity, awakened all the ardour of an impassioned soul; and the bosom of that beauteous creature palpitated with hope, with joy, and with excitement, as she gazed upon the future through the mirror presented by Stephens to her view.

She was now exactly in a frame of mind suited to his purpose.

Without allowing her ardour time to abate, and while she was animated by the delicious aspirations which he had conjured up, as it were by an enchanter's spell, in her breast, he took her by the hand, and led her up to the mantel-piece; then, pointing to the portrait of her brother, he said in a low, hurried, and yet solemn tone,—"The fortune which must be wrested from the grasp of cupidity this day, would have belonged to your brother; and no power on earth could have deprived him of it; for, had he lived, he would yesterday have attained his twenty-first year! His death is unknown to him who holds this money: but, by a miserable legal technicality, you—*you*, his sister, and *in justice* his heiress—*you* would be deprived of that fortune by the man who now grasps it, and who would chuckle at any plan which made it his own. Now do you comprehend me? You have but to say that your name is *Walter*, instead of *Eliza*,—and you will recover your just rights, defeat the wretched chicanery of the law, and enter into possession of those resources which belong to you in the eyes of God, but which, if you shrink, will be for ever alienated from you and your's!"

"In one word," said the lady, "I am to personate my brother?"

"Precisely! Do you hesitate?" demanded Stephens: "will you allow the property of your family to pass into the hands of a stranger, who possesses not the remotest right to its enjoyment? or will you by one bold effort—an effort that cannot fail—direct that fortune into its just, its proper, and its legitimate channel?"

"The temptation is great," said the lady, earnestly contemplating the portrait of her brother; "but the danger—the danger?" she added hastily: "what would be the result if we were detected?"

"Nothing—nothing, save the total loss of the entire fortune," answered Stephens: "and, therefore, you perceive, that want of nerve—hesitation—awkwardness—blushes—confusion on your part, would ruin all. Be firm—be collected—be calm and resolute—and our plans *must* be crowned with unequivocal success!"

"Oh! if I proceed farther, I will pass through the ordeal with ease and safety," exclaimed the lady: "I can nerve my mind to encounter any danger, when it is well defined, and I know its extent;—it is only when it is vague, uncertain, and indistinct, that I shrink from meeting it. Yes," she continued, after a few moments' reflection, "I will follow your counsel in all respects: you *do* know—you *must* know how much we risk, and how far we compromise ourselves;—and when I see you ready to urge on this matter to the end, how can I fear to accompany you? Yes," she added, after another pause, much longer than the preceding one,—"I will be Walter Sydney throughout this day at least!"

"My dear friend," ejaculated Stephens, in a transport of joy, "you act in a manner worthy of your noble-hearted brother, I see—he smiles upon you even in his picture-frame."

"I will retrieve from the hands of strangers that which is thine, dear brother," said the lady, addressing herself to the portrait as if it could hear the words which she pronounced with a melancholy solemnity: then, turning towards Stephens, she exclaimed, "But you must acquaint me with the ceremonies we have to fulfil, and the duties which I shall have to perform, in order to accomplish the desired aim."

"I need not instruct you now," returned Stephens: "the forms are nothing, and explain themselves, as it were;—a few papers to sign at a certain person's house in Grosvenor Square—then a ride to the Bank—and all is over. But we must now take our departure: the hackney-coach that brought us hither is waiting to convey us to the West End."

Stephens and Sydney issued from the house together. The former gave certain directions to the coachman; and they then commenced their memorable journey.

Mr. Stephens did not allow his companion a single moment for calm and dispassionate reflection. He continued to expatiate upon the happiness which was within her reach amidst the rural scenery of Switzerland:—he conjured up before her mental vision the most ravishing and delightful pictures of domestic tranquillity, so congenial to her tastes:—he fed her imagination with all those fairy visions which were calculated to attract and dazzle a mind tinged with a romantic shade;—and then he skilfully introduced those specious arguments which blinded her as to the real nature of the deceit in which she was so prominent an agent. He thus sustained an artificial state of excitement, bordering upon enthusiasm, in the bosom of that confiding and generous-hearted woman; and not for one moment during that long ride, did she repent of the step she had taken. In fact, such an influence did the reasoning of Stephens exercise upon her mind, that she ceased to think of the possibility of either incurring danger or doing wrong;—she knew not how serious might be the consequences of detection;—she believed that she was combating the chicanery of the law with a similar weapon, the use of which was justified and rendered legitimate by the peculiar circumstances of the case.

The hackney-coach proceeded by way of the New Road, and stopped to take up Mr. Mac Chizzle at his residence near Saint Pancras New Church. The vehicle then proceeded to Grosvenor Square, where it stopped opposite one of those princely dwellings whose dingy exteriors afford to the eye of the foreigner accustomed to the gorgeous edifices of continental cities, but little promise of the wealth, grandeur, and magnificence which exist within.

The door was opened by a footman in splendid livery.

This domestic immediately recognised Mr. Stephens, and said, "His lordship expects you, sir."

The three visitors alighted from the coach: and as Stephens walked with the disguised lady into the hall of the mansion, he said in a hurried whisper, "Courage, my dear Walter: you are now about to appear in the presence of the Earl of Warrington!"

The servant led the way up a wide staircase, and conducted the visitors into a library fitted up in the most luxurious and costly manner. Cases filled with magnificently bound volumes, statues of exquisite sculpture, and pictures of eminent artists, denoted the taste of the aristocratic possessor of that lordly mansion.

Two individuals were seated at a table covered with papers and legal documents. One was a fine, tall, middle-aged man, with a noble and handsome countenance, polished manners, and most kind and affable address:—the other was an old gentleman with a bald head, sharp features, and constant smile upon his lips when he addressed the personage just described.

The first was the Earl of Warrington; the other was his solicitor, Mr. Pakenham.

The Earl rose and greeted Mr. Stephens cordially; then, turning towards Walter, he shook her kindly by the hand, and said, "I need not ask if you are the young gentleman to whom I am to be introduced as Mr. Walter Sydney."

"This is my ward, your lordship," said Mr. Stephens, smiling. "I think it is scarcely necessary to call your lordship's attention to the striking resemblance which he bears to his lamented father."

"Yes—it would be impossible to mistake him," said his lordship hastily, while a cloud passed over his brow. "But sit down—pray sit down; and we will proceed to business. I presume that gentleman is your professional adviser?"

"Mr. Mac Chizzle," observed Stephens, introducing the lawyer. "Mr. Pakenham, I have had the pleasure of seeing you before," he added, addressing the nobleman's attorney with a placid smile.

Mr. Pakenham acknowledged the salutation with a bow; and his eye wandered for a moment, with some surprise, towards Mac Chizzle,—as much as to say, "I am astonished to see a person like you employed in so important an affair."

When every one was seated, the Earl of Warrington referred to some papers placed before him, and said, "The object of this meeting is known to everyone present. The duty that devolves upon me is to transfer to Walter Sydney, the only son and heir of the late Stanford Sydney, upon being satisfied with respect to the identity of the claimant, the sum of forty-one thousand pounds now invested in certain stocks in the Bank of England."

"It is needless, I presume," said Mr. Pakenham, "to enter into the particulars of this inheritance. We on our side admit our liability to pay the amount specified by his lordship, to the proper claimant."

"Quite satisfactory," observed Mac Chizzle, to whom these observations were addressed.

"The proofs of identity are, then, all that your lordship now requires?" said Mr. Stephens.

"And I only require them as a mere matter of necessary form and ceremony, Mr. Stephens," returned the Earl of Warrington. "I am well aware of your acquaintance with the late Mrs. Sydney, and of the fact that the deceased lady left her children to your care."

"My lord, here are the various certificates," said Stephens, placing a small packet of papers before the Earl. "In the first instance you have the marriage certificate of Stanford Sydney and Letitia Hardinge, the natural daughter of the late Earl of Warrington, your lordship's uncle."

"Well—well," exclaimed the nobleman, somewhat impatiently, as if he were anxious to get rid as soon as possible of a business by no means pleasant to him. "That certificate is beyond all dispute."

"Here," continued Stephens, "is the certificate of the birth of

Eliza Sydney, born October 12th, 1810; and here is the certificate of her death, which took place on the 14th of February, 1831."

"This certificate is not necessary," observed Mr. Pakenham; "as in no case, under the provisions of these deeds," he added, pointing to a pile of documents before him, "could that young lady have instituted even a shadow of a claim to this money."

"We had better possess one deed too many, than one too few," said Mr. Stephens, with another bland smile.

"Oh! certainly," exclaimed the Earl. "And this precaution shows the exact condition of the late Mr. Stanford Sydney's family. The daughter is no more: the son lives, and is present."

"Here, then, my lord," continued Stephens, "is the certificate of the birth of Walter Sydney, on the 25th day of November, 1814."

The nobleman examined this document with far more attention than he had devoted to either of the former. He then handed it to Mr. Pakenham, who also scrutinized it narrowly.

"It is quite correct, my Lord," said this gentleman. "We now require two witnesses as to identity."

"I presume his Lordship will receive me as one," observed Mr. Stephens, "considering my intimate acquaintance with all—"

"Oh certainly—certainly," interrupted the Earl hastily.

"And Mr. Mac Chizzle will tender his evidence in the other instance," said Stephens.

"I have known this young gentleman for the last six years," exclaimed Mac Chizzle, pointing towards Walter, "and I knew his mother also."

"Is your Lordship satisfied?" enquired Mr. Pakenham, after a short pause.

"Perfectly," answered the nobleman, without hesitation. "I am, however, in your hands."

"Oh! as for me," returned Mr. Pakenham, "I have no objection to offer. Your Lordship is acquainted with Mr. Stephens."

"Yes—yes," again interrupted the Earl; "I have known Mr. Stephens for some years—and I know him to be a man of honour."

"Then there is nothing more to be said," observed Pakenham.

"No—nothing," added Mac Chizzle; "but to complete the business."

"I will now read the release," said Mr. Pakenham.

The solicitor settled himself in a comfortable manner in his chair, and taking up a deed consisting of several folios, proceeded to make his hearers as much acquainted with its contents as the multifarious redundancies of law terms would allow.

The disguised lady had now time for reflection. She had been more or less prepared for the assertion of Mr. Stephens that Eliza Sydney was dead, and that Walter was living:—but the bare-faced falsehood uttered by Mac Chizzle (who, so far from having been acquainted with her for years, had never seen her until that morning), shocked and astounded her. She had also just learnt for the first time, that her late mother was the natural daughter of an Earl; and she perceived that she herself could claim a distant kinship with the nobleman in whose presence she then was. This circumstance inspired her with feelings in his favour, which were enhanced by the urbanity of his manners, and the readiness with which he admitted all the proofs submitted to him by Mr. Stephens. She had expected, from the arguments used by this gentleman to convince her that she should not hesitate to fight the law with its own weapons, &c., that every obstacle would be thrown in the way of her claims by him on whom they were to be made;—and she was astonished when she compared all the specious representations of Stephens with the readiness, good-will, and alacrity manifested by the Earl in yielding up an enormous sum of money. Now also, for the first time, it struck her as remarkable that Stephens had promised her ten thousand pounds only—a fourth part of that amount to which, according to his own showing, she alone was justly entitled.

All these reflections passed rapidly through her mind while the lawyer was reading the deed of release, not one word of which was attended to by her. She suddenly felt as if her eyes were opened to a fearful conspiracy, in which she was playing a conspicuous part:—she trembled, as if she were standing upon the edge of a precipice;—and yet she knew not how to act. She was bewildered: but the uppermost idea in her mind was that she had gone too far to retreat.

This was the impression that ruled her thoughts at the precise moment when Mr. Pakenham brought the reading of the long wearisome document to a termination. The buzzing, droning noise which had filled her ears for upwards of twenty minutes, suddenly ceased;—and she heard a voice say in a kind tone, "Will you now please to sign this?"

She started—but immediately recovered her presence of mind, and, taking the pen from the lawyer's hand, applied the signature of *Walter Sydney* to the document. It was next witnessed by Pakenham, Stephens, and Mac Chizzle, and handed to the Earl.

The nobleman then took several papers—familiar to all those who have ever possessed Bank Stock—from an iron safe in one corner of the library, and handing them to the disguised lady, said, "Mr. Walter Sydney, I have much pleasure in putting you in possession of this fortune; and I can assure you that my best—my very best wishes for your health and prosperity, accompany the transfer."

Walter received the documents mechanically as it were and murmured a few words of thanks and gratitude.

"Perhaps, Mr. Stephens," said the Earl, when the ceremony was thus completed, "you and your friends will do me the honour to accept of a slight refreshment in an adjoining room. You will excuse my absence; but I have a few matters of pressing importance to transact with my solicitor, and which cannot possibly be postponed. You must accept this as my apology; and believe in my regret that I cannot keep you company."

The Earl shook hands with both Stephens and Sydney, and bowed to Mac Chizzle. These three individuals then withdrew.

An elegant collation was prepared for them in another apartment; but Mac Chizzle was the only one who seemed inclined to pay his respects to it. Walter, however, gladly swallowed a glass of wine; for she felt exhausted with the excitement she had passed through. Stephens was too highly elated either to eat or drink, and too anxious to complete the business in the City, to allow Mac Chizzle to waste much time over the delicacies of which the collation consisted.

They were, therefore, all three soon on their way to the Bank of England.

"Well, I think we managed the job very correctly," said Mac Chizzle.

"Everything passed off precisely as I had anticipated," observed Mr. Stephens. "But you, Walter—you are serious."

"I do not look upon the transaction in the same light as I did a couple of hours since," answered she coldly.

"Ah! my dear friend," cried Stephens, "you are deceived by the apparent urbanity of that nobleman, and the mildness of his solicitor.

They assumed that appearance because there was no help for them;—they had no good to gain by throwing obstacles in our way."

"But the certificate of *my* death was a forgery," said Walter, bitterly.

"A necessary alteration of names—without which the accomplishment of our plan would have been impossible," answered Stephens. "But let me ease your mind in one respect, my dear Walter. That nobleman is a relation of yours—and yet until this day his name has never been mentioned to you. And why? Because he visits upon you the hatred which he entertained for your deceased mother! Did you not observe that he interrupted me when I spoke of her? did you not notice that he touched with extreme aversion upon the topics connected with your revered parents?"

"I did!—I did!" exclaimed Walter.

"He hates you!—he detests you!" continued Stephens, emphatically; "and he will not countenance any claim which you might advance towards kinship with him. His duties as a nobleman and a gentleman dictated the outward civility with which he treated you; but his heart gave no echo to the words of congratulation which issued from his lips."

"I believe you—I know that you are speaking the truth," cried Walter. "Pardon me, if for a moment I ceased to look upon you as a friend."

Stephens pressed the hand of the too-confiding being, over whom his dangerous eloquence and subtle reasoning possessed an influence so omnipotent for purposes of evil; and he then again launched out into glowing descriptions of the sources and means of happiness within her reach. This reasoning, aided by the hope that in a few hours she should be enabled to quit London for ever, restored the lady's disposition to that same easy and pliant state, to which Stephens had devoted nearly five years to model it.

At length the hackney-coach stopped at the Bank of England. Stephens hurried to the rotunda to obtain the assistance of a stockbroker, for the purpose of transferring and selling out the immense sum which now appeared within his reach, and to obtain which he had devoted his time, his money, and his tranquillity!

Walter and the lawyer awaited his return beneath the porch of the entrance. After the lapse of a few moments he appeared, accompanied by a broker of his acquaintance. They then all four proceeded together to the office where the business was to be transacted.

The broker explained the affair to a clerk, and the clerk, after consulting a huge volume, received the documents which Lord Warrington had handed over to Sydney. Having compared those papers with the entries in the book, the clerk made a sign to three men who were lounging at the upper end of the office, near the stove, and who had the appearance of messengers, or porters.

These men moved hastily forward, and advanced up to Stephens, Mac Chizzle, and Walter Sydney.

A deadly pallor spread over the countenance of Stephens; Mac Chizzle appeared alarmed; but Walter remained still unsuspicious of danger.

"Those are the persons," said the clerk, significantly, as he pointed to the three conspirators, to whom he observed, almost in the same breath, "Your plans are detected—these men are officers!"

"Officers!" ejaculated Sydney; "what does this mean?"

"We are here to apprehend you," answered the foremost of these functionaries. "Resistance will be vain: there are others outside in readiness."

"Merciful heavens!" cried Walter, joining her hands in agony: "Oh! Stephens, to what have you brought me!"

That unhappy man hung down his head, and made no reply. He felt crushed by this unexpected blow, which came upon him at the very instant when the object of his dearest hopes seemed within his reach.

As for Mac Chizzle, he resigned himself with dogged submission to his fate.

The officers and their prisoners now proceeded to the Mansion House, accompanied by the clerk and the stockbroker.

Sydney—a prey to the most dreadful apprehensions and painful remorse—was compelled to lean for support upon the arm of the officer who had charge of her.

Sir Peter Laurie[1] sat for the Lord Mayor.

The worthy knight is the terror of all swindlers, mock companies, and bubble firms existing in the City of London: wherever there is fraud, within the jurisdiction of the civic authorities, he is certain

1 Sir Peter Laurie was a real person, who was born in East Lothian, Scotland, in 1780. Barrister-at-Law, Magistrate for the City of Westminster, and, as Reynolds mentions, Alderman for the City of London, Sir Peter lived in some style at 24 Park Square, Marylebone, just south of Regent's Park.

to root it out. He has conferred more benefit upon the commercial world, and has devoted himself more energetically to protect the interests of the trading community, than any other alderman. Unlike the generality of the city magistrates, who are coarse, vulgar, ignorant, and narrow-minded men, Sir Peter Laurie is possessed of a high range of intellect, and is an enlightened, an agreeable, and a polished gentleman.

It was about three o'clock in the afternoon, when Stephens, Mac Chizzle, and Sydney were placed in the dock of the Mansion House Police-office.

The solicitor of the Bank of England attended for the prosecution.

"With what do you charge these prisoners?" demanded the magistrate.

"With conspiring to obtain the sum of forty-one thousand pounds from the hands of the Earl of Warrington, and the Governor and Company of the Bank of England."

"Is his lordship present?"

"Your worship, he is, at this moment, unaware of the diabolical fraud that has been contemplated, and in part perpetrated upon him. He has given up to the prisoners certain documents, which constituted their authority for transferring and selling out the sum I have mentioned. By certain means the intentions of the prisoners were discovered some time ago; and secret information was given to the Bank directors upon the subject. The directors were not, however, permitted to communicate with the Earl of Warrington, under penalty of receiving no farther information from the quarter whence the original warning emanated. Under all circumstances, I shall content myself with stating sufficient to support the charge to-day, so that your worship may remand the prisoners until a period when the attendance of the Earl of Warrington can be procured."

"State your case."

"I charge this prisoner," said the solicitor, pointing towards Sydney, "with endeavouring to obtain the sum of forty-one thousand pounds from the Governor and Company of the Bank of England, under pretence of being one Walter Sydney, a man—whereas the prisoner's name is Eliza Sydney, and she is a woman!"

An immense sensation prevailed in the justice-room at this announcement.

The disguised lady moaned audibly, and leant against the bar of the dock for support.

"And I charge the other prisoners, Robert Stephens and Hugh Mac Chizzle, with aiding and abetting in the crime," added the solicitor, after a pause.

The unhappy lady, yielding to emotions and feelings which she was now no longer able to contain, threw herself upon her knees, clasped her hands together in an agony of grief, and exclaimed, "It is true! I am not what I seem! I have been guilty of a fearful deception—a horrible cheat: but it was he—he," she cried, pointing to Stephens, "who made me do it!"

There was an universal sentiment of deep sympathy with the female prisoner, throughout the court; and the worthy alderman himself was affected.

"You must remember," he said, in a kind tone, "that anything which you admit here, may be used against you elsewhere."

"I am anxious to confess all that I have done, and all that I know," cried the lady; "and in so doing, I shall in some measure atone for the enormity of my guilt, which I now view in its true light!"

"Under these circumstances," said the alderman, "let the case stand over until to-morrow."

The prisoners were then removed.

In another hour they were inmates of the Giltspur-street Compter.

And how terminated the 26th of November for Walter Sydney? Instead of being in possession of an ample fortune, and about to visit a clime where she hoped to enjoy all the blessings of domestic tranquillity, and the charms of rural bliss, she found herself a prisoner, charged with a crime of deep dye!

Oh! what a sudden reverse was this!

Still, upon that eventful day, there was one hope of hers fulfilled. She threw aside her masculine attire, and assumed the garb adapted to her sex. A messenger was despatched to the villa, to communicate the sad tidings of the arrest to Louisa, and procure suitable clothing for her wretched mistress.

But, alas! that garb in which she had so ardently desired to appear again, was now doomed to be worn, for the first time, in a prison:—the new epoch of her life, which was to be marked by a return to feminine habits, was commenced in a dungeon!

Still that new period had begun; and from henceforth we shall know her only by her real name of Eliza Sydney.

CHAPTER XXXI.

EXPLANATIONS.

WITH the greatest forethought and the best taste, Louisa had forwarded to her mistress the most simple and unassuming garb which the boudoir contained, amongst its miscellaneous articles of female attire.

Dressed in the garments which suited her sex, Eliza was a fine and elegant woman—above the common female height, yet graceful in her deportment, and charming in all her movements. Her shoulders possessed that beautiful slope, and the contours of her bust were modelled in that ample and voluptuous mould, which form such essential elements of superb and majestic loveliness.

Although so long accustomed to masculine attire, there was nothing awkward—nothing constrained in her gait; her step was free and light, and her pace short, as if that exquisitely turned ancle, and long narrow foot had never known aught save the softest silken hose, and the most delicate prunella shoes.

In a word, the beauty of Eliza Sydney was of a lofty and imposing order;—a pale high brow, melting hazle eyes, a delicately-chiselled mouth and nose, and a form whose matured expansion and height were rendered more commanding by its exquisite symmetry of proportions.

The morning journals published an account of the extraordinary attempt at fraud detected at the Bank on the previous day; and the utmost curiosity was evinced by an immense crowd that had collected to obtain a view of the prisoners, especially the female one, as they alighted from the separate cabs in which they were conveyed to the Mansion House for re-examination. Eliza's countenance was flushed and animated, and the expression of her eyes denoted profound mental excitement: Stephens was ghastly pale:—the lawyer maintained a species of sullen and reserved composure.

The police-office at the Mansion House was crowded to excess. Sir Peter Laurie presided; and on his right hand was seated the Earl of Warrington. Mr. Pakenham was also present, in company with the solicitor of the Bank of England.

The moment the prisoners appeared in the dock, Eliza in a firm tone addressed the magistrate, and intimated her intention of making the most ample confession, in accordance with her promise of the preceding day. She was accommodated with a chair, and the chief clerk proceeded to take down the narrative which detailed the origins and progress of this most extraordinary conspiracy.

Alas! that so criminal a tale should have been accompanied by the music of that flute-like voice; and that so foul a history should have emanated from so sweet a mouth. Those words of guilt which trembled upon her lips, resembled the slime of the snail upon the leaf of the rose.

When the confession of Eliza Sydney was fully taken down, and signed by her, the Earl of Warrington's solicitor entered into a statement which placed the magistrate in full possession of the facts of the case.

We shall now proceed to acquaint our readers with the complete history formed by these revelations.

"The late Earl of Warrington was a man of eccentric and peculiar habits. An accident in his infancy had rendered his person deformed and stunted his growth, and, being endowed with tender feelings and acute susceptibilities, he could not bear to mingle in that society where his own physical defects were placed in strong contrast with the fine figures, handsome countenances, and manly forms of many of his aristocratic acquaintances. He possessed a magnificent estate in Cambridgeshire; and in the country seat attached to that domain did he pass the greater portion of his time in solitude.

"The bailiff of the Warrington estate was a widower, and possessed an only child—a daughter. Letitia Hardinge was about sixteen years of age when the Earl first took up his abode in Cambridgeshire, in the year 1790. She was not good looking; but she possessed a mild and melancholy expression of countenance, and an amiability of disposition, which rendered her an object of interest to all who knew her. She was fond of reading; and the library at the neighbouring mansion was always open to her inspection.

"The reserved and world-shunning Earl soon became attracted towards Letitia Hardinge. He found that she possessed a high order of intellect; and he delighted to converse with her. By degrees he experienced a deep attachment towards a being whose society often relieved the monotonous routine of his life; and the gratitude which Letitia entertained towards the Earl for his kindness to her, soon partook of a more tender feeling. She found herself interested in a nobleman of high rank and boundless wealth, who was compelled to avoid the great world where the homage shown to his proud name appeared to him to be a mockery of his physical deformity; she ministered to him with all a woman's devotedness, during a tedious and painful malady which seized upon him shortly after his arrival in Cambridgeshire; and at length her presence became as it were necessary to him.

"They loved: and although no priest blessed their union, they entertained unalterable respect and affection for each other. That dread of ridicule which had driven the Earl from society, and which with him was a weakness amounting almost to folly, prevented the solemnization of his nuptials with the woman he loved. She become pregnant; and the day that made the Earl the father of a daughter, robbed him of the mother of that innocent child who was thus born in sin!

"Letitia Hardinge, the Earl's natural child, grew up in health and beauty. The father was dotingly attached to her, and watched her growth with pride and adoration. She was sixteen years of age, when Frederick, the Earl's nephew and heir presumptive to the title and vast estates of the family, arrived in Cambridgeshire to pay his respects to his uncle, on his emancipation from college. The young man's parents had both died in his infancy, and he was entirely dependant upon the Earl.

"Letitia Hardinge passed as the niece of the Earl of Warrington. Frederick was acquainted with the real history of the young lady; and, previous to his arrival at the mansion of his uncle, he was not prepared to treat her with any excess of civility. He was brought up in that aristocratic school which looks upon pure blood as a necessary element of existence, and as alone entitled to respect. But he had not been many days in the society of Miss Hardinge, before his ideas upon this subject underwent a complete change, and he could not help admiring her. Admiration soon led to love:—he became deeply enamoured of her!

"The Earl beheld this attachment on his part, and was rejoiced. An union between the two cousins would secure to his adored daughter that rank and social position, which he was most anxious for her to occupy. As the wife of the heir presumptive to the richest Earldom in the realm, her origin would never be canvassed nor thought of. But Letitia herself returned not the young man's love. By one of those extraordinary caprices, which so often characterise even the strongest female minds, she had taken a profound aversion to her suitor; and being of a high and independent disposition, not even the dazzling prospect of wealth and title could move her heart in his favour.

"There was a farmer upon the Earl's estate, of the name of Sydney. He had a son whose Christian name was Stanford—a handsome but sickly youth, and by no means comparable to the polished and intellectual Frederick. Nevertheless, Letitia entertained for this young man an affection bordering upon madness. The Earl discovered her secret, and was deeply afflicted at his daughter's predilection. He remonstrated with her, and urged the necessity of conquering her inclinations in this respect. It was then that she showed the temper and the spirit of *a spoiled child*, and declared that she would follow the dictates of her own mind in preference to every other consideration. The Earl swore a most solemn oath, *that if she dared marry Stanford Sydney, neither she nor her husband should ever receive one single shilling from him!*

"Reckless of this threat—indifferent to the feelings of that father who had cherished her so fondly, the perverse girl one morning abandoned the paternal home, and fled with Stanford Sydney, on whom she bestowed her hand. The blow came like a thunderbolt upon the head of the old Earl. He was naturally of a delicate and infirm constitution; and this sudden misfortune proved too much for his debilitated frame. He took to his bed; and a few hours before his death he made a will consistent with his oath. He left all his property to his nephew, with the exception of forty-one thousand pounds—the amount of his savings since he had inherited the title. This will ordained that his nephew should enjoy the interest of this amount; but that, should Letitia bear a male child to Stanford Sydney, such issue should, upon attaining the age of twenty-one years, receive as his portion the above sum of forty-one thousand pounds. Such was the confidence which the old Earl possessed in his nephew, that he left the execution of this provision to him. It was also enacted by that will, that should the said Letitia die without bearing a son to the said Stanford Sydney; or should a son born of her die previously to attaining his twenty-first year, then the sum alluded to should become the property of Frederick.

"The old man died, a prey to the deepest mental affliction—indeed, literally heart-broken—shortly after making this will. Frederick, who was honour and integrity personified, determined upon fulfilling all the instructions of his uncle to the very letter.

"The fruits of the union of Stanford Sydney and Letitia Hardinge were a daughter and a son. The name of the former was Eliza: that of the latter was Walter. Eliza was a strong and healthy child; Walter was sickly and ailing from his birth. Shortly after the birth of Walter, the father, who had long been in a deep decline, paid the debt of nature. Letitia was then left a widow, with two young children, and nothing but a small farm for her support. Her high spirit prevented her from applying to the Earl of Warrington—the man whose love she had slighted and scorned; and thus she had to struggle with poverty and misfortune in rearing and educating her fatherless progeny. The farm which she tenanted was situated in Berkshire, whither she and her husband had removed immediately after the death of the father of Stanford. This farm belonged to a gentleman of the name of Stephens—a merchant of respectability and property, in the City of London.

"It was in the year 1829 that Robert Stephens appeared at the farm-house, to announce the death of his father and his inheritance of all the landed property which had belonged to the deceased. The widow was considerably in arrears of rent: Stephens inquired into her condition and prospects, and learnt from her lips her entire history—that history which, from motives of disappointed pride, she had religiously concealed from her children. She was well aware of the provisions of the late Earl's will; but she had determined not to acquaint either Eliza or Walter with the clause relative to the fortune, until the majority of the latter. Towards Stephens she did not manifest the same reserve, the revelation of that fact being necessary to convince him that she possessed good perspective chances of settling those long arrears, which she was in the meantime totally unable to liquidate.

"Robert Stephens was immediately attracted towards that family.

It was not the beauty of Eliza which struck him:—he was a cold, calculating man of the world, and considered female loveliness as mere dross compared to sterling gold. He found that Walter was an amiable and simple-hearted youth, and he hoped to turn to his own advantage the immense inheritance which awaited the lad at his majority. He accordingly treated Mrs. Sydney with every indulgence, forgiving her the arrears already accumulated, and lowering her rent in future. He thus gained an immense influence over the family; and when a sudden malady threw the widow upon her death-bed, it was to Stephens that she recommended her children.

"Stephens manifested the most paternal attention towards the orphans, and secured their unbounded gratitude, attachment, and confidence. But his designs were abruptly menaced in an alarming manner. The seeds of consumption, which had been sown by paternal tradition in the constitution of Walter, germinated with fatal effect; and on the 14th of February, 1831, he surrendered up his spirit.

"Scarcely had the breath left the body of the youth, when Stephens, by that species of magic influence which he had already begun to exercise over Eliza, induced her to assume her brother's garb; and she was taught to believe, even by the very side of his corpse, that immense interests were connected with her compliance with his wish. An old woman was the only female attendant at the farm-house; and she was easily persuaded to spread a report amongst the neighbours that it was the daughter who was dead. Eliza did not stir abroad: Stephens managed the funeral, and gave instructions for the entry in the parish register of the burial of Eliza Sydney; and, as Eliza immediately afterwards repaired to the Villa at Clapton, the fraud was not suspected in the neighbourhood of the Berkshire farm.

"Stephens duly communicated the deaths of Mrs. Sydney and Eliza to the Earl of Warrington, and obtained an introduction to this nobleman. He called occasionally in Grosvenor Square, during the interval of four years and nine months which occurred between the reported death of Eliza and the 26th of November, 1835; and invariably took care to mention not only that Walter was in good health, but that he was residing at the Villa. His lordship, however, on no occasion expressed a wish to see the young man: for years had failed to wipe away the impression made upon Frederick's mind by the deceased Letitia Hardinge!

"When Stephens introduced the disguised Eliza to the nobleman, as Walter Sydney, upon the morning of the 26th of November, the Earl entertained not the least suspicion of fraud. He knew that Stephens was the son of an eminent merchant, and that he was well spoken of in society; and he was moreover anxious to complete a ceremony which only recalled painful reminiscences to his mind. Thus, so far as his lordship was concerned, the deceit was managed with the most complete success; and there is no doubt that the entire scheme might have been carried out, and the secret have remained for ever undiscovered, had not a private warning been communicated in time to the Bank of England."

Such was the complete narrative formed by the statement of the Earl of Warrington, through his solicitor, and the confession of Eliza Sydney. The history excited the most extraordinary interest in all who heard it; and there was a powerful feeling of sympathy and commiseration in favour of Eliza. Even Lord Warrington himself looked once or twice kindly upon her.

The examination which elicited all the facts detailed in the narrative, and the evidence gone into to prove the attempt to obtain possession of the money at the Bank of England, occupied until four o'clock in the afternoon; when the magistrate committed Robert Stephens, Hugh Mac Chizzle, and Eliza Sydney to Newgate, to take their trials at the approaching session of the Central Criminal Court.

CHAPTER XXXII.

THE OLD BAILEY.

The sessions of the Central Criminal Court commenced.

The street of the Old Bailey was covered with straw; and the pavement in the neighbourhood of the doors of the court on one side, and of the public-houses on the other, was crowded with policemen, the touters of the barristers and attornies practising criminal law, and the friends of the prisoners whose trials were expected to come on that day.

The press-yard, which is situate between the solid granite wall of Newgate and the Court-house, was also flooded with living waves, which rolled onwards from the street to the flight of steps leading into the gallery of the Old Court. In former times, prisoners who refused to plead, were pressed beneath immense weights, until they would consent to declare themselves guilty or not guilty. This odious punishment was inflicted in that enclosure: hence its name of the press-yard.

It cannot be necessary to describe the court-house, with its dark sombre walls, and its huge ventilator at the top. Alas! the golden bowl of hope has been broken within those walls, and the knell of many a miserable wretch has been rung upon its tribunals from the lips of the judge!

The street of the Old Bailey presents quite an animated appearance during the sessions;—but it is horrible to reflect that numbers of the policemen who throng in that thoroughfare upon those occasions, have trumped up the charges for which prisoners have been committed for trial, in order to obtain a holiday, and extort from the county the expenses of attending as witnesses.

At the time of which our tale treats, the sheriffs were accustomed to provide two dinners for the judges every day; one at three, and the other at five o'clock, so that those who could not attend the first, were enabled to take their seats at the second. Marrow puddings, beef-steaks, and boiled rounds of beef, invariably formed the staple commodities of these repasts; and it was the duty of the ordinary chaplains of Newgate to act as vice-presidents at both meals. This ceremony was always performed by those reverend gentlemen: the ecclesiastical gourmands contrived, during sessions, to eat two dinners every day, and wash each down with a very tolerable allowance of wine.

We said that the Sessions commenced. On the Monday and Tuesday, the Recorder in the Old Court, and the Common Sergeant in the New, tried those prisoners who were charged with minor offences: on the Wednesday the Judges upon the *rota* took their seats on the bench of the Old Court.

Richard Markham's name stood first for trial upon the list on that day. He was conducted from Newgate by means of a subterraneous passage, running under the Press-yard, into the dock of the Court.

The Hall was crowded to excess, for the case had produced a profound sensation. The moment Markham appeared in the dock, every eye was fixed upon him. His countenance was very pale; but his demeanour was firm. He cast one glance around, and then looked only towards the twelve men who were to decide upon his fate. Close by the dock stood Mr. Monroe: Whittingham was in the gallery;—the Baronet, Chichester, and Talbot lounged together near the reporters' box.

The Jury were sworn, and the counsel for the prosecution stated the case. He observed that the prisoner at the bar was a young man who, upon his majority, would become possessed of a considerable fortune; but that in the mean time he had no doubt fallen into bad company, for it would be proved that he was arrested by the police at a common gambling house in the evening of the very same day on which he had committed the offence with which he was now charged. It was but natural to presume that this young man had imbibed the habit of gaming, and, having thereby involved himself in pecuniary embarrassments, had adopted the desperate and fatal expedient of obtaining money by means of forged Bank-notes, rather than communicate his situation to his guardian. Where he procured these forged notes, it was impossible to say: it would, however, be satisfactorily proved to the jury that he passed a forged note for five hundred pounds at the banking-house of Messrs. ———, and that when he was arrested a second note for fifty pounds was found upon his person. Several concurrent circumstances established the guilt of the prisoner. On the evening previous to his arrest, the prisoner dined with Sir Rupert Harborough, Mr. Chichester, and Mr. Talbot; and when these gentlemen proposed a walk after dessert, the prisoner requested them to accompany him to a common gaming-house in the Quadrant. They refused; but finding him determined to visit that den, they agreed to go with him, with the friendly intention of taking care that he was not plundered of his money, he being considerably excited by the wine he had been drinking. Ere he set out, the prisoner enquired if either of his companions could change him a fifty pound note; but neither gentleman had sufficient gold to afford the accommodation required. Now was it not fair to presume that the prisoner intended to pass off upon one of his friends the very forged fifty-pound note subsequently found upon him! On the following day, the prisoner—the moment he was released from custody on the charge of being found in a common gaming-house—hurried home, and ordered his servants to prepare for his immediate departure for the continent. He moreover wrote two letters, which would be read to the jury,—one to a lady, and the other to his guardian,—and both containing unequivocal admission of his guilt. The learned counsel then read the letters, and commented upon their contents at some length. There were several expressions (he said) which clearly tended to self-crimination.—*"Circumstances of a very peculiar nature, and which I cannot at present explain, compel me to quit London thus abruptly." "I could not have remained in London another minute with safety to myself." "I conceive it to be my duty—in consequence of rumours which may shortly reach you concerning me—to inform you that I have this moment only awoke to the fearful perils of the career in which I have for some weeks past been blindly hurrying along, till at length yesterday———." "I am penitent, deeply penitent: let this statement induce you to defend and protect my reputation."* The last paragraph but one which concluded so abruptly with the words, *"till at length yesterday——"* clearly pointed to the crime with which the prisoner was now charged; and the last paragraph of all undeniably implored Mr. Monroe, the young man's guardian, to hush up the matter the moment it should reach his ears.

The clerk at the banking-house, who changed the five hundred pound note for the prisoner, then gave his evidence.

At length Sir Rupert Harborough was called into the witness-box; and he deposed that the prisoner had dined with him on the evening previous to his arrest; that he very pressingly solicited him (Sir Rupert), and Mr. Chichester, and Mr. Talbot, to accompany him to the gambling-house; and that he moreover, enquired if either of them could accommodate him with change for a fifty pound note.

Mr. Chichester was called next. He stated the line of defence adopted by the prisoner at Bow-street, and positively denied having ever given the prisoner any notes to change for him.

Markham's counsel cross-examined this witness with great severity.

"What are you, sir?"

"A private gentleman."

"What are your means of subsistence?"

"I receive an allowance from my father."

"Who is your father? Now, take care, sir, how you answer that question."

"He is a commercial man, sir."

"Is he not a tradesman?"

"Well,—he is a tradesman, then—if you like it."

"Yes,—I do like it. Now—upon your oath—is he not a pawnbroker in Brick-lane, Bethnal Green?"

"He is a goldsmith in a large way of business, and lends money occasionally——"

"Ha!" complacently observed the counsel for the defence. "Go on, sir: *lends money occasionally—*"

"Upon real security, I suppose," added Chichester, taken considerably aback by these questions.

"Upon deposits; let us give things their proper names. He lends money upon flannel petticoats—watches—flat-irons, &c." observed the barrister, with withering sarcasm. "But I have not done with you yet, sir. Was your father—this very respectable pawnbroker—ever elevated to the peerage?"

"He was not, sir."

"Then how come you by the distinction of *Honourable* prefixed to your name?"

Mr. Chichester hung down his head, and made no reply. The counsel for the prisoner repeated the question in a deliberate and emphatic manner. At length, Mr. Chichester was fairly bullied into a humble acknowledgment "that he had no right to the distinction, but that he had assumed it as a convenient West-End appendage." The cross examination then proceeded.

"Did you not travel under the name of Winchester?"

"I did—in Germany."

"With what motive did you assume a false name?"

"I had no particular motive."

"Did you not leave England in debt? and were you not afraid of your bills of exchange following you abroad?"

"There is some truth in that; but the most honourable men are frequently involved in pecuniary difficulties."

"Answer my questions, sir, and make no observations. You will leave me to do that, if you please. Now sir—tell the jury whether you were not accompanied by a valet or coachman in your German trip?"

"I am always accustomed to travel with a domestic."

"A man who runs away from his creditors should have more delicacy than to waste his money in such a manner. When you were at

Baden-baden, were you not involved in some gambling transactions which compelled you to quit the Grand-Duchy abruptly?"

"I certainly had a dispute with a gentleman at cards: and I left the town next morning."

"Yes—and you left your clothes and your servant behind you—and your bill unpaid at the hotel?"

"But I have since met my servant, and paid him more than double the wages then due."[1]

"You may stand down, sir," said the counsel for the defence—a permission of which the witness availed himself with surprising alacrity.

The counsel for the prosecution now called Mr. Whittingham. The poor butler ascended the witness-box with a rueful countenance; and, after an immense amount of badgering and baiting, admitted that his young master had meditated a sudden and abrupt departure from England, the very day upon which he was arrested. In his cross-examination he declared that the motives of the journey were founded upon certain regrets which Richard entertained at having permitted himself to be led away by Messrs. Chichester and Talbot, and Sir Rupert Harborough.

"And, my Lords," ejaculated the old domestic, elevating his voice, "Master Richard is no more guilty of this here circumwention than either one of your Lordships; but the man that did it all is that there Chichester, which bilked his wally-de-shamble, and that wulgar fellow, Talbot, which called me a *tulip*."

This piece of eloquence was delivered with much feeling; and the Judges smiled—for they appreciated the motives of the honest old domestic.

The officer who arrested Markham, proved that he found upon his person, when he searched him at Bow Street, a pocket-book, containing between thirty and forty pounds, in notes and gold, together with a note for fifty pounds.

A clerk from the Bank of England proved that both the note for five hundred pounds changed at the bankers, and the one for fifty just alluded to, were forgeries.

---

1 In 1848, a letter to the Home Secretary accused Reynolds himself of precisely this crime. It was sent by a Captain Andrew Atkinson Vincent, of Walmer, in Kent, a friend of Reynolds's godfather, Duncan McArthur. Whether it was true, and Reynolds used the experience here, or whether Vincent took it from the *Mysteries*, is unclear.

The case for the prosecution here closed; and the Judges retired to partake of some refreshment.

Markham had leisure to think over the proceedings of the morning. He was literally astounded when he contemplated the diabolical perjury committed by Sir Rupert Harborough and Mr. Chichester; but he entertained the most sanguine hope that the discredit thrown upon the character of the latter would render his testimony worthless. He shuddered when he reflected how ingeniously the counsel for the prosecution had grouped together those circumstances which told against him; and then again a ray of satisfaction animated his countenance, when he remembered that his counsel would speedily show those circumstances in a new light.

The Judges returned: silence prevailed throughout the hall; and the prisoner's counsel rose for the defence. Richard seated himself in the dock, and prepared to listen with the greatest attention to the speech of his advocate; and Whittingham placed his hand in a curved position behind his ear, in order to assist that organ on the present important occasion.

The counsel for the defence began by giving some account of the family and social position of the prisoner, who was born of parents accustomed to move in the first rank of life, and who was the heir to a fortune of no inconsiderable amount. During his minority, his guardian, who was then present, had promised to allow the prisoner six hundred pounds a-year. With these pecuniary advantages, it was absurd to suppose that young man of education—a young man whose noble and honourable feelings had been the object of remark on the part of all his friends, and who had only to express a want to his guardian, in order to receive its immediate gratification—it was absurd to imagine that such an individual would either enter into a conspiracy with others, or plan by himself, for the purpose of raising money upon forged notes. No—this young man was one of a most generous and confiding disposition; and, as he had seen but little of the world, he was totally unacquainted with its wiles and artifices. Thus was he made the dupe of some designing villains, at his very outset upon life. The whole history of the present transaction was to be summed up in a few words. A gang of conspirators had hit upon the desperate mode of passing forged notes, in order to retrieve their ruined fortunes. Not as magnanimous as the highwayman who perils his own existence while he perpetrates a crime, these men required a tool of whom they might make use, and who could be at any time sacrificed to save them. This instrument—this scapegoat, was the prisoner at the bar. The witness, whose real name was Chichester, but who, by his own confession, had travelled on the Continent under another denomination, was not a person on whom the Jury could place any reliance. He had assumed a distinction to which he was by no means entitled—he had affected all the arrogance and importance of a man of rank and fashion,—whereas he was the son of a pawnbroker in the refined locality of Brick-Lane, Bethnal Green! Endowed with much impudence, clever in imitating the manners of his superiors, and well versed in all the intricacies and subtleties of the world, this possessor of assumed distinctions—this swaggering imitator of a class far above him—this adventurer, with fascinating conversation, ready wit, amusing anecdote, and fashionable attire,—this *roué* of the present day, with jewellery about his person, and gold in his pocket—allowing ever an engaging smile to play upon his lips, and professing unmitigated disgust at the slightest appearance of vulgarity in another,—this individual—this Mr. Chichester was the principal witness whom the counsel for the prosecution had brought forward. But no English Jury would condemn a fellow creature upon such testimony—the testimony of one who was compelled to fly ignominiously and precipitately from Baden, on account of some rascality at cards, and who left his domestic in a strange land, pennyless, ignorant of the language, and surrounded by the odium which also attached itself to the name of his master. The prisoner had no motive in passing forged notes, because he was wealthy;—but Mr. Chichester had a motive, because he evidently lived far beyond the means which his father could allow him.

The learned counsel here related the manner in which Richard had been induced to change the larger note, and had become possessed of the smaller.

He then proceeded to observe, that the letters addressed to Mrs. Arlington and Mr. Monroe related to the fact that the prisoner's eyes had been suddenly opened to the characters of his associates, and to the career of dissipation in which they were leading him. The phrase upon which so much stress had been laid—*"till at length yesterday——"* alluded to the suicide of a young officer, which had taken place while the prisoner was at the gambling-house, whither he had been inveigled instead of inveigling others. "*He could not have remained in London another minute with safety to himself.*" And why? because these associates whom he had accidentally picked up, would not leave him quiet. They regularly beset him. "*He was penitent;*" and he hoped that Mr. Monroe would "*defend and protect his reputation.*" Yes—when the newspaper reports conveyed to the knowledge of that gentleman the fact that his ward had been arrested in a common gambling-house, and fined for being there. The letters were written hurriedly, and were ambiguous: thus they were susceptible of more than one interpretation. Let the jury interpret them in favour of the prisoner. It was better to send a dozen guilty men back again into society, terrible as that evil would be, than to condemn *one* innocent person. Then, with regard to the precipitate departure: the witness Whittingham had shown, in his cross-examination, that the prisoner's object was to escape from the three men whose characters were suddenly unveiled to him. It was said, that the prisoner had requested those three individuals to accompany him to the gaming-house, and that they at first refused. Oh! amazing fastidiousness—especially on the part of Mr. Arthur Chichester, who had been compelled to decamp from Baden, for cheating at cards! Then it was stated that the prisoner asked for change for a fifty-pound note; and it was said, that he would have availed himself of that accommodation to pass a forged note. Why—he (the learned counsel) had already explained how that fifty-pound note came into the prisoner's possession—his own gold having been transferred by Mr. Chichester to Sir Rupert Harborough's writing desk! The learned counsel concluded, by asking how it happened that no other forged Bank of England notes—no copper-plates to print them with—no materials for such a fraud, were found at the prisoner's house? Could it be supposed that a young man with his prospects would risk his reputation and his safety for a few hundreds of pounds? The idea was preposterous. The prisoner's counsel entered into a few minute points of the evidence which told in favour of his client, and wound up with a powerful appeal to the jury in his behalf.

Richard followed, with absorbing interest, the able defence made for him by his counsel; and his soul was filled with hope as each fact and argument in his favour was divested of all mystery, and lucidly exhibited to the consideration of the court.

Mr. Monroe was summoned to the witness box, and he proved the statements made by the prisoner's counsel relative to the pecuniary position of his ward. Snoggles, the ostler, followed, and very freely stated all the particulars of his late master's precipitate decampment from Baden.

Thus terminated the case for the defence.

The counsel of the prosecution—according to that odious right which gives the accusing party the last word in those instances where the defendant has called witnesses—rose to reply. He stated that neither the wealth nor the social position of an individual afforded a certain guarantee against crime. Besides, the law must not always be swayed by the apparent absence of motives; because some of the most extraordinary deeds of turpitude upon record had never been traced to a source which could satisfactorily account for their origin. The *perpetration* was the object which the jury had to keep in view; and the use of evidence was to prove or deny that perpetration by some particular individual. A forgery had been committed, and money obtained by the prisoner at the bar through the agency of that forgery. The defence had not attempted to deny that the prisoner was the individual who had thus obtained the money. The point to be considered was, whether the prisoner knew the note to be a forged one; and he (the learned counsel) considered that an assemblage of circumstances of a most unequivocal nature stamped the prisoner with that guilt. Mr. Chichester's evidence went to show that he himself never gave any notes to the prisoner. Even if Chichester were proved to be a disreputable person, there was nothing beyond the prisoner's mere assertion (made through his counsel) to prove that he had received the two notes from Chichester. Mr. Chichester had certainly assumed another name during his German tour, but it was for the purpose of avoiding arrest in a foreign land upon bills of exchange which might have been sent from England after him. He had, moreover, assumed the distinction of *Honourable*—a foolish vanity, but by no means a crime; for half the Englishmen who were called *Captain*, were no more captains than he (the learned counsel) was.

The senior judge now summed up the evidence to the jury; and the most profound interest was still manifested by all present in the proceedings. The learned judge occupied nearly two hours in his charge to the jury, whom he put in possession of all the points of the case which it was necessary to consider.

The jury retired, and debated for a considerable a time upon their verdict.

This was the dread interval of suspense. Richard's countenance was deadly pale; and his lips were firmly compressed in order to prevent any sudden ebullition of feeling—a weakness to which he seemed for a moment inclined to yield. Mr. Monroe did not entertain much hope; the summing up of the judge had been unfavourable to Markham. As for Whittingham, he shook his head dolefully from time to time, and murmured, loud enough to be heard by those near him, "Oh! Master Richard, Master Richard! who would ever have propulgated an opinion that you would have been brought into such a fixture as this? It's all along of them fellers which call butlers *tulips!*"

How singularly reckless is the mind of man with regard to the destinies of those to whom he is not connected by any ties of blood or friendship! While the jury were absent, discussing their verdict, the various barristers assembled round the table, began chattering together, and laughing, and telling pleasant anecdotes, as if the fate of a fellow-creature was by no means compromised at that moment. The counsel for the prosecution, who had done his duty by exerting all his talents, all his energies, and all his eloquence, to obtain the conviction of a youth who had never injured him, and whom he had never seen before, coolly took up a newspaper and perused it with evident gratification; while, at a little distance from him, stood the individual whom he had so zealously and earnestly sought to render miserable for life!

How strange!—how horribly depraved and vitiated must be that state of society in which hundreds of talented men are constantly employed, with large recompense, in procuring the condemnation of their fellow-creatures to the scaffold, the hulks, or eternal banishment! And what an idea must we entertain of our vaunted condition of consummate civilization, when we behold these learned men calling to their aid every miserable chicanery, every artificial technicality, and every possible exaggeration, to pursue the accused prisoner either to the platform of the gibbet, to loathsome dungeons, or to the horrors of Norfolk Island. Does society avenge?—or does it merely make examples of the wicked to warn others from sin? If the enquirer who asks himself or us these questions, would only attend the Central Criminal Court, he would hear the barristers for the prosecution imploring, coaxing, and commanding the jury to return such a verdict as will either condemn a human being to the scaffold, or separate him for ever from home, wife, children, kindred, and friends! He would find men straining every nerve, availing themselves of every miserable legal quirk and quibble, torturing their imaginations to find arguments, calling subtlety and mystification to their aid, shamefully exaggerating trivial incidents into important facts, dealing in misrepresentation and false deduction, substituting and dovetailing facts to suit their purposes, omitting others which tell against their own case, almost falling upon their knees to the jury, and staking their very reputation on the results,—and all these dishonourable, disgraceful, vile, and inhuman means and efforts exerted and called into action for the sake of sending a fellow-creature to the scaffold, or separating him for ever from the family that is dependant upon him, and that will starve without him!

O God! is it possible that man can have been made for such sad purposes? is it possible that the being *whom thou hast created after thine own image*, should be so demon-like in heart?

Oh! if the prisoner standing in the dock had inflicted some terrible injury upon the honour or the family of the barrister who holds a brief against him, then were it easy to comprehend that profound anxiety on the part of this barrister, to send the trembling criminal to the gallows! But, no—that barrister has no revenge to gratify—no hatred to assuage—no malignity to appease; he toils to take away that man's life, with all his strength, with all his talent, and with all his energy, because he has received gold to do his best to obtain a conviction!

Ah! what a hideous traffic in flesh and blood!

And if any one were to say to that barrister, "Thou art a bloodthirsty and merciless wretch," he would answer coolly and confidently, "No: on the other hand, I subscribe to philanthropic institutions!"

The jury returned; and the feeling uppermost in their minds was satisfaction at the prospect of being so speedily dismissed to their respective homes, where they would pursue their efforts after wealth, and speedily forget the youth whom they had condemned to punishment, and whose prospects they had blasted.

For their verdict was *Guilty!*

And the judges hastened to terminate the proceedings.

Richard was commanded to rise, and receive the sentence of the court. He obeyed with a kind of mechanical precision—for his mental energies were entirely prostrated. The voice of the judge addressing him rang like the chimes of distant bells in his ears;—the numerous persons whom he beheld around, appeared to be all moving and agitating like an immense crowd assembled to witness an execution.

He stood up as he was commanded; and the Judge proceeded to pass sentence upon him. He said that the court took his youth into consideration, and that there were circumstances which would render a very lenient sentence satisfactory to that society which had been outraged. The court accordingly condemned him to two years' imprisonment in the Giltspur Street Compter, without hard labour.

"That's all!" said the spectators to each other; and they appeared disappointed!

The audience then separated.

CHAPTER XXXIII.

ANOTHER DAY AT THE OLD BAILEY.

Richard was conveyed back to Newgate in a state of mind which can be more easily imagined than described. The Judges returned in their handsome carriages, to their splendid abodes;—the prosecuting barrister, that zealous and enthusiastic defender of social morality, hastened to the Temple to entertain a couple of prostitutes in his chambers;—and the various lawyers engaged about the court, hurried to their respective homes to prepare writs relating to fresh cases of turpitude and crime for the morrow.

Richard had shaken hands with Monroe and Whittingham over the parapet of the dock—he would not be allowed to see them again for three months! They still believed in his innocence—although twelve men that afternoon had declared their conviction of his guilt!

On the ensuing morning the trial of Eliza Sydney, Robert Stephens, and Hugh Mac Chizzle took place. As on the preceding day, the court was crowded from floor to roof. The bench was filled with the ladies and daughters of the aldermen; there was a full attendance

of barristers; and extra reporters occupied the box devoted to the gentlemen of the press. The case had created an extraordinary sensation, not only in consequence of the immensity of the stake played for by the prisoners, but also on account of the remarkable fraud practised by one of the most lovely women that had ever breathed the air of this world.

Eliza was dressed with extreme simplicity, but great taste. A straw bonnet with a plain riband, enclosed her pale but charming countenance: there was a soft and bewitching melancholy in her eyes; and her moist red lips were slightly apart as if she breathed with difficulty. She was a woman of a strong mind, as we have said before; and she endeavoured to restrain her emotions to the utmost of her power. She did not condescend to cast a look upon her fellow prisoners; nor during the trial were her glances once turned towards them.

Stephens appeared to be suffering with acute mental pain: his countenance was cadaverous, so pale and altered was it;—even his very lips were white. Mac Chizzle still retained an air of dogged sullenness, approaching to brutal indifference.

The Earl of Warrington was in attendance.

When called upon to plead, Stephens and the lawyer replied *Not Guilty*: Eliza answered *Guilty* in a firm and audible voice.

As the entire facts of the case are known to the readers, we need not enter into any fresh details. Suffice it to say, that when the Jury had delivered their verdict of *Guilty* against the two male prisoners, the Earl of Warrington rose, and in a most feeling and handsome manner interceded with the court in behalf of Eliza Sydney. Eliza herself was quite overcome with this unexpected generosity, and burst into a flood of tears.

The foreman of the jury also rose and observed that, though the female prisoner had taken her case out of their hands by pleading guilty, the jury were nevertheless unanimous in recommending her to the favourable consideration of the court.

The Judge proceeded to pass sentence. He said, "Robert Stephens, you have been guilty of one of the most serious attempts at fraud, which, in a commercial country and a civilised community, could be perpetrated. You have moreover availed yourself of your influence over a young and confiding woman—an influence obtained by a series of kind actions towards her mother, her late brother, and herself—to convert her into the instrument of your guilty designs. The court cannot pass over your case without inflicting the severest penalty which the law allows. The sentence of the Court is that you be transported beyond the seas for the term of your natural life."

The culprit staggered, and leant against the dock for support. A momentary pause ensued, at the expiration of which he partially recovered himself and said, "My Lord, I acknowledge the justice of my sentence: but permit me to observe that the female prisoner Eliza

Sydney is innocent of any attempt to defraud. Up to a few hours before we called upon the Earl of Warrington to sign the release and obtain the bank receipts, she was ignorant of the real object which I had in view. Even then, when I unveiled my designs, she shrank from the part she had to perform; and I was compelled to make use of all the specious arguments and all the sophistry I could call to my aid, to blind her as to the real nature of the transaction. My Lord, I make these few observations in justice to her; I have nothing now to lose or gain by this appeal in her behalf."

Stephens sank back exhausted in a chair which had been placed in the dock for the accommodation of Eliza Sydney; and the lady herself was melted to fresh tears by this proof of latent generosity on the part of the man who had been the means of placing her in her present sad position.

The Judge continued: "Hugh Mac Chizzle, you have been found guilty of aiding and abetting, at the last moment, in the consummation of a deed of almost unpardonable fraud. You have taken advantage of a profession which invests him who practises it with an appearance of respectability and gives him opportunities of perpetrating, if he be so inclined, enormous breaches and abuses of confidence. You stand second in degree of culpability to the prisoner Stephens. The sentence of the court, therefore, is, that you be transported beyond the seas for the term of fifteen years."

There was another momentary pause; and the Judge then proceeded as follows, while the most breathless silence prevailed:—

"Eliza Sydney, your share in this unfortunate and guilty business has been rather that of an instrument than a principal. Still you had arrived, when you first assumed a masculine disguise, at the years of discretion, which should have taught you to reflect that no deceit can be designed for a good purpose. Your readiness to confess your guilt—the testimony of your fellow prisoner in your behalf—the recommendation of the jury—and the intercession of the prosecutor, however, weigh with the court. Still a severe punishment must be awarded you; for if we were to admit the plea that a person between twenty and thirty is not responsible for his or her actions, justice would in numerous cases be defeated, and crime would find constant apologies and extenuation. The sentence of the court is that you be imprisoned for the space of two years in her Majesty's gaol of Newgate."

Eliza had anticipated transportation—she had made up her mind to banishment for at least seven years, from her native clime. The observation of the Judge that "a severe punishment must be awarded her," had confirmed her in that impression. The concluding words of that functionary had therefore taken her by surprise—a surprise so sudden that it overcame her. She tottered, and would have fallen; but she felt herself suddenly supported in the arms of a female, who conducted her to a seat in the dock, and whispered kind and consolatory words in her ear.

Eliza raised her eyes towards the countenance of this unexpected friend; and, to her astonishment, encountered the soft and sympathising glance of Diana Arlington.

"Do not be alarmed, Miss Sydney," whispered the Enchantress: "the Earl of Warrington will do more for you than you may anticipate. He will use his influence with the Home Secretary, and obtain a mitigation of your sentence."

"Oh! how kind in him thus to interest himself in my behalf," murmured Eliza; "and I—who am so unworthy of his commiseration!"

"Do not say that! we have made enquiries, and we have found how you have been deceived. We have seen your faithful servant Louisa; and she has told us enough to convince us that you was more to be pitied than blamed. One thing I have to communicate which will console you—I have taken Louisa into my service!"

"A thousand thanks, my dear madam," said Eliza. "The thought of what was to become of her has made me very unhappy. This is indeed one subject of comfort. But I saw Louisa yesterday: why did she keep me in the dark in this respect?"

"We enjoined her to maintain the strictest silence," returned Mrs. Arlington. "We were determined to see how you would act up to the very last moment in this distressing business, ere we allowed you to know that you had friends who cared for you."

"And how have I obtained this generous sympathy?" enquired Eliza, pressing Diana's hand with an effusion of gratitude.

"The Earl loved your mother, and blames himself for his neglect of her children, whose welfare would have been dear to his deceased uncle," said Diana gravely. "And for myself," she added, blushing—"anything which interests the Earl, also interests me."

"Believe me, I shall never forget this kindness on your

part:—neither shall I ever be able to repay it," observed Eliza. "I am now going to a protracted incarceration, in a terrible prison," she continued mournfully,—"and God only knows whether I may survive it. But until the day of my death shall I pray for you and that good nobleman who forgives, pities, and consoles me."

"He does—he does," said Mrs. Arlington, deeply affected: "but fancy not that your confinement will pass without being relieved by the visits of friends. I shall call and see you as often as the regulations of the prison will permit; and I again renew the promise which the Earl has authorised me to make relative to his intercession with the Secretary of State in your favour."

Eliza again poured forth her gratitude to Diana, and they then separated. The former was conveyed back to Newgate: the latter hastened to the humble hackney-coach which she had purposely hired to take her to the Old Bailey.

As soon as the case of Stephens, Mac Chizzle, and Eliza Sydney was disposed of, William Bolter was placed at the bar to take his trial for the murder of his wife.

"The miscreant"—as the newspapers had called him all along—wore a sullen and hardened appearance; and pleaded *Not Guilty* in a brutal and ferocious manner. The only feature of interest in the case was the examination of his son—his little son—as a witness against him. The poor boy seemed to comprehend the fearful position in which his father was placed; for he gave his evidence with the utmost reluctance. There was, however, a sufficiency of testimony, direct and circumstantial, to induce the jury to find the prisoner guilty without a moment's hesitation.

The Judge put on the black cap, and proceeded to pass upon the culprit the awful sentence of the law. Having expatiated upon the enormity of the prisoner's guilt, and admonished him to use the little time that remained to him in this world for the purpose of making his peace with heaven, he sentenced William Bolter *to be taken back again to the place from whence he came, and thence to a place of execution, where he was to be hanged by the neck until he should be dead*. "And may the Lord," added the Judge solemnly, "have mercy upon your soul."

There was some years ago, amongst ruffians of the very worst description, a custom of abusing the Judge, or "blackguarding the Beak," as it was called, when they received the award due to their crimes, in the felon's dock. This miserable and vain bravado—an affectation of recklessness which even the most hardened could scarcely feel—was revived by Bill Bolter upon the present occasion. "Taking a sight" at the Judge, the murderer commenced a string of horrible abuse—laden with imprecations and epithets of a most shocking and filthy nature. A shudder passed through the audience as if it were one man, at that revolting display on the part of a wretch who stood upon the edge of the tomb!

The officers of the court speedily interfered to put an end to the sad scene; and the convict, after a desperate resistance, was carried back to Newgate, where he was lodged in one of the condemned cells.

While these important cases were being disposed of in the Old Court, two others, which it is necessary to notice, were adjudicated upon in the New Court before the Recorder. The first was that of Thomas Armstrong, who was fortunate enough to be acquitted for want of evidence, George Montague, a principal witness against him, not appearing;—the other was that of Crankey Jem and the Resurrection Man. It is needless to enter into particulars in this matter: suffice it to say that the former was convicted of a daring burglary, upon the testimony of the latter who turned King's evidence. Crankey Jem was sentenced to transportation for life, he having been previously convicted of serious offences; and the Resurrection Man was sent back to Newgate to be discharged at the termination of the sessions.

The business of the Court was concluded in a few days; and Richard was removed to the Giltspur Street Compter. There he was dressed in the prison garb, and forced to submit to a *régime* peculiarly trying to the constitution of those who have been accustomed to tender nurture. The gruel, which constituted his principal aliment, created a nausea upon his stomach; the thin and weak soup was far from satisfying the cravings of the appetite; the bread was good, but doled out in miserably small quantities; and the meat seemed only offered to tantalise or provoke acuteness of hunger.

The Resurrection Man was set at liberty.

Stephens, Mac Chizzle, and Crankey Jem were removed to the hulks at Woolwich, previous to the sailing of a convict-ship for New South Wales.

Eliza Sydney remained in Newgate.

Bill Bolter, the murderer, also stayed for a short season in the condemned cell of that fearful prison.

CHAPTER XXXIV.

THE LESSON INTERRUPTED.

THE moment the trial of Richard Markham was concluded, Sir Rupert Harborough and Mr. Chichester bade a cold and hasty adieu to Mr. Talbot, and left the court together.

They wended their way up the Old Bailey, turned into Newgate Street, and thence proceeded down Butcher-hall Lane towards Bartholomew Close; for in that large dreary Square did Mr. Chichester now occupy a cheap lodging.

This lodging consisted of a couple of small and ill-furnished rooms on the second floor. When the two gentlemen arrived there, it was past five o'clock—for the trial had lasted the entire day—and a dirty cloth was laid for dinner in the front apartment. Black-handled knives and forks, a japanned pepper-box, pewter salt-cellar and mustard pot, and common white plates with a blue edge, constituted the "service." The dinner itself was equally humble, consisting of mutton-chops and potatoes, flanked by a pot of porter.

The baronet and the fashionable gentleman took their seats in silence, and partook of the meal without much appetite. There was a damp upon their spirits: they were not so utterly depraved as to be altogether unmindful of the detestable part they had played towards Markham; and their own affairs were moreover in a desperate condition.

A slip-shod, dirty, familiar girl cleared away the dinner things; and the gentlemen then took to gin-and-water and cigars. For some minutes they smoked in silence; till at length the baronet, stamping his foot impatiently upon the floor exclaimed, "My God! Chichester, is nothing to be done?"

"I really don't know," answered that individual. "You heard how deucedly I got exposed to-day in the witness-box; and after that I should not dare show up at the west-end for weeks and months to come—even if the sheriff's officers weren't looking out for me."

"Well, something must be done," observed the baronet. "Here

am I, playing at hide-and-seek as well as you—all my horses sold—my furniture seized—my carriages made away with—my plate pawned—and not a guinea—not a guinea left!"

"What should you say to a trip into the country?" demanded Chichester, after a pause. "London is too hot for both of us—at least for the present; indeed my surprise is that we were not arrested on those infernal bills, coming out of the court. But, as I was saying—a trip into the country might do more good. To be sure, this is no time for the watering places: we might, however, pay a visit to Hastings, Bath, and Cheltenham on a venture."

"And what could we do for ourselves there?"

"Why—pick up flats, to be sure!"

"You know, Chichester, that I am not able to work the cards and dice as you can."

"Then you must learn, as I did."

"And who will teach me?"

"Why—myself, to be sure! Could you have a better master than Arthur Chichester?"

"But it would take so long to understand all these manœuvres—I should never have the patience."

"Oh! nonsense, Harborough. Come—what do you say? Three days' practice, and we will be off?"

"But the money—the funds to move with?" cried the baronet, impatiently. "I am literally reduced to my last guinea."

"Oh! as for that," returned Chichester, "I will engage to get a twenty pound note from my father to-morrow; and with that supply we can safely start off on our expedition."

"Well—if you can rely upon doing this," observed the baronet, "we will put your plan into execution. So let us lose no time; but please to give me my first lesson."

"That's what I call business," cried Chichester, rising from his seat and drawing the curtains, while the baronet lighted the two tallow candles that adorned the wooden mantel-piece.

Chichester locked the door of the room, and then produced from his writing-desk the necessary implements of a gambler—packs of cards, dice-boxes, and dice.

Having reseated himself, he took up a pair of dice and a box, and said, "Now, my dear fellow, be a good boy, and learn your lesson well. You will soon meet with your reward."

"I am all attention," observed the baronet.

"In the first place I shall show you how to *secure*," continued Chichester; "and as you know the game of *Hazard* well enough, I need say but little more on that head. There are two ways of *securing*. The first is to hold one of the dice between the fore and middle fingers, or the middle and third fingers, against the side of the box, so that one finger must cover the top of the die—in this way, you see."

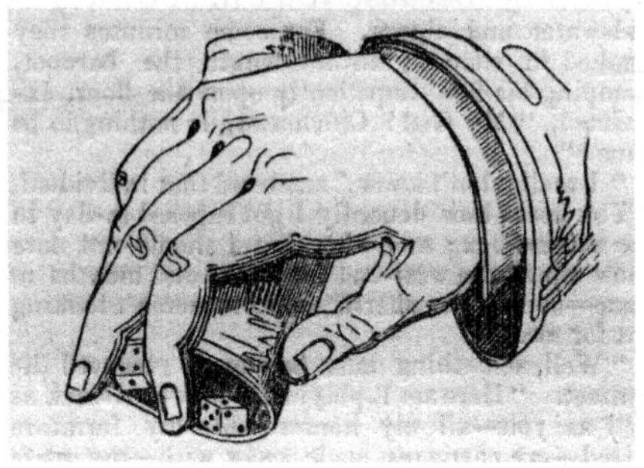

"I understand," said the baronet, attentively watching the proceedings of his companion, who by certain clever and adroit manipulations with the dice-box, illustrated his oral descriptions.

"This system is not so easy as the second, which I shall presently show you," continued Chichester; "because the die must be kept cleverly inside the box, so as not to be seen. The second way of *securing* is by taking hold of one of the dice by the little finger, and keeping it firm against the palm of the hand while you shake the box, so as to be able to drop it skilfully upon the table at the proper moment, when it will seem as if it came from the box along with the other. This is the way."

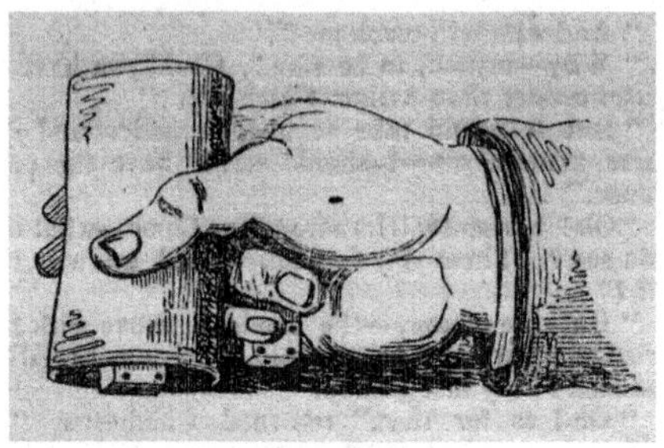

"I shall soon understand," said the baronet. "Of course by being able to *secure* one die, you may make it turn up any number you choose."

"When you mean to practise this dodge," continued Chichester, "call five for *a main*; because you can *secure* the four, and there is only the six on the loose die that can come up against you. If you have a good stake to get, *secure* a five every time because when the *main* is six to five, or seven to five, or eight to five, or nine to five, or ten to five, you must win every time, because you can't possibly throw out while the five is *secured*."

"But will not the ear tell the *pigeon* that there is only one die rattling in the box?" demanded the baronet.

"Look at this box," exclaimed Chichester. "It has two rims cut inside, near the bottom: the one die shaking against them produces the sound of two dice."

"Are there not some peculiarities about these dice?" asked Sir Rupert, pointing to a pair which Chichester had placed apart from the rest.

"Yes—those are *unequal dice*, and are so well made that no one, except a regular sharper, could detect them. They are bigger at one end than the other, and the sixes are placed on the smaller squares, because you must play with these dice to win upon high numbers, which are on those smaller squares. The dice will in nine cases out of ten fall upon the larger squares, and thus show the high numbers uppermost."

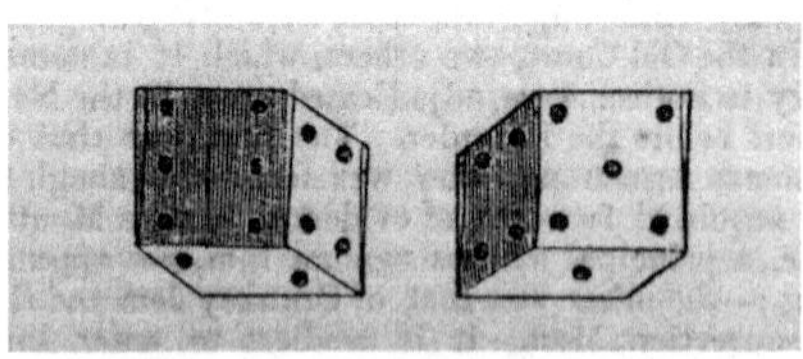

"And these dice?" enquired the baronet, taking up two others.

"Loaded ones," replied Chichester. "These are to throw low; and so the two sides which have got four and five on them are loaded."

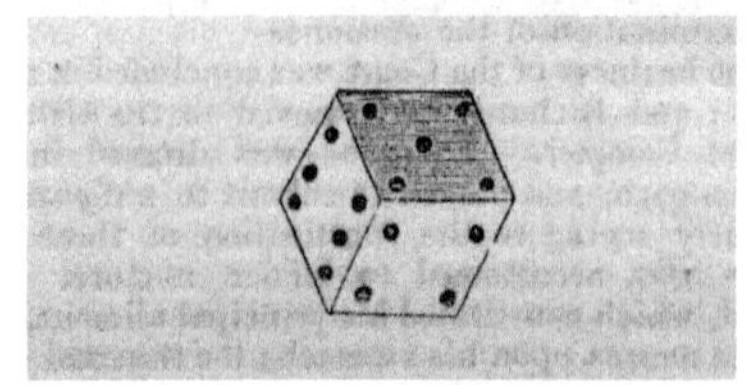

"How are they loaded?" asked Sir Rupert.

"The corner pip of the four side, next to the five side, is bored very neatly to a certain depth; the same is done to the corner pip of the five side adjoining the four side. Thus the two holes, so bored, meet each other at right angles. One of the holes is covered over with some strong cement; quicksilver is then poured in; and the other hole is covered over with the cement. The spots are blackened; and your dice are ready for use. These being intended to throw low, you must call a main and take the odds accordingly."

"Well," said the baronet, "I think I can now safely say that I know enough of the elements of your grammar to enable me to practise myself. Let us devote half an hour to the working of cards."

"The ways of managing the cards," said Chichester, taking up a pack, and shuffling them, "are numerous. These, for instance, are *Longs and Shorts*. All the cards above the eight, are the least thing longer than those below it. I have a machine which was invented on purpose to cut them accurately. Nothing under an eight can be cut, you see, with these cards, lengthways."

"And that pack so carefully wrapped up in the paper?"

"Oh! these are my *Concaves* and *Convexes*. All from the two to the seven are cut concave; and all from the eight to the king are cut convex. By cutting the pack breadthways a convex card is cut; by cutting it lengthways, a concave one is secured."

"I have often heard of *the bridge*," said Sir Rupert; "what does that mean?"

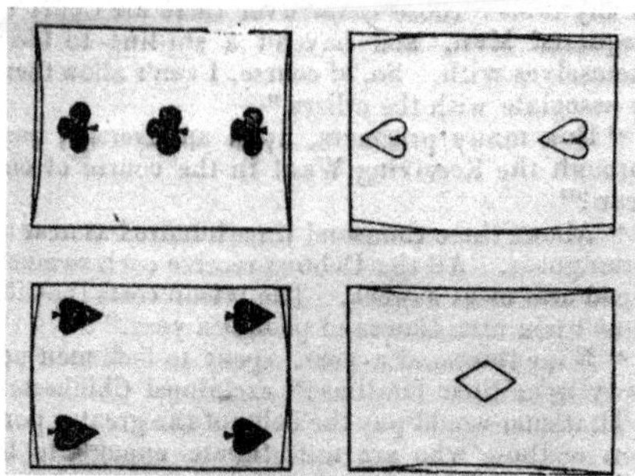

"Oh! *the bridge* is simply and easily done," replied Chichester, shuffling the pack which he held in his hand. "You see it is nothing but slightly curving a card, and introducing it carelessly into the pack.

Shuffle the cards as your opponent will, you are sure to be able to cut the bridged one."

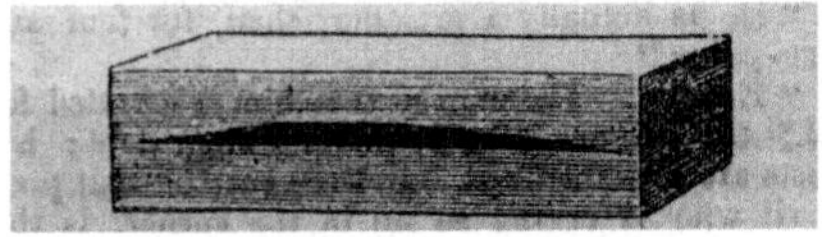

"I could do that without study," observed Sir Rupert Harborough. "Is my initiation now complete?"

"There are several other schemes with the cards," answered Chichester, "but I think that I have taught you enough for this evening. One famous device, however, must not be forgotten. You have heard of the way in which Lord de Roos lately attempted to cheat his noble companions at the club? The plan practiced by him is called *sauter la coupe*, and enables the dealer to do what he chooses with one particular card, which of course he has selected for his purpose. Now look how it is done; for I can better show practically than explain verbally."

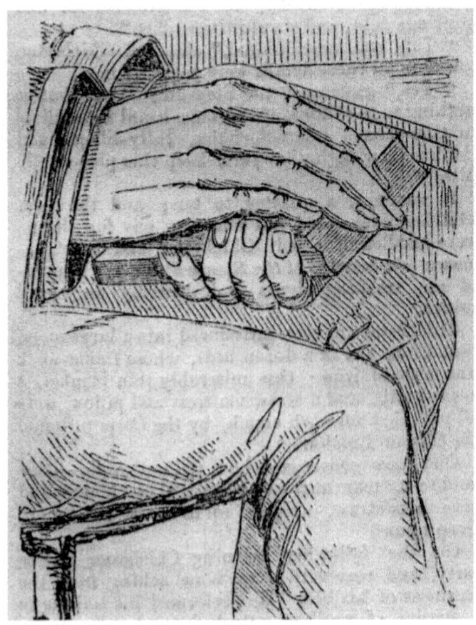

Scarcely was this portion of the lesson accomplished, when steps were heard ascending the stairs; and immediately afterwards a heavy fist knocked with more violence than courtesy at the parlour door.

The baronet and Chichester both turned pale.

"They can't have found us out here?" murmured the one to the other in a hoarse and tremulous tone.

"What shall we do?"

"We must open—happen what will."

Chichester unlocked the door: two ill-looking men entered the room.

"Mr. Arthur Chichester?" said one.

"He isn't here—we don't know him. My name is Davis—ask the landlady if it is not," cried Chichester hurriedly, and in a manner which only served to convince the officer that he was right.

"Come—come, none of that there gammon," said the bailiff. "I knows you well enough: my name's Garnell; and I'll stand the risk of your being Chichester. Here's execution out against you for four hundred and forty-seven pounds. I don't suppose that you can pay—so you'd better come off at once."

"Where to?" demanded Chichester, seeing that it was no use disputing his own identity any longer.

"Where to!" cried the officer; "why—to Whitecross, to be sure! Where the devil would you go to?"

"Can I not be allowed to sleep in a sponging-house?"

"No—this is an execution, and a large sum, mind. I don't dare do it."

"Well, then—here goes for Whitecross Street!" said Chichester; and after exchanging a few words in a whisper with the baronet, he left the house with the sheriff's officers.

CHAPTER XXXV.

WHITECROSS-STREET PRISON.

A COLD drizzling rain was falling, as Chichester proceeded along the streets leading to the debtors' prison. The noise of pattens upon the pavement; the numbers of umbrellas that were up; the splashing of horses' feet and carriage-wheels in the kennels; the rush of cabs and the shouting of omnibus-cads, were all characteristic of a wet night in a crowded metropolis.

Chichester shivered—more through nervousness than actual cold;

and he felt an oppressive sensation at the bottom of his stomach, as well as at the chest.

The officer endeavoured to console him, by observing that "it was lucky he had been taken so close to the prison on such a rainy night."

The ruined young man envied many a poor wretch whom he passed on his way; for he knew that it was far easier to get into a debtors' gaol than to get out of it.

At length they arrived at the prison.

It was now nine o'clock; and the place, viewed by the flickering light of the lamp at the gate of the governor's house, wore a melancholy and sombre appearance. The prisoner was introduced into a small lobby, where an elderly turnkey with knee-breeches and gaiters, thrust a small loaf of bread into his hand, and immediately consigned him to the care of another turnkey, who led him through several alleys to the staircase communicating with the Receiving Ward.

The turnkey pulled a wire, which rang a bell on the first floor.

"Who rings?" cried a voice at the top of the stairs.

"Sheriff's debtor—Arthur Chichester—L. S.," replied the turnkey, in a loud sing-song voice.

Chichester afterwards learnt that he was mentioned as a sheriff's prisoner, in contra-distinction to one arrested by a warrant from the Court of Requests, and that L. S. meant *London side*—an intimation that he had been arrested in the City of London, and not in the County of Middlesex.

Having ascended a flight of stone steps, Chichester was met at the door of the Receiving Ward by the steward thereof. This steward was himself a prisoner, but was considered a trustworthy person, and had therefore been selected by the governor to preside over that department of the prison.

The Receiving Ward was a long low room, with windows secured by bars, at each end. There were two grates, but only one contained any fire. The place was remarkably clean—the floor, the deal tables, and the forms being as white as snow.

The following conversation forthwith took place between the new prisoner and the steward:—

"What is your name?"

"Arthur Chichester."

"Have you got your bread?"

"Yes."

"Well—put it in that pigeon-hole. Do you choose to have sheets to-night on your bed?"

"Certainly."

"Then that will be a shilling the first night, and sixpence every night after, as long as you remain here. You can, moreover, sleep in the inner room, and sit up till twelve o'clock. Those who can't afford to pay for sheets sleep in a room by themselves, and go to bed at a quarter to ten. You see we know how to separate the gentlemen from the riff-raff."

"And how long shall I be allowed to stay up in the Receiving Ward?"

"That depends. Do you mean to live at my table? I charge sixpence for tea, the same for breakfast, a shilling for dinner, and four-pence for supper."

"Well—I shall be most happy to live at your table."

"In that case, write a note to the governor to say you are certain to be able to settle your affairs in the course of a week; and I will take care he shall have it the very first thing to-morrow morning."

"But I am sure of not being able to settle in a week."

"Do as you like. You won't be allowed to stay up here unless you do."

"Oh! in that case I will do so at once. Can you oblige me with a sheet of writing-paper?"

"Certainly. Here is one. A penny, if you please."

Chichester paid for the paper, wrote the letter, and handed it to the Steward.

He then cast a glance round the room; and saw three or four tolerably decent-looking persons warming themselves at the fire, while fifteen or sixteen wretched-looking men, dressed for the most part as labourers, were sitting on the forms round the walls, at a considerable distance from the blazing grate.

The Steward, perceiving that the new prisoner threw a look of inquiry towards him, said,—"Those *gentlemen* at the fire are Sheriff's Debtors, and live at my table: those *chaps* over there are Court of Requests' Men, and haven't a shilling to bless themselves with. So, of course, I can't allow them to associate with the others."

"How many prisoners, upon an average, pass through the Receiving Ward in the course of one year?"

"About three thousand three hundred as near as I can guess. All the Debtors receive each so much bread and meat a-week. The prison costs the City close upon nine thousand pounds a year."

"Nine thousand a-year, spent to lock men up, away from their families!" exclaimed Chichester. "That sum would pay the debts of the greater portion of those who are unfortunate enough to be brought here."

"You may well say *that*," returned the Steward. "Why, half the prisoners who come here are poor working-men, snatched away from their labour, and obliged to know that their wives and children will starve during their absence. That man over there, with the little bundle tied up in a blue cotton handkerchief, is only arrested for 8d. The costs are three and sixpence."

"He is actually a prisoner, then, for four and two-pence."

"Exactly. The man next to him is arrested for 3d., the balance of a chandler's shop debt; his costs are five shillings. But the case of that poor devil who is crying so up in the corner, is the worst. It appears that he had an account at a tally-shop, and paid one shilling a-week towards its liquidation. He was in full work, and earned eighteen shillings a week; and so he regularly gave his wife the money every Saturday night to put away for the tally-man. But the woman is fond of tippling, and she spent the money in gin. Well, the tally-man takes out a *summons* from the Court of Requests; the wife receives it, and is afraid to tell her husband. Next week comes the *Rule*: this the woman also hides, hoping, somehow or another, to get together the debt and costs, and settle it unknown to her husband. But no such thing: so this morning, as the poor fellow was going home to dinner, he was arrested for four shillings debt, and six shillings costs."

"This was cruel indeed," observed Chichester, to whom all these details were perfectly new.

"Yes," continued the Steward; "but that is nothing to the things that I have heard men tell up in this room. Loan-Societies, Tally-Shops, and the low pettifogging lawyers, keep this place well-filled."

It was now a quarter to ten; and the poor wretches who could not afford to pay for sheets, were huddled off to bed. Chichester, and the *"gentlemen who boarded at the Steward's table,"* remained up, smoking cigars and drinking ale, until twelve.

Chichester was then introduced into a large room containing ten or a dozen beds, whose frame-work was made of iron. One miserably thin blanket, a horse-cloth, and a straw mattress and pillow, were all provided for each couch, by the Corporation of the City of London!

Oh! how generous—how philanthropic—how noble; to tear men away from their homes and give them straw, wrapped up in coarse ticking, to sleep upon!

On the following morning Chichester awoke early, and rose with every bone aching from the hardness of his bed. He performed his toilette in a species of scullery attached to the Receiving Ward; and the enjoyment of this luxury was attended with the following disbursements:—Towel, 2d.; Use of Soap, 1d.; Loan of Razor and Lather-box, 1d.

Breakfast, consisting of coffee and dry toast, was then served up.

Those who boarded with the steward sate down and commenced a desperate assault upon the provisions; and those who fancied an egg or a rasher of bacon with their meal, paid twopence extra. The conversation was entirely associated with the prison affairs; it appeared as if those men, when once they set foot in the prison, discarded all thoughts of the great world without, from which they have been snatched away. Even when the morning newspaper came in, attention was first directed, by a strange kind of sympathy, to the list of Bankrupts and to the Law Notices, the latter of which afforded them the pleasing and interesting intelligence of who were that day to appear before the Commissioners of the Insolvent Court.

At five minutes past nine, a violent ring at the bell called the Steward in haste to the door. This was the summons of a turnkey who came to remove new prisoners to the respective departments of the establishment to which they belonged. Thus they were classified into Middlesex Sheriffs' Debtors, London Sheriffs' Debtors, and City Freemen who were also Sheriffs' Debtors; and London Court of Requests' Debtors, and Middlesex Court of Requests' Debtors.

Chichester was ordered to remove to the Poultry Ward, on the London side, the governor declining to comply with the request contained in his letter.

It will be seen from what we have already said, that Whitecross-street prison is essentially different from the Bench, descriptions of which have been given in so many different works, and the leading features of which are so familiar to a large portion of the community, either from hearsay or experience. If a man cannot muster four or five pounds to transfer himself from the custody of the Sheriffs to that of the Judges, by a *habeas corpus* writ, he must remain in Whitecross-street prison, while the more wealthy debtor enjoys every luxury and privilege in the Bench. And yet, we are constantly assured that there is the same law for the poor as there is for the rich!

The system of imprisonment for debt is in itself impolitic, unwise, and cruel in the extreme:—it ruins the honest man, and destroys the little remnant of good feeling existing in the heart of the callous one. It establishes the absurd doctrine, that if a man *cannot* pay his debts while he is allowed the exercise of his talents, his labour, and his acquirements, he *can* when shut up in the narrow compass of a prison, where his talents, his labour, and his acquirements are useless. How eminently narrow-sighted are English legislators! They fear totally to abolish this absurd custom, because they dread that credit will suffer. Why—credit is altogether begotten in confidence, and never arises from the preconceived intention on the part of him who gives it, to avail himself of this law against him who receives it. Larceny and theft are punished by a limited imprisonment, with an allowance of food; but debtors, who commit no crime, may linger and languish—and *starve in gaol*.

The Poultry Ward was a long, dark, low room, with seven or eight barred windows on each side, sawdust upon the stone floor, and about a dozen or fourteen small tables arranged, like those of a coffee-house, around the walls. The room was full of debtors of all appearances—from the shabby-genteel down to the absolutely ragged. Here a prisoner was occupied in drawing up his schedule for the Insolvent Debtors' Court;—there an emaciated old man was writing a letter, over which he shed bitter and scalding tears;—at another table a young farmer's labourer-looking man was breakfasting off bread and cheese and onions, which he washed down with porter;—close by was a stout, seedy-looking person with grey hair, who did not seem to have any breakfast at all;—in this nook a poor pale wretch was reading a newspaper;—in that corner another individual was examining a pile of letters;—several were gathered round the fire in the scullery or kitchen attached to the Ward, preparing their breakfasts;—and others were lounging up and down the room, laughing, and talking over the amusements of the preceding night up in the sleeping rooms.

The steward of the Poultry Ward had just finished his breakfast when the turnkey introduced Mr. Chichester.

"Well, Mr. Thaynes," said the Steward, quite delighted to see the new prisoner, "I began to think we should have had none down this morning. Pray take a seat, sir."

This invitation was addressed to Chichester, who sat down accordingly.

The Steward, after exchanging a few observations with the turnkey, produced a book from a drawer in the table, and addressing himself in a semi-mysterious tone to Mr. Chichester, said—"These are our rules and regulations. Every new member is required to pay an entrance fee of one pound and sixpence; and this goes towards the fund for paying the officers and servants of the ward, providing coals, and administering generally to the comforts of the place."

"I am quite satisfied with the justice of the charge," said Chichester; and he paid it accordingly.

"I suppose you will live at my table?" enquired the Steward. "Same charges as up stairs in the Receiving Ward."

"Oh! certainly," answered Chichester. "Have you any body here of any consequence at all?"

"Not particularly at this moment. Lord William Priggins stayed a couple of days with us, and went over to the Bench yesterday morning."

"Who is that gentleman walking up and down the narrow court outside?" enquired Chichester, glancing towards a window, through which might be seen a tall slim young man, with black moustachios, a long faded cotton dressing gown, a dingy velvet skull cap, and pantaloons hanging low and loose, because the owner had forgotten his braces.

"Oh! that is Count Pichantoss—a celebrated Russian nobleman, who was cleaned out some weeks since at a West-end Hell, and got put into prison for his hotel bill."

"And who is that respectable old gentleman with the bald head, and dressed in black?"

"That is a clergyman, the Rev. Henry Sharpere; he is an excellent preacher, they say—and the best securer of a die that I ever saw in my life."

"And that very sickly pale-faced youth, who seems to be scarcely twenty?"

"He is only twenty-one and a month. He was arrested the day after he came of age for blank acceptances which he had given, during his minority, to the tune of three thousand pounds, and for which he never received more than three hundred."

"And that quiet-looking old gentleman at the table opposite?"

"He is a Chancery prisoner—committed for contempt. It appears that he was one morning walking by the Auction Mart, and saw large posting-bills announcing the immediate sale of an estate consisting of thirteen houses somewhere in Finsbury, under a decree of the Court of Chancery. My gentleman hadn't a guinea in his pocket, nor the means of raising one at the time. Nevertheless he walked into the Mart as bold as brass, strode up stairs to the auctioneer's rooms, and bid for the estate. There were plenty of competitors; but he didn't care—he bid away: and at last the estate was knocked down to him for four thousand three hundred pounds. When sales are effected under an order of the Chancellor, no deposit-money is required. This may seem strange to you, but it is not the less a fact. So off walks my gentleman, quite rejoiced at his bargain. The first thing he does is to go and collect all the arrears of rent he can from the tenants of the houses, and to distrain upon those who couldn't or wouldn't pay. Lord! what a game he did play, to be sure! He called into request the services of half the brokers in Finsbury, and made the tenants cash up to the very last farthing that was due. Well, the lawyers employed for the sale of the estate, drew up the deeds of conveyance and the abstract of the title; but my gentleman never meant paying—so at last the Chancery Court, getting tired of his excuses, and finding that he would not disgorge the amount he had already received for rents, nor yet come down with a shilling towards the purchase-money, clapt him into limbo under some form or another;—and so here he is."

In this manner did the steward of the Poultry Ward render the new prisoner familiar with the leading characters of that department of the prison. In addition to the few instances of flagrant dishonesty, or culpable extravagance which were pointed out to Chichester, information was given him of many—very many cases of pure and unadulterated misfortune. The churchyard has known no sorrow—the death-chamber has known no anguish equal to that acute and poignant suffering which many an inmate endures within the walls of that prison. If he be an affectionate father, he thinks of his absent little ones—and he feels shocked at the cold cruelty of the rules which only permit children to visit their incarcerated sire twice a week—on Wednesday and Sunday—and then only for three hours each time. If he be a kind husband, and possesses a tender and a loving wife, he dreads the fatal hour of five of the evening, which is the signal for all strangers and visitors to leave these walls. Misery—lank, lean, palpable misery—is the characteristic of Whitecross Street prison.

The legislature says—"We only allow men to be locked up in order to prevent them from running away without paying the debts they owe."—Then why treat them as felons? Why impose upon them rules and regulations, the severity of which is as galling to their souls as the iron chains of Newgate are to the felons' flesh? Why break their spirits and crush their good and generous feelings by compelling them all to herd together—the high and the low—the polite and the vulgar—the temperate and the drunkard—the cleanly and the filthy—the religious and the profane—the sedate and the ribald?

O excellent legislators! do you believe that a man ever went out of the debtor's gaol more moral and better disposed than he was when he went in? The answer to this question will, in one word, teach you the efficacy of Imprisonment for Debt.

Chichester walked out into a large stone-paved court attached to the ward, and bearing the attractive but somewhat illusive name of the "Park." At twelve o'clock the beer men from the public-houses in Whitecross Street were allowed admittance; and then commenced the debauchery of the day. The seats round the "Park" were soon crowded with prisoners and visitors, drinking, smoking, laughing, and swearing.

Many poor wretches, who could not boast of much strength of mind, but were in reality well disposed, took to this occupation *to kill care*.

And who will blame them? Not you, proud peer, who bury your vexations in crystal goblets sparkling with the choicest juice of Epernay's grape—nor you, fine gentleman, who seek in gaming at your club a relief from the anxieties and petty troubles which now and then interrupt the otherwise even tenure of your way!

In the course of the day Mr. Chichester wrote a very penitent letter to his father, the pawnbroker, lamenting past follies, and promising future good conduct. The postscript contained an intimation that prison was bad enough when one possessed plenty of money; but that it was ten thousand times worse when associated with empty pockets. This precious epistle succeeded in inducing the "old gentleman," as Chichester denominated his father, to loosen his purse strings, and remit a few pounds to supply immediate wants.

Chichester was thus enabled to live at the Steward's table, and smoke his cigars and drink his ale to his heart's content. In a small community like that of a ward in Whitecross Street, as well as in the great world without, he who has the most money is the most "looked up to"—which is a phrase perfectly understood, and almost synonymous with "respected;" and thus Mr. Chichester very speedily became the "star" of that department of the prison to which he had been assigned.

CHAPTER XXXVI.

THE EXECUTION.

From the moment that Bill Bolter had been removed to the condemned cell, after his trial at the Old Bailey for the murder of his wife, he preserved a sullen and moody silence.

Two turnkeys sat up with him constantly, according to the rules of the prison; but he never made the slightest advances towards entering into conversation with them. The Chaplain was frequent in his attendance upon the convict; but no regard was paid to the religious consolations and exhortations of the reverend gentleman.

The murderer ate his meals heartily, and enjoyed sound physical health: he was hale and strong, and might, in the common course of nature, have lived until a good old age.

By day he sate, with folded arms, meditating upon his condition. He scarcely repented of the numerous evil deeds of which he had been guilty: but he trembled at the idea of a future state!

One night he had a horrid dream. He thought that the moment had arrived for his execution, and that he was standing upon the drop. Suddenly the board gave way beneath his feet—and he fell. An agonising feeling of the blood rushing with the fury of a torrent and with a heat of molten lead up into his brain, seized upon him: his eyes shot sparks of fire; and in his ears there was a loud droning sound, like the moan of the ocean on a winter's night. This sensation, he fancied, lasted about two minutes—a short and insignificant space to those who feel not pain, but an age when passed in the endurance of agony the most intense. Then he died: and he thought that his spirit left his body with the last pulsation of the lungs, and was suddenly whirled downwards, with fearful rapidity, upon the wings of a hurricane. He felt himself in total darkness; and yet he had an idea that he was plunging precipitately into a fearful gulf, around the sides of which hideous monsters, immense serpents, formidable bats, and all kinds of slimy reptiles were climbing. At length he reached the bottom of the gulf; and then the faculty of sight was suddenly restored to him. At the same moment, he felt fires encircling him all around; and a horrible snake coiled itself about him. He was in the midst of a boundless lake of flame; and far as his eyes could reach, he beheld myriads of spirits all undergoing the same punishment—writhing in quenchless fire and girt by hideous serpents. And he thought that neither himself nor those spirits which he beheld around, wore any shape which he could define; and yet he saw them plainly—palpably. They had no heads—no limbs; and yet they were something more than shapeless trunks,—all naked and flesh-coloured, and unconsumed and indestructible amidst that burning lake, which had no end. In a few moments this dread scene changed, and all was again dark. The murderer fancied that he was now groping about in convulsive agonies upon the bank of a river, the stream of which was tepid and thick like blood. The bank was slimy and moist, and overgrown with huge osiers and dark weeds amidst which loathsome reptiles and enormous alligators were crowded together. And it was in this frightful place that the murderer was now spiritually groping his way, in total and coal-black darkness. At length he slipped down the slimy bank—and his feet touched the river, which he now knew to be of blood. He grasped convulsively at the osiers to save himself from falling into that horrible stream; a huge serpent sprung from the thicket, and coiled itself about his arms and neck;—and at the same moment an enormous alligator rose from the river of blood, and seized him in the middle between its tremendous jaws. He uttered a fearful cry—and awoke.

This dream made a deep impression upon him. He believed that he had experienced a foretaste of Hell—of that hell, with all its horrors, in which he would be doomed for ever and ever—without hope, without end.

And yet, by a strange idiosyncracy of conduct, he did not court the consolation of the clergyman: he breathed no prayer, gave no outward and visible sign of repentance: but continued in the same sullen state of reserve before noticed.

Still, after that dream, he dreaded to seek his bed at night. He was afraid of sleep; for when he closed his eyes in slumber, visions of hell, varied in a thousand horrible ways presented themselves to his mind.

He never thought of his children: and once when the clergyman asked him if he would like to see them, he shook his head impatiently.

Death! he shuddered at the idea—and yet he never sought to escape from its presence by conversation or books. He sat moodily brooding upon death and what would probably occur hereafter, until he conjured up to his imagination all the phantasmagorical displays of demons, spectres, and posthumous horrors ever conceived by human mind.

On another occasion—the Friday before the Monday on which he was executed—he dreamt of heaven. He thought that the moment the drop had fallen from beneath his feet, a brilliant light, such as he had never seen on earth, shone all around him:—the entire atmosphere was illuminated as with gold-dust in the rays of a powerful sun. And the sun and moon and stars all appeared of amazing size—immense orbs of lustrous and shining metal. He fancied that he winged his way upwards with a slow and steady motion, a genial warmth prevailing all around, and sweet odours delighting his senses. In this manner he soared on high until at length he passed sun, moon, and stars, and beheld them all shining far, far beneath his feet. Presently the sounds of the most ravishing sacred music, accompanied by choral voices hymning to the praise of the Highest, fell upon his ear. His soul was enchanted by these notes of promise, of hope, and of love; and, raising his eyes, he beheld the shining palaces of heaven towering above vast and awe-inspiring piles of clouds. He reached a luminous avenue amidst those clouds, which led to the gates of paradise. He was about to enter upon that glorious and radiant path, when a sudden change came over the entire spirit of his dream; and in a moment he found himself dashing precipitately downwards, amidst darkness increasing in intensity, but through which the sun, moon, and planets might be seen, at immense distances, of a lurid and ominous red. Down—down he continued falling, until he was pitched with violence upon the moist and slimy bank of that river of tepid blood, whose margin was crowded with hideous reptiles, and whose depths swarmed with wide-mouthed alligators.

Thus passed the murderer's time—dread meditations by day, and appalling dreams by night.

Once he thought of committing suicide, and thus avoiding the ignominy of the scaffold. He had no shame; but he dreaded hanging on account of the pain—whereof he had experienced the dread sensations in his dreams. Besides, death is not quite so terrible when inflicted by one's own hand, as it is when dealt by another. He was, however, closely watched; and the only way in which he could have killed himself was by dashing the back of his head violently against the stone-wall. Then he reflected that he might not do this effectually;—and so he abandoned the idea of self-destruction.

On the last Sunday of his life he attended the Chapel. A condemned sermon was preached according to custom. The sacred fane was filled with elegantly dressed ladies—the wives, daughters, and friends of the City authorities. The Clergyman enjoined the prisoner to repentance, and concluded by assuring him *that it was not even then too late to acknowledge his errors and save his soul. God would still forgive him!*

If God could thus forgive him,—why could not Man? Oh! wherefore did that preacher confine his observations to the mercy of the Almighty? why did he not address a terrible lecture to bloodthirsty and avenging mortals? Of what use was the death of that sinner? Surely there is no moral example in a public execution? "There is," says the Legislature. We will see presently.

Oh! why could not the life of that man—stained with crime and red with blood though it were—have been spared, and he himself allowed to live to see the horror of his ways, and learn to admire virtue? He might have been locked up for the remainder of his existence: bars and bolts in English gaols are very strong; there was enough air for him to be allowed to breathe it; and there was enough bread to have spared him a morsel at the expense of the state!

We cannot give life: we have no right to take it away.

On the Sunday afternoon, the murderer's children were taken to see him in the condemned cell. He had not asked for them: but the authorities considered it proper that *they* should take leave of *him*.

The poor little innocents were dressed in the workhouse garb. The boy understood that his father was to be hanged on the following morning; and his grief was heart-rending. The little girl could not understand why her parent was in that gloomy place, nor what horrible fate awaited him;—but she had an undefined and vague sense of peril and misfortune; and she cried also.

The murderer kissed them, and told them to be good children;—but he only thus conducted himself because he was *ashamed* to appear so unfeeling and brutal as he knew himself to be, in the presence of the Ordinary,[1] the Governor, the Sheriffs, and the ladies who were admitted to have a glimpse of him in his dungeon.

* * * * *

The morning of the second Monday after the Sessions dawned.

This was the one fixed by the Sheriffs for the execution of William Bolter, the murderer.

At four o'clock on that fatal morning the huge black stage containing the drop, was wheeled out of a shed in the Press Yard, and stationed opposite the debtors' door of Newgate. A carpenter and his assistant then hastily fitted up the two perpendicular spars, and the one horizontal beam, which formed the gibbet.

There were already several hundreds of persons collected to witness these preliminary arrangements; and from that hour until eight o'clock multitudes continued pouring from every direction towards that spot—the focus of an all-absorbing interest.

Man—that social, domestic, and intelligent animal—will leave his child crying in the cradle, his wife tossing upon a bed of pain and sickness, and his blind old parents to grope their way about in the dark, in order to be present at an exhibition of a fellow creature's disgrace, agony, or death. And the law encourages this morbid taste in all countries termed civilised,—whether it be opposite the debtors' door of Newgate, or around the guillotine erected at the Barriere Saint Jacques of Paris,—whether it be in the midst of ranks of soldiers,

---

1 The Ordinary: the chief Anglican chaplain of Newgate. He had the right to publish the 'Ordinary's Account' of the last days and sufferings of condemned criminals, from which he made a great deal of money.

drawn up to witness the abominable infliction of the lash in the barracks of Charing Cross, or the buttons cut off a deserter's coat in the Place Vendome,—whether it be to see a malefactor broken on the wheel in the dominions of the tyrant who is called "Europe's Protestant Sovereign,"[1] or to behold the military execution of a great general at Madrid,—whether it be to hear an English judge in the nineteenth century, unblushingly condemn a man to be hanged, drawn, and quartered, and his dissected corpse disposed of according to the will of our Sovereign Lady the Queen; or to witness some miserable peasant expire beneath the knout in the territories of the Czar.

But the Law is vindictive, cowardly, mean, and ignorant. It is *vindictive* because its punishments are more severe than the offences, and because its officers descend to any dirtiness in order to obtain conviction. It is *cowardly*, because it cuts off from the world, with a rope or an axe, those men whose dispositions it fears to undertake to curb. It is *mean*, because it is all in favour of the wealthy, and reserves its thunders for the poor and obscure who have no powerful interest to protect them; and because itself originates nearly half the crimes which it punishes. And it is *ignorant*, because it erects the gibbet where it should rear the cross,—because it makes no allowance for the cool calculating individual who commits a crime, but takes into its consideration the case of the passionate man who assassinates his neighbour in a momentary and uncontroulable burst of rage,—thus forgetting that the former is the more likely one to be led by reflection to virtue, and that the latter is a demon subject to impulses which he can never subdue.

From an early hour a glittering light was seen through the small grated window above the debtors' door; for the room to which that door belongs is now the kitchen.

These was something sinister and ominous in that oscillating glare, breaking through the mists of the cold December morning, and playing upon the black spars of the gibbet which stood high above the already dense but still increasing multitudes.

Towards eight o'clock the crowd had congregated to such an

---

1 Gustavus IV of Sweden. One of this king's first acts was to supervise the public impalement of Ankarstrom, who had assassinated his father and predecessor Gustavus Adolphus, despite the latter's having publicly pardoned the killers.

extent that it moved and undulated like the stormy ocean. And, oh! what characters were collected around that gibbet. Every hideous den, every revolting hole—every abode of vice, squalor, and low debauchery, had vomited forth their horrible population. Women, with young children in their arms,—pickpockets of all ages,—swell-mobsmen,—prostitutes, thieves, and villains of all degrees and descriptions, were gathered there on that fatal morning.

And amidst that multitude prevailed mirth, and laughter, and gaiety. Ribald language, obscene jokes, and filthy expressions, were heard around, even to the very foot of the gallows; and even at that early hour intoxication was depicted upon the countenances of several whom the Law had invited thither to derive an example from the tragedy about to be enacted!

Example, indeed! Listen to those shouts of laughter: they emanate from a group collected round a pickpocket only twelve years old, who is giving an account of how he robbed an elderly lady on the preceding evening. But, ah! what are those moans, accompanied with horrible oaths and imprecations? Two women fighting: they are tearing each other to pieces—and their husbands are backing them. In another direction, a simple-looking countryman suddenly discovers that his handkerchief and purse are gone. In a moment his hat is knocked over his eyes; and he himself is cuffed, and kicked, and pushed about in a most brutal manner.

Near the scaffold the following conversation takes place:—

"I wonder what the man who is going to be hanged is doing at this moment."

"It is now half-past seven. He is about receiving the sacrament."

"Well—if I was he, I'd send the old parson to the devil, and pitch into the sheriffs."

"Yes—so would I. For my part, I should like to live such a life as Jack Sheppard[1] or Dick Turpin[2] did, even if I did get hanged at last."

1 John Sheppard, known as Jack (1702-1724) housebreaker and thief, but a popular hero on account of his brilliant and daring escapes from Newgate and the Round-House. He was betrayed by Jonathan Wild and hanged at Newgate on 16 November 1724.

2 Richard Turpin, known as Dick (1705-1739), highwayman, murderer, horse-thief, and chicken-killer. Born in Hempstead, Essex, Turpin was apprenticed to a butcher in Whitechapel, before taking to a career of crime which has been told too many times to need repeating here. A disgusting, vicious criminal, Turpin became, almost beyond belief, the most popular criminal figure since Robin Hood. The final form of

"There is something noble and exciting in the existence of a highwayman: and then—at last—what admiration on the part of the crowd—what applause when he appears upon the drop!"

"Yes. If this fellow Bolter had contented himself with being a burglar, or had only murdered those who resisted him, I should have cheered him heartily;—but to kill his wife—there's something cowardly in that; and so I shall hiss him."

---

the legend was given to him by W. H. Ainsworth in *Rookwood* (1834), but it had been in circulation long before. Turpin was finally arrested for shooting a neighbour's cockerel; by his handwriting he was recognised as the infamous Turpin, and he was hanged at York on 7 April 1739.

"And so shall I."

"A quarter to eight! The poor devil's minutes are pretty well numbered."

"I wonder what he is about now."

"The pinioning will begin directly, I dare say."

"That must be the worst part."

"Oh! no—not a bit of it. You may depend upon it that he is not half so miserable as we are inclined to think him. A man makes up his mind to die as well as to anything else. But what the devil noise is that?"

"Oh! only some fool of a fellow singing a patter song about a man hanging, and imitating all the convulsions of the poor wretch. My eyes! how the people do laugh!"

"Five minutes to eight! They won't be long now."

At this moment the bell of Saint Sepulchre's church began to toll the funeral knell—that same bell whose ominous sound had fallen upon the ears of the wretched murderer, where he lay concealed in the vault of the Old House.

The laughing—the joking—the singing—and the fighting now suddenly subsided; and every eye was turned towards the scaffold. The most breathless curiosity prevailed.

Suddenly the entrance of the debtor's door was darkened by a human form; the executioner hastily ascended the steps, and appeared upon the scaffold.

He was followed by the Ordinary in his black-gown, walking with slow and measured pace along, and reading the funeral service—while the bell of Saint Sepulchre continued its deep, solemn, and foreboding death-note.

The criminal came next.

His elbows were bound to his sides, and his wrists fastened together with thin cord. He had on a decent suit of clothes, supplied by the generosity of Tom the Cracksman; and on his head was a white night-cap.

The moment he appeared upon the scaffold, a tremendous shout arose from the thousands and thousands of spectators assembled to witness his punishment.

He cast a hurried and anxious glance around him.

The large open space opposite the northern wing of Newgate

seemed literally paved with human faces, which were continued down the Old Bailey and Giltspur Street, as far as he could see. The houses facing the prison were crammed with life—roof and window.

It seemed as if he were posted upon a rock in the midst of an ocean of people.

Ten thousand pairs of eyes were concentrated in him. All was animation and interest, as if a grand national spectacle were about to take place.

"Hats off!" was the universal cry: the multitudes were determined to lose nothing! The cheapness of an amusement augments the pleasure derived from it. We wonder that the government has never attempted to realise funds by charging a penny a-piece for admission to behold the execution at Newgate. In such a country as England, where even religion is made a compulsory matter of taxation, the dues collected at executions would form a fund calculated to thrive bravely.

While the executioner was occupied in fixing the halter round the convict's neck, the Ordinary commenced that portion of the Burial Service, which begins thus:—

"Man that is born of a woman hath but a short time to live, and is full of misery. He cometh up, and is cut down like a flower: he fleeth as it were a shadow, and never continueth in one stay."

The executioner having attached the rope, and drawn the night-cap over the criminal's face, disappeared from the scaffold, and went beneath the platform to draw the bolt that sustained the drop.

"In the midst of life we are in death; of whom may we seek for succour, but of thee, O Lord who—"

Here the drop fell.

A dreadful convulsion appeared to pass through the murderer's frame; and for nearly a minute his hands moved nervously up and down. Perhaps during those fifty seconds, the horrors of his dream were realised, *and he felt the blood rushing with the fury of a torrent and with a heat of molten lead up into his brain; perhaps his eyes shot sparks of fire; and in his ears was a loud droning sound, like the moan of the ocean on a winter's night!*

But the convulsive movement of the hands soon ceased, and the murderer hung a lifeless corpse.

The crowd retained its post till nine o'clock, when the body was cut down: then did that vast assemblage of persons, of both sexes and all ages, begin to disperse.

The public-houses in the Old Bailey and the immediate neighbourhood drove a roaring trade throughout that day.

CHAPTER XXXVII.

THE LAPSE OF TWO YEARS.

SHAKSPEARE said, "All the world is a *stage*:" we say, "All the world is an *omnibus*."

The old and young—the virtuous and wicked—the rich and the poor, are invariably thrown and mixed up together; and yet their interests are always separate. Few stretch out a hand to help a ragged or decrepit man into the vehicle; and the well-dressed draw back and avert their heads as the impoverished wretch forces his way with difficulty past them up to the vacant seat in the farthest corner. The moment a well-dressed individual mounts the steps of the omnibus, every hand is thrust out to help him in, and the most convenient seat is instantaneously accorded to him. And then the World's omnibus hurries along, stopping occasionally at the gates of a church-yard to put down one of its passengers, and calling at some palace or some cottage indiscriminately to fill up the vacant seat.

Away—away thunders the World's omnibus again, crushing the fairest flowers of the earth in its progress, and frequently choosing rough, dreary, and unfrequented roads in preference to paths inviting, even, and pleasant. Sometimes, by the caprice of the passengers, or by the despotic commands of the masters of the World's omnibus, the beggar and the rich man change garments and places; and then the former becomes the object of deference and respect, while the latter is treated with contempt and scorn. In the World's omnibus *might* makes *right*;—but *cunning* frequently secures a more soft and comfortable seat than either.

If a dispute ensues, and the question at issue is referred to the conductor for arbitration, he glances at the personal appearance of the complainant and defendant, and decides in favour of him who wears the better coat. When stones or other impediments obstruct the way of the World's omnibus, the poor and the ragged passengers are commanded to alight and clear them away; and yet, when the vehicle stops for dinner at the inn by the way side, the well-dressed and the affluent appropriate to themselves the luxuries, while those who cleared away the stones and who grease the wheels, get only a sorry crust—and sometimes nothing at all.

And then, away—away the World's omnibus goes again, amidst noise, dust, and all variations of weather. In the inclement seasons extra garments are given to the well-dressed and the rich, but none to the ragged and the poor:—on the contrary, their very rags and tatters are frequently taken from them to pay the prices of the hard crusts at the road-side inns. So goes the World's omnibus; and the moment the driver and conductor, who are its masters and owners, are deposited in their turn at the gates of some cemetery, their sons succeed them, whether competent or not—whether infants in swaddling-clothes, or old men in their dotage. And few—very few of those drivers know how to hold the reins;—and thus is it that the World's omnibus is frequently hurried at a thundering rate over broken ground, even unto the very verge of some precipice, down which it would be inevitably dashed, did not some bold intrepid passenger emerge from his obscurity in the corner, rush upon the box, hurl the incompetent driver from his seat, and assume the reins in his stead. But mark the strange opinions of those who journey in the World's omnibus! The passengers, instead of being grateful to him who has thus rescued them from ruin, pronounce him the usurper of a seat to which he has no hereditary claim, and never rest till they have succeeded in displacing him, and restoring the incompetent driver to his functions.

So goes the World's omnibus! None of the passengers are ever contented with their seats even though they may have originally chosen those seats for themselves. This circumstance leads to a thousand quarrels and mean artifices; and constant shiftings of positions take place. One passenger envies the seat of another; and, when he has succeeded in working his way into it, he finds to his surprise that it is not so agreeable as he imagines, and he either wishes to get back to his old one or to shove himself into another. The passengers in the World's omnibus are divided into different sects and parties, each party professing certain opinions for the authority of which they have no better plea than "the wisdom of their forefathers." Thus one party hates and abhors another; and each confidently imagines itself to be in the right, and all other parties to be in the wrong. And for those differences of opinion the most sanguinary broils ensue; and friendship, honour, virtue, and integrity are all forgotten in the vindictive contention.

But the World's omnibus rolls along all the same; and the Driver and Conductor laugh at the contests amongst the passengers, which they themselves have probably encouraged, and which somehow or another always turn to their individual benefit in the long run.

So goes the World's omnibus;—so it has always hurried onwards;—and in like manner will it ever go!

Oh! say not that Time has a leaden wing while it accompanies the World's omnibus on its way!

Two years elapsed from the date of the Old Bailey trials described in preceding chapters.

It was now the beginning of December, 1837.

The morning was dry, fine, and bright: the ground was as hard as asphalte; and the air was pure, cold, and frosty.

From an early hour a stout, elderly man—well wrapped up in a large great coat, and with a worsted "comforter" coming up to his very nose, which was of a purple colour with the cold—was seen walking up and down the front of the Giltspur Street Compter, apparently dividing his attention between the prison entrance and the clock of Saint Sepulchre's church.

At a quarter to ten o'clock, on that same morning, a private carriage, without armorial bearings upon the panels, and attended by two domestics, whose splendid liveries were concealed beneath drab great-coats, drove up to the door of the house inhabited by the Governor of Newgate. Inside that carriage was seated a lady—wrapped up in the most costly furs, and with a countenance whose beauty was enhanced by the smile of pleasure and satisfaction which illuminated it.

Precisely as the clock of Saint Sepulchre's Church struck ten, the doors of the Compter and Newgate opened simultaneously, and with a similar object.

From the Compter issued Richard Markham:—the portal of Newgate gave freedom to Eliza Sydney.

They were both restored to liberty upon the same day—the terms of their imprisonment dating from the commencement of the sessions during which they were tried.

The moment Richard set foot in the street, he was caught in the arms of the faithful Whittingham, who welcomed him with a kind of paternal affection, and whimpered over him like a child.

Eliza Sydney entered the carriage awaiting her at the door of Newgate, and was clasped to the bosom of Mrs. Arlington. The vehicle immediately drove rapidly away in a north-easterly direction.

"Mr. Monroe is waiting for you at your own house at Holloway," said Whittingham to his young master, when the first ebullition of joy was over. "He has been ailing lately—and he thought that this happy and fortitudinous event would be too much for his nerves."

"Let us make haste home, my excellent friend," observed Markham. "I am dying to behold once more the haunts of my childhood."

Whittingham summoned a cab; and he and his young master were soon rolling along the road which led to *home*.

Two years' imprisonment had produced a great effect upon Richard Markham. The intellectual cast and faultless beauty of his countenance still remained; but the joyous expression, natural to youth, had fled for ever; and in its place was a settled melancholy which proclaimed an early and intimate acquaintance with misfortune. His spirit was broken; but his principles were not undermined:—his heart was lacerated to its very core, but his integrity remained intact. Even though the gate of his prison had closed behind him, he could not shake off the idea that his very countenance proclaimed him to be a *Freed Convict*.

At length the cab reached Markham Place.

Richard glanced, with a momentary gleam of satisfaction upon his pale countenance, towards the hill on which stood the two trees—the rallying point for the brothers who had separated, more than six years back, beneath the foliage. Tears started to his eyes; and the ray of sunshine upon his brow gave place to a cloud of deep and sombre melancholy. He thought of what he was when he bade adieu to his brother at that period, and what he was at the present moment. *Then* all was blooming and encouraging in his path; and *now* he felt as if the mark of Cain were upon him!

He alighted from the vehicle, and entered the library, where Mr. Monroe awaited him. He and his guardian were at length alone together.

But how altered was Monroe since Richard had last seen him! His form was bowed down, his countenance was haggard, his eyes were sunken, and his brow was covered with wrinkles. He glanced furtively and anxiously around him the instant the young man entered the room; and instead of hastening forward to welcome him, he sank upon a chair, covering his face with his hands. The tears trickled through his fingers; and his breast was convulsed with deep sobs.

"In the name of heaven, what ails you, sir?" demanded Richard.

"My boy—you have come back at last," exclaimed the old gentleman, scarcely able to articulate a word, through the bitterness of his grief;—"and this much-dreaded day has at length arrived!"

"Much-dreaded day," repeated Markham, in unfeigned astonishment. "I should have thought, sir," he added coldly, "that *you*, who professed yourself so convinced of my innocence, would have received me with a smile of welcome!"

"My dear—dear boy," gasped the old man, "God knows I am rejoiced to hail your freedom; and that same Almighty power can also attest to my sincere conviction of your innocence. Believe me, I would go through fire and water to serve you,—I would lay down my life, miserable and valueless as it is, to benefit you;—but, oh! I cannot—cannot support your presence!"

And the old gentlemen seemed absolutely convulsed with agony as he spoke.

"I presume," said Richard, leaning over him, so as to be enabled to whisper in his ear, although there was none else at hand to listen,—"I presume that you scorn the man who has been convicted of felony? It is natural, sir—it is natural; but such a demonstration of aversion is not the less calculated to wound one who never injured you."

"No—no, Richard; you never injured me; and that makes me feel the more acutely now. But—hear me. I take God to witness that I love you as my own son, and that I am above such unnatural conduct as that which you would impute to me."

"My God!" cried Markham, impatiently, "what does all this mean? Are you ill? Has anything unpleasant occurred? If so, we will postpone all discussion upon my affairs until a period more agreeable to yourself."

As Markham uttered these words, he gently disengaged the old man's hands from his countenance, and pressed them in his own. He was then for the first time struck by the altered and care-worn features of his guardian; and without thinking of the effect his words might produce, he exclaimed, "My dear sir, you have evidently been very—very ill!"

"Ill!" cried the old man, bitterly. "When the mind suffers, the body is sympathetically affected; and this has been my case! If you have suffered much, Richard, during the last two years—so have I; and we have both only the same consolation—our innocence!"

"You speak in enigmas," ejaculated Markham. "What can you have to do with innocence or guilt—you who never wronged a human being?"

So strange became the expression of the old man's countenance, as Richard uttered these words, that the young man was perfectly astonished, and almost horrified; and undefined alarms floated through his brain. He was in a painful state of suspense; and yet he was afraid to ask a question.

"Richard!" suddenly exclaimed the old man, now looking our hero fixedly and fearlessly in the face, "I have a terrible communication to make to you."

"A terrible communication!" repeated Markham: "is it in respect to my brother? If so, do not keep me in suspense—let me know the worst at once—I can bear anything but suspense!"

"I have never heard *from* nor *of* your brother," answered Mr. Monroe; "and cannot say whether he is dead or living."

"Thank God, you have nothing terrible to communicate relative to *him*," exclaimed Markham; for he always had, and still entertained a presentiment that the appointment on the hill, beneath the two trees, would be punctually kept;—and this hope had cheered him during his horrible imprisonment.

"But I will not keep you in suspense, Richard," said the old man; "it is better for me to unburthen my mind at once. You are ruined!"

"Ruined!" said Markham starting as that dread word fell upon his ears; for the word *ruin* does not express one evil, like other words such as sickness, poverty, imprisonment; but it comprises and expresses an awful catalogue of all the miseries which can be supposed to afflict humanity. "Ruined!" he cried;—then catching at a straw, he added, "Aye! ruined in reputation, doubtless; but rich in the possessions which this world principally esteems. My property was all vested in you by my deceased father—I was not of age when I was condemned—and consequently the law could not touch my fortune when it filched from me my good name!"

"Ruined—ruined in property and all!" returned Mr. Monroe, solemnly. "Unfortunate speculations on *my* part, but in *your* interest, have consumed the vast property entrusted to me by your father!"

Markham fell into an arm chair; and for a moment he thought that every fibre in his heart would break. A terrible load oppressed his chest and his brain;—he was the victim of deep despair. As one looks forth into the darkness of midnight, and sees it dense and motionless, so did he now survey his own prospects. The single consolation which, besides the hope of again meeting his brother,—the real, the present, the tangible consolation, as it might be called, which would have enabled him to forget a portion of his sufferings and his wrongs,—this was now gone; and, a beggar upon the face of the earth, he found that he had not even the advantage of a good name to help him onwards in his career. Hope was quenched within him!

A long pause ensued.

At its expiration Markham suddenly rose from the arm-chair, approached his guardian, and said in a low and hollow voice, "Tell me how all this has happened: let me know the circumstances which led to this calamity."

"They are brief," said Monroe, "and will convince you that I am more to be pitied than blamed. Long previous to your unfortunate trial I commenced a series of speculations with my own property, all of which turned out unhappily. The year 1832 was a fatal one to many old-established houses; and mine was menaced with absolute ruin. In an evil hour I listened to the advice of a Mr. Allen, a merchant who had been reduced by great losses in America trading; and by his counsel, I employed a small portion of *your* property with the view of recovering my own, and augmenting your wealth at the same time. Allen acted as my agent in these new speculations. At first we were eminently successful: I speedily released myself from difficulty, and doubled the sum that I had borrowed from your fortune. At the beginning of 1836 Mr. Allen heard of a gentleman who required the loan of a considerable sum of money to work a patent which was represented to be a perfect mine of gold. Mr. Allen and I consulted upon the eligibility of embarking money in this enterprise: in a word, we were dazzled by the immense advantages to be derived from the speculation. At that time—it was shortly after your trial and sentence, Richard—I was ill and confined to my bed. Mr. Allen therefore managed this for me; and it is an extraordinary fact that I have never once seen the individual to whom I lent an enormous sum of money—for I *did* advance the sum required by that person; and I drew largely upon your fortune to procure it! Oh! Richard—had this speculation succeeded, I should have been a wealthy man once more, and your property would have been more than doubled. But, alas! this individual to whom I advanced that immense amount, and whose securities I had fancied unexceptionable, defrauded me in the most barefaced manner! And yet the law could not touch him, for he had contrived to associate Allen's name with his own as a partner in the enterprise. Rendered desperate by this appalling loss, I embarked in the most extravagant speculations with the remainder of your money. The infatuation of the gambler seized upon me: and I never stopped until the result was ruin—total ruin to me and comparative ruin to you!"

"Comparative ruin—only *comparative* ruin!" ejaculated Markham, his countenance suddenly brightening up at these words: "is there any thing left from the wrecks of my property—is there any thing available still remaining? Speak;—and if you answer me in the affirmative—if you announce the existence of never so small a pittance, I will yet forgive you all!"

"This house and the small estate attached to it are left," answered the old man, "and totally unincumbered. I neither could nor would touch your paternal possessions."

Markham felt indescribable relief from this statement; and he wrung his guardian's hand with the same gratitude which he would have shown had he that day received his inheritance entire.

"Thank God, I am not totally ruined!" cried Markham. "I can at least bury myself in this retreat;—I can daily ascend that hill where the memorials of fraternal affection stand;—and I can there hope for the return of my brother! My dear sir, what has been done cannot be recalled: reproaches, even were I inclined to offer any, would be useless; and regrets would be equally unavailing. This estate will produce me a small income—but enough for my wants. Two hundred pounds a-year are certainly a beggar's pittance, when compared with the inheritance which my father left me;—but I am still grateful that even the means of subsistence are left. And you, Mr. Monroe—upon what are you subsisting?"

"I still attend to the wrecks of my affairs," replied the old man; "and then I have my daughter Ellen—who earns a little with her needle——"

"You shall come and take up your abode with me—you and your daughter—and share my income," interrupted the generous young man, who saw not before him an individual that had deprived him of a large fortune, but an old—old man, bent down by the weight of numerous and deep afflictions.

Monroe wept at this noble conduct on the part of his ward, and strenuously refused to accept the proffered kindness and hospitality. Markham urged, begged, and entreated;—but the old man would not accede to his wish.

"You have not told me what became of your friend Mr. Allen," said Richard, after a pause.

"He was an honourable and an upright man," was the reply; "and the ruin which he had been the means of entailing, though innocently, upon me, broke his heart. He died three months ago."

"And what became of the infamous cheat whose schemes have thus killed one person and ruined two others?"

"I know not," answered Mr. Monroe. "I never saw him myself; nor did he even know that there was such a person as myself connected with the loan which he received. Certain commercial reasons—too long to be explained now—made me put forward Allen as the person who advanced the money, and conducted the entire business as a principal, and not as an agent. Thus no communication ever took place between me and this George Montague."

"George Montague!" ejaculated Richard.

"Yes—he was the villain who has plundered us."

"George Montague again!" murmured Richard, as he paced the room with hurried and uneven steps. "Why is it that this name should constantly obtrude itself upon my notice? wherefore should I be perpetually condemned to hear it uttered, and always coupled with epithets of abhorrence and reproach? and why should I be amongst the number of that miscreant's victims? Strange combination of circumstances!"

"Are you acquainted with this Montague?" demanded his guardian: "the name seemed to produce a singular effect upon you."

"I am not acquainted with him: like you, I have never even seen him," said Markham. "But I have heard much concerning him; and all that I *have* heard is evil. Surely—surely justice will some day overtake a miscreant who is constantly preying upon society, and who enriches himself at the expense of his fellow-creatures' happiness!"

Some time longer was devoted to conversation upon topics of interest to Markham and his guardian; and when the former had partially succeeded in tranquillising the mind of the latter, the old man was suffered to take his departure.

CHAPTER XXXVIII.

THE VISIT.

We purpose to follow the history of Richard Markham a little farther, ere we return to Eliza Sydney, whose adventures, after her release from Newgate, will, it is believed, excite the liveliest interest in the minds of the readers.

As soon as Mr. Monroe had taken his departure, Richard made Whittingham acquainted with his altered prospects; and they two together settled certain economical alterations in the establishment at the Place which were calculated to meet the limited means of its master,—who, it will be remembered, was now of age, and, consequently invested with the control of the little property that the villany of George Montague had left him.

Markham then proceeded, attended by Whittingham, to visit the various apartments of the old mansion from which he had been so long absent; and each recalled to his mind reminiscences that circumstances had made painful. In one apartment he had been wont to sit with his revered father of an evening, and survey the adjacent scenery and the mighty city from the windows. In another he had pursued his studies with the dearly loved brother whom he had lost: whichever way he turned, visions calculated to oppress his mind rose before him. He felt like a criminal who had disgraced an honourable name; and even the very pictures of his ancestors appeared to frown upon him from their antique and dust-covered frames.

But when he entered the room where the spirit of his father had taken its leave of this world, his emotions almost overpowered him. He wept aloud; and even the old butler did not now endeavour to comfort him. He had returned, branded with shame, to a house where he had received an existence that was full of hope and honour;—he had come back to a dwelling in the rooms of which were hung the portraits of many great and good men, who were his ancestors, but amongst whom his own likeness could never take a place, for fear that some visitor to that mansion should write the words *"Freed Convict"* upon the frame.

For though conscience reproached him not for guilt, the world would not believe his innocence.

That night he could not sleep; and he hailed the dawn of morning as the shipwrecked mariner upon the raft beholds the signal of assistance in the horizon. He rose, and hastened to the hill, where he seated himself upon the bench between the two trees. There he gave free vent to his tears; and he was relieved.

Suddenly his eye caught sight of letters carved upon the bark of his brother's tree. He looked closer; and, to his indescribable joy, he beheld these characters rudely but deeply cut on the tree:—

EUGENE.
Dec. 25, 1836.

"Thank God! my brother lives!" exclaimed Richard, clasping his hands together. "This is an intimation of his remembrance of me! But—oh! why did he desert me in my need? wherefore came he not to see me in my prison? Alas! years must yet elapse ere I clasp him to my heart! Let me not repine—let me not reproach him without hearing his justification! He has revisited the hill; and he chose a sacred day for what he no doubt deemed a sacred duty! It was on the anniversary of the nativity of the Saviour that he came back to the scenes of his youth! Oh, Eugene! I thank thee for this: it is an assurance that the appointment on the 10th of July, 1843, will be punctually kept!"

From the moment when his eyes rested upon the memorial of his lost brother thus carved upon the bark of the tree, Richard's mind became composed, and, indeed, comparatively happy. His habits, however, grew more and more secluded and reserved; and he seldom ventured into that mighty Babylon whose snares had proved so fatal to his happiness.

One day—it was about the middle of March, 1838—Richard was surprised by the arrival of a phaeton and pair at his abode; and he eagerly watched from the window to ascertain who could have thought of paying him a visit. In a few minutes he was delighted to see Mr. Armstrong, the political martyr with whom he had become acquainted in Newgate, alight from the vehicle.

Richard hastened to welcome him with the most unfeigned sincerity.

"You see I have found you out, my dear young friend," said Armstrong. "I miscalculated the date of your release from that abominable hole, and a few weeks ago was waiting for hours one day in Giltspur Street to welcome you to freedom. At length I did what I ought to have done at first—that is, inquired of the turnkeys whether you were to be released that day or not: and, behold—I found that the bird had flown."

"I should have written to you," said Richard, "for you were kind enough to give me your address; but really my mind has been so bent upon solitude——"

"From which solitude," interrupted Armstrong, smiling, "I am come to drag you away. Will you allow me to dispose of the next ten days for you?"

"How do you mean, my good friend?" inquired Markham.

"I mean that you shall pass that time with me at the house of a friend at Richmond. Solitude and seclusion will never wean you from the contemplation of your past sorrows."

"But you know that I cannot go into society again," said Richard.

"This is absurd, Markham. I will hear no apologies: you must and shall place yourself at my disposal," returned the old gentleman, in a kind and yet positive manner.

"But to whom do you wish to introduce me?" inquired Markham.

"To an Italian emigrant, who has only just arrived in this country, with his family, but the honour of whose friendship I have enjoyed for many, many years. I must tell you that I have travelled much; and that Italy has always been a country which has excited my warmest sympathy. It was at Montoni, the capital of the Grand Duchy of Castelcicala that I first met Count Alteroni; and his extremely liberal political opinions, which completely coincide with my own, were the foundation of a staunch friendship between us. Ten years ago he was compelled to fly from his native land; and he sought refuge in England. His only child—a beautiful girl, of the name of Isabella—thus obtained an English education and speaks the language with fluency. Two years ago, he was allowed to return to Castelcicala; but a few months back fresh political events in that state forced him once more to become an exile. He arrived in England a month ago, and has taken a small but commodious and picturesque residence at Richmond. His means are ample, but not vast; and he therefore lives in comparative seclusion—other reasons, moreover, inducing him to avoid the pomp and ostentation which noblemen of his rank usually maintain. Thus, in addressing him, you must drop the formality of *My Lord*; and remember also that his daughter chooses to be called simply, *Miss Isabella*, or the *Signora Isabella*."

"And how can I venture to present myself to this nobleman of high rank, and his wife and daughter, knowing that but a few weeks ago I was liberated from a gaol?" demanded Richard, somewhat bitterly.

"The count has not heard of your misfortune, and is not likely to do so," answered Armstrong. "He pressed me yesterday to pass a few days with him; and I happened to mention that I was about to visit a young friend—meaning yourself—in whom I felt a deep interest. I then gave him such an account of you that he expressed a desire to form your acquaintance. Thus, you perceive, that I am taking no unwarranted liberty in introducing you to his house. As for the danger which you incur of your history being known, that cannot be avoided; and it is a point which you may as well risk now as upon any future occasion. A man of the world must always be prepared for reverses of this kind, and I think that I am not mistaken in you, Markham, when I express my opinion that you would know how to vindicate your character and assert your innocence in a manner which would disarm resentment and conquer prejudice. At least, assume as cheerful an appearance as possible; and, believe me, you will find yourself right welcome at the dwelling of Count Alteroni."

Reassured by remarks of this nature, and warmed by the generous friendship displayed towards him by the Republican writer, Markham's countenance again wore a smile; and he felt more at ease than he had done ever since his misfortune. The presence of one who took an interest in his welfare—the prospect of enjoying pleasant society—and the idea of change of scene, combined to elevate his spirits and create new hopes in his breast. He began to think that he was not altogether the solitary, deserted, and sorrow-doomed being he had so lately considered himself.

It was about four o'clock in the afternoon that the phaeton, in which rode Markham and his friend the Republican, entered a spacious shrubbery, through which a wide avenue led to the front-door of a very beautiful country residence near Richmond. The dwelling was not large; but its external appearance seemed to bear ample testimony to its interior comfort.

A domestic, in a plain and unpretending livery, appeared at the door the moment the phaeton stopped; and the count himself met his visitors in the hall, to welcome their arrival.

The nobleman shook hands with Armstrong in the most cordial manner; and, when Richard was introduced to him, he received him with a courtesy and warm affability which showed how much any friend of Armstrong's was valued by the Italian exile.

The guests were ushered into the drawing-room, where the countess and her daughter, and two gentlemen who were also visitors, were seated.

But while we allow Richard time to get acquainted with the family of the Italian noble, we must give the reader a brief description of the new characters now introduced upon the stage.

Count Alteroni was about forty years of age. His hair and whiskers, originally of a deep black, were tinged prematurely with grey; but his moustachios were of the darkest jet. His complexion was of a clear olive. In figure he was tall, well formed, and muscular, though slight. His countenance was expressive of great dignity—one would almost say of conscious superiority; but this softness of aspect and the nobility of demeanour which distinguished him, failed to produce any unpleasant impression, inasmuch as every one who approached the count was charmed by the affability of his manners and the condescending kindness of his tone.

The countess was about two years younger than her husband, and was of a complexion and cast of countenance which denoted her northern origin. In fact, she was a German lady of high birth; but she spoke Italian, French, and English with as much facility as her own tongue.

But what of Isabella? To say that she was beautiful were to say nothing. Her aspect was resplendent with all those graces which innocence lavishly diffuses over the lineaments of loveliness. She was sixteen years old; and her dark black eyes were animated with all the fire of that impassioned age, when even the most rugged paths of life seem adorned and strewed with flowers. Her mouth was small; but the lips were full and pouting, and revealed, when she smiled, a set of beautifully white and even teeth. Her hair was dark as the raven's wing, and was invariably arranged in the most natural and simple manner. Her brows were exquisitely pencilled; and as her large black eyes were the mirror of her pure and guileless soul, when she glanced downwards, and those expressive orbs were concealed by their long black fringes, it seemed as if she were drawing a veil over her thoughts. Her complexion was that of a brunette; but the pure, red blood shone in her vermilion lips and her rose-tinted nostrils, and mantled her pure brow with a crimson hue when any passion was excited. Her sylph-like figure was modelled with the most perfect symmetry. Her waist was so delicate, and her hands and feet so small, that it was easy to perceive she came of patrician blood; and the swell of her bosom gave a proper roundness to her form, without expanding into proportions that might be termed voluptuous.

In manners, disposition, and accomplishments, Isabella was equally calculated to charm all her acquaintances. Having finished her education in England, she had united all the solid morality of English manners, with the sprightliness and vivacity of her native clime; and as she was without levity and frivolity, she was also entirely free from any insipid and ridiculous affectations. She was artlessness itself; her manners commanded universal respect; and her bearing alone repressed the impertinence of the libertine's gaze. With a disposition naturally lively, she was still attached to serious pursuits; and her mind was well stored with all useful information, and embellished with every feminine accomplishment.

The two gentlemen who were present in the drawing room when Armstrong and Richard arrived, were two young *beaux*—members of the aristocracy; and this was their only recommendation. It was not, however, on this account that they had obtained a footing in the count's abode; but because they were nearly related to a deceased English general who had taken part with the Italians against the French, during the career of Napoleon, and had been of essential service to the family to which the count belonged. With regard to their exterior, suffice it to say, that they were dressed in the extreme of fashion: one was very effeminate in appearance, having neither whiskers nor the slightest appearance of a beard; and the other was rather good-looking, sported an incipient moustachio, and wore an undress military uniform.

The effeminate young gentleman was introduced to Armstrong and Markham by the name of Sir Cherry Bounce, and the moustachioed one as the Honourable Smilax Dapper, a captain (at the age of twenty) in His Majesty's —th Regiment of Hussars.

During the hour which intervened between the arrival of the new guests and the announcement of dinner, a conversation ensued which will serve to throw some light upon the characters of those inmates of the hospitable abode, whom we have as yet only partially introduced to our readers.

"You reside in a very pleasant and healthy part of London, Mr. Markham," said the count; "I am well acquainted with the situation of your mansion and grounds, from the description which my friend Armstrong has given me. The house stands close by a hill, on the summit of which there are two trees."

"Ah, indeed!" ejaculated Sir Cherry Bounce. "The other day I wode by there for the firtht time in my life; and I remember the houth ith veway beautifully thithuate in the neighbourwood of the hill dethwibed by the count, and with two ath tweeth on the top."

"That is my house," said Richard. "But it is an antiquated, gloomy-looking pile; but ——"

"Oh! I beg your pardon, thir; it is the thweeteth little plaith I ever thaw. I never thaw it but that time, and wath thwuck with the weway wemarkable appearanth of the hill and the tweeth."

"Those trees were planted many years ago by my brother and myself," said Markham, a deep shade of melancholy suddenly overclouding his countenance; "and they yet remain there as the trysting-mark for a strange appointment."

"Indeed!" said the count; and as Richard saw that Isabella was also interested in his observations, he determined to gratify the sentiment of curiosity which he had excited.

"It is nearly seven years since that event took place. My elder brother disputed with my father, and determined to leave home and choose some career for himself, which he hoped might lead to fortune. He and I parted upon that hill, beneath those trees, with the understanding that in twelve years we were to meet again upon that same spot, and then compare our respective fortunes and worldly positions. On the 10th of July, 1843, that appointment is to be kept."

"And during the seven years which have already elapsed, have you received no tidings of your brother?" inquired Isabella.

"None direct," answered Markham. "All that I know is that on Christmas-day, 1836, he was alive; for he went to the hill, while I was absent from home, and carved his name upon the tree that he himself planted."

"Strike me stupid, if that isn't the most romantic thing I ever heard of!" exclaimed Captain Dapper, caressing his moustachio.

"You ought to wite a copy of vertheth upon the wemarkable inthident, in Mith Ithabella's *Album*," observed Sir Cherry Bounce.

"So I would, strike me! if I was half such a good poet as you, Cherry," returned the captain.

"You wote thum veway pwetty poetry the other day upon the *Great Thea Therpenth*, Smilax," said the effeminate baronet; "and I don't know why you thouldn't do the thame by the two ath tweeth."

"Yes; but—strike me ugly! Miss Isabella would not let me insert them in her *Album*," observed the captain; "and that was very unkind."

"Bella says that you undertook to finish a butterfly and spoilt it," exclaimed the count laughing.

"And now it theemth for all the world like an enormouth fwog," said Sir Cherry.

"Now, really, Bounce, that is too bad!" drawled the captain, playing with his moustachio. "I appeal to the Signora herself, whether the butterfly was so very—very bad?"

"Considering it to be your first attempt," said the young lady, "it was not so very much amiss; and I must say that I preferred the butterfly to the lines upon the Sea Serpent."

"Well, may I perish," cried the hussar, "if I think the lines were so bad. But we will refer them to Mr. Markham;—not that I dispute Miss Isabella's judgment: I'd rather have my moustachios singed than do that! But ——"

"The vertheth! the vertheth!" cried Sir Cherry.

"I am afraid that my talent does not justify such a reference to it," said Markham; "and I should rather imagine that Miss Isabella's decision will admit of no appeal."

"My dear thir, we will have your opinion. The vertheth were composed in a hurway; and they may not be quite tho exthellent and faultleth ath they might be."

"I only devoted half an hour to them, strike me if I did!"

"Let'th thee—how do they begin?" continued the effeminate young baronet of nineteen. "Oh! I wemember—the opening ith thimple but ekpwethive:

"Thwough the thea the therpenth wollth,
Moving ever 'thwixth the polth,
Fwightning herwinth, pwath, and tholth,
        In hith pwogweth rapid;—
Thwallowing up the mighty thipth,
By the thuction of hith lipth,
Onward still the monthtwer twipth,
        Like ——"

"Well, strike me!" interrupted the captain, "if ever I heard poetry spouted like that before. Please listen to *me*, Mr. Markham. This is the way the poem opens:—

"Through the sea the serpent rolls
Moving ever 'twixt the poles,
Fright'ning herrings, sprats, and soles,
        In his progress rapid;—
Swallowing up the mighty ships,
By the motion of his lips,
Onward still the monster trips,
        Like ——"

"No, that ithn't the way," cried Sir Cherry.

"Well, strike me, if I'll say another word more then," returned the captain of hussars, apparently very much inclined to cry.

"I am sure Miss Isabella was wrong not to have inserted these verses in her album," said Armstrong, with a smile of good-natured satire. "But I know that my young friend, Mr. Markham, has a more refined taste with regard to poetry than he chose just now to admit."

"Indeed!" said the beautiful Isabella; "I should be delighted to hear Mr. Markham's sentiments upon the subject of poetry; for I confess that I myself entertain very singular notions in that respect. It is difficult to afford a minute definition of what poetry is; for, like the unearthly visitants which the fears of superstition have occasionally summoned to the world, poetry fascinates the senses, but eludes the grasp of the beholder, and stands before him visible, powerful, and yet impalpable!"

"I concur with your views, Miss Isabella," said Markham, delighted to hear, amidst the frivolity of the conversation, remarks which exhibited sound sense and judgment. "It is impossible to set forth, in any array of words, the subtlety and peculiarity of poetry, which soars above the powers of language and defies the reach of description."

"Yes," said Isabella; "the painter cannot place the rainbow or the glittering dew-drop upon his canvass; the sculptor cannot invest his image with a soul; and it seems equally difficult to define poetry."

"We know of what we are speaking when we allude to it; but there are no definitions which give us views of it sufficiently comprehensive."

"Well, strike me! If I didn't think that every thing with rhymes, or in lines of a certain length, was poetry," observed the captain of hussars.

"My daughter can explain the mystery to you," said the countess, surveying Isabella with pride and maternal enthusiasm.

Isabella blushed deeply. She feared that she had intruded her remarks on the company, and dreaded to be considered vain or anxious for display. Markham immediately perceived the nature of her thoughts, and skilfully turned the conversation to the poetry of her native land, and thence to the leading characteristics and features of Italian life.

Dinner was at length announced, and Richard had the felicity of conducting the lovely daughter of the count to the dining-room, and of occupying a seat by her side during the banquet.

CHAPTER XXXIX.

THE DREAM.

THREE weeks passed away in a most agreeable manner, and Richard frequently expressed his gratitude to Armstrong for the pleasure he had procured him by this visit.

The more he saw of Count Alteroni's daughter, the more he was compelled to admire her personal and mental qualifications. But he felt somewhat annoyed when he discovered that Captain Smilax Dapper was paying his addresses to her: for he was interested in so charming a young lady, and would have regretted to see her throw herself away on such a coxcomb. He did not however find that Isabella gave the captain any encouragement: on the contrary he had frequently seen an erratic smile of contempt upon her lips when the military aspirant to her hand uttered an absurdity or indulged in an air of affectation.

By the constant and unvaried respect, and the absence of all familiarity on the part of Dapper towards the lovely Italian, Markham also argued that he had not as yet declared his sentiments, because had he been a favoured suitor, the truth would have betrayed itself in some trifling manner or another. Moreover, as Isabella conducted herself in only just the same friendly way towards Captain Dapper as she manifested towards her father's other guests, Richard saw no reason to believe that this passion was reciprocal.

Markham was thrown much in the signora's society during his visit at her father's house. He soon perceived that she preferred a conversation upon edifying and intellectual subjects to the frivolous chit-chat of Sir Cherry Bounce and Captain Dapper; and he frequently found himself carrying on a lengthened discourse upon music, poetry, painting and Italian literature, while the others were amusing themselves in the billiard or smoking-rooms. But Isabel was no blue-stocking; she was full of vivacity and life, and her conversation was sprightly and agreeable, even when turning upon those serious subjects.

In a few days after Richard's arrival, it was always he who turned the leaves of Isabella's music-book, "because Captain Dapper didn't know when;" she always took his arm when they walked round the shrubbery and garden after breakfast, "because Captain Dapper was constantly leaving her to play Sir Cherry some trick;" and somehow or another at meal-times, Richard and Isabella were invariably seated next to each other.

Such was the state of things at the expiration of three weeks, to which extent, although contrary to the original proposal of Armstrong, the visit had already extended; and Captain Smilax Dapper more than once fancied that he saw a rival in Richard Markham. At length he determined to communicate his suspicions to his friend Sir Cherry Bounce—a resolution which he carried into effect in the following manner.

"Cherry, my dear fellow," said he, one morning, taking the effeminate young baronet with him into the garden, up the gravel walks of which he walked in a very excited state; "Cherry, my dear fellow, I have something upon my mind, strike me! and I wish to unburden myself to you."

"Do you, Thmilackth? What can pothibly be the matter?" demanded the youth, turning very pale. "Ith it veway terwible? becauth if it ith, I had better call the count, and he will bwing hith blunderbuth."

"Strike me an idiot, Cherry, if you ain't a fool with your counts and blunderbusses. Now listen to me! I love Isabella, and have been doing the agreeable to her——"

"On my thoul I never could thee it!"

"I dare say not! strike me, if I didn't keep it so precious snug and quiet! However I love the girl; and curse me if I don't have her too—that's more! She shall be Mrs. Smilax Dapper, as sure as she's born, and I hope the mother of a whole regiment of little Smilaxes. And then Cherry, you shall stay a month or six weeks with us at a time, and fondle the little ones on your knees, you shall, and every thing will go on comfortable and smooth."

"Oh! veway thmooth!" cried Sir Cherry Bounce, making a slight grimace at the pleasing prospect of fondling the little Dappers upon his knees.

"And I suppose I am not presumptuous in aspiring to the hand of Isabella? My father is a peer—and my uncle is a peer—and I have three thousand a-year of my own, beside expectations. Strike me, if I'm a man to be sneezed at!"

"Who thinkth of thneething at you?"

"I don't know exactly. And then I am not such a very bad looking fellow either. You are not ugly, Cherry, you are not—that is, not particularly ugly, although you have got pink eyes and white lashes, and a pug nose;—but I'm more athletic, strike me!"

"I'm thure I don't dithpute what you thay."

"Well then—acknowledging all this," proceeded the captain, "how should I treat a fellow who endeavours to cut me out?"

"Thallenge him to fight with thword and pithtol," answered Sir Cherry. "But who ith he?"

"That upstart fellow, Markham, who was brought here by that odious, republican, seditious, disloyal scoundrel Armstrong, and who talks all day about poetry and music, and God knows what. However, I can't say I admire that plan of yours," continued the hussar; "swords and pistols, you know are so very dangerous; and—and—"

"And what elth?"

"Why, you're a fool, Cherry. I thought you would have hit upon some plan to enable me to secure the prize."

"Well then—thuppothing we carwy the girl off, to Wochethter for inthanth."

"Deuce take Rochester! my regiment is quartered at Chatham."

"Well—to Canterbuwy then?"

"Yes—that will do—strike me blind if it won't!" ejaculated the captain. "But if I could only get rid of this Markham somehow or another, I should prefer it. The fellow——"

Captain Smilax Dapper stopped short: for at that moment, as he and his companion were turning the angle of a summer-house, they ran against Richard Markham.

"It wathn't me—it wathn't me who thpoke!" ejaculated Sir Cherry Bounce; and having uttered these words, he very fairly took to his heels, leaving his friend the captain to settle matters as best he might.

"Who was taking a most unwarrantable liberty with my name?" demanded Richard, walking straight up to Captain Smilax Dapper.

"I certainly made an observation," answered the captain, turning mighty pale, "and I do not hesitate to say, sir——"

"What, sir?"

"Why, sir—that I feel, sir—that strike me, sir!"

"Yes, sir—I *shall* strike you," very coolly answered Markham; "and that will teach you not to speak lightly of one, who is a comparative stranger to you, on another occasion."

As he uttered these words, he seized the captain by the collar, and gave him a couple of boxes on the ears. Dapper endeavoured to pluck up a spirit and resist; but the ceremony was performed before he could release himself from his assailant's clutches; and he then returned to the house, muttering threats of vengeance.

That same afternoon Markham took leave of his new friends.

On his return home, he found his dwelling more lonely and cheerless than ever. He felt that he was isolated in the world; and his heart seemed to be pierced with a red-hot iron when the remembrance of all his wrongs returned to his imagination.

Oh! if we would but study the alphabet of fate, and remember that each leaf which falls, each flower that dies, is but the emblem of man's kindred doom, how much of the coldness, the selfishness, the viciousness of life would be swept away, and earth would be but a proof-sheet of heaven's fairer volume—with errors and imperfections, it is true, but still susceptible of correction and amendment, ere its pages be unfolded before the High Chancery of heaven!

Spring now asserted its tranquil reign once more; and May strewed the earth with flowers, and covered the trees with foliage.

One evening Richard sate in his library reading until a very late hour. Night came, and found him at his studies; and the morning dawned ere he thought of retiring to slumber.

He hastened to his bed-room, with the intention of seeking his couch; but he felt no inclination to sleep. He walked up to the window, drew aside the curtain, and gazed forth into the open air. The partial obscurity seemed to hang like a dusky veil against the windows: but by degrees the darkness yielded to the grey light of the dawn.

He glanced in the direction of the hill upon the summit of which stood the two trees; and he thought of his brother. He wondered, for the thousandth time, whether the appointment would be eventually kept, and why Eugene came not to revisit the home of his birth.

He was in the midst of cogitations like these, when his eyes were suddenly struck by an object which seemed to be moving between the trees upon the top of the hill. A superstitious fear seized upon Richard's mind. In the first moment of his surprise he imagined that the apparition of his brother had been led back to the trysting-place by those leafy banners that proclaimed the covenant of the heart. But he speedily divested himself of that momentary alarm, and smiled at his folly in believing it to be extraordinary that any one should visit the hill at that early hour.

The object was still there—it was a human being—and, as the morning gradually grew brighter, he was enabled to distinguish that it was a man.

But that was the hour at which labourers went to their daily toils:—still, why should one of those peasants linger upon the top of the hill, to reach which he must have gone out of his way?

Markham felt an indescribable curiosity to repair to the hill;—but he was ashamed to yield to the superstitious impulse under the influence of which he still more or less laboured;—and the sudden disappearance of the object of his anxiety from the hill confirmed him in his resolution to remain in his chamber. He accordingly closed the blind, and retired to his couch, where he shortly sank into a deep slumber.

Markham was now plunged into the aërial world of dreams. First he saw himself walking by the side of Isabella in a cool and shady grove, where the birds were singing cheerily in the trees; and it seemed to him that there reigned a certain understanding between himself and his fair companion which allowed him to indulge in the most delightful and tender hopes. He pressed her hand—she returned the token of affection and love. Suddenly this scene was rudely interrupted. From a deep recess in the grove appeared a wretch, covered with rags, dirty and revolting in appearance, with matted hair, parched and cracked lips, wild and ferocious eyes, and a demoniac expression of countenance. Isabella screamed: the wretch advanced, grasped Richard's hand, gave utterance to a horrible laugh, and claimed his friendship—the friendship of Newgate! It seemed to Richard that he made a desperate effort to withdraw his hand from that rude grasp;—and the attempt instantly awoke him.

He opened his eyes;—but the horror experienced in his dream was now prolonged, for a human countenance was bending over him!

It was not, however, the distorted, hideous, and fearful one which he had seen in his vision,—but a countenance handsome, though very pale, and whose features were instantly familiar to him.

"Eugene, my brother—Eugene, dearest Eugene!" ejaculated Richard; and he stretched out his arms to embrace him whom he thus adjured.

But scarcely had his eyes opened upon that countenance, when it was instantly withdrawn; and Richard remained for a few moments in his bed, deprived of all power of motion, and endeavouring to assure himself whether he was awake or in a vision.

A sudden impulse roused him from his lethargy;—he sprang from his couch, rushed towards the door, and called aloud for his brother.

The door was closed when he reached it; and no trace seemed to denote that any visitor had been in that chamber.

He threw on a dressing-gown, hurried down stairs, and found all the doors fast closed and locked as usual at that hour. He opened the front-door and looked forth,—but no one was to be seen. Bewildered and alarmed, he returned to his bed-chamber, and once more sought his couch. He again fell asleep, in the midst of numerous and conflicting conjectures relative to the incident which had just occurred; and when he awoke two hours afterwards, he was fain to persuade himself that it was all a dream.

He dressed himself, and walked towards the hill. On his arrival at the top, he instinctively cast his eyes upon the name and date carved in the bark of his brother's tree. But how great was his surprise—how ineffable his joy, when he beheld fresh traces of the same hand imprinted on that tree. Beneath the former memento—and still fresh and green, as if they had only been engraved a few hours—were the words—

EUGENE.
May 17th, 1838.

"My God!" exclaimed Richard, "it was then no dream!"

He threw himself upon the seat between the two trees and wept abundantly.

CHAPTER XL.

THE SPECULATION.—AN UNWELCOME MEETING.

Five months elapsed; and in the middle of October Richard received an invitation to pass a few days at the abode of Count Alteroni.

He contemplated change of scene with unfeigned delight, and lost no time in repairing to Richmond.

The count received him with the utmost cordiality: the countess expressed a regret that he should wait to be solicited to honour them with his company; and Isabella's countenance wore a smile and a blush as she extended her hand towards him.

"I was anxious to see you again," said the count, after dinner, before the ladies had retired, "if it were only to joke you about the fright into which you threw poor Bounce the last time you were here. Isabella apprehended a duel between you and Dapper; but we never could learn the origin of your dispute."

"Indeed, I scarcely dreaded such an event," said Isabella; "for however capable Mr. Markham may be of fighting, I felt perfectly well convinced that Captain Dapper would not be induced to commit such a breach of the peace."

"Our dispute was a mere trifle," said Markham; "and I am sorry it should have reached your ears."

"The Trojan war sprung from a trifle," cried the count: "but these trifles are frequently very interesting."

"The truth is," said Richard, "that I overheard Captain Dapper abuse me to his companion, heaven only knows why! Sir Cherry Bounce started away; and I was compelled to give the young officer a couple of boxes upon the ears to teach him courtesy in future."

Isabella laughed heartily at this anecdote; and Markham felt indescribably happy when he thus received a convincing proof that the lovely Italian was in no way interested in that aspirant to her hand.

"I shall not invite those gentlemen here very readily again," observed the count. "I thought that they would have helped to pass away the time agreeably; but one was such a fool, and the other such a fop, that I was really glad to get rid of them. However, I have now something else to occupy my attention."

"The count is going to speculate in an English Company," said the countess. "We foreigners, you know, Mr. Markham, are struck with the facility with which enormous fortunes are built up in your country."

"Italy has lost all her commerce," added the count, with a sigh: "poor Italy!"

"With all due deference to your experience," said Markham, "I should counsel you to be particularly careful how you allow yourself to be deluded by visionaries and adventurers."

"Oh! the gentleman who has proposed to me certain schemes for the realization of an immense fortune, is a man of probity and honour. The truth is, that the political condition of Italy may possibly compel me to remain an exile from my native land for the rest of my existence; and I am anxious to turn the means now within my reach to the best advantage for my daughter."

"You know, my dear father," said Isabella, her eyes filling with tears, "that I can be contented with a little—a very little."

"I think I have before informed you that I lost a considerable portion of my own property through the nefarious speculations of an adventurer," observed Richard; "and I must confess that I look with a suspicious eye upon all schemes which induce us to change realities for chances. You possess, count, all that you require to make you happy during your exile;—why should you sigh and languish after immense wealth?"

The signora bestowed a glance of gratitude upon Markham, who also rose considerably in the estimation of the countess. Indeed, both the ladies were very much averse to the count's ideas of speculating; and they were delighted to find in their visitor so able an advocate of their opinions.

"I consider," resumed the count, "that a man is bound to do the best he can to increase the property he has to leave his offspring; and as my own estate in Castelcicala is confiscated, and I have nothing to rely upon but a certain sum of ready-money, I am determined to vest the greater portion of it in an enterprise which will produce immense returns."

"And what may the nature of the undertaking be?" inquired Markham.

"A line of steam-packets between London and Montoni, the

capital of Castelcicala. Such an enterprise would absorb all the commerce now enjoyed by Leghorn and Civita Vecchia; and Montoni would be the great mercantile port of Italy."

"The scheme certainly seems plausible," observed Richard; "and, guided by your experience, may realize your expectations. I would rather see you embarking money in such an undertaking than in those desperate and outrageous ones which have nothing but their originality to recommend them."

The count smiled with triumph and satisfaction at having thus disarmed the opposition of his young friend to the projected speculation.

On the following day Count Alteroni repaired to London, and did not return home until dinner-time.

After dinner, when he and Richard were sitting alone together, sipping their claret, the count said in a semi-mysterious and confidential manner, "I have this morning broken the ice: indeed, I have made the first plunge. I have confided the necessary funds to Mr. Greenwood—that is the name of the gentleman with whom I am to cooperate—and he will immediately busy himself with the foundation of the enterprize. I shall not, however, mention this to the countess and Isabella for a few days; for in commercial matters ladies always entertain apprehensions which give one what you English call the 'blue-devils.'"

Richard made an observation. The evil—if evil it were—was done; and he did not choose to fill the count with apprehensions which might eventually prove to be unfounded. The conversation upon the subject accordingly dropped for the present; and the two gentlemen joined the ladies in the drawing-room.

Several weeks glided away; and Markham still remained at Richmond. His acquaintance with the count's family rapidly expanded into an intimacy which gave him unfeigned pleasure. The count treated him as a near relative—almost as a son; the countess was charmed with him because he could converse upon German literature and history;—and where the parents were so encouraging, how could the daughter be reserved? Isabella was naturally of a frank and confiding disposition; and she soon learned to consider Markham as a very intimate friend of the family. Whenever he hinted at the necessity of returning to his own home, he expressed his fears that he was intruding upon the hospitality of his kind hosts, Isabella always had some cause ready to delay his departure, as soon as her father and mother had concluded their own entreaties for him to prolong his visit. Markham had nothing to occupy his attention elsewhere; and he was thus easily induced to remain in a mansion where he received so much kindness, and where there was an attraction that daily disclosed new charms and revealed fresh spells.

It was in the middle of December that Markham was walking, on a fine frosty morning, with Isabella along the high road in the immediate vicinity of the count's dwelling, when he noticed a strange and repulsive looking individual following them at a short distance. At first he supposed that the man's way lay in the same direction which he and his fair companion were pursuing; he accordingly turned with Isabella into another path, and, to his misfortune and annoyance, found that he was still followed by the stranger whose dilapidated appearance, long black matted hair, week's beard, filthy person, and sinister expression of countenance, filled him with alarming suspicions.

He remembered his dream; and a shudder passed through his frame.

Determined to ascertain the motive of this man's perseverance in dogging him thus, he conducted Isabella by a short cut back to the house, and retraced his steps to encounter the person who was still following him.

The man advanced towards him with a dogged and determined air, and yet downcast eyes, which were buried beneath his projecting temples and shaggy brows.

"Holloa, my fine fellow!" he exclaimed, when he came within a few yards of Richard; "you don't mean to say that you have forgotten an old pal?"

"What, Anthony—is this you?" said Markham, turning deadly pale as he recognised one of his fellow-prisoners in Newgate.

It was the Resurrection Man.

"Yes—it is me—poor Tony Tidkins. But now permit me to ask you a question or two. What are you doing now? Who lives there? And what young girl was that you were walking about with?"

"And by what right do you dare put those insolent queries to me?" cried Markham, surveying the ruffian with mingled indignation and disgust.

"Oh! if you don't choose to answer my questions, I can precious soon ascertain all the truth for myself," coolly replied the Resurrection Man, who never once looked Markham in the face—then, having uttered these words, he advanced a few paces as if he were about to seek the count's dwelling.

"Wretch! what do you mean to do?" ejaculated Richard, hurrying after him and detaining him by the arm: "you do not know that that abode is sacred—that it is the residence of probity, innocence, and honour—that if you were to breathe a hint who and what you are, you would be spurned from the door?"

"Ah! I am accustomed to *that* in this Christian land—in this land of Bibles and Missionary Societies," said the Resurrection Man bitterly;

then, resuming his dogged surliness of tone, he added, "But at all events I can first ask for alms and a morsel of bread at that house, and thereupon state that the gentleman who was just now walking with the young lady belonging to the house was a companion of mine in Newgate—a communication which will tend to preserve the innocence, honour, probity, and all the rest of it, of that family."

With these words he again set off in the direction of the count's abode.

"Confusion!" exclaimed Markham: "this man will now effect my ruin!"

A second time did he stop the Resurrection Man as he advanced towards the residence of the Italians.

"Well—what now? Isn't a man at liberty to walk which way he chooses?"

"You cannot be so base as to betray me? you would not ruin my happiness for ever?" said Richard, in whose mind the particulars of his dream were now uppermost.

"And why should I have any regard for you, since you receive and treat me as if I was a dog?"

"I really did not mean——"

"Oh! bother to all apologies," cried the Resurrection Man, ferociously.

"My God! what do you want of me? what can I do for you?" exclaimed Richard, uncertain how to act, and his mind a prey to the most painful emotions; for he already fancied that he saw himself exposed—banished from the count's hospitable roof—separated from Isabella, without a chance of reconciliation—and reproached for having intruded himself upon the society of a virtuous and untainted family.

The mere anticipation of such an afflicting series of incidents was more than he could bear; and he was prepared to make any sacrifices to avert so terrible an occurrence.

"I may obtain from your fears what I should not have got from your generosity," exclaimed the Resurrection Man: "but it doesn't matter what motive produces it, so long as I get it."

"And what is it that you require?" asked Richard hastily. "But let us walk aside—they may see us from the windows."

"And what do I care if they do?" brutally demanded the Resurrection Man. "I suppose I shan't suffer in character by talking to a companion in former misfortunes?" he added, in a sarcastic tone.

There was something peculiarly revolting about that man;—his death-like countenance, jet-black whiskers, shaggy brows, averted glances, and horrible nick-name, all combined to render him a loathsome and disgusting object.

The contact of such a wretch was like plunging one's hand amidst the spawn of toads.

But the savage irony of this monster—oh! that was utterly intolerable. Richard writhed beneath it.

"Now I tell you what it is," said the Resurrection Man, who probably by this time saw that he had reduced the young man to a pliability suitable to his purposes; "if you will only be civil I'll accommodate you to the utmost of my power. Let us walk away from the house—we can then talk more at our ease."

Richard accompanied the miscreant a short distance; and then they again stopped,—but no longer within view of the count's residence.

"You can, doubtless, suppose what I want!" said the Resurrection Man, turning suddenly round upon Markham, and looking him full in the face for the first time.

"Money, I presume," replied Richard.

"Yes—money. I know that you were in expectation of a great fortune when you were in Newgate; and I suppose you have not run through it all yet."

"I was almost totally ruined, during my imprisonment, by the unfortunate speculations in which my guardian engaged," answered Markham mournfully.

"That's all my eye! Nevertheless, I won't be hard upon you: I know that you have got a splendid house and a grand estate close by——"

"A few acres of land, as heaven is my witness!"

"Well—you may try it on as much as you like; but I tell you plainly it won't do for me. Let us cut this matter devilish short, and come to some understanding at once. I am hard up—I don't know what to turn my hand to for a moment; and I can't get orders for the stiff 'uns as I used to do."

"All that I have told you about the loss of my property is quite true," said Markham; "and I have now but little more than a bare two hundred a-year to live upon."

"Well, I will be generous and let you off easy," said the Resurrection Man. "You shall give me for the present——"

"For the present!" repeated Markham, all the terror of his mind again betraying itself; "if I make any arrangement with you at all, it would be upon the express condition that you would never molest me more."

"Be it so," said the Resurrection Man, whom the promise cost nothing, and who knew that there was nothing to bind him to its implicit performance; "give me five hundred pounds, and I will never seek you out again."

"Five hundred pounds!" exclaimed Richard: "I cannot command the money!"

"Not a mag less will I take," said the extortioner with a determined air and voice.

"I really cannot comply with the proposal—I have not the money—I do not know where to get it. Why do you persecute me in this way? what harm have I ever done to you? why should you seek to ruin me, and to annihilate all my hopes of again establishing myself in an honourable position in society? Tell me—by what right, by what law, do you now endeavour to extort—vilely, infamously extort—this money from me?"

No pen could describe—no painter depict the singular expression of countenance which the Resurrection Man wore as these words fell upon his ears. He knew not whether to burst out into a fit of laughter, or to utter a volley of imprecations against his former companion in Newgate; and so, not to be wrong by doing one and omitting the other, he did both. His ironical and ferocious laugh fell horribly upon the ears of Markham, who was at the same time assailed by such a string of oaths and blasphemies, that he trembled.

"You want to know by what law and right I demand money of you," cried the wretch, when he had indulged in this out-pouring of laughter and imprecations to his heart's content: "well—I will tell you. My law is that practised by all the world—*the oppression of the weak by the strong*; and my right is also that of universal practice—*the right of him who takes what will not dare to be refused*. Now, then, you understand me; and if not, hear my resolution."

"Speak," said Richard, now thoroughly cooled and disarmed; "and let me know the worst at once."

"You have confirmed my suspicion that you are courting the young girl I saw you walking with: you have confirmed that suspicion by your manner and your words. Now, I require five hundred pounds; and if you are anxious that your fair one should remain in ignorance of your Old Bailey adventures, you had better comply with my terms."

"I positively declare that I have not the money," said Richard.

"Make it."

"But how?"

"Borrow it of the young lady's father or mother, or uncle, or aunt."

"Never—impossible!"

"You say that you have a few acres of land left. I believe you have more; but let's take your own statement. Upon those few acres you can easily borrow the money I require."

"And diminish my miserable income still more?"

"Yes—or no, without further wrangling? You must be well aware that this sacrifice is necessary if the girl is worth having."

"In the name of heaven, allude not to—to—to—Miss —— to the young lady with whom you saw me ere now;—allude not to her in this disgraceful manner!" cried Markham; for when the lips of that horrible man framed a sentiment which bore reference to Isabella, it seemed to Richard as if a loathsome serpent was pouring its slimy venom on a sweet and blooming flower.

"Will you give me the money?" demanded the Resurrection Man.

"I will give you two hundred pounds—I have no more—I can get no more—I will not raise any more upon my property."

"Can't be done," returned the ruffian. "I will have the five hundred, or nothing."

"It will take some days to procure the money," said Markham, yielding gradually.

"Never mind. Give me what you have about you for my present purposes, and name the day and place for me to receive the rest."

Markham took his purse from his pocket, and examined its contents. There were seventeen sovereigns at that moment at his command. He retained two, and handed fifteen to the Resurrection Man, who pocketed them with savage glee.

"Now this looks like business," said he, "and an earnest that you will do the thing that's right. Where and when for the remainder?"

"In a fortnight I will meet you at any place you may name in London," answered Markham.

"Well, make it a fortnight. Do you know the *Dark House*, in Brick Lane, Bethnal Green?"

"What is it?" asked Richard, shuddering at the name.

"A public-house. Any one will tell you where it is. This day fortnight I shall expect to find you there at eight o'clock in the evening. If I don't happen to be punctual, you can wait for me; and if I don't come that night, I shall the next. Remember how much depends upon your fulfilment of the contract."

"I shall not fail," answered Richard, with a sinking of the heart which none can understand who have not been placed in a similar position. "And you, on your part, will adhere to your side of the agreement?"

"Mute as a mouse," said the Resurrection Man; "and should I afterwards meet you by accident, I shall not know you. Farewell."

With these words the Resurrection Man turned away, and pursued his course towards London.

Markham followed him with his eyes until he turned an angle of the road and was no longer to be seen.

Then only did Richard breathe freely.

CHAPTER XLI.

MR. GREENWOOD.

About six o'clock in the evening—ten days after the incident which concluded the preceding chapter,—a handsome cabriolet drove up to the door of a house in Spring Gardens.

Down jumped the tiger—an urchin not much bigger than a walking stick—and away went the knocker, rat-tat-tat, for upwards of fifteen seconds. A servant in livery opened the door, and an elegantly-dressed gentleman, about six or seven and twenty years of age, alighted from the vehicle.

This gentleman rushed up stairs to his study, drew forth his cheque-book, wrote an order upon his banker for a thousand pounds, enclosed it in an envelope, and immediately despatched the letter to

Lord Tremordyn by one of his numerous domestics. He had that afternoon lost the money to his lordship in some sporting-bet; and, "as it was a debt of honour," he could not possibly think of sitting down to dinner, or even pulling off his boots (which, being fashionable, pinched him excessively) without settling it.

As soon as he had done this, another servant entered the room, and said, "If you please, sir, Mrs. Mangles has called, and is waiting below to see you. She has been here these three hours, and wishes very much to say a few words to you, sir."

"What! that bothering upholsterer's wife!" ejaculated the gentleman, in a tone of indignation which would have induced a stranger to believe that he was the most persecuted man in the world. "Why—her husband's account hasn't been owing quite a year yet; and here she is boring from morning to night."

"Please, sir, she says that her husband is locked up in a spunging-house."

"Serve him right!"

"But he is a hard-working sober man——"

"He shouldn't run into debt."

"And he has five children."

"It is really disgusting! these lower orders literally swarm with children!"

"And if you would only pay a quarter of the money, he would get out to-night."

"I won't pay a sixpence till January."

"Then he will be totally ruined, sir, his wife says."

"Well—he must be ruined, then. Go and turn her out, and send up Lafleur."

And the fashionable gentleman, who would not owe a *debt of honour* for half an hour, thought no more of the sum which was due to a tradesman, which had been already owing for nearly a year, and which he could have immediately settled without the slightest inconvenience to himself.

For this man was rich; and, having got his money in the City (God knows how), had now come to the West End to make the most of it.

"Lafleur," said the fashionable gentleman to the French valet, "you must dismiss that fellow John to-morrow morning."

"Yes, sir."

"He actually had the impertinence to bring me a message from a dun, while I was in a hurry to get dressed for dinner."

"Indeed, sir—you don't say so sir!" ejaculated the valet, who had as much horror of a dun as an overseer has of a pauper. "Yes, sir—I will dismiss him to-morrow, sir—and without a character too."

"Do, Lafleur. And now to dress. Are the company come?"

"Mr. Chichester and Sir Rupert Harborough are in the drawing-room, sir."

"Oh!" said Mr. Greenwood—for such was the gentleman's name—"very well!"

Having carelessly perused three or four letters which he found upon his table, he repaired to his dressing-room, where he washed his hands in a silver basin, while the poor upholsterer's wife returned to her husband in the lock-up house, to say that their last hope had failed, and that nothing but a debtor's gaol awaited them. Accordingly, while the poor man was being carried off to Whitecross Street Prison, Mr. Greenwood repaired to his elegantly furnished drawing-room to welcome the guests whom he had invited that day to dinner.

"My dear Sir Rupert," said Mr. Greenwood, "I am delighted to see you. Chichester, how are you? Where have you both been for the last six months? Scarcely had I the pleasure of forming your acquaintance, when you were off like shots: and I have never seen nor heard of you till this morning."

"Upon my honour, I hardly know what we have been doing—or indeed, what we have *not* been doing," ejaculated the baronet. "We have been in Paris and Brussels, and enjoyed all the pleasures of the Continent."

"And we found our way into the good graces of the Parisian ladies, and the purses of their husbands," observed Chichester, with a complacent smile.

"Ah! ah!" said Mr. Greenwood, laughing. "Trust you both for allowing yourselves to starve in a land of plenty."

"And so here we are, come back to England quite fresh and ready for new sport," said Chichester. "You see that it is useful to go abroad for a season every now and then. Immediately after I passed through the Insolvents' Court, two years ago, I went to Paris for six months, and came home again with a new reputation, as it were."

"By the bye, Sir Rupert," exclaimed Mr. Greenwood, "I lost a cool thousand to your father-in-law this afternoon at Tattersall's."

"What! does the old lord do things in so spirited a way as that?" cried the baronet.

"Yes—now and then. I believe you and he are not on very good terms? When I asked him after you a month or two ago, he appeared to evade the conversation."

"The fact is," said the baronet, "old Lord and Lady Tremordyn pretend that I treat their daughter with neglect—just because I cannot and will not be tied to my wife's apron strings. I did not want to marry her; but Lady Tremordyn intrigued to catch me; and the old lord came down handsome—and so the match was made up."

The baronet did not think of informing his friend that he had stipulated for twenty thousand pounds to pay his debts, ere he would do justice to the young and beautiful creature whom he had seduced, and whose pathetic appeal to her mother has been already laid before the reader in the chapter which treats of the *Black Chamber* of the General Post Office.

"Do you know what has become of your old flame Diana Arlington?" inquired Mr. Greenwood of the baronet, after a pause.

"And was she not *your* old flame too?" said Sir Rupert, laughing. "I believe that when you were plain Mr. George Montague, instead of Mr. Montague Greenwood——"

"Oh! I have assumed the name of Greenwood, remember, because a relation of that name has left me a considerable fortune."

"Well—that is a very good story to tell the world, but not friends, my dear fellow," said the baronet, coolly. "But we were talking of the Enchantress. I presume she is still under the protection of the Earl of Warrington?"

"So I understand," replied Greenwood.

"Well—I must say," continued the baronet, "I always liked Diana; and I dare say we should have been together up to the present moment, if it had not been for that infernal affair of Markham's."

"Ah! Richard Markham!" ejaculated Mr. Greenwood hastily. "I have heard of him—but never seen him."

"I and Mr. Chichester were compelled to sacrifice him to save ourselves," observed Harborough.

"Yes—yes—it was a pity—a great pity," cried Greenwood, poking the fire violently.

"I wonder what has become of that same Markham?" said Chichester.

"I understand that he lost the greater portion of his property by some unfortunate speculation or another, but the nature of which I have never learnt," replied Greenwood.

"And what about this Steam-Packet Company of which you were speaking this morning?" inquired Sir Rupert Harborough.

"The fact is, I have got a certain Italian count in tow, and I intend to make him useful. He is an emigrant from the Grand Duchy of Castelcicala, having been concerned in some treasonable proceedings with Prince Alberto, who is the Grand Duke's nephew, and who has also been compelled to fly to some other country. Be it as it may, this Count Alteroni and I became acquainted; and, in the course of conversation, he observed that a fortune might be made by the establishment of a line of steam-packets between London and Montoni, the capital of Castelcicala. He added that he should be very willing to embark his own capital in such an enterprise. '*How extraordinary!*' I immediately exclaimed: '*I had myself entertained the very same idea!*' The count was enchanted; and he has already advanced a considerable sum."

At this moment dinner was announced; and the three gentlemen proceeded to the apartment in which it was served up. The repast consisted of all the luxuries *in* season, and many *out* of season: the choicest wines were produced; and justice was done to each and all, while wit and humour flowed as freely, and sparkled as brightly as the juice of the grape itself. The baronet was more affable than ever;—Mr. Chichester related several amusing anecdotes of midnight sprees, policemen, knockers, station-houses, and magistrates;—and Mr. Greenwood explained his plans relative to the steam-packets.

"I should very much like to have you both in the Direction," said Mr. Montague Greenwood, when he had terminated his elucidations: "but I have learnt that this Richard Markham, of whom we have been talking, is acquainted with the count; and if he saw your names connected with the affair, he would instantly blow upon it. I should then have the count upon me for the fifteen thousand pounds he has already lodged in my hands."

"Let us write an anonymous letter to the count, and inform him that Markham has been convicted at the Old Bailey," suggested Chichester.

"No—no," ejaculated Greenwood emphatically: "you have injured that young man enough already."

"And what do you care about him?" cried Chichester. "You said just now that you had never seen him."

"I did—and I repeat the assertion," answered Greenwood; then, in a very serious tone, he added, "and I will beg you both to remember, gentlemen, that if you wish to co-operate with me in any of those speculations which I know so well how to manage, you will leave Mr. Richard Markham alone; for I have certain private reasons for being rather anxious to do him a service than an injury."

"Well, I will not in any way interfere with your good intentions," said the baronet.

"Nor I," observed Chichester.

"And as it is impossible for you to enter my Steam-Packet Company," added Mr. Greenwood, "I will let you into another good thing which I have in view, and in which a certain banker is concerned. To tell you the real truth, this banker has been insolvent for some time; and if his father had not advanced him about fifty thousand pounds three years ago, he would most undoubtedly have gone to smash. As it was, the Lords of the Treasury got hold of his real position, by some means or another—he never could divine how; and they refused a tender which he sent in for a certain money contract—I don't know exactly what. *Now* his position is more desperate than ever, and he and I are going to do an admirable stroke of business. I will let you both into it."

We need scarcely remind the reader that the banker now alluded to was the writer of one of the letters perused by the Examiner's clerks in the *Black Chamber*.

The conversation between the three gentlemen was proceeding very comfortably, when a servant entered the room, and, handing his master a card upon a silver tray, said, "This gentleman, sir, requests to be allowed to see you, if perfectly convenient."

"The Count Alteroni!" exclaimed Mr. Greenwood. "What the devil could have brought him to London at this time of night? John—show him into the study—there is a good fire for him; and if that won't warm his heart, perhaps a bottle of Burgundy will."

The servant left the room; and in a few moments Mr. Greenwood hastened to join the count in the elegant apartment which was denominated "the study."

"My dear sir, I have to apologise for calling thus late," said the count; "but the truth is that I had a little business which brought me up to town to-day, and in this neighbourhood too; and I thought——"

"Pray offer no excuses, my dear count," interrupted Mr. Greenwood. "The truth is, I wished to see you very particularly—upon a matter not altogether connected with our enterprise——"

"Indeed," said the count; "you interest me. Pray explain yourself."

"In the first place, allow me to ask whether the ladies are yet acquainted with the undertaking in which you have embarked?"

"Yes—I acquainted them with the fact this very morning."

"And do they approve of it?"

"They approve of every thing of which I think well, and disapprove of all that I abhor."

"And do they know that I am the projector and principal in the enterprise?" demanded Greenwood.

"They are acquainted with every thing," answered the count. "Indeed, they have formed of you the same exalted opinion which I myself entertain. It would be strange if they had not. We met you at the house of Lord Tremordyn; and that nobleman spoke in the highest possible terms of you. But what connection exists between all those questions which you have put to me, and the matter concerning which you desired to see me?"

"I am not sure that I ought to explain myself at present, nor to *you* in the first instance," was the answer, delivered with some embarrassment of manner: "at all events I should wish you to know a little more of me, and to have some reason to thank me for the little service which I shall have the means of rendering you, in enabling you to treble your capital."

The count appeared mystified; and Mr. Greenwood continued:—

"I had the pleasure of seeing the amiable countess and her lovely daughter many times last summer at the house of Lord Tremordyn; and no one could know the Signora Isabella without being forcibly struck by her personal and mental qualifications. To render myself agreeable to Miss Isabella would be the height of my earthly happiness. You will pardon my presumption; but——"

Mr. Greenwood ceased, and looked at the count to ascertain the effect which his words had produced.

The honourable and open-hearted Italian was not averse to this proposition. He considered his own affairs and prospects in Castelcicala to be so desperate that he was bound to make the best provision he could for his daughter in a free, enlightened, and hospitable nation. Mr. Greenwood was good looking, moving in the best society, well spoken of by a peer of the realm (who, by the way, merely judged of Greenwood's character by the punctuality with which he paid his gambling debts), and evidently immensely rich:—his manners were elegant, and his taste refined;—and, in a word, he might be called a most eligible suitor for the hand of the count's daughter. Not being over-well skilled in affairs of the heart himself, the count had not noticed the attachment which decidedly existed between Isabella and Richard Markham; and it never for a moment struck him that his daughter might manifest the most powerful repugnance to Mr. Greenwood.

"I have no doubt," said he, after a long pause, "that Isabella will feel highly flattered by your good opinion of her. Indeed, I shall inform her without delay of the manner in which you have expressed yourself."

"My dear sir," interrupted Greenwood hastily, "in the name of heaven tell the signora nothing at all about our present conversation. Her delicacy would be offended. Rather give me an opportunity of making myself better known to your daughter."

"I understand you. Come and pass a week or two with us at Richmond. We have not a soul staying with us at the present moment, Mr. Markham, who was our last guest, having returned to his own abode about ten days ago."

"This is a busy time with me," began Mr. Greenwood; "and I could scarcely spare a week with justice to yourself and my own interests——"

"True," interrupted the count. "I will bring the ladies up to town at the beginning of the new year. We have a very pressing invitation from the Tremordyns, and I will avail myself of it."

Mr. Greenwood expressed his gratitude to the count for the favour which his suit thus received; and in a few minutes the Italian noble took his leave, more than ever convinced of the honour, wealth, and business-like habits of Mr. Greenwood.

"There," said the man of the world, as he once more seated himself at the table in the dining-room, where he had left the baronet and Chichester, "I have not passed the last hour unprofitably. I have not only demanded the hand of the count's lovely daughter, but have also persuaded the count to pay a few weeks' visit to your father-in-law, Lord Tremordyn," he added, addressing Sir Rupert.

"And what good do you propose by the latter arrangement?" demanded the baronet.

"I shall get the count's family at a house which Richard Markham stands no chance of visiting: for even if the count asked him to call upon him there, Markham would refuse, because he is sure to have read or heard that you, Sir Rupert, have married Lady Cecilia Huntingfield, and he would be afraid of meeting *you* at Lord Tremordyn's residence."

"And why should you be so anxious to separate the count from Markham, since Chichester and I are not to be in the Steam-packet concern?"

"Because I myself could not, for certain reasons, visit the count's family if I stood the chance of meeting that same Richard Markham."

Mr. Greenwood then immediately changed the conversation, and pushed the bottle briskly about.

CHAPTER XLII.

"THE DARK HOUSE."

MARKHAM did not forget his appointment with the Resurrection Man. Having obtained the necessary sum from his solicitor, he determined to sacrifice it in propitiating a miscreant who possessed the power of wounding him in a tender and almost vital point. Accordingly we find him, on the evening agreed upon, threading his way on foot amidst the maze of narrow streets and crooked alleys which lie in the immediate neighbourhood of Spitalfields Church.

There is not probably in all London—not even in Saint Giles's nor the Mint—so great an amount of squalid misery and fearful crime huddled together, as in the joint districts of Spitalfields and Bethnal Green. Between Shoreditch Church and Wentworth Street the most intense pangs of poverty, the most profligate morals, and the most odious crimes, rage with the fury of a pestilence.

Entire streets that are nought but sinks of misery and vice,—dark courts, fœtid with puddles of black slimy water,—alleys, blocked up with heaps of filth, and nauseating with unwholesome odours, constitute, with but little variety, the vast district of which we are speaking.

The Eastern Counties' Railway intersects Spitalfields and Bethnal Green. The traveller upon this line may catch, from the windows of the carriage in which he journeys, a hasty, but alas! too comprehensive glance of the wretchedness and squalor of that portion of London. He may actually obtain a view of the interior and domestic misery peculiar to the neighbourhood;—he may penetrate, with his eyes, into the secrets of those abodes of sorrow, vice, and destitution. In summer time the poor always have their windows open, and thus the hideous poverty of their rooms can be readily descried from the summit of the arches on which the railroad is constructed.

And in those rooms may be seen women half naked,—some employed in washing the few rags which they possess,—others ironing the linen of a more wealthy neighbour,—a few preparing the sorry meal,—and numbers scolding, swearing, and quarrelling. At many of the windows, men out of work, with matted hair, black beards, and dressed only in filthy shirts and ragged trousers,—lounge all the day long, smoking. From not a few of the open casements hang tattered garments to dry in the sun. Around the doors children, unwashed, uncombed, shoeless, dirty, and uncared for—throng in numbers,—a rising generation of thieves and vagabonds.

In the districts of Spitalfields and Bethnal Green the police are but little particular with regard to street-stalls. These portable shops are therefore great in number and in nuisance. Fish, fresh and fried,—oysters, sweet-stuff, vegetables, fruit, cheap publications, sop-in-the-pan, shrimps and periwinkles, hair-combs, baked potatoes, liver and lights, curds and whey, sheep's heads, haddocks and red-herrings, are the principal comestibles which find vendors and purchasers in the public street. The public-houses and the pawnbrokers also drive an excellent trade in that huge section of London.

In a former chapter we have described the region of Saffron Hill: all the streets and courts of that locality are safe and secure when compared with many in Bethnal Green and Spitalfields. There are lanes and alleys between Shoreditch and Church Street, and in the immediate neighbourhood of the Railway east of Brick Lane, through which a well-dressed person would not wander with a gold chain round his neck, at night, were he prudent.

Leading from the neighbourhood of Church Street[1] up into the Hackney Road, is a sinuous thoroughfare, composed of Tyssen Street,[2] Turk Street,[3] Virginia Street, and the Bird-cage Walk;[4] and in the vicinity of these narrow and perilous ways are the Wellington Road (bordered by a ditch of black mud) and several vile streets, inhabited by the very lowest of the low, the most filthy of the squalid, and the most profligate of the immoral.

We defy any city upon the face of the earth to produce a district equal in vice, dirt, penury, and fear-inspiring dens, to these which we are now describing.

The *Dark House* was a tavern of the lowest description in Brick Lane, a little north of the spot where the railway now intersects the street. The parlour of the *Dark House* was dirty and repulsive in all respects; the gas-lights formed two enormous black patches upon the ceiling; the tables were occupied by ill-looking men, whose principal articles of consumption were tobacco and malt liquor, and the atmosphere was filled with a dense volume of smoke. Markham was ashamed to be seen in such a place and in such society; but he consoled himself with the idea that neither he nor his business was known to those present; and as very little notice was taken of him as he proceeded to seat himself in the most retired and obscure corner, he speedily divested himself of the momentary embarrassment which had seized upon him.

Having satisfied himself by a glance that the Resurrection Man was not there, Richard ordered a glass of spirits and water, and resolved to await with patience the arrival of the extortioner.

By degrees he fell into a train of reflections in which he had never been involved before. He was about to purchase the silence of a villain who had menaced him with exposure to a family whose good opinion he valued. We have said elsewhere that he was a young man of the strictest honour, and that he was ever animated with the most

1 Church Street: now the eastern part of Bethnal Green Road, before its junction with Brick Lane.

2 Tyssen Street: now the northern part of Brick Lane, after its junction with Bethnal Green Road.

3 Turk Street: formerly, a continuation of Tyssen Street.

4 Now Columbia Road, leading up to the City Farm.

scrupulous integrity of purpose. He could no longer conceal from himself the fact that he entertained a sincere and deep attachment for the Signora Isabella, and he flattered himself that he was not disagreeable to her in return. His transient passion for Mrs. Arlington had faded away with reflection, and he now comprehended the immense difference between an evanescent flame of that nature,—a flame kindled only by animal beauty, and unsustained by moral considerations,—and the pure, chaste, and sacred affection he experienced towards the charming Isabella. From the moment of his release from confinement, he had never inquired after Diana—much less sought after her; he knew not where she was, nor what had become of her, and his heart was totally independent of any inclination in her favour. He now asked himself whether he was pursuing an honourable part in concealing the antecedent adventures of his life from her whose pure and holy love he was so anxious to retain, whose confidence he would not lose for worlds, and whose peace of mind he would not for a moment sacrifice to his own passion or interest?

He had not satisfactorily answered the question which he had thus put to himself, when he was aroused from his reverie by the sound of a voice at the further end of the room, which appeared familiar to him.

Glancing in that direction, he immediately recognised the well-known form and features of Mr. Talbot, the vulgar companion of Sir Rupert Harborough and Mr. Chichester.

But how had the mighty fallen! The charitable gentleman now seemed to require the aid of charity himself. His hat, which was originally a gossamer at four-and-nine, was now so fully ventilated about the crown, that it would have fetched nothing at a Jews' auction, even though George Robins himself had put it up for sale.[1] His coat was out at the elbows, his trousers out at the knees, and his shoes out at the toes; he was out of *cash* and out of *spirits*; and as he had none of the former, he trusted to the kindness of the frequenters of the *Dark House* parlour to supply him with some of the latter, diluted with hot water, and rendered more agreeable by means of sugar. Indeed, at the moment when his voice fell upon Markham's ear, he was just about to apply his lips to a tumbler of gin-punch which a butcher had ordered for his behoof.

1 George Robins, celebrated auctioneer and huckster, one of the early advocates of 'salesmanship' as an art in itself.

"Well, Mr. Pocock," (this was Talbot's real name), said the butcher, "how does the world use you now?"

"Very bad, indeed, Mr. Griskin," was the reply. "For the last three year, come Janivary, I havn't known, when I got up in the morning, where the devil I should sleep at night;—and that is God's Almighty's truth."

"I'm sorry to hear your affairs don't mend," said the butcher. "For my part, I'm getting on blooming. I was a bankrupt only seven weeks ago."

"A strange manner of being successful in business," thought Markham.

"But all my goods was seized by the landlord," added the butcher, in a triumphant tone of voice, "and so they was saved from the messenger of the Court, when he come down to take possession."

"Ah! I suppose your bankruptcy has put you all right again," said Pocock. "Nothing like a bankruptcy now-a-days—it makes a man's fortune."

"Yes—and no going to quod neither. I made a lot of friends of mine creditors, and so I got my certificate the wery same day as I passed my second examination; and now I'm as right as a trivet. But what ails you, though, old feller, that you can't contrive to get on?"

"The fact is," said Pocock, sipping his gin-and-water, "I was led into bad company about three or four years ago, and I don't care before who I say it, or who knows what infernal scrapes I was partly the means of getting a nice young fellow into."

"I suppose you fell in with flash company?" observed the butcher.

"I did indeed! I went out of my element—out of my proper sphere, as I may say; and when a man does that without the means of keeping in it, he's d——d and done for at once. I fell in with a baronet and a swell cove of the name of Chichester, or Winchester, and, who after all turned out to be the son of old Chichester the pawnbroker down the street here. They made a perfect tool of me. I was fed and pampered, and lived on the fat of the land; and then, when the scheme fell through, I was trundled off like a hoop of which a charity school-boy is tired. I fell into distress; and though I've met this here baronet and that there Chichester riding in their cabs, with tigers behind and horses before, they never so much as said, '*Talbot*,' or '*Pocock, my tulip, here is a quid for you*.'"

"Willanous," ejaculated the butcher. "But of what natur' was the scheme you talk of?"

"Why, I'll tell you that too. I shall certainly proclaim my own crimes; but I don't hesitate to say that I was led away by those two thieves. My name, as you well know, is Bill Pocock, and they made me take the name of Talbot. I was brought up as an engraver, and did pretty well until some four years ago, when I lost my wife and got drinking, and then every thing went wrong. One day I fell in with this Chichester, and he lent me some money. He then began telling me how he knew the way of making an immense fortune with very little trouble, and no risk or expense to myself."

"So far, so good," said the butcher.

"I was hard up—I was rendered desperate by the death of my wife, and, to tell the truth, I wanted to live an idle life. I had got attached to public-house parlours, and couldn't sit down to work with the graver. So I bit at Chichester's proposal, and he introduced me to the baronet."

"Another glass, Pocock," interrupted the butcher, winking to the other inmates of the parlour, who were now all listening with the greatest attention to this narrative—but none with more avidity nor with deeper interest than Richard Markham, who sate unperceived by Pocock in his obscure corner.

"The scheme was certainly a very ingenious one," continued Talbot, "and deserved success. It was nothing more nor less than making bank-notes. I was used to engraving plates of that kind; and so I undertook the job. I don't care if any one here present goes and informs against me; perhaps I should be better off in a prison than out of one. But what goes to my heart—and what I can never forget, and shall reproach myself for as long as I live, was the getting of a nice young fellow into a scrape, and making him stand Moses for the punishment, as you do, Griskin, for the grog."

"And who was this young chap?" demanded the butcher.

"One Markham. You must recollect his case. He was tried just about this time three years ago, and sentenced to two years' imprisonment."

"Can't say I recollect."

"Well—this Markham was as innocent about the notes, as the child unborn!" added Pocock emphatically.

"I raly don't see that you need take on so," remarked the butcher, "for after all, you'd better let another feller get into trouble than be locked up in lavender yourself."

"It was an unfortunate event," said Pocock, shaking his head solemnly, "and nothing has prospered with me since. But what vexes me as much as all the rest, is to think of the conduct of those two chaps, Chichester and the baronet. They pretended not to know who I was, when I one day stopped them in Regent Street, and wanted to borrow a few pounds of them. The baronet turns round, and says to his pal, '*Who the devil is that fellow?*' and Chichester puts up his eyeglass, stares at me through it for five minutes, and says, '*My good man, we never give alms to people unless they have certificates of good character to show.*'"

"Perhaps you wasn't over swell in your toggery?" said the butcher.

"Why—no: I don't think I was so well dressed then as I am now."

"The devil you wasn't! Well then, it ain't no wonder if so be they slighted you; for one wouldn't think as how you was titivated off at present to go to the Queen's le-*vee*."

"Come, no joking," exclaimed Pocock. "I have told you my story, and if you think it is a good one, and are inclined to do me a service, you can just order in a chop or a steak, for I think I could manage to eat a bit."

"With all my heart," said the butcher, who was a good-natured man in his way, and who, having realised a considerable sum by his late bankruptcy, was disposed to be generous: "you shall have as good a supper, and as much lush as you can stow away. Here, Dick," he cried, addressing himself to the waiter, "run round to my shop, and ask the old 'ooman for a nice steak; and then get it fried for me along with some inguns. And, Dick, let's have some taturs."

The waiter disappeared to execute these orders, and the conversation was then resumed upon the former topic.

Pocock entered into all the details with which the reader is already acquainted; and Markham, who had made up his mind how to act, was determined to allow him to disclose spontaneously as much as he thought fit, before he should reveal himself. He sate in his obscure corner, shading his face with his hands, and affecting to be deeply interested in the columns of the *Morning Advertiser*, which lay the wrong way upwards before him.

The moment Pocock had begun to speak upon matters which so deeply interested him, Richard had become an attentive listener, and, as that individual proceeded, and he found within his reach a means of establishing his innocence, his brain seemed to be excited with joy—even to delirium. His pulse throbbed violently—his heart palpitated audibly. Much as he had loathed that den when he first entered it, he would now have fallen down, and kissed its dirty, saw-dust covered floor.

Hour after hour had passed away; the clock had struck eleven, and still the Resurrection Man did not make his appearance.

The butcher and Pocock were discussing their supper, and Markham was just thinking of accosting the latter, when the door was suddenly opened with great violence, and two persons muffled up in pea-coats, carrying enormous sticks, and smoking cigars, precipitated themselves into the parlour of the *Dark House*.

"D—n me, what a lark!" ejaculated one, flinging himself upon a seat, and laughing heartily: "but we're quite safe in here. I know this place; and the policeman lost sight of us, before we reached the door."

"Upon my honour, I cannot say that I admire frolics of this kind," observed the other; "it is really ridiculous to break lamps up at this end of the town. But, my God! what a neighbourhood you have brought me into! I couldn't have suspected that there was such a district in London."

"I told you that you would do good if you would come with me to my father," said the first speaker. "The old boy was quite delighted at the idea of a baronet condescending to sup with him; and you saw how he shelled out the blunt to me when he had imbibed his third glass of the punch."

The latter portion of this conversation was uttered in whispers, and the two gentlemen again laughed heartily—doubtless because they had succeeded in the business which had that evening brought them to the eastern regions of London.

In the midst of that second burst of hilarity, Mr. Pocock rose from his seat and advanced slowly towards the two new-comers.

"Well, gentlemen," he exclaimed, "this *is* an honour which you do us poor folks in Spitalfields. Come—you needn't stare so confounded hard at me. How are you, Chichester? Been to see the old gentleman at the sign of the Lombardy Arms—three balls, eh? Two chances to one that the things put up the spout will never come down again, eh?"

The butcher burst out into a roar of laughter, which was echoed by several other inmates of the room.

"Who the devil are you?" demanded Chichester, recovering his presence of mind sooner than the baronet; for both were astounded at this unexpected and very embarrassing encounter.

"Upon my honour, the man must be mistaken," murmured Sir Rupert Harborough.

"So far from being mistaken," cried Pocock, "you were the very fellows I was talking about just now. Gentlemen," he added, turning towards the people seated at the various tables, "these are the two swells that led me into the scrape I told you about just now. And now they pretend not to know me!"

"What does the fellow mean?" said Chichester, in an impudent tone: "do you know, Harborough?"

"'Pon my honour, not I!"

"Then I will tell you who I am," ejaculated the engraver. "I am the man who forged the plates from which the bank-notes were struck, that got poor Richard Markham condemned to two years' imprisonment in the Compter; and you know as well as possible that *he* suffered for *our* crime."

Chichester and the baronet were stupefied by the sudden and unexpected exposure.

They knew not what to say or do; and their countenances betrayed their guilt.

"Yes, gentlemen," resumed Pocock, growing excited, "these are the men whom some extraordinary chance—some providential or devilish design—has brought here this evening to confirm all I have told you."

"Devil take this impudence!" cried Chichester, now once more recovering his wonted self-possession, and determining to brave the accusation out: "my name isn't Chichester—you're quite mistaken, my good fellow—I can assure you that you are."

"Liar!" cried the engraver, furiously: "I should know you both amongst a million!"

"And so should I," calmly observed Markham, now advancing

from his obscure corner, and appearing in the presence of those who so little expected to see him there.

A tremendous sensation now prevailed in the room, and those who were spectators anxiously awaited the result of this strange drama.

"Yes—there are indeed the villains to whom I am indebted for all the miseries I have endured," continued Markham. "But say not that a lucky accident brought *us* all here together this night,—think not that a mere chance occasioned the present meeting of the deceivers and the deceived:—no; it was the will of the Almighty, to establish the innocence of an injured man!"

A solemn silence succeeded these words, which were delivered in a tone which produced an impression of awe upon all who heard them. Even the depraved and hardened men that were present on this occasion, in the parlour of the *Dark House*, gazed with respect upon the young man who dared to speak of the Almighty in that den of dissipation.

Markham continued after a short pause:—

"Were it not that I should be involving in ruin a man who has spontaneously come forward to proclaim his own guilt, to declare his repentance, and to assert my innocence—without hope of reward from me, and even without knowing that God had sent me hither to overhear every word he uttered—were it not that I should be inflicting upon *him* the deepest injury, I would this moment assign you to the custody of the police, as the instigators of the diabolical fraud in which Talbot was your tool, and I your scape-goat. But though I shall take no steps to punish you, heaven will not allow you to triumph in your career of turpitude!"

"Well spoken," said Mr. Chichester, perceiving that he was in no danger, and therefore assuming an air of bravado.

"Upon my honour, I can't comprehend all this," muttered the baronet. "Let us go, my dear fellow—I do not admire your Spitalfields' riff-raff."

"Yes—go—depart!" cried Markham; "or else I shall not be able to restrain my indignation."

"They shan't go without a wolloping, however," said the butcher, very coolly taking off his apron, and turning up the sleeves of his blue stuff jacket. "I'll take one—who'll take the other?"

"I will," cried a barber's boy, laying aside his pipe, taking a long pull at the porter, and then advancing towards the two adventurers with clenched fists.

"Stop—stop, I implore you!" ejaculated Markham. "I ask not for such vengeance as this—no violence, I beseech you."

"Let's give it 'em in true John Bull style, and knock all that cursed dandy nonsense out of 'em," cried the butcher; and before Richard could interfere farther, he felled the baronet with one blow of his tremendous fist.

The barber forthwith pitched into the fashionable Mr. Chichester, who struggled in vain to defend himself. The baronet rose; and the butcher instantly took his head "into chancery,"[1] and pummelled him to his heart's content.

As soon as Chichester and Sir Rupert were so severely thrashed that they were covered all over with bruises, and could scarcely stand upon their legs, the butcher and the barber kicked them into the open air, amidst the shouts and acclamations of all the inmates of the *Dark House* parlour.

When order was once more restored, Markham addressed himself to the two champions who had avenged him in their own peculiar style, and not only thanked them for their well-meant though mistaken kindness, but also gave them munificent proofs of his bounty.

"And now," said Richard, turning towards Pocock, "are you willing to sign a declaration of my innocence?"

"On condition that the paper shall never be used against me," answered the engraver.

"Could I not this moment give you into custody to the police, upon your own confession of having forged the plate from which the bank-notes were printed?"

"Certainly: I was wrong to make any conditions. You are a man of honour."

Markham proceeded to draw up the declaration referred to; and Pocock signed it with a firm and steady hand.

This ceremony being completed, Richard placed Bank of England notes for fifty pounds in the engraver's hand.

"Accept this," he said, "as a token of my gratitude and a proof of my forgiveness; and, believe me, I regret that my means do not allow me to be more liberal. Endeavour to enter an honest path; and should you ever require a friend, do not hesitate to apply to me."

Pocock wept tears of gratitude and repentance—the only acknowledgment he could offer for this sudden and most welcome aid. His emotions choked his powers of utterance.

Markham hurried from the room, and took his departure from the establishment which possessed such an ominous name, but which had proved the scene of a great benefit to him that evening.

He was hurrying up Brick Lane in a northerly direction—that is to say, towards Church Street, when he was suddenly stopped by an

1 A prize-fighter's expression: he took Sir Rupert in an arm-lock around his neck, and hit his head repeatedly.

individual whom he encountered in his way, and who carried a large life-preserver in his hand.

"I suppose you were tired of waiting for me," said the Resurrection Man—for it was he.

"I certainly imagined you would not come to-night," answered Richard.

"Well, better late than never. It is fortunate that we met: it will save you another journey to-morrow night, you know."

"Yes—I am glad that we have met, as my time is now too valuable to waste."

"In that case, we can either return to the *Dark House*, which is open all night; or you can give me the money in the street. You don't require any receipt, I suppose?"

"No: neither will you require to give me any."

"So I thought: honour among thieves, eh? Excuse the compliment. But, in the first place, have you got the tin?"

"I had the whole amount just now, in my pocket, when I first went to the *Dark House*."

"Then I suppose it is all there still?"

"Not all. I have parted with fifty pounds out of it."

"The deuce you have! And how came you to do that?" demanded the Resurrection Man gruffly. "I gave you fair warning that I would take nothing less than the entire sum."

"I obtained, in a most extraordinary manner, a proof of my innocence; and I think I purchased it cheaply at that rate. I would have given all I possessed in the world," added Markham, "to procure it."

"The devil!" cried the Resurrection Man, who grew uneasy at the cold and indifferent way in which Markham spoke. "Well, I suppose I must take what you have got left. You can easily leave the remainder for me at the *Dark House*."

"Not a shilling will you now obtain from me," ejaculated Richard firmly; "and I have waited to tell you so. I have made up my mind to reveal the entire truth, without reserve, to those from whom I was before foolishly and dishonourably anxious to conceal it."

"This gammon won't do for me," cried the Resurrection Man. "You want to stall me off; but I'm too wide awake. Give me the tin, or I'll start off to-morrow morning to Richmond, and see the count upon—*you* know what subject. Before I left that neighbourhood the other day, I made all the necessary inquiries about the people of the house which the young lady went into."

"You may save yourself that trouble also," said Markham; "for I shall reveal all that you would unfold. But, in a word, you may do what you choose."

"Come now," ejaculated the Resurrection Man, considerably crest-fallen; "assist an old companion in difficulties—lend me a hundred or so."

"No," returned Richard in a resolute manner: "had you asked me in the first instance to assist you, I would have done so willingly;—but you have endeavoured to extort a considerable sum of money from me—much more than I could spare; and I should not now be justified in yielding to the prayers of a man who has found that his base menaces have failed."

"You do not think I would have done what I said?" cried the Resurrection Man.

"I believe you to be capable of any villany. But we have already conversed too long. I was anxious to show you how a virtuous resolution would enable me to triumph over your base designs;—and I have now nothing more to say to you. Our ways lie in different directions, both at present and in future. Farewell."

With these words Markham continued his way up Brick Lane; but the Resurrection Man was again by his side in a moment.

"You refuse to assist me?" he muttered in a hoarse and savage tone.

"I do. Molest me no further."

"You refuse to assist me?" repeated the villain, grinding his teeth with rage: "then you may mind the consequences! I will very soon show you that you will bitterly—bitterly repent your determination. By God, I will be revenged!"

"I shall know how to be upon my guard," said Markham.

He then walked rapidly on, without looking behind him.

The Resurrection Man stood still for a moment, considering how to act: then, apparently struck by a sudden idea, he hastened stealthily after Richard Markham.

CHAPTER XLIII.

THE MUMMY.

THE district of Spitalfields and Bethnal Green was totally unknown to Markham. Indeed, his visit upon the present occasion was the first he had ever paid to that densely populated and miserable region.

It was now midnight; and the streets were nearly deserted. The lamps, few and far between, only made darkness visible, instead of throwing a useful light upon the intricate maze of narrow thoroughfares.

Markham's object was to reach Shoreditch as soon as possible; for he knew that opposite the church there was a cab-stand where he might procure a vehicle to take him home. Emerging from Brick Lane, he crossed Church Street, and struck into that labyrinth of dirty and dangerous lanes in the vicinity of Bird-cage Walk, which we alluded to at the commencement of the preceding chapter.

He soon perceived that he had mistaken his way; and at length found himself floundering about in a long narrow street, unpaved, and here and there almost blocked up with heaps of putrescent filth.[1] There was not a lamp in this perilous thoroughfare: no moon on high irradiated his path;—black night enveloped every thing above and below in total darkness.

Once or twice he thought he heard footsteps behind him; and then he stopped, hoping to be overtaken by some one of whom he might inquire his way. But either his ears deceived him, or else the person whose steps he heard stopped when he did.

There was not a light in any of the houses on either side; and not a sound of revelry or sorrow escaped from the ill-closed casements.

Richard was bewildered; and—to speak truly—he began to be alarmed. He remembered to have read of the mysterious

---

1 Following Markham's route north from the *Dark House*, we have reached roughly the vicinity of Wellington Road, which is still there, though mightily changed. In the previous chapter, Reynolds describes Wellington Road as '(bordered by a ditch of black mud) and several vile streets, inhabited by the very lowest of the low, the most filthy of the squalid, and the most profligate of the immoral.' From this, it is not a bad guess that the Resurrection Man's house is in Wellington Road.

disappearance of persons in the east end of the metropolis, and also of certain fell deeds of crime which had been lately brought to light in the very district where he was now wandering;[1]—and he could not help wishing that he was in some more secure and less gloomy region.

He was groping his way along, feeling with his hands against the houses to guide him,—now knee-deep in some filthy puddle, now stumbling over some heap of slimy dirt, now floundering up to his ankles in the mud,—when a heavy and crushing blow fell upon his hat from behind.

He staggered and fell against the door of a house. Almost at the same instant that door was thrust open, and two powerful arms hurled the prostrate young man down three or four steps into a passage. The person who thus ferociously attacked him leapt after him, closing the door violently behind him.

All this occupied but a couple of seconds; and though Markham was not completely stunned by the blow, he was too much stupefied by the suddenness and violence of the assault to cry out. To this circumstance he was probably indebted for his life; for the villain who had struck him no doubt conceived the blow to have been fatal; and therefore, instead of renewing the attack, he strode over Markham and entered a room into which the passage opened.

Richard's first idea was to rise and attempt an escape by the front door; but before he had time to consider it even for a moment, the murderous ruffian struck a light in the room, which, as well as a part of the passage, was immediately illuminated by a powerful glare.

Markham had been thrown upon the damp tiles with which the passage was paved, in such a manner that his head was close by the door of the room. The man who had assailed him lighted a piece of candle in a bright tin shade hanging against the wall; and the reflection produced by the metal caused the strong glare that fell so suddenly upon Richard's eyes.

Markham was about to start from his prostrate position when the interior of that room was thus abruptly revealed to him; but for a few moments the spectacle which met his sight paralyzed every limb, and

---

1 Probably a reference to the murder of 'the Italian Boy,' in 1831, by Bishop, Williams and May. For a fascinating account of this, see Sarah Wise, *The Italian Boy* (London: Jonathan Cape, 2004). Nova Scotia Gardens, where the murder took place, was only a few yards from Wellington Road.

rendered him breathless, speechless, and motionless with horror.

Stretched upon a shutter, which three chairs supported, was a corpse—naked, and of that blueish or livid colour which denotes the beginning of decomposition!

Near this loathsome object was a large tub full of water; and to that part of the ceiling immediately above it were affixed two large hooks, to each of which hung thick cords.

In one corner of the room were long flexible iron rods, spades, pickaxes, wooden levers, coils of thick rope, trowels, saws, hammers, huge chisels, skeleton-keys, &c.

But how great was Richard's astonishment when, glancing from the objects just described towards the ruffian who had hurled him into that den of horrors, his eyes were struck by the sombre and revolting countenance of the Resurrection Man.

He closed his eyes for a moment, as if he could thus banish both thought and danger.

"Now, then, Mummy," ejaculated the Resurrection Man; "come and hold this light while I rifle the pockets of a new subject."

Scarcely had he uttered these words, when a low knock was heard at the front door of the house.

"D—n the thing!" cried the Resurrection Man, aloud: "here are these fellows come for the stiff 'un."

These words struck fresh dismay into the soul of Richard Markham; for it instantly occurred to him that any friends of the Resurrection Man, who were thus craving admittance, were more likely to aid than to frustrate that villain's designs upon the life and property of a fellow-creature.

"Here, Mummy," cried the Resurrection Man, once more; and, hastily returning into the passage, he reiterated his summons at the bottom of a staircase at the further end; "here, Mummy, why the hell don't you come down?"

"I'm a comin', I'm a comin'," answered a cracked female voice from the top of the staircase; and in another moment an old, blear-eyed, shrivelled hag made her appearance.

She was so thin, her eyes were so sunken, her skin was so much like dirty parchment, and her entire appearance was so horrible and repulsive, that it was impossible to conceive a more appropriate and expressive nickname than the one which had been conferred upon her.

"Now come, Mummy," said the ruffian, in a hasty whisper; "help me to drag this fellow into the back room; there's good pickings here, and the chaps have come for the stiff 'un."

Another knock was heard at the door.

Markham, well aware that resistance was at present vain, exercised sufficient control over himself to remain motionless, with his eyes nearly closed, while the Resurrection Man and the Mummy dragged him hastily into the back room.

The Mummy turned the key in the lock, while the Resurrection Man hurried to the street door, and admitted two men into the front apartment.

One was Tom the Cracksman; the other was a rogue of the same stamp, and was known amongst his confederates in crime by the name of the Buffer. It was this man's boast that he never robbed any one without stripping him to the very skin; and as a person in a state of nudity is said to be "in buff," the origin of his pseudonym is easily comprehended.

"Well," said the Cracksman, sulkily, "you ain't at all partikler how you keep people at your door—you ain't. For twopence, I'd have sported it[1] with my foot."

"Why, the old Mummy was fast asleep," returned the Resurrection Man; "and I was up stairs trying to awake her. But I didn't expect you till to-morrow night."

"No; and we shouldn't have come either," said the Cracksman, "if there hadn't been thirty quids to earn to-night."

"The devil there is!" cried the Resurrection Man. "Then you ain't come for the stiff 'un to-night?"

"No sich a thing; the Sawbones[2] that it's for don't expect it till to-morrow night; so its no use taking it. But there's t'other Sawbones, which lives down by the Middlesex Hospital, will meet us at half-past one at the back of Shoreditch church——"

"What, to-night!" ejaculated the Resurrection Man.

"To-night—in half an hour—and with all the tools," returned the Cracksman.

"Work for the inside of the church," he says, added the Buffer. "Thirty quids isn't to be sneezed at; that's ten a-piece. I'm blowed if

1 Burst it open. [Reynolds's note.]

2 Surgeon. [Reynolds's note.]

I don't like this here resurrection business better than cracking cribs. What do you say, Tom?"

"Anythink by vay of a change; partikler as when we want a stiff 'un by a certain day, and don't know in which churchyard to dive for one, we hit upon the plan of catching 'em alive in the street."

"It was my idea, though," exclaimed the Buffer. "Don't you remember when we wanted a stiff 'un for the wery same Sawbones which we've got to meet presently, we waited for near two hours at this house-door, and at last we caught hold of a feller that was walking so comfortable along, looking up at the moon?"

"And then I thought of holding him with his head downwards in a tub of water," added the Cracksman, "till he was drownded. That way don't tell no tales;—no wound on the skin—no pison in the stomach; and there ain't too much water inside neither, cos the poor devils don't swaller with their heads downwards."

"Ah! it was a good idea," said the Buffer; "and now we've reduced it to a reg'lar system. Tub of water all ready on the floor—hooks and cords to hold the chaps' feet up to the ceiling; and then, my eye! there they hangs, head downwards, jest for all the world like the carcasses in the butchers' shops, if they hadn't got their clothes on."

"And them we precious soon takes off. But I say, old feller," said the Cracksman, turning to the Resurrection Man, who had remained silent during the colloquy between his two companions; "what the devil are you thinking of?"

"I was thinking," was the answer, "that the Sawbones that you've agreed to meet to-night wants some particular body."

"He does," said the Cracksman; "and the one he wants is buried in a vault."

"Well and good," exclaimed the Resurrection Man; "he is too good a customer to disappoint. We must be off at once."

The Resurrection Man did not for a moment doubt that Richard Markham had been killed by the blow which he had inflicted upon him with his life-preserver; and he therefore did not hesitate to undertake the business just proposed by his two confederates. He knew that, whatever Richard's pockets might contain, he could rely upon the *honesty* of the Mummy, who—horrible to relate—was the miscreant's own mother. Having therefore given a few instructions, in a whisper, to the old woman, he prepared to accompany the Cracksman and the Buffer.

The three worthies provided themselves with some of the long flexible rods and other implements before noticed; and the Resurrection Man took from a cupboard two boxes, each of about six inches square, and which he gave to his companions to carry. He also concealed the tin shade which held the candle, about his person; and, these preliminaries being settled, the three men left the house.

Let us now return to Richard Markham.

The moment he was deposited in the back room and the door had closed behind the occupants of that fearful den, he started up, a prey to the most indescribable feelings of alarm and horror.

What a lurking hole of enormity—what a haunt of infamy—what a scene of desperate crime—was this in which he now found himself! A feculent smell of the decomposing corpse in the next room reached his nostrils, and produced a nauseating sensation in his stomach. And that corpse—was it the remains of one who had died a natural death, or who had been most foully murdered? He dared not answer the question which he had thus put to himself; he feared lest the solution of that mystery might prove ominous in respect to his own fate.

Oh! for the means of escape! He must fly—he must fly from that horrible sink of crime—from that human slaughter-house! But how? the door was locked—and the window was closed with a shutter. If he made the slightest noise, the ruffians in the next room would rush in and assassinate him!

But, hark! those men were talking, and he could overhear all they said. Could it be possible? The two who had just come, were going to take the third away with them upon his own revolting business! Hope returned to the bosom of the poor young man: he felt that he might yet be saved!

But—oh, horror! on what topic had the conversation turned? Those men were rejoicing in their own infernal inventions to render murder unsuspected. The object of the tub of water, and the hooks and cords upon the ceiling, were now explained. The unsuspecting individual who passed the door of that accursed dwelling by night was set upon by the murderers, dragged into the house, gagged, and suspended by his feet to these hooks, while his head hung downwards in the water. And thus he delivered up his last breath; and the wretches kept him there until decomposition commenced, that the corpse might not appear too fresh to the surgeon to whom it was to be sold!

Merciful heavens! could such things be? could atrocities of so appalling a nature be perpetrated in a great city, protected by thousands of a well-paid police? Could the voice of murder—murder effected with so much safety, cry up to heaven for vengeance through the atmosphere of London?

At length the three men went out, as before described; and Markham felt an immense weight suddenly lifted from off his mind.

Before the Resurrection Man set out upon his excursion with the Cracksman and the Buffer, he had whispered these words to the Mummy: "While I'm gone, you can clean out the swell's pockets in the back room. He has got about four or five hundred pounds about him—so mind and take care. When you've searched his pockets, strip him, and look at his skull. I'm afraid I've fractured it, for my life-preserver came down precious heavy upon him; and he never spoke a word. If there's the wound, I must bury him to-morrow in the cellar: if not, wash him clean, and I know where to dispose of him."

It was in obedience to these instructions that the Mummy took a candle in her hand, and proceeded to the back-room, as soon as her son and his two companions had left the house.

The horrible old woman was not afraid of the dead: her husband had been a resurrection man, and her only son followed the same business,—she was therefore too familiar with the sight of death in all its most fearful as well as its most interesting shapes to be alarmed at it. The revolting spectacle of a corpse putrid with decomposition produced no more impression upon her than the pale and beautiful remains of any lovely girl whom death had called early to the tomb, and whose form was snatched from its silent couch beneath the sod ere the finger of decay had begun its ravages. That hideous old woman considered corpses an article of commerce, and handled her wares as a trader does his merchandise. She cared no more for the sickly and fetid odour which they sent forth, than the tanner does for the smell of the tan-yard, or the scourer for the fumes of his bleaching-liquid.

The Mummy entered the back-room, holding a candle in her hand.

Markham started forward, and caught her by the wrist.

She uttered a sort of growl of savage disappointment, but gave no sign of alarm.

"Vile wretch!" exclaimed Richard; "God has at length sent me to discover and expose your crimes!"

"Don't do me any harm—don't hurt me," said the old woman—"and I will do any thing you want of me."

"Answer me," cried Markham: "that corpse in the other room——"

"Murdered by my son," replied the hag.

"And the clothes? where are the clothes? They may contain some papers which may throw a light upon the name and residence of your victim."

"Follow me—I will show you."

The old woman turned and walked slowly out of the room. Markham went after her; for he thought that if he could discover who the unfortunate person was that had met his death in that accursed dwelling, he might be enabled to relieve his family at least from the horrors of suspense, although he should be the bearer of fatal news indeed.

The Mummy opened the door of a cupboard formed beneath the staircase, and holding forward the light, pointed to some clothes which hung upon a nail inside.

"There—take them yourself if you want them," said the old woman; "I won't touch them."

With these words she drew back, but still held the candle in such a way as to throw the light into the closet.

Markham stepped forward to reach the clothes, and, in extending his hand to take them from the peg, he advanced one of his feet upon the floor of the closet.

A trap-door instantly gave way beneath his foot: he lost his balance, and fell precipitately into a subterranean excavation.

The trap-door, which moved with a spring, closed by itself above his head, and he heard the triumphant cackling laugh of the old hag, as she fastened it with a large iron bolt.

The Mummy then went and seated herself by the corpse in the front room; and, while she rocked backwards and forwards in her chair, she crooned the following song:—

THE BODY-SNATCHER'S SONG.

In the churchyard the body is laid,
There they inter the beautiful maid:
  "Earth to earth" is the solemn sound!
Over the sod where their daughter sleeps,
The father prays, and the mother weeps:
  "Ashes to ashes" echoes around!

Come with the axe, and come with the spade,
Come where the beautiful virgin's laid:
  Earth from earth must we take back now!
The sod is damp, and the grave is cold:
Lay the white corpse on the dark black mould.
  That the pale moonbeam may kiss its brow!

Throw back the earth, and heap up the clay;
This cold white corpse we will bear away,
  Now that the moonlight waxes dim;
For the student doth his knife prepare
To hack all over this form so fair,
  And sever the virgin limb from limb!

At morn the mother will come to pray
Over the grave where her child she lay,
  And freshest flowers thereon will spread;
And on that spot will she kneel and weep,
Nor dream that we have disturbed the sleep
  Of her who lay in that narrow bed.

We must leave the Mummy singing her horrible staves, and accompany the body-snatchers in their proceedings at Shoreditch Church.

CHAPTER XLIV.

THE BODY-SNATCHERS.

The Resurrection Man, the Cracksman, and the Buffer hastened rapidly along the narrow lanes and filthy alleys leading towards Shoreditch Church. They threaded their way in silence, through the jet-black darkness of the night, and without once hesitating as to the particular turnings which they were to follow. Those men were as familiar with that neighbourhood as a person can be with the rooms and passages in his own house.

At length the body-snatchers reached the low wall surmounted with a high railing which encloses Shoreditch churchyard. They were now at the back part of that burial ground, in a narrow and deserted street, whose dark and lonely appearance tended to aid their designs upon an edifice situated in one of the most populous districts in all London.

For some minutes before their arrival an individual, enveloped in a long cloak, was walking up and down beneath the shadow of the wall.

This was the surgeon, whose thirst after science had called into action the energies of the body-snatchers that night.

The Cracksman advanced first, and ascertained that the surgeon had already arrived, and that the coast was otherwise clear.

He then whistled in a low and peculiar manner; and his two confederates came up.

"You have got all your tools?" said the surgeon in a hasty whisper.

"Every one that we require," answered the Resurrection Man.

"For opening a vault inside the church, mind?" added the surgeon, interrogatively.

"You show us the vault, sir, and we'll soon have out the body," said the Resurrection Man.

"All right," whispered the surgeon; "and my own carriage will be in this street at three precisely. We shall have plenty of time—there's no one stirring till five, and it's dark till seven."

The surgeon and the body-snatchers then scaled the railing, and in a few moments stood in the churchyard.

The Resurrection Man addressed himself to his two confederates and the surgeon, and said, "Do you lie snug under the wall here while I go forward and see how we must manage the door." With these words he crept stealthily along, amidst the tomb-stones, towards the church.

The surgeon and the Cracksman seated themselves upon a grave close to the wall; and the Buffer threw himself flat upon his stomach, with his ear towards the ground. He remained in this position for some minutes, and then uttered a species of low growl as if he were answering some signal which caught his ears alone.

"The skeleton-keys won't open the side-door, the Resurrection Man says," whispered the Buffer, raising his head towards the surgeon and the Cracksman.

He then laid his ear close to the ground once more, and resumed his listening posture.

In a few minutes he again replied to a signal; and this time his answer was conveyed by means of a short sharp whistle.

"It appears there is a bolt; and it will take a quarter of an hour to saw through the padlock that holds it," observed the Buffer in a whisper.

Nearly twenty minutes elapsed after this announcement. The

surgeon's teeth chattered with the intense cold; and he could not altogether subdue certain feelings of horror at the idea of the business which had brought him thither. The almost mute correspondence which those two men were enabled to carry on together—the methodical precision with which they performed their avocations—and the coolness they exhibited in undertaking a sacrilegious task, made a powerful impression upon his mind. He shuddered from head to foot:—his feelings of aversion were the same as he would have experienced had a loathsome reptile crawled over his naked flesh.

"It's all right now!" suddenly exclaimed the Buffer, rising from the ground. "Come along."

The surgeon and the Cracksman followed the Buffer to the southern side of the church where there was a flight of steps leading up to a side-door in a species of lobby, or lodge. This door was open; and the Resurrection Man was standing inside the lodge.

As soon as they had all entered the sacred edifice, the door was carefully closed once more.

We have before said that the night was cold: but the interior of the church was of a chill so intense, that an icy feeling appeared to penetrate to the very back-bone. The wind murmured down the aisle; and every footstep echoed, like a hollow sound in the distance, throughout the spacious pile.

"Now, sir," said the Resurrection Man to the surgeon, "it is for you to tell us whereabouts we are to begin."

The surgeon groped his way towards the communion-table, and at the northern side of the railings which surrounded it he stopped short.

"I must now be standing," he said, "upon the very stone which you are to remove. You can, however, soon ascertain; for the funeral only took place yesterday morning, and the mortar must be quite soft."

The Resurrection Man stooped down, felt with his hand for the joints of the pavement in that particular spot, and thrust his knife between them.

"Yes," he said, after a few minutes' silence: "this stone has only been put down a day or two. But do you wish, sir, that all traces of our work should disappear?"

"Certainly! I would not for the world that the family of the deceased should learn that this tomb has been violated. Suspicion would immediately fall upon me; for it would be remembered how earnestly I desired to open the body, and how resolutely my request was refused."

"We must use a candle, then, presently," said the Resurrection Man; "and that is the most dangerous part of the whole proceeding."

"It cannot be helped," returned the surgeon, in a decided tone. "The fact that the side-door has been opened by unfair means must transpire in a day or two; and search will then be made inside the church to ascertain whether those who have been guilty of the sacrilege were thieves or resurrection-men. You see, then, how necessary it is that there should remain no proofs of the violation of a tomb."

"Well and good, sir," said the Resurrection Man. "You command—we obey. Now, then, my mates, to work."

In a moment the Resurrection Man lighted a piece of candle, and placed it in the tin shade before alluded to. The glare which it shed was thereby thrown almost entirely downwards. He then carefully, and with surprising rapidity, examined the joints of the large flagstone which was to be removed, and on which no inscription had yet been engraved. He observed the manner in which the mortar was laid down, and noticed even the places where it spread a little over the adjoining stones or where it was slightly deficient. This inspection being completed, he extinguished the light, and set to work in company with the Cracksman and the Buffer.

The eyes of the surgeon gradually became accustomed to the obscurity; and he was enabled to observe to some extent the proceedings of the body-snatchers.

These men commenced by pouring vinegar over the mortar round the stone which they were to raise. They then took long clasp-knives, with very thin and flexible blades, from their pockets; and inserted them between the joints of the stones. They moved these knives rapidly backwards and forwards for a few seconds, so as effectually to loosen the mortar, and moistened the interstices several times with the vinegar.

This operation being finished, they introduced the thin and pointed end of a lever between the end of the stone which they were to raise and the one adjoining it. The Resurrection Man, who held the lever, only worked it very gently; but at every fresh effort on his part, the Cracksman and the Buffer introduced each a wedge of wood into the space which thus grew larger and larger. By these means, had the lever suddenly given way, the stone would not have fallen back into its setting. At length it was raised to a sufficient height to admit of its being supported by a thick log about three feet in length.

While these three men were thus proceeding as expeditiously as possible with their task, the surgeon, although a man of a naturally strong mind, could not control the strange feelings which crept upon him. It suddenly appeared to him as if he beheld those men for the first time. That continuation of regular and systematic movements—that silent perseverance, faintly shadowed forth amidst the obscurity of the night, at length assumed so singular a character, that the surgeon felt as if he beheld three demons disinterring a doomed one to carry him off to hell!

He was aroused from this painful reverie by the Resurrection Man, who said to him, "Come and help us remove the stone."

The surgeon applied all his strength to this task; and the huge flagstone was speedily moved upon two wooden rollers away from the mouth of the grave.

"You are certain that this is the place?" said the Resurrection Man.

"As certain as one can be who stood by the grave for a quarter of an hour in day-light, and who has to recognise it again in total darkness," answered the surgeon. "Besides, the mortar was soft——"

"There might have been another burial close by," interrupted the Resurrection Man; "but we will soon find out whether you are right or not, sir. Was the coffin a wooden one?"

"Yes! an elm coffin, covered with black cloth," replied the surgeon. "I gave the instructions for the funeral myself, being the oldest friend of the family."

The Resurrection Man took one of the long flexible rods which we have before noticed, and thrust it down into the vault. The point penetrated into the lid of a coffin. He drew it back, put the point to his tongue, and tasted it.

"Yes," he said, smacking his lips, "the coffin in this vault is an elm one, and is covered with black cloth."

"I thought I could not be wrong," observed the surgeon.

The body-snatchers then proceeded to raise the coffin, by means

of ropes passed underneath it. This was a comparatively easy portion of their task; and in a few moments it was placed upon the flag-stones of the church.

The Resurrection Man took a chisel and opened the lid with considerable care. He then lighted his candle a second time; and the glare fell upon the pale features of the corpse in its narrow shell.

"This is the right one," said the surgeon, casting a hasty glance upon the face of the dead body, which was that of a young girl of about sixteen.

The Resurrection Man extinguished the light; and he and his companions proceeded to lift the corpse out of the coffin.

The polished marble limbs of the deceased were rudely grasped by the sacrilegious hands of the body-snatchers; and, having stripped the corpse stark naked, they tied its neck and heels together by means of a strong cord. They then thrust it into a large sack made for the purpose.

The body-snatchers then applied themselves to the restoration of the vault to its original appearance.

The lid of the coffin was carefully fastened down; and that now tenantless bed was lowered into the tomb. The stone was rolled over the mouth of the vault; and one of the small square boxes previously alluded to, furnished mortar wherewith to fill up the joints. The Resurrection Man lighted his candle a third time, and applied the cement in such a way that even the very workman who laid the stone down after the funeral would not have known that it had been disturbed. Then, as this mortar was a shade fresher and lighter than that originally used, the Resurrection Man scattered over it a thin brown powder, which was furnished by the second box brought away from his house on this occasion. Lastly, a light brush was swept over the scene of these operations, and the necessary precautions were complete.

The clock struck three as the surgeon and the body-snatchers issued from the church, carrying the sack containing the corpse between them.

They reached the wall at the back of the churchyard, and there deposited their burden, while the Cracksman hastened to see if the surgeon's carriage had arrived.

In a few minutes he returned to the railing, and said in a low tone, "All right!"

The body was lifted over the iron barrier and conveyed to the vehicle.

The surgeon counted ten sovereigns into the hands of each of the body-snatchers; and, having taken his seat inside the vehicle, close by his strange freight, was whirled rapidly away towards his own abode.

The three body-snatchers retraced their steps to the house in the vicinity of the Bird-cage Walk; and the Cracksman and Buffer, having deposited the implements of their avocation in the corner of the front room, took their departure.

The moment the Resurrection Man was thus relieved from the observation of his companions, he seized the candle and hastened into the back room, where he expected to find the corpse of Richard Markham stripped and washed.

To his surprise the room was empty.

"What the devil has the old fool been up to?" he exclaimed: then, hastening to the foot of the stairs, he cried, "Mummy, are you awake?"

In a few moments a door on the first floor opened, and the old woman appeared in her night gear at the head of the stairs.

"Is that you, Tony?" she exclaimed.

"Yes! who the hell do you think it could be? But what have you done with the fresh 'un?"

"The fresh 'un came alive again——"

"Gammon! Where is the money? how much was there? and is his skull fractured?" demanded the Resurrection Man.

"I tell you that he came to his senses," returned the old hag: "and that he sprung upon me like a tiger when I went into the back room after you was gone."

"Damnation! what a fool I was not to stick three inches of cold steel into him!" ejaculated the Resurrection Man, stamping his foot. "So I suppose he got clear away—money and all?—gone, may be, to fetch the traps!"

"Don't alarm yourself, Tony," said the old hag, with a horrible cackling laugh; "he's safe enough, I'll warrant it!"

"Safe! where—where?"

"Where his betters have been 'afore him," answered the Mummy.

"What!—in the well in the yard?" exclaimed the Resurrection Man, in a state of horrible suspense.

"No—in the hole under the stairs."

"Wretch!—drivelling fool!—idiot that you are!" cried the Resurrection Man in a voice of thunder: "you decoyed him into the very place from which he was sure to escape!"

"Escape!" exclaimed the Mummy, in a tone of profound alarm.

"Yes—escape!" repeated the Resurrection Man. "Did I not tell you a month or more ago that the wall between the hole and the saw-pit in the empty house next door had given way!"

"No—you never told me! I'll swear you never told me!" cried the old hag, now furious in her turn. "You only say so to throw all the blame on me: it's just like you."

"Don't provoke me, mother!" said the Resurrection Man, grinding his teeth. "You know that I told you about the wall falling down; and you know that I spoke to you about not using the place any more!"

"It's false!" exclaimed the Mummy.

"It's true; for I said to you at the time that I must brick up the wall myself some night, before any new people take the carpenter's yard, or they might wonder what the devil we could want with a place under ground like that; and it would be the means of blowing us!"

"It's a lie! you never told me a word about it," persisted the old harridan doggedly.

"Perdition take you!" cried the man. "The affair of this cursed Markham will be the ruin of us both!"

The Resurrection Man still had a hope left: the subterranean pit beneath the stairs was deep, and Markham might have been stunned by the fall.

He hastened to the trap-door, and raised it. The vivid light of his candle was thrown to the very bottom of the pit by means of the bright reflector of tin.

The hole was empty.

Maddened by disappointment—a prey to the most terrible apprehensions—and uncertain whether to flee or remain in his den, the Resurrection Man paced the passage in a state of mind which would not have been envied by even a criminal on his way to execution.

CHAPTER XLV.

THE FRUITLESS SEARCH.

When Richard Markham was precipitated into the hole beneath the stairs, by the perfidy of the Mummy, he fell with his head against a stone, and became insensible.

He lay in this manner for upwards of half an hour, when a current of air which blew steadily upon his face, revived him; and he awoke to all the horrors of his situation.

He had seen and passed through enough that night to unhinge the strongest mind. The secrets of the accursed den in a subterranean dungeon of which he now lay,—the atrocious mysteries revealed by the conversation of the body-snatchers ere they set out on their expedition to Shoreditch Church,—the cold corpse of some unfortunate being most inhumanly murdered, and all the paraphernalia of a hideous death, in the front-room of that outpost of hell,—haunted his imagination, and worked him up to a pitch of excitement bordering upon frenzy.

He felt that if he did not escape from that hole, he should dash his head against the wall, or go raving mad.

He clenched his fists and struck them against his forehead in an access of despair.

And then he endeavoured to reason with himself, and to look the perils that beset him, in the face.

But he could not remain cool—he could not control his agonising emotions.

"O God!" he exclaimed aloud; "what have I done to be thus afflicted? What sin have I committed to be thus tortured? Have I not served thee in word and deed to the best of my ability? Do I not worship—venerate—adore thee? O God! why wilt thou that I should die thus early—and die, too, so cruel a death? Is there not room on earth enough for a worm like me? Have I not been sufficiently tried, O my God? and in the hour of my deepest—bitterest anguish, did I ever deny thee? Did I repine against thy supreme will when false men encompassed me to destroy me in the opinion of the world? Hear me, O God—hear me! and let me not die this time;—let me not perish, O Lord, thus miserably!"

Such was the fervent, heart-felt prayer which Markham breathed to heaven, in the agony and despair of his soul.

He extended his arms, with his hands clasped together, in the ardour of his appeal; and they encountered an opening in the wall.

A ray of hope penetrated to his heart; and when upon further search, he discovered an aperture sufficiently wide for him to creep through, he exclaimed, "O Lord! I thank thee, thou hast heard my prayer! Pardon—oh! pardon my repinings;—forgive me that I dared to question thy sovereign will!"

At all risks he determined to pass through the opening—lead whithersoever it might; for he knew that he could scarcely be worse off; and he felt a secret influence which prompted him thus to act, and for which he could not wholly account.

He crept through the hole in the partition-wall, and found himself upon a soft damp ground.

Every thing was veiled in the blackest obscurity.

He groped about with his hands, and stepped cautiously forward, pausing at every pace.

Presently his foot encountered what appeared to be a step: to his infinite joy he ascertained, in another moment, that he was at the bottom of a flight of stone stairs.

He ascended them, and came to a door, which yielded to his touch. He proceeded slowly and cautiously along a passage, groping his way with his hands; and, in a few moments he reached another door, which opened with a latch.

He was now in the open street!

Carefully closing the door behind him, he hurried away from that accursed vicinity as if he were pursued by blood-hounds.

He ran—he ran, reckless of the deep pools of stagnant water, careless of the heaps of thick mud through which he passed,—indifferent to the bruises which he sustained against the angles of houses, the corners of streets, and the stone-steps of doors,—unmindful of the dangers which he dared in threading thus wildly those rugged and uneven thoroughfares amidst the dense obscurity which covered the earth.

He ran—he ran, a delirium of joy thrilling in his brain, and thanksgiving in his soul; for now that he had escaped from the peril which so lately beset him, it appeared to his imagination a thousand times more frightful than when it actually impended over him. Oh! he was happy—happy—thrice happy, in the enjoyment of liberty, and the security of life once more;—and he began to look upon the scenes of that eventful night as an accumulation of horrors which could have possibility only in a dream!

He ran—he ran, amidst those filthy lanes and foul streets, where a nauseating atmosphere prevailed;—but had he been threading a labyrinth of rose-trees, amongst the most delicious perfumes, he could not have experienced a more burning—ardent—furious joy! Yes—his delight was madness, frenzy! On, on—splashed with mud—floundering through black puddles—knee-deep in mire,—on, on he went—reckless which direction he pursued, so long as the rapidity of his pace removed him afar from the accursed house that had nearly become his tomb!

For an hour did he thus pursue his way.

At length he stopped through sheer exhaustion, and seated himself upon the steps of a door over which a lamp was flickering.

He collected his scattered ideas as well as he could, and began to wonder whither his wild and reckless course had led him: but no conjecture on his part furnished him with any clue to solve the mystery of his present whereabouts. He knew that he must be somewhere in the eastern district of the metropolis; but in what precise spot it was impossible for him to tell.

While he was thus lost in vain endeavours to unravel the tangled topographical skein which perplexed his imagination, he heard footsteps advancing along the street.

By the light of the lamp he soon distinguished a policeman, walking with slow and measured steps along his beat.

"Will you have the kindness to tell me where I am?" said Richard, accosting the officer: "I have lost my way. What neighbourhood is this?"

"Ratcliff Highway," answered the policeman: "in the middle of Wapping, you know."

"In the midst of Wapping?" ejaculated Markham, in a tone of surprise and vexation.

And, truly enough, there he was in the centre of that immense assemblage of dangerous streets, cut-throat lanes, and filthy alleys, which swarm with crimps ever ready to entrap the reckless and generous-hearted sailor; publicans who farm the unloading of the colliers, and compel those whom they employ to take out half their wages in vile adulterated beer; and poor half-starved coal-heavers whose existence alternates between crushing toil and killing intoxication. It was in this neighbourhood that Richard Markham now was!

Heaven alone can tell what tortuous path and circuitous routes he had been pursuing during the hour of his precipitate flight; but his feet must have passed over many miles of ground from the instant that he emerged from the murderers' den until he sank exhausted on the steps of a house in Ratcliff Highway.

He was wet and covered with mud, and very cold. But he suddenly remembered that there was a duty which he owed to society—an imperative duty which he dared not neglect. He was impressed with the idea that Providence had that night favoured his escape from the jaws of death, in order that he might become the means of rooting up a den of horrors.

There was not a moment to be lost: the three miscreants, unconscious of peril, had repaired to Shoreditch Church to exercise the least terrible portion of their avocations in that sacred edifice:—it might yet be time to secure them there!

The policeman was still standing near him.

"Which is the way to the station-house?" suddenly exclaimed Markham. "I have matters of the deepest importance to communicate to the police,—I can place them upon the scent of three miscreants—three demons in human form——"

"And how came you to know about them?" asked the officer.

"Oh! it is too long to tell you now—we shall only be wasting time; and the villains may escape," cried Richard, in a tone of excitement and with a wildness of manner which induced the officer to fancy that his brain was turned.

"Well, come along with me," said the policeman; "and you can tell all you know to the Superintendent."

Markham signified his readiness to accompany the officer; and they proceeded to the station-house in the neighbourhood.

There Richard was introduced to the Superintendent.

"I have this night," said the young man, "escaped from the most fearful perils. I was proceeding along a dark, narrow, and dirty street somewhere in the neighbourhood of Shoreditch Church, when I was knocked down, and carried into a house where murder—yes, murder," added Markham, in a tone of fearful excitement, "seems to be committed wholesale. At this moment there is a corpse—the corpse of some unfortunate man who has been assassinated in a most inhuman manner—lying stretched out in that house! I could tell you how the miscreants who frequent that den dispose of their victims,—how they pounce upon those who pass their door, and drag them into that human slaughter-house,—and how they make away with them;—I could tell you horrors which would make your hair stand on end;—but we should lose time; for you may yet capture the three wretches whose crimes have been this night so providentially revealed to me!"

"And where can we capture these men?" inquired the Superintendent, surveying Markham from head to foot in a strange manner.

"They are at this moment at Shoreditch Church," returned the young man; "they are engaged in exhuming a corpse for a surgeon whom they were to meet at half-past one at the back of the burial ground."

"And it is now three o'clock," said the Superintendent. "I dare say they have got over their business by this time. You had much better sit down here by the fire and rest yourself; and when it is day-light some one shall see you home to your friends."

"Sit here tranquilly, when justice claims its due!" ejaculated Markham; "impossible! If you will not second my endeavours to expose a most appalling system of wholesale murder——"

"My dear sir," interrupted the Superintendent, "do compose yourself, and get such horrid thoughts out of your head. Come—be reasonable. This is London, you know—and it is impossible that the things you have described could be committed in so populous a city."

"I tell you that every word I have uttered is the strict truth," cried Markham emphatically.

"And how came you to escape from such a place?" demanded the Superintendent.

"The villain who attacked me thought me dead—he fancied that I was killed by the blow; but it had only stunned me for a few moments——"

"Just now there were three murderers," whispered one policeman to another: "now there is only one. He is as mad as a March-hare."

"Then I was decoyed into a deep pit," continued Markham; "and I escaped through an aperture opening into another pit, with stone steps to it, in the next house."

The two policemen turned round to conceal their inclination to laugh; and the Superintendent could scarcely maintain a serious countenance.

"And now will you come with me to Shoreditch Church, and capture the villains?" cried Markham.

"We had better wait till morning. Pray sit down and compose yourself. You are wet and covered with mud—you have evidently been walking a great distance."

"Oh! now I understand the cause of your hesitation," ejaculated Markham: "you do not believe me—you fancy that I am labouring under a delusion. I conjure you not to suffer justice to be defeated by that idea! The tale is strange; and I myself, had it been communicated to me as it now is to you, should look upon it as improbable. No doubt, too, my appearance is strange; and my manner may be excited, and my tone wild;—but, I swear to you by the great God who hears us, that I am sane—in the possession of my reason,—although, heaven knows! I have this night passed through enough to unhinge the strongest intellects!"

"Can you lead us to the house where you allege that these enormities are committed?" demanded the Superintendent, moved by the solemnity and rationality with which Markham had uttered this last appeal to him.

"No, I cannot," was the reply: "I had lost my way amongst those streets with which I was totally unacquainted: the night was dark—dark as it is now;—and therefore I could not guide you to that den of such black atrocities. But, I repeat: the murderers left that house a little after one to commit a deed of sacrilege in Shoreditch Church. You say that it is now three: perhaps their resurrection-labours are not terminated yet; and you might then capture them in the midst of their unholy pursuits."

"And if we do not find that Shoreditch Church has been broken open?" said the Superintendent, "you will admit ——"

"Admit that I am mad—that I have deceived you—that I deserve to be consigned to a lunatic asylum," exclaimed Markham, in a tone which inspired the Superintendent with confidence.

That officer accordingly gave instructions to four constables to accompany Markham to Shoreditch Church.

The little party proceeded thither with all possible expedition; but the clock struck four just as they reached the point of destination.

They hastily scaled the railings around the burial-ground, and proceeded to the very door from which the body-snatchers had emerged an hour previously.

One of the policemen tried the door; and it immediately yielded to his touch. At the same moment his foot struck against something upon the top step. He picked it up:—it was a padlock with the semicircular bolt sawed through.

The policemen and Markham entered the church; and the former commenced a strict search by means of their bull's-eye lanterns.

"There's no doubt that the gentleman was right and all he said was true," observed one of the officers; "but the birds have flown—that's clear."

"Well—they must have done their work pretty cleverly if they haven't left a trace," said another.

"I have heard it stated," remarked Richard, "that resurrection-men are so expert at their calling, that they can defy the most acute eye to discover the spot upon such they have been operating."

"Well, if we don't find out which vault they have opened, it's no matter. We have seen enough to convince us that you were right, sir, in all you told us."

"And as the body-snatchers are not here," added another police-officer, "we had better get back as quick as we can and report the church's having been broke open to our Superintendent."

"And I will return with you," said Markham; "for when it is light I may perhaps be enabled to conduct you to within a short distance of the street—even if not into the very street itself—where the den is situated which those monsters frequent or inhabit."

The officers and Richard accordingly returned to the station-house whence they came; and as soon as the Superintendent heard that the church had really been broken open, he apologised to Markham for his former incredulity.

"You will, however, admit, sir," said this functionary, "that your narrative was calculated to excite strange suspicions relative to the condition of the intellects of the person who told it."

"I presume you fancied that I had escaped from a madhouse?" observed Markham.

"To tell you the truth, I did," answered the Superintendent: "you were in such a dreadful condition! And that reminds me that you are all wet and covered with mud: please to step into my private room, and you will find every thing necessary to make you clean and comfortable."

* * * * *

Day dawned shortly after seven; and at that time might be seen Richard Markham, accompanied by an officer in plain clothes, and followed by others at a distance, threading the streets and alleys in the neighbourhood of the Bird-cage Walk.

The sun rose upon that labyrinth of close, narrow, and wretched thoroughfares, and irradiated those sinks of misery and crime as well as the regal palace and the lordly mansion at the opposite end of London.

But the search after the house in which Markham had witnessed such horrors and endured such intense mental agony on the preceding night, was as vain and fruitless as if its existence were but a dream.

There was not a street which Markham could remember having passed through; there was not a house to which even his suspicions attached.

And yet, may be, he and his official companions proceeded up the very street, and went by the door of the very house, which they sought.

After a useless search throughout that neighbourhood for nearly four hours, Markham declared that he was completely at fault.

The police accordingly abandoned any further proceedings on that occasion. It was however agreed between them and Markham that the strictest secresy should be preserved relative to the entire business, in order that the measures to be subsequently adopted with a view to discover the den of the murderers, might not be defeated by the tattle of busy tongues.

CHAPTER XLVI.

RICHARD AND ISABELLA.

Richard Markham had determined to lose no time in revealing to Count Alteroni those adventures which had rendered him an inmate of the Giltspur Street Compter for two years.

And yet it was hard to dare the destruction of the bright visions which had dawned upon him in respect to the Signora Isabella: it was cruel to dash away from his lips the only cup of enjoyment which he had tasted for a long time.

He knew not how the count would receive such a narrative as he had to tell. Doubtless it would alarm him: "for society," thought Richard, "was too apt to judge rashly by outward appearances." Should the count nobly and generously rise above the prejudices of the world, and believe the statement of Markham's innocence, corroborated as it was by the document signed by Talbot, *alias* Pocock, much would have been gained by a candid and honourable confession. But if the reverse ensued, and the count banished Richard from his friendship, the young man felt that he himself would only have performed a melancholy duty, and broken asunder of his own accord those bonds which, were he to remain silent, an accident might one day snap abruptly and rudely.

"I feel happy," said Markham to himself, as he arose in the morning after the day on which the fruitless search mentioned in the preceding chapter took place,—"I feel happy even while about to consummate a sacrifice which may destroy the most golden of my dreams! The Infinite Being has declared that the days of our life shall be marked with sorrow; and they are—as I can well testify! But the afflictions to which we are subject are attended with blessed antidotes;—moral sources of enjoyment are given to us, as fruits and flowers for the soul; and the teachings of interest, as well as the impulses of gratitude, should lead us to consider with attention those duties we owe each other, for the sake of the bounties the Almighty showers upon us."

So reasoned Richard Markham.

That evening he arrived at the count's abode near Richmond, a few minutes before dinner.

A kind welcome awaited him on the part of the count and countess; and the eyes of Signora Isabella expressed the satisfaction she experienced at his return.

When Markham was seated with the count after dinner, he determined to commence the explanation which he had resolved to give.

He was just about to broach the subject, when the count observed, "By the bye, I am happy to inform you that I received letters from Greenwood this morning; and he assures me that the speculation looks admirably."

"I am delighted to hear it," returned Richard. "But the chief object of my present visit ——"

"Was to speak about this Steam Packet business, no doubt," interrupted the count. "Well, if you like to take shares in it, it is not too late. But what do you think? I am going to tell you a secret. You know that I look upon you as a friend of the family; besides, I am well aware that you respect Isabel and love her like a brother——"

"What did you say, count?" stammered Markham.

"I was going to tell you that Mr. Greenwood—who is immensely rich—has taken a liking to Isabella——"

"Indeed!"

"Yes—and I gave him some little encouragement."

"What! without previously ascertaining whether the Signora's feelings are reciprocal?" cried Richard.

"As for that, my dear Markham, remember that a dutiful daughter knows no will and no inclination save those of her parents."

"This is not an English doctrine," said Markham, "so far as the principle applies to affairs of the heart."

"It is nevertheless an Italian doctrine," exclaimed the count, somewhat haughtily; "and I have no doubt that Isabella will ever recognise the authority of her parents in this as in all other matters."

As the count uttered these words, he rose and led the way to the drawing-room; and thus deprived Markham of that opportunity of making the confession he had intended.

Richard was unhappy and dispirited. He perceived that the count was inclined to favour Mr. Greenwood's suit; and he now felt how dear Isabella was to him—how profoundly seated was his love for the beauteous Italian!

Misfortunes never come alone. Richard was destined to receive a crushing blow, although innocently inflicted, the moment he entered the drawing-room.

The countess was conversing with her daughter upon her own family connections.

"Do not let us interrupt your conversation," said the count, as he took his seat upon the sofa near his wife.

"We were only talking about the Chevalier Guilderstein, whose death was mentioned in yesterday's newspaper," observed the countess. "I was saying that I remembered how delighted I was when I discovered a few years ago that the chevalier was not related to our family, as he had always pretended to be."

"And why so?" inquired the count.

"Because the father of the chevalier was put to death in Austria for coining—or rather upon a charge of coining," answered the countess; "and although his innocence was discovered and proclaimed a few years after his death, I should not like to have amongst my ancestors a man who had been criminally convicted, however innocent he may in reality have been."

"Certainly not," said the count. "I should be very sorry for any one whose character had ever been tainted with suspicion, to have the slightest connection with our family."

"I cannot say that I agree with you," observed Isabel. "There can be no disgrace attached to one who has suffered under a false accusation: on the contrary—such a person is rather deserving of our deepest sympathy and——"

"Heavens, Mr. Markham!" ejaculated the Countess; "are you ill? Bella, dear—ring the bell—get Mr. Markham a glass of water——"

"It is nothing—nothing, I can assure you," stammered Richard, whose countenance was as pale as that of a corpse. "Miss Isabella, do not give yourself any trouble! It was only a sudden faintness—a spasm: but it is over now."

With these words Markham hurried to the bed-chamber which was always allotted to him when he visited the count's residence.

All the horrible tortures which man can conceive, harassed him at that moment. He threw himself upon his couch—he writhed—he struggled, as if against a serpent which held him in its embraces. His eyes seemed as if they were about to start from their sockets; his teeth were fast closed—he wrung his hair—he beat his breast—and low moans escaped from his bosom. The *fiat* of the count had gone forth. He who would claim or aspire to connection with his family must be like the wife of Cæsar—beyond all suspicion. It was not enough that such an one should be innocent of any crime: he must never have even been accused of one. Such was the disposition of the count—elicited by an accident and unexpectedly; and Markham could now divine the nature of the treatment which he would be likely to experience, were he to reveal his misfortunes to a nobleman who entertained such punctilious and extremely scrupulous notions!

"But I was mad to imagine that Isabella would ever become mine," thought Markham within himself, as soon as he became somewhat more tranquillised. "It was folly—supreme folly—rank, idiotic, inconceivable folly, in me to have cherished a hope which could never be realised! All that now remains for me to do, is to abandon myself to my adverse fate—to attempt no more struggles against the destinies that await me,—to leave this house without delay—to return home, and bury myself in a solitude from which no persuasions nor attractions shall henceforth induce me to emerge! Would that I could leave this house this very evening;—but appearances compel me to remain at least until to-morrow! I must endeavour to assume that ease of manner—that friendly confidence, which is reciprocal here:—for a few hours I must consent to act the hypocrite; and to-morrow—to-morrow, I shall be relieved from that dread necessity.—I shall be compelled to bid adieu to Isabella for ever! No avowal of my past sufferings is now required—since I shall to-morrow leave this hospitable mansion, never to return!"

A flood of tears relieved the unfortunate young man; and he descended once more to the drawing-room—very pale, but as calm and tranquil as usual. Isabella glanced towards him from time to time with evident anxiety; and, in spite of all his endeavours to appear cheerful and at his ease, he was embarrassed, cool, and reserved. Isabella was wounded and mortified by his conduct:—she attempted to rally him, and to ascertain whether he was really chilling in his manners on purpose, or only melancholy against his will: but she received frigid and laconic replies, which annoyed and disheartened the poor girl to such an extent that she could scarcely refrain from tears. Markham felt that, as an honourable man, he could no longer aspire to the hand of the signora, after the expression of opinion accidentally conveyed to him by the count and countess; and he therefore forbore from any attempt to render himself agreeable, or to afford the slightest testimony of his passion. Acting with these views, and endeavouring to seem only properly polite, he fell into the opposite extreme, and grew cold and reserved. The count and countess imagined that he was unwell, and were not therefore annoyed by his conduct;—but poor Isabella, who was deeply attached to him, set down his behaviour to indifference. This idea on her part was confirmed, when Markham, in the course of conversation, intimated his intention of returning home on the following day.

"Return home! and what for?" ejaculated the count. "You have no society there, and here you have some—unamusing and tedious though it may be."

"Never did I pass a happier period of my existence than that which I have spent in your hospitable abode," said Richard.

"Then remain with us at least ten days or a fortnight," cried the count. "We shall then be visiting London ourselves, for we have promised to pass a few weeks with Lord and Lady Tremordyn."

"Lord Tremordyn!" exclaimed Richard.

"Yes—do you know him?"

"Only by name. But did not his daughter marry Sir Rupert

Harborough?" said Markham, shuddering as he pronounced the abhorred name.

"The same. Sir Rupert treats her shamefully—neglects her in every way, and passes whole months away from his home. He has, moreover, expended all the fortune she brought him, and is again, I understand, deeply involved in debt."

"Poor Lady Cecilia!" ejaculated Isabella. "She is deeply to be pitied!"

"But to return to this sudden resolution of yours to depart to-morrow," said the count.

"Which resolution is very suddenly taken," added the signora, affecting to be engaged in contemplating a book of prints which lay upon the table before her, while her beautiful countenance was suffused with a deep blush.

"My resolution is sudden, certainly," observed Richard. "Circumstances over which I have no control, and which it would be useless to communicate to you, frequently compel me to adopt sudden resolutions, and act up to them. Be assured, however, that the memory of your kindness will always be dear to me."

"You speak as if we were never to meet again," exclaimed the count.

"We cannot dispose of events in this world according to our own will," said Markham, emphatically. "Would to God we could!"

"But there are certain circumstances in which we seem to be free agents," said Isabella, still holding down her head; "and remaining in one place, or going to another, appears to be amongst those actions which depend upon our own volition."

At this moment a servant entered the room and informed the count that the private secretary of the envoy of the Grand Duke of Castelcicala to the English court desired to speak with him in another apartment.

"Oh! I am interested in this," exclaimed the countess; and, upon a signal of approval on the part of her husband, she accompanied him to the room where the secretary was waiting.

Markham was now alone with Isabella.

This was a probable occurrence which he had dreaded all that evening. He felt himself cruelly embarrassed in her presence; and the silence which prevailed between them was awkward to a degree.

At length the signora herself spoke.

"It appears that you are determined to leave us, Mr. Markham?" she said, without glancing towards him, and in a tone which she endeavoured to render as cool and indifferent as possible.

"I feel that I have been too long here already, signora," answered Richard, scarcely knowing what reply to make.

"Do you mean to tax us with inattention to your comfort, Mr. Markham?"

"God forbid, signora! In the name of heaven do not entertain such an idea!"

"Mr. Markham has been treated as well as our humble means would admit; and he leaves us with an abruptness which justifies us in entertaining fears that he is not comfortable."

"How can I convince you of the injustice of your suspicions?"

ejaculated Markham. "You would not wantonly wound my feelings, Miss Isabella, by a belief which is totally unfounded? No! that is not the cause of my departure. My own happiness—my own honour—every thing commands me to quit a spot where—where I shall, nevertheless, leave so many reminiscences of joy and tranquil felicity behind me! I dare not explain myself farther at present; perhaps *never* will you know the cause—but, pardon me, signora—I am wandering—I know not what I say!"

"Pray compose yourself, Mr. Markham," said Isabella, now raising her head from the book, and glancing towards him.

"Compose myself, Isabella—signora, I mean," he exclaimed: "*that* is impossible! Oh! if you knew *all*, you would pity me! But I dare not now reveal to you what I wish. A word which this day dropped from your father's lips has banished all hope from my mind. Now I am wandering again! In the name of heaven, take no notice of what I say; I am mad—I am raving!"

"And what was it that my father said to annoy you?" inquired Isabella timidly.

"Oh! nothing—nothing purposely," answered Markham. "He himself was unaware that he fired the arrow from his bow."

"Am I unworthy of your confidence in this instance?" asked Isabella; "and may I not be made acquainted with the nature of the annoyance which my father has thus unintentionally caused you to experience?"

"Oh! why should I repeat words which would only lead to a revelation of what it is now useless to reveal. Your father and mother both delivered the same sentiment—a sentiment that destroys all hope. But, oh! you cannot understand the cause of my anxiety—my grief—my disappointment!"

"And why not entrust me with that cause? I could sympathise with you as a friend."

"As a friend! Alas, Isabella, is it useless for me now to deplore the visions which I had conjured up, and which have been so cruelly destroyed? You yourself know not what is in store for you—what plans your father may have formed concerning you!"

"And are you acquainted with those plans?" asked the beauteous Italian, in a tone of voice rendered almost inaudible by a variety of emotions—for the heart of that innocent and charming being fluttered like a bird in the net of the fowler.

"Do not question me on that head, Isabella! Let me speak of myself—for it is sweet to be commiserated by such as you! My life for some time past has been a scene of almost unceasing misery. When I came of age I found my vast property dissipated by him to whom it was entrusted. And other circumstances gave a new and unpleasant aspect to those places which were dear to me in my childhood. What wild hopes, in early life, had I there indulged,—what dreams for the future had there visited my mind in its boyhood!—what vain wishes, what strong yearnings, what ambitious aspirations had there first found existence! When I returned to those spots, after an absence of two years, and thought of the feelings that there once agitated my bosom, and contrasted them with those which had displaced them,—when I traced the history of each hope from its inception there, and followed it through the vista of years until its final extinction,—when I thought how differently my course in life had been shaped from that career which I had there marked out, and how vain and futile were all the efforts and strivings which I exerted against the tide of events and the force of circumstances,—I awoke, as it were from a long dream,—I opened my eyes upon the path which I should thenceforth have to pursue, and judged of it by the one I had been pursuing;—I saw the nothingness of men's lives in general, and the utter vanity of the main pursuits which engross their minds, and waste their energies;—and I then felt convinced that I was indeed but an instrument in the hands of another, and that the ends which I had obtained had not been those for which I had striven, but which the Almighty willed!—So is it with me now, Isabella. I had planned a dream—a dream of Elysium, with which to cheer and bless the remainder of my existence; and, behold! like all the former hopes and aspirations of my life, this one is also suddenly destroyed!"

"How know you that it is destroyed?" inquired Isabella, casting down her eyes.

"Oh! I am unworthy of you, Isabella—I do not deserve you; and yet it was to your hand that I aspired;—you were the star that was to irradiate the remainder of my existence! Oh! I could weep—I could weep, Isabella, when I think of what I might have been, and what I am!"

"You say that you aspired to my hand," murmured the lovely Italian maiden, casting down her large dark eyes and blushing deeply; "you did me honour!"

"Silence, Isabella—silence!" interrupted Richard. "I dare not now hear the words of hope from *your* lips! But I love thee—I love thee—God only knows how sincerely I love thee!"

"And shall I conceal my own feelings with regard to you, Richard?" said Isabella, approaching him and laying her delicate and beautifully modelled hand lightly upon his wrist.

"She loves me in return—she loves me!" ejaculated Markham, half wild with mingled joy and apprehensions;—and, yielding to an impulse which no mortal under such circumstances could have conquered, he caught her in his arms.

He kissed her pure and chaste brow—he felt her fragrant breath upon his cheek—her hair commingled with his own—and he murmured the words, "You love me?"

A gentle voice breathed an affirmative in his ear; and he pressed his lips to hers to ratify that covenant of two fond hearts.

Suddenly he recollected that Count Alteroni had declared that no one against whom there was even a suspicion of crime should ever form a connection with his family. Markham's high sense of honour told him in a moment that he had no right to secure the affections of a confiding and gentle girl whose father would never yield an assent to their union: his brain, already excited, now became inflamed almost to madness;—he abruptly turned aside from her who had just avowed her attachment to him, he muttered some incoherent words which she did not comprehend, and rushed out of the room.

He hurried to the garden at the back of the house, and walked rapidly up and down a shady avenue of trees which ran along the wall that bounded the enclosure on the side of the public road.

By degrees he grew calm and relaxed the speed of his pace. He then fell into a long and profound meditation upon the occurrences of the last half hour.

He was beloved by Isabella, it was true;—but never might he aspire to her hand;—never could it be accorded to him to lead her to the altar where their attachment might be ratified and *his* happiness confirmed! An inseparable barrier seemed to oppose itself to his wishes; and he felt that no alternative remained to him but to put his former resolution into force, and take his departure homewards on the ensuing morning.

Thus was it that he now reasoned.

The moon shone brightly; and the heavens were studded with stars.

As Markham was about to turn for the twentieth time at that end of the avenue which was the more remote from the house, the beams of the moon suddenly disclosed to him a human face peering over the wall at him.

He started, and was about to utter an exclamation of alarm, when a well-known voice fell upon his ears.

"Hush!" was the word first spoken; "I have just one question to ask you, and then one thing to tell you; and the last will just depend upon the first."

"Wretch—miscreant—murderer!" exclaimed Richard; "nothing shall now prevent me from securing you on the behalf of justice."

"Fool!" coolly returned the Resurrection Man—for it was he; "who can catch me in the darkness and the open fields?"

"True!" cried Markham, stamping his foot with vexation. "But God grant that the day of retribution may come!"

"Come, come—none of this nonsense, my dear boy," said the Resurrection Man, with diabolical irony. "Now, answer me—will you give me a cool hundred and fifty? If not, then I will get the swag in spite of you."

"Why do you thus molest and persecute me? I would sooner handle the most venomous serpent, than enter into a compromise with a fiend like you!"

"Then beware of the consequences!"

The moon shone full upon the cadaverous and unearthly countenance of the Resurrection Man, and revealed the expression of ferocious rage which it wore as he uttered these words. That vile and foreboding face then suddenly disappeared behind the wall.

"Who are you talking to, Markham?" cried the voice of the count, who was now advancing down the avenue.

"Talking to?" repeated Richard, alarmed and confused.

"Yes—I heard your voice, and another answering you," said the count.

"It was a man in the road," answered Markham.

"I missed you from the drawing-room on my return; and Bella said she thought you were unwell, and had gone to walk in the garden for the fresh air. The news I have received from Castelcicala, through the Envoy's secretary, are by no means favourable to my hopes of a speedy return to my native land. You therefore see that I have done well to lay out my capital in this. But we will not discuss matters of business now; for there is company up stairs, and we must join them. Who do you think have just made their appearance?"

"Mr. Armstrong and other friends?" said Markham inquiringly.

"No—Armstrong is on the Continent. The visitors are Sir Cherry Bounce and Captain Smilax Dapper; and I am by no means pleased with their company. However, my house *must* always remain open to them in consequence of the services rendered to me by their deceased relative."

Markham accompanied the count back to the drawing-room, where Captain Smilax Dapper had seated himself next to the signora; and Sir Cherry Bounce was endeavouring to divert the countess with an account of their journey that evening from London. They both coloured deeply and bowed very politely when Richard entered the apartment.

"Well, ath I wath thaying," continued Sir Cherry, "one of the twatheth bwoke at the bottom of the hill, and the hortheth took to fwight. Thmilakth thwore like a twooper; but nothing could thwop the thaithe till it wolled thlap down into a dwy dith. Dapper then woared like a bull; and I——"

"And Cherry began to cry, strike me if he didn't!" ejaculated the gallant hussar, caressing his moustache. "A countryman who passed by asked him if his mamma knew he was out: Cherry thought that the fellow was in earnest, and assured him that he had her permission to undertake the journey. I never laughed so much in my life!"

"Oh! naughty Dapper to thay that I cwied! That really ith too cwuel. Well, we got the thaithe lifted out of the dith, and the twathe mended."

"You are the heroes of an adventure," said the count.

"I intend to put it into verse, strike me ugly if I don't!" cried the young officer; "and perhaps the signora will allow me to copy it into her *Album*?"

"Oh! I must read it first," said Isabella, laughing. "But since you speak of my *Album*, I must show you the additions I have received to its treasures."

"This is really a beautiful landscape," observed Captain Dapper, as he turned over the leaves of the book which the beautiful Italian presented to him. "The water flowing over the wheel of the mill is quite natural, strike me! And—may I never know what fair woman's smiles are again, if those trees don't seem actually to be growing out of the paper!"

"Thuperb!" ejaculated Sir Cherry Bounce. "The wiver litewally wollth along in the picthure. The cowth and the theepe are walking in the gween fieldth. Pway who might have been the artitht of thith mathleth producthion?"

"That is a secret," said the signora. "And now read these lines."

"Read them yourself, Bella," said the count. "No one can do justice to them but you."

Isabella accordingly read the following stanzas in a tone of voice that added a new charm to the words themselves:—

LONDON.

'Twas midnight—and the beam of Cynthia shone
  In company with many a lovely star,
Steeping in silver the huge Babylon
  Whose countless habitations stretch afar,
Plain, valley, hill, and river's bank upon,
  And in whose mighty heart all interests jar!—
O sovereign city of a thousand towers,
What vice is cradled in thy princely bowers!

If thou would'st view fair London-town aright,
  Survey her from the bridge of Waterloo;
And let the hour be at the morning's light,
  When the sun's earliest rays have struggled through
The star-bespangled curtain of the night,
  And when Aurora's locks are moist with dew:
Then take thy stand upon that bridge, and see
London awake in all her majesty!

Then do her greatest features seem to crowd
  Down to the river's brink:—then does she raise
From off her brow the everlasting cloud,
  (Thus with her veil the coquette archly plays)
And for a moment shows her features, proud
  To catch the Rembrandt light of the sun's rays:—
Then may the eye of the beholder dwell
On steeple, column, dome, and pinnacle.

Yes—he may reckon temple, mart, and tower—
The old historic sites—the halls of kings—
The seats of art—the fortalice of power—
The ships that waft our commerce on their wings;—
All these commingle in that dawning hour;
And each into one common focus brings
Some separate moral of life's scenes so true,
As all those objects form one point of view!

The ceaseless hum of the huge Babylon
Has known no silence for a thousand years;
Still does her tide of human life flow on,
Still is she racked with sorrows, hopes, and fears;
Still the sun sets, still morning dawns upon
Hearts full of anguish, eye-balls dimmed with tears;—
Still do the millions toil to bless the few—
And hideous Want stalks all her pathways through!

"Beautiful—very beautiful!" exclaimed Captain Dapper. "Strike me if I ever heard more beautiful poetry!"

"Almotht ath good ath your lineth on the Thea Therpent. Wath the poem witten by the thame perthon that painted the landthcape?"

"The very same," answered Isabella. "His initials are in the corner."

"R. M. Who can that be?" exclaimed Dapper.

"Robert Montgomery, perhaps?" said Isabella, smiling with charmingly arch expression of countenance.

"No—Wichard Markham!" cried Sir Cherry; and then he and his friend the hussar captain were excessively annoyed to think that they had been extolling to the skies the performance of an individual who had frightened the one out of his wits, and boxed the ears of the other.

Thus passed the evening; but Markham was reserved and melancholy. It was in vain that Isabella exerted herself to instil confidence into his mind, by means of those thousand little attentions and manifestations of preference which lovers know so well how to exhibit, but which those around perceive not. Richard was firm in those resolutions which he deemed consistent with propriety and honour; and he deeply regretted the explanation and its consequences into which the enthusiasm of the moment had that evening led him.

At length the hour for retiring to rest arrived.

Richard repaired to his chamber—but not to sleep. His mind was too much harassed by the events of the evening—the plans which he had pursued, and those which he intended to pursue—the love which he bore to Isabel, and the stern opposition which might be anticipated from her father—the persecution to which he was subject at the hands of the Resurrection Man—and the train of evil fortune which appeared constantly to attend upon him;—of all these he thought; and his painful meditations defied the advance of slumber.

The window of his bed-chamber overlooked the garden at the back of the house; from which direction a strange and alarming noise suddenly broke in upon his reflections. He listened—and all was quiet: he therefore felt convinced that his terror was unfounded. A few moments elapsed; and he was again alarmed by a sound which seemed like the jarring of an unfastened shutter. A certain uneasiness now took possession of him; and he was determined to ascertain whether all was safe about the premises. He leapt from his bed, raised the window, and looked forth. The night was now pitch dark; and he could distinguish nothing. Not even were the outlines of the trees in the garden discernible amidst that profound and dense obscurity. Markham held his breath; and the whispering of voices met his ears. He could not, however, distinguish a word they uttered:—a low hissing continuous murmur, the nature of which it was impossible to mistake, convinced him that some persons were talking together immediately beneath his window. In a few moments the jarring of a door or shutter, which he had before heard, was repeated; and then the whispering ceased.

By this time his eyes had become accustomed to the darkness; and he could now faintly discern the outlines of three human forms standing together at the back door of the house. He could not, however, distinguish the precise nature of their present employment. It was, nevertheless, evident to him that they were not there with any honest intention in view; and he resolved to adopt immediate measures to defeat their burglarious schemes. He hastily threw on his clothes, struck a light, and issued from his room.

Cautiously advancing along a passage was the count, only half-dressed, with a pistol in each hand, and a cutlass under his arm.

"This is fortunate!" whispered the count: "I was coming to alarm you: there are thieves breaking in. You and I can manage them; it is of no use to call Bounce or Dapper. Take this cutlass and let us descend gently. Here come the men-servants."

The count hurried down stairs, followed by Markham, and the three male domestics of the household.

A noise was heard in the pantry, which was situate at the back of the house on the same level with the hall.

"Douse the darkey, blow the glim, and mizzle," cried a hoarse gruff voice, as the count, Richard, and the servants approached the pantry: "there's five on 'em—it's no use——"

The count rushed forward, and burst open the door of the pantry, closely followed by Markham, holding the candle.

Two of the burglars made a desperate push down the kitchen stairs and escaped: the third was captured in an attempt to follow his companions.

The light of the candle fell upon the villain's countenance, which was literally ghastly with a mingled expression of rage and alarm.

Richard shuddered: for the captured burglar was no other than the Resurrection Man.

"Wretch!" exclaimed Markham, recovering his self-command: "the law will at length reach you."

"What! do you know this fellow?" demanded the count, somewhat surprised by the observation.

"Know me!" cried the Resurrection Man: "of course he does. But supposing some one was to tell you a piece of valuable information, count—about a matter closely concerning yourself and family—would you be inclined to be merciful?"

"Of what nature is that information? It must be very valuable indeed, if you think that I will enter into any compromise with such as you."

"Pledge me your word that you will let me go scot free, and I will tell you something that concerns the peace and happiness—perhaps the honour of your daughter."

"Miscreant!" cried Markham: "profane not that lady by even alluding to her!"

"Stay—curse the fellow's impudence," said the count: "perhaps he may really have somewhat worth communicating. At all events, I will try him. Now, then, my man, what is it that you have to say? If your statement be worth hearing, I swear that I will neither molest you, nor suffer you to be molested."

"Hold count," exclaimed Markham: "make no rash vow—you know not what a wretch——"

"Silence, my dear friend," said the count authoritatively: "I will hear the man, let him be who or what he may!"

"And you will do well to hear me, sir," continued the Resurrection Man. "You harbour a villain in your house; and that villain is now before you. He boasts of having secured the affections of your daughter, and hopes to gull you into allowing him to marry her."

"Miscreant—murderer!" exclaimed Markham, no longer able to contain his indignation: "pollute not innocence itself by these allusions to a lady whose spotless mind ——"

"Hush!" said the count. "Let us hear patiently all this man has to say. I can soon judge whether he be speaking the truth; and if he deceives me, I will show him no mercy."

"But, count—allow me one word—I myself will unfold ——"

"Excuse me, Markham," interrupted the Italian noble, with dignified firmness: "I will hear this man first. Proceed!"

"The villain I allude to is of course that Markham," continued the Resurrection Man. "It was him, too, that induced me and my pals, the Cracksman and the Buffer, to make this attempt upon your house to-night."

"What foul—what hideous calumny is this!" almost screamed the distracted Markham, as this totally unexpected and unfounded accusation met his ears.

The count himself was shocked at this announcement; for he suddenly recollected Richard's moody, embarrassed, and thoughtful manner the whole evening, and his sudden intention of departing the next day.

"Go on," said the count.

"I met that man," continued the body-snatcher, pointing contemptuously towards Markham, "a little more than a fortnight ago in this neighbourhood: he was walking with your daughter, and it was in consequence of certain little arrangements with me that he went back to London next day. Oh! I am well acquainted with all his movements."

"And you sought my life in a manner the most base——" began Markham, unable to restrain his feelings.

"Silence, Markham!" exclaimed the count, still more authoritatively than before. "Your time to speak will come."

"We planned this work while he was in London," continued the Resurrection Man; "and this very evening he told me over the garden wall that all was right."

"Merciful God!" cried the count: "this is but too true!"

"Yes, sir—I certainly spoke to him," said Richard,—"and from the garden too——"

"Mr. Markham, this continued interruption is indecent," exclaimed the count emphatically, while a cold perspiration burst out upon his forehead, for he had recalled to mind the incident respecting the garden.

"I have little more to add, count," said the Resurrection Man. "This Markham told me that you had plenty of plate and money always in the house, and as he had lost nearly all his property, he should not be displeased at an opportunity of getting hold of a little swag. It was agreed that we should meet in London to arrange the business; and so we did meet at the *Dark House* in Brick Lane, where we settled the affair along with the Cracksman and the Buffer, who have just made off. This is all I have to say—unless it is that me and your friend Markham first got acquainted in Newgate——"

"Newgate!" ejaculated the count, with a thrill of horror.

"Yes—Newgate; where he was waiting to be tried for forgery, for which he got two years in the Compter. And that's all. Let him deny it if he can."

Scarcely were these terrible words uttered by the Resurrection Man, when a loud—long—and piercing scream was heard, coming from the direction of the staircase; and then some object instantly fell with violence upon the marble floor of the hall.

"Isabella! Isabella!" ejaculated Markham, turning hastily round to hurry to her assistance.

"Stop, sir—seek not my daughter," cried the count, in a stern voice, as he caught Richard's arm, and held him back. "Let not a soul stir until my return!"

There was a noble and dignified air of command about Count Alteroni, as he uttered these words, which could not escape the notice of Richard Markham, even amidst the crushing and overwhelming circumstances that surrounded him.

The count took the candle from Markham's hand, and hastened to the aid of his daughter, who, half-dressed, was lying upon the cold marble of the hall. He hastened to raise her; and at that moment the countess appeared upon the stairs, followed by a lady's-maid bearing a lamp.

The count reassured her in respect to the safety of the house, consigned Isabella to her care, and then returned to the pantry, where his presence was awaited in silence.

"Have you any thing more to say?" demanded the count of the Resurrection Man.

"Nothing. Have not I said enough?"—and he glanced with fiendish triumph towards Markham.

"Now, sir," said the count, turning to Richard; "is the statement of this man easy to be refuted?"

"Alas! I am compelled to admit that, the victim of the most extraordinary circumstantial evidence ever known to fix guilt upon an innocent man, I was a prisoner in Newgate and the Compter; but——"

"Say no more! say no more! God forgive me that I should have allowed such a man to become the friend of my wife and daughter!"

The count uttered these words in a tone of intense agony.

"Count Alteroni, allow me one word of explanation," said Richard. "Only cast your eyes over this paper, and you will be convinced of my innocence!"

Markham handed the document signed by Talbot, *alias* Pocock, to the count; but the nobleman tossed it indignantly on the floor.

"You have confessed that you have been an inmate of the felons' gaols: what explanation can you give that will wipe away so foul a stain? Depart—begone! defile not my house longer with your presence!"

Vainly did Markham endeavour to obtain a hearing. The count silenced him with an air of command and an imposing dignity of manner that struck him with awe. Never did the Italian nobleman appear more really noble than when he was thus performing that which he considered to be an imperious duty. His fine form was drawn up to its full height—his chest expanded—his cheeks were flushed—and his eyes flashed fire. Yes—even beneath his dark complexion was the rich Italian blood seen mantling his countenance.

"Go, sir—hasten your departure—stay not another minute here! A man accused of forgery—condemned to an infamous punishment,—a liberated felon—a freed convict in my family dwelling——Holy God! I can scarcely restrain myself within the bounds of common patience when I think of the indignity that myself, my wife, and my innocent daughter have endured."

With these words the count pushed Markham rudely from the pantry, and ordered a servant to conduct him to the front door.

The blood of the young man boiled in his veins at this ignominious treatment;—and yet he dared not rebel against it!

The Resurrection Man took his departure at the same time by the garden at the back of the house.

As Markham turned down the shrubbery, a window on the third floor of the count's dwelling was thrown open; and the voices of Sir Cherry Bounce and the Honourable Captain Dapper were heard loading him with abuse.

Bowed down to the earth by the weight of the misfortune which had just fallen upon his head,—crushed by unjust and unfounded suspicions,—and sinking beneath a sense of shame and degradation, which all his innocence did not deprive of a single pang,—Markham dragged himself away from the house in which he had passed so many happy hours, and where he left behind him all that he held dear in this life.

He seated himself upon a mile-stone at a little distance from the count's mansion, to which he turned his eyes to take a last farewell of the place where Isabella resided.

Lights were moving about in several rooms;—perhaps she was ill?

Most assuredly she had heard the dread accusations which had issued from the lips of the Resurrection Man against her lover;—and she would haply believe them all?

So thought Richard. Human language cannot convey an adequate idea of the heart-rending misery which the poor oppressed young man endured as he sate by the road-side, and pondered upon all that had just occurred.

Shame upon shame—degradation upon degradation—mountain upon mountain rolled on his breast, as if he were a modern Titan, to crush him and keep him down—never more to rise;—this was now *his* fate!

At length, afraid of being left alone with his own thoughts, which seemed to urge him to end his earthly woes in the blood of a suicide, he rose from the cold stone, turned one last sorrowful and lingering glance towards the mansion in the distance, and then hurried along the road to Richmond as if he were pursued by bloodhounds.

And not more fearful nor more appalling would those bloodhounds have been than the horrible and excruciating thoughts which haunted him upon his way, and of which he could not divest himself; so that at length a species of delirium seized upon him as he ran furiously onward, the mark of Cain appearing to burn like red-hot iron upon his brow, and a terrible voice thundering in his ear—"FREED CONVICT!"

CHAPTER XLVII.

ELIZA SYDNEY.

THE reader will remember that the events already related have brought us up to the close of 1838.

Thus three years had elapsed since the memorable trial which resulted in the condemnation of Eliza Sydney to an imprisonment of twenty-four long months in Newgate; and a year had passed since her release from that dread abode.

We therefore return to her again in December, 1838—about the same time that those incidents occurred which we detailed in the last few chapters.

Probably to the surprise of the reader, we again find Eliza Sydney the mistress of the beautiful villa at Upper Clapton.

Yes: on the evening when we once more introduce ourselves to her, she was sitting alone in the drawing-room of that house, reading by the side of a cheerful fire.

She was now twenty-eight years of age; and, although somewhat more inclining to *embonpoint* than when we first described her, she was still a lovely and fascinating woman. That slightly increased roundness of form had given her charms a voluptuousness the most ravishing and seductive, but the effects of which upon the beholder were attempered by the dignity that reigned upon her high and noble brow, and the chaste expression of her melting hazel eyes.

She was one of those fine creatures—one of those splendid specimens of the female sex, which are alone seen in the cold climates of the north; for it appears to be a rule in nature that the flowers of our species expand into the most luscious loveliness in the least genial latitudes.

There was a soft melancholy in the expression of her countenance, which might have been mistaken for languor, and which gave an additional charm to her appearance; for it was easy to perceive her mind was now at ease, that delicate shade of sadness being the indelible effect of the adventures of the past.

Her mind was at ease, because she was pure in heart and virtuous in intention,—because she knew that she had erred innocently when she lent herself to the fraud for which she had suffered,—because she possessed a competency that secured her against care for the present and fear for the future,—and because she dwelt in that strict solitude and retirement which she loved, and which was congenial to a soul that had seen enough of the world to learn to dread its cruel artifices and deceptive ways.

We said that it was evening when we again introduce Eliza to the readers. A cold wind whistled without; and a huge Christmas log burnt at the back of the grate, giving an air of supreme comfort to that liberally-furnished room.

The French porcelain time-piece upon the mantel proclaimed the hour of eight.

Scarcely had the silvery chime ceased, when Louisa entered the room in great haste and excitement.

"Oh, ma'am! who do you think is here?" she cried, closing the door carefully behind her.

"It is impossible for me to guess, Louisa," said Eliza, smiling.

"Mr. Stephens!" exclaimed the servant: "and he earnestly implores to see you!"

"Mr. Stephens!" echoed Eliza. "Impossible!"

"It is him, flesh and blood: but so pale—so ghostly pale—and so altered!"

"Mr. Stephens!" repeated Eliza. "You must be mistaken—you must be dreaming; for you are aware that, in accordance with his sentence, he must be very—very far from England."

"He is here—he is in London—he is at your door!" said Louisa emphatically; "and as far as I could see by the light of the candle that I had with me when I answered his knock, he is in rags and tatters."

"And he wishes to see me?" said Eliza, musing.

"Yes, ma'am."

There was a pause of a few moments.

"I will see him," exclaimed Eliza, in a decided tone, after some consideration. "He may be in want—in distress; and I cannot forget that he proclaimed my innocence in the dock of the Old Bailey."

Louisa left the room: and in another minute the convict Stephens stood in the presence of Eliza Sydney.

Altered! he was indeed altered. His eyes were sunken and lustreless—his cheeks wan and hollow—his hair prematurely tinged with grey—and his form thin and emaciated. He was moreover clad in rags—absolute rags.

"My God!" ejaculated Eliza: "in what a condition do you return to your native land!"

"And heaven alone knows what sacrifices I have made, and what hardships I have undergone to come back!" said Stephens in a hollow voice.

"You are pardoned, then?"

"Oh, no! crimes like mine are not so readily forgiven. I escaped!"

"Escaped!" exclaimed Eliza: "and are you not afraid of being recaptured?"

"I must run that risk," replied Stephens, sorrowfully. "But give me food—I am hungry—I am starving!"

The unhappy man sank upon a chair as he uttered these words; and Eliza summoned Louisa to bring refreshments.

The servant placed a tray laden with provisions upon the table, and retired.

Stephens then fell ravenously upon the food thus set before him; while tears stood in Eliza's eyes when she thought that the miserable wretch had once commanded in that house where he now craved a morsel of bread!

At length the convict terminated his meal.

"I had eaten nothing," he said, "since yesterday afternoon, when I spent my last penny to procure a roll. Last night I slept in a shed near the docks, a large stone for my pillow. All this day I have been wandering about the most obscure and wretched neighbourhoods of

London—not knowing whither to go, and afraid to be seen by any one who may recognise me. Recognise me!" he added, in a strange satirical manner: "that would perhaps be difficult;" then, sinking his voice almost to a whisper, he said in a tone of profound and touching melancholy, "Do you not find me much—very much altered?"

"You have doubtless suffered deeply," said Eliza, wiping away the tears from her eyes; for at that moment she remembered not the injury brought by that man upon herself—she saw and knew of nought save the misery of the hapless being before her.

"You weep, Eliza," exclaimed Stephens, "you weep for me who am unworthy even of your notice!"

"Forget the past: I prefer dwelling upon the kindnesses rather than the injuries I have experienced at your hands."

"Excellent woman!" cried the convict, deeply affected. "Oh! you know not what I have endured—what dangers I have incurred—what hardships I have undergone—what privations I have experienced! Compelled to work my passage back to England as a common sailor—a prey to the brutality of a tyrannical and drunken captain—exposed to all the inclemencies of the weather,—no tongue can tell what I have gone through! But I will not weary you with my complaints. Rather let me hear how you yourself have fared."

"My tale is short," answered Eliza. "The two years in Newgate passed away. God knows how they passed away—but they *did* pass! Of that I will say no more—save that the most powerful interest was exerted to obtain a mitigation of my sentence—but in vain! The Secretary of State assured the Earl of Warrington that he could not interfere with the very lenient judgment awarded by the court relative to myself. One more circumstance I must mention. Every three months, when the prison regulations allowed the admission of the friends of those confined, a lady visited me; and though that lady be the mistress of the Earl of Warrington, I would rejoice to call her *sister*."

"Oh! how rejoiced I am to know that you were not without friends!" exclaimed Stephens.

"The Earl of Warrington sent me by this lady assurances of his forgiveness, and even of his intention to befriend me, for the sake of my dear departed mother. But, oh! who could have anticipated the noble—the generous conduct pursued towards me by that nobleman? The day of my liberation dawned. Mrs. Arlington came in the earl's private travelling carriage, and received me at the door of the prison. The carriage rolled away; and, when I had recovered from the first emotions of joy at leaving that horrible place, I found we were proceeding along the Hackney Road. I cast a glance of surprise at Mrs. Arlington; she only smiled, and would not gratify my curiosity. At length we came in sight of the villa, and my astonishment increased. Still Mrs. Arlington only smiled. In a few minutes more the carriage entered the enclosure, and drove up to this door. Mrs. Arlington seemed to enjoy my surprise—and yet tears glistened in her eyes. Oh! the admirable woman: they were tears of joy at the grateful task which the earl had imposed upon her. The front door opened, and Louisa ran forward to welcome me. Mrs. Arlington took my hand, and led me into the dining-room. The furniture was all entirely new. She conducted me over the house: every room was similarly renovated. At length I felt exhausted with pleasure, hope, and alarm, and sank upon the sofa in this apartment. 'My dear Eliza,' said Mrs. Arlington, 'all that you survey is yours. The very house itself is your own property. The Earl of Warrington has purchased it for you; and his solicitor, Mr. Pakenham, will call upon you to-morrow with the title-deeds.'—I fainted through excess of happiness and gratitude."

"How noble!" exclaimed Stephens. "I knew that the Earl of Warrington had purchased this estate; for I had already mortgaged it to its full value previous to that fatal epoch when all my hopes failed! My brother, who resided in Liverpool, left England six months after my departure, and went out to settle in New South Wales. He told me that the person who had lent me the money upon this property, had disposed of it to the earl. My brother's object was to settle at Sydney, and procure me to be allotted to him as his servant. I should then have been free. But, alas! scarcely had he set foot in the island, when he was seized with a malignant fever, which proved fatal."

"Misfortunes never come singly," said Eliza. Then, after a pause, she added. "Neither do blessings! And if I have been greatly afflicted—I have also enjoyed some happiness. In reference to my own narrative, I must add that Mr. Pakenham called on the following day, as Mrs. Arlington had promised; and he placed the deeds in my hand. I desired him to retain them in his care for me. He then informed me that the Earl of Warrington had purchased for me an annuity of four hundred pounds a-year. Oh! such generosity overwhelmed me. I begged to be allowed to hasten and throw myself at the feet of that excellent nobleman; but Mr. Pakenham intimated that his lordship was averse to an interview. In a word, he made me understand that I might never hope to thank my benefactor to his face, and that a letter expressing my feelings would be equally unwelcome. The good lawyer, however, tranquillised my mind on one point: the earl has no aversion to me—entertains no animosity against me; but he cannot bear to contemplate the offspring of the woman whom he himself loved so madly!"

"Thus you are happy, and blest with kind friends; and I——I am an outcast!" said Stephens, in a tone of bitter remorse. "Oh! what would I give to be able to recall the past! Blessed, however, be that strange and unaccountable curiosity which led me into this neighbourhood to-night! I say, blessed be it—since it has been the unexpected means for me to hear and know that you at least are happy. Oh! conceive my astonishment when, on approaching the villa, I inquired of a peasant, '*Who dwells there, now?*' and he replied, '*Miss Sydney!*' I could not mistake that announcement: I was already prepared by it for the narrative which you have given me of the Earl of Warrington's generosity."

"Without him, what should I be at this moment?" said Eliza. "He has been more than a friend to me,—his kindness was rather that of a father or a brother! And that angel Mrs. Arlington, who visited me in prison—who poured consolation into my soul, and sustained me with hopes that have been more than realised,—oh! how deep a debt of gratitude do I owe to her also. She did not conceal from me her true position in reference to the Earl of Warrington: she detailed to me the narrative of her sorrows; and I learnt that George Montague was the base deceiver who first taught her to stray from the paths of virtue."

"George Montague!" exclaimed Stephens. "What has become of that man? He is artful, talented, designing, and might perhaps be able to serve me if he would."

"He has assumed, I am told, the name of Greenwood, and dwells in a magnificent house in Spring Gardens. This I learnt from Mrs. Arlington, who called here a few days ago. She also informed me that Montague had circulated a report amongst his acquaintances, that the death of a distant relation had put him in possession of considerable property, and rendered the assumption of the name of Greenwood an indispensable condition of its enjoyment."

"And thus has Montague risen," said Stephens; "while I am humbled to the dust! His intrigues and machinations have enriched him; and the story of the death of a wealthy relation is no doubt the apology for the sudden display of the treasures he has been amassing for the last four or five years. Have you seen him lately?"

"He called here a few days after my release from imprisonment," said Eliza, with a slight blush; "but I did not choose to see him. I love solitude—I prefer retirement."

"And my visit has most disagreeably intruded upon your privacy," observed Stephens.

"I could have wished to have seen you in a more prosperous state, for your own sake," answered Eliza; "but as I observed just now, I would rather remember the kindnesses I have received at your hands, than the miseries which have resulted from your guilty deception. If with my modest and limited means I can assist you, speak! What do you propose to do?"

"My object is to proceed to America, where I might be enabled to obtain an honest livelihood by my mercantile experience and knowledge. Every moment that I prolong my stay in England is fraught with increased peril to my safety; for were I captured, I should be sent back to that far-off clime where so many of my fellow-countrymen endure inconceivable miseries, and where my lot would become terrible indeed."

"I will assist you in your object," said Eliza. "Mr. Pakenham, who acts as my banker, has a hundred pounds of mine in his hands: to-morrow I will draw that amount; and if it will be of any service towards the accomplishment of your plans——"

"Oh, Eliza! how can I sufficiently express my gratitude?" interrupted Stephens, joy and hope animating his care-worn countenance and firing his sunken eyes.

"Do not thank me," said Eliza. "I shall be happy if I can efface one wrinkle from the brow of a fellow-creature. For your present necessities take this,"—and she handed him her purse. "To-morrow evening I shall expect you to call again; and I will then provide you with the means to seek your fortune in another quarter of the world."

Stephens shed tears as he received the purse from the fair hand of that noble-hearted woman.

He then took his departure with a heart far more light than when he had knocked humbly and timidly at the door of that villa an hour before.

CHAPTER XLVIII.

MR. GREENWOOD'S VISITORS.

Mr. Greenwood was seated in his study the morning after the event which occupied the last chapter.

He was dressed *en negligé*.

A French velvet skull-cap, embroidered with gold, sate upon his curled and perfumed hair: a sumptuous brocade silk dressing-gown was confined around the waist by a gold cord with large tassels hanging almost to his feet: his shirt collar was turned down over a plain broad black riband, the bow of which was fastened with a diamond broach of immense value; and on his fingers were costly rings, sparkling with stones of corresponding kind and worth.

On the writing-table an elegant French watch attached to a long gold chain, lay amidst a pile of letters, just as if it had been carelessly tossed there. A cheque, partly filled up for a thousand guineas,—several bank-notes, and some loose gold, were lying on an open writing-desk; and, at one end of the table lay, in seeming confusion, a number of visiting cards bearing the names of eminent capitalists, wealthy merchants, peers, and members of Parliament.

All this pell-mell assemblage of proofs of wealth and tokens of high acquaintance, was only apparent—and not real. It was a portion of Mr. Greenwood's system—one of the principles of the art which he practised in deceiving the world. He knew none of the capitalists, and few of the aristocrats whose cards lay upon his table: and his own hand had arranged the manner in which the watch, the cheque-book, and the money were tossing about. Never did a coquet practise a particular glance, attitude, or mannerism, more seriously than did Mr. Greenwood these little artifices which, however trifling they may appear, produced an immense effect upon those with whom he had to deal, and who visited him in that study.

Every thing he did was the result of a calculation, and had an aim: every word he spoke, however rapid the utterance, was duly weighed and measured.

And yet at this time the man who thus carried his knowledge of human nature even to the most ridiculous niceties, was only in his twenty-eighth year. How perverted were great talents—how misapplied an extraordinary quickness of apprehension in this instance!

Mr. Greenwood contemplated the arrangements of his writing-table with calm satisfaction; and a smile of triumph curled his lip as he thought of the position to which such little artifices as those had helped to raise him. He despised the world: he laughed at society; and he cared not for the law—for he walked boldly up to the extreme verge where personal security ceased and peril began; but he never over-stepped the boundary. He had plundered many—he had enriched himself with the wealth of others—he had built his own fortunes upon the ruins of his fellow men's hopes and prospects: but still he had so contrived all his schemes that the law could never reach him, and if one of his victims accused him of villany he had a plausible explanation to offer for his conduct.

If a person said to him, "Your schemes have involved me in utter ruin, and deprived me of every penny I possessed,"—he would unblushingly reply, "What does the man mean? He forgets that I suffered far more than he did; and that where he lost hundreds I lost thousands! It is impossible to control speculations: some turn up well, some badly; and this man might as well blame the keeper of a lottery-office because his ticket did not turn up a prize, as attempt to throw any odium upon me!"

And this language would prove satisfactory and seem straight-forward to all by-standers, save the poor victim himself, who nevertheless would be struck dumb by the other's assurance.

Greenwood had commenced his ways of intrigue and pursuits of duplicity in the City, where he was known as George Montague. The moment he had obtained a considerable fortune, he repaired to the West End, added the name of Greenwood to his other appellations, and thus commenced, as it were, a new existence in a new sphere.

He possessed the great advantage of exercising a complete control over all his feelings, passions, and inclinations—save with respect to women. In this point of view he was a complete sensualist—a heartless voluptuary. He would spare neither expense nor trouble to gratify his amorous desires, where he formed a predilection; and if in any case he would run a risk of involving himself in the complexities of civil or criminal law, the peril would be encountered in an attempt to satisfy his lustful cravings. There are many men of this stamp in the world,—especially in great cities—and, more especially still, in London.

Mr. Greenwood, having completed the arrangements of his study in the manner described, rang the bell.

His French valet Lafleur made his appearance in answer to the summons. Mr. Greenwood then threw himself negligently into the arm-chair at his writing-table, and proceeded to issue his instructions to his dependant.

"Lafleur, the Count Alteroni will call this morning. When he has been here about ten minutes, bring me in this letter."

He handed his valet a letter, sealed, and addressed to himself.

"At about twelve o'clock Lord Tremordyn will call. Let him remain quietly for a quarter of an hour with me; and then come in and say, '*The Duke of Portsmouth has sent round, sir, to know whether he can positively rely upon your company to dinner this evening.*' Do you understand?"

"Perfectly, sir," answered Lafleur, without the slightest variation of countenance; for he was too politic and too *finished* a valet to attempt to criticise his master's proceedings by means of even a look.

"So far, so good," resumed Mr. Greenwood. "Sir Rupert Harborough will call this morning: you will tell him I am not at home."

"Yes, sir."

"Lady Cecilia Harborough will call at one precisely: you will conduct her to the drawing-room."

"Yes, sir."

"And all the time she is here I shall not be at home to a soul."

"No, sir."

"At four o'clock I shall go out in the cab: you can then pay a visit to Upper Clapton and ascertain by any indirect means you can light upon, whether Miss Sydney still inhabits the villa, and whether she still pursues the same retired and secluded mode of existence as when you last made inquiries in that quarter."

"Yes, sir."

"And you can ride round by Holloway and find out—also by indirect inquiries, remember—whether Mr. Markham is at home, and any other particulars relative to him which you can glean. I have already told you that I have the deepest interest in being acquainted with all that that young man does—his minutest actions even."

"I will attend to your orders, sir."

"To-night, you will dress yourself in mean attire and repair to a low public-house on Saffron-hill, known by the name of the *Boozing Ken* by the thieves and reprobates of that district. You will inquire for a man who frequents that house, and who is called Tom the Cracksman. No one knows him by any other name. You will tell him who your master is, and that I wish to see him upon very particular business. He must be here to-morrow night at nine o'clock. Give him this five-pound note as an earnest of good intentions."

"Yes, sir."

"And now take these duplicates and that bank-note for five hundred pounds, and just go yourself to V——'s the pawnbroker's in the Strand, and redeem the diamonds mentioned in these tickets. You will have time before any one comes."

"Yes, sir."

"And should Lord Tremordyn happen to be here when you return, hand me the packet, which you will have wrapped up in white paper, saying '*With the Duke's compliments, sir.*'"

"Yes, sir."

Thus ended the morning's instructions.

The valet took the letter (which Mr. Greenwood had written to himself,) the duplicates, and the bank notes; and retired.

In half an hour he returned with a small purple morocco case containing a complete set of diamonds, worth at least twelve hundred guineas.

He again withdrew, and returned in a few minutes;—but this time it was to usher in Count Alteroni.

Mr. Greenwood received the Italian noble with more than usual affability and apparent friendship.

"I am delighted to inform you, my dear count," he said, when they were both seated, "that our enterprise is progressing well. I yesterday received a letter from a certain capitalist to whom I applied relative to the loan of two hundred thousand pounds which I informed you it was necessary to raise to carry out our undertaking, in addition to the capital which you and I have both subscribed; and I have no doubt that I shall succeed in this point. Indeed, he is to send me his decision this very morning."

"Then I hope that at length the Company is definitively formed?" said the count.

"Definitively," answered Mr. Greenwood.

"And the deed by which you guarantee to me the safety of the money I have embarked, let the event be what it may?" said the count.

"That will be ready to-morrow evening. Can you dine with me to-morrow, and terminate that portion of the business after dinner? My solicitor will send the deed hither by one of his clerks at half-past eight o'clock."

"With pleasure," said the count, evidently pleased at this arrangement.

"There has been some delay," said Mr. Greenwood; "but really the fault has not existed with me."

"You will excuse my anxiety in this respect: indeed, I have probably pressed you more than I ought for the completion of that security; but you will remember that I have embarked my all in this enterprise."

"Do not attempt an apology. You have acted as a man of prudence and caution; and you will find that I shall behave as a man of business."

"I am perfectly satisfied," said the count. "I should not have advanced my money unless I had been so perfectly satisfied with your representations; for—unless events turn up in my favour in my own country, I must for ever expect to remain an exile from Castelcicala. And that good fortune will shine upon me from that quarter, I can scarcely expect. My liberal principles have offended the Grand-Duke and the old nobility of that state; and now that the aristocracy has there gained the ascendancy, and is likely to retain it, I can hope for nothing. I would gladly have aided the popular cause, and obtained for the people of Castelcicala a constitution; but the idea of representative principles is odious to those now in power."

"I believe that you were a staunch adherent of the Prince of Castelcicala, who is the nephew of the reigning Grand-Duke and the heir-apparent to the throne," said Mr. Greenwood.

"You have been rightly informed; but if the Pope and the Kings of Naples and Sardinia support the aristocracy of Castelcicala, that prince will be excluded from his inheritance and a foreigner will be placed upon the grand-ducal throne. In this case, the prince will be an exile until his death—without even a pension to support him; so irritated are the old aristocracy against him."

"I believe that Castelcicala is a fine state?"

"A beautiful country—extensive, well-cultivated, and productive. It contains two millions of inhabitants. The capital, Montoni, is a magnificent city, of a hundred thousand souls. The revenues of the Grand-Duke are two hundred thousand pounds sterling a-year; and yet he is not contented! He does not study his people's happiness."

"And where at the present moment is that gallant prince who has thus risked his accession to the throne for the welfare of his fellow-countrymen?" inquired Greenwood.

"That remains a secret," answered the count. "His partisans alone know."

"Of course I would not attempt to intrude upon matters so sacred," said Greenwood, "were I not deeply interested in yourself, whom I know to be one of his most staunch adherents."

At that moment the door opened; and Lafleur entered, bearing a letter, which he handed to Mr. Greenwood. He then retired.

"Will you excuse me?" said Greenwood to the count; then, opening the letter, he appeared to read it with attention.

At the expiration of a few moments, he said, "This letter is from my capitalist. He gives me both good and bad news. He will advance the loan; but he cannot command the necessary amount for three months."

"Then there will be three months' more delay?" exclaimed the count in a tone of vexation.

"Three months! and what is that? A mere nothing!" cried Mr. Greenwood. "You can satisfy yourself of my friend's sincerity."

With these words he handed to the count the letter which he had written to himself in a feigned hand, and to which he had affixed a fictitious name and address.

The count read the letter and was satisfied.

He then rose to depart.

"To-morrow evening, at seven o'clock punctually, I shall do myself the pleasure of waiting upon you. In a few days, you remember, I and my family are coming up to town to pass some time with Lord Tremordyn."

"And I shall then be bold and presumptuous enough," said Greenwood, "to endeavour to render myself acceptable to the Signora Isabella."

"By the bye," exclaimed the count, "I forgot to inform you of the villany of that Richard Markham, whom I received into the bosom of my family, and treated as a son, or a brother."

"His villany!" ejaculated Greenwood, in a tone of unfeigned surprise.

"Villany the most atrocious!" cried the count. "He is a man branded with the infamy of a felon's gaol!"

"Impossible!" said Greenwood, this time affecting the astonishment expressed by his countenance.

"It is, alas! too true. The night before last, he invited thieves to break into my dwelling: and to those miscreants had he boasted of his intentions to win the favour of my daughter!"

"Oh! no—no," said Greenwood emphatically; "you must have been misinformed!"

"On the contrary, I have received evidence only too corroborative of what I tell you. But when I come to-morrow evening, I will give you the details."

The count then took his departure.

"Thank God!" said Mr. Greenwood to himself, the moment the door had closed behind the Italian nobleman: "I have succeeded in putting off that bothering count for three good months. Much may be done in the mean time; and if I can secure his daughter—all will be well! I can then pension him off upon a hundred and fifty pounds a year—and retain possession of his capital. But this deed—he demands the deed of guarantee: he presses for that! I must give him the security to show my good-will; and then neutralise that concession on my part, in the manner already resolved upon. How strange was the account he gave me of Richard Markham! That unhappy young man appears to be the victim of the most wonderful combination of suspicious circumstances ever known; for guilty he could not be—oh! no—impossible!"

Mr. Greenwood's meditations were interrupted by the entrance of Lord Tremordyn.

This nobleman was a short, stout, good-tempered man. Being a large landholder, he exercised considerable influence in his county, of which he was lord-lieutenant; and he boasted that he could return six members to parliament in spite of the Reform-bill. His wife was moreover allied to one of the richest and most important families in the hierarchy of the aristocracy; and thus Lord Tremordyn—with no talent, no knowledge, no acquirements to recommend him, but with certain political tenets which he inherited along with the family estate, and which he professed for no other reason than because they were those of his ancestors,—Lord Tremordyn, we say, was a very great man in the House of Lords. He seldom spoke, it is true; but then he *voted*—and dictated to others *how to vote*; and in this existed his power. When he *did* speak, he uttered an awful amount of nonsense; but the reporters were very kind—and so his speeches read well. Indeed, he did not know them again when he perused them in print the morning after their delivery. Moreover, his wife was a blue-stocking, and dabbled a little in politics; and she occasionally furnished her noble husband with a few hints which might have been valuable had he clothed them in language a little intelligible. For the rest, Lord Tremordyn was a most hospitable man, was fond of his bottle, and fancied himself a sporting character because he kept hounds and horses, and generally employed an agent to "make up a book" for him at races, whereby he was most amazingly plundered.

"My dear lord," exclaimed Mr. Greenwood, conducting his noble visitor to a seat; "I am delighted to see your lordship look so well. So you have parted with *Electricity*? I heard of it yesterday at Tattersalls'."

"Yes—and a good price I had for him. But, by the way, my dear Greenwood, I must not forget to thank you for the Hock you sent me. It is superb!"

"I am delighted that your lordship is pleased with it. Have you seen Sir Rupert Harborough lately?"

"My scapegrace son-in-law? I wish I had never seen him at all!" ejaculated his lordship. "He is over head and ears in debt again: and I swear most solemnly that I will do nothing more for him—not to the amount of a penny-piece! Cecilia, too, has quarrelled with her mother; and, even if she had not, Lady Tremordyn is the last woman on earth to advance them a shilling."

"It is a pity—a great pity!" said Mr. Greenwood, apparently musing; then, after a brief pause, he added, "You never can guess, my dear lord, why I wished to see your lordship so particularly this morning?"

"About the match between *Electricity* and *Galvanism*? The odds are three to four."

"That was not exactly my business," said Greenwood, with a bland smile: "the fact is, the representation of Rottenborough will be vacant in a few weeks. I know positively, that the present member intends to accept the Chiltern Hundreds."[1]

"I have received a similar intimation," observed his lordship.

"At present the matter is a profound secret."

---

1 Being servants of the Crown, Members of Parliament cannot resign their positions. Instead, they apply for an office of gain under the Crown, which disqualifies them from being Members. The usual office is the Stewardship of the Chiltern Hundreds, from which they immediately resign.

"Yes—a profound secret: known only to the member's friends, and me and my friends, and you and your friends," added the nobleman, seriously meaning what he said without any attempt at irony or satire.

"Of course there will be an election in February, shortly after the Houses meet," continued Greenwood. "I was going to observe to your lordship that I should be most happy to offer myself as a candidate——"

"You, Greenwood! What—are you a politician?"

"Not so profound nor so well versed as your lordship; but I flatter myself that, aided by your lordship's advice——"

"Lady Tremordyn would never consent to it!"

"And by Lady Tremordyn's suggestions——"

"It would never do! She *will* have a man of rank and family; and—excuse me, Greenwood—although you are no doubt rich enough for a lord, and well educated, and clever, and so on—the deuce of it is that we don't know who the devil you are!"

"An excellent family—an excellent family, my dear lord," exclaimed Mr. Greenwood; "and although nothing equal to your own, which I know to be the most ancient in England——"

"Or Scotland, or Ireland, either."

"Or Scotland, or Ireland, or even Europe—still——"

"No—it cannot be done, Greenwood;—it cannot be done," interrupted the nobleman. "I would do any thing to oblige you;—but——"

At that moment the door opened, and Lafleur entered the study.

"If you please, sir," said the French valet, "the Duke of Portsmouth has sent round to know whether he can positively rely upon your company to dinner this evening?'

"My best compliments to his grace, Lafleur," said Mr. Greenwood, affecting to meditate upon this message for a moment, "and I will do myself the honour of waiting on his grace at the usual hour."

"Very good, sir."

And Lafleur retired.

"Well, after all," resumed Lord Tremordyn, who had not lost a word of this message and the answer, "I think I might undertake to arrange the Rottenborough business for you. You have high acquaintances—and they often do more good than high connexions. So we will consider that matter as settled."

"I am deeply obliged to your lordship," said Greenwood, with the calmness of a man who had never entertained a fear of being ultimately enabled to carry his point: "you will see that I shall imitate in the Lower House your lordship's admirable conduct in the Upper, to the very best of my ability."

"Of course you will always support the measures I support, and oppose those which I may oppose?"

"Oh! that is a matter of course! What would become of society—where should we be, if the Commons did not obey the great landholders who allow them to be returned?"

"Ah! what indeed?" said the nobleman, shaking his head ominously. "But really, Greenwood, I wasn't at all aware that you were half so clever a politician as I see you are."

"Your lordship does me honour. I know how to value your lordship's good opinion," said Greenwood, in a meek and submissive manner: then, after a moment's silence, he added, "By the bye, I understand that our mutual friend Alteroni, and his amiable wife, and beautiful daughter, are going to pass the first few weeks of the new year with your lordship and Lady Tremordyn?"

"Yes: we shall be very gay. The signora must pick up a husband amongst the young nobles or scions of great families whom she will meet this winter in London."

"Do you not know, my lord," said Greenwood, sinking his voice to a mysterious whisper, "that Count Alteroni detests gaiety? are you not aware that he and the ladies have accepted your kind invitation under the impression that they will enjoy the pleasing society of your lordship and Lady Tremordyn, and a few select friends only?"

"I am glad you have told me that!" exclaimed the nobleman. "We will have no gaiety at all."

"The count has honoured me with his utmost confidence, and his sincere friendship," said Greenwood.

"Oh! of course you will be welcome on all occasions: do not wait for invitations—I give you a general one."

"I am more than ever indebted to your lordship."

After a little more conversation in the same strain, the nobleman took his leave, more pleased with Mr. Greenwood than ever.

This gentleman, the moment he was alone, threw himself into his chair, and smiled complacently.

"Gained all my points!" he said, musing. "I shall be a member of parliament—the fair Isabella will stand no chance of captivating some wealthy and titled individual who might woo and win her—and I have obtained a general invitation to Lord Tremordyn's dwelling! I alone shall therefore have an opportunity of paying court to this Italian beauty."

The French valet entered the room.

"Lady Cecilia Harborough is in the drawing room, sir."

Mr. Greenwood thrust the morocco case containing the diamonds into the pocket of his dressing-gown; and then proceeded to the apartment where the lady was waiting.

Lady Cecilia Harborough was about two-and-twenty, and very beautiful. Her hair was auburn, her eyes blue, and her features regular. Her figure was good; but she was very slightly made—a perfect sylph in symmetry and model. Nursed amidst fashionable pleasure and aristocratic dissipation, she was without those principles which are the very basis of virtue. If she were true and faithful to her husband, it was only because she had not been strongly tempted to prove otherwise: if she had never indulged in an intrigue, it was simply because one to her taste had never come in her way. Her passions were strong—her disposition decidedly sensual. Thus was it that she had become an easy prey to Sir Rupert Harborough; and when she had discovered that she was in a way to become a mother in consequence of that amour, she only repented of her conduct through dread of shame, and not for the mere fact of having deviated from the path of virtue. Her disgrace was concealed by a patched-up marriage with her seducer, a trip to the Continent, and the death of the child at its birth; and thus there was no scandal in society attached to the name of Lady Cecilia Harborough.

Mr. Greenwood had not made her wait many moments when he entered the drawing-room.

Lady Cecilia rose, and hastening towards him, said, "Oh! Mr. Greenwood, what can you think of me after the imprudent step I have taken in coming alone and unattended?"

"I can only think, Lady Cecilia," said Greenwood, handing her to a seat, and taking a chair near her, "that you have done me an honour, the extent of which I can fully appreciate."

"But why insist upon this visit to you? why could you not have called upon me?" inquired the lady impatiently.

"Your ladyship wishes to consult with me upon financial affairs: and every capitalist *receives* visits, and does not *pay* them, when they refer to business only."

"Thank you for this apology for my conduct. I fancied that I was guilty of a very great imprudence; you have reassured me upon that head;"—and a smile played upon the fair patrician's lips.

"In what manner can I be of service to your ladyship? You perceive that I will save you the trouble of even introducing a disagreeable subject."

"Well, Mr. Greenwood," said Lady Cecilia, with that easy familiarity which is always shown towards those who are confidants in cases of pecuniary embarrassment,—"you are well aware of Sir Rupert's unfortunate situation; and of course his position is also mine. We are literally without the means of paying the common weekly bills of the house, and the servants' wages. I have quarrelled with my mother; and my father will not advance another sixpence."

"Your ladyship is well aware that Sir Rupert Harborough has no security to offer; and if he had, I would scarcely advance money to *him*—since I know that *your ladyship* seldom profits by any funds which he may possess."

"Oh! that is true, Mr. Greenwood!" ejaculated Lady Cecilia, emphatically. "Would you believe it—even my very diamonds are gone? Sir Rupert has made away with them!"

"In plain terms he pawned them."

"He did:—but that is such a horrid avowal to make! When one thinks that it is generally supposed that the poor alone have recourse to such means, and that *we* in the upper class do not even know what is meant by a pawnbroker's——Oh! how false is that idea! how erroneous is that impression!"

"It is, indeed," said Greenwood. "The jewels of half the high-born ladies in London have been deposited at different times in the hands of the very pawnbroker where yours were."

Lady Cecilia stared at Mr. Greenwood in profound astonishment: then, as a sudden idea seemed to flash across her brain, she added, "But Sir Rupert must have told you of this?"

"He did."

"Do you know," continued the lady, "that I have actually lost the receipts or duplicates—or whatever you call them—which the pawnbroker gave when Harborough sent the diamonds by a trusty servant of ours."

"Those duplicates Sir Rupert Harborough handed over to me," said Greenwood. "I lent him a hundred pounds upon them yesterday morning!"

"Oh! how ungrateful he is—how unworthy of one particle of affection!" exclaimed Lady Cecilia. "He knew how distressed—literally distressed I was for ready money; and he never offered me a guinea!"

"Are you so distressed as that?" inquired Mr. Greenwood, drawing his chair closer to that of his fair visitor.

"Why should I conceal any thing from you, when I come to consult you upon my embarrassments?" said Lady Cecilia, tears starting into her eyes. "I am literally disgraced! I cannot go to court, nor appear at any grand *réunion*, for the want of my jewels; and I am indebted to old Lady Marlborough to the amount of two hundred pounds which she lent me. Yesterday she wrote for the sixth time for the money, and actually observed in her letter that she considered my conduct unlady-like in the extreme. If I do not pay her this day, I shall be ruined—exposed—ashamed to show my face in any society whatever!"

"You would therefore make any sacrifice to relieve yourself from these embarrassments?" said Greenwood interrogatively.

"Oh! any sacrifice! To obtain about eight hundred or a thousand pounds, to redeem my jewels and pay my most pressing debts—Lady Marlborough's, for instance—I would do any thing!"

"You would make any sacrifice? You would do any thing, Lady Cecilia?" repeated Greenwood emphatically. "That is saying a great deal; and an impertinent coxcomb—like me, for instance—might perhaps construe your words literally, and be most presumptuous in his demands."

"My God, Mr. Greenwood—what do you mean?" exclaimed the lady, a slight flush appearing upon her cheeks. "My case is so very desperate—I have no security to offer at present—and yet I require money,—money I must have! Tell me to throw myself into the Thames a year hence, so that I have money to-day, and I would willingly subscribe to the contract. I could even sell myself to the Evil One, like Dr. Faustus—I am so bewildered—so truly wretched!"

"Since you have verged into the regions of romance, and mentioned improbabilities, or impossibilities," said Mr. Greenwood, "suppose another strange case;—suppose that a man threw himself at your feet—declared his love—sought yours in return—and proffered you his fortune as a proof of the sincerity of his heart?"

"Such generous and noble-minded lovers are not so easily found now-a-days," returned Lady Cecilia: "but, if I must respond to your question, I am almost inclined to think that I should not prove very cruel to the tender swain who would present himself in so truly romantic a manner."

Greenwood caught hold of Lady Cecilia's hand, fell at her feet, and presented her with the purple morocco case containing the diamonds.

"Heavens!" she exclaimed, half inclined to suppose that this proceeding was a mere jest,—"what do you mean, Mr. Greenwood? Surely you were not supposing a case in which you yourself were to be the principal actor?"

"Permit me to lay my heart and fortune at your feet!" said Greenwood. "Nay—you cannot repulse me now: you accepted the alternative; your own words have rendered me thus bold, thus presumptuous!"

"Ah! Mr. Greenwood," exclaimed the fair patrician lady, abandoning her left hand to this bold admirer, and receiving the case of diamonds with the right; "you have spread a snare for me—and I have fallen into the tangled meshes!"

"You can have no compunction—you can entertain no remorse in transferring your affections from a man who neglects you, to one who will study your happiness in every way."

"But—merciful heavens! you would not have me leave my husband altogether? Oh! I could not bear the *éclat* of an elopement: no—never—never!"

"Nor would I counsel such a proceeding," said Greenwood, who was himself astonished at the ease with which he had obtained this victory: "you must sustain appearances in society; but when we *can* meet—and when we are together—oh! then we can be to each other as if we alone existed in the world—as if we could indulge in all the joys and sweets of love without fear and without peril!"

"Yes—I will be yours upon these terms—I will be yours!"

murmured Cecilia. "And—remember—you must be faithful towards me; and you must never forget the sacrifice I make and the risk I run in thus responding to your attachment! But—above all things—do not think ill of me—do not despise me! I want something to love—and some one to love me;—and you sympathise with my distress—you feel for my unhappiness—you offer me your consolations: oh! yes—it is you whom I must love—and you will love me!"

"For ever," answered the libertine; and he caught that frail but beauteous lady in his arms.

* * * * * *

An hour elapsed: Lady Cecilia had taken her departure, richer in purse but poorer in honour;—and Greenwood had returned to his study.

The flush of triumph was upon his brow; and the smile of satisfaction was upon his lip.

Lafleur entered the room.

"While you were engaged, sir," said the valet, "Sir Rupert Harborough called. He was most anxious to see you. I assured him that you were not at home. He said he would call again in an hour."

"You can then admit him."

The valet bowed and withdrew.

Mr. Greenwood then wrote several letters connected with the various schemes which he had in hand. His occupation was interrupted by the entrance of Sir Rupert Harborough.

With what ease and assurance—with what unblushing confidence did the libertine receive the man whose wife he had drawn into the snares of infamy and dishonour!

"You really must excuse my perseverance in seeing you this day," said Sir Rupert, who perceived by Greenwood's attire that he had not been out of the house that morning; "but I am in such a mess of difficulties and embarrassments, I really know not which way to turn."

"I was particularly engaged when you called just now," said Greenwood; "and you are aware that one's valet always answers '*Not at home*' in such cases."

"Oh! deuce take ceremony," exclaimed Sir Rupert. "See if you can do any thing to assist me. Lord Tremordyn has literally cut me;

and Lady Tremordyn is as stingy as the devil. Besides, she and Lady Cecilia have quarrelled; and so there is no hope in that quarter."

"I really cannot assist you any farther—at present," observed Greenwood. "In a short time I shall be enabled to let you into a good thing, as I told you a little while ago; but for the moment—"

"Come, Greenwood," interrupted the baronet; "do not refuse me. I will give you a *post-obit*[1] on the old lord: he is sure to leave me something handsome at his death."

"Yes—but he may settle it upon your wife in such a manner that you will not be able to touch it."

"Suppose that Lady Cecilia will join me in the security?"

"Insufficient still. Lord Tremordyn may bequeath her ladyship merely a life interest, without power to touch the capital."

"Well—what the devil can I do?" exclaimed the baronet, almost distracted. "Point out some means—lay down some plan—do any thing you like—but don't refuse some assistance."

Mr. Greenwood reflected for some minutes; and this time his thoughtful manner was not affected. It struck him that he might effect a certain arrangement in this instance by which he might get the baronet completely in his power, and lay out some money at an enormous interest at the same time.

"You see," said Mr. Greenwood, "you have not an atom of security to offer me."

"None—none," answered Sir Rupert: "I know of none—if you will not have the *post-obit*."

"The only means I can think of for the moment," pursued Mr. Greenwood, "is this:—Get me Lord Tremordyn's acceptance to a bill of fifteen hundred pounds at three months, and I will lend you a thousand upon it without an instant's delay."

"Lord Tremordyn's acceptance! Are you mad, Greenwood?"

"No—perfectly sane and serious. Of course I shall not call upon him to ask *if it be his acceptance*—neither shall I put the bill into circulation. It will be in my desk until it is due; and then—if you cannot pay it——"

"What then?" said the baronet, in a subdued tone, as if he breathed with difficulty.

"Why—you must get it renewed, that's all!" replied Mr. Greenwood.

1 A promise to pay on the death of someone.

"I understand you—I understand you," exclaimed Sir Rupert Harborough: "it shall be done! When can I see you again?"

"I shall not stir out for another hour."

"Then I shall return this afternoon."

And the baronet departed to forge the name of Lord Tremordyn to a bill of exchange for fifteen hundred pounds.

"I shall hold him in iron chains," said Greenwood to himself, when he was again alone. "This bill will hang constantly over his head. Should he detect my intrigue with his wife, he will not dare open his mouth; and when I am tired of that amour and care no more for the beautiful Cecilia, I can obtain payment of the entire amount, with interest, from Lord Tremordyn himself; for his lordship will never allow his son-in-law to be ruined and lost for fifteen or sixteen hundred pounds."

Again the study door opened; and again did Lafleur make his appearance.

"A person, sir, who declines to give his name," said the valet, "solicits an interview for a few minutes."

"What sort of a looking person is he?"

"Very pale and sallow; about the middle height; genteel in appearance; respectably clad; and I should say about forty years of age."

"I do not recollect such a person. Show him up."

Lafleur withdrew, and presently introduced Stephens.

For a few moments Greenwood surveyed him in a manner as if he were trying to recollect to whom that pale and altered countenance belonged; for although Stephens had made considerable improvement in his attire, thanks to the contents of Eliza's purse, he still retained upon his features the traces of great suffering, mental and bodily.

"You do not know me?" he said, with a sickly smile.

"Stephens! is it possible?" exclaimed Greenwood, in an accent of the most profound surprise.

"Yes—it is I! No wonder that you did not immediately recognise me: were I not fearfully altered I should not dare thus to venture abroad by daylight."

"Ah! I understand. You have escaped?"

"I have returned from transportation. That is the exact truth. Had it not been for an angel in human shape, I should have died last night of starvation. That generous being who relieved me was Eliza Sydney."

"Eliza Sydney!" cried Greenwood. "She received you with kindness?"

"She gave me food, and money to obtain clothes and lodging. She moreover promised to supply me with the means to reach America. I am to return to her this evening, and receive a certain sum for that purpose."

"And she told you that I was residing here?" said Greenwood inquiringly.

"Yes. I thought that you might be enabled to assist me in my object of commencing the world anew in another quarter of the globe. I shall arrive there with but little money and no friends;—perhaps you can procure me letters of introduction to merchants in New York."

"I think I can assist you," said Greenwood, musing upon a scheme which he was revolving in his mind, and which was as yet only a few minutes old: "yes—I think I can. But, would it not be better for you to take out a few hundred pounds in your pocket? How can you begin any business in the States without capital?"

"Show me the way to procure those few hundreds," said Stephens, "and I would hold myself ever your debtor."

"And perhaps you would not be very particular as to the way in which you obtained such a sum?" demanded Greenwood, surveying the returned convict in a peculiar manner.

"My condition is too desperate to allow me to stick at trifles," answered Stephens, not shrinking from a glance which seemed to penetrate into his soul.

"We understand each other," said Greenwood. "I have money—and you want money: you are a returned transport, and in my power. I can serve and save you; or I can ruin and crush you for ever."

"You speak candidly, at all events," observed Stephens, somewhat bitterly. "Try promises first; and should they fail, essay threats."

"I merely wished you to comprehend your true position with regard to me," said Greenwood, coolly.

"And now I understand it but too well. You require of me some service of a certain nature—no matter what: in a word, I agree to the bargain."

"The business regards Eliza Sydney," proceeded Greenwood.

"Eliza Sydney!" exclaimed Stephens, in dismay.

"Yes; I love her—and she detests me. I must therefore gratify two passions at the same moment—vengeance and desire."

"Impossible!" cried Stephens. "You can never accomplish your schemes through my agency!"

"Very good:" and Mr. Greenwood moved towards the bell.

"What would you do?" demanded Stephens, in alarm.

"Summon my servants to hand a returned convict over to justice," answered Greenwood, coolly.

"Villain! you could not do it!"

"I *will* do it:" and Greenwood placed his hand upon the bell-rope.

"Oh! no—no—that must not be!" exclaimed Stephens. "Speak—I will do your bidding."

Mr. Greenwood returned to his seat.

"I must possess Eliza Sydney—and you must be the instrument," he said in his usual calm and measured tone. "You are to return to her this evening?"

"I am. But I implore you—"

"Silence! This evening I am engaged—and to-morrow evening also. The day after to-morrow I shall be at liberty. You will invent some excuse which will enable you to postpone your departure; and you will contrive to pass the evening after to-morrow with Eliza Sydney. Can you do this?"

"I can, no doubt: but, again, I beg—"

"No more of this nonsense! You will adopt some means to get her faithful servant Louisa out of the way; and you will open the front-door of the villa to me at midnight on the evening appointed."

"You never can effect your purpose!" cried Stephens emphatically. "Were you to introduce yourself to her chamber, she would sooner die herself, or slay you, than submit to your purpose!"

"She must sleep—sleep profoundly!" said Greenwood, sinking his voice almost to a whisper, and regarding his companion in a significant manner.

"My God! what an atrocity!" ejaculated Stephens, with horror depicted upon his countenance.

"Perhaps you prefer a return to the horrors of transportation,—the miseries of Norfolk Island?" said Greenwood satirically.

"No—death, sooner!" cried Stephens, striking the palm of his right hand against his forehead.

Greenwood approached him, and whispered for some time in his ear. Stephens listened in silence and when the libertine had done, he signified a reluctant assent by means of a slight nod.

"You understand how you are to act?" said Greenwood aloud.

"Perfectly," answered Stephens.

He then took his departure.

Scarcely had he left the house when Sir Rupert Harborough returned.

The baronet was deadly pale, and trembled violently. Greenwood affected not to observe his emotions, but received the bill of exchange which the baronet handed to him, with as much coolness as if he were concluding a perfectly legitimate transaction.

Having read the document, he handed a pen to the baronet to endorse it.

Sir Rupert affixed his name at the back of the forged instrument with a species of desperate resolution.

Mr. Greenwood consigned the bill to his desk, and then wrote a cheque for a thousand pounds, which he handed to the baronet.

Thus terminated this transaction.

When the baronet had taken his departure, Mr. Greenwood summoned Lafleur, and said, "You need not institute any inquiries relative to Miss Sydney, at Upper Clapton. My orders relative to Mr. Markham remain unchanged; and mind that the fellow known as Tom the Cracksman is here to-morrow evening at nine o'clock."

Mr. Greenwood having thus concluded his morning's business, partook of an elegant luncheon, and then proceeded to dress for his afternoon's ride in the Park.

CHAPTER XLIX.

THE DOCUMENT.

THE more civilization progresses, and the more refined becomes the human intellect, so does human iniquity increase.

It is true that heinous and appalling crimes are less frequent;—but every kind of social, domestic, political, and commercial intrigue grows more into vogue: human ingenuity is more continually on the rack to discover the means of defrauding a neighbour or cheating the world;—the sacred name of religion is called in to aid and further the nefarious devices of the schemer;—hypocrisy is the cloak which conceals modern acts of turpitude, as dark nights were trusted to for the concealment of the bloody deeds of old: mere brute force is now less frequently resorted to; but the refinements of education or the exercise of duplicity are the engines chiefly used for purposes of plunder. The steel engraver's art, and the skill of the calligrapher, are mighty implements of modern misdeed:—years and years are expended in calculating the chances of cards and dice;—education, manners, and good looks are essential to the formation of the adventurers of the present day;—the Bankruptcy Court itself is a frequent avenue to the temple of fortune;—and, in order to suit this new and refined system of things, the degrees of vices themselves are qualified by different names, so that he who gambles at a gaming-table is a scamp, and he who propagates a lie upon the Exchange and gambles accordingly, and with success, is a respectable financier. Chicanery, upon a small scale, and in a miserable dark office, is a degradation;—but the delicate and elaborate chicanery of politics, by which a statesman is enabled to outwit parties, or deceive whole nations, is a masterpiece of human talent! To utter a falsehood in private life, to suit a private end, is to cut one's-self off from all honourable society:—but to lie day and night in a public journal—to lie habitually and boldly in print—to lie in a manner the most shameless and barefaced in the editorial columns of a newspaper, is not only admissible, but conventional, and a proof of skill, tact, and talent.

Thus is modern society constituted:—let him deny the truth of the picture who can!

London is filled with Mr. Greenwoods: they are to be found in numbers at the West End. Do not for one moment believe, reader, that our portrait of this character is exaggerated.

In pursuing the thread of a narrative like this, there will naturally be found much to alarm, to astonish, and to shock: but however appalling the picture, it teaches lessons which none can regret to learn. The chart that would describe the course to virtue must point out and lay bare the shoals, the quicksands, and the rocks of vice which render the passage perilous and full of terrors.

With these few remarks, we pursue our history.

At seven o'clock in the evening of the day following the one on which we have seen Mr. Greenwood conducting his multifarious schemes and transactions with the precision of a minister of state, Count Alteroni arrived at that gentleman's house in Spring Gardens. He was shown into the elegantly furnished drawing-room, where Mr. Greenwood received him. The count was, however, the only one of all the financier's visitors who did not seem dazzled by the proofs of wealth and luxury that prevailed around. The Italian nobleman remarked these indications of great riches, and considered them the guarantees of Mr. Greenwood's prosperous position in the world: but, apart from this view of the splendour and sumptuousness of the mansion, he neither appeared astonished nor struck with admiration. The truth was, that Mr. Greenwood's abode, with all its magnificent decorations and ornaments, its costly furniture, and its brilliant display of plate, was a mere hovel compared to the count's own palace at Montoni, the capital city of Castelcicala.

Mr. Greenwood and the count had not exchanged many words, ere dinner was announced. The banquet, although only provided for the founder of the feast and his one guest, was of a most magnificent description, every luxury which London could produce appearing upon the table.

At half-past eight o'clock, the clerk of Mr. Greenwood's solicitor arrived, and was introduced into the dining-room. He had brought with him a deed by which Greenwood bound himself to be answerable to Count Alteroni for the sum of fifteen thousand pounds, which the latter had placed in the hands of the former for the purpose of speculation in a certain Steam-packet Company, Greenwood recognising his responsibility towards the count to the above extent whether the Company should succeed or not, it having been originally agreed that he (Greenwood) should incur all risks, as he had undertaken the sole direction of the enterprise. This deed was signed by George M. Greenwood, witnessed by the attorney's clerk, and handed to Count Alteroni.

The clerk then withdrew.

Mr. Greenwood ordered a bottle of the very best Burgundy to be opened, and drank a bumper to the health of the Signora Isabella.

Scarcely was this toast disposed of, when Lafleur entered the room, and said, "A courier with despatches from your correspondents in Paris, sir, has just arrived, and requests to see you instantly. I have shown him into the study."

"Very good," exclaimed Mr. Greenwood, suddenly assuming a business air. "Will you excuse me, count, for a few minutes?"

"I shall take my leave, since you are likely to be much occupied," said the nobleman.

"On the contrary—pray remain—I insist upon it! I shall not be long with this messenger," cried Mr. Greenwood: "and we must empty another bottle before I allow you to take your departure."

The count suffered himself to be over-ruled; and Mr. Greenwood repaired to his study, well-knowing that, instead of a courier from Paris, he should there find Tom the Cracksman.

Nor was he mistaken. That individual was sitting very comfortably in an arm-chair near the fire, gazing around him, and wondering, amongst other things, where the master of the house kept his strong-box.

"You are known, I believe," said Greenwood, carefully closing the door, "as the Cracksman?"

"That's my title, sir—for want of a better," answered the villain.

"You are, perhaps, astonished that I have sent for you here," continued Greenwood: "but I wish a certain service performed this very night, and for which I will pay you liberally."

"What's the natur' of the sarvice?" demanded the Cracksman, darting a keen and penetrating glance at Greenwood.

"A highway robbery," coolly answered this individual.

"Well, that's plain enow," said the Cracksman. "But first tell me how you come to know of me, and where I was to be seen: because how can I tell but what this is all a plant of yours to get me into trouble?"

"I will answer you candidly and fairly. A few years ago, when I first entered on a London life, I determined to make myself acquainted with all the ways of the metropolis, high or low, virtuous or vicious. I disguised myself on several occasions, in very mean clothes, and visited all the flash houses and patter-cribs—amongst others, the boozing-ken in Great Saffron-hill. There you were pointed out to me; and your skill, your audacity, and your extraordinary luck in eluding the police, were vaunted by the landlord of that place in no measured terms."

"Well—this is singular—blow me if it ain't!" cried the Cracksman. "Another person found me out jist in the same way this wery morning, only, and *he* wants a little private job done for him. But that's for to-morrow night. Howsomever, I never blab to one, of what I have done or am going to do for another. You to-night—him to-morrow night! Arter all, the landlord's a fool to talk so free: how did he know you wasn't a trap in disguise?"

"Because I told him that my object was merely to see life in all its shapes: and I was then so very young I could scarcely have been considered dangerous. However, I have occasionally indulged in such rambles, even very lately; and only a few weeks ago I looked in at the boozing-ken dressed as a poor countryman. There I saw you again; and I overheard you say to a friend of yours whom you called the Buffer, that you were generally there every evening to see what was going on."

"All right!" cried the Cracksman. "Now what's the robbery, and what's the reward?"

"Are you man enough to do it alone?"

"I'm man enow to try it on; but if so be the chap is stronger than me——"

"He is a tall, powerful person, and by no means likely to surrender without a desperate resistance."

"Well, all that can be arranged," said the Cracksman, coolly. "Not knowing what you wanted with me, I brought two of my pals along with me, and they're out in the street, or in the alley leading into the park. If there'd been anythink wrong on your part, they would either have rescued me, or marked you and your house for future punishment."

"I am glad that you have your companions so near. Of course they will assist you?"

"In anythink. The Resurrection Man and the Buffer will stick to me like bricks."

"Very good. I will now explain to you what I want done. Between eleven and twelve o'clock a gentleman will leave London for Richmond. He will be in his own cabriolet, with a tiger, only twelve years old, behind. The cab is light blue—the wheels streaked with white. This is peculiar, and cannot be mistaken. The horse is a tall bay, with silver-mounted harness. This gentleman must be stopped; and every thing his pockets contain—every thing, mind—must be brought to me. Whatever money there may be about him shall be yours; and I will add fifty guineas to the amount:—but all that you find about his person, save the money, must be handed over to me."

"I understand," said the Cracksman. "Does he carry pistols?"

"I should imagine not."

"Never mind: the Resurrection Man has got a couple of barkers. But supposing he shouldn't come at all—what then?"

"You shall have twenty guineas for your loss of time. Here are ten as an earnest."

"That's business," said the Cracksman. "Any more instructions?"

"No. I need scarcely say that no unnecessary violence is to be used?"

"Leave all that to me. You will sit up and wait for me?"

"Yes. Give a low single knock at the door, and the same servant who sought you out last night, and let you in just now, will admit you again."

The Cracksman gave a significant nod and took his departure.

Mr. Greenwood returned to the dining-room, where he had left the count.

"My news from Paris is of the most satisfactory nature," he observed. "My correspondents in that city, moreover, promise me their best support in our new enterprise."

"I am delighted to hear that your letters have pleased you," said the count.

The two gentlemen then broached another bottle of Burgundy; and Mr. Greenwood conversed with even more sprightliness than usual. Indeed, the count fancied that he had never found his host so agreeable and entertaining.

At eleven o'clock precisely, the count's cabriolet was announced; and the nobleman took his departure, with the conviction, that, under his present circumstances, Mr. Greenwood was the most eligible suitor for the hand of Isabella that was likely to present himself.

As soon as the count had taken his departure, Mr. Greenwood rang for his slippers and dressing-gown, drew close to the cheerful fire that burnt in the grate, and ordered Lafleur to make him a tumbler of the best pine-apple rum-punch. This exhilarating beverage and a fragrant Havannah cigar enabled Mr. Greenwood to pass the time away in a most comfortable and soul-soothing manner.

And it was thus that he mused as he watched the pale blue

transparent smoke of his cigar wreathing upwards to the ceiling:—

"I began the world without a shilling, and at an age when I had no experience in the devious ways of society;—and what am I now? The possessor of sixty thousand pounds! A few years ago I slept in coffee-houses, paying eight-pence a night for my bed: I breakfasted for three-pence halfpenny; dined for ten-pence; and supped for two-pence. Now the luxuries of the four quarters of the world tempt my palate at every meal. At the outset of my career, my transactions were petty rogueries: now I play my false cards to produce me thousands at a stake. I once purchased my coat for twelve shillings in Holywell-street; there is not now a tailor at the west-end who will not give credit to George Greenwood. My wealth purchases me every kind of pleasure. I can afford to bestow a thousand guineas upon the woman, who, daughter of a peer, and wife of a baronet, throws herself into my arms. One single scheme produces me ten times that amount. And Isabella—beauteous Isabella shall be my wife. I shall receive no dowry with her, it is true—because I have obtained all her father's fortune in advance;—but I shall be proud to introduce a lovely wife—the daughter of a Count, and descended from a long line of ancestry, in that fashionable sphere to which I must henceforth belong. I shall be a member of parliament: Lord Tremordyn can easily obtain for me a baronetcy in due time;—and then, the peerage is not a height *too* difficult to aspire to! Oh! if with a coronet upon my brow, and Isabella by my side, I can drive in my chariot to——"

Lafleur entered the room at this moment, and handed a letter to his master. Greenwood opened it, and read as follows:—

"I have done your bidding in every particular up to the present moment. Louisa set off this afternoon for Birmingham, having received a letter stating that her only sister is at the point of death in that town. You will of course understand by whom that letter was written. I have, moreover, invented an excuse, relative to the date of the departure of the New York packets from Liverpool, by which means I am enabled to remain in London without exciting the suspicions of Eliza. I shall pass to-morrow evening with her. You may rely upon being admitted at midnight."

Greenwood full well understood the meaning of this note without a signature; and its contents tended to augment that happiness which the success of his schemes infused into his breast.

Hour after hour passed away;—at length, midnight sounded; and all the servants, save Lafleur, were dismissed to their sleeping apartments.

The cigars, the rum-punch, and the pleasurable reflections into which the financier plunged, made the time elapse rapidly. One o'clock struck; and he had not found a single moment tedious. He was not anxious, nor a prey to suspense, as other men would have been; he felt certain that his wishes would be accomplished, and he was therefore as composed as if he had already been assured of their success.

The clock struck two; and a low knock was heard at the front door. Lafleur answered the summons; and in a few moments introduced the Cracksman to the room where his master was sitting.

"All right, sir," said that worthy, the moment Lafleur had withdrawn.

"And no violence, I hope?" cried Greenwood.

"Not a bit," returned the Cracksman. "We was as gentle as lambs. We on'y pitched the small boy into a dry ditch that was by the side of the road; and as for the gentleman, I just tapped him over the head with the butt of a pistol to keep him quiet; but I did it myself to make sure that it wasn't done too hard."

"You surely have not murdered him?" said Greenwood, his whole countenance suddenly convulsed with horror.

"Don't be afeard; he was on'y stunned—you may take my word for that," returned the Cracksman, coolly. "But here's all the papers we found in his pocket; and as for his purse—it had but a few pounds in it."

Mr. Greenwood received the papers from the hands of the Cracksman, and observed with a glance that amongst them was the document which he had given a few hours previously to guarantee the safety of the fifteen thousand pounds placed in his hands by Count Alteroni.

"You are sure," he said, with some uneasiness depicted upon his countenance, "that there is no danger to be apprehended from the blow——"

"Danger be d——d!" cried the Cracksman; "I know from experience exactly what kind o' blow will stun, or break a limb, or kill outright. I'll forfeit my reputation if there's any harm in that there whack which I gave to-night."

"We must hope that you are right in your conjecture," said Greenwood;—then, taking his purse from his pocket, he counted down forty-two sovereigns upon the table, adding, "That will make up the fifty guineas promised."

The Cracksman consigned the money to his fob, and then took leave of his employer, hoping *"that he should have his custom in future."*

The moment he was gone, Greenwood thrust the document, which he had thus got back by a crime of an infamous nature, into the fire. When it was completely consumed, he proceeded to examine the other papers. These consisted chiefly of letters written in cypher, addressed to Count Alteroni, and bearing the post-mark of Montoni, Castelcicala: the rest were notes and memoranda of no consequence whatever.

Mr. Greenwood, being unable to unriddle the letters written in cypher, and considering that they were upon political subjects with which he had little or no interest, consigned the entire packet of papers to the flames.

He then retired to rest, and slept as soundly as if his entire day had been passed in virtuous deeds.

At about ten o'clock in the morning he received the following letter from Richmond:—

"My Dear Mr. Greenwood,

"As I was on my way home last evening, I was suddenly attacked by three villains in a dark and lonely part of the road. One of the miscreants stunned me with the blow of a pistol, and threw the little jockey into a ditch. Fortunately we are neither of us seriously injured. The robbers plundered me of every thing I had about my person—my purse containing thirty-four sovereigns, and all my papers, amongst which was the security I had received from your hands a few hours before. You will perhaps have another drawn.

"I do not think it is worth while to make any disturbance relative to the matter, as, in consequence of the darkness of the night, I should be totally unable to recognise the miscreants.

"Yours faithfully,

"Alteroni."

"Thank heavens, there is no danger in that quarter!" exclaimed Mr. Greenwood, when he had perused this letter. "He is not hurt—and he will not adopt any means to detect the culprits. As for having another document drawn up—I can take my time about that, and he will not dare press me for it as he did for the first. Besides, he will consider my honourable intentions in the matter fully proved by having given the one which he has lost! Thus have I obtained fifteen thousand pounds without much trouble—thus have I thrown dust into the eyes of this count, and still do I retain his confidence. And his lovely daughter—the beautiful Isabella, with her large black eyes, her raven hair, her sweet red lips, and her sylph-like form,—she shall be mine! I shall lead her to the altar—that charming Italian virgin, whose very looks are heavens. Everything progresses well: success attends all my plans; and to-night—to-night," he added, "to-night will ensure me the gratification of my desires and my vengeance with regard to that haughty fair one of the villa!"

CHAPTER L.

THE DRUGGED WINE-GLASS.

Return we once more to the villa at Upper Clapton.

Eliza Sydney's household consisted only of Louisa and a peasant girl of about fifteen. She no longer kept horses and dogs, as she was compelled by Stephens to do during the time of her disguise, previously to her imprisonment. She therefore required no male retainers, save an old gardener who lived in one of the out-houses.

A fictitious letter had caused the faithful Louisa to set out on a long journey; and thus the principal obstacle to the atrocious scheme of the conspirators against Eliza's peace and honour was removed.

At ten o'clock on the evening fixed for the perpetration of the foul deed, the servant-girl carried the supper-tray to the dining-room where Eliza and Stephens were seated. The domestic spread the table with the materials for the most sociable of all meals, and, having placed two decanters upon the hospitable board, withdrew.

The countenance of Stephens was particularly calm, considering the part he had undertaken to play towards a woman whose loveliness alone was sufficient to disarm the hand of enmity, and obtain the friendship of the most lawless. She had, moreover, already suffered so much through him,—she had extended towards him the hand of forgiveness and succour in his dire need,—and she possessed the most generous, the most noble, and the most confiding of dispositions.

Oh! should not all these considerations have moved that man in her favour?

He had received from Eliza the hundred pounds which she had promised him. With that sum he might have found his way to America, and still had a considerable balance in his pocket. But he had determined to add to it the two hundred pounds more which Greenwood had promised him.

Although calm, he was very thoughtful.

"You seem unhappy?" said Eliza, observing the pensive air of her guest. "Surely you cannot regret your approaching departure from a land where your safety is so fearfully compromised?"

"And yet the land of which you speak is the one of my birth; and when once I have left it, I may reckon upon being destined to see it never again."

"Yes—it is hard to bid an eternal adieu to one's native country. And yet," continued Eliza, "there is but little to wed the sensitive mind to England. Since my release I have passed nearly all my time in reading; and I am shocked to perceive, from the information I have gleaned, that England is the only civilized country in the world where death from starvation—literal starvation, is common. Indeed, it is an event of such frequent occurrence, that it actually ceases to create astonishment, and almost fails to excite dismay. There must be something radically wrong in that system of society where all the wealth is in the hands of a few, and all the misery is shared by millions."

"You would then, quit England without much regret?" said Stephens.

"For myself," answered Eliza, "I abhor a country in which poverty and destitution prevail to such an extent, while there is so much to spare in the hands of the favoured few. I sometimes look forth from the window, and survey that mighty city which stretches over plain, hill, and valley, and which is ever extending its mighty arms—as if in time it would embrace the entire island:—I gaze upon it at that hour in the morning when the eternal cloud is raised for a little space from its brow; and, as I mark the thousand spires which point up into the cool clear sky, I tremble—I feel oppressed as with a weight, when I reflect upon the hideous misery, the agonising woe, the appalling sorrow that want entails upon the sons and daughters of toil in that vast Babylon."

"And do you not suppose that the same destitution prevails in the other great cities of Europe?"

"Certainly not. Were a person to die of actual starvation in Paris, the entire population would rise up in dismay. With all our immense and cumbersome machinery of Poor Laws, there is more real wretchedness in these islands than in any other country upon the face of the earth, not even excepting the myriads who dwell upon the rivers in China."

"The topic is calculated to distress you, because you enter so deeply and feelingly into it," said Stephens. "Take a glass of wine—it will compose you."

Stephens filled two glasses with Port wine; and almost at the same moment he exclaimed, "What a bad light the lamp gives this evening." Then, in a feigned attempt to raise the wick, he turned the screw the wrong way, and extinguished the light.

"How awkward I am!" he cried; and, while Eliza hastened to relight the lamp, he poured a few drops from a phial into one of the glasses of wine.

The lamp was lighted once more; and Eliza had resumed her seat.

Stephens handed her the fatal glass.

"May all health and happiness attend you," he said: "and may God reward you for your generosity towards me."

The words did not stick in his throat as he gave them utterance.

"And may you prosper in another clime," exclaimed Eliza in a tone which proved that the wish came from the bottom of her heart.

She then drank a portion of the wine in her glass.

The countenance of Stephens did not change as Eliza imbibed the soporific fluid. He contemplated her beauteous face with as much calmness as if he had just administered to her a potion calculated to embellish her charms, and add to her health and happiness.

"Either my taste deceives me," said Eliza, placing the half-emptied glass upon the table; "or this wine has some defect which I cannot understand."

"No—it is excellent," returned Stephens.

"I drink so little that I scarcely know the proper taste," observed Eliza. "The pure spring water is my favourite beverage."

"It is considered an unlucky omen to leave unfinished the glass in which you pledge the health of one who is about to traverse the ocean," said Stephens.

"In that case," answered Eliza, with a smile, "I will relieve your superstitious fears;" and she drained her glass.

Half an hour passed in conversation; and Eliza felt an irresistible drowsiness coming over her. She endeavoured to rally against it—but in vain; and at length she would have fallen from her chair fast asleep, had not Stephens rushed forward and caught her.

He then rang the bell for the servant.

"Your mistress is unwell—she has been complaining all the evening; and she has now fallen into a profound sleep. I will assist you to convey her up stairs to her chamber."

Stephens and the servant carried the entranced lady to the boudoir.

Having placed her upon the bed, Stephens left the servant to undress her, and hastily descended to the hall. He opened the front door with caution, and whistled.

Two men emerged from the total darkness without, and glided into the hall. Stephens conducted them into a back parlour, and gave them the key to lock themselves in.

He himself then returned to the dining room, where he tranquilly awaited the arrival of Mr. Greenwood.

Midnight was proclaimed at length.

A low knock at the front door fell upon Stephens's ear.

He hastened to obey the summons, and admitted Greenwood into the house.

They repaired to the dining-room together.

"Your wishes have been obeyed in all respects," said Stephens. "Eliza is in your power: the servant has retired to her own room. Give me my reward—for I am in a hurry to leave a dwelling to which my presence will have brought so much misery."

And yet this man did not seem appalled nor horror-struck at the infernal nature of the crime for which he thus demanded the recompense.

"You will await me here five minutes," said Greenwood; and he left the room.

At the expiration of that interval he returned, the fire of triumph and lust flashing from his eyes.

"It is all well—you have not deceived me," he observed in a tone of joy and exultation; "I have seen her, buried in a profound sleep—stretched like a beauteous statue in her voluptuous bed! The light of a lamp plays upon her naked bosom: the atmosphere of her chamber is soft, warm, and perfumed. Such charms are worth a kingdom's purchase! She is mine—she is mine: here is your reward!"

Greenwood handed a bank-note to his accomplice—or rather instrument in this atrocious proceeding; and Stephens then took his departure.

But as he passed through the hall, he thrust a letter, addressed to Eliza Sydney, beneath the carpet that covered the stairs.

The moment Greenwood was alone, he paced the dining-room for a few minutes, to feast his imagination with the pleasures of love and triumph which he now beheld within his reach.

"Yes—she is mine," he said: "she is mine—no power on earth can now save her! Oh! how will I triumph over the proud and haughty beauty, when to-morrow she awakes and finds herself in my arms. She will thrust her hand beneath the pillow for her long sharp dagger; it will not be there! She will extend her arm towards the bell-rope; it will be cut! And then she may rave—and weep—and reproach—and pray; I shall smile at her grief—her eyes will be more beautiful when seen through her tears! I shall compel her then to crave to be my mistress—she who refused to be my wife! Oh! what a triumph is within my reach!"

He paused; filled a tumbler half full of wine—and drank the contents at a draught.

"Now for my victory—now for the fruits of my intrigue!" he resumed. "But let me wait one moment longer! let me ask myself whether it be really true that the lovely Eliza Sydney will shortly bless my arms—that she is at this moment in my power. It is—it is; and I shall now no longer delay the enjoyment of that terrestrial paradise!"

With these words, he left the dining-room, and crossed the hall towards the staircase.

He was now about to ascend to the boudoir.

His foot was upon the first step, when he was rudely seized from behind, and instantly gagged with a pocket-handkerchief.

Turning his head partially round, in a vain effort to escape from the powerful grasp in which he found himself, he encountered, by the light of the lamp that hung in the hall, the glance of the Cracksman.

"The deuce!" exclaimed the burglar in a low and subdued tone:

"this is a rum go! Working *for* you last night, and *against* you to-night! But, never mind: we must fulfil our agreement, let it be what it will. I can however tell you for your satisfaction that we don't mean to hurt you. So come along quiet; and all will be right."

"What's the meaning of this, Tom?" said the Cracksman's companion, who was no other than the Resurrection Man: "you don't mean to say that you know this fellow?"

"He's the one that we did the job for last night on the Richmond road," answered the Cracksman.

"And he's got plenty of tin," added the Resurrection Man significantly. "We can perhaps make a better bargain with him than what Stephens has promised us for this night's business."

"Yes—but we can't talk here," returned the Cracksman: "so come along. I've got my plan all cut and dry."

Greenwood conveyed several intimations, by means of signs, that he wished to speak; but the two ruffians hurried him out of the house.

They conducted him across the fields to an empty barn at a distance of about a mile from the villa. During the journey thither they conversed together in a flash language altogether unintelligible to their captive, who was still gagged. A difference of opinion evidently seemed to subsist between the two men, relative to the plan which they should pursue with regard to Greenwood; but they at length appeared to agree upon the point.

With regard to Greenwood himself, he was a prey to a variety of painful feelings,—disappointment in his designs upon Eliza at the moment when he appeared to stand upon the threshold of success,—bitter malignity against Stephens who had thus duped him,—and alarm at the uncertainty of the fate which might await him at the hands of the villains in whose power he thus strangely found himself.

The night was pitch-dark; but the moment the two ruffians with their captive entered the barn, a lantern in the hands of the Cracksman was suddenly made to throw a bright light forwards.

That light fell upon the countenance of Stephens, who was standing in the middle of the shed.

"All right," said the Cracksman. "We pinioned the bird without trouble; and he ain't a strange one, neither."

"What! do you mean that you know him?" demanded Stephens.

"That's neither here nor there," replied the Cracksman. "We don't tell secrets out of school, 'cos if we did, there'd be no reliance put in us; and we does a great many pretty little jobs now and then for the swell folks. But here is your bird—delivered at this werry spot, accordin' to agreement."

"Well and good," said Stephens. "Tie him hand and foot."

The Cracksman and the Resurrection Man instantly obeyed this command: they threw Greenwood upon a truss of straw, and fastened his hands together, and then his feet, with strong cord.

"Here is your reward," said Stephens, as soon as this was accomplished. "I have now no more need of your services."

He handed them some money as he thus spoke; and, having counted it, the two villains bade him good night and left the barn, which was now enveloped in total darkness.

"Montague Greenwood," said Stephens, as soon as he was alone with his prisoner, "your design upon Eliza Sydney was too atrocious for even a man who has been knocked about in the world, as I have, to permit. You dazzled me with the promise of a reward which my necessities did not permit me to refuse;—and you moreover secured my co-operation by means of menaces. But I was determined to defeat your treacherous designs—to avenge myself for the threats which you uttered against me—and to obtain the recompense you had promised me, at the same time. How well I have succeeded you now know. The whole of yesterday morning did I wander amongst the sinks of iniquity and haunts of crime in Clerkenwell, and the neighbourhood of Saffron Hill; and accident led me into a low public house where I encountered two men who agreed to do my bidding. I tell you all this to convince you that never for a moment was I villain enough—bad though I may be—to pander to infamy of so deep a dye as that which you meditated. I have taken measures to acquaint the noble-hearted woman whose ruin you aimed at, with the entire history of this transaction, so that she may be upon her guard in future. With reference to you, here I shall leave you: in a few hours the labourers of the farm will no doubt discover you, and you will be restored to liberty when Eliza has awakened from her torpor, and I shall be far beyond the danger of pursuit."

Stephens ceased; and taking a long rope from the corner of the barn where he had concealed it, he fastened it to the cord which already confined the hands and feet of Greenwood. He then attached the ends firmly to one of the upright beams of the barn, so as to prevent the captive from crawling away from the place.

This precaution being adopted, Stephens took his departure.

It would be impossible to describe the rage, vexation, and disappointment which filled the breast of Greenwood while Stephens addressed him in the manner described, and then bound him with the cord. Yet during this latter process he lay perfectly quiet,—well aware that any attempt at escape on his part would at that moment be totally unavailing.

Five minutes elapsed after Stephens had left the barn, and Greenwood was marvelling within himself how long he should have to remain in that unpleasant position—bound with cords, and gagged in such a way that he could only breathe through his nostrils,—when the sounds of footsteps fell upon his ear, and the light of the Cracksman's lantern again flashed through the barn.

"Well, sir," said the Cracksman, "your *friend* is gone now; and so we can have a word or two together. You see, we couldn't help you afore, 'cos we was obliged to fulfil our agreement with the man which hired us for the evening. Now it is just likely that you may have to remain here for some hours if so be we don't let you loose; so tell us what you'll give us for cutting them cords."

The Cracksman removed the gag from Greenwood's mouth, as he uttered these words.

"I will give you my purse," exclaimed the discomfited financier, "if you will release me this moment. It contains ten or a dozen guineas."

"Thank'ee kindly," said the Cracksman, drily; "we've got that already. We helped ourselves to it as we came across the fields. Don't you see, we always make it a rule to have the plucking of all pigeons which we're hired to snare. You told us we might take all we found on the swell in the sky-blue cab; and that man with the sallow complexion that hired us to do this here business to-night, said, 'I will give you twenty pounds, and you can help yourselves to all you find about the gentleman you're to operate on.'"

"Call upon me to-morrow, and I will give you another twenty pounds to free me from these bonds," said Greenwood.

"That's only the price of a good corpse," said the Resurrection Man. "Make it thirty."

"Yes—make it thirty," added the Cracksman.

"Well—I will give you thirty guineas," cried Greenwood: "only delay not another instant. My limbs are stiffening with the cold and with the confinement of these accursed cords."

"Let it be thirty, then," said the Cracksman. "Here, Tony," he added, turning towards his companion, "hold this here light while I cut the cords. And while I think of it, Mr. Greenwood, I shan't call upon you for the money; but you'll send it to the landlord of the Boozing-ken, where your servant came and found me. Mind it's there by to-morrow night, or else you'll repent it—that's all. Blowed if we haven't had two good nights' work on it, Tony. But, my eye! wasn't I surprised yesterday when the man with the sallow face which hired us for to-night, told me that we was to come to that there willa yonder, and I found out as how it was the same that I'd cracked three year ago along with Bill Bolter and Dick Flairer. Arter all, there's been some curious things about all these matters—partickler our having to tackle to-night the wery gentleman which we served last night."

"Come—don't talk so much, Tom," said the Resurrection Man; "but let's make haste and be off."

"There—it's done," exclaimed the Cracksman: "the cords is all cut: you can get up, sir."

Greenwood arose from the straw upon which he had been lying, and stretched his limbs with as much pleasure as if he had just recovered from a severe cramp.

He then reiterated his promise to the two men relative to the reward to be paid for the service just rendered him; and, having inquired of them which was the nearest way to the West End, he set out upon his long and lonely walk home, depressed, disappointed, and hesitating between plans of vengeance against Stephens and fears of exposure in his own vile and defeated machinations with regard to the beautiful Eliza Sydney.

CHAPTER LI.

DIANA AND ELIZA.

On the morning following the events just narrated, Mrs. Arlington was seated at breakfast in a sweet little parlour of the splendid mansion which the Earl of Warrington had taken and fitted up for her in Dover Street, Piccadilly.[1]

It was about eleven o'clock; and the Enchantress was attired in a delicious *deshabillé*. With her little feet upon an ottoman near the fender, and her fine form reclining in a luxurious large arm-chair, she divided her attention between her chocolate and the columns of the *Morning Herald*. She invariably prolonged the morning's repast as much as possible, simply because it served to wile away the time until the hour for dressing arrived. Then visits received, filled up the interval till three or four o'clock, when the carriage came round to the door. A drive in the park, or shopping (according to the state of the weather) occupied the time until six or seven. Then another toilet

1 Dover Street runs off Piccadilly, but is more properly in Mayfair. For those unused to the semiotics of London, it is a very desirable street indeed: the very opposite of Wellington Street, Brick Lane.

in preparation for dinner. In the evening a *tête-à-tête* with the Earl of Warrington, who had, perhaps, arrived in time for dinner,—or a visit to a theatre, the Opera, or a concert,—and to bed at midnight, or frequently much later.

Such was the routine of the Enchantress's existence.

The Earl of Warrington behaved most liberally towards her. On the first day of every month he enclosed her a cheque upon his banker for two hundred guineas. He supplied her cellar with wine, and frequently made her the most splendid presents of jewellery, plate, cachmeres, &c. The furniture for her mansion had cost fifteen hundred pounds; and all the bills were paid in her name. She was not extravagant, as women in her situation usually are; and therefore, so far from incurring debts, she saved money.

We cannot say that the Earl of Warrington positively *loved* her. His first affections in life had experienced such a blight, that they might almost be said to have been interred in the grave of defeated hopes and aspirations. He could therefore never *love* again. But he *liked* Mrs. Arlington; and he had every reason to believe that she was faithful to him. He was charmed with her conversation and her manners: he saw in her a woman who gave herself no airs, but, on the contrary, exerted herself in every way to please him;—she never attempted to excite his jealousy, nor affected gusts of passion merely for the sake of asserting her independence or of proving the hold which she possessed over him;—and in her society he forgot the cares of politics (in which he was profoundly interested) and all those other little annoyances, real or imaginary, to which every one in this world is subject, be his condition never so prosperous!

And Diana *was* faithful to him. She was a woman naturally inclined to virtue:—circumstances had made her what she was. She looked upon the Earl of Warrington as a benefactor; and, although she did not actually *love* him more than he loved her, she *liked* him upon pretty nearly the same principles that he liked her. Her vanity was flattered by having captivated and being able to retain a handsome man, whose wealth and high rank rendered him an object of desire on the part of all ladies situated as was Diana;—she moreover found him an agreeable companion, kind, and indulgent;—and thus their *liaison* continued upon a basis which nothing appeared to threaten, nor even to weaken.

They never spoke of love in reference to their connection. The earl was never upon his knees at the feet of his mistress; nor did he repeat vows of constancy and fidelity every time he saw her. She acted on the same principle towards him. There was a great amount of real friendship and good feeling between those two;—but not an atom of mawkish sentimentality. The earl could *trust* Diana: he consulted her upon many of his plans and proceedings, whether in regard to his political career or the management of his estate; and she invariably tendered him the advice which appeared most consistent with his interests. He therefore placed the fullest confidence in her;—and hence have we seen her carrying out all his generous plans with reference to Eliza Sydney.

But to continue.

Mrs. Arlington was seated at breakfast, as we have before stated, when a servant entered and informed her that Miss Sydney requested a few minutes' conversation with her. Diana immediately ordered Eliza to be admitted.

"Pardon this early and unceremonious visit, my dear friend," said Eliza, affectionately grasping the hand that was stretched out to welcome her.

"I am always at home to you, Eliza," answered the Enchantress. "But how pale you are! Come—sit down here—close by me—and tell me in what way I can be of service to you."

"My dear friend," continued Eliza, "I have a secret to reveal to you—and a deed of infamy to narrate——"

"Oh! you alarm me, Eliza! Has any harm happened to yourself?"

"No, thank heavens! The compunction of one man saved me from disgrace and ruin. But read this—it will explain all."

With these words, Eliza handed to Mrs. Arlington the letter which Stephens had thrust under the stair-carpet at the villa on the preceding evening.

Diana perused the letter with attention; and a flush of indignation animated her fine countenance, as she thus made herself acquainted with the atrocious plot contrived by Greenwood against the honour of Eliza Sydney.

"Such is the villany of George Montague!" cried Diana at the termination of the perusal of that letter.

"Forgive me, dearest friend," said Eliza, taking the hand of Mrs.

Arlington and pressing it between her own;—"forgive me if I have kept back one secret of my life from your knowledge. That George Montague—I once loved him!"

"You!" exclaimed Mrs. Arlington in surprise.

"Yes, Diana—I once loved that man—before the fatal exposure which led to my imprisonment;—but he behaved like a villain—he endeavoured to take advantage of my affection;—and I smothered the feeling in my bosom!"

"Oh! you did well—you did well thus to triumph over a passion which would have been fatal to your happiness;—for never would your hopes have been fulfilled—with honour to yourself," added Mrs. Arlington, sinking her voice almost to a whisper.

"Alas! you are right! I stood upon the brink of a precipice—I escaped;—but Montague, or Greenwood,—whichever he may choose to call himself,—pursues me with a view of accomplishing my dishonour."

"The crimes of that man are unlimited, and his perseverance is unwearied," said Diana.

"What plan can I adopt," demanded Eliza, "to escape his machinations? What system can I pursue to avoid his persecution? Conceive my affright when upon awaking this morning, I remembered that I had not retired to bed last evening of my own accord—that I could think of nothing that had occurred since supper-time! Then I found that the bell-rope in my sleeping-room was cut, and that a weapon which I have been in the habit of keeping beneath my pillow ever since I first dwelt in the villa, had disappeared! Oh! I was alarmed—I shuddered, although it was broad day-light, and every thing was calm and silent around. At length I summoned the servant—and she entered, bearing a letter which she had discovered a few moments before beneath the stair-carpet. That letter is the one you read ere now;—and it explained all. Tell me—tell me, Diana, how am I to avoid the persecution, and combat the intrigues of this man?"

"Alas! my dear friend," replied Mrs. Arlington, after a few minutes' consideration, "I know of no effectual method save that of leaving London."

"And if I leave London, I will leave England," said Miss Sydney. "But I can do nothing without the consent of him to whom I am under such deep obligations."

"You mean the Earl of Warrington," observed Mrs. Arlington. "I admire the sentiment of gratitude which animates you. The earl will do all he can to forward your views and contribute to your happiness. You shall pass the day with me, Eliza; here at least you are safe;—and I will immediately write a note to the earl, and request him to call upon me without delay."

"His lordship will be perhaps annoyed——"

"Fear nothing, Eliza. I will see the earl in another room. And let not this disinclination to meet you on his part, cause you pain: you well know the motive of his conduct. The memory of your mother——"

"I am well aware he can have no antipathy towards me, on my own account," interrupted Eliza; "else he could not have acted towards me in a way which claims all my gratitude!"

Mrs. Arlington dispatched the note to Lord Warrington, and then hastened to dress to receive him.

In an hour the earl arrived.

He and Mrs. Arlington were then closeted together for a considerable time.

It was four o'clock when the nobleman took his departure, and Diana returned to the room where she had left Eliza Sydney.

"The Earl of Warrington," said the Enchantress, whose countenance was animated with joy, "has listened with attention to the tale of atrocity which I have related to him in respect to George Montague Greenwood. His lordship and myself—for he does me the honour to consult me—have debated upon the best means of ensuring your tranquillity and safety; and we have decided that you had better quit England for a time. The perseverance of that bold bad man, backed by his wealth, may succeed in effecting your ruin—you yourself remaining innocent of guilty participation! The earl has recommended Italy as the country most likely to please you—and the more so because he himself possesses a charming villa in the State of Castelcicala."

"How kind of his lordship!" exclaimed Eliza, tears of gratitude starting into her eyes.

"Some years ago," continued Diana, "the earl set out upon a continental tour, and passed two years at Montoni, the capital of the Grand Duchy of Castelcicala. So charmed was he with that delightful city, that he purchased a small estate in the suburbs, with the idea of spending the summer from time to time amidst Italian scenery and beneath an Italian sky. The idea has, however, been displaced by others arising from new occupations and fresh interests; and for a long period has the villa at Montoni remained uninhabited, save by an old porter and his wife. The house is situate upon the banks of the river which flows through Montoni, and commands the most delicious views. That villa is to be your residence so long as it may be agreeable; and the earl will make arrangements with his London bankers so that your income may be regularly paid you by their agents at Montoni. His lordship has moreover instructed me to supply you with the necessary funds for your travelling expenses."

"Oh! my dearest friend, how can I ever testify my gratitude——"

"Not a word—not a word!" interrupted Mrs. Arlington, playfully closing Eliza's lips with her hand. "The earl conceives that he is performing a duty, sacred to the memory of his deceased uncle, in thus caring for you, who are the offspring of that uncle's daughter; and, on my part, Eliza—on my part, it is a pleasure to do you a service. But I have not yet finished. The earl has gone straight to Richmond, to call upon a certain Count Alteroni—a noble exile from the Grand Duchy of Castelcicala—with whom it appears the earl was acquainted in Italy. His object is to obtain for you a few letters of introduction to some of the best families of Montoni, so that you may not want society."

"I shall live in so retired a manner," said Eliza, "that this additional act of kindness was scarcely necessary."

"The earl will have his own way; and perhaps those letters may prove useful to you—who can tell?" exclaimed Mrs. Arlington. "But I must observe that I cannot think of parting with you any more until you leave England altogether. In three or four days the necessary preparations for your journey will be completed: meantime you must remain here as my guest. The earl himself recommended this step; that is," added Mrs. Arlington, "if my house be agreeable to you, and my society——"

"Oh! how can you entertain a doubt on that head?" cried Eliza, embracing Diana with the most grateful fervour. "Ah! it is but a few hours since I said how happy I should be to call you by the endearing name of *Sister*?"

"And would you not blush, Eliza, to call me your sister?" said Mrs. Arlington, in a tone deeply affected.

"Blush to call you my sister!" exclaimed Miss Sydney, as if she repelled the idea with indignation: "Oh! no—never, never! You are the most noble-hearted of women, and as such, I love—I revere you!"

"We will then be sisters in heart, although not in blood," said Diana, warmly returning her friend's embrace; "and perhaps our affection towards each other will be more sincere than that existing between many who are really the offspring of the same parents."

Mrs Arlington gave directions to her servant that she was not "at home" to a soul, save the Earl of Warrington; and the ride in the park—the shopping—the theatre in the evening—all were sacrificed by Diana to the pleasure of Eliza's society.

Miss Sydney dispatched a note to the villa at Upper Clapton, announcing her intention of staying a few days with Mrs. Arlington. In the evening, Louisa, who had just returned from the journey on which the fictitious letter written by Stephens had sent her, made her appearance in Dover Street, with clothes, &c. for her mistress, and she then received instructions relative to the intended departure for the Continent.

CHAPTER LII.

THE BED OF SICKNESS.

Return we to the dwelling of Richard Markham on the same day that Eliza Sydney sought her friend Mrs. Arlington, as related in the preceding chapter.

Richard awoke as from a long and painful dream.

He opened his eyes, and gazed vacantly around him. He was in his own bed, and Whittingham was seated by his side.

"The Lord be praised!" ejaculated the faithful old domestic;—and conceiving it necessary to quote Scripture upon the occasion of this happy recovery, he uttered, in a loud and solemn voice, the first sentence which presented itself to his memory,—"My tongue is the pen of a ready writer!"

"How long have I been ill, Whittingham?" demanded our hero, in a faint tone.

"Four blessed days have you been devoided of your sensations, Master Richard," was the reply; "and most disastrous was my fears that you would never be evanescent no more. I have sustained my vigils by day and my diaries by night at your bedside, Master Richard; and I may say, without mitigating against truth, that I haven't had my garments off my back since you was first brought home."

"Indeed, Whittingham, I am deeply indebted to you, my good friend," said Richard, pressing the faithful old domestic's hand. "But have I really been so very ill?"

"Ill!" exclaimed Whittingham; "for these four days you have never opened your eyes, save in delirium, until this moment. But you have been a ravaging in your dreams—and sobbing—and moaning so! I suppose, Master Richard, you haven't the most remotest idea of how you come home again?"

"Not in the least, Whittingham. All I recollect was, running along the Richmond Road, in the middle of the night—with a whirlwind in my brain—"

"And you must have fallen down from sheer fatigue," interrupted the butler; "for two drovers picked you up, and took you to a cottage close by. The people at the cottage searched your pockets and found your card, so they sent off a messenger to your own house, and I went in a po-shay, and fetched you home."

"And I have been ill four whole days!" cried Markham.

"Yes, but you don't know yet what has happened during that period," said the butler, with a solemn shake of the head.

"Tell me all the news, Whittingham: let me know what has passed during my illness."

"I'll repeat to you allegorically all that's incurred," resumed Whittingham, preparing to enumerate the various incidents upon his fingers. "In the first place—let me see—yes, it *was* the first incurrence of any consequence—the old sow littered. That's annygoat the first. Then come a terrible buffoon—a tifoon, I mean—and down tumbled the eastern stack of chimbleys. That's annygoat the second. Third, the young water-cress gal was confined with a unlegitimated child; and so I told her mother never to let her call here again, as we didn't encourage immoral karikters. That's annygoat the third. Next, there's poor Ben Halliday, who wouldn't pay the pavement rate at Holloway, 'cause he hasn't got any pavement before his house, sold up, stick and stock; and so I gave him a couple of guineas. Annygoat the fourth. And last of all, a gentleman's livery servant—not that villain Yorkminster's, or whatever his name was—come with a horse and shay and left your pokmanty, without saying a word. That's anny—"

"My portmanteau!" exclaimed Richard, whose countenance was now suddenly animated with a ray of hope: "and have you unpacked it?"

"Not yet: I haven't had no time."

"Bring it to the bed-side, place it upon a couple of chairs, and open it at once," said Markham hastily. "Bestir yourself, good Whittingham: I am anxious to see if there be any note—any letter—any—"

While Richard uttered these words with a considerable degree of impatience, the butler dragged the portmanteau from beneath the bed, where he had deposited it, and placed it close to his master's right hand. It was speedily opened, unpacked, and examined throughout; the clothes and linen were unfolded; and Richard's eyes followed the investigation with the most painful curiosity. But there was no letter—no note from any inmate of the count's abode.

A sudden reminiscence entered his mind. Was the document signed at the *Dark House* amongst his papers? He recollected having handed it to the count; but he could not call to mind what had afterwards become of it. A moment's examination convinced him that it had not been returned to him. At first he was grievously annoyed by this circumstance;—in another minute he was pleased, for it struck him that, after all, its contents might have been perused by the count and his family when the excitement of that fatal night had worn off. But how to wipe away the dread suspicion raised by the Resurrection Man, relative to the burglary—oh! that was the most painful, and yet the most necessary task of all!

Markham sank back upon his pillow, and was lost in thought, when a low knock was heard at the door of his chamber. Whittingham answered it, and introduced Mr. Monroe.

The old man was the very picture of care and wretchedness:—the mark of famine was, moreover, upon his sunken cheeks. His eyes were dead and lustreless;—his neck, his wrists, and his hands—seemed nothing but skin and bone. In spite of the cleanliness of his person, the thread-bare shabbiness of his clothes could not escape the eye of even the most superficial observer.

Markham had not seen him for some months; and now, forgetting his own malady and his own cares, he felt shocked at the dreadful alteration wrought upon the old man's person during that interval. On his part, Mr. Monroe was not less surprised to find Richard upon a bed of sickness.

"My dear sir," said Markham, "you are ill—you are suffering—and you do not come to me to—"

"What! you have penetrated my secret, Richard!" exclaimed the old man bitterly. "Well—I will conceal the truth no longer: yes—myself and my poor daughter—we are dying by inches!"

"My God! and you were too proud to come to me! Oh! how sincerely—how eagerly would I have offered you the half of all I possess—"

"How could I come to you, Richard," interrupted the old man, bursting into tears, "when I had already ruined you?"

"No—not you—not you," said Markham: "you were the victim of a scoundrel; and, in acting for the best, you lost all!"

"God knows how truly you speak!" cried the old man fervently. "But tell me—what ails you? and how long have you been upon a bed of sickness?"

"A day or two;—it is nothing! Never mind me—I am now well—at all events, much better:—let us talk of yourself and your own affairs."

"My fate, Richard, is a melancholy one—my destiny is sad, indeed! From the pinnacle of wealth and prosperity I have been dashed down to the lowest abyss of destitution and misery! But it is not for myself that I complain—it is not for myself that I suffer! I am by this time inured to every kind of disappointment and privation:—but my daughter—my poor Ellen! Oh! my God—it was for her sake that I came to you this morning to implore the wherewith to purchase a loaf of bread!"

"Merciful heavens, Mr. Monroe! are you reduced to this?" cried Richard, horror-struck at the piteous tale thus conveyed to him in a few words.

"It is true:—we are starving!" answered the old man, sinking into a chair, and sobbing bitterly.

Whittingham walked towards the window, and wiped his eyes more than once.

"Ah! I am glad you have come to me at last," said Markham. "I will assist you to the utmost of my power—I will never let you want again! Oh! that villain Montague! how many hearts has he already broken—how many more will he yet break!"

"He is the cause of all this deep—deep misery," observed Monroe. "But not alone by me is his name mentioned with loathing and horror: others have doubtless been, and will yet be, his victims. I have learnt—by the merest accident—that he has changed his name, and is now pursuing at the West End, the same course he so successfully practised in the City."

"Changed his name!" ejaculated Markham. "And what does he call himself now?"

"Greenwood," answered Mr. Monroe.

"Greenwood! George Montague and Greenwood one and the same person!" cried Richard, suddenly recalling to mind the name of the individual to whom the count had entrusted his capital. "Ah! you talk of new victims—I know one, whose ruin is perhaps by this time consummated. Quick—quick, Whittingham, give me writing materials: I will send a warning—although I am afraid it is already too late!"

While Whittingham was arranging his master's portfolio upon the coverlid of the bed, Markham reflected upon the best means of communicating to Count Alteroni the character of the man to whom he had confided his fortune, and whom he thought of favourably as a suitor for his daughter's hand. Anonymous letters were detestable to the honourable and open disposition of Richard, and he hesitated at the idea of sending a note direct from himself, fearing that it might be thrown into the fire the moment its signature should be perceived, and thus fail in its proposed aim. To call upon the count was impossible: to send Mr. Monroe was disagreeable. To communicate the important intelligence was imperiously necessary. But how was it to be conveyed? An idea struck across his brain in this perplexity:—he would write to the countess, and trust to the natural curiosity of the female disposition to ensure the perusal of his letter. He accordingly penned the ensuing epistle:—

"Madam,

"Although calumniated in the presence of Count Alteroni, without being permitted to justify myself, and although ruined in your estimation, without the freedom of explanation,—believe me, I have still the welfare of your family most sincerely at heart. As a proof of this assertion, allow me to inform you that the Mr. Greenwood, to whom Count Alteroni has entrusted his capital, is an adventurer and a villain. I on several occasions casually mentioned to you that I was plundered of all my property, before I became of an age entitled to enjoy it. My guardian Mr. Monroe, employed a certain Mr. Allen to speculate for him; and this Mr. Allen was mercilessly robbed of all he possessed, and all he could raise, and all his friends who backed him could provide him with, by a miscreant of the name of Montague. These particulars, which I never mentioned to you before, I now deem it requisite to acquaint you with. Madam, that same George Montague is your Mr. Greenwood!

"I remain, Madam, your obedient servant,

"Richard Markham."

This letter was dispatched that same evening to Richmond.

CHAPTER LIII.

ACCUSATIONS AND EXPLANATIONS.

It was seven o'clock in the evening.

Count Alteroni was sipping his claret; the countess was reading a new German novel; and the Signora Isabella was sitting in a pensive and melancholy mood, apparently occupied with some embroidery or other fancy-work, but in reality bent only upon her own painful reflections.

The air of this charming girl was languishing and sorrowful; and from time to time a tear started into her large black eye. That crystal drop upon the jet fringe of her eye-lid, seemed like the dew hanging on the ebony frame of a window.

The delicate hue of the rose which usually coloured her cheeks, and appeared as it were beneath the complexion of faint bistre which denoted her Italian origin, had fled; and her sweet vermilion lips were no longer wreathed in smiles.

"Isabel, my love," said the count, "you are thoughtful this evening. What a silly girl you are to oppose that tyrannical little will of your own to my anxious hopes and wishes for your welfare—especially as I must know so much better than you what is for your good and what is not."

"I think," answered Isabella, with a deep sigh, "that I oppose no tyrannical will to your lordship's commands."

"Lordship's commands!" repeated the count, somewhat angrily. "Have I not ordered our rank and station to be forgotten here—in England? And as for commands, Bella," added the nobleman, softening, "I have merely expressed my wish that you should give Mr. Greenwood an opportunity of proving his disinterested affection and securing your esteem—especially on the occasion of our approaching visit to our friends the Tremordyns."

"My dear papa," answered the signora, "I have faithfully promised you that if Mr. Greenwood should gain my affections, he shall not sue in vain for my hand."

"That is a species of compromise which I do not understand," exclaimed the count. "Have you any particular aversion to him?"

"I have no aversion—but I certainly have no love," replied Isabella firmly; "and where there is not love, dear father, you would not have me wed?"

"Oh! as for love," said the count, evading a direct reply to this query, "time invariably thaws away those stern resolves and objections which young ladies sometimes choose to entertain, in opposition to the wishes of their parents."

"My lord, I have no power over volition," exclaimed Isabella, with difficulty restraining her tears.

"This is very provoking, Isabella—very!" said the count, drinking his claret with rapidity. "This man is in every way worthy of you—rich, genteel, and good-looking. As for his rank—it is true that he has no title: but of what avail to us are rank and title—exiled as we are from our native land—"

"Oh! my dear father!" cried Isabella, wiping her eyes; "do not fancy so ill of me as to suppose that I languish for rank, or care for honour! No—let me either possess that title which is a reflection of your own when in Castelcicala;—or let me be plain Signora Isabella in a foreign land. Pomp and banishment—pride and exile, are monstrous incongruities!"

"That is spoken like my own dear daughter," exclaimed the count. "The sorrows of my own lot are mitigated by the philosophy and firmness with which you and your dear mother support our change of fortunes;—and, alas! I see but little chance of another re-action in our favour. O my dear country! shall I ever see thee more? Wilt thou one day recognise those who really love thee?"

A profound silence ensued: neither of the ladies chose to interrupt the meditations of the patriot; and he himself rose and paced the room with agitated steps.

"And it is this despair when I contemplate my future prospects," continued the nobleman, after a long pause, "that induces me to wish to see you speedily settled and provided for, my dearest Isabella. What other motive can I have but your good?"

"Oh! I know it—I know it, my dear father," cried the charming girl; "and it is that conviction which makes me wretched when I think how reluctant I am to obey you in this instance. But do not grieve yourself, my dear father—and do not be angry with me! I will be as civil and friendly as I can to this Mr. Greenwood; and if—and if——"

The beautiful Italian could say no more: her heart was full—almost to bursting; and throwing herself into her mother's arms, she wept bitterly.

The count, who was passionately attached to his daughter, was deeply affected and greatly shocked by this demonstration of her feelings. He had flattered himself that her repugnance to Mr. Greenwood was far from being deeply rooted, and was merely the result of a young girl's fears and anxieties when she found that she was not romantically attached to her suitor. But he little suspected that she cherished a sincere and tender passion for another—a passion which she might essay in vain to conquer.

"Bella, my darling," he exclaimed, "do not give way to grief: you cannot think that I would sacrifice you to gold—mere gold? No—never, never! Console yourself—you shall never be dragged a victim to the altar!"

"My dearest father," cried Isabella, turning towards the count and embracing him fondly,—"God, who reads all my actions, knows that I would make any sacrifice to please you—to spare you one pang—to forward your views! Oh! believe me, I am too well aware of the deep responsibility under which I exist towards my parents—too deeply imbued with gratitude for all your kindness towards me, not to be prepared to obey your wishes!"

"I will exact no sacrifice, dearest girl," said the count. "Compose yourself—and do not weep!"

At that moment a loud double knock at the front door resounded through the house; and scarcely had Isabella recovered her self-possession, when Mr. Greenwood was announced.

"Ladies, excuse this late visit," said the financier, sailing into the room with his countenance wreathed into the blandest smiles; "but the truth is, I had business in the neighbourhood, and I could not possibly pass without stopping for a few moments at a mansion where there are such attractions."

These last words were addressed pointedly to Isabella, who only replied to the compliment by a cold bow.

"Count," said Mr. Greenwood, now turning towards the nobleman, "I have not seen you since your adventure upon the highway! But I was delighted to learn that you had received no injury."

"My only regret is that I did not shoot the villains," answered the count. "Have you had another deed prepared, to replace the one stolen from me on that occasion?"

"I have given my solicitors the necessary instructions," answered Greenwood. "In a few days——"

"Every thing with you is in a few days, Greenwood," interrupted the count, somewhat pointedly. "That deed would not occupy one day to engross, now that the copy is at your attorney's office; and it would have been a mark of goodwill on your part—"

"Pray do not blame me!" exclaimed the financier, smiling so as to display his very white teeth, of which he seemed not a little proud. "I believe that for a man who has so much business upon his hands, and the interests of so many to watch and care for, I am as punctual to my appointments as most people."

"I do not speak of want of punctuality in keeping appointments," said the nobleman: "but I allude to the neglect of a matter which to you may appear trivial, but which to me is of importance."

"Oh! my dear count—we will repair this little error the day after to-morrow—or the next day," answered Mr. Greenwood: "I wish that every body was as regular and as punctual with me, as I endeavour to be with others; and that punctuality on my part, my dear sir, has been the origin of my fortune. I do not like to speak of myself, ladies—I hate egotism—but really," he added with another smile, "when one is attacked, you know——"

At that moment a domestic entered the room, and handed a letter to the countess, who immediately opened it, glanced towards the signature, and exclaimed almost involuntarily, "From Richard Markham!"

"Richard Markham!" cried Mr. Greenwood: "I thought I understood you that that gentleman has ceased to visit or correspond with you?"

"So I said—and so I shall maintain!" exclaimed the count. "My dear, we will return that letter without reading it."

"But I have already commenced the perusal of it," said the countess, without taking her eyes off the paper: "and——"

"Then read no more," cried the count, angrily.

"Excuse me—I shall read it all," answered the countess significantly: "and so will you."

"What means this?" ejaculated the count. "Have I lost all authority in my own house? Madam, I command you——"

"There—I have finished it, and I implore you to read it yourself. Its contents are highly important, and do not in any way relate to certain recent events. Indeed he has purposely avoided any thing which may appear obtrusive, either in the shape of explanation or apology."

The count took the letter with a very ill grace, and requested Mr. Greenwood's permission to read it. This was of course awarded; and the nobleman commenced the perusal. He had not, however, read many lines, before he gave a convulsive start, and looked mistrustfully upon Mr. Greenwood (who noticed his emotion), and hastily ran his eye over the remainder of the letter's contents.

He then folded up the letter, and appeared to be absorbed in deep thought for several moments. Mr. Greenwood saw that the note bore some allusion to himself, and prepared his mind for any explanation, or any storm.

The countess sate, pale and unhappy, in deep meditation; and the eyes of Isabella wandered anxiously from one to the other.

At length the count, in a tone which showed with how much difficulty he suppressed an outbreak of his irritated feelings, turned abruptly towards Mr. Greenwood, exclaiming, "Pray, sir, how long is it since you were acquainted with one George Montague?"

Mr. Greenwood was not taken at all aback. This was a question to which he was always liable, and for which he was constantly prepared. He accordingly answered, with his usual smile of complaisance, in the following manner:—

"Oh! my dear sir, I presume you are acquainted with the fact that my name was once Montague, since you ask me that question. I may also suppose that some one has communicated that circumstance to you with a desire to prejudice me in your opinion; but I can assure you that I have not changed my name for any sinister purpose. My only motive was the request of an old lady, who left me a considerable property some time ago, upon that condition."

"And you can also explain, perhaps, the nature of your dealings with a certain Mr. Allen?" demanded the count, staggered at the assurance with which Mr. Greenwood met an accusation that the nobleman imagined would have overwhelmed him with confusion.

"My dear sir," replied the financier, very far from betraying any embarrassment, whatever he might have felt, "I can explain that and every other action of my life. I was myself misled—I was duped—I was involved in an enterprise which entailed ruin upon myself and all connected with me. I suffered along with the others, and gave up all to the creditors. I have, however, been enabled to build up my fortunes again by means of the property left to me, and a series of successful operations. All people in commercial and financial affairs are liable to disappointment and embarrassment: the most cautious may over-speculate or miscalculate, and how can I be blamed more than another?"

"I will admit that a particular enterprise may fail," said the count: "but the writer of this letter explained to me on one or two occasions, enough to enable me to comprehend the whole machinery of fraud which you put into motion to obtain money from the public; and though he never mentioned any names until to-day, in his letter, I might——"

"Every man has his enemies," said Mr. Greenwood, calmly: "I cannot hope to be without mine. They may assert what they choose: upright and impartial men never listen to one-sided statements. But perhaps the writer of that letter——"

"He is the Mr. Markham of whom I have often spoken to you, and concerning whom you were always asking me questions. I could not conceive," proceeded the count, "why you were so curious to pry into his affairs, especially as when I mentioned you to him by the name of Greenwood, he did not seem to know any thing about you. But I can now well understand why *you* should wish to know something of a man whom you ruined!"

"I ruined!" cried Mr. Greenwood, now excited for the first time since the commencement of this dialogue, and speaking with an air of unfeigned astonishment. "There must be some mistake in this! I never had any dealings with him in my life, which could either cause his ruin or establish his prosperity."

"You took very good care, it would appear, not to do the latter," said the count. "But probably Mr. Markham's letter will explain to you that which you appear to have forgotten."

Count Alteroni handed the letter to Mr. Greenwood, who perused its contents with intense interest and anxiety.

The count, the countess, and the signora watched his countenance as he read it. Proficient in the art of duplicity as he was,—skilled in all the wiles of hypocrisy and deceit, he could not conceal his emotions now. There was something in that letter which chased the colour from his cheeks, and convulsed his whole frame with extreme agony.

"This is indeed singular!" he murmured, turning the letter over and over in his hand. "Who would have suspected that Allen was merely an agent? who could have foreseen *where that blow was to strike?* Strange—unaccountable concatenation of unfortunate circumstances!"

"Is the writer of that letter correct in his statement?" demanded the count imperiously.

"The information given to you by Mr. Markham, relative to the losses experienced by a certain Mr. Allen, is correct," returned Mr. Greenwood, apparently labouring under considerable excitement. "But, I take my God to witness, that, until this moment, I was unaware that either Mr. Monroe or Mr. Markham were in the remotest way connected with that affair; and I also solemnly protest that I would have given worlds sooner than have been the means of injuring either of them!"

"You admit, then, that you defrauded the people who at that time placed their funds in your hands?" said the count.

"I admit nothing of the kind," returned the financier, now recovering his presence of mind: "I admit nothing so base as your insinuation implies."

"Then wherefore were you so agitated when you perused that letter from Mr. Richard Markham?"

"Count Alteroni, I am not aware that I owe you any explanation of my own private feelings. It is true, I *was* agitated—and I *am* still deeply grieved, to think that my want of judgment and foresight in a certain speculation should have involved in ruin those whom I wish well! But I suffered as well as they—I lost as many thousands as they did," continued Mr. Greenwood, passing once more into that system of plausible, specious, and deceptive reasoning, which lulled so many suspicions, and closed the eyes of so many persons with regard to his real character: "and although I have done nothing for which I can be blamed by the world, I may still reproach myself when I find that others whom I care for have suffered by my speculations."

The count was staggered at this expression and honourable manifestation of feeling on the part of one whom he had a few minutes ago begun to look upon as a selfish adventurer, callous to all humane emotions and philanthropic sentiments.

Mr. Greenwood continued:—

"When that unfortunate speculation of mine took place, I was not so experienced in the sinuosities of the commercial and financial worlds as I am now. I lost my all, and poverty stared me in the face."

Mr. Greenwood's voice faltered, although he was now once more uttering a tissue of falsehoods.

"But by dint of some good fortune and much hard toil and unwearied application to business, I retrieved my circumstances. Now, answer me candidly, Count Alteroni; is there any thing dishonourable in my career? Will you judge a man upon an *ex-parte* statement? Is not one story very good until another be told? Why, if all persons viewed their affairs constantly in the same light, would there be any business for the civil tribunals? Do not plaintiff and defendant invariably survey the point at issue between them under discrepant aspects? If they did not, wherefore do they go to law? You may allow Mr. Markham and Mr. Monroe to entertain their views; you will also permit me to enjoy mine?"

"Mr. Greenwood," said the count, "I am afraid I have been too severe—nay, even rude in my observations. You will forgive me?"

"My dear sir, say not another word," ejaculated the financier, chuckling inwardly at the triumphant victory which he had thus gained over the suspicions of the Italian nobleman.

At that moment a servant entered the room, and informed Count Alteroni "that the Earl of Warrington was in the drawing-room, and requested an interview, at which his lordship would not detain the count above ten minutes."

The count, having desired Mr. Greenwood not to depart until his return, and apologising for his temporary absence, proceeded to the drawing-room, where the Earl of Warrington awaited him.

The earl rose when the count entered the apartment; and that proud, wealthy, and high-born English peer wore an air of profound respect and deference, as he returned the salutation of the Italian exile.

"Your lordship," said the earl, "will, I hope, pardon this intrusion at so unseemly an hour——"

"The Earl of Warrington is always welcome," interrupted Count Alteroni; "and if I cannot give him so princely a reception in England as I was proud to do in Italy, it is my means and not my will, which is the cause."

"My lord, I beseech you not to allude to any discrepancy in that respect—a discrepancy which I can regret for your lordship only, and not for myself," said the earl. "Indeed, I am so far selfish on the present occasion, that I am come to ask a favour."

"Name the matter in which my poor services can avail your lordship," returned the count, "and I pledge myself in advance to meet your wishes."

"My lord," said the Earl of Warrington, "I must inform your lordship that I am somewhat interested in a cousin of mine of the name of Eliza Sydney. This lady loved a man who was unworthy of her—a wretch whose pursuits are villany, and who enriches himself at the expense of the unwary and confiding. The heartless scoundrel to whom I allude, and the full measure of whose infamy was only exposed to me this day, has endeavoured to possess himself of the person of Eliza in a manner the most atrocious and cowardly. My lord, he employed a confederate to administer soporific drugs to her; but Providence moved that confederate's heart, and frustrated the damnable scheme."

"And can such conduct go unpunished in this land of excellent laws and unerring justice?" inquired the count.

"Ah! my lord," replied the earl, "this man is possessed of great wealth, and consequently of great influence; for, in England, *money is power!* Moreover, the complete chain of evidence is wanting; and then exposure to the female in such a case is almost equal to a stigma and to shame! To continue my brief tale, my lord—this man, with a demon heart, is one who will persecute my cousin Eliza to the very death. A lady of my acquaintance, who can also tell a tale of the unequalled villany of this George Montague Greenwood——"

"What!" ejaculated the count; "do I hear aright? or do my ears deceive me? What name did you give the miscreant who administered opiate drugs to a woman with the foulest of motives?"

"George Montague Greenwood," repeated the earl.

"O God!" ejaculated the count, sinking back in his chair, and covering his face with his hands; "I thank thee that thou hast intervened ere it was too late to prevent that fearful sacrifice of my daughter!"

"Pardon me, my lord," exclaimed the earl, "if I have awakened any disagreeable reminiscences, or produced impressions——"

"Your lordship has done me an infinite service, in fully opening my eyes to the villany of a man whose damnable sophistry glosses over his crimes with so deceptive a varnish, that the sight is dazzled when contemplating his conduct."

As the count uttered these words he wrung the hands of the English peer with the most friendly and grateful warmth.

"Another time, my lord," continued the Italian noble, "I will explain to you the cause of my present emotions. You will then perceive how confirmed a miscreant is this Greenwood. In the meantime tell me how I can aid your lordship?"

"I was about to inform you, my lord," continued the Earl of Warrington, "that Miss Sydney, alarmed and appalled at the persecution of this man, who seems to spare neither expense nor crime to accomplish any purpose upon which he has once set his mind, has determined to sojourn for a time upon the Continent. Your lordship is aware that I possess a humble villa in the suburbs of Montoni——"

"A beautiful residence, on the contrary," said the count, "and where," he added with a sigh, "in happier times I have partaken of your hospitality."

"Yes, your lordship has honoured me with your society at that retreat," said the earl, with a low and deferential bow. "It is to that villa that I now propose to despatch my cousin, in order that she may escape the persecutions and the plots of this vile Greenwood. The object of my present visit is to solicit your lordship for a few letters of introduction for Miss Sydney to some of those families in Montoni with whom she may experience the charms of profitable and intellectual society."

"With much pleasure," answered the count. "When does Miss Sydney propose to leave England?"

"The day after to-morrow, my lord."

"To-morrow evening your lordship shall receive the letters which Miss Sydney requires. They will of course be unsealed—both in observance of the rules of etiquette, and on account of the customhouse officers in the continental states; but your lordship will take care that they be not opened in England."

"I comprehend you, my lord. The incognito which your lordship chooses to preserve in this country shall not be disturbed by any indiscretion on the part of myself or of those connected with me."

The Earl of Warrington then took his leave.

The moment he had departed, the count rang the bell, and said to the servant who answered the summons, "Request Mr. Greenwood to favour me with his company in this room—*here!*"

In another minute the financier was introduced into the saloon which the count was pacing with uneven and agitated steps.

"Mr. Greenwood," said the Italian nobleman, "I think you recollect the subject of our conversation when I was called away by the visit of the Earl of Warrington?"

"Perfectly," answered the financier, who perceived that there was again something wrong. "I remember that you made many accusations against me, all of which I most satisfactorily explained—insomuch that you very handsomely apologised for the severity of your language."

"Then, sir," continued the count, with difficulty restraining his impatience while Mr. Greenwood thus delivered himself, "if you be really such an honourable and such an injured man as you would represent, and if you be really grieved when you hear that a fellow-creature has been ruined by the failure of your speculations, have the kindness to return to me the money which I have confided to you, and I shall be inclined to think of you as you choose to think of yourself. To tell the truth, I am already sick of the uncertainty of speculation; and I would rather withdraw from the enterprise altogether."

"Really, my dear sir," said Mr. Greenwood, "this demand is so very irregular—so exceedingly unbusiness-like——"

"We will not place it upon the footing of *business*, sir," interrupted the count emphatically; "we will place it upon the basis of *honour*."

"Honour and business with me, my dear sir, are synonymous," said the financier with a smile.

"So much the better!" ejaculated the count: "I see that we shall not dispute over this matter. The whole is summed up in a few words: return me the money I have placed in your hands."

"These things cannot be done in a hurry, my dear sir," said Mr. Greenwood, playing with a very handsome gold guard-chain which festooned over his waistcoat.

"Either you have made away with my money, or you have it in your possession still," exclaimed the count. "If you have it, give me a cheque upon your banker for the amount: if you have placed it out at interest, give me security."

"I must observe to you that the whole proceeding is most irregular," said Mr. Greenwood: "and the business requires mature reflection. Moreover, all my funds are locked up for the moment."

"Then how would you carry out the enterprise for which I embarked my capital?" demanded the count.

"You must be aware," replied the financier, "that capitalists—like me—always lay out their cash to the greatest advantage, and make use of bills and negotiable paper of various descriptions. Thus, I could build a dozen steam-packets in a few weeks, and pay for them all without actually encroaching upon my capital!"

"I understand you, sir," said the count: "and in order to meet your convenience, I am ready to receive the securities you mention, payable at early dates, instead of specie."

"Oh! well—that alters the question," cried Mr. Greenwood, an idea apparently striking him at that moment. "I am acquainted with one of the richest bankers in London—intimately acquainted with him:—would you have any objection for him to take my place in respect to you, and become the holder of your capital—say for a period of six months?"

"Who is the banker?" asked the count.

"James Tomlinson," answered the financier.

"I know the name well. Are you serious in your proposal?"

"Call upon me to-morrow at twelve o'clock, and we will proceed together to Mr. Tomlinson's banking house in the city. I will have the whole affair arranged for you in the course of an hour after our arrival at his establishment."

"I rely upon your word, Mr. Greenwood," returned the count.

The financier then took his departure.

CHAPTER LIV.

THE BANKER.

The native of London is as proud of the City as if it were his own property. He can afford to be called a cockney for having been born within the sound of Bow bells, for there are merchant-princes, and the peers and monopolists of the commerce of the world, who bear the nickname as well as he.

And well may the Londoner be proud of his city in numerous respects. It is the richest and the most powerful that the world has ever seen! The dingy back parlours in Lombard Street, the upstairs business rooms in Cheapside, and the warehouses with shutters half up the windows in Wood Street and its neighbourhood, are the mysterious places in which the springs of the finance and trade of a mighty empire are set in motion? Half a dozen men in the City can command in an hour more wealth than either Rome or Babylon had to boast of at the respective periods of their greatest prosperity. And neither Rome nor Babylon possessed drapers who cleared their fifty thousand a-year by selling gowns and shawls, nor sugar-bakers with a million in hard cash, nor grocers with a plum in each hand, nor brewers to whom the rise or fall of one halfpenny per pot in the price of beer makes a difference of forty thousand pounds *per annum!* Rome, Babylon, Thebes, and Carthage, could all have been purchased by the East India Company—with perhaps a mortgage upon the India Docks!

But the reader must not imagine that all which glitters is gold. Amongst the most splendid establishments in London, and those most wealthy in appearance, there are some in a hopeless state of insolvency. To one of these we shall now introduce those who may choose to accompany us thither.

The well-known banking-house of James Tomlinson was situated in Lombard Street. The establishment was not extensive; nor were there a great many clerks, because it did little agency business for country banks, but was chiefly a house of deposit. It enjoyed a high reputation, and was considered as safe as the presumed wealth, integrity, and experience of its proprietor were likely to render it. It was moreover believed that the father of James Tomlinson was a sleeping partner; and as the old gentleman had retired from the business of oilman with an immense fortune, the bank was presumed to possess every guarantee of stability. It had existed for upwards of sixty years, having been founded and most successfully carried on by an uncle of James Tomlinson. James himself had originally entered the establishment as a clerk, whence he rose to be a partner, and finally found himself at the head of the concern at his uncle's death.

James Tomlinson was not an extravagant man; but he was not possessed of the ability and experience for which the world gave him credit. In the year 1826, and at the age of forty, he found himself at the head of a flourishing and respectable establishment. He was indeed the sole proprietor, for his father was in reality totally unconnected with it as a partner. James was intimately acquainted with the mechanical routine of the bank business; but he was deficient in those powers of combination and faculties of foresight which were necessary to enable him to lay out to the best advantage the moneys deposited in his hands. With good intentions, he lacked talent. He was an excellent head clerk or junior partner; but he was totally unfitted for supreme management. Thus was it that in two or three years he experienced serious reverses; and, although he carefully concealed the failure of his operations from all human eyes, the very safety of his establishment was seriously compromised. The French Revolution of 1830 ruined a Paris house to which Tomlinson had advanced a considerable sum; and this blow consummated the insolvency of his bank.

He was then compelled to make a confidant of his cashier, an old and faithful servant of his uncle, and of frugal habits, and kind but eccentric disposition. Michael Martin was this individual's name. He was of very repulsive appearance, stooping in his gait, blear-eyed, and dirty in person. He took vast quantities of snuff; but as much lodged upon his shirt-frill and waistcoat as was thrust up his nose. Thus his linen was invariably filthy in the extreme. His dress was a suit of seedy black; and the right thigh of his trousers was brown and grimy with the marks of snuff—for upon that part of his attire did he invariably wipe his finger and thumb after taking a pinch of his brown rappee.

Such was the individual whom Tomlinson took into his confidence, when the affairs of the bank grew desperate. Old Martin was as close and reserved as if he were both deaf and dumb; and he was moreover possessed of a peculiar craftiness and cunning which admirably fitted him for the part that he was now to enact. Although it was next to impossible to retrieve the affairs of the bank, so great was the deficiency, still Michael Martin assured his master that it was quite probable that they might be enabled to carry on the establishment for a length of time—perhaps even many years, the chances that the draughts upon the bank would not equal the deposits being in their favour.

Thus was this insolvent and ruined establishment carried on, with seeming respectability and success, by the perseverance of Tomlinson, and the skill and craft of old Martin.

We shall now introduce our readers into the parlour of the bank, at ten o'clock in the morning after the incidents related in the preceding chapter.

James Tomlinson had just arrived, and was standing before the fire, glancing over the City Article of *The Times*. He was a fine, tall, good-looking man, plainly dressed, and without the slightest affectation either in manner or attire. The bluntness and apparent straightforwardness of his character had won and secured him many friends amongst a class of men who regard frankness of disposition and plainness of demeanour as qualities indicative of solidity of position and regular habits of business. Then he was always at his post—always to be seen; and hence unlimited confidence was placed in him!

Having glanced over the newspaper which he held in his hand, he rang the bell. A clerk responded to the summons.

"Is Mr. Martin come yet?"

"Yes, sir."

"Tell him to step this way."

The clerk withdrew; and the old cashier entered the room, the door of which he carefully closed.

"Good morning, Michael," said the banker. "What news?"

"Worse and worse," answered the old man, with a species of savage grunt. "We have had a sad time of it for the last three months."

"For the last seven or eight years, you may say," observed Tomlinson, with a sigh; and then his countenance suddenly wore an expression of ineffable despair—as evanescent as it was poignant.

"At first the work was easy enough," said Michael: "a little combination and tact enabled us to struggle on; but latterly the concern has fallen into so desperate a condition, that I really fear when I come in the morning that it will never last through the day."

"My God! my God! what a life!" exclaimed Tomlinson. "And there are hundreds and thousands who pass up the street every day, and who say within themselves. '*How I wish I was James Tomlinson!*' Heavens! I would that I were a beggar in the street—a sweeper of a crossing—a pauper in a workhouse——"

"Come—this is folly," interrupted the old cashier, impatiently. "We must go on to the end."

"What is the state of your book this morning?" demanded the banker, putting the question with evident alarm—almost amounting to horror.

"Three thousand four hundred pounds, eighteen shillings, in specie—sixteen hundred and thirty-five in notes," answered the cashier.

"Is that all!" ejaculated Tomlinson. "And this morning we have to pay Greenwood the two thousand pounds he lent me six weeks ago."

"We can't part with the money," said the cashier rudely. "Greenwood knows the circumstances of the bank, and must give time."

"You know what Greenwood is, Michael," exclaimed the banker. "If we are not punctual with him, he will never lend us another shilling; and what should we have done without him on several occasions?"

"I know all that. But look at the interest he makes you pay," muttered the cashier.

"And look at the risk he runs," added the banker.

"He finds it worth his while. I calculated the other day that we paid him three thousand pounds last year for interest only: we can't go on much longer at that rate."

"I had almost said that the sooner it ends the better," cried Tomlinson. "What low trickery—what meanness—what abominable craft, have we been compelled to resort to! Oh! if that affair with the Treasury three years ago had only turned up well—if we could have secured the operation, we should have retrieved all our losses, enormous as they are—we should have built up the fortunes of the establishment upon a more solid foundation than ever!"

"That was indeed a misfortune," observed the cashier, taking a huge pinch of snuff.

"And how the Chancellor of the Exchequer obtained his information about me—at the eleventh hour—after all previous inquiries were known to be satisfactory," continued Tomlinson, "I never could conjecture. At that time the secret was confined to you and me, and my father, to whom I communicated it, you remember, in that letter which I wrote to him soliciting the fifty thousand pounds."

"Which sum saved the bank at that period," observed Michael.

"Never shall I forget the day when I called at the Treasury for the decision of the government relative to my proposal," returned

Tomlinson. "The functionary who received me, said in so pointed a manner, '*Mr. Tomlinson, you have not dealt candidly with us relative to your true position; your secret is known to us; but rest assured that, although we decline any negotiation with you, we will not betray you.*' This announcement came upon me like a thunder-stroke: I was literally paralysed. The functionary added with a sort of triumphant and yet mysterious smile, '*There is not a secret connected with the true position of any individual of any consequence in the City which escapes our knowledge. The government, sir, is omniscient!*' God alone can divine the sources of this intimate acquaintance with things locked up, as it were, in one's own bosom!" added the banker, thoughtfully.

"And this is not the only case in which such secrets have been discovered by the government," said the old cashier, again regaling his nose with a copious pinch of snuff.

"Yes, I myself have heard of other instances," observed the banker, with a shudder. "I have known great firms expend large sums of money to obtain particular information from Paris, Frankfort, and Madrid, by means of couriers; and this information has been despatched by letter to their agents at Liverpool and Manchester, and elsewhere, to answer certain commercial or financial purposes. Well, that information has been known to government within a few hours, and the government broker has bought or sold stock accordingly!"

"But how *could* the government obtain that information?" demanded Martin. "Some treachery——"

"No—impossible! The government has gleaned its knowledge when every human precaution against treachery and fraud was adopted. Look at my own case!" continued Tomlinson. "You, my father, and myself alone, knew *my* secret. On you I can reckon as a man can reckon upon his own self: my father was incapable of betraying me; and I of course should not have divulged my own ruin. And yet the secret became known to the government. I shudder, Michael—oh! I shudder when I think that we dwell in a country which vaunts its freedom, yet where there exists the secret, dark, and mysterious element of the most hideous despotism!"

At this moment a clerk entered, and informed the cashier that he was wanted in the public office.

As soon as Michael had disappeared, the banker walked up and down his parlour, a prey to the most maddening reflections. There were but five thousand pounds left in the safe; two thousand were to be paid to Greenwood; and every minute a cheque, or two or three cheques might be presented, which would crush the bank at one blow.

"One hundred and eighty thousand pounds of liability," murmured Tomlinson to himself, "and five thousand pounds to meet it!"

Ah! little thought those who passed by the banking-house at that moment, what heart-felt, horrible tortures were endured by the master of the establishment in his own parlour!

At length Martin returned.

His countenance never revealed any emotions; but he took snuff wholesale—and that was a fearful omen.

"Well?" said Tomlinson, in a hoarse and hollow voice.

"Alderman Phipps just drawn for twelve hundred pounds, and Colonel Brown for eight hundred," replied the cashier.

"Two thousand gone in a minute!" ejaculated the banker.

"Shall I pay any more?" asked the cashier.

"Yes—pay, pay up to the last farthing!" answered Tomlinson. "An accident—a chance may save us, as oftentimes before! And yet methinks, Michael, that we never stood so near the verge of ruin as we do to-day."

"Never," said the old man coldly.

"And is there no expedient by which we can raise a few thousands, or even a few hundreds, for immediate wants?"

"None that I know of," returned Martin, taking more snuff.

At that moment Mr. Greenwood was announced, and Michael withdrew from the parlour.

"You have called for your two thousand pounds?" said the banker, after the usual interchange of civilities.

"Yes: I require that sum particularly this morning, replied the financier; "for I am pledged to pay fifteen thousand at twelve o'clock to Count Alteroni."

"This is very unfortunate," observed Tomlinson. "I am literally in this position—take the money, and I must stop payment the next moment."

"That is disagreeable, no doubt," said Greenwood; "but the count is urgent, and I cannot put him off."

"My God!" cried Tomlinson; "what can I do? Greenwood—my

good friend—I know you are rich—I know you can raise any amount you choose: pray do not push me this morning."

"What am I to do, my dear fellow?" said the financier: "I must satisfy this count—and I really cannot manage without the two thousand. I could let you have them again in a fortnight."

"A fortnight!" ejaculated the banker, clenching his fists; "to-morrow it might be too late. Can you suggest no plan? can you devise no scheme? Let me keep these two thousand pounds for six weeks longer—a month longer; and ask me—ask me what you will! I am desperate—I will do anything you bid me!"

"Tell me how I can satisfy this ravenous Italian," said Greenwood, "and I will let you keep the money for six months."

"You say you have to settle with this count for fifteen thousand pounds?" inquired the banker.

Greenwood nodded an affirmative.

"And does he require it all in hard cash?"

"No—he will take the security of any responsible person, or apparently responsible person," added the financier, with a significant smile, "payable in six months."

Tomlinson appeared to reflect profoundly.

His reverie was interrupted by the entrance of old Martin, taking snuff more vehemently than ever.

The cashier whispered something in the banker's ear, and then again retired.

"Seven hundred and fifty more gone!" cried Tomlinson; "and now, Greenwood, there remains in the safe but a fraction more than your two thousand pounds. Dictate your own terms!"

This was precisely the point to which the financier was anxious to arrive.

"Listen," he said, playing with his watch-chain. "This Count Alteroni will accept of you as his debtor instead of me. Take the responsibility off me on to your own shoulders, and I make you a present of the two thousand pounds!"

"What!" ejaculated Tomlinson; "incur a liability of fifteen thousand to this count! Greenwood, you never can be serious?"

"I never was more serious in my life," returned the financier coolly. "If you fail before the six months have elapsed, fifteen thousand more or less on your books will be nothing: if you contrive to carry on the establishment until the expiration of that period, I will help you out of the dilemma."

"You are not reasonable—you are anxious to crush me at once!" cried Tomlinson. "Well, be it so, Mr. Greenwood! Take your two thousand pounds——"

"And leave you to put up a notice on your doors—eh?" said Greenwood, still playing with his watch-chain.

"Ah! my God—has it come to this?" exclaimed the banker. "Ruin—disgrace—and beggary, all in one day! But better that than submit to such terms as those which you dictate."

With these words he rang the bell violently.

Old Martin immediately made his appearance.

"Mr. Martin," said Tomlinson, affecting a calmness which he was far from feeling, "bring two thousand pounds for Mr. Greenwood."

"It can't be done," growled Michael, taking a huge pinch of snuff.

"Can't be done?" ejaculated the banker.

"No," answered the old man, doggedly: "just paid away four hundred and sixty-five more. There isn't two thousand in the safe."

Tomlinson walked once up the room; then, turning to Greenwood, he said, "I will accept your proposal. Mr. Martin," he added, addressing the cashier, "you can retire: I will settle this matter with Mr. Greenwood."

The old man withdrew.

"When, where, and how is this business to be arranged?" demanded Tomlinson, after a short pause.

"The count is to call at my house at twelve. I have left a note to request him to come on hither."

"You had, then, already arranged this matter in your mind?" said the banker, ironically.

"Certainly," answered Greenwood, with his usual coolness. "I knew you would relieve me of this obligation; because I shall be enabled in return to afford you that assistance of which you stand so much in need."

"I must throw myself upon your generosity," said Tomlinson. "It is now twelve: the count will soon be here."

Half an hour passed away; and the Italian nobleman made his appearance.

"You see that I have kept my word, count," exclaimed Mr.

Greenwood, with an ironical smile of triumph. "Mr. Tomlinson holds in his hands certain funds of mine, which, according to the terms of agreement between us, he is to retain in his possession and use for a period of six months and six days from the present day, at an interest of four per cent. If you, Count Alteroni, be willing to accept a transfer of fifteen thousand pounds of such funds in Mr. Tomlinson's hands from my name to your own, the bargain can be completed this moment."

"I cannot hesitate, Mr. Greenwood," said the count, "to accept a guarantee of such known stability as the name of Mr. Tomlinson."

"Then all that remains to be done," exclaimed the financier, "is for you to return me my acknowledgment for the amount specified, and for Mr. Tomlinson to give you his in its place. Mr. Tomlinson has already received my written authority for the transfer."

The business was settled as Mr. Greenwood proposed. The count returned the financier his receipt, and accepted one from the banker.

"Now, that this is concluded, count," said Mr. Greenwood, placing the receipt in his pocket-book, "I hope that our friendship will continue uninterrupted."

"Pardon me, sir," returned the count, his features assuming a stern expression: "although I am bound to admit that you have not wronged me in respect to money, you have dared to talk to me of my daughter, who is innocence and purity itself."

"Count Alteroni," began Mr. Greenwood, "I am not aware——"

"Silence, sir!" cried the Italian noble, imperatively: "I have but one word more to say. Circumstances have revealed to me your profligate character; and never can I be too thankful that my daughter should have escaped an alliance with a man who bribes his agents to administer opiate drugs to an unprotected female for the vilest of purposes. Mr. Tomlinson," added the count, "pardon me for having used such language in your apartment, and in your presence."

Count Alteroni bowed politely to the banker, and, darting a withering glance of mingled contempt and indignation upon the abashed and astounded Greenwood, took his departure.

"He talks of things which are quite new to me," said Greenwood, recovering an outward appearance of composure, though inwardly he was chagrined beyond description.

Tomlinson made no reply: he was too much occupied with his own affairs to be able to afford attention to those of others.

Greenwood shortly took his leave—delighted at having effectually settled his pecuniary obligation with the count, in such a manner that it could never again be the means of molestation in respect to himself,—but vexed at the discovery which the Italian nobleman had evidently made in respect to his conduct towards Eliza Sydney.

Immediately after Mr. Greenwood had left the bank-parlour, old Michael entered. This time he carried his snuff-box open in his left hand; and at every two paces he took a copious pinch with the forefinger and thumb of his right. This was a fearful omen; and Tomlinson trembled.

"Well, Michael—well?"

"Not a deposit this morning. Draughts come in like wild-fire," said the old cashier. "There is but a hundred pounds left in the safe!"

"A hundred pounds!" ejaculated the banker, clasping his hands together: "and is it come to this at length, Michael?"

"Yes," said the cashier, gruffly.

"Then let us post a notice at once," cried Tomlinson: "the establishment must be closed without another moment's delay."

"Will you write out the notice of stoppage of payment, or shall I?" inquired Michael.

"Do it yourself, my good old friend—do it for me!" said the banker, whose countenance was ashy pale, and whose limbs trembled under him, as if he expected the officers of justice to drag him to a place of execution.

The old cashier seated himself at the table, and wrote out the announcement that the bank was unfortunately compelled to suspend its payments. He then read it to the ruined man who was now pacing the apartment with agitated steps.

"Will that do?"

"Yes," answered the banker; "but, in mercy, let me leave the house ere that notice be made public."

Tomlinson was about to rush distractedly out of the room, when the cashier was summoned into the public department of the establishment.

Five minutes elapsed ere his return—five minutes which appeared five hours to James Tomlinson.

At length the old man came back; and this time he did not carry his snuff-box in his hand.

Without uttering a word, he took the "notice of stoppage" off the table, crushed it in his hand, and threw it into the fire.

"Saved once more," he murmured, as he watched the paper burning to tinder; and when it was completely consumed, he took a long and hearty pinch of snuff.

"Saved!" echoed Tomlinson: "do you mean that we are saved again?"

"Seven thousand four hundred and sixty-seven pounds just paid in to Dobson and Dobbins's account," answered the cashier, coolly and leisurely, as if he himself experienced not the slightest emotion.

In another hour there were fifteen thousand pounds in the safe; and when the bank closed that evening at the usual time, this sum had swollen up to twenty thousand and some hundreds.

This day was a specimen of the life of James Tomlinson, the banker.

Readers, when you pass by the grand commercial and financial establishments of this great metropolis, pause and reflect ere you envy their proprietors! In the parlours and offices of those reputed emporiums of wealth are men whose minds are a prey to the most agonising feelings—the most poignant emotions.

There is no situation so full of responsibility as that of a banker—no trust so sacred as that which is confided to him. When he fails, it is not the ruin of one man which is accomplished: it is the ruin of hundreds—perhaps thousands. The effects of that one failure are ramified through a wide section of society: widows and orphans are reduced to beggary—and those who have been well and tenderly nurtured are driven to the workhouse.

And yet the law punishes not the great banker who fails, and who involves thousands in his ruin. The petty trader who breaks for fifty pounds is thrown into prison, and is placed at the tender mercy of the Insolvents' Court, which perhaps remands him to a debtor's gaol for a year, for having contracted debts without a reasonable chance of paying them. But the great banker, who commenced business with a hundred thousand pounds, and who has dissipated five hundred thousand belonging to others, applies to the Bankruptcy Court, never sees the inside of a prison at all, and in due time receives a certificate, which clears him of all his liabilities, and enables him to begin the world anew. The petty trader passes a weary time in gaol, and is then merely emancipated from his confinement—but not from his debts. His future exertions are clogged by an impending weight of liability. One system or the other is wrong:—decide, O ye legislators who vaunt "the wisdom of your ancestors," which should be retained, and which abolished,—or whether both should be modified!

* * * * * * *

In the course of the evening the Earl of Warrington called upon Mrs. Arlington, with whom he passed a few minutes alone in the drawing-room.

When his lordship had taken his departure, Diana returned to Eliza whom she had left in another apartment, and, placing a quantity of letters, folded, but unsealed, in her hands, said, "These are the means of introduction to some of the first families in Montoni. They are written, I am informed, by an Italian nobleman of great influence, and whose name will act like a talisman in your behalf. They are sent unsealed according to usage; but the earl has earnestly and positively desired that their contents be not examined in this country. He gave this injunction very seriously," added Diana, with a smile, "doubtless because he supposed that he has to deal with two daughters of Eve whose curiosity is invincible. He, however, charged me to deliver this message to you as delicately as possible."

"These letters," answered Eliza, glancing over their superscriptions, "are addressed to strangers and not to me; and although I know that they refer to me, I should not think of penetrating into their contents, either in England or elsewhere. But did you express to the earl all the gratitude that I feel for his numerous and signal deeds of kindness?"

"The earl is well aware of your grateful feelings," replied Mrs. Arlington. "Can you suppose that I would forget to paint all you experience for what he has already done, and what he will still do for you? He will see you for a moment ere your departure to-morrow, to bid you farewell."

"I appreciate that act of condescension on his part," observed Eliza, affected even to tears, "more than all else he has ever yet done for me!"

* * * * * * *

On the following day Eliza Sydney, accompanied by the faithful Louisa, and attended by an elderly valet who had been for years in the service of the Earl of Warrington, took her departure from London, on her way to the Grand Duchy of Castelcicala.

CHAPTER LV.

MISERRIMA!!!

We now come to a sad episode in our history—and yet one in which there is perhaps less romance and more truth than in any scene yet depicted.

We have already warned our reader that he will have to accompany us amidst appalling scenes of vice and wretchedness:—we are now about to introduce him to one of destitution and suffering—of powerful struggle and unavailing toil—whose details are so very sad, that we have been able to find no better heading for our chapter than *miserrima*, or "very miserable things."

The reader will remember that we have brought our narrative, in preceding chapters, up to the end of 1838:—we must now go back for a period of two years, in order to commence the harrowing details of our present episode.

In one of the low dark rooms of a gloomy house in a court leading out of Golden Lane, St. Luke's, a young girl of seventeen sate at work. It was about nine o'clock in the evening; and a single candle lighted the miserable chamber, which was almost completely denuded of furniture. The cold wind of December whistled through the ill-closed casement and the broken panes, over which thin paper had been pasted to repel the biting chill. A small deal table, two common chairs, and a mattress were all the articles of furniture which this wretched room contained. A door at the end opposite the window opened into another and smaller chamber: and this latter one was furnished with nothing, save an old mattress. There were no blankets—no coverlids in either room. The occupants had no other covering at night than their own clothes;—and those clothes—God knows they were thin, worn, and scanty enough!

Not a spark of fire burned in the grate;—and yet that front room in which the young girl was seated was as cold as the nave of a vast cathedral in the depth of winter.

The reader has perhaps experienced that icy chill which seems to strike to the very marrow of the bones, when entering a huge stone edifice:—the cold which prevailed in that room, and in which the young creature was at work with her needle, was more intense—more penetrating—more bitter—more frost-like than even that icy chill!

Miserable and cheerless was that chamber: the dull light of the candle only served to render its nakedness the more apparent, without relieving it of any of its gloom. And as the cold draught from the wretched casement caused the flame of that candle to flicker and oscillate, the poor girl was compelled to seat herself between the window and the table, to protect her light from the wind. Thus, the chilling December blast blew upon the back of the young sempstress, whose clothing was so thin and scant:—so very scant!

The sempstress was, as we have before said, about seventeen years of age. She was very beautiful; and her features, although pale with want, and wan with care and long vigils, were pleasing and agreeable. The cast of her countenance was purely Grecian—the shape of her head eminently classical—and her form was of a perfect and symmetrical mould. Although clothed in the most scanty and wretched manner, she was singularly neat and clean in her appearance; and her air and demeanour were far above her humble occupation and her impoverished condition.

She had, indeed, seen better days! Reared in the lap of luxury by fond, but too indulgent parents, her education had been of a high order; and thus her qualifications were rather calculated to embellish her in prosperity than to prove of use to her in adversity. She had lost her mother at the age of twelve; and her father—kind and fond, and proud of his only child—had sought to make her shine in that sphere which she had then appeared destined to adorn. But misfortunes came upon them like a thunderbolt: and when poverty—grim poverty—stared them in the face—this poor girl had no resource, save her needle! Now and then her father earned a trifle in the City, by making out accounts or copying deeds;—but sorrow and ill-health had almost entirely incapacitated him from labour or occupation of any kind;—and his young and affectionate daughter was compelled to toil from sun-rise until a late hour in the night to earn even a pittance.

One after another, all their little comforts, in the shape of furniture and clothing, disappeared; and after vainly endeavouring to maintain a humble lodging in a cheap but respectable neighbourhood, poverty compelled them to take refuge in that dark, narrow, filthy court leading out of Golden Lane.

Such was the sad fate of Mr. Monroe and his daughter Ellen.

At the time when we introduce the latter to our readers, her father was absent in the City. He had a little occupation in a counting-house, which was to last three days, which kept him hard at work from nine in the morning till eleven at night, and for which he was to receive a pittance so small we dare not mention its amount! This is how it was:—an official assignee belonging to the Bankruptcy Court had some heavy accounts to make up by a certain day: he was consequently compelled to employ an accountant to aid him; the accountant employed a petty scrivener to make out the balance-sheet; and the petty scrivener employed Monroe to ease him of a portion of the toil. It is therefore plain that Monroe was not to receive much for his three days' labour.

And so Ellen was compelled to toil and work, and work and toil—to rise early and go to bed late—so late that she had scarcely fallen asleep, worn out with fatigue, when it appeared time to get up again;—and thus the roses forsook her cheeks—and her health suffered—and her head ached—and her eyes grew dim—and her limbs were stiff with the chill!

And so she worked and toiled, and toiled and worked.

We said it was about nine o'clock in the evening.

Ellen's fingers were almost paralysed with cold and labour; and yet the work which she had in her hands must be done that night; else no supper then—and no breakfast on the morrow; for on the shelf in that cheerless chamber there was not a morsel of bread!

And for sixteen hours had that poor girl fasted already; for she had eaten a crust at five in the morning, when she had risen from her hard cold couch in the back chamber. She had left the larger portion of the bread that then remained, for her father; and she had assured him that she had a few halfpence to purchase more for herself—but she had therein deceived him! Ah! how noble and generous was that deception;—and how often—how very often did that poor girl practise it!

Ellen had risen at five that morning to embroider a silk shawl with eighty flowers. She had calculated upon finishing it by eight in the evening; but, although she had worked, and worked, and worked hour after hour, without ceasing, save for a moment at long intervals to rest her aching head and stretch her cramped fingers, eight had struck—and nine had struck also—and still the blossoms were not all embroidered.

It was a quarter to ten when the last stitch was put into the last flower.

But then the poor creature could not rest:—not to her was it allowed to repose after that severe day of toil! She was hungry—she was faint—her stomach was sick for want of food; and at eleven her father would come home, hungry, faint, and sick at stomach also!

Rising from her chair—every limb stiff, cramped, and aching with cold and weariness—the poor creature put on her modest straw bonnet with a faded riband, and her thin wretched shawl, to take home her work.

Her employer dwelt upon Finsbury Pavement; and as it was now late, the poor girl was compelled to hasten as fast as her aching limbs would carry her.

The shop to which she repaired was brilliant with lamps and gas-lights. Articles of great variety and large value were piled in the windows, on the counters, on the shelves. Upwards of twenty young men were busily employed in serving the customers. The proprietor of that establishment was at that moment entertaining a party of friends up stairs, at a champagne supper!

The young girl walked timidly into the vast magazine of fashions, and, with downcast eyes, advanced towards an elderly woman who was sitting at a counter at the farther end of the shop. To this female did she present the shawl.

"A pretty time of night to come!" murmured the shopwoman. "This ought to have been done by three or four o'clock."

"I have worked since five this morning, without ceasing," answered Ellen; "and I could not finish it before."

"Ah! I see," exclaimed the shopwoman, turning the shawl over, and examining it critically; "there are fifty or sixty flowers, I see."

"Eighty," said Ellen; "I was ordered to embroider that number."

"Well, Miss—and is there so much difference between sixty and eighty?"

"Difference, ma'am!" ejaculated the young girl, the tears starting into her eyes; "the difference is more than four hours' work!"

"Very likely, very likely, Miss. And how much do you expect for this?"

"I must leave it entirely to you, ma'am."

The poor girl spoke deferentially to this cold-hearted woman, in order to make her generous. Oh! poverty renders even the innocence of seventeen selfish, mundane, and calculating!

"Oh! you leave it to me, do you?" said the woman, turning the shawl over and over, and scrutinising it in all points; but she could not discover a single fault in Ellen's work. "You leave it to me? Well, it isn't so badly done—very tolerably for a girl of your age and inexperience! I presume," she added, thrusting her hand into the till under the counter, and drawing forth sixpence, "I presume that this is sufficient."

"Madam," said Ellen, bursting into tears, "I have worked nearly seventeen hours at that shawl—"

She could say no more: her voice was lost in sobs.

"Come, come," cried the shopwoman harshly,—"no whimpering here! Take up your money, if you like it—and if you don't, leave it. Only decide one way or another, and make haste!"

Ellen took up the sixpence, wiped her eyes, and hastily turned to leave the shop.

"Do you not want any more work?" demanded the shopwoman abruptly.

The fact was that the poor girl worked well, and did not "shirk" labour; and the woman knew that it was the interest of her master to retain that young creature's services.

Those words, "Do you not want any more work?" reminded Ellen that she and her father must live—that they could not starve! She accordingly turned towards that uncouth female once more, and received another shawl, to embroider in the same manner, and at the same price!

Eighty blossoms for sixpence!

Sixteen hours' work for sixpence!!

A farthing and a half per hour!!!

The young girl returned to the dirty court in Golden Lane, after purchasing some food, coarse and cheap, on her way home.

On the ground-floor of a house in the same court dwelt an old woman—one of those old women who are the moral sewers of great towns—the sinks towards which flow all the impurities of the human passions. One of those abominable hags was she who dishonour the sanctity of old age. She had hideous wrinkles upon her face; and as she stretched out her huge, dry, and bony hand, and tapped the young girl upon the shoulder, as the latter hurried past her door, the very touch seemed to chill the maiden even through her clothes.

Ellen turned abruptly round, and shuddered—she scarcely knew why—when she found herself confronting that old hag by the dim lustre of the lights which shone through the windows in the narrow court.

That old woman, who was the widow of crime, assumed as pleasant an aspect as her horrible countenance would allow her to put on, and addressed the timid maiden in a strain which the latter scarcely comprehended. All that Ellen could understand was that the old woman suspected how hardly she toiled and how badly she was paid, and offered to point out a more pleasant and profitable mode of earning money.

Without precisely knowing why, Ellen shrank from the contact of that hideous old hag, and trembled at the words which issued from the crone's mouth.

"You do not answer me," said the wretch. "Well, well; when you have no bread to eat—no work—no money to pay your rent—and nothing but the workhouse before you, you will think better of it and come to me."

Thus saying, the old hag turned abruptly into her own den, the door of which she banged violently.

With her heart fluttering like a little bird in its cage, poor Ellen hastened to her own miserable abode.

She placed the food upon the table, but would not touch it until her father should return. She longed for a spark of fire, for she was so cold and so wretched—and even in warm weather misery makes one shiver! But that room was as cold as an icehouse—and the unhappiness of that poor girl was a burden almost too heavy for her to bear.

She sate down, and thought. Oh! how poignant is meditation in such a condition as hers. Her prospects were utterly black and hopeless.

When she and her father had first taken those lodgings, she had obtained work from a "middle-woman." This middle-woman was one who contracted with great drapery and upholstery firms to do their needle-work at certain low rates. The middle-woman had to live, and was therefore compelled to make a decent profit upon the work. So she gave it out to poor creatures like Ellen Monroe, and got it done for next to nothing.

Thus for some weeks had Ellen made shirts—with the collars, wristband, and fronts all well stitched—for four-pence the shirt.

And it took her twelve hours, without intermission, to make a shirt: and it cost her a penny for needles, and thread, and candle.

She therefore had three-pence for herself!

Twelve hours' unwearied toil for three-pence!!

One farthing an hour!!!

Sometimes she had made dissecting-trousers, which were sold to the medical students at the hospitals; and for those she was paid two-pence halfpenny each.

It occupied her eight hours to make one pair of those trousers!

At length the middle-woman had recommended her to the linen-draper's establishment on Finsbury Pavement; and there she was told that she might have plenty of work, and be well paid.

Well paid!

At the rate of a farthing and a half per hour!!

Oh! it was a mockery—a hideous mockery, to give that young creature gay flowers and blossoms to work—she, who was working her own winding-sheet!

She sate, shivering with the cold, awaiting her father's return. Ever and anon the words of that old crone who had addressed her in the court, rang in her ears. What could she mean? How could she—stern in her own wretchedness herself and perhaps stern to the wretchedness of others—how could that old hag possess the means of teaching her a pleasant and profitable mode of earning money? The soul of Ellen was purity itself—although she dwelt in that low, obscene, filthy, and disreputable neighbourhood. She seemed like a solitary lily in the midst of a black morass swarming with reptiles!

The words of the old woman were therefore unintelligible to that fair young creature of seventeen:—and yet she intuitively reproached herself for pondering upon them. Oh! mysterious influence of an all-wise and all-seeing Providence, that thus furnishes warnings against dangers yet unseen!

She tried to avert her thoughts from the contemplation of her own misery, and of the tempting offer made to her by the wrinkled harridan in the adjoining house; and so she busied herself with thinking of the condition of the other lodgers in the same tenement which she and her father inhabited. She then perceived that there were others in the world—as wretched and as badly off as herself; but, in contradiction to the detestable maxim of Rochefoucauld—she found no consolation in this conviction.

In the attics were Irish families, whose children ran all day, half naked, about the court and lane, paddling with their poor cold bare feet in the puddle or the snow, and apparently thriving in dirt, hunger, and privation. Ellen and her father occupied the two rooms on the second floor. On the first floor, in the front room, lived two families—an elderly man and woman, with their grown-up sons and daughters; and with one of those sons were a wife and young children. Eleven souls thus herded together, without shame, in a room eighteen feet wide! These eleven human beings, dwelling in so swine-like a manner, existed upon twenty-five shillings a week, the joint earnings of all of them who were able to work. In the back chamber on the same floor was a tailor, with a paralytic wife and a complete tribe of children. This poor wretch worked for a celebrated "Clothing Mart," and sometimes toiled for twenty hours a-day—never less than seventeen, Sunday included—to earn—what?

Eight shillings a week.

He made mackintoshes at the rate of one shilling and three-pence each; and he could make one each day. But then he had to find needles and thread; and the cost of these, together with candles, amounted to nine-pence a week.

He thus had eight shillings remaining for himself, after working like a slave, without recreation or rest, even upon the sabbath, seventeen hours every day.

A week contains a hundred and sixty-eight hours.

And he worked a hundred and nineteen hours each week!

And earned eight shillings!!

A decimal more than three farthings an hour!!!

On the ground floor of the house the tenants were no better off. In the front room dwelt a poor costermonger, or hawker of fruit, who earned upon an average seven shillings a week, out of which he was compelled to pay one shilling to treat the policeman upon the beat where he took his stand. His wife did a little washing, and perhaps earned eighteen-pence. And that was all this poor couple with four children had to subsist upon. The back room on the ground floor was occupied by the landlady of the house. She paid twelve shillings a week for rent and taxes, and let the various rooms for an aggregate of twenty-one shillings. She thus had nine shillings to live upon, supposing that every one of her lodgers paid her—which was never the case.

Poor Ellen, in reflecting in this manner upon the condition of her neighbours, found herself surrounded on all sides by misery. Misery was above—misery below: misery was on the right and on the left. Misery was the genius of that dwelling, and of every other in that court. Misery was the cold and speechless companion of the young girl as she sate in that icy chamber: misery spread her meal, and made her bed, and was her chambermaid at morning and at night!

Eleven o'clock struck by St. Luke's church; and Mr. Monroe returned to his wretched abode. It had begun to rain shortly after Ellen had returned home; and the old man was wet to the skin.

"Oh! my dear father!" exclaimed the poor girl,—"you are wet, and there is not a morsel of fire in the grate."

"And I have no money, dearest," returned the heart-broken father, pressing his thin lips upon the forehead of his daughter. "But I am not cold, Nell—I am not cold!"

Without uttering a word, Ellen hastened out of the room, and begged a few sticks from one lodger, and a little coal from another. It would shame the affluent great, did they know how ready are the miserable—miserable poor to assist each other!

With her delicate taper fingers—with those little white hands which seemed never made to do menial service, the young girl laid the fire; and when she saw the flame blazing cheerfully up the chimney, she turned towards the old man—and smiled!

She would not for worlds have begged any thing for herself—but for her father—oh! she would have submitted to any degradation!

And then for a moment a gleam of something like happiness stole upon that hitherto mournful scene, as the father and daughter partook of their frugal—very frugal and sparing meal together.

As soon as it was concluded, Ellen rose, kissed her parent affectionately, wished him "good night," and retired into her own miserable, cold, and naked chamber.

She extinguished her candle in a few moments, to induce her father to believe that she had sought repose; but when she knew that the old man was asleep, she lighted the candle once more, and seated herself upon the old mattress, to embroider a few blossoms upon the silk which had been confided to her at the establishment in Finsbury.

From the neighbouring houses the sounds of boisterous revelry fell upon her ears. She was too young and inexperienced to know that this mirth emanated from persons perhaps as miserable as herself, and that they were only drowning care in liquor, instead of encountering their miseries face to face. The din of that hilarity and those shouts of laughter, therefore made her sad.

Presently that noise grew fainter and fainter; and at length it altogether ceased. The clock of St. Luke's church struck one; and all was then silent around.

A lovely moon rode high in the heavens; the rain had ceased, and the night was beautiful—but bitter, bitter cold.

Wearied with toil, the young maiden threw down her work, and, opening the casement, looked forth from her wretched chamber. The gentle breeze, though bearing on its wing the chill of ice, refreshed her; and as she gazed upwards to the moon, she wondered within herself whether the spirit of her departed mother was permitted to look down upon her from the empyrean palaces on high. Tears—large tears trickled down her cheeks; and she was too much overcome by her feelings even to pray.

While she was thus endeavouring to divert her thoughts from the appalling miseries of earth to the transcendant glories of heaven, she was diverted from her mournful reverie by the sound of a window opening in a neighbouring house; and in a few moments violent sobs fell upon her ears. Those sobs, evidently coming from a female bosom, were so acute, so heart-rending, so full of anguish, that Ellen was herself overcome with grief. At length those indications of extreme woe ceased gradually, and then these words—"Oh my God! what will become of my starving babes!" fell upon Ellen's ears. She was about to inquire into the cause of that profound affliction, when the voice of a man was heard to exclaim gruffly, "Come—let's have no more of this gammon: we must all go to the workus in the morning—that's all!" And then the window was closed violently.

The workhouse! That word sounded like a fearful knell upon Ellen's ears. Oh! for hours and hours together had that poor girl meditated upon the sad condition of her father and herself, until she had traced, in imagination, their melancholy career up to the very door of the workhouse. And there she had stopped: she dared think no more—or she would have gone mad, raving mad! For she had heard of the horrors of those asylums for the poor; and she knew that she should be separated from her father on the day when their stern destinies should drive them to that much-dreaded refuge. And to part from him—from the parent whom she loved so tenderly, and who loved her so well;—no—death were far preferable!

The workhouse! How was it that the idea of this fearful home—more dreaded than the prison, less formidable than the grave—had taken so strong a hold upon the poor girl's mind? Because the former tenant of the miserable room which now was hers had passed thence to the workhouse: but ere she went away, she left behind her a record of her feelings in anticipation of that removal to the pauper's home!

Impelled by an influence which she could not control—that species of impulse which urges the timid one to gaze upon the corpse of the dead, even while shuddering at the aspect of death—Ellen closed the window, and read for the hundredth time the following lines, which were pencilled in a neat hand upon the whitewashed wall of the naked chamber:—

"I HAD A TENDER MOTHER ONCE.

I HAD a tender mother once,
Whose eyes so sad and mild
Beamed tearfully yet kindly on
Her little orphan child.
A father's care I never knew;
But in that mother dear,
Was centred every thing to love,
To cherish, and revere!

I loved her with that fervent love
Which daughters only know;
And often o'er my little head
Her bitter tears would flow.
Perhaps she knew that death approached
To snatch her from my side;
And on one gloomy winter day
This tender mother died.

They laid her in the pauper's ground,
And hurried o'er the prayer:
It nearly broke my heart to think
That they should place her there.
And now it seems I see her still

Within her snowy shroud;
And in the dark and silent night
My spirit weeps aloud.

I know not how the years have passed
Since my poor mother died;
But I too have an orphan girl,
That grows up by my side.
O God! thou know'st I do not crave
To eat the bread of sloth:
I labour hard both day and night,
To earn enough for both!

But though I starve myself for her,
Yet hunger wastes her form:—
My God! and must that darling child
Soon feed the loathsome worm?
'Tis vain—for I can work no more—
My eyes with toil are dim;
My fingers seem all paralyzed,
And stiff is every limb!

And now there is but one resource;
The pauper's dreaded doom!
To hasten to the workhouse, and
There find a living tomb.
I know that they will separate
My darling child from me;
And though 't will break our hearts, yet both
Must bow to that decree!

Henceforth our tears must fall apart,
Nor flow together more;
And from to-day our prayers may not
Be mingled as before!
O God! is this the Christian creed,
So merciful and mild?
The daughter from the mother snatched,
The mother from her child!

Ah! we shall ne'er be blessed again
Till death has closed our eyes,

And we meet in the pauper's ground
  Where my poor mother lies.—
Though sad this chamber, it is bright
  To what must be our doom;
The portal of the workhouse is
  The entrance of the tomb!

Ellen read these lines till her eyes were dim with tears. She then retired to her wretched couch; and she slept through sheer fatigue. But dreams of hunger and of cold filled up her slumbers;—and yet those dreams were light beside the waking pangs which realised the visions!

The young maiden slept for three hours, and then arose unrefreshed, and paler than she was on the preceding day. It was dark: the moon had gone down; and some time would yet elapse ere the dawn. Ellen washed herself in water upon which the ice floated; and the cold piercing breeze of the morning whistled through the window upon her fair and delicate form.

As soon as she was dressed, she lighted her candle and crept gently into her father's room. The old man slept soundly. Ellen flung his clothes over her arm, took his boots up in her hand, and stole noiselessly back to her own chamber. She then brushed those garments, and cleaned those boots, all bespattered with thick mud as they were; and this task—so hard for her delicate and diminutive hands—she performed with the most heart-felt satisfaction.

As soon as this occupation was finished, she sate down once more to work.

Thus that poor girl knew no rest!

CHAPTER LVI.

THE ROAD TO RUIN.

About two months after the period when we first introduced Ellen Monroe to our readers, the old woman of whom we have before spoken, and who dwelt in the same court as that poor maiden and her father, was sitting at work in her chamber.

The old woman was ill-favoured in countenance, and vile in heart. Hers was one of those hardened dispositions which know no pity, no charity, no love, no friendship, no yearning after any thing proper to human fellowship.

She was poor and wretched;—and yet *she*, in all her misery, had a large easy chair left to sit upon, warm blankets to cover her at night, a Dutch clock to tell her the hour, a cupboard in which to keep her food, a mat whereon to lay her feet, and a few turves burning in the grate to keep her warm. The walls of her room were covered with cheap prints, coloured with glaring hues, and representing the exploits of celebrated highwaymen and courtezans; scenes upon the stage in which favourite actresses figured, and execrable imitations of Hogarth's "Rake's Progress." The coverlid of her bed was of patchwork, pieces of silk, satin, cotton, and other stuffs, all of different patterns, sizes, and shapes, being sewn together—strange and expressive remnants of a vicious and faded luxury! Upon the chimney-piece were two or three scent-bottles, which for years had contained no perfume, and in the cupboard was a champagne-bottle, in which the hag now kept her gin. The pillow of her couch was stuffed neither with wool nor feathers—but with well-worn silk stockings, tattered lace collars, faded ribands, a piece of a muff and a boa, the velvet off a bonnet, and old kid gloves. And—more singular than all the other features of her room—the old hag had a huge Bible, with silver clasps, upon a shelf!

This horrible woman was darning old stockings, and stooping over her work, when a low knock at the door of her chamber fell upon her ear. That knock was not imperative and commanding, but gentle and timid; and therefore the old woman did not hurry herself to say, "Come in!" Even after the door had opened and the visitor had entered the room, the old hag proceeded with her work for a few moments.

At length raising her head, she beheld Ellen Monroe.

She was not surprised: but as she gazed upon that fair thin face whose roundness had yielded to the hand of starvation, and that blue eye whose fire was subdued by long and painful vigils, she said, "And so you have come at last? I have been expecting you every day!"

"Expecting me! and why?" exclaimed Ellen, surprised at these words, which appeared to contain a sense of dark and mysterious import that was ominous to the young girl.

"Yes—I have expected you," repeated the old woman. "Did I not tell you that when you had no money, no work, and no bread, and owed arrears of rent, you would come to me?"

"Alas! and you predicted truly," said Ellen, with a bitter sigh. "All the miseries which you have detailed have fallen upon me;—and more! for my father lies ill upon the *one mattress* that remains to us!"

"Poor creature!" exclaimed the old woman, endeavouring to assume a soothing tone; then, pointing to a foot-stool near her, she added, "Come and sit near me that we may talk together upon your sad condition."

Ellen really believed that she had excited a feeling of generous and disinterested sympathy in the heart of that hag; and she therefore seated herself confidently upon the stool, saying at the same time, "You told me that you could serve me: if you have still the power, in the name of heaven delay not, for—for—we are starving!"

The old woman glanced round to assure herself that the door of her cupboard was closed; for in that cupboard were bread and meat, and cheese. Then, turning her eyes upwards, the hag exclaimed, "God bless us all, dear child! I am dying of misery myself, and have not a morsel to give you to eat!"

But when she had uttered these words, she cast her eyes upon the young girl who was now seated familiarly as it were, by her side, and scanned her from head to foot, and from foot to head. In spite of the wretched and scanty garments which Ellen wore, the admirable symmetry of her shape was easily descried; and the old woman thought within herself how happy she should be to dress that sweet form in gay and gorgeous garments, for her own unhallowed purposes.

"You do not answer me," said Ellen. "Do not keep me in suspense—but tell me whether it is in your power to procure me work?"

The old hag's countenance wore a singular expression when these last words fell upon her ears. Then she began to talk to the poor starving girl in a manner which the latter could not comprehend, and which we dare not describe. Ellen listened for some time, as if she were hearing a strange language which she was endeavouring to make out; and then she cast a sudden look of doubt and alarm upon the old hag. The wretch grew somewhat more explicit; and the poor girl burst into an agony of tears, exclaiming, as she covered her blushing cheeks with her snow-white hands—"No: never—never!"

Still she did not fly from that den and from the presence of that accursed old hag, because she was so very, very wretched, and had no hope elsewhere.

There was a long pause; and the old hag and the young girl sate close to each other, silent and musing. The harridan cast upon her pale and starving companion a look of mingled anger and surprise; but the poor creature saw it not—for she was intent only on her own despair.

Suddenly a thought struck the hag.

"I can do nothing for you, miss, since you will not follow my advice," she said, after a while: "and yet I am acquainted with a statuary who would pay you well for casts of your countenance for his Madonnas, his actresses, his Esmeraldas, his queens, his princesses, and his angels."

These words sounded upon the ears of the unhappy girl like a dream; and parting, with her wasted fingers, the ringlets that clustered round her brow, she lifted up her large moist eyes in astonishment towards the face of the aged hag.

But the old woman was serious in her offer.

"I repeat—will you sell your countenance to a statuary?" she said. "It is a good one; and you will obtain a handsome price for it."

Ellen was literally stupefied by this strange proposal; but when she had power to collect her ideas into one focus, she saw her father pining upon a bed of sickness, and surrounded by all the horrors of want and privation;—and she herself—the unhappy girl—had not tasted food for nearly thirty hours. Then, on the other side, was her innate modesty;—but this was nothing in the balance compared to the poignancy of her own and her parent's sufferings.

So she agreed to accompany the old hag to the house of the statuary in Leather Lane, Holborn. But first she hurried home to see if her father required any thing—a vain act of filial tenderness, for if he did she had nothing to give. The old man slept soundly—worn out with suffering, want, and sorrowful meditation; and the landlady of the house promised to attend to him while Ellen was absent.

The young maiden then returned to the old woman; and they proceeded together to the house of the statuary.

Up two flights of narrow and dark stairs, precipitate as ladders, did the trembling and almost heart-broken girl follow the hag. They then entered a spacious depository of statues modelled in plaster of

Paris. A strange assembly of images was that! Heathen gods seemed to fraternize with angels, Madonnas, and Christian saints; Napoleon and Wellington stood motionless side by side; George the Fourth and Greenacre occupied the same shelf; William Pitt[1] and Cobbett[2] appeared to be contemplating each other with silent admiration; Thomas Paine[3] elbowed a bishop; Lord Castlereagh[4] seemed to be extending his hand to welcome Jack Ketch;[5] Cupid pointed his arrow at the bosom of a pope; in a word, that strange pell-mell of statues was calculated to awaken ideas of a most wild and ludicrous character, in the imagination of one whose thoughts were not otherwise occupied.

The statuary was an Italian; and as he spoke the English language imperfectly, he did not waste much time over the bargain. With the cool criticism of a sportsman examining a horse or a dog, the statuary gazed upon the young maiden; then, taking a rule in his hand, he measured her head; and with a pair of blunt compasses he took the dimensions of her features. Giving a nod of approval, he consulted a large book which lay open upon a desk; and finding that he had orders for a queen, an opera-dancer, and a Madonna, he declared that he would take three casts of his new model's countenance that very morning.

The old woman whispered words of encouragement in Ellen's ear,

---

1 William Pitt, father and son. William Pitt the Elder (1708-1778) was Prime Minister in 1761, and again from 1766 to 1768. He was made Earl of Chatham. His son, William Pitt the Younger (1759-1806) was Prime Minister, at the age of 24, from 1784 to 1801, and from 1804 to 1806.

2 William Cobbett (1762-1835), English Radical politician and writer.

3 Thomas (Tom) Paine (1737-1809), Radical politician. The son of a Norfolk Quaker, he was briefly a customs man in Reynolds's home-town of Sandwich. A prolific writer and pamphleteer, his *Common Sense* is reputed to have sparked the American War of Independence. He went to France, became a naturalised French citizen and was elected to the Assemblée Nationale; but he opposed the execution of Louis XVI, and was imprisoned during the Terror. He returned to America, where he died.

4 Robert Stewart, Viscount Castlereagh (1769-1822), Secretary for War (1805-1809), and Foreign Secretary (1809). An intensely unpopular minister, his death moved Byron to song: 'Posterity will ne'er survey / A nobler tomb than this, / Here lie the bones of Castlereagh; / Pause, Traveller; and piss.'

5 A generic term for a hangman. The original of the name was John Price, called Jack Ketch; although himself a hangman, he was hanged for the murder of Elizabeth White, an elderly pastry-seller, whom he beat to death in the street. He was executed in Bunhill Fields on 31 May, 1718.

as they all three repaired to the workshop, where upwards of twenty men were employed in making statues. Some were preparing the clay models over which the plaster of Paris was to be laid: others joined legs and arms to trunks;—some polished the features of the countenances: others effaced the seams that betrayed the various joints in the complete statues. One fixed wings to angels' backs—another swords to warriors' sides: a third repaired a limb that had been broken; a fourth stuck on a new nose in the place of an old one knocked off.

Ellen was stretched at full length upon a table; and a wet cloth was placed over her face. The statuary then covered it with moist clay;—and the process was only complete when she was ready to faint through difficulty of breathing. She rested a little while; and then the second cast was taken. Another interval to recover breath—and the third and last mould was formed.

The statuary seemed well pleased with this trial of his new model;

and placing a sovereign in the young maiden's hand, he desired her to return in three days, as he should require her services again. The poor trembling creature's eyes glistened with delight as she balanced the gold in her little hand; and she took her departure, accompanied by the hag, with a heart comparatively light.

"You will have plenty to do there," said the old woman, as they proceeded homewards: "I have introduced you to a good thing. You must therefore divide your first day's earnings with me."

Ellen really felt grateful to the selfish harridan; and having changed her gold for silver coin at a shop where she stopped to buy provisions, she counted ten shillings in the withered and sinewy hand which the hag thrust forth.

Thus for three months did Ellen earn the means of a comfortable subsistence, by selling her countenance to the statuary. And that countenance might be seen belonging to the statues of Madonnas in catholic chapels; opera dancers, and actresses in theatrical clubs; nymphs holding lamps in the halls of public institutions; and queens in the staircase windows of insurance offices.

She never revealed to her father the secret spring of that improved condition which soon restored him to health; but assured him that she had found more needle-work, and was well paid for it. The old man had too good an opinion of his daughter to suspect her of crime or frailty; and he believed her innocent and well-meant falsehood the more readily, inasmuch as he saw her constantly engaged with her needle when he was at home.

Three months passed away; and already had a little air of comfort succeeded to the former dismal aspect of those two chambers which the father and daughter occupied, when the statuary died suddenly.

Ellen's occupation was once more gone; and, after vainly endeavouring to obtain needle-work—for that which she did in the presence of her father was merely a pretence to make good her tale to him—she again repaired to the abode of the old hag who had introduced her to the statuary.

The aged female was, if possible, more wrinkled and hideous than before; the contrast between her and her fair young visitant was the more striking, inasmuch as the cheeks of the latter had recovered their roundness, and her form its plumpness by means of good and sufficient food.

"You have come to me again," said the hag. "Doubtless I should have never seen you more if you had not wanted my services."

"The statuary is dead," returned Ellen, "and has left behind him an immense fortune. His son has therefore declined the business, and has discharged every one in the employment of his late father."

"And what would you have me do for you, miss?" demanded the old woman. "I am not acquainted with another statuary."

Ellen heaved a deep sigh.

The hag contemplated her for some time in silence, and then exclaimed, "Your appearance has improved; you have a tinge of the carnation upon your cheeks; and your eyes have recovered their brightness. I know an artist of great repute, who will be glad of you as a copy for his shepherdesses, his huntresses, his sea-nymphs, and heathen goddesses. Let us lose no time in proceeding to his residence."

This proposal was far more agreeable to the maiden than the one which had led her into the service of the statuary; and she did not for a moment hesitate to accompany the old woman to the abode of the artist.

The great painter was about forty years of age, and dwelt in a splendid house in Bloomsbury Square. The rooms on the third floor were his *studio*, as he required a clear and good light. He accepted the services of Ellen Monroe as a copy, and remunerated the old woman out of his own pocket, for the introduction. But he required the attendance of his copy every day from ten till four; and she was accordingly compelled to tell her father another story to account for these long intervals of absence. She now assured him that she was engaged to work at the residence of a family in Bloomsbury Square; and the old man believed her.

Her countenance having embellished statues, was now transferred to canvass. Her Grecian features and classic head appeared surmounted with the crescent of Diana, the helmet of Minerva, and the crown of Juno. The painter purchased dresses suitable to the characters which he wished her to adopt; and, although she was frequently compelled to appear before him, in a state which at first was strongly repugnant to her modesty—with naked bust, and naked arms, and naked legs—the feeling of shame gradually wore away. Thus, though in body she remained pure and chaste, yet in soul was she gradually hardened to the sentiments of maiden delicacy and female reserve!

It is true that she retained her virtue—because it was not tempted. The artist saw not before him a lovely creature of warm flesh and blood; he beheld nothing but a beautiful and symmetrical statue which served as an original for his heathen divinities and pastoral heroines. And in this light did he treat her.

He paid her handsomely; and her father and herself were enabled to remove to better lodgings, and in a more respectable neighbourhood, than those which had been the scene of so much misery in Golden Lane.

The artist whom Ellen served was a portrait-painter as well as a delineator of classical subjects. When he was employed to paint the likeness of some vain and conceited West End daughter of the aristocracy, it was Ellen's hand—or Ellen's hair—or Ellen's eyes—or Ellen's bust—or some feature or peculiar beauty of the young maiden, in which the fashionable lady somewhat resembled her, that figured upon the canvass. Then when the portrait was finished, the artist would assemble his friends at the same time that the lady and her friends called to see it; and the artist's friends—well tutored beforehand—would exclaim, one, "How like is the eye!" another, "The very mouth!" a third, "The hair to the life itself!" a fourth, "The exact profile!"—and so on. And all the while it was Ellen's eye, or Ellen's mouth, or Ellen's hair, or Ellen's profile, which the enthusiasts admired. Then the lady, flattering herself that *she* alone was the original, and little suspecting that the charms of another had been called in to enhance the beauty of *her* portrait, persuaded her fond and uxorious husband to double the amount of the price bargained for, and had the picture set in a very costly frame, to hang in the most conspicuous place in her mansion.

It happened one day that the artist obtained the favour of a marchioness of forty-six by introducing into her portrait the nose, eyes, and mouth of that fair young maiden of seventeen. The great lady recommended him to the Russian Ambassador as the greatest of English painters; and the ambassador immediately retained him to proceed to St. Petersburgh to transfer to canvass the physiognomy of the Czar.

Ellen thus lost her employment once more; and again did she repair to the den of the old hag who had recommended her to the statuary and the artist.

The step of the maiden was less timid than formerly; and her look was more confident. She was also dressed in a style which savoured of coquetry, for her occupation at the artist's had taught her the value of her charms, and prompted her how to enhance them. She had imbibed the idea that her beauty was worth much, and should at least produce her a comfortable livelihood, even if it did not lay the foundation for a fortune. She therefore occupied all her leisure time in studying how to set it off to the greatest advantage. Thus dire necessity had compelled that charming young creature to embrace occupations which awoke all the latent female vanity that had slumbered in her bosom throughout the period of her pinching poverty, and that now shone forth in her manner—her gait—her glance—her speech—and her attire.

The old hag observed this change, and was not surprised—for she was a woman of the world; but she muttered to herself, "A little while, my dear—and you will suit my purposes altogether."

"I am come again, you see," said Ellen, seating herself without waiting to be asked. "My artist has left England suddenly, and I am once more without occupation."

"Have you any money?" demanded the old hag.

"I have three sovereigns left," replied Ellen.

"You must give me two," said the woman; "and you must promise me half your first week's earnings, for the new introduction which I shall presently give you."

Ellen placed two sovereigns in the hand of the beldame; and the old wretch opened her table drawer to search for something which she required.

That drawer contained a strange incongruity of articles. Old valentine letters, knots of faded riband, cards, prophetic almanacs; tooth powder boxes, and scented oil bottles, all alike empty; the visiting cards of several noblemen and gentlemen, play-bills, theatrical journals, masquerade tickets never used, pieces of music, magazines of fashion, a volume of the "Memoirs of Harriett Wilson," immoral prints, a song book, some leaves torn from the "Newgate Calendar," medical drugs wrapped up in papers, a child's caul, pieces of poetry in manuscript, amatory epistles on sheets of various tints, writs from the Court of Requests, summonses from police courts, &c. &c. The contents of that filthy drawer furnished a complete history of that old hag's former life.

The object of the old woman's search was a card, which, having found it, she handed to the young maiden, saying, "Here is the address of an eminent sculptor: he requires a model of a bust for the statue of a great lady who may be said to have no bust at all. You will suit him."

Ellen received the card, and hastened to Halkin Street, Belgrave Square, where the sculptor resided. She was shown first into a parlour upon the ground floor, then, when the object of her visit was made known, she was requested to walk up stairs to the *studio* of the great man. She found him contemplating with profound satisfaction a head which he had already cut from the top part of a block of marble. He was an old man of sixty, and he stooped in his gait; but his eyes were dark and piercing.

A bargain between the sculptor and Ellen was soon terminated; and the next morning she entered upon her new employment. Stripped to the waist, she had to stand in a certain position, for several hours each day, in the presence of the sculptor. The old man laboured diligently at his statue, and allowed her little rest; but he paid her munificently, and she was contented.

The lady, whose statue was thus *supposed* to be in progress, called daily, and remained at the sculptor's house for hours. She always came alone, and sate in the *studio* the whole time during which her call lasted: it was therefore imagined by all her friends that she really formed the model of the statue which was to bear her name. But Ellen's neck—and Ellen's shoulders—and Ellen's bosom—and Ellen's arms were in truth the pattern of the bust of that statue which was to be a great sculptor's masterpiece, and to hand down the name of a great lady to posterity!

The very day upon which Ellen was to leave the sculptor's employment, her services as a model being no longer required, this great lady happened to observe that she was in want of a nursery governess for her two young daughters. Ellen ventured to offer herself as a candidate for the situation. The lady raised her eyes and hands to heaven in astonishment, exclaiming, "*You*, miss, a companion for my children! a girl who gets her livelihood by standing half naked in the presence of any body, as a model!" And the lady was compelled to have recourse to her scent-bottle to save herself from fainting. She forgot that she would have herself stood to the sculptor if she had possessed a good bust!

The answer and the behaviour of this lady opened the eyes of Ellen to the nature of the opinion which the world must now form of her. She suddenly comprehended the real position which she occupied in society—about one remove above the unfortunate girls who were the avowed daughters of crime. Were she now to speak to the world of her virtue, that world would laugh insultingly in her face. Thus the dire necessity which had urged her upon this career, began by destroying her sense of female delicacy and shame: it now destroyed, in her estimation, every inducement to pursue a virtuous career.

Again she sought the dwelling of the old hag: for the fourth time she demanded the assistance of the beldame.

"It seems, my child," said the old woman, "that my advice has produced beneficial consequences. Each time that you cross my threshold I observe that you are freer and lighter in step, and more choice in your apparel."

"You know that I am not detestably ugly, mother," answered Ellen, with a smile of complacence; "and surely it is as cheap to have a gown well made as badly made, and a becoming bonnet as one altogether out of date."

"Ah! I see that you study the fashions," exclaimed the old woman with a sigh—for she recalled to mind the pleasures and pursuits of her own youthful days, over which she retrospected with regret:—then, after a pause, she said, "How old are you?"

"Eighteen and a half," replied Ellen.

"And, with all that beauty, is your heart still unoccupied by the image of some favoured suitor?"

"Oh!" ejaculated Ellen, laughing heartily, so as to display her brilliant teeth, "I have not thought of *that* yet. I have lately read a great deal about love in novels and romances—for I never do any needlework now,—but I have not experienced the passion. I dare say my time will come sooner or later;"—and again she laughed. "But, hasten, mother—I am losing my time: tell me, do you know of farther employment for me?"

"I am acquainted with a French gentleman of science at the West End," answered the hag, "who has invented a means of taking likenesses by the aid of the sun. I do not know what the process is: all that concerns me and you is that the Frenchman requires a beautiful woman to serve as a pattern for his experiments."

"Give me his address," said Ellen, "and if he engages me I will pay you liberally. You know that you can rely upon me."

The old woman once more had recourse to her filthy drawer, in which her present memoranda were mingled with the relics of the luxury of former days; and taking thence a letter which she had only received that same morning, she tore off the address for the use of the young maiden.

Ellen, who a few months previously had been accustomed to work for seventeen or eighteen hours without ceasing, now took a cab to proceed from the neighbourhood of St. Luke's to Leicester Square. The French scientific experimentalist was at home; and Ellen was conducted up four flights of stairs to a species of belvidere, or glass cabinet, built upon the roof of the house. The windows of this belvidere, and the paper with which the wood-work of the interior was covered, were of a dark blue, in order to mitigate the strength of the sun's rays.

Within this belvidere the Frenchman was at work. He was a short, middle-aged, sallow-faced, sharp featured person—entirely devoted to matters of science, and having no soul for love, pleasure, politics, or any kind of excitement save his learned pursuits. He was now busily employed at a table covered with copper plates coated with silver, phials of nitric acid, cotton wool, pounce, a camera obscura, several boxes, each of about two feet square, and other materials necessary for photography.

The Frenchman spoke English tolerably well; and eyeing his fair visitant from head to foot, he expressed himself infinitely obliged to the person who had sent her. He then entered into particulars; and Ellen found, to her surprise, that the photographer was desirous of taking full-length female portraits in a state of nudity. She drew her veil over her countenance, and was about to retire in disgust and indignation, when the Frenchman, who was examining a plate as he spoke, and therefore did not observe the effect his words had produced upon her, mentioned the price which he proposed to pay her. Now the artist paid better than the statuary; the sculptor better than the artist; and the photographer better than the sculptor. She therefore hesitated no longer; but entered the service of the man of science.

We shall not proceed to any details connected with this new

avocation to which that lovely maiden lent herself. Suffice it to say, that having sold her countenance to the statuary, her likeness to the artist, and her bust to the sculptor, she disposed of her whole body to the photographer. Thus her head embellished images white and bronzed; her features and her figure were perpetuated in divers paintings; her bust was immortalized in a splendid statue; and her entire form is preserved, in all attitudes, and on many plates, in the private cabinet of a photographer at one of the metropolitan Galleries of Practical Science.

At length the photographer was satisfied with the results of his experiments regarding the action of light upon every part of the human frame, and Ellen's occupation was again gone.

A tainted soul now resided in a pure body. Every remaining sentiment of decency and delicacy was crushed—obliterated—destroyed by this last service. Pure souls have frequently resided in tainted bodies: witness Lucretia after the outrage perpetrated upon her:—but here was essentially a foul soul in a chaste and virgin form.

And what dread cause had consummated this sad result? Not the will of the poor girl—for when we first saw her in her cold and cheerless chamber, her mind was spotless as the Alpine snow. But dire necessity—that necessity which became an instrument in the old hag's hands to model the young maiden to her purposes. For it was with ulterior views that the designing harridan had introduced the poor girl to that career which, without being actually criminal, led step by step towards criminality. The wretch knew the world well, and was enabled to calculate the influence of exterior circumstances upon the mind and the passions. After the first conversation which she had with Ellen, she perceived that the purity of the virgin was not to be undermined by specious representations, nor by dazzling theories, nor by delusive sophistry: and the hag accordingly placed the confiding girl upon a path which, while it supplied her with the necessaries of life, gradually presented to her mind scenes which were calculated to destroy her purity of thought and chastity of feeling for ever!

When Ellen left the service of the photographer, she repaired for the fifth time to the dwelling of the hag.

The old woman was seated as usual at her work; and she was humming to herself an opera air, which she remembered to have heard many—many years back.

"The Frenchman requires my services no longer," said Ellen. "What next can you do for me?"

"Alas! my poor child," answered the old woman, "the times were never so bad as they are at present! What is to become of us? what is to become of us?"

And the hag rocked herself backwards and forwards in her chair, as if overcome by painful reflections.

"You can, then, do nothing for me?" observed Ellen, interrogatively. "That is a pity! for I have not a shilling left in the world. We have lived up to the income which my occupations produced. My poor old father fancies up to the present moment that I have been working at dress-making and embroidery at the houses of great families and he will wonder how all my engagements should so suddenly cease. Think, mother: are you not acquainted with another artist or sculptor?"

"Why, my child, do you pitch upon the artist and the sculptor?" inquired the hag, regarding Ellen fixedly in the face.

"Oh!" answered the young maiden, lightly, "because I do not like to have my countenance handled about by the dirty fingers of the statuary; and you cannot suppose that out of the four services I should voluntarily prefer that of the photographer?"

The old woman looked disappointed, and muttered to herself, "Not quite yet! not quite yet!"

"What did you say, mother?" inquired Ellen.

"I say," replied the hag, assuming a tone of kindness and conciliation, "that you must come back to me in ten days; and in the meantime I will see what is to be done for you."

"In ten days," observed Ellen: "be it so!"

And she took her departure, downcast and disappointed, from the old hag's abode.

CHAPTER LVII.

THE LAST RESOURCE.

Poverty once again returned—with all its hideous escort of miseries—to the abode of Monroe and his daughter. The articles of comfort which they had lately collected around them were sent to the pawnbroker: necessaries then followed to the same destination.

Ellen no longer sought for needle-work: she had for some time past led a life which incapacitated her for close application to monotonous toil; and she confidently reposed upon the hope that the old woman would procure her more employment with an artist or a sculptor.

But at the expiration of the ten days, the hag put her off for ten days more; and then again for another ten days. Thus a month passed away in idleness for both father and daughter, neither of whom earned a shilling.

They could no longer retain the lodgings which they had occupied for some time in a respectable neighbourhood; and now behold them returning to the very same cold, miserable, and cheerless rooms which we saw them occupying in the first instance in the court leading out of Golden Lane!

What ups and downs constitute existence!

Two years had now passed away since we first introduced the reader to that destitute lodging in Golden Lane. We have therefore brought up this portion of our narrative, as well as all the other parts of it, to the close of the year 1838.

Misery, more grinding, more pinching, and more acute than any which they had yet known, now surrounded the father and daughter. They had parted with every thing which would produce the wherewith to purchase food. They lay upon straw at night; and for days and days they had not a spark of fire in the grate. They often went six-and-thirty hours together without tasting a morsel of food. They could not even pay the pittance of rent which was claimed for their two chambers: and if it had not been for their compassionate neighbours they must have starved altogether.

Monroe could obtain no employment in the City. When he had failed, during the time of Richard Markham's imprisonment, he lost all his friends, because they took no account of his misfortunes, and looked only to the fact that he had been compelled to give up business. Had he passed through the Bankruptcy Court, and then opened his counting-house again to commence affairs upon credit, he would have found admirers and supporters. But as he had paid his creditors every farthing, left himself a beggar, and spurned the idea of entering upon business without capital of his own, he had not a friend to whom he could apply for a shilling.

At length the day came when the misery of the father and the daughter arrived at an extreme when it became no longer tolerable. They had fasted for forty-eight hours; and their landlady threatened to turn them out of their empty rooms into the street, unless they paid her the arrears of rent which they owed. They had not an article upon which they could raise the price of a loaf:—it was the depth of a cold and severe winter, and Ellen had already parted with all her undergarments.

"My dear child," said the heart-broken father, embracing his daughter affectionately, on the morning when their misery thus reached its utmost limit, "I have one resource left—a resource to which I should never fly save in an extreme like this!"

"What mean you?" inquired the daughter, anxiously glancing in the pale and haggard countenance of her sire.

"I mean that I will apply to Richard Markham," said the old man. "He does not suspect our appalling state of destitution, or he would seek us out—he would fly to our succour."

"And you will apply to him who has already suffered so much by you?" said the daughter, shaking her head. "Alas! he will refuse you the succour you require!"

"No—no—not he!" ejaculated the old man. "Be of good cheer, Ellen—I shall not be long absent; and on my return thou shalt have food, and fire, and clothes!"

"God grant that it may be so!" cried Ellen, clasping her hands together.

"I have moreover a piece of news relative to that villain Montague to communicate to him," added Monroe; "and for that reason—if for none other—should I have called at his residence to-day. While I was roving about in the City yesterday to endeavour to procure employment I accidentally learnt that Montague is pursuing his old game at the West End, under the name of Greenwood."

"Ah! why do you not rather call upon this man," cried Ellen, "and represent to him the misery to which his villany has reduced us? He is doubtless wealthy, and might be inclined to give a few pounds to one whom he robbed of thousands."

"Alas! my dear Ellen, you do not know the world as I know it! I have no means of convincing Montague, or Greenwood, that I lost money by him. He only knew Allen in the entire transaction: he never saw me in his life—nor I him,—at least to my knowledge. Allen is dead;—how then can I present myself to this man, whom villany has no doubt rendered hard-hearted and selfish, with mere assertions of losses through his instrumentality? He would eject me ignominiously from his abode! No—I shall repair to Richard Markham; he is my last and only hope!"

With these words the old man embraced his daughter affectionately, and left the room.

The moment he was gone Eliza said to herself, "My father has undertaken a hopeless task! It is not probable that Markham, whom he has reduced to a miserable pittance, will spare from that pittance aught to relieve our necessities. What is to be done? There are no more artists or sculptors who require my services—no more statuaries or photographers who need my aid. And yet we cannot starve! When I last saw the old woman, she spoke out plainly—her meaning could not be misunderstood. I rushed away from her presence, as if she were a venomous reptile! Fool that I was. Starvation is undermining those charms which I have learnt to value: hunger is defacing that beauty which gave me bread for nearly two years, and which may give me bread again in the same way. I am clothed in rags, and shiver with the cold! My hands, once so white, are becoming red: my form, lately so round and plump, is losing its fulness and its freshness; my cheeks grow thin and hollow. And in a few hours my poor old father will return home, wasted with fatigue, and overwhelmed with famine and disappointment. O my God!" she continued, clasping her hands together in an ebullition of intense agony; "pardon—pardon—I can hesitate no longer!"

And straightway she proceeded to the dwelling of the old hag.

* * * * * * * * *

It was about two o'clock in the afternoon when Mr. Monroe returned to the court in Golden Lane.

His countenance was animated with an expression of joy, as he encountered the landlady upon the threshold of the house in which he resided.

"Miss Monroe is not come in yet," said the woman roughly. "Here is the key of your lodgings—not that I think there is much worth the locking up. However, this key you don't have again till my rent is paid."

"Here—pay yourself—pay yourself!" cried the old man, taking a handful of gold and silver from his pocket.

The woman's manner instantly changed into cringing politeness. She was not now pressed for the rent. She could wait till it was convenient. She always knew that she had to deal with a gentleman. What did it matter to her when she was paid, since she felt convinced the money was safe?

Monroe cut short her compliments by settling the arrears due, and sending the landlady out to purchase some food. The old man was determined to be extravagant that day—he was so happy! Markham had declared that he and his daughter should never know want again;—and then—he had such a surprise for Ellen. They were to proceed next day to take up their abode with Richard: the young man had insisted upon it—Whittingham had supported the proposal;—and so it was all resolved upon. No more poverty—no more cold—no more hunger!

It was for this that the old gentleman was resolved to be extravagant. He was anxious to provide a delicate little treat for his daughter;—and he was glad that she was not at home when he returned. He felt convinced that she had gone out to seek for work, and hoped that she would not be long ere she returned.

By means of the landlady he procured a cold fowl, a piece of ham, and a bottle of cheap wine; and his own thin and meagre hands spread the dainties upon the table, while the landlady lighted a fire in the grate.

When these arrangements were complete, Monroe dispatched the now obsequious mistress of the house to redeem from pledge the various articles which had been pawned during this latter period of destitution; and when she returned, laden with the necessaries and the comforts which had thus been temporarily disposed of, Monroe felt pleasure in arranging them in such a way that they might strike Ellen's eyes the moment she should return.

The poor old man was so joyful—so happy, as he executed his task, that he did not observe the lapse of time. Six o'clock struck, and the candle had been burning for some time upon the mantelpiece, ere Monroe began to wonder what could keep his daughter so long away.

Another half-hour passed; and her well-known step was heard ascending the staircase. The door opened; and Ellen rushed into the room, exclaiming, "My dear father, here is gold! here is gold!"

"This then appears to be a day of good fortune," said the old man, glancing triumphantly around him. "I also have gold—and these are the fruits of the first use which I have made of it!"

"What!" exclaimed Ellen, gazing wildly upon the well-spread table and the various articles redeemed from the pawnbroker; "Richard Markham——"

"Is an angel!" cried Monroe. "He never will let us know want again!"

"Oh! my God!" ejaculated Ellen, throwing herself upon a chair, and burying her face in her hands: "why did I not wait a few hours? why did I not have patience and hope until your return?"

"Ellen, what mean those words?" demanded the old man: "speak—tell me——"

"Simply, my dear father," she answered, raising her head, and at the same time exercising an almost superhuman control over her inward emotions, "that I have consented to receive work at a price which will scarcely find us in bread; and——"

"You shall not hold to your bargain, dearest," interrupted Monroe. "The money which you may have received in advance,—for you said, I think, that you had money,—shall be returned to those who would condemn you to a slavery more atrocious than that endured by the negroes in the West Indies! Take courage my beloved Ellen—take courage: a brighter day will yet dawn upon us."

Ellen made no reply: but her countenance wore so singular an expression, that her father was alarmed.

"My dearest daughter," he exclaimed, "you have no longer any hope! I see by your looks that you despair! God knows that we have encountered enough to teach us to place but little reliance upon the smiles of fortune: nevertheless, let us not banish hope altogether from our bosoms! To-morrow we shall leave this dismal abode, and repair to the house of our young benefactor, Markham."

"Markham!" cried Ellen, the very name appearing to arouse

agonizing emotions in her mind: "have you promised Mr. Richard Markham that we will reside with him?"

"Yes, dearest Ellen; and in so doing I had hoped to give thee pleasure. You have known each other from infancy. Methinks I see thee now, a little child, climbing up that hill in company with Richard and his brother——"

"His brother!" repeated Ellen, a cold shudder passing over her entire frame.

"My dearest girl, you are not well," said the old man; and, pouring some wine into a glass, he added, "drink this, Ellen; it will revive thee."

The young lady partook of the exhilarating beverage, and appeared refreshed. Her father and herself then seated themselves at the table, and partook of the meal.

Ellen ate but little. She was pensive and melancholy; and every now and then her countenance wore an expression of supreme horror, which denoted intense agony of feeling within her bosom. She, however, contrived to veil from her father's eyes much of the anguish which she thus experienced; and the old man's features were animated with a gleam of joy, as he sate by the cheerful fire and talked to his daughter of brighter prospects and happier days.

On the following morning they took leave of those rooms in which they had experienced so much misery, and repaired to the dwelling of Richard Markham.

CHAPTER LVIII.

NEW YEAR'S DAY.

It was the 1st of January, 1839.

The weather was cold and inclement;—Nature in nakedness appeared to recline upon the turfless grave of summer.

The ancient river which intersects the mightiest city upon the surface of the earth, was swollen; and in the country through which it wound its way, the fields were flooded in many parts.

The trees were stripped of their verdure: the singing of birds had ceased.

Gloomy and mournful was the face of nature, sombre and lowering the aspect of the proud city.

So pale—so faint were the beams of the mid-day sun, that the summit of Saint Paul's, which a few months back was wont to glitter as if it were crowned with a diadem of gold, was now veiled in a murky cloud; and the myriad pinnacles of the modern Babylon, which erst were each tipped as with a star, pointed upwards to a sky ominous and foreboding.

Nevertheless, the ingenuity and wonderous perseverence of man had adopted all precautions to expel the cold from the palaces of the rich and powerful, and to surround the lordly owners of those splendid mansions with the most delicious wines and the most luxurious food, in doors, to induce them to forget that winter reigned without.

Soft carpets, thick curtains—satin, and velvet, and silk,—downy beds beneath gorgeous canopies,—warm clothing, and cheerful fires, combined to defy the approach of winter, and to render the absence of genial summer a matter of small regret.

Then, when the occupants of these palaces went abroad, there was no bold exertion required for them to face the nipping cold; for they stepped from their thresholds into carriages thickly lined with wool, and supplied with cushions, soft, luxurious, and warm.

But that cold which was thus expelled from the palaces of the rich took refuge in the dwellings of the poor; and there it remained, sharp as a razor, pitiless as an executioner, inexorable as a judge, and keen as the north-western wind that blows from the ice-bound coasts of Labrador.

No silks, nor satins, nor velvets, nor carpets, nor canopies, nor curtains, had the dwellings of the poor to defy, or even mitigate the freezing malignity of that chill which, engendered in the arctic regions of eternal snow, and having swept over the frozen rivers and the mighty forests of America, had come to vent its collected spite upon the islands of Europe.

Shivering, starving, in their miserable hovels, the industrious many, by the sweat of whose brow the indolent few were supplied with their silks, and their satins, and their velvets, wept bitter—bitter tears over their suffering and famished children, and cursed the day on which their little ones were born.

For the winter was a very hard one; and bread—bread was very dear!

Yes—bread, which thou, Almighty God! hast given to feed those whom thou didst create after thine own image,—even bread was too dear for the starving poor to buy!

How long, O Lord! wilt thou permit the few to wrest every thing from the many—to monopolize, accumulate, gripe, snatch, drag forth, cling to, the fruits of the earth, for their own behoof alone?

How long shall there exist such spells in the privilege of birth? how long must all happiness and all misery be summed up in the words—

WEALTH. | POVERTY.

We said that it was New Year's Day, 1839.

In the palaces of the great were rejoicings, and music, and festivity; and diamonds glittered—and feathers waved—and silks rustled;—the elastic floors bent beneath the steps of the dancers; the wine flowed in crystal cups; and the fruits of summer were amongst the dainties spread to tempt the appetite of the aristocracy.

Ah! there was happiness indeed, in thus welcoming the new year; for those who there greeted its presence, were well assured that it would teem with the joys and blandishments which had characterized the one that had just sunk into the grave of Time!

And how was it with the poor of this mighty metropolis—the imperial city, to whose marts whole navies waft the commerce of the world!

The granaries were full; the pastures had surrendered up fat oxen to commemorate the season; the provision-shops teemed with food of the most luxurious and of the humblest kinds alike. A stranger walking through this great city would have wondered where the mouths were that could consume such vast quantities of food.

And yet thousands famished for want of the merest necessaries of life.

The hovels of the poor echoed not to the sounds of mirth and music—but to the wail of hunger and the cry of misery. In those sad abodes there was no joviality to welcome a new year;—for a new year was a curse—a mere prolongation of the acute and poignant horrors of the one gone by.

Alas! that New Year's Day was one of strange contrasts in the social sphere of London.

And as London is the heart of this empire, the disease which prevails in the core is conveyed through every vein and artery over the entire national frame.

The country that contains the greatest wealth of all the territories of the universe, is that which also knows the greatest amount of hideous, revolting, heart-rending misery.

In England men and women die of starvation in the streets.

In England women murder their children to save them from a lingering death by famine.

In England the poor commit crimes to obtain an asylum in a gaol.

In England aged females die by their own hands, in order to avoid the workhouse.

There is one cause of all these miseries and horrors—one fatal scourge invented by the rich to torture the poor—one infernal principle of mischief and of woe, which has taken root in the land—one element of a cruelty so keen and so refined, that it outdoes the agonies endured in the Inquisition of the olden time.

And this fertile source of misery, and murder, and suicide, and crime, is—

THE TREATMENT OF THE WORKHOUSE.

Alas! when the bees have made the honey, the apiarist comes and takes all away, begrudging the industrious insects even a morsel of the wax!

Let us examine for a moment the social scale of these realms:

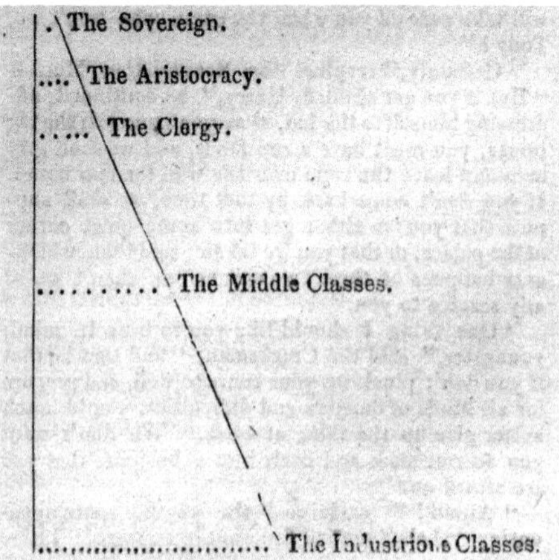

The lowest step in the ladder is occupied by that class which is the most numerous, the most useful, and which ought to be the most influential.

The average annual incomes of the individuals of each class are as follows:—

The Sovereign ....£500,000.
The member of the Aristocracy ...... £30,000.
The Priest .... £7,500.
The member of the middle classes .... £300.
The member of the industrious classes... £20.

Is this reasonable? is this just? is this even consistent with common sense?

It was New Year's Day, 1839.

The rich man sate down to a table crowded with every luxury: the pauper in the workhouse had not enough to eat. The contrast may thus be represented:—

Turtle, venison, turkey, hare, pheasant, perigord-pie, plum-pudding, mince-pies, jellies, blanc-manger, trifle, preserves, cakes, fruits of all kinds, wines of every description.	½ lb. bread 4 oz. bacon ½ lb. potatoes 1½ pint of gruel.

And this was New Year's Day, 1839!

But to proceed.

It was five o'clock in the evening. Three persons were conversing together on Constitution Hill, beneath the wall of the Palace Gardens.

Two of them, who were wrapped up in warm pilot coats, are well known to our readers: the third was a young lad of about sixteen or seventeen, and very short in stature. He was dressed in a blue jacket, dark waistcoat of coarse materials, and corduroy trousers. His countenance was effeminate and by no means bad-looking; his eyes were dark and intelligent; his teeth good. The name of this youth was Henry Holford.

"Well, my boy," said the Resurrection Man, for he was one of the lad's companions, the other being the redoubtable Cracksman,—"well, my boy, do you feel equal to this undertaking?"

"Quite," answered Holford in a decided tone.

"If we succeed, you know," observed the Cracksman, "it will be a jolly good thing for you; and if you happen to get nabbed, why—all the beaks can do to you will be to send you for a month or two upon the stepper. In that there case Tony and me will take care on you when you come out—won't we, Tony?"

"Certainly," replied the Resurrection Man.—"But if you get scented, Harry," he continued, addressing himself to the lad, "as you approach the big house, you must have a run for it, and we shall stay here and leave the rope over the wall for two hours. If you don't come back by that time, we shall suppose that you've either got into some quiet corner of the palace, or that you're taken; and then, whichever happens of these two events, we shan't be of any service to you."

"One thing I should like you to bear in mind, youngster," said the Cracksman, "and that is, that if you don't pluck up your courage well, and prepare for all kinds of dangers and difficulties, you'd much better give up the thing at once. We don't want you to run neck and heels into a business that you're afeard on."

"Afraid!" exclaimed the youth, contemptuously: "I shall not fail for want of courage. I have made up my mind to risk the venture; and let the result be what it will, I shall go through with it."

"That's what I call speaking like a man," said the burglar, "though you are but a boy. Take a drop of brandy before you begin."

"Not a drop," answered Holford: "I require a clear head and quick eye, and dare not drink."

"Well, as you will," said the Cracksman; and he took a tolerably long draught from a case-bottle which he had produced from his pocket.

He then handed the bottle to the Resurrection Man, who also paid his respects to it with a hearty good will.

"I am ready," said Holford; "there is no use in delay."

"Not a bit," observed the Cracksman. "Tony and me will help you over the wall in a jiffey."

By the aid of the Resurrection Man and the burglar, the youth scaled the wall of the Palace Gardens, and ere he dropped upon the

inner side, he said in a low but firm tone, "Good night."

Holford was now within the enclosure of the royal demesne. The evening was very dark; but at a distance the windows of the palace shone with effulgence.

Thitherward did he proceed, advancing cautiously along, for he knew that there was a piece of water in the pleasure-grounds. This small lake he soon left on his right hand; and he was shortly within fifty yards of the back part of Buckingham Palace.

At that moment he was suddenly startled by hearing voices close to him. He stood still, and listened. Steps approached, and he heard a gardener issue some instructions to a subordinate. There was a tuft of trees near at hand: Holford had not a moment to lose;—he darted into the thicket of evergreens, where he concealed himself.

"What was that?" said the gardener, stopping short.

"I heard nothing," answered the man.

"Yes—there was a rustling of those trees."

"A cat, perhaps."

"Or one of the aquatic birds."

All was still, and the gardener, accompanied by his man, proceeded on his way. The sounds of their footsteps were soon lost in the distance; and Holford emerged from his hiding-place. Without any farther alarm he reached the back premises of the palace.

He now became involved in a maze of out-houses and offices, and was at a loss which direction to take. He was going cautiously along the wall of one of those buildings, when he suddenly ran against a man who was advancing rapidly in a contrary direction.

"Holloa! who the devil is this?" cried the man; and clutching hold of Holford's collar, he dragged him a few paces, until he brought him beneath a window whence streamed a powerful light. "I suppose you're the new boy that the head-gardener hired this morning?"

"Yes, sir," answered Holford, gladly availing himself of an excuse thus so conveniently suggested by the error of the man who had collared him.

"Then mind which way you go in future, young brocoli-sprout," exclaimed the other; and, dismissing the youth with a slight cuff on the head, he passed on.

Holford hastened away from the light of the window; and, crossing a small court, reached a glass door opening into the back part of the palace. The adventurous lad laid his hand upon the latch: the door was not locked; and he hesitated not a moment to enter the royal abode.

He was now in a low vestibule, well lighted, and at the extremity of which there was a staircase. In one corner of the vestibule was a marble table, on which lay several cloaks, the skirts of which hung down to the ground. This circumstance was particularly fortunate for the safety of the intruder, inasmuch as he had scarcely entered the vestibule, when the sound of footsteps, rapidly descending the staircase, fell upon his ears. He hastened to conceal himself beneath the table, the cloaks serving effectually to veil his person.

Two footmen in gorgeous liveries shortly made their appearance in the vestibule.

"Where did you say her majesty is?" demanded one.

"In the Roman drawing-room," replied the other. "The Sculpture Gallery is to be lighted up this evening. You can attend to that duty at once, if you will."

"Very well," said the first speaker; and he left the vestibule by means of a door on the right-hand side, but which door he neglected to close behind him.

The other servant advanced straight up to the marble table, and, sweeping off the cloaks, threw them all over his left arm. Holford's person was now exposed to the eyes of any one who might happen to glance beneath that table. The domestic was, however, a tall and stately individual, and kept his head elevated. Having taken the cloaks from the table, he slowly retraced his steps up the stairs, and disappeared from Holford's view.

The young adventurer started from his hiding-place. The door, by which one of the servants had left the vestibule for the purpose of repairing to the Sculpture Gallery, was open. It communicated with a long passage, only feebly lighted. Holford hesitated not a moment, but proceeded in this direction.

He advanced to the end of the passage, and entered a narrow corridor, branching off to the right, and lighted by lamps sustained in the hands of two tall statues. Again the sound of footsteps fell upon Holford's ears; and he had scarcely time to slip behind one of these statues, when the domestic whom he had before seen enter that part of the building, appeared at the end of the corridor. The servant passed without observing him; and the youthful intruder emerged from his lurking-place.

He now pursued his way, without interruption, through several passages and rooms, until he reached a magnificent marble hall, at the farther extremity of which were numerous dependants of the palace, grouped together, and conversing in a low tone. Holford instantly shrank back into the passage by which he had reached the hall. Exactly opposite was the entrance to the Sculpture Gallery. To retrace his steps was useless: he determined to proceed. But how was he to cross the hall? A few moments' reflection suggested to him an expedient. He walked boldly across the hall; and his presence excited no suspicion, it being impossible for the dependants collected together at the other end to observe the nature of his garb at that distance.

He now gained access to the Sculpture Gallery; but there he found no means of concealment. He determined to explore elsewhere, and speedily found himself in a magnificent saloon, adjoining the library, and where he beheld sofas, with the drapery hanging down to the carpet.

It was beneath one of these downy sofas that the daring intruder into the royal dwelling took refuge; and there, comfortably extended at full length, he chuckled triumphantly at the success which had, up to this moment, attended his adventurous undertaking. We have before said that he was of very small stature; he was moreover thin and delicate, and easily packed away.

Some time passed, and no one appeared to interrupt the reflections of Henry Holford. Hour after hour glided by; and at length this palace-clock struck nine. Scarcely had the last chime died away, when the folding doors were thrown open, and a gorgeous procession of nobles and ladies entered the apartment. The magnificence of the dresses worn by England's peeresses and high-born dames—the waving plumes, the glittering jewels, the sparkling diamonds,—combined with a glorious assemblage of female loveliness, formed a spectacle, at once awe-inspiring, ravishing, and delightful. A little in advance of that splendid *cortège*,—conversing easily with the ladies who walked one pace behind her on either hand, and embellished with precious stones of regal price,—moved the sovereign of the mightiest empire in the universe.

Upon her high and polished brow, Victoria wore a tiara of diamonds: diamonds innumerable, and of immense value, studded her stomacher; diamond pendants adorned her ears; and diamonds also glistened upon her wrists. She walked with grace and dignity; and her noble bearing compensated for the shortness of her stature.

The queen advanced to the very sofa beneath which Holford lay concealed and seated herself upon it. The ladies and nobles of the court, together with the guests present upon the occasion, stood at a respectful distance from the sovereign. The splendour of the scene was enhanced by the brilliant uniforms of several military officers of high rank, and the court-dresses of the foreign ambassadors. The blaze of light in which the room was bathed, was reflected from the diamonds of the ladies, and the stars and orders which the nobles wore upon their breasts.

At that time Victoria was yet a virgin-queen. If not strictly beautiful, her countenance was very pleasing. Her light brown hair was worn quite plain; her blue eyes were animated with intellect; and when she smiled, her lips revealed a set of teeth white as Oriental pearls. Her bust was magnificent, and her figure good, in spite of the lowness of her stature. Her manner was distinguished by somewhat of that impatience which characterised all the family of George the Third, and which seemed to result from a slightly nervous temperament. She appeared to require answers to her questions more promptly than court etiquette permitted those around her to respond to her inquiries. With regard to the condition of the humbler classes of her subjects, she was totally ignorant: she knew that they were suffering *some* distress; but the fearful amount of that misery was carefully concealed from her. She only read the journals favourable to the ministry; and they took care to report nothing which might offend or wound her. Thus, she who should have known every thing relative to her people, in reality scarcely knew any thing!

Foremost amid the chiefs of foreign diplomacy was the Ambassador from the court of Castelcicala. He was a man of advanced years; and on his breast glittered the stars of all the principal orders of knighthood in Europe—the Cross and Bath of England, the Legion of Honour of France, the Golden Fleece of Spain, the Black Eagle of Prussia, the Sword of Sweden, the Crescent of Turkey, Saint Nepomecenus of Austria, and the Lion Rampant of Castelcicala. The Ambassadors of France and Austria were also present upon this occasion,—Count Sebastiani, the representative of Louis-Philippe, being clad in the splendid uniform of a General in the French army, and wearing the grand cordon of the Legion of Honour,—and Prince Esterhazy, the Austrian Minister, and himself the possessor of estates more extensive than many a German principality, wearing a court dress covered with lace and glittering with stars.

Several members of the English Cabinet were also present. There was one whose good-tempered and handsome countenance, gentlemanly demeanour, stout and sturdy form, and complacent smile, would hardly have induced a stranger to believe that this was Viscount Melbourne, the Prime Minister of England.[1] Next was a short person-

---

1 William Lamb, Viscount Melbourne (1779-1848), Prime Minister in 1834, and from 1835 to 1841, he was the political mentor of Queen Victoria.

age, with a refined and intelligent, though by no means an imposing air,—a something sharp and cunning in the curl of the mouth, and the flash of the eye,—and a weak disagreeable voice, frequently stammering and hesitating at a long sentence: this was Lord John Russell, the Secretary for the Home Department.[1] Near Lord John Russell was a tall man of about fifty,—very good-looking, with dark and well-curled locks, glossy whiskers, and an elegant figure,—but excessively foppish in his attire, and somewhat affected in manner;—and this was Lord Palmerston, Secretary for Foreign Affairs.[2] Conversing with this nobleman was a personage with pale and sallow cheeks, luxuriant and naturally-curling locks,—dark and interesting in appearance, and in the prime of life,—whose conversation denoted him to be a man of elegant taste, and whose manners were those of a finished gentleman; but who little suited the idea which a stranger would have formed of a great viceroy or a responsible minister:—nevertheless, this was the Marquis of Normanby, lately Lord-Lieutenant of Ireland, and at the time of which we are speaking, Secretary for the Colonies.[3]

The conversation turned upon the specimens of art in the gallery of sculpture, which the noble company had just visited. In this manner an hour passed away; and at the expiration of that period, the queen and her numerous guests repaired to the drawing-rooms on the first floor, where arrangements had been made for a grand musical entertainment.

The entire pageantry was viewed with ease, and the conversation plainly heard, by the plebeian intruder upon that scene of patrician splendour, and glory, and wealth. The musical tones of the queen's

---

1 John Russell, 1st Earl Russell (1792-1878), Prime Minister from 1846 to 1852 and from 1865 to 1866; also Foreign Secretary, from 1852 to 1855 and from 1860 to 1865. He was a radical Free-Trader, opposing all restraints on finance and business, whatever the social cost. Reynolds and Russell clashed personally on at least one occasion, which is described at length in *The Household Narrative of Current Events*, June 1850, p. 136.

2 Henry Temple, Viscount Palmerston (1784-1865) was Foreign Secretary from 1830 to 1831, and from 1846 to 1851. He was Prime Minister from 1855 to 1858, and again from 1859 to his death in 1865. Staunchly pro-business, his anti-French and anti-Russian policies helped to bring about the Crimean War. He is most famous nowadays for his apocryphal last words: 'Die, Doctor? That is the last thing that I shall do.'

3 Constantine Henry Phipps, Marquess of Normanby (1797-1855), Lord Lieutenant of Ireland, 1835-1839. He was briefly Colonial Secretary and Home Secretary in Melbourne's government. A liberal Whig, he gained much respect for his support of Catholic Emancipation.

voice had fallen upon his ears: he had listened to the words of great lords and high-born ladies. At that moment how little, how contemptible did he feel himself to be! Never had he entertained so humble an opinion of his own worth and value in society as he did at that period. He—a common pot-boy in a public-house—had for an hour been the unseen companion of a queen and her mightiest paladins and loveliest dames;—and had he been discovered in his retreat, he would have been turned ignominiously forth, like the man in the parable who went to the marriage-feast without a wedding-garment.

For two more mortal hours did Holford remain beneath the sofa, cramped by his recumbent and uneasy position, and already more than half inclined to regret the adventure upon which he had so precipitately entered.

At length the palace grew quiet, and servants entered the room in which Holford was concealed, to extinguish the lights. The moment that this duty was performed, and the domestics had withdrawn, Holford emerged from beneath the sofa, and seated himself upon it. He was proud to think that he now occupied the place where royalty had so lately been. The voice of the queen still seemed to ring in his ears; and he felt an unknown and unaccountable species of happiness in recalling to mind and pondering upon all that had fallen from her lips. At that moment how he envied those peers and high-born dames who were privileged to approach the royal presence and bask beneath the smile of the sovereign;—how he wished that his lot had been cast in a different sphere! But—no! it was useless to regret what could not be remedied; and, although he was now in a palace, and seated upon the very cushion which a few hours previously had been pressed by royalty, he was not one atom less Henry Holford, the pot-boy!

The reverie of this extraordinary youth was long. Visions the most wild and fantastical sustained a powerful excitement in his imagination. At length the clock struck two. Holford awoke from his strange meditations, and collected his scattered ideas.

He now felt the cravings of hunger, and determined to explore the palace in search of food. He had already seen enough of its geography to be enabled to guess the precise position of the servants' offices; and thither he now directed his steps. He reached the great marble hall, which was lighted by lamps: there was no one there. He crossed it, and proceeded along those passages which he had already threaded a few hours before. After wandering about for some time, and, to his infinite surprise and joy, without encountering a soul, he reached the servants' offices. A short search conducted him to a well-stored larder. Some of the dishes had evidently been put away in a hurry, for silver spoons and forks had been left in them. Holford might have possessed himself of property of considerable value: but such an idea never for a moment entered his head. He moreover contented himself with the simplest food he could find; then, remembering that four-and-twenty hours might elapse ere he should be enabled to return to the larder, he supplied himself with a sufficient amount of provender to last during that interval.

Having adopted this precaution, he stole back again to the room where the friendly sofa had already afforded a secure hiding-place. He once more crept beneath the costly drapery, extended himself upon his back, and fell asleep.

CHAPTER LIX.

THE ROYAL LOVERS.

HOLFORD awoke with a start.

At that moment the time-piece upon the mantel struck five. It was still quite dark.

The young man felt cold and nervous. He had dreamt that he was discovered and ejected from the palace amidst the jeers and taunts of the servants. He now suddenly recollected that the domestics would most probably soon arrive to cleanse and arrange the apartment; and detection in that case must be certain.

It struck him that he had better endeavour to escape at once from the royal dwelling. Then he thought and fondly flattered himself that the same good fortune which had hitherto attended him in this adventure would still follow him. This idea has caused many a hesitating mind to decide upon pursuing a career of crime, or folly, or peril. So was it with Holford; and he resolved to remain in the palace at least a short time longer.

But he perceived the absolute necessity of seeking out a secure place of concealment; and it struck him that the highest storeys of the building were those best calculated for this purpose. Leaving the apartment in which he had availed himself of the friendly sofa, and which, as before stated, was in the immediate vicinity of the Sculpture Gallery upon the ground-floor, he passed through the Library, and returned to the great hall. Ascending a magnificent marble staircase, he reached the Picture Gallery. Every here and there lamps were burning, and thus he was enabled to inspect all the scenes of magnificence and splendour through which he passed.

The Picture Gallery in Buckingham Palace is immediately over the Sculpture Gallery, and forms a wide passage separating the Green Drawing Room, the Throne Room, and other state apartments from the Roman, the Yellow, and the little drawing rooms. The Yellow Drawing Room is the largest and most splendid of the suite. The furniture is all richly carved, and is overlaid with burnished gilding and covered with yellow satin. The wall is surrounded by polished pillars of syenite marble; and on each panel is painted a portrait of some royal personage.

The Dining Room also leads out of the Picture Gallery. This gallery itself is decorated and adorned upon classic models. The frames of the pictures are very plain, but neat, and appropriated to the style of the architecture. There is nothing gorgeous in this gallery—every thing is in good taste; and yet the mouldings and fretwork of the ceiling are of the most elaborate description. The pictures in the gallery are all originals by eminent masters, and are the private property of the sovereign.

It may be here observed that the queen is passionately attached to the Fine Arts, in which, indeed, she is a proficient. In every room of the palace there are some excellent paintings; and in each apartment occupied by the queen, with the exception of the Throne Room, there is a grand pianoforte.

With a lamp in his hand, Henry Holford proceeded through those magnificent apartments which communicated with the Picture Gallery. He was astonished at the assemblage of wealth and splendour that met his eyes on every side. From time to time he seated himself upon the softest ottomans, and in the gilded chairs—in every place where he deemed it probable that the queen might have rested. At length he reached the Throne Room. The imperial seat itself was covered over with a velvet cloth, to protect it against the dust. Holford removed the cloth; and the splendours of the throne were revealed to him.

He hesitated for a moment: he felt as if he were committing a species of sacrilege;—then triumphing over this feeling—a feeling which had appeared like a remorse—he ascended the steps of the throne;—he placed himself in the seat of England's monarch.

Had the sceptre been there he would have grasped it;—had the crown been within his reach, he would have placed it upon his head!

But time pressed; and he was compelled to leave those apartments in which a strange and unaccountable fascination induced him to linger. He ascended a staircase leading to another storey; and now he proceeded with extreme caution, for he conceived that he must be in the immediate vicinity of the royal sleeping apartments. He hastened up to the highest storey he could reach, and entered several passages from which doors opened on either side. One of these doors was ajar: the light of a lamp in the passage enabled him to ascertain that the chamber into which it led was full of old furniture, trunks, boxes, bedding, and other lumber. This was precisely the place which suited the adventurous pot-boy; and he hastened to conceal himself amidst a pile of mattresses which formed a secure, warm, and comfortable berth.

Here he again fell asleep; and when he awoke the sun was shining brightly. He partook of his provisions with a good appetite, and then deliberated within himself what course he should pursue. He felt madly anxious to be near the person of the queen once more: he longed to hear her voice again;—he resolved to risk every thing to gratify these inclinations.

He began to understand that the vast extent of the palace, and the many different ways of reaching the various floors and suites of apartments, constituted the elements of his safety, and greatly diminished the risk of encountering any of the inmates of the royal dwelling. He was insane enough, moreover, to believe that some good genius or especial favour of fortune protected him; and these impressions were sufficiently powerful to induce him to attempt any fresh enterprise within the walls of the palace.

While he was debating within himself how he should proceed in order to satisfy his enthusiastic curiosity, the door suddenly opened, and two female servants of the royal household entered the lumber-room.

Holford's heart sank within him: his limbs seemed paralysed; his breath failed him.

"The entertainment takes place in the Yellow and Roman Drawing Rooms this evening," said one.

"The prince is expected at five o'clock," observed the other. "He and his father the Duke of Saxe Coburg Gotha, are to land at Woolwich between two and three."

"So I heard. The royal carriages have already left to meet her Majesty's guests."

"Have you ever seen the prince?"

"Once. He was in England, I remember, a short time previous to the accession of her Majesty."

"Is he good looking?"

"Very. Of course you believe as I do, and as every one else does that Prince Albert of Saxe Coburg will——"

"Soon be Prince Albert of England."

"Hush! walls have ears!"

The servants having discovered the article of furniture which was the object of their search, left the room—greatly to the relief of Henry Holford, whose presence they never for a moment suspected.

Holford had thus accidentally learnt some information which served to guide his plans. The evening's entertainment was to take place in the Yellow Drawing Room—an apartment which he could not fail to recognise by the colour, as one which he had visited before day-break that morning. He had heard of Prince Albert, whom rumour had already mentioned as the happy being who had attracted the queen's favour. Every circumstance now lent its aid to induce the enthusiastic lad to resolve upon penetrating into the Yellow Drawing Room, by some means or another, during the afternoon.

It struck the intruder that if the queen intended to receive company in the Yellow Drawing-room in the evening, she would most probably welcome her illustrious guests from Germany in some other apartment. He knew, from the conversation of the two female servants, that the Grand Duke of Saxe-Coburg Gotha and Prince Albert, were to arrive at five; he presumed that the inmates of the palace would assemble in those points where they could command a view of the ducal *cortège*; and he came to the conclusion that the coast would be most clear for his purposes at five o'clock.

Nor was he wrong in his conjectures; for scarcely had two minutes elapsed after the clock had proclaimed the hour of five, when Henry Holford was safely ensconced beneath a sofa in the Yellow Drawing Room.

At eight o'clock the servants entered and lighted the lamps. The colour of the paper and the satin of the furniture enhanced the splendour of the effulgence thus created in that magnificent saloon.

At half-past nine the door opened again and Holford's heart beat quickly, for he now expected the appearance of the sovereign and her guests. But, no—not yet. Two ladies attached to the court, entered the drawing-room, and seated themselves upon the sofa beneath which Holford lay concealed.

"Well—what think you of the young prince?" said one. "Your grace was seated next to him."

"Very handsome—and so unassuming," was the reply.

"Does your grace really believe that her Majesty is smitten?"

"No doubt of it. How fortunate for the family of the Grand Duke of Saxe-Coburg!"

"Yes—fortunate on the score of alliance."

"And in a pecuniary point of view."

"Not so much as your grace thinks. There has been an absurd report in circulation that the grand duke's revenues are so small, none of his family could venture to appear at the court of Vienna: and also, that the means of education for the younger branches were always excessively restricted."

"And are not these reports correct, countess?"

"By no means. Your grace probably is aware that the earl and myself visited Germany the year before last; and we remained six weeks at Gotha. The Duke of Saxe-Coburg possesses a considerable civil list, and a large private fortune. His brother Ferdinand espoused the wealthy Princess Kohary of Hungary; and another brother, Leopold, married our lamented Princess Charlotte. It has been stated that Prince Leopold himself was a simple major in the Austrian service, with nothing but his pay, when he was fortunate enough to obtain the favour of the Princess Charlotte: this is so far from being correct, that he never was in the Austrian service at all, but was a general officer in the Russian army, enjoying, in addition to his full pay, a princely allowance from his country."

"Your ladyship has greatly pleased me with these elucidations."

"Your grace honours me with this mark of satisfaction. Prince Albert was educated at Bonn, on the Rhine. His mental qualifications are said to be of a very high order; his disposition is amiable; and he has obtained the affections of all who know him in Germany."

"It is to be hoped that her most gracious Majesty will enjoy a long, prosperous, and happy reign," said the duchess, in a tone of unfeigned sincerity.

"Long and prosperous it may be," returned the countess, with a strange solemnity of voice and manner; "but happy for her—happy for the sovereign whom we all so much love,—no—that is impossible!"

"Alas! I know to what you allude," observed the duchess, her tone also changing. "Merciful heavens! is there, then, no perfect happiness in this world?"

"Where shall perfect happiness be found?" exclaimed the countess, in a voice of deep melancholy, and with a profound sigh. "Never did any sovereign ascend the throne under more favourable circumstances than Victoria. Enshrined in a nation's heart—beloved by millions of human beings—wearing the proudest diadem in the universe, and swaying the sceptre of a dominion extensive as that of Rome, in her most glorious days,—oh! why should not Victoria be completely happy? Alas! she can command the affections of her people by her conduct:—the valour of her subjects, the prowess of her generals, and the dauntless courage of her admirals, can preserve her empire from all encroachment—all peril;—wealth can surround her with every luxury, and all the potentates of the earth may seek her friendship;—but no power—no dominion—no wealth—no luxury—no love, can exterminate the seeds——"

"Ah! countess—for God's sake, talk not in this manner!" ejaculated the duchess: "you make me melancholy—so melancholy, that I shall be dispirited the entire evening."

"Pardon me, my dear friend; but I know not how our discourse gradually turned upon so sad a subject. And yet the transition must have been natural," added the countess, in a mournful and plaintive voice; "for, most assuredly, I should not have voluntarily sought to converse upon so sad a theme."

"Sad!" cried the duchess; "it is sufficient to make one's heart bleed.

To think that a young creature whom millions and millions of beings idolize and adore—whose name is upon every lip—whose virtues and qualifications are the theme of every pen—whose slightest wish amounts to a command,—oh! to think that this envied and amiable being should be haunted, day and night—alone, or when surrounded by all that is most noble or most lovely in England's aristocracy,—haunted by that dread fear—that appalling alarm—that dismal apprehension;—oh! it is intolerable!"

"Alas!" said the countess; "what poor—what miserable creatures are we! The hand of the Deity mingles gall with the cup of nectar which is drunk by his elect! There is no situation in life without its vexations."

"Yes—vexations of all kinds!" echoed the duchess; "for those annoyances which are mere trifles to the lower classes, are grievous afflictions to us. But——"

At that moment the time-piece upon the mantel proclaimed the half-hour after ten; and the two ladies rose from the sofa, observing to each other, that it was time to hasten to attend upon the person of their royal mistress. They then withdrew.

It may be supposed that Holford had not lost one word of the above conversation. He had greedily drunk in every word;—but the concluding portion of it had filled him with the most anxious curiosity, and with wonder. To what did those dark, mysterious hints bear reference? And how could the happiness of the sovereign be incomplete? Those two noble ladies had detailed all the elements of felicity which formed the basis of the queen's position; and surely sufficient had been enumerated to prove the perfection of her happiness. And yet, allusion was made to one source of perpetual fear—one cause of unmixed alarm—one object of ever-present dread, by which the queen was haunted on all occasions. What could this be? Conjecture was vain—imagination could suggest nothing calculated to explain this strange mystery.

Shortly after eleven o'clock the doors were thrown open, and the royal train made its appearance. On the queen's right hand walked Prince Albert, the sovereign leaning gently upon his arm. He was dressed in a court-garb, and wore a foreign order upon his breast. Of slight form and slender make, his figure was wanting in manliness; but his deportment was graceful. His eyes beamed kindness;

and there was something peculiarly sweet and pleasant in his smile. His countenance was expressive of intellect; his conversation was amusing. He was evidently a very pleasant companion; and when Victoria and Albert walked down the saloon together, there appeared a certain fitness in their union which was calculated to strike the most common beholder.

The queen and the prince seated themselves upon the sofa beneath which the pot-boy was concealed; and their conversation was plainly overheard by him. The noble and beauteous guests—the lords and the ladies of the court—withdrew to a distance; and the royal lovers—for such already were Victoria and Albert—enjoyed the pleasures of a *tête-à-tête*. We shall not record any portion of their discourse—animated, interesting, and tender though it were: suffice it to say, that for a short time they seemed to forget their high rank, and to throw aside the trammels of court etiquette, in order to give vent to those natural feelings which the sovereign has in common with the peasant.

This *tête-à-tête* lasted for nearly an hour; music and dancing then ensued; and the entertainment continued until two o'clock in the morning.

The company retired—the lights were extinguished in the state apartments—and profound silence once more reigned throughout the palace.

Holford paid another visit to the larder, and then retraced his steps unobserved to the lumber-room, where he slept until a late hour in the morning.

CHAPTER LX.

REVELATIONS.

FROM the very first moment that Victoria was called to the throne, she manifested a strict determination to exact a scrupulous observance of all the rules, regulations, and precedents which related to court-etiquette and official dignity. The Presence Chamber is never entered by any one who is not fully conversant with the laws of the court, and the mode of conduct and demeanour which they enforce. The rigid maintenance of these rules is nevertheless calculated to render the queen an isolated being, as it were, amidst her court; for no one is permitted to commence a conversation nor make a remark until first addressed by her Majesty. Then every word must be so measured—every syllable so weighed, that the mere fact of conversing with royalty would be deemed a complete labour, and even a perilous undertaking by those not conversant with the routine of a court.

Holford had seen much to surprise and astonish him. The image of the queen ever haunted his imagination: her voice ever rang in his ears. He disliked Prince Albert: that low, vulgar, uneducated, despised, obscure pot-boy, entertained a feeling of animosity,—he scarcely knew wherefore—against the young German who was evidently destined to become the husband of England's queen. Again and again did he ponder upon the mysterious conversation between the two ladies of the court, which he had overheard;—and he felt an ardent and insuperable longing to fathom their meaning to the bottom. But how was this to be done? He determined to obtain access to the drawing-room once more, and trust to the chapter of accidents to elucidate the mystery.

Accordingly, he contrived that same afternoon, to obtain access to the royal apartments, without detection, once more; and once more, also, did he conceal himself beneath the sofa. Fortune appeared to favour his views and wishes. Not many minutes had elapsed after he had ensconced himself in his hiding-place, when the two ladies, whose conversation had so much interested him on the preceding day, slowly entered the Yellow Drawing-Room.

The following dialogue then took place:—

"How very awkward the viscount was last evening, my dear duchess. He would insist upon turning the pages for me when I sate at the grand pianoforte; and he was always too soon or too late; although he pretended to read the *fantasia* which I played, bar by bar."

"That is very provoking!" said the duchess. "I believe there is to be a Drawing-Room to-morrow, at St. James's?"

"Yes: your grace must have forgotten that her Majesty decided last evening upon holding one."

"How many a young heart is fluttering now with anxiety and eager anticipation of to-morrow!" observed the duchess. "A Drawing-Room is most formidable to the novice in court affairs. But the most entertaining portion of the embarrassment of the novice, is the fear that the gentleman who bears the name of the *Court Circular*, and who is invariably stationed in the Presence Chamber, may omit to mention her presence in the report which he draws up for the newspapers."

"George the Third and his consort held Drawing-Rooms weekly, for many years," said the countess. "George the Fourth held Drawing-Rooms but very seldom. William and Adelaide usually held about five or six in a season. And, after all, what can be more magnificent—what more eminently calculated to sustain the honour and dignity of the crown,[1] than a British Court Drawing-Room? The tasteful dresses of the ladies—the blaze of diamonds—the waving ostrich plumes and lappets—the gold net—the costly tulle, constitute rather the

1 The author begs it to be fully understood that his own sentiments relative to courts and court etiquette, &c., must not be identified with the opinions of these ladies who are now conversing together. [Reynolds's note.]

characteristics of an oriental fiction than the reality of the present day."

"The most magnificent Drawing-Rooms, in my opinion," observed the duchess, "are those which we call *Collar Days*. The appearance of the Knights of the Garter, St. Patrick, the Thistle, the Cross of Bath, and all English orders, in their respective collars and jewels, in the presence of the sovereign, is splendid in the extreme."

"And how crowded upon Drawing-Room days are all the passages and corridors of St. James's Palace," continued the countess. "On the last occasion many of the peers and peeresses of the highest rank were compelled thus to wait for nearly three hours before their carriages could reach the palace-gates."

"The most beautiful view of splendid equipages is found in a glance upon the Ambassador's Court at Saint James's, the carriages of the foreign ministers being decidedly the finest and most tasteful that are seen in the vicinity of the palace on those occasions."

"Of a truth, this must be the most splendid court in the world," said the countess, "since France became half republican (how I hate the odious word *Republic!*), and since Spain was compelled to copy France."

"Yes—our court is the most splendid in the world," echoed the duchess, in a tone of triumph, as if her grace were well aware that of that court she herself formed a brilliant ornament; "and more splendid still will it be when the queen shall have conferred her hand upon the interesting young prince who arrived yesterday."

"Have you heard when the royal intentions to contract an union with his Serene Highness Prince Albert, will be communicated to the country?"

"Not until the close of the year; and the marriage will therefore take place at the commencement of 1840. The prince will pay but a short visit upon this occasion, and then return to Germany until within a short period of the happy day."

"God send that the union may be a happy one!" ejaculated the countess. "But——"

"Oh! my dear friend, do not relapse again into those gloomy forebodings which rendered me melancholy all yesterday evening," interrupted the duchess.

"Alas! your grace is well aware of my devoted attachment to our royal mistress; and if there be times when I tremble for the consequences of——"

"Breathe it not—give not utterance to the bare idea!" cried the duchess, in a tone of the most unfeigned horror. "Providence will never permit an entire empire to experience so great a misfortune as this!"

"Maladies of that kind are hereditary," said the countess, solemnly;—"maladies of that species descend through generations—unsparing—pitiless—regardless of rank, power, or position;—oh! it is horrible to contemplate!"

"Horrible—most horrible!" echoed the duchess. "The mind that thus labours under constant terror of the approach of that fearful malady, requires incessant excitement—perpetual change of scene; and this restlessness which we have observed on the part of our beloved Sovereign—and those intervals of deep gloom and depression of spirits, when that craving after variety and bustle is not indulged——"

"Are all——"

"Oh! I comprehend you too well."

"And marriage in such a case——"

"Perpetuates the disease! Yes—yes—we must surround our sovereign with all our love, all our affection, all our devotion—for bitter, bitter are the moments of solitary meditation experienced at intervals by our adored mistress."

"Such is our duty—such our desire," said the countess. "The entire family of George the Third has inherited the seeds of disease—physical and mental——"

"Scrofula and insanity," said the duchess, with a cold shudder.

"Which were inherent in that monarch," added the countess. "Did your grace ever hear the real cause and spring of that development of mental alienation in George the Third?"

"I know not precisely to what incident your ladyship alludes," said the duchess.

"That unhappy sovereign," resumed the countess, "when Prince of Wales, fell in love with a beautiful young Quakeress, whose name was Hannah Lightfoot, and whom he first beheld at the window of a house in Saint James's Street. For some time his Royal Highness and the young lady met in secret, and enjoyed each other's society. At length the passion of the prince arrived at that point when he discovered that his happiness entirely depended upon his union with Hannah Lightfoot. His Royal Highness confided his secret to his next brother Edward, to Dr. Wilmot (who was really the author of the letters of Junius), and to my mother. Those personages were the only witnesses of the legal marriage of the Prince of Wales with Hannah Lightfoot, which was solemnized by Dr. Wilmot, in Curzon Street Chapel, May Fair, in the year 1759."[1]

"I have heard that such a connection existed," said the duchess; "but I never thought until now that it was of so serious and solemn a nature."

"Your grace may rely upon the truth of what I now tell you. Not long after the prince came to the throne, the Ministers discovered his connection with the Quakeress. The 'Royal Marriage Act' was ultimately framed to prevent such occurrences with regard to future princes; but it did not annul the union between George the Third and Hannah Lightfoot."

"Was there any issue from this marriage?" inquired the duchess.

"There *was* issue," answered the countess solemnly, a deep gloom suddenly passing over her countenance. "At my mother's death I discovered certain papers which revealed to me many, many strange events connected with the court of George the Third; and in which she was a confidant. But the history of Hannah Lightfoot is a sad one—a very melancholy one; and positively can I assert that it led to the subsequent mental aberration of the king."

"And there was issue resulting from that union, your ladyship says?" exclaimed the duchess, deeply interested in these disclosures.

"Yes—there was, there was!" returned the countess. "But do not question me any more at present—on a future occasion I will place in the hands of your grace the papers which my deceased mother left behind her, and which I have carefully treasured up in secret—unknown even to my husband!"

---

1 This and the following are all perfectly true, and a matter of public record. Hannah Lightfoot was born 12 October 1730 in Wapping, London. On 17 April 1759 she married George, Prince of Wales, in Keith's Chapel, Curzon Street, Mayfair. Two years later George married Princess Sophia Charlotte of Mecklenburg-Strelitz, without Hannah dying in the meantime, and without the formality of a divorce. Hannah went to America, where she died in Greene County, Pennsylvania, in 1778. There is no doubt that she was George's legitimate wife, and that his marriage to Sophia was bigamous; and, thus, that his subsequent children were illegitimate.

"And are the revelations so very interesting?" demanded the duchess.

"The events which have taken place in the family of George the Third would make your hair stand on end," replied the countess, sinking her voice almost to a whisper. "But, pray—question me no more at present. Another time—another time," she added hastily, "you shall know all that I know!"

There was something so exceedingly mysterious and exciting in the tone and manner of the countess, that the duchess evidently burned with curiosity to make further inquiries. But her fair companion avoided the subject with terror and disgust; and the conversation accordingly reverted to the engagement existing between Prince Albert and Queen Victoria. Nothing more was, however, said which we deem it necessary to record;—but when the two ladies had retired from the apartment, Holford had plenty of food for mental digestion. He had discovered the fatal drawback to the perfect happiness of his sovereign; and he now perceived that those who dwell in palaces, and wear diadems upon their brows, are not beyond the reach of the sharpest arrows of misfortune.

During the remainder of that evening Holford was the uninterrupted possessor of the Yellow Drawing-Room. There was a grand ball in another suite of apartments; but it was not until between three and four o'clock in the morning that the pot-boy considered it safe to quit his hiding-place.

He was now undecided whether to beat a retreat from the royal dwelling, or to favour it with his presence a little longer. The last conversation which he had overheard between the duchess and the countess, had excited within him the most lively interest; and he was anxious to hear more of those strange revelations connected with the family of George the Third, a continuation of which the countess had appeared to promise her noble friend. He was moreover emboldened by the success which had hitherto attended his adventures in the palace; and he consequently resolved upon prolonging his stay in a place where a morbid taste for the romantic encountered such welcome food.

Upon leaving the Yellow Drawing-Room, at about half-past three in the morning, as before stated, Holford proceeded to the pantry to lay in a supply of provender, as usual. He was so pressed with hunger upon this occasion, that he commenced an immediate attack upon the provisions; and was thus pleasantly engaged when, to his horror and dismay, he beheld the shadow of a human form suddenly pass along the wall—for he was standing with his back to the lamp that was burning in the passage.

He turned round—and his eyes encountered the cadaverous and sinister countenance of the Resurrection Man.

"Well this *is* fortunate," said the latter.

"What! you here!" ejaculated Holford, trembling from head to foot.

"Yes—certainly: why not?" said the Resurrection Man. "It struck me that as you never came near me and the Cracksman, you must be still in the royal crib; and I considered that to be a sign that all was right. So I mustered up my courage, and came to look after you. The Cracksman's waiting on the hill."

"Then let us leave this place immediately," cried Holford. "We can do nothing at present—I was going to take my departure within an hour. Come—let us go; and I will tell you every thing when we are in a place of security."

"What's the meaning of this?" demanded the Resurrection Man. "You can't have been here all this time without having found out where the plate is kept."

"Listen for one moment," said Holford, a sudden idea striking him: "the queen leaves for Windsor the day after to-morrow—then will be the time to do what you require; and I can give you all the information you will want. At present nothing can be done—nothing; and if we stay here much longer, we shall be discovered."

"Well," said the Resurrection Man; "provided that some good will result from your visit——"

"There will—there will."

"Then I must follow your advice; for of course you are better able to judge of what can be done and what can't be done in this crib, than me."

The Resurrection Man glanced around him; but fortunately there was no plate left upon the shelves on this occasion. Holford felt inwardly pleased at this circumstance; for the idea of abstracting anything beyond a morsel of food from the palace was abhorrent to his mind.

The Resurrection Man intimated that he was ready to depart; and the pot-boy was only too glad to be the means of hurrying him away.

They left the palace, and entered the gardens, which they threaded in safety. A profound silence reigned around: the morning air was chill and piercing. The fresh atmosphere was nevertheless most welcome and cheering to the young pot-boy, who had passed so many hours in close and heated rooms.

They reached the wall on Constitution Hill in safety, and in a few moments were beyond the enclosure of the royal domains.

CHAPTER LXI.

THE "BOOZING KEN" ONCE MORE.

MORNING dawned upon the great metropolis.

The landlord and landlady of the "Boozing-Ken" on Saffron Hill were busily employed, as we have seen them upon a former occasion, in dispensing glasses of "all sorts" to their numerous customers. The bar was surrounded by every thing the most revolting, the most hideous, and the most repulsive in human shape.

"Well, Joe," said the landlord to a man dressed like a butcher, and whose clothes emitted a greasy and carrion-like smell, "what news down at Cow Cross?"

"Nothink partikler," answered the man, who followed the pleasant and agreeable calling of a journeyman-knacker. "We have been precious full of work lately—and that's all I knows or cares about. Seventy-nine horses I see knocked down yesterday; and out of them, fifty-three was so awful diseased and glandered when they was brought in, that we was obleeged to kill 'em and cut 'em up with masks and gloves on. It was but three weeks ago that we lost our best man, Ben Biddle;—you recollects Ben Biddle?"

"I knowed him well," said the landlord. "He took his 'morning' here reglar for sixteen years, and never owed a penny."

"But do you know how he died?" demanded the knacker, staring the landlord significantly in the face.

"Can't say that I do."

"He died of a fearful disease which is getting more and more amongst human creeturs every day," continued the knacker:—"he died of the glanders!"

"The glanders!" ejaculated the landlady, with a shudder; and all the persons who were taking their "morning" at the bar crowded around the knacker to hear the particulars of Ben Biddle's death.

"You see," resumed the knacker, now putting on a very solemn and important air, "there is more diseased horses sold in Smithfield-Market than sound 'uns. The art of doctoring a dying horse so that he looks as lively and sound as possible to any one which ain't wery knowing in them matters, is come to sich a pitch, that I'm blowed if the wisest ain't taken in at times. We have horses come into our yard that was bought the same morning in Smithfield, and seemed slap-up animals; but in a few hours the effects of the stimulants given to 'em goes off, the plugs falls out of their noses, and there they are at the point of death. Why—if a horse has got four white feet, they'll paint three, or perhaps all on 'em black; and *that part* of the deception isn't never found out till they're flayed in our yard."

"But about poor Biddle?" said the landlord.

"Well, in comes a horse one day," continued the knacker; "and although we saw he was dead lame and altogether done up, we never suspected that he had the glanders. So Ben Biddle had the killing on him. He drives the pole-axe into the animal's skull; and he takes the wire and thrusts it into the brain as business-like as possible. While he was stooping over the beast, his hat falls off his head, and his handkerchief, which he always carried in his hat, fell just upon the horse's mouth. The brute snorted out a last groan at the wery moment that Ben picks up his handkerchief. So Ben puts the handkerchief again into his hat, and puts his hat upon his head; and away we all goes to the public-house to have a drop of half-and-half."

"Very right too," said the landlord, who no doubt spoke feelingly.

"Well," proceeded the knacker, "Ben drinks his share, and presently he takes his handkerchief out of his hat quite permiscuous like, and wipes his face. In a few minutes he feels a strange pain in the eyes just as if some dust had got in;—but he didn't think much on it, and so we all goes back to the yard. In a few hours Ben was taken so bad he was obliged to give up work; and by eight or nine o'clock we was forced to take him to Bartholomew's Hospital. He was seized with dreadful fits of womiting; and matter come out of his nose, eyes, and mouth. By the morning his face was all covered over with sores; holes appeared in his eyes, just for all the world as if they had got a most tremendous small-pox in 'em; and his nose fell off. By three o'clock in the arternoon he was a dead man; and I heerd say that he died in the most awful agonies."

"And that was the glanders?" said the landlady.

"Yes he got 'em by wiping his face with the pocket-handkerchief that had fallen on the horse's nostrils."

"How shocking!" ejaculated several voices.

"And is the glanders increasing?" asked the landlord.

"The glanders *is* increasing," answered the knacker; "and I feel convinced that it will soon become a disease as reglar amongst human beings as the small-pox or measles; 'cos the authorities doesn't do their duty in preventing the sale of diseased animals."

"And how would you remedy the evil?"

"I would have the Lord Mayor and Corporation appoint a proper veterinary surgeon as Inspector in Smithfield Market—a man of great experience and knowledge, who won't let himself be humbugged or gammoned by any of those infernal thieves that gets a living—aye, and makes fortunes too, by selling diseased animals doctored up for the occasion."

"Yes—that's certainly a capital plan of your'n," said the landlord approvingly. "But what becomes of all the flesh of the horses that go to your yards?"

"You may divide the horses that's killed by the knackers into three sorts," answered the man: "that is—first, those horses that is quite healthy but that has met with accidents in their limbs; second, those that is perhaps the least thing diseased, or in the wery last stage through old age; and third, those that is altogether rotten. The flesh of the first is bought by men whose business it is to boil it carefully, and sell it to the sassage-makers: it makes the sassages firm, and is much better than beef. There isn't a sassage shop in London that don't use it. Then the tongues of these first-rate animals goes to the butchers, who salts and pickles 'em; and I'm blow'd if any one could tell 'em from the best ox-tongues."

"Well, I'll never eat sassages or tongues again!" cried the landlady.

"Oh! nonsense—it's all fancy!" exclaimed the knacker. "Half the tongues that is sold for ox-tongues is horses' tongues. A knowing hand may always tell 'em, 'cos they're raything longer and thinner: for my part, I like 'em just as well—every bit."

"And the flesh of the second sort of horses?"

"That goes to supply the cat's-meat men in the swell neighbourhoods; and the third sort, that is altogether putrid and rotten, is taken up by the cat's-meat men in the poor neighbourhoods."

"And do you mean to say that there's a difference even in cat's-meat between the rich and the poor customers?" demanded the landlord.

"Do I mean to say so?" repeated the knacker, in a tone which showed that he was surprised at the question being asked: "why, of course I do! The poor may be pisoned—and very often is too—for what the rich cares a fig. I can tell you more too: some of the first class horses'-meat—the sound and good, remember—is made into what's called *hung-beef*; some is potted; some is sold to the boarding-schools round London, where they takes in young gen'lemen and ladies at a wery low rate; and some is disposed of—but, no—I don't dare tell you—"

"Yes—do tell us!" said the landlady, in a coaxing tone.

"Do—there's a good fellow," cried the landlord.

"Come, tell us," exclaimed a dozen voices.

"No—no—I can't—I should get myself into a scrape, perhaps," said the knacker, who was only putting a more keen edge upon the curiosity which he had excited, for he intended to yield all the time.

"We won't say a word," observed the landlady.

"And I'll stand a quartern of blue ruin," added the landlord, "with three outs—for you, me, and the missus."

"Well—if I must, I must," said the knacker, with affected reluctance. "The fact is," he continued slowly, as if he were weighing every word he uttered, "some of the primest bits of the first-rate flesh that goes out of the knackers' yards of this wast metropolis is sent to the workuses!"

"The workhouses!" ejaculated the landlady: "oh, what a horror!"

"An abomination!" cried the landlord, filling three wine-glasses with gin.

"It is God's truth—and now that I've said it, I'll stick to it," said the knacker.

"It's a shame—a burning shame!" screamed a female voice. "My poor old mother's in the Union, after having paid rates and taxes for forty-two year; and if they make her eat horse's-flesh, I'd like to know whether this country is governed by savages or not."

"And my brother's in a workus too," said a poor decrepit old man; "and he once kept his carriage and dined in company with George the Third at Guildhall, where he'd no end of turtle and venison. But, lack-a-daisy! this is a sad falling off, if he's to come down to horse-flesh in his old age."

"What's the use of all this here whining and nonsense, eh?" exclaimed the knacker. "Don't I tell you that good horse-flesh answers all the purposes of beef, and is eaten by the rich in the shape of sassages and tongues? What's the use, then, of making a fuss about it? How do you suppose the sassage-shops can afford to sell solid meat, without bone, at the price they do, if they didn't mix it with horses'-flesh? They pays two-pence a-pound for the first-class flesh—and so it must be good."

"Never mind," ejaculated a voice: "it's a shame to give paupers only a few ounces of meat a-week, and let *that* be horses'-flesh. It's high time these things was put an end to. Why don't the people take their own affairs in their own hands?"

"Come, now," said the knacker, assuming a dictatorial air, and placing his arms akimbo; "perhaps you ain't aweer that good first-class horses'-flesh is better than half the meat that is sold in certain markets—I shan't say which—for the benefit of the poor. Now you toddle out on Sunday night, on the Holloway, Liverpool, Mile End, and Hackney roads, and see the sheep, and oxen, and calves, coming into London for the next morning's market. Numbers of the poor beasts fall down and die through sheer fatigue. They're flayed and cut up all the same for the butcher's market. And what do you think becomes of all the beasts that die of disease and so on, in the fields? Do you suppose they're wasted? No such a thing! *They* are all cut up *too* for consumption. Just take a walk on a Saturday night through a certain market, *after* the gas is lighted—not *before*, mind—and look at the meat which is marked cheap. You'll see beef at two-pence half-penny a pound, and veal at three-pence. But what sort of stuff is it? Diseased—rotten! The butchers rub it over with fresh suet or fat, and that gives it a brighter appearance and a better smell. Howsomever, they can't perwent the meat from being quite thin, shrunk, poor, and flabby upon the bone."

"I'll bear witness to the truth of all wot you've been saying this last time," said a butcher's lad, stepping forward.

"Of course you can," exclaimed the knacker, casting a triumphant glance around him. "And do you know," he continued, "that half the diseases and illnesses which takes hold on us without any visible cause, and which sometimes puzzles the doctors themselves, comes from eating this bad meat that I've been talkin' about. Now, tell me—ain't a bit out of a good healthy horse, that was killed in a reg'lar way, with the blood flowing, better than a joint off a old cow that dropped down dead of the yallows in a field during the night, and wasn't found so till the morning?"

With these words the knacker took his departure, leaving his hearers disgusted, indignant, and astonished at what they had heard.

As the clock struck nine, the Resurrection Man and the Cracksman entered the "Boozing Ken." They repaired straight into the parlour, and seemed disappointed at not finding there some one whom they evidently expected.

"He ain't come yet, the young spark," said the Cracksman. "And yet he's had plenty of time to go home and get a change o' linen and that like."

"May be he has turned into bed and had a good snooze," observed the Resurrection Man. "He is not so accustomed to remain up all night as we are."

"I think his head is reg'lar turned with what he has seen in the great crib yonder. He seemed to give sich exceeding vague answers to the questions we put to him as we walked through the park this morning. I've heard say that the conwersation of great people is very gammoning, and that they can't always understand each other: so, if young Holford has been listening to their fine talk, it's no wonder he's got crankey."

"Humbug!" ejaculated the Resurrection Man, sulkily. "Let's have some egg-flip, and we'll wait for him. If he comes he shall give us all the information we want; and if he doesn't, we will lay wait for him, carry him off to the crib, and let the Mummy take care of him till he chooses to speak."

"Yes—that'll be the best plan," said the Cracksman. "But don't you think it's a wery likely thing he wants to have the whole business to himself?"

"That's just what I *do* think," answered the Resurrection Man; "he'll find himself mistaken, though—I rather fancy."

"So do I," echoed the Cracksman. "But let's have this egg-flip."

With these words he ordered the beverage, and, in due time a quart pot filled with the inviting compound, with a foaming head, and exhaling a strong odour of spices, was brought in by a paralytic waiter, who had succeeded the slip-shod girl mentioned on a former occasion.

"Good stuff this," said the Cracksman, smacking his lips. "I wonder whether poor Buffer has got anythink half so good this morning."

"What's to-day? Oh! Friday," mused the Resurrection Man, as he sipped his quantum of flip from a tumbler, with a relish equal to that evinced by his companion: "let's see—what's the fare to-day in Clerkenwell Prison?"

"Lord! don't you recollect all that?" cried the Cracksman; and taking a piece of chalk from his pocket, he wrote the Dietary Table of Clerkenwell New Prison upon the wall:—

	Soup.	Gruel.	Meat.	Bread.
	Pint.	*Pint.*	*Ounces.*	*Ounces.*
Monday	..	2½	..	20
Tuesday	..	1½	6	20
Wednesday	..	2½	..	20
Thursday	..	2½	..	20
Friday	1	1½	..	20
Saturday	..	1½	6	20
Sunday	1	1½	..	20
Total Weekly Allowance	2	13½	12	140

"That's a nice allowance for a strong healthy fellow!" exclaimed the Resurrection Man contemptuously. "One month upon that will make his flesh as soft and flabby as possible. It's a shame, by heavens! to kill human beings by inches in that way!"

"What a precious fool the Buffer *has* made of himself!" said the Cracksman after a pause.

"The Buffer!" ejaculated the paralytic waiter, who had been affecting to dust a table as an excuse to linger in the room with the chance of obtaining an invitation to partake of the flip: "is any thing wrong with the Buffer?"

"Safe in lavender," answered the Cracksman, coolly; "and ten to one he'll swing for it."

"My eyes! I'm very sorry to hear that," cried the waiter. "He was a capital fellow, and never took the change when he gave me a joey[1] to pay for his three-penn'orth of rum of a morning."

"Well, he's done it brown at last, at all events," continued the Cracksman.

"What *has* he done?" asked the waiter.

"Why—what he isn't likely to have a chance of doing again," answered the Cracksman. "I suppose you know that he married Moll Flairer, the sister of her as was killed by Bill Bolter at the Old House in Chick Lane, three years or so ago? Well—he had a child by Moll; and a very pretty little creetur it was. Even a fellow like me that can't be supposed to have much feeling for that kind of thing, used to love to play with that little child. It was a girl; and I never did see such sweet blue eyes, and soft flaxy hair. The moment she was born, off goes the Buffer and subscribes to half a dozen *burying clubs*. The secretaries and treasurers was all exceedin' glad to see him, took his tin, and put down his name. This was about two year ago. He kept up all his payments reg'lar; and he was also precious reg'lar in keeping up such a system of ill-treatment, that the poor little thing seemed sinking under it. Now, as I said before, I'm not the most remarkablest man in London for feeling; but I'm blow'd if I couldn't have cried sometimes to see the way in which the Buffer and Moll would use that child. I've seen it standing in a pail of cold water, stark naked, in the middle of winter, when the ice was floating on the top; and because it cried, its mother would take a rope, half an inch thick, and belabour its poor back. Then they half starved it, and made it sleep on the bare boards. But the little thing loved its parents for all that; and when the Buffer beat Moll, I've seen that poor child creep up to her, and say in such a soft tone, *'Don't cry, mother?'* Perhaps all the reward it got for that was a good weltering. How the child stood it all so long, I can't say: the Buffer thought she never would die; so he determined to put an end to it at once. And yet he didn't want money, for we had had some good things lately, what with one thing and another. All I know is that he first takes the little child and flings it down stairs; he then puts it to bed, and sends his wife to the doctor's for some medicine, and into the medicine he pours some laudanum. The little creature went to sleep smiling at him; and never woke no more. This was two days ago. Yesterday the Buffer goes round to all the *burying clubs*, and gives

1 Four-penny piece. [Reynolds's note.]

notice of the death of the child. But some how or another the thing got wind; one of the secretaries of a club takes a surgeon along with him to the Buffer's lodgings, and all's blown."

"Well—I never heard of such a rig as that before," exclaimed the waiter.

"As for the rig," observed the Cracksman, coolly, "that is common enough. Ever since the *burial societies* and *funeral clubs* came into existence, nothink has been more common than these child-murders. A man in full work can very well afford to pay a few halfpence a-week to each club that he subscribes to, even supposing he puts his name down to a dozen. Then those that don't kill their children right out, do it by means of exposure, neglect, and all kinds of horrible treatment; and so it's easy enough for a man to get forty or fifty pounds in this way at one sweep."

"So it is—so it is," said the waiter: "*burial clubs* afford a regular premium upon the murder of young children. Ah! London's a wonderful place—a wonderful place! Every thing of that kind is invented and got up first in London. I really do think that London beats all other cities in the world for matters of that sort. Look, for instance, what a blessed thing it is that the authorities seldom or never attempt to alter what they call the *low neighbourhoods*: why, it's the low neighbourhoods that make such gentlemen as you two, and affords you the means of concealment, and existence, and occupation, and every thing else. Supposing there was no boozing-kens, and patter-cribs like this, how would such gentlemen as you two get on? Ah! London is a fine place—a very fine place; and I hope I shall never live to see the day when it will be spoilt by improvement!"

"Come, there's a good deal of reason in all that," exclaimed the Resurrection Man. "Here, my good fellow," he added, turning to the waiter, "drink this tumbler of egg-hot for your fine speech."

The waiter did not require to be asked twice, but imbibed the smoking beverage with infinite satisfaction to himself.

"I never heard any thing more true than what that fellow has just said," observed the Resurrection Man to his companion in iniquity. "Only suppose, now, that all Saint Giles's, Clerkenwell, Bethnal Green, and the Mint were *improved*, as they call it, where the devil would crime take refuge?—for no one knows better than you and me that we should uncommon soon have to give up business if we hadn't dark and narrow streets to operate in, cribs like this ken to meet and plan in, and the low courts and alleys to conceal ourselves in. Lord! what indeed would London be to us if it was all like the West-End?"

"And so the fact is that the authorities very kindly leave in existence and undisturbed, those very places which give birth to you gentlemen in the first instance," said the waiter, "and sustain you afterwards."

"Well, you ain't very far wrong, old feller," exclaimed the Cracksman. "But, blow me, if this ever struck me before."

"Nor me, neither," said the Resurrection Man, "till the flunkey started the subject."

"Ah! there's a many things that has struck me since I've been in the waiter-line in flash houses of this kind," observed the paralytic attendant, shaking his head solemnly; "but one curious fact I've noticed,—which is, that in nine cases out of ten the laws themselves make men take to bad ways, and then punish them for acting under their influence."

"I don't understand that," said the Cracksman.

"I do, though," exclaimed the Resurrection Man; "and I mean to say that the flunkey is quite right. We ain't born bad: something then must have made us bad. If I had been in the Duke of Wellington's place, I should be an honourable and upright man like him; and if he had been in my place, he would be—what I am."

"Of course he would," echoed the waiter.

"Now I understand," cried the Cracksman.

"I tell you what we'll do," said the Resurrection Man, after a few moments' reflection; "this devil of a Holford doesn't appear to hurry himself, and the rain has just begun to fall in torrents;—so we'll have another quart of flip, and the flunkey shall sit down with us and enjoy it; and I will just tell you the history of my own life, by way of passing away the time. Perhaps you may find," added the Resurrection Man, "that it helps to bear out the flunkey's remark, *that in nine cases out of ten the laws themselves make us take to bad ways, and then punish us for acting under their influence.*"

The second supply of flip was procured; the door of the parlour was shut; room was made for the paralytic waiter near the fire; and the Resurrection Man commenced his narrative in the following manner.

CHAPTER LXII.

THE RESURRECTION MAN'S HISTORY.

"I WAS born thirty-eight years ago, near the village of Walmer, in Kent. My father and mother occupied a small cottage—or rather hovel, made of the wreck of a ship, upon the sea-coast. Their ostensible employment was that of fishing: but it would appear that smuggling and body-snatching also formed a portion of my father's avocations. The rich inhabitants of Walmer and Deal encouraged him in his contraband pursuits, by purchasing French silks, gloves, and scents of him: the gentlemen, moreover, were excellent customers for French brandy, and the ladies for dresses and perfumes. The clergyman of Walmer and his wife were our best patrons in this way; and in consequence of the frequent visits they paid our cottage, they took a sort of liking to me. The parson made me attend the national school regularly every Sunday; and when I was nine years old he took me into his service to clean the boots and knives, brush the clothes, and so forth. I was then very fond of reading, and used to pass all my leisure time in studying books which he allowed me to take out of his library. This lasted till I was twelve years old, when my father was one morning arrested on a charge of smuggling, and taken to Dover Castle. The whole neighbourhood expressed their surprise that a man who appeared to be so respectable, should turn out such a villain. The gentlemen who used to buy brandy of him talked loudly of the necessity of making an example of him: the ladies, who were accustomed to purchase gloves, silks, and *eau-de-cologne*, wondered that such a desperate ruffian should have allowed them to sleep safe in their beds; and of course the clergyman and his wife kicked me ignominiously out of doors. As all things of this nature create a sensation in a small community, the parson preached a sermon upon the subject on the following Sunday, choosing for his text '*Render unto Cæsar the things that are Cæsar's, and unto God the things that are God's,*' and earnestly enjoining all his congregation to unite in deprecating the conduct of a man who had brought disgrace upon a neighbourhood till then famed for its loyalty, its morality, and its devotion to the laws of the country.

"My father was acquitted for want of evidence, and returned

home after having been in prison six months waiting for his trial. In the mean time my mother and myself were compelled to receive parish relief: not one of the fine ladies and gentlemen who had been the indirect means of getting my father into a scrape by encouraging him in his illegal pursuits, would notice us. My mother called upon several; but their doors were banged in her face. When I appeared at the Sunday School, the parson expelled me, declaring that I was only calculated to pollute honest and good boys; and the beadle thrashed me soundly for daring to attempt to enter the church. All this gave me a very strange idea of human nature, and set me a-thinking upon the state of society. Just at that period a baronet in the neighbourhood was proved to be the owner of a smuggling vessel, and to be pretty deep in the contraband business himself. He was compelled to run away: an Exchequer process, I think they call it, issued against his property; and every thing he possessed was swept away. It appeared that he had been smuggling for years, and had defrauded the revenue to an immense amount. He was a widower: but he had three children—two boys and a girl, at school in the neighbourhood. Oh! then what sympathy was created for these *'poor dear bereaved little ones,'* as the parson called them in a charity sermon which he preached for their benefit. And there they were, marshalled into the parson's own pew, by the beadle; and the parson's wife wept over them. Subscriptions were got up for them;—the mayor of Deal took one boy, the banker another, and the clergyman's wife took charge of the girl; and never was seen so much weeping, and consoling, and compassion before!

"Well, at that time my mother had got so thin, and weak, and ill, through want and affliction, that her neighbours gave her the name of the *Mummy*, which she has kept ever since. My father came home, and was shunned by every body. The baronet's uncle happened to die at that period, and left his nephew an immense fortune:—the baronet paid all the fines, settled the Exchequer matters, and returned to Walmer. A triumphal reception awaited him: balls, parties, concerts, and routs took place in honour of the event;—and the mayor, the banker and the clergyman and his wife were held up as the patterns of philanthropy and humanity. Of course the baronet rewarded them liberally for having taken care of his children in the hour of need.

"This business again set me a-thinking; and I began to comprehend that birth and station made an immense difference in the views that the world adopted of men's actions. My father, who had only higgled and fiddled with smuggling affairs upon a miserably small scale, was set down as the most atrocious monster unhung, because he was one of the common herd; but the baronet, who had carried on a systematic contraband trade to an immense amount, was looked upon as a martyr to tyrannical laws, because he was one of the upper classes and possessed a title. So my disposition was soured by these proofs of human injustice, at my very entrance upon life.

"Up to this period, in spite of the contemplation of the lawless trade carried on by my father, I had been a regular attendant at church and at the Sunday-school; and I declare most solemnly that I never went to sleep at night, nor commenced my morning's avocations, without saying my prayers. But when my father got into trouble, the beadle kicked me out of church, and the parson drove me out of the school; and so I began to think that if my religion was only serviceable and available as long as my father remained unharmed by the law, it could not be worth much. From that moment I never said another prayer, and never opened a bible or prayer-book. Still I was inclined to labour to obtain an honest livelihood; and I implored my father, upon my knees, not to force me to assist in his proceedings of smuggling and body-snatching, to both which he was compelled by dire necessity to return the moment he was released from gaol. He told me I was a fool to think of living honestly, as the world would not let me; but he added that I might make the trial.

"Pleased with this permission, and sincerely hoping that I might obtain some occupation, however menial, which would enable me to eat the bread of honest toil, I went round to all the farmers in the neighbourhood, and offered to enter their service as a plough-boy or a stable-boy. The moment they found out who I was, they one and all turned me away from their doors. One said, '*Like father, like son;*'—another asked if I was mad, to think that I could thus thrust myself into an honest family;—a third laughed in my face;—a fourth threatened to have me taken up for wanting to get into his house to commit a felony;—a fifth swore that there was gallows written upon my countenance;—a sixth ordered his men to loosen the bull-dog at me;—and a seventh would have had me ducked in his horse-pond, if I had not run away.

"Dispirited, but not altogether despairing, I returned home. On the following day, I walked into Deal, (which almost joins Walmer) and called at several tradesmen's shops to inquire if they wanted an errand-boy. My reception by these individuals was worse than that which I had met with at the hands of the farmers. One asked me if I thought he would run the risk of having his house indicted as the receptacle for thieves and vagabonds;—a second pointed to his children, and said, *'Do you suppose I want to bring them up in the road to the gallows?'*—a third locked up his till in affright, and threatened to call a constable;—and a fourth lashed me severely with a horse-whip.

"Still I was not totally disheartened. I determined to call upon some of those ladies and gentlemen who had been my father's best customers for his contraband articles. One lady upon hearing my business, seized hold of the poker with one hand and her salts-bottle with the other;—a second was also nearly fainting, and rang the bell for her maid to bring her some *eau-de-cologne*—the very *eau-de-cologne* which my father had smuggled for her;—a third begged me with tears in her eyes to retire, or my very suspicious appearance would frighten her lap-dog into fits;—and a fourth (an old lady, who was my father's best customer for French brandy), held up her hands to heaven, and implored the Lord to protect her from all sabbath-breakers, profane swearers, and drunkards.

"Finding that I had nothing to expect from the ladies, I tried the gentlemen who had been accustomed to patronise my father previous to his *misfortune*. The first swore at me like a trooper, and assured me that he had always prophesied I should go wrong:—the second spoke civilly, and regretted that his excellent advice had been all thrown away upon my father, whom he had vainly endeavored to avert from his wicked courses (it was for smuggling things for this gentleman that my father had been arrested);—and the third made no direct answer, but shook his head solemnly, and wondered what the world was coming to.

"I was now really reduced to despair. I, however, resolved to try some of the very poorest tradesmen in the town. By these miserable creatures I was received with compassionate interest; and my case was fully comprehended by them. Some even gave me a few halfpence; and one made me sit down and dine with him, his wife, and his children. They, however, one and all declared *that they could not take me into their service, for, if they did, they would be sure to offend all their customers*. Thus was it that the overbearing conduct and atrocious tyranny of the more wealthy part of the community, compelled the poorer portion to smother all sympathy in my behalf.

A sudden thought now struck me. I resolved to call next day upon the very baronet who had himself suffered so much in consequence of the customs-laws. Exhilarated by the new hope awakened within me, I repaired on the following morning to the splendid mansion which he now inhabited. I was shown into a magnificent room, where he received me, lounging before a cheerful fire. He listened very patiently to my tale, and then spoke, as nearly as I can recollect, as follows:—'My good lad, I have not the slightest doubt that you are anxious to eat the bread of honesty, as you very properly express it. But that bread is not within the reach of every body; and if we were all to pick and choose in this world, my God! what would become of us? My dear young man, I occupy a prominent position amidst the gentry of these parts, and I have also a duty to fulfil towards society. Society has condemned you—unheard, I grant you: nevertheless, society *has* condemned you. Under these circumstances I have no alternative, but to decline taking you into my service; and I must moreover request you to remember that if you are ever found loitering upon my grounds, I shall have you put in the stocks. I regret that my duty to society compels me thus to act.'

"You may conceive with what feelings I heard this long tirade. I was literally confounded, and retired without venturing upon a remonstrance. I knew not what course to adopt. To return home and inform my parents that I could obtain no work, was to lay myself under the necessity of becoming a smuggler and a body-snatcher at once. As a desperate resource I thought of calling upon the clergyman, and explaining all my sentiments to him. I hoped to be able to convince him that although my father was bad, or supposed to be bad, yet I abhorred vice in all its shapes, and was anxious only to pursue honest courses. As a Christian minister, he could not, I imagined, be so uncharitable as to infer my guilt in consequence of that of my parent; and, accordingly, to him did I repair. He had just returned to his own house from a funeral, and was in a hurry to be off on a shooting excursion, for he had on his sporting-garb beneath his surplice. He listened to me with great impatience, and asked if my father still pursued his contraband trade. Seeing that I hesitated how to reply, he exclaimed, turning his eyes up to heaven, '*Speak the truth, young man, and shame the devil!*' I answered in the affirmative; and he then said carelessly, 'Well, go and speak to my wife; she will act in the matter as she chooses.' Rejoiced at this hopeful turn in the proceeding, I sought his lady, as I was desired. She heard all that I had to say, and then observed, 'Not for worlds could I receive you into my house again; but if your father has any silks and gloves, very cheap and very good, I do not mind purchasing them. And remember,' she added, as I was about to depart, 'I do not want these things; I only offer to take them for the purpose of doing you a service. My motive is purely a Christian one.'

"I returned home. 'Well,' said my father, 'what luck this morning?'—'None,' I replied.—'And what do you mean to do, lad?'—'To become a smuggler, a body-snatcher, or any thing else that you choose,' was my reply; 'and the sooner we begin, the better, for I am sick and tired of being good.'

"So I became a smuggler and a resurrection man.

"You have heard, perhaps, that Deal is famous for its boatmen and pilots. It is also renowned for the beauty of the sailors' daughters. One of those lovely creatures captivated my heart—for I can even talk sentimentally when I think of those times; and she seemed to like me in return. Her name was Katharine Price—Kate Price, as she was called by her acquaintance; and a prettier creature the sun never shone upon. She was good and virtuous, too—and she alone understood my real disposition, which, even now that I had embarked in lawless pursuits, still panted to be good and virtuous also. At this time I was nineteen, and she was one year younger. We loved in secret—and we met in secret; for her parents would not for one moment have listened to the idea of our union. My hope was to obtain a good sum of money by one desperate venture in the contraband line, and run away with Kate to some distant part of the country, where we could enter upon some way of business that would produce us an honest livelihood. This hope sustained us!

"At this time there were a great many sick sailors in Deal Hospital, and numerous funerals took place in the burial-ground of that establishment. My father and I determined to have up a few of the corpses, for we always knew where to dispose of as many *subjects* as we could obtain. By these means I proposed to raise enough money to purchase in France the articles that I meant to smuggle into England and thereby obtain the necessary funds for carrying out the plans upon which Kate and myself were resolved.

"Good luck attended upon my father and myself in respect to the body-snatching business. We raised thirty pounds; and with that we set sail for France in the boat which we always hired for our smuggling expeditions. We landed at Calais, and made our purchases. We bought an immense quantity of brandy at tenpence a quart; gloves at eightpence a pair; three watches at two pound ten each; and some *eau-de-cologne*, proportionately cheap. Our thirty pounds we calculated would produce us a hundred and twenty. We put out to sea again at about ten o'clock at night. The wind was blowing stiff from the nor'east; and by the time we had been an hour at sea it increased to a perfect hurricane. Never shall I forget that awful night. The entire ocean was white with foam; but the sky above was as black as pitch. We weathered the tempest until we reached the shore about a mile to the south'ard of Walmer, at a place called Kingsdown. We touched the beach—I thought every thing was safe. A huge billow broke over the stern of the lugger; and in a moment the boat was a complete wreck. My father leapt on shore from the bow at the instant this catastrophe took place: I was swallowed up along with the ill-fated bark. I was, however, an excellent swimmer; and I combated, and fought, and struggled with the ocean, as a man would wrestle with a savage animal that held him in his grasp. I succeeded in gaining the beach; but so weak and enfeebled was I that my father was compelled to carry me to our hovel, close by.

"I was put to bed: a violent fever seized upon me—I became delirious—and for six weeks I lay tossing upon a bed of sickness.

"At length I got well. But what hope remained, for me? We were totally ruined—so was the poor fisherman whose boat was wrecked upon that eventful night. I wrote a note to Kate to tell her all that had happened, and to make an appointment for the following Sunday evening, that we might meet and talk over the altered aspect of affairs. Scarcely had I despatched this letter to the care of Kate's sister-in-law, who was in our secret, and managed our little correspondence, when my father came in and asked me if I felt myself well enough to accompany him on a little expedition that evening. I replied in the affirmative. He then told me that a certain surgeon for whom we did business, and who resided in Deal, required a particular subject which had been buried that morning in Walmer Churchyard. I did not ask my father any more questions; but that night I accompanied him to the burial-ground between eleven and twelve o'clock. The surgeon had shown my father the grave in the afternoon; and we had a cart waiting in a lane close by. The church is in a secluded part, surrounded by trees, and at some little distance from any habitations. There was no danger of being meddled with:—moreover, we had often operated in the same ground before.

"To work we went in the usual manner. We shovelled out the soil, broke open the coffin, thrust the corpse into a sack, filled up the grave once more, and carried our prize safe off to the cart. We then set off at a round pace towards Deal, and arrived at the back door of the surgeon's house by two o'clock. He was up and waiting for us. We carried the corpse into the surgery, and laid it upon a table. 'You are sure it is the right one?' said the surgeon.—'It is the body from the grave that you pointed out,' answered my father.—'The fact is,' resumed the surgeon, 'that this is a very peculiar case. Six days ago, a young female rose in the morning in perfect health; that evening she was a corpse. I opened her, and found no traces of poison; but her family would not permit me to carry the examination any further. They did not wish her to be hacked about. Since her death some love-letters have been found in her drawer; but there is no name attached to any of them.'—I began to feel interested, I scarcely knew why; but this was the manner in which I was accustomed to write to Kate. The surgeon continued: 'I am therefore anxious to make another and more searching investigation than on the former occasion, into the cause of death. But I will soon satisfy myself that this is indeed the corpse I mean.'—With these words the surgeon tore away the shroud from the face of the corpse. I cast an anxious glance upon the pale, cold, marble countenance. My blood ran cold—my legs trembled—my strength seemed to have failed me. Was I mistaken? could it be the beloved of my heart—'Yes; that is Miss Price,' said the surgeon, coolly. All doubt on my part was now removed. I had exhumed the body of her whom a thousand times I had pressed to my sorrowful breast—whom I had clasped to my aching heart. I felt as if I had committed some horrible crime—a murder, or other deadly deed!

"The surgeon and my father did not notice my emotions, but

settled their accounts. The medical man then offered us each a glass of brandy. I drank mine with avidity, and then accompanied my father from the spot—uncertain whether to rush back and claim the body, or not. But I did not do so.

"For some days I wandered about scarcely knowing what I did—and certainly not caring what became of me. One morning I was roving amidst the fields, when I heard a loud voice exclaim,—'I say, you fellow there, open the gate, will you?' I turned round, and recognised the baronet on horseback. He had a large hunting whip in his hand.—'Open the gate!' said I; 'and whom for?' 'Whom for!' repeated the baronet; 'why, for me, to be sure, fellow.'—'Then open it yourself,' said I. The baronet was near enough to me to reach me with his whip; and he dealt me a stinging blow across the face. Maddened with pain, and soured with vexation, I leapt over the gate and attacked the baronet with a stout ash stick which I carried in my hand. I dragged him from his horse, and thrashed him without mercy. When I was tired, I walked quietly away, he roaring after me that he would be revenged upon me as sure as I was born.

"Next day I was arrested and taken before a magistrate. The baronet appeared against me, and—to my surprise—swore that I had assaulted him with a view to rob him, and that he had the greatest difficulty in protecting his purse and watch. I told my story and showed the mark of the baronet's whip across my face. The justice asked me if I could bring forward any witnesses to character. The baronet exclaimed, 'How can he? he has been in Dover Castle for smuggling.'—'Never!' I cried emphatically.—'Well, your father has, then,' said the baronet. This I could not deny.—'Oh! that's just the same thing!' cried the magistrate; and I was committed to gaol for trial at the next Maidstone assizes.

"For three months I lay in prison. I was not, however, completely hardened yet; nor did I associate with those who drank, and sang, and swore. I detested vice in all its shapes; and I longed for an opportunity to be good. It may seem strange to you, who know me *now*, to hear me speak thus;—but you are not aware what I was *then!*

"I was tried, and found guilty. The next two years of my life I passed at the hulks at Woolwich, dressed in dark grey, and wearing a chain round my leg. Even there I did not grow so corrupted, but that I sought for work the moment I was set at liberty again. I resolved not to return home to my parents, for I detested the ways into which they had led me. Turned away from the hulks one fine morning at ten o'clock, without a farthing in my pocket nor the means of obtaining a morsel of bread, my prospects were miserable enough. I could not obtain any employment in Woolwich: evening was coming on—and I was hungry. Suddenly I thought of enlisting. Pleased with this idea, I went to the barracks, and offered myself as a recruit. The regiment stationed there was about to embark for the East Indies in a few days and wanted men. Although certain of being banished, as it were, to a most unhealthy climate for twenty-one years, I preferred that to the life of a vagabond or a criminal in England. The sergeant was delighted with me, because I could read and write well; but the surgeon would not pass me. He said to me, 'You have either been half-starved for a length of time, or you have undergone a long imprisonment, for your flesh is as flabby as possible.' Thus was this hope destroyed.

"Now what pains had the law taken to make me good—even supposing, that I was really bad at the time of my condemnation? The law locked me up for two years, half-starved me, and yet exacted from me as much labour as a strong, healthy, man could have performed: then the law turned me out into the wide world, so weak, reduced, and feeble, that even the last resource of the most wretched—namely, enlisting in a regiment bound for India—was closed against me!

"Well—that night I wandered into the country and slept under a hedge. On the following morning I was compelled to satisfy the ravenous cravings of my hunger with Swedish turnips plucked from the fields. This food lay so cold upon my stomach that I felt ready to drop with illness, misery, and fatigue. And yet, in this Christian land, even that morsel, against which my heart literally heaved, was begrudged me. I was not permitted to satisfy my hunger with the food of beasts. A constable came up and took me into custody for robbing the turnip field. I was conducted before a neighbouring justice of the peace. He asked me what I meant by stealing the turnips? I told him that I had fasted for twenty-four hours, and was hungry. 'Nonsense, hungry!' he exclaimed; 'I'd give five pounds to know what hunger is! you kind of fellows eat turnips by way of luxury, you do—and not because you're hungry.' I assured him that I spoke the truth.—'Well, why don't you go to work?' he demanded.—'So I will, sir, with pleasure, if you will give me employment.' I replied.—'Me give you employment,' he shouted; 'I wouldn't have such a fellow about me, if he'd work for nothing. Where did you sleep last night?'—'Under a hedge, sir,' was my answer.—'Ah! I thought so,' he exclaimed: 'a rogue and vagabond evidently.' And this excellent specimen of the 'Great unpaid' committed me forthwith to the treadmill for one month *as a rogue and vagabond*.

"The treadmill is a horrible punishment: it is too bad even for those that are really rogues and vagabonds. The weak and the strong take the same turn, without any distinction; and I have seen men fall down fainting upon the platform, with the risk of having their legs or arms smashed by the wheel, through sheer exhaustion. Then the miserable fare that one receives in prison renders him more fit for an hospital than for the violent labour of the treadmill.

"I had been two years at the hulks, and was not hardened: I had been a smuggler and a body-snatcher, and was not hardened:—but this one month's imprisonment and spell at the treadmill *did* harden me—and hardened me completely! I could not see any advantage in being good. I could not find out any inducement to be honest. As for a desire to lead an honourable life, that was absurd. I now laughed the idea to scorn; and I swore within myself that whenever I *did* commence a course of crime, I would be an unsparing demon at my work. Oh! how I then detested the very name of virtue. 'The rich look upon the poor as degraded reptiles that are born in infamy and that cannot possibly possess a good instinct,' I reasoned within myself. 'Let a rich man accuse a poor man before a justice, a jury, or a judge, and see how quick the poor wretch is condemned! The aristocracy hold the lower classes in horror and abhorrence. The legislature thinks that if it does not make the most grinding laws to keep down the poor, the poor will rise up and commit the most unheard-of atrocities. In fact the rich are prepared to believe any infamy which is imputed to the poor.' It was thus that I reasoned; and I looked forward to the day of my release with a burning—maddening—drunken joy!

"That day came. I was turned adrift, as before, without a shilling and without a crust. That alone was as bad as branding the words *rogue and vagabond* upon my forehead. How could I remain honest, even if I had any longer been inclined to do so, when I could not get work and had no money—no bread—no lodging? The legislature

does not think of all this. It fancies that all its duty consists in punishing men for crimes, and never dreams of adopting measures to prevent them from committing crimes at all. But I now no more thought of honesty: I went out of prison a confirmed ruffian. I had no money—no conscience—no fear—no hope—no love—no friendship—no sympathy—no kindly feeling of any sort. My soul had turned to the blackness of hell!

"The very first thing I did was to cut myself a good tough ash stick with a heavy knob at one end. The next thing I did was to break into the house of the very justice who had sentenced me to the treadmill for eating a raw turnip; and I feasted jovially upon the cold fowl and ham which I found in his larder. I also drank success to my new career in a bumper of his fine old wine. This compliment was due to him: he had made me what I was!

"I carried off a small quantity of plate—all that I could find, you may be sure—and took my departure from the house of the justice. As I was hurrying away from this scene of my first exploit, I passed by a fine large barn, also belonging to my friend the magistrate. I did not hesitate a moment what to do. I owed him a recompense for my month at the treadmill; and I thought I might as well add *Incendiary* to my other titles of *Rogue* and *Vagabond*. Besides, I longed for mischief—the world had persecuted me quite long enough, the hour of retaliation had arrived. I fired the barn and scampered away as hard as I could. I halted at a distance of about half a mile, and turned to look. A bright column of flame was shooting up to heaven! Oh! how happy did I feel at that moment. Happy! this is not the word! I was mad—intoxicated—delirious with joy. I literally danced as I saw the barn burning. I was avenged on the man who would not allow me to eat a cold turnip to save me from starving:—that one cold turnip cost him dear! The fire spread, and communicated with his dwelling-house; and there was no adequate supply of water. The barn—the stacks—the out-houses—the mansion were all destroyed. But that was not all. The only daughter of the justice—a lovely girl of nineteen—was burnt to death. I read the entire account in the newspapers a few days afterwards!

"And the upper classes wonder that there are so many incendiary fires: my only surprise is, that there are so few! Ah! the Lucifer-match is a fearful weapon in the hands of the man whom the laws, the aristocracy, and the present state of society have ground down to the very dust. I felt all my power—I knew all my strength—I was aware of all my importance as a man, when I read of the awful extent of misery and desolation which I had thus caused. Oh! I was signally avenged!

"I now bethought me of punishing the baronet in the same manner. He had been the means of sending me for two years to the hulks at Woolwich. Pleased with this idea, I jogged merrily on towards Walmer. It was late at night when I reached home. I found my mother watching by my father's deathbed, and arrived just in time to behold him breathe his last. My mother spoke to me about decent interment for him. I laughed in her face. Had he ever allowed any one to sleep quietly in his grave? No. How could *he* then hope for repose in the tomb? My mother remonstrated: I threatened to dash out her brains with my stout ash stick; and on the following night I sold my father's body to the surgeon who had anatomised poor Kate Price! This was another vengeance on my part.

"Not many hours elapsed before I set fire to the largest barn upon the baronet's estate. I waited in the neighbourhood and glutted myself with a view of the conflagration. The damage was immense. The next day I composed a song upon the subject, which I have never since forgotten. You may laugh at the idea of me becoming a poet; but you know well enough that I received some trifle of education—that I was not a fool by nature—and that in early life I was fond of reading. The lines were these:—

"THE INCENDIARY'S SONG.

"The Lucifer-match! the Lucifer-match!
'Tis the weapon for us to wield.
How bonnily burns up rick and thatch,
And the crop just housed from the field!
The proud may oppress and the rich distress,
And drive us from their door;—
But they cannot snatch the Lucifer-match
From the hand of the desperate poor!

"The purse proud squire and the tyrant peer
May keep their Game Laws still;
And the very glance of the overseer
May continue to freeze and kill.
The wealthy and great, and the chiefs of the state,
May tyrannise more and more;—
But they cannot snatch the Lucifer-match
From the hand of the desperate poor!

"'*Oh! give us bread?*' is the piteous wail
That is murmured far and wide;
And echo takes up and repeats the tale—
But the rich man turns aside.
The Justice of Peace may send his Police
To scour the country o'er;
But they cannot snatch the Lucifer-match
From the hand of the desperate poor!

"Then, hurrah! hurrah! for the Lucifer-match;

'Tis the weapon of despair.—
How bonnily blaze up barn and thatch—
The poor man's revenge is there!
For the *worm* will turn on the feet that spurn—
And surely a *man* is more?—
Oh! none can e'er snatch the Lucifer match
From the hand of the desperate poor!

"The baronet suspected that I was the cause of the fire, as I had just returned to the neighbourhood; and he had me arrested and taken before a justice; but there was not a shadow of proof against me, nor a pretence to keep me in custody. I was accordingly discharged, with an admonition '*to take care of myself*'—which was as much as to say, '*If I can find an opportunity of sending you to prison, I will.*'

"Walmer and its neighbourhood grew loathsome to me. The image of Kate Price constantly haunted me; and I was moreover shunned by every one who knew that I had been at the hulks. I accordingly sold off all the fishing tackle, and other traps, and came up to London with the old Mummy.

"I need say no more."

"And there's enough in your history to set a man a-thinking," exclaimed the waiter of the boozing-ken; "there is indeed."

"Ah! I b'lieve you, there is," observed the Cracksman, draining the pot which had contained the egg-flip.

The clock struck mid-day when Holford entered the parlour of the boozing-ken.

CHAPTER LXIII.

THE PLOT.

"WELL, young blade," cried the Cracksman, "you haven't kept us waiting at all, I suppose?"

"And do you fancy that I could wake myself up again in a minute when I had once laid down?" demanded the lad, sulkily.

"Oh! bother to the laying down, Harry," said the Cracksman. "Don't you think me and Tony wants sleep as well as a strong hearty young feller like you? and we haven't put buff in downy[1] since the night afore last."

"Well, never mind chaffing about *that*," cried the Resurrection Man impatiently: then, having dismissed the waiter, he continued, "Now, about this business at the palace? We must have no delay; and when we make appointments in future, they must be better kept. But I won't speak of this one now, because there's some allowance to be made for you, as you were up the best part of the night, and you ain't accustomed to it as we are. But to the point. How is this affair to be managed?"

"I don't see how it is to be managed at all," answered Holford, firmly.

"The devil you don't," cried the Cracksman. "Then what was you doing all that time in the palace?"

"Running a thousand risks of being found out every minute——"

"So we all do at times."

"And sneaking about at night-time to find food."

"I think you managed to discover the right place for the grist," said the Resurrection Man, his cadaverous countenance wearing an ironical smile; "for you must recollect that I found you in the pantry."

"And the pantry's a good neighbourhood: it can't be far from where the plate's kept," observed the Cracksman.

"The plate is kept where no one can get at it," said Holford.

"How do you know that, youngster?"

"I overheard the servants count it, lock it up in a chest, and take it up to the apartments of—of—the Lord Steward, I think they call him."

"The deuce!" ejaculated the Cracksman, in a tone of deep disappointment.

"Now I tell you what it is, young fellow," said the Resurrection Man; "I think that for some reason or another you're deceiving us."

"You think so?" cried the lad. "And why should you fancy that I am deceiving you?"

"Because your manners tell me so."

"In that case," said Holford, rising from his seat, "it is not of any use for us to talk more upon the subject."

"By G—d, it is of use, though!" exclaimed the Cracksman. "You

[1] "We have not gone to bed." [Reynolds's note.]

shall tell us the truth by fair means or foul;" and he produced from his pocket a clasp-knife, the murderous blade of which flew open by means of a spring which was pressed at the back.

Holford turned pale, and resumed his seat.

"Now, you see that it is no use to humbug us," said the Resurrection Man. "Tell us the whole truth, and you will of course get your reg'lars out of the swag. You told me that the Queen was going to Windsor in a day or two; and that was as much as to say that the affair would come off then."

"I told you the Queen was going to Windsor—and I tell you so again," replied Holford. "But I can't help it if they lock up the plate: and I don't know what else there is for you to carry off."

The Resurrection Man and the Cracksman exchanged glances of mingled rage and disappointment. They did not precisely believe what the lad told them, and yet they could not see any motive which he was likely to have for misleading them—unless it were to retain all the profits of his discoveries in the palace for his own sole behoof.

"Now, Holford, my good fellow," said the Cracksman, shutting up his clasp-knife, and returning it to his pocket, "if you fancy that you are able to go through this business alone, and without any help, you are deucedly mistaken."

"I imagine no such thing," returned Holford; "and to prove to you that I am convinced there is nothing to be got by the affair, in any shape or way, do you and Tidkins attempt it alone together. He found his way to the pantry as well as I did, and can tell you what he saw there."

"That's true," said the Resurrection Man, apparently struck by this observation. "So I suppose we must give the thing up as a bad job?"

"I suppose we must," added the Cracksman, grinding his teeth. "But, by G—d, if I thought this younker was humbugging us, I'd plant three inches of cold steel in him, come what would."

"Thank you for your kindness," said Holford, not without a shudder. "Another time, get some person to act for you whose word you will believe. And now," he continued, turning to the Resurrection Man, "please to recollect the terms we agreed upon—a third of all we could get if successful, or five pounds for me in case of failure."

"Well, I shall keep my word," returned the Resurrection Man.

"Blow me if I would, though," exclaimed the Cracksman, fiercely.

"Yes—fair play's a jewel," said the Resurrection Man, darting a significant glance at his companion; then, feeling in his pocket, he added, "Holford is entitled to his five pounds, and he shall have them; but, curse me! if I have enough in my pocket to pay him. I tell you what it is, my lad," he continued, turning towards the young man, "you must meet me somewhere this evening, and I'll give you the money."

"That will do," cried Holford. "Where shall I meet you?"

"Where?" repeated the Resurrection Man, affecting to muse upon the question: "Oh! I will tell you. You know the *Dark-House* in Brick Lane, Spitalfields?"

"I have heard of it, but was never there."

"Well—meet me there to-night at nine o'clock, Harry," said the Resurrection Man, in as kind a tone as he could assume, "and I'll tip you the five couters."

"At nine punctually," returned Holford. "I would not press you, but I have lost my place in consequence of being absent all this time without being able to give any account of myself; and so I am regularly hard up. I'm going to look after a situation up somewhere beyond Camden Town this afternoon, that I heard of by accident: but I am afraid I shall not get it, as I can give no reference for character;—and even if I could, it would be to the public-house where I was pot-boy, and the place I'm going to try for is to clean boots and knives, and make myself generally useful in a gentleman's house. So I am afraid that I am not likely to get the situation."

"I hope you may, my lad, for your sake," cried the Resurrection Man. "At all events the five quids will keep you from starving for the next two months to come; so mind and be punctual this evening at nine."

"I shall not fail," answered Holford; and with these words he departed.

"Well, blow me, if I can make out now what you're up to," exclaimed the Cracksman, as soon as he and his companion in infamy were alone together.

"You never thought that I should be fool enough to give him five couters for doing nothing but humbug us?" said the Resurrection Man. "No—no: catch a weasel asleep—but not Tony Tidkins! Don't you see that he has been making fools of us? I remember what a devil of a hurry he was in to get me away from the palace, when I lighted upon him in the pantry, and, altogether, I am convinced he has been doing his best to stall us off from the business."

"So I think," said the Cracksman.

"Well," resumed the Resurrection Man, "we'll just try what a few days of the pit under the staircase in my crib will do for him. I have mended up the hole that opens into the saw-pit next door; and there is no chance of his escaping. We must make him drink a glass at the *Dark House*, and drug the grog well, and we needn't fear about being able to get him up into my street."

"Ah! now I understand you," observed the Cracksman: "only see what it is to have a head like your'n. The pit will soon make him tell us the real truth."

"And if not—if he remains obstinate—" mused the Resurrection Man, aloud;—"why—in that case—"

"We shall know what to do with him," added the Cracksman.

And the two miscreants exchanged glances of horrible significancy.

CHAPTER LXIV.

THE COUNTERPLOT.

On the same day that the above conversation took place in the parlour of the boozing-ken on Saffron Hill, Markham was seated in his library, with several books before him. His countenance was pale, and bore the traces of recent illness; and an air of profound melancholy reigned upon his handsome features. He endeavoured to fix his attention on the volume beneath his eyes; but his thoughts were evidently far away from the subject of his studies. At length, as if to compose his mind, he turned abruptly towards his writing-desk, and took thence a note which he had already perused a thousand times, and every word of which was indelibly stamped upon his memory.

We can suppose a traveller upon Saara's burning desert,—sinking beneath fatigue, and oppressed by a thirst, the agony of which becomes maddening. Presently he reaches a well: it is deep and difficult of access;—nevertheless, the traveller's life or death reposes at the bottom of that well. In like manner did Markham's only hope lay in that letter.

No wonder, then, that he read it so often; no marvel that he referred to it when his mind was afflicted, and when the wing of his spirit was oppressed by the dense atmosphere of despair.

And yet the contents of that letter were simple and laconic enough:

"Richmond.

"The Countess Alteroni presents her compliments to Mr. Markham, and begs to acknowledge Mr. Markham's letter of yesterday's date.

"The Countess expresses her most sincere thanks for a communication which prevented an arrangement that, under the circumstances disclosed, would have proved a serious family calamity."

"Yes—Isabella is saved!" said Markham to himself, as his eyes wandered over the contents of that most welcome note, which he had received some days previously: "it is impossible to mistake the meaning of that last sentence. She is saved—and I have been the instrument of her salvation! I have rescued her from an union with a profligate, an adventurer, a man of infamous heart! Surely—surely her parents will admit that I have paid back a portion of the debt of gratitude which their kindness imposed upon me! Yes—the countess herself seems to hold out a hope of reconciliation;—that note bids me hope! It is more than coldly polite—it is confidential:—it gives me to understand the results of my own letter denouncing the miscreant George Montague Greenwood."

Richard's countenance brightened as he reasoned thus within himself. But in a few moments, a dark cloud again displaced that gleam of happiness.

"Enthusiastic visionary that I am!" he murmured to himself. "I construe common politeness into a ground of hope: I fancy that every bird I see—however ill-omened—is a dove of promise, with an olive-branch in its mouth! Alas! mine is a luckless fate—and God alone can tell what strange destinies yet await me."

He rose from his chair, and walked to the window. The rain, which had poured down in torrents all the morning, had ceased; and the afternoon was fine and unusually warm for the early part of January. He glanced towards the hill, whereon the two trees stood, and thought of his brother—that much-loved brother, of whose fate he was kept so cruelly ignorant!

While he was standing at the window, buried in profound thought, and with his eyes fixed upon the hill, he heard a light step near him; and in a moment Ellen Monroe was by his side.

"Do I intrude, Richard?" she exclaimed. "I knocked twice at the door; and not receiving any reply, imagined that there was no one here. I came to change a book. But you—you are thoughtful and depressed."

"I was meditating upon a topic which to me is always fraught with distressing ideas," answered Markham: "I was thinking of my brother!"

"Your brother," ejaculated Ellen; and her countenance became ashy pale.

"Yes," continued Richard, not observing her emotion; "I would rather know the worst—if misfortunes have really overtaken him—than remain in this painful state of suspense. If he be prosperous, why should he stay away? if poor, why does he not seek consolation with me?"

"Perhaps," said Ellen, hesitatingly, "perhaps he is—in reality—much better off than—than—any one who feels interested in him."

"Heaven knows!" ejaculated Markham. "But ere now you observed that I was melancholy and dispirited; and I have told you wherefore. Ellen, I must make the same charge against you."

"Against me!" cried the young lady, with a start, while at the same time a deep blush suffused her cheeks.

"Yes, against you," continued Richard, now glancing towards her. "You may think that I am joking—but I never was more serious in my life. For the few days that you have been in this house, you have been subject to intervals of profound depression."

"I!" repeated Ellen, the hue of her blushes becoming more intensely crimson, as her glances sank confusedly beneath those of Markham.

"Alas! Ellen," answered Richard, "I have myself been too deeply initiated in the mysteries of adversity and sorrow,—I have drunk too deeply of the cup of affliction,—I have experienced too much bitter, bitter anguish, not to be able to detect the presence of unhappiness in others. And by many signs, Ellen, have I discovered that you are unhappy. I speak to you as a friend—I do not wish to penetrate into your secrets;—but if there be any thing in which I can aid you—if there be aught wherein my poor services or my counsels may be rendered available,—speak, command me!"

"Oh! Richard," cried Ellen, tears starting into her eyes, "how kind—how generous of you thus to think of me—you who have already done so much for my father and myself!"

"Were you not the companion of my childhood, Ellen? and should I not be to you as a brother, and you to me as a sister? Let me be your brother, then—and tell me how I can alleviate the weight of that unhappiness which is crushing your young heart!"

"A brother!" exclaimed Ellen, almost wildly: "yes—you shall—you must be a brother to me! And I will be your sister! Ah there is consolation in that idea!"—then, after a moment's pause, she added, "But the time is not yet come when I, as a sister, shall appeal to you as a brother for that aid which a brother alone can give! And until then—ask me no more—speak to me no farther upon the subject—I implore you!"

Ellen pressed Richard's hand convulsively, and then hurried from the room.

Markham had scarcely recovered from the astonishment into which these last words had thrown him,—words which, coming from the lips of a young and beautiful girl, were fraught with additional mystery and interest,—when Whittingham entered the library.

"A young lad, Master Richard," said the old butler, "has called about the situation which is vacated in our household. I took the percaution of leaving word yesterday with the people at a public of most dubitable respectability called the *Servants' Arms*, where I call now and then when I go into town; and it appears that this young lad having called in there quite perspicuously this morning heard of the place."

"Let him step in, Whittingham," said Markham. "I will speak to him—although, to tell you the truth, I do not admire a public-house recommendation."

Whittingham made no reply, but opening the door, exclaimed, "Step in here, young man; step in here."

And Henry Holford stood in the presence of Richard Markham.

Whittingham retired.

"I believe you are in want of a young lad, sir," said Holford, "to assist in the house."

"I am," answered Markham. "Have you ever served in that capacity before?"

"No, sir; but if you would take me and give me a trial, I should feel very much obliged. I have neither father or mother, and am totally dependant upon my own exertions."

These words were quite sufficient to command the attention and sympathy of the generous-hearted Richard. The lad was moreover of superior manners, and well-spoken; and there was something in his appeal to Markham which was very touching.

"What have you been before, my good lad?"

"To tell you the truth, sir," was the reply, "I have been a simple pot-boy in a public-house."

"And of course the landlord will give you a character?"

"Yes—for honesty and industry, sir; but—"

"But what?"

"I do not think it is of any use to apply to that landlord for a character, because—"

"Because what?" demanded Markham, seeing that the young man again hesitated. "If you can have a character for honesty and industry, you need not be afraid of anything else that could be said of you."

"The truth is, sir," answered Holford, "I absented myself without leave, and remained away for two or three days: then, when I returned this morning at a very early hour I refused to give an account of my proceedings. That is the whole truth, sir; and if you will only give me a trial—"

"There is something very straightforward and ingenuous about you," said Markham: "perhaps you would have no objection to tell me how you were occupied during your absence."

"That, sir, is impossible! But I declare most solemnly that I did nothing for which I can reproach myself—unless," added Holford, "it was in leading a couple of villains to believe that I would do a certain thing which I never once intended to do."

"Really your answers are so strange," cried Richard, "that I know not what to say to you. It however appears from your last observation that two villains tempted you to do something wrong—that you led them to believe you would fall into their plans—and that you never meant to fulfil your promise."

"It is all perfectly true, sir. They proposed a certain scheme in which I was to be an agent: I accepted the office they assigned to me, because it suited my disposition, and promised to gratify my curiosity in a way where it was deeply interested."

"And how did you explain your conduct to the two men whom you speak of?" inquired Richard, not knowing what to think of the young lad, but half inclining to believe that his brain was affected.

"I invented certain excuses, sir," was Holford's reply, "which completely damped their ardour in the matter alluded to. And now, sir, will you give me a trial? I feel convinced you will: had I not thought so from the very beginning, I should not have spoken so freely as I have done."

"I am disposed to assist you—I am desirous to meet your wishes," said Markham. "Still, your representations are rather calculated to awaken fears than clear up doubts concerning you. What guarantee can you offer that you will never see those two villains again? what security—"

"Sir," said Holford, "your own manner is so frank and kind—so very condescending, indeed, to a poor lad like me—that I would not deceive you for the world. I *had* promised to meet those men tonight—for the last time—"

"To meet them again?"

"Yes, sir—to receive the reward promised for the service which I undertook—"

"Ah! young man," cried Markham, "this is most imprudent—if not actually criminal! and where was this precious interview to take place?"

"At the *Dark-House*, sir—"

"The *Dark-House!*" ejaculated Markham: "what—a low tavern in Brick Lane, Spitalfields?"

"The same, sir."

"And the names of the two men?" demanded Richard hastily.

"Their right names and those by which they are commonly known amongst their own set, are very different," said Holford.

"How are they known? what are they called in their own infamous sphere?" cried Markham, his impatience amounting almost to a fever: "speak!"

"I do not know whether I shall be doing right," said Holford, hesitating,—"perhaps I have already told you too much—"

"Speak, I say!" cried Richard, taking Holford by the collar of his jacket; "speak. You do not know—you cannot guess how necessary it is for me to have my present suspicions cleared up! Speak—I swear no harm shall happen to you: on the contrary—I will reward you, if it should turn out as I suppose. Once more, who are these villains?"

"They are called—"

"What? speak—speak!"

"The Resurrection Man—"

"Ah!"

"And the Cracksman."

"Then I am right—my suspicions are confirmed!" ejaculated Markham, relinquishing his hold upon Holford's jacket, and throwing himself upon a chair. "Sit down, my good lad—sit down: you and I have not done with each other yet."

The young man appeared alarmed by Richard's exclamations and manners, and seemed undecided whether to remain where he was or attempt to escape.

Richard divined what was passing in the lad's bosom, and hastened to reassure him.

"Sit down—and fear nothing. I swear most solemnly that no harm shall happen to you, be you who or what you may: for I cannot suppose that you are a participator in the crimes of these miscreants. You would not have come to me to tell me all this—Oh! no; Providence has sent you hither this day."

Holford took a seat, wondering how this extraordinary scene was to terminate.

"Are you aware of the pursuits of those two men whom you have named—I mean the full extent of the atrocity of their pursuits?" demanded Richard, after a few moments' pause.

"I know that they are body-snatchers and burglars, sir," answered Holford: "indeed it was a burglary of which they would have made me the instrument; but, oh! sir—believe me, I am incapable of such a crime; and the representations I have made to them have induced them to abandon all idea of it."

"And you are not aware, then," continued Richard, "that they are more than body-snatchers and burglars?"

"More, sir!" repeated Holford in a tone of unfeigned surprise: "Oh! no, sir—how can they be more than that?"

"They are more—far more," rejoined Markham with a shudder: "they are murderers!"

"Murderers!" ejaculated Holford, starting from his chair with mingled emotions of horror and alarm.

"Yes—murderers of the most diabolical and cold-blooded description," said Markham. "But it is too long a tale to tell you now. Let it suffice for you to know that I was myself upon the point of becoming a victim to that most infernal of all miscreants, the Resurrection Man; and I should conceive that the other whom you named is in all respects as bad as he!"

"Murderers!" repeated Holford, his mental eyes fixed, by a horrible and snake-like fascination, upon the fearful idea now suddenly engendered in his imagination.

"Murderers," echoed Markham solemnly; "and through you must they be surrendered up to justice!"

"Through me!" cried Holford.

"Yes—through you. If you be really imbued with such honourable feelings as you ere now professed, you will not hesitate for one moment in discharging this duty towards society."

"But it would be an odious act of treachery on my part," said Holford, "let the men be what they may."

"If you manifest such a reluctance to rid the metropolis of two murderers," cried Markham angrily, "I shall conceive that you are more intimately connected with them than you choose to admit. But if you imagine that these villains are more innocent than I describe them—if you fancy that some motive prompts me to exaggerate their infamy, I will tell you that no language can enhance their guilt—no vengeance be too severe. Have you not heard that men have disappeared in a most strange and mysterious manner within the last year, at the eastern end of the metropolis,—disappeared without leaving a trace behind them,—men who were not in that situation which hurries the despairing wretch on to suicide? You must have heard of this! If not, learn the dismal fact now from my lips! But the assassins—the dark and secret assassins of these numerous victims, are the wretches whom we shall this night lodge in the grasp of justice!"

"As you will, sir," said Holford, awe-inspired by the solemnity of Markham's voice, and the impressiveness of his manner. "I was to meet them at the *Dark-House* at nine o'clock: do you take measures to secure them."

"Most assuredly I will," returned Markham emphatically. "And when I think of all that you have told me, my good lad," continued Richard, "I am inclined to believe that you yourself would have been a victim to those wretches."

"Me!" exclaimed Holford, horror-struck at the mere idea.

"Yes—such is now my conviction. They made an appointment with you at the *Dark-House*, to give you a sum of money you say?"

"Yes, sir."

"Foolish boy! Do such men pay their agents or accomplices who fail to fulfil their designs, or who deceive them? do such men part with their money so readily—that money which they encounter so many perils to obtain? And that *Dark-House*—the place of your appointment,—that *Dark-House* is in the immediate neighbourhood of the head-quarters of their crimes! Yes—there cannot be a doubt: *you* also were to be a victim!"

"My God! what a fearful danger have I incurred!" ejaculated Holford, shuddering from head to foot, as Markham thus addressed him; then, when he called to mind the ferocity with which the Cracksman menaced him with his knife, and the coaxing manner in which the Resurrection Man had engaged him to form the appointment for the evening, he felt convinced that the dread suspicion was a correct one.

"You say that the hour of meeting is fixed for nine?" cried Markham, after a few minutes' reflection.

"Yes, sir; and now let me thank you with the most unfeigned sincerity for having thus saved me from a dreadful death. Your kindness and condescension have led to a lengthy conversation between us; and accident has made me reveal to you those particulars which have led you to form that conclusion relative to the fate destined for myself. You must not imagine for a moment that I would league with such villains in any of their diabolical plans. No, sir—I would sooner be led forth to the place of execution this minute. Although I consented to do their bidding in one respect, I repeat—that I had mine own curiosity to gratify—that is, my own inclinations to serve: but when they wished to make me their instrument and tool in forwarding their unholy motives, I shrank back in dismay. Oh! yes, sir—now I comprehend the entire infamy of those men's characters: I see from what a fearful abyss I have escaped."

There was again something so sincere and so natural in the manner and emphasis of this young lad, that Markham surveyed him with sentiments of mingled interest and surprise. Then all the thoughts of our hero were directed towards the one grand object he had in view—that of delivering a horde of ruffians over to justice.

"The gang may be more numerous than I imagine," said Markham; "indeed, I know that there are a third man and a hideous woman connected with those two assassins whom you have already named. It will therefore be advisable to lay such a trap that will lead to the capture of them all."

"Oh! by all means, sir," exclaimed Holford, enthusiastically: "I do not wish to show them any mercy now!"

"We have no time to lose: it is now four o'clock," said Markham; "and we must arrange the plan of proceeding with the police. You will accompany me on this enterprise."

"Mr. Markham," returned Holford, respectfully but firmly, "I have no objection to aid you in any shape or way in capturing these miscreants, and rooting out their head quarters; but I must beg of you not to place me in a position where I shall be questioned how I came to make this appointment for to-night with those two wretches. It would compel me to make a revelation of the manner in which I employed my time during the last few days; and *that*—for certain reasons—I could not do!"

Markham appeared to reflect profoundly.

"I do not see how your presence can be dispensed with," he observed at the expiration of some minutes. "In order to discover the exact spot where the murderers dwell, it will be advisable for you to allow yourself to be inveigled thither, and myself and the police would be close behind you."

"Oh! never—never, sir!" cried Holford, turning deadly pale. "Were you to miss us only for a moment—or were you to force an entrance a single instant too late—my life would be sacrificed to those wretches."

"True—true," said Markham: "it would be too great a risk in a dark night—in narrow streets, and with such desperadoes as those. No—I must devise some other means to detect the den of this vile gang. But first of all I must communicate with the police. You can remain here until my return. To-morrow inquiry shall be made relative to your honesty and industry; and, those points satisfactorily ascertained, I will take you into my service, without asking any farther questions."

Holford expressed his gratitude for this kindness on the part of Markham, and was then handed over to the care of Whittingham.

Having partaken of some hasty refreshment, and armed himself with a brace of pistols, in preparation for his enterprise, Richard proceeded with all possible speed into London.

CHAPTER LXV.

THE WRONGS AND CRIMES OF THE POOR.

THE parlour of the *Dark-House* was, as usual, filled with a very tolerable sprinkle of queer-looking customers. One would have thought, to look at their beards, that there was not a barber in the whole district of the Tower Hamlets; and yet it appears to be a social peculiarity, that the lower the neighbourhood, the more numerous the shaving-shops. Amongst the very rich classes, nobles and gentlemen are shaved by their valets: the males of the middle grade shave themselves; and the men of the lower orders are shaved at barbers' shops. Hence the immense number of party-coloured poles projecting over the pavement of miserable and dirty streets, and the total absence of those signs in wealthy districts.

The guests in the *Dark-House* parlour formed about as pleasant an assemblage of scamps as one could wish to behold. The establishment was a notorious resort for thieves and persons of the worst character; and no one who frequented it thought it worth while to shroud his real occupation beneath an air of false modesty. The conversation in the parlour, therefore, usually turned upon the tricks and exploits of the thieves frequenting the place; and many entertaining autobiographical sketches were in this way delivered. Women often constituted a portion of the company in the parlour; and they were invariably the most noisy and quarrelsome of all the guests. Whenever the landlord was compelled to call in the police, to have a clearance of the house—a proceeding to which he only had recourse when his guests were drunk and penniless, and demanded supplies of liquor upon credit,—a woman was sure to be at the bottom of the row; and a virago of Spitalfields would think no more of smashing every window in the house, or dashing out the landlord's brains with one of his own pewter-pots, than of tossing off a tumbler of raw gin without winking.

On the evening of which we are writing there were several women in the parlour of the *Dark-House*. These horrible females were the "blowens" of the thieves frequenting the house, and the principal means of disposing of the property stolen by their paramours. They usually ended by betraying their lovers to the police, in fits of jealousy; and yet—by some strange infatuation on the part of those lawless men—the women who acted in this way speedily obtained fresh husbands upon the morganatic system. For the most part, these females are disfigured by intemperance; and their conversation is far more revolting than that of the males. Oh! there is no barbarism in the whole world so truly horrible and ferocious—so obscene and shameless—as that which is found in the poor districts of London!

Alas! what a wretched mockery it is to hold grand meetings at Exeter Hall, and proclaim, with all due pomp and ceremony, how many savages in the far-off islands of the globe have been converted to Christianity, when here—at home, under our very eyes—even London itself swarms with infidels of a more dangerous character:—how detestable is it for philanthropy to be exercised in clothing negroes or Red Men thousands of miles distant, while our own poor are cold and naked at our very doors:—how monstrously absurd to erect twelve new churches in Bethnal Green, and withhold the education that would alone enable the poor to appreciate the doctrines enunciated from that dozen of freshly-built pulpits!

But to return to the parlour of the *Dark-House*.

In one corner sate the Resurrection Man and the Cracksman, each with a smoking glass of gin-and-water before him. They mingled but little in the conversation, contenting themselves with laughing an approval of any thing good that fell upon their ears, and listening to the discourse that took place around them.

"Now, come, tell us, Joe," said a woman with eyes like saucers, hair like a bundle of tow, and teeth like dominoes, and addressing herself to a man who was dressed like a coal-heaver,—"tell us, Joe, how you come to be a prig?"

"Ah! do, Joe—there's a good feller," echoed a dozen voices, male and female.

"Lor' it's simple enough," cried the man thus appealed to: "every poor devil must become a thief in time."

"That's what you say, Tony," whispered the Cracksman to the Resurrection Man.

"Of course he must," continued the coal-heaver, "more partickler them as follows my old trade—for though I've got on the togs of a whipper, I ain't one no longer. The dress is convenient—that's all."

"The Blue-bottles don't twig—eh?" cried the woman with the domino teeth.

"That's it: but you asked me how I come to be a prig—I'll tell you. My father was a coal-whipper, and had three sons. He brought us all up to be coal-whippers also. My eldest brother was drownded in the pool one night when he was drunk, after only drinking about two pots of the publicans' beer: my other brother died of hunger in Cold-Bath Fields prison, where he was sent for three months for taking home a bit of coal one night to his family when he couldn't get his wages paid him by the publican that hired the gang in which he worked. My father died when he was forty—and any one to have seen him would have fancied he was sixty-five at least—so broke down was he with hard work and drinking. But no coal-whipper lives to an old age: they all die off at about forty—old men in the wery prime of life."

"And why's that?" demanded the large-toothed lady.

"Why not?" repeated the man. "Because a coal-whipper isn't a human being—or if he is, he isn't treated as such: and so I've always thought he must be different from the rest of the world."

"How isn't he treated like any one else?"

"In the first place, he doesn't get paid for his labour in a proper way. Wapping swarms with low public-houses, the landlords of which act as middle-men between the owners of the colliers and the men that's hired to unload 'em. A coal-whipper can't get employment direct from the captain of the collier: the working of the collier is farmed by them landlords I speak of; and the whipper must apply at their houses. Those whippers as drinks the most always gets employment first; and whether a whipper chooses to drink beer or not, it's always sent three times a-day on board the colliers for the gangs. And, my eye! what stuff it is! Often and often have we throwed it away, 'cos we couldn't possibly drink it—and it must be queer liquor that a coal-whipper won't drink!"

"I should think so too. But go on."

"Well, I used to earn from fifteen to eighteen shillings a-week; and out of that, eight was always stopped for the beer; and if I didn't spend another or two on Saturday night when I received the balance, the landlord set me down as a stingy feller and put a cross agin my name in his book."

"What was that for?"

"Why, not to give me any more work till he was either forced to do so for want of hands, or I made it up with him by standing a crown bowl of punch. So what with one thing and another, I had to keep myself, my wife, and three children, on about seven or eight shillings a-week—after working from light to dark."

"And now your wife and children is better purvided for?" said the woman with the huge teeth.

"Yes—indeed! in the workus," answered the man, sharply. "So now you see what a coal-whipper's life is. He can't be a sober man if he wishes to—because he must pay for a certain quantity of drink; and so of course he won't throw it away, unless it's so bad he can't keep it on his stomach."

"And was that often the case?"

"Often and often. Well—he can't be a saving man, because he has no chance of getting his wages under his own management. He is the publican's slave—the publican's tool and instrument. Negro slavery is nothing to it. No tyranny is equal to the tyranny of them publicans."

"And why isn't the plan altered?"

"Ah! why? What do the owners of the colliers, or the people that the cargo's consigned to, care about the poor devils that unload? The publicans takes the unloading on contract, and employs the whippers in such a way as to get an enormous profit. Talk of appealing to the owners—what do they care? There has been meetings got up to change the system—and what's the consekvence? Why, them whippers as attended them became marked men, never got no more employment, and drownded themselves in despair, or turned prigs like me."

"Ah! that's better than suicide."

"Well—I don't know, now! But them meetings as I was a-speaking of, got up deputations to the Court of Aldermen, and the matter was referred to the Coal and Corn Committee—and there was, as usual, a great talk, but nothink done. Then an application was made to some Minister—I don't know which; and he sent back a letter with a seal as big as a crown-piece, just to say that he'd received the application, and would give it his earliest attention. Some time passed away, and no more notice was ever taken of it in that quarter; and so, I s'pose, a Minister's earliest attention means ten or a dozen years."

"What a shame to treat people so."

"It's only the poor that's treated so. And now I think I have said enough to show why I turned prig, like a many more whippers from the port of London. There isn't a more degraded, oppressed, and brutalised set of men in the world than the whippers. They are born with examples of drunken fathers afore their eyes; and drunken fathers makes drunken mothers; and drunken parents makes sons turn out thieves, and daughters prostitutes;—and that's the existence of the coal-whippers of Wapping. It ain't their fault: they haven't edication and self-command to refuse the drink that's forced upon them, and that they must pay for;—and their sons and daughters shouldn't be blamed for turning out bad. How can they help it? And yet one reads in the papers that the upper classes is always a-crying out about the dreadful immorality of the poor!"

"The laws—the laws, you see, Tony," whispered the Cracksman to his companion.

"Of course," answered the Resurrection Man. "Here we are, in this room, upwards of twenty thieves and prostitutes: I'll be bound to say that the laws and the state of society made eighteen of them what they are."

"Nobody knows the miseries of a coal-whipper's life," continued the orator of the evening, "but him that's been in it his-self. He is always dirty—always lurking about public-houses when not at work—always ready to drink—always in debt—and always dissatisfied with his own way of living, which isn't, however, his fault. There's no hope for coal-whippers or their families. The sons that don't turn out thieves must lead the same terrible life of cart-horse labour and constant drinking, with the certainty of dying old men at forty;—and the daughters that don't turn out prostitutes marry whippers, and draw down upon their heads all the horrors and sorrows of the life I have been describing."

"Well—I never knowed all this before!"

"No—and there's a deal of misery of each kind in London that isn't known to them as dwells in the other kinds of wretchedness: and if these things gets represented in Parliament, the cry is, '*Oh! the people's always complaining; they're never satisfied!*'"

"Well, you speak of each person knowing his own species of misery, and being ignorant of the nature of the misery next door," said a young and somewhat prepossessing woman, but upon whose face intemperance and licentiousness had made sad havoc; "all I can say is, that people see girls like us laughing and joking always in public—but they little know how we weep and moan in private."

"Drink gin then, as I do," cried the woman with the large teeth.

"Ah! *you* know well enough," continued the young female who had previously spoken, "that we *do* drink a great deal too much of that! My father used to sell *jiggered* gin in George Yard, Whitechapel."

"And what the devil is jiggered gin?" demanded one of the male guests.

"It's made from molasses, beer, and vitriol. Lor', every one knows what jiggered gin is. Three wine glasses of it will make the strongest man mad drunk. I'll tell you one thing," continued the young woman, "which you do not seem to know—and that is, that the very, very poor people who are driven almost to despair and suicide by their sorrows, are glad to drink this jiggered gin, which is all that they can afford. For three halfpence they may have enough to send them raving; and then what do they think or care about their miseries?"

"Ah! very true," said the coal whipper. "I've heard of this before."

"Well—my father sold that horrid stuff," resumed the young woman; "and though he was constantly getting into trouble for it, he didn't mind; but the moment he came out of prison, he took to his old trade again. I was his only child; and my mother died when I was about nine years old. She was always drunk with the jiggered gin; and one day she fell into the fire and was burnt to death. I had no one then who cared any thing for me, but used to run about in the streets with all the boys in the neighbourhood. My father took in lodgers, and sixteen or seventeen of us, boys and girls all huddled together, used to sleep in one room not near so big as this. There was fifteen lodging houses of the same kind in George Yard at that time; and it was supposed that about two hundred and seventy-five persons used to sleep in those houses every night, male and female lodgers all pigging together. Every sheet, blanket, and bolster, in my father's house was marked with STOP THIEF, in large letters. Well—at eleven years old I went upon the town; and if I didn't bring home so much money every Saturday night to my father, I used to be well thrashed with a rope's end on my bare back."

"Serve you right too, a pretty girl like you."

"Ah! you may joke about it—but it was no joke to me! I would gladly have done anything in an honest way to get my livelihood—"

"Like me, when I was young," whispered the Resurrection Man to his companion.

"Exactly. Let's hear what the gal has got to say for herself," returned the Cracksman; "the lush has made her sentimental;—she'll soon be crying drunk."

"But I was doomed, it seemed," continued the young woman, "to live in this horrible manner. When I was thirteen or fourteen my father died, and I was then left to shift for myself. I moved down into Wapping, and frequented the long-rooms belonging to the public-houses there. I was then pretty well off; because the sailors that went to these places always had plenty of money and was very generous. But I was one night suspected of hocussing and robbing a sailor, and—though if I was on my death-bed I could swear that I never had any hand in the affair at all—I was so blown upon that I was forced to shift my quarters. So I went to a *dress-house*[1] in Ada Street, Hackney Road. All the remuneration I received there was board and lodging; and I was actually a slave to the old woman that kept it. I was forced to walk the streets at night with a little girl following me to see that I did not run away; and all the money I received I was forced to give up to the old woman. While I was there, several other girls were turned out of doors, and left to die in ditches or on dunghills, because they were no longer serviceable. All this frightened me. And then I was so ill-used, and more than half starved. I was forced to turn out in all weathers—wet or dry—hot or cold—well or ill. Sometimes I have hardly been able to drag myself out of bed with sickness and fatigue—but, no matter, out I must go—the rain perhaps pouring in torrents, or the roads knee-deep in snow—and nothing but a thin cotton gown to wear! Winter and summer, always flaunting dresses—yellow, green, and red! Wet or dry, always silk stockings

1 dress-house: a brothel.

and thin shoes! Cold or warm, always short skirts and a low body, with strict orders not to fasten the miserable scanty shawl over the bosom! And then the little girl that followed me about was a spy with wits as sharp as needles. Impossible to deceive her! At length I grew completely tired of this kind of life; and so I gave the little spy the slip one fine evening. I was then sixteen, and I came back to this neighbourhood. But one day I met the old woman who kept the dress-house, and she gave me in charge for stealing wearing apparel—the clothes I had on my back when I ran away from her!"

"Always the police—the police—the police, when the poor and miserable are concerned," whispered the Resurrection Man to the Cracksman.

"But did the inspector take the charge?" demanded the coal-heaver.

"He not only took the charge," answered the unfortunate girl, "but the magistrate next morning committed me for trial, although I proved to him that the clothes were bought with the wages of my own prostitution! Well, I was tried at the Central Criminal Court—"

"And of course acquitted?"

"No—found *Guilty*——"

"What—by an English jury?"

"I can show you the newspaper—I have kept the report of the trial ever since."

"Then, by G—d, things are a thousand times worse than I thought they was!" ejaculated the coal-whipper, striking his clenched fist violently upon the table at which he was seated.

"But the jury recommended me to mercy," continued the unfortunate young woman, "and so the Recorder only sentenced me to twenty-one days' imprisonment. His lordship also read me a long lecture about the errors of my ways, and advised me to enter upon a new course of life; but he did not offer to give me a character, nor did he tell me how I was to obtain honest employment without one."

"That's the way with them beaks," cried one of the male inmates of the parlour: "they can talk for an hour; but supposing you'd said to the Recorder, '*My Lord, will your wife take me into her service as scullery-girl?*' he would have stared in astonishment at your imperence."

"When I got out of prison," resumed the girl who was thus sketching the adventures of her wretched life, "I went into Great Titchfield Street. My new abode was a dress-house kept by French people. Every year the husband went over to France, and returned with a famous supply of French girls, and in the mean time his wife decoyed young English women up from the country, under pretence of obtaining situations as nursery-governesses and lady's-maids for them. Many of these poor creatures were the daughters of clergymen and half-pay officers in the marines. The moment a new supply was obtained by these means, circulars was sent round to all the persons that was in the habit of using the house. Different sums, from twenty to a hundred pounds—"

"Ah! I understand," said the coal-whipper. "But did you ever hear say how many unfortunate gals there was in London?"

"Eighty thousand. From Titchfield Street I went into the Almonry, Westminster. The houses there are all occupied by *fences*, prigs, and gals of the town."

"And the parsons of Westminster Abbey, who is the landlords of the houses, does nothink to put 'em down," said the coal-whipper.

"Not a bit," echoed the young woman, with a laugh. "We had capital fun in the house where I lived—dog-fighting, badger-baiting, and drinking all day long. The police never visits the Almonry—"

"In course not, 'cos it's the property of the parsons. They wouldn't be so rude."

This coarse jest was received with a shout of laughter; and the health of the Dean and Chapter of Westminster was drunk amidst uproarious applause, by the thieves and loose women assembled in the *Dark-House* parlour.[1]

---

1 The causes which produce prostitution are as follows:

I. Natural causes:—1. Licentiousness of inclination. 2. Irritability of temper. 3. Pride and love of dress. 4. Dishonesty, and desire of property. 5. Indolence.

II. Accidental causes:—1. Seduction. 2. Inconsiderate and ill-sorted marriages. 3. Inadequate remuneration for female work. 4. Want of employment. 5. Intemperance. 6. Poverty. 7. Want of proper looking after their servants on the part of masters and mistresses. 8. Ignorance. 9. Bad example of parents. 10. Harsh and unkind treatment by parents and other relations. 11. Attendance on evening dancing schools, and dancing parties. 12. Theatre-going. 13. The publication of improper works, and obscene prints. 14. The countenance and reward given to vice. 15. The small encouragement given to virtue.

The proportions amongst those females who have deviated from the path of virtue may be quoted as follows:—

1. One-fourth from being servants in taverns and public-houses, where they have been seduced by men frequenting these places of dissipation and temptation.

2. One-fourth from the intermixture of the sexes in factories, and those employed

"Well, go on, my dear," said the coal-whipper, when order was somewhat restored.

"I never was in a sentimental humour before to-night—not for many, many years," resumed the young woman; "and I don't know what's making me talk as I am now."

"'Cos you haven't had enough gin, my dear," interrupted a coarse-looking fellow, winking to his companions.

Scarcely was the laughter promoted by this sally beginning to subside, when a short, thick-set, middle-aged man, enveloped in a huge great-coat, with most capacious pockets at the sides, entered the parlour, took his seat near the door, and called for a glass of hot gin-and-water.

---

in workhouses, shops, &c.

3. One-fourth by procuresses, or females who visit country towns, markets, and places of worship, for the purpose of decoying good-looking girls of all classes.

4. One-fourth may be divided into four classes:—1. Such as being indolent, or possessing bad tempers, leave their situations. 2. Those who are driven to that awful course by young men making false promises. 3. Children who have been urged by their mothers to become prostitutes for a livelihood. 4. Daughters of clergymen, half pay officers, &c., who are left portionless orphans. [Reynolds's note.]

CHAPTER LXVI.

THE RESULT OF MARKHAM'S ENTERPRISE.

THE reader at all acquainted with German literature may probably remember some of those old tales of demonology and witchcraft, in which assemblies of jovial revellers are frequently dismayed and overawed by the sudden entrance of some mysterious stranger—perhaps a knight in black armour, with his vizor closed, or a monk with his cowl drawn over his countenance. If the recollection of such an episode in the sphere of romance recur to the reader's mind, he will have no difficulty in comprehending us when we state that the presence of the short, thick-set, middle-aged stranger caused an immediate damp to fall upon the spirits of the company in the *Dark-House* parlour.

The stranger seemed to take no notice of any one present, but drank his grog, lighted his cigar, and settled himself in his seat, apparently with the view of making himself very comfortable.

Still there was something sinister and mysterious about this man, which did not exactly please the other inmates of the room; and as we cannot suppose that the consciences of these persons were over pure, the least appearance of ambiguity to them was an instantaneous omen of danger. Like the dog that scents the corpse of the murdered victim, even when buried deep in the earth, those wretches possessed an instinct marvellously sensitive and acute in perceiving the approach or presence of peril.

And yet, to a common beholder, there was nothing very remarkable about that stranger. He was a plain-looking, quiet, shabbily dressed person, and one who seemed anxious to smoke his cigar in peace, and neither speak nor be spoken to.

Good reader—it was the reserve of this man,—his staid and serious demeanour—his tranquil countenance—and his exclusive manner altogether, that created the unpleasant impression we have described. Had he entered the room with a swagger, banged the door behind him, sworn at the waiter, or nodded to one single individual present, he would have produced no embarrassing sensation whatever. But he was unknown:—what, then, could he do there, where all were well known to each other?

However, he continued to smoke, with his eyes intently fixed upon the blueish wreaths that ascended slowly and fantastically from the end of his cigar; and for five minutes after his entrance not a word was spoken.

At length the coal-whipper broke silence.

"Well, my dear," he said, addressing himself to the unfortunate girl who had already narrated a portion of her adventures, "you haven't done your story yet."

"Oh! I do not feel in the humour to go on with it to-night," she exclaimed, glancing uneasily towards the stranger. "Indeed, I recollect—I have an appointment—close by—"

She hesitated; then, apparently mustering up her courage, cried "Good-night, all," and left the room.

"Who the deuce is that feller, Tony?" demanded the Cracksman, in a whisper, of his companion. "I can't say I like his appearance at all."

"Oh! nonsense," answered the Resurrection Man: "he is some quiet chap that doesn't like to smoke and talk at the same time."

"But don't it seem as how he's throwed a damp on the whole party?" continued the Cracksman, in the same subdued tone.

"Do you take me for a child that's frightened at a shadow?" said the Resurrection Man savagely. "I suppose you're afraid that this young Holford will play us false. Why—what could he do to us? Any thing he revealed would only implicate himself. He knows nothing about our games up by the Bird-cage Walk there."

"I forgot *that*;—no more he doesn't," cried the Cracksman. "There's nobody can do us any harm, that I know on."

"One—and one only," answered the Resurrection Man, sinking his already subdued tone to the lowest possible whisper,—"one only, I say, can injure us; and he will not dare to do it!"

"Who the devil do you mean?" demanded the Cracksman.

"I mean the only man that ever escaped out of the crib up by the walk after he had received a blow from my stick," answered the Resurrection Man.

"You don't mean to say, Tony," whispered the Cracksman, his countenance giving the most unequivocal signs of alarm, "that there's a breathing soul which ever went in the door of that crib an intended wictim, and come out alive agin!"

"Never do you mind now. We shall make all the people stare at us if we go on whispering in this way. Supposing any one *did* mean to nose upon us—haven't we got our barkers in our pocket?"

"Ah! Tony," said the Cracksman, in whose mind these words of his companion seemed to arouse a sudden and most disagreeable idea,—"talking about *nosing* makes me remember someot that I was told a few days ago up in Rat's Castle in the Rookery."

"And what was that?" asked the Resurrection Man, surveying his friend with his serpent-like eyes in a manner that made him actually quail beneath the glance.

"What was it?" repeated the Cracksman, who appeared to hesitate whether he should proceed, or not: "why—I heard a magsman say that you nosed upon poor Crankey Jem, and that was the reason he got lagged and you was acquitted three year ago at the Old Bailey."

"And what did you say to that?" demanded the Resurrection Man, looking from beneath his bushy brows at the Cracksman, as the ghole in eastern mythology may be supposed to gaze on the countenance of him whom he marks for his victim.

"What did I say?" answered the Cracksman in a hoarse whisper: "why—I knocked the fellow down to be sure."

"And you did what you ought to do, and what I should have done if any one had told me *that* of you," said the Resurrection Man in a tone of the most perfect composure.

While this conversation took place, hurriedly and in whispers, the mysterious stranger continued to smoke his cigar without once glancing around him; and the other inmates of the *Dark-House* parlour, recovering a little from their panic at the entrance of that individual, made a faint attempt to renew the discourse.

But although the eyes of the stranger were apparently occupied in watching the wreaths of smoke, as they curled upwards to the ceiling, they were in reality intent upon the parlour window, the lower part of which alone was darkened by the sliding shutter that lifted up and down. There was a bright lamp over the front door of the public-house; and thus the heads of all the passengers in the street might be descried, as they passed the window, by the inmates of the parlour.

"I say, Ben," exclaimed one reveller to another, "have you heerd that they're a goin' to lay out a park up by Bonner's Road and Hackney Wick?"

"Yes—the Wictoria Park," was the reply. "On'y fancy giving them poor devils of Spitalfields weavers a park to walk in instead o' filling their bellies. But I s'pose they'll make a preshus deep pond in it."

"What for?" demanded the first speaker.

"Why—for the poor creturs to drown theirselves in, to be sure."

At this moment the countenance of a man in the street peered for a single instant over the shutter, and was then immediately withdrawn; but not before a significant glance had been exchanged with the stranger sitting in the neighbourhood of the door.

All this, however, remained entirely unnoticed by the male and female revellers in the parlour.

"Well, it's gone nine," whispered the Cracksman to his companion, "and this fellow Holford don't come. It's my opinion he ain't a-going to."

"We'll give him half an hour's grace," returned the Resurrection Man. "The young fool is hard up, and won't let the hope of five couters slip through his brain quite so easy."

"Half an hour's grace, as you say, Tony," whispered the Cracksman; "and then if he don't come: we'll be off—eh?"

"Oh! just as you like," growled the Resurrection Man. "You seem quite chicken-hearted to-night, Tom."

"I don't know how it is," answered the Cracksman; "but I've got a persentiment—as they calls it—of evil. The sight of that there feller there——" and he nodded towards the stranger.

"Humbug!" interrupted the Resurrection Man. "you haven't had grog enough—that's it."

He accordingly ordered the waiter to supply fresh tumblers of hot liquor; and the next half hour slipped away rapidly enough; but no Henry Holford made his appearance.

At a quarter to ten the two villains rose, and, having settled their score, departed.

Scarcely had the parlour door closed behind them, when the short thick-set stranger also retreated precipitately from the room.

Disappointed and in an ill-humour, the Resurrection Man and the Cracksman hurried away from the *Dark-House* towards the den situate in the immediate vicinity of the Bird-cage Walk.

The streets were ankle-deep in mud: a thin mizzling rain was falling; and neither moon nor stars appeared upon the dark and murky field of heaven.

The two men walked one a little in advance of the other, until they reached the top of Brick Lane, where they separated for the purpose of proceeding by different routes towards the same point—a precaution they invariably adopted after quitting any public place in each other's company.

But so well were the arrangements of the police concocted, that while the Resurrection Man continued his way along Tyssen Street, and the Cracksman turned to the right in Church Street until he reached Samuel Street, up which he proceeded, an active officer followed each: while in the neighbourhood of Virginia Street and the Bird-cage Walk numerous policemen were concealed in dark alleys, lone courts, and obscure nooks, ready to hasten to any point whence the spring of rattles might presently emanate.

Also concealed in a convenient hiding-place, and anxiously awaiting the result of the various combinations effected to discover the den of the murderers, Richard Markham was prepared to aid in the operations of the night.

Meantime, the Resurrection Man pursued one route, and the Cracksman another, both converging towards the same point; but neither individual suspected that danger was on every side! They advanced as confidently as the flies that work their way amidst the tangled web of the spider.

At length the Resurrection Man reached his house; and almost at the same moment the other ruffian arrived at the door.

"All right, Tom."

"All right, Tony."

And the Resurrection Man opened the door, by simply pressing his foot forcibly against it in a peculiar manner.

He entered the passage, followed by the Cracksman, which latter individual turned to close the door, when it was burst wide open and half a dozen policemen rushed into the house.

"Damnation!" cried the Resurrection Man; "we are sold!"—and, darting down the passage, he rushed into the little back room, the door of which he succeeded in closing and fastening against the officers.

But the Cracksman had fallen into the hands of the police, and was immediately secured. Rattles were sprung; and the sudden and unexpected din, breaking upon the solemn silence of the place and hour, startled the poor and the guilty in their wretched abodes.

"Break open the door there!" cried the serjeant who commanded the police, and who was no other than the mysterious stranger of the *Dark-House* parlour: "break open that door—and two of you run up stairs this moment!"

As he spoke, a strong light shone from the top of the staircase. The officers cast their eyes in that direction, and beheld a hideous old woman scowling down upon them. In her hand she carried a candle, the light of which was thrown forward in a vivid flood by the reflection of a large bright tin shade.

This horrible old woman was the Mummy.

Already were two of the officers half-way up the staircase,—already was the door of the back room on the ground floor yielding to the strength of a constable,—already were Richard Markham and several officers hurrying down the street towards the spot, obedient to the signal conveyed by the springing of the rattles,—when a terrific explosion took place.

"Good God!" ejaculated Markham: "what can that mean?"

"There—there!" cried a policeman near him: "it is all over with the serjeant and my poor comrades!"

Immediately after the explosion, and while Markham and the officer were yet speaking, a bright column of fire shot up into the air:—millions and millions of sparks, glistening vividly, showered down upon the scene of havoc;—for a moment—a single moment—the very heavens seemed on fire;—then all was black—and silent—and doubly sombre.

The den of the assassins had ceased to exist: it had been destroyed by gunpowder.

The blackened remains and dismembered relics of mortality were discovered on the following morning amongst the ruins, or in the immediate neighbourhood;—but it was impossible to ascertain how many persons had perished on this dread occasion.

CHAPTER LXVII.

SCENES IN FASHIONABLE LIFE.

Two months elapsed from the date of the preceding event.

It was now the commencement of March; and bleak winds had succeeded the hoary snows of winter.

The scene changes to the house of Sir Rupert Harborough, in Tavistock Square.

It was about one o'clock in the afternoon. The baronet was pacing the drawing-room with uneven steps, while Lady Cecilia lounged upon the sofa, turning over the pages of a new novel.

"Now this is most provoking, Cecilia," exclaimed the baronet: "I never was so much in want of money in my life; and you refuse to adopt the only means which——"

"Yes, Sir Rupert," interrupted the lady impatiently; "I refuse to give you my diamonds to pledge again—and all your arguments shall never persuade me to do so."

"Your heart is too good, Cecilia——"

"Oh! yes—you may try what coaxing will do; but I can assure you that I am proof against both honied and bitter words. Neither will serve your turn now."

"And yet, somehow or another, you *have* the command of money, Cecilia," resumed the baronet, after a pause. "You paid all the tradesmen's bills and servants' wages about two months ago: you found out—though God only knows how—that Greenwood had the duplicate of your diamonds;—you redeemed the ticket from him, and the jewels themselves from V——'s; and from that moment you have never seemed embarrassed for a five-pound note."

"All *that* is perfectly true, Sir Rupert," said Lady Cecilia, blushing slightly, and yet smiling archly,—and never did she seem more beautiful than when the glow of shame thus mantled her cheek and poured a flood of light into those eyes that were so expressive of a voluptuous and sensual nature.

"Well, then," continued the baronet, "if you can thus obtain supplies for yourself, surely you can do something in the same way for me."

"I have no ready money at present," said Lady Cecilia; "and I have determined not to part with my jewels. There!"

"Perhaps you think that I am fool enough to be the dupe of your miserable and flimsy artifices, Cecilia?" cried the baronet impatiently: "but I can tell you that I have seen through them all along."

"You!" ejaculated the lady, starting uneasily while her heart palpitated violently, and she felt that her cheeks were crimson.

"Yes—I, Lady Cecilia," answered the baronet. "I am not quite such a fool as you take me for."

"My God, Sir Rupert! what—how—who——" stammered the guilty wife, a cold tremor pervading every limb, although her cheeks appeared to be on fire.

"There! you see that all my suspicions are confirmed," cried the baronet; "your confusion proves it!"

"You cannot say that—that—I have ever given you any cause, Sir Rupert——"

"What? to doubt your word? Oh! no—I can't say that you are in the habit of telling falsehoods generally; but——"

"Sir Rupert!"

"Nay—I will speak out! The fact is, you pretend to have quarrelled with Lady Tremordyn; and it is all nonsense. Your mother supplies you with as much money as you require—and that is the secret!"

"Oh! Sir Rupert—Sir Rupert!" exclaimed Lady Cecilia, suddenly relieved from a most painful state of apprehension, and now comprehending the error under which he was labouring.

"You cannot deny what I affirm, Cecilia. And now that I bethink me, it is most probable that Greenwood himself told Lord Tremordyn (with whom he was intimate at that time, although they have since quarrelled, God only knows what about) of my having placed the duplicate of the diamonds in his hands, and so your father arranged that matter with Greenwood. It is a gross system of duplicity, Cecilia—a gross system; a pretended quarrel merely to prevent me from visiting at the house of my father-in-law. But, by God! I will stand it no longer!"

"What will you do, then?" demanded Lady Cecilia, ironically.

"What will I do? I will go straight off to Lord and Lady Tremordyn, and tell them my mind."

"And Lord and Lady Tremordyn will tell you theirs in return."

"And what can they say, madam, against me?"

"Nay—Sir Rupert, rather ask what they can say for you."

"Oh! you wish to irritate me, madam—you are anxious to quarrel with me," cried the baronet.—"Well—be it so! As for your father and mother, I will tell them that they do not act honourably, nor even prudently, in allowing their son-in-law to live by his wits and be compelled to raise money where he can."

"And they will tell you in reply, that you did not act honourably nor prudently to squander the large sum they gave you when you married their daughter."

"The devil they will!" exclaimed the baronet. "Then, in that case, I shall remind them of the consideration for which the large sum you allude to was given."

"Monster—coward!" cried Lady Cecilia: "do you dare to throw in my teeth the weakness of which I was guilty through excess of love for you?"

"I am sure you need not be so fastidious, Cecilia. To talk of love now, between a man of the world like me and a woman of the world like you, is an absurdity;—and as for the little weakness of which you speak, I repaired it."

"Yes," said the lady, bitterly. "When you saw me kneeling in despair at your feet—and when my mother implored you to save her daughter's honour, you turned a deaf ear to our entreaties—you scorned our prayers: but when my father offered a golden argument——"

"Lady Cecilia—silence, I command you!"

"When he offered a golden argument, I say," continued the lady, with withering scorn,—"when he produced his cheque-book, Sir Rupert Harborough pretended to yield to my entreaties; and as he raised me from the ground—condescendingly—raised me—me, the daughter of a peer—with one hand,—with the other he clutched the bribe! Ah! Sir Rupert—you spoilt a good heart—you trampled a confiding disposition in the dust—when you would not allow yourself to be purchased by my love, but still consented to sell yourself to me for my father's gold! Oh! it was the vile instance of a man prostituting himself for gain, as poor weak woman has so often been doomed to do!"

"Lady Cecilia—I am astonished—I am amazed at the terms in which you allow yourself to address me!" said Sir Rupert Harborough, humiliated and put to shame by these words of keenly cutting satire.

"And now," continued the indignant lady,—"now you solicit me to ruin myself for you—to part with my very ornaments to supply your extravagances,—you, who had no pity upon my tears, no feeling for my anguish, no respect for my honour! No, Sir Rupert Harborough: I have assisted you once—assisted you twice—assisted you thrice—assisted you a hundred times already; and what return have you made me? When you are penniless, you remain at home: when you are in the possession of funds, you remain absent for weeks and weeks together. You may love me no longer, it is true;—and, with regard to myself, I confess that your conduct has long—long ago destroyed all the romance of affection in my bosom. Still a woman cannot endure neglect—at least I thought so a few months ago;—but now—*now*," she added emphatically, as her thoughts wandered to Greenwood, "I am indifferent alike as to your attention or your neglect!"

"At least, Lady Cecilia, you are candid and explicit," said Sir Rupert, biting his lips. "But perhaps you have something more to observe."

"No—nothing," answered the lady coldly; and, with these words, she rose and left the room.

Not many minutes had elapsed since the termination of this "scene," when Mr. Chichester was announced.

"Well, what news with the old man?" demanded the baronet hastily.

"My father will not advance me another shilling until June," answered Chichester, throwing himself upon the sofa; "and as for your bill—he won't look at it. Any thing good with you?"

"Nothing. Lady Cecilia positively refuses to part with the jewels again," said the baronet, stamping his foot with rage.

"And can't you——"

"Can't I what?"

"Can't you help yourself to them in spite of her?" demanded Chichester.

"Impossible!" returned Harborough. "She keeps them under lock and key in her own room; and the door of that room she always locks when she goes out."

"How provoking! If we only had some ready money at this moment," observed Chichester, "we might make a little fortune."

"Yes—town is full—and such opportunities as we might have! By Jove, we *must* raise the wind somewhere."

"You do not think that Greenwood——"

"Oh! no—not for a moment!" cried the baronet, turning very pale as the idea of the forged acceptance of Lord Tremordyn, which would be due in another month, flashed across his mind: "no—I cannot apply to Greenwood for a shilling."

"And after all the pains I have taken in perfecting you in the new dodges with the cards and dice, ready for this season," said Mr. Chichester, in a most lachrymose tone; then, taking a small parcel from his pocket, he continued, "Here are the implements we want, too: every thing prepared—except the money."

"Ah!" exclaimed the baronet, "you have got the things, then, at last?"

"Yes," returned Chichester, opening the parcel and displaying its contents upon the table. "Here are the *scratched dice*, you see. These must be used upon a bare table, because it is necessary to judge by

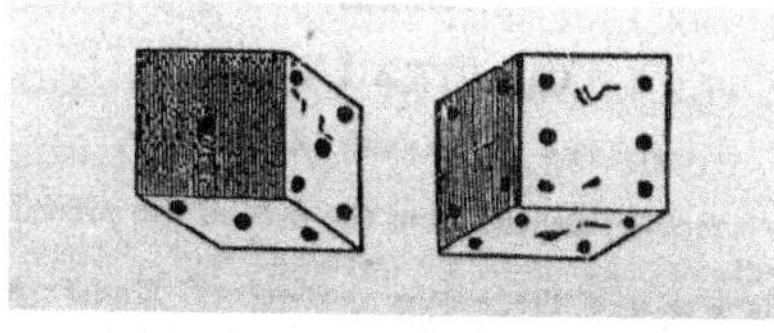

the sound of the dice in the box whether they are on the scratched side or not. You understand that a hole has been drilled in the centre pip of the five in this die, and in the ace of the other: a piece of ebony is then inserted, with a very small portion projecting. These dice cannot, therefore, fall perfectly flat, when the five side of the one and the ace of the other are underneath on the table; and it is very easy for the thrower just to move the box the least thing before he lifts it, so that the sound may tell him whether the scratched side is down or not. But you are to recollect that a man must be very drunk when you can use them with any degree of safety."

"I should think so, indeed," said Sir Rupert.

"I can assure you that no implements of our craft are, on certain occasions, more destructive than these," observed Chichester.

"And what is the use of these slight scratches upon the dice?"

"To assist the eye in manipulating them. But here," continued Chichester, holding up a dice-box, and surveying it with a species of paternal admiration,—"here is a famous antidote to fair dice. Don't you see that when fair dice are used, you must introduce an unfair box. Many a greenhorn may have heard of loaded dice, and so on; but very few know that there is such a thing as the *Doctor Dice-box*. Honour to the man, say I, who invented it. If you judge by the outside of this box, it is a very fair-looking one; but just put your finger into it, and you will feel that no less than three-quarters of the inside are filled up, so that there is now only just space enough left in the middle for the dice to fit in. Towards the top the sides grow larger and smoother. The dice, you see, rattle by rising up and down, when shaken briskly, but do not change their position. All that you have to do is to put them in, in the first instance, with a view to the way in which you want them to come up."

"So that if you want to throw a six and a five, put the dice into the box with the ace and the two uppermost," said the baronet.

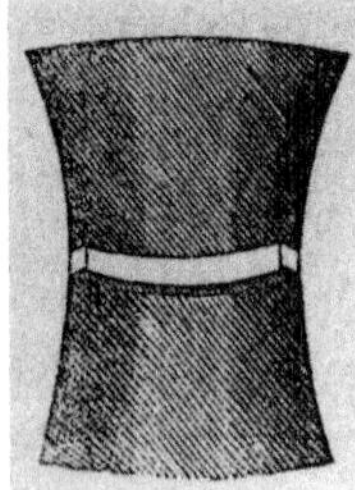

"Precisely," answered Chichester. "A fair box, you know as well as I do, has one or more rims inside, against which the dice must turn in coming out."

"By the bye," said the baronet, "what is the *Gradus*, Chichester? you promised to show me a great many times, and have forgotten it; but now that we are upon the subject, you may as well enlighten me."

"Certainly, my dear fellow," returned this very complacent Mentor; then, taking up a pack of cards, he said, "nothing is more easy than the *Gradus*, or Step. It is often much safer than *Bridging*, too. *Bridging* is known by every snob about town who pretends to set up for a *Greek*. All that you have to do for the *Gradus* is to let any particular card you fancy project a little in this way, so as to make sure that

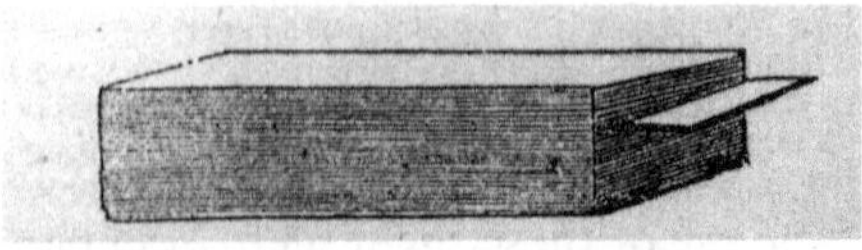

your opponent will turn it up, at whist or ecarté, as the case may be."

"Excellent! I like the plan better than any other you ever yet showed me for effecting the same object."

"*Palming* may sometimes be done successfully," continued

Chichester: "but you must have the small French cards to do it. There—all that there is to do is to secrete a particular card under the palm and partially up the sleeve till it is required. When your opponent is well primed, you can easily introduce a *fifth king*, or *fifth ace*, in this way. There is a great deal of art, too, in shuffling, or *Weaving*. At ecarté or whist, always watch which tricks taken up have the best cards; then, when you take up all the cards to shuffle them again, *weave* in the good tricks to suit your purposes."

"I heard a gentleman say the other night," observed the baronet, "that he had been most gloriously fleeced by a fellow who used *pricked cards*."

"Ah! they are capital weapons," exclaimed Chichester. "Just lay the high cards flat on their backs, and then prick them with a very fine needle,—so as to raise the slightest possible pimple in the world upon the backs down in one of the corners; but mind, the cards are not to be punctured quite through. The fellow who told me how to do this dodge, used some chemical preparation to the ball of his thumb, which made that part almost raw, and consequently so very sensitive that he could feel the smallest possible pimple on the card with the greatest ease."

"And what have you got there?" demanded Sir Rupert, pointing to a pack of cards which Chichester had just taken from his parcel.

"These are *Reflectors*," replied the Mentor. "They are French cards, you perceive, and are only manufactured in France. They cost two guineas a pack; but then—only think of their utility! Look at the backs of these cards: instead of being plain, they are figured. Now this to a common observer is nothing, most of the French cards being, you

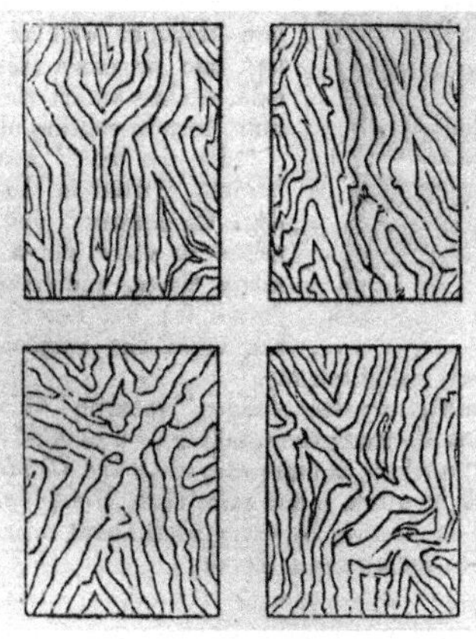

know, variegated with flowers or other designs at the back. But to the initiated, the lines upon these cards are every thing. Mark how they run. All the high cards have semicircles in the corners, while all the low cards have the ends of the lines meeting in the corners. Then, by a more minute study still of these cards, it is easy to know kings, queens, knaves, and aces, by the manner in which the lines run upon the back. I hope these weapons are dangerous enough for you?"

"They are decidedly the most efficient I have yet seen," answered the baronet. "I think we now know all the mysteries of the gaming world and considering how many *flats* there are in London and the watering places, it would be astonishing indeed if we could not pick up a handsome living."

"Of course it would," said Mr. Chichester. "The mania for play is most extraordinary. The moment a young man enters upon life, he fancies that it is very fine to frequent gambling-houses or lose his loose gold at private play: indeed he imagines that he cannot be a *man of the world* without it. There is our advantage. That anxiety to be looked upon as a *fine dashing fellow* is the real cause of the immense increase of gaming propensities. Young men do not begin to play in the first instance because they like it: they commence, simply to gratify their vanity; and then they imbibe the taste and acquire the habit. What they began through pride, they continue through love. There, again, I say, is our pull:—there always will be flats ready to throw themselves head and shoulders into the nets that sharps spread out for them."

"All that is very true, Chichester," said the baronet. "But we don't want a homily on the vice of gambling this afternoon: what we require is the needful to enable us to put our plans into execution. The old tricks that you taught me more than three years ago in that very respectable lodging which you occupied in Bartholomew Close, are well-nigh worn out: we have now studied fresh ones;—but we are totally deficient in the steam to set our new engines in motion."

Chichester was about to reply when a carriage drove up to the front door, and Mr. Greenwood alighted.

CHAPTER LXVIII.

THE ELECTION.

"WELL—it is all right!" exclaimed Mr. Greenwood, the moment he entered the drawing-room, his countenance radiant with joy, and his eyes expressive of triumph.

"What is all right?" demanded both the baronet and Chichester in the same breath.

"Why—have you not heard that the election for Rottenborough took place yesterday?" said Greenwood.

"Oh! to be sure—I forgot that!" observed the baronet. "But you surely never have beaten Lord Tremordyn's candidate?"

"Yes—I was returned triumphantly—814 against 102," said Greenwood.

"I wish you joy, my dear fellow," exclaimed Chichester. "I suppose you astonished the natives of Rottenborough? but how the devil did you manage this victory?"

"I will give you a brief sketch of the whole proceeding," said Greenwood, throwing himself upon the sofa, and playing with his elegant guard-chain. "The fact is, I learnt in the latter part of December that the representative of Rottenborough intended to accept the Chiltern Hundreds when the Houses met in February. You know that I was at that time very intimate with Lord Tremordyn, your worthy and much revered father-in-law, Sir Rupert——"

"Ah! worthy, indeed!" ejaculated the baronet impatiently.

"I accordingly spoke to Lord Tremordyn," continued Greenwood; "and, after a little delicate manœuvring, received his promise to support me,—in fact, to get me in for Rottenborough. It had been arranged that Count Alteroni and his family were to pass the month of January and a portion of February with Lord and Lady Tremordyn; but in the mean time, the count learned something about me, as I before told you, which he did not like; and he rejected me as a suitor for his daughter's hand. That did not grieve me much. My only motives for making up to the signora at all were, because I really liked the girl, and because she is a nobleman's daughter. But the count did not stop there. He sent his apology to Lord and Lady Tremordyn, and declined the invitation. Off goes his lordship to Richmond, and calls upon the count. The count spoke so ill of me, it appears, that his lordship determined to cut me. There seemed at first an insurmountable obstacle to my hopes relative to Rottenborough."

"Yes—but you are never dismayed at any thing," said Chichester.

"Never. There is no such word as *impossible* in my vocabulary," returned Greenwood; "and as for *improbable*—that is a word which can only intimidate cowards. I made up my mind to exert all my energies to obtain the gratification of my wishes. I had set my mind upon becoming an M.P. I had dreamt of it—thought upon it for hours together—and had even based certain calculations and schemes upon the event. I was not to be disappointed. I immediately went down to Rottenborough, and put up at the principal inn. I looked about me for a day or two, and at length saw something that suited me—an old mansion in such a ruined and dilapidated state, that it would require three or four thousand pounds to restore it to a habitable and comfortable condition. It belonged to the banker of the place. I bought it without haggling, and thus made a friend of him. I then set all the masons, carpenters, decorators, and upholsterers in the place to work, paid a considerable sum into the banker's hands, and appointed the head solicitor in the town to be my agent. I moreover gave him certain secret instructions relative to my ultimate views, and returned to London. Every Saturday I went down to Rottenborough—it is only twenty-four miles from London, you know—and paid all the bills without demanding discount. I also sent fifty pounds to the clergyman of the parish to lay out in purchasing blankets for the poor; and paid the coal merchant for fifty tons of coals also for charitable distribution. I always remained at Rottenborough until Monday morning, and went to church three times on the Sundays. No one spoke the responses louder than I did—no one dwelt with such holy delight upon the clergyman's sermons as myself. I moreover won the hearts of the churchwardens, by placing a ten-pound note in the plate, after a charity sermon; and I secured the overseer by visiting the workhouse with him, tasting the soup, and pronouncing the dietary-scale to amount to absolute luxuries. In this manner, I was soon talked about. 'Who is this Mr. Greenwood?' was the universal question. 'A wealthy capitalist of London,' answered the lawyer. Thus, every thing progressed well."

"So I should imagine," observed the baronet.

"Well—parliament met—the representative of Rottenborough resigned his seat; and the next morning by eight o'clock, my lawyer-agent had secured every inn, tavern, and public-house in Rottenborough in my name. Placards were posted all over the town, announcing my intention to come forward in the liberal interest, Lord Tremordyn having always supported the opposite side. Down goes Lord Tremordyn with his candidate, and is quite astonished to see all the walls and houses covered with posters, on which the name of Greenwood appeared in monster-type. But if he were surprised at first, how much more was he compelled to marvel, and how deeply was he annoyed, when not an inn—not a tavern—not even a public-house, would receive him, or his horses. His lordship drove to the rector's. The parson 'was excessively glad to see his lordship, and hoped his lordship would make his (the rector's) house his home; but he (the rector) could not think of entertaining the Conservative candidate also, as he had promised his vote to a gentleman who intended to settle in the place, and who had already done a vast amount of good there.' Lord Tremordyn was astounded. He went to the banker's. Precisely the same answer. The brewer, the coal-merchant, the Chairman of the Board of Poor Law Guardians (who had heard that I admired the soup and considered gruel at nineteen out of twenty-one meals every week, to be actually encouraging in the poor a taste for luxuries) all spoke well of me. Lord Tremordyn grew livid with rage; and he was compelled to take up his quarters, with the new candidate, at the house of the undertaker, whose services I had neglected to secure, not having known upon what possible pretence to order a few coffins."

"Capital!" ejaculated Sir Rupert: "I am glad the old lord was taken in at last—he who fancied himself omnipotent at Rottenborough."

"Every engine of Tory tactics was now put into execution by Lord Tremordyn, his candidate, and his agents. All his tenants who had not paid up their arrears of rent, were menaced with executions and ejectments if they did not vote for the Conservative. My lawyer knew how to counteract this influence. He found out all the tenants who were in arrears, and proffered them loans payable at very distant dates. This accommodation was gladly accepted; and they were of course given to understand that the assistance emanated from me. 'At the same time,' said my lawyer, 'you must not think that this is a mere electioneering manœuvre to secure your support. No—remain free and independent electors. Mr. Greenwood's wishes and objects were merely to defeat tyranny and annihilate intimidation.' In this way we completely weaned his own tenants away from Lord Tremordyn and his cause."

"All this must have cost you a great deal of money," said Chichester.

"Not near so much as you would fancy. But, whatever it was, it was well spent. The position of an M. P. to me is worth thousands and thousands:—I know how to avail myself of it."

"I wish I had your head, Greenwood," exclaimed Sir Rupert Harborough, with a sigh.

"My dear baronet, if you had my head and lacked my perseverance, my industry, and my power of self-command, you would be but little benefited. Let me, however, continue my narrative of the electioneering proceedings. There was now nothing but placarding and counter-placarding. My canvassers were most eloquent in my cause. 'Do not look,' said they, 'to whether a man be Whig or Tory—Radical or Conservative: ascertain whether he will benefit the town—whether he will be charitable to the poor, will support the tradesmen, and will dwell during the recess amongst the inhabitants of Rottenborough. What good have the candidates of the Tremordyn interest ever done for ye, O Rottenboroughers? Has the present candidate an account at the banker's? has he given away blankets and coals wholesale? has he come regularly on Sundays to attend divine service in our parish church three times? has he employed the greater portion of the tradesmen of the town? No—he appears amongst you as a stranger—making fine promises, but having given an earnest of nothing. Look at Greenwood—a man of enormous wealth—known probity—vast experience—high character—splendid qualifications—unlimited charity—and undoubted piety.'"

"I suppose you wrote out all that for your canvassers?" said Chichester.

"No: my lawyer copied a character for me out of an old romance; and it seemed to be admirably appreciated. At length the eventful day—yesterday—came. You may depend upon it, I was up early. My band and colours commenced parading about the town at seven o'clock; and my lawyer had very prudently hired the clown and pantaloon of Richardson's Theatre to attend the band, and amuse the people with their antics during the intervals between the different airs. This told wonderfully well, and, as I afterwards learnt, won thirty-three votes away from Lord Tremordyn's candidate."

"A fact which speaks volumes in favour of the intellectual qualifications of the people of Rottenborough," observed the baronet.

"But the beauty of it was," continued Greenwood, "that my lawyer had the clown in the Guildhall, when my opponent addressed the electors; and the fellow imitated the gesticulations and the facial contortions of Lord Tremordyn's candidate so well, that the speech was drowned in roars of laughter."

"And I suppose that your speech was listened to with the greatest attention?" said Chichester.

"The very greatest," returned Greenwood; "and I can assure you that I pitched them the gammon in the very finest possible style. 'Gentlemen,' I said, 'it is well known that not a single town in this empire contains a more enlightened, intellectual, and independent population than Rottenborough. The inhabitants of Rottenborough are the envy of surrounding cities, and the admiration of the universe. History has ever been busy with the name of Rottenborough; and never has a gallant Rottenborougher disgraced his name, his country, or his cause. This is the chosen home of freedom: if you seek for independence, you will find it in the peaceful groves and delicious retreats of Rottenborough. Famous also is this town for the loveliness and virtue of its women; and beauteous and faithful wives make their husbands and sons good and great. Oh! supremely blessed is the town of Rottenborough, situate in its happy valley, and through whose streets sweep balmy gales, laden with perfume and delicious odour.'—At this moment, the voice of some purblind Tory exclaimed, 'What do you say to the putrid black ditch at the back of the church?' Of course one of my own supporters smashed this ruffian's hat over his eyes; and I then proceeded thus: 'Gentlemen, free and independent electors of Rottenborough! I offer myself as your representative! I throw myself into your arms! I undertake your cause! Tory influence has long blunted your energies: Tory machinations have for years dimmed the bright and brilliant intellects of the Rottenboroughers. Do you ask me what are my principles? I will tell you. I am a liberal in every sense of the word. I am anxious that every free and independent elector of Rottenborough shall have his beef and beer for nothing—which shall be the case to-morrow, if I am returned to-day. I am desirous that the industrious classes should be improved in condition—that they should have more food and less treadmill, and be supplied with flannel to expel the bleak and nipping cold of winter. This want it shall be my duty to supply. But that is not all: I hope to see the day arrive when every pauper in the workhouse at Rottenborough shall thank God for his happy condition, and receive an extra half ounce of bacon for the dinner of the Sabbath! These are my fond aspirations—these are my aims! If I seem to promise much—I am ready to perform it all. Trust me—try me—place me in a condition to be useful to you. I have now expounded to you all my views—I have laid bare my secret soul to your eyes; and heaven can attest the sincerity of my intentions. Under these circumstances I confidently claim your suffrage;—but if it should happen that I am disappointed—if I am forced to shut up the mansion which I have purchased in this neighbourhood, suspend all the works, and fly for ever from the peaceful retreats and delicious haunts of Rottenborough, I shall at least——' Here it was arranged between my lawyer and me that my voice was to falter and that I should seem as if I was about to faint. I accordingly wound up the farce with a little bit of melodrama: and from that instant the cause of my opponent was desperate beyond all chances of redemption."

"You deserved success, after that brilliant speech," said Chichester, laughing heartily at this narrative.

"The polling was continued briskly until four o'clock, when the mayor closed the books and announced that *George Greenwood, Esquire, Gentleman, was duly returned to serve in Parliament as the representative of Rottenborough*."

"When shall you 'take your oaths and your seat,' as the papers say?" demanded Chichester.

"This evening," answered Greenwood.

"And of course you will range yourself amongst the liberals?"

"How can you fancy that I shall be guilty of such egregious folly?" cried the new Member of Parliament. "The reign of the Liberals is drawing to a close: a Tory administration within a year or eighteen months is inevitable."

"But you stood forward as a Liberal, and were returned as such."

"Very true—very true, my dear fellow. But do you imagine that I became a Member of Parliament to meet the interests and wishes of a pack of strangers, or to suit my own?"

"And at the next election——"

"I shall be returned again. Mark my word for that. A politician is not worth a fig who has not a dozen excuses ready for the most flagrant tergiversation; and money—money will purchase all the free and independent electors of Rottenborough."

Lady Cecilia Harborough returned to the drawing-room at this moment. She scarcely noticed Chichester—who was "her aversion"—but welcomed Greenwood in the most cordial manner. The baronet observed "that he should leave Mr. Greenwood to amuse Lady Cecilia with an account of his electioneering exploits;" and then withdrew, accompanied by his "shadow" Mr. Chichester.

"You have succeeded, George?" said Lady Cecilia, the moment they were alone together.

"To my heart's content, dearest Cecilia," answered Greenwood, placing his arm around the delicate waist of the frail fair one, and drawing her close to him as they stood before the fire.

"I am delighted with this result," said Lady Cecilia; "although my own father has sustained a defeat in the person of his candidate."

"All fair in the political world, dear Cecilia," replied the new Member of Parliament. "But you have not yet appeared to understand that I came hither the moment I returned from Rottenborough,—to bear to you, first and foremost, the news of my success."

"Ah! dearest George, how can I ever sufficiently testify my gratitude to thee for all thy proofs of ardent love?" whispered Lady Cecilia, in a soft and melting tone.

"Yes—I love you—I love you well," answered Greenwood, who in a moment of tenderness declared with the lips far more than he really felt with the heart;—and he imprinted a thousand kisses upon her mouth, her cheeks, and her brow.

She returned them, while her countenance glowed with a deep crimson dye;—but neither the kisses nor the blushes were those of a pure and sacred affection; they were the offspring of a licentious and illicit flame.

A slight noise in the room startled the guilty pair.

They hastily withdrew from each other's embrace, and glanced around.

Mr. Chichester was advancing towards the table in the middle of the apartment.

Lady Cecilia uttered a faint cry, and sank upon the sofa.

"I beg you a thousand pardons," said Chichester, affecting the utmost indifference of manner, "but I had left this parcel behind me;"——and, taking up the small package containing his dice and cards, he withdrew.

"Merciful heavens!" ejaculated Lady Cecilia: "we are discovered—we are betrayed! That wretch will ruin us!"

"Do not fear—do not alarm yourself, sweetest lady," returned Greenwood: "I will undertake to stop that man's mouth! One moment—and I return."

He hurried after Mr. Chichester, whom he overtook half-way down the stairs.

"Chichester, one word with you," said Greenwood.

"A dozen, if you like, my dear fellow."

"You came into the drawing-room a minute ago—unexpectedly——"

"And I apologised for my rudeness."

"Yes—but you are not the less possessed of a secret which involves the honour of a lady—the happiness of an entire family——"

"Greenwood, I am a man of the world: you can rely upon me," interrupted Chichester. "Fear nothing on that score. You have now asked your favour, and obtained it of me: let me request one of you."

"Command me in any way you choose."

"I am at this moment embarrassed for a hundred pounds or so——"

"Say no more: they are yours," returned Greenwood; and he forthwith handed a bank-note for the amount mentioned, to Mr. Chichester.

"Thank you," said that individual; and he hastened to rejoin the baronet, who was waiting for him in the square.

"Well—have you found your implements?" said Sir Rupert, as he took his friend's arm.

"Yes—and a hundred pounds into the bargain," returned Chichester drily.

"A hundred pounds! Impossible!"

"There is the bank-note. It is just what we required."

"But how——"

"Greenwood was coming down stairs, and I mustered up courage to ask him for a loan. He complied without a moment's hesitation. Indeed," added Chichester, with a sneer, "I almost think that I shall be enabled, in case of emergency, to obtain another supply from the same quarter."

"This is fortunate—most fortunate!" exclaimed Harborough. "Let us go and dine at Long's or Stephen's this evening, and see if we can pick up a flat."

CHAPTER LXIX.

THE "WHIPPERS-IN."

HAVING reassured Lady Cecilia Harborough relative to the alarm inspired by the intrusion of Chichester at so critical a moment, Mr. Greenwood returned to his own residence in Spring Gardens.

"Any one called, Lafleur?" he said to his favourite valet, as he ascended to his study.

"Two gentlemen; sir. Their cards are upon your desk. They both declared that they would call again to-day."

Mr. Greenwood hastened to inspect the cards of his two visitors. One contained the following name and address:—

THE HON. V. W. Y. SAWDER, M.P.
Reform-Club.

The other presented the annexed superscription to view:—

SIR T. M. B. MUZZELHEM, BART., M.P.
Carlton-Club.

"Ah! ha!" exclaimed Mr. Greenwood, chuckling audibly: "I understand what this means. Already at work, eh? No time to be lost, I see." Then turning towards Lafleur, he added, "You see, my good fellow, that when a man like me—a man of—of—consideration, in a word—becomes entrusted with the interests of a free, enlightened, and independent constituency, like that of Rottenborough, the Ministerial party and the Opposition each endeavour to secure me to their cause—you understand, Lafleur—eh?"

"Perfectly, sir," answered the imperturbable valet, with his usual bow.

"Well, then, Lafleur," continued Mr. Greenwood, "you must know farther that each party has its whipper-in. The whippers-in keep lists of those who belong respectively to their own parties, and collect them together when their support is absolutely necessary on a division of the House. In fact, the whippers-in are the huntsmen of the pack; and the members all collect at the sound of their bugles. Do you comprehend, Lafleur?"

"Yes, sir—thank you, sir."

"I must therefore see both these gentlemen—but separately, mind. If they should happen to call at the same time, show one into the drawing-room while I receive the other here."

"Yes, sir."

"And now, Lafleur," proceeded Mr. Greenwood, "while we are upon the subject, I may as well give you a few instructions relative to that deportment which my altered position renders necessary."

Lafleur bowed.

"Placed in a situation of high responsibility and trust, by the confidence of an intelligent and enlightened constituency," resumed Mr. Greenwood, "I am bound to maintain a position which may inspire respect and confidence. In the first place, as it cannot be supposed that I shall receive many epistolary communications until my opinions upon particular measures and questions become known through my parliamentary conduct,—and as, at the same time, it would be disgraceful for the neighbourhood to imagine that my correspondence is limited, you must take care that the two-penny postman never passes my door without leaving a letter."

"Yes, sir. I will have a letter, addressed to you, posted every two hours, sir, so that you cannot fail to receive one by each delivery."

"Good, Lafleur; and you can tell the postman," added Mr. Greenwood, "to knock louder than he has been in the habit of doing——"

"Yes, sir; because it is difficult to hear from the servants' offices."

"Precisely, Lafleur. And you can tell our newsman to bring me all the *second editions* of the newspapers whenever there are any; and mind you always keep the news-boy waiting a long time at the door. Tell him, moreover, to bawl out '*second edition*' of whatever paper it may be, as loud as he can."

"I will take care he shall do so, sir," answered Lafleur.

"And once a week, or so," proceeded Greenwood, after a pause, "let an express-courier gallop at full speed up to the house, and ring and knock furiously until the door is opened. But, mind that he comes from at least three or four miles distant, so that his horse may be covered with foam, and himself with mud or dust, according to the state of the weather."

"I understand, sir."

"Moreover, Lafleur, at least three or four times a week, go to Leadenhall Market and purchase the game and poultry which we may require for the house, and send it home by the London Parcels Delivery Company, so that the neighbours may say, '*More presents for Mr. Greenwood. Dear me! how popular he must be with his constituents!*'"

"I fully comprehend, sir."

"You can send fish home, too,—and haunches of venison in the same manner," continued the new Member of Parliament; "but mind that the feathers of the pheasants, the tails of the fish, and the feet of the haunches always hang out of the baskets in which they are packed."

"Oh! certainly, sir."

"If you could possibly get a charity-school to wait upon me some morning, to solicit me to become a patron, or any thing of that sort, it would do good, and I should make a handsome donation to the funds."

"That can be managed, sir. I can safely promise that seventy boys and ninety girls shall wait upon you in procession any day you choose to appoint."

"Well and good, Lafleur. And mind that they are kept standing for three quarters of an hour in the street before they are admitted."

"As a matter of course, sir."

"And now I will just mention a few things," continued Mr. Greenwood, "that you must manage with very great nicety. Indeed, I know I can rely upon you in every thing."

Lafleur bowed.

"You must turn away all Italian organ-players. The moment one shows himself under our windows, let one of the footmen rush out and order him off. It is not proper to encourage such vagabonds: the aristocracy don't like them."

"Certainly not, sir."

"Organ-playing is a thing I am determined to put an end to. There is also the hoop nuisance. Give any boy into charge, whatever may be his age, who is caught trundling a hoop in Spring Gardens. That is another thing I am resolved to put an end to. Ballad-singers and broom-girls you will of course have taken into custody without hesitation. In fact you had better give the policeman upon the beat general instructions upon this head; and you can slip a guinea into his hand at the same time."

"Very good, sir."

"At the same time we must be charitable, Lafleur—we must be charitable."

"Decidedly, sir."

"You must find out some decent woman with half a dozen children, to whom the broken victuals can be given every day at about three o'clock, when there are plenty of people in the street;—a woman who does not exactly want the food, but who will not refuse it. The respectability of her appearance will be set down to my benevolence, Lafleur; and she must be careful always to come with her children. By these means we shall gain the reputation of being judiciously particular in respect to vagabonds and impostors, but charitable in the extreme to the deserving poor."

"Just so, sir."

"One word more, Lafleur. When any person calls whom you know I do not want to see, say, '*Mr. Greenwood is engaged with a deputation from his constituents;*' or else, '*Mr. Greenwood has just received very important dispatches, and cannot be disturbed;*'—or, again, '*Mr. Greenwood has just stepped down as far as the Home Office.*' You fully comprehend."

"Perfectly, sir."

"Then you may retire, Lafleur. But—by the bye—Lafleur!"

"Yes, sir?"

"I shall add twenty guineas a year to your wages from this date, Lafleur," said Mr. Greenwood.

"Thank you, sir," answered the valet; and, with a low bow, he retired.

"Another step gained in the ladder of ambition!" said Greenwood to himself, when he was alone. "A Member of Parliament—and in spite of Lord Tremordyn! ha! ha! ha! In spite of Lord Tremordyn! Oh! most intelligent and independent electors of Rottenborough: I bought your suffrages with gold, with fine words, with clowns and mountebanks, and with pots of beer! Free and enlightened electors! ha! ha! I shall turn against the very interest in which I was elected; but if my constituents grumble, I will silence them with more gold;—if they reproach, I will use all the sophistry of which language is capable—and that is not a little;—if they repine, I will win them back to good humour with fresh sights, and buffoons, and galas;—if they grow dry with talking against me, I will have whole pipes of wine and butts of beer broached in their streets! Yes—I must join the Tory interest: I see that it is now upon the rise. And yet I know—I feel in my heart—I have the conviction that the popular cause is the true one, the just one. But what of that? I stood forward as a candidate to suit myself, and not for the sake of the free and independent electors of Rottenborough! Yes, all goes well with me! An occasional annoyance—such as my failure in obtaining possession of the person of Eliza Sydney, and of the hand of Isabella, the lovely Italian—cannot be avoided;—but in all great points—in all my important views, I am successful! And yet, Isabella—Isabella! Upon her the eye that is wearied with the contemplation of the rude and discordant scenes of life, could rest—could rest with unfeigned, with ineffable delight! O Isabella, there are times when thine image comes before me, like the vision of a holy and chaste Madonna to the sleep-bound mind of the pious Catholic;—and there have been solitary hours in which the whole earth has seemed to me to be covered with flowers beneath the sweet sunlight of thine eyes! And yet—who knows? The day may come when even thou shalt be mine! I longed to languish in the arms of Diana Arlington;—and I had my wish. I coveted the patrician loveliness of Cecilia Harborough;—and, behold! my wealth purchased it. I sought for change; and accident—a strange accident—surrendered to my embraces *another*—yes, *another*—whom I have never seen since that day—now more than two months ago,—but who, I have since learnt through the medium of my faithful Lafleur, dwells in the same house with—"

Mr. Greenwood's reverie was interrupted by the entrance of his valet, who introduced the Honourable Mr. Sawder into the study. The new Member of Parliament received the Whig whipper-in with his usual courtesy of manner; and, when they were both seated, Mr. Sawder felicitated Mr. Greenwood upon the successful result of the Rottenborough election.

"The liberal cause triumphed most signally," said Mr. Sawder: "the result was hailed with enthusiasm at the Reform Club, I can assure you."

"I have no doubt," answered Mr. Greenwood, already adopting

the method of evasion so much in vogue amongst diplomatic and political circles,—"I have no doubt that every true lover of his country must be rejoiced at the victory achieved by straightforward conduct over the system of bribery, intimidation, and corruption practised by the nominee of Lord Tremordyn and his agents."

"Oh! certainly—certainly," returned Mr. Sawder. "The object of my present visit is to ascertain whether you will permit me to introduce you to the House this evening?"

"It is my intention to take the oaths and my seat this evening," answered Mr. Greenwood.

"And my services as *chaperon*—"

"You really confer a great honour upon me."

"Then I may consider that you accept—"

"My dear sir, how can I sufficiently thank you for this kind interest which you take in my behalf?"

"Pray do not mention it, Mr. Greenwood."

"No, Mr. Sawder, I will not allude to it; since it is the more to be appreciated, inasmuch as I never had the pleasure of being known to you previous to this occasion."

"I am therefore to understand," said the whipper-in, who could not precisely fathom the new member through the depths of these ambiguous phrases, "that you will allow me the honour of introducing you—"

"The honour, my dear sir, would be with me," observed Mr. Greenwood, with a gracious bow.

"At what hour, then, will you be prepared—"

"My time shall henceforth always be devoted to the interests of my constituents."

"A very noble sentiment, my dear Mr. Greenwood," said the whipper-in. "Shall we then fix the ceremony for five o'clock?"

"Five o'clock is an excellent hour, Mr. Sawder—an excellent hour. I know no hour that I like more than five o'clock," exclaimed Mr. Greenwood.

"Be it five, then," said the whipper-in. "And now, relative to the Reform Club—when will it please you to be proposed a member?"

"It will please me, my dear sir, at any time, to join that fraternity of honourable gentlemen with whom I shall in future co-operate."

"Well and good, my dear sir," said Mr. Sawder; and he slowly and reluctantly took his leave, not knowing what to make of the new member for Rottenborough, nor whether to calculate upon his adhesion to the Whig cause, or not.

Scarcely had the Honourable Mr. V. W. Y. Sawder, M. P., driven away in his beautiful cabriolet from Mr. Greenwood's door, when Sir T. M. B. Muzzlehem, Bart., M. P. arrived in his brougham at the same point. But if Mr. Greenwood were evasive and ambiguous to the Whig whipper-in, he was clear and lucid to the Tory one.

Sir T. Muzzlehem began by felicitating him upon his election, and in a verbose harangue, expressed his hopes that Mr. Greenwood would support that cause "the object of which was to maintain the glorious old constitution inviolate, and uphold the Established Church in its unity and integrity."

"Those are precisely my intentions," said Mr. Greenwood.

"I am delighted to hear you say so, my dear sir," resumed the Tory whipper-in; "but I have one deep cause of uneasiness, which is that you may not entertain precisely the same views of what is necessary to maintain these honourable and ancient institutions, as the men who would gladly lay down their lives to benefit their country."

"I believe, Sir Thomas Muzzlehem," answered Mr. Greenwood, "that I shall act according to the wishes of my constituents, the dictates of my own conscience, and the views of the illustrious men of whom you speak."

"In which case, my dear Mr. Greenwood, I am of course to understand that you will be one of *us*—one of the true defenders of the Throne, the Constitution, and the Church—"

"In other words, a Conservative," added Mr. Greenwood.

"Bravo!" ejaculated the whipper-in, unable to conceal his joy at this unexpected result of a visit whose object he had at first deemed certain of defeat: then, shaking Mr. Greenwood heartily by the hand, he said, "At what hour shall I have the pleasure of introducing you this evening?"

"At a quarter to five precisely," replied Mr. Greenwood.

"And of course you will become a member of the Carlton?" added the whipper-in.

"Of course—whenever you choose—as early as possible," said Mr. Greenwood.

Sir Thomas Muzzlehem again wrung the hand of the new member, and then took his leave.

The moment he had departed, Lafleur repaired to the study, and said, "A lady, sir, is waiting to see you in the drawing-room."

"A lady!" ejaculated Mr. Greenwood: "who is she?"

"I do not know, sir. She refused to give me her name; and I have never seen her before."

"How did she come?"

"On foot, sir. She is neatly, but plainly dressed; and yet her manners seem to indicate that she is a lady."

"Strange! who can she be?" murmured Greenwood, as he hastened to the drawing-room.

CHAPTER LXX.

THE IMAGE, THE PICTURE, AND THE STATUE.

Upon the sofa in Mr. Greenwood's elegantly-furnished drawing-room was seated the young lady who so anxiously sought an interview with the owner of that princely mansion.

Her face was very pale: a profound melancholy reigned upon her countenance, and was even discernible in her drooping attitude; her eyes expressed a sorrow bordering upon anguish; and yet, through that veil of dark foreboding, the acute observer might have seen a ray—a feeble ray of hope gleaming faintly, so faintly, that it appeared a flickering lamp burning at the end of a long and gloomy cavern.

Her elbow rested upon one end of the sofa, and her forehead was supported upon her hand, when Greenwood entered the room.

The doors of that luxurious dwelling moved so noiselessly upon their hinges, and the carpets spread upon the floors were so thick, that not a sound, either of door or footstep, announced to that pale and mournful girl the approach of the man whom she so deeply longed to see.

He was close by her ere she was aware of his presence.

With a start, she raised her head, and gazed steadfastly up into his countenance; but her tongue clave to the roof of her mouth, and refused utterance to the name which she would have spoken.

"Ellen!" ejaculated Greenwood, as his eyes met hers.—"What has brought you hither?"

"Can you not imagine it possible that I should wish to see you again?" answered Miss Monroe—for she was Mr. Greenwood's visitor upon the present occasion.

"But why so much mystery, Ellen? why refuse to give the servant your name? why adopt a course which cannot fail to render your visit a matter of suspicion to my household?" said Greenwood, somewhat impatiently.

"Forgive me—forgive me, if I have done wrong," exclaimed Ellen, the tears gushing to her eyes. "Alas! misfortunes have rendered me so suspicious of human nature, that I feared—I feared lest you should refuse to see me—that you would consider me importunate—"

"Well—well, Ellen: do not cry—that is foolish! I am not angry now; so cheer up, and tell me in what I can serve thee?"

As Greenwood uttered these words, he seated himself upon the sofa by the side of the young lady, and took her hand. We cannot say that her tears had moved him—for his was a heart that was moved by nothing regarding another: but she had looked pretty as she wept, and as her eyes glanced through their tears towards him; and the apparent kindness of his manner was the mechanical impulse of the libertine.

"Oh! if *you* would only smile thus upon me—now and then—" murmured Ellen, gazing tenderly upon him,—"how much of the sorrow of this life would disappear from before my eyes."

"How can one gifted with such charms as you be unhappy?" exclaimed Greenwood.

"What! do you imagine that beauty constitutes felicity?" cried Ellen, in an impassioned tone. "Are not the loveliest flowers exposed to the nipping frosts, as well as the rank and poisonous weeds? Do not clouds obscure the brightest stars, as well as those of a pale and sickly lustre? You ask me if I can be unhappy? Alas! it is now long—long since I knew what perfect happiness was! I need not tell you—*you*—how my father's fortune was swept away;—but I may detail to you the miseries which the loss of it raised up around him and me—and chiefly *me!*"

"But why dwell upon so sad a theme, Ellen? Did you come hither to divert me with a narrative of sorrows which must now be past, since—according to what I have heard—your father and yourself have found an asylum—"

"At Markham Place!" added Miss Monroe, emphatically. "Yes—we have found an asylum there—*there*, in the house of the individual whom my father's speculations and your agency—"

"Speak not of that—speak not of that, I conjure you!" hastily exclaimed Greenwood. "Tell me, Ellen—tell me, you have not breathed a word to your father, nor to that young man—"

"No—not for worlds!" cried Ellen, with a shudder: then, after a pause, during which she appeared to reflect deeply, she said, "But you ask me why I wish to narrate to you the history of all the miseries I have endured for two long years, and upwards: you demand of me why I would dwell upon so sad a theme. I will tell you presently. You shall hear me first. But pray, be not impatient: I shall not detain you long;—and, surely—surely, you can spare an hour to one who is so very—very miserable."

"Speak, Ellen—speak!"

"The loss of our fortune plunged us into the most frightful poverty. We were not let down gradually from affluence to penury;—but we fell—as one falls from a height—abruptly, suddenly, and precipitately into the depths of want and starvation. The tree of our happiness lost not its foliage leaf by leaf: it was blighted in an hour. This made the sting so much more sharp—the heavy weight of misfortune so much less tolerable. Nevertheless, I worked, and worked with my needle until my energies were wasted, my eyes grew dim, and my health was sinking fast. Oh! my God, I only asked for work;—and yet, at length, I lost even that resource! Then commenced a strange kind of life for me."

"A strange kind of life, Ellen—what mean you?" exclaimed Greenwood, now interested in the recital.

"I sold myself in detail," answered Ellen, in a tone of the deepest and most touching melancholy.

"I cannot understand you," cried Greenwood. "Surely—surely your mind is not wandering!"

"No: all I tell you is unhappily too true," returned the poor girl, shaking her head; then, as if suddenly recollecting herself, she started from her thoughtful mood, and said, "You have a plaster of Paris image as large as life, in the window of your staircase?"

"Yes—it is a Diana, and holds a lamp which is lighted at night," observed Greenwood. "But what means that strange question—so irrelevant to the subject of our discourse?"

"More—more than you can imagine," answered Ellen, bitterly: "That statue explains one phase in my chequered life;"—then, sinking her tone almost to a whisper, grasping Greenwood's hand convulsively, and regarding him fixedly in the countenance, while her own eyes were suddenly lighted up with a strange wildness of expression, she added, "The face of your beautiful Diana is my own!"

Greenwood gazed upon her in speechless astonishment: he fancied that her reason was unhinged; and—he knew not why—he was afraid!

Ellen glanced around, and her eyes rested upon a magnificent picture that hung against the wall. The subject of this painting, which had no doubt struck her upon first entering that room, was a mythological scene.

Taking Greenwood by the hand, Ellen led him towards the picture.

"Do you see any thing that strikes you strangely there?" she said, pointing towards the work of art.

"The scene is Venus rising from the ocean, surrounded by nereids and nymphs," answered Greenwood.

"And you admire that picture much?"

"Yes—much; or else I should not have purchased it."

"Then have you unwittingly admired me," exclaimed Ellen; "for the face of your Venus is my own!"

Greenwood gazed earnestly upon the picture for a few moments; then, turning towards Ellen, he cried, "True—it is true! There are your eyes—your mouth—your smile—your forehead—your very hair! How strange that I never noticed this before! But—no—it is a dream: it is a mere coincidence! Tell me—how could this have taken place;—speak—is it not a mere delusion—an accidental resemblance which you noticed on entering this room?"

"Come with me," said Ellen in a soft and melancholy tone.

Still retaining him by the hand, she led him into the landing place communicating with the drawing-room and leading to the stairs.

A magnificent marble statue of a female, as large as life, stood in one corner. The model was naked down to the waist, one hand gracefully sustaining the drapery which enveloped the lower part of the form.

"Whence did you obtain that statue!" demanded Ellen, pointing towards the object of her inquiry.

"The ruin of a family long reputed rich, caused the sale of all their effects," answered Greenwood; "and I purchased that statue, amongst other objects of value which were sold, for a mere trifle."

"The lady has paid dearly for her vanity!" cried Ellen: "her fate—or rather the fate of her statue is a just reward for the contempt, the scorn—the withering scorn with which she treated me, when I implored her to take me into her service."

"What do you mean, Ellen?"

"I mean that the bust of your marble statue is my own," answered the young lady, casting down her eyes, and blushing deeply.

"Another enigma!" cried Greenwood.

They returned to the drawing-room, and resumed their seats upon the sofa.

A long pause ensued.

"Will you tell me, Ellen," at length exclaimed Greenwood, deeply struck by all he had heard and seen within the last half hour,—"will you tell me, Ellen, whether you have lost your reason, or I am dreaming?"

"Lost my reason!" repeated Ellen, with fearful bitterness of tone; "no—that were perhaps a blessing; and naught save misery awaits me!"

"But the image—the picture—and the statue?" exclaimed Greenwood impatiently.

"They are emblems of phases in my life," answered Ellen. "I told you ere now that my father and myself were reduced to the very lowest depths of poverty. And yet we could not die;—at least I could not see that poor, white-haired, tottering old man perish by inches—die the death of starvation. Oh! no—that was too horrible. I cried for bread—bread—bread! And there was one—an old hag—you know her—"

"Go on—go on."

"Who offered me bread—bread for myself, bread for my father—upon strange and wild conditions. In a word I sold myself in detail."

"Again that strange phrase!" ejaculated Greenwood. "What mean you, Ellen?"

"I mean that I sold my face to the statuary—my likeness to the artist—my bust to the sculptor—my whole form to the photographer—and——"

"And—" repeated Greenwood, strangely excited.

"And my virtue to you!" added the young woman, whose tone, as she enumerated these sacrifices, had gradually risen from a low whisper to the wildness of despair.

"Ah! now I understand," said Greenwood, whose iron heart was for a moment touched: "how horrible!"

"Horrible indeed!" ejaculated Ellen. "But what other women sell first, I sold last: what others give in a moment of delirium, and in an excess of burning, ardent passion, I coolly and deliberately exchanged for the price of bread! But you know this sad—this saddest episode in my strange history! Maddened by the sight of my father's sufferings, I flew to the accursed old hag: I said, '*Give me bread, and do with me as thou wilt!*' She took me with her. I accompanied her, reckless of the way we went, to a house where I was shown into a chamber that was darkened; there I remained an hour alone, a prey to all the horrible ideas that ever yet combined to drive poor mortal mad, and still failed to accomplish their dread aim;—the hour passed—a man came—you know the rest!"

"Say no more, Ellen, on that head: but tell me, to what does all this tend?"

"One word more. Hours passed away, as you are well aware: you would not let me go. At length I returned home. My God! my poor father was happy! He had met an angel, while I had encountered a devil——"

"Ellen! Ellen!"

"He had gold—he was happy, I say! He had purchased a succulent repast—he had spread it with his own hand—he had heaped up his luxuries, in his humble way, to greet the return of his dear—his darling child. Heavens! how did I survive that moment? how dared I stand in the presence of that old man—that good, that kind old man—whose hair was so white with many winters, and whose brow was so wrinkled with many sorrows? I cannot say how passed the few hours that followed my return! Flower after flower had dropped from the garland of my purity—that purity in which he—the kind old man—had nurtured me! And then there was the dread—the crushing—the overwhelming conviction that had I retained my faith in God for a few hours more—had I only exercised my patience until the evening of that fatal day, I had been spared that final guilt—that crowning infamy!"

Ellen covered her face with her hands, and burst into an agony of tears. Deep sobs convulsed her bosom; she groaned in spirit; and never had the libertine by her side beheld female anguish so fearfully exemplified before.

Oh! when fair woman loses the star from her brow, and yet retains the sense of shame, where shall she seek for comfort? whither shall she fly to find consolation?

Greenwood was really alarmed at the violence of the poor girl's grief.

"Ellen, what can I do for you? what would you have with me?" he said, passing his arm around her waist.

She drew hastily away from his embrace, and turning upon him her tearful eyes, exclaimed, "If you touch me under the influence of the sentiment that made you purchase my only jewel, lay not a finger on me—defile me not—let my sorrows make my person sacred! But if you entertain one spark of feeling—one single idea of honour, do me justice—resign me not to despair!"

"Do you justice, Ellen?"

"Yes—do me justice; for I was pure and spotless till want and misery threw me into your arms," continued Ellen, in an impassioned tone; "and if I sinned—if I surrendered myself up to him who offered me a price—it was only that I might obtain bread—bread for my poor father!"

"Ellen, what would you have me do?"

"What would I have you do!" she repeated, bitterly: "oh! cannot you comprehend what I would have you do to save my honour? It is in your power to restore me to happiness;—it is you who this day—this hour—must decide my doom! You ask me what I would have you do? Here, upon my knees I answer you—here, at your feet I implore you, by all your hopes of prosperity in this world and salvation in the next—by all you hold dear, solemn, and sacred—I implore you to bestow a father's honourable name upon the child which I bear in my womb!"

She had thrown herself before him—she grasped his hands—she bedewed them with her tears—she pressed them against her bosom that was convulsed with anguish.

"Rise, Ellen—rise," exclaimed Greenwood: "some one may come—some one may—"

"Never will I rise from this position until your tongue pronounces my fate!"

"You do not—you cannot mean——"

"That you should marry me!" exclaimed Ellen. "Yes—that is the prayer which I now offer to you! Oh! if you will but restore me to the path of honour, I will be your slave. If my presence be an annoyance to you, I will never see you more from the moment when we quit the altar: but if you will admit me to your confidence—if you will make me the partner of your hopes and fears, your joys and sorrows, I will smile when you smile—I will console you when you weep. I will serve you—upon my knees will I serve you;—I will never weary of doing your bidding. But—O God! do not, do not refuse me the only prayer which I have now to offer to mortal man!"

"Ellen, this is impossible! My position—my interest—my plans render marriage—at present—a venture in which I cannot embark."

"You reject my supplication—you throw me back into disgrace and despair," cried Ellen: "Oh! reflect well upon what you are doing!"

"Listen to me," said Mr. Greenwood. "Ask me any thing that money can purchase, and you shall have it. Say the word, and you shall have a house—a home—furnished in all imaginable splendour; and measures shall be taken to conceal your situation from the world."

"No—this is not what I ask," returned Ellen. "The wealth of the universe cannot recompense me if I am to pass as Mr. Greenwood's pensioned mistress!"

"Then what, in the name of heaven, do you now require of me?" demanded the Member of Parliament impatiently.

"That you should do me justice," was the reply, while Ellen still remained upon her knees.

"Do you justice!" repeated Greenwood: "and how have I wronged you? If I deliberately set to work to seduce you—if, by art and treachery, I wiled you away from the paths of duty—if, by false promises, I allured you from a prosperous and happy sphere,—then might you talk to me of justice. But no: I knew not whom I was about to meet when the old hag came to me that day, and said——"

"Enough! enough! I understand you," cried Ellen, rising from her suppliant position, and clasping her hands despairingly together. "You consider that you purchased me as you would have bought any poor girl who, through motives of vanity, gain, or lust, would have sold her person to the highest bidder! Oh—now I understand you! But, one word, Mr. Greenwood! If there were no such voluptuaries—such heartless libertines as you in this world, would there be so many poor unhappy creatures like me? In an access of despair—of folly—and of madness, I rushed upon a path which men like you alone open to women placed as I then was! Perhaps you consider that I am not worthy to become your wife? Fool that I was to seek redress—to hope for consolation at your hands! Your conduct to others—to my father—to—"

"Ellen! I command you to be silent! Remember our solemn compact on that day when we met in so strange and mysterious a manner;—remember that we pledged ourselves to mutual silence—silence with respect to all we know of each other! Do you wish to break that compact?"

"No—no," ejaculated Ellen, convulsively clasping her hands

together: "I would not have you publish my disgrace! Happily I have yet friends who will—but no matter. Sir, I now leave you: I have your answer. You refuse to give a father's name to the child which I bear? You may live to repent your decision. For the present, farewell."

And having condensed all her agonising feelings into a moment of unnatural coolness—the awful calmness of despair—Ellen slowly left the room.

But Mr. Greenwood did not breathe freely until he heard the front door close behind her.

CHAPTER LXXI.

THE HOUSE OF COMMONS.

The building in which the representatives of the nation assemble at Westminster, is about as insignificant, ill-contrived, and inconvenient a place as can be well conceived. It is true that the edifices appropriated to both Lords and Commons are both only temporary ones;[1] nevertheless, it would have been easy to construct halls of assembly more suitable for their purposes than those that now exist.

The House of Commons is an oblong, with rows of plain wooden benches on each side, leaving a space in the middle which is occupied by the table, whereon petitions are laid. At one end of this table is the mace: at the other, sit the clerks who record all proceedings that require to be noted. Close behind the clerks, and at one extremity of the apartment, is the Speaker's chair: galleries surround this hall of assembly;—the one for the reporters is immediately over the Speaker's chair; that for strangers occupies the other extremity of the oblong; and the two side ones are for the use of the members. The ministers and their supporters occupy the benches on the right of the speaker: the opposition members are seated on those to the left of that functionary. There are also cross-benches under the strangers' gallery, where those members who fluctuate between ministerial and opposition opinions, occasionally supporting the one side or the other according to their pleasure or convictions, take their place.

At each extremity of the house there is a lobby—one behind the cross-benches, the other behind the Speaker's chair, between which and the door of this latter lobby there is a high screen surmounted

1 The old Houses of Parliament were burned down in 1834.

by the arms of the united kingdom. When the House divides upon any question, those who vote for the motion or bill pass into one lobby, and those who vote against the point in question proceed to the other. Each party appoints its *tellers*, who station themselves at the respective doors of the two lobbies, and count the members on either side as they return into the house.

The house is illuminated with bude-lights, and is ventilated by means of innumerable holes perforated through the floor, which is covered with thick hair matting.

According to the above-mentioned arrangements of benches, it is evident that the orator, in whatever part he may sit, almost invariably has a considerable number of members behind him, or, at all events, sitting in places extremely inconvenient for hearing. Then, the apartment itself is so miserably confined, that when there is a full attendance of members, at least a fourth cannot obtain seats.

It will scarcely be believed by those previously unaware of the fact, that the reporters for the public press are only allowed to attend and take notes at the proceedings *upon sufferance*. Any one member can procure the clearance of both the reporters' and the strangers' galleries, without assigning any reason whatever.[1]

---

1 "The process of parliamentary reporting, and the qualifications of those by whom the task is performed, cannot be adequately described within the narrow limits of this article; but it is hoped that the reader may be enabled to form some idea of both from the following brief outline. Every publication not copying from or abridging any other, but giving original reports, keeps one of a series of reporters constantly in the gallery of the lords, and another in the commons. These, like sentinels, are at stated periods relieved by their colleagues, when they take advantage of the interval to transcribe their notes, in order to be ready again to resume the duty of note-taking, and afterwards that of transcription for the press. A succession of reporters for each establishment is thus maintained; and the process of writing from their notes is never interrupted until an account of the whole debates of the evening has been committed to the hands of the printer. There are only seven publications for which a reporter is constantly in attendance; and these include the London morning papers, from which all others that give debates are under the necessity of copying or abridging them. The number of reporters maintained by each varies from ten or eleven to seventeen or eighteen. They are for the most part gentlemen of liberal education—many have graduated at the Universities of Oxford, Cambridge, Edinburgh, Glasgow, or Dublin; and they must all possess a competent knowledge of the multifarious subjects which come under the consideration of Parliament. The expedition and ability with which their duties are performed must be admitted by every one who attends a debate and afterwards reads a newspaper, while the correctness and rapidity with which their manuscript is put in type and printed, has long been a subject of surprise and admiration."—*The Parliamentary Companion*. [Reynolds's note.]

At half-past four o'clock the members began to enter the house pretty thickly.

Near the table stood a portly happy-looking man, with a somewhat florid and good-natured countenance, grey eyes, and reddish hair. He was well dressed, and wore enormous watch-seals and a massive gold guard-chain. He conversed in an easy and complacent manner with a few members who had gathered around him, and who appeared to receive his opinions with respect and survey him with profound admiration: this was Sir Robert Peel.[1]

One of his principal admirers on this (as on all other occasions) was a very stout gentleman, with dark hair, prominent features, a full round face, eyes of a sleepy expression, and considerable heaviness of tone and manner: this was Sir James Graham.[2]

Close by Sir James Graham, with whom he exchanged frequent signs of approval as Sir Robert Peel was conversing, was a small and somewhat repulsive looking individual, with red hair, little eyes that kept constantly blinking, a fair complexion, and diminutive features,—very restless in manner, and with a disagreeable and ill-tempered expression of countenance. When he spoke, there was far more of gall than honey in his language; and the shafts of his satire, though dealt at his political opponents, not unfrequently glanced aside and struck his friends. This was Lord Stanley.[3]

Shortly before the Speaker took the chair, a stout burly man, accompanied by half-a-dozen representatives of the Emerald Isle, entered the house. He was enveloped in a cloak, which he proceeded to doff in a very leisurely manner, and then turned to make some observation to his companions. They immediately burst out into a hearty laugh—for it was a joke that had fallen upon their ears—a

1 Sir Robert Peel (1788-1850), Conservative Chancellor from 1834-35, and Prime Minister from 1841-46. He is most famous for introducing the Metropolitan Police Force in 1829, and for repealing the Corn Laws in 1846. He effectively split the Tory Party, and after his death his liberal followers left and joined the Liberals.

2 Sir James Graham (1792-1861), Home Secretary under Peel from 1841-46. He was extremely unpopular, not least because of the scandal when he was found to be detaining and opening letters sent in the Royal Mail. Criticised after the Crimean War for his part in that fiasco, he resigned from office in 1857.

3 Edward George Geoffrey Smith-Stanley, 14th Earl of Derby (1799-1869) First elected as a Whig, he broke with them over what he considered their radical policies and went into opposition with (among others) James Graham. He formed a minority Tory government in 1852.

joke, too, purposely delivered in the richest Irish brogue, and, accompanied by so comical an expression of his round good-natured countenance that the jest was altogether irresistible. He then proceeded slowly to his seat, saying something good-natured to his various political friends as he passed along. His broad-brimmed hat he retained upon his head, but of his cloak he made a soft seat. His adherents immediately crowded around him; and while he told them some rich racy anecdote, or delivered himself of another jest, his broad Irish countenance expanded into an expression of the most hearty and heart-felt good-humour. And yet that man had much to occupy his thoughts and engage his attention; for he of whom we now speak was Daniel O'Connell.[1]

Close by Mr. O'Connell's place was seated a gentleman of most enormously portly form, though little above the middle height. On the wrong side of sixty, he was as hale, robust, and healthy-looking a man as could be seen. His ample chest, massive limbs, ponderous body, and large head denoted strength of no ordinary kind. His hair was iron-grey, rough, and bushy; his eyes large, grey, and intelligent; his countenance rigid in expression, although broad and round in shape. This was Joseph Hume.[2]

Precisely at a quarter to five the Speaker took the chair; Mr. Greenwood was then introduced by the Tory whipper-in, and (as the papers said next morning) "took the oaths and his seat for Rottenborough."

The Whig whipper-in surveyed him with a glance of indignant disappointment; but Mr. Greenwood affected not to notice the feeling which his conduct had excited. On the contrary, he passed over to the Opposition benches (for it must be remembered that the Whigs then occupied the ministerial seat) where his accession to the Tory ranks

---

1 Daniel O'Connell (1775-1847), Irish politician. Widely celebrated as 'the Liberator,' and as the chief mover of Catholic emancipation, O'Connell in fact achieved the right of Catholics to sit in Parliament; and since an MP was necessarily a wealthy man, the achievement was limited. After emancipation (1829) he tended towards conservative politics, and was a particular bugbear of the later Chartists such as Feargus O'Connor.

2 Joseph Hume (1777-1855) Scottish doctor and politician. Elected for a rotten borough in 1812, as a Tory, he was a friend of the Utilitarian philosopher Jeremy Bentham, and of the Radical Francis Place. He was instrumental in abolishing the Combinations Acts (against Trades Unions), and also against flogging as a military punishment and 'pressing' men into the Navy. A philanthropic man, he helped found schools for the working classes, and savings banks.

was very warmly greeted—being the more pleasant as it was totally unexpected—by Sir Robert Peel and the other leaders of that party.

Mr. Greenwood was not a man to allow the grass to grow under his feet. He accordingly delivered his "maiden speech" that very evening. The question before the House was connected with the condition of the poor. The new member was fortunate enough to catch the Speaker's eye in the course of the debate; and he accordingly delivered his sentiments upon the topic.

He declared that the idea of a diminution of duties upon foreign produce was a mere delusion. The people, he said, were in a most prosperous condition—they never were more prosperous; but they were eternal grumblers whom nothing could satisfy. Although some of the most enlightened men in the kingdom devoted themselves to the interests of the people—he alluded to the party amongst whom he had the honour to sit—the people were not satisfied. For his part, he thought that there was too much of what was called *freedom*. He would punish all malcontents with a little wholesome exercise upon the tread-mill. What presumption, he would like to know, could be greater than that of the millions daring to have an opinion of their own, unless it were the audacity of attempting to make that opinion the rule for those who sate in that House? He was astounded when he heard the misrepresentations that had just met his ears from honourable gentlemen opposite relative to the condition of the working classes. He could prove that they ought to put money in the savings'-banks, and yet it was coolly alleged that in entire districts they wanted bread. Well—why did they not live upon potatoes? He could demonstrate, by the evidence of chemists and naturalists that potatoes were far more wholesome than bread; and for his part he was much attached to potatoes. Indeed, he often ate his dinner without touching a single mouthful of bread. There was a worthy alderman at his right hand, who could no doubt prove to the house that bread spoilt the taste of turtle. Was it not, then, a complete delusion to raise such a clamour about bread? He (Mr. Greenwood) was really astonished at honourable gentlemen opposite; and he should give their measure his most strenuous opposition at every stage.

Mr. Greenwood sat down amidst loud cheers from the Tory party; and Sir Robert Peel turned round and gave him a patronising nod of most gracious approval. Indeed his speech must have created a very powerful sensation, for upwards of fifty members who had been previously stretched upon the benches in the galleries, comfortably snoozing, rose up in the middle of their nap to listen to him.

The Conservative papers next morning spoke in raptures of the brilliancy of the new talent which had thus suddenly developed itself in the political heaven; while the Liberal prints denounced Greenwood's language as the most insane farrago of anti-popular trash ever heard during the present century.

Mr. Greenwood cared nothing for these attacks. He had gained his aims: he had already taken a stand amongst the party with whom he had determined to act;—he had won the smiles of the leader of that party; and he chuckled within himself as he saw baronetcies and sinecures in the perspective.

That night he could not sleep. His ideas were reflected back to the time when, poor, obscure, and friendless, he had commenced his extraordinary career in the City of London. A very few years had passed;—he was now rich, and in a fair way to become influential and renowned. The torch of Fortune seemed ever to light him on his way, and never to shine obscurely for him in the momentous affairs of life:—like the fabled light of the Rosicrucian's ever-burning lamp, the halo of that torch appeared constantly to attend upon his steps.

Whether he thus prospered to the end, the sequel of our tale must show.

CHAPTER LXXII.

THE BLACK CHAMBER AGAIN.

It was now the beginning of April, and the bleak winds had yielded to the genial breath of an early spring.

At ten o'clock, one morning, an elderly gentleman, with a high forehead, open countenance, thin white hair falling over his coat collar, and dressed in a complete suit of black, ascended the steps of the northern door, leading to the Inland Letter Department of the General Post Office, Saint Martin's-le-Grand.

He paused for a moment, looked at his watch, and then entered the building. Having ascended a narrow staircase, he stopped at a door in that extremity of the building which is the nearer to Aldersgate

Street. Taking a key from his pocket, he unlocked the door, glanced cautiously behind him, and then entered the *Black Chamber.*

Having carefully secured the door by means of a bolt and chain, he threw himself into the arm-chair which stood near the large round oaken table.

The Examiner—for the reader has doubtless already recognised him to be the same individual whom we introduced in the twenty-ninth chapter of our narrative—glanced complacently around him; and a smile of triumph curled his thin pale lips. At the same time his small, grey, sparkling eyes were lighted up with an expression of diabolical cunning: his whole countenance was animated with a glow of pride and conscious power; and no one would have supposed that this was the same old man who meekly and quietly ascended the steps of the Post-Office a few minutes ago.

Bad deeds, if not the results of bad passions and feelings, soon engender them. This was the case with the Examiner. He was the agent of the Government in the perpetration of deeds which disgraced his white hair and his venerable years;—he held his appointment, not from the Postmaster-General, but direct from the Lords of the Treasury themselves;—he filled a situation of extreme responsibility and trust;—he knew his influence—he was well aware that he controlled an engine of fearful power—and he gloated over the secrets that had been revealed to him in the course of his avocation, and which he treasured up in his bosom.

He had risen from nothing; and yet his influence with the Government was immense. His friends, who believed him to be nothing more than a senior clerk in the Post-Office, were surprised at the great interest which he evidently possessed, and which was demonstrated by the handsome manner in which all his relatives were provided for. But the old man kept his secret. The four clerks who served in his department under him, were all tried and trustworthy young men; and their fidelity was moreover secured by good salaries. Thus every precaution was adopted to render the proceedings of the Black Chamber as secret as possible;—and, at the time of which we are writing, the uses to which that room was appropriated were even unknown to the greater number of the persons employed in the General Post-Office.

The Examiner was omnipotent in his inquisitorial tribunal. There alone the authorities of the Post-Office had no power. None could enter that apartment without his leave:—he was responsible for his proceedings only to those from whom he held his appointment. At the same time, he was compelled to open any letters upon a warrant issued and directed to him by the Secretaries of State for the Home and Foreign Departments, and for the Colonies, as well as in obedience to the Treasury. Thus did he superintend an immense system of *espionnage*, which was extended to every class of society, and had its ramifications through every department of the state.

It must be observed that, although the great powers of Europe usually communicated with their representatives at the English court by means of couriers, still the agency of post-offices was frequently used to convey duplicates of the instructions borne by these express-messengers; and many of the minor courts depended altogether upon the post-office for the transport of their despatches to their envoys and ambassadors. All diplomatic correspondence, thus transmitted, was invariably opened, and notes or entire copies were taken from the despatches, in the Black Chamber. Hence it will be perceived that the English Cabinet became possessed of the nature of the greater part of all the instructions conveyed by foreign powers to their representatives at the court of Saint James's.

But the Government carried its proceedings with regard to the violation of correspondence, much farther than this. It caused to be opened all letters passing between important political personages—the friends as well as the enemies of the Cabinet; and thus detected party combinations against its existence—ascertained private opinions upon particular measures—and became possessed of an immense mass of information highly serviceable to diplomatic intrigue and general policy.

Truly, this was a mighty engine in the hands of those who swayed the destinies of the British Empire;—but the secret springs of that fearfully complicated machine were all set in motion and controlled by that white-headed and aged man who now sat in the Black Chamber!

Need we wonder if he felt proud of his strange position? can we be astonished if he gloated, like the boa-constrictor over the victim that it retains in its deadly folds, over the mighty secrets stored in his memory?

That man knew enough to overturn a Ministry with one word.

That man could have set an entire empire in a blaze with one syllable of mystic revelation.

That man was acquainted with sufficient to paralyze the policy of many mighty states.

That man treasured in his mind facts a mere hint at which would have overwhelmed entire families—aye, even the noblest and highest in the land—with eternal disgrace.

That man could have ruined bankers—hurled down vast commercial firms—levelled mercantile establishments—destroyed grand institutions.

That man wielded a power which, were it set in motion, would have convulsed society throughout the length and breadth of the land.

Need we wonder if the government gave him all he asked? can we be astonished if all those in whom he felt an interest were well provided for?

When he went into society, he met the possessors of vast estates, whom he could prostrate and beggar with one word—a word that would proclaim the illegitimacy of their birth. He encountered fair dames and titled ladies, walking with head erect and unblushing brow, but whom he could level with the syllable that should announce their frailty and their shame. He conversed with peers and gentlemen who were lauded as the essence of honour and of virtue, but whose fame would have withered like a parched scroll, had his breath, pregnant with fearful revelations, only fanned its surface. There were few, either men or women, of rank and name, of whom he knew not something which they would wish to remain unknown.

Need we wonder if bad passions and feelings had been engendered in his mind? Can we be astonished if he had learnt to look upon human nature as a fruit resembling the apples of the Dead Sea, fair to gaze upon, but ashes at the heart?

Presently a knock at the door was heard. The Examiner opened it, and one of his clerks entered the room. He bowed respectfully to his superior, and proceeded to take his seat at the table. In like manner, at short intervals, the other three subordinates arrived; but the one who came last, brought with him a sealed parcel containing a vast number of letters, which he had received from the President of one of the sorting departments of the establishment. These letters were now heaped upon the table before the Examiner; and the business of this mysterious conclave commenced.

The entire process of opening the letters has been described in detail in the twenty-ninth chapter. We shall therefore now content ourselves, with a record of those letters which were examined upon the present occasion.

The first was from Castelcicala to the representative of that Grand Duchy at the English court, and was marked "Private." It ran as follows:—

"City of Montoni, Castelcicala.

"The undersigned is desired by his lordship the Marquis of Gerrano, his Serene Highness's Secretary of State for Foreign Affairs, to inform your Excellency that your despatches marked L1, M2, and N3, were received in due course. His Lordship regrets to find that Prince Alberto positively refuses to renounce his claims to the ducal crown of Castelcicala at the death of the reigning Grand Duke, whom God preserve for many years! His lordship is surprised that Prince Alberto should reject the compromise offered; inasmuch as, by complying with the terms thereof, he would receive a pension of twenty thousand pounds sterling *per annum*; whereas, by obstinately refusing the proposals made by the government of Castelcicala, he will obtain nothing. Moreover, it must be apparent to Prince Alberto that his claims will be set aside by the government of Castelcicala; and that a foreign prince will receive an invitation to accept the ducal crown at the death of his present Serene Highness the reigning Grand Duke. It would be well to make fresh representations to Prince Alberto; and assure him that he would act wisely to accept offers made in perfect good will, and that he may probably regret his obstinacy when too late. If the Prince cherishes the idea of enforcing his claims by arms, at the death of the reigning Grand Duke, your Excellency would do well to undeceive him; inasmuch, as his Majesty the King of Naples and his Holiness the Pope, holding in abhorrence the liberal notions entertained by the Prince, will support the government of Castelcicala in its determination to place a foreign prince upon the ducal throne at the death of his Serene Highness now reigning.

"The undersigned is moreover instructed by his lordship the Marquis of Gerrano, to request your Excellency to pay prompt and full attention to the following instructions:—An English lady, of the name of Eliza Sydney, arrived a month ago at Montoni. She is apparently about twenty-seven or twenty-eight years of age, very beautiful, and unmarried. She travelled in a handsome carriage, attended by one female servant and an elderly valet.

Although arrived at that mature age, she has preserved all the brashness of her youthful charms—a circumstance which renders her presence here the more dangerous, for certain reasons which the undersigned will detail to your Excellency on a future occasion. This charming English woman brought letters of introduction to certain noble families at Montoni, and immediately obtained admittance into the very first society of this capital. She has taken up her residence at the villa possessed by the Earl of Warrington, in the suburbs of Montoni, and is, it is believed, nearly related to that English nobleman. The service now required of your Excellency is to ascertain all particulars that can be gleaned concerning her. This is of the utmost—the very utmost importance. As a guide to your proceedings, it may be as well to mention that Miss Sydney this morning sent a letter to the post-office addressed to a Mrs. Arlington, residing in Dover Street, London.

"The undersigned avails himself of this note to renew to your Excellency assurances of his most perfect consideration.

"*March* 15, 1839. BARON RUPERTO,

"Under Secretary of State for Foreign affairs, &c."

"Eliza Sydney!" exclaimed the Examiner. "That is the same young lady whose plot with one Stephens, to defraud the Earl of Warrington, was discovered through the medium of the Black Chamber, and revealed to the solicitor of the Bank of England."

"The very same, no doubt, sir," observed the first clerk.

"Then the letter which Eliza Sydney has sent from Montoni to Mrs. Arlington in London, must be amongst this packet of correspondence," continued the Examiner, glancing at the pile of letters before him, "since it left Castelcicala by the same mail as the document of Lord Ruperto."

The Examiner turned over the letters; and, at length, extracted a particular one from the heap, observing, "Here it is." He then passed it to the clerks, by whom it was opened. The contents were as follows:—

"*Montoni*, *15th March*, 1839

"Exactly a month ago, my dearest Diana, I wrote to you a hasty note to state my safe arrival in this city, after a very pleasant journey through the delicious climes of France, Switzerland, and Northern Italy. It was at about three o'clock in the afternoon of the 13th of February that the carriage reached the brow of a hill from whence the eye commanded a magnificent view of a vast plain, rich with fertility, bounded at the further extremity by the horizon, and on the right hand stretching down to the sea, the blue of which seemed a pure reflection of the cloudless heavens above. At the mouth of a superb river, which, after meandering through that delicious plain, amidst groves and pleasant meadows, flowed into the calm and tranquil sea, the tall towers and white buildings of Montoni met my eyes. It is impossible to conceive any thing more charming or picturesque than the sight of this peerless city of Italy. The river's verdant banks are dotted with magnificent villas and mansions, with which are connected beautiful gardens teeming with the choicest fruits and flowers, even at this season of the year! For here, my dear Diana, it is perfect summer! I ordered the carriage to stop for at least a quarter of an hour upon the hill, that I might enjoy the magnificent view of the vast plain and the beautiful city. Far above the edifices around, rose the two towers of the ancient cathedral of St. Theodosia—their dark and gloomy masses forming a striking contrast with the extensive white buildings of the ducal palace in the immediate foreground. The port of the city was crowded with shipping, the flags of all nations waving from the forest of masts that indicated the existence of an extensive commerce. While I was yet gazing upon the scene, the roar of distant artillery reached my ears. The Grand Duke (as I afterwards learnt) was just coming back from a water excursion in his beautiful yacht, a small steamer rigged as a frigate; and the batteries of the port, and the ships of war in the offing thundered forth a salute in honour of the royal return. Two line-of-battle ships, one French and the other English, and three frigates of the Castelcicalan navy, had all their yards manned, and displayed their gayest colours. Altogether the scene was one of the most enchanting and exhilarating that I have ever yet beheld.

"In three quarters of an hour my carriage entered Montoni by the suburb of Saint Joanna. If I had admired the city from a distant point, how was I enraptured when I could survey it close at hand. It more nearly resembles the Chaussée d'Antin (a fashionable quarter of Paris, which city I had an opportunity of seeing during the four days that I remained there on my way hither) than any other place which I have ever yet beheld. The streets of Montoni are wide, and the buildings elegant. There are numerous fountains, and all the principal mansions, even in the very heart of the town, have gardens attached to them. At length I reached the fashionable quarter, and, having passed the magnificent dwellings of the Ministers of Foreign Affairs and the Interior, I passed through the immense arena, on one side of which stands the ducal palace. At that moment a regiment of Horse Guards was returning to its barracks close to the royal residence. The superb black chargers, the glittering helmets and cuirasses of the men, the waving plumes, the clang of armour, and the braying of trumpets, formed a *tout ensemble* so inspiring, that I almost wished I was a man to be able to serve in such a corps.

"The carriage proceeded, crossed the river over a suspension bridge, and, having passed the official dwellings of the Ministers of War, Commerce, Marine, and Finance, entered the southern suburbs of the metropolis of Castelcicala. I could not have conceived that any city could have possibly equalled London or Paris in the magnificence of its shops and the amount of wealth displayed in their windows;—but certainly, Montoni is a miniature counterpart of the finest portions of either the English or French capital.

"At length I reached the villa so generously placed at my disposal by the Earl of Warrington, whom I can never sufficiently thank for all his kindness towards me. The servants, already advertised of my intended visit by letters which his lordship had written from England at the time of my departure, were prepared to receive me. I was immediately comfortable—immediately *at home*. Oh! how deliciously did I sleep that night;—but before I closed my eyes, how fervently did I pray for the welfare and happiness of the Earl of Warrington and of Diana Arlington!

"And the Earl told you that it was a little villa, Diana! It is a superb mansion. The rooms are magnificently furnished; the gardens are spacious and full of all that is delicious in the shape of fruit or enchanting in the guise of flowers. I wandered for hours in those inviting grounds the morning after my arrival. But would you have me depict my new abode? Listen:—

"Imagine a river half as broad as the Thames at Richmond, and far, far more lovely in its scenery. At a distance of about fifty yards from the stream, on a gentle acclivity rising from its very edge, stands a large square mansion, built of white free-stone. The villa is two storeys high: and the windows on the lower floor open like folding doors down to the ground. The hall and magnificent staircase are of the finest marble. And will you humour me in attending to all my minor details?—I have fitted up my own boudoir in precisely the same style as that in which I passed many happy hours at Clapton! A grove of myrtles almost surrounds the villa, and is musical with the warblings of a thousand birds. A gravel walk, margined with flowers, leads down to the river's bank. Behind the mansion extend the gardens, the acclivity still rising gently, until the summit of the verdant amphitheatre is on a level with the first floor windows. There is a marble basin in the middle of the grounds, filled with crystal water, in which gold and silver fish disport joyously beneath the shade of the overhanging fruit trees on one side, or, on the other, play with their glistening fins, in the brilliant flood of sunlight. Oh! in truth it is a charming spot, and seems as if its barriers could for ever exclude the footsteps of sorrow!

"When I had rested myself for two or three days, and completely recovered from the fatigues of travelling, I delivered my letters of introduction to the families to whom they were addressed. And here I have another instance of the Earl of Warrington's noble conduct to record. The letters all represented me as the near relation of the Earl of Warrington! I was received with open arms by all to whom I was thus introduced; and each kind Italian family seemed only anxious to make me happy! Oh! what virtue there must have been in those letters, which Count Alteroni had written, no doubt according to the dictation of the Earl. But, ah! Diana, relative to those letters there is a secret, which I do not choose to trust to paper, but which the Earl has perhaps already explained to you. Oh! I do not wonder now that I was not to seek to penetrate their contents, in England (neither did I myself ever open them at all); nor is it a matter of marvel that those recommendations should prove such strong passports to the favour of those to whom they were addressed!

"One of those letters was directed to General Grachia, the colonel of that very regiment of Horse Guards which I so much admired on my first entrance into Montoni. He and his amiable family, consisting of a wife and three lovely daughters, overwhelmed me with kindness. But now I am going to state something that will surprise you. A few days after I first became known to this delightful family, there was a grand review in the palace-square. General Grachia commanded the troops, which mustered to the number of about seven thousand. The ladies insisted that I should accompany them in their open carriage to see the manœuvres. The review was to be a very brilliant one, as the Grand Duke himself intended to inspect the troops. I accordingly assented; and, to the review we went. Never have I beheld a more magnificent sight. The road around the square was lined with carriages filled with all the rank and beauty of Montoni. The troops presented a splendid appearance—being the choice regiments of the Castelcicalan army, which, I have understood, is seventeen thousand strong. At length the Grand Duke Angelo III., attended by a brilliant staff, arrived upon the arena. He is a fine-looking man for his age, which must be at least sixty. He was dressed in a Field Marshal's uniform, and wore, amongst other orders, the insignia of the English Garter, of which he is a knight. He rode a little in advance of the great officers of state, who attended upon him; and when the troops presented arms, and the band struck up the national air, he took his heron plumed hat completely off, thus remaining bare-headed until the royal salute was ended. He then passed along the lines; but the troops received him in silence, for, to tell you the truth, his Serene Highness is far from popular, in consequence of certain political reasons with which I shall not trouble you at present.

"When the review was over, the Duke, attended by his staff, rode round the square, and graciously replied to the salutations which awaited him on all sides. When he drew near the carriage in which General Grachia's family and myself were seated, he rode up to it and entered into conversation with the General's lady. Presently he glanced toward me, and immediately bent down and whispered to Signora Grachia. The result was my formal introduction to the Grand Duke of Castelcicala. He inquired very kindly after the Earl of Warrington, whom he remembered perfectly. I blushed deeply as I answered his questions, for I was ashamed of the imperfect manner in which I speak the Italian language—for all that I know, as well as the little French with which I am acquainted, I taught myself during my residence at the villa at Clapton. The Grand Duke, however, seemed to comprehend me perfectly. Having conversed with us at least a quarter of an hour, he again whispered something to General Grachia's lady; and then rode on.

"It appeared that there was to be a grand ball and reception at the ducal palace on the following evening; and this second whisper expressed a positive wish—amounting, you know, on the part of royalty, to a command—that I should accompany General Grachia's family. I could not avoid obedience to this invitation. I therefore expressed my readiness to comply with it. And now, my dearest Diana, pardon a woman's vanity;—but it struck me that I never looked so well as on that evening, when I was dressed for the ducal ball!

"I need scarcely say that the entertainment itself was magnificent. Such a blaze of beauty I never saw before. Oh! what charming creatures are the Italian women; and Montoni is justly famed for its female loveliness! The Grand Duke is a widower, and has no children. The honours of the evening were entrusted to the lady of the Minister of the Interior, who is also the President of the Council. The Duke opened the ball with that lady. You may laugh at the idea of a prince of sixty dancing: but in Italy everybody dances. I was invited by the major of General Grachia's regiment for the first quadrille, and by Baron Ruperto, under secretary of state for Foreign Affairs, for the second. The third and fourth I declined dancing, being somewhat overcome with the heat of the apartments. But the fifth quadrille I danced: *this time* I could not refuse. No—it was not *an invitation* that I received—it was *a command!* I danced with the Grand Duke of Castelcicala!

"I found, on this occasion, that his highness speaks English well. He emigrated, it appears, to England, when the French armies occupied Italy, and resided in London for some years. We accordingly conversed in English. He expressed a hope that I should make a long stay in Montoni, and observed that he should be very angry with General Grachia's lady if she did not always bring me to court with her on the evenings of reception. I was at a loss how to express myself in return for so much condescension; and I am afraid, my dear Diana, that I was very awkward.

"On the following morning, one of the Duke's attendants arrived at the villa with a present of the choicest fruits and flowers for me. He informed me that they were sent by order of his highness, and the messenger was expressly commanded to make inquiries concerning my health. I thanked him most sincerely for this act of kindness on the part of his illustrious master; and when he had taken his departure, I sate in a delicious summer-house the entire morning, wondering to what circumstance I could have been indebted for such a token of royal favour.

"A few days elapsed; and the same messenger returned, bringing me a quantity of the most select Italian works, all beautifully bound, and with the ducal arms printed on the fly-leaf. Beneath this blazonry, were the words—'FROM ANGELO III. TO MISS ELIZA SYDNEY.' And now I asked myself, 'What can all this mean?'

"Two days more passed, when I received an intimation from Signora Grachia that there was to be a select *conversazione* in the evening at the palace, and that I was specially invited. I accompanied General Grachia's family; and the moment we entered the room, the Grand Duke accosted us. After conversing with us for a few moments, he offered me his arm, saying that he would conduct me to inspect his sculpture-gallery. This splendid museum communicated with the apartment wherein the company (which was by no means numerous on the occasion) was assembled. His Highness led me into the gallery, and explained all its curiosities. The works of art, by some of the most eminent masters, are very valuable. His Highness evidently prolonged the inspection as much as possible, and his language was occasionally interspersed with a compliment calculated to flatter me—nay, Diana, to make me very vain! When we returned to the drawing-rooms, the Duke led me to a sofa, seated himself by me, and conversed with me for a considerable time. He asked me many questions relative to my family—whether my father and mother were still living, whether I had any brothers or sisters, and in what degree of relationship I stood towards the Earl of Warrington? He then asked me how it was that I had not as yet launched my fortunes in the bark of matrimony? I blushed deeply at this question, and replied that I had never as yet encountered any one with whom I had chosen to link my destinies. He then spoke of the peculiar position of princes, observing with a deep sigh, that they could not always follow the bent of their inclinations, nor obey the natural dictates of their affections. During the remainder of the evening I was the object of universal attention—I could not *then* conceive wherefore—on the part of the noble and beauteous guests assembled. Every one manifested the most respectful courtesy towards me; and General Grachia's family were more kind to me than ever. Ah! a vague suspicion darted across my mind:—could it be possible? Oh! no—no! that were the height of the most insane presumption!

"Day after day passed; and frequent were the tokens of the Grand Duke's favour which I received—but all of the most delicate description,—flowers, fruits, and books. I was also compelled to accompany the Grachias to all the ducal *soirées* and receptions; and on each occasion, the Duke paid me marked attention. Oh! my dear friend, my heart beats when I remember that only last evening his Serene Highness pressed my hand, and said to me in a low but impressive tone. '*Would that I were not a prince, or that you were a princess!*'

"I can say no more at present, dearest Diana; but you shall speedily hear again from your sincerely attached and ever deeply grateful

"ELIZA SYDNEY."

"No wonder," said the Examiner, drily, "that Baron Ruperto has desired the Envoy of Castelcicala at the English court to make inquiries relative to Miss Eliza Sydney. Let the contents of both letters be duly noted, and forwarded to her Majesty's Secretary of State for Foreign Affairs."

CHAPTER LXXIII.

CAPTAIN DAPPER AND SIR CHERRY BOUNCE.

THE verdure of the early spring re-clothed the trees with their gay garments, and gave back its air of cheerfulness to the residence of Count Alteroni.

It was about mid-day; and the sun beamed brightly from a heaven of unclouded blue. Nature appeared to be reviving from the despotism of winter's rule; and the primrose peeped bashfully forth to welcome the return of the feathered chorister of the grove.

The count and countess, with their lovely daughter, were seated in the breakfast-parlour. The two ladies were occupied with their embroidery; the noble Italian exile himself was reading the *Montoni Gazette*, which that morning's post had brought him.

Suddenly he uttered an exclamation of surprise, and then appeared to read with additional interest and attention.

"What news from Castelcicala?" inquired the countess.

"You remember that the Earl of Warrington applied to me between three and four months ago for letters of introduction on behalf of a lady of the name of Eliza Sydney?" said the count.

"And who was about to visit Castelcicala in order to escape the persecution of that vile man who aspired to the hand of Isabella," added the countess.

"The very same. She is a cousin of the Earl of Warrington; and it appears that her presence has created quite a sensation in Montoni.

The *Gazette* of the 15th of last month contains the following passage:—'*The fashionable circles of Montoni have lately received a brilliant addition in the person of Miss Eliza Sydney, a near relative of the Earl of Warrington, the noble Englishman who purchased some years ago the beautiful villa at the extremity of the suburbs of Petrarca. Miss Sydney has taken up her abode at the villa; and during the month that she has already honoured our city with her presence, her agreeable manners, amiable qualities, and great personal attraction, have won all hearts. It is even rumoured that the highest person in the land has not remained indifferent to the attractions of this charming foreigner.*'

"Surely this latter sentence cannot allude to the duke?" exclaimed the countess.

"It can allude to none other," answered the count: "'*the highest person in the land.*' Of course it means the duke. But, after all, it is probably only one of those idle reports which so frequently obtain vogue in the fashionable circles of all great cities—"

"Or one engendered in the fertile brain of a newspaper editor," said the countess. "Still it would be strange if, through *your* letters of introduction—"

"Oh! it is too absurd to speculate upon," interrupted the count, impatiently.

"And yet your lordship is not unaccustomed to judge now and then by the mere superficial appearances of things," said the countess severely.

"I!" ejaculated the Italian noble.

"Decidedly," answered the countess. "You believed Mr. Greenwood to be an honest man without examining into his real position—"

"Ah! that one foolish step of mine!"

"And you pronounced Mr. Markham a villain without according him an opportunity of giving an explanation," added the countess.

"Always Richard Markham!" cried the count angrily. "Why do you perpetually throw his name in my teeth?"

"Because I think that you judged him too hastily," said the countess.

"Not at all! did he not admit that he had been in Newgate?"

A cold shudder crept over Isabella's frame.

"Yes; and so has our friend Mr. Armstrong, whom you value so highly, and whose letter from Germany gave you so much pleasure yesterday morning."

"Certainly I was pleased to receive that letter, because I had not heard from Armstrong so long: I fancied that something had happened to him. But, to return to what you were saying," continued the count; "Armstrong was incarcerated merely for a political offence; and there is something honourable in that."

"Mr. Markham may have been more unfortunate than guilty," said the countess. "At all events you have condemned without giving him a fair hearing. I have even asked you to refer to the newspapers of the period and read his case; but you refuse to give him a single chance."

"Your ladyship is very quick to blame," said the count, somewhat sarcastically; "but you forget how rejoiced you were some years ago to discover that the chevalier Gilderstein, whose father was executed for coining, was no relation of our family, as you had long deemed him to be: and yet the chevalier was himself innocent of his father's offence."

"I certainly have expressed myself more than once in the way you mention," returned the countess; "but I had so spoken without due consideration. Now that a case is immediately present to my view, I am inclined to feel and act more charitably."

"But how could Mr. Markham justify himself?" exclaimed the count. "Was not that attempt at burglary in this house so very glaring?"

"Oh!" cried Isabella, colouring deeply; "let Mr. Markham be guilty in other respects, I would pledge my existence he never, *never* could have been a participator in that!"

"You speak warmly, Signora," said the count, whose brow contracted. "You forget that I myself overheard him talking with some one over the wall of the garden only a few hours before the entrance of the burglars——"

"We have many cases upon record," interrupted Isabella enthusiastically, "in which men have been unjustly convicted on an almost miraculous combination of adverse circumstances. Suppose that Mr. Markham was, in the first instance, made the victim of rogues and villains, and sacrificed by them to screen their own infamy,—suppose he underwent his punishment in Newgate, being innocent,—will you sympathise with and commiserate him? or will you scorn and repulse him? Oh! my dear father, no kindness would be too great towards a being who has suffered through the fallibility of human laws!

Suppose that one of the villains who plunged him—innocent—into all that misery, repented of the evil, and signed a confession of his own enormity and of Mr. Markham's guiltlessness;—then would you remain thus prejudiced? Oh! no—my dear father, you never would! your nature is too noble!"

"My dearest Isabella, let us drop this conversation. In the first place, it is not likely that your romantic idea of one of the villains whom you bring upon your fanciful stage, signing such a confession——"

"Oh! my dear father," exclaimed Isabella, a ray of joy flashing from her large black eyes; "if such were the case——"

"Well—if such were the case," added the count impatiently, "the entire mystery of the burglary remains to be cleared up to my satisfaction; and therefore, with your permission, we will leave this subject—now, and for ever!"

Isabella's head dropped upon her bosom; and her countenance wore an expression of the most profound disappointment and grief.

Scarcely had the conversation thus received a rude check and the count resumed the perusal of his paper, when Sir Cherry Bounce and Captain Smilax Dapper were announced.

"Here we are—the two inseparables, strike me!" ejaculated the gallant hussar. "How is the signora this morning? somewhat melancholy—blow me!"

"It seems that you have nothing to make you melancholy, Captain Dapper," said the count, who did not experience the greatest possible amount of delight at the arrival of the two young gentlemen, although he was far too well bred to show his annoyance.

"Beg pardon, count—on the contrary, smite me!" returned Captain Dapper: "I have a great deal to be melancholy for. I lost six hundred pounds last night at cards—blow me for a fool that I was! I must confess, however, that I wasn't half awake."

"Yeth—and Thmilackth inthithted upon my thitting down and playing too; and I lotht thwenty poundth."

"And got scolded by your mamma into the bargain, for sitting up too late," said the captain.

"Nonthenth, Thmilackth!" exclaimed Sir Cherry; "I dare thay my mother allowth me ath gweat a lithenth ath your'th."

"Well we won't quarrel, Cherry," said the officer. "But what do you think, count? I and Cherry dined together at the Piazza,

Covent-Garden, where we got the most unexceptionable turtle and the most approved venison. The iced punch was superlative—the charges, of course, comparative. Well, in the evening, while I and Cherry were sipping our claret—and Cherry was admitting confidentially to me that he really hates claret, and only drinks because it is fashionable——"

"Oh! naughty Thmilackth!"

"Hold your tongue, Cherry. Well—a couple of gentlemen came into the coffee-room. There was no one else there besides me and Cherry and the new comers. So they began whispering together for a few moments; and at length one of them rushes forward, catches Cherry in his arms, and cries out, *'Oh! my dear Smith—my friend Smith—how glad I am to meet with you again!'* Cherry coloured up to the eyes——"

"Oh! what an infamouth falthhood!"

"You did, and you were so frightened you could not speak a word. I was obliged to tell the loving gentleman that your name was not Smith; and then he begged pardon, and said he never saw in his life such a resemblance to an old school-fellow of his as Cherry was. Well, we laughed over the mistake: the two gentlemen rang for claret; and we all sate down to the same table together. We drank several bottles of wine, and then adjourned to another place to sink it all with brandy-and-water. Cherry was quite top-heavy; but I was as sober as a judge—"

"Why did you woll in the mud, then?"

"Why? because I tripped against a stone. Well, then we were foolish enough to go to a gambling-house with these gentlemen; and there I lost, and Cherry lost."

"And the two gentlemen won, I suppose?" said the count, drily.

"Oh! of course," answered Captain Dapper.

"How foolish of two mere boys like you to think of going to a gambling-house," exclaimed the count. "Do you not see that the two *gentlemen* who accosted you in so strange a manner in the coffee-room of an hotel, perceived you to be a couple of greenhorns?"

"They might have thought so of Cherry," cried the captain, colouring deeply, and twirling his moustachios; "but they couldn't have formed such an opinion of me—an officer in her majesty's service—strike, smite, and blow me!"

"I'm thure I don't look tho veway gween ath you think," said Sir Cherry Bounce, now falling into a sulky fit with his friend the officer.

"Oh! I know perfectly well that they were regular gentlemen," continued the captain; "for they gave us their cards; and one was Sir Rupert Harborough. The other was Mr. Chichester."

"Sir Rupert Harborough and Mr. Chichester!" exclaimed Isabella, on whom the mention of these names produced a strange effect.

"Yes," answered Captain Dapper; "and so you see that they were proper gentlemen, and it was all luck. But strike such luck as mine!"

Isabella's countenance was suddenly irradiated with a gleam of the purest and most heart-felt joy;—the tears started to her eyes—but they were tears of happiness;—and, fearful that her emotions would be observed, she hurried from the room.

"Ah! but you didn't hear Cherry's adventure about the bird, did you, count?" demanded Dapper, still continuing the conversation.

The count shook his head.

"Why, this was it," said the gallant captain of hussars. "A waggish friend of mine, whose name is Dawson, dined with me and Cherry the other day; and the conversation turned upon birds. Cherry said he was very fond of choice birds; and Dawson immediately observed, 'If you like to accept of it, I will make you a present of a very beautiful and curious bird. I bought it the other day at Snodkins's, the bird-fancier's in Castle Street; and you may have it:—it is still there. All you have to do is to take a cage with you, call, and ask for Mr. Dawson's *Poluphloisboio*.' Of course Cherry was quite delighted;—indeed, he almost hugged my friend Dawson; and all the rest of the evening he could think and talk of nothing but the bird with a hard name. At length he thought of asking how large a cage he ought to take with him. 'The largest you have got,' replied Dawson. So the evening passed away; and next morning, before the clock struck nine, there was Cherry, rattling up Regent Street as fast as he could in a hack-cab, with a huge parrot-cage jolting on his knees. Well, he reached Castle Street, found out Snodkins's, and said, 'Pleathe, I have come for Mithter Dawthon'th *Poluphloithboio*.'—'For Mr. Dawson's what?' cried Snodkins.—'For Mithter Dawthon'th *Poluphoithboio*,' repeated Cherry.—'And what the devil is that? and who the deuce are you?' roared Snodkins, who thought that Cherry had come to make a fool of him.—'The thing ith a bird; and my name ith Thir

Cherway Bounthe,' was the reply.—'And my name is Snodkins,' said the fellow; 'and I don't understand being made a fool of by you.'—'Mithter Dawthon bought a bird here a few dayth ago,' persisted Cherry; 'and he thayth I may have it. Here'th the cage: tho give me the bird.'—Snodkins was now inclined to believe that it was all right; so he brought down the bird, put it into the cage, and Cherry drove triumphantly home with it. His mamma was sitting at breakfast when he entered with the cage in his hand. 'Here, ma,' said Cherry——"

"I don't thay *Ma* more than you do, Thmilackth," interrupted the youthful baronet.

"Yes, you do, Cherry," returned Dapper: "I have heard you a hundred times. But let me tell the story out. Well—Cherry's mamma exclaims, 'Lor, boy, what have you got there?'—'A *Poluphloithboio*, ma, that my fwiend Dawthon gave me.'—'A what, Cherry!' shrieks the old lady.—'A *Poluphloithboio*, ma,' answers Cherry, bringing the cage close up to his ma.—'A *Poluphloisboio!*' ejaculates mamma: 'why, you stupid boy, it is nothing more or less than a hideous old owl!'—and so it was: and there the monster sate upon the perch, blinking away at a furious rate and looking as stupid as—as Cherry himself—smite him!"

Isabella had returned to the apartment and resumed her seat a few moments before this story was finished; and Captain Dapper appeared very much annoyed and surprised that she did not condescend to laugh at the recital.

"By the by," he observed, after a moment's pause, "I have something to tell you all—strike me!"

"Oh! yeth—about Wichard Markham," said Sir Cherry.

The count made a movement of impatience; the countess looked up from her embroidery; and a deep blush mantled upon the cheek, and a sudden tremor passed through the frame, of the lovely Isabella.

"Yes—about Richard Markham," continued the hussar officer. "I and Cherry were riding in the neighbourhood of his house the other day——"

"And we thaw the two ath tweeth."

"Yes—and something else too;—for we saw one of the sweetest, prettiest, most interesting young ladies—the signora herself excepted—walking in the garden—"

"Well, well," said the count impatiently; "perhaps Mr. Markham is married, and you saw his wife—that is all."

"No," continued Dapper; "for she was close by the railings that skirt the side of the road running behind his house; and we saw an old butler-looking kind of a fellow go up to her, and I heard him call her '*Miss.*'"

"Mr. Markham and his affairs are not of the slightest interest to us, Captain Dapper," said the count: "we do not even wish to hear his name mentioned. Isabella, my love, let us have some music."

But no reply was given to the request of the count, who was seated in such a way that he could not see his daughter's place at the work-table.

Isabella had again left the room.

Of what nature were the emotions which agitated the bosom of that beauteous—that amiable creature?

Wherefore had she first sought her own chamber to conceal tears of joy?

And why had she now retired once more, to hide the out-pourings of an intense anguish?

CHAPTER LXXIV.

THE MEETING.

WHEN Isabella retired to her chamber the second time, she hastily put on her bonnet and shawl, and then hurried to the garden at the back of the mansion; for she felt the necessity of fresh air, to cool her burning brow.

She walked slowly up and down for a few minutes, her mind filled with the most distressing thoughts, when the sounds of voices fell upon her ears. She listened; and the consequential tone of the hussar-captain, alternating with the childish lisp of Sir Cherry Bounce, warned her that the two young coxcombs had also directed their steps towards the garden.

She felt in no humour to listen to their chattering gossip—wearisome at all times, but intolerable in a moment of mental affliction; still she could not return to the house without encountering them in her way. A thought struck her—the gardener had been at work all the morning; and the back-gate of the enclosure had been left open for his convenience. Perhaps it was not locked again? Thither did she hurry; and, to her joy, the means of egress into the fields were open to her.

The delicate foot of that beauteous creature of seventeen scarcely made an impression upon the grass, nor even crushed the daisy, so light was her tread! And yet her heart was heavy. Grief sate upon her brow; and her bosom was agitated with sighs.

She walked onward; and, turning the angle of a grove, was now beyond the view of any one in her father's garden. She relaxed her speed, and moved slowly and mournfully along the outskirts of the grove, vainly endeavouring to conquer the sorrowful ideas that obtruded themselves on her imagination.

But Woe is an enemy that knows no remorse, gives no quarter, while it retains poor mortal in its grasp; and when its victim is a young and innocent girl, whose heart beats with its first, its virgin love,—that direful enemy augments its pangs in proportion to the tenderness and sensibility of that heart which it thus ruthlessly torments.

Isabella's reverie was suddenly interrupted by a deep sigh.

She turned her head; and there, on her left hand—seated upon the trunk of a tree that had been blown down by the late winds,—with his face buried in his hands, was a gentleman apparently absorbed in reflections of no pleasurable nature.

He sighed deeply, and his lips murmured some words, the sound of which, but not the meaning, met her ears.

She was about to retrace her steps, when her own name was pronounced by the lips of the person seated on the tree,—and in a tone, too, which she could not mistake.

"Oh! Isabella, Isabella, thou knowest not how I love thee!"

An exclamation of surprise—almost of alarm—burst from the lips of the beautiful Italian; and she leant for support against a tree.

Richard Markham—for it was by *his* lips that her name had been pronounced—raised his head, and gave vent to a cry of the most wild, the most enthusiastic joy.

In a moment he was by her side.

"Isabella!" he exclaimed: "to what good angel am I indebted for this unexpected joy—this unmeasurable happiness?"

"Oh! Mr. Markham—forgive me if I intruded upon you—but, accident—"

"Call it not accident, Isabella: it was heaven!—heaven that

prompted me to seek this spot to-day, for the first time since that fatal night—"

"Ah! that fatal night," repeated the signora, with a shudder.

Markham dropped the hand which he had taken—which he had pressed for a moment in his: and he retreated a few paces, his entire manner changing as if he were suddenly awakened to a sense of his humiliating condition.

"Signora," he said, in a low and tremulous tone, "is it possible that *you* can believe me guilty of the terrible deed which a monster imputed to me?"

"Oh! no, Mr. Markham," answered the young lady hastily; "I never for an instant imagined so vile—so absurd an accusation to be based upon truth."

"Thank you, signora—thank you a thousand times for that avowal," exclaimed Richard. "Oh! how have I longed for an opportunity to explain to you all that has hitherto been dark and mysterious relative to myself:—how have I anticipated a moment like this, when I might narrate to you the history of all my sorrows—all my wrongs, and part with you—either bearing away the knowledge of your sympathy to console me, or of your scorn to crush me down into the very dust!"

"Oh! Mr. Markham, I cannot hear you—I dare not stay another moment here," said Isabella, excessively agitated. "My father's anger—"

"I will not detain you, signora," interrupted Richard, coldly. "Obey the will of your parents; and if—some day—you should learn the narrative of my sorrows from some accidental source, then—when you hear how cruelly circumstances combined, and how successfully villains leagued to plunge me into an abyss of infamy and disgrace,—then, signora, then reflect upon my prayer to be allowed to justify myself to you to-day—a prayer which obedience to your parents compels you to reject."

"To me, Mr. Markham, no explanation is necessary," said Isabella, timidly, and with her eyes bent towards the ground so that the long black fringes reposed upon her cheeks.

"Oh! fool that I was to flatter myself that you would hear me—or to hope that you would listen to aught which I might say to justify myself!" ejaculated Markham. "Pardon me, signora—pardon my

presumption; but I judged your heart by mine—I measured your sympathy, your love, by what I feel;—and I have erred—yes, I have erred;—but you will pardon me! Oh! how could the *freed convict* dare to hope that the daughter of a noble—a lady of spotless name, and high birth—should for a moment stoop to him? Ah! I indulged in a miserable delusion! And yet how sweet was that dream in my solitary hours! for you must know, lady, that I have fed myself with hopes—with wild, insane hopes—until my soul has been comforted, and for a season I have forgotten my wrongs, deep—ineffaceable though they be! I thought to myself—'There is one being in this cold and cheerless world who will not put faith in all that calumny proclaims against me,—one being who, having read my heart, will know that I have suffered for a deed which I never committed, and from which my soul revolts,—one being who can understand how it is possible for me to have been unfortunate but never criminal,—one being whose sympathy follows me amidst the hatred and scorn of others,—one being, in a word, who would not refuse to hear from my lips a sad history, and who would be prepared to find it filled with sorrows, but not stained with infamy!'—Such were my thoughts—such was my hope—such was my delusive dream: O God! that I had never yielded to so bright a vision! It is now dissipated; and I can well understand, lady—now—that no explanation is indeed necessary!"

"Mr. Markham," said Isabella, in a voice scarcely audible through deep emotion,—"Mr. Markham—you misunderstand me—I did not mean that I would hear no explanation;—Oh! very far from that—"

"But that it would be now useless!" exclaimed Markham, his tone softening, for he saw that the lovely idol of his heart was deeply touched. "You mean, signora, that all explanation would be now too late; that, whether innocent or guilty of the crime for which I suffered two years' cruel imprisonment, I am so surrounded by infamy—my name is so encrusted with odium, and scorn, and disgrace, that to associate with me—to be seen for a moment near me, is a moral contagion—a plague—a pestilence—"

"Oh! spare me—spare me these reproaches," cried Isabella, now weeping bitterly; "for reproaches they are—and most unjust ones, too!"

"Unjust ones!" exclaimed Richard; "what mean you, signora?"

"That by me at least they are undeserved, Mr. Markham," returned the lovely girl.

"How undeserved? how unjust?" said Richard, eagerly catching at the first straw which presented itself upon the ocean that had wrecked all his hopes; "did you not say that no explanation was now necessary?"

"Nor was it ever," answered Isabella, whose voice was almost entirely subdued by her emotions; "for I never—never believed the accusations which you seek to explain away!"

"My God! do I hear aright? or am I again the sport of a delusive vision?" cried Richard; then, advancing towards Isabella, he took her hand, and said, "Signora, repeat what you ere now averred, that I may believe my own ears! You believe that I was the victim of villains, and not a vile—degraded—base criminal?"

"Such has been, and ever would have been my belief—even without a proof," replied Isabella.

"A proof!" ejaculated Markham: "what mean you?"

"The confession of one of the wretches who wronged you—the narrative of the man named Talbot!" answered the Italian, casting a glance of sympathy—of tender sympathy—upon her lover.

"And now, O God, I thank thee!" said Markham, his eyes filling with tears, and his heart a prey to feelings of an indescribable nature: "O God, I thank thee—how sincerely, devoutly I thank thee, thou well knowest, for thou canst read the secrets of my soul! And you, Isabella—dearest Isabella—Oh! can you forgive me, that I dared for a moment to suspect your generous soul—that I doubted your noble disposition?"

"Forgive you, Richard!" exclaimed the charming girl, smiling through her tears: "Oh! how can you ask me?"

"And thus, my Isabella, you know all!"

"I know all—how deeply you were wronged, how fearfully you have suffered."

"Isabella, you are an angel!" cried Markham, rapturously.

"Nay—do not flatter me," said the signora. "I have but obeyed the dictates of my own convictions—and—"

"Speak, Isabella—speak!"

"And of my own heart," she added, casting down her eyes, and blushing. "You left the confession of that Talbot behind you—on the fatal night——"

"Oh! I remember now; and since then, how often have I deplored its loss."

"My own maid found it, and gave it to me on the following morning. Since then, I have read it very—very often!" said Isabella. "But now—I will return it to you—I will find some opportunity to forward it you."

"Not for worlds, Isabella!" cried Markham. "If you still love me—if you still deem me worthy of your regard—keep it, keep it as a pledge that you believe me to be innocent!"

"Yes, Richard, I will keep it—keep it for you," said Isabella. "But do not think that your cause is without advocates at our abode. My mother believes that you were wronged, and not guilty—"

"Oh, Isabella! then there is yet hope!"

"But my father—my father," continued the signora, mournfully; "he will not hear our arguments in your favour. It was only an hour ago that my mother and myself reasoned with him upon the subject; but, alas! he—who is so good and so just in all other respects,—*he* is obdurate and inexorable in this!"

"Time, sweetest girl, will do much; and now my soul is filled with hope! Oh! how I rejoice that accident should have thrown in your way the very proof that confirmed the opinion which your goodness suggested in my favour."

"And not that proof alone," said Isabella; "for even this very morning, a circumstance confirmed the assertion, that the two men who were associated with Talbot in making you the blind instrument of their infamous schemes, are characters of the very worst description. Captain Dapper and his young friend were plundered by Sir Rupert Harborough and Mr. Chichester last evening at a gambling-house."

"Oh! there is no enormity of which those villains are not capable!" said Markham.

"But while I speak of Captain Dapper," observed Isabella, suddenly assuming an air of restraint and embarrassment, "I am reminded of another piece of information which he gave me, and which nearly concerns yourself."

"Concerns me, Isabella! What can it be?"

"Nay—I know not whether it would be discreet—indeed, I am confident that——"

"Speak, Isabella—speak unreservedly. Do you wish any explanation from me? have you heard any further aspersions upon my character? Speak, Isabella—speak: your own noble confidence merits an equally unreserved frankness on my part."

"No, Richard—dear Richard," said the lovely Italian, in a bewitching tone of tenderness; "I was wrong—very wrong to allude to so idle, so silly an assertion;—and yet—and yet it grieved me—deeply at the moment."

"My dearest Isabella, I implore you to speak. Let there be no secrets between you and me."

"No—Richard—I will not insult you—"

"Insult me, Isabella? Impossible!"

"Yes—insult you with a suspicion—"

"Ah! some falsehood of that Captain Dapper," exclaimed Markham. "Pray give me an opportunity of explaining away any impression—"

"Oh! no impression, Richard;—only a moment's uneasiness;—and, if you will compel me to tell you—even at the risk of appearing a jealous, suspicious creature in your eyes—"

"Ah, Isabella, if it be nothing but jealousy," said Richard, with a smile of satisfaction, "I am well pleased; for there would not be jealousy without love; and thus, the former is a proof of the latter."

"Then, Captain Dapper observed that he was riding near your abode the other day; and he saw a young and very beautiful lady in your garden——"

"And he said truly, Isabella," interrupted Markham: "he, no doubt, saw Miss Monroe, who, with her venerable father, is residing at my house—through charity, Isabella—through charity! No tongue can tell the miseries which those poor creatures had endured, until I forced them to come and take up their abode with me. Mr. Monroe was my guardian—and by his speculations did I lose my fortune;—but never have I borne him ill-will—and now—"

"Say no more, Richard," exclaimed Isabella: "you have a noble heart—and never, never will I mistrust it!"

"And you love me, Isabella? and you will ever love me? and you will never be another's?"

"Do you require oaths, and vows, and protestations, Richard?" said the young lady, tenderly: "if so, you shall have them. But my own feelings—my own sentiments are the best guarantee of my actions towards you!"

"Oh! I believe you—dearest, dearest Isabella!" cried the young man, enthusiastically, his handsome countenance irradiated with a glow of animation which set off his proud style of male beauty to its fullest extent; "I believe you; and you have rendered me supremely happy, for you have taught me to have confidence in myself—you have led me to believe that I am worthy of even such an angel as you! Oh! dearest Isabella, you know not how sweet it is to be beloved by a pure and virgin heart like yours! If my wrongs—my injuries—my sufferings—have taught thee to feel one particle of sympathy the more for me, then am I proud of the sad destinies that have so touched that tender heart of thine! But say, Isabella—say, when shall we meet again?"

"Richard," answered the Italian lady, "you know how sincerely—how fondly I love you; you know that you—and you alone shall ever accompany me to the altar. But, never—never, dear Richard, can I so far neglect my duty to my father, as to consent to a clandestine meeting. And you, Richard—you possess a soul too noble, and too good, to urge me to do that which would be wrong. The woman who has been a disobedient daughter, may be a disobedient wife; and much as I love you, Richard—much as I dote upon every word that falls from your lips—much as I confide in your own affection for me, I cannot—I dare not—will not diminish myself in my own opinion, nor stand the chance of incurring a suspicion of levity in yours, by a course which is contrary to filial duty. No, Richard—do not ask me to meet you again. Something tells me that all will yet be well: we are young—we can hope;—and God—that God in whom we both trust—will not forget us!"

"Now, Isabella—now," exclaimed Richard, "I comprehend all that is great and noble in your disposition. Yes—it shall be as you say, my ever dear Isabella; and the mental contemplation of your virtue will teach me to appreciate the love of such a heart as yours."

"We must now separate, dear Richard," said Isabella: "I have already remained too long away from home! But one word ere you depart:—that miscreant who made so fearful an accusation against you on the fatal night when you left my father's dwelling——"

"He is no more, Isabella," answered Markham: "at least I have every reason to believe that when the police, instructed by me, discovered his dwelling, three months ago, the villain terminated his existence in a manner that corresponded well with the whole tenour of his life. The den of infamy which he inhabited, was blown up with gunpowder, the moment after the officers of justice entered it; and there can be no doubt that he, together with one of his accomplices, perished in the ruin that was produced by his own hand. Several constables met their death at the same time; and, according to information gathered from the neighbours, an old woman—believed to be the miscreant's mother—was also in the house at the time of the explosion."

"How fearful are the ways of crime!" said Isabella, with a shudder. "May God grant that in future you will have no enemies to cross your path! And now, farewell, Richard—farewell. We shall meet again soon—Providence will not desert us!"

Richard pressed his lips to those of that charming girl, and bade her adieu.

She tore herself—how reluctantly!—away from him, and hastily retraced her steps towards the mansion.

But ere she passed the angle of the grove, she turned and waved her handkerchief to her lover.

The young man kissed his hand fondly to the idol of his heart: and in another moment Isabella was out of sight.

That one half-hour of bliss, which Richard had thus passed with the Italian lady, was a reward for weeks—months—years of anguish and of sorrow!

CHAPTER LXXV.

THE CRISIS.

During the ensuing three months nothing occurred worthy of record, in connexion with any character that has figured upon the stage of our narrative.

The month of July arrived: and found Tomlinson, the banker, more deeply involved in difficulties than ever. The result was that the consultations between him and old Michael, the cashier, were of very frequent occurrence; and the latter grew more morose, more dirty, and more addicted to snuff in proportion as the affairs of the bank became the more desperate.

One morning, in the first week of July, Tomlinson arrived at the banking-house half an hour earlier than usual. He had taken home the cash-books with him on the preceding evening, for the purpose of ascertaining his true position; and he brought them back again in the morning before any of the clerks had arrived, with the exception of old Michael Martin, who was already waiting for him when he entered the parlour.

"Well, Michael, my old friend," said Tomlinson, on whose countenance the marks of care and anxiety were now too visibly traced, "I am afraid that the establishment cannot possibly exist many days longer. Mr. Greenwood will be here presently: and he is my only hope."

"Hope indeed!" growled Martin, plunging his fore-finger and thumb into his capacious snuff-box: "how he left you to shift for yourself after you gave that security to Count Alteroni."

"Which security fell due a few days ago; and a note from the count, received yesterday, tells me that he shall call upon me next Saturday at twelve o'clock for the amount."

"He is very welcome to call—and so are a good many others," said Michael; "but they will go back as empty as they came."

"Good God! can nothing be done?" exclaimed Tomlinson, with an expression of blank despair upon his countenance. "Say, Michael—is there any resource? do you know of any plan? can you suggest any method—"

"Not one. You must go to the Bankruptcy Court, and I must go to the workhouse;"—and the old man took a huge pinch of snuff.

"To the workhouse!" cried Tomlinson; "no—impossible! Do not say that, my good old friend."

"I do say it, though;"—and two tears rolled slowly down the cashier's cheeks.

This was the first time that Tomlinson had ever beheld any outward and visible sign of emotion on the part of his faithful clerk.

Tomlinson was not naturally a bad man—at all events, not a bad-hearted man: the cashier had served him with a fidelity rarely equalled; and that announcement of a workhouse-doom in connexion with the old man touched him to the soul.

"Michael," he said, taking the cashier's hand, "you do not mean to tell me that you are totally without resources for yourself? Your salary has been six hundred a year for a long time; and surely you must have saved something out of that—you, who have no family encumbrances of any kind, and whose expenses are so very limited."

The old man slowly opened one of the cash-books, pointed to the page at the head of which stood his own name, ran his finger down a column of payments made to himself, and stopping at the total, said, "That amount runs over nine years; and the amount is £540."

"What—is it possible?" cried Tomlinson: "you have only paid yourself £60 a year."

"And that was too much for the state of the bank," said the cashier drily, taking a pinch of snuff at the same time.

"Now of all things which combine to make me wretched at this moment," said Tomlinson, "your position is the most afflicting."

"Don't think of me: I'm not worth it," returned Michael. "What will you do yourself?"

"What shall we both do?" cried the banker. "But so long as I have a crust, you shall not want."

"Well—well, there's enough of that," almost growled the cashier, though his furrowed cheeks were still moist with tears. "I am an old man, and my wants are few. A bit of bread and a pinch of snuff are enough for me. But you—you, who have always lived like a gentleman—how can *you* stand it?"

"And is it literally come to this? Is there no resource?"

"Do you see any? I do not. Will your father help you?"

"Not with another sixpence."

"Will Greenwood?"

"Here he comes to answer for himself."

Mr. Greenwood entered the parlour, and old Michael, taking his cash-books under his arm, withdrew.

The member of parliament threw himself into a chair, and observed what a beautiful morning it was.

Tomlinson made a movement of impatience, and yet dared not ask the question that trembled upon his tongue, and the answer to which would decide his fate.

"Yes," continued Greenwood, "it is a lovely morning: all nature seems enlivened, and every body is inspired with a congenial feeling."

"What nonsense is this, Greenwood?" cried the banker. "Do you come to taunt a man upon the brink of ruin, with the happiness of others?"

"Oh! I beg your pardon, my dear Tomlinson. I really was waiting for you to question me upon matters of business; and in the mean time made use of some observations of common courtesy and politeness."

"The fact is, that since you obtained a seat in Parliament your manners have altogether changed. But please to put me out of suspense at once:—have you considered my proposal?"

"I have—maturely."

"And what is your decision?"

"That I cannot agree to it."

"I thought as much," said Tomlinson. "Well—now I have no alternative. I must close the bank and appear in the *Gazette*."

"And when you are cleared by a certificate, I will enable you to set up in business again."

"Upon that promise, Mr. Greenwood," said Tomlinson severely, "I place no reliance—no reliance whatever."

"Just as you please," returned Greenwood coolly.

"How can I?" cried the banker. "When I gave my security for you to Count Alteroni, and relieved you of a burden of fifteen thousand pounds, you faithfully promised to assist me. Did you keep your word?"

"Did I not forgive you a debt which would have ruined you that very day?"

"True. But you were an immense gainer! You obtained twelve thousand pounds by the transaction. However, I shall be compelled to give an account of the transaction to the Bankruptcy Court."

"An avowal which will do you no good, and will only expose me," observed Greenwood, alarmed by this declaration.

"And why should I have any regard for you?" demanded Tomlinson, with that moroseness which men in his desperate condition are so frequently known to manifest towards intriguers more fortunate than themselves.

"I will tell you why you should have some regard for me," answered Greenwood. "In the first place, the mere fact of your having so long carried on this bank when in a helpless state of insolvency, thereby increasing your liabilities in a desperate manner, and receiving deposits the eventual repayment of which each day became less likely, will so irritate the mass of your creditors that you will never obtain your certificate. Secondly, unless you have a friendly trade-assignee, you will obtain no allowance out of the wrecks of the property, and you will find it difficult, considering the state your books *must* be in, to make up a balance sheet that would stand the remotest chance of passing."

"True—true," said Tomlinson: "my condition is really desperate."

"Not so desperate as you imagine," resumed Greenwood: "I will be your friend—I will save you, if you only follow my counsel."

"Ah! my good friend," cried the despairing man, "forgive me the expressions which fell from my lips just now."

"Do not mention that circumstance; I make every allowance for the irritated state of your feelings. In the first place, then, you can make me a creditor to the amount of thirty thousand pounds, and two or three of my friends creditors to an equal amount in the aggregate. We shall be enabled to give you your certificate, together with those persons who will not bear you animosity or whom we can talk over. In the second place, I can apply to be appointed trade-assignee; and I flatter myself—considering my position, representing as I do a free, enlightened, and independent constituency—my nomination will not be opposed."

"If you could only contrive *that*," said Tomlinson. "I might pass my second examination in even a creditable manner; and afterwards—"

"And afterwards open as a stock-broker," added Greenwood. "That is the invariable resource of all bankrupt bankers; and what is more extraordinary, they obtain confidence and succeed too. Tradesmen who are unfortunate, always take to the wine, coal, or discount business, each of which can be commenced without a shilling; but your aim must be a broker's profession. It is so genteel—so comfortable; a hole of an office in the City, and a villa at Clapham or Kensington;—a mutton-chop at the Dining-rooms in Hercules Passage at one, and turtle and venison at home at six. Ah! the life of a stock-broker is a very pleasant one!"

"I am sure the life of an insolvent banker is not," said Tomlinson, again rendered rather impatient by Mr. Greenwood's discursiveness.

"A thousand pounds will set you up comfortably again," continued Greenwood; "and that you shall have. Only follow my advice—and I will be the making of you. In the meantime, you had better not struggle against fortune any longer in this position. What is to-day? Thursday. Very well. I will strike a docket against you this very afternoon; the *fiat* can be opened to-morrow morning; and to-morrow evening you can be in the *Gazette*. Is that agreed?"

"Agreed!" exclaimed Tomlinson bitterly: "I have no resource left but that! Yes—it shall be as you say. But for God's sake, talk not in so cold and heartless a manner of the mode of procedure."

"Cold and heartless, my dear fellow!" repeated Greenwood: "I speak of your affairs just as I would speak of my own. Keep up your spirits, and come and dine with me this evening. You shall then give me the necessary securities to enable me to prove as your creditor for the amount agreed upon. Meantime, give me a bill for a thousand or so, ante-dated about four months, and due a month ago, so that I may strike the docket upon it presently. Then, as you are not to know that these proceedings are in operation against you, you must keep the bank open until the messenger comes down to-morrow afternoon from the Bankruptcy Court the moment the *fiat* is lawfully proclaimed before the Commissioner. Of course you will pretend to be struck with surprise, and instantly proceed to the Court to obtain your *protection*. Is that agreed upon?"

"I am in your hands," said Tomlinson. "Your advice shall now guide me altogether. But when I think upon the ruin and desolation my failure will cause—the widows and the orphans whom it will reduce to beggary—the poor tradesmen whom it will involve in inextricable difficulties,—it is enough to drive me mad."

"Pooh! pooh! my good fellow," said Greenwood; "these little things happen every day. As for the widows and the orphans, allow me to remind you that the wisdom and goodness of the legislative bodies—to one of which I have the honour to belong as the representative of an intelligent and independent constituency—have established asylums for the reception of persons so reduced, and where they enjoy every comfort, upon the trifling condition of doing a little needle-work, or breaking a few stones."

"Greenwood—Greenwood, do not speak in this heartless manner! Oh! the idea that my failure will render your words literally true—that numbers will be thereby reduced to the workhouse of which you speak,—it is this, it is this that overwhelms me!"

"You are very silly to give way to your feelings in this manner. Why do you know (and I may as well mention it by way of consolation in respect to the widows and orphans whose fate you deplore)—that the workhouses are conducted at present upon the most liberal principle possible? Do you know that the female inmates are handsomely remunerated for the shirts which they make—that they can make a shirt in a day and a half, and that they receive one farthing for each? That is their pocket-money—their little perquisites, my dear fellow;—so you perceive that the workhouse is not such a bad place after all."

Tomlinson was pacing the bank-parlour in an abstracted mood, and paid not the slightest attention to this tirade from the lips of the newly-fledged politician.

Mr. Greenwood saw that his observations were unheeded, and accordingly rose to take his departure. Tomlinson gave him a bill for a thousand pounds to enable him to strike a docket against him; and Mr. Greenwood then withdrew.

The moment he was gone, old Michael entered the room; and Tomlinson communicated to him all that had passed. The cashier made no reply, but took the largest pinch of snuff he had ever yet abstracted from his box or conveyed to his nose.

He had not yet broken silence, when the door opened, and Mr. Greenwood returned. Michael was about to withdraw; but the capitalist stopped him, saying, "Stay—three heads are better than two. I was just entering my cabriolet, when an idea—a brilliant idea struck me."

"An idea!" exclaimed Tomlinson: "what—to save me?"

"To render your failure legitimate—to make you appear an honourable, but an unfortunate man—to avert all blame from you—"

"Ah! if that could be done," interrupted the banker, his countenance animated with hope, "I might yet be spared the execrations of the widow and the orphan!"

"Ever your widows and orphans, my dear fellow," said Greenwood: "you are really quite sickening."

"Well—well—the idea?"

"Nothing is more simple," continued Greenwood. "You leave the bank this afternoon at five, as usual: Michael sees all safe, and takes his departure also. You leave fifty thousand pounds in specie and notes in the strong box, together with securities of foreign houses at Leipzig, Vienna, Turin, New York, Rio Janeiro, Calcutta, Sydney——"

"Greenwood, have you come back to mock a miserable—ruined man?"

"Quite the contrary. Listen! You leave money and securities to the amount of ninety-two thousand, three hundred, and forty-seven pounds—or any odd sum, to look well—safe in the strong box, together with the cash-books. You and Michael come in the morning—or perhaps it would be better to allow one of the clerks to arrive first,—and, behold! the bank has been broken into during the night—the money, the securities, and the books are all gone—and the bank stops as a natural consequence!"

"Impossible—impossible!" exclaimed Tomlinson: "it could never be done! I could not proclaim such a fraud without a blush that would betray me. What say you, Michael?"

The old cashier answered only with a grunt, and took snuff as it were by handfuls.

"What say you, Michael?" repeated Tomlinson, impatiently.

"I say that it *can* be done—ought to be done—and must be done," replied the old man. "I would sooner die than see the honour of the house lost—and *that* will save it."

"Well said, Michael," exclaimed Greenwood. "Now, Tomlinson, your decision?"

"It is a fearful alternative—and yet—and yet, it is preferable to infamy—disgrace——"

"Then you agree?"

"And if I agree—where are the means of executing the scheme? Who will rob—or affect to rob the premises?"

"That must be arranged by yourselves. The back of this house looks upon a court. The thieves can have effected their entrance through these parlour windows: the parlour doors will be found forced; the safe will have been broken open. Nothing can be more simple."

"Yes—I know how to manage it all," exclaimed old Martin, who had been ruminating more seriously than ever for the last few moments. "Mr. Greenwood, you have saved the honour of the bank, which I love as if it was my own child;"—and the cashier wrung the hand of the member of Parliament with a warmth indicative of an amount of feeling which he had never been known to demonstrate before.

"Well—I have given you the hint—do you profit by it," said Greenwood; and with these words he departed.

And as he drove back to the West-End, he said to himself, "Tomlinson will now be completely in my power, and will never dare confess the real nature of the transaction relative to Count Alteroni's fifteen thousand pounds. According to the first arrangement proposed, a bullying counsel or an astute Commissioner might have wormed out of him the exact truth; whereas, now—now his lips are silenced on that head for ever!"

The moment Greenwood had left the bank-parlour, old Michael accosted Tomlinson, and said, "Have you full confidence in me?"

"I have, Michael: but why do you ask me that question?"

"Will you place yourself in my hands?"

"I will—in every way."

"Then you will leave the establishment as usual at five this evening;

and trust to me to manage every thing. I have my plan ready arranged; but you shall know nothing to-day:—to-morrow—to-morrow——"

The old man stopped short, and had recourse to his snuff-box.

"Be it as you say, Michael," cried Tomlinson, always bewildered by the terrors of his situation, and still half shrinking from the daring plot which Greenwood had opened to his view; "I know that you are my faithful friend—my best, my only friend:—it shall be as you desire!"

CHAPTER LXXVI.

COUNT ALTERONI'S FIFTEEN THOUSAND POUNDS.

On the Saturday morning following the Thursday on which the above-mentioned conversation took place, the count and his family were seated at breakfast.

The morning paper was late; and his lordship was one of those persons who cannot enjoy their repast without the intellectual association of a journal.

At length the wished-for print arrived; and the count was soon buried in the preceding night's debate in the House of Commons—for he felt deeply interested in all political affairs, no matter to which country they referred.

"Really this Greenwood is a very clever man," he observed, after a long interval of silence. "He acquitted himself well last evening, notwithstanding the erroneous course he is pursuing in the political sphere. The Tories of this country have obtained a powerful auxiliary in him. It is a pity he is so unprincipled a villain—for, I repeat, he is really very clever."

"It is astonishing how men of his stamp contrive to push themselves forward in the world," said the countess, "while those of honest principles and upright minds are either misunderstood, or vilely persecuted."

"And yet vice only prospers for a time," observed Isabella; "and virtue becomes triumphant at last. Those who are misunderstood to-day will be comprehended and honoured to-morrow."

She thought of Markham as she uttered these words: indeed, the image of her lover was ever uppermost in the mind of the charming and affectionate girl.

"I am afraid," said the count, after a pause, "that the moral you have just advanced, Bella, is rather that of the stage and the romancist than of real life. And yet," he added fervently, "to entertain such an idea as mine is to question the goodness and the justice of Providence. Yes—I must believe in earthly rewards and punishments. You are right, my child—you are right: the wicked man will not ever triumph in his turpitude; nor may the virtuous one be oppressed until the end."

"No—or else were there small hope for us," said the countess solemnly. "The great men of Castelcicala must some day perceive who is their real friend."

"Alas!" exclaimed Isabella, "it is hard to be mistaken and suspected by those whose good opinions we would fain secure."

The count resumed the perusal of the newspaper; but his eyes had not dwelt many minutes upon the page ere he uttered a loud exclamation of mingled astonishment and alarm.

The ladies looked towards him in a state of the most painful suspense: and this feeling was not immediately removed, for the count, with an ashy pale face, continued to read the article that had caught his eyes, for some moments, ere he explained the cause of his emotion.

"Heavens!" exclaimed the countess, "are there any bad tidings from Italy?"

"No—the hand which strikes the blow which ruins us, is not so far distant," answered the nobleman; throwing the paper upon the table. "Ah! we were premature," he continued bitterly, "in founding our hopes upon the justice with which virtue is rewarded and vice punished!"

"The blow which ruins us?" said the countess, a prey to the most acute anxiety.

"Yes—Tomlinson has stopped payment," cried the Italian exile; "and—and we are ruined!"

"My dear father," said Isabella, hastening to fling her arms around the neck of her much-loved sire, "all may not be so bad as you imagine!"

"Ruined!" repeated the countess; and, taking up the newspaper, the following article instantly met her eyes:—

"ROBBERY AND STOPPAGE OF TOMLINSON'S BANK.

"The City was yesterday morning thrown into a state of the greatest fermentation by a rumour which prevailed at about eleven o'clock, that the above-mentioned old-established and well-known banking establishment had been plundered to an enormous amount, and had suspended its payments. Unfortunately the rumour was but too true; and our reporter, upon repairing to Lombard Street, found an immense crowd collected in front of the bank. The doors were closed; and the following notice was posted up:—'JAMES TOMLINSON *is under the painful necessity of suspending the affairs of the bank, at least for the present. The flight of the cashier, with money and securities to an amount bordering upon a hundred thousand pounds, is the cause of this unfortunate step. Further particulars will be made known as speedily as possible.'* It is impossible to describe the dismay which was depicted upon the countenances of those amongst the crowd who are sufferers by this calamity; and many very painful scenes took place. One widow lady who had placed her little all in the concern, and who arrived upon the spot, to draw her half-yearly interest, only a few moments after the doors were closed, was taken away in a state of madness. We have since learnt that the unfortunate lady has entirely lost her reason.

"Our reporter upon prosecuting his inquiries, gleaned the following particulars of the occurrence which led to the stoppage of the bank; and we have every reason to believe that the narrative which they furnish may be relied upon.

"It appears that the cashier, whose name was Michael Martin, is a very old man, and has been for many years in the service of the present and late proprietors of the bank. His presumed integrity, his known experience, and his general conduct, had led to his elevation to the post of head cashier—a situation which he has filled for upwards of ten years, without exciting a suspicion relative to his proceedings. It is, however, supposed that he must have been pursuing a most nefarious course for a considerable length of time, for reasons which we shall state presently. On Thursday evening, Mr. Tomlinson, who, it appears, is the sole proprietor of the establishment, although the business has been all along carried on under its original denomination of *Tomlinson & Co.*, quitted the bank at five o'clock, as usual, leaving the cashier to see all safe, and close the establishment for the day, according to custom. When Mr. Sanderson, one of the clerks, arrived at the bank at nine o'clock yesterday morning, he was surprised to find that the doors were not yet opened. The other clerks arrived shortly afterwards, and their surprise at length turned into alarm. Still the integrity of the cashier was not for a moment suspected; it was, however, imagined that something must have happened to him—an idea that was strengthened by the fact that the cashier occupied a room in the establishment, and there was consequently no reason to account for the doors remaining closed. The char-woman, who waited upon the cashier and swept out the bank, &c., came up to the door while the clerks were thus deliberating, and stated that she had not been able to obtain admission that morning as usual. It was now determined by Mr. Sanderson to obtain the assistance of a policeman, and force an entrance. This was done; and egress was obtained by breaking through the windows and shutters (which close inside) of the bank parlour. Mr. Sanderson and the constable immediately proceeded to the cashier's private room, which is on the ground-floor, and in which the iron safe was kept. The bed had not been slept in during the night. Attention was then directed to the safe, when it was found that it was open, and its contents had been abstracted. The front door of the bank was opened, and the clerks admitted. Mr. Tomlinson was then immediately sent for. That gentleman arrived by ten o'clock; and a farther investigation took place under his directions. The result of this search was a discovery that not only had the specie, notes, and securities disappeared, but even the cash-books, and all the papers that could throw any light upon the financial affairs of the establishment. It is this circumstance which induces a belief that the cashier must have carried on a system of plunder for a considerable length of time.

"We regret to state that the shock was so great that Mr. Tomlinson was conveyed to his residence in a state bordering upon distraction."

"FURTHER PARTICULARS.

"A reward of £3000 has been offered for the apprehension of the cashier; and a description of his person has been forwarded to all the principal seaports. [For *Description* see our advertising columns.] Our reporter learnt last evening that Mr. Tomlinson was more composed, and had even exerted himself to consult with some friends upon the best course to pursue. It, however, appears that so entirely did he confide in his cashier, that he is only able to give a vague and meagre account of the nature of the securities abstracted. They were, however, the bills and bonds of several great foreign and colonial mercantile houses. We regret to hear that Mr. G. M. Greenwood, M.P., had paid a considerable sum of money into the bank, on Thursday morning. It appears that upwards of fifty thousand pounds in specie and notes (the numbers of which are now unknown, they having been entered in one of the books taken away) and forty-four thousand in securities have disappeared.

"There is every reason to suppose that the delinquent will be speedily captured, as it is impossible for him to travel with a large amount of specie without exciting suspicion."

"LATEST PARTICULARS.

"In order to institute the fullest and most complete investigation into the affairs of the bank, it was resolved, at a late hour last evening, at a meeting of the principal creditors, Mr. Greenwood in the chair, that a docket should be struck against Mr. Tomlinson. At the same time, it is our duty to observe that this is done with no ill-feeling towards that gentleman, who is deserving only of universal sympathy, and, in no way, of blame."

"The name of that man Greenwood, in connexion with this affair," said the count, "impresses me with the idea that all is not right. Moreover, how could the cashier have removed a large quantity of specie without attracting attention in a thoroughfare so frequented at all hours as Lombard Street? There is something wrong at the foundation of this history of the robbery."

"Alas! little does it matter now to us, whether Mr. Tomlinson be a false or an unfortunate man," said the countess; "there is one thing certain—we are ruined!"

"Yes—my dearest wife, my beloved daughter," exclaimed the count, "we are in a pitiable situation—in a foreign land! It is true that I have friends: the Earl of Warrington—Lord Tremordyn, both of whom know our secret, and have faithfully kept it—would gladly assist me; but I would not—could not apply to them—even though it be to settle the few debts which I owe!"

"Still there remains one course," said the countess, hesitating, and regarding her husband with anxious timidity.

"One course!" ejaculated the count. "Ah! I know full well to what you allude; but never, never will I sell my rights for gold! No, my dear wife—my beloved daughter—we must prepare ourselves to meet our misfortunes in a becoming manner."

"Dear father," murmured Isabella, "your goodness has conferred upon me an excellent education: surely I might turn to advantage some of those accomplishments—"

"You, my sweetest girl!" cried the nobleman, surveying with feelings of ineffable pride the angelic countenance of the lovely being that was leaning upon his shoulder: "you—my own darling girl—a lady of your high rank become a governess! no—never, never!"

"Isabella, you are worthy of your noble sire," said the countess enthusiastically.

And, even in the hour of their misfortune, that exiled—ruined family found inexpressible solace in the sweet balm of each other's love!

CHAPTER LXXVII.

A WOMAN'S SECRET.

IT was now seven months since Ellen Monroe became the victim of George Greenwood.

She bore in her bosom the fruit of that amour; and until the present time she had managed to conceal her situation from those around her.

She now began to perceive the utter impossibility of veiling her disgrace much longer. Her health was failing, and her father and Markham were constantly urging upon her the necessity of receiving medical advice. This recommendation she invariably combated to the utmost of her power; and in order to give a colour to her assurance that she suffered only from some trivial physical ailment, she was compelled to affect a flow of good spirits which she was far—very far from experiencing.

Markham had frequently questioned her with the most earnest and friendly solicitude relative to the causes of those intervals of deep depression which it was impossible for her to conceal;—he had implored her to open her mind to him, as a sister might to a brother;—he had suggested to her change of scene, diversion, and other means of restoring her lost spirits;—but to all he advanced she returned evasive replies.

Richard and the aged father of the young lady frequently conversed together upon the subject, and lost themselves in conjectures relative to the cause of that decaying health and increasing unhappiness for which the sufferer herself would assign no feasible motive. At times Mr. Monroe was inclined to believe that the privations and vicissitudes which his daughter had experienced during the two years previous to their reception at the hospitable dwelling of Richard Markham, had engendered a profound melancholy in a mind that had been so painfully harassed, and had implanted the germs of a subtle malady in a system never constitutionally strong. This belief appeared the more reasonable when the old man called to mind the hours of toil—the wearisome vigils—and the exposure to want, cold, and inclement weather, which had been endured by the poor girl in the court in Golden Lane; and Markham sometimes yielded to the same impression relative to the causes of a mental and physical decline which every day became more apparent.

Then, again, Richard thought that the fresh air of the healthy locality where she now dwelt, and the absence of all care in respect to the wherewithal to sustain life, would have produced a beneficial effect. He enjoined her father to question her whether she cherished some secret affection—some love that had experienced disappointment; but to this demand she returned a positive negative: and her father assured his young friend that Ellen had had no opportunity of obtaining the affection of another, or of bestowing her own upon any being who now slighted it. Of course her true position was never suspected for a moment; and thus the cause of Ellen's unhappiness remained an object of varied and conflicting conjectures.

Seven months had now passed since that fatal day when the accursed old hag, whose name we have not allowed to defile these pages, handed her over to the arms of a ruthless libertine;—seven months of mental anguish and physical suffering had nearly flown;—the close of July was at hand;—and as yet Ellen had decided upon no plan to direct her future proceedings. She sometimes thought of returning to Greenwood, and endeavouring to touch his heart;—but then she remembered the way in which they had parted on the occasion of her visit to his house in Spring-Gardens;—she recalled to mind all she knew of the character of the man;—and she was compelled to abandon this idea. She felt that she would sooner die than accept his succour in the capacity of a mistress;—and there were, moreover, moments when she entertained sentiments of profound hatred, and experienced a longing for revenge, against the man who refused to do her justice. Then, again, she recollected that he was the father of the child which she bore in her bosom; and all her rancorous feelings dissolved in tears.

At other times she thought of throwing herself at her father's feet, and confessing all. But what woman does not shudder at such a step? Moreover, frail mortals invariably place reliance in the chapter of accidents, and entertain hopes, even in situations where it is impossible for those hopes to be realised.

To Richard Markham she would not—dared not breathe a syllable that might lead him to infer her shame;—and yet where was she to find a friend save in the person of her father and her benefactor?

Most pitiable was the situation of this poor girl. And yet she already felt a mother's feeling of love and solicitude for her unborn babe. Often—often in the still hour of night, when others slept, did she sit up and weep in her chamber;—often—often, while others forgot their cares in the arms of slumber, was she a prey to an agony of mind which seemed to admit of no solace. And then, in those hours of intense wretchedness, would the idea of suicide steal into her mind—that idea which suggests a last resource and a sure relief as a term for misery grown too heavy for mortal endurance. But, oh! she trembled—she trembled in the presence of that dread thought, which each night assumed a shape more awfully palpable, more fearfully defined to her imagination. She struggled against the idea: she exclaimed, in the bitterness of her agony, "Get thee behind me, tempter;"—and yet there the tempter stood, more plainly seen, more positive in its allurement than ever! That poor, helpless girl balanced in her mind whether she should dare human scorn, or in one mad moment resign her soul to Satan!

There was a piece of water at the back of the house close by the main road; and thither would her footsteps lead her—almost unvoluntarily, for the tempter pushed her on from behind;—thither would she repair at noon, to contemplate the sleeping waters of the lake within whose depths lurked one pearl more precious in the eyes of the unhappy than the brightest ornaments set in regal diadems,—the pearl of Oblivion! Thither did the lost one stray: upon the margin of that water did she hover like the ghost of one who had sought repose beneath that silver surface;—and, oh! how she longed to plunge into the shining water—and dared not.

At eve, too, when the sun had set, and every star on the dark vault above was reflected on the bosom of the lake, and the pure argent rays of the lovely moon seemed to fathom its mysterious depths,—then again did she seek the bank; and as she stood gazing upon the motionless pool, she prepared herself to take the one fatal leap that should terminate her sorrows—and dared not.

No—she shrank from suicide; and yet the time had now come when she must nerve herself to adopt some decided plan; for a prolonged concealment of her condition was impossible.

Markham's household consisted of Whittingham, Holford, and a female domestic of the name of Marian. This woman was a widow, and had been in the service of our hero only since his release from incarceration. She was between forty and fifty; and her disposition was kind, easy, and compassionate.

One night—about an hour after the inmates of the place had retired to their chambers—Ellen was sitting, as usual, mournfully in her room, pondering upon her unhappy condition, and dreading to seek a couch where her ideas assumed an aspect which made her brain reel as if with incipient madness,—when she heard a low knock at her door. She hastened to open it; and Marian instantly entered the room.

"Hush, my dear young lady," she said in a whisper: "do not be alarmed;"—and she carefully closed the door behind her.

"What is the matter, Marian?" exclaimed Ellen: "has any thing happened? is my father ill?"

"No, Miss—do not frighten yourself, I say," replied the servant. "I have come to console you; for I can't bear to see you pining away like this—dying by inches."

"What do you mean, Marian?" said Ellen, much confused.

"I mean, my dear Miss," continued the servant, "that if you won't think me impertinent, I might befriend you. The eyes of a woman are sharp and penetrating, Miss; and while every body else in the house is wondering what can make you so pale, and ill, and low-spirited, I do not want to conjecture to discover the cause."

"My God, Marian!" ejaculated the young lady, sinking into a chair; "you—you really frighten me: you mistake—you—"

And Ellen burst into tears.

The servant took her hand kindly, and said "Miss, forgive my boldness; but I am a woman—and I cannot bear to see one of my own sex suffer as you do. Besides, you are so good and gentle—and when I was ill a few weeks ago, you behaved with so much kindness to me, that my heart bleeds for you—it does indeed. I was coming down to you last night—and the night before—and the night before that too; but I didn't like to intrude upon you. And to-day I saw how very much you was altered; and I could restrain myself no longer. So, Miss, if I have done wrong, forgive me; for I have come with a good intention—and would go a hundred miles to serve you. In a word, Miss, you require a friend—a faithful friend; and if you will confide in me, Miss, I will give you the best advice, and help you in the best way I can."

"Marian, this is very kind of you—very kind," answered Ellen, to whose ear these words of female sympathy came ineffably sweet; "but I shall be better soon—I shall get well—"

"Ah! Miss," interrupted Marian, soothingly, "don't hesitate to confide in me. I know what ails you—I understand your situation; and I feel for you deeply—indeed, indeed I do."

"Marian—"

"Yes, Miss: you cannot conceal it from others much longer. For God's sake take some step before you kill yourself and your child at the same time."

"Marian—Marian, what do you say?" exclaimed Ellen, sobbing violently, as if her heart would break.

"Miss Monroe, you will shortly become a mother!"

"Ah! my God—kill me, kill me! Save me from this deep degradation—this last disgrace!"

"Calm yourself, Miss—calm yourself; and I will be your friend," said Marian. "I have been thinking of your condition for some time past—and I have already settled in my mind a plan to save you!"

"To save me—to save me!" exclaimed Ellen. "Oh, how can I ever repay you for this kindness?"

"I am but a poor ignorant woman, Miss," answered Marian; "but I hope that I do not possess a bad heart. At all events I can feel for *you*."

"A bad heart, Marian!" repeated Ellen. "Oh! no—you are goodness itself. But you said you had some plan to save me, Marian?"

"Yes, Miss. I have a sister, who is married and lives with her husband a few miles off. He is a market-gardener; and they have a nice little cottage. They will be delighted to do all they can for you."

"But how can I leave this house and remain absent for weeks without acquainting my benefactor Mr. Markham, and my poor old father? You forget, Marian—you forget that were I to steal away, and leave no trace behind me, it would break my father's heart."

"Then, Miss, you had better throw yourself at your father's feet, and tell him all."

"Never—never, Marian!" ejaculated Ellen, clasping her hands together, while her bosom heaved convulsively.

"Trust in Mr. Markham, Miss—let me break the truth to him?"

"Impossible, Marian! I should never dare to look him in the face again."

"And the person—the individual—the father of your child, Miss—" said the servant, hesitatingly.

"Mention not him—allude not to him," cried Ellen; then, after a pause, she added in a low and almost despairing tone, "No!—hope exists not there!"

"And yet, Miss," continued Marian, "you must make up your mind to something—and that soon. You cannot conceal your situation another fortnight without danger to yourself and the little unborn innocent. Besides, you have made no preparations, Miss; and if any sudden accident—"

"Ah! Marian, you remind me of my duty," interrupted Ellen. "I must not sacrifice the life of that being who has not asked me to give it existence—who is the innocent fruit of my shame,—I must not sacrifice its life to any selfish scruples of mine! Thank you, Marian—thank you! You have reminded me of my duty! come to me again to-morrow night, and I will tell you what step I have determined to take without delay!"

The servant then retired; and Ellen remained alone—alone with the most desolating, heart-breaking reflections.

At length her ideas produced a mental agony which was beyond endurance. She rose from her chair, and advanced towards the window, against the cold glass of which she leant her brow—her burning brow, to cool it. The moon shone brightly, and edged the clouds of night with silver. The eyes of the wretched girl wandered over the landscape, the outlines of which were strongly marked beneath the lustre of the moon; and amongst other objects, she caught sight of the small lake at a little distance. It shone like a pool of quicksilver, and seemed to woo her to its bosom.

Upon that lake her eye rested long and wistfully; and again the tempter stood behind her, and urged her to seek repose beneath that shining surface.

She asked herself for what she had to live? She did not seek to combat the arguments of the secret tempter; but she collected into one focus all her sorrows; and at length the contemplation of that mass of misery strengthened the deep anxiety which she felt to escape from this world for ever.

And all the while she kept her eyes fixed upon the lake that seemed sleeping beneath the moonlight which kissed its bosom.

But her poor father! and the babe that she bore in her breast! oh! no—she dared not die! Her suicide would not comprise one death only;—but it would be the death of a second, and the death of a third,—the death of her father, and the death of her still unborn child!

She turned away from the window, and hastened to seek her couch. But slumber did not visit her eyes. She lay pondering on the best course for her to pursue; but the more she reflected upon her condition, the farther off did she seem to wander from any settled point. At length she sank into an uneasy sleep; and her grief pursued her in her dreams.

She rose late; and when she descended to the breakfast-room she learnt that Richard Markham was about to depart immediately for the Continent. Whittingham was busily occupied in packing his master's baggage in the hall; and Holford had been despatched into town to order a post-chaise.

Markham explained this sudden movement on his part by placing a letter in Ellen's hand, saying at the same time, "This is from a man who has been a friend to me: I cannot hesitate a moment to obey his summons."

Ellen cast her eyes over the letter and read as follows:—

"Boulogne-sur-Mer, France,
"July 24, 1839.

"MY DEAR YOUNG FRIEND,

"If you can possibly dispose of your time for a few days, come to me at once. A severe accident—which may prove fatal—renders it prudent that I should attend to my worldly affairs; and to this end I require the assistance of a friend. Such I know you to be.

"THOMAS ARMSTRONG."

"The accident which my friend has met with must have been a serious one," said Markham, "or his letter would be more explicit. I feel deeply anxious to know the whole truth; for it was he who gave me courage to face the world, and taught me how to raise my head again, after my release from imprisonment;—he also introduced me to *one*——"

Markham ceased: and for some moments his thoughts were bent wholly on Isabella.

At length the post-chaise arrived, and Richard departed on his journey, after bidding adieu to Mr. Monroe and Ellen, and having received a special request from the faithful Whittingham "to mind and not to be conglomerated by any such fellers as Kidderminster and them wulgar chaps which called butlers *tulips*."

CHAPTER LXXVIII.

MARIAN.

In the evening Ellen retired early to her apartment, for she felt very unwell; and certain sensations which she had experienced during the day had alarmed her.

A short time after she had withdrawn to the security of her own chamber, the faithful and kind-hearted Marian made her appearance.

"This is very good of you, Marian," said Ellen. "I never felt the want of some one to talk to and console, so much as I do to-night."

"You look very pale and ill, Miss," observed the servant: "had you not better retire to rest?"

"Yes," said Ellen. "I wish to struggle against a sense of weariness and oppression which comes over me; and I cannot."

"Heavens, Miss!—If any thing was to happen to you to-night—"

"It cannot be that, Marian; but I feel very, very ill."

Marian aided Miss Monroe to divest herself of her garments; and the young lady retired to her couch.

"How do you feel now, Miss?"

"Alas! I am not better, good Marian. I feel—I feel—"

"My God, Miss! you are about to become a mother this very night. Oh! what is to be done? what is to be done?"

"Save me, save me, Marian—do not suffer me to be exposed!" cried Ellen wildly.

"Why did I not speak to you before last night? We might have made some arrangement—invented some plan: but now—now it is impossible!"

"Do not say it is impossible, Marian—do not take away every remaining hope—for I am wretched, very wretched."

"Poor young lady!" said Marian, advancing towards the bed, and taking Ellen's hand.

"It is not for myself that I care so much," continued the unhappy girl; "it is for my poor father. It would break his heart—oh! it would break his heart!"

"And he is a good, kind old gentleman," observed Marian.

"And he has tasted already so deeply of the bitter cup of adversity," said Ellen, "that a blow like this would send him to his grave. I know him so well—he would never survive my dishonour. He has loved me so tenderly—he has taken such pride in me, it would kill him! Do you hear, Marian?—it would kill him. Ah! you weep—you weep for me, kind Marian!"

"Yes, Miss: I would do any thing I could to serve you. But now—it is too late—"

"Say not that it is too late!" ejaculated Ellen, distractedly: "say not that all chance of avoiding exposure has fled! take compassion on me, Marian; take compassion on my poor old father! Ah! these pains—"

"Tell me how I can serve you, Miss—"

"Alas! I cannot concentrate my ideas, Marian; I am bewildered—I am reduced to despair! Oh! if men only knew what bitter, bitter anguish they entail upon poor woman, when they sacrifice her to their desires—"

"Do not make yourself miserable, dear young lady," interrupted Marian, whose eyes were dimmed with tears. "Something must be done! How do you feel now?"

"I cannot explain my sensations. My mental pangs are so great that they almost absorb my bodily sufferings; and yet, it seems as if the latter were increasing every moment."

"There can be no doubt of it, Miss," said Marian. "Do you know that when I heard this morning of Mr. Markham's intended departure for France it struck me at the moment that Providence interfered in your behalf. I do not know why such an idea should have come across me; for I could not foresee that you would be so soon overtaken with—"

"I feel that I am getting worse, Marian; can nothing be done? must my poor father know all? Oh! think of his grey hairs—his wrinkles! Think how he loves me—his only child! Alas! can nothing be done to save me from disgrace? How shall I ever be able to meet Mr. Markham again? Ah! Marian, you would not desert me in such a moment as this?"

"No, dear young lady—not for worlds!"

"Thank you, Marian! And yet forgive me if I say again, do not desert me—do not expose me! Oh! let me die rather than have my shame made known. Think, Marian—do you not know of any means of screening me?"

"I am bewildered," exclaimed the poor woman. "How do you feel now?"

"My fears augment, that—"

"Ah! it is premature, you see, Miss! What is to be done? what shall we do?"

"Marian, I beseech you—I implore you not to expose me!" said Ellen, in a tone of such intense agony, that the good-hearted woman was touched to the very soul.

A sudden idea seemed to strike her.

"I know a young surgeon in the village—who is just married, and has only set up in business a few weeks—he is very poor—and he does not know where I am now in service."

"Do any thing you choose, Marian—follow the dictates of your own mind—but do not expose me! Oh! my God! what misery—what misery is this!"

"Yes," continued Marian, musing, "there is no other resource. But, Miss," she added, turning towards the suffering girl, "if I can save you from exposure, you must part with your child, should it be born alive!"

"I am in your hands: save me from exposure—for my poor old father's sake! That is all I ask."

"This, then," said Marian, "is the only alternative; there is nothing else to be done! And perhaps even *he* will not consent—"

"To whom do you allude?" demanded Ellen impatiently.

"To the young surgeon of whom I spoke. But I must try: at all events his assistance must be had. Miss, my plan is too long to tell you now: do you think it is safe to leave you alone for three quarters of an hour?"

"Oh! yes—if it be for my benefit, kind—good Marian," said Ellen. "But I must not be exposed—even to the surgeon!"

"The room must then be quite dark," observed Marian. "Do you mind that?"

Ellen shook her head.

"Then, take courage, Miss—and I think I can promise—but we shall see."

The servant then hastily extinguished the lights and left the room.

She hurried up to her own chamber, took from her box a purse containing forty sovereigns—all her little savings, put on her bonnet and shawl, concealed her face with a thick black veil, and then stole carefully down stairs.

All was quiet; and she left the house by the back door.

* * * * * *
* * * * *
* * * * * *

In three quarters of an hour two persons advanced together up the garden at the back of the house.

One was a woman; and she led a man, whose eyes were blindfolded with a black handkerchief.

"Your hand trembles," said Marian—for she was the female alluded to.

"No," answered the surgeon. "But one word—ere I proceed farther."

"Speak—do not delay."

"You gave me forty pounds for this night's work. What guarantee do you offer me that the child—should it survive—will not be left on my hands, altogether unprovided for?"

"Trust to paternal affection, sir," answered Marian. "I can promise you that the child will not even remain long with you."

"Well, I will venture it," said the surgeon. "Your money will save me from being compelled to shut up my establishment after an unsuccessful struggle of only a few weeks; and I ought not to ask too many questions."

"And you remember your solemn promise, sir, not to attempt to obtain any clue to the place to which I am conducting you."

"On my honour as a man—on my solemn word as a gentleman."

"Enough, sir. Let us proceed."

Marian led the surgeon onward, and admitted him into the house by the back door.

All was still quiet.

We have said on a previous occasion that the mansion was a

spacious one. Ellen's apartment was far removed from that in which her father slept; and the rooms occupied by Whittingham and Holford were on the uppermost storey. There consequently existed little chance of disturbing any one.

Marian led the surgeon very cautiously up the staircase to Ellen's chamber, which they entered as noiselessly as possible.

Upon advancing into the room, which was quite dark, the surgeon struck against a chest of drawers, and uttered a slight ejaculation of pain; but not loud enough to reach the ears of those from whom it was necessary to conceal this nocturnal proceeding.

Ellen was in the pangs of maternity when Marian and the surgeon came to her assistance; and in a few moments after their arrival, she was the mother of a boy.

Oh! who can express her feelings when the gentle cry of the child fell upon her ears—that child from whom she was to part in a few minutes, perhaps for ever?

* * * * * * *
* * * * * *

Half an hour afterwards Marian and the surgeon were again threading the garden;—but this time their steps led them away from the house.

Beneath her thick shawl, carefully wrapped up, the servant carried Ellen's child.

She conducted the surgeon to within a short distance of his own abode, placed the child in his arms, and hurried rapidly away.

She returned to the Place, and ascended to Ellen's chamber without disturbing the other inmates.

"Ah! Marian," said Ellen, "how can I ever sufficiently thank you for your kindness of this night?"

"Silence, my dear young lady. Do not mention it! You must keep yourself very tranquil and quiet; and in the morning I must say that you are too unwell to rise."

"And that surgeon—"

"I know what you would ask, Miss," interrupted Marian. "All is safe and secret—the bandage was never raised from the surgeon's eyes from the moment he left his own house until he was far away from here again; nor did he once catch a glimpse of my face, for

when I first went to explain the business to him and engage his assistance, he came down from his bed-chamber and spoke to me in the passage where it was quite dark. Moreover, I had taken my thick black veil with me by way of precaution. Therefore, he can never know me again."

"But the means of securing his assistance? how did you contrive that, Marian?"

"Well, Miss, if you must know," said the servant, after some hesitation, "I had saved up forty pounds—"

"And you gave him all!" exclaimed Ellen. "Oh! this was truly noble! However—I shall know how to repay you fourfold."

"We will speak of that another time, Miss," answered Marian. "You must now endeavour to obtain some sleep;—and I shall sit with you all night."

"Tell me one thing, Marian," said Ellen, with tears in her eyes;—"the child—"

"Will be well taken care of, Miss. Do not alarm yourself about that. And now you must try and obtain some repose."

In a few moments the young mother was overtaken by a profound sleep—the first she had enjoyed for many, many weeks. But even this slumber was not attended by dreams of unmixed pleasure: the thoughts of her child—her new-born child, entrusted to the care of strangers, and severed from the maternal bosom—followed her in her visions.

She awoke, considerably refreshed, at about seven o'clock in the morning.

The faithful Marian was still watching by her side, and had prepared her some refreshment, of which Ellen partook.

The young mother then asked for writing materials; and, in spite of the remonstrances of Marian, sate up in her bed, and wrote a letter.

When she had sealed and addressed it, she spoke in the following manner:

"Marian, I have now one favour to ask you. You have already given me such proofs of friendship and fidelity, that I need not implore you to observe the strictest secrecy with respect to the request that I am about to make. At the same time, I shall feel more happy if you will promise me, that under any circumstances—whether my shame remain concealed, or not—you will never disclose, without my consent, the name of the person to whom this letter is addressed, and to whom you must carry it as speedily as possible."

"You know, Miss, that I will do anything I can to make you happy. Your secret is safe in my keeping."

"Thank you, Marian! My father would curse me—Mr. Markham would scorn me, did they know that I held communication with this man;"—and she showed the address upon the letter to Marian.

"Mr. Greenwood!" exclaimed the servant. "Ah! now I recollect—Whittingham has told me that he is the person who ruined your poor father, and robbed Mr. Markham of nearly all his property."

"And yet, Marian," said Ellen, "that man—that same Mr. Greenwood, who reduced my poor father to beggary, and plundered Mr. Markham—that very same individual is the father of my child!"

"Ah! Miss, now I understand how impossible it was for you to reveal your condition to your father, or to Mr. Markham. The blow would have been too severe upon both!"

"Yes, Marian—Mr. Greenwood is the father of my child; and more than that—he is—but no matter," said Ellen, suddenly checking herself. "You now know my secret, Marian; and you will never reveal it?"

"Never, Miss, I promise you most solemnly."

"And you will take this letter to him to-day—and you will wait for his reply."

"I will go this afternoon, Miss; and will obey your wishes in every way."

"And now, Marian, hasten to tell my father that I am unwell; and resist any desire on his part to obtain medical assistance."

"Leave that to me, Miss. You already appear so much better that the old gentleman will easily be induced to suppose that a little rest is all you require."

"Ah! Marian—how can I ever reward you for all your goodness towards me?"

CHAPTER LXXIX.

THE BILL.—A FATHER.

NOTHING could be more business-like than the study of Mr. Greenwood. The sofa was heaped up with papers tied round with red tape, and endorsed, some "Corn-Laws," others "New Poor Law," a third batch "Rottenborough Union," a fourth "Select Committee on Bribery at Elections;" and so on.

Piles of letters lay upon one table; piles of newspapers upon another; and a number of Reports of various Committees of the House of Commons, easily recognised by their unwieldy shapes and blue covers, was heaped up on the cheffonier between the windows.

The writing-table was also arranged, with a view to effect, in the manner described upon a former occasion; and in his arm-chair lounged Mr. Greenwood, pleasantly engaged in perusing the daily newspaper which contained the oration that he had delivered in the House on the preceding evening.

It was about three o'clock in the afternoon. Mr. Greenwood had risen late, for the House had not separated until half-past two in the morning, and the member for Rottenborough was a man of too decidedly business-habits to leave his post in the middle of a debate.

Lafleur entered, and announced Sir Rupert Harborough.

"I have called about that bill again," said the baronet. "When it came due at the end of March, we renewed it for four months. It will be due again to-morrow."

"I am aware of it," said Greenwood. "What do you propose to do?"

"I am in no condition to pay it," answered the baronet.

"You must provide a portion, and renew for the remainder," said Greenwood.

"It is impossible, my dear fellow!" exclaimed Sir Rupert. "I am completely at low water-mark again, upon my honour!"

"And yet I have heard that you and Chichester have not been altogether unsuccessful in the play-world during the last few months," observed Greenwood.

"Not so prosperous as you may fancy," returned the baronet. "Come, what shall we say about this bill?"

"I have told you. The bill was originally given for fifteen hundred pounds—"

"For which I only had a thousand."

"I don't recollect now. At all events, it fell due; and fortunately I had not passed it away."

"Of course not. You promised to retain it in your portfolio."

"I don't recollect. You could not pay it; and I agreed to renew it—"

"On condition of making it sixteen hundred," said the baronet.

"I don't recollect," observed Greenwood again. "Now you come to me, and tell me that you can do nothing towards it. Things cannot go on so."

"But you knew very well, Greenwood, when you took it, that the day of payment might be rather distant."

"I don't recollect. You must bring me the six hundred, and I will renew for the thousand—without interest. There!"

"And where the devil am I to find six hundred pounds on a sudden like this?" exclaimed Sir Rupert.

"I am sure I am not aware of your private resources, my good sir," answered Greenwood, coolly. "You must be well aware that I cannot afford to remain without my money in this manner; and since it would appear you do not wish Lord Tremordyn to know that you have not paid the acceptance which he so kindly lent you—"

"Lent me!" ejaculated Sir Rupert, now really alarmed.

"Of course. He could not possibly have owed you the amount."

"Greenwood, what do you mean by this?" cried the baronet. "Upon my honour, one would almost suppose that you had forgotten the real nature of the transaction."

"Possibly I may not recall to mind some of the minor details. One thing is, however, certain: I have in my possession a bill bearing your endorsement and accepted by Lord Tremordyn, for sixteen hundred pounds; and I offer you the most easy terms I can think of for its payment."

"Greenwood, you cannot have forgotten—"

"Forgotten what?"

"Forgotten that the acceptance—"

"Well?"

"Is not Lord Tremordyn's."

"The acceptance not Lord Tremordyn's!" cried Mr. Greenwood, affecting to be quite confounded by this statement.

"Certainly not," answered the baronet. "You yourself suggested to me—"

"I suggested!" cried Greenwood, now pretending indignation. "Sir Rupert Harborough, what are you aiming at? to what point would you arrive?"

"Oh! if I were not in the power of this man!" thought the baronet, actually grinding his teeth with rage; but suppressing his feelings, he said, "My dear Greenwood, pray renew this bill for four months more, and it shall be paid at maturity."

"No, Sir Rupert Harborough," replied the capitalist, who had not failed to notice the emotions of concentrated rage which filled the mind of the baronet. "I am decided: give me six hundred pounds, and I renew for the thousand; otherwise—"

"Otherwise," repeated Sir Rupert mechanically.

"I shall pay the bill into my banker's this afternoon, and it will be presented for payment at Lord Tremordyn's agent's to-morrow morning."

"You would not wish to ruin me, Greenwood!"

"Such a course will not ruin you: Lord Tremordyn will of course honour his acceptance."

"Greenwood, you drive me mad!"

"I am really very sorry to hear it; but if every one who could not meet his bills were driven mad by being asked for payment of them, every third house in the street would become a lunatic-asylum."

"You can spare your raillery, Mr. Greenwood," said the baronet. "Do you wish to have me transported?"

"Certainly not. I want a proper settlement in this respect."

"And how can I settle the bill? Where am I to procure six hundred pounds at a moment's warning?"

"A moment's warning! you have had four clear months."

"But I fancied—I hoped you would renew the bill from time to time until I could pay it. You said as much when you lent me the money upon it."

"I don't recollect."

"You did indeed; and upon the faith of that promise, I—"

"I don't recollect."

"My God! what am I to do?" cried Sir Rupert, despairingly. "I have no means of raising half the sum you require."

"Then why did you take my money seven months ago?"

"Why did I take the money? why did I take it? Because you yourself proposed the transaction. You said, '*Bring me the acceptance of Lord Tremordyn for fifteen hundred pounds, and I will lend you a thousand upon it immediately.*'"

"I don't recollect."

"And you said emphatically and distinctly that *you should not call upon Lord Tremordyn to inquire if it were his acceptance.*"

"Of course not. Amongst gentlemen such a proceeding would be unpardonable."

"Oh! Greenwood, you affect ignorance in all this! and yet it was you who put the infernal idea into my head—"

"Sir Rupert Harborough," said the capitalist, rising from his chair; "enough of this! I put no infernal ideas into any one's head. Settle the bill in the way I propose; or it shall take its course."

"But—my God! you will send me to the Old Bailey!" cried the baronet, whose countenance was actually livid with rage and alarm.

"And did you not send Richard Markham thither?" said

Greenwood, fixing his piercing dark eyes upon Sir Rupert Harborough in so strange a manner that the unhappy man shrank from that fearful glance.

"But what matters that to you?" cried the baronet. "In one word, will you ruin me? or will you give me time to pay this accursed bill?"

"I have stated my conditions: I will not depart from them," replied Greenwood in a determined manner. "You have plenty of time before you. I will keep the bill back until to-morrow morning at twelve o'clock."

"Very good, sir," said the baronet, scarcely able to repress his rage.

Sir Rupert Harborough then withdrew, a prey to feelings more easily imagined than described.

"Why should I allow this gambler to retain my money without even paying me the interest?" said Greenwood to himself, when he was again alone. "I can keep him in my power as well with a forged bill for a thousand, as for sixteen hundred pounds. As for his wife, the beautiful Cecilia—I am now wearied of that intrigue, which, moreover, becomes too expensive! Lady Cecilia's extravagance is unbounded. I must put an end to that connexion without delay!"

Lafleur entered the room at this moment, and said, "A female, sir, desires to see you upon particular business."

"Is it anybody whom you know?"

Lafleur replied in the negative.

"Never mind! I will see her," said Greenwood; and, unaware who she might be, he seated himself at his writing-table, where he appeared to be profoundly occupied with some deeds that were lying before him.

In a few moments Marian entered the room.

"Well, my good woman, what is the object of your call?" demanded Greenwood.

"I am the bearer of a letter, sir, from Miss Monroe," was the reply.

"From Miss Monroe!" ejaculated Greenwood, and he hastened to peruse the letter which the servant placed in his hand.

Its contents ran thus:—

"You are the father of a boy. The excellent woman who bears this will explain every thing to you. I should not recall myself to your memory—if you have forgotten the mother of your child—did not a sacred duty towards the female whom I have above alluded to, and towards the helpless infant who perhaps will never know a parent's care, compel me thus to address you. The kind woman who will give you this, expended forty pounds—all her little savings—to save me from disgrace. The surgeon to whose care the child is entrusted, must receive a small allowance for its support. If you ever entertained one generous feeling towards me, relieve my mind on these two subjects.

"ELLEN MONROE."

For some minutes Mr. Greenwood appeared to be absorbed in thought.

He then questioned Marian relative to the particulars of Ellen's accouchement; and she detailed to him every particular with which the reader is already acquainted.

"You managed the matter admirably," said Greenwood. "There are two points to which Miss Monroe directs my attention in this note. In the first place, she speaks of your most disinterested services. Accept this as a trifling mark of my gratitude:"—and he placed six Bank-notes for ten pounds each in Marian's hand.

"I do not desire any remuneration, sir," said the kind-hearted woman. "I will take my forty pounds; but the other two notes I must beg to return."

"No—keep them," exclaimed Greenwood.

"I thank you, sir, most sincerely," said the servant firmly; "but I would rather not. I rendered Miss Monroe that service which one female should afford another in such a case and I cannot think of accepting any recompense."

With these words she laid two of the notes upon the table.

"You are really a most extraordinary woman," cried Greenwood, who was perfectly astonished at the idea of any one in her class of life refusing money. "Will you not permit me to offer you a ring—a watch—or some trinket—"

"No, sir," replied Marian, with severe firmness of tone and manner. "Miss Monroe is so kind—so good—so gentle, I would go to the end of the world to serve her."

"Well—you must have your own way," said Mr. Greenwood. "The next point in Miss Monroe's letter is a provision for her child. What sum do you suppose would content the surgeon and his wife who have taken care of it?"

"They are poor people, sir—struggling against difficulties—and having their way to make in the world—"

"Suppose we say forty pounds a year for the present?" interrupted Greenwood.

"Oh! sir—that will be ample!" exclaimed Marian: "and Miss Monroe will be so rejoiced! Ah! sir—what consolation to the poor young lady."

"What is the address of the surgeon?" demanded Greenwood.

"*Mr. Wentworth, Lower Holloway*," was the reply.

"My servant shall call upon that gentleman this very evening, and carry him the first quarter's payment," continued Greenwood. "You can say to Miss Monroe—but stay: I will write her a few lines."

"Oh! do sir. Who knows but it may console her?" ejaculated the kind-hearted Marian.

Mr. Greenwood wrote as follows:—

"Your wishes are attended to on every point. The existence of the child need never be known to either Mr. Monroe or Mr. Richard Markham. Keep faithfully *all the secrets* which are treasured in your bosom; and I will never desert the child. I will watch over its welfare from a distance: trust to me. You were wrong to hesitate to apply to me. My purse is at all times at your disposal—so long as those secrets remain undivulged.

"G. M. G."

Marian, prompted by that inherently kind feeling which had influenced her entire conduct towards Ellen, hesitated for a few moments, after receiving this letter, and seemed anxious to speak. She would have pleaded in behalf of the young mother: she would have implored Greenwood to make her his own in the sight of heaven, and acknowledge their child. But her tongue clave to the roof of her mouth;—and she at length retired, unable to give utterance to a single word in favour of poor Ellen.

As soon as she was gone, Greenwood rang for his faithful French valet.

"Lafleur," said he, "you will take these ten pounds, and proceed without delay to the house of Mr. Wentworth, a surgeon residing in Lower Holloway. You will say to him, '*The father of the child which was entrusted to you last night in so mysterious a manner, will allow you forty pounds a year for its support. As it grows older, and the expenses it incurs augment, this allowance will be proportionately increased. But should you endeavour to find out who are the parents of that child, it will instantly be removed to the care of others who may possess less curious dispositions.'*—You will pay him those ten pounds: you will tell him that every three months you will call with a similar sum; and you will see the child. Remember, you will see the child. If it have any peculiar mark about it, notice that mark: at all events, study it well, that you may know it again. You will moreover direct that its Christian name be *Richard*: its surname is immaterial. In a word, you will neither say nor do a whit more nor less than I have told you."

"I understand, sir," answered Lafleur. "Any further commands?"

"No—not at present. Be cautious how you conduct this business. It is delicate."

"You may depend upon me, sir."

And Lafleur retired.

"Thus far it is well," said Greenwood to himself, when he was again alone. "I am relieved of a subject of frequent annoying reflection and suspense. Ellen's shame is unknown to those from whom I was most anxious it should be concealed. It can never transpire now!"

The clock struck six; and Mr. Greenwood repaired to his dressing-room to arrange his toilet for dinner.

CHAPTER LXXX.

THE REVELATION.

THAT same evening Mr. Chichester dined with his friend Sir Rupert Harborough, at the dwelling of the latter in Tavistock Square.

Whenever her husband invited this guest, Lady Cecilia invariably made it a rule to accept an invitation elsewhere.

The baronet and his friend were therefore alone together.

"This is awkward—very awkward," said Chichester, when the cloth was removed, and the two gentlemen were occupied with their wine.

"Awkward! I believe you," exclaimed the baronet. "Upon my honour, that Greenwood ought to be well thrashed!"

"He is an insufferable coxcomb," said Chichester.

"A conceited humbug," added the baronet.

"A self-sufficient fool," remarked Chichester.

"A consummate scoundrel," cried Sir Rupert.

"So he is," observed Chichester.

"But all this will not pay my bill," continued the baronet; "and where to obtain six hundred pounds, the deuce take me if I can tell."

"No—nor I either," said Chichester; "unless we get a couple of horses and ride down towards Hounslow upon a venture."

"You never can be serious, Chichester? What! turn highwaymen!"

"I was only joking. But do you really think that Greenwood will press you so hard?"

"He will send the bill to Lord Tremordyn's banker's to-morrow. Oh! I can assure you he was quite high about it, and pretended to forget all the circumstances that had led to the transaction. To every word I said, it was '*I don't recollect.*' May the devil take him!"

"And so he has got you completely in his power?"

"Completely."

"And you would like to have your revenge?"

"Of course I should. But what is the use of talking in this manner? You know very well that I can do him no injury!"

"I am not quite so sure of that," said Chichester.

"What do you mean?" demanded the baronet. "I can see that there is something in your mind."

"I was only thinking. Suppose we accused him of something that he would not like exposed, and could not very well refute—an intrigue with any particular lady, for instance—"

"Ah! if we could—even though it were with my own wife," exclaimed the baronet. "And, by the bye, he is very intimate with Lady Cecilia."

"Of course he is," said Chichester drily. "Have you never noticed that before."

"It never struck me until now," observed the baronet.

"But it has struck me—frequently," added Chichester.

"And when I think of it," continued Sir Rupert Harborough, "he has often been here for an hour or two together; for I have gone out and left him with Lady Cecilia in the drawing-room; and when I have come back, he has been there still."

"Greenwood is not the man to waste his time at a lady's apron-strings for nothing."

"Chichester—you do not mean—"

"Oh! no—I mean nothing more than you choose to surmise."

"And what would you have me surmise?"

"I do not suppose," said Chichester, "that you care very much for Lady Cecilia."

"You are well aware of my feelings with regard to her."

"And out of all the money she has had lately—an affluence that you yourself have noticed more than once—she has never assisted you."

"No—never. And I have often puzzled myself to think whence came those supplies."

"You cannot suppose that either Lord or Lady Tremordyn replenish her purse?"

"Yes—I have thought so."

"Oh! very well; you know best;" and Chichester sipped his wine with an affected indifference which was in itself most eloquently significant.

"My dear fellow," said the baronet, after a pause, "I feel convinced that you have got some plan in your head, or else that you know more than you choose to say. In either case, Lady Cecilia is concerned. I have told you that I care not one fig about her—on my honour! Have the kindness, then, to speak without reserve."

"And then you may be offended," said Chichester.

"How absurd! Speak."

"What if I was to tell you that Lady Cecilia—"

"Well?"

"Is Greenwood's mistress!"

"The proof! the proof!" ejaculated the baronet.

"I myself saw them in each other's arms."

Sir Rupert Harborough's countenance grew deadly pale, and his lips quivered. He now revolted from the mere idea of what he had just before wished to be a fact.

"You remember the day that Greenwood called to acquaint us with his success at Rottenborough in March last?" said Chichester, after a pause. "You and I had been practising with the dice and cards; and we went out together."

"I recollect," exclaimed the baronet; "and you returned for the dice-boxes which you had left behind."

"It was upon that occasion. Greenwood followed me out of the drawing-room, and gave me a hundred pounds to keep the secret."

"True! you produced a hundred pounds immediately afterwards; and you said that Greenwood had lent you the amount. Why did you never tell me of this before?"

"The deuce! Is it a pleasant thing to communicate to a friend, Harborough? Besides, it always struck me that the discovery would one day or another be of some use."

"Of use indeed!" ejaculated the baronet. "And Lady Cecilia is Greenwood's mistress! Ah! that explains the restoration of her diamonds, as well as the improved condition of her finances. The false creature!"

"You must admit, Harborough," said Chichester, "that you have never been over attentive to your wife; and if—"

"Nonsense, my good fellow," interrupted the baronet sharply. "That is no excuse for a woman. A man may do what he chooses; but a man's wife—"

"Come, come—no moralizing," said Chichester. "It is all your own fault. Not one woman out of fifty would go wrong, if the husband behaved properly. But now that I have told you the secret, think what use you can make of it."

"I cannot see how the circumstance can serve me, without farther proof," remarked the baronet. "Ah! Lady Cecilia—what duplicity! what deceit!"

"Why not search her drawers—her boxes?" said Chichester. "She is absent; no one can interrupt you; and perhaps you may find a letter—"

"Excellent thought!" cried Sir Rupert; and, seizing a candle, he hurried from the room.

Twenty minutes elapsed, during which Mr. Chichester sate drinking his wine as comfortably as if he had done a good action, instead of revealing so fearful a secret to his friend.

At length Sir Rupert Harborough returned to the dining-room.

He was very pale; and there was something ghastly in his countenance, and sinister in the expression of his eyes.

"Well—any news?" inquired Chichester.

"No proof—not a note, not a letter," answered the baronet. "But I have found something," he added, with an hysterical kind of laugh, "that will answer my purpose for the moment better still."

"What is that?" asked his friend.

"Lady Cecilia's diamonds and other trinkets—presents, most likely, from Greenwood—together with ninety pounds in notes and gold."

"Capital!" cried Chichester. "You can now settle with Greenwood."

"Yes—I will pay him his six hundred pounds, renew for the remainder for three or four months, and then devise some plot to obtain undeniable proof of his amour with Lady Cecilia. But when I think of that woman, Chichester—not that she is any thing to me—still she is my wife—"

"Nonsense! It is fortunate for you that I told you of the affair, or else you would never have thought of using her property for the purpose of raising the sum you require."

"Ah! I will be revenged on that Greenwood!" cried Sir Rupert, in whose mind one idea was uppermost, in spite of his depraved and selfish disposition: "I will have the most signal vengeance upon the seducer of my wife! But remember, Chichester—I care nothing for *her*;—still the outrage—the dishonour—the perfidy! Yes—by God!" he added, dashing his clenched fist upon the table; "I will be avenged!"

"And in the mean time convert the diamonds and jewels into money," said Chichester. "It is only seven o'clock; we have plenty of time for the pawnbroker's."

"Come," cried the baronet, whose manner continued to be excited and irritable; "I am ready."

The two friends emptied their glasses, and took their departure, the baronet having carefully secured about his person the booty he had plundered from his wife. They then bent their steps towards the pawnbroking-establishment of Mr. V——, in the Strand.

What a strange type of all the luxury, dissipation, extravagance, profligacy, misery, ruin, and want, which characterise the various classes of society, is a pawnbroker's shop! It is the emporium whither go the jewels of the aristocrat, the clothes of the mechanic, the ornaments of the actress, and the necessaries of the poor. Genteel profligacy and pining industry seek, at the same place—the one the means for fresh extravagance, the other the wherewith to purchase food to sustain life. Two broad and direct roads branch off from the pawnbroker's shop in different directions; the first leading to the gaming-table, the second to the gin-palace; and then those paths are carried onwards, past those half-way houses of destruction, and converge to one point, at which they meet at last, and whose name is Ruin.

Two working men have been seen standing at the corner of a street, whispering together: at length one has taken off his coat, gone to the pawnbroker's, come out with the proceeds, and accompanied the other to the nearest gin-shop, where they have remained until all the money raised upon the garment was expended. Again, during the absence from home of the hard-working mechanic, his intemperate wife has collected together their few necessaries, carried them to the pawnbroker's, and spent the few shillings, thus procured, on gin. The thief, when he has picked a pocket of a watch, finds a ready means of disposing of it at the pawnbroker's. Hundreds of working-men pledge their Sunday garments regularly every Monday morning, and redeem them again on Saturday night.

Are pawnbrokers' shops a necessary evil? To some extent they are. They afford assistance to those whom some pressing urgence suddenly overtakes, or who are temporarily out of work. But are not the facilities which they thus present to all classes liable to an abuse more than commensurate with this occasional advantage? Decidedly. They supply a ready means for drink to those who would hesitate before they sold their little property out-and-out; for every one who pawns, under such circumstances, entertains the hope and intention of redeeming the articles again. The enormous interest charged by pawnbrokers crushes and effectually ruins the poor. We will suppose that a mechanic pledges his best clothes every Monday morning, and redeems them every Saturday night for wear on the Sabbath: we will presume that the pawnbroker lends him one pound each time:—they will thus be in pawn 313 days in each year, for which year he will pay 3*s*. 8*d*. interest, and 4*s* 4*d*. for duplicates—making a total of 8*s*. Thus he pays 8*s*. for the use of his own clothes for 52 days!

If the government were really a paternal one—if it had the welfare of the industrious community at heart, it would take the system of lending money upon deposits under its own supervision, and establish institutions similar to the Mont de Piété in France. Correctly managed, demanding a small interest upon loans, such institutions would become a blessing:—now the shops of pawnbrokers are an evil and a curse!

Sir Rupert Harborough entered the pawnbroker's shop by the front door, while Mr. Chichester awaited him in the Lowther Arcade.

The baronet was well known in that establishment; and he accordingly entered into a friendly and familiar chat with one of the young men behind the counter.

"That is a very handsome painting," said Sir Rupert, pointing to one suspended to the wall.

"Yes, sir. It was pledged fifteen months ago for seven pounds, by a young nobleman who had received it along with fifty pounds in cash the same morning by way of discount for a thousand pound bill."

"And what do you expect for it?"

"Eighty guineas," answered the young man coolly. "But here is one much finer than that," continued the pawnbroker's assistant, turning towards another painting. "That expired a few days ago. It was only pledged for thirty guineas."

"And how much have you the conscience to ask for it?"

"One hundred and twenty," whispered the young man. "There is something peculiar connected with that picture. It belonged to an upholsterer who was once immensely rich, but who was ruined by giving credit to the Duke of York."

"To the Duke of York—eh?"

"Oh! yes, sir: we have received in pledge the goods of many, many tradesmen who were once very wealthy, but who have been reduced to absolute beggary—starvation—by his late Royal Highness. We call the pillar in Saint James's Park the Column of Infamy."

"Well, it was too bad not to pay his debts before they built that monument," said the baronet carelessly. "But, come—give me a cool six hundred for these things."

"What! the diamonds again?" exclaimed the assistant.

"Oh yes—they come and go, like good and bad fortune—'pon my honour!" said Sir Rupert.

"Like the jewels of many others at the West End," added the assistant; and, having made out the duplicates, he handed Sir Rupert over the sum required.

On the following morning the baronet paid Mr. Greenwood the six hundred pounds, and gave a new bill for a thousand at four months, for which the capitalist was generous enough not to charge him any interest.

There was nothing in the baronet's conduct to create a suspicion in Mr. Greenwood's mind that his intrigue with Lady Cecilia was detected; but when the transaction was completed, Sir Rupert hastened to consult with his friend Chichester upon some plan for obtaining positive evidence of that amour.

CHAPTER LXXXI.

THE MYSTERIOUS INSTRUCTIONS.

At the expiration of ten days from the mysterious accouchement of Ellen Monroe, Richard Markham returned home.

It was late at night when he alighted at his dwelling; but, as he had written two days previously to say when his arrival might be expected, Mr. Monroe and Whittingham were sitting up to receive him.

Richard's countenance was mournful; and he wore a black crape round his hat.

"You have lost a kind friend, Richard," said Mr. Monroe. "Your hasty letter acquainted us with the fact of Mr. Armstrong's death; but you gave us no details connected with that event."

"I will now tell you all that has occurred," said Richard. "You need not leave the room, Whittingham: you knew Mr. Armstrong, and will be, no doubt, interested in the particulars of his last moments."

"I knowed him for a staunched and consisting man in his demmy-cratical opinions," answered Whittingham; "and what's more com-portant, he thought well of you, Master Richard."

"He was an excellent man!" observed Markham, wiping away a tear.

"Worth a thousand Ilchesters, and ten thousand wulgarians which calls butlers *tulips*," added Whittingham, dogmatically.

"I will tell you the particulars of his death," continued Richard, after a pause. "You remember that I received a letter from Mr. Arm-strong, written in a hurried manner, and desiring me to repair to him in Boulogne, where he was detained by an accident which, he feared, might prove fatal. I posted to Dover, which town I reached at about five in the evening; and I found that no packet would leave for France until the following morning. The condition of my friend, as I judged of it by his note, seemed too serious to allow me to delay: I accordingly hired a vessel, and proceeded without loss of time to

Boulogne, where I arrived at eleven that same night, after a tolerably rough passage. I hurried to the hotel at which my friend was staying, and the card of which he had enclosed in his letter. I found him in bed, suffering from a fearful accident caused by the overturning of the chaise in which he had arrived at Boulogne from Paris, on his way to England. No limbs were broken: but he had sustained internal injuries of a most serious nature. A nurse was seated at his bed-side; and his medical attendant visited him every two or three hours. He was delighted to see me—wept—and said frequently, even up to the moment of his decease, 'Richard, this is very—very kind of you.' I sate up with him all that night, in spite of his entreaties that I would retire to rest; and from the first moment that I set my eyes upon him in that room, I felt convinced he would never leave it alive. I need not tell you that I did all I could to solace and render comfortable the man who had selected me, of all his acquaintances, to receive his last breath. I considered myself honoured by that mark of friendship; and I moreover remembered that he had believed in my innocence when I first told him my sad tale within the walls of Newgate. I never left him, save for one hour, from the instant I arrived in Boulogne until that of his death."

"Poor Master Richard," said Whittingham, surveying the young man with affectionate admiration.

"I said that I left him for one hour," continued Markham: "that was the evening before his death. Five days after my arrival, he called me to his bed-side, and said, 'Richard, I feel that my hours are numbered. You heard what my physician observed ere now; and I am not the man to delude myself with vain and futile hope. I repeat—my moments are now numbered. Leave me alone, Richard, for one hour; that I may commune with myself.' This desire was sacred; and I immediately obeyed it. But I remained away only just one hour, and then hastened back to him. He was very faint and languid; and I saw, with much surprise, that he had been writing. I sate down by his bed-side, and took his emaciated hand. He pressed mine, and said in a slow and calm tone,—'Richard, I need not recall to your mind under what circumstances we first met. I heard your tale; I knew that you were innocent. I could read your heart. In an hour I understood all your good qualities. I formed a friendship for you; and in the name of that friendship, listen to the last words of a dying man.' He paused for a few moments, and then continued thus:—'When I am no more, you will take possession of the few effects that I have with me here. In my desk you will find a sum sufficient to pay all the expenses incurred by my illness and to meet the cost of my interment. I desire to be buried in the Protestant cemetery in the neighbourhood of Boulogne: you and the physician will attend me to my grave. The funeral must be of the most humble description. Do not neglect this desire on my part. I have been all my life opposed to pomp and ostentation, and shall scarcely wish any display to mark my death.' He paused again; and I gave him some refreshing beverage. He then proceeded:—'Beneath my pillow, Richard, there is a paper in a sealed envelope. After my death you will open that envelope and read what is written within it. And now I must exact from you a solemn promise—a promise made to a dying man—a promise which I am not ashamed to ask, and which you need not fear to give, especially as it relates eventually to yourself. I require you to pledge yourself most sacredly that you will obey to the very letter the directions which are written within that envelope, and which relate to the papers that the envelope contains.' I readily gave the promise required. He then directed me to take the sealed packet from beneath his pillow, and retain it safely about my person. He shortly after sank into a deep slumber—from which he never awoke. His spirit glided imperceptibly away!"

"Good old man!" exclaimed Whittingham, applying his snow-white handkerchief to his eyes.

"According to the French laws," continued Richard, "interments must take place within forty-eight hours after death. The funeral of Thomas Armstrong was humble and unostentatious as he desired. The physician and myself alone followed him to the tomb. I then inspected his papers; but found no will—no instructions how his property was to be disposed of; and yet I knew that he was possessed of ample means. Having liquidated his debts with a portion of the money I found in his desk, and which amounted to about a hundred pounds, I gave the remainder to an English charity at Boulogne. And now you are no doubt anxious to know the contents of that packet so mysteriously delivered to me. When I broke the seal of the envelope, I found a letter addressed thus:—'*To my dear friend Richard Markham.*' This letter was sealed. I then examined the envelope. You shall yourselves see what was written within it.

Markham took a paper from his pocket, and handed it to Monroe, who read its contents aloud as follows:—

"Richard, remember your solemn promise to a dying man; for when I write this, I know you will not refuse to give me that sacred pledge which I shall ask of you.

"When you are destitute of all resources—when adversity or a too generous heart shall have deprived you of all means of subsistence—and when your own exertions fail to supply your wants, open the enclosed letter.

"But should no circumstances of any kind deprive you of the little property which you now possess,—and should you not be plunged into a state of need from which your own talents or exertions cannot relieve you—then shall you open this letter upon the morning of the 10th, of July, 1843, on which day you have told me that you are to meet your brother.

"These directions I charge you to observe faithfully and solemnly.

"THOMAS ARMSTRONG."

"How very extraordinary!" ejaculated Monroe. "Nevertheless, I have a presentiment that these mysterious instructions intend some eventual good to you, Richard."

"It's a fortin!—a fortin! depend upon it," said the old butler.

"Upon that head it is useless to speculate," observed Richard. "I shall obey to the very letter the directions of my late friend, be their tendency what it may. And now that I have told you all that concerns myself, allow me to ask how fares it with you here. Does Ellen's health improve?"

"For the last ten days she has been confined to her bed," answered Monroe, tears starting to his eyes.

"Confined to her bed!" cried Markham. "I hope you have had proper medical advice?"

"I wished to call in the aid of a physician," said Monroe, "but Ellen would not permit me. She declared that she should soon be better; she assured me that her illness was produced only by the privations and mental tortures which she had undergone, poor creature! previous to our taking up our abode in your hospitable dwelling; and then Marian was so kind and attentive, and echoed every thing which Ellen advanced, so readily, that I suffered myself to be over-persuaded."

"You did wrong—you did wrong, Mr. Monroe," exclaimed Markham. "Your daughter should have had medical advice; and she shall have it to-morrow."

"She appears to be mending in health, though not in spirits," observed Monroe. "But my dear young friend, you shall have your own way; and I thank you sincerely for the interest you show in behalf of one who is dear—very dear to me."

Richard pressed the hand of the old man, and retired to his chamber, to seek that repose of which he stood so much in need after his journey. But ere he sought his couch, he sate down and wrote the following note to Count Alteroni, that it might be despatched to Richmond without delay in the morning:—

"Mr. Markham regrets to be the means of communicating news of an afflicting nature to Count Alteroni; nor should he intrude himself again upon Count Alteroni's notice, did he not feel himself urged by a solemn duty to do so in the present instance. Count Alteroni's old and esteemed friend, Thomas Armstrong, is no more. He departed this life four days ago, at Boulogne-sur-Mer. Mr. Markham had the melancholy honour of closing the eyes of a good man and true patriot, and of following his remains to the tomb."

CHAPTER LXXXII.

THE MEDICAL MAN.

In the morning, when Ellen awoke at about eight o'clock, the first news she heard from Marian's lips was the return of Richard Markham.

The first sentiment which this announcement excited in the mind of the young lady, was one of extreme joy and thankfulness that her accouchement should have occurred so prematurely, and thus have happened during his absence; but this feeling was succeeded by one of vague alarm and undefined dread, lest by some means or other her secret should transpire.

This fear she expressed to Marian.

"No, Miss—that is impossible," said the faithful attendant. "The child is provided for; and the surgeon is totally ignorant of the house to which he was brought the night the poor infant was born. How could Mr. Markham discover your secret?"

"It is perhaps my conscience, Marian, that alarms me," returned Ellen; "but I confess that I tremble. Do you think that Mr. Wentworth is to be relied upon, even if he should suspect or should ever discover—"

"Mr. Greenwood has purchased his silence, Miss. Do not be down-hearted. I declare you are quite white in the face—and you seem to tremble so, the bed shakes. Pray—dear Miss—don't give way to these idle alarms!"

"I shall be more composed presently, Marian."

"And I will just step down stairs and get up your breakfast."

When Ellen was alone, she buried her face in the pillow and wept bitterly; and from time to time her voice, almost choked with sobs, gave utterance to the words—"My child! my child!"

Oh! how happy would she have been, could she have proclaimed herself a mother without shame and have spoken of her child to her father and her friend without a blush.

In a few minutes Marian returned to the room; and Ellen hastened to assume an air of composure. She wiped away her tears, and sate up in the bed supported by pillows—for she was yet very weak and sickly—to partake of some refreshment.

"Mr. Markham is up and has already gone out," said Marian, as she attended upon her lovely young patient. "He left word with Whittingham to tell me that he should come up, and see you on his return in half an hour."

"I would that this first interview were over, Marian," exclaimed Ellen.

"So you said, Miss, in the morning after your accouchement, when your father was coming up to see you; and yet all passed off well enough."

"Yes—but I felt that I blushed, and then grew deadly pale again, at least ten times in a minute," observed Ellen.

Marian said all she could to re-assure the young mother; and when the invalid had partaken of some tea, the kind-hearted servant left her, in order to attend to her own domestic duties down stairs.

Ellen then fell into a mournful reverie, during which she reviewed all the events of the last two years and a half of her life. She pondered upon the hideous poverty in which she and her father had been plunged in the court leading out of Golden Lane; she retrospected upon the strange services she had rendered the statuary, the artist, the sculptor, and the photographer; she thought of the old hag who had induced her to enter upon that career;—and then she fixed her thoughts upon Greenwood and her child.

She was thus mentally occupied when she heard footsteps ascending the staircase; and immediately afterwards some one knocked at her door.

In a faint voice she said, "Come in."

The door opened, and Richard Markham entered the apartment; but, as he crossed the threshold, he turned and said to some one who remained upon the landing, "Have the kindness to wait here one moment."

He then advanced towards the bed, and took the young lady's thin white hand.

"Ellen," he exclaimed, "you have been very ill."

"Yes—very ill, Richard," returned the invalid, casting down her eyes; "but I am better—oh! much, very much better now; and, in a day or two, shall be quite well."

"And yet you are very pale, and sadly altered," said Markham.

"I can assure you that I am recovering fast. Indeed, I should have risen to-day; but Marian persuaded me to keep my bed a short time longer."

"And you have had no medical advice, Ellen. I told your father that he had done wrong—"

"Oh! no, Richard," interrupted Ellen eagerly; "he was anxious to call in the aid of a physician; but I was not so ill as he thought."

"Not ill!" ejaculated Markham. "You must have been very—very ill."

"But Marian was so kind to me."

"No doubt! Nevertheless I have no confidence in the nostrums and prescriptions of old servants and nurses; and human existence is too serious a thing to be tampered with."

"I assure you, Richard, that Marian has treated me most judiciously; and I am now very nearly quite well."

"Ah! Ellen," cried Markham, "I can read your heart!"

"You, Richard!" exclaimed the young lady, with a cold shudder that seemed to terminate in a death-chill at the heart.

"Yes," continued Markham, his voice assuming a tone of melancholy interest; "I can well appreciate your motives in combating the desire of your father to procure medical aid. You were afraid of burdening me with an expense which you feared my restricted means would not permit me to afford;—Oh! I understand your good feeling!

But this was wrong, Ellen; for I did not invite you to my house to deny to either yourself or father the common attentions which I would bestow upon a stranger who fell sick under my roof. No—thank God! I have yet enough left to meet casualties like these."

"Ah! Richard, how kind—how generous you are," said Ellen; "but I am now really much better;—and to-morrow—to-morrow I shall be quite well."

"No—Ellen, you are very far from well," returned Markham; "but you shall be well soon. I have been myself this morning to procure you proper advice."

"Advice?" repeated Ellen, mechanically.

"Yes: there is a medical gentleman now waiting to see you."

With these words Richard hastened to the door, and said, "Miss Monroe, sir, is now ready to receive you. I will leave you with her."

The medical man then entered the chamber; and Markham immediately retired.

The votary of Æsculapius was a man of apparently five-and-twenty years of age—pale, but good-looking, with light hair, and a somewhat melancholy expression of countenance. He was attired in deep black. His manners were soft and pleasing; but his voice was mournful; and his utterance slow, precise, and solemn.

Approaching the couch, he took the hand of the invalid, and, placing his fingers upon the pulse, said, "How long have you been ill, Miss?"

"Oh! sir—I am not ill now—I am nearly well—I shall rise presently—the fresh air will do me good," exclaimed Ellen, speaking with a rapidity, and almost an incoherence, which somewhat surprised the medical man.

"No, Miss," he said calmly, after a pause, "you cannot leave your bed yet: you are in a state of fever. How long have you been confined to your couch?"

"How long? Oh! only a few days—but, I repeat, I am better now."

"How many days, Miss?" asked the medical man.

"Ten or twelve, sir; and, therefore, you see that I have kept my bed long enough."

"What do you feel?" demanded the surgeon, seating himself by the side of the invalid with the air of a man who is determined to obtain answers to his questions.

"I did feel unwell a few days ago, sir," said Ellen; "but now—oh! now I am quite recovered."

"Perhaps, miss, you will allow me to be the judge of that. You are very feverish—your pulse is rapid. Have you been taking any medicine?"

"No—that is, a little cooling medicine which the servant who attends upon me purchased. But why all these questions, since I shall soon be well?"

"Pardon me, Miss: you must have the kindness to answer all my queries. If, however, you would prefer another medical adviser, I will at once acquaint Mr. Markham with your desire, and will relieve you of my presence."

"No, sir—as well you as another," cried Ellen, scarcely knowing what she said, and shrinking beneath the glance of mingled curiosity and surprise which the surgeon cast upon her.

"During your illness were you at all delirious?" inquired the medical adviser.

"Oh! no—I have not been so ill as you are led to suppose. All I require is repose—rest—tranquillity——"

"And professional aid," added the surgeon. "Now, I beg of you, Miss Monroe, to tell me without reserve what you feel. How did your illness commence?"

"Ah! sir, I scarcely know," replied Ellen. "I have experienced great mental affliction; and that operated upon my constitution, I suppose."

"And you say that you have been confined to your bed nearly a fortnight?"

"Oh! no—not so long as that," said Ellen, fearful of confirming the surgeon's impression that she had been very ill, and consequently stood greatly in need of professional assistance: "not so long as that! Ten days exactly."

"Ten days!" repeated the medical man, as if struck by the coincidence of this statement with something which at that moment occurred to his memory; then glancing rapidly round the room, he started from his chair, and said, "Ten days ago, Miss Monroe! And at what hour were you taken ill?"

"At what hour?" repeated the unhappy young lady, who trembled for her secret.

"Yes—at what hour?" demanded the surgeon, the slow solemnity

of his tone changing to a strange rapidity of utterance: "was it not a little before midnight?"

"Sir—what do you mean? why do you question me thus?"

"On that night," continued the surgeon, gazing fixedly upon Ellen's countenance, "a man with his eyes blind-folded—"

"His eyes blindfolded?" repeated Ellen mechanically, while a fearful shudder passed through her frame.

"Led by a servant wearing a black veil—"

"A black veil?"

"Entered this room—"

"Ah! my God—spare me!"

"And delivered a lady of a male child."

"How do you know it, sir? who told you?"

"That man was myself!" cried the surgeon emphatically.

"Oh! kill me—kill me!" exclaimed Ellen; and covering her face with her hands, she burst into an agony of tears and heart-wrung sobs.

"Yes," continued the surgeon, pacing the room, and glancing rapidly on all sides: "there is the chest of drawers against which I dashed my foot—here stood the bed—here the table—I sate down in this chair—Oh! now I remember all!"

And for some moments he walked up and down the room in profound silence.

Suddenly Ellen started up to a sitting posture in the bed, and exclaimed. "My child, sir? Tell me—have you taken care of my child?"

"Yes—Miss—Madam," replied Mr. Wentworth; "the little boy thrives well, although deprived of his natural nourishment."

"Thank you, sir—thank you at least for that assurance," said Ellen. "Oh! sir—you cannot understand how deeply a mother feels to be separated from her child!"

"Poor girl," said the surgeon, in a compassionate tone; "you have then suffered very much?"

"God alone knows what I have endured for months past, mentally and bodily!" cried Ellen, clasping her hands together. "And now you know all, sir—will you betray me? say, sir—will you betray me?"

Mr. Wentworth appeared to reflect deeply for some moments.

Ellen awaited his reply in a state of the most agonising suspense.

"Miss Monroe," at length said Mr. Wentworth, speaking in his usual solemn and grave tone, "you know your own affairs better than I; but would it not be well to confide in those friends by whom you are surrounded?"

"I would die first—die by my own hand!" answered Ellen emphatically. "If you tell me that you will betray me—if you leave this room to communicate my secret to Mr. Markham, who brought you hither, or to my father—I will not hesitate a moment—I will throw myself from the window—"

"Calm, yourself, Miss Monroe. Your secret is safe in my hands."

"Oh! thank you, sir—a thousand times I thank you," exclaimed Ellen. "There are circumstances which render it necessary that this secret should not transpire—circumstances, not altogether connected with my own shame, which I cannot, dare not reveal to you."

"Enough, Miss Monroe—I do not seek to penetrate into those mysteries. Your child is with me—I will be a father to him!"

"And heaven will bless you!" said Ellen pressing the surgeon's hand with the warmth of the most fervent gratitude.

"In time you will be able to call at my house," observed Mr. Wentworth; "and you can see your son—you can watch his growth—mark his progress—"

"How kind you are! Oh! now I am rejoiced that you know all!"

"And no one will ever suspect the real motive of your visits," continued the surgeon. "Mrs. Wentworth shall call upon you in a few days; and thus an acquaintance may be commenced. With reference to my visit of this morning, I shall inform Mr. Markham that you will be convalescent in a few days."

Ellen once more expressed her sincere and heartfelt thanks to the surgeon, who shortly took his leave of her, after strictly recommending her to take the medicaments which he should send in the course of the day.

And now the recovery of the young invalid progressed rapidly; and her own mind, relieved of many sources of anxiety and alarm, aided nature in conducting her to convalescence; for she longed to behold and caress her child!

CHAPTER LXXXIII.

THE BLACK CHAMBER AGAIN.

A FEW days after the incidents just narrated, the following letters were opened in the Black Chamber of the General Post-Office.

The first was from the Under Secretary for Foreign Affairs of Castelcicala to the representative of that state at the British court:—

"Montoni, Castelcicala.

"The undersigned is desired by his lordship the Marquis of Gerrano, Minister of Foreign Affairs, to inform your excellency that the information you forwarded relative to the Englishwoman Eliza Sydney, has failed to produce the desired effect. Your excellency stated that Mrs. Arlington, the correspondent of the said Eliza Sydney, was the mistress of the Earl of Warrington; and that Eliza Sydney herself had been confined for two years in a criminal prison in England. Your excellency moreover forwarded the English newspapers of the time, containing a full and detailed report of her crime and trial. These statements have failed to produce any effect in a certain quarter, in consequence of the infatuation of a high personage in respect to this Eliza Sydney, and the apparent frankness (as the Marquis of Gerrano has learnt) with which she avowed the entire history of her past life to the high personage alluded to. It is now of the greatest consequence that your excellency should ascertain whether Eliza Sydney's conduct has ever been tainted with incontinence; whether, in a word, she has not indulged in immoral and vicious courses. The result of your excellency's inquiries must be forwarded by courier without delay; as you will perceive, by the inclosed copy of a ducal ordinance issued this morning, that the infatuation above alluded to grows to a very dangerous point.

"The undersigned avails himself of this opportunity to state that the Marquis of Gerrano is greatly afflicted at the perverse and obstinate conduct of the Prince Alberto, in steadily refusing the offers of a pension for life made by the Government of his reigning Highness through your Excellency. The Marquis of Gerrano desires your Excellency to redouble your assiduity in inducing the Prince to accept the terms proposed, for which purpose a farther delay of three months will be granted; and should his reply then continue unfavourable, the Government of his Highness will adopt measures to ensure the succession to the ducal throne of Castelcicala to a Neapolitan Prince.

"The undersigned renews his expressions of perfect consideration toward your Excellency.

"Baron Ruperto,
"Under Secretary of State for Foreign Affairs.

"*July* 13, 1839."

The following is a copy of the ducal ordinance to which reference was made in the above letter:—

"ANGELO III., BY THE GRACE OF GOD, GRAND DUKE OF CASTELCICALA.

"To all present and to come, Greeting:

"We have ordered and do order that which follows:—

"I. The style and title of Marchioness of Ziani are conferred upon the Signora Eliza Sydney.

"II. A pension of one thousand ducats annually shall be paid to the Marchioness of Ziani from the public treasury.

"III. Our Minister Secretary of State for the Department of the Interior will execute the first article of this ordinance; and our Minister Secretary of State for the Department of Finance will execute the second article.

"*By the Grand Duke*, ANGELO III.

"MARQUIS OF VINCENZA,
"Minister of the Interior.
"COUNT OF MARCOTTI,
"Minister of Finance.

"July 13, 1839."

The next letter, read in the Black Chamber upon this occasion, ran as follows:—

"*Montoni, Castelcicala.*

"I received your charming letters, my dearest Diana, and return you my most sincere thanks for the kind expressions of love and friendship which they contain, and for the advice which you proffer me. You moreover inform me that you have shown my letters of March, April, and May, to the Earl of Warrington; and that his lordship approves of the cautious manner in which I have acted, and recommends me to accept the honourable offer of marriage made to me by his Highness Angelo III. I assured you that his highness never once insulted me by hinting at the possibility of a connexion upon any other terms than those of marriage; and when he proposed a morganatic union, it was merely in accordance with the practice of many European sovereigns. I however expressed myself firmly to his serene highness upon this head, stating that, although a morganatic marriage was perfectly valid so far as the religious ceremonies went, still it was not strictly legal, and would not please those who wished me well in England.

"In my last letter I informed you that some one had represented to the Grand Duke my misfortunes in England. Happily this announcement failed to produce any change in his conduct or views with regard to me, as I had previously made him acquainted with all those particulars of my own accord.

"In a word, my dearest Diana, his Serene Highness has offered me his hand,—offered to raise me to a seat by his side on the ducal throne,—offered to make me his bride in sight of the world. Could I refuse? or why should I? You ask me if I can love his Serene Highness? Ah! how can I help revering one who shows such love for me? And then, human nature has its weak points; and rank, honour, wealth, and distinction cannot fail to attract even one naturally so retiring as myself. Oh! how pleasant will it be to possess riches and influence for the mere purpose of doing good!

"Well, then—all is decided: I am to be Grand Duchess of Castelcicala. The marriage is to take place in six weeks from the present date. The daughters of General Grachia are to be my bridesmaids. As a preliminary step towards this high honour, the Grand Duke has conferred upon me a title and a pension. To the world I am now the Marchioness of Ziani: to you, Diana, I am still, and always shall be—Eliza Sydney.

"I was surprised to learn from you that the villain Montague Greenwood has succeeded in obtaining a seat in the English Parliament. Ever since I have had power and wealth in the prospective, I have meditated upon the best means of protecting others from that villany which he designed against me, but which Providence so signally frustrated. At length I thought of a plan, and despatched a trusty person to England a few days ago to execute it. This person has instructions from me to call upon you on his arrival in England, and communicate to you my scheme. He is also the bearer of a trifling token of my sincere friendship and gratitude towards you, dear Diana, and which little token I hope you will accept for my sake.

"I need scarcely say that you will oblige me by tendering my best thanks to the Earl of Warrington for the kind advice he sent me through you, and renew to him the expression of my eternal gratitude for all he has done for me.

"You shall hear again shortly from your devoted and attached

"ELIZA SYDNEY.

"*July* 13, 1839."

The third letter read upon this occasion, was addressed to Count Alteroni, Richmond, and ran in the following manner:—

"*Montoni, Castelcicala,*
"*July* 13, 1839.

"Things, my lord, are growing towards a crisis in this country. No. 29 is literally infatuated with No. 1. He has this morning created her a marchioness; and in a month or six weeks he will, it is said, espouse her. There is no possibility of preventing this, No. 29 being quite despotic; and now his foolish ministers see their mistake in having maintained him in his absolutism, and refused the country a constitution."

"Number 29, you will understand," interrupted the Examiner, "evidently means the Grand Duke; and No. 1 represents Eliza Sydney. Proceed."

The clerk who read the letter continued as follows:—

"The ministers know not what to do. They are at their wits' end. I know for a fact that they obtained from England certain information relative to No. 1, which proved that she had been in a criminal gaol; but No. 29 made no account of it. No. 1 is very beautiful; fascinating in manners; somewhat shy and reserved; and yet amiable. She is also accomplished. When she first came to Montoni she spoke the Italian language imperfectly: she now speaks it fluently;—and this knowledge she has acquired in a few months. There can be no doubt that she will exercise an immense influence over No. 29, if she choose to make use of it. And who knows what a woman, suddenly rising from private life to the first ducal throne in the world, may do? She does not, however, seem to be ambitious. Nevertheless, something ought to be done. If this marriage take place, you are well aware that issue may follow, for No. 1 is young; and in that case * * * * I really think that if your lordship were to land suddenly upon the Castelcicalan coast, without delay, this union might be prevented. I hinted to your lordship in my last letter the immense ascendancy gained by No. 1 over No. 29: your lordship's reply astonished me. Your lordship states that if No. 29 choose to marry according to his fancy, no human power has a right to control him. With due deference, is not this carrying liberality of opinion a little too far? Your lordship expresses a determination to trust to the issue of events, and do nothing that may stand the chance of plunging the country into a civil war. These self-denying sentiments are no doubt highly patriotic and noble;—but is it in human nature to resign without a struggle? * * * * In any case I am your lordship's faithful servant, and am anxious only to execute your lordship's wishes. I therefore await your lordship's instructions.

"NUMBER 17."

"You have taken copies of these letters?" said the Examiner.

"Yes, sir," replied the clerk thus addressed.

"Then let them be immediately conveyed to the office of the Secretary of State for Foreign Affairs, as their contents are highly important."

"Yes, sir."

And this order was forthwith obeyed.

CHAPTER LXXXIV.

THE SECOND EXAMINATION.—COUNT ALTERONI.

FORTY-TWO days after the appearance of Mr. Tomlinson's name in the *Gazette*, among the category of Bankrupts, the second examination of this gentleman took place at the Bankruptcy Court in Basinghall Street.

In an arm-chair, behind a desk raised upon a species of dais, sate the commissioner, embellished with a wig and gown. Close under the desk was placed the registrar, also with wig and gown; and two or three barristers, who were retained in the case, were similarly adorned. In a sort of pew on the right of the commissioner sate the official assignee, with a pile of books and papers before him. About two hundred persons thronged the room—most of whom, by their sullen and sinister looks, might be easily recognised as the creditors of the bankrupt. At a distance from the box in which witnesses were placed during examination, stood Count Alteroni, with folded arms and severe countenance.

A few moments before eleven o'clock a bustle was heard near the door; and a whisper of "Here's the trade assignee," ran through the crowd.

Mr. Greenwood entered the court with a patronising smile upon his countenance, and an easy kind of gait, as if he were by no means dissatisfied with himself. He was dressed in the most elegant manner; and his left hand played negligently, as usual, with the costly gold chain that festooned over his waistcoat.

As he passed through the crowd of his friend's creditors, many of whom were known to him, he addressed a few words in an off-hand and patronising manner to those whom he recognised at the moment.

"Fine day, Mr. Styles. How are Mrs. Styles and those dear children?" (Mr. Styles was an old batchelor.)—"Ah! Mr. Milksop, how are you? quite delighted to see you! Why, upon my word, you are getting quite stout." (Poor Mr. Milksop was as thin as a lath.) "But every thing prospers with you, I suppose!—Well, Mr. Chivers, how do *you* do? Any thing new on the Stock-Exchange? I believe you don't suffer much by this business of Tomlinson's, do you?"

"Only three thousand—that's all!" returned Mr. Chivers, with a smile which would have turned new milk sour.

"Oh! a mere song!" exclaimed Greenwood, tossing up his head. "Well, Vokes, are you here?—you don't mean to say that you're wasting your time in this manner, eh?—Ah! Tullett, my good friend—delighted to see you. Why, how well you do look, to be sure!" (Mr. Tullett was in a rapid decline; and he "grinned horribly a ghastly smile" at this salutation.)

In this manner did Mr. Greenwood work his way through the crowd, until he reached the desk of the official assignee, by the side of whom he took a seat.

"Where's the bankrupt?" exclaimed the clerk of the court in a loud and imperious tone of voice, while Mr. Greenwood bestowed one of his patronising smiles upon the Commissioner.

"Here," replied Tomlinson; and he stood forward close by the witness-box.

He was pale and altered; and the marks of care and anxiety were visible upon his countenance. The glance he cast around him, as he took his stand in the presence of the Commissioner, was hurried and fearful:—he almost dreaded that the face of Michael Martin would meet his eyes as he thus hastily scanned the crowd by whom he was surrounded. But his alarm was without foundation: the old cashier was not there.

The examination of the bankrupt then commenced.

In answer to the questions put to him, he stated that he had delivered in to the assignee as full and complete a statement of his affairs as the loss of his books (which had been abstracted by the cashier at the time of the robbery) would permit.

Mr. Greenwood observed that the accounts were highly satisfactory, and would doubtless please every creditor present. It was, however, unfortunate that the estate would not pay a single farthing in the pound.

"Very unfortunate indeed," growled a creditor.

"I would much rather have heard that there was a dividend, than that the accounts are so very satisfactory," murmured another.

"Mr. Tomlinson's creditors cannot complain of him, your Honour," said Mr. Greenwood to the Commissioner: "on the contrary, they have every reason to be perfectly satisfied with him. He has given up every thing—"

"Why, there was nothing left to give up!" ejaculated Mr. Vokes.

"Nothing left to give up!" cried Mr. Greenwood, casting a stern glance upon the unfortunate creditor; "permit me, sir, as the trade-assignee duly chosen at the last meeting—permit me, sir, to inform you that there were the desks, counters, stools, and various fixtures of the bank—all of which Mr. Tomlinson surrendered in the most honourable and straightforward manner, and which have realized a

hundred and eighty-one pounds, seventeen shillings, and sixpence, for the benefit of the estate."

"Well—and what has become of that sum?" demanded Mr. Vokes.

"Consumed by the expenses of the *fiat*," answered Mr. Greenwood coolly. "But, as I was observing, your Honour, when I was interrupted—interrupted in a most indecent manner—the position of Mr. Tomlinson is a most honourable one—"

"Perhaps it is even enviable," said the consumptive creditor, drily.

"And I for one," added Mr. Greenwood, "shall certainly sign his certificate."

"Have no tidings been heard of the cashier who absconded?" inquired the Commissioner.

"None, sir," answered the official assignee and Mr. Greenwood simultaneously.

"What has become of the bankrupt's furniture at his private residence?" demanded a creditor.

"His landlord issued a distress for a year's rent the moment the bank stopped," answered Greenwood. "The amount due to this most hard-hearted and unfeeling landlord is a hundred and twenty pounds, and the furniture would not fetch more at an auction. I therefore, with the full concurrence of the official assignee, allowed that very harsh man to keep the goods."

A barrister, who had been retained for one of the creditors, then proceeded to examine Mr. Tomlinson.

"You allege that about ninety-four thousand pounds were abstracted from the bank by the fugitive cashier?"

"I do—or as nearly as I can guess."

"And yet, by this balance-sheet, I perceive that your liabilities are two hundred thousand pounds. Were you not insolvent when the robbery was perpetrated?"

"It would appear so, certainly."

"Then how do you account for that immense deficiency?"

"I can account for it in no other manner than by presuming that my cashier had carried on a systematic mode of plunder for some years past; but as I placed implicit reliance on him, I was never led to an investigation of my actual position."

"Do you mean to say that your cashier embezzled many thousand pounds every year?"

"I am afraid that such was the fact."

The barrister asked no farther questions.

Another opposing counsel interrogated the bankrupt relative to his affairs; but Tomlinson's replies were given in a manner which afforded no scope for suspicion.

Ah! none divined how much it cost that unhappy man thus to heap shame and infamy upon the head of a faithful old clerk, who had never wronged him of a shilling!

The case terminated by the declaration of the Commissioner that the bankrupt had passed his second examination.

Tomlinson was glad to escape from the frightful ordeal to which his feelings had been subjected for two mortal hours; and, while he hurried home to conceal his emotions from every eye, and meditate upon his condition in private, Mr. Greenwood busied himself in obtaining signatures for his certificate. This was an easy matter to a man of the financier's powers of persuasion; and that very afternoon the names of four-fifths of the bankrupt's creditors were attached to the parchment which was to relieve him of all past embarrassments.

When Greenwood took the certificate to Tomlinson in the evening, he said, "My dear fellow, you will soon be a new man. In one-and-twenty days this document will have passed the Lord Chancellor and the Court of Review, and be duly registered in Basinghall Street. I will then lend you a thousand pounds, *at only twenty per cent.*, to start you as a stock-broker. You see how well I have managed your business. You have passed through the Court—and you have kept your furniture."

"Which I would have given up to my creditors, had you permitted me," said Tomlinson sorrowfully.

"Nonsense, my dear fellow! Never give away what you can keep by a little manœuvring. Your landlord can now withdraw his friendly seizure, and all will be well."

"Nothing will render me happy until I find out that poor old man who has so nobly, so generously sacrificed himself for me," observed Tomlinson in a tone of deep dejection. "What can have become of him?"

"Oh! do not bother yourself about him," cried Greenwood impatiently. "He will turn up one of these days; and then you can remunerate him handsomely."

"Ah! that would indeed be a moment of supreme happiness for me!" ejaculated Tomlinson.

"Yes," continued Greenwood, musing: "a five-pound note will recompense the old fellow well for his conduct."

"A five-pound note!" repeated Tomlinson. "Can you be in earnest, Greenwood?"

"Well, if you think it is too much, give him a couple of sovereigns," said Greenwood, coolly. "But I must take leave of you now: I am compelled to devote a couple of hours this evening to the interests of that free and enlightened body whom I have the honour to represent in parliament. So, adieu, Tomlinson; and when your certificate is registered, come to me."

Mr. Greenwood then took his departure from the bankrupt's abode.

"The heartless villain!" cried Tomlinson, when the door had closed behind the financier; then, after a long pause, he added, "and yet his ingenuity has saved me from eternal degradation and shame!"

In the mean time Count Alteroni returned to his dwelling at Richmond. He reached home at about five o'clock in the evening, and found his wife and daughter anxiously awaiting his arrival. The moment he entered the drawing-room, the ladies cast a timid and yet inquiring glance towards him; and their hearts sank within them when their eyes caught sight of his severe and sombre expression of countenance.

"My dear wife—my beloved daughter," he said, advancing towards them, and taking the hand of each in his own, "my worst fears are confirmed. The bank will not pay one sixpence of dividend: Greenwood has contrived to get his fellow-conspirator clear of the tribunal; and the creditors have not a hope left. It was with the greatest difficulty that I could so far master my feelings as to avoid an interference in those most iniquitous proceedings. But my position—my rank forbade me from attempting aught to expose those villains. And now, my dear wife—now, my charming Isabella—prepare yourselves to hear the worst. We are ruined!"

"Ruined!" exclaimed both the countess and her daughter at the same moment.

"Oh! no," added Isabella: "we have many friends, my dear father."

"To whom I will not apply," said the Count, proudly. "No—we must wrestle with our evil fortunes, and trust to the advent of better times. At present every thing seems to conspire to crush us; and should that contemplated marriage take place in Castelcicala——"

"My dearest husband," interrupted the Countess, "do not aggravate present griefs by the apprehension of those which as yet only menace us. It is scarcely possible that the Grand Duke will perpetrate such a folly."

"And that title of Marchioness of Ziani—and that pension,—do they not speak volumes?" cried the count bitterly. "Oh! there are moments when I feel inclined to listen to the representations of those faithful friends in my own country with whom I correspond, and who are ever counselling me to——"

"Ah! my dearest father," exclaimed Isabella, bursting into tears; "would you endanger that life which is so precious to my mother and myself? would you plunge your native land in the horrors of a civil war? Oh! let us bear all our present ills with firmness and resolution; and if there be a guardian Providence—as I devoutly believe—he will not allow us to be persecuted for ever!"

"Noble girl!" cried the count; "you teach me my duty;"—and he embraced his lovely daughter with the utmost warmth and tenderness.

"Yes," said the countess, fondly pressing her husband's hand, "we are crushed only for a time. Our course is now clear:—we must give up our present establishment; and—as we have, thank God! no debts——"

"Ah! it is that which cuts me to the very soul!" interrupted the count. "You are not yet acquainted with the extent of our misfortunes. A brave fellow countryman of mine, who supported me in all the plans which I endeavoured to carry out for the welfare of the Castelcicalans, and who was driven into exile on my account, was imprisoned in London a few months ago for a considerable sum of money. I could not leave him to perish in a gaol. I became answerable for him—and the creditor is now pressing me for the payment of the debt."

"And what is the amount of this liability?" inquired the countess, hastily.

"Eighteen hundred pounds," was the reply.

"Do not suffer that to annoy you, my dearest father," exclaimed Isabella. "My jewellery and superfluous wardrobe will produce——"

"Alas! my dearest child," interrupted the count, "all that we possess would not realize any thing like that sum. But, happen what will, our first step must be to give up this furnished mansion, and retire to a more humble dwelling. That will not cost us many pangs. We shall still be together; and our love for each other constitutes our greatest happiness."

"Yes, my dearest husband," said the countess; "even a prison should not separate us."

"Where my beloved father is—where my parents are—there am I happy," murmured Isabella, the pearly tears trickling down her cheeks.

Oh! in that hour of his sorrow, how sweet—how sweet upon the ears of that noble Italian sounded the words, "husband" and "father," which, coupled with tender syllables of consolation, came from the lips of the two affectionate beings who clung to him so fondly. The lovely countenance of his daughter—so beautiful, that it seemed rather to belong to the ethereal inhabitants of heaven than to a mortal denizen of earth—was upturned to him; and her large black eyes, shining through her tears, beamed with an ineffable expression of tenderness and filial love.

Charming, charming Isabella—how ravishing, how enchanting wast thou at that moment when thou didst offer sweet consolation to thy father! The roses dyed thy cheeks beneath the delicate tinge of transparent bistre which proclaimed thee a daughter of the sunny south;—thy moist red lips apart, disclosed thy teeth white as the orient pearl;—thy young bosom heaved beneath the gauze which veiled it;—purity sat upon thy lofty brow, like a diadem which innocence confers upon its elect! Very beautiful wast thou, Isabella—charming exotic flower from the sweet Italian clime!

"Yes, my beloved wife—my darling daughter," said the Count; "we are ruined by my mad confidence in that villain Greenwood. You know that there is one means by which I could obtain wealth and release us from this cruel embarrassment. But never would either of you wish to see me sell my claims and resign my patriotism for gold! No—dearest partakers of my sad destinies, that may not be! I shall ever reject the offers of my persecutors with scorn; and until fortune may choose to smile upon us, we must learn to support her frowns with resignation."

"That same Almighty power which afflicts and chastises, can also restore gladness, and multiply blessings," said Isabella, solemnly.

A servant now entered the room to announce that dinner was served in another apartment.

Assuming a cheerful air, the count led his wife and daughter to the dining-room, and partook of the repast with a forced appetite, in order to avoid giving pain to those who watched all his movements and hung upon all his words with such tender solicitude.

After dinner, the count, still pondering upon the scene in which a tender wife and affectionate daughter had administered to him such sweet consolation, and experiencing a delicious balm in the domestic felicity which he enjoyed, said to Isabella, "Read me from your *Album*, my dear girl, those lines which a poet is supposed to address to his wife, and which always possess new charms for me."

Isabella hastened to obey her father's wishes, and read, in a soft and silver tone, the following stanzas:—

THE POET TO HIS WIFE.

WHEN far away, my memory keeps in view,
Unweariedly, the image of my wife;
This tribute of my gratitude is due
To her who seems the angel of my life—
The guiding star that leads me safely through
The eddies of this world's unceasing strife;—
Hope's beacon, cheering ever from afar,
How beautiful art thou, my guiding star!

Our children have thy countenance, that beams
With love for him who tells thy virtues now;—
Their eyes have caught the heavenly ray which gleams
From thine athwart the clouds that shade my brow,
Like sunshine on a night of hideous dreams!—
The first to wean me from despair art thou;
For all th' endearing sentiments of life
Are summed up in the words *Children* and *Wife*.

The mind, when in a desert state, renews
Its strength, if by Hope's purest manna fed;
As drooping flowers revive beneath the dews
Which April mornings bountifully shed.
Mohammed taught (let none the faith abuse)
That echoes were the voices of the dead
Repeating, in a far-off realm of bliss,
The words of those they loved and left in this.

My well beloved, should'st thou pass hence away,
Into another and a happier sphere,
Ere death has also closed my little day,
And morn may wake no more on my career,—
"I love thee," are the words that I shall say
From hour to hour, during my sojourn here,
That thou in other realms may'st still be found
Prepared to echo back the welcome sound.

Scarcely had Isabella finished these lines, when a servant entered the room, and announced a Mr. Johnson, "who had some pressing business to communicate, and who was very sure that he shouldn't be considered an intruder."

Mr. Johnson—a queer-looking, shabby-genteel, off-hand kind of man—made his appearance close behind the servant, over whose shoulder he leered ominously.

"I b'lieve you're Count Alteroni, air you?" was Mr. Johnson's first question.

"I am. What is your business with me?"

"I'm come from Rolfe, the attorney, in Clement's Inn," was the reply: "he—"

"Oh! I suppose he has sent you to say that he will accord me the delay I require?" interrupted the count.

"Not quite that there neither," said the man; then, sinking his voice to a mysterious whisper, and glancing towards the ladies with an air of embarrassment, he added, "The fact is, I've got a execution agin your person—a *ca-sa*, you know, for eighteen hundred and costs."

"A writ—a warrant!" ejaculated the count aloud. "You do not mean to say that you are come to take me to prison?"

"Not exactly that either," replied Mr. Johnson. "You needn't go to quod, you know. You can come to our lock-up in the New-Cut, Lambeth, where you'll be as snug as if you was in your own house, barring liberty."

"I understand you," said the count; then, turning to his wife and daughter, he added, "My dears, the evil moment is arrived. This person is a bailiff come to arrest me; and I must go with him. I implore you not to take this misfortune to heart:—it was sure to happen; and it might just as well occur to-day as a week or a month hence."

"And whither will they take you?" asked the countess, bursting into tears. "Cannot we be allowed to accompany you?"

"You can come, ma'am, and see his lordship to-morrow," said the bailiff; "and you can stay with him from ten in the morning till nine in the evening—or may-be till half-arter ten as a wery partick'lar faviour—for which you'll on'y have to pay half a sufferin extray. But there's my man."

A sneaking kind of knock—something more than a single one, not so much as a double one, and by no means as bold as a postman's—had been heard the moment before the bailiff uttered these last words; and while he went in person to inform his acolyte that the caption was made, and that he might wait in the hall, the count endeavoured to soothe and console the two afflicted ladies, who now clung to him in the most impassioned and distracted manner.

"To-morrow, my dear father—to-morrow, the moment the clock strikes ten, we will be with you," said Isabella. "Oh! how miserably will pass the hours until that period!"

"Will you not *now* permit me, my dearest husband, to see the Envoy of Castelcicala, and—"

"No," answered the Count firmly. "Did we not agree ere now to support with resignation all that fortune might have in store for us?"

"Ah! pardon me—I forgot," said the countess, "I am overwhelmed with grief. Oh! what a blow—and for *you!*"

"Show yourselves worthy of your high rank and proud name," cried the nobleman; "and all will yet be well."

At this moment the bailiff returned to the room.

"I am now ready to accompany you," said the count.

"So much the better," cried Mr. Johnson. "Me and my man Tim Bunkins come down in a omnibus; I don't know which vay you'd like to go, but I've heerd say you keeps a wery tidy cabrioily."

"It would be a monstrous mockery for any one to proceed to a prison in his own luxurious vehicle," said the count sternly. "As you came, so may you return. I will accompany you in an omnibus."

The count embraced his wife and daughter tenderly and with much difficulty tore himself away, in order to leave a comfortable home for a miserable sponging-house.

CHAPTER LXXXV.

A FRIEND IN NEED.

Ten days after the arrest of Count Alteroni, a young lady was proceeding, at about eleven o'clock in the forenoon, down the Blackfriars Road.

She was dressed plainly, but with that exquisite taste which denotes a polished mind, and is in itself an aristocracy of sentiment. She looked neither to the right nor to the left: her pace was somewhat rapid, as if she were anxious to arrive at her destination:—and though there was something timid in her manner as she threaded her way along the crowded thoroughfare, few who passed her could help turning round to obtain another glimpse of the sylph-like form of that unassuming girl.

From the opposite direction advanced a young man of tall and handsome appearance, neatly dressed, and with a shade of melancholy upon his countenance.

In a few moments he met the young lady, and was about to pass her, when his eyes happened to catch a glimpse of her lovely features.

He started with surprise, exclaiming, "Signora! is it possible? Do we indeed meet again? Ah! it seems to me that it is an age since I saw you, dearest Isabella!"

"And since we last met, Richard, many unfortunate events have happened. My poor father—"

"Your father! what can have happened to him?" cried Markham, struck by the mournful tone of the beauteous Italian.

"He is in the Queen's Bench Prison," replied Isabella, her eyes filling with tears.

"In the Queen's Bench! And you are going to him now? Oh! Isabella, you must tell me how all this happened: I will escort you a little way;"—and with these words, Richard offered his arm to the signora, who accepted it with a ready confidence in him whom she loved, and whose presence was by no means displeasing to her at that moment when she stood so much in need of consolation.

"You are aware," resumed Isabella, "that my father entrusted a considerable sum of money to Mr. Greenwood."

"The villain!" ejaculated Markham warmly.

"I cannot explain to you exactly how it was that my father accepted the security of Mr. Tomlinson, the banker, for that amount, as I am not acquainted with matters of business;—but he did so, and released Mr. Greenwood."

"And Tomlinson failed—and your father lost all!"

"Alas! he did;—and he is now imprisoned for a sum for which he had become answerable to serve a friend," said Isabella.

"How long has the count been in—in—"

"In prison," added the signora mournfully. "He was arrested ten days ago; and, by the advice of a solicitor, he removed on the following day from the bailiff's private house to the Bench."

"And the countess?"

"My mother is very unwell to-day, and could not leave her room; and I am now on my way to visit my poor father. We have left Richmond altogether; and my mother and myself occupy lodgings in the Blackfriars Road, near the bridge."

"Ten days ago this happened, Isabella," said Richard reproachfully; "and you did not acquaint me with what had occurred?"

"Ah! Richard—you know well that circumstances forbade me;—or else—"

"Or else? Speak—dearest Isabella."

"Or else I believe you would have given my father the best advice how to proceed. He is too proud to apply to his friends; and he cannot—he must not remain in prison. His health would sink under the idea of degradation that has taken possession of him."

"That villain Greenwood!" said Markham, musing. "When will the day of retribution arrive for him?"

"We must now part, Richard," observed Isabella, as they came in view of the dingy wall of the Queen's Bench Prison, crowned by *chevaux-de-frise*.

"Yes—we must part again," said Markham mournfully. "But how happy should I have been had we met this morning under other circumstances! How I should have blessed the accident that brought me thus early this morning on some business of my own, to this neighbourhood! Oh! Isabella, you know not how constantly I think of you—how unceasingly I dwell upon your dear image!"

"And can you suppose, Richard, that I never devote a thought to you?" said Isabella, in a low and plaintive tone. "But we must not talk upon such a subject at present. Let us hope for happier times."

With these words the young lady returned the pressure of her lover's hand, and hurried towards the Queen's Bench.

Markham loitered about the spot for five minutes, and then proceeded to the lobby of the prison. There he inquired into the particulars of Count Alteroni's detention; and ascertained that he had been arrested for eighteen hundred pounds, with costs.

He then left the gloomy precincts of the debtors' gaol, and retraced his steps towards the City.

"Eighteen hundred pounds would procure the count's liberation," he said to himself: "eighteen hundred pounds, which he does not possess, and which he is too proud to borrow,—eighteen hundred pounds, which would restore him to his family, and make Isabella happy! My property is worth four thousand pounds:—if I raise two thousand pounds upon it, I shall curtail my income by exactly one half. I shall have one hundred pounds a-year remaining. But my education was good—my acquirements are not contemptible: surely I can turn them to some account?"

Then it suddenly struck him that he had already raised five hundred pounds upon his estate at the period when the Resurrection Man endeavoured to extort that sum from him; and half of this sum had already disappeared in consequence of the amount given to Talbot (*alias* Pocock) in the *Dark-House*—the assistance rendered to Monroe and Ellen—his journey to Boulogne—and other claims. Then there would be the expenses of deeds to reckon. If he raised two thousand pounds more, his property would only remain worth to him about fifteen hundred pounds. His income would therefore be reduced to seventy-five pounds *per annum*.

But not for one moment did this noble-hearted young man hesitate relative to the course he should pursue; and without delay he proceeded to the office of Mr. Dyson, his solicitor, in the City.

There the business was speedily explained and put in train. It would, however, require, said the solicitor, four days to terminate the affair; but Markham did not leave him until he had fixed the precise moment when the deeds were to be signed and the money paid over.

Richard returned home in a state of mind more truly happy than he had known for some time past. He had resolved upon an immense sacrifice, to benefit those whom he esteemed or loved; and he was prepared to meet any consequences which it might produce. This is human nature. We may inure ourselves to the contemplation of any idea, however appalling or alarming it may appear at first sight, without a shudder and almost without a regret. The convict, under sentence of death in the condemned cell, and his ears ringing with the din of the hammers erecting the scaffold, does not experience such acute mental agony as the world are apt to suppose. We all have the certainty of death, at some date more or less near, before our eyes; and yet this conviction does not trouble our mental equanimity. The convict who is doomed to die, is only worse off than ourselves inasmuch as the precise day, hour, and moment of his fate are revealed to him; but his death, which is to be sudden and only of a moment's pain, must be a thousand times preferable to the long, lingering, agonising throes of sickness which many of those who pity him are eventually doomed to endure before their thread of existence shall be severed for ever!

Yes—we can bring our minds to meet every species of mortal affliction with resignation, and even with cheerfulness;—and there is no sorrow, no malady, no pang, which issued from Pandora's box, that did not bear the imprint of hope along with it!

True to the appointed time, Richard proceeded to the office of Mr. Dyson, on the fourth day from the commencement of the business.

He signed the papers and received two thousand pounds.

The lawyer shook his head, implying his fears that his client was improvident and wasteful.

He was, however, speedily undeceived.

"Will you have the kindness to accompany me in a cab?" said Markham. "You can render me a service in the way in which I am about to dispose of this money."

"Certainly," returned Mr. Dyson. "Are you going far?"

"Not very," answered Richard; and when they were both seated in the vehicle, he told the driver to proceed towards the Queen's Bench Prison, but to stop at some distance from the gates.

These directions were obeyed.

"Now, Mr. Dyson," said Richard, "will you have the kindness to repair to the office of the prison, and inquire the amount of debts for which a certain Count Alteroni is detained in custody?"

Mr. Dyson obeyed the instructions thus given to him, and in ten minutes returned from the prison with a *copy of causes* in his hand.

"Count Alteroni is a prisoner for eighteen hundred and twenty-one pounds," said the lawyer.

"Are there any fees or extra expenses beyond the sum specified in that paper?" asked Richard.

"Yes—merely a few shillings," replied the solicitor.

"I wish, then, that every liability of Count Alteroni be settled in such a way that he may quit the prison without being asked for a single shilling. Here is the necessary amount: pay all that is due—and pay liberally."

"My dear sir," said the lawyer, hesitating, "I hope you have well reflected upon what you are about to do."

"Yes—yes," answered Richard impatiently: "I have well reflected, I can assure you."

"Two thousand pounds—or nearly so—is a large sum, Mr. Markham."

"I have weighed all the consequences."

"At least, then, you have received ample security—"

"Not a scrap of paper."

"Had I not better call and see this nobleman, and obtain from him a warrant of attorney or cognovit—"

"So far from doing any such thing," interrupted Markham, "you must take especial care not to mention to a soul the name of the person who has employed you to effect the count's release—not a syllable must escape your lips on this head; nor need you acquaint the clerks whom you may see, with your own name. In a word, the affair must be buried in profound mystery."

"Since you are determined," said Mr. Dyson, "I will obey your instructions to the very letter. But, once again, excuse me if I request you to reflect whether—"

"My dear sir, I have nothing more to reflect upon; and you will oblige me by terminating this business as speedily as possible."

The solicitor returned to the prison; and Markham, whom he now considered to be foolish or mad, instead of improvident and extravagant, threw himself back in the vehicle, and gave way to his reflections. His eyes were, however, turned towards the road leading to the Bench; for he was anxious to watch for the re-appearance of his agent.

Ten minutes had elapsed, when his attention was directed to two ladies who passed by the cab, and advanced towards the prison-gate.

He leant forward—he could not be mistaken:—no—it was indeed she—the idol of his adoration—the being whom he loved with a species of worship! She was walking with the countess. They were on their way to visit the count in his confinement; but Richard could not catch a glimpse of their countenances—though he divined full well that they wore not an expression of joy. It was not, however, necessary for him to behold Isabella's face, in order to recognise her—he knew her by her symmetrical form, the elegant contours of which even the ample shawl she wore could not hide: he knew her by her step—by her graceful and dignified gesture—by her lady-like and yet unassuming gait.

Oh! how speedily, thought he within himself, were she and her parents to be restored to happiness again!

In about a quarter of an hour after the ladies had entered the prison, Dyson returned to his client.

"Is it all settled?" demanded Markham.

"Every thing," answered the lawyer.

"And when can the count leave the prison?"

"Almost immediately," replied Dyson, as he entered the vehicle once more.

Markham then ordered the driver to return to the City.

In the mean time the countess and Isabella repaired to the room which the noble exile occupied in the prison. As they ascended the steep stone stair-case which led to it, they wondered within themselves when he whom they loved so tenderly would be restored in freedom to them.

The count was seated at a table covered with books and papers, and was busily occupied in arranging the latter when the countess and signora entered the room. They were instantly welcomed with the most affectionate warmth by the noble prisoner; and he endeavoured to assume a cheerful air in their presence.

"Any letters?" said the count, after the usual inquiries concerning health and comfort.

"None this morning," answered the countess. "And now, my dear husband, tell me—have you settled any plan to effect your release?"

"No," said the count. "I must trust to events. Were Armstrong alive, I should not hesitate to accept a loan from him;—but to none other would I apply."

At this moment a knock at the door of the prison chamber was heard; and the two inseparables, Captain Smilax Dapper and Sir Cherry Bounce, made their appearance.

"My dear count, you don't mean to say that it is really true, and that you are here on your own account—strike me!" ejaculated the gallant hussar.

"The newth wath twue—too twue, you thee, Thmilackth," said Sir Cherry, shuddering visibly, and without any affectation too as he glanced around him.

"True indeed!" cried the count bitterly.

"I wonder whether they will let uth out again?" said Sir Cherry, gazing from the window. "But, I declare, they have got wacket-gwoundth here, and no leth than thwee pumpth. What can the pwithonerth want with tho muth water?"

"What, indeed—confound me!" exclaimed the captain. "For my part, I always heard that they lived upon beer. But tell me—how much is there against you?"

"Yeth—how muth?" echoed Sir Cherry Bounce.

"A mere trifle," answered the count evasively. "I have been cruelly robbed, and my present position is the result."

"Well," continued the captain, with remarkable embarrassment of manner, "we are all here together—and so there is no harm in speaking openly, you know—and Cherry isn't anybody, strike him!—I was thinking that a very satisfactory arrangement might be made. Always strike when the iron's hot! I have long entertained a high respect for your family, count: my late uncle the general, who introduced me and Cherry to you, always spoke in the best possible terms of you, although he never said much about your past life, and even hinted that there was some mystery—"

"To what is all this to lead, Captain Dapper?" exclaimed the count, somewhat impatiently.

"Simply that—why do you stand there, laughing like a fool, Cherry?"

"Me, Thmilackth?"

"Yes—you. Well, as I was saying when Cherry interrupted me—I have always entertained the highest possible opinion of your family, count, and especially of the signora; and if she would accept my hand and heart—why, strike me! an arrangement could be made in four-and-twenty hours—"

"Captain Dapper," interrupted the count, "no more of this. I believe that you would not wantonly insult either my daughter or myself; but I cannot listen to the terms to which you allude."

"My dear count—"

"Silence, sir! No more of this!" exclaimed the noble Italian.

There was a pause, which was broken by the entrance of one of the turnkeys.

"Sir, I have the pleasure to inform you that you are discharged," said that functionary.

"Discharged!" ejaculated the count: "impossible! How could I be discharged?"

The countess and Isabella surveyed the turnkey with looks of the most intense and painful anxiety.

"A stranger has sent his solicitor to pay every thing against you at the gate; and all the fees and the little donations to us and the criers are paid also."

"You are bantering me, sirrah!" cried the count. "You are mistaken. The Envoy from my native land, who alone of all my acquaintances is capable of doing an action of this generous nature, and in so delicate a manner, has been absent from London for the last ten days, and is even unaware of my situation. Who then could have paid my debts?"

A name trembled upon Isabella's tongue; but the word died upon her lips. She dared not pronounce that name—although her heart told her that her surmise was correct, and that Richard Markham was the secret friend to whom her father was indebted for his liberty. Richard! the reward of thy good deed had already commenced by the feelings which now changed the love that the beauteous girl had hitherto experienced for thee, into an adoration and a worship!

"Well, sir," said the turnkey, "we don't know who has done this, and it wasn't our business to inquire. All I can say is, that the debt is paid, the fees settled, and you may leave the place as soon so you like."

"Dapper, this is your doing," cried the count, after a moment's pause. "And yet—"

"No—strike me!—I had nothing to do with it—I wish I had *now*."

We shall not attempt to describe the delight of the Italian family, when they found that the joyful tidings were indeed true; but all the count's conjectures, to fix this generous and noble deed upon any particular member of his acquaintance, were alike unsatisfactory and unavailing:—Isabella alone divined the truth.

CHAPTER LXXXVI.

THE OLD HAG.

MARKHAM was not the man to remain idle now that his circumstances were so desperately reduced. He had a taste for literary pursuits, and he resolved to devote his talents to some advantage. His income was totally insufficient to support his establishment, and yet he knew not how to effect any very great economy in the mode of conducting it. He would not for worlds allow Mr. Monroe and Ellen to leave his house, and again enter upon a struggle with the world. With Whittingham nothing could have induced him to part;—Marian was the only female domestic he kept, and he could not dispense with her services. Holford alone was an incumbrance of which he thought of relieving himself. But before he adopted any measure of economical reform, he summoned the faithful Whittingham to a consultation with him in the library.

When Markham had made the butler acquainted with his altered circumstances, the old man shook his head and observed—

"Well, Master Richard, all this here ruination—and when I make use of the paragraph *ruination*, I mean to express the common sentence, *flooring*—has been brought round about by your over generosity, and good disposition towards others. I can't a-bear, Master Richard, to see you circumlocuted and circumwented in this manner; and now all your property has gone to the canine species—or, wulgarly speaking, *to the dogs*."

"What is done, is done, Whittingham," said Richard; "nor did I send for you to criticise my conduct."

"Ah! Master Richard; don't go for to scold me—me that saw you bred and born," exclaimed the old butler, tears starting into his eyes. "I wouldn't be an ominous burden to you for all the world; so I'll get employment somewhere else—"

"No—no, my faithful friend," cried Richard, taking the old man's hand, "I would not allow you to leave me on any account. As long as I have a crust you shall share it. My present object is to acquaint you with the necessity of introducing the most rigid economy into our household."

"Ah! now I understand you, Master Richard. And talking of this reminds me that a gentleman in the neighbourhood requires a young youth of the natur' of Holford; and so the lad might step quite permiscuous, as the saying is, into a good situation at once."

"Well, let him seek for another place, Whittingham; but tell him that he may stay here until he can succeed in finding one."

Markham and Whittingham then arranged other little methods of economy, and the debate terminated. Fortunately for these plans, Holford procured the place alluded to by Whittingham, and repaired to his new situation in the course of a few days.

Notwithstanding the solicitude with which Markham endeavoured to conceal his altered circumstances from Mr. Monroe and Ellen, the quick perception of the latter soon enabled her to penetrate into the real truth; and she immediately reflected upon the best means of turning her own acquirements to some good purpose. She did not mention to her father her suspicion that they were a burden upon Markham's resources; but she took an early opportunity of hinting to Richard her anxiety to avail herself of her education and accomplishments, in order to add to the general resources of the household. The young man was struck by the delicate manner in which she thus made him comprehend that she was not blind to the limited nature of his means; but he assured her that his property was quite commensurate with his expenditure. Ellen appeared to be satisfied; but she nevertheless determined within herself to lose no time in seeking for profitable employment for her leisure hours.

But where was she to seek for occupation? She knew the miserable rate at which the labours of the needle-women were paid; and she shuddered at the idea of returning to the service of a statuary, an artist, a sculptor, or a photographer. And yet she was resolved not to remain idle. She could not bear the thought that her father and herself were a burden upon the slender resources of their generous and noble-hearted benefactor:—she saw with pain that while Markham forced her father to partake of his wine as usual, he himself now invariably invented an excuse to avoid joining in the indulgence;—she saw that Richard rose earlier than heretofore, and remained in his library the greater portion of the day;—she learned from Marian that the surplus garden produce was sold;—in a word, she beheld a system of the most rigid economy introduced into the establishment, and which was only relaxed on behalf of her father and herself. All this gave her pain; and she was resolved to do somewhat to enable her to contribute towards the resources of the household—even though she should be compelled to return to the service of a statuary, an artist, a sculptor, or a photographer.

At one moment she thought of applying to Greenwood:—but he had already done all she asked in respect to their child. And then, even if she were to obtain money from him, in what manner could she account to her father and to Markham for its possession? for there was a secret—a terrible secret connected with Greenwood, which she dared not reveal—even though such confession were to save her from a death of lingering tortures!

Thus thought Ellen Monroe. Was it extraordinary if the idea of applying to the old hag—that nameless woman—dwelling in a nameless court in Golden Lane, and exercising a nameless avocation—often entered the young lady's imagination? Was it strange that she should gradually overcome her repugnance to seek the presence of the filthy-souled harridan, and at length look upon such a step as the only means through which her ardent desire to obtain employment could be gratified?

It was decided! she would go.

Accordingly, one morning, she dressed herself in the most simple manner, and proceeded by an omnibus into the City. It was mid-day when she reached Golden Lane.

With what strange feelings did she proceed along the narrow and dirty thoroughfare! Pure and spotless was she when, nearly three years back, she had first set foot in that vile lane;—how much had she seen—how much passed through—how much endured since that period? Dishonoured—unwedded—she was a mother. Her virgin purity was gone for ever—the evidence of her shame was living, and could at any moment be brought forward to betray her. And if she now pursued a virtuous course, it was scarcely for virtue's sake, but through dread of the consequences of a fresh fault. The innate chastity of her soul had dissolved, like snow before the mid-day sun's effulgence, beneath the glances of the statuary, the artist, the sculptor, and the photographer. It was true that she looked upon her services to those masters with disgust; but the feeling had little reference to pure and unadulterated feminine modesty. Still she was of a proud spirit in one respect;—she detested a life of slothful dependence upon an individual who had not enough for himself!

Such was Ellen Monroe when she retraced her way, on the present occasion, to the dwelling of the old hag—that way which had led her to so frightful a precipice before!

The old woman was sitting in her great easy chair, watching the steam that rose from a large saucepan upon the hob. That saucepan contained the harridan's dinner—tripe and cow-heel stewing with onions, and filling the close apartment with a sickly odour. But the hag savoured that smell with a hideous expression of delight; to her nostrils it was a delicious perfume. From time to time she glanced—almost impatiently—towards her Dutch clock, as if anxious for the arrival of the happy moment when she might serve up her mess. She was just spreading a filthy napkin upon one corner of her table, when a knock was heard at her door.

Instead of inviting the visitor, whoever it might be, to enter, the hag hastened to answer the summons by opening the door a few inches. She was already afraid that some poor neighbour might seek a portion of her dainty meal!

But when she recognised Ellen Monroe, a gleam of joy suddenly illumined her lowering countenance, and the young lady immediately obtained admittance, for the hag thought within herself—"There is gold yet to be gained by her!"

Re-assured as to the undivided enjoyment of the stew, and having satisfied herself with a glance that Ellen was above immediate want, the old woman conducted her fair visitant to a seat, saying—

"My bird of beauty, you have come back to me again; I have been waiting for your return a long, long time."

"Waiting for me?" cried Ellen, with surprise.

"Yes, miss—certainly. I know the world—and I felt convinced that you could not always contrive for yourself, without me."

"I am at a loss to understand you," said Ellen.

"Well—well, no matter!" exclaimed the hag, lifting off the lid of her saucepan, and ogling the stew. "At all events," she continued, after a pause, "you require my services now—else why are you come?"

"Yes—I require your services," answered the young lady. "I want employment—can you tell me of any thing likely to suit me?"

"In what way?" demanded the hag, with an impudent leer.

Ellen remained silent—absorbed in thought. That question recalled to her mind the difficulties of her position, and convinced her how little scope there was for the exercise of choice in respect to employment.

The old woman surveyed her fair visitant with attention; the sardonic expression of her countenance changed into one of admiration, as she contemplated that lovely girl. Her head was so gracefully inclined the least thing over one shoulder as she sat wrapt up in her reflections;—there was a shade of such bewitching melancholy upon her classic countenance: the long, dark fringes that shadowed her deep blue eyes, gave so Murillo-like a softness to her cheek as she glanced downwards; her bust, since she had become a mother, had expanded into such fine proportions, yet without destroying the perfect symmetry of her shape;—and her entire air had something so languishing—something of an only partially-subdued voluptuousness—that the old hag regarded her with mingled sentiments of admiration, envy, and pleasure.

"In what way can I serve you?" said the harridan again, after a long time.

"Alas! I have scarcely made up my mind how to answer the question," replied Ellen, smiling in spite of her melancholy thoughts. "I am not actually in want; but my father and myself are dependent upon the bounty of one who is by no means able to support us in idleness. My father can do nothing; he is old—infirm, and broken down by affliction. It therefore remains for me to do some thing to earn at least a trifle."

"A young lady of your beauty cannot be at a loss for friends who will treat her nobly," said the old woman, affecting to busy herself with her stew, but in reality watching Ellen's countenance with a reptile-like gaze as she spoke.

"Ah! I know that I am not the ugliest person in existence," exclaimed the young lady, smiling once more; "but I am anxious," she added, her countenance suddenly assuming a serious expression, "to live a quiet—an honourable—and a virtuous life. I know there is nothing to be gained by the needle. I dislike the menial and degrading situation of a copy or a model:—are you aware of no other occupation that will suit me?"

"Have you any money in your pocket?" demanded the hag, after a few moments' reflection.

"I have three sovereigns and a few shillings," answered Ellen, taking her purse from her reticule.

"I know of an employment that will suit you well," continued the old woman; "and my price for putting it in your way will be the three sovereigns in your purse."

"Of what nature is the employment?" asked Ellen.

"That of patient to a Mesmerist," was the reply.

"Patient to a mesmerist!" exclaimed the young lady: "I do not understand you."

"There is a French gentleman who has lately arrived in London, and who lectures upon Animal Magnetism at the West End," said the hag. "He has created a powerful sensation; and all the world are running after him. But he requires patients to operate upon, and the photographer, with whom he is acquainted, recommended him to apply to me. You will answer his purpose; and you well know that I have always performed my promises to you hitherto, so you need not be afraid to pay me my price at once. I will then give you the mesmerist's card."

"First explain the nature of the services that will be demanded of me," said Ellen.

"You will be placed in a chair, and the magnetiser will pass his hands backwards and forwards in a particular way before your eyes; you will then have to fall asleep—or pretend to do so, whichever you like; and the professor will ask you questions, to which you must reply. This is the main business which he will require at your hands."

"But it is a gross deception," said Ellen.

"You may embrace or refuse my offer, just as you choose. If you are so very particular, Miss," added the old woman ironically, "why do you not obtain the situation of a governess, or go out and give lessons in music and drawing?"

"Because I should be asked for references, which I cannot give;—because there would be a perpetual danger of my former occupations transpiring; and because——"

"Because—because you do not fancy that employment," exclaimed the hag impatiently. "See now—my dinner is ready—you are wasting my time—I have other business to attend to anon. Do you refuse or accept my offer?"

"What remuneration shall I be enabled to earn?" demanded Ellen, hesitatingly.

"Thirty shillings a-week."

"And how long shall I be occupied each day?"

"About two hours at the evening lectures three times a week; and perhaps an hour every day to study your part."

"Then I accept your offer," said Ellen; and she placed three sovereigns upon the table.

The eyes of the old woman glistened at the sight of the gold, which she clutched hastily from the table for fear that Ellen might suddenly repent of her bargain. She wrapped the three pieces carefully up in a piece of paper, and hastened to conceal them in the interior of her old Dutch clock. She then opened her table-drawer, and began to rummage, as on former occasions when Ellen visited her, amongst its filthy contents.

The search occupied several minutes; for the old woman had numerous cards and notes scattered about in her drawer.

"You see that I have a good connexion," she observed, with a horrible smile of self-gratulation, as she turned the cards and notes over and over with her long bony hands: "all the fashionable young men about town know me, and do not hesitate to engage my services on particular occasions. Then they recommend me, because I give them satisfaction; and so I always have enough to do to give me bread. I am not idle, my dear child—I am not idle, I can assure you. Day and night I am at the beck and call of my patrons. I help gentlemen to mistresses, and ladies to lovers. But, ah! the pay is not what it used to be—it is not what it used to be!" repeated the old hag, shaking her head dolefully. "There is a great competition, even in my profession, miss—a very great competition. The shoemakers, the tailors, the publicans, the butchers, the bakers, all complain of competition;—but they have not half so much right to complain as I have. Now and then I pick up a handsome sum in one way;—and, while I think of it, miss, I may as well mention to you—for who can tell what may happen?—you are young, and beautiful, and warm—and such a thing is almost sure to befall you as well as any other woman. But, as I was saying, miss—I may as well mention to you, that if you should happen—in consequence of a fault—to——"

The old woman leant forward, and whispered something in Ellen's ear.

The young lady started; and an exclamation of mingled disgust and horror escaped her lips.

"Do not alarm yourself, my dear child," said the old hag, resuming her search with the most imperturbable coolness: "I did not mean to offend you. I can assure you that many a young lady, of higher birth than yours, and dwelling in the most fashionable quarters of London, has been glad to avail herself of my services. What would often become of the indiscreet miss if it wasn't for me? what, indeed?—what, indeed?"

"Haste and give me the card," exclaimed Ellen, in a tone of ill concealed disgust and aversion; "I am in a hurry—I can wait no longer."

"There it is, my dear," said the old hag. "I know the situation will suit you. When you require another, come to me."

Miss Monroe received the card, and took her departure without another moment's delay.

As soon as the young lady had left that den, the old hag proceeded to serve up her stew, muttering to herself all the while, "One of my stray sheep come back home again! This is as it should be. There is yet much gold to be made by that girl: she cannot do long without me!"

Then the horrible wretch fetched from the cupboard the champagne-bottle which contained her gin; and she seated herself cheerfully at the table covered with the dainties that she loved.

CHAPTER LXXXVII.

THE PROFESSOR OF MESMERISM.

Ellen had already been long enough from home to incur the chance of exciting surprise or alarm at her absence; she was therefore compelled to postpone her visit to the Professor of Mesmerism until the following day.

On her return to the Place, after an absence of nearly three hours, her fears were to some extent realised, her father being uneasy at her disappearance for so long a period. She availed herself of this opportunity to acquaint Mr. Monroe with her anxiety to devote her talents to some useful purpose, in order to earn at least sufficient to supply them both with clothes, and thus spare as much as possible the purse of their benefactor. Her father highly approved of this laudable aim; and Ellen assured him that one of the families, for whom she had once worked at the West End, had promised to engage her as a teacher of music and drawing for a few hours every week. It will be recollected that the old man had invariably been led to believe that his daughter was occupied in private houses with her needle, when she was really in the service of the statuary, the artist, the sculptor, and the photographer: he therefore now readily put faith in the tale which Ellen told him, and even undertook not only to communicate her intention to Markham, but also to prevent him from throwing any obstacle in its way. This task the old man accomplished that very day; and thus Ellen triumphed over the chief difficulty which she had foreseen—namely, that of accounting for the frequent absence from home which her new pursuits would render imperative. And this duplicity towards her sire she practised without a blush. Oh! what a wreck of virtue and chastity had the mind of that young female become!

The Professor of Mesmerism occupied a handsome suite of apartments in New Burlington Street. He was a man of about fifty, of prepossessing exterior, elegant manners, and intelligent mind. He spoke English fluently, and was acquainted with many continental languages besides his own.

It was mid-day when Miss Monroe was ushered into his presence.

The Professor was evidently struck by the beauty of her appearance; but he held her virtue at no high estimation, in consequence of the source of her recommendation to him. Little cared he, however, whether she were a paragon of moral excellence, or an example of female degradation: his connexion with her was to be based upon a purely commercial ground; and he accordingly set about an explanation of his views and objects. Ellen listened with attention, and agreed to become the patient of the mesmerist.

Thus, having sold her countenance to the statuary, her likeness to the artist, her bust to the sculptor, her entire form to the photographer, and her virtue to a libertine, she disposed of her dreams to the mesmerist.

Several days were spent in taking lessons and studying her part, under the tutelage of the Professor. She was naturally of quick comprehension; and this practice was easy to her. Her initiation was therefore soon complete; and the Professor at length resolved upon giving a private exhibition of "the truths of Mesmerism practically

illustrated" to a few friends. Ellen took a feigned name; and all the preliminary arrangements were settled.

The memorable evening arrived; and by eight o'clock the Professor's drawing-room was filled with certain select individuals, all of whom were favourably inclined towards the "science of Mesmerism." Some of them, indeed, were perfectly enthusiastic in behalf of this newly-revived doctrine. The reporters of the press were rigidly excluded from this meeting, with two or three exceptions in favour of journals which were known to be friendly to the principle of Animal Magnetism.

When the guests were thus assembled, Ellen was led into the apartment. She was desired to seat herself comfortably in an easy arm-chair; and the Professor then commenced his manipulations, "with a view to produce *coma*, or mesmeric sleep." In about five minutes Ellen sank back, apparently in a profound sleep, with the eyes tightly closed.

The Professor then expatiated upon the truths of the science of Mesmerism; and the assembled guests eagerly drank in every word he uttered. At length he touched upon *Clairvoyance*, which he explained in the following manner:—

"*Clairvoyance*," he said, "is the most extraordinary result of Animal Magnetism. It enables the person magnetised to foretell events relating both to themselves and others; to describe places which they have never visited, and houses the interior of which they have never seen; to read books opened and held behind their heads; to delineate the leading points of pictures in a similar position; to read a letter through its envelope; to describe the motions or actions of a person in another room, with a wall intervening; and to narrate events passing in far distant places."

The Professor then proposed to give practical illustrations of the phenomena which he had just described.

The visitors were now all on the tiptoe of expectation; and the reporters prepared their note-books. Meantime Ellen remained apparently wrapped up in a profound slumber; and more than one admiring glance was turned upon her beautiful classic features and the exuberant richness of her bust.

"I shall now question the patient," said the Professor, "in a manner which will prove the first phenomenon of *clairvoyance*; namely, *the power of foretelling events relative to themselves and others*."

He paused for a moment, performed a few more manipulations, and then said, "Can you tell me any thing in reference to future events which are likely to happen to myself?"

"Within a week from this moment you will hear of the death of a relation!" replied Ellen in slow and measured terms.

"Of what sex is that relation?"

"A lady: she is now dangerously ill."

"How old is she?"

"Between sixty and seventy. I can see her lying upon her sick-couch with two doctors by her side. She has just undergone a most painful operation."

"It is perfectly true," whispered the Professor to his friends, "that I have an aunt of that age; but I am not aware that she is even ill—much less at the point of death."

"It is wonderful—truly wonderful!" exclaimed several voices, in a perfect enthusiasm of admiration.

"Let us now test her in reference to the second phenomenon I mentioned," said the Professor; "which will show *the power of describing places she has never visited, and houses whose interiors she has never seen.*"

"Ah! that will be curious, indeed," cried several guests.

"Perhaps you, Mr. Wilmot," said the Professor, addressing a gentleman standing next to him, "will have the kindness to examine the patient relative to your own abode."

"Certainly," replied Mr. Wilmot; then, turning towards Ellen, he said, "Will you visit me at my house?"

"With much pleasure," was her immediate answer.

"Where is it situated?"

"In Park Lane."

"Come in with me. What do you see?"

"A splendid hall, with a marble table between two pillars on one side, and a wide flight of stairs, also of marble, on the other."

"Come with me into the dining room of my house. Now what do you see?"

"Seven large pictures."

"Where are the windows?"

"There are three at the bottom of the room."

"What colour are the curtains?"

"A rich red."

"What is the subject of the large picture facing the fire-place?"

"The battle of Trafalgar."

"How do you know it is that battle?"

"Because I can read on the flag of one of the ships the words, '*England expects that every man will do his duty.*'"

"I shall not ask her any more questions," said Mr. Wilmot, evidently quite amazed by these answers. "Every one of her replies is true to the very letter. And I think," he added, turning towards the other guests, "that you all know me well enough to believe me, when I declare most solemnly that this young person has never, to my knowledge, been in my house in her life."

A murmur of satisfaction arose amongst the guests, who were all perfectly astounded at the phenomena now illustrated—although they had come, as before said, with a predisposition in favour of Mesmerism.

"We will have another proof yet," said the Professor. "Perhaps Mr. Parke will have the kindness to question the patient."

Mr. Parke stepped forward, and said, "Will you do me the favour to walk with me to my house."

"Thank you, I will," answered Ellen, still apparently remaining in a profound mesmeric sleep.

"Where is my house?"

"In Mortimer Street, Cavendish Square."

"How many windows has it in front?"

"Thirteen."

"Where are the two statues of Napoleon?"

"In the library."

"What else do you see in that room?"

"Immense quantities of books on shelves in glass cases."

"Are there any pictures?"

"Yes—seven."

"What is the subject of the one over the mantelpiece?"

"A beautiful view of London, by moonlight, from one of the bridges."

"Wonderful!" ejaculated Mr. Parke. "All she has said is perfectly correct. It is not necessary to ask her any more questions on this subject."

"Gentlemen," said the Professor, casting a triumphant glance around him, "I am delighted to perceive that you are satisfied with this mode of illustrating the phenomena of *clairvoyance*. I will now prove to you that the patient *can read a book held open behind her head*."

He then performed some more manipulations to plunge his patient into as deep a mesmeric sleep as possible, although she had given no symptom of an inclination to awake throughout the preceding examination. Having thus confirmed, as he said, her perfect state of *coma*, the Professor took up a book—apparently pitched upon at random amongst a heap of volumes upon the table; and, holding it open behind the head of the patient, he said, "What is this?"

"A book," was the immediate reply.

"What book?"

"Milton's *Paradise Lost*."

"At what page have I opened it?"

"I can read pages 110 and 111."

"Read a few lines."

Ellen accordingly repeated the following passage in a slow and beautifully mellifluous tone:—

"Now morn, her rosy steps in th' eastern clime
Advancing, sowed the earth with orient pearl,
When Adam waked, so 'customed, for his sleep
Was airy light, from pure digestion bred,
And temperate vapours bland, which th' only sound
Of leaves and fuming rills, Aurora's fan,
Lightly dispersed, and the shrill matin song
Of birds on every bough."[1]

"That is sufficient," cried several voices. "Do not fatigue her. We are perfectly satisfied. It is really marvellous. Who will now dare to doubt the phenomena of *clairvoyance*?"

"Let us take a picture," said the Professor; *"and she will delineate all the leading points in it."*

The mesmerist took an engraving from a portfolio, and held it behind Ellen's head.

"What is this?" he demanded.

"A picture."

"What is the subject?"

"I do not know the subject; but I can see two figures in the foreground, with a camel. The back-ground has elevated buildings. Oh! now I can see it plainer: it is a scene in Egypt; and those buildings are the pyramids."

"Extraordinary!" cried Mr. Wilmot.

"And that little hesitation was a proof of the fact that she could really see the picture," added Mr. Parke.

"Wonderful! extraordinary!" exclaimed numerous voices.

At this moment a servant entered the room and delivered a letter to his master, the Professor, stating that it had just been left by a friend from Paris.

The mesmerist was about to open it, when a sudden idea seemed to strike him.

"Gentlemen," he exclaimed, throwing the letter upon the table, "the arrival of this missive affords me an opportunity of proving

1 Commencement of Book V. [Reynolds's note.]

another phenomenon belonging to *clairvoyance. The patient shall read this letter through the envelope.*"

"But if its contents be private?" said a guest.

"Then I am surrounded by gentlemen of honour, who will not publish those contents," returned the professor with a smile.

A murmur of approbation welcomed this happy compliment of the Frenchman.

The mesmerist held the letter at a short distance from Ellen's countenance, and said, "What is this?"

"A letter," she replied. "It is written in French."

"Read it," cried the mesmerist.

"The writing is obscure, and the lines seem to cross each other."

"That is because the letter is in an envelope and folded," said the Professor. "But try and read it."

Ellen then distinctly repeated the contents of the letter, of which the following is a translation:—

"*Paris.*

"HONOURED SIR,—I have to acquaint you with the alarming illness of my beloved mistress, your aunt Madame Delabarre. She was taken suddenly ill four days ago. Two eminent physicians are in constant attendance upon her. It is believed that if she does not get better in a few days, the medical attendants will perform an operation upon her. Should your leisure and occupation permit, you would do well to hasten to France to comfort your venerable relative.

"Your humble servant,

"FELICIE SOLIVEAU."

"Ah! my poor aunt! my poor aunt!" cried the Professor: "she is no more! It was her death that the patient foretold ere now! Yes—the two physicians—the painful operation—Oh! my poor aunt!"

The mesmerist tore open the letter, hastily glanced over it, and handed it to the gentleman who stood nearest to him. This individual perused it attentively, and, turning towards the other guests, said,—"It is word for word as the patient read it."

The enthusiasm of the disciples of mesmerism present was only damped by the grief into which the Professor was now plunged by the conviction of the death of his venerable aunt. They, therefore, briefly returned their best thanks for the highly satisfactory illustrations of the truths of mesmeric phenomena which they had witnessed upon the occasion, and took their leave, their minds filled with the marvels that had been developed to them.

The moment the guests and the reporters had taken their departure, the Professor hastened up to Ellen, took her by the hand, and exclaimed in a transport of joy, "You may rise, my good young lady; it is all over! You acquitted yourself admirably! Nothing could be better. I am delighted with you! My fortune is made—my fortune is made! These English blockheads bite at anything!"

Ellen rose from the chair in which she had feigned her mesmeric sleep, and was by no means displeased with the opportunity of stretching her limbs, which were dreadfully cramped through having remained an hour in one unchanged position. The Professor compelled her to drink a glass of wine to refresh her; and in a few minutes she was perfectly at her ease once more.

"Yes," repeated the mesmerist; "you conducted yourself admirably. I really could not have anticipated such perfection at what I may call a mere rehearsal of your part. You remembered every thing I had told you to the very letter. By cleverly selecting to examine you, those persons whose houses I have visited myself, and the leading features of which I am able to explain to you beforehand, I shall make you accomplish such wonders in this respect, that even the most sceptical will be astounded. You have an excellent memory; and that is the essential. Moreover, I shall never mislead you. The book and the print agreed upon between us during the day, shall always be chosen for illustration at the lecture. By the bye, your little hesitation about the engraving was admirable. You may always introduce that *piece of acting* into your *part*: it appears true. The part then is not over-done. I give you great credit for the idea. In a few days I shall tell all my friends that I have received a letter announcing my aunt's death; and that her demise took place at the very moment when you beheld her death-bed in your mesmeric slumber. This will astound them completely. On the next occasion we must introduce into our comedy the scene of *the patient describing what takes place in another room with a wall intervening*; and as we will settle before-hand all that I shall do in another apartment, upon the occasion, that portion of the task will not be difficult."

"But suppose, sir," said Ellen, "that a gentleman, concerning whose house you have given me no previous description, should wish to examine me,—what must I do in such a case?"

"Remain silent," answered the Professor.

"And would not this excite suspicion?"

"Not a bit of it. I have my answer ready:—'*There is no magnetic affinity, no mesmeric sympathy, between you and your interlocutor.*' That is the way to stave off such a difficulty; and it applies equally to a stranger holding books or prints for you to read with the back of your head."

"I really can scarcely avoid laughing when I think of the nature of the farce," observed Ellen.

"And yet this is not the only doctrine with which the world is duped," said the Professor. "But it is growing late; and you are doubtless anxious to return home. I am so well pleased with you, that I must beg you to accept this five-pound note as an earnest of my liberal intentions. You were very perfect with the poetry and the letter—the letter, by the bye, from my poor old aunt, whose existence is only in my own imagination!—Indeed, altogether, I am delighted with you!"

Ellen received the money tendered her by the mesmerist, and took her departure.

Thus successfully terminated her first essay as a patient to a Professor of Animal Magnetism!

CHAPTER LXXXVIII.

THE FIGURANTE.

The wonders performed by the Professor of Mesmerism produced an immense sensation. The persons who had been admitted to the "private exhibition," did not fail to proclaim far and wide the particulars of all that they had witnessed; and, as a tale never loses by repetition, the narrative of those marvels became in a very few days a perfect romance. The reporters of the press, who had attended the exhibition, dressed up a magnificent account of the entire proceedings, for the journals with which they were connected; and the fame of the Professor, like that of one of the knights of the olden time, was soon "bruited abroad through the length and breadth of the land."

At length a public lecture was given, and attended with the most complete success. Ellen had an excellent memory; and her part was enacted to admiration. She recollected the most minute particulars detailed to her by the Mesmerist, relative to the interior of the houses of his friends, the contents of letters to be read through envelopes, the subjects of prints, and the lines of poetry or passages of prose in the books to be read when placed behind her. Never was a deception better contrived: the most wary were deluded by it; and the purse of the Professor was well filled with the gold of his dupes.

But all things have an end: and the deceit of the Mesmerist was not an exception to the rule.

One evening, a gentleman—a friend of the Professor—was examining Ellen, who of course was in a perfect state of *coma*, respecting the interior of his library. The patient had gone through the process of questioning uncommonly well, until at length the gentleman said to her, "Whereabouts does the stuffed owl stand in the room you are describing?"

In the abstract there was nothing ludicrous in this query: but, when associated with the absurdity of the part which Ellen was playing, and entering as a link into the chain of curious ideas that occupied her mind at the moment, it assumed a shape so truly ridiculous that her gravity was completely overcome. She burst into an immoderate fit of laughter: her eyes opened wide—the perfect state of coma vanished in a moment—the *clairvoyance* was forgotten—the catalepsy disappeared—and the patient became unmesmerised in a moment, in total defiance of all the prescribed rules and regulations of Animal Magnetism!

Laughter is catching. The audience began to titter—then to indulge in a half-suppressed cachinnation;—and at length a chorus of hilarity succeeded the congenial symphony which emanated from the lips of the patient.

The Professor was astounded.

He was, however, a man of great presence of mind: and he instantaneously pronounced Ellen's conduct to be a phenomenon in Mesmerism, which was certainly rarely illustrated, but for which he was by no means unprepared.

But all his eloquence was useless. The risible inclination which now animated the great majority of his audience, triumphed over the previous prejudice in favour of Mesmerism; the charm was dissolved—the spell was annihilated—"the pitcher had gone so often to the well that it got broken at last"—the voice of the Professor had lost its power.

No sooner did the hilarity subside a little, when it was renewed again; and even the friends and most staunch adherents of the Professor looked at each other with suspicion depicted upon their countenances.

What reason could not do, was effected by ridicule: Mesmerism, like the heathen mythology, ceased to be a worship.

The Professor grew distracted. Confusion ensued; the audience rose from their seats; groups were formed; and the proceedings of the evening were freely discussed by the various different parties into which the company thus split.

Ellen took advantage of the confusion to slip out of the room; and in a few moments she left the house.

Her occupation was now once more gone; and she resolved to pay another visit to the old hag.

Accordingly, in a few days she again sought the miserable court in Golden Lane.

It was about three o'clock in the afternoon, when the young lady entered the apartment in which the old hag dwelt. The wrinkled wretch was seated at the table, working. She had bought herself a new gown with a portion of the money which she had received from Ellen on the occasion of recommending the latter to the Mesmerist; and the old woman's looks were joyful—as joyful as so hideous an expression of countenance would allow them to be—for she thought of being smart once more, even in her old age. Vanity only ceases with the extinction of life itself.

"Well, my child," said the old woman, gaily; "you have come back to me again. Surely you have not already finished with your Mesmerist?"

"Yes," replied Ellen. "The bubble has burst, and I am once more in search of employment."

"And in such search, miss, will you ever be, until you choose to settle yourself in a manner suitable to your beauty, your accomplishments, and your merits," said the old woman.

"In what way could I thus settle myself?"

"Do you ask me so simple a question? May you not have a handsome house, a carriage, servants, money, rich garments, jewels, and a box at the Opera, for the mere asking?"

"I do not require so much," answered Ellen, with a smile. "If I can earn a guinea or two a week, I shall be contented."

"And do you not feel anxious to set off your charms to the greatest advantage?" demanded the old woman. "How well would pearls become your soft and shining hair! how dazzling would your polished arms appear when clasped by costly bracelets! how lovely would be your little ears with brilliant pendants! how elegant would be your figure when clad in rustling silk or rich satin! how the whiteness of your bosom would eclipse that of the finest lace! Ah! miss, you are your own enemy—you are your own enemy!"

"You forget that I have a father," said Ellen,—"a father who loves me, and whom I love,—a father who would die if he knew of his daughter's disgrace."

"Fathers do not die so easily," cried the old hag. "They habituate themselves to every thing, as well as other people. And then—think of the luxuries and comforts with which you could surround the old man."

"We will not talk any more upon that subject," said Ellen firmly. "I well understand your meaning; and I am not prudish nor false enough to affect a virtue which I do not possess. But I have my interests to consult; and it does not suit my ideas of happiness to accept the proposal implied by your language. In a word, can you find me any more employment?"

"I know no more Mesmerists," answered the old hag, in a surly tone.

"Then you can do nothing for me?"

"I did not say that—I did not say that," cried the hag. "It is true I can get you upon the stage; but perhaps that pursuit will not please you."

"Upon the stage!" ejaculated Ellen. "In what capacity?"

"As a *figurante*, or dancer in the ballet, at a great theatre," replied the old woman.

"But I should be known—I should be recognised," said Ellen.

"There is no chance of that," returned the hag. "Dressed like a sylph, with rouge upon your cheeks, and surrounded by a blaze of light, you would be altogether a different being. Ah! it seems that I already behold you upon the stage—the point of admiration for a thousand looks—the object of envy and desire, and of every passion which can possibly gratify female vanity."

For some moments Ellen remained lost in thought. The old

woman's offer pleased her: she was vain of her beauty; and she contemplated with delight the opportunity thus presented to her of displaying it with brilliant effect. She already dreamt of success, applause, and showers of nosegays; and her countenance gradually expanded into a smile of pleasure.

"I accept your proposal," she said: "but—"

"Why do you hesitate?" demanded the old woman.

"Oh! I was only thinking that the introduction would be better——"

"If it did not come from me?" added the old woman, her wrinkled face becoming more wrinkled still with a sardonic grin. "Well, make yourself easy upon that score. I am only aware that a celebrated manager has a vacancy in his establishment for a figurante, and you may apply for it."

"But I am ignorant of the modes of dancing practised upon the stage," said Ellen.

"You will soon learn," answered the old woman. "Your beauty will prove your principal recommendation."

"And what shall I give you for your suggestion?" asked Ellen, taking out her purse.

When a bailiff makes a seizure in a house, he assures himself with a glance around, whether there be sufficient property to pay at least *his* expenses;—when a debtor calls upon his creditor to ask for time, the latter surveys the former for a moment, to ascertain by his countenance if he can be trusted;—the wholesale dealer always "takes stock," as it were, of the petty detailer who applies to him for credit;—and thus was it that the old woman scrutinized with a single look the capacity of Ellen's purse, so that she might thereby regulate her demand. And all the while she appeared intent only on her work.

"You can give me a couple of guineas now," the old woman at length said; "and if your engagement proves a good one, you can bring or send me three more in the course of the month."

This arrangement was immediately complied with, and Ellen took leave of the old hag, with the fervent hope that she should never require her aid any more.

On the following day Miss Monroe called upon the manager of the great national theatre where a figurante was required.

She was ushered into the presence of the theatrical monarch, who received her with much urbanity and kindness; and he was evidently pleased with her address, appearance, and manners, as she explained to him the nature of her business.

"Dancing in a ball-room, and dancing upon the stage, are two very different things," said the manager. "You will have to undergo a course of training, the length of which will depend upon your skill and your application. I have known young ladies become proficient in a month—others in a year—many never, in spite of all their exertions. Most of the figurantes have been brought up to their avocation from childhood; but I see no reason why you should not learn to acquit yourself well in a very short time."

"I shall exert myself to the utmost, at all events," observed Ellen.

"How are you circumstanced?" inquired the manager. "Excuse the question; but my object is to ascertain if you can support yourself during your apprenticeship, as we may term the process of study and initiation?"

"I have a comfortable home, and am not without resources for my present wants," answered Ellen.

"So far, so good," said the manager. "I do not seek to pry into your secrets. You know best what motives induce you to adopt the stage: my business is to secure the services of young, handsome, and elegant ladies, to form my *corps de ballet*. It is no compliment to you to say that you will answer my purpose, provided your studies are successful."

"With whom am I to study, sir?"

"My ballet-master will instruct you," replied the manager. "You can attend his class. If you will come to the theatre to-morrow morning at ten o'clock, you can take your first lesson."

Ellen assented to the proposal, and took leave of the manager. They were mutually satisfied with this interview: the manager was pleased with the idea of securing the services of a young lady of great beauty, perfect figure, and exquisite grace;—and, on her side, Ellen was cheered with the prospect of embracing an avocation which, she hoped, would render her independent of the bounty of others.

And now her training commenced. In the first place her feet were placed in a groove-box, heel to heel, so that they formed only one straight line, and with the knees turned outwards. This process is called "*se tourner.*" At first the pain was excruciating—it was a perfect martyrdom; but the fair student supported it without a murmur; and in a very few days her feet accustomed themselves, as it were, to fall in dancing parallel to each other.

The second lesson in the course of training consisted of resting the right foot on a bar, which Ellen was compelled to hold in a horizontal line with her left hand. Then the left foot was placed upon the bar, which was in this case held up by the right hand. By these means the stiffness of the feet was destroyed, and they were rendered as pliant and elastic as if they had steel springs instead of bones. This process is denominated *"se casser."*

Next, the student had to practise walking upon the extreme points of the toes, so that the foot and the leg formed one straight line. Then Ellen had to practise the flings, capers, caprioles, turns, whirls, leaps, balances, borees, and all the various cuts, steps, positions, attitudes, and movements of the dance. During the caprioles the student had to train herself to perform four, six, and even eight steps in the air; and the fatigue produced by these lessons was at times of the most oppressive nature.[1]

When Ellen was perfected in these portions of her training, she had to practise the tricks of the stage. At one time she was suspended to lines of wires; at another she was seated on paste-board clouds; then she learned to disappear through traps, or to make her exit by a window. Some of these manœuvres were of a very dangerous nature; indeed, in some, the *danseuse* actually risked her life—and all, her limbs. The awkwardness of an underling in shifting a trap-door at the precise moment would have led her to dash her head against a plank with fearful violence.

The art of theatrical dancing is divided into two schools, called *Ballonné* and *Tacqueté*. The former is the branch in which Taglioni shines; the latter is that in which Fanny Ellsler excels.[2] The style of the *Ballonné* takes its name from the airiness of the balloon; it combines lightness with grace, and is principally characterized by a breezy and floating appearance of the figure. The *Tacqueté* is all vivacity and

1 The French terms for the various steps and features of the ballet-dance are—*jetés, balances, rondes de jambes, fouettes, cabrioles, pirouettes sur le coude-pied, sauts de basques, pas de bourrés*, and *entre-chats à quatre, à six* and *à huit*. [Reynolds's note.]

2 Maria Taglioni (1804-1884), ballet dancer, inventor of dancing on 'points;' Fanny Elssler (Franziska Elßler) (1810-1884). The *ballonné* style was slow and lyrical, the *tacqueté* fast, vivacious, and jerky.

rapidity, distinguished by sparkling steps and twinkling measures, executed with wonderful quickness upon the point of the feet. In both these schools was Ellen instructed.

So intense was the application of Miss Monroe—so unwearied was she in her practice, so quick in comprehending the instructions of the master—so resolute in surmounting all obstacles, that in the short space of two months she was a beautiful dancer. The manager was perfectly astonished at her progress; and he pronounced a most favourable opinion upon her chance of achieving a grand triumph.

Her form became all suppleness and lightness; her powers of relaxation and abandonment of limb were prodigious. When attired in the delicate drapery of the ballet, nothing could be more beautiful—nothing more sylph-like, than the elastic airiness of her rich and rounded figure. The grace of her attitudes—the charm of her dance—the arrangement of that drapery, which revealed or exhibited the exquisite contours of her form—the classic loveliness of her countenance—the admirable symmetry of her limbs—and the brilliant whiteness of her skin, formed a whole so attractive, so ravishing, that even the envy of her sister-figurantes was subdued by a sentiment of uncontrollable admiration.

In obedience to a suggestion from the manager, Ellen agreed to adopt a well-sounding name. She accordingly styled herself Miss Selina Fitzherbert. She then learned that at least two-thirds of the gentlemen and ladies constituting the theatrical company, had changed their original patronymics into convenient pseudonyms. Thus Timothy Jones had become Gerald Montgomery; William Wilkins was announced as William Plantagenet; Simon Snuffles adopted the more aristocratic nomenclature of Emeric Gordon; Benjamin Glasscock was changed into Horatio Mortimer; Betsy Podkins was distinguished as Lucinda Hartington; Mary Smicks was displaced by Clara Maberly; Jane Storks was commuted into Jacintha Runnymede; and so on.

In her relations with the gentlemen and ladies of the corps, Ellen (for we shall continue to call her by her real name) found herself in a new world. Every thing with her present associates might be summed up in the word—*egotism*. To hear them talk, one would have imagined that they were so many princes and princesses in disguise, who had graciously condescended to honour the public by appearing upon the stage. The gentlemen were all descended (according to their own accounts) from the best and most ancient families in the country; the ladies had all brothers, or cousins, or uncles highly placed in the army or navy;—and if any one ventured to express surprise that so many well-connected individuals should be compelled to adopt the stage as a profession, the answer was invariably the same—

"I entered on this career through preference, and have quarrelled with all my friends in consequence. Oh! if I chose," would be added, with a toss of the head, "I might have any thing done for me; I might ride in my carriage; but I am determined to stick to the stage."

Poor creatures! this innocent little vanity was a species of reward, a sort of set-off, for long hours of toil, the miseries of a precarious existence, the moments of bitter anguish produced by the coldness of an audience, and all the thousand causes of sorrow, vexation, and distress which embitter the lives of the actor and actress.

With all their little faults, Ellen found the members of the theatrical company good-natured creatures, ever ready to assist each other, hospitable and generous to a fault. In their gay moments, they were sprightly, full of anecdote, and remarkably entertaining. Many of them were clever, and exhibited much sound judgment in their remarks and critical observations upon new dramas and popular works.

At length the evening arrived when Ellen was to make her first appearance upon the stage in public. The house was well attended; and the audience was thrown into a remarkably good humour by the various performances which preceded the ballet. Ellen was in excellent spirits, and full of confidence. As she surveyed herself in the glass in her little dressing-room a few moments before she appeared, a smile of triumph played upon her lips, and lent fire to her eyes. She was indeed ravishingly beautiful.

Her success was complete. The loveliness of her person at once produced an impression in her favour; and when she executed some of the most difficult measures of the Ballonné school, the enthusiasm of the audience knew no bounds. The eyes of the ancient libertines, aided by opera-glasses and *lorgnettes*, devoured the charms of that beautiful girl;—the young men followed every motion, every gesture, with rapturous attention;—the triumph of the *debutante* was complete.

There was something so graceful and yet so voluptuous in her style of dancing,—something so bewitching in her attitudes and so captivating in her manner, that she could not have failed to please. And then she had so well studied all those positions which set off her symmetrical form to its best advantage,—she had paid such unwearied attention to those measures that were chiefly calculated to invoke attention to her well-rounded, and yet light and elastic limbs,—she had so particularly practised those pauses which afforded her an opportunity of making the most of her fine person, that her dancing excited pleasure in every sense—delighting the eye,—producing an effect as of a musical and harmonious feeling in the mind, and exciting in the breasts of the male portion of the spectators passions of rapture and desire.

She literally wantoned in the gay and voluptuous dance; at one moment all rapidity, grace, and airiness; at another suddenly falling into a pause expressive of a soft and languishing fatigue;—then again becoming all energy, activity, and animation,—representing, in all its phases, the soul—the spirit—the very poetry of the dance!

At length the toils of her first performance ended. There was not a dissenting voice, when she was called for before the curtain. And then, as she came forward, led by the manager, flowers fell around her—and handkerchiefs were waved by fair hands—and a thousand enthusiastic voices proclaimed her success. Her hopes were gratified—her aspirations were fulfilled:—she had achieved a brilliant triumph!

CHAPTER LXXXIX.

THE MYSTERIOUS LETTER.

AND now commenced a gay and busy life for Ellen Monroe. To account for her long absence each day from home, was an easy matter; for her father was readily satisfied, so implicit was the confidence he placed in his daughter's discretion; and Markham was always buried amongst his books in his study, save during the intervals occupied by meals.

Ellen's salary was considerable; and to dispose of it in a manner that was not calculated to excite the suspicion of her parent and benefactor, required more duplicity. She took home with her a small amount weekly; and the remainder she placed in the hands of a man of business, recommended to her by the manager.

Numerous attempts were made by certain young noblemen and gentlemen, who frequented the theatre, to ascertain where she resided. But this secret was unknown to every one save the manager, and he kept it religiously.

Nevertheless, Ellen was persecuted by amatory letters, and by proposals of a tender nature. A certain favoured few, of the youthful fashionables above alluded to, were permitted to lounge behind the scenes during the hours of performance; and with them Ellen was an object of powerful attraction—indeed, *the* object of undivided attention and interest. They perceived that she was as beautiful when surveyed near as she seemed when viewed from a distance. But, although she would lend a willing ear to the nonsense and small talk of her wooers, she gave them no direct encouragement; and, though somewhat free, her manners never afforded a pretence even for the most daring to overstep the bounds of decency towards her. The most brilliant offers were conveyed to her in the most delicate terms; but they were invariably declined with firmness, when oral—and left unanswered, when written.

A species of mystery appeared to hang around the charming *danseuse*, and only served to render her the more interesting. No one knew who she was, or whence she came. Her residence was a secret; and she was seen only at the theatre. There she was reported to be a very paragon of virtue, and had refused the offers of titled and wealthy men. These circumstances invested her with those artificial attractions which please the public, and which, when united with her real qualifications, raised her to a splendid degree of popularity.

Although her time was fully occupied, she now and then found leisure to call at the house of Mr. Wentworth, the surgeon, and pass half an hour in the company of her child. The little being throve apace; and Ellen felt for it all a mother's tenderness—a love which was not impaired by that callousness towards virtue for virtue's sake, which we have before noticed, and which had been produced in her by the strange scenes through which she had passed.

One evening, a short time before she was to appear in the ballet, the manager informed her that a gentleman desired to speak with her alone in the green-room.

To that apartment did Ellen immediately repair, and, to her surprise, she found herself in the presence of Mr. Greenwood.

"Ah! I am not then mistaken," exclaimed that gentleman, with one of his blandest smiles. "I saw you last night for the first time; and the moment you appeared upon the stage I knew you—that is, I felt almost convinced that it was you. But how happened this strange event in your life?"

"My benefactor, *Richard Markham*," answered Ellen, with singular and mysterious emphasis upon the name, "is not wealthy—*you* best know why; my father is irretrievably ruined—*you* also know how:—and, with all my faults, I could not endure the idea of eating the bread of dependence and idleness."

"But why did you not apply to me?" demanded Greenwood. "I would have placed you above want."

"No—I would not for worlds be dependent upon you," replied Ellen warmly. "I appealed to you to support my child—*our* child; and you did so. There was only one way in which you could have manifested a real generosity towards me—and you refused. The service I asked you once upon my knees—with tears and prayers—you rejected:—I implored you to give a father's honourable name to your child—I besought you to save the reputation of her whose father was ruined through you, and who herself became your victim by a strange combination of circumstances. You refused! What *less* could I accept at *your* hands? Do you think that I have not my little sentiments of pride as well as you? I could not live idly:—I embraced the stage; and my exertions have been crowned with success."

"And your father—and Richard—do they know of your present avocation?" demanded Greenwood, somewhat abashed by the bitterness of the undercurrent of reproach which had characterised the last speech of the figurante.

"God forbid!" cried Ellen. "And yet," she added, after a moment's thought, "I need not be ashamed of earning my bread by my own honourable exertions."

"And now, Ellen—one more question," said Greenwood. "The child—is he well! Is he taken care of?"

"He is well—and he is duly cared for," was Ellen's reply; and as she delivered it, she felt an emotion—almost of tenderness—in favour of the man who thus inquired, with embarrassment of manner, after the welfare of *their* child.

Greenwood's quick eye noticed the feeling that animated the young mother's bosom. He took her hand, and drew her towards him. She was so exquisitely beautiful—so inviting in the light gauze garb which she wore, that Greenwood's passions were fired, and he longed to make her his mistress.

Her hand lingered in his;—he pressed it gently. She did not seem to notice the circumstance; her eyes were cast down—she was absorbed in thought.

Greenwood imprinted a kiss upon her spotless forehead.

She started, hastily withdrew her hand, and cast upon him a look of mingled curiosity and reproach.

"Are you astonished that I should bestow a mark of kind feeling upon the mother of my child?" asked Greenwood, assuming a soft and tender tone of voice.

"That mother," answered Ellen, "whom you abandoned to shame and dishonour!"

"Do not reproach me for what is past," said Greenwood.

"Would you not act in the same manner over again?" inquired Ellen, darting a searching glance at the member of Parliament.

"Why this question, Ellen?" exclaimed Greenwood. "Will you not believe me if I tell you that I am attached to you? Will you not give me credit for sincerity, when I declare that I would gladly exert all the means in my power to make you happy? Why do you look so coldly upon me? Listen for a moment, Ellen, to what I am about to say. A few miles from London there is a delicious spot—a perfect Paradise upon earth, a villa surrounded by charming grounds, and commanding views of the most lovely scenery. That property is for sale: say but the word—I will purchase it—it shall be yours; and all the time that I can spare from my numerous avocations shall be devoted to Ellen and to love."

"The way to that charming villa, so far as you and I are concerned," said Ellen, "must lead through the church. Is it thus that you understand it?"

"Why destroy the dream of love and happiness which I had formed, by allusion to the formal ceremonies of this cold world?" exclaimed Greenwood.

"That is the language of every libertine, sir," replied Ellen, with bitter irony. "Do not deceive yourself—you cannot deceive me. I would accept the title of your wife, for the sake of our child;—but to be your mistress—no, never—never."

With these words Ellen left the green-room; and in a few minutes she appeared upon the stage—gay, animated, radiant with beauty and with smiles—the very personification of the voluptuous dance in which she shone with such unrivalled splendour.

Five or six evenings after the one on which she had this interview with Greenwood, Ellen received a note by the post. It was addressed to her at the theatre, by the name which she had assumed; and its contents ran as follows:—

"A certain person who is enamoured of you, and who is not accustomed to allow trivial obstacles to stand in the way of his designs, has determined upon carrying you forcibly off to a secluded spot in the country. He knows where you reside, and has ascertained that you return every evening from the theatre in a hackney cab to within a short distance of your abode. His plan is to way-lay you during your walk from the place where you descend from the vehicle, to your residence. If your suspicions fall upon any person of your acquaintance, after a perusal of this note, beware how you tax him with the vile intent;—beware how you communicate this warning, for by any imprudence on your part, you may deprive the writer of the means of counteracting in future the infamous designs which the individual above alluded to may form against yourself or others."

This note was written in a neat but curious hand, which seemed to be that of a foreigner. The reader can well imagine the painful surprise which its contents produced upon the young figurante. She however had no difficulty in fixing upon Greenwood as the person who contemplated the atrocity revealed in that note.

He alone (save the manager, who was an honourable and discreet man) knew where she lived; unless, indeed, some other amatory swain had followed her homeward. This idea perplexed her—it was possible; and yet she could not help thinking that Greenwood was the person against whom she was thus warned.

But who had sent her that friendly notice? Who was the mysterious individual that had thus generously placed her upon her guard? Conjecture was useless. She must think only of how she ought to act!

Her mind was speedily made up. She resolved to ride in the vehicle of an evening up to the very door of Markham's house, and trust to her ingenuity for an excuse to satisfy her father relative to this apparent extravagance on her part. Both Richard and Mr. Monroe put implicit confidence in her word;—she had already satisfactorily accounted for the late hours which her attendance at the theatre compelled her to keep, by stating that she was engaged to attend private concerts and musical conversaziones at the West End—sometimes, even, at Blackheath, Kensington, and Clapham—where she presided at the piano, in which she was a proficient. Then, when she was compelled to be present at rehearsals at the theatre, she stated that she had morning concerts to attend; and as she was not absent from home every day (her engagement with the manager being merely to appear three nights a-week) this system of deception on her part readily obtained credit with both Markham and her father, neither of whom could seriously object to what they were induced to believe was the legitimate exercise of her accomplishments. Accordingly, when, on the morning after the receipt of the mysterious letter, she casually mentioned that she should no longer return home of an evening by the omnibus, as she disliked the lonely walk from the main-road, where it set her down, to the Place, and that her emoluments would now permit her to enjoy the comfort and safety of a cab, both Richard and her father earnestly commended her resolution.

And why did she not tell the truth at once? wherefore did she not acknowledge the career which she was pursuing, and reveal the triumph which she had achieved?

Because she knew that both her father and Markham would oppose themselves to the idea of her exercising the profession of a dancer;—because she had commenced a system of duplicity, and was almost necessitated to persevere in it;—and because she really loved—ardently loved—the course upon which she had entered. The applause of crowded audiences—the smiles of the manager—the adulation of the young nobles and gentlemen who, behind the scenes, complimented her upon her success, her talents, and her beauty,—these were delights which she would not very readily abandon.

CHAPTER XC.

MARKHAM'S OCCUPATIONS.

Since the period when Markham had made so great a sacrifice of his pecuniary resources, in order to effect the liberation of Count Alteroni from a debtor's prison, he had devoted himself to literary pursuits. He aspired to the honours of authorship, and composed a tragedy.

All young authors, while yet nibbling the grass at the foot of Parnassus (and how many never reach any higher!) attempt either poetry or the drama. They invariably fix upon the most difficult tasks; and yet they did not begin learning Greek with Euripides, nor enter upon their initiation into the mysteries of the Latin tongue with Juvenal.

There is also another fault into which they invariably fall;—and that is an extraordinary tendency to those meretricious ornaments which they seem to mistake for fine writing. Truth and nature may be regarded as a noble flock, furnishing the richest fleece to mankind; but when a series of good writers have exhausted their fleece in weaving the fabrics of genius, their successors are tempted to have recourse to swine for a supply of materials; and we know, besides, that in this attempt, as in the rude dramas called "Moralities" in the middle ages, there is great cry and little wool. It is also liable to the objection that no skill in the workmanship, or adjustment in the machinery, can give it the beauty and perfection of the raw material which nature has appropriated to the purpose of clothing her favoured offspring.

Too many writers of the present day, instead of attempting to rival their predecessors in endeavouring to fabricate the genuine fleece derived from this flock of truth and nature, into new and exquisite forms, are engaged in shearing the swine. In this labour they can obtain, at best, nothing more than erroneous principles of science, worthless paradoxes, unnatural fictions, tinsel poetry and prose, and unnumbered crudities.

Richard Markham was not exempted from these faults. He wrote a tragedy—abounding in beauties, and abounding in faults.

The most delicious sweets, used in undue proportions with our food and drink, soon become in a high degree offensive and disgusting. Markham heaped figure upon figure—crammed his speeches with metaphors—and travelled many thousands of miles out of his way in search of a similitude, when he had a much better and more simple one close at hand. Nevertheless, his tragedy contained proofs of a brilliant talent, and, with much judicious pruning, every element of triumphant success.

Having obtained the address of the private residence of the manager of one of the principal metropolitan theatres, Richard sent his tragedy to the great man. He, however, withheld his real name, for he had determined to commence his literary career under a feigned one; so that, in case he should prove unsuccessful, his failure might not become known to his friends the Monroes, or reach the ears of his well-beloved Isabella. For the same reason he did not give his proper address in the letter which accompanied the drama; but requested that a reply might be sent to *Edward Preston, to the care of Mr. Dyson* (his solicitor).

He did not mention to a single soul—not even to Monroe or the faithful Whittingham—the circumstance of his authorship. He reflected that if he succeeded, it would then be time to communicate his happiness; but, that if he failed, it would be useless to wound others by imparting to them his disappointments. He had ceased to be sanguine about any thing in this world; for he had met with too many misfortunes to anticipate much success in life; and his only ambition was to obtain an honourable livelihood.

Scarcely a week had elapsed after Markham had sent his drama to the manager, when he received a letter from this gentleman. The contents were laconic enough, but explicit. The manager "had perused the tragedy with feelings of extreme satisfaction;"—he congratulated the writer upon "the skill which he had made his combinations to produce stage effect;"—he suggested "a few alterations and considerable abbreviations;" and concluded by stating that "he should be most happy to introduce so promising an author to the public." A postscript appointed a time for an interview at the manager's own private residence.

At eleven o'clock the next morning Markham was ushered into the presence of the manager.

The great man was seated in his study, dressed in a magnificent Turkish dressing-gown, with a French skull-cap upon his head, and red morocco slippers upon his feet. He was a man of middle age—gentlemanly and affable in manner—and possessed of considerable literary abilities.

"Sit down, sir—pray, sit down," said the manager, when Markham was introduced. "I have perused your tragedy with great attention, and am pleased with it. I am, moreover, perfectly willing to undertake the risk of bringing it out, although tragedy is at a terrible discount now-a-days. But, first and foremost, we must make arrangements about terms. What price do you put upon your manuscript?"

"I have formed no idea upon that subject," replied Markham. "I would rather leave myself entirely in your hands."

"Nay—you must know the hope you have entertained in this respect?" said the manager.

"To tell you the candid truth, this is my first essay," returned Markham; "and I am totally unacquainted with the ordinary value of such labour."

"If this be your first essay, sir," said the manager, surveying Markham with some astonishment, "I can only assure you that it is a most promising one. But once again—name your price."

"The manner in which you speak to me shows that if I trust to your generosity, I shall not do wrong."

"Well, Mr. Preston," cried the manager, pleased at this compliment, "I shall use you in an equally liberal manner. You must be informed that you will have certain pecuniary privileges, in respect to any provincial theatres at which your piece may be performed should it prove successful; and you will also have the benefit of the publication of the work in a volume. What, then, should you say if I were to give you fifty guineas for the play, and five guineas a-night for every time of its performance, after the first fortnight?"

"I should esteem your offer a very liberal one," answered Richard, overjoyed at the proposal.

"In that case the bargain is concluded at once, and without any more words," said the manager; then, taking a well-filled canvass bag from his desk, he counted down fifty guineas in notes, gold, and silver.

Markham gave a receipt, and they exchanged undertakings specifying the conditions proposed by the manager.

"When do you propose to bring out the piece?" inquired Richard, when this business was concluded.

"In about six weeks," said the manager. "Shall you have any objection to attend the rehearsals, and see that the gentlemen and ladies of the company fully appreciate the spirit of the parts that will be assigned to them?"

"I shall not have the least objection," answered Markham; "but I am afraid that my experience——"

"Well, well," said the manager, smiling, "I will not press you. Leave it all to me—I will see justice done to your design, which I think I understand pretty well. If I want you I will let you know; and if you do not hear from me, you will see by the advertisements in the newspapers for what night the first representation will be announced."

Markham expressed his gratitude to the manager for the kindness with which he had received him, and then took his leave, his heart elated with hope, and his mind relieved from much anxiety respecting the future.

When he left the manager's residence he repaired to an adjacent tavern to procure some refreshment; and there, while engaged in the discussion of a sandwich and a glass of sherry, he cast his eyes over *The Times* newspaper.

A particular advertisement arrested his attention.

A gentleman—a widower—required a daily tutor for his two

young sons, whom he was desirous of having instructed in Latin, history, drawing, arithmetic, &c. The boys were respectively nine and eleven years old. The advertiser stated that any individual who could himself teach the various branches of education specified, would be preferred to a plurality of masters, each proficient only in one particular study. Personal application was to be made between certain hours.

The residence of the advertiser was in Kentish Town; and this vicinity to Markham's own abode induced him to think seriously of offering his services. He did not feel disposed to pursue his literary labours until after the representation of his drama, as he was as yet unaware of the reception it might experience at the hands of the public;—and he was also by no means inclined to remain idle. The occupation of daily tutor in a respectable family appeared congenial to his tastes; and he resolved to proceed forthwith to the residence of Mr. Gregory, in Kentish Town.

Arrived at the house, he was admitted into the presence of a gentleman of about fifty, with a serious and melancholy countenance, prepossessing manners, and a peculiar suavity of voice that gave encouragement to the applicant.

Markham told him in a few words that he was once possessed of considerable property, the greater portion of which he had lost through the unfortunate speculations of his guardian, and that he was now anxious to turn the excellent education which he had received to some advantage.

Mr. Gregory had only lately arrived in London with his family, from a very distant part of the country, where he had a house and small estate; but the recent death of a beloved wife had rendered the scenes of their wedded happiness disagreeable to him;—and this was the cause of his removal and his settlement in London. He lived in a very retired manner, and had previously known nothing of Markham—not even his name. He was therefore totally ignorant of Richard's trial and condemnation for forgery. The young man felt the greatest possible inclination to reveal the entire facts to Mr. Gregory, whose amiable manners gave him confidence; but he restrained himself—for it struck him that others were dependent upon him—that he ought not to stand in his own light—and that his innocence of the crime imputed to him, and the consciousness of those upright and honourable intentions which on all occasions filled his breast, were a sufficient extenuation for this silence.

Mr. Gregory, who was himself a highly-educated man, soon saw that Markham was competent to teach his children all that it was desirable for them to acquire; and he agreed to engage the applicant as his sons' tutor. Richard offered to give him a reference to his solicitor; but Mr. Gregory declined to take it, saying, "Your appearance, Mr. Markham, is sufficient."

On the following day Richard entered upon his new avocation. He was engaged to attend at Mr. Gregory's house from ten till three every day. The employment was a pleasant one; and the pecuniary terms were liberal in the extreme.

Gustavus and Lionel Gregory were two intelligent and handsome youths; and they soon became greatly attached to their tutor.

From the mere fact of having never been accustomed to tuition, Richard took the greater pains to explain all difficult subjects to them; and so well did he adapt his plan of instruction to their juvenile capacities, that in the short space of a month, Mr. Gregory was himself perfectly astonished at the advance which his sons had made in their studies. He then determined that the advantages of the tutor's abilities should be extended to his daughter, in respect to drawing; and Miss Mary-Anne Gregory was accordingly added to the number of Markham's pupils.

Mary-Anne was, at the time of which we are writing, sixteen years of age. Delicate in constitution, and of a sweet and amiable disposition, she was an object of peculiar interest to all who knew her. Her long flaxen hair, soft blue eyes, pale countenance, and vermilion lips, gave her the appearance of a wax figure; and her light and airy form, flitting ever hither and thither in obedience to the innocent gaiety and vivacity of her disposition, seemed that of some fairy whose destinies belonged not to the common lot of mortals.

Although she was sixteen, she was considered but a mere girl; and she romped with her brothers, and with the young female friends who occasionally visited her, with all the joyousness and glee of a child of ten years old.

The animation of her countenance was on those occasions radiant and brilliant in the extreme:—a spectator could have snatched her to his arms and embraced her fondly,—not with a single gross desire—not with the shadow of an unhallowed motive; but, in the same way as a man, who, being a parent himself, is attached to children, suddenly seizes upon a lovely little boy or girl of two or three years old, and covers its cheeks with kisses.

Mary-Anne was by no means beautiful—not even pretty; and yet there was something altogether unearthly in the whole character and expression of her countenance. It was a face of angelic interest—indicative of a mental amiability and serenity truly divine.

Without possessing the ingredients of physical beauty—without regularity of feature or classical formation of head,—there was still about her an abstract loveliness, apart from shape and features, which was of itself positive and distinct, and seemed an emanation of mental qualities, infantine joyousness, and winning manners. It produced a sort of atmosphere of light around her—enveloping her as with a halo of innocence.

Her face was as pale—as colourless as the finest Parian marble, but also, like the surface of that beautiful material, spotless and devoid of blemish. Her pure forehead was streaked with small azure veins: her lips were thin, and of the brightest vermilion; and these hues placed in contrast with that delicate complexion, gave a sentiment and expression to her countenance altogether peculiar to itself.

Her eyes, of a light and yet too positive a blue to be mistaken for grey, were fringed with long dark lashes, which imparted to them—ever gay and sparkling as they were—a magic eloquence as powerful as that of the most faultless beauty. And, again, in strange contrast with those dark lashes was her flaxen hair, the whole of which fell in ringlets and in waves over her shoulders and her back, no portion of it being collected in a knot behind.

Then her form—it was so slight as to appear almost etherealised, and yet there was no mistaking the symmetry of its proportions.

Thus—without being actually beautiful—Mary-Anne was a creature of light and joy who was calculated to interest, fascinate, and win, in a manner which produced feelings of admiration and of love. Her appearance therefore produced upon the mind an impression that she *was* beautiful—very beautiful; and yet, if any one had paused to analyse her features, she would have been found to possess no real elements of physical loveliness. She was charming—fascinating—bewitching—interesting; therefore lovely in one sense, and loveable in all respects!

Mary-Anne was a very difficult pupil to teach. In the midst of the most serious study, that charming and volatile creature would start from her chair, run to her piano, and commence a lively air, which she would leave also unfinished, and then narrate some sprightly anecdote, or utter some artless sally, which would create a general laugh.

The seriousness of the tutor would be disturbed in spite of himself: and even her father, if present, could not find it in his heart to scold.

The drawing would at length be resumed; and for half an hour, the application of Mary-Anne would be intense. Then away would be flung the pencil; and a new freak must be accomplished before the study would be resumed.

Richard could not help liking this volatile, but artless and innocent creature,—as a man likes his daughter or his sister; and she, on her part, appeared to become greatly attached to her tutor.

Although Mr. Gregory followed no profession, being a man of considerable independent property, he was nevertheless much from home, passing his time either at the library of the British Museum or at his Club. Richard and Mary-Anne were thus much together,—too much for the peace of that innocent and fascinating girl!

She speedily conceived a violent passion for her tutor, which he, however, neither perceived nor returned.

She was herself unaware of the nature of her own feelings towards him;—she knew as much of love and its sensations as a beauteous savage girl, in some far-off isle, knows of Christianity;—and hers was an attachment which could only be revealed to herself by some accident, which might excite her jealousy or awaken her grief.

One morning, before the usual lessons of the day commenced, Mr. Gregory entered the study, and, addressing himself to Markham, said, "We must now give the young people a holiday for a short time. Proper relaxation is as necessary to their bodily welfare as education to their mental well-being. We will suspend their studies for a month, if you be agreeable, Mr. Markham. I shall, however, be always pleased to see you as often as you choose to call during that interval; and every Sunday, at all events, we shall expect the pleasure of your company to dinner as usual."

"What!" cried Mary-Anne; "is Mr. Markham to discontinue his daily visits for a whole month?"

"Certainly, my dear," said her father. "Mr. Markham requires a holiday as well as you."

"I want no holiday," exclaimed Mary-Anne, pouting her lip, in a manner that was quite charming, and which might remind the reader of the *petite moue* that Esmeralda was accustomed to make in Victor Hugo's admirable novel *Notre Dame de Paris*.

"But *you* always take a holiday, my dear," returned her father with a smile; "and therefore you fancy that others do not require a temporary relaxation. Gustavus and Lionel want a holiday; and Mr. Markham cannot be always poring over books and drawings."

"Well, I wish Mr. Markham to take the trouble to come every morning and give me my drawing lesson," said the young lady, with a little air of decision and firmness, which was quite comic in its way; "and if he will not," she added, "then I will never learn to draw any more—and that is decided."

Mr. Gregory surveyed his daughter with an air of astonishment.

Probably he half penetrated *the* secret—for her passion could not be called *her* secret, because she was totally unconscious of the nature of her feelings, and sought to conceal nothing.

Had she been aware of the real sentiment which she experienced, she would have at once revealed it; for she was guileless and unsuspicious—ignorant of all deceit—devoid of all hypocrisy—and endowed with as much simplicity and artlessness as a child of six years old.

"Mr. Markham must have a holiday, my dear," said Mr. Gregory, at length, with a peculiar emphasis; "and I beg that no further objection may be offered."

Mary-Anne instantly burst into tears, exclaiming, in a voice almost choked with sobs, "Mr. Markham *may* have *his* holiday, if he likes; but I will not learn any thing more of him when the studies begin again."

And she retired in a pet to another apartment.

Markham was himself astonished at this singular behaviour on the part of his interesting pupil.

He was, however, far from suspecting the real cause, and took his leave with a promise to return to dinner on the following Sunday, until which time there was then an interval of five days.

Three days after the one on which the above conversation took place, Markham was about to issue from his dwelling to proceed into town for the purpose of calling upon the manager, as he had that morning seen his drama advertised for early representation,—when Whittingham informed him that a young lady desired to speak to him in the drawing-room.

The idea of Isabella instantly flashed through the mind of Richard:—but would *she* call upon him, alone and unattended? No—for Isabella was modesty and prudence personified.

Then, who could it be?

Markham asked this question of his butler.

"A remarkable sweet creatur," said Whittingham; "and come quite spontaneous like. Beautiful flaxy hair—blue eyes—pale complexion—"

"Impossible! you do not say *that*, Whittingham?" cried Markham, on whom a light now broke.

"Do I look like a man that speaks evasiously, Master Richard?" demanded the butler, shifting his inseparable companion—the white napkin—from beneath one arm to the other.

Markham repaired to the drawing-room:—his suspicions were verified;—the moment he entered the apartment, he beheld Miss Gregory seated upon the sofa.

"Well, Mr. Markham," she said, extending to him her hand, and smiling so sweetly with her vermilion lips, which disclosed a set of teeth not quite even, but as white as ivory, that Richard could not find it in his heart to be angry with her; "I was resolved not to pass the day without seeing you; and as you would not come to me, I was compelled to come to you."

"But, Miss Gregory," said Markham, "are you not aware that you have taken a most imprudent step, and that the world would highly censure your conduct?"

"Why?" demanded Mary-Anne, in astonishment.

"Because ladies, no matter whether single or married, never call upon single gentlemen; and society has laid down certain rules in this respect, which—"

"My dear Mr. Markham, you are not giving me a lesson now, remember, in my father's study," interrupted Mary-Anne, laughing heartily. "I know nothing about the rules of society in this respect, or that respect, or any other respect. All I know is, that I cried all night long after you left us the other day; and I have been very miserable until this morning, when I suddenly recollected that I knew your address, and could come and call on you."

"If your father were to know that you came hither," said Richard, "he would never forgive you, nor ever see me again."

"Well, then, all we have to do is not to tell my father any thing about the matter," said Mary-Anne, with considerable ingenuousness. "But how cross you look; and I—I thought," she added, ready to cry, "that you would be as pleased to see me as I am to see you."

"Yes, Miss Gregory—I *am* pleased to see you—I am always pleased to see you," answered Markham, by way of soothing the poor girl; "but you must allow me to assure you that this step is the most imprudent—the most thoughtless in the world. I really tremble for the consequences—should your father happen to hear of it."

"I tell you over and over again," persisted Miss Gregory, "that my papa shall never know any thing at all about the matter. Now, then, pray don't be cross; but tell me that you are glad to see me. Speak, Mr. Markham—are you glad to see me?"

"How shall I ever be able to convince this artless young creature of the impropriety of her conduct?" murmured Richard within himself. "To argue with her too long and too forcibly upon the subject would be to instruct her innocent mind in the evils and vices of society, and to imbue her with ideas which are as yet like a foreign and a strange tongue to her! Innocence, then, is not a pearl of invaluable price to its possessor, in this world,—since it can so readily prepare the path which *might* lead to ruin!"

"You do not answer me—you are thoughtful—you will not speak to me," said Mary-Anne, rising from the sofa, with tears in her eyes, and preparing—or rather affecting an intention to depart.

Markham still gave her no reply.

He was grieved—deeply grieved to wound her feelings; but he thought that it would be better to allow her to return home at once, with sentiments of pique and wounded pride which would prevent a repetition of the same step, than to initiate her into those social mysteries which would only give an impulse to her lively imagination that would probably prove morally injurious to her.

But Mary-Anne was incapable of harbouring resentment; and she burst into an agony of grief.

"Oh! how unkind you are, Mr. Markham," she exclaimed, "after all my endeavours to please you! I thought that you would have experienced as much joy to see me, as I felt when I saw you enter the room. Since the day that I lost my dear mother—upwards of nine years ago—I have never loved any one so much as I love you—no, not even my father; for I feel that at this moment I could dare even *his* anger, if you were to shelter me! I have long thought that I had no friend but God, to whom I could communicate my little secrets; and now I feel as if I could bestow all my confidence upon you. Since the death of my mother I have never sought my couch without resigning my soul into the hands of God, and without demanding of him an insight into truth and virtue. But now I would rather entrust my safety to you; and I would rather learn all I should know from your lips than from those of another! You ought, therefore, to treat me with more kindness and consideration than you have done up to this moment;—you should bestow upon me an additional share of your attention and notice,—because I am anxious to please you—I would do any thing to save you pain—I would lay down my life to ensure a prolongation of yours!"

Mary-Anne had never spoken so seriously, nor in so impassioned a manner, in her life before. She was even astonished herself at the very ideas which she was now expressing for the first time, and which seemed to flow from some inward fountain whose springs she could not check.

Markham was astounded.

He suddenly comprehended the true situation of the innocent and artless girl in respect to himself.

A pang shot through his heart when he considered the impossibility of her happiness ever being ensured by his means; and he thought within himself, "Alas! poor child, she does not rightly comprehend the state of her own mind!"

But how could this love of hers be stifled? how could that passion be suppressed?

All the remedies yet essayed to quench and annihilate love, have changed into poisons;—even violent and unexpected lessons will not always make the heart reflect.

The more the slave bends, the heavier becomes the yoke: the more a man employs an unjust force, the more will injustice become necessary to his views. No one should attempt to exercise tyranny upon proud souls; for he will readily learn that it is not easy to triumph over and trample on a noble love. Error succeeds error—outrage follows upon outrage—and bitterness increases like a torrent whose embankments have given way. Who can define the termination of these ravages? Will not the tender and affectionate woman, whose love man may endeavour to stifle by coldness or neglect, perish in the ruin? *She* will succumb to tears and to devouring cares—even while the *love* which she cherishes still preserves all its vigour, and loses nothing of its ardour through intense suffering!

Markham knew not how to reply to that affectionate girl, whose spirit he dared not break by his unkindness,—whose passion he could not return, because his heart was devoted to another,—and whose mind he was afraid to enlighten with regard to those social duties which originated in reasons and motives totally unknown to her.

"Mr. Markham," said Mary-Anne, wiping away her tears, "tell me that you are not angry with me for calling: and, as you say it is not right, I will never come again."

"Angry with you, Miss Gregory, I cannot be," exclaimed Markham. "But I ought to tell you that you must not give way to that feeling of—of—preference towards me—"

"Oh! I suppose that the rules of society also prevent a single lady from liking a single gentleman?" interrupted Mary-Anne pettishly.

"No rules can control volition, Miss Gregory," said Richard, cruelly embarrassed how to explain himself to the young lady; "but if you tell me that you prefer me to your father—"

"And so I do," exclaimed Mary-Anne quickly.

"Then you are wrong," returned Markham.

"Wrong, indeed! and yet you have just told me that no rules can control volition."

"True; but we must endeavour to conquer those feelings. You say that you like me?—suppose that we were never to meet again; would you not then learn to forget that you ever knew such a being?"

"Impossible! never—never!" cried Mary-Anne enthusiastically. "I am always thinking of you!"

"But the time must come, some day or another—whether now, or a year, or ten years hence—when we must cease to meet. I may be married—or you yourself may marry—"

"Married!" ejaculated Mary-Anne: "do you think of marrying, then, Mr. Markham?"

"I am certainly attached to a young lady," replied Richard; "but there are circumstances which—"

"You are attached to a young lady? Is she beautiful—very beautiful?"

"Very beautiful," answered Richard.

Mary-Anne remained silent for some moments: she appeared to reflect profoundly.

A sudden glow of animation flushed her cheek:—was it a light that dawned in upon her soul?

Richard sincerely hoped so.

"Mr. Markham," said Mary-Anne, rising from her seat, and speaking in a tone so serious that Richard could scarcely believe he was now listening to the once volatile, sprightly, thoughtless, and playful creature he had known,—"Mr. Markham, I have to apologise most sincerely for the trouble I have given you, and the intrusion of which I have been guilty. A veil has suddenly fallen from my eyes; and I now comprehend the impropriety of my conduct. Ah! I see what you mean by the laws of society. But God—and you also, Mr. Markham, well know the innocence of my motives in calling this morning upon you; and if my friendship for you has betrayed me into error, I beseech you to forget that such a scene has ever taken place."

She shook hands with Richard with her usual cordiality and warmth, and then took her departure—no longer skipping like the young fawn, but with steady and measured pace.

And still that young girl did not dream that love had influenced her conduct;—she continued to believe that the sentiment she experienced was one of friendship. The idea of Richard's marriage with another had only enlightened her in respect to those laws which, as social and sympathetic beings, we have conventionally enacted.

On the ensuing Sunday Markham dined, according to engagement, with Mr. Gregory.

Mary-Anne was present; and striking was the change which had taken place in her!

Her manners were no longer gay, joyous, confiding, and full of animation. As sickness chases from the cheek the flush of hoyden health, so had a new sentiment banished that sprightliness of disposition and that liveliness of temperament which so lately had characterised this *child of nature*.

Love, then, is omnipotent, if he can effect such changes as these! Alas! Love can work much for our unhappiness, but little for our felicity:—he may make the gladsome companion melancholy and serious; but he seldom covers the countenance of the morose one with smiles!

Mary-Anne endeavoured to seem as reserved as possible with Richard; and yet, from time to time, when she thought he did not notice her, she fixed her eyes upon him with an expression of such heart-devoted tenderness, that it seemed as if she were pouring forth her entire soul to the divinity whom she worshipped.

In the grotesque and colossal sculptures, and the mountainous architectural piles of the East we seem to behold the products of an imagination struggling with conceptions too vast for its compass, and hence endeavouring to make some approximation to the reality by heaping up the irregular and huge invisible forms; and thus did the tortured and embarrassed mind of this poor girl, unacquainted with the precise nature of the sentiment it cherished, maintain a conflict with the feelings which oppressed it and offer up an idolatry of its own invention to the object of its unbounded veneration.

Mr. Gregory could not but perceive this change in his daughter's behaviour, and he was more or less at a loss to conceive the cause.

He had entertained for a few days previously, a faint suspicion that Mary-Anne had peradventure formed an attachment, which would thus account for her altered demeanour; for since her call upon Markham, had her manners changed. But the good-hearted father was still loth to believe that his daughter's young heart had been smitten—and for the simple reason because he did not wish it to be so.

Although he respected Markham, he was like all parents who, possessing fortunes themselves, are anxious that the suitors for their daughters' hands should also be enabled to produce a modicum of this world's lucre.

He was therefore unwilling to admit in his own mind the conviction that his suspicion was well-founded: he fancied that change of scene or amusement would probably operate favourably upon his daughter's mind, and bring her spirits back to their proper tone; and in this resolution was he confirmed, when in the course of that Sunday evening, he saw the confirmation of his suspicion. He could no longer doubt:—a thousand little incidents proved to him, the attachment of his daughter to Richard Markham; and his quick glance convinced him—that she was *not* loved by her tutor in return.

That night Mr. Gregory lay awake, pondering upon the best course to pursue. At one moment he thought of communicating to Markham the state of his daughter's heart (for he could not suppose that Richard was aware of the passion of which he was the object), and permitting the young couple to look upon each other as destined to be one day united:—at another moment, he imagined that it would be better to allow things to take their chance for a short time and thereby ascertain whether the attachment gained ground on the part of his daughter, and whether it would become mutual (for he was entirely ignorant of Markham's love for another); and at length he resolved upon dispensing with the services of Richard, and trusting to time to eradicate the seeds of the unfortunate passion from the heart of Mary-Anne.

This plan Mr. Gregory put into execution in the course of a few days—indeed, the very next time that Richard called at his house.

"Mr. Markham," said the father, "I deeply regret that certain circumstances, which it is not necessary for me to explain to you, compel me to dispense with your farther attendance upon my children."

"I hope," said Markham, "that I have given you no cause——"

"Not at all—not in the least," interrupted Mr. Gregory, shaking Richard cordially by the hand: then, in a serious tone, he added, "my daughter's health requires rest—repose—and quiet. I shall see no visitors for some time."

Markham was satisfied. Mr. Gregory had heard nothing prejudicial to his character; but he had evidently penetrated into the state of Mary-Anne's feelings. Richard was delighted to be thus dismissed from a house where his presence was only calculated to destroy the more profoundly the peace of one of its inmates:—indeed, he himself had already entertained serious ideas of severing his connexion with that family.

"If I can at any time be of service to you, Mr. Markham, in any way, you may command me," said Mr. Gregory, when the former rose to depart; "and do not think that I am merely uttering a cold ceremonial phrase, when I desire you to make use of me as a friend, should you ever require one."

Richard thanked Mr. Gregory for his kindness, and took leave of him. He also bade adieu to Gustavus and Lionel, both of whom were deeply affected at the idea of losing the visits of their tutor:—but Mary-Anne had been purposely sent to pass a few days with some friends in the country.

CHAPTER XCI.

THE TRAGEDY.

At length the evening, upon which the tragedy was to be represented for the first time, arrived.

Markham in the mean time had seen little of the manager, and had not attended a single rehearsal, his presence for that purpose not having been required. Moreover, true to his original intentions, he had not acquainted a soul with his secret relative to the drama. The manager still knew him only as Edward Preston; and the advertisements in the newspapers had announced the "forthcoming tragedy" as one that had "emanated from the pen of a young author of considerable promise, but who had determined to maintain a strict *incognito* until the public verdict should have been pronounced upon his piece."

A short time before the doors opened, Richard proceeded to the theatre, and called upon the manager, who received him in his own private apartment.

"Well, Mr. Preston," said the theatrical monarch, "this evening will decide the fate of the tragedy. A few hours, and we shall know more."

"I hope you still think well of it," returned Markham.

"My candid opinion is that the success will be triumphant," said the manager. "I have spared no expense to get up the piece well; and I am very sanguine. Besides, I have another element of success."

"What is that?" inquired Richard.

"My principal ballet-dancer, who is a beautiful creature and a general favourite—Miss Selina Fitzherbert—"

"I have heard of her fame," said Markham, "but have never seen her. Strange as it may appear, I never visit theatres—I have not done so for years."

"You will visit them often enough if your productions succeed," observed the manager with a smile. "But, as I was saying, Miss

Fitzherbert has lately manifested a passionate desire to shine in tragedy; and she will make her *debut* in that sphere to-night, in your piece. She will play the *Baron's Daughter*."

"Which character does not appear until the commencement of the third act," said Markham.

"Precisely," observed the manager. "But time is now drawing on. Where will you remain during the performance?"

"I shall proceed into the body of the house," returned Markham, "and take my seat in one of the central boxes—I mean those precisely fronting the stage. I shall be able to judge of the effect better in that part of the house than elsewhere."

"As you please," said the manager. "But mind and let me see you after the performance."

Richard promised compliance with this request, and then proceeded into the house, where he took a seat in the centre of the amphitheatre.

The doors had been opened a few minutes previously, and the house was filling fast. By half-past six it was crowded from pit to roof. The boxes were filled with elegantly-dressed ladies and fashionable gentlemen: there was not room to thrust another spectator into any one point at the moment when the curtain drew up.

The overture commenced. How long it appeared to Markham, passionately fond of music though he was!

At length it ceased; and the First Act commenced.

For some time a profound silence pervaded the audience:—not a voice, not a murmur, not a sigh, gave the slightest demonstration of either approbation or dislike.

But, at length, at the conclusion of a most impressive soliloquy, which was delivered by the hero of the piece, one universal burst of applause broke forth; and the theatre rang with the sounds of human tongues and the clapping of hands. When the First Act ended, the opinion of the audience was decisive in favour of the piece; and the manager felt persuaded that "it was a hit."

This was one of the happiest moments of Markham's existence—that existence which had latterly presented so few green spots to please the mental eye of the wanderer in the world's desert. His veins seemed to run with liquid fire!—a delirium of joy seized upon him—he was inebriated with excess of bliss.

Around him the spectators were expressing their opinions of the first act, little suspecting that the author of the piece was so near. All those sentiments were unequivocally in favour of the tragedy.

The Second Act began—progressed—terminated.

No pen can describe the enthusiasm with which the audience received the development of the drama, nor the interest which it seemed to excite.

Inspired by the applause that greeted them, the performers exerted all their efforts; and the excellence of the tragedy, united with the talent of the actors and the beauty of the scenery, achieved a triumph not often witnessed within the walls of that or any other theatre.

The Third Act commenced. Selina Fitzherbert appeared upon the stage; and her presence was welcomed with rapturous applause.

She came forward, and acknowledged the kindness of the audience with a graceful curtsey.

Markham surveyed her with interest, in consequence of the manner in which her name had been mentioned to him by the manager;—but that interest grew more profound, and was gradually associated with feelings of extreme surprise, suspense, and uncertainty, for he fancied that if ever he saw Ellen Monroe in his life, there was she—or else her living counterpart—before him—an actress playing a part in his own drama!

He was stupefied;—he strained his eyes—he leant forward—he borrowed the opera-glass of a gentleman seated next to him;—and the more he gazed, the more he felt convinced that he beheld Ellen Monroe in the person of Selina Fitzherbert.

At length the actress spoke: wonder upon wonder—it was Ellen's voice—her intonation—her accent—her style of speaking.

Markham was amazed—confounded.

He inquired of his neighbour whether Selina Fitzherbert was the young lady's real name, or an assumed one.

The gentleman to whom he spoke did not know.

"How long has she been upon the stage?"

"Between two and three months; and, strange to say, it is rumoured that she only took two months to render herself so proficient a dancer as she is. But she now appears to be equally fine in tragedy. Listen!"

Markham could ask no more questions; for his neighbour became all attention towards the piece.

Richard reviewed in a moment, in his mind, all the principal appearances and characteristics of Ellen's life during the last few months,—the lateness of her hours—the constancy of her employment—and a variety of circumstances, which only now struck him, but which tended to ratify his suspicion that she was indeed Selina Fitzherbert.

His attention was withdrawn from his own piece; and he determined to convince himself at once upon this head.

Taking advantage of the termination of the first scene in the third act, he left the box, and proceeded behind the scenes of the theatre. But while he was on his way thither, it struck him that if his suspicions were correct, and if he appeared too suddenly in the presence of Ellen, he would perhaps so disconcert her as to render her unfit to proceed with the part entrusted to her. He accordingly concealed himself in a dark corner, behind some scene-boards, and whence he could see plainly, but where he himself could not be very readily discovered.

He did not wait long ere his doubts were cleared up. In a few minutes after he had taken his post in the obscure nook, Ellen passed close by him. She was conversing with another actress.

"Have you seen the author?" said the latter.

"No—not yet," replied Ellen. "But the manager has promised us that pleasure when the curtain falls."

"He has made a brilliant hit."

"Yes," said Ellen. "He need not have been so bashful if he had known his own powers, or foreseen this success. The greatest mystery has been preserved about him: he never once came to rehearsal and the prompter who copied out my part for me from the original manuscript, tells me that he is convinced the author is quite a novice in dramatic composition, by the way in which the piece was written—I mean, there were not in the manuscript any of those hints and suggestions which an experienced writer would have introduced."

"I really quite long to see him," said Ellen's companion: "he must be quite——"

The two ladies passed on; and Richard heard no more.

His doubts were, however, cleared up:—Ellen Monroe was a figurante and an actress!

He was not so annoyed at this discovery as Ellen had imagined he would have been when she took such precautions to conceal the fact from the knowledge of him and her father. Richard could not help admiring the independent spirit which had induced her to seek the means of earning her own livelihood, and which he now fully comprehended:—at the same time, he was sorry that she had withheld the truth, and that she had embraced the stage in preference to any other avocation. Alas! he little suspected what scenes that poor girl had passed through:—he knew nothing of her connexion with the statuary, the artist, the sculptor, the photographer, Greenwood, and the mesmerist!

Having satisfied himself that Selina Fitzherbert and Ellen Monroe were one and the same person, and still amazed and bewildered by the discovery, Markham returned to the body of the theatre; but, instead of proceeding to his former seat, he repaired to the "author's box," which he found unoccupied, and which, being close to the stage, commanded a full view of the scene.

The tragedy proceeded with unabated success: the performance of Ellen was alone sufficient to give it an extraordinary *éclat*. Her beautiful countenance—the noble and dignified manner in which she carried her classic head—her elegant form—the natural grace and suavity of her manners—her musical voice—and the correct appreciation she evinced of the character in which she appeared,—these were the elements of an irresistible appeal to the public heart. The tragedy would have been eminently successful by reason of its own intrinsic merits, and *without* Ellen:—but *with* her, that success was brilliant—triumphant—unparalleled in the annals of the modern stage!

The entire audience was enraptured with the charming woman who shone in two ways so essentially distinct, who had first captivated the sense as a dancer, and who now came forth a great tragic actress. Her lovely person and her talents united, formed a passport to favour which not a dissentient voice could question;—and when the curtain fell at the close of the fifth act, the approbation of the spectators was expressed with clapping of hands, waving of handkerchiefs, and shouts of applause—all prolonged to an unusual length of time, and frequently renewed with additional enthusiasm.

The moment the curtain fell Markham hastened behind the scenes, and encountered Ellen in one of the slips.

Hastily grasping her by the hand, he said in a low but hurried tone, "Do not be alarmed—I know all—I am here to thank you—not to blame you."

"Thank *me*, Richard!" exclaimed the young actress, partially recovering from the almost overwhelming state of alarm into which the sudden apparition of Markham had thrown her: "why should you thank *me*?"

"Thank you, Ellen—Oh! how can I do otherwise than thank you?" said Markham. "You have carried my tragedy through the ordeal—"

"*Your* tragedy, Richard?" cried Miss Monroe, more and more bewildered.

"Yes, *my* tragedy, Ellen—it is mine! But, ah! there is a call for you—"

A moment's silence had succeeded the flattering expression of public opinion which arose at the termination of the performance; and then arose a loud cry for Selina Fitzherbert.

This was followed by a call for the author, and then a thousand voices ejaculated—"Selina Fitzherbert and the Author! Let them come together!"

The manager now hastened up to the place where Ellen and Richard were standing, and where the above hurried words had been exchanged between them.

"You must go forward, Miss Fitzherbert—and you too, Mr. Preston—"

Ellen glanced with an arch smile towards Richard, as much as to say, "*You* also have taken an assumed name."

Markham begged and implored the manager not to force him upon the stage;—but the call for "Selina Fitzherbert and the Author" was peremptory; and the "gods" were growing clamorous.

Popular will is never more arbitrary than in a theatre.

Markham accordingly took Ellen's hand:—the curtain rose, and he led her forward.

The appearance of that handsome couple—a fine dark-eyed and genteel young man leading by the hand a lovely woman,—a successful author, and a favourite actress,—this was the signal for a fresh burst of applause.

Richard was dazzled with the glare of light, and for some time could see nothing distinctly.

Myriads of human countenances, heaped together, danced before him; and yet the aspect and features of none were accurately delineated to his eyes. He could not have selected from amongst those countenances, even that of his long-lost brother, or that of his dearly beloved Isabella, had they been both or either of them prominent in that multitude of faces.

And Isabella *was* there, with her parents—impelled by the curiosity which had taken so many thither that evening.

Her surprise, and that of her father and mother, may therefore well be conceived, when, in the author of one of the most successful and beautiful dramatic compositions of modern times, they recognised Richard Markham!

The applause continued for three or four minutes—uninterrupted and enthusiastic—as if some mighty conqueror, who had just released his country from the thraldom of a foreign foe, was the object of adulation.

At length this expression of approbation ceased; and the spectators awaited in suspense, and with curiosity depicted upon their countenances, the acknowledgment of the honours showered upon the author.

At that moment the manager stepped forward, and said, "Ladies and gentlemen, I have the honour to inform you that Mr. Edward Preston is the author of the successful tragedy upon which you have been pleased to bestow your approval. I consider it to be my duty to mention a name which the author's own modesty—modesty which you will agree with me in pronouncing to be unnecessary under such circumstances—would not probably have allowed him to reveal to you."

The manager bowed and retired.

Fresh applause welcomed the announcement of the tragic author's name; and a thousand voices exclaimed, "Bravo, Edward Preston!"

By this time Markham had recovered his presence of mind and self-possession: and his joy was extreme when he suddenly recognised Isabella in a box close by the stage.

Oh! that was a glorious moment for him: *she* was there—*she* beheld his triumph—and doubtless *she* participated in his own happy feelings.

"Bravo, Edward Preston!" was re-echoed through the house.

And then a dead silence prevailed.

All were anxious to hear Richard speak.

But just at the moment when he was about to acknowledge the honour conferred upon him and his fair companion by the audience, a strange voice broke upon the stillness of the scene.

"It is false! his name is not Preston——"

"Silence!" cried numerous voices.

"His name is——"

"Turn out that brawler! turn him out!"

"His name is——"

"Hold your tongue!"

"Silence!"

"Turn him out! turn him out!"

"His name is Richard Markham—the Forger!"

A burst of indignation, mingled with strong expressions of incredulity, rose against the individual, who, from an obscure nook in the gallery, had interrupted the harmony of the evening.

"It is true—I say! he is Richard Markham who was condemned to two years' imprisonment for forgery!" thundered forth the hoarse and unpleasant voice.

A piercing scream—the scream of a female tone—echoed through the house: all eyes were turned towards the box whence it issued; and a young lady with flaxen hair and pale complexion, was seen to sink senseless in the arms of the elderly gentleman who accompanied her.

And in another part of the house a young lady also sank, pale, trembling, and overcome with feelings of acute anguish, upon her father's bosom.

So deeply did that dread accusing voice affect the sensitive and astonished Mary-Anne, and the faithful Isabella!

All was now confusion. The audience rose from their seats in all directions; and the theatre suddenly appeared to be converted into a modern Babel.

Overwhelmed with shame, and so bewildered by this cruel blow, that he knew not how to act, Markham stood for some moments like a criminal before his judges. Ellen, forgetting where she was, clung to him for support.

At length, the unhappy young man seized Ellen abruptly by the hand, and led her from the public gaze.

The curtain fell as they passed behind the scenes.

The audience then grew more clamorous—none scarcely knew why. Some demanded that the man who had caused the interruption should be arrested by the police; but those in the gallery shouted out that he had suddenly disappeared. Others declared that the accusation ought to be investigated;—people in the pit maintained that, even if the story were true, it had nothing to do with the success of the accused as a dramatic author;—and gentlemen in the boxes expressed their determination never to support a man, in a public institution and in a public capacity, who had been condemned to infamous penalties for an enormous crime.

Thus all was noise, confusion, and uproar,—argument, accusation, and recrimination,—the buzzing of hundreds of tongues,—the clamour of thousands of voices.

Some called "Shame!" upon the manager for introducing a

discharged convict to the notice of Englishmen's wives and daughters,—although the persons who thus clamoured did not utter a reproach against the immoral females who made no secret of their profligacy, and who appeared nightly upon the stage as its brightest ornaments—nor did they condescend to recall to mind the vicinity of that infamous saloon which vomited forth numbers of impure characters to occupy seats by the sides of those wives and daughters, whose purity was now supposed to be tainted because a man who had undergone an infamous punishment, but who could *there* set no bad example, had contributed to their entertainment!

And then commenced a riot in the theatre. The respectable portion of the audience escaped from the scene with the utmost precipitation:—but the occupants of the upper region, and some of the tenants of the pit, remained to exhibit their inclination for what they were pleased to term "a lark." The benches were torn up, and hurled upon the stage:—hats and orange-peel flew about in all directions;—and serious damage would have been done to the theatre, had not a body of police succeeded in restoring order.

In the mean time Markham and Ellen had been conducted to the Green Room, where a glass of wine was administered to each to restore their self-possession.

The manager was alone with them; and when Richard had time to collect his scattered ideas, he seemed to awake as from a horrible dream. But the ominous countenance of the manager met his glance;—and he knew that it was all a fearful reality.

Then did Markham bury his face in his hands, and weep bitterly—bitterly.

"Alas! young man," said the manager, "it was an evil day for both you and me, when you sought and I accorded my patronage. This business will no doubt injure me seriously. You are a young man of extraordinary talent;—but it will not avail you in this sphere again. You have enjoyed one signal triumph—you have experienced a most heart-rending overthrow. Never did defeat follow upon conquest so rapidly. The power of your genius will not vanquish the opinion of the public. I do not blame you: you were not compelled to communicate your former history to me;—and it was I who forced you to go forward."

Markham was consoled by the language of the manager, who spoke in a kind and sympathising tone of voice.

Thus the only man who would suffer in a pecuniary point of view—or, at least, he who would suffer most—by the fatal occurrence of that evening,—was also the only one who attempted to solace the unhappy Markham.

As for poor Ellen—she was overwhelmed with grief.

"You gave me fifty guineas for that fatal—fatal drama," said Richard, after a long pause. "The money shall be returned to you to-morrow."

"No, my young friend,—that must not be done!" exclaimed the manager, taking Richard's hand. "Your noble conduct in this respect raises you fifty per cent. in my opinion."

"Yes—he is noble, he is generous!" cried Ellen. "He has been a benefactor to myself and my father: it is at his house that we live; and never until this evening were we aware of each other's avocations in respect to the stage."

"How singular a coincidence!" exclaimed the manager. "But I hope that I shall not lose the services of the principal attraction of my company?"

"Yes," said Ellen firmly: "I shall never more appear in public in that capacity of which I was lately so enamoured, but for which I have suddenly entertained an abhorrence."

"A few days' repose and rest will induce you to change your mind, I hope?" said the manager, who was really alarmed at the prospect of losing a figurante of such talent and an actress of such great promise.

"We shall see—I will reflect," returned Ellen, unwilling to add to the annoyances of the kind-hearted manager.

"You must not desert me," said this gentleman,—"especially at a time when I shall require all the attractions possible to restore the reputation of my house."

Markham now rose to take his departure.

"I should not advise you to leave the house together," said the manager. "There may be a few mal-contents in the street;—and, at all events, it will be as well that the ladies and gentlemen of my company should not know of your intimate acquaintance with each other. Such a proceeding might only compromise Miss Fitzherbert."

Markham cordially acceded to this suggestion; and it was agreed that he should depart by the private door, and that Ellen should return home in the usual manner by herself.

But before they separated, the two young people agreed with each other that the strictest silence should be preserved at the Place, not only with respect to the events of that evening, but also in regard to the nature of the avocations in which they had both lately been engaged.

Markham succeeded in escaping unobserved from the theatre;—and, humiliated, cast down, heart-broken,—bending beneath an insupportable burden of ignominy and shame,—with the fainting form of Isabella before his eyes, and the piercing shriek of Mary-Anne, whom he had also recognised, in his ears,—he pursued his precipitate retreat homewards.

But what a dread revelation had been made to him that evening! His mortal enemy—his inveterate foe had escaped from the death which, it was hitherto supposed, the miscreant had met in the den of infamy near Bird-Cage Walk some months previously:—his ominous voice still thundered in Markham's ears;—and our unhappy hero once more saw all his prospects ruined by the unmitigated hatred of the Resurrection Man.

CHAPTER XCII.

THE ITALIAN VALET.

Ellen retired to her private dressing-room, and hastily threw aside her theatrical garb.

She assumed her usual attire, and then stole away from the establishment, without waiting to say farewell either to the manager or any of her acquaintances belonging to the company.

As she left the private door of the theatre, she saw several persons loitering about—probably in hopes of catching a glimpse of the author who had been so signally disgraced that evening, and whose previous departure from the house was unperceived.

She drew her veil closely over her countenance; but not before one fellow, more impudent than the rest, and whose cadaverous countenance, shaggy eye-brows, and sinister expression, struck a momentary terror into her soul, had peered beneath her bonnet.

Fortunately, as Ellen considered it, a cab was close by; and the driver was standing on the pavement with his hand grasping the door-latch, as if he were expecting some one.

"Cab, ma'am?" said he, as Ellen approached.

Ellen answered in the affirmative, mentioned her address, and stepped into the vehicle.

The driver banged the door, and mounted his box.

The man with the cadaverous countenance watched Ellen into the vehicle, and exchanged a sign of intelligence with the driver.

The cab then drove rapidly away.

Another cab was standing at a little distance; and into this the man with the cadaverous countenance stepped. There was already an individual in it, who, when the former opened the door, said, "All right?"

"All right," was the reply.

This second cab, containing these two individuals, then followed rapidly in the traces of the first.

Meantime Ellen had thrown herself back in the vehicle, and had given way to her reflections.

The events of that memorable evening occupied her attention. A coincidence, of a nature fitted only for the pages of a romance, had revealed to Markham and herself the history of each other's pursuits. While she had been following the occupation of a figurante, he was devoting his time to dramatic composition. He had retained his employment a secret: she had dissembled hers. He had accidentally applied for the patronage of the same manager who had taken her by the hand. He had assumed a false name: so had she. Chance led her to take a part in his drama;—her talent had materially contributed to its success. A triumph was achieved by each;—and then came the overwhelming, crushing denunciation which turned his joy to mourning—his honour to disgrace—his glory to shame. She felt as if she were identified with his fate in this one respect:—he was her benefactor; she esteemed him: and she seemed to partake in his most painful emotions as she pondered upon the incidents of that evening.

And then she retrospected over the recent events which had chequered her own life. The cast of her countenance embellished statues;—her likeness lent its attraction to pictures;—her bust was preserved in marble;—her entire form feasted the eyes of many a libertine in the private room of the photographic department of a gallery of science;—her virtue had become the prey of one who gave her a few pieces of paltry gold in exchange for the inestimable jewel of her purity;—her dreams had been sold to a mesmerist;—her dancing had captivated thousands;—her tragic talent had crowned the success of a drama. What remained for her now to sell? what talent did she possess which could now be turned to advantage? Alas! she knew not!

Her meditations were painful; and some time elapsed ere she awoke from her reverie.

At length she glanced towards the window: the night was beautifully clear, though piercing cold—for it was now the month of December; and the year 1839 was drawing to a close.

The vehicle was proceeding along a road skirted only by a few leafless trees, and wearing an aspect strange and new to her.

The country beyond, on either side, seemed to present to her view different outlines from those which frequent passage along the road leading to Markham Place had rendered familiar to her eyes. Again she gazed wistfully forth:—she lowered the window, and surveyed the adjacent scenery with redoubled interest.

And now she felt really alarmed; for she was convinced that the driver had mistaken the road.

She called to him, and expressed her fears.

"No—no, ma'am," he exclaimed, without relaxing the speed at which the vehicle was proceeding; "there's more ways than one of reaching the place where you live. Don't be afraid, ma'am—it's all right."

Ellen's fears were hushed for a short time; but as she leant partially out of the window to survey the country through which she was passing, the sounds of another vehicle behind her own fell upon her ears.

At any other time this circumstance would not have produced a second thought; but on this occasion Ellen felt a presentiment of evil. Whether the mournful catastrophe of the evening, or her recent sad reflections,—or both united, had produced this morbid feeling, we cannot say. Sufficient is it for us to know that such was the state of her mind; and then she remembered the warning contained in the letter so mysteriously sent to her a short time previously at the theatre.

Again she addressed the cabman; but this time he made no answer; and in a few minutes he drove up to the door of a small house which stood alone by the side of that dreary road.

Scarcely had he alighted from his box, when the second cab came up and stopped also.

"Where am I?" demanded Ellen, now seriously alarmed.

An individual, who had alighted from the second cab, hastened to open the door of the first, and assist Ellen to alight.

"You must get down here, Miss," he said, in a dialect and tone which denoted him to be a foreigner.

Ellen saw at a glance that he was a tall elderly man, with a dark olive complexion, piercing black eyes, but by no means an unpleasant expression of countenance. He was dressed in black, and wore a large cloak hanging loosely over his shoulders.

"Get down here!" repeated Ellen. "And why? where am I? who are you? Speak."

"No harm will happen to you, Miss," replied the tall stranger. "A gentleman is waiting in this house to see you."

"A gentleman!" cried Ellen. "Ah! can it be Mr. Greenwood?"

"It is, Miss: you need fear nothing."

Ellen was naturally of a courageous disposition; and the circumstances of her life had tended to strengthen her mind. It instantly struck her that she was in the power of her persecutor's myrmidons, and that resistance against them was calculated to produce effects much less beneficial for her than those which remonstrance and firmness might lead to with their employer.

She accordingly accompanied the tall stranger into the house.

But what was the astonishment of the poor creature when she encountered in the hall the very old hag whom she had known in the court in Golden-lane, and who had originally introduced her to the embraces of Mr. Greenwood!

The horrible wrinkled wretch grinned significantly, as she conducted Ellen into a parlour very neatly furnished, and where a cheerful fire was burning in the grate.

Meantime the tall stranger issued forth again, and ordered the driver of the cab in which Ellen had arrived to await further instructions. He then accosted the cadaverous looking man who had accompanied him in the second cab, and who was now loitering about in front of the house.

"Tidkins," said he, "we do not require your services any further. The young lady made no resistance, and consequently there has been no need for the exercise of your strong arm. Here is your reward. You can return to London in the same cab that brought you hither."

"Thank you, my friend," exclaimed the Resurrection Man. "Your master knows my address, the next time he requires my services. Good night."

"Good night," said the tall man: and when he had seen the second cab depart, he re-entered the house.

In the hall he met Mr. Greenwood.

"Well, Filippo—all right, eh?" said this gentleman, in a whisper.

"All right, sir. We managed it without violence; and the lady is in your power."

"Ah! I thought you would do the business genteelly for me. Lafleur is a faithful fellow, and would do any thing to serve me; but he is clumsy and awkward in an intrigue of this kind. No one can manage these little matters so well as a foreigner. A Frenchman is clever—but an Italian incomparable."

"Thank you, sir, for the compliment," said Filippo, with a low bow.

"Oh! it is no compliment," returned Greenwood. "Three or four little things that I have entrusted to you since you have been in my service, were all admirably managed so far as you were concerned; and though they every one failed afterwards, yet it was no fault of yours. I am well aware of that."

The Italian bowed.

"And now I must present myself to this haughty beauty," said Greenwood.

"Am I to dismiss the vehicle which brought her hither, sir?" demanded Filippo.

"Yes: you will stay here to-night."

The Italian valet bowed once more, and returned to the driver of the vehicle that brought Ellen thither.

"My good fellow," said Filippo, in a hurried tone, "here is your money for the service rendered up to this moment. Are you now disposed to earn five guineas in addition?"

"Certainly, sir," replied the man.

"Then drive to the bend in the road yonder," continued Filippo. "There you will find a large barn, belonging to my master's property here. You can house your horse and cab comfortably there. But do not unharness the animal. There is a pond close by; and you will find a bucket in the barn. There is also hay for your horse. Wait there patiently till I come to you."

The cabman signified acquiescence; and Filippo returned to the house.

Meantime the old hag, as before stated, had conducted Ellen to a parlour, where the young lady threw herself upon a sofa, her mind and body being alike fatigued with the events and anxieties of the evening.

"We meet again, Miss," said the old woman, lingering near the table, on which refreshments of several luxurious kinds were placed. "You came no more to visit me in the court; and yet I watched from a distance the brilliancy of your career. Ah! what fine things—what fine things I have introduced you to, since first I knew you."

"If you wish to serve me," said Ellen, "help me away from this place, and I will recompense you largely."

"For every guinea that you would give me to let you go, I shall receive two for keeping you in safe custody," returned the hag.

"Name the price that you are to have from your employer," cried Ellen; "and I will double it."

"That you cannot do, Miss. Besides, have I not your interests to consider? Do I not know what is good for you? I tell you that you may become a great lady—ride in a magnificent carriage—have fine clothes and sparkling jewels—and never know again what toil is. I should not be so squeamish if I were you."

"Silence, wretch!" cried Ellen, exasperated more at the cool language of calculation in which the old woman spoke, than with the prospects she held out and the arguments she used.

"Ah! Miss," resumed the hag, nothing discomfited, "I am not annoyed with you, for the harsh way in which you speak to me. I have seen too much of your stubborn beauties in my life to be abashed with a word. Lack-a-day! they all yield in time—they all yield in time!"

And the old hag shook her head seriously, as if she had arrived at some great moral conclusion.

Ellen paid no attention to her.

"Ah! Miss," continued the hag, "I was once young like you—and as beautiful too, wrinkled and tanned as I now appear. But I was not such a fool to my own interests as you. I lived luxuriously for many, many years—God knows how many—I can't count them now—I don't like to think of those happy times. I ought to have saved money—much money; but I frittered it all away as quick as I got it. Now, do you take my advice: accept Mr. Greenwood's offers;—he is a handsome man, and pays like a prince."

The argument of the old hag was cut short by the entrance of the individual of whom she was just speaking.

She left the room; and Ellen was now alone with Greenwood.

"Sir, are you the author of this cowardly outrage which has been perpetrated upon me?" demanded Ellen, rising from the sofa, and speaking in a firm but cold tone.

"Call it not an outrage, dearest Ellen——"

"It is nothing else, sir; and if you have one spark of honour left—one feeling of respect for the mother of your child," added Miss Monroe, sinking her voice, "you will allow me to depart without delay. On that condition I will forget all that has transpired this evening."

"My dear girl, you cannot think that I have taken all this trouble to be thwarted by a trifling obstacle at the end, or that I have merely had you brought hither to have the pleasure of letting you depart again after one minute's conversation. No, Ellen: listen to me! I have conceived a deep—profound—a fervent affection for you——"

"Cease this libertine's jargon, Mr. Greenwood," interrupted Ellen. "You must know that your sophistry cannot deceive me as it has done so many—many others."

"Then in plain terms, Ellen, you shall be mine—wholly and solely mine—and I will remain faithful to you until death."

"I will become your wife, for the sake of my child: on no other terms will I consort with you. As surely as you attempt to force me to compliance with your will, so certainly will I unmask you sooner or later. I will expose you—I will tell the world who you are—I will proclaim how you obtained your fortune by the plunder of your own—"

"Silence, Ellen!" thundered Greenwood, his face becoming purple with indignation. "Remember that the least word calculated to betray my secret, would lead to a revelation of yours; and the result would be the execrations of your father showered down upon your devoted head."

"I care not for that catastrophe—I care not for mine own past dishonour—I care not for the existence of that child of whom you are the father," exclaimed Ellen in a rapid and impassioned tone. "I will not be immolated to your desires—I will not succumb to your wishes, without revenge! Oh! full well do I comprehend you—full well do I know how you calculated when you resolved to perpetrate this outrage. You thought that I must suffer every thing at your hands, and not dare proclaim my wrongs:—you fancied that my lips are sealed against all and every thing connected with *you!* Mark me, you have reckoned erroneously upon the extent of my dread of my father and my benefactor! There is one thing that will make me fall at their feet and reveal all—and that is the consummation on your part of this vile outrage upon me!"

"Be it so, Ellen," said Greenwood. "I am as determined as you. I will use no force against you; but I will keep you a prisoner here; and believe me—for I know the world well—your stern resolves will soon melt in the presence of solitude and monotony. You will then solicit me to come to you—if it be only to bear you company! Escape is impossible—my spies are around the house. Day and night will you be watched as if you were a criminal. And when you consent to become mine, in all save the vain ties which priestcraft has invented, and the shackles of which shall never curb my proud spirit,—then will I surround you with every luxury, gratify your slightest wishes, study your pleasures unceasingly, and do all to make you cling to me more fervently than if I were your husband according to monkish ceremony. This is my resolve. In the mean time, if you choose to console your father for your absence, write a note telling him that you are happy, but that circumstances at present compel you to withhold from him the place of your residence; and that letter shall be delivered to-morrow morning at Markham Place. I now leave you. This is your sitting-room; your sleeping apartment is above. The servant—the old woman whom you know so well," added Greenwood, in a tone slightly ironical, "will attend upon you. The house contains every luxury that may gratify the appetite; all your wishes shall be complied with. But, again I say, think not of escape; that is impossible. And if you feel inclined to write the note of which I have spoken, do so, and give it to your attendant. It is now late—the clock has struck one: I leave you to yourself."

Ellen made no reply; and Greenwood left the room.

The moment she was alone, Ellen rose and hastened to the window. She drew aside the curtain, and was somewhat surprised to perceive that the casements were not barred; for she had expected to find every precaution against escape adopted after the confident manner in which Greenwood had spoken upon that head. But her heart sank within her; for she remembered his assurance that the house was surrounded by spies. She therefore made up her mind, after some reflection, to remain quiet until the next day, and then regulate her endeavours to escape by the aspect of the house and its locality when seen by day-light.

She felt exhausted and wearied, and partook of a slight refreshment. She then took a candle from the table, and proceeded upstairs to the bed-room prepared for her. Having carefully bolted the door, she sate down to reflect upon the propriety of writing to her father the note suggested by Greenwood. She felt most acutely on the old man's account; and she knew that she would not be permitted to communicate with him in terms more explicit than those mentioned by her persecutor. Such terms were too vague and equivocal to be satisfactory;—and she concluded in her own mind that silence was the better alternative of the two.

Having once more satisfied herself that the room was safe against all chances of intrusion, she thought of retiring to rest. She laid aside her bonnet and shawl, which she had hitherto kept on, and then took off her gown. She approached a long Psyche, or full-length mirror, that stood near the dressing-table (for the room was elegantly furnished), and for a moment contemplated herself with feelings of pride and pleasure—in spite of the vexatious position in which she found herself. But vanity was now an essential ingredient of her character. It had been engendered, nurtured, and matured by the mode of life she had been compelled to adopt.

And, assuredly, hers were charms of which she had full right to be proud. The mirror reflected to her eyes a countenance that had been deemed worthy to embellish a Venus on the canvass of a great painter. In that same faithful glass was also seen a form the beautiful undulations and rich contours of which were perfectly symmetrical, and yet voluptuously matured. The delicate white corset yielded with docile elasticity to the shape which no invention of art could improve. The form reduced that corset to suit its own proportions; and in no way did the corset shape the form. Those swelling globes of snow, each adorned as with a delicate rose-bud, needed no support to maintain them in their full and natural rotundity;—the curvatures which formed the waist, were not drawn nearer to each other by the compression of the stay;—the graceful swell of the hips required no art to improve or augment its copiousness. Ellen smiled—in spite of herself,—smiled complacently—smiled almost proudly, as she surveyed her perfect form in that mirror.

But, hark! what sound is that which suddenly falls upon her ear?

She starts—looks round—and listens.

Again!—that sound is repeated.

This time she comprehends its source: some one is tapping gently at the side window of the room.

Ellen hastily put on her gown once more, and advanced to the casement.

She raised the blind, and beheld the dark form of a man mounted upon a ladder, at the window. A second glance convinced her that he was the tall Italian whom she had before seen.

She approached as closely as possible, and said, in a low tone, "What do you require? what means this strange proceeding?"

"I am come to save you," answered Filippo, in a voice so low, that his words were scarcely intelligible. "Do not be afraid—I am he who wrote the warning letter, which——"

Without a moment's farther hesitation, Ellen gently raised the window.

"I am he who wrote the warning letter which you received at the theatre," repeated Filippo. "Although ostensibly compelled to serve my master, yet privately I counteract all his vile schemes to the utmost of my power."

"I believe you—I trust you," said Ellen, overjoyed at the arrival of this unlooked-for succour. "What would you have me do?"

"Tie the sheets of the bed together—fasten one end to the bed-post, and throw the other outside," returned Filippo, speaking in a rapid whisper.

In less than a minute this was done; and Ellen once more assumed her bonnet and shawl.

By the directions of Filippo she then stepped upon the window-sill: he received her in his arms, and bore her in safety to the ground.

Then, taking the ladder on his shoulders, he desired her to follow him without speaking a word.

They passed behind the house, and stopped for a moment at a

stable where Filippo deposited the ladder. He then led the way across a field adjoining the garden that belonged to the house.

"Lady," said the Italian, when they were at some distance from the dwelling, "if you consider that you owe me any gratitude for the service I am now rendering you, all the recompense I require is strict silence on your part with respect to the real mode of your escape."

"Rest well assured that I shall never betray you," answered Ellen. "But how is it that so bad a man as your master can possess so honest and generous a follower as you?"

"That, lady, is a mystery which it is by no means difficult to explain," replied Filippo. "Chosen by a noble-hearted lady, who by this time doubtless enjoys a sovereign rank in another clime, to counteract the villanies of Greenwood, I came to England; and fortunately I learnt that he required a foreign valet. I applied for the situation and obtained it. He believes me faithful, because I appear to enter heart and soul into all his schemes; but I generally succeed eventually in defeating or mitigating their evil effects upon others. This is the simple truth, lady; and you must consider my confidence in you as implicitly sacred. Any revelation—the slightest hint, on your part, would frustrate the generous purposes of my mistress. And think not, lady, that I am merely acting the part of a base spy:—I mean Mr. Greenwood no harm—I shall do him none: all I aim at is the prevention of harm springing from his machinations in regard to others. But we are now at the spot where a vehicle waits to convey you back to London."

Filippo opened the door of a barn, which they had just reached; and the cabman responded to his summons.

In a few minutes the vehicle was ready to depart. Ellen offered the Italian a recompense for his goodness towards her; but he drew himself up haughtily, and said, "Keep your gold, lady: I require no other reward than *silence* on your part."

He then handed Miss Monroe into the vehicle; and ordered the driver to conduct the lady whithersoever she commanded him.

Ellen desired to be taken home to Markham Place; the Italian raised his hat respectfully; and the cab drove rapidly away towards London.

Miss Monroe now began to reflect profoundly upon the nature of the excuse which she should offer to her father and Richard Markham, to account for her prolonged absence. We have before said that she had ceased to shrink from a falsehood; and she had certain cogent reasons for never associating her own name with that of Greenwood;—much less would she acquaint her father or Richard with an outrage which would only induce them to adopt means to punish its perpetrator, and thus bring them in collision with him.

At length she resolved upon stating that she had been taken ill at a concert where she had been engaged for the evening: this course would be comprehended by Markham, who would only have to substitute the word "theatre" for "concert" in his own imagination; and it would also satisfy her father.

We need merely add to this episode in our eventful history that Ellen reached home safely at four o'clock in the morning, and that the excuse was satisfactory to both Markham and her father, who were anxiously awaiting her return.

CHAPTER XCIII.

NEWS FROM CASTELCICALA.

Return we once more to Diana Arlington, who still occupied the splendid mansion in Dover Street, which had been fitted up for her by the Earl of Warrington.

The routine of the life of the Enchantress continued the same as we have described it in Chapter LI.

The Earl of Warrington was unremitting in his attention, and unchanged in his liberality towards his beautiful mistress; and, on her part, Diana was the faithful friend and true companion who by her correct conduct maintained the confidence which she had inspired in the heart of her noble protector.

We must again introduce our readers to the Enchantress at the hour of breakfast, and in the little parlour where we have before seen her.

But on this occasion, instead of being occupied with the perusal of the *Morning Herald*, her entire attention was absorbed in the contents of a letter, which ran as follows:—

"*Montoni, December* 3, 1839.

"I sit down, my dearest Diana, to inform you that the ceremony of my union with his Serene Highness Angelo III. was solemnized yesterday.

"You are aware that this ceremony was to have taken place some months ago; but the intrigues of certain persons holding high and influential offices in the state, delayed it. Calumny after calumny against me was whispered in the ears of the Grand Duke; and, although his Highness believed not a word of those evil reports, I steadily refused to accept the honour he was anxious to confer upon me, until he had satisfied himself of the falsity of each successive calumny. At length I implored his Highness to address an autograph letter to the Earl of Warrington, with whom his Highness was acquainted during the residence of that good English nobleman in Castelcicala. His Highness complied with my request, and despatched his letter so privately that none of those who surround him suspected his proceeding. The Earl of Warrington, as you know, dearest Diana, hastened to reply. His answer was so satisfactory, so frank, so generous, so candid, that the Duke declared he would visit with his severest displeasure any one who dared breathe a word of calumny against me or my friends in England, in future.

"The next step adopted by his Serene Highness was to dismiss the Marquis of Gerrano from the office of Minister of Foreign Affairs. Baron Ruperto, the Under Secretary in that Department, retired with his superior. The Duke adopted this measure in consequence of the intrigues of those noblemen to thwart his Highness's intentions of raising to the ducal throne the woman whom he loved. You may suppose how grieved—how vexed—how distressed I have been through the conviction that I myself was the cause of these heart-burnings, jealousies, and intrigues; and although I was innocently the source of such disagreeable proceedings, my sorrow and annoyance were but little mitigated by this impression. I implored the Grand Duke to allow me to leave the country, and retire to Switzerland; but his Serene Highness remained firm, and assured me that, although he had many difficulties to overcome, he was not disheartened. Then he declared that his entire happiness was centred in me, and he thus over-ruled my scruples.

"At length the duke remodelled his cabinet (a fact to which I alluded above) by appointing the Count of Friuli (who is deeply attached to His Highness, and favourable to our union) to the Foreign Office, in place of the Marquis of Gerrano. Signor Pisani, another faithful dependant of His Highness, was appointed Under-Secretary in the place of Baron Ruperto. The Minister of War also retired, and was succeeded by General Grachia. When these changes were effected, his Serene Highness communicated to the council of ministers his intention to unite himself to *Eliza Marchioness of Ziani on the 2d of December of the present year.*

"This decision was made known on the 19th of last month. I did not write to communicate the important fact to you, because I was apprehensive of new delays; and as I had already misled you once (though unintentionally on my part) I was unwilling to deceive either you or myself a second time. I know your friendship for me, Diana,—I know that you entertain a sister's love for me, the same that I feel for you,—and I also know that you anxiously watch the progress of my fortunes, as, under similar circumstances, I should yours. I therefore resolved to acquaint you with no more of my hopes, until they should have been realised. That result has now been attained; and I need preserve a cold silence no longer.

"In the evening of the 19th of November, the Grand Chancellor of Castelcicala, the President of the Council (the Marquis of Vincenza), and the Archbishop of Montoni, visited me at the villa to acquaint me with the royal decision. I endeavoured—and I hope succeeded—to convince their lordships of the profound sense which I entertained of the high honour intended to be conferred upon me, and my conviction that no merit which I possessed could render me worthy of such distinction; at the same time I declared my readiness to accept that honour, since it was the will and pleasure of a sovereign Prince to bestow it upon me.

"I can scarcely tell you the nature of the varied emotions and feelings which filled—indeed agitated—my bosom when the memorable morning dawned. That was yesterday! I awoke at an early—a very early hour—before six, and walked in the garden with the hope that the fresh air and the charming tranquillity of the scene would compose me. I could scarcely believe that I was on the point of entering upon such high destinies; that a diadem was so soon to encircle my brow; that the thrilling words *Highness* and *Princess* would in a few hours be addressed to me! I could not reconcile with my former obscure lot the idea that I was shortly to sit upon a sovereign throne—command the allegiance of millions of human beings,—and share the fortunes of a potentate of Europe! Was it possible that I—I who was the daughter of a poor farmer, and who had seen so much of the vicissitudes of life,—I who had thought myself happy with the competence which I enjoyed through the Earl of Warrington's bounty at Clapton,—I who conceived myself to be one of the most fortunate of individuals when, by the goodness of that same excellent peer, I arrived in this State, and took possession of the villa which he had placed at my disposal,—I who had then no more elevated aspirations than to dwell in tranquillity and peace—no loftier hope than to deserve that kind nobleman's benefits by my conduct—was it possible that I was in a few hours to become the Grand Duchess of Castelcicala? I could not fix my mind to such a belief; the idea seemed an oriental fiction—a romantic dream. And yet, I remembered, I had already received an earnest of this splendid promise of fortune; I had already been elevated from a lowly condition to an exalted rank; the distinction of a Marchioness was mine; for months had I been accustomed to the sounding title of *Your Ladyship*; and for months had I been enrolled amongst the peeresses of Castelcicala. Yes—I thought: it was true,—true that a Prince—a powerful Prince—intended to raise me to a seat upon his own ducal throne!

"At seven precisely the three lovely daughters of General Grachia arrived at the villa to assist me in my toilette—my nuptial toilette. They informed me that, if it were my pleasure, they were to remain in attendance upon me after my marriage. I embraced them tenderly, and assured them that they should always be near me as friends. When the toilette was completed, I bade adieu to the villa. I wept—wept tears of mingled joy and sorrow as I said farewell to that abode where I had passed so many happy, happy hours! At length I entered General Grachia's carriage, which was waiting; and, accompanied by my three amiable friends, repaired to their father's private dwelling (not his official palace of the War Department) in Montoni.

"Here my letter must terminate. Enclosed is an account of the entire ceremony, translated into English by my private secretary (who is well acquainted with my native tongue) from the *Montoni Gazette*. Fain would I have erased those passages which are favourable—too favourable to myself; but I fancied that my friend—my sister Diana would be pleased to read the narrative in its integrity.

"In conclusion, let me say—and do you believe it as devoutly as I say it sincerely—that, in spite of my rank and fortunes,—in spite of the splendours that surround me, to you I am in heart, and always shall remain, the same attached and grateful being, whom you have known as

"ELIZA SYDNEY."

It would be impossible to describe the feelings of delight with which Mrs. Arlington perused the latter portion of this letter. Pass we on, therefore, to the Bridal Ceremony, as it was described in the translated narrative which accompanied the communication of the Grand Duchess:—

"THE MARRIAGE OF THE GRAND DUKE.

"Yesterday morning were celebrated the nuptials of his Serene Highness Angelo III. and Eliza Marchioness of Ziani.

"From an early hour the capital wore an appearance of unusual gaiety and bustle. The houses looking on the Piazzetta of Contarini, leading to the ancient Cathedral of Saint Theodosia, were decorated in a most splendid manner with banners, garlands, festoons of flowers, and various ornaments and devices appropriate to the occasion. The balconies were fitted up as verdant bowers and arbours, and the lovely characteristics of the country were thus introduced into the very heart of the city. The Town-Hall was hung with numerous banners; and the royal standard waved proudly over the Black Tower of the Citadel. The shops in those streets through which the procession was to pass were fitted up with seats which were let to those who were willing to pay the high prices demanded for them. In other parts of the city the shops and marts of trade were all closed, as was the Exchange. A holiday was observed at the Bank of Castelcicala; and the business of the General Post Office closed at eleven o'clock in the forenoon. Nor was the port less gay than the city. All the vessels in the harbour and docks, as well as those in the roadstead, were decked with innumerable flags. The royal standard floated from the main of the ships of war of the Castelcicalan navy. The sight was altogether most imposing and lively.

"At seven o'clock the bells of Saint Theodosia and all the other churches in Montoni rang out merry peals and the troops of the garrison got under arms. At a quarter before eight the Mayor and Corporation of the city, arrayed in their robes of green velvet edged with gold, proceeded to the palace and presented an address of congratulation on the auspicious day, to his Serene Highness, who was pleased to return a most gracious answer. It being generally understood that the Marchioness of Ziani would in the first instance alight at the dwelling of General Grachia, the Minister of War, a crowd of highly respectable and well-dressed persons had collected in that neighbourhood. At nine o'clock the General's private carriage, which had been sent to convey the future Grand Duchess from her own abode to the General's mansion, drove rapidly up the street, attended by two outriders. We shall never forget the enthusiasm manifested by the assembled multitude upon that occasion. All political feelings appeared to be forgotten; and a loud, hearty, and prolonged burst of welcome met the ear. The object of this ebullition of generous feeling bowed gracefully to the crowds on either side; and the cheering continued for some moments after the carriage had entered the court-yard of the General's mansion.

"At half-past ten o'clock the President of the Council, the Grand Chancellor, and the Intendant of the Ducal Civil List arrived in their carriages at General Grachia's abode, preceded by one of the royal equipages, which was sent to convey the bride and her ladies-in-waiting to the palace. In a few minutes the President of the Council handed the bride, who was attended by the lady and three lovely daughters of General Grachia, into the ducal carriage. The procession then repaired to the palace, the crowds that lined the streets and occupied the windows and balconies by which it passed, expressing their feelings by cheers and the waving of handkerchiefs. To these demonstrations the bride responded by graceful bows, bestowed in a manner so modest and yet evidently sincere, that the conduct of this exalted lady upon the occasion won all hearts.

"The procession entered the palace-square; and the Grand Duke, attended by the great officers of state and a brilliant staff, received his intended bride at the foot of the great marble staircase of the western pavilion. The illustrious company then entered the palace. Immediately afterwards the five regiments of household troops, commanded by that noble veteran the Marshal Count of Galeazzo, marched into the square, and formed into three lines along the western side of the palace. At half-past eleven the royal party appeared at the foot of the marble staircase, and entered the numerous carriages in waiting. The bride occupied the carriage which had conveyed her to the palace, and was accompanied by the ladies in attendance upon her. His Serene Highness, attended by the President of the Council and the Grand Chancellor, entered the state carriage. The procession then moved onwards to the Cathedral of Saint Theodosia.

"This was the signal for the roar of artillery from all points. The citadel, and the ships of war in the roadstead thundered forth the announcement that His Serene Highness had just left the palace. The bells rang blithely from every steeple; the troops presented arms; the military bands played the national hymn; and the procession was welcomed with joyous shouts, the waving of handkerchiefs, and the smiles of beauty. The windows and balconies of the houses overlooking the streets through which it passed, were crowded with elegantly dressed ladies, brilliant with their own beauty, gay with waving plumes, and sparkling with diamonds. The only indication of political feeling which we observed upon the occasion, was on the part of the troops; *and they were silent*.

"The bride was naturally the centre of all interest and attraction. Every one was anxious to catch a glimpse of her charming countenance. And certainly this lovely lady never could have appeared *more lovely* than on the present occasion. She was attired in a dress of the most costly point-lace over white satin. Her veil was of the first-mentioned material, and of the richest description. She was somewhat pale; but a charming serenity was depicted upon her countenance. She bowed frequently, and in the most unpretending and affable manner, as the procession moved along.

"At length the cavalcade reached the cathedral, where the Archbishop of Montoni, assisted by the Bishops of Trevisano and Collato, was in attendance to perform the solemn ceremony. The sacred edifice was thronged by the *élite* and fashion of the capital, who had been admitted by tickets. When the royal party had entered the Cathedral, the doors were closed; and the holy ceremony was solemnized. The roar of the artillery was again heard, as the royal party returned to their carriages. This time the Grand Duchess was handed by his Serene Highness into the state carriage. The return to the palace was distinguished by demonstrations of satisfaction on the part of the spectators more enthusiastic, if possible, than those which marked the progress of the cavalcade to the cathedral. A glow of animation was visible upon the countenance of her Serene Highness; and the Grand Duke himself looked remarkably well and cheerful. In a short time the Sovereign conducted his lovely bride into that palace which in future is to be her home.

"Thus ended a ceremony which, in a political point of view, may probably be attended with important results to the interests of Castelcicala. Should male issue proceed from this marriage, the contentions of rival parties in the state will be at once annihilated. The supporters of the Prince of Castelcicala, who is now an exile in England, are naturally indignant and annoyed at the marriage of his Serene Highness Angelo III. with a lady young enough to encourage hopes that the union may not remain unfruitful. It is even evident that many of the former friends of the exiled Prince pronounced in favour of this marriage, the moment it was contemplated some months previously to its solemnization. This sentiment of approval will account for the entrance of General Grachia, who was notorious for his adhesion to the popular cause espoused by the Prince, into the Ministry. Probably the best friends of their country, aware that it was neither natural nor legal to attempt to control the inclinations and affections of his Serene Highness Angelo III., looked upon this marriage as the best means of securing peace and internal tranquillity to Castelcicala, inasmuch as it gives a prospect of an heir to the ducal throne—an heir whose right and title none could dispute. This is the view we ourselves take of the case, and we therefore hail the event as one of a most auspicious nature in our annals."

Scarcely had the Enchantress terminated this narrative of the ceremony which elevated her friend to a ducal throne,—a narrative which she had perused with the liveliest feelings of satisfaction, and the most unadulterated pleasure—when the Earl of Warrington was announced.

Diana hastened to communicate to him the tidings which she had received; and the nobleman himself read Eliza's letter, and the extract from the *Montoni Gazette*, with an interest which showed how gratified he felt in the high and exalted fortunes of the daughter of her whom he had once loved so tenderly.

"Yes, indeed," said the earl, when he had terminated the perusal of the two documents, "Eliza Sydney now ranks amongst the queens and reigning princesses of the world: from a humble cottage she has risen to a throne."

"And this exalted station she owes to your lordship's goodness," remarked Diana.

"Say to my justice," observed the earl; "for I may flatter myself that I have behaved with justice to the child of my departed uncle's daughter. And this remarkable exaltation of Eliza Sydney shows us, Diana, that we should never judge of a person's character by one fault. Eliza has always been imbued with sentiments of virtue and integrity, although she was led into one error by that villain Stephens; and she has now met with a reward of a price high almost beyond precedent. But, ah!" exclaimed the earl, who was carelessly turning the letter of the Grand Duchess over and over in his hands as he spoke, "this is very singular—very remarkable;"—and he inspected the seal and postmarks of the letter with minute attention.

"What is the matter?" inquired Diana.

"Some treachery has been perpetrated here," answered the earl, still continuing his scrutiny: "this letter had been opened before it was delivered to you."

"Opened!" cried Diana.

"Yes," said the Earl of Warrington; "here is every proof that the letter has been violated. See—there is the English post-mark of *yesterday morning*; and over it has been stamped *another mark*, of this morning's date. Then contemplate the seal. There are two kinds of wax, the one melted over the other: do you not notice a shade different in their colours?"

"Certainly," said Diana: "it is apparent. But who could have done this? Perhaps the Grand Duchess herself; for the ducal arms are imprinted upon the upper layer of wax."

"The persons who opened this letter, Diana," said the earl, in a serious—almost a solemn tone, "are those who know full well how to take the imprint of a seal. But have you not other letters from Castelcicala?"

"Several," replied Diana; and she hastily unlocked her writing-desk, where she produced all the correspondence she had received from Eliza Sydney.

The earl carefully inspected the envelopes of those letters; and his countenance grew more serious as he proceeded with his scrutiny.

"Yes," he exclaimed, after a long pause; "the fact is glaring! Every one of these letters was opened *somewhere* ere they were delivered to you. The utmost caution has been evidently used in re-sealing and re-stamping them;—nevertheless, there are proofs—undoubted proofs—that the whole of this correspondence has been violated in its transit from the writer to the receiver."

"But what object—what motive——"

"I have long entertained suspicions," said the Earl of Warrington, interrupting his fair mistress, "that there is one public institution in England which is made the scene of proceedings so vile—so detestable—so base as to cast a stain upon the entire nation. Those suspicions are now confirmed."

"What mean you?" inquired Diana: "to which institution do you allude?"

"*To the General Post-office*," replied the Earl of Warrington.

"The General Post-office!" cried Mrs. Arlington, her countenance expressing the most profound astonishment.

"The General Post-office," repeated the earl. "But this is a matter of so serious a nature that I shall not allow it to rest here. You will lend me these letters for a few hours? I am more intimately acquainted with the Home Secretary than with any other of her Majesty's Ministers; and to him will I now proceed."

The earl consigned the letters to his pocket, and, with an air of deep determination, took a temporary leave of Mrs. Arlington.

Scarcely had the earl left the house, when Mr. Greenwood's valet, Filippo, was introduced.

"I have called, madam," said the Italian, "to inform you that I last night counteracted another of my master's plots, and saved a young female from the persecution of his addresses."

"You have done well, Filippo," exclaimed Mrs. Arlington. "Does your master suspect you?"

"Not in the remotest degree, madam. I contrived matters so well, that he believed the young person alluded to had escaped by her own means, and without any assistance, save that of a pair of sheets which enabled her to descend in safety from the window of the room in which she was confined."

"I am delighted to hear that your mission to England has been so successful, in thwarting the machinations of that bad man," observed Mrs. Arlington. "Have you heard any news from Castelcicala?"

"I have this morning received a Montoni newspaper, announcing the nuptials of the Grand Duke and the Marchioness of Ziani," replied Filippo.

"And I also have heard those happy tidings," said Mrs. Arlington. "But have you any farther information to give me relative to the schemes of your master? I am always pleased to learn that his evil designs experience defeat through your agency."

"I have nothing more to say at present, madam," answered Filippo; "except, indeed," he added, suddenly recollecting himself, "that I overheard, a few days ago, a warm contention between my master and a certain Sir Rupert Harborough."

"Sir Rupert Harborough!" ejaculated Diana, a blush suddenly overspreading her cheeks.

"Yes, madam. From what I could learn, there was a balance of about a thousand pounds due from Sir Rupert Harborough to Mr. Greenwood, on a bill that purported to be the acceptance of Lord Tremordyn, but which was in reality a forgery committed by Sir Rupert himself."

"A forgery!" cried Diana.

"A forgery, madam. Sir Rupert bitterly reproached Mr. Greenwood with having suggested to him that mode of raising money, whereas Mr. Greenwood appeared to deny with indignation any share in the part of the transaction imputed to him. The matter ended by Mr. Greenwood declaring that if the bill were not paid to-morrow, when it falls due (having, it appears, been renewed several times), Sir Rupert Harborough should be prosecuted for forgery."

"And what said Sir Rupert Harborough to that?" inquired Diana.

"He changed his tone, and began to implore the mercy of Mr. Greenwood: but my master was inexorable; and Sir Rupert left the house with ruin and terror depicted upon his countenance."

"This battle you must allow them to fight out between themselves," said Diana, after a moment's hesitation. "I know Sir Rupert Harborough—know him full well; but I do not think that he is so thoroughly black-hearted as your master. He was once kind to me—once," she added, musing to herself rather than addressing the Italian valet: then, suddenly recollecting herself, she said, "However, Filippo—that affair does not regard you."

"Very good, madam," replied the valet; and he then took his departure.

The moment he was gone, Mrs. Arlington threw herself into her comfortable arm-chair, and became wrapt up in deep thought.

CHAPTER XCIV.

THE HOME OFFICE.

In a well furnished room, on the first-floor of the Home Office, sate the Secretary of State for that Department.

The room was spacious and lofty. The walls were hung with the portraits of several eminent statesmen who had, at different times, presided over the internal policy of the country. A round table stood in the middle of the apartment; and at this table, which groaned beneath a mass of papers, was seated the Minister.

At the feet of this functionary was a wicker basket, into which he threw the greater portion of the letters addressed to him, and over each of which he cast a glance of such rapidity that he must either have been a wonderfully clever man to acquire a notion of the contents of those documents by means of so superficial a survey, or else a very neglectful one to pay so little attention to affairs which were associated with important individual interests or which related to matters of national concern.

The time-piece upon the mantel struck twelve, when a low knock at the door of the apartment elicited from the Minister an invitation to enter.

A tall, thin, middle-aged, sallow-faced person, dressed in black, glided noiselessly into the room, bowed obsequiously to the Minister, and took his seat at the round table.

This was the Minister's private secretary.

The secretary immediately mended a pen, arranged his blotting-paper in a business-like fashion before him, spread out his foolscap writing paper, and then glanced towards his master, as much as to say, "I am ready."

"Take that pile of correspondence, if you please," said the Minister, "and run your eye over each letter."

"Yes, my lord," said the Secretary; and he glanced cursorily over the letters alluded to, one after the other, briefly mentioning their respective objects as he proceeded. "This letter, my lord, is from the chaplain of Newgate. It sets forth that there is a man of the name of William Lees at present under sentence of death in that prison;

that William Lees, in a fit of unbridled passion, which bordered upon insanity, murdered his wife; that the conduct of the deceased was sufficient to provoke the most temperate individual to a similar deed; that he had no interest in killing her; and that he committed the crime in a moment over which he had no control."

"Do you remember anything of the case?" demanded the Home Secretary. "For my part, I have no time to read trials."

"Yes, my lord," replied the Secretary. "This William Lees is a barber; and his wife was of vile and most intemperate habits. He murdered her in a fit of exasperation caused by the discovery that she had pledged every thing moveable in the house, to obtain the means of buying drink."

"Oh! a barber—eh?" said the Home Secretary, yawning.

"Yes, my lord. Your lordship will remember that young Medhurst, who assassinated a school-fellow in a fit of passion, was only condemned to three years' imprisonment."

"Ah! but that was quite a different thing," exclaimed the Minister. "Medhurst was a gentleman; but this man is only a barber."[1]

"True, my lord—very true," said the Secretary. "I had quite forgotten that."

"Make a memorandum, that the law in the case of William Lees must take its course."

"Yes, my lord;"—and the Secretary, having endorsed the note upon the letter, referred to another document. "This, my lord, is a petition from a political prisoner confined in a county gaol, and who sets forth that he is compelled to wear the prison dress, associate with felons of the blackest character, and eat the prison allowance. He humbly submits—"

"He may submit till he is tired," interrupted the Minister. "Make a memorandum to answer the petition to the effect that her Maj-

---

1 Francis Hastings Medhurst was convicted on 13 April 1839 of the manslaughter of Joseph Alsop, his fellow pupil at the Rev. Sturmer's academy in Hayes, Middlesex. William Lees, a barber, was convicted on 25 November 1839 for the murder of Elizabeth Lees, and was executed the same year. Lees was clearly suffering from a form of mental illness, and though guilty should never have been hanged under the law as it stood; Medhurst killed Alsop for no better reason than that Alsop had broken the glass in his watch, but received a lenient sentence because, as the transcript of the trial states, "Several highly respectable witnesses deposed to the prisoner's good character."

esty's Secretary of State for the Home Department does not see any ground for interfering in the matter."

"Very good, my lord. This letter is from a pauper in the —— Union, stating that he has been cruelly assaulted, beaten, and ill-used by the master; that he has applied in vain to the Poor Law Commissioners for redress; and that he now ventures to submit his case to your lordship."

"Make a note to answer that the fullest inquiries shall be immediately instituted," said the Minister.

"Shall I give the necessary instructions for the inquiry, my lord?" asked the Secretary.

"Inquiry!" repeated the Minister: "are you mad? Do you really imagine that I shall be foolish enough to permit any inquiry at all? Such a step would be almost certain to end in substantiating the pauper's charge against the master; and then there would be a clamour from one end of the country to the other against the New Poor Laws. We must smother all such affairs whenever we can; but by writing to say that the fullest inquiries shall be instituted, I shall be armed with a reply to any member who might happen to bring the case before Parliament. My answer to the charge would then be *that her Majesty's Government had instituted a full inquiry into the matter, and had ascertained that the pauper was a quarrelsome, obstreperous, and disorderly person, who was not to be believed upon his oath.*"

"True, my lord," said the Secretary, evidently struck by this display of ministerial wisdom. "The next letter, my lord, is from a clerk in the Tax Office, Somerset House. He complains that his income is too small, and that the Commissioners of Taxes refuse to augment it. He states in pretty plain terms, that unless he receives an augmentation, he shall not hesitate to publish the fact, that the Dividend Books of the Bank of England are removed to the Tax-Office every six months, in order that an account of every fundholder's stock in the government securities may be taken for the information of the Treasury and the Tax Commissioners: he adds that such an announcement would convulse the whole nation with alarm at the awful state of *espionnage* under which the people exist; and he states these grounds as a reason for purchasing his silence by means of an increase of salary."

"This is serious—very serious," said the Minister: "but the letter should have been addressed to the Chancellor of the Exchequer. You must enclose it to my colleague."

"Yes, my lord," replied the Secretary.

At this moment a gentle knock was heard at the door of the apartment.

The Secretary hastened to respond to the summons, and admitted two persons dressed in plain but decent attire. One was a short, stout, red-faced, consequential-looking man: the other was a tall, raw-boned, ungainly person, and seemed quite confounded at the presence in which he found himself.

The former of these individuals was an inspector of police: the latter was a common police-officer. Indeed, the reader has been already introduced to them, in the fourteenth chapter of this narrative.

Having ushered these individuals into the room, the private

secretary hastened to breathe a few words in an under tone to the ear of his master.

"Oh! these are the men, are they?" said the Minister aloud.

"Yes, my lord," replied the Secretary; then, addressing the police-officers, he exclaimed, "Step forward, my men—step forward. There—that's right: now sit down at that side of the table, and let the one who can write best make notes of the instructions that will be immediately given to you."

Both the Minister and Secretary were cautious enough not to give those instructions in their own handwriting.

The men sate down, as they were desired; and the inspector whispered to his companion an order to assume the duties of amanuensis on the occasion.

"You are aware, my good fellows," said the Minister, "that there is to be a great political meeting to-morrow evening somewhere in Bethnal Green?"

"Yes, my lord," replied the inspector.

"It is necessary to the purposes of her Majesty's Government," continued the Minister, "that discredit should be thrown upon all political meetings where very liberal sentiments are enunciated."

"Yes, my lord," said the inspector. "Shall Crisp put that down, my lord?"

"There is no necessity to make a note of my observations, only of my instructions," answered the Minister, with a smile. "The best method of throwing discredit upon those meetings is to create a disturbance. You, Mr. Inspector, will therefore take care and have at least a dozen of your men in plain clothes at the assembly to-morrow evening."

"Yes, my lord. Put that down, Crisp."

"You will direct your men, Mr. Inspector, to applaud most vehemently all the inflammatory parts of the speeches made upon the occasion."

"Yes, my lord. Put that down, Crisp."

"You will contrive that Mr. Crisp, whom my secretary states to be a proper man for the purpose, shall himself make a speech to-morrow evening."

"Yes, my lord. Put that down, Crisp."

"This speech must be of the most violent and inflammatory kind:

it must advocate the use of physical force, denounce the aristocracy, the government, and the parliament in the most blood-thirsty terms; it need not even spare her most gracious Majesty. Let the cry be *Blood*; and let your men, Mr. Inspector, applaud with deafening shouts, every period in this incendiary harangue."

"Yes, my lord. Put that down, Crisp."

"The well-disposed portion of the audience will remonstrate. Your men in plain clothes can thus readily pick a quarrel; and a quarrel may be easily made to lead to blows. Then let a posse of constables in uniform rush in, and lay about them with their bludgeons most unsparingly. The more broken heads and limbs, the better. Be sure to have some of the audience taken into custody; and on the following morning, appear against them before the police-magistrate."

"Yes, my lord. Put that down, Crisp."

"You will take especial care to denounce the individuals so captured, as the ringleaders of the riot, and the ones who made themselves most conspicuous in applauding the inflammatory speeches uttered on the occasion—especially those which advocated rebellion, bloodshed, and death to monarchy and aristocracy."

"Yes, my lord. Put that down, Crisp."

"If the magistrate asks you—as he will be certain to do," continued the Minister, "whether you are acquainted with the prisoners at the bar, you can say that they are well known to the police as most dangerous and disorderly characters."

"Yes, my lord. Put that down, Crisp."

"You see," said the Minister, turning towards his own private secretary, "it is ten to one that the individuals so arrested will be respectable tradesmen; and as they will thus obtain a taste of the treadmill (for we must send our private instructions to the magistrates at Lambeth Street, to that effect) the warning will be a most salutary one throughout the whole district—especially at a moment when the Spitalfields weavers are reduced to desperation by their dreadfully distressed condition."

"Of course, my lord," replied the Secretary. "Such a proceeding will sicken men of political meetings. Has your lordship any farther instructions for these officers?"

"None," said the Minister. "I may, however, add, that if they acquit themselves well in this respect, the inspector shall become a superintendent, and the constable a serjeant."

"Thank your lordship," exclaimed the inspector. "You may put that down, too, Crisp—and express your gratitude to his lordship for his kindness."

Mr. Crisp acted in all respects as he was desired; and having each made an awkward bow, the two officers retired.

"Now proceed with the correspondence," said the Minister.

"Yes, my lord," replied the Secretary. "Here is a letter from the mayor of ——, stating that the experiment of making the prisoners, tried and untried, who are confined in the gaol of that town, wear black masks whenever they are compelled to mingle together, works well. The mayor moreover states, that out of two hundred prisoners subjected to the *solitary system*, since the introduction of the plan into the gaol, only nineteen have gone mad, and of those only three have died raving. He therefore recommends the solitary system. He adds that all personal identity is now destroyed in the prison, and prisoners are known by *numbers* instead of by their *names*. He concludes by inquiring whether these regulations shall continue in force?"

"Most assuredly," answered the Minister. "Make a note that a reply is to be sent to that effect. I am glad the system of solitary confinement, black cloth masks, and numbers instead of names, works well. I shall gradually apply it to every criminal prison in England. At the same time, I must endeavour to throw the odium of the introduction of that system upon the justices in quarter sessions assembled—in case I should be assailed on the subject in the House."

"Certainly, my lord. This letter is from the secret agent, sent down to Manchester to inquire into the constitution and principles of the Independent Order of Rechabites. He obtained admission into a lodge, and was regularly initiated a member of the Brotherhood. He finds that the Rechabites are about eighty thousand in number, having lodges in all the great cities and towns of England, with the head-quarters at Manchester. The Order is not political; but is formed of sections of the Teetotal Societies. The government need not entertain any fears of this combination. The agent sends up a detailed account of the secrets and signs connected with the Order, accompanied by a copy of the rules and regulations."

"These Teetotalers must not be encouraged. They are seriously injuring the Excise-revenues. Proceed."

"This letter, my lord, is from the principal agent sent down into the mining districts, to encourage a spirit of discontent amongst the pitmen. He says that he has no doubt of being enabled to produce a disturbance in the north, and thus afford your lordship the wished-for opportunity of sending more troops in that direction. When once over-awed by the presence of a formidable number of bayonets, the pitmen will be compelled to submit to the terms dictated by the coal-mine proprietors; and your lordship's aims will be thus accomplished."

"I am glad of that. The coal-mine proprietors are rich and influential men, whom it is necessary to conciliate," said the Minister. "What next?"

"Here is a letter, my lord," continued the Secretary, "from Sir Joseph Gosborne, stating that his daughter, Miss Gosborne, was taken into custody yesterday morning on an accusation of stealing a jar of anchovies from an oilman's shop. The magistrate refused to take bail, and remanded the young lady until next Monday. Sir Joseph is anxious that his daughter should be admitted to bail, because, in that case, should he fail to settle with the prosecutor, he can keep his daughter out of the way when the day of trial arrives, and pay the money for the estreated recognizances. He is moreover desirous that the case should be sent to the Sessions, because, if by any accident the matter *should* go to trial, a verdict of acquittal is certain at the hands of a Clerkenwell jury, but by no means sure with an Old Bailey one."

"Make a memorandum to write to the magistrate who will hear the case next Monday, to take bail—*moderate bail*, mind—and to refer the matter to the Sessions. We must not refuse to oblige Sir Joseph Gosborne."

While the private secretary was still writing, a servant entered and informed the Minister that Mr. Teynham was waiting, and solicited an audience.

"Ah! the new magistrate at Marlborough Street," exclaimed the Home Secretary. "Show him in."

Mr. Teynham, a middle-aged gentleman attired in black, was introduced accordingly. He bowed very low to the Minister, and, when desired to take a chair, obsequiously seated himself upon the very edge.

"I have recommended you to Her Majesty, Mr. Teynham," said the Minister, "as a fit and proper person to fill the situation of police-magistrate and justice of the peace at the Marlborough Street Court; and her Majesty has been most graciously pleased to confirm the appointment."

Mr. Teynham bowed very low, and became entangled in a labyrinth of acknowledgments, with which "deep gratitude"—"sense of duty"—"impartial distribution of justice," and such like phrases were blended.

"It is necessary," said the Minister, after a pause, "that I should give you a few instructions with respect to the functions upon which you are about to enter. You are aware, Mr. Teynham, that the young gentlemen of the aristocracy are occasionally addicted to wrenching off knockers, pulling down bells, and other innocent little pranks of a similar nature. These are delicate cases to deal with, Mr. Teynham;—but I need scarcely inform you that the treadmill is *not* for the aristocracy."

"I understand, my lord. A trifling fine, with a reprimand—and a little wholesome advice—"

"Precisely, Mr. Teynham—precisely!" cried the Minister: "I see that you understand your business well. The nice discrimination which you possess will always teach you whether you have a gentleman to deal with, or not. If a low person choose to divert himself with aristocratic amusements, punish him—do not spare him—send him to the treadmill. In the same way that game is preserved for the sport of the upper classes, so must the knockers and the bells be saved from spoliation by the lower orders."

"I fully comprehend your lordship," said the newly-made magistrate. "I should like, however, to know your lordship's sentiments in one respect."

"Speak, Mr. Teynham," said the Minister, with the most condescending affability, or the most affable condescension—whichever the reader likes best.

"Suppose, my lord, that a young nobleman or well-born gentleman wrenches off a knocker, and throws it into the street; then suppose, my lord, that a poor man, passing by, picks up the knocker and carries it off to a marine-store dealer's to sell it for old iron, in order to procure his family a meal; and then if your lordship will be kind enough to suppose that both those persons are brought up before me—the nobleman for wrenching off the knocker and throwing it away, and the poor man for picking it up and selling it,—how am I to act in such a case?"

"Very ingenious—very ingenious, indeed, Mr. Teynham,"—said the Minister: "you will make an excellent magistrate! Your course in the case propounded is clear; the nobleman is fined five shillings for being drunk and disorderly—because all noblemen and gentlemen who wrench off knockers *are* drunk and disorderly; and the poor man must be committed to the House of Correction for three months. Nothing is plainer, Mr. Teynham."

"Nothing, my lord. Has your lordship any farther instructions?"

"Oh! decidedly," returned the Minister. "When any individual connected with a noble or influential family gets into a scrape, and is brought before you, hear the case in private, and exclude the reporters. Again, never commit such a person for trial, unless you are absolutely compelled. Let him go upon bail: it will be ten to one if you are ever troubled any more with the case. There is another point to which I must direct your attention. The practice of shoplifting among ladies has increased lately to a fearful degree. But, after all, it is only a *little eccentricity*—indeed one might almost call it an *amiable weakness*. The fact is, that many ladies will go into a shop, purchase a hundred-guinea shawl, and secrete an eighteen-penny pair of gloves. Prudent husbands and fathers avert the tradesman, with whom their wives and daughters deal, beforehand; and these trifling abstractions are duly entered in the running accounts; but now and then a lady *does* get taken up. In such a case you must show her every possible distinction. Order her a chair in the dock; and before the business comes on, permit her to remain with her friends in the 'magistrates' private room.' Then, if the prosecutor hesitates in giving his evidence, fly into a passion, tell him that he is prevaricating and not worthy to be believed upon his oath, and indignantly dismiss the case. The accused lady can then step into her carriage, and drive off comfortably home."

"Your lordship's instructions shall be complied with to the very letter," said Mr. Teynham.

"In a word," continued the Minister, "you must always shield the upper classes as much as possible; and in order to veil their little peccadilloes, bring out the misdeeds of the lower orders in the boldest relief. This is the only way to support the doctrine that the poor *must* be governed by the rich. Whenever young boys or girls appear as witnesses, ask them if they know the value of an oath; and if they reply in the negative, expatiate upon the frightful immorality prevalent among the poorer classes, so that the reporters may record your observations. This does good—and enables the Bishops to make long speeches in the House of Lords on the necessity of religious instruction, and the want of more churches. If you attend to these remarks of mine, Mr. Teynham, you will make an excellent magistrate."

"Your lordship may rely upon me," was the submissive answer.

"There is one more point—I had almost forgotten it," said the Home Secretary. "You must invariably take the part of the police. Remember that the oath of one police-officer is worth the oaths of a dozen defendants. This only applies to the collision of the police with the lower orders, mind. As a general rule, remember that the police are always *in the right* when the poor are concerned, and always *in the wrong* when the rich are brought before you. And now, Mr. Teynham, I have nothing more to say."

The newly-made magistrate rose, bowed several times, and withdrew, walking obsequiously upon the points of his toes for fear his boots should creak in the awful presence of the Home Secretary.

But if "his worship" were thus meek and lowly before his patron, he afterwards avenged himself for that constraint, when seated in the magisterial chair, upon the poor devils that appeared before him!

The private secretary was about to proceed with the correspondence addressed from different quarters to the Minister, when a servant entered the room, and placed a card upon the table before this great officer of state.

"The Earl of Warrington?" said the Minister. "I will receive him."

The servant withdrew, and the private secretary retired to an inner apartment.

In a few moments the Earl of Warrington was announced.

When the usual civilities had been exchanged between the two noblemen, the Earl of Warrington said, "I have called, my lord, upon a matter which, I hope from the knowledge I have of your lordship's character, will be considered by you as one of importance to the whole nation."

"The estimate your lordship forms of any business can be no mean guide to my own opinion," answered the Minister.

"I am not quite aware whether I am acting in accordance with official etiquette, to bring the matter alluded to under the notice of your lordship, or whether it would have been more regular in me to have addressed myself direct to the Postmaster-General or the Prime Minister; but as I have the honour of being better acquainted with your lordship than with any of your colleagues in the administration, I made up my mind to come hither."

"I shall be most happy to serve your lordship in any way in my power," said the Minister.

"Then I shall at once come to the point," continued the Earl of Warrington. "A friend of mine—a lady who resides in London—has corresponded for some months past with a lady living in the state of Castelcicala; and there is every reason to believe that the letters addressed to my friend in London have been opened during the transit."

"Indeed," said the Minister, not a muscle of whose countenance moved as he heard this communication. "May I ask what is the nature of the proofs that such is the fact?"

"I believe," returned the Earl of Warrington, "that the letters have been opened at the English Post-office."

"The English Post-office!" ejaculated the Minister, with an air of great surprise—whether real or affected, we must leave our readers to determine.

"Yes, my lord—the English Post-office," said the Earl of Warrington, firmly. "The proofs are these;"—and, extracting the letters from his pocket, he pointed out to the Minister the same appearances which he had ere now explained to Mrs. Arlington.

"On this last letter," said the Minister, "I perceive the ducal arms of Castelcicala."

"The present Grand Duchess of that State is the correspondent of Mrs. Arlington, to whom, your lordship may perceive, these letters are addressed."

"And her Serene Highness is a relative of your lordship, I believe?" observed the Minister inquiringly.

"Which circumstance, united with my friendship for Mrs. Arlington, has determined me to inquire into this matter—nay, to sift it to the very bottom."

"Your lordship can scarcely suppose that the contents of letters are violated by the sanction of the Post-Master General?" said the Minister, darting a keen glance upon the earl.

"I will not take upon myself to accuse any individual directly," was the answer.

"Nor is it worth while to scrutinise a matter which will probably terminate in the discovery that the impertinent curiosity of some clerk has led to the evil complained of," said the Minister.

"No, my lord—this violation of private correspondence has been conducted too systematically to be the work of a clerk surrounded by prying eyes and hurried with the fear of detection every moment. Here are two distinct coats of wax on several of the letters; and yet the impressions of the original seals are retained. Those impressions were not taken by official process in an instant, nor without previous preparation."

"Then whom does your lordship suspect?" inquired the Minister, with a trifling uneasiness of manner.

"I come to ask your lordship to furnish me with a clue to this mystery, and not to supply one. Were I acquainted with the real truth, I should know what course to pursue."

"And what course would that be?"

"In the next session of Parliament, I would rise in my place in the House of Lords, and proclaim to the whole nation—nay, to the entire world—the disgraceful fact, that England, the land of vaunted freedom, possesses an institution where the most sacred ties of honour are basely violated and trampled under foot."

"But suppose, my lord—I only say suppose," cried the Minister, "that her Majesty's government should consider it vitally important to English interests to be acquainted with the contents of certain letters,—suppose, I say, my lord, that such were the case,—would you then think it necessary to publish your discovery,—presuming that your lordship has made such discovery,—of that necessary proceeding on the part of her Majesty's government?"

"I am afraid that your lordship has now afforded me a clue to the mystery which has perplexed me," said the Earl of Warrington coldly.

"And as a nobleman devoted to your country, your lordship must recognise the imperious necessity of adopting such a course, at times, as the one now made known to you."

"As a nobleman devoted to my country," exclaimed the Earl of Warrington proudly, "I abhor and detest all underhand means of obtaining information which serves as a guide for diplomatic intrigue, but which in nowise affects the sterling interests of the state."

"Your lordship speaks warmly," said the Minister.

"And were I in my place in Parliament, I should speak more warmly—far more warmly still. I am, however, here in your lordship's apartment, and the laws of courtesy do not permit me to express my feelings as I elsewhere *should* do—and as I elsewhere *shall* do."

"Your lordship will reflect," said the Minister, now really alarmed,—"your lordship will reflect—maturely—seriously——"

"It requires no reflection to teach me my duty."

"But, my dear earl——"

"My lord?"

"The peace of the country frequently depends upon the information which we acquire in this manner."

"Then had the peace of the country better be occasionally menaced, than that the sacred envelope of a letter should be violated?"

"Your lordship is too severe," said the Minister.

"No—my lord: I am not, under the circumstances, severe enough. Behold the gross injustice of the system. The law forbids us to transmit sealed letters through any other medium than the Post-office; and yet that very Post-office is made the scene of the violation of those sacred missives. My lord, it is impossible to defend so atrocious a proceeding. Now, my lord, I have spoken as warmly as I feel."

"Really, my dear earl, you must not permit this little business to go any further. You shall have for your friends every satisfaction they require: their correspondence shall be strictly inviolate in future. And now, my lord," continued the Minister, with a smile whose deceptive blandness Mr. Greenwood would have envied, "let me request attention to another point. The Premier has placed your lordship's name on the list of peers who are to be raised to a more elevated rank ere the opening of the next session; and your lordship may exchange your coronet of an earldom against that of a marquisate."

"Her Majesty's government," replied the earl with chilling—freezing *hauteur*, "would do well to reserve that honour in respect to me, until it may choose to reward me when I shall have performed a duty that I owe my country, and exposed a system to express my full sense of which I dare not *now* trust my tongue with epithets. Good morning, my lord."

And the Earl of Warrington walked proudly from the room.

On the following day a cabinet council was held at the Home Office.

CHAPTER XCV.

THE FORGER AND THE ADULTERESS.

It was evening; and Lady Cecilia Harborough was seated alone in the drawing-room of the house which she and her husband occupied in Tavistock Square.

A cheerful fire blazed in the grate: the lamp upon the table diffused a soft and mellow lustre through the apartment.

Lady Cecilia's manner was pensive: a deep shade of melancholy overspread her countenance; and at times her lips quivered, and her bosom heaved convulsively.

She was evidently attempting to struggle with feelings of a very painful nature.

"Slighted—neglected—perhaps despised!" she at length murmured. "Oh! what an indignity! To have yielded myself up entirely to that man—and now to be cast aside in this manner! For months past have I observed that his conduct grew more and more cool towards me;—his visits became less frequent;—he made appointments with me and did not keep them;—he remonstrated with me for what he called my extravagance, when I asked him for money! Ah! how I endeavoured to close my eyes to the truth:—I forced myself to put faith in his excuses for absence—I compelled myself to be satisfied with his apologies for not keeping his engagements. Fool that I have been! Had I reproached—wept—stormed—and quarrelled, as other women would have done, he would yet be my slave: but I was too pliant—too easy—too docile—and he has ended by contemning me! I wanted spirit—I was deficient in courage—I practised no artifice. I should have refused him my favours when he was most impassioned; I should have tantalised him—acted with caprice—set a high value upon the pleasures which he enjoyed in my arms. Oh! it is cruel—cruel! I have been the pensioned harlot of that man! He commanded the use of my person as he would that of the lowest prostitute in the street. I was too cheap—too willing—too ready to meet him half way in the dalliance of love! I caught a fine bird—and by leaving his cage open, have allowed him an opportunity to fly away! The indignity is insufferable! For weeks I had not asked him for a shilling—for weeks I had not spoken to him on the subject of money. And now—to-day—when I require a hundred guineas for urgent matters, to be refused! to be denied that paltry sum! Oh! it is monstrous! And not to come himself to explain,—but to send a cool note, expressing a regret that the numerous demands he has had upon him lately render it impossible for him to comply with my request! A worn-out excuse—a wretched apology! And for him, too, who absolutely rolls in riches! I never could have believed it. Even now it appears a dream! Ah! the ungrateful monster! It is true that he has supplied me at times in the most generous manner,—that he redeemed my jewels for me a second time, some months ago, when Rupert played me that vile trick by plundering me during my absence;—but, alas! the jewels have returned to their old place—and who is to redeem them *now?*"

Lady Cecilia paused, and compressed her lips together.

She felt herself slighted—perhaps for some rival: and whose sufferings are more acute than those of a neglected woman? who experiences mental pangs more poignant?

Lady Cecilia felt herself degraded. She now comprehended that she had been made the instrument of a heartless libertine's pleasures; and that he coolly thrust her aside when literally satiated with her charms.

This was a most debasing conviction—debasing beyond all others, for a patrician lady!

Never did she seem so little in her own estimation: she felt polluted;—she saw that she had sold herself for gold: she remembered how willingly, how easily she surrendered herself on the first occasion of her criminality; and she despised herself, because she felt that Greenwood despised her also!

She had no virtue—but she had pride.

The highest bidder might enjoy her person, so voluptuous was she by nature—so ready also was she to make any sacrifice to obtain the means of gratifying her extravagance.

Love with her was not a refinement—it was a sensuality.

Still she had her pride—her woman's pride; for even the most degraded courtesan has *that*; and it was her pride that was now so deeply wounded.

She knew not what course to pursue.

Should she endeavour to bring Greenwood back to her arms?

Or should she be revenged?

If she resolved upon the former, what wiles was she to adopt—what artifices to employ?

If she decided upon the latter, what point in her neglectful lover was vulnerable—what weapon could she use?

A woman does not like to choose the alternative of vengeance, because such a proceeding implies the absence of all hope and of all power of recalling the faithless one.

And yet what was Lady Cecilia to do? That refusal of the money which she had requested, appeared expressive of Mr. Greenwood's determination to break off the connexion.

In that case nothing remained to her but vengeance.

Such were her thoughts.

Her reverie was interrupted by the sudden entrance of her husband Sir Rupert Harborough. His face was flushed with drinking—for he had dined, with his friend Chichester, at a tavern; and his cares had forced him to apply with even more than usual liberality to the bottle.

He threw himself into a chair opposite to his wife, and said, "Well, Cecilia, I have got very bad news to tell you."

"Indeed, Sir Rupert?" she said, in a tone which signified that *she* also had her annoyances, and would rather not be troubled with *his*.

"I have, on my honour!" cried the baronet. "In fact, Cecilia, I must find a thousand pounds to-morrow by twelve o'clock."

Lady Cecilia only laughed ironically.

"You make merry, madam, at my misfortunes," said Sir Rupert; "but I can assure you that the present is no laughing matter."

"And I unfortunately have no more diamonds and jewellery for you to rob me of," returned the lady.

"No, Cecilia—but you are my wife; and the disgrace that falls upon your husband would redound on yourself."

"Oh! if you be afraid of rusticating in the Queen's Bench prison for a season, I would advise you to make yourself easy on that head; because—"

"Because what, Cecilia?"

"Because I can assure all your friends and acquaintances that you are merely passing the winter in Paris."

"Ridiculous!" cried the baronet impatiently.

"Not so ridiculous as you imagine," returned Lady Cecilia. "You are accustomed, you know, to leave home for weeks and months together."

"Lady Cecilia, this is no time for either ill-feeling or sarcasm. If we have no love for one another, at least let us sit down and converse calmly upon the urgency of our present situation."

"*Our* situation?" ejaculated Cecilia.

"Yes—*ours*," repeated the baronet emphatically. "In one word, Cecilia, can you possibly raise a thousand pounds?"

To a person who had not the means of obtaining even the tenth part of that sum, and who had herself been disappointed that very evening in her endeavour to procure a hundred guineas, the question put by the baronet appeared in so ridiculous a light, that—in spite of her own annoyances—Lady Cecilia threw herself back in her chair, and burst into a loud and hearty laugh.

Sir Rupert rose and paced the room in an agitated manner; for he was totally at a loss what course to pursue. His only hope was in his wife; and yet he knew not how to break the fatal news to her.

"My God! Cecilia," he exclaimed, after a pause, during which he resumed his seat, "you will drive me mad!"

"You have become very sensitive of late, Sir Rupert; and yet I was not aware that you were so weak-minded as to tremble upon the verge of insanity. Certainly your conduct has never led me to suppose that you were over sane."

"My dear Cecilia, cease this raillery, in the name of every thing sacred," cried the baronet. "I tell you that ruin hangs over me—ruin of the most fearful nature—ruin in which your own name, as that of my wife, will be compromised—"

"Then tell me at once what you dread, and I will tell you whether I can assist you; for I know perfectly well that you require me to do something."

"Do not ask me what it is, Cecilia; but say—can you procure from any quarter—*from any quarter*, mind—a thousand pounds?"

"Absurd! Sir Rupert," answered the lady. "I have no means of helping myself at this moment—much less of providing so large a sum to supply your extravagance. This is a debt of honour, I presume—a debt contracted at the gambling table."

"No—it is far more serious than that, Cecilia; and you *must* exert yourself. If I do not have that amount by twelve to-morrow, the consequences will be most fatal. I know you can borrow the money for me—you have resources, no matter where or how—I ask no questions—I do not wish to pry into your secrets—"

"You are really very considerate, Sir Rupert. You do not wish to pry into my secrets: but you would not hesitate to pry into my drawers and boxes, if you thought there was any thing in them worth taking."

And as she uttered these words, a smile of superb contempt curled her vermilion lips.

Sir Rupert was maddened by this behaviour on the part of his wife; and with difficulty could he restrain his feelings of rage and hatred.

"Madam," he exclaimed, "I ask you to throw aside your raillery, and converse with me—for once—in a serious manner."

"I am willing to do so, Sir Rupert," answered Cecilia; "but you really appear to be joking me yourself. You speak in enigmas about the ruin that hangs over *you* and will involve *me*,—you refuse to entrust me with more of your secret than is necessary to serve as a preface for your demand;—and that demand is a thousand pounds! A thousand pounds are required in a few hours of a person who has no diamonds to pledge—no friends to apply to—"

"Stay, Cecilia," cried the baronet. "You cannot be without friends. For a year past you have been well supplied with funds—you have redeemed your diamonds twice—you have satisfied many of our creditors—the servants' wages and the rent have been regularly paid—"

"And all this has been done without the contribution of one shilling on the part of my husband towards the household expenses," added Lady Cecilia.

"I am glad you have mentioned that point," exclaimed Sir Rupert: "it proves that you *have* friends—that perhaps your father and mother assist you in private,—in a word, that you have some resources. Now what those resources may be, I do not ask you: all I require is assistance—now—within a few hours—before twelve to-morrow."

"Even if I could raise the sum you require," said Cecilia, "I would not think of giving it to you without knowing for what destination it was intended."

"And can you procure the sum, if I reveal to you—if I tell you——"

"I promise nothing," interrupted Lady Cecilia drily.

"But you will do your best?" persisted the baronet.

"I will do nothing without being previously made aware of the real nature of your difficulties."

"I will then keep you in the dark no longer. The cause of my embarrassment is a bill of exchange, for a thousand pounds, now lying in Greenwood's hands, and due to-morrow."

"That is but a simple debt; and, methinks, Sir Rupert, that your acquaintance with bills is not so slight as to render you an alarmist respecting the consequences."

"Were it only a simple matter of debt, I should care but little," said Sir Rupert, still compelled to support the biting raillery of his wife: "but unfortunately—in an evil hour—I know not what demon prompted me at the moment——"

"Speak, Sir Rupert—tell me the truth at once," cried Lady Cecilia, now really alarmed.

"I say that in an evil hour—in a moment of desperation—in an excess of frenzy—I committed a forgery!"

"A forgery!" repeated Lady Cecilia, turning deadly pale. "Ah! what a disgrace to the family—what shame for me——"

"I told you that my ruin would redound upon yourself, Cecilia. But there is more yet for you to hear. The acceptance that I forged——"

"Well?"

"Was that of Lord Tremordyn——"

"My father!"

"And now you know all. Can you assist me?"

"Sir Rupert, I have no means of raising one tenth part of the sum that you need to cover this infamous transaction."

"And yet you seemed to say that if I told you the nature of my difficulties——"

"I was curious to learn your secret; and as you appeared resolved to keep it from *me*, I thought I would see if there were no means of wheedling it out of *you*."

"And you therefore have no hope to give me?" said the baronet, in a tone of despair.

"None. Where could I raise one thousand pounds? how am I to obtain such a sum? It is for you either to pacify Mr. Greenwood, or to throw yourself at my father's feet and confess all."

"Mr. Greenwood is resolute; and you know that your father would spurn me from his presence. So far from me being able to help myself, it is for you to help me. Perhaps Mr. Greenwood would listen to your representations; or else Lord Tremordyn would accord to you what he would never concede to me."

"You cannot suppose that I can have any influence upon Mr. Greenwood," began Lady Cecilia: "and as for—"

"On the contrary," said Sir Rupert, fixing his eyes in a significant manner upon his wife's countenance; "I have every reason to believe that your influence over Mr. Greenwood is very great; and I will now thank you to exercise it in my behalf."

"What do you mean, Sir Rupert?" exclaimed Cecilia, a deep blush suffusing her face, and her eyes sinking beneath her husband's expressive look.

"Do not force me to explanations, Cecilia," returned the baronet. "I know more than you imagine—I have proofs of more than you fancy I could even suspect. But of that no matter: relieve me from this embarrassment—and I will never trouble you about *your* pursuits."

"What would you have me do?" asked the guilty wife, in a trembling voice.

"Go to Greenwood and settle this business for me," said the baronet, in an authoritative tone.

"I cannot—I dare not—I have no right to demand such a favour of him—I should be certain to experience a refusal—I—"

"Lady Cecilia," interrupted the baronet, speaking in a slow and emphatic manner, "Mr. Greenwood is too gallant a man to refuse a mere trifle to a lady who has refused nothing to him."

"Sir Rupert—you cannot suppose—you—"

"I mean what I say, madam," added the baronet sternly. "Mr. Greenwood is your paramour, and you can surely use your influence with him to save your husband."

"My God! what do I hear?" ejaculated Cecilia. "What proof have you, Sir Rupert—what testimony—what ground—"

"Every proof—every testimony—every ground," interrupted the baronet impatiently. "But, again I say, I do not wish to ruin your reputation, if you will save mine."

"Impossible!" cried Lady Cecilia. "I do not deny that Mr. Greenwood has accommodated me with an occasional loan—upon interest—"

"Interest indeed!" said the baronet, whose turn to assume a tone of raillery had now arrived: "interest paid from the bank of my honour!"

"Upon legal and commercial terms has he lent me money," continued Lady Cecilia; "and this very evening has he refused to advance me another shilling!"

"Is that true, Cecilia?" demanded Sir Rupert.

"Nay—satisfy yourself," said the lady; and drawing a note from her bosom, she handed it to her husband.

The correspondence that passed between Mr. Greenwood and Lady Cecilia was always of a laconic and most guarded nature: there was consequently nothing in the letter now communicated to Sir Rupert Harborough, to confirm his belief in his wife's criminality. Indeed, the epistle was neither more nor less than any gentleman might write upon a matter of business to any lady.

"I see that Mr. Greenwood is tired of you, Cecilia," said the baronet, throwing the note upon the table, "and that he is anxious to break off the connexion. Now I will tell you how you must be kind enough to act," he continued, in a tone of command. "You must proceed at once to Mr. Greenwood; you must tell him that I have discovered all—that I have positive proofs—that since the day when Chichester discovered him with his arm round your neck in my drawing-room—"

"Oh! that villain Chichester!" murmured Lady Cecilia.

"That ever since that day," continued the baronet, "Chichester and myself have watched your proceedings—have seen you, Cecilia, repair to the appointments agreed upon with your paramour—"

"But this is atrocious!" ejaculated the lady, now dreadfully excited.

"Nay—do not interrupt me," said Sir Rupert in an imperative manner. "You must tell Mr. Greenwood that I and my witness have followed you both to an hotel at Greenwich—that we have been in the next room and have overheard your conversation—that we have been aware of the moments of your amorous dalliance—"

"Ah! Sir Rupert—do you want to kill me?" cried Cecilia, bursting into an agony of tears.

"Nonsense!" ejaculated the baronet: "I only want you to save me, and I will screen you. Go, then, to Greenwood—tell him all this—assure him that I know all—that for months have I been watching you—and that I should obtain from him damages far more important than the amount of this acceptance, but that I am willing to compromise the business by the destruction of that document."

"And why could you not have acquainted Mr. Greenwood with all this when you last saw him?" demanded Lady Cecilia, drying her tears, and endeavouring to compose herself, now that the worst was known.

"I did not intend to mention my knowledge of your criminality at all," said Sir Rupert; "and had you consented in the first instance to use your influence with Greenwood to obtain the money to settle the bill, you would not have forced me to these revelations."

"Say rather, Sir Rupert Harborough," exclaimed the lady, "that you would have me obtain for you the means to pay this forged bill; and when once you were freed from the power of Greenwood, you would have brought your action against him, and exposed your wife. But as you have failed in making me—the wife whom you would thus expose—the instrument of procuring that sum,—and as the danger now stares you in the face, you proclaim your knowledge of our connexion, and use it as a means to compromise the forgery."

"Cecilia, you do not think me capable——"

"I think you capable of any thing," interrupted his wife indignantly; and it was singular to see that adulterous woman—that criminal wife—that profligate female now putting her husband to the blush, by exposing his base designs.

"Well—after all," exclaimed Sir Rupert, "recriminations will do no good. Go to Greenwood—settle the affair—and the past shall be buried in oblivion."

"And what guarantee do you offer to ensure eternal secresy on your part, provided Mr. Greenwood will give up this forged bill?"

"I will sign any paper he may require," replied the baronet. "But time presses—it is now nearly ten o'clock—and to-morrow morning——"

"I will go to Mr. Greenwood," said Lady Cecilia, rising from her seat: "I will go to him—and endeavour to compromise this affair to the best of my power."

Sir Rupert rang the bell and ordered wine to be brought up while Lady Cecilia hastened to her boudoir to attire herself for going out; and in the mean time a servant was despatched to procure a cab.

The vehicle arrived and Lady Cecilia was already upon the threshold of the front door of the house, when a servant in a handsome livery ascended the steps, presented a letter, and said "For Sir Rupert Harborough."

Lady Cecilia received the letter; and the servant who delivered it immediately took his departure.

The lady was about to send in the letter by her own domestic to her husband, when the superscription on the envelope caught her eyes by the light of the hall-lamp. The writing was in the delicate hand of a female; and, without a moment's hesitation, Cecilia consigned the epistle to her reticule.

She then stepped into the vehicle, and ordered the driver to take her to Spring Gardens.

There were two bright lamps fixed in front of the cab; and by these means was Lady Cecilia enabled to examine the contents of the letter intended for her husband.

Without the least hesitation she opened the letter, and to her ineffable surprise discovered that it contained a Bank of England note for one thousand pounds.

This treasure was accompanied by a letter, the contents of which were as follows:—

"An individual who once received some kindness at the hands of Sir Rupert Harborough, has learnt by a strange accident that Sir Rupert Harborough has a pressing need of a sum of money to liquidate a debt due to Mr. George Montague Greenwood. The individual alluded to takes leave to place the sum required at Sir Rupert Harborough's disposal."

No name—no date—no address were appended to this mysterious note. The writing was in a delicate female hand;—and a servant in a handsome livery had delivered the letter. These circumstances, combined with the handsome manner in which the money was tendered, refuted the suspicion that some female, with whom Sir Rupert was illicitly connected, had thus befriended him.

Lady Cecilia was bewildered: the pain of conjecture and doubt was however absorbed in the pleasurable feelings excited by the possession of so large a sum of money.

The cab now stopped at Mr. Greenwood's residence.

CHAPTER XCVI.

THE MEMBER OF PARLIAMENT'S LEVEE.

"You have doubtless called, my dear Cecilia," said Mr. Greenwood, as he handed the fair visitant to a seat in his elegant drawing-room,—"you have doubtless called to remonstrate with me respecting my note of this evening."

"No," answered Cecilia coldly: "I come on a more momentous affair than that: Sir Rupert knows all!"

"Ah!" cried Greenwood; "is it possible that the villain Chichester—"

"Has betrayed us," added the lady. "Moreover, Sir Rupert and his inseparable friend have been watching and dogging all our movements for months past."

"This is awkward—very awkward," observed Greenwood. "However, Sir Rupert will not dare show his teeth against me, nor venture to give publicity to the affair."

"Because you hold his bill, with a forged acceptance, for one thousand pounds," said Lady Cecilia.

"Ah! he has told you that much—has he?" exclaimed Greenwood. "Well—you perceive, my dearest Cecilia, that he is completely in my power."

"The most remarkable part of the entire business," observed the lady, "is that I am actually deputed by Sir Rupert to negotiate the amicable settlement of the affair with you."

"Indeed!" cried Greenwood. "He could not have chosen a more charming plenipotentiary."

"His proposal is this:—you are to give up the acceptance, and he will sign any paper you choose to guarantee you against legal proceedings on his part."

"I do not see, fair ambassadress," said Greenwood, who did not treat the business with so much serious attention as Lady Cecilia had anticipated—"I do not see that I should benefit myself by such an arrangement. So long as the bill remains in my possession, it is impossible for Sir Rupert Harborough to commence civil proceedings against me, because he knows full well that were he to have process issued against me, I should that moment hand him over to the officers of justice."

"Then, for my sake, Mr. Greenwood," said Lady Cecilia, cruelly hurt by this cold calculation on the part of a man the slave of whose passions she had so completely been,—"for my sake, compromise this affair amicably."

"A thousand pounds is a large sum to fling into the street, my dear Cecilia," observed Greenwood.

"And suppose that, by some accident my husband should raise that amount and pay the bill—"

"It never was my intention to allow him to pay all," interrupted Greenwood. "I imagined that by threatening him, I should obtain five or six hundred on account, and I should still hold the bill for the balance. That balance I would not receive, were he to offer it, because by retaining the bill, I keep him in my power."

"Then, once again, for my sake—*for my sake,*" repeated Lady Cecilia, "consent to the proposal made to you this evening—settle the affair in an amicable manner."

"To oblige you, my dear Cecilia, I will assent to Sir Rupert Harborough's proposal. Let him draw up and sign a document in which he acknowledges that he has discovered the—the—"

"Criminal conversation between his wife and Mr. George Greenwood," said Cecilia: "we will not mince words in a negotiation of this kind," she added, ironically.

"Precisely," exclaimed Greenwood, coolly; "and that he has received full satisfaction for the same. In this manner the business can be disposed of to the satisfaction of all parties."

"To-morrow morning at eleven o'clock I will call with the paper," said Lady Cecilia.

"And I will give you up the forged bill," returned the Member of Parliament. "And now, my dear Cecilia, allow me to make an observation relative to the answer I sent you this evening to your little note. The truth is, that representing as I do an enlightened and independent constituency—"

"Pardon me," said Lady Cecilia, rising, "we will not talk of any other business until this most painful affair be settled."

The fair patrician lady then took her leave, and returned to her husband, who awaited Greenwood's decision in a state of the most painful suspense.

Cecilia communicated to him the particulars of the interview; and, ere he retired to rest, the baronet drew up the document which was to save himself by the compromise of his honour.

"So far, so good," said Sir Rupert, as he handed the paper to his wife. "I have now a proposal to make to you, Cecilia—and I have little doubt that you will accept it."

"Proceed," said Cecilia.

"After the explanation which has taken place between us this evening, it is impossible that we can ever entertain much respect for each other again. You know me to be a forger—I know you to be unfaithful to my bed. If it suits you, we will agree to live together beneath the same roof as hitherto—to have our separate apartments—to maintain an appearance of enjoying domestic tranquillity—and each to follow his own pursuits without leave or remonstrance on the part of the other. You will never interfere with me—I will never interfere with you. If you hear that I have a mistress, you will take no notice of it: if I know that you have a lover, I shall be equally blind and dumb. Does this please you?"

"Perfectly," answered Lady Cecilia. "Shall we commit this compact to writing?"

"Oh! with much pleasure," returned Sir Rupert. "I will draw up two agreements, embodying the conditions of our compact, immediately. You can retain one; and I will keep the other."

The baronet set to work, and, in a most business-like manner, wrote out the compact. He then read it to Lady Cecilia, who signified her approval of its terms. A counterpart was written; and the husband and wife signed the papers that released them from all the moral obligations of their marriage-vows!

They then retired to their separate apartments, better pleased with each other, perhaps, than they had been for a long—long time.

The reader need scarcely be informed that Lady Cecilia said nothing to her husband relative to the mysterious letter containing the Bank note for a thousand pounds.

On the following morning Lady Cecilia repaired to the abode of Mr. Greenwood. When she arrived in Spring Gardens, she found the street completely blocked up with a train of charity children—boys and girls, marshalled by the parish beadle, and accompanied by the schoolmaster and school-mistress. The girls were attired in their light blue dresses, plain straw bonnets, white collars, and pepper-and-salt coloured cloaks; and their arms, red with the cold, were only half covered with their coarse mittens. The boys wore their muffin caps, short coats, and knee-breeches; and each was embellished with a large tin plate, or species of medal, affixed like a badge of honour, to the breast. Their meagre countenances, their thin arms, and lanky legs, did not speak much in favour of the quantity of food which constituted their diurnal meals.

Lady Cecilia was conducted to the drawing-room by the Italian valet, who informed her that Mr. Greenwood would wait upon her the moment he had dismissed the charity children.

Lafleur, in the mean time threw open the door of the mansion, and admitted the procession into the spacious hall, after having kept the poor creatures shivering in the cold for nearly a quarter of an hour. The beadle took his station upon the steps, with awful dignity, and watched the boys and girls as they defiled past him in military order into the hall. It was very evident from the timid glances which the little scholars cast towards the countenance of this functionary, that they believed him to be one of the most important personages on the face of the earth; and perhaps they were even perplexed to decide, in their own minds, whether the parish beadle whom they saw before them, or Mr. Greenwood, M.P., whom they were about to see, was the greater man of the two.

At length the procession had entirely cleared the threshold of the mansion, and then only did the beadle enter. He doffed his enormous cocked hat out of respect to the owner of the dwelling in which he now found himself, and made his long staff ring upon the marble pavement of the hall with a din that electrified the children and called looks of solemn importance to the countenances of the schoolmaster and mistress.

In a few moments a side door opened, and Mr. Greenwood appeared.

The beadle struck his stick upon the hall floor once more; and the children, duly tutored to obey the signal, saluted the great man, the girls with low curtseys, and the boys by doffing their muffin caps, bobbing their heads forward, and kicking back their left legs.

"Well, Mr. Muffles," said the Member of Parliament to the beadle, with one of his usual affable smiles; "brought your little family—eh?"

"These children, sir," responded Muffles in a self-sufficient and important tone, glancing at the same time in a patronising manner upon the groups of juveniles around—"these children, sir, has come, as in dooty bounden, to hoffer up the hincense of their most gratefullest thanks to you, sir, as their kind paytron which supplied 'em with pea-soup, blankets, and religious tracts, to keep their bodies and souls both warm and comfortable, as one may say."

"I am delighted, Mr. Muffles," replied the Member of Parliament, in a most condescending manner, "to receive this little mark of gratitude on the part of those for whom I entertain a deep interest, and I am the more pleased because this visit on their part was quite spontaneous, and on mine totally unlooked for."

Mr. Greenwood did not think it necessary to state his knowledge that the whole affair had been got up by Lafleur, in obedience to his own commands.

"Representing as I do," continued Mr. Greenwood, "an enlightened, independent, and important constituency, I cannot do otherwise than feel interested in the welfare of the rising generation; and when I glance upon the happy countenances of these dear children, I thank God for having given me the means to contribute my mite towards the maintenance of the schools of the parish wherein I have the honour to reside."

Mr. Muffles' stick was here rapped upon the floor with tremendous violence; and the boys and girls immediately burst forth into shrill cries of "Hear! hear!"

When silence was once more restored, the beadle in due form presented the schoolmaster and school-mistress to Mr. Greenwood.

"This gen'leman, sir," said the parish functionary, "is Mr. Twiggs, the parochial perceptor—as worthy a man, sir, as ever broke bread. He's bin in his present sitivation thirteen year come Janivary—"

"Febivary, Mr. Muffles," said the schoolmaster, mildly correcting the beadle.

"Oh! Febivary, be it, Mr. Twiggs?" exclaimed the parish authority. "And this, sir, is Mrs. Twiggs, a lady well known for her excellent qualities in teaching them blessed young gals, and taking care o' their linen."

"Delighted to see your scholars looking so well, Mr. Twiggs," said Greenwood, bowing to the master: "quite charmed, Mrs. Twiggs, to behold the healthy and neat appearance of your girls," he added, bowing to the mistress.

"Would you be kind enough, sir," said Mr. Twiggs, in a meek and fawning tone, "to question any of them lads on any pint of edication?"

"Perhaps I might as well, Mr. Twiggs," returned Greenwood; "in case I should ever have to allude to the subject in the House of Commons."

The mere idea of any mention of the parochial school being made in Parliament, produced such an impression upon the beadle that he banged his staff most earnestly on the hall floor; and the children, taking it for a signal which they had been previously tutored to observe, again yelled forth "Hear! Hear!"

"Silence!" thundered Mr. Muffles; and the vociferations instantly ceased.

"Now, my boy," said Mr. Greenwood, addressing the one who stood nearest to him, "I will ask you a question or two. What is your name?"

"Jem Blister, sir," was the prompt reply.

"James Blister—eh? Well—who gave you that name?"[1]

"Father and mother, please, sir."

"Blister, for shame!" ejaculated Mr. Twiggs, with a terrific frown: then, by way of prompting the lad, he said, "*My Godfathers and—*"

"*My Godfathers and Godmother in my baptism,*" hastily cried the boy, catching at the hint; and after a pause, he added, "*I mean an outward and wisible sign of an inward—*"

"Blister, I am raly ashamed of you!" again exclaimed Mr. Twiggs. "Stand back, sir; and let the boy behind you stand for'ard."

Another urchin stepped forth from the rank, and stood, blushing up to his very hair, and fumbling about with his cap, in the presence of Mr. Greenwood.

"My good boy," said the Member of Parliament, condescendingly patting him upon the head, "what is *your* name?"

"M. or N. as the case may be, please, sir," replied the boy.[2]

"I should observe, sir," said the schoolmaster, "that this lad only began his Catechism yesterday."

"Oh very well, Mr. Twiggs," exclaimed Greenwood: "that accounts for his answer! I will ask him something else, then. My good lad, who was Adam?"

"The fust man, sir."

"Very good, my boy. And who was Eve?"

"The fust 'ooman, sir."

"Very good indeed," repeated Mr. Greenwood. "Now tell me what is the capital of England?"

"This boy is not in geography, sir," said Mr. Twiggs. "He's jest begun cyphering."

"Oh very good. Can you say your multiplication table, my boy?"

---

1 The reference is to the Catechism in the 1660 *Book of Common Prayer*.

2 The Catechism in the *Book of Common Prayer* begins: "What is your name?" and the answer is given in the form, "N. or M." This stands supposedly for "Nicholas or Mary," as being the commonest boy's and girl's name of the time; but the real reason is a mystery.

"Twice one's two; twice two's three; twice three's eight; twice four's ten; twice five's fourteen—"

The boy was rattling on at a furious pace, when the ominous voice of Mr. Twiggs ejaculated, "Garlick, I am ashamed of you!"

And Master Garlick began to cry most piteously.

"Come, it is not so bad, though," said Mr. Greenwood, by way of soothing the discomfited schoolmaster and restoring the abashed beadle to confidence; "he evidently knows his Bible very well—and that is the essential."

The Member of Parliament then delivered himself of a long harangue in favour of a sound religious education and in praise of virtue; and thus ended the solemn farce.

The great man bowed and withdrew: the beadle rapped his staff upon the floor; Lafleur opened the door; and the procession filed slowly out of the mansion.

Mr. Greenwood, having thus gone through a ceremony an account of which was to appear in the papers on the following morning, hurried up to the drawing-room where Lady Cecilia awaited him.

"My dear Cecilia," he exclaimed, as he entered the room, "a thousand pardons for keeping you; but the fact is that the position in which an intelligent and independent constituency has placed me, entails upon me duties—"

"A truce to that absurdity with me," interrupted the baronet's wife, in a more peremptory tone than Mr. Greenwood had ever yet heard her use. "I am come according to appointment to settle a most unpleasant business. Here is my husband's acknowledgment, drawn up as you desired: please to deliver up to me the bill."

Mr. Greenwood ran his eye over the document, and appeared satisfied. He then drew forth the bill from his pocket-book, and handed it to Lady Cecilia.

There was a flush upon the lady's delicately pale countenance; and her eyes sparkled with unusual vivacity. She was dressed in a very neat, but plain and simple manner; and Mr. Greenwood fancied that she had never seemed so interesting before.

As he delivered the bill into her keeping, he took her hand and endeavoured to convey it to his lips.

She drew back with an air of offended dignity, which would have well become a lady that had never surrendered herself to the pleasures of an illicit love.

"No, Mr. Greenwood," she said, in a firm, and even haughty tone: "all *that* is ended between you and me. You are a heartless man, who cannot appreciate the warmth with which a confiding woman yields herself up to you;—you have treated me—the daughter of a peer—like a pensioned mistress. But I let that now pass:—I have made you acquainted with the nature of my thoughts—and I am satisfied."

"I am at a loss to understand how I should have deserved these harsh words, Cecilia," replied Greenwood, with a somewhat supercilious smile; "but perhaps my inability to supply you with the means of gratifying your extravagances has given you offence."

"Your cool indifference of late has indeed given me a bitter lesson," said Lady Cecilia.

"And yet I manifested every disposition to serve you, madam," rejoined Greenwood haughtily, "when I consented to compromise your husband's felony."

"Yes—you generously abandoned your claim to a thousand pounds," exclaimed Cecilia, with cutting irony, "in order to hush up an intrigue with the wife of the man whom you had inveigled into your net. But think not, Mr. Greenwood, that I attempt to justify my husband's conduct: I know him to be a heartless—a bad—an unprincipled man; and yet Mr. Greenwood, I do not conceive that *you* would shine the more resplendently by being placed in contrast with *him*. One word more. Had you refused to deliver up that bill, I was prepared to pay it. Some unknown friend had heard of this transaction—heaven alone knows how; and that friend forwarded last evening the means wherewith to liquidate this debt. Here is the letter which contained a Bank-note for a thousand pounds: it fell into my hands, and my husband knows naught concerning it;—can you say whose writing that is?"

Greenwood glanced hastily at the letter, and exclaimed, "Yes—I know that writing well—Mrs. Arlington is your husband's generous friend!"

"Mrs. Arlington!" exclaimed Cecilia: "Oh!—now I recollect that rumour points to that woman as having once been my husband's mistress."

"The same," said Greenwood, struck by this noble act on the part of the fair one whom he himself had first seduced from the paths of virtue.

"It would now be difficult to decide," observed Cecilia, in a tone of profound contempt, "which has acted the more noble part—the late mistress of his Rupert Harborough, or the late lover of his wife."

Greenwood only answered with a satirical curl of the lip.

Lady Cecilia rose from her seat, bowed coldly to the capitalist, and withdrew.

Thus terminated the amours of the man of the world and the lady of fashion—ending, as such illicit loves usually do, in a quarrel.

But the reader must not suppose that the same sentiments of pride which had thus induced Lady Cecilia to break off abruptly a connexion which her paramour had been for some time dissolving by degrees, influenced her in the use to which she appropriated the handsome sum supplied for an especial purpose by Mrs. Arlington. The lady knew no compunction in this respect, and she therefore devoted the thousand pounds so generously forwarded by her husband's late mistress, to her own wants!

* * * * * * *

The Italian valet had overheard the entire conversation between Lady Cecilia Harborough and Mr. Greenwood, which we have just described.

In the course of the day the whole details of that interview were communicated to Mrs. Arlington, who thus learnt that Lady Cecilia had intercepted the money intended for Sir Rupert Harborough, and had settled the forged bill without being compelled to disburse it.

CHAPTER XCVII.

ANOTHER NEW YEAR'S DAY.

It was the 1st of January, 1840.

The tide of Time rolls on with the same unvarying steadiness of motion, wearing off the asperities of barbarism, as the great flood of ocean smooths the sharp edges of rugged rocks.

But as the seasons glide away, vainly may we endeavour to throw a veil upon the past;—vainly do we lament, when Winter comes, that our Spring-dreams should be faded and gone, too beautiful to endure;—vainly, vainly do we pray that the waves of a Lethean sea may overwhelm the memories of those years when Time cast flowers from his brow, and diamonds from his wing!

Time looks down upon the world from the heights of the Pyramids of Egypt; and, as he surveys the myriad cities of the universe swarming with life,—marks the mighty armies of all states, ready to exterminate and kill,—views the navies of great powers riding over every sea,—as he beholds all these, Time chuckles, for he knows that they are his own!

For the day must come when the Pyramids themselves, the all but immortal children of antiquity, shall totter and fall; and Time shall triumph over even these.

The strongest edifices crumble into dust, and the power of the mightiest nations fritters into shreds, beneath the hand of Time.

The glories of Sesostris are now a vague dream—the domination of Greece and Rome has become an uncertain vision: the heroes of the Crusades have long since mouldered in the earth;—the crescent of the Ottomans menaces Christendom no more: the armadas of Spain are extinct;—the thrones that Napoleon raised are cast down: of the millions that he led to conquest, during his meteor-like career, what numbers have left this busy scene for ever; and how varied are the climes in which they have found their graves!

Oh, Time! what is there that can strive with thee—thou that art the expression of the infinite existence of God himself!

Alas! if Time were a spirit endowed with intellect to comprehend, and feelings to sympathise, how would he sorrow over the woes of that human existence, which has now occupied nearly sixty centuries!

Year after year rolls away; and yet how slowly does civilization accomplish its task of improving the condition of the sons and daughters of toil.

For in the present day, as it was in the olden time, the millions labour to support the few, and the few continue to monopolize the choicest fruits of the earth.

The rights of labour are denied; and the privileges of birth and wealth are dominant.

And ever, when the millions, bowed down by care, and crushed with incessant hardships, raise the voice of anguish to their taskmasters, the cry is, *"Toil! toil!"*

And when the poor labourer, with the sweat standing in large drops upon his brow, points to his half-starved wife and little ones, and demands that increase of his wages which will enable him to feed them adequately, and clothe them comfortably, the only response that meets his ears is still, *"Toil! toil!"*

And when the mechanic, pale and emaciated, droops over his loom, and in a faint tone beseeches that his miserable pittance may be turned into a fair remuneration for that hard and unceasing work which builds up the fortunes of his employer, the answer to his pathetic prayer is, *"Toil! toil!"*

And when the miner, who spends his best days in the bowels of the earth, hewing the hard mineral in dark subterranean caves at the peril of his life, and in positions which cramp his limbs, contract his chest, and early prostrate his energies beyond relief,—when *he* exalts his voice from those hideous depths, and demands the settlement of labour's rights upon a just basis, the only echo to his petition is, *"Toil! toil!"*

Yes—it is ever *"Toil! toil!"* for the millions, while the few repose on downy couches, feed upon the luxuries of the land and water, and move from place to place in sumptuous equipages!

It was the 1st of January, 1840.

Another New Year's Day—commemorated with feasting by those who had no reason to repine, but marked as the opening of another weary epoch of care and sorrow by those who had nothing for which to be grateful, either to heaven or to man!

The first day of January, 1840, was inclement and severe. The air was piercing cold, and the rain fell in torrents. The streets of the great metropolis were swept by a wintery wind that chased the poor houseless wanderers beneath the coverings of arches and doorways, and sent the shivering mendicants to implore an asylum at the workhouse.

It was evening; and the lamps diffused but an uncertain light in the great thoroughfares. The courts and alleys of the poor neighbourhoods were enveloped in almost total darkness; for every shutter was closed, and where there were no shutters, blinds were drawn down, or rags were stretched across the windows, to expel the bitter cold.

We must now request our readers to accompany us to a district of London, which is most probably altogether unknown to the aristocrat, even by name, and with which many of that class whose occupations lead them into an intimate acquaintance with the metropolis, are by no means familiar.

Situate to the east of Bethnal Green,—bounded on the north by Bonner's Fields, on the south by the Mile End Road, and on the east by the Regent's Canal,—and intersected by the line of the Eastern Counties Railway, is an assemblage of narrow streets and filthy lanes, bearing the denomination of Globe Town.

When compared with even the worst districts of the metropolis,—when placed in contrast with Saint Giles's or Saffron Hill,—Globe Town still appears a sink of human misery which civilization, in its progress, has forgotten to visit.

The majority of the streets are unpaved, rugged, and broken. The individual who traverses them in the summer is blinded by the dust, or disgusted by heaps of putrescent offal, the rotting remains of vegetables and filth of every description, which meet the eye at short intervals; and, in winter, he wallows, knee-deep, in black mud and stagnant water. But even in the summer itself, and in the very midst of the dog-days, there are swamps of mire in many of the streets of Globe Town, which exhale a nauseating and sickly odour, like that of decomposing dead bodies.

In the winter time Globe Town is a complete marsh. Lying low, in the vicinity of the canal, and on a naturally swampy soil, the district is unhealthy in the extreme. Nor do its inhabitants endeavour, by any efforts of their own, to mitigate the consequences of these local disadvantages. They seem, for the most part, to cling with a sort of natural tenacity, to their rags and filth. Perhaps it is the bitterness of their poverty which makes them thus neglectful of the first duties of cleanliness: perhaps their pinching indigence reduces them to a state of despair that allows them no spirit and no heart to do any thing that may conduce to their comfort. Whatever be the cause, it is nevertheless a fact that, with the exception of one or two streets, Globe Town is a district which necessity alone could compel a person of cleanly habits and domestic propriety to reside in.

And yet Globe Town contains streets delighting in aristocratic names. There is Grosvenor Place, in which a carriage and pair would have some trouble to turn; there is Parade Street, where a corporal's guard could not find space to manœuvre; there is Park Street, whose most gorgeous establishment is the sign of a mangle; there is Chester

Place, formed by two rows of miserable shops; and, there are Essex Street and Digby Street, where single men may obtain lodgings at the rate of threepence a night.

How strange is this affection for fine names to distinguish horrible neighbourhoods! In the lowest parts of Whitechapel we find Pleasant Row, Queen Street, Flower Street, Duke Street, and Rose Lane. In Bethnal Green, a place inhabited by the poorest of the poor is denominated Silver Street; and, in the same district, a filthy thoroughfare is christened Pleasant Street.

Globe Town and its immediate vicinity abound in cemeteries. To the north there is the Eastern London Cemetery; and to the south there are two Jews' burial grounds, and two other places of sepulture. With the exception of the first-mentioned one, which has only been recently opened, and is a large airy space neatly planted with shrubs, those cemeteries are so crowded with the remains of mortality, that it is impossible to drive a spade into the ground without striking against human bones.

When you once merge from the Cambridge Road, pass the new church in Bethnal Green, and plunge into Globe Town, it seems as if you had left London altogether,—as if you were no longer within the limits of the metropolis, but had suddenly dropped from the clouds into a strange village strangely peopled. You encounter but few persons in the streets; and those whom you do meet are, for the most part, squalid, emaciated, pale, and drooping. The only sounds of mirth which meet your ear, emanate from the casements of the public-houses, or from the urchins that play half-naked in the mud. With these exceptions, Globe Town is silent, gloomy, and sombre.

The shop-windows are indicative of the poverty of the inhabitants. The butcher's shed displays a few slices of liver stretched upon a board, sheep's heads of no very inviting appearance, and hearts, lungs, and lights, all hanging together, like a Dutch clock with its weights against a wall. The poor make stews of this offal. The fish-stalls present "for public competition," as George Robins would say, nothing but the most coarse and the cheapest articles—such as huge Dutch plaice, haddocks, &c. In the season the itinerant venders of fresh-herrings and sprats drive a good trade in Globe Town. In a word, every thing in that district denotes poverty—poverty—nothing but pinching poverty.

The inhabitants of Globe Town are of two kinds; being weavers, and persons who earn their livelihood by working at the docks or on the canal, on the one hand; and thieves, prostitutes, and vagrants, on the other. When a burglar or a pickpocket finds St. Giles's, Clerkenwell, the Mint, or Bethnal Green too hot to hold him, he betakes himself to Globe Town, where he buries himself in some obscure garret until the storms that menaced him be blown over. Globe Town has thus acquired amongst the fraternity of rogues of all classes, the expressive denomination of the "Happy Valley."

In one of the narrowest, dirtiest, and most lonely streets at the eastern extremity of Globe Town, there was a house of an appearance more dilapidated than the rest. It was only two storeys high, and was built in a very singular manner. From the very threshold of the front door a precipitate staircase, more nearly resembling a ladder, led to the upper apartments; so that when any one entered that house from the street, he had to thread no passage nor corridor, but immediately began to ascend those steep steps. The staircase led to a landing, from which two doors opened into small, dirty, and dark chambers. These rooms had a door of communication pierced in the wall that separated them; but there were no stairs leading down into the lower apartments of the house. The only way of obtaining access to the rooms on the ground-floor, was by means of a door up an alley leading from the street, and running along one side of the house into a court formed by other dwellings. Thus the upper and lower parts of this strange building might be said to constitute two distinct tenements. The windows of the ground-floor rooms were darkened with shutters, at the upper part of which holes in the shape of hearts had been cut to admit a few straggling rays of light.

The rooms on the upper floor were furnished in a tolerably comfortable manner; but every article was wretchedly begrimed with dirt. The front apartment served as a sitting-room for the inmates of this strangely-built house; and the back chamber was fitted up as a bed-room.

It was evening, as we before said; and thick curtains were drawn over the two windows of the front-room to which we have alluded. A candle with a long flaring wick, stood upon the table. On a good fire a kettle was just beginning to boil. The table was set out with glasses, bottles, sugar, lemons, pipes, and tobacco. The inmates of that room were evidently preparing for a carouse, while the rain beat in torrents, against the windows, and the wind swept down the street like a hurricane.

But who *were* the inmates of that room?

We will proceed to inform our readers.

Lolling in an arm-chair, the covering of which was torn in many places, and spotted all over with grease, was a female, who in reality had scarcely numbered five-and-twenty years, but to whom the ravages of dissipation and evil passions gave the appearance of five-and-thirty. She had once been good-looking; and her features still retained the traces of beauty: but there was a deep blue tint, beneath the eyes, which joined the dark thick brows, and thus seemed to inclose the orbs themselves in a dingy circle. The faded cheeks were coloured with rouge; but the dye had been so clumsily plastered on, that the effect could not deceive the most ignorant in such matters. This woman wore a faded light silk gown, cut very low in front, and disclosing a considerable portion of a thin and shrivelled neck. In a word, she had the air of being what she really was—a faded courtezan of a low order. Her proper name was Margaret Flathers; but her acquaintance, for brevity's sake, called her Meg; and, in addition to these appellations, the name of *The Rattlesnake* had been conferred upon her, from the circumstance that she was fond of dressing in silks or satins, which she had a habit of rustling as much as possible when she walked.

On the other side of the fire-place was seated a man of cadaverous countenance, which was over-shadowed by a quantity of tangled black hair, and whose expression was vile and sinister to a degree.

"Half-past eight," said the woman, glancing towards a huge silver-watch which hung by a faded blue riband to a nail over the mantel.

"Yes—they can't be long now," returned her companion, who was no other than the Resurrection Man. "But because they're late, Meg, it's no reason why we shouldn't have a drop of blue ruin. The night's precious cold; and the kettle's just on the boil. Pour out the daffy, Meg."

The woman drew two tumblers towards her, and half filled each with gin. She then added sugar and lemon; and in a few moments the Resurrection Man poured the boiling element upon the liquor.

"Good, isn't it, Tony?" said the Rattlesnake.

"Capital, Meg. You're an excellent girl to judge of the proportions in a glass of lush."

"And I think, Tony," said the woman coaxingly, "that you have had no reason to complain of me in other respects. Twelve months all but a few days that we've been together, and I have done all I could to make you comfortable."

"And so you ought," answered the Resurrection Man. "Didn't I take you out of the street and make an independent lady of you? Ain't you the mistress of this crib of mine? and don't you live upon the fat of the land?"

"Very true, Tony," said the Rattlesnake. "But what would you have done without me? When that business took place down by the Bird-cage Walk, and you was obliged to come and hide yourself in the Happy Valley, you wanted some one you could rely upon to go out and buy your things, take care of the place, and get information whether the blue-bottles had fallen on any scent."

"All right, my girl," cried the Resurrection Man. "I *did* want such a person, and the moment after I escaped that night when I blew the old crib up, I went to you and told you just what I required. You agreed to come and live with me, and I agreed to treat you well. We have both kept our bargain; and I am satisfied if you are."

"Oh! you know I am, Tony dear," exclaimed the Rattlesnake. "But sometimes you have been so cross and quarrelsome, that I didn't know what to make of it."

"And was there no excuse, Meg?" cried the Resurrection Man. "Did I not see my old mother and the Cracksman perish before my very eyes—and by my own hand too? But I do not accuse myself of having wilfully caused their death. There was no help for it. We should have all three been taken to Newgate, and never have come out of the jug again but twice—once to be tried, and the second time to be hung."

"Could they have proved any thing against you?" demanded the Rattlesnake.

"Yes, Meg," answered the Resurrection Man—"there was a stiff 'un in the front room at the very moment when the police broke into the house. We had burked him on the preceding evening; and he was still hanging head downwards to the ceiling."

"It was much better, then, to blow the place up, as you did," observed the Rattlesnake.

"Of course it was, Meg. Don't you see," continued the Resurrection Man, after a pause, during which he imbibed a considerable quantity of the exhilarating fluid in his glass,—"don't you see that I was too old a bird not to be always prepared for such an event as that which happened at last? I had got together a great quantity of gunpowder in the back-room of the crib, and had stowed it away in brown paper parcels in a cupboard. This cupboard stood between the fire-place and the back wall of the house. So I had made a hole through the wall, and had introduced a long iron pipe into the cupboard. This pipe was ten or twelve feet in length, and ran all along the wall that divided my yard from the next. The pipe, so placed, was protected by a wooden cover or case; and any one who saw it, must have thought it was only a water-pipe. It was, however, filled with excellent gunpowder, and there was nothing to do but to put a match to the farthest end of the pipe to blow up the whole place."

"Capital contrivance!" exclaimed the Rattlesnake. "Had you put up that pipe long before the police broke into the house?"

"Oh! yes—some months," answered the Resurrection Man; "and very lucky it was, too, that the pipe was water-tight, so that the rain had never moistened the powder in the least. Well, when the bluebottles broke in, I rushed into the back-room, locked the door, leapt through the window, flew to the end of the pipe, tore out the plug, applied the match, and in a moment all was over."

"And for a long time even your old pals at the Boozing-ken on Saffron Hill, fancied you had been blown up with the rest," said the Rattlesnake.

"Of course they did, because the newspapers, which you always used to go and fetch me to read, said there was no doubt that every one of the gang in the house at the time had perished."

"And they also spoke of the way in which the police had followed you and the Cracksman to the house," said the Rattlesnake.

"Yes—and that was how I came to learn that the man who had hunted me almost to death, was Richard Markham," exclaimed the Resurrection Man, his countenance suddenly wearing an expression of such concentrated—vile—malignant rage, as to render him perfectly hideous.

"Now don't begin to brood over that," cried the Rattlesnake hastily; "for I am almost afraid of you when you get into one of those humours, dear Tony."

"No—I shan't give way now," said the villain: "I have prepared the means for revenge; and then I shall be happy. Ah! Meg, you cannot conceive how I gloated over the wretch the other night when I denounced him in the theatre! That man has been the means of making me stay in this infernal prison—for it has been nothing better—for weeks and months; he was the cause of the loss of my best friend, the Cracksman, and of my old mother, who was very useful in her way: and he prevented me from getting that young fellow into my power, who went and explored the Palace. When I think of all that I have suffered through this infernal Richard Markham, I am ready to go mad;—and I should have gone mad, too, if it hadn't been that I always thought the day of vengeance would come!"

"And my little attentions helped to console you, Tony," said the Rattlesnake, in a wheedling manner that seemed peculiar to her.

"Oh! as for that, Meg, a man like me can be consoled by nothing short of revenge in such a case. I have told you the history of my life over and over again; and I think you must have learnt from it, that I am not a person to put up with an injury. I have often thought of doing to Markham as I did to the justice of the peace and the baronet—setting his house on fire; but then he might not learn who was the incendiary, or he might even think that it was an accident. My object is for him to know who strikes him, that he may writhe the more."

"And do you think that the Buffer and Moll are to be depended upon?" asked Margaret Flathers.

"To the back-bone," replied the Resurrection Man. "How could the Buffer possibly betray *me*, when *he* was one of the gang, as the newspapers called it? Besides, wasn't he laid by the heels in Clerkenwell Gaol for making away with the bantling to cheat the Burying Society? and didn't he escape? How could he go and place himself in contact with the police by giving information against me? And what good would it be to him to deceive me? He knows that I have got plenty of tin, and can pay him well. Indeed, how has he lived in the Happy Valley for the last eleven months and more, since he escaped out of Clerkenwell? Haven't I been as good as a brother to him, and lent him money over and over again?"

"Very true," said the Rattlesnake. "I only spoke on your account."

"I shall be able to let the Buffer in for several good things, now that I am determined to commence an active life again," continued the Resurrection Man. "I have been idle quite long enough; and I am not going to remain so any more. Why, Greenwood alone ought to be as good as an annuity to me. He can always find employment for a skilful and daring fellow like me."

"And he pays like a prince, doesn't he?" demanded the Rattlesnake.

"Like a prince," repeated the Resurrection Man. "Five guineas the other night for just attending the carrying off of the young actress. That is the way to make money, Meg."

"And you have got plenty, Tony, I know?" said the woman, in a tone more than half interrogatively, and only partially expressing a conviction.

"What's that to you?" cried the Resurrection Man, brutally; at the same time eyeing his mistress in a somewhat suspicious manner.

"Oh! only because you needn't have any secrets from me, Tony," returned the Rattlesnake, affecting a tone of indifference. "You have been out every night lately—and only for a short time—"

"Now I tell you what it is, Meg," exclaimed Tidkins, striking his fist upon the table, "you have asked me about my money a great many times lately; and I tell you very candidly, I don't like it. It looks suspicious; but, by heavens! if you attempt to play me false—"

"Why should you say that, Tony? Have I not given you every proof of fidelity?"

"Yes—you have; or else I should have known what to do in a very few moments. But why do you bother yourself about the money that I have got? It is very little, I can tell you; but where it is, it's safe enough; and if I ever catch you attempting to follow me or spy upon me when I go into the rooms down stairs, I'll make you repent it."

"Now, Tony dear, don't put yourself into a passion," said the Rattlesnake, turning pale, and assuming her usual wheedling tone: "I didn't mean to annoy you. All that I wanted to know was whether there was a chance of running short or not."

"Don't frighten yourself, Meg," returned the Resurrection Man. "Whenever I run low, I know how to get more. And now, that we mayn't have to talk upon this subject again, recollect once for all that I won't have you prying into any thing that I choose to keep to myself. You know that I am not a man to be trifled with; and if any one was to betray me—I don't mean to say that you ever had such an idea—I only mean you to understand that if anybody *did*—"

"Well—what?" said the Rattlesnake in a tone of alarm.

"I would not be taken alive," added the Resurrection Man; "and those who came to take me at all, would probably travel the same road that the police, the Cracksman, and the Mummy have gone already."

"Tony," exclaimed the woman, a deadly pallor overspreading her countenance, "you don't mean to say that this house is provided with a pipe like the one—"

"I don't mean to say any thing at all about it,—one way or another," interrupted the Resurrection Man coolly. "All I want you to do is to remain quiet—attend to my wishes—keep a close tongue in your head—and have no eyes for any thing that I don't tell you to look at,—and then we shall go on as pleasant as before. Otherwise—"

At this moment a knock at the street door was heard.

The Rattlesnake hastened to answer the summons, and returned accompanied by the Buffer and his wife.

CHAPTER XCVIII.

DARK PLOTS AND SCHEMES.

The Buffer was one of the most unmitigated villains that ever disgraced the name of man. There was no species of crime with which he was not familiar; and he had a suitable helpmate in his wife, who was the sister of Dick Flairer—a character that disappeared from the stage of life in the early part of this history.

In person, the Buffer was slight, short, and rather well-made,—extremely active, and endowed with great physical power. His countenance was by no means an index to his mind; for it was inexpressive, stolid, and vacant.

His wife was a woman of about five-and-twenty, being probably ten years younger than her husband. She was not precisely ugly; but her countenance—the very reverse of that of the Buffer—was so indicative of every evil passion that can possibly disgrace womanhood, as to be almost repulsive.

The two new-comers seated themselves near the fire, for their clothes were dripping with the rain, which continued to pour in torrents. The warmth of the apartment and a couple of glasses of smoking grog soon, however, put them into good humour and made them comfortable; and the Resurrection Man then proposed that they should "proceed to business."

"In the first place, Jack," said the Resurrection Man, addressing himself to the Buffer, "what news about Markham?"

"He will attend to the appointment," was the answer.

"He will?" exclaimed the Resurrection Man, as if the news were almost too good to be true: "you are sure?"

"As sure as I am that I've got this here glass in my mawley," said the Buffer.

"To-morrow night?"

"To-morrow night he'll meet his brother at Twig Folly," answered the Buffer, with a laugh.

"Tell me all that took place," cried the Resurrection Man; "and then I shall be able to judge for myself."

"As you told me," began the Buffer, "I made myself particklerly clean and tidy, and went up to Holloway this morning at about eleven o'clock. I knocked at the door of the swell's crib; and an old butler-like looking feller, with a port-wine face, and a white napkin under his arm, came and opened it. He asked me what my business was. I said I wanted to speak to Mr. Markham in private. He asked me to walk in; and he showed me into a library kind of a place, where I see a good-looking young feller sitting reading. He was very pale, and seemed as if he'd been ill."

"Fretting about that business at the theatre, no doubt," observed the Resurrection Man.

"What business?" cried the Buffer.

"No matter—go on."

"Well—so I went into this library and see Mr. Markham. The old servant left us alone together. 'What do you want with me, my good man?' says Markham in a very pleasant tone of voice.—'I have summut exceeding partickler to say to you, sir,' says I.—'Well, what is it?' he asks.—'Have you heerd from your brother lately, sir?' says I, throwing out the feeler you put me up to. If so be he had said he had, and I saw that he really knew where he was, and every thing about him, I should have invented some excuse, and walked myself off; but there was no need of that; for the moment I mentioned his brother, he was quite astonished.—'My brother!' he says in a wery excited tone: 'many years has elapsed since I heard from him. Do you know what has becomed on him?'—'Perhaps I knows a trifle about him, sir,' says I; 'and what is wery trifling indeed. In a word,' I says, 'he wants to see you.'—'He wants to see me!' cries my gentleman: 'then why doesn't he come to me? But where is he? tell me, that I may fly to him.'—So then I says, 'The fact of the matter is this, sir; your brother has got his-self into a bit of a scrape, and don't dare show. He's living down quite in the east of London, close by the Regent's Canal; and he has sent me to say that if so be you'll meet him to-morrow night at ten o'clock at Twig Folly, he'll be there.'—Then Mr. Markham cries out, 'But why can I not go to him now? if he is in distress or difficulty, the sooner he sees me the better.'—'Softly, sir,' says I. 'All I know of the matter is this, that I'm a honest man as airns his livelihood by running on messages and doing odd jobs. A gentleman meets me on the bank of the canal, close by Twig Folly, very early this morning and says, '*Do you want to airn five shillings?*' Of course I says '*Yes.*'—'*Then,*' says the gentleman, '*go up to Markham Place without delay, and ask to see Mr. Markham. He lives at Holloway. Tell him that you come from his brother, who is in trouble, and can't go to him; but that his brother will meet him to-morrow night at ten o'clock on the banks of the canal, near Twig Folly. And,*' says the gentleman, '*if he should ask you for a token that you're tellin' the truth, say that this appointment must be kept instead of the one on the top of the hill where two ash trees stands planted.*'—Well, the moment I tells Mr. Markham all this, he begins to blubber, and then to laugh, and to dance about the room, crying, 'Oh! my dear—dear brother, shall I then embrace you so soon again?' and suchlike nonsense. Then he gives me half a sovereign his-self, and sends me into the kitchen, where the cook makes me eat and drink till I was well-nigh ready to bust. The old butler was rung for; and I've no doubt that his master told him the good news, for when he come back into the kitchen, he treated me with the greatest civility, but asked me a lot of questions about *Master Eugene*, as he called him. I satisfied him in all ways; and at last I rises, takes my leave of the servants, and comes off."

"Well done!" cried the Resurrection Man, whose cadaverous countenance wore an expression of superlative satisfaction. "And you do not think he entertained the least suspicion?"

"Not a atom," returned the Buffer.

"Nor the old butler?" asked the Resurrection Man.

"Not a bit. But do jest satisfy me on one point, Tony; how come you to know that anythink about this young feller's brother would produce such a powerful excitement?"

"Have I not before told you that this Richard Markham was a fellow-prisoner with me in Newgate some four years and more ago? Well, I often overheard him talking about his affairs to another man that was also there, and whose name was Armstrong. Markham and this Armstrong were very thick together; and Markham spoke quite openly to him about his family matters, his brother, and one thing or another. That's the way I came to hear of the strange appointment made between the two brothers."

"Well, there's no doubt that the fish has bit and can be hooked to-morrow night," said the Buffer.

"Yes—he is within my reach—and now I shall be revenged," exclaimed the Resurrection Man, grinding his teeth together. "I will tell you my plans in this respect presently," he added. "Let us now talk about the old man that your wife nurses."

"Or *did* nurse, rather," cried Moll, with a coarse laugh.

Both the Resurrection Man and Margaret Flathers turned a glance of inquiry and surprise upon the Buffer's wife.

"The old fellow's dead," she added, after a moment's pause.

"Dead already!" exclaimed Tidkins.

"Just as I tell you," answered Moll. "He seemed very sinking and low this morning; and so I was more attentive to him than ever."

"But the money?" said the Resurrection Man.

"All a dream on her part," cried the Buffer, sulkily, pointing towards his wife.

"Now don't you go for to throw all the blame on me, Jack," retorted the woman; "for you know as well as I do that you was as sanguine as me. And who wouldn't have taken him for an old miser? Here you and me," she continued, addressing herself to her husband, "go to hire a lodging in a house in Smart Street, about three months ago, and we find out that there's an old chap living overhead, on the first floor, who had been there three months before that time, and had always lived in the same regular, quiet way—never going out except after dusk, doing nothing to earn his bread, paying his way, and owing nobody a penny. Then he was dressed in clothes that wasn't worth sixpence, and yet he had gold to buy others if he chose, because he used to change a sovereign every week, when he paid his rent. Well, all these things put together, made me think he was a miser, and had a store somewhere or another; and when I said to you——"

"I know what you said, fast enough," interrupted the Buffer, sulkily: "what's the use of telling us all this over again?"

"Just to show that if I was deceived, you was too. But it's always the way with you: when any thing turns out wrong, you throw the blame on me. Didn't you say to me, when the old fellow was took ill a month ago: '*Moll*,' says you, '*go and offer your services to nurse the old gentleman; and may be if he dies he'll leave you something; or at all events you may worm out of him the secret of where he keeps his money, and we can get hold of it all the same.*' That's what you said—and so I did go and nurse the old man; and he seemed very grateful, for at last he began to like me almost as much as he did his snuff-box—and that's saying a great deal, considering the quantity of snuff he used to take, and the good it seemed to do him when he was low and melancholy."

"Well—what's the use of you and the Buffer wrangling?" cried the Resurrection Man. "Tell us all about the old fellow's death."

"As I was saying just now," continued Moll, "the old gentleman was took wery bad this morning soon after Jack left to go up to Holloway; and the landlady, Mrs. Smith, insisted on sending for a doctor. The old gentleman shook his head, when he heard Mrs. Smith say so, and seemed wery much annoyed at the idea of having a medical visit. But Mrs. Smith was positive, for she said that she had lost her husband and been left a lone widder through not having a doctor in time to him when he was ill. Well, a doctor *was* sent for, and he said that the old gentleman was very bad indeed. He asked me and Mrs. Smith what his name was, and whether he'd any relations, as they ought to be sent for; but Mrs. Smith said that she never knowed his name at all, and as for relations no one never come to see him and he never went to see no one his-self. The doctors orders him to have mustard poultices put to his feet; but it wasn't of no use, for the old fellow gives a last gasp and dies at twenty minutes past two this blessed afternoon."

"Well," said the Resurrection Man; "and then, I suppose, you had a rummage in his boxes?"

"Boxes, indeed!" cried Moll, with an indignant toss of her head. "Why, when he first come to the house, Mrs. Smith says that all he had was a bundle tied up in a blue cotton pocket handkercher—a couple of shirts, and a few pair of stockings, or so. She didn't like to take him in, she says; but he offered to pay a month's rent in advance; and so she was satisfied."

"Then you found nothing at all?" exclaimed the Rattlesnake.

"Not much," returned Moll. "The moment we saw he was dead, we began to search all over the room, to see what he had left behind him. For a long time we could find nothing but a dirty shirt, two pair of stockings, and a jar of snuff; and yet Mrs. Smith said she knew there must be money, for she had heard him counting his gold one day before he was took ill. Besides, during his illness, whenever money was wanted to get any thing for him, he never gave it at first, but sent me or Mrs. Smith out of the room with some excuse; and when we went back, he always had the money in his hand. Well, me and Mrs. Smith searched and searched away, and at last Mrs. Smith bethinks herself of looking behind the bed. We moved the bed away from the wall as well as we could, for the dead body lying upon it made it precious heavy; and then we saw that a hole had been made down in the corner of the room. Mrs. Smith puts in her finger, and draws out an old greasy silk purse. I heard the gold chink; but I saw that the purse was not over heavy. '*Well,*' says Mrs. Smith, '*I'm glad I've got a witness of what the poor gentleman left behind him; or else I might get into trouble some day or another, if any inquiries should be made.*' So she pours out the gold into her hand, and counts thirty-nine sovereigns."

"And that was all?" cried the Resurrection Man.

"Every farthing," replied the Buffer's wife. "Well, I asked Mrs. Smith what she intended to do with it; and she says, '*I shall bury the poor old gentleman decently: that will be five pounds. Then there is a pound for the doctor, as I must get him to follow the funeral; and here is two pounds for you for your attention to the old gentleman in his illness.*' So she gives me the two pounds; and I asks her what she is going to do with the rest, because there was still thirty-one pounds left."

"And what did she say to that?" demanded the Rattlesnake.

"She began a long ditty about her being an honest woman, though a poor one, and that dead man's gold would only bring ill-luck into her house."

"The old fool!" cried the Resurrection Man.

"And then she said she should ask the parson, when she had buried the old man, what she ought to do with the thirty-one pounds."

"Why didn't you propose to split it between you and hold your tongues?" asked the Resurrection Man.

"So I did," answered Moll; "and what do you think the old fool said? She up and told me that she always thought that me and my husband was not the most respectablest of characters, and she now felt convinced of it."

"Well, we must have those thirty yellow boys, old fellow," said the Resurrection Man to the Buffer.

"Yes—if we can get them," answered the latter; "and I know of no way to do it but to cut the old woman's throat."

"No—that won't do," ejaculated the Resurrection Man. "If the old woman disappeared suddenly, suspicion would be sure to fall on you; and the whole Happy Valley would be up in arms. Then the blue-bottles might find a trace to this crib here; and we should all get into trouble."

"But if you mean to put the kyebosh upon young Markham to-morrow night," said the Buffer, "won't that raise a devil of a dust in the neighbourhood?"

"Markham disappears from Holloway, which is a long way from the Happy Valley," replied the Resurrection Man.

"And the old butler, who is certain to know that the appointment was made for Twig Folly," persisted the Buffer, "won't he give information that will raise the whole Valley in arms, as you call it?"

"No such thing," said the Resurrection Man. "Markham falls into the canal accidentally, and is drowned. There's no mark of violence on his body, and his watch and money are safe about his person. Now do you understand me?"

"I understand that if you mean me to jump into the canal and help to hold him in it till he's drowned, you're deucedly out in your reckoning, for I ain't going to risk drowning myself, 'cause I can't swim better than a stone."

"You need not set foot in the water," said the Resurrection Man, somewhat impatiently. "But I suppose you could hold him by the heels fast enough upon the bank?"

"Oh! yes—I don't mind *that*," replied the Buffer: "but how shall we get the thirty-one couters from this old fool of a landlady, unless we use violence?"

The Resurrection Man leant his head upon his hand, his elbow being supported by the table, and reflected profoundly for some moments.

So high an opinion did the other villain and the two women entertain of the ingenuity, craft, and cunning of the Resurrection Man, that they observed a solemn silence while he was thus occupied in meditation,—as if they were afraid of interrupting a current of ideas which, they hoped, would lead to some scheme beneficial to them all.

Suddenly the Resurrection Man raised his head, and, turning towards the Buffer's wife, said, "Do you know whether the old woman has spoken to any one yet about the funeral?"

"She said she should let it be till to-morrow morning, because the weather was so awful bad this afternoon."

"Excellent!" ejaculated the Resurrection Man. "Now, Moll, do you put on your bonnet, take the large cotton umbrella there, and go and do what I tell you without delay."

The woman rose to put on her bonnet and cloak which she had laid aside upon first entering the room; and the Resurrection Man wrote a hurried note. Having folded, wafered, and addressed it, he handed it to the Buffer's wife, saying, "Go down as fast as your legs will carry you to Banks, the undertaker, in Globe Lane, and ask to see him. Give him this; but mind and deliver it into his hand only. If he is not at home, wait till he comes in."

The woman took the note, and departed on the mysterious mission entrusted to her.

"What's in the wind now?" demanded the Buffer, as soon as the door had closed behind his wife.

"You shall see," replied the Resurrection Man. "Now let us fill our glasses, and blow a cloud till Moll comes back."

The Rattlesnake mixed fresh supplies of grog; and the two men lighted their pipes.

"How the rain does beat down," observed the Buffer, after a pause.

"And the wind sweeps along like a hurricane," said the Resurrection Man. "By the by, this is New Year's Day. What different weather it is from what it was last New Year's Day."

"Do you recollect what sort of weather it was last New Year's Day?" demanded the Buffer.

"Perfectly well," answered the Resurrection Man; "because it was on that evening that I and the poor Cracksman helped young Holford over the Palace wall."

"And that venture turned out no go, didn't it?" asked the Buffer.

"It failed because the young scamp either turned funky or played us false, I never could make out which. But I have an account to settle with him too; and the first time I meet him I'll teach him what it is to humbug a man like me."

There was a pause, during which the two men smoked their pipes with all the calmness of individuals engaged in virtuous and innocent meditation; and the Rattlesnake added fresh fuel to the fire, the flames of which roared cheerfully up the chimney.

"Come, sing us a song, Meg," cried the Buffer, breaking a silence which had lasted several minutes.

"I have got a cold, and can't sing," replied the woman.

"Well, then, Tony," said the Buffer, "tell us some of your adventures. They'll amuse us till Moll comes back."

"I am quite tired of telling the same things over and over again," answered the Resurrection Man. "We've never heard you practise in that line yet; so the sooner you begin the better. Come, tell us your history."

"There isn't much to tell," said the Buffer, refilling his pipe; "but such as it is, you're welcome to it."

With this preface, the Buffer commenced his autobiography, in the record of which we have taken the liberty of correcting the grammatical solecisms that invariably characterised this individual's discourse; and we have also improved the language in which the narrative was originally clothed.

CHAPTER XCIX.

THE BUFFER'S HISTORY.

"You are well aware that my name is really John Wicks, although very few of my pals know me by any other title than the Buffer.

"My father and mother kept a coal and potatoe shed in Great Suffolk Street, Borough. I was their only child; and as they were very fond of me, they would not let me be bothered and annoyed with learning. For decency's sake, however, they made me go to the Sunday-school, and there I just learnt to read, and that's all.

"When I was twelve years old, I began to carry out small quantities of coals and potatoes to the customers. We used to supply a great many of the prisoners in the Bench; and whenever I went into that place, I generally managed to have a game of marbles, and sometimes rackets, with the young blackguards that lurked about the prison to pick up the racket balls, run on messages, and so on. At length I got to play for money; and as I generally lost, I had to take the money which I received from the customers to pay my little gambling debts. I was obliged to tell my father and mother all kinds of falsehoods to account for the disappearance of the money. Sometimes I said that I had lost a few halfpence; then I declared that a beggar in the street had snatched a sixpence out of my hand, and ran away; or else I swore that the customers had not paid me. This last excuse led to serious misunderstandings; for sometimes my father went himself to collect the debts owing to him; and then, when the prisoners declared they had paid me, I stuck out that it was false; and my father called them rogues and swindlers. At length, he began seriously to suspect that his son was robbing him and one day he found it out in a manner which I could not deny. I was then fourteen, and was pretty well hardened, I can tell you. So I turned round, and told my father that he had brought it all on himself, because he had instructed me how to cheat the customers in weight and measure, and had therefore brought me up in wrong principles.

"You must understand that the usual mode of doing business in coal-sheds is this: all the weights only weigh one half of what they are represented to weigh. For instance, the one which is used as the fifty pound weight is hollow, and is, therefore, made as large in outward appearance as the real fifty pound weight; whereas, in consequence of being hollow, it actually only weighs twenty-five pounds. This is the case with all the weights; the pound weight really weighs only half a pound, and so on. You may ask why the weights are thus exactly one half less than they are represented to be,—neither more nor less than one half. I will tell you: when the leet jury comes round and points, for instance, to the weight used for fifty pounds, the answer is, 'Oh, that is the twenty-five pound weight;' and, upon being tested, the assertion is found to be correct. So there is never any danger of being hauled over the coals by the leet jury; but if the weights were each an odd number of ounces or pounds short, they could not be passed off to the jury as weights of a particular standard, and then the warehouseman would get into a scrape. It is just the same with the measures. The bushel contains a false bottom, and is really half a bushel; and when the leet jury calls, it is stated to be the half bushel measure, whereas to customers it is passed off as the bushel. This will also account to you for the way in which costermongers in the streets are able to sell fruit (cherries particularly) and peas, in the season, for just one half of the price at which they can be bought at respectable dealers. The poor dupe who gives twopence for *a pound* of cherries of a costermonger in the street, only obtains half a pound; and the housewife who thinks that she can save a hundred per cent. by buying her peas in the same way, only gets half a peck instead of a peck.

"My father had thirty barrows, which he let out to the costermongers at the rate of eighteen pence a day each; and some of those men could clear eight or ten shillings a day by their traffic. But they are so addicted to drinking that they spend all they get; and in the winter season they starve. Now and then a costermonger would disappear with the barrow, for the loan of which my father never required any security, as the poor souls had none to give; and then my father offered a reward for the apprehension of the absentee. He was generally caught, and my father always had him taken before the magistrate and punished—as a warning, he said, to the rest. I used to think he behaved very harshly in this respect, as the poor wretch whom he thus got sent to the treadmill had most probably paid for the barrow over and over again.

"But to return to my story. When my father discovered that I had robbed him, I threw in his teeth the use he made of false weights and measures. He was alarmed at this, because I threatened to inform the neighbours; and so he did not give me the thrashing which he had at first promised. He, however, resolved to send me away from home, and in the course of a few days got me a place at a friend's of his, who kept a sweet-stuff shop, in Friar Street, Blackfriars. There I was initiated into all the mysteries of that trade. I found that the white-sugar articles were all largely adulterated with plaster of Paris; and that immediately accounted to me for the pernicious—often fatal—effects produced by this kind of trash upon children. If parents, who really care for their children, were only commonly prudent, they would never allow them to eat any white-sugar sweet-stuff at all. Then I discovered that the articles passed off as burnt almonds, really contained the kernels of fruits; for the kitchen-maids in wealthy families and hotels collect and sell the stones of the peaches, apricots, and nectarines, eaten at the dinner-tables of their masters, as regularly as cooks dispose of their bones and grease. In fact, the most deleterious ingredients enter into the composition of sweet-stuff. The sugar-refiners sell all their scum to the sweet-stuff makers; and this scum is composed of the lime, alum, bullock's blood, charcoal, acetate of soda, and other things used for fining sugar. Oxide of lead is also mixed with the small proportions of sugar used in making sweet-stuff; and thus you may perceive what filthy and poisonous substances are given to children in the shape of sugar-plums. I hope that I do not weary you with this description; and if you should be surprised that I can now recollect the chemical names of the ingredients used, I must tell you that I went so often to the sugar-refiners, and to the chemists, for my master, that I soon became familiar with every thing at all relating to the business.

"I now came to more interesting matters. I had been with my master about six years, and was then going on for twenty-one, when my father died. My mother sent for me home to help her in the business; and I now had the command of money. The taste for gambling which I had imbibed in my boyhood, returned with additional force; and I sought every opportunity of gratifying my inclination in this respect. I frequented a notorious public-house in Suffolk Street, where gaming was carried on to a great extent; and my ill-luck seemed unvaried. My mother did all she could to check the progress of this infatuation; but it was invincible; and in the course of three years I had completely ruined both my mother and myself. An execution was put into the house for rent, and my mother died of a broken heart. I shed a few tears, and then looked round me for some occupation.

"One of the persons who frequented the public-house in Suffolk Street offered to recommend me to a friend of his, who kept an auction-room in the City. I gladly accepted the proposal, and was engaged as 'a bidder,' at that establishment. I will tell you what I had to do: the auction was carried on in an open warehouse in a great thoroughfare. The articles put up for sale were all of the most worthless description—razors, made (like Peter Pindar's) to sell, and not to cut; pen-knives, that would inflict no damage upon a piece of wood; decanters, that would scarcely resist the pressure of the most delicate lady's hand; candlesticks, made of a metal that would melt if held too close to the fire; urns, that sprang a leak the moment hot water was poured into them; watches, that were never known to go beyond the first four-and-twenty hours; scissors, that would not sever a thread; snuffers, that merely crushed without diminishing the wick; tea-pots, made of polished pewter, and warranted as silver; in a word, every species of domestic rubbish of this kind, occupied the counters and tables in the auction-room. Myself and three others were hired as bidders. Our duty was to offer a price for every article put up, and buy it in if it appeared likely to go to a stranger at too low a price—although, indeed, few prices were too low for the articles on which they were put. Then, when a greenhorn entered the mart, we were to puff off the articles amongst ourselves in his hearing—never talking *to* him, but talking *at* him. The master was perched up behind a high desk, using his hammer with exemplary alacrity, and knocking down article after article to the flat that came in and bid. Sometimes the dupes would come back the following day, and demand the return of their money, as they had ascertained that the goods for which they had parted with it were worthless: it was then our duty to hustle such obstreperous claimants, bonnet them, or, in extreme cases, knock them down, and then give them into custody for creating a disturbance.

"In this situation I remained for three years. The master was very good to us, and gave us a present every time he effected large sales by our means. One afternoon an elderly gentleman entered the mart, and stood bidding for some cut decanters. They had been invoiced to the proprietor of the establishment for six shillings, and the lowest price at which they were to be knocked down was two pounds ten. The bidding was rather slow; and I retreated a pace or two behind the old gentleman, to avoid having the appearance of being anxious to make myself conspicuous. In that position I observed the corner of a red pocket-book peeping out of his coat tail. I glanced around: no one noticed me; and in a moment I abstracted the inviting object. This was the first theft I ever committed; and bad as I already was, the moment I had that pocket-book safe in my possession, I would have given the world for it to have been back again in its former place. The deed was however done; and I evaporated from the auction mart with the rapidity of thought.

"I was not such an idiot as to return to my lodgings; but I hastened into the vicinity of Smithfield, and entered a public-house in Chick Lane. The parlour—a little slip, with a single window looking upon the street—was fortunately empty; and I immediately examined my treasure. And true enough it was a treasure! It contained eight hundred pounds in Bank of England notes, together with bills of exchange to the amount of three thousand. There were also letters and cards of address, which showed me who the old gentleman was.

He was a rich landholder in the county of Hants. I enclosed the bills of exchange and the letters in a sheet of paper, and returned them through the post to their owner. The Bank notes I kept. But I was now at a loss how to act; for I fancied that if the notes had been stopped, there would be danger in attempting to pass them. After I had put the letter in the post, I returned to the public-house in Chick Lane, and meditated upon the best course to pursue. While I was sitting in the parlour, over a glass of brandy-and-water, pondering upon this very difficult matter, a man entered, sate down, called for some liquor, and got into conversation with me. By degrees we grew confidential; and he let me know that he was a member of the swell-mob. I opened my heart to him; and he immediately offered to take me to a place where I could change my notes.

"I thankfully accepted his proposal; and he led me into Field Lane. There he entered a shop where they sold salt fish, herrings, haddocks, and oysters. He asked a dirty-looking girl if Israel Moses was at home; and, receiving an affirmative answer, led the way up a narrow, dark, and dirty staircase, to a room where an old Jew, with a face almost completely concealed by grisly white hair, was sitting at a table covered with papers. My guide immediately communicated to him the object of my visit; and the old Jew questioned me closely relative to the way in which I had obtained the Bank notes. My companion advised me to tell him the exact truth, which I did; and the Jew then offered me six hundred pounds in gold for my eight hundred pounds' worth of notes. He explained to me that he should be compelled to send them to his agents in Paris, Hamburgh, and Amsterdam, to get rid of them; and that he could therefore afford to give me no more. I accepted his proposal, received the gold, and departed, accompanied by my new friend, who was no other than Dick Flairer.

"I made him a handsome present for his counsel and assistance, and was about to part from him, when he told me that I had better take care of myself for a few days until the hue and cry concerning the pocket-book should be over. He asked me to accompany him to his lodgings in Castle Street, Saffron Hill. I agreed; and there I first met his sister Mary. In the evening Dick went out, to ascertain, as he said, 'how the wind blew.' He came back at a late hour, and brought me a copy of a hand-bill that had been printed and circulated, and which gave not only a full description of the robbery, but also a most painfully accurate account of my person. Dick assured me that I was not safe in his lodgings, as he himself was a suspicious character in the neighbourhood; and he advised me to hide myself in a certain house which he knew in Chick Lane. I followed his advice, and proceeded to the Old House, where I lay concealed in that horrid dungeon under ground for a mortal fortnight. Mary brought me my food every other day, and gave me information of what was going on outside. She told me that the newspapers had published an account of the return of the bills of exchange and letters by post; and that the same organs stated that the old gentleman who had been robbed was unwilling to proceed any farther on that very account. At length Dick came himself, and assured me that I might leave the dungeon; but that it would be better for me to remain quiet in some snug place for a few weeks. I proposed to him a trip into the country: he agreed; and Mary accompanied us.

"We went down to Canterbury, and took lodgings on the Herne Bay road, close by the barracks. Dick and I used to visit all the neighbouring towns, and see what we could pick up; but we led a jovial life, spending much more than we got, and thus making desperate inroads into my funds. My old habits of gambling returned; and the gold which I had received from the Jew was disappearing very rapidly. We had left London for upwards of eight months, when we thought of returning to our old haunts. Mary seemed quite averse to the proposal, and was most anxious to remain a short time longer where she was. To this Dick agreed; and he and I came up to town. We went to the Boozing-ken on Saffron Hill, and there took up our quarters. Dick introduced me to Bill Bolter; and as it happened that our funds were all low, we resolved upon adopting some means to replenish our purses. Happening to take up the *Times*, I saw an advertisement, according to which a wealthy jeweller and goldsmith in the Strand required a porter. I made a remark which led Dick Flairer to observe, that if I chose to take the situation, he could get me a reference, as he knew one of the largest linen-drapers in Norton Folgate, who was in the habit of buying stolen goods of the cracksmen of Dick's gang, and would not dare refuse to perform the part required. The plan was settled: I applied for the situation, gave the reference, and in two days entered the service of the rich goldsmith. In less than a fortnight I had obtained all the information I required; and stepping out one evening, I hastened to the boozing-ken, where I met the pals, and appointed the following night for the enterprise. I then returned to my master's residence.

"On the ensuing night, precisely as the clock struck twelve, I stole softly down from my bed-room, and entered the shop by means of a skeleton key. I then cautiously opened the front door, and admitted Dick Flairer and Bill Bolter. We immediately set to work to pack up all the most valuable and most portable articles; in which occupation we were engaged when a cry of '*Fire, fire!*' was heard in the street outside; and almost at the same moment a tremendous knocking at the front door began. For an instant we were paralysed; but the noise of steps descending the stairs hurried us into action; and, opening the doors, we darted from the house with the speed of wild animals, leaving all the booty behind us. The cry of '*Fire!*' was instantly succeeded by that of '*Thieves!*' and several persons began to pursue us hotly. We gained Wellington Street, and hastened towards Waterloo Bridge, intending to get into the Borough with the least possible delay. On we went—through the great gate, without waiting to pay the toll at the entrance of the footway—the pursuers gaining upon us. Suddenly I recollected that the cornice along the outside of the parapet was very wide; and without hesitating a moment I sprang over the parapet, alighted on the cornice, and only saved myself from falling into the river by catching hold of the gas-pipe which runs along the outer side of the bridge. Scarcely had I thus accomplished a most dangerous feat, when I distinctly saw a man, a few yards a-head, mount the parapet, and precipitate himself into the river. Then arose the sounds of voices on the bridge, crying, '*He is over!*' '*He has leaped in!*' '*He will be drowned.*' '*They have all three escaped.*' '*But where the devil could the other two have got to*?' and such-like exclamations, which convinced me that my companions were safe. There I remained, a prey to a thousand painful reflections and horrid ideas, for upwards of an hour; till at length I grew so dizzy that I was every moment on the point of falling into the river. The bridge was now completely silent; and I ventured to leave my hiding-place. I passed over the bridge to the Surrey side, without molestation, and proceeded by a circuitous route to the Old House in Chick Lane, where, to my astonishment, I found Bill Bolter. I then learnt that it was Dick Flairer who had leapt into the river, and was no doubt drowned; and that Bolter had only escaped by concealing himself in the deep shade of one of the recesses of the bridge, when totally overcome by fatigue, until his pursuers had passed, when he retraced his steps, and quietly gained the Strand.

"We were greatly grieved to think that our enterprise in the jeweller's house should have failed, and that we had lost so excellent a fellow as Flairer; but in the midst of our lamentations, the door opened and Dick himself entered the room. Pale, dripping, and exhausted, he fell upon a seat, and would most probably have fainted—if not died—had we not forced some brandy down his throat. He then revived; and, having changed his clothes, was soon completely recovered from the effects of his bath, and the desperate exertions he had made to swim to a wharf communicating with the Commercial Road.

"We staid for the remainder of the night at the Old House; and on the following morning Dick Flairer went up to the boozing-ken, where he procured a newspaper. He then returned to us; and we perceived by the journal that the curtains of the bed-room which I had occupied at the jeweller's house had caught fire, and created the alarms which had interrupted us in the midst of our employment in the shop. I moreover ascertained that I was of course suspected of having admitted thieves into the premises, and that a reward was offered for my apprehension. I was accordingly compelled to remain concealed for some weeks in the Old House, while Bolter and Flairer, being unsuspected, were enabled to go abroad. I did not upon this occasion conceal myself in the dungeon of the Old House, for I could not bear the solitude of that living tomb; and as Bolter and Flairer were constantly visiting me, the time did not hang so very heavily on my hands. At length I left the Old House, and I and Dick returned to Canterbury.

"When we arrived there, after an absence of two months, we made a most unpleasant discovery—unpleasant to Dick as the brother, and to me who was enamoured of Mary. She was in a way to become a mother; her situation was too palpable to be concealed. Dick flew into a most ungovernable rage; and Mary tried to deny it. But the fact was glaring, and she was obliged to confess that she had been seduced by a serjeant of the regiment stationed at Canterbury. Her attachment to that man, and the hope that he would do her justice, were the reasons that had induced her to remain at Canterbury, when we went to London. The serjeant had recently treated her with neglect and indifference, and she longed for revenge. Dick and I swore that she should have it. She told us that the serjeant was very fond of angling, and that every morning early he indulged in his favourite sport in the river Stour, which flowed close by the barracks.

"Next morning Dick and I went down to the river, and there we saw the serjeant preparing his tackle. From the description we had received of him, we knew him to be the man we wanted; but there was a large water-mill close by, and we dared not attack him in a spot that was so overlooked. We accordingly returned home, and consulted together how we should proceed. At length we resolved that Mary should endeavour to get him to grant her an interview on the banks of the river. She sent him a note, saying that she was to leave Canterbury in a few days, and that she wished to see him once more. She concluded by begging him to meet her that evening or the next between nine and ten o'clock, close by the bridge of Kingsford's water-mill.[1] He consented, and appointed the evening of the next day for the interview.

"The hour drew nigh, and Mary went to the place agreed upon. Dick and I followed her at a little distance. The night was dark; it was in the month of April; and the air was very cold. As we drew near the bridge as noiselessly as we could, we distinguished the forms of two persons standing upon the bridge, and leaning in earnest conversation upon the low railing that overhung the huge wheel which was revolving beneath, the torrent pouring over it through the sluices of the dam upon the top of which the bridge stood. We advanced closer; and could then perceive that the two forms were those of Mary and her seducer. We proceeded to the bridge. When we reached the middle, Dick went up to the serjeant, and said, '*This is my sister; do you mean to do her justice?*'—'*No,*' cried Mary; '*he has just told me that I need have no hope in that respect.*' '*Then there is nothing more to be said,*' exclaimed Dick Flairer; and at the same moment we precipitated ourselves upon the serjeant. Dick Flairer pressed his hand upon his mouth; the poor wretch struggled violently; but in an instant we hurled him over the bridge-railing. He fell upon the wheel; the roar of the torrent, and the din of the ponderous machine drowned his last cry of agony, and the crushing of his bones. '*Now, Mary,*' said I,

1 Thomas Kingsford's establishment at Barton Mill, Canterbury.

'you are revenged.' She pressed my hand convulsively, without uttering a word; and we returned to our lodgings.

"Next day, the body of the serjeant was found, fearfully crushed and mutilated, a mile below the mill, entangled in a bed of osiers. It was carried to the barracks: an inquest was called and a verdict of *'Found Drowned'* was recorded. Not a suspicion was entertained that the man had been murdered, it being evident from the surgical examination that he had been crushed by the wheel of the mill, upon which it was supposed he had accidentally fallen, over the bridge-railing, which was only about three feet high.

"The moment the verdict was returned, and we saw that no suspicion attached to any body in reference to the murder, we left Canterbury, and repaired to London. In the course of a few weeks, Mary became the mother of a still-born child; and in due time I assured her that I would overlook her fault, and marry her if she would have me. She was pleased with the proposal; and Dick readily agreed to it. But before we could be spliced, I one day met the goldsmith of the Strand in the street; and he gave me into custody. I was taken before the magistrates, and fully committed for an attempt to rob my employer. While I was in Newgate, waiting for my trial, I was greatly alarmed lest the old gentleman, whom I had robbed at the auction mart, should prefer an indictment against me; but my fears in this respect were unfounded. At length the sessions commenced, and I was put upon my trial. The Sheriffs had supplied me with counsel, for I was completely without funds when I was arrested. The barrister thus retained in my behalf, advised me to plead guilty, as I should then stand a good chance of escaping transportation. I followed his recommendation, and expressed my contrition for the offence. The Recorder read me a long lecture, and condemned me to seven years' transportation, which sentence was commuted to two years' imprisonment in Newgate.

"During that time I seriously thought of mending my ways, when I should be once more at liberty. But I could not conceive what on earth I should do for a livelihood if I did not steal. I knew that I should be turned adrift without a penny in my pocket; and I had no friends but those with whom I could only pursue my old career. When the chaplain spoke to me upon the errors of my past life, and the necessity of reformation, I used to say to him, *'Show me, reverend sir, how*

I am to obtain an honest living when I leave these walls, and I never shall sin again.' But he always gave an evasive reply. In fact, what could he say? If he had required a man-servant—a groom—an errand-boy—a menial scrub to black his boots and brush his clothes, would he have taken me? No. If he had known any friend who wanted a man to take care of his hounds—never enter his house—but sleep in the kennels along with the dogs, would the chaplain have recommended me? No. If the governor of Newgate had needed a man to sweep the dirt away from the front of the prison, would the reverend gentleman have spoken a kind word in favour of me? No. Of what use, then, is it for these gaol chaplains to preach penitence and reformation, when by their very actions they say, '*We do not believe that you can possibly change for the better?*' Of what benefit is it for these salaried moralists to declaim upon the advantages of a virtuous course, when they know perfectly well that the old maxim is invariably correct,—'*Give a dog a bad name and hang him!*' Virtue must be fed; but Virtue, upon leaving the walls of a criminal prison, can obtain no food. Must Virtue, then, die of starvation? Human nature revolts against this self-destruction—this systematic suicide; and, sooner than submit to it, Virtue will allow itself to be changed by circumstances into Vice. Virtue in this case has no option but to become Vice.

"I often thought, when I was in prison, that if there was a workshop, established by the government to receive persons whom the criminal gaols daily vomit back upon society, many a miserable creature would in reality reform, and be saved from a re-plunge into the sea of crime. But all that the government does is to punish. I mentioned these thoughts to the chaplain. And what did he say? He endeavoured to get rid of the necessity of giving a decisive opinion, by throwing himself headlong into a mass of argument and reasoning, half religious and half political, which I could not understand. Thus do those men invariably extricate themselves from perplexing topics. In my opinion there is no mockery more abominable—no hypocrisy more contemptible—no morality more baseless than the attributes of a gaol-chaplain!

"If good and pious men attended criminal prisons of their own free will, and talked in a plain homely manner to the inmates,—a manner which those inmates could understand,—how much benefit might result! But when you think that the chaplain only troubles himself about you because he is paid,—that he doles out his doctrine in proportion to the income which he receives,—and that he says the same to you to-day which he said to another yesterday, and will say to a third to-morrow,—his office is mean, contemptible, and degrading.

"It does not do for me to hold forth in this manner; I know *that*: but I cannot help expressing the thoughts that occupied me when I was in Newgate. They are often present in my memory; and, sometimes, when I am dull and in low spirits, I console myself by the conviction that if I am bad now, it is because there is no door open for me to be good. So a truce to these ideas. They do not often come from my lips; and even now I scarcely wish to recall them.

"Well—I passed my two years in Newgate; and when I was released, I stood still by the lamp-post at the top of the Old Bailey, thinking which way I should go. I had not a penny in my pocket; and I knew that in the course of a few hours I should be hungry. As true as I am sitting here, tears rolled down my cheeks as I contemplated the necessity of returning to my old pursuits,—yes—burning tears—tears of agony—such tears as I never shed before, and shall never shed again!

"Suddenly a thought struck me. I would go to the workhouse. The idea consoled me; and, fearful lest my good intentions should grow cool, I turned back past the door of Newgate again, and directed my steps down the Old Bailey towards Blackfriars' Bridge. In the course of an hour, I knocked at the door of the ——— Workhouse, with an order for admission from the overseer.

"It was about twelve o'clock in the day when I entered the Workhouse. The porter conducted me into the office, where the master took down my name, age, &c. He then sent me to the bath-room, where I was cleansed. When I came from the bath I put on the coarse linen, grey suit, and thick shoes which constitute the workhouse garb—the livery of poverty. The dress differed but little from the one I had worn in Newgate—so small is the distinction in this blessed country between a felon and a pauper! My old clothes were put up together in a bundle, labelled with my name, and conveyed to the storeroom, to be returned to me when I chose to leave the place. As soon as I was dressed, I was allotted to the *able-bodied men's department* of the Workhouse. The scale of food for this class of persons was just this:—

	Bread.	Gruel.	Meat.	Bacon.	Potatoes.	Soup.	Cheese.	Suet Pudding.
	Oz.	Pints.	Oz.	Oz.	Oz.	Pints.	Oz.	
Monday ..	14	1½	..	..	..	1½	2	..
Tuesday ..	21	1½	..	..	..	..	4	..
Wednesday.	14	1½	..	..	..	1½	2	..
Thursday..	14	1½	..	4	8	..	2	..
Friday	14	1½	..	..	..	..	2	14
Saturday ..	14	1½	.	..	..	1½	2	..
Sunday....	14	1½	5	..	8	1½	..	..
Total Weekly Allowance	105	10½	5	4	16	6	14	14

So you see that we had only five ounces of cooked meat and five ounces of bacon, in the shape of animal food, in the course of each week! And yet we had to work—to keep the grounds in order, to do various jobs in the establishment, and to pick four pounds of oakum each, every day, the Sabbath excepted. Felons are better off;[1] for in the prison one has more meat, more bread, and more gruel (which is certainly nourishing) than in the workhouse!

"We had nothing to drink with our dinners and suppers but water—and of that they could not very well stint us, because it cost nothing. The able-bodied women had much *less* than the able-bodied men. The infirm paupers had each one ounce of tea and seven ounces of sugar weekly, instead of gruel, for breakfast! Fancy one ounce of tea for seven meals!

"We were divided into messes, or tables of ten each; and each mess elected a carver. The duty of the carver was to go to the kitchen and fetch the provision allotted to the individuals at his particular table, and then to distribute it in equal proportions. What fighting

---

1 [Reynolds's note:] The Dietary Table of Clerkenwell New Prison, already quoted at page 529, is as follows:—

	Soup.	Gruel.	Meat.	Bread.
	Pints.	Pints.	Ounces.	Ounces.
Monday	..	2½	..	20
Tuesday	..	1½	6	20
Wednesday . . .	..	2½	..	20
Thursday . .	..	2½	..	20
Friday . . .	1	1½	..	20
Saturday . . .	..	1½	6	20
Sunday . . .	1	1½	..	20
Total Weekly Allowance	2	13½	12	140

and wrangling always took place at meal times! On meat days, one had too much fat, and another's morsel was too under-done:—on bacon days, one had too much lean, and another had the rind given to him. Then one declared that he had been cheated out of a potatoe; and so on. It was a scene of perpetual selfishness—of human beings quarrelling for a crumb! But who can wonder? A potatoe or a cubic inch of bread was a considerable portion of a meal; and where all were ravenous, who could afford to lose even a potatoe or a crumb?[1]

1 It is too frequently the habit to throw the blame of the diabolical nature of some of the clauses of the New Poor Law upon the masters of workhouses; whereas the whole vituperation should be levelled against the guardians who issue the dietary-tables, from the conditions of which the masters dare not deviate. We have no doubt that there are many masters of workhouses who are humane and kind-hearted men. Indeed, having inspected several of those establishments for the purpose of collecting information to aid us in the episode to which this note is appended, we have been

"Neither of you have ever been in a workhouse, I know; and therefore you cannot imagine the change it produces in its inmates. They grow discontented with the world, and look upon their superiors with abhorrence. An army of able-bodied men, recruited from all the Unions in the kingdom, would make the finest republican soldiers imaginable. They would proceed with a good heart to level throne, aristocracy, and every institution which they believed oppressive to the industrious classes.

"But that is no business of mine—and I care nothing for politics of any kind. Of an evening, we used to gather round the fire till bed-time, and talk of our past lives. Many—many of my companions had, like myself, seen better days; and it actually made one's heart ache to hear them compare their former positions with their present ones. And after all, what can be more inhuman—what more cruel, than the very principles of the workhouse system? Old couples, who have lived together for years and years, are separated when they go to the workhouse. Mothers are debarred from the society of their little ones:—no ties of kindred are respected *there!*

"I remember one man—he was about sixty, and much better behaved than the rest—who had been a writer, or something of that kind, in his time. The men used to get him now and then, when he was in the humour, to recite poems—some of which he had composed in better days, and others since he had been in the Union. Those of his palmy years were all about love, and friendship, and sweet spring, and moonlight scenes, and so on;—but from the moment that he set foot in the workhouse, he bade farewell to love and friendship; and he never more was destined to know the enjoyments or charming seasons and tranquil hours! One of his late poems made such an impression on me, that I learnt it by heart. It was a workhouse scene. I remember it now; and will repeat it:—

---

enabled to ascertain that such is really the fact. Amongst others, we must signalize the Edmonton and Tottenham Union House, the master of which is Mr. Barraclough. This gentleman is a man of a most benevolent heart, and exerts himself in every way to ameliorate the condition of those entrusted to his charge. The guardians of that particular Union are, moreover, worthy, liberal-minded and considerate men, who sanction and encourage Mr. Barraclough in his humane endeavours to make the inmates of the workhouse as little sensible of their degraded condition as possible. Would that all boards of guardians merited the same encomium! [Reynolds's note.]

"THE SONG OF THE WORKHOUSE.

"Stooping over the ample grate,
Where burnt an ounce of fuel,
That cheered not the gloom
Of the workhouse room,
An aged and shivering female sate,
Sipping a pint of gruel:
And as she sopped a morsel of bread
In that liquid thin and poor,
With anguish she shook her aching head,
And thought of the days that were o'er

"Through the deep mists of years gone by
Her mental glances wandered;
And the warm blood ran
To her features wan;
And fire for a moment lighted her eye,
As o'er the past she pondered.
For she had once tripped the meadow green
With a heart as blithe as May;
And she had been crowned the village-queen
In times that were far away!

"She'd been the pride of parents dear,
And plenty banished sorrow;
And her love she gave
To a yeoman brave;
And a smiling offspring rose to cheer
Hearts that feared not for the morrow.
Oh! why should they fear? In the sweat of their brow
They ate their daily bread;
And they thought, 'The earth will e'er yield as now
The fruits whereon we're fed!'

"But when their hair grew silvery white,
Sorrow their cot invaded,
And ravaged it then
As armies of men
Sack the defenceless town by night:—
Thus all Hope's blossoms faded!

From their little farm the stock was swept
By the owner of their land;
And the very bed on which they slept,
Was snatched by the bailiff's hand.

"One hope—one fond hope now was all
Each tender heart dared cherish—
That they might remain
Still linked by one chain,
And 'midst the sorrows that might befal,
Together live or perish.
But Want drove them on to the workhouse gate;
And when the door was pass'd
They found themselves doomed to separate—
To separate at last!

"And he fell sick:—she prayed in vain
To be where he was lying;
She poured forth her moan
Unto hearts of stone;
Never admittance she could gain
To the room where he was dying!
Then into her brain the sad thoughts stole
That brain with anguish reeling—
That the great ones, judging by their own soul,
Think that paupers have no feeling.

"So, thus before the cheerless grate,
Watching the flick'ring ember
She rocked to and fro,
Her heart full of woe;
For into that heart the arrow of fate
Pierced like the cold of December.
And though she sopped a morsel of bread,
She could not eat for crying;
'Twas hard that she might not support the head
Of her much-lov'd husband dying!

"I stayed in the workhouse six weeks; and could stand it no longer. I had to labour, and was half-starved. So one morning I went to the Master, demanded my clothes, and was speedily retracing my steps towards my old haunts. That evening I supped with Dick Flairer at the boozing-ken on Saffron Hill; and the same night we broke into a watchmaker's shop in the City. We got seventeen pounds in money, and a dozen watches and other trinkets, which we sold to the 'fence' in Field Lane for thirty guineas. That was a good bargain for him! I then went and took up my quarters with Dick Flairer at his lodgings; and in a few weeks I married his sister Mary. Six or eight months afterwards poor Dick was killed; and—"

CHAPTER C.

THE MYSTERIES OF THE GROUND-FLOOR ROOMS.

The Buffer was interrupted at this point by the return of his wife, who in spite of the protection of the Resurrection Man's umbrella, was dripping wet.

We must observe that we have taken the liberty of altering and improving the language, in which the Buffer delivered his autobiography, to the utmost of our power: we have moreover embodied his crude ideas and reduced his random observations into a tangible shape. We should add that the man was not deficient in intellectual sharpness, in spite of the stolid expression of his countenance; and thus the observations which he made relative to prison discipline and the neglect of government to adopt means of *preventing* crime in preference to *punishing* it when committed, need excite no astonishment in those who peruse them.

But to return to the thread of our narrative.

When the Buffer's wife had taken a warm seat by the fire, and comforted herself with a tolerably profound libation of steaming gin-and-water, she proceeded to give an account of her mission.

"I went down to Globe Lane," she said; "and a miserable walk it was, I can assure you. The rain falls in torrents, and the wind blows enough to carry the Monument into the Thames. By the time I got down to the undertaker's house I was drenched. Then Banks wasn't at home; but his wife asked me to stop till he came in; and as I thought that the business was pressing, I agreed. I waited—and waited till I was tired: one hour passed—then half an hour more; and I was just coming back when Banks walks in."

"And so you gave him the note," said the Resurrection Man, who had listened somewhat impatiently to this prelude.

"Yes—I gave him the note," continued Moll Wicks; "and he put on a pair of spectacles with round glasses as big as the bottoms of wine-glasses. When he had read it, he said he would attend to it, and should call his-self on you to-morrow morning by nine o'clock."

"Well and good," exclaimed the Resurrection Man.

"What are you going to do, Tony?" demanded the Rattlesnake.

"Never do you mind now," answered the Resurrection Man. "I will tell you all to-morrow."

"But I haven't quite done yet," cried the Buffer's wife. "Just as I came out of the undertaker's shop I met the surgeon that attended upon the old gentleman at Mrs. Smith's. He beckoned me under an archway, and asked when the old gentleman was going to be buried? I told him that I knew nothing about it. He hesitated, and was going away; and then he turned round suddenly, and said, 'Do you think your husband would mind a job that would put ten pounds into his pocket?' I don't know whether he had ever seen Jack, or not——"

"To be sure he has," interrupted the Buffer. "Didn't I go to him when I cut my hand with the hatchet, chopping wood one day?"

"Ah! I forgot that," said Moll. "Well, so I told him that my husband wasn't at all the man to refuse a ten pun' note; and even then he didn't seem to like to trust me. But after a little more hesitation, he says, says he, 'I should like to know what that old gentleman died of; I can't make out at all. I wonder whether his friends would have any objection to my opening the body; for I spoke to Mrs. Smith, and she won't hear of it.' I told him that the poor old feller had no friends; but I saw very well what the sawbones wanted; and so I says, 'Why don't you have him up again if so be you want so partickler to know what he died of?'—'That's just the very thing,' he says. 'Do you think your husband would do the job? I once knew a famous feller,' he says, 'one Anthony Tidkins'——"

"And so do I know him," interrupted the Resurrection Man. "Doesn't he live in the Cambridge Road, not far from the corner of Bethnal Green Road?"[1]

"The same," answered the Buffer's wife.

1 In 1841, Reynolds and his family lived in Suffolk Place, on the corner of Cambridge Heath Road and Bethnal Green Road.

"Well—what took place then?"

"He only told me to tell my husband to call upon him—and that was all."

"Here's more work, you see, Jack," said the Resurrection Man. "Leave this business to me. I'll take care and manage it. When we meet to-morrow night, I'll explain all my plans about the money this old fellow has left behind him; and then I'll tell you what arrangement I've made with this surgeon. You must mind and be with me at nine to-morrow night, Jack; because we won't keep young Markham waiting for us."

These last words were uttered with a low chuckle and an expression of countenance that indicated but too well the diabolical hopes and intentions of the Resurrection Man.

The Buffer and his wife then took leave of their friends, and departed to their own abode.

"Now, Meg," said the Resurrection Man, "it is nearly twelve o'clock; and you may get ready to go to bed. I am just going out for a few minutes—"

"As usual, Tony," cried the Rattlesnake, impatiently. "Why do you always go out now—every night?"

"I have told you over and over again not to pry into my secrets," returned the Resurrection Man, furiously. "You mind your own business, and only meddle in what I tell you to take a part; or else—"

"Well, well, Tony—don't be angry now," said the Rattlesnake, in her most wheedling tone. "I will never ask you any more questions. Only I thought it strange that you should have gone out every night for the last three weeks—no matter what weather—"

"And you may think it strange a little longer if you like," once more interrupted the terrible Resurrection Man, with a sinister lowering of his countenance which checked the reply that was rising to the lips of his companion.

The Rattlesnake lighted a candle, and passed into the adjoining apartment.

The Resurrection Man poured some raw spirits into a wine glass, tossed it off, and putting on his hat, left the room.

He descended the precipitate staircase leading to the front door of the house, and in another moment reached the street.

Simply closing, without locking, the door behind him, he turned sharply round into the dark alley which ran beneath a sombre and narrow arch, along one side of the house.

But his footsteps, on this occasion, were closely followed by the Rattlesnake.

Unable to restrain her curiosity any longer—and, *perhaps*, influenced by other motives of a less superficial nature,—Margaret Flathers had determined to follow her paramour this night; and, scarcely had he closed the street door, when she was already at the bottom of the staircase.

The moment she stepped into the street, she saw the dark form of the Resurrection Man turn down the alley above mentioned; and she muttered to herself, "I thought so! and now perhaps I shall find out why he never would allow me to set foot in the rooms of the lower storey."

The Resurrection Man passed half-way up the alley, and taking a key from his pocket, proceeded to open a door that communicated with the ground-floor of his singularly-built house.

He entered, and the Rattlesnake hurried up to the door. She applied her ear to the key-hole—listened—and heard his footsteps echoing upon the boarded floor of the back-room. In a few moments the grating of a lucifer-match upon the wall met her ear; and applying her eye for a moment to the key-hole, she saw that there was now a light within.

Impelled by an invincible curiosity, or other motives of a powerful nature,—if not both,—the Rattlesnake cautiously raised the latch, and opened the door to the distance of nearly a foot.

With the utmost care, she now ventured to look into the interior of that part of the house, in respect to which a species of Blue-beard restriction had existed for her ever since she first became the companion of the Resurrection Man in that mysterious abode.

Glancing cautiously in, we say, she saw a small passage communicating with two rooms—one at each end, front and back. The door of the front room was closed: that of the back one was open. She accordingly directed all her attention to the back-room.

Against the wall facing the door was a candle, burning in a bright tin shade or reflector; and in the middle of the room, between the door and the light, stood the Resurrection Man. He had his back towards the Rattlesnake; but she could watch all his proceedings with the greatest facility.

And how strange were those proceedings!—The Resurrection Man enveloped himself in a large dark cloak, and fixed a black cloth mask over his countenance. He then advanced towards a cupboard, which he opened, and whence he took several articles, the precise nature of which the Rattlesnake could not ascertain, in consequence of the position in which her paramour was then standing. She however observed that he placed those articles in a basket at his feet; and when this task was accomplished, he lifted the basket in his hand, and turned so abruptly round to leave the room, that the Rattlesnake trembled from head to foot lest he should have caught a glimpse of her head protruded through the opening of the door.

She drew herself back and pulled the door towards her. For a moment she felt inclined to beat a precipitate retreat to her own quarters; but curiosity compelled her to remain.

What could mean that strange disguise?—Why that cloak?—Wherefore that mask?—And what were the objects which the Resurrection Man had consigned to his basket?—Lastly, whither was he going?

With the most extreme caution she again pushed the door partly open, and again did she glance into the interior of that mysterious division of the house.

But all was now dark; the light had disappeared, or was extinguished, and the place was involved in total obscurity.

Nevertheless, all was not silent. The measured tread of receding footsteps fell upon the woman's ear: those sounds seemed to come from heavy feet descending stone stairs.

Fainter and fainter became the sounds, until at length they merged into the low wind, which whistled gloomily and monotonously through the lower part of the house.

Margaret Flathers felt alarmed: she scarcely knew why.

Was it that being aware of the diabolical character of the Resurrection Man, she naturally associated his present strange proceedings with some deed of darkness whose very mystery made her shudder?

Was it that she trembled at the idea of being in the power of a miscreant whose ability to work evil seemed as unbounded as his inclination?

Suddenly her thoughts received an interruption which was by no means calculated to tranquillize her mind.

A scream, apparently coming from the very bowels of the earth, echoed through the lower part of that house—a scream expressive of an agony so intense, an anguish so acute, that it smote even her hardened and ruthless heart!

That scream was not repeated; but its echoes rang long throughout the place, and vibrated in a strange and terrible manner on the ears of the Rattlesnake.

Then followed low mutterings, in a hoarse and subdued tone; but as they gradually grew louder, she could recognise the menacing voice of the Resurrection Man.

Fear now completely triumphed over the motives which had induced the woman to seek to penetrate into the secrets of her paramour. The dark cloak—the black mask—the basket—the piercing scream—and the threatening voice, all combined to bewilder her imagination, and fill her with vague but not less terrible alarms.

Hastily closing the door, she retreated with precipitate speed from the dark alley, and ascended the steep staircase leading to the upper rooms of the house.

To throw off her clothes and betake herself to rest was the occupation of but a few minutes: nevertheless, as she laid aside her garments, she cast timid and furtive glances behind her—as if she were afraid that her eyes would encounter some horrible spectre—or some masked figure of appalling aspect.

In a quarter of an hour after she had returned from the contemplation of those mysterious proceedings that had filled her mind with such ineffable horror, the Resurrection Man entered the bed-room.

A light was burning upon the table, and when the door opened the Rattlesnake glanced with profound terror in that direction—for she feared lest he should appear in his long dark cloak and black mask. She was inured to crime;—but it was that crime which she could contemplate face to face; and thus the idea that she was in a house where deeds of unknown horror and machinations of an undefined degree of blackness were the business of the terrible man with whom her fortunes were now linked, prostrated all her courage, and filled her with alarms the more profound, because so ominously vague.

In order to avoid the risk of betraying her trepidation to the Resurrection Man, she soon affected to fall asleep; and, when at length slumber really overtook her, her dreams were filled with gaunt forms clad in long black cloaks, and wearing upon their countenances dark masks, through the holes of which their eyes glared with fearful brightness.

CHAPTER CI.

THE WIDOW.

THE cold January morning struggled into existence, amidst rain and sleet, and seemed cradled in dense masses of clouds of tempestuous blackness.

It appeared as if the sun had taken leave of the earth for ever; and it would not have been surprising had the ignorant inquired whence came the gloomy light that just seemed to guide them to their toil.

Miserable indeed was the aspect of the eastern district of the metropolis. Emaciated women, wrapt in thin and scanty shawls, crept along the streets, through the pouring rain, to purchase at the chandlers' shops the morsel that was to serve for the morning's meal,—or, perhaps, to pledge some trifling article in their way, ere they could obtain that meal! Half-starved men,—poor wretches who never made a hearty meal, and who were yet compelled to work like horses,—unhappy beings, who flew to the public houses in despair, and then were reproached by the illiberal and intolerant for their immorality,—black sheep of Fortune's flock, to whom verdant pastures were unknown,—friendless outcasts, who in sickness knew no other consolation than that of the hospital, and in destitution, no asylum save the workhouse,—luckless mortals, who cursed the day they knew the power of love, and execrated that on which they pronounced the marriage vows, because therefrom had sprung children who pined for want before their face,—such men as these were seen dragging themselves along to their labours on the railroad, the canal, or at the docks.

It was about eight o'clock on this miserable morning, when a man, dressed in a shabby suit of black, and wearing a very dirty white neckcloth, the long ends of which hung, damp and lanky, over the front of his closely-buttoned body-coat, walked slowly along Smart Street—a thoroughfare in the eastern part of Globe Town.

This individual was in reality verging upon sixty; but as he dyed his hair and whiskers in order to maintain an uniform aspect of funereal solemnity, he looked ten years younger. His manner was grave and important; and, although the rain was descending in torrents, he would not for the world depart from that measured pace which was habitual to him. He held an old umbrella above his head, to protect a battered hat, round which a piece of crape was sewn in three or four clumsy folds; but the torrent penetrated through the cotton tegument, and two streams poured from the broad brims of his hat adown his anti-laughter-looking and rigidly demure countenance.

When he arrived at about the middle of Smart Street, he halted, examined the numbers of the houses, and at length knocked at the door of one of them.

An elderly woman, dressed in a neat but very homely garb, responded to the summons.

"Does Mrs. Smith live here, ma'am?" demanded the individual in black.

"My name's Smith, sir," answered the widow.

"Very good, ma'am. I'll have a little conversation with you, if you please,"—and the stranger stepped into the passage.

Mrs. Smith conducted him into her little parlour, and inquired his business.

"Mine, ma'am," was the answer, "is a professional visit—entirely a professional visit, ma'am. Alas! ma'am," continued the stranger, casting his eyes upwards in a most dolorous manner, and taking a dirty white handkerchief from his pocket,—"alas ma'am, I understand you have had a sad loss here?"

"A lodger of mine, sir, is dead," said Mrs. Smith, somewhat surprised at the display of sorrow which she now beheld, and very naturally expecting that her visitor would prove to be a relation of the deceased.

"Ah! ma'am, we're all mortal!" exclaimed the stranger, with a mournful shake of the head, and a truly pitiful turning up of the whites of his eyes, "we're all mortal, ma'am; and howsomever high and mighty we may be in this life, the grave at last must have our carkisses!"

"Very true, sir," said the good woman, putting the corner of her apron to her eyes; for the reflection of the stranger called to her mind the loss she had experienced in the deceased Mr. Smith.

"Alas! it's too true, ma'am," continued the stranger, applying his handkerchief to his face, to suppress, as the widow thought, a sob: "but it is to be hoped, ma'am, that your lodger has gone to a better speer, where there's no cares to wex him—and no rent to pay!"

"I hope so too, most sincerely, sir," said Mrs. Smith, wondering when the gentleman would announce the precise terms of relationship in which he stood to the deceased. "But, might I inquire—"

"Yes, ma'am, you may inquire anything you choose," said the stranger, with another solemn shake of his head—in consequence of which a great deal of wet was thrown over Mrs. Smith's furniture; "for I know you by name, Mrs. Smith—I know you well by reputation—as a respectable, kind-hearted, and pious widder; and I feel convinced that your treatment to the poor lamented deceased—" here the stranger shook his head again, and groaned audibly—"was everything that it ought to be in this blessed land of Christian comfort!"

Mrs. Smith now began to suspect that she was honoured with the visit of a devout minister of some particular sect to which the deceased had probably belonged. But before she had time to mention her supposition, the stranger resumed his highly edifying discourse.

"My dear madam," he said, turning up his eyes, "the presence of death in this house—this wery house—ought to make us mindful of the uncertain leasehold of our own lives; it ought to make us prayerful and church-loving. But madam—my dear madam," continued the stranger, apparently on the point of bursting out into a perfect agony of grief, "there are attentions to be paid to the body as well as cares to entertain for the soul; and the least we can do is to show a feeling of weneration for our deceased friends by consigning them in a decent manner to the grave."

"On that point, sir," said Mrs. Smith, "I think as you do; and I s'pose you're come to superintend the funeral. If so, I am sure I am very thankful, for it's a great tax on a poor lone body like me to have such a undertaking to attend to."

"I'll *undertake* the undertaking—out of respect to the poor dear deceased, ma'am," observed the stranger, in a tone of deep solemnity. "And now, ma'am," he continued, rising, "I must request you to command those feelings which is so nat'ral under such circumstances, and show me into the room where the blessed departed lays."

Mrs. Smith, thinking within herself that the visitor must have

some legitimate authority for his present proceeding, and presuming that he would condescend to impart to her the nature of that authority ere he took his leave, conducted him with very little hesitation to the room where the deceased lay stretched upon the bed.

The corpse was covered with a clean white sheet; for every thing, though excessively homely, was still neat and decent in the widow's dwelling.

"I see, ma'am," said the stranger, advancing solemnly up to the bed, and drawing the sheet away from the corpse,—"I see that you know how to pay proper respect to the last remnants of mortality. Ah! ma'am, it's all wanity and wexation of spirit!"

With these words the extraordinary stranger drew a rule gravely from his pocket, and proceeded to measure the corpse, saying at the same time, "Ah! my dear madam, heaven will reward you for all your goodness towards our dear deceased friend!"

"Was he a friend of yours, then, sir?" demanded the widow, somewhat astounded at the process of measurement which was now going on before her eyes.

"Are we not all friends and brethren, ma'am?" said the stranger: "are we not all Christian friends and Christian brethren? Yes, ma'am, we are—we must be."

"May I ask, sir, why—"

"Yes, ma'am, ask any thing—I implore you to ask any thing. I am so overcome by the idea of your goodness towards the blessed defunct, and by the sense of the dooty which my profession—"

"What profession, sir?" asked Mrs. Smith, point-blank.

"Ah! my dear madam," answered the stranger, with a shake of the head more solemn than any he had yet delivered himself of, "I exercise the profession of undertaker."

"Undertaker!" ejaculated the widow, a light breaking in upon her as she thought of the systematic measurement of the body.

"Undertaker and furnisher of funerals, ma'am, on the most genteel and economic principles."

"Well—I raly took you for a minister," said Mrs. Smith, somewhat disappointed.

"Excellent woman! your goodness flatters me," ejaculated the undertaker. "But here is my card, ma'am—*Edward Banks*, you perceive—*Globe Lane*. Ah! my dear madam, I knew your dear deceased husband well! Often and oft have we chanted the same hymn together in the parish church; and often have we drunk together out of the same pewter at the *Spotted Dog*."

Mournful, indeed, was the shake of the head that accompanied this latter assurance; and the undertaker once more had recourse to his dingy pocket-handkerchief.

The widow used the corner of her apron.

Mr. Banks saw the advantage he had gained, and hastened to clench the object of his visit.

"Yes, my dear madam, no man respected your dear husband more than me: in fact, I wenerated that man. Poor dear Thomas Smith—"

"Matthew, sir," said the widow mildly.

"Ah! so it was, ma'am—Matthew Smith! Good fellow—charming

companion—excellent man—gone, gone—never to come back no more!"

And Mr. Banks sobbed audibly.

"Well," observed the widow, wiping her eyes, "it's wery strange that poor dear Mat never should have mentioned your name to me, considering you was so intimate."

"Our friendship, ma'am, was a solemn compact—too solemn to be made a matter of idle conversation. But since I have made myself known to you, my dear madam, do, pray, let me take this unpleasant business off your hands, and conduct the funeral of your lamented lodger."

"Well, sir," said the widow, after a moment's reflection, "since you are in the undertaking line, and as you've called so polite and all, I shall be wery much obleeged—"

"Say no more, my dear Mrs. Smith," exclaimed Mr. Banks. "I will do the thing respectable for you—and wery moderate charges. You need not bother yourself about it in any way. We will bury the dear departed in one of the Globe Lane grounds and I will even provide the clergyman."

"Do you know a good—pious—sincere minister that you can recommend, Mr. Banks?" asked the widow.

"I do, ma'am—a godly, dewout, prayerful man—meek and humble," answered the undertaker.

"I rather want a little advice in one way—quite private," continued Mrs. Smith; "and I should take it as a favour if your friend the minister would just step round—or shall I call upon him?"

"No, Mrs. Smith—certainly not. He shall pay his respects to you. Gentlemen always waits upon ladies," added Mr. Banks.

Though he uttered a compliment, he did not smile; but Mrs. Smith was flattered; and, leading the way down stairs to her little parlour, she invited Mr. Banks to take "a thimble-full of something short to keep out the damp that cold morning."

Mr. Banks accepted the civility; and the costs of the funeral were duly settled. The undertaker engaged to inter the deceased lodger for five pounds, and pay all expenses. At length he took his leave; and Mrs. Smith felt quite relieved from any anxiety respecting the obsequies of the deceased.

From Mrs. Smith's humble abode, the respectable Mr. Banks

proceeded to the dwelling of the Resurrection Man, who had just returned from a visit to the surgeon that had attended upon the deceased. The success of this visit will be related hereafter; for the present, let us hasten to inform our readers that Mr. Banks acquainted his friend Mr. Tidkins with every particular respecting his call upon the widow in Smart Street.

CHAPTER CII.

THE REVEREND VISITOR.

WHEN Mr. Banks had taken his leave of the widow in Smart Street, Globe Town, the latter seated herself in her little parlour to reflect upon what had passed during the interview.

"Well," she said to herself, "that certainly is a very singular man. To have knowed my husband so well, and for me never to have knowed *him!* P'raps, after all, my poor Mat was fond of the public-house, and didn't like to speak of the acquaintances he met there. That accounts for his never mentioning Mr. Banks's name. But for a man like Mr. Banks to come here whimpering and crying over a corpse, which he never see living, shows a excellent heart. Mr. Banks must be a wery amiable man. And yet I always heerd say that butchers and undertakers was the most unfeelingest of men. They never let butchers set on juries; but I'm sure if undertakers is so milk-hearted, *they* may set on juries, or up in pulpits, or any where else, for my part. Mr. Banks is a wery respectable man—and a wery pious one too. I'm sure I thought he was going to sing a hymn—'specially after the dodger of gin he took. The minister that he said he'd send to me must be a holy man: I shall put confidence in him—and foller his advice."

A tap at the parlour door interrupted Mrs. Smith's reverie; and the Buffer's wife entered the room.

"How do you do this morning, ma'am?" said Moll Wicks. "I thought I heerd that you had company just now?"

"Only Mr. Banks, the undertaker, Mrs. Wicks."

"Oh! Mr. Banks, was it?" ejaculated the Buffer's wife, who now began to comprehend a part of the Resurrection Man's plan: "and a highly respectable individual he is too."

"Do you know any thing of him, Mrs. Wicks?"

"Certainly I do, ma'am. He buried my grandfather and grandmother, my great uncle and my lame aunt, and never took no more than expenses out of pocket," answered Moll—although be it well remembered, she had never seen nor heard of Mr. Banks before the preceding evening.

"Ah! well—I thought I couldn't be wrong," observed the widow, extremely satisfied with this information.

"And so I suppose, ma'am, you've made the arrangements with him for the funeral?"

"Just so," responded Mrs. Smith; "and in the course of the day I expect a wery pious minister of Mr. Banks's acquaintance."

Scarcely were these words uttered, when a modest double knock at the front door was heard—a summons which Mrs. Wicks volunteered to answer.

The moment she opened the door, an ejaculation of surprise was about to issue from her tongue; but the individual whom she saw upon the threshold put his finger to his lips to impose silence.

The Buffer's wife responded with a significant nod, and introduced the visitor into the widow's parlour.

Moll Wicks then withdrew to her own room.

Meantime the visitor stood in the presence of Mrs. Smith, who beheld before her a short man, with a pale face, dark piercing eyes, shaggy brows, and long straggling black hair. He was dressed in a respectable suit of mourning, and wore a clean white cravat.

"Pardon me, ma'am, if I intrude," said the visitor; "but my friend Mr. Banks—"

"Oh! sir, you are quite welcome," ejaculated the widow. "Pray sit down, sir. I presume you are the reverend minister—"

"I am a humble vessel of the Lord," answered the visitor, casting down his eyes with great meekness: "and I am come to see in what way I can be useful to a respectable widow of whom my friend, the excellent Mr. Banks, has spoken so very highly."

"The truth is, reverend sir," said the widow, sinking her voice, and drawing her chair closer up to her sanctified visitor, "I want some good advice how to act in a wery partickler matter."

"It is my business to give good advice," was the reply.

"I thought so, reverend sir; and if Mat had been alive, I should have told him that I thought so. Howsomever, this is what I want to know about. An old gentleman dies yesterday morning in my house; and he leaves a little money—thirty or forty pounds, or so—behind him. He always paid his way with me; and so I don't start no claim to a farthing of it. He has no name—no friends—no relations—no nothing: now the question is, sir, what am I to do with this here money that he's left behind him?"

"You are a very honest woman, Mrs. Smith," answered the reverend gentleman; "and you conduct yourself in a most creditable way in this respect. Many people would have put the money into their own pockets."

"And that's just what a female lodger of mine wanted me to do, reverend sir," exclaimed the landlady. "But I know myself better. Dead man's money never did no one no good unless it was properly left, as the saying is. Mrs. Wicks would have had me keep it all quiet; and I must say that I was surprised at the perposal. But, between you and me, sir, I don't think overmuch of my lodgers, although they do pay their rent pretty reg'lar. The man doesn't seem to have any work or employment; and yet they live on the best—biled beef one day, steaks the next, bacon and greens the next—and so on. I know that *I* can't do it on nothing. And then they have their ale at dinner, and their gin of an evening. For my part I can't understand it. The man keeps late hours too; and the woman swears like a trooper when she's got a drop too much. But then, as I said, they pays their way; and a lone widder like me doesn't dare ask no questions."

"Of course not," said the reverend gentleman. "I think you stated that the name of the lodgers you allude to is Wicks?"

"Yes, sir—Wicks."

"I know them—by reputation only. They have an annuity of eighty pounds a-year, and are very respectable people. Their only fault is that they are rather fond of company—and that, perhaps, makes them stay out late now and then."

"Well, sir, if a pious gentleman like you thinks well on them, it isn't for a poor ignorant creatur' like me to say black's the white of their eye. They pays their way; and that's all I ought to bother myself about. But, as I was a-saying, the old gentleman which lodged with me dies and leaves some money behind him. There ain't kith or kin to claim it. Now what had I better do with it?"

"The ecclesiastical law—"

"Sir?"

"The law of Doctors' Commons, I mean, is very particular on this head," said the reverend visitor. "There are only two things to do."

"And which be they, sir?" asked the widow.

"Either to go and put the money into the Chancery Court, or to bury it in the coffin along with the deceased."

"And suppose I put it into the Chancery Court, sir?"

"Then no one will ever get it out again—that's all."

"But if some relation comes for'ard?"

"Then he'll just have to pay two pounds costs for every pound he draws out."

"Lack-a-daisy me!" ejaculated the widow. "I raly think it would be best to bury the money in the poor old gentleman's coffin."

"I am sure it would be," said the reverend adviser; "and although you would be giving up a treasure in this life, you would be laying up for yourself a treasure in heaven."

"Ah! well-a-day, sir—we must all think of that. I shall foller your advice, and bury the money with the poor man in his coffin."

"Without mentioning the business to a soul except Mr. Banks," said the saintly man, in an impressive tone.

"Or else his rest might be disturbed—eh, sir?" demanded the widow, sinking her voice to a whisper. "But do you think there are such people as resurrection men now-a-days?"

"Resurrection men!" ejaculated the reverend visitor, bursting out into a laugh; "no, my dear madam—society has got rid of those abominations."

"Then where do surgeons get corpses from, sir?"

"From the hulks, the prisons, and the workhouses," was the answer.

"What! poor creatures which goes to the workus!" cried Mrs. Smith, revolting at the idea.

"Yes—ma'am; but the surgeons don't like them as subjects, because they're nothing but skin and bone."

"Well, for my part," exclaimed the widow, wiping away a tear, "I think it's wery hard if, after paying rates and taxes for a many—many year, I should be obleeged to go to the workus, and then be cut up in a surgeon's slaughter-house at last."

"Ah! my dear ma'am, these are sad times—very sad times," said the sanctified gentleman. "But a woman who does her duty to her fellow creatures as you do, need fear nothing; heaven will protect you!"

With these words the holy man rose from his seat, and prepared to depart.

"I hope Mr. Banks has engaged you to perform the service over my poor deceased lodger, sir?" said the widow, as she conducted him to the door.

"He has, ma'am," was the reply; and the reverend minister took his leave of Mrs. Smith, from whose mind a considerable load was removed by the suggestion she had received relative to the disposal of the money of her defunct lodger—a suggestion which she now determined to follow to the very letter.

In the mean time the Rattlesnake had been left alone at the mysterious dwelling which she and her terrible paramour inhabited.

Before the Resurrection Man went out, after the call of Mr. Banks, he threw aside his every-day garb, and put on a complete suit of black. He performed the ceremony of his toilet somewhat hurriedly; and the Rattlesnake perceived with the most unfeigned delight that he forgot to transfer the contents of the pockets of his old garments to those of his new ones. At length he went out; and the Rattlesnake instantly commenced a strict examination of the clothes which he had just put off.

There were a few papers and dirty letters, but of those the woman took no notice. Neither did her fingers clutch greedily the three or four sovereigns which were contained in a greasy purse. A bunch of keys—the principal object of her search—rivetted all her attention—engrossed all her interest.

Without a moment's delay, she descended the stairs, and issued from the house. She darted up the narrow alley, paused at the side door, and tried the lock with the different keys. The last of all was the one which opened the door.

The heart of the Rattlesnake beat with joy as she entered the passage, and closed the door carefully behind her.

She first peeped into the front room, and by the faint light that was admitted through the heart-shaped holes in the shutters, she beheld only the implements peculiar to the avocation of a resurrection man; namely, flexible iron rods to sound the depths of graves, and long poles with hooks at the ends to drag up bodies, together with saws, spades, pickaxes, trowels, ropes, skeleton-keys, &c. &c.

The Rattlesnake then entered the back room, which was small, damp, and in a dilapidated condition. The plaster of the walls had given way in several places; and the whole appearance of the chamber seemed to indicate that it had not been inhabited for many years.

A table, a chair, and a cupboard were all the furniture which the room contained. On the table lay the mask, and over the chair hung the cloak in which the Resurrection Man had disguised himself on the preceding night. The basket, which she had seen him use on the same occasion, and which was of the kind that housewives take to market to hold their purchases, lay upon the floor.

The contents and appearance of the room were visible by means of the light admitted through the shutters.

The door of the cupboard was locked, but one of the keys which the Rattlesnake had with her speedily unlocked it. There, however, was nothing either to excite or allay her curiosity—for it was empty.

She now proceeded to examine the chamber more carefully, expecting to find some secret communication with a subterranean excavation; for she was still impressed with the idea that she had heard the steps of the Resurrection Man descend a flight of stairs on the preceding evening; and she was also convinced that the scream she had then heard had proceeded from a greater distance or lower depth than the small back chamber in which she now found herself.

But all her attempts to penetrate this mystery were unavailing; and, fearful that the Resurrection Man might return and detect her proceedings, she hastened away from the ground floor of this strange house.

Carefully locking the doors after her, she succeeded in reaching the upper story and replacing the keys where she had found them, some time ere she heard the steps of the Resurrection Man ascending the staircase.

When he entered the bed-room to change his clothes once more, he found her busily engaged in some domestic occupation; and, as she welcomed him in her usual manner, not a suspicion of her proceedings entered his mind.

"Well," he said, as he assumed his common garb, "I have managed this business. I have played the parson to some purpose; and the old woman has consented to bury the yellow boys along with the old fellow. I shall now sit down and write a letter to a certain Mr. Chichester, which letter you must take to the post yourself. That being done, I can remain quiet until the evening; and then," he added, with a ferocious leer, "*then* for Richard Markham!"

CHAPTER CIII.

HOPES AND FEARS.

We must now go back to the preceding day, and introduce our readers to Markham Place, immediately after the Buffer had called upon Richard in the manner already described.

Richard had received him in the library, and had there heard the exciting news of which the Buffer was the bearer.

Dismissing the man to the kitchen to partake of some refreshment, Richard hastened to the parlour, where Mr. Monroe and Ellen were seated.

The past sorrows and anxieties which the young man had experienced were now all forgotten: forgotten also was the dread exposure which he had so recently received at the theatre,—an exposure which had deprived him of the honourable renown earned by his own talent,—an exposure, too, which had induced Ellen to abandon that career wherein she excelled so pre-eminently.

The idea of meeting his well-beloved brother now alone occupied his mind:—the hope of seeing and even succouring the wanderer banished every other consideration.

His cheek, lately so pale, was flushed with a glow of animation, and his eyes glistened with delight, as he rushed into the room where Ellen and her father were seated.

"Eugene is returned—my brother has come back at last!" he exclaimed.

"Your brother!" repeated Ellen, a deadly pallor overspreading her countenance.

"Eugene!" cried Mr. Monroe, in a tone of deep interest.

"Yes—Eugene is in London—is returned," answered Richard, not noticing the strange impression which his words had made, and still produced upon Ellen, who now sat incapable of motion in her chair, as if she were suddenly paralyzed: "Eugene is in London! A man has just been to tell me this welcome news; and I am to see my brother to-morrow evening."

"To-morrow evening!" said Mr. Monroe. "And why not now—at once?"

"Alas! my brother is in some difficulty, and dares not appear at the dwelling of his forefathers. I am not aware of the nature of that dilemma, but I am assured that he has need of my help."

"Where are you to meet him?" inquired Monroe, somewhat surprised by the singularity of this announcement.

"At the eastern extremity of London—on the banks of the canal, near some place called Twig Folly."

"And at what hour?" demanded the old man.

"To-morrow night, at ten precisely," was the reply.

"Do you know the man who brought you this message? or have you received a letter?" asked Ellen, who now began to breathe more freely.

"No, I never saw the man before; nor have I any letter. But, surely, you cannot suppose that any one is deceiving me in so cruel a manner?"

"I feel convinced of it," said Ellen, with peculiar emphasis on her words and warmth in her manner.

"No—no—impossible!" cried Markham, unwilling to allow the hope which had a moment ago appeared so bright, to be obscured by the mists of doubt: then, acting upon a sudden impulse, he rang the bell violently.

Whittingham speedily made his appearance.

"The man that I have just sent below," said Richard, hastily, "has come to inform me that my brother is in London—"

"Master Eugene in London!" ejaculated the old butler, forgetting his gravity, and literally beginning to dance with joy.

"And he has appointed to meet me to-morrow evening in a very distant and lonely part of London," continued Markham. "This circumstance seems suspicious—strange;—at least so Miss Monroe thinks—"

"Nay—I do not *think*, Richard: I am *sure*," exclaimed Ellen, with the same emphasis which had marked her previous declaration.

"At all events, Whittingham," said Markham, "do you return to the kitchen, get into conversation with the man, and then give us your opinion."

The old butler withdrew to execute these orders.

Markham then began to pace the room in an agitated manner.

"I cannot think who could be cruel enough to practise such a vile cheat upon me," he said, "if a cheat it really be. No one would benefit by so doing. Besides—the man spoke of the appointment which my brother made when we parted on yonder hill; he spoke of that appointment as a token of his sincerity—as a proof of the veracity of his statement—as an evidence that he came direct from Eugene!"

"Many persons are acquainted with the fact of that appointment," said Ellen. "There is not an individual in this neighbourhood who is ignorant of the meeting that is named for the 10th of July, 1843, between the ash-trees on that hill."

"True!" exclaimed Markham. "The mere mention of that appointment is scarcely a sufficient evidence. And yet my brother might deem that it would prove sufficient: Eugene may not know how suspicious the deceits of this world are calculated to render the mind that has been their victim."

"I have no doubt that Eugene is by this time as well acquainted with the world as you can be, Richard," persisted Ellen; "and I am also convinced that if he were to send such a message to you as this stranger has brought—making an appointment at a strange place and at a very lonely hour—he would have been careful to accompany it with some undeniable token of its genuineness."

"You reason sensibly, Ellen," said Markham; "and yet I am by no means inclined to surrender up the hope that was just now so consoling to my heart—wounded as that heart is by many misfortunes!"

"I reason consistently with your interests," returned Ellen. "Nothing could persuade me that your brother would fail to write a line to you in such a case as this is represented to be."

"What say you, Mr. Monroe?" inquired Richard.

"I am hesitating between the two arguments," answered the old man: "I know not whether to encourage the hope to which you cling—or to suffer myself to be persuaded by the reasoning of Ellen."

At this moment Whittingham returned to the parlour.

"The enwoy-plentipotent-and-hairy is gone," said Whittingham; "and, although he didn't show his credentials, my firm compression is that he was raly the representation of the court he said he come from."

"You questioned him closely?" asked Markham.

"You know, Master Richard, I can put a poser or two now and then; and if this man had been a compostor, I should have circumwented him pretty soon, I can assure you."

"He answered your questions in a straightforward manner, then?" persisted Richard.

"He couldn't have been more straightfor'ard," replied Whittingham. "I'm sure he's a honest, simple-hearted, well-meaning man."

"Then it is decided!" ejaculated Richard: "I will go to this appointment. Who knows in what peril my poor brother may be? who can say from what dangers I may save him? who can explain what powerful motives he may have for the nature of the appointment he has made, and the caution he has adopted in making it? I should be wrong to allow a suspicion to interfere with a duty. Were any thing serious to happen to Eugene, through the want of a friend at this moment, how should I ever after reproach myself? I will not incur such a chance: I will go to-morrow evening to the spot named, and to the hour appointed!"

Whittingham withdrew; and Ellen once more endeavoured to deter Richard from his resolution.

"In the name of God, reflect," she exclaimed, with an earnestness which, had he not been otherwise preoccupied, would have struck him by its peculiarity, for it seemed rather the impassioned expression of a conviction based on indisputable grounds, than a doubt which might be based on truth or error;—"in the name of God, reflect, Richard, ere you endanger your life, perhaps, by going at a suspicious hour to a lonely place. Remember, you have enemies: recollect how nearly you met your death at the hands of *one villain* in the neighbourhood of Bird-Cage Walk—the narrative of which occurrence and your miraculous escape you have so often related to us;—reflect that *that* was not the only occasion on which the same miscreant has sought to injure you—"

"I know to what you allude, Ellen," said Markham, significantly; "and I thank you sincerely for your interest in my behalf. But, believe me, there is no Resurrection Man in the present matter: all is straightforward—I feel convinced of it."

Markham uttered these words in a tone which left no scope for further argument or remonstrance; and Ellen threw herself back in her chair, a prey to reflections of the most painful nature.

At length she retired to her chamber to meditate in secret upon the incident of the morning.

"What can I do," she mused aloud, "to convince Richard Markham that he is nursing a delusion? I tremble lest some enemy should meditate treachery against him. Perhaps even his life may be threatened? Oh! the plots—the perfidies—the villanies which are engendered in this London! But how warn him? how prove to him that he is deceived? Alas! that is impossible; unless, indeed—"

But she shook her head impatiently, as if to renounce as impracticable the idea which had for a moment occupied her mind.

"No," she continued, "that were madness indeed! And yet what can be done? He must not be allowed to rush headlong and blindly into danger—for that danger awaits him, I feel convinced. Perhaps that terrible man, from whose power he once escaped, and who denounced him at the theatre, may be the instigator of all this? And, if such be the fact, then who knows where the atrocity of that miscreant may stop? Murder—cold-blooded, ruthless murder may be the result of this mysterious appointment. And the murder of whom?" said Ellen, a shudder passing, like a cold chill, over her entire frame: "the murder of my benefactor—of the noble-minded, the generous-hearted young man who gave us an asylum when all the world forsook us! Oh! no—no—it must not be! I dare not tell him all I know; but I can do somewhat to protect him!"

She smiled, in spite of the unpleasant nature of the emotions that agitated her bosom—she smiled, because a wild and romantic idea had entered her imagination.

Without further hesitation,—and acting under the sudden impulse of that idea,—she sate down and wrote a short note.

When she had sealed and addressed it, she rang the bell.

In a few moments Marian answered the summons.

"My faithful friend," said Ellen, "I am about to put your goodness to another test. But before I explain what I require of you, I beseech that you will not now endeavour to penetrate my motives. You shall know all the day after to-morrow."

"Speak, Miss; I am always ready to do any thing I can for you," said Marian.

"In the evening," continued Ellen, "you must find a pretence to go out for two or three hours. In the first instance you must call at Mr. Greenwood's house—"

"Mr. Greenwood's?" ejaculated Marian.

"Yes—but your business is not this time with him. On the contrary, he must not know the real motive of your visit, which is to deliver this note into the hands of his Italian valet Filippo. You have never seen Filippo—for he entered the service of Mr. Greenwood since you called there some months ago. You cannot, however, mistake him. He is a tall, dark man, with long black curling hair. Moreover, he speaks English with a strong foreign accent."

"The description is sufficient, Miss," said Marian; "I shall not be mistaken."

"This note is to be delivered into his hand—and his only," continued Ellen. "Should you meet Mr. Greenwood by accident, you may say, *'I come from Miss Monroe to inform you that your child is well and thriving.'* This will be an excuse; I must leave the rest to you; but I implore you to do all you can to obtain an interview with Filippo."

"I will follow your wishes, Miss, to the utmost of my power," returned Marian.

"And when you know the motives of my present proceeding," said Ellen, "you will be satisfied with the part you have taken in it."

"I do not doubt you, Miss," observed Marian. "Have you seen the dear little baby lately?"

"I saw him yesterday," answered Ellen. "I called at Mr. Wentworth's: the excellent man's wife was nursing my little Richard. I took him in my arms and fondled him; but, alas! he cried bitterly. Of course he does not know me: he will learn to look up to a stranger as his mother! Oh! Marian, that idea pierced like a dagger to my very heart!"

"Cheer up, Miss!" exclaimed Marian, in a kind tone; "better days will come."

"But never the day, Marian," added Ellen, solemnly, "when I can proclaim myself the mother of that child, nor blush to mention its father's name!"

CHAPTER CIV.

FEMALE COURAGE.

HOLYWELL STREET was once noted only as a mart for second-hand clothing, and booksellers' shops dealing in indecent prints and volumes. The reputation it thus acquired was not a very creditable one.

Time has, however, included Holywell Street in the clauses of its Reform Bill. Several highly respectable booksellers and publishers have located themselves in the place that once deserved no better denomination than "Rag Fair." The unprincipled venders of demoralizing books and pictures have, with few exceptions, migrated into Wych Street or Drury Lane; and even the two or three that pertinaciously cling to their old temples of infamy in Holywell Street, seem to be aware of the incursions of respectability into that once notorious thoroughfare, and cease to outrage decency by the display of vile obscenities in their windows.[1]

The reputation of Holywell Street has now ceased to be a by-word: it is respectable; and, as a mart for the sale of literary wares, threatens to rival Paternoster Row.

It is curious to observe that, while butchers, tailors, linen-drapers, tallow-manufacturers, and toy-venders, are gradually dislodging the booksellers of Paternoster Row, and thus changing the once exclusive nature of this famous street into one of general features, the booksellers, on the other hand, are gradually ousting the old-clothes dealers of Holywell Street.

As the progress of the American colonist towards the far-west drives before it the aboriginal inhabitants, so do the inroads of the bibliophiles menace the Israelites of Holywell Street with total extinction.

Paternoster Row and Holywell Street are both losing their primitive features: the former is becoming a mart of miscellaneous trades; the latter is rising into a bazaar of booksellers.

Already has Holywell Street progressed far towards this consummation. On the southern side of the thoroughfare scarcely a clothes shop remains; and those on the opposite side wear a dirty and miserably dilapidated appearance. The huge masks, which denote the warehouse where masquerading and fancy-attire may be procured on sale or hire, seem to "grin horribly a ghastly smile," as if they knew that their occupation was all but gone. The red-haired ladies who stand

1 Reynolds is being disingenuous. Holywell Street ran north of and parallel to Strand, coming off of St. Clement Danes church. It had the reputation for pornographic and seditious books: one of the latter kind being Reynolds's own first work, the grandiosely claiming *Errors of the Christian Religion Exposed*.

at their doors beneath a canopy of grey trousers with black seats, and blue coats with brown elbows—a distant imitation of Joseph's garment of many colours—seem dispirited and care-worn, and no longer watch, with the delighted eyes of maternal affection, their promising offspring playing in the gutters. Their glances are turned towards the east—a sure sign that they meditate an early migration to the pleasant regions which touch upon the Minories.

Holywell Street is now a thoroughfare which no one can decry on the score of reputation: it is, however, impossible to deny that, were the southern range of houses pulled down, the Strand would reap an immense advantage, and a fine road would be opened from the New Church to Saint Clement Danes.

It was about half-past seven in the evening that Ellen Monroe, dressed in the most simple manner, and enveloped in a large cloak, entered Holywell Street.

Her countenance was pale; but its expression was one of resolution and firmness.

She walked slowly along from the west end of the street towards the eastern extremity, glancing anxiously upon the countenances of those traders who stood in front of the second-hand clothes shops.

At length she beheld a female—one of the identical ladies with red hair above alluded to—standing on the threshold of one of those warehouses.

Ellen looked upwards, and perceived all kinds of articles of male attire suspended over the head of this female, and swinging backwards and forwards, like so many men hanging, upon the shop-front.

Ellen paused—glanced wistfully at the Jewess, and appeared to hesitate.

Her manner was so peculiar, that, although the clothes venders do not usually solicit the custom of females, the Jewess immediately exclaimed in a sharp under-tone, "Sell or buy, ma'am?"

Ellen turned, without another moment's hesitation, into the shop.

"I wish to purchase a complete suit of male attire—for myself," said Miss Monroe. "Serve me quickly—and we shall not dispute about the price."

These last words denoted a customer of precisely the nature that was most agreeable to the Jewess. She accordingly bustled about her, ransacked drawers and cupboards, and spread such a quantity of coats, trousers, and waistcoats, before Ellen, that the young lady was quite bewildered.

"Select me a good suit which you think will fit me," said Miss Monroe, after a moment's hesitation; "and allow me to try it on in a private room."

"Certainly, ma'am," answered the Jewess; and, having looked out a suit, she conducted Ellen up stairs into her own sleeping-apartment.

"And now I require a hat and a pair of boots," said Ellen;—"in a word, every thing suitable to form a complete male disguise. I am going to a masquerade," she added, with a smile.

The Jewess made no reply: it did not concern her, if her customer chose to metamorphose herself, so long as *she* was paid; and she accordingly hastened to supply all the remaining apparel necessary to complete the disguise.

She then left Ellen to dress herself at leisure.

And soon that charming form was clothed in the raiment of the other sex: those delicate feet and ankles were encased in heavy boots; thick blue trousers hampered the limbs lately so supple in the voluptuous dance; a coarse shirt and faded silk waistcoat imprisoned the lovely bosom; a collar and black neckcloth concealed the swan-like neck and dazzling whiteness of the throat; and a capacious frock coat concealed the admirable symmetry of the faultless figure. The hair was then gathered up in a manner which would not betray the sex of the wearer of those coarse habiliments, especially when the disguise was aided by the darkness of the night, and when that luxuriant mass was covered with the broad-brimmed and somewhat slouching hat which the Jewess had provided for the purpose.

Ellen's toilette was thus completed, and she then descended to the shop.

The Jewess—perhaps not altogether unaccustomed to such occurrences—made no comment, and took no impertinent notice of the metamorphosed lady. She contented herself with asking a handsome price for the clothes and accommodation afforded; and Ellen paid the sum without a murmur, merely observing that she should send for her own apparel next day.

Miss Monroe then left the shop, and issued from Holywell Street just as the church clocks in the neighbourhood struck eight.

The reader has, doubtless, seen enough of her character to be well aware that she had acquired a considerable amount of fortitude and self-possession from the various circumstances in which she has been placed: she was not, therefore, now likely to betray any diffidence or timidity as she threaded, in male attire, the crowded streets of the metropolis. She threw into her gait as much assurance as possible; and thus, without exciting any particular notice, she pursued her way towards the eastern districts of the great city.

The weather was cold and damp; but the rain, which had fallen in torrents the day before, had apparently expended its rage for a short interval. A sharp wind, however, swept through the streets; and Ellen pitied the poor shivering, half-naked wretches, whom she saw huddling upon steps, or crouching beneath archways, as she passed along.

Ellen walked rapidly, and having gained Bishopsgate Street, proceeded as far as the terminus of the Eastern Counties Railway.

There she halted, and glanced anxiously around her.

In a few minutes, a tall man, wrapped up in a large cloak, came up to the spot where she was standing.

"Is that you, Filippo?" said Ellen.

"Yes, Miss; I am here in obedience to your commands," returned Mr. Greenwood's Italian valet. "I promised your servant yesterday evening that I would be punctual to the hour—half-past eight—to-night; and I have kept my word."

"I owe you a debt of gratitude, which I never shall be able to repay," said Ellen. "Your generous behaviour towards me on a former occasion emboldened me to write to you when I required a friend. I told you in my note not to be surprised if you should find me disguised in male attire; I moreover requested you to arm yourself with pistols. Have you complied with this desire on my part?"

"I have, Miss," answered Filippo. "Conceiving it to be impossible that you could wish me to aid you in any dishonourable service, I have attended to your commands in every respect. I mentioned to you when we last met that my mission to England is from a lady now enjoying a sovereign rank, and that it is devoted to good and liberal purposes. Under those circumstances, I am ready to assist you in any manner consistent with my own principles and with the real objects of my mission."

"You will this night be the means of rendering an essential service to a fellow-creature," said Ellen, in an impressive tone. "A foul conspiracy against him,—whether to take his life or for other purposes of villany, I know not,—has been devised; and he has blindly fallen into the snare that has been spread for him. At ten o'clock he is to attend an appointment on the banks of the canal at a place called Twig Folly. We must proceed thither: we must watch at a little distance; and, if need be, we must interpose to save him."

"A more simple plan, Miss," said the Italian, "would be to warn this individual of his danger."

"I have done so; but he will not believe that treachery is intended," returned Ellen.

"Then another effectual manner to counteract the designs of villains in such a case is to obtain the assistance of the police."

"No, Filippo; such a proceeding would lead to inquiries and investigations whence would transpire circumstances that must not be made known."

"Miss Monroe, this proceeding on your part is so mysterious, that I hesitate whether to accompany you further," said the Italian.

While thus conversing, they had pursued their way, Ellen being the guide, along Church Street into the Bethnal Green Road.

"Come with me—do not hesitate—I implore you," exclaimed Ellen. "If you persist in penetrating my motives for acting in this strange manner, I will tell you all, rather than you should retreat at a moment when it is too late for me to obtain other succour. And be your resolve as it may," added Ellen, hastily, "nothing shall induce *me* to turn back. Desert me—abandon me if you will, Filippo—but, in the name of every thing sacred, lend me the weapons which you carry with you."

The Italian made no reply for some moments, but continued to walk rapidly along by the side of the disguised lady.

"I will believe, Miss Monroe," he said, at length, "that your motives are excellent; but are you well advised?"

"Listen," exclaimed Ellen. "The individual, whose life we may perhaps this night save, is Richard Markham—the generous young man who has been a son to my father, and a brother to myself."

"I have heard Mr. Greenwood mention his name many times," observed Filippo.

"He believes that he is to meet his brother, from whom he has been for many years separated, this night on the banks of the canal," continued Ellen.—"For certain reasons I know most positively that the idea of such an appointment can only be a plot on the part of some enemies of Richard Markham. And yet I dared not communicate those reasons to him—Oh! no," added Ellen, with a shudder, "that was impossible—impossible!"

"I do not seek to penetrate further into your secrets, Miss," said Filippo, struck by the earnestness of the young lady's manner, and naturally inclined to admire the heroism of her character, as developed by the proceeding in which he was now bearing a part.

"And the necessity of keeping those *certain reasons* a profound secret," continued Ellen, "has also prevented me from procuring the intervention of the police. In the same way, should the result of our present expedition introduce you to the notice of Mr. Markham, it would be necessary for you to retain as a profound secret who you are—how you came to accompany me—and especially your connexion with Mr. Greenwood. Not for worlds must the name of Greenwood be mentioned in the presence of Richard Markham! If it should be necessary to enter into explanations with him, leave that task to me; and contradict nothing that you may hear me state. I have my motives for all I do and all I say—motives so grave, so important, that, did you know them all, you would applaud and not doubt me. And now are you satisfied?"

"Perfectly," returned Filippo: "I will not ask another question, nor hesitate another moment."

"My everlasting gratitude is your due," said Ellen. "And now, one more favour have I to ask."

"Name it," answered the Italian.

"Give me one of your pistols."

"But, Miss Monroe—"

"Pray do not refuse me! I am not a coward; and I must inform you that I learnt to fire a pistol at the theatre."

The Italian handed the young lady one of his loaded weapons.

She concealed it beneath the breast of her coat; and her heart palpitated with pride and satisfaction.

Ellen and the Italian then quickened their pace, and proceeded rapidly towards Globe Town.

CHAPTER CV.

THE COMBAT.

IN spite of the suspicions entertained by Mr. Monroe and Ellen concerning the genuineness of the appointment for which Markham was engaged, the young man was too devotedly attached to the memory of his brother not to indulge in the most wild and sanguine hopes.

Thus, as he proceeded to the place of meeting near Twig Folly, he communed with himself in the following manner:—

"If my brother be involved in pecuniary difficulties,—or if he have committed any imprudence, from the results of which money may release him,—how gladly will I dispose of the remainder of my small income—how joyfully will I devote all I possess to aid him! And then, when I have no other resources, I will open the mysterious document which Thomas Armstrong placed in my hands ere he breathed his last; and I feel convinced that I shall at least receive therefrom good advice—if not pecuniary succour—to guide me in future. O Eugene! is it possible that I am now about to meet you once more? On the 10th of July, 1831, did we part on the summit of the hill which overlooks the mansion of our ancestors. This is the 2d of January, 1840. Eight years and a half have now elapsed since the day of our separation. Ah! I know the proud—the haughty—the independent disposition of my brother! Were he prosperous—were he successful in his pursuits, (be those pursuits what they may,) he would not seek me now. He would wait until the accomplishment of the twelve years: he would not seek me until the 10th of July, 1843. *Then* should we compare notes, and ascertain who was the more prosperous! Yes—this would be my brother's mode of conduct. And therefore he is unhappy—he is unfortunate, that he seeks me ere the time be elapsed: he is perhaps poor—in want—who knows? Oh! how sincerely I hope that this is no delusion; that my unfortunate star will not pursue me even unto the point of so terrible a disappointment! No—I feel that this is no deception—that Eugene indeed awaits me. Who could wish to injure *me?* who would desire to take *my* life? who could hope to obtain a treasure by laying a plot to rob *me?* The idea is preposterous! Yes—the appointment is a genuine one: I am about to meet my brother Eugene!"

Such were the meditations of Richard Markham as he proceeded towards the place of appointment.

He was considerably before his time; for hope cannot brook delay.

When he reached the banks of the canal, he was struck by the lonely and deserted nature of the spot. The sward was damp and marshy with the late heavy rains: the canal was swollen, and rolled, muddy and dark, between its banks, the pale and sickly moon vainly wooing its bosom to respond to the caresses of its beams by a reflective kiss.

The bank on which Markham now walked backwards and forwards, and which constituted the verge of the region of Globe Town, was higher than the opposite one; and the canal, swollen by the rains, had deluged many parts of that latter shore.

In the place where Markham now found himself, several ditches and sluices had been cut; and these, added to the uneven and swampy nature of the soil, rendered his ramble in that quarter not only unpleasant, but even dangerous.

Nevertheless, Markham continued to pace backwards and forwards on the bank where he expected to meet one who was so dear to him.

He had been at his post about half an hour when footsteps suddenly fell upon his ears.

He stopped, and listened.

The steps approached; and in a few moments he beheld, through the obscurity of the night, a person advancing towards him.

"True to your appointment, sir," said the individual, when he came up to the spot where Richard was standing.

"I told you that I should not fail," answered Markham, who had immediately recognised the voice of the man that had borne him the message making the present appointment. "But what of my brother? will he come? is he near? Speak!"

"He will be here in a few moments," said the man, who, as our readers well know, was none other than the Buffer.

"Are you sure?" demanded Markham. "Why has he sent you first? could he suspect treachery from his own brother?"

"Not a bit of it," replied the Buffer. "Only—but here he comes, sure enow."

Approaching footsteps were heard; and in a minute or two another form emerged from the gloom of night.

Markham's heart palpitated violently.

"Here is your brother, sir," said the Buffer.

"Eugene—dear Eugene!" cried Richard, springing forward to catch his brother in his arms.

"Brother indeed!" muttered the ominous voice of the Resurrection Man; and at the same moment Richard was pinioned from behind by the Buffer, who skilfully wove a cord around his arms, and fastened his elbows together.

"Villains!" ejaculated Richard, struggling with all his might—but vainly, for the Resurrection Man, whose voice he had immediately recognised but too well, threw him violently upon the damp sod.

"Now, my lad," cried the Resurrection Man, "your fate is decided. In a few minutes you'll be at the bottom of the canal, and then—"

He said no more—for at that moment another person appeared upon the scene; and, quick as thought, the Resurrection Man was felled by the butt end of a pistol.

But the instant the miscreant touched the ground, he caught a desperate hold of the person who had so suddenly and unexpectedly appeared upon the spot; and Filippo—for it was he—also rolled on the damp sward.

The Resurrection Man leapt upon him, and caught hold of his throat with such savage violence, that the Italian would have been suffocated in a few moments, had not the flash of a pistol close by the head of the Resurrection Man turned the fortune of the combat.

The pistol so aimed only flashed in the pan; but the sudden glare singed the Resurrection Man's hair, and caused him to abandon his victim and spring upon his feet with an alacrity that resembled a galvanic effect.

The Buffer, alarmed by the first attack on the part of Filippo, had relinquished his hold of the rope that confined Richard's arms; and Markham, encouraged by this sudden and unexpected assistance, disengaged himself from the coil with the rapidity of lightning. He then sprang upon the Buffer, hurled him to the ground, and, placing his knee upon the ruffian's chest, kept him fast in that prostrate condition on the very verge of the canal.

The Resurrection Man, with eagle glance, beheld the situation

of affairs. He saw his confederate powerless, and desperate odds leagued against himself—for, in the darkness of the night, he could not observe that one of his opponents was a female in disguise.

The moment that he sprang from the ground, in consequence of the flash of the pistol close by his ear, he cast this comprehensive look over the field of action.

There was no time for hesitation.

Pushing Ellen violently aside, and dashing Filippo furiously back again upon the ground from which he was rising, the Resurrection Man darted upon Richard Markham.

In another moment there was a splash of water—a cry of horror issued from the lips of Ellen; the Resurrection Man shouted "Run! run!"—but neither the young lady nor Filippo thought of interrupting the flight of the miscreants.

"The villains!—they have drowned him!" exclaimed Filippo; and, without an instant's hesitation, he plunged into the canal.

"Brave man!" cried Ellen. "Save him—oh! save him!"

As she uttered these words, she stumbled over the coil of rope which had been used to confine Markham's hands, and which the miscreants had left behind them.

Instantly twining one end round her delicate wrist, she cast the other into the canal; and creeping so far down the bank as nearly to touch the water, she exclaimed, "Here is a rope, Filippo! Richard, try and catch the rope. Speak, Filippo—can you save him? If not, I will myself plunge into the stream—and—"

"He is lost—he is gone!" said Filippo, who was swimming about on the surface of the water as skilfully as if it were his native element.

"Oh, God! do not say that! do not—"

"I see him—I see him, Miss—yonder—down the stream—struggling desperately—"

At that moment a faint cry for help echoed over the bosom of the canal.

Ellen scrambled up the bank, and darted along the margin with the speed of the fawn, dragging the long coil of rope after her.

In a few moments she beheld a black object appear on the surface of the water—then disappear again in an instant.

But Filippo had already gained that part of the stream; and Ellen directed him with her voice to the spot where the object had sunk.

The brave Italian, though well-nigh exhausted, dived fearlessly; and to the infinite joy of Ellen, re-appeared upon the surface, exclaiming, "He is saved—he is saved!"

Supporting Markham's head above the water, Filippo swam to the bank; and, aided by Ellen and the rope, succeeded in landing his burden as well as himself.

Markham was insensible; but Filippo placed his hand upon the young man's breast, and said, "He lives!"

"Heaven be thanked!" ejaculated Ellen, solemnly.

She then chafed his temples; while the Italian rubbed the palms of his hands.

In a few minutes Richard moaned.

The attentions of those who hung over him were redoubled; and Filippo was about to propose to convey him to the nearest dwelling, when he gasped violently, and murmured, "Where am I?"

"Saved!" answered Ellen. "None but friends are near you."

A quarter of an hour had not elapsed from the moment that he was rescued from the water when he was so far recovered as to sit up on the bank, and all fears on the part of Ellen relative to his complete resuscitation had vanished.

"Ellen—is that you? can this be you? was it your voice that I heard?" he said, in a faint tone: "or is it a vision?"

"It is no vision, Richard—it is indeed Ellen, who owes you so much, and who has been the humble instrument—aided by this brave man—of saving your life."

"And who is this brave man?" asked Markham "Tell me his name, that I may pour forth my gratitude to him, as well as to you, kind Ellen—my sister!"

"His sister!" murmured Ellen; while an emotion, like an electric shock, agitated her to the very heart's core.

But those words—"his sister!"—were not heard by either Markham or Filippo.

"Do not fatigue yourself by speaking now," said Ellen, after a moment's pause. "Suffice it for the present to tell you that I was afraid of treachery towards you—I had my misgivings—a presentiment of evil haunted me! I owed you so much, that I was determined to watch over your safety—weak and powerless as I am. Hence this strange attire. Fortunately I met this brave man—a total stranger to me—near the spot; and, when I communicated my object to him, he generously offered to bear me company."

"Excellent girl!—generous stranger!" cried Richard; "I owe you my life. Oh! how can I ever express my gratitude?"

"We must not speak on that subject now, sir," said Filippo. "The chief point to be considered is how to get you home."

"And he lives so far from here, too," hastily exclaimed Ellen, laying her hand at the same time, but unseen by Markham, on Filippo's arm.

The Italian took the hint, which was to remind him that he must not seem to know the place of residence, or indeed any other particular concerning the affairs, of Richard Markham.

"Oh! this bitter disappointment—this vile treachery!" cried the young man, whose thoughts were now reflected back to the cause of the perils from which he had just escaped.

"Compose yourself," said Ellen, with peculiar and touching kindness of manner: "compose yourself, Richard; and do not excite yourself by unpleasant reflections. Let us rather think how we are to convey you home. There is no vehicle to be obtained in this neighbourhood."

"I feel myself able to walk," said Markham,—"at least as far as the nearest place where we can procure conveyance."

"Wrap yourself up in my cloak," cried Filippo. "It is close at hand—I took it off and concealed it under yonder tree, before the conflict began."

Filippo hastened to fetch the cloak, in which Markham enveloped himself.

Then, leaning on the arms of those to whom he was indebted for his rescue from the murderous designs of his enemies, he walked slowly away from the spot where he had hoped to meet a brother, but where he had encountered fiends in human shape.

In this manner they traversed Globe Town, and reached Bethnal Green New Church. In that neighbourhood they procured a cab, into which Markham and Ellen stepped.

"I shall now take leave of you, sir," said Filippo, "and I most sincerely hope that you will soon recover from the effects of this night's maltreatment."

"Generous man!" cried Markham, "tell me your name that I may—"

But Filippo had already disappeared.

"How strange!" said Markham. "That noble-hearted foreigner makes light of his own good deeds. He has left me no opportunity of expressing my gratitude more fully than by mere words."

"He is evidently a man of lofty feelings and generous disposition," observed Ellen calmly. "It was fortunate that I happened to encounter him in that lonely spot."

She then informed the driver whither he was to proceed; and the vehicle rolled quickly away.

CHAPTER CVI.

THE GRAVE-DIGGER.

Three days after the events related in the preceding chapter,—and at that hour in the cold wintry morning when the dawn breaks in fitful gleams through a dense atmosphere of a dark neutral dye,—a labouring-man, with a shovel and pickaxe upon his shoulder, entered one of the cemeteries in the immediate vicinity of Globe Lane.

This cemetery was only partly enclosed by houses; on the remaining sides there was a low wall.

The soil was damp; and a nauseous odour, emanating from it, impregnated the air. When the sun lay for several days upon the place, even in the depth of winter,—and invariably throughout the summer,—the stench was so intolerable that not a dwelling in the neighbourhood was seen with a window open. Nevertheless, that sickly, fetid odour penetrated into every house, and every room, and every inhabited nook or corner, in that vicinity; and the clothes of the poor inmates smelt, and their food tasted, of the damp grave!

The cemetery was crowded with the remains of mortality. The proprietors of the ground had only one aim in view—namely, to crowd the greatest possible quantity of corpses into the smallest space. But even this economy of room did not prevent the place from being so filled with the dead, that in a given quantity of the soil it was difficult to say whether earth or decayed human remains predominated. Still the cemetery was kept open for interments; and when there was no room for a new-comer, some recently-buried tenant of a grave was exhumed to afford the required space.

In one part of the ground was a rude brick-building, denominated a Bone-House. This hovel was provided with a large fire-place; and seldom did a day pass without smoke being seen to issue from the chimney. On those occasions,—when the furnace was lighted,—the stench from the cemetery was always more powerful than at other times.

Some of the poor inhabitants of the adjoining houses had remonstrated with the parochial authorities on the subject of this nuisance being tolerated; but the only reply the applicants could obtain was, "Well, prefer an indictment at the session, if you don't like it!"

The idea of men in the receipt of eight or ten shillings a week preferring an indictment! Such a process is only accessible to those possessed of ample means; for the legislature has purposely rendered law,—that is, the power of obtaining justice, enforcing rights, or suppressing nuisances,—a luxury attainable only by money. The poor, indeed! who ever thought of legislating for the poor? Legislate *against* them, and it is all well and good: heap statute upon statute—pile act upon act—accumulate measure upon measure—encumber the most simple forms with the most intricate technicalities—diversify readings and expand in verbiage until the sense becomes unintelligible—convert the whole legal scheme into a cunning web, so that the poor man cannot walk three steps without entangling his foot in one of those meshes of whose very existence he was previously unaware, and whose nature he cannot comprehend even when involved therein;—do all this, and you are a wise and sound statesman; for this is legislating *against* the poor—and who, we repeat, would ever think of legislating *for* them?

But to continue.

The grave-digger entered the cemetery, and cast a glance around him.

That glance well expressed the man's thoughts; for he mentally asked himself, "Whose grave must I disturb now to make room for the new one?"

At length he advanced towards a particular spot, considered it for a moment, and then struck his spade into the soil, as much as to say, "This will do."

The place where he had now halted was only a few yards from the Bone-House. Taking a key from his pocket, he proceeded to unlock the door of that building.

Entering the Bone-House he took from amongst a quantity of implements in one corner, a long flexible iron rod similar to those which we have already described as being used by the body-snatchers.

Returning to the grave, he thrust the rod into the ground. It met with a little resistance from some substance a little harder than the soil; but the man pushed it downwards with a strong arm; and it sank at least twelve feet into the ground.

Satisfied with this essay of the nature of the spot, the grave-digger drew back the rod; and from the deep but narrow aperture thus formed, issued a stench more pestiferous than that which ever came from the lowest knacker's yard.

The man retreated rapidly to the Bone-House; that odour was too powerful even for one who had passed the greater portion of his life in that very grave-yard.

He now proceeded to light a fire in the Bone-House; and when he saw the huge logs which he heaped on the grate, blazing brightly, he covered them with coke. The current of air from the open door fanned the flames, which roared up the chimney; and the grave-digger felt invigorated and cheered by the genial warmth that issued from the ample grate.

After lingering for a few minutes in the Bone-House, the grave-digger returned to the spot which he had previously marked for excavation.

Baring his brawny arms to the very shoulders, he now set himself vigorously to work to dig the grave which was to receive a new-comer that afternoon.

Throwing the earth up on either side, he had digged to a depth of about two feet, when his spade encountered a coffin. He immediately took his pickaxe, broke the coffin to pieces, and then separated with his shovel the pieces of wood and the human bones from the damp earth. The coffin was already so soft with decay that the iron rod had penetrated through it without much difficulty; and it therefore required but little exertion to break it up altogether.

But the odour which came from the grave was now of the most nauseating kind—fetid, sickly, pestiferous—making the atmosphere heavy, and the human breath thick and clammy, as it were—and causing even that experienced grave-digger to retch as if he were about to vomit.

Leaping from the grave, he began to busy himself in conveying the pieces of the broken coffin and the putrid remains of mortality into the Bone-House, where he heaped them pell-mell upon the fire.

The flesh had not completely decayed all away from the bones; a thick, black, fatty-looking substance still covered those human relics; and the fire was thus fed with a material which made the flames roar and play half up the chimney.

And from the summit of that chimney came a smoke—thick, dense, and dark, like the smoke of a gasometer or a manufactory, but bearing on its sable wing the odour of a pestilence.

The man returned to the grave, and was about to resume his labour, when his eyes caught sight of a black object, almost embedded in the damp clay heaped up by the side. He turned it over with his spade: it was the upper part of the skull, with the long, dark hair of a woman still remaining attached to it. The grave-digger coolly took up the relic by that long hair which perhaps had once been a valued ornament; and, carrying it in this manner into the Bone-House, threw it upon the fire. The hair hissed for a moment as it burnt, for it was damp and clogged with clay; then the voracious flames licked up the thin coat of blackened flesh which had still remained on the skull; and lastly devoured the bone itself.

The grave-digger returned to his toils; and at a depth of scarcely one foot below the coffin thus exhumed and burnt, his shovel was again impeded for a moment—and by another coffin!

Once more was the pickaxe put into requisition—a second coffin was broken up; another decomposing, but not entirely decomposed, corpse was hacked, and hewed, and rent to pieces by the merciless implement which was wielded by a merciless arm;—and in a few moments, the fire in the Bone-House burnt cheerfully once more, the mouth of the chimney vomiting forth its dense and pest-bearing breath, the volume of which was from time to time lighted with sparks and flakes of fire.

Thus was it that this grave-digger disposed of the old tenants of the cemetery in order to make room for new ones.

And then fond, surviving relations and friends speak of the *last home* and the *quiet resting-place* of the deceased: they talk with affectionate reverence of those who *sleep in the grave*, and they grow pathetic in their eulogies of the *tranquil slumber of the tomb!*

Poor deluded creatures! While they are thus engaged in innocent discourse,—a discourse that affords them solace when they ponder upon the loss which they have sustained,—the *last home* is invaded—the *quiet resting-place* is rudely awakened with sacrilegious echoes—the *sleep of the grave* is disturbed by the thunder of a pickaxe—and the corpse is snatched from the *tranquil slumber of the tomb* to be cast into the all-devouring furnace of the Bone-House.

The grave-digger proceeded in his task; and a third coffin was speedily encountered. Each successive one was more decayed than that which had preceded it; and thus the labour of breaking them up diminished in severity.

But the destination of one and all was the same—the fire of the Bone-House.

No wonder that the cemetery continued to receive so many fresh tenants, although the neighbours knew that it must be full:—no wonder that the stench was always more pestiferous when the furnace of the Bone-House was lighted!

And that man—that grave-digger performed his task—his odious task—without compunction, and without remorse: he was fulfilling the commands of his employers—his employers were his superiors—and "surely his superiors must know what was right and what was wrong!"

And so the grave-digger worked and toiled—and the fire in the Bone-House burnt cheerfully—and the dark, thick smoke was borne over the whole neighbourhood, like a plague-cloud.

Two hours had passed away since the man had commenced his work; and he now felt hungry.

Retiring to the Bone-House, he took a coffee-pot from the shelf, and proceeded to make some coffee, the material for which was in a cupboard in a corner of the building. Water he took from a large pitcher, also kept in that foul place; and bread he had brought with him in his pockets.

He drew a stool close to the fire; and, when the coffee boiled, commenced his meal.

The liquid cheered and refreshed him; but he never once recollected that it had been heated by flames fed with human flesh and bones!

While he was thus occupied, he heard footsteps approaching the Bone-House; and in a few moments Mr. Banks, the undertaker, appeared upon the threshold.

"Mornin', sir," said the grave-digger. "Come to have a look at the size of the grave, s'pose? You've no call to be afeard; I'll be bound to make it big enow."

"I hope it won't be a very deep one, Jones," returned the undertaker. "Somehow or another the friends of the blessed defunct are awerse to a deep grave."

"My orders is to dig down sixteen feet and shore up the sides as I deepens," said Jones. "Don't you see that I shall throw the earth on wery light, so that it won't take scarcely no trouble to shovel it out agin; 'cos the next seven as comes to this ground must all go into that there grave."

"Sixteen feet!" ejaculated the undertaker, in dismay. "It will never do, Jones. The friends of the dear deceased wouldn't sleep quiet in their beds if they thought he had to sleep so deep in his'n. It won't do, Jones—it won't do."

"My orders is sich from the proprietors, sir," answered the grave-digger, munching and drinking at intervals with considerable calmness.

"Now I tell you what it is, Jones," continued the undertaker, after a moment's pause, "not another grave will I ever order in this ground, and not another carkiss that I undertake shall come here, unless you choose to comply with my wishes concerning this blessed old defunct."

"Well, Mr. Banks, there isn't a gen'leman wot undertakes in all Globe Town, or from Bonner's Fields down to Mile End Gate, that I'd sooner obleege than yourself," said Jones, the grave-digger; "but if so be I transgresses my orders—"

"Who will know it?" interrupted Banks. "You have whole and sole charge of the ground; and it can't be often that the proprietors come to trouble you."

"Well, sir, there is summut in that—"

"And then, instead of five shillings for yourself, I should not hesitate to make it ten—"

"That's business, Mr. Banks. How deep must the grave be?"

"How deep is it already?"

"A matter of nine feet, sir," said Jones.

"Then not another hinch must you move," cried the undertaker, emphatically; "and here's the ten bob as an earnest."

Mr. Banks accordingly counted ten shillings into the hands of the grave-digger.

"When's the funeral a-coming, sir?" asked Jones, after a pause.

"At two precisely," replied Mr. Banks.

"Rale parson, or von of your men as usual?" continued the grave-digger, inquiringly.

"Oh, a friend of mine—a wery pious, savoury, soul-loving wessel, Jones—a man that it'll do your heart good to hear. But, I say, Jones," added the undertaker, "you're getting uncommon full here."

"Yes, full enow, sir; but I makes room."

"I see you do," said Banks, glancing towards the fire: "what a offensive smell it makes."

"And would you believe that I can scarcely support it myself sometimes, Mr. Banks?" returned Jones. "But, arter all, our ground isn't so bad as some others in London."

"I know it isn't," observed the undertaker.

"Now ain't it a odd thing, sir," continued the grave-digger, "that persons which dwells up in decent neighbourhoods like, and seems exceedin' proud of their fine houses and handsome shops, shouldn't notice the foul air that comes from places only hid by a low wall or a thin paling?"

"It is indeed odd enough," said Mr. Banks.

"Well, I knows the diggers in some o' the yards more west," continued Jones, "and I've heard from them over and over agin that they pursues just the wery same course as we does here—has a Bone House or some such conwenient place, and burns the coffins and bones that is turned up."

"I suppose it is necessary, Jones?" observed Mr. Banks.

"Necessary, sir? in course it be," exclaimed the grave-digger. "On'y fancy wot a lot of burials takes place every year in London; and room must be made for 'em somehow or other."

"Ah! I know something about that," said the undertaker. "Calkilations have been made which proves that the average life of us poor weak human creeturs is thirty-five years; so, if London contains a million and a half of people, a million and a half of persons dies, and is buried in the course of every thirty-five years. Isn't that a fine thing for them that's in the undertaking line? 'cause it's quite clear that there's a million and a half of funerals in every thirty-five years in this blessed city."

"And a million and a half of graves or waults rekvired," said Jones. "Well, then, who the deuce can blame us for burning up the old 'uns to make room for the new 'uns?"

"Who, indeed?" echoed Mr. Banks. "T'other day I had an undertaking, which was buried in Enon Chapel, Saint Clement's Lane,—down there by Lincoln's Inn, you know. The chapel's surrounded by houses, all okkipied by poor people, and the stench is horrid. The fact is, that the chapel's divided into two storeys: the upper one is the preaching place; and the underneath one is the burial place. There's only a common boarded floor to separate 'em. You go down by a trap-door in the floor; and pits is dug below for the coffins. Why, at one end the place is so full, that the coffins is piled up till they touch the ceiling—that is, the floor of the chapel itself, and there's only a few inches of earth over 'em. The common sewer runs through the place; so, what with that and the coffins and carkisses, it's a nice hole."

"Wuss than this?" said Jones.

"Of course it is," returned Banks; "'cause at all ewents this *is* out in the open air, while t'other's shut up and close. But I'll tell you what it is, Jones," continued the undertaker, sinking his voice as if he were afraid of being overheard by a stranger, "the people that lives in that densely-populated quarter about Saint Clement's Lane, exists in the midst of a pestilence. Why they breathe nothing but the putrid stench of the Enon burial-place, the Green Ground in Portugal Street, and the Alms-House burying ground down at the bottom of the Lane."

"All that'll breed a plague von o' these days in the werry middle of London," observed Jones.

"Not a doubt of it," said the undertaker. "But I haven't done yet all I had to say about that quarter. Wery soon after a burial takes place at Enon Chapel, a queer-looking, long, narrow, black fly crawls out of the coffin. It is a production of the putrefaction of the dead body. But what do you think? Next season this fly is succeeded by another kind of insect just like the common bug, and with wings. The children that go to Sunday-school at the Chapel calls 'em '*body bugs*.' Them insects is seen all through the summer flying or crawling about the Chapel. All the houses that overlooks the Chapel is infested with rats; and if a poor creetur only hangs a bit of meat out of his window in the summer time, in a few hours it grows putrid."[1]

"Well, Mr. Banks, sir," said Jones, after reflecting profoundly for some moments, "it's wery lucky that you ain't one o' them chaps which writes books and nonsense."

---

1 During 1841, the Enon Chapel was regularly booked for meetings of the London United Temperance Association. This body published a weekly journal, *The Teetotaler*, whose editor was none other than G. W. M. Reynolds.

"Why so, Jones?"

"'Cos if you was to print all that you've been tellin' me, you'd make the fortunes of them new cemetries that's opened all round London, and the consekvence would be that the grounds *in* London would have to shut up shop."

"Very true, Jones. But what I'm saying to you now is only in confidence, and by way of chat. Why, do you know that the people round about the burying grounds in London—this one as well as any other—have seen the walls of their rooms covered at times with a sort of thick fatty fluid, which produces a smell that's quite horrid! Look at that burying place in Drury Lane. It's so full of blessed carkisses, that the ground is level with the first-floor windows of the houses round it."

"Well, it's a happy thing to know that the world don't trouble themselves with these here matters," said Jones. "Thank God! in my ground I clears and clears away, coffins and bodies both alike, as quick as I turns 'em up. Lord! what a sight of coffin nails I sells every month to the marine-store dealers; and yet people passes by them shops and sees second-hand coffin furniture put out for sale, and never thinks of how it got there, and where it come from."

"Of course they don't," cried Banks. "What the devil do you think would become of a many trades if people always wondered, and wondered how they supported theirselves?"

"You speaks like a book, Mr. Banks, sir," said Jones. "Arter all, I've often thought wot a fool I am not to sell the coffin-wood for fuel, as most other grave-diggers does in grounds that's obleeged to be cleared of the old 'uns to make room for the new 'uns. But, I say, Mr. Banks, sir, I've often been going to ask you a question about summut, and I've *always* forgot it; but talkin' of these things puts me in mind of it. What's the reason, sir, that gen'lemen in the undertaking line wery often bores holes right through the coffins?"

"That's what we call '*tapping the coffin*,' Jones," answered Mr. Banks; "and we do it whenever a body a going to remain at home two or three days with the coffin-lid screwed down, before the funeral takes place. Poor people generally buries on Sunday: well, p'raps the coffin's took home on Wednesday or Thursday, and then the body's put in and the lid's screwed tight down at once to save trouble when

Sunday comes. Then we tap the coffin to let out the gas; 'cause there *is* a gas formed by the decomposition of dead bodies."[1]

"Well, all that's a cut above me," said Jones. "And now I must get back to work—"

"Not at *that* grave, mind," interrupted the undertaker. "It musn't be another hinch deeper."

"Not a bit, sir—I ain't a goin' to touch it: but I've got another place to open; so here goes."

With these words the grave-digger rose from his seat, and walked slowly out of the Bone-House.

"At two o'clock, Jones, I shall be here with the funeral," said Mr. Banks.

"Wery good, sir," returned Jones.

The undertaker then left the burial-ground; and the grave-digger proceeded to open another pit.

CHAPTER CVII.

A DISCOVERY.

At two o'clock precisely the funeral entered the cemetery.

Four villanous-looking fellows supported a common coffin, over which was thrown a scanty pall, full of holes, and so ragged at the edges that it seemed as if it were embellished with a fringe.

Mr. Banks, with a countenance expressing only a moderate degree of grief, attended as a mourner, accompanied by the surgeon and the Buffer. The truth is that Mr. Banks had a graduated scale of funeral expressions of countenance. When he was uncommonly well paid, his physiognomy denoted a grief more poignant than that of even the nearest relatives of the deceased: when he was indifferently paid, as he considered himself to be in the present case, he could not afford

1 The products of ordinary combustion are sufficiently poisonous. The gases produced by the decomposition of the dead are partially soluble in water; and a fatty pellicle is instantly formed in large quantities. The wood, saturated with these dissolved gases, and used as fuel (a frequent occurrence in poor neighbourhoods, and in the vicinity of metropolitan graveyards), must diffuse, in addition to the exhalations constantly given off from bodies in vaults, and on the earth's surface, vast volumes of gaseous poison. Hence many of those maladies whose source, symptoms, and principle defy medical experience either to explain or cure. [Reynolds's note.]

tears, although he was not so economical as to dispense with a white pocket-handkerchief.

In front of the procession walked the Resurrection Man, clad in a surplice of dingy hue, and holding an enormous prayer-book in his hand. This miscreant performed one of the most holy—one of the most sacred of religious rites!

Start not, gentle reader! This is no exaggeration—no extravagance on our part. In all the poor districts in London, the undertakers have their own men to solemnise the burial rites of those who die in poverty, or who have no friends to superintend their passage to the grave.

The Resurrection Man,—a villain stained with every crime—a murderer of the blackest dye—a wretch whose chief pursuit was the violation of the tomb,—the Resurrection Man read the funeral service over *the unknown* who was now consigned to the grave.

The ceremony ended; and Jones hastened to throw the earth back again into the grave.

The surgeon exchanged a few words with the Resurrection Man, and then departed towards his home.

Mr. Banks and the Buffer accompanied the Resurrection Man to his own abode, where they found a copious repast ready to be served up to them by the Rattlesnake. The Buffer's wife was also there; and the party sat down with a determination to enjoy themselves.

To accomplish this most desirable aim there were ample means. A huge round of beef smoked upon the board, flanked with sundry pots of porter; and on a side-table stood divers bottles of "Booth's best."

"Well," said Mr. Banks, "the worst part now is over. We have got the body under ground—"

"And we must soon get it up again," added the Resurrection Man drily. "You are sure the old woman put the money in the coffin?"

"I see her do it," answered the undertaker. "She wrapped it up in a old stocking which belonged to the blessed defunct—"

"Blessed defunct indeed!" said the Rattlesnake, with a coarse laugh.

"You see, ma'am, I can't divest myself of my professional lingo," observed Mr. Banks. "It comes natural to me now. But as I was a saying, I see the old woman wrap the thirty-one quids up in the toe of a stocking, and put it on his breast—"

"On the shroud, or underneath?" demanded the Resurrection Man eagerly.

"Underneath," replied Banks: "I took good care of that. I knowed very well that you'd want to draw the body up by the head, and that the money must be so placed as to come along with it."

"Of course," said the Buffer; "or else we should have to dig out all the earth, and break open the lid of the coffin; and that takes twice as long as to do the job t'other way."

"At what time is the sawbones coming down to the grave-yard?" asked Banks.

"He isn't coming at all," returned the Resurrection Man: "but I promised that we would be at his place at half-past one o'clock to-night."

"Too early!" exclaimed the Buffer. "We can't think of beginning work afore twelve. The place ain't quiet till then."

"Well, and an hour will do the business," said the Resurrection Man. "Besides, the saw-bones will set up for us. Now then, Meg, clear away, and let's have the blue ruin and hot water. I must just write a short note to a gentleman with whom I have a little business of a private nature; and you can run and take it to the post presently."

The Resurrection Man seated himself at a little side-table, and penned a hasty letter, which he folded, sealed, and addressed to "ARTHUR CHICHESTER, ESQ., *Cambridge Heath, near Hackney.*"

Margaret Flathers took it to the post-office, which was in the immediate neighbourhood.

On her return, the Resurrection Man said, "Now you and Moll try your hands at some punch,—and make it pretty stiff too—just as you like it yourselves."

This command was obeyed; and the three men betook themselves to their pipes, while the women set to work to brew a mighty jorum of gin-punch in an earthenware pitcher that held about a gallon and a half. The potent beverage was speedily served up; and the conversation grew animated. Even the moroseness of the Resurrection Man partially gave way before the exhilarating fluid; and he narrated a variety of incidents connected with the pursuits of his criminal career.

Then the women sang songs, and Mr. Banks told a number of anecdotes showing how he was enabled to undertake funerals at a cheaper rate than many of his competitors, because he had always taken care to league himself with body-snatchers, to whom he gave information of a nature serviceable to them, and for which they were well contented to pay a handsome price. Thus, whenever he was intrusted with the interment of a corpse which he fancied would make a "good subject," he communicated with his friends the resurrectionists, and in a night or two the body was exhumed for the benefit of some enterprising surgeon.

In this manner the time slipped away;—hour after hour passed; supper was served up; "another glass, and another pipe," was the order of the evening; and although these three men sate drinking and smoking to an immoderate degree, they rose from their chairs, at half-past eleven o'clock, but little the worse for their debauch.

The Resurrection Man filled a flask with pure gin, and consigned it to his pocket.

"We must now be off," he said. "You, Banks, can go home and get the cart ready: the Buffer and me will go our way."

"At what time shall I come with the cart?" demanded the undertaker.

"At a quarter past one to a second—neither more nor less," answered Tidkins.

Banks then took his departure.

"Are you going to stay here with Meg, or what?" asked the Buffer of his wife.

"I shall go to bed," said the Rattlesnake hastily. "Tony can take the key with him."

"Then I shall be off home," observed Moll. "Besides, Mrs. Smith may think it odd if we both remain out so late."

The Buffer's wife accordingly took her leave.

"Now come, Jack," said the Resurrection Man. "We have no time to lose. There's the tools to get out."

The two men descended the stairs, and issued from the house. They hastened up the little alley: the Resurrection Man opened the door of the ground-floor rooms; and they entered that part of the house together.

"Bustle about," said Tidkins, when they found themselves in the front room; and having lighted a candle, he hastily gathered together the implements which they required.

Laden with the tools, the two men were about to leave the room, when the Buffer suddenly exclaimed, "What the devil was that? I could have sworn I heard some one moaning."

"Nonsense," said the Resurrection Man; but, as he spoke, he observed by the glare of the candle, that the countenance of his companion had suddenly become ashy pale.

"Well, I never was more deceived in my life," observed the Buffer.

"You certainly never was," answered the Resurrection Man: then, hastily extinguishing the light, he pushed the Buffer into the alley, and locked the door carefully behind himself.

The two body-snatchers then proceeded to the scene of their midnight labour.

We take leave of them for a short space, and follow the movements of the Rattlesnake.

It was not without an object that this woman had got rid of the company of the Buffer's wife, by declaring that she was about to retire to rest.

She permitted ten minutes to elapse after the Resurrection Man and his companion had left the room; then, deeming that sufficient time had been allowed for them to provide themselves with the implements necessary for their night's work, she started from her chair, involuntarily exclaiming aloud, "Now for the great secret!"

From an obscure corner of a shelf in the bed-room she drew forth a bunch of skeleton keys, which she had procured on the preceding day.

She then provided herself with a dark-lantern, and descended to the alley.

In five minutes she lighted upon a key, after many vain attempts with the others, which turned in the lock. The door opened, and she entered the ground floor.

Having closed the door, she immediately proceeded into the back room, the appearance of which was the same as when she last visited it. The mysterious cloak and mask were there; but in the cupboard, which was before empty, were now a loaf and a bottle of water.

"Then there *is* a human being concealed somewhere hereabouts!" she said to herself: "or else why that food! And it must have been the supply of bread and water that I saw *him* put into his basket the other night."

She listened; but no sound fell upon her ear. Then she carefully examined the room, to discover any trap-door or secret means of communication with a dungeon or subterranean place. She knew, by the situation of the house in respect to those on either side of it, that there could be no inner room level with the ground-floor; she therefore felt convinced that if there were any secret chamber or cell connected with the premises, it must be underneath.

She scrutinized every inch of the floor, and could perceive no signs of a trap-door. The boards were all firm and tight. She advanced towards the chimney, which was divested of its grate; and suddenly she felt the hearth-stone move with a slight oscillation beneath her feet.

Her countenance became animated with joy; she felt convinced that her perseverance in examining that room was about to be rewarded.

She placed the lantern upon the floor, and endeavoured to raise the stone; but it seemed fixed in its setting, although it trembled as she touched it.

Still she was not disheartened. She scrutinized the boards in the immediate vicinity of the stone; but her search was unavailing. No evidence of a concealed lock—no trace of a secret spring met her eyes. Yet she was confident that she was on the right scent. As she turned herself round, while crawling upon her hands and knees the better to pursue her examination, her rustling silk dress disturbed a portion of the masonry in the chimney, where a grate had once been fixed.

A brick fell out.

The heart of the Rattlesnake now beat quickly.

She approached the lantern to the cavity left by the dislodged brick; and at the bottom of the recess she espied a small iron ring.

She pulled it without hesitation; the ring yielded to her touch, and drew out a thick wire to the distance of nearly a foot.

The Rattlesnake now tried once more to raise the stone, and succeeded. The stone was fixed at one end with stout iron hinges to one of the beams that supported the floor, and thus opened like a trapdoor.

When raised, it disclosed a narrow flight of stone steps, at the bottom of which the most perfect obscurity reigned.

The Rattlesnake now paused—in alarm.

She longed to penetrate into those mysterious depths—she panted to dive into that subterranean darkness; but she was afraid.

All those terrible reminiscences which were associated with her knowledge of the Resurrection Man, rushed to her mind; and she trembled to descend into the vault at her feet, for fear she should never return.

These terrors were too much for her. She, moreover, recalled to mind that nearly an hour had now elapsed since the Resurrection Man and the Buffer had departed; and she knew not how speedily they might conclude their task. Besides, some unforeseen accident or sudden interruption might compel them to beat a retreat homewards; and she knew full well that if she were discovered *there*, death would be her portion.

She accordingly determined to postpone any further examination into the mysteries of that house until some further occasion.

Having closed the stone trap-door and replaced the brick in the wall of the chimney, she hastened back to the upper-floor, where she speedily retired to bed.

We may as well observe that during the time she was in the lower room, no sound of a human tongue met her ears.

But perhaps the victim slept!

CHAPTER CVIII.

THE EXHUMATION.

The night was fine—frosty—and bright with the lustre of a lovely moon.

Even the chimneys and gables of the squalid houses of Globe Town appeared to bathe their heads in that flood of silver light.

The Resurrection Man and the Buffer pursued their way towards the cemetery.

For some minutes they preserved a profound silence: at length the Buffer exclaimed, "I only hope, Tony, that this business won't turn out as bad as the job with young Markham three nights ago."

"Why should it?" demanded the Resurrection Man, in a gruff tone.

"Well, I don't know why," answered the Buffer. "P'rhaps, after all, it was just as well that feller escaped as he did. We might have swung for it."

"Escape!" muttered the Resurrection Man, grinding his teeth savagely. "Yes—he did escape *then*; but I haven't done with him yet. He shall not get off so easy another time."

"I wonder who those chaps was that come up so sudden?" observed the Buffer, after a pause.

"Friends of his, no doubt," answered Tidkins. "Most likely he suspected a trap, or thought he would be on the right side. But the night was so plaguy dark, and the whole thing was so sudden, it was impossible to form an idea of who the two strangers might be."

"One on 'em was precious strong, I know," said the Buffer. "But, for my part, I think you'd better leave the young feller alone in future. It's no good standing the chance of getting scragged for mere wengeance. I can't understand that sort of thing. If you like to crack his crib for him and hive the swag, I'm your man; but I'll have no more of a business that's all danger and no profit."

"Well, well, as you like," said the Resurrection Man, impatiently. "Here we are; so look alive."

They were now under the wall of the cemetery.

The Buffer clambered to the top of the wall, which was not very high; and the Resurrection Man handed him the implements and tools, which he dropped cautiously upon the ground inside the enclosure.

He then helped his companion upon the wall; and in another moment they stood together within the cemetery.

"Are you sure you can find the way to the right grave?" demanded the Buffer in a whisper.

"Don't be afraid," was the reply: "I could go straight up to it blindfold."

They then shouldered their implements, and the Resurrection Man led the way to the spot where Mrs. Smith's anonymous lodger had been buried.

"I'm afeard the ground's precious hard," observed the Buffer, when he and his companion had satisfied themselves by a cautious glance around that no one was watching their movements.

The eyes of these men had become so habituated to the obscurity of night, in consequence of the frequency with which they pursued their avocations during the darkness which cradled others to rest, that they were possessed of the visual acuteness generally ascribed to the cat.

"We'll soon turn it up, let it be as hard as it will," said the Resurrection Man, in answer to his comrade's remark.

Then, suiting the action to the word, he began his operations in the following manner.

He measured a distance of five paces from the head of the grave. At the point thus marked he took a long iron rod and drove it in an oblique direction through the ground towards one end of the coffin. So accurate were his calculations relative to the precise spot in which the coffin was embedded in the earth, that the iron rod struck against it the very first time he thus sounded the soil.

"All right," he whispered to the Buffer.

He then took a spade and began to break up the earth just at that spot where the end of the iron rod peeped out of the ground.

"Not so hard as you thought," he observed. "The fact is, the whole burial-place is so mixed up with human remains, that the clay is too greasy to freeze very easy."

"I s'pose that's it," said the Buffer.

The Resurrection Man worked for about ten minutes with a skill and an effect that would have astonished even Jones the grave-digger himself, had he been there to see. He then resigned the spade to the Buffer, who took his turn with equal ardour and ability.

When *his* ten minutes elapsed, the resurrectionists regaled themselves each with a dram from Tidkins' flask; and this individual then applied himself once more to the work in hand. When he was wearied, the Buffer relieved him; and thus did they fairly divide the toil until the excavation of the ground was completed.

This portion of the task was finished in about forty minutes. An oblique channel, about ten feet long, and three feet square at the mouth, and decreasing only in length, as it verged towards the head of the coffin at the bottom, was now formed.

The Resurrection Man provided himself with a stout chisel, the handle of which was covered with leather, and with a mallet, the ends of which were also protected with pieces of the same material. Thus the former instrument when struck by the latter emitted but little noise.

He then descended into the channel which terminated at the very head of the coffin.

Breaking away the soil that lay upon that end of the coffin, he inserted the chisel into the joints of the wood, and in a very few moments knocked off the board that closed the coffin at that extremity.

The wood-work of the head of the shell was also removed with ease—for Banks had purposely nailed those parts of the two cases very slightly together.

The Resurrection Man next handed up the tools to his companion, who threw him down a strong cord.

The end of this rope was then fastened under the armpits of the corpse as it lay in its coffin.

This being done, the Buffer helped the Resurrection Man out of the hole.

"So far, so good," said Tidkins: "it must be close upon one o'clock. We have got a quarter of an hour left—and that's plenty of time to do all that's yet to be done."

The two men then took the rope between them, and drew the corpse gently out of its coffin—up the slope of the channel—and landed it safely on the ground at a little distance from the mouth of the excavation.

The moon fell upon the pale features of the dead—those features which were still as unchanged, save in colour, as if they had never come in contact with a shroud—nor belonged to a body that had been swathed in a winding-sheet!

The contrast formed by the white figure and the black soil on which it was stretched, would have struck terror to the heart of any one save a resurrectionist.

Indeed, the moment the corpse was thus dragged forth from its grave, the Resurrection Man thrust his hand into its breast, and felt for the gold.

It was there—wrapped up as the undertaker had described.

"The blunt is all safe, Jack," said the Resurrection Man; and he secured the coin about his person.

They then applied themselves vigorously to shovel back the earth; but, when they had filled up the excavation, a considerable quantity of the soil still remained to dispose of, it being impossible, in spite

of stamping down, to condense the earth into the same space from which it was originally taken.

They therefore filled two sacks with the surplus soil, and proceeded to empty them in different parts of the ground.

Their task was so far accomplished, when they heard the low rumble of wheels in the lane outside the cemetery.

To bundle the corpse neck and heels into a sack, and gather up their implements, was the work of only a few moments. They then conveyed their burdens between them to the wall overlooking the lane, where the well-known voice of Mr. Banks greeted their ears, as he stood upright in his cart peering over the barrier into the cemetery.

"Got the blessed defunct?" said the undertaker interrogatively.

"Right and tight," answered the Buffer; "and the tin too. Now, then, look sharp—here's the tools."

"I've got 'em," returned Banks.

"Look out for the stiff 'un, then," added the Buffer; and, aided by the Resurrection Man, he shoved the body up to the undertaker, who deposited it in the bottom of his cart.

The Resurrection Man and the Buffer then mounted the wall, and got into the vehicle, in which they laid themselves down, so that any person whom they might meet in the streets through which they were to pass would only see one individual in the cart—namely, the driver. Otherwise, the appearance of three men at that time of night, or rather at that hour in the morning, might have excited suspicion.

Banks lashed the sides of his horse; and the animal started off at a round pace.

Not a word was spoken during the short drive to the surgeon's residence in the Cambridge Road.

When they reached his house the road was quiet and deserted. A light glimmered through the fan-light over the door; and the door itself was opened the moment the cart stopped.

The Resurrection Man and the Buffer sprang up; and, seeing that the coast was clear, bundled the corpse out of the vehicle in an instant; then in less than half a minute the "blessed defunct," as the undertaker called it, was safely lodged in the passage of the surgeon's house.

Mr. Banks, as soon as the body was removed from his vehicle, drove rapidly away. His portion of the night's work was done; and he knew that his accomplices would give him his "reg'lars" when they should meet again.

The Resurrection Man and the Buffer conveyed the body into a species of out-house, which the surgeon, who was passionately attached to anatomical studies, devoted to purposes of dissection and physiological experiment.

In the middle of this room, which was about ten feet long and six broad, stood a strong deal table, forming a slightly inclined plane. The stone pavement of the out-house was perforated with holes in the immediate vicinity of the table, so that the fluid which poured from subjects for dissection might escape into a drain communicating with the common sewer. To the ceiling, immediately above the head of the table, was attached a pulley with a strong cord, by means of which a body might be supported in any position that was most convenient to the anatomist.

The Resurrection Man and his companion carried the corpse into this dissecting-room, and placed it upon the table, the surgeon holding a candle to light their movements.

"Now, Jack," said Tidkins to the Buffer, "do you take the stiff 'un out of the sack, and lay him along decently on the table ready for business, while I retire a moment to this gentleman's study and settle accounts with him."

"Well and good," returned the Buffer. "I'll stay here till you come back."

The surgeon lighted another candle, which he placed on the window-sill, and then withdrew, accompanied by the Resurrection Man.

The Buffer shut the door of the dissecting-room, because the draught caused the candle to flicker, and menaced the light with extinction. He then proceeded to obey the directions which he had received from his accomplice.

The Buffer removed the sack from the body, which he then stretched out at length upon the inclined table, taking care to place its head on the higher extremity and immediately beneath the pulley.

"There, old feller," he said, "you're comfortable, at any rate. What a blessin' it would be to your friends, if they was ever to find out that you'd been had up again, to know into what skilful hands you'd happened to fall!"

Thus musing, the Buffer turned his back listlessly towards the corpse, and leant against the table on which it was lying.

"Let me see," he said to himself, "there's thirty-one pounds that was buried along with *him*, and then there's ten pounds that the sawbones is a paying now to Tony for the *snatch*; that makes forty-one pounds, and there's three to go shares. What does that make? Threes into four goes once—threes into eleven goes three and two over—that's thirteen pounds a-piece, and two pound to split—"

The Buffer started abruptly round, and became deadly pale. He thought he heard a slight movement of the corpse, and his whole frame trembled.

Almost at the same moment some object was hurled violently against the window; the glass was shivered to atoms; the candle was thrown down and extinguished; and total darkness reigned in the dissecting-room.

"Holloa!" cried the Buffer, turning sick at heart; "what's that?"

Scarcely had these words escaped his lips when he felt his hand suddenly grasped by the cold fingers of the corpse.

"O God!" cried the miscreant; and he fell insensible across the body on the table.

CHAPTER CIX.

THE STOCK-BROKER.

Upon a glass-door, leading into offices on a ground floor in Tokenhouse Yard, were the words "James Tomlinson, *Stock-broker.*"

It was about eleven o'clock in the morning.

A clerk was busily employed in writing at a desk in the front office. The walls of this room were covered with placards, bills, and prospectuses, all announcing the most gigantic enterprises, and whose principal features were large figures expressing millions of money.

These prospectuses were of various kinds. Some merely put forth schemes by which enormous profits were to be realised, but which had not yet arrived to that state of maturity (the point at which the popular gullibility has been laid hold of,) when Directors, Secretaries, and Treasurers can be announced in a flaming list. Others denoted that the projectors had triumphed over the little difficulty of obtaining good names to form a board; and the upper part of this class of prospectuses was embellished with a perfect array of M.P.'s, Aldermen, and Esquires.

The prospectuses, one and all, set forth, with George-Robins-flourishes and poetico-hyperbolical flowers of rhetoric, the unparalleled and astounding advantages to be reaped from the enterprises respectfully submitted to public consideration and to the monied world especially. The face of the globe was a complete paradise according to those announcements. The interior of Africa was represented to be a perfect mine of gold by the projectors of a company to trade to those salubrious parts; the cannibals of the South Sea Islands became intelligent and interesting beings in the language of another association of speculators; the majestic scenery of the North Pole and the phenomena of the aurora borealis were held out by a colonizing company as inducements to families to emigrate to Spitzbergen; the originators of a scheme for forming railways in Egypt expatiated upon the delights of travelling at the rate of sixty miles an hour through a land famous for its antiquarian remains, and along the banks of a river where the young alligators might be seen disporting in the sun; and numerous other prospectuses of majestic enterprises developed their original principles and prospective benefits to the astounded reader.

One would have imagined that any individual with a five-pound note in his pocket, had only just to step into Mr. Tomlinson's office, take five shares in as many enterprises, pay one pound deposit upon each, and walk out again a man of vast wealth.

Mr. Tomlinson himself was seated in a decently furnished room, which constituted the "private office." He was looking well, but somewhat careworn, and not quite so comfortable as a man who had passed through the Bankruptcy Court, got his certificate, and was in business once more, might be expected to look. In a word, he had a hard struggle to make his way respectably, and was compelled to meddle in many things that shocked his somewhat sensitive disposition.

A short, well-dressed, good-humoured man, with a small quick eye, was sitting on one side of the fire, conversing with the stock-broker.

"Well, Mr. Tomlinson," he said, "on those conditions I will lend my name to the Irish Railway Company proposed. But, remember, I require fifty shares, and I am not to pay a farthing for them."

"Oh, of course," cried Tomlinson; "that is precisely the proposal I was instructed to make to you. The fact is, between you and me, the projectors are all men of straw—one came out of Whitecross Street Prison a few weeks ago, and another has been a bankrupt twice and an insolvent seven times; and so they must raise heaven and earth to get good names."

" 'Tis their only plan—their only plan," answered the gentleman; "and I flatter myself," he added, drawing himself up, "that the countenance of Mr. Sheriff Popkins is not to be sneezed at."

"On the contrary, my dear Mr. Popkins," said Tomlinson, "your name will soon bring a host of others."

"I should think so, Mr. Tomlinson—I should think so," was the self-sufficient reply.

"Well, then, Mr. Popkins, shall I make an appointment for you to meet Messrs. Bubble and Chouse to-morrow morning at my office?"

"If you please, my dear sir. And now I wish you to do a little matter for me. The fact is, I have been fool enough to take thirty shares in a certain railway company, and I have been elected a director. The company is in a most flourishing condition, and so I mean to make them purchase my shares of me. You will accordingly have the kindness to let it be known on 'Change that you have my shares to sell; but you must mind and not part with them. The thing will get to the Company's ears, and they will be terribly alarmed at the prospect of the injury which may be done to the enterprise by a director offering his shares for sale. They will then send and negotiate with you privately, and you can make a good bargain with them."

"I understand," said Tomlinson. "I shall only breathe a whisper about the shares being offered for sale, in a quarter whence I know the rumour will immediately fly to the Directors of the Company."

"Good," observed Mr. Sheriff Popkins. "Here is the scrip: you can tell me what you have done when I call to-morrow morning to meet Messrs. Bubble and Choose."

The worthy sheriff then withdrew, and Mr. Alderman Sniff was announced.

"Mr. Tomlinson," said this gentleman, "I wish you to do your best for a new Joint Stock-Company which I have just founded. This is the prospectus."

The stock-broker glanced over it, and said, in a musing manner, "Ah! very good indeed—excellent! *'British Marble Company.'* Famous idea! *'Capital Two Hundred Thousand Pounds in Ten Thousand Shares of Twenty Pounds Each.'* Good again. *'Deposit One Pound per Share.'* That will do. Then comes the Board of Directors—all good names. I see you have made yourself Managing Director: well, that's quite fair! Then, again, *'Auditor, Mr. Alderman Sniff; Treasurer, Mr. Alderman Sniff; Secretary, Mr. Alderman Sniff.'* But who sells the quarry to the Company? Oh! I see, *'Mr. Alderman Sniff.'"*

"Well, what do you think of it?" demanded the alderman.

"You ask me candidly, my dear sir?"

"Certainly," replied the alderman.

"I think the plan is excellent. The only drawback to its success, is—shall I speak openly?"

"I wish you to do so."

"Then I am of opinion that you have given yourself too many

situations," continued Tomlinson. "In the first place you found the Company, and you make yourself Managing Director. Well and good. But then you also sell the quarry *to* the Company. Now, as Managing Director, you have to award to yourself a sum for that quarry; as Treasurer you pay yourself; as Secretary you draw up the agreements; and as Auditor you confirm your own accounts!"

"Perfectly correct, Mr. Tomlinson. Is it not a rule that Joint-Stock Companies are never to benefit any one save the founder?"

"Oh! no one denies *that*," answered the stock-broker. "What I am afraid of is, that the public will not *bite*, when they see one man occupying so many situations in the Company."

"Nonsense, my dear fellow! The name of an alderman will carry every thing before it. Does not the world believe that the Aldermen of the City of London are all as rich as Crœsus?"

"Whereas, between you and me," returned Tomlinson with a sly laugh, "there is scarcely one of them who has got a penny if his affairs came to be wound up."

"And yet we live gloriously, ha! ha!" chuckled Mr. Alderman Sniff. "But to return to my business: what can you do for me?"

"I can certainly recommend the enterprise," answered Tomlinson. "But where can the marble be seen?"

"At my office," said the alderman. "I went and bought the finest piece that was ever imported from Italy; and there it is in my counting-house, labelled 'British Marble' in letters at least half a foot high."

"Where is the quarry situated?" inquired Tomlinson.

"Oh! I haven't quite made up my mind about *that* yet," was the answer given by Mr. Alderman Sniff. "The truth is, I am going down into Wales this week, and I shall buy the first field I can get cheap in some rude part of the country. That is the least difficulty in the whole enterprise."

"Your plans are admirable, my dear sir," exclaimed Tomlinson. "I will do all I can for you. Will you take a glass of wine and a biscuit?"

"No, I thank you—not now," said the Alderman. "I have promised a colleague to sit for him to-day at Guildhall police-court. Last week I was on the rota for attendance there, and I remanded a man who was brought up on a charge of obtaining three and sixpence under false pretences."

"Indeed?" ejaculated Tomlinson, whose eyes were fixed upon the

"Two Hundred Thousand Pounds" in the alderman's prospectus.

"Yes," continued Mr. Sniff; "and I am going to sit to-day because that fellow comes up again. I mean to clear the City of all such rogues and vagabonds. I shall give him a taste of the treadmill for two months. So, good morning. By the by, call as you pass my office and have a look at the marble; and mind," he added, sinking his voice, "you don't let out that it came from Italy. It is pure Welsh marble, remember!"

Alderman Sniff chuckled at this pleasant idea, and then hastened to Guildhall, where he fully justified his character of being the most severe magistrate in the City of London.

A few minutes after Mr. Alderman Sniff had taken his departure, Mr. Greenwood was announced.

"My dear Tomlinson, I am delighted to see you," said the capitalist. "It is really an age—a week at least—since I saw you. How do matters get on?"

"I have prospects of doing an excellent business," answered Tomlinson. "The numberless bubble companies that are started every day, are the making of us stock-brokers. We dispose of shares or effect transfers, and obtain our commission, let the result be what it may to the purchasers."

"And I hope that you have conquered those ridiculous qualms of conscience which always made a coward of you, when you were in Lombard Street?" said Greenwood.

"Needs must when the devil drives," observed Tomlinson drily.

"For my part," continued Greenwood, "I take advantage of this mania on the part of the English for speculation in joint-stock companies and railway shares. A day of reaction will come and the effects will be fearful. Thousands and thousands of families will be involved in irretrievable ruin. That day may not occur for one year—two years—five years—or even ten years;—but come it will; and the signal for it will be when the House of Commons is inundated with railway and joint-stock company business, and when it is compelled to postpone a portion of that business until the ensuing session. Then confidence will receive a shock: an interval for calm meditation will occur; and the result will be awful. Every one will be anxious to sell shares, and there will be no buyers. Now mark my words, Tomlinson; and, if you speculate on your own account, speculate accordingly. *I* do so."

"And you are not likely to go wrong, I know," said Tomlinson. "But stock-brokers do not risk any money of their own: they have plenty of clients, who will do that for them."

"Then you are really thriving?" asked Greenwood.

"I am earning a living, and my business is increasing. But I feel hanging like a mill-stone round my neck the thousand pounds which you lent me at twenty per cent.—"

"Yes—*only* twenty per cent."

"*Only* at twenty per cent.," continued Tomlinson with a sigh: "and I am unable to return you more than one hundred at present, although I agreed to pay you two hundred every four months."

"The hundred will do," said Greenwood; and he wrote out a receipt for that amount.

Tomlinson handed him over a number of notes, which Greenwood counted and then consigned to his pocket.

"There is a pretty business to be done in the City now," said the capitalist, after a pause. "I contrive to snatch an hour or two now and then from the time which I am compelled to devote to the enlightened and independent body that returned me to Parliament; and I seldom come into the City on those occasions without lending a few hundreds to some poor devil who has over-bought himself in shares."

"I have no doubt that you thrive, Greenwood," said the stock-broker. "Every man who takes advantage of the miseries of others must get on."

"To be sure—to be sure," cried the Member of Parliament. "I hope that you will act upon that principle."

"I have no reason to complain of the business that I am now doing: I act as honestly as I can—and that principle deprives me of many advantageous affairs. Then I experience annoyance from a constant reminiscence of that poor old man who so nobly sacrificed himself for me."

"The eternal cry!" ejaculated Greenwood. "If you are so very anxious to find him out, put an advertisement in the *Times*—"

"And if he saw it, he would believe it to be a stratagem of the police to arrest him. You know that there is a warrant out against him. The official assignee took that step."

"Well, let him take his chance; and if he should happen to be captured, we will petition the Home Secretary to diminish the period for which he will be sentenced to transportation. Not that such a step would benefit him much, because his age—"

"Let us drop this subject, Greenwood," said Tomlinson, evidently affected.

"With all my heart. I must admit that it moves one's feelings; and if I met the old man in the street, I should not hesitate to give him a guinea out of my own pocket."

"A guinea!" cried Tomlinson—and a smile of contempt curled his lips. "Perhaps you would recommend me to bestow a five-pound note upon that poor Italian nobleman whom you cheated out of his fifteen thousand pounds."

"You need not call him a poor nobleman," answered Greenwood. "He is now worth ten thousand pounds a-year."

"Indeed! A great change must have taken place, then, in his fortunes?" exclaimed Tomlinson.

"The fact, in a few words, is this. A young lady, whom I knew well," said Greenwood, "obtained letters of introduction from Count Alteroni to certain friends of his in Montoni, the capital of Castelcicala, to which state she repaired for the benefit of her health, or some such frivolous reason. She had the good fortune to captivate the Grand Duke—"

"Miss Eliza Sydney, you mean?" said Tomlinson.

"The same. Did you know her?"

"Not at all. But I read in the newspapers the account of her marriage with Angelo III. Proceed."

"The moment she married the Grand Duke, a pension of ten thousand a-year was granted to Count Alteroni, by way of indemnification, I have heard, for his estates, which were confiscated after he had fled the country in consequence of political intrigues."

"How did you learn all this?"

"My valet Filippo happens to be a native of Montoni, and he seems well acquainted with all that passes in Castelcicala. Count Alteroni and his family have returned to the villa which they formerly inhabited at Richmond."

"I am delighted to hear this good news. You have taken a considerable weight off my mind; the transaction with that nobleman was always a subject of self-reproach."

"I dare say," observed Mr. Greenwood ironically; then, drawing his chair closer to Tomlinson's seat, he added, "You are no doubt the most punctilious and conscientious of all City men. I have something to communicate to you, and must do it briefly, as I am compelled to return to Spring Gardens, to meet a deputation from the Rottenborough Agricultural Society, at one o'clock precisely—and I never keep such people waiting more than an hour!"

"That is considerate on your part," said the stock-broker.

"Don't you think it is? But I did not come here for the sole purpose of chatting. The fact is, a gentleman with whom I am acquainted wants a stock-broker for a very delicate and important business—for a business," added Greenwood, sinking his voice to a whisper, "which requires a man who will be content to put five hundred pounds into his pocket for the service that will be required of him, and perform that service blindfold, as it were."

"I will do nothing to compromise my safety," said Tomlinson.

"You will not be required to do so," answered Greenwood. "However, the gentleman I allude to will call upon you in the course of the day, I dare say; and he will then explain to you the service he has to demand at your hands."

"What is the name of your friend?" inquired Tomlinson.

"Mr. Chichester—Arthur Chichester," was the reply.

"Chichester—Chichester," said the stock-broker, musing; "surely I have heard you mention that name before? Ah! now I remember! Did you not complain to me a few days ago that he had been making mischief between you and a certain Sir Rupert Harborough?"

"I did," answered Greenwood; "and I certainly had good cause for anger against this same Arthur Chichester. But I had become his confidant and adviser in a certain affair a few weeks before I discovered that he had acquainted Sir Rupert Harborough with circumstances which he had better have kept to himself; and I am therefore compelled to continue my assistance and counsel to him until the affair alluded to be brought to a successful termination. Besides, as Sir Rupert and I have settled our little differences, there is no use in bearing malice, especially when something is to be gained by forbearance."

"I thought you would make that admission," said Tomlinson, laughing. "Well, I shall see your friend, and if, with safety, I can earn five hundred pounds, certainly, in my position, I cannot afford to lose such an opportunity."

"That is speaking like a reasonable man," observed Greenwood. "Never stick at trifles. What should I be now, if I had hesitated at every step I took? Should I possess a hundred thousand pounds, in good securities? should I be enabled to gratify every wish, caprice, or desire, whose object money can accomplish? should I be the representative of one of the most independent and intelligent constituencies in England? Ah, my dear fellow, think of me and my position when you hesitate; and always make money after the well-authorised system—*honestly*, if you can; *but, at all events, make money*."

With these words, Mr. Greenwood took his departure.

"Yes," mused Tomlinson, when he was alone once more, "that man is right! Make money, honestly, if you can; but, at all events, *make money*. That is the burden of *his* song; why should it not be the *chorus* of mine? When I look around me, I see every one making money upon the same plan. Sheriff Popkins does not hesitate to lend his name to a bubble; and Alderman Sniff concocts one! And they are men of reputation—holding important offices—appearing at Court—wielding power—exercising influence. This is indeed a wide field for contemplation. Why, Greenwood, in his bold, dashing manner, gains more in a day than I, in my miserable, droning fashion, earn in a month. To be afraid to touch the gold that is thrown in one's way in this wonderful city, is to be a coward—a very coward. Yes—I see it all! Greenwood is right. Make money—honestly, if you can; but, at all events, make money!"

Mr. Tomlinson's soliloquy had arrived at this very pleasing conclusion, just as the door of his office opened, and a clerk entered to acquaint his master that a gentleman of the name of Chichester desired to speak to him.

"Show Mr. Chichester in," said Tomlinson.

Mr. Chichester was dressed in his usually fashionable manner; and his gait had lost nothing of the care-nothing-for-anybody kind of swagger which characterised him when he was first introduced to the reader.

Having thrown himself listlessly upon a chair, he said, "I presume our mutual friend Greenwood has mentioned my name to you, Mr. Tomlinson?"

"He has. I was prepared for your visit."

"But not for its object, perhaps?" said Chichester.

"I am as yet ignorant on that head," was the reply.

"Mr. Greenwood then told you nothing—"

"Nothing, save an intimation that my services were required in a certain delicate and important matter, and that five hundred pounds would be my remuneration."

"Perfectly correct," answered Mr. Chichester. "Are you disposed to aid me on the proposed terms?"

"I must first learn the nature of the business in which my interference is needed."

"And if you should then decline?"

"You shall have my solemn assurance that what you confide to me remains buried in my own bosom."

"That is what I call a proper understanding," exclaimed Chichester. "You must know, then, that some three months ago I wooed, and won, a widow lady, not very ugly, certainly, but whose principal attraction consisted of the sum of sixteen thousand pounds in the three and a half per cents. She was five and twenty years of age, and possessed of a sweet little house in the neighbourhood of the Cambridge Heath gate. I met her one evening in July or August last at a party at my father's house—when I was doing the amiable to the old gentleman in order to sound his pockets; and my father whispered to me that I ought to make up to Mrs. Higgins. Certainly the name was not very aristocratic; but then her Christian name was Viola; and I thought that Viola Chichester would be pretty enough. I accordingly flirted with the widow on that occasion, and we seemed tolerably pleased with each other. I called next day—and every now and then, when I had time; but I, really, scarcely entertained serious thoughts of making her an offer, until one day when I was desperately hard up, and I saw my friend Harborough involved in such difficulties that we could not do any good together. So I got into an omnibus in Bishopsgate Street, went down to Cambridge Heath, called upon Mrs. Higgins, and then and there offered her my heart and hand. She accepted me. We had a pleasant little chat about money matters: she stated that her late husband, a wealthy builder, had left her sixteen thousand pounds; and, of course, I could not make myself out a pauper. Besides, she knew that my father was tolerably well off. I assured her that I was possessed of a few thousands, and that the old gentleman allowed me three hundred a-year into the bargain. She stipulated that all her own money should be settled upon herself. I demurred to this proposal; but she was obstinate; and I then discovered that Mrs. Viola Higgins had a very determined will and a very positive temper of her own. I thought to myself, '*Here is a charming widow who throws herself into my arms, and who possesses a decent fortune; it would be madness to neglect so golden an opportunity of enriching myself. Besides,*' I reasoned, '*when once we are married, it will be very easy for me to wheedle the affectionate creature out of any money that I may require.*' Well, I consented to the settlement of all her property upon herself; and in due course we were married. I did not mention the matter to any of my West-End friends, because I did not like to invite them to the wedding—I was afraid their offhand manners would alarm the bride, and give her an unfavourable opinion with regard to myself. So the business was kept very snug and quiet; and we passed the honey-moon at my wife's sister and brother-in-law's, very decent people in their way, and dwelling at Stratford-le-Bow. On our return to London, I thought it time to break the ice in respect to my own pecuniary situation. The truth was, that I had not a penny-piece of my own, and that my father had long since withdrawn his support, in consequence of the immense drains I had made upon his purse. I was moreover encumbered with debts; and some of my tradesmen had found me out and began to call at the house at Cambridge Heath. They even used menaces. My position was truly critical. I did not marry the widow merely with a view to take her out for a walk, sit by the fire-side chatting, or read a book while she worked. I wanted money,—money to pay my debts,—money to enjoy myself with. Accordingly I broke the ice by very candidly avowing that I had not a shilling. I, however, swore that her beauty and accomplishments had alone induced me thus to deceive her. But—oh! the vixen! She flew into such a passion that I thought she would tear my eyes out. She raved and wept—and wept and raved—and then reproached and taunted,—until I wished one of us at the devil, and scarcely cared which went there. The scene ended in Viola's falling into a fit of hysterics; and she was compelled to go to bed. I was most assiduous to her; and my attentions evidently softened her. In a few hours she grew calm, and then said, '*Arthur, you have deceived me grossly; but I can forgive you. I do not regret the loss of the wealth and income which you led me to believe were yours; I am only sorry that you should have thought it necessary to practise such a measure to induce me to marry you. But let what is past be forgotten. The income derived from my property is sufficient for us; and, if you will be kind and good to me, this deception shall never more trouble our happiness.*'"

"I think Mrs. Chichester spoke like a generous, sensible, and noble-hearted woman," observed Tomlinson, who was, nevertheless, at a loss to conceive how all these details could be connected with the service which Mr. Chichester required at his hands.

"Ahem!" exclaimed that gentleman, who did not seem to relish the remark particularly well. "However, all that fine feeling was mere outward show with my wife," he continued; "for she was inexorable in her refusal to sell out or mortgage any of her funded property for my use. I told her that I had debts. '*Give a list to my solicitor,*' she said, '*and he shall compromise with your creditors.*' I assured her that I could make a better bargain with them myself. She would not believe me. I then declared point-blank that I did not mean to remain tied to her apron-strings; that she must at least settle half the property upon me; that I desired to keep a horse and cab, and introduce my friends to my wife; and that I was resolved we should live as people of property ought to live. It was then that she showed her inveterate obstinacy, and manifested the worst shades of an infamous temper. She agreed to allow me one hundred a-year for my clothes and pocket-money, but would not give me any control over her property. As for horses, cabs, and West End friends, she ridiculed the idea. I prayed, threatened, and reasoned by turns: she was as immoveable as Mount Atlas. Several days were passed in perpetual arguments upon the subject; but the more I prayed, threatened, and reasoned, the more obstinate she grew. One morning we had a desperate quarrel. I swore that I would be revenged—that I would extort from her by violence or other means, what she refused to yield to argument. Nothing, however, could move her: she said that she would not ruin herself to gratify my extravagances. This was nearly a month ago. I bounced out of the house, and hurried up to the West End of the town, as fast as I could go, to see and consult my friend Sir Rupert Harborough. But, as I was on my way thither—for I actually had not even money in my pocket to pay a cab—I accidentally met Greenwood. He saw that I was annoyed and vexed, and inquired the reason. I told him all. He reflected for some moments, and then said, '*Do not consult Harborough in this matter. He cannot assist you. There is only one course to adopt with such a woman as this. You must put her under restraint.'* I told him that nothing would please me better; but that I should have all her friends upon me if I threw her into a lunatic asylum; and that I was, moreover, without the means to take a single step. Greenwood and I went into a tavern, and discussed the business over a bottle of wine. He then laid down a certain plan, made certain stipulations respecting remuneration for himself, and offered to back me in carrying the matter to the extreme. Of course I assented to all he proposed. The whole affair was managed in such a manner as—"

"As none but Greenwood *could* manage it," observed Tomlinson.

"Exactly," returned Chichester. "Indeed, he *is* a thorough man of business! He procured two surgeons to call at separate times, at the house at Cambridge Heath, ostensibly to see me. I took care to be at home. They also saw my wife; and the result was that they granted the certificates I required."

"Certificates of an unsound state of mind?" inquired Tomlinson.

"Certificates of an unsound state of mind," repeated Chichester, affirmatively. "Greenwood managed it all—keeping himself, however, entirely in the back-ground. He found the surgeons—provided me with money to fee them—and then recommended to me a keeper of a lunatic asylum, who is not over particular. These proceedings occupied two or three days, during which I was on my very best behaviour with my wife; but if ever I hinted to her the propriety of acceding to my wishes in respect to the disposal of her property, she cut me short by the assurance that her decision was irrevocable. I really wished to avoid extreme measures; but with such a disobedient, self-willed, obstinate woman, leniency was an impossibility. Accordingly, I one evening allured her, during a walk, into the immediate vicinity of the lunatic asylum: the streets were lonely and deserted; and it was already dark. The keeper of the mad-house had been prepared for the execution of the project that evening; and he was at his post. As we slowly passed by his house, he sprang forward from some recess or dark nook, and fixed a plaster over my wife's mouth. Thus not a cry could escape her lips. At the same moment we seized her, and conveyed her into the asylum."

"That was three weeks ago?" inquired Tomlinson.

Chichester nodded an assent.

"And she has not come to her senses yet?"

"She has at length," was the answer. "I received a letter yesterday from the keeper of the asylum, stating that her spirit is broken, and that she is now ready to obey her husband in all things. The keeper wrote to me a few days ago to state that his *mode of cure* was producing a favourable result; and yesterday he intimated to me by another letter that the *mode* alluded to had proved completely successful."

"What course do you now intend to pursue?" demanded Tomlinson, who began to suspect the manner in which his services were to be made available.

"I immediately communicated the important contents of this second letter to Greenwood," continued Chichester, "and he recommended me to apply to you to aid me in completing the business. My wife now sees her folly, and is willing to devote one half of her property—namely, eight thousand pounds, to the use and purposes of her lawful husband; and I am generous enough to be satisfied with that sum, instead of insisting upon having the whole."

"I understand you," said Tomlinson: "you require a stock-broker to effect the transfer of eight thousand pounds from the name of your wife into your own name."

"And to sell out the amount when so transferred," added Chichester.

"It will be necessary for me to obtain the signature of your wife to a certain paper," observed Tomlinson.

"Greenwood has told me all this. In one word, will you accompany me to the asylum where my wife is confined, and obtain her signature?"

"If she be willing to give it, I am willing to receive it—*as a matter of business*," answered Tomlinson. "But, are you sure—in a word, what guarantee have you that she will not denounce the whole proceeding to the officers of justice—rally her friends around her—appeal to the law—and punish every one concerned in the business?"

"Listen. The document which she agrees to sign is a general power on my behalf over eight thousand pounds in the Bank of England: this power will be dated two months back—a month after our marriage. We must be supposed to have called at your office on a particular day at that period, on which occasion she signed the power in your presence. It being a general power of transfer, it would not seem extraordinary that I did not use it until now—that is, two months after it was given. This night must she sign the deed: to-morrow you must transfer and sell out the money. Then to-morrow night, she shall be conveyed back to the house at Cambridge Heath. The two servants whom we keep are bribed to my interest: they are ready, in case of need, to prove the existence of those symptoms of insanity which justified the certificates of the surgeons and the restraint under which my wife has been placed. How, then, can she do us an injury? If she proclaim her *'wrongs'*—as she may call them, *you* can prove that the power of transfer could not have been extorted from her in a mad-house, as it was signed two months ago at your office! Then, if she were to speak of the *mode of treatment* adopted by the keeper of that mad-house to curb her haughty spirit, the accusation would be indignantly denied; and her statements would be set down to a disordered imagination, and *would justify further restraint*. Be you well assured, that she will never say or do any thing that may endanger her liberty again! No—the fact is simply this: we divide the property, and separate for ever. She will be glad to get rid of a husband like me: I shall not be sorry to dissolve—as far as we can dissolve it—a connexion with a woman of her mean, griping, and avaricious disposition."

"This is Greenwood's scheme throughout," said Tomlinson. "No other man living could plot such admirable combinations to effect a certain object, without danger to any one."

"Do you consent to act in this matter, on consideration of retaining for yourself five hundred pounds of the money which you will have to transfer and sell out to-morrow?"

"I do consent," replied Tomlinson, after a few moments' reflection, during which he muttered to himself, "*Make money—honestly, if you can; but, at all events, make money.*"

"To-night—at ten o'clock, will you come to me at my house at Cambridge Heath?" inquired Chichester.

"I will," was the answer. "But let me ask you one question:—what excuse have you made to your wife's friends for this absence of three weeks?"

"In the first place," said Chichester, "her only relations consist of a sister and this sister's husband at Stratford-le-Bow; and they are so immersed in the cares of business, that they have not called once at Cambridge Heath ever since our marriage. Secondly, my wife always lived in a very retired manner, and has very few acquaintances or friends besides my father's family. It was therefore easy to satisfy the one or two persons who *did* call, with the excuse that Mrs. Chichester had gone on a short visit to some relatives in the country."

"And you feel convinced your precautions are so wisely taken, that she will never open her lips relative to the past?" said Tomlinson.

"I am confident that she will not breathe a word that may lead to her return to the place where she now is," answered Chichester, with a significant look and emphatic solemnity of tone.

"Then I will not hesitate to serve you in this business," said Tomlinson. "To-night—at ten o'clock."

"To-night—at ten o'clock," repeated Chichester; and with these words he departed.

When he was gone, Tomlinson paced his office in an agitated manner.

"The die is cast—I am now about to plunge into crime!" he said. "And yet how could I avoid—how could I long procrastinate this step? These mean tricks—these dishonourable dealings—these deceptive schemes in which we brokers are compelled to bear a part, only serve to prepare the way for more daring and more criminal pursuits. Five hundred pounds at one stroke! That is a little fortune to a man, struggling against the world, like me! Four hundred will I pay to Greenwood—the other hundred will swell my little account at the bankers'; for who can hope to do any extent of business in this city without a good name at his bankers'?"

Tomlinson ceased, and sate down calm and collected. Alas! how easy is it to reason oneself into a belief of the existence of a necessity for pursuits of dishonesty or crime!

The clerk entered the private office, and said, "Sir, there is a person, who refuses to give his name, waiting to speak to you."

"Let him come in," replied Tomlinson.

The clerk ushered in a man of cadaverous countenance, bushy brows, and large whiskers, and who was dressed in a suit of black.

"Your business, sir?" said the stock-broker, who did not much like the appearance of his visitor.

"Your name's Tomlinson?" remarked the man, coolly taking a chair.

"Yes. What would you with me?"

"James Tomlinson," continued the man, referring to a scrap of paper, which he took from his waistcoat pocket, "late banker in Lombard Street?"

"The same," said Tomlinson, impatiently.

"Then I took it down right, although he did speak in such a confused manner," observed the man, muttering rather to himself than to Mr. Tomlinson.

"What do you mean?" demanded the stock-broker.

"I mean that there's a person who wants to see you," answered the stranger. "I don't know that I'm exactly right in saying *wants*, because he is in such a state that he can neither want nor care about any thing. At the same time, I think it would be as well if *you* was to see *him*."

"Who is this person?" cried Tomlinson.

"A man that seems to know you well enough, if I can understand his ravings."

"Ravings!" repeated the stock-broker, already influenced by a slight misgiving.

"Ravings, indeed! and enough to make him rave! To be laid out as dead for four days, then put in a coffin, buried, and be had up again within ten or a dozen hours:—if that wouldn't make a man rave—what the devil would?"

"Have the goodness to explain yourself. Every word you utter is an enigma to me."

"But it wasn't an enigma to my poor friend when the stiff 'un suddenly put a cold hand upon his. However, in two words, do you know a person called Michael Martin?"

"Michael Martin!" cried the stock-broker. "Speak—what has become of him?"

"He has been ill—"

"Ill! poor old man! and I not to know it!"

"Worse than that! He died—"

"Died! Where—when?"

"Died—and was buried."

"Trifle not with me. When did he die? where is he buried?"

"He died—was buried—and came to life again!" said the stranger, with the most provoking coolness.

"Sir," exclaimed Tomlinson, advancing towards his visitor, and speaking in a firm and emphatic manner, "if you have called to tell me any thing concerning Michael Martin, speak without mystification."

"Well, sir," returned the stranger, "the plain truth is this:—An old man, without a name, took up his abode in a by-street in Globe Town some months ago. He was taken ill, and, to all appearance, died. He was buried. A surgeon fancied him as a subject, and hired me and a friend of mine to have him up again. We resurrectionized him, and took him in a cart last night to the surgeon's house. He was conveyed into the dissecting-room, and stretched on the table. The doctor and I went into the surgery to settle the expenses; and, in the mean time, my friend was left alone with the stiff 'un. It seems that a neighbour, suspecting that the surgeon now and then got a subject for his experiments, saw the cart stop at the door, and immediately understood what was going on. He went into his garden, which joins the yard where the dissecting-house stands, and seeing a light in the window of the dissecting-house, he felt sure that his suspicions were well founded, although he could not see into the place, because there was a dark blind drawn down over the window. However, the neighbour was resolved to clear up his doubts; so he took up a brick-bat, and threw it as hard as he could against the window. The glass was broken, and the light extinguished. My friend, who was left alone with the stiff 'un, was somewhat startled at this occurrence; but how much more was he alarmed when he suddenly felt the body stretch out its hand and catch hold of one of his?"

"Then Michael Martin was not dead?" ejaculated Tomlinson, in a tone which expressed alike the tenderness of deep emotion and also the bitterness of disappointment; for, perhaps, all circumstances considered, the ex-banker would rather have heard a confirmation of the death, than an account of the resuscitation of his late clerk.

"No—the old man is not dead. The doctor and myself were in the surgery, when we heard the smash of the window and the cry of the Buf—of my friend, I mean."

"Of your brother resurrectionist, I suppose," continued Tomlinson, in a tone of ineffable disgust. "Well, go on."

"We went into the dissecting-room with a lamp, and there we found the light put out, and my comrade insensible on the floor. But what was more extraordinary still, we saw the corpse gasping for breath. '*He is not dead!*' cried the surgeon; and in a moment a lancet was stuck into his arm. The blood would not flow at first, but the surgeon chafed his temples and hands by turns; and in a few moments the blood trickled out pretty freely. Meantime I had recovered my companion, and explained to him the nature of the phenomenon that had taken place. When he heard the real truth, he was no longer alarmed, because he knew very well that people are often buried in a trance. In fact, one night, about eighteen months ago, he and I went to Old Saint Pancras church-yard to get up a stiff 'un, and when we opened the coffin, we found that the body had turned completely round on its face; it was, however, stone dead when we got it up—and never shall I forget what a countenance it had! But of that no matter."

"Have the goodness to keep to your present narrative," said Tomlinson, scarcely able to conceal his disgust at the presence of a resurrectionist—an avowed body-snatcher.

"Well," continued the man with the cadaverous countenance, "in a very few minutes we completely recovered the old gentleman.

I obeyed all the directions of the surgeon, and ran backwards and forwards to the pharmacy for God only knows what salts and what ammonia. At last the subject gave a terrible groan, opened his eyes, and exclaimed, '*Where am I?*' The surgeon assured him that he was in safety—that he had been very ill—that he was now much better—and so on. Meantime, by the surgeon's orders, I had called up his housekeeper, (for he is a bachelor,) and she had got a bed prepared and warmed, and some hot water ready, and every thing comfortable. Well, we carried the old gentleman up to bed; the doctor gave him a little warm brandy and water; and in another half hour, he was able to speak a few words in a comprehensible manner. But his brain seemed confused, and all we could learn was that his name was '*Michael Martin,*' and that he raved after a gentleman, whom he called '*James Tomlinson, the banker.*'"

"Ah! he said that—did he?" cried Tomlinson, rising, and pacing the room with agitated steps.

"He did," was the reply. "And then we began to think that we had heard those names before; and, in a few minutes, I—who know every thing," added the man, fixing his serpent-like eyes upon the stock-broker with a kind of fiendish leer,—"I," he continued, "remembered that Michael Martin was the man who had been the cashier in the bank of Tomlinson and Company, Lombard Street."

"But did he say—did he—" began the stock-broker, gasping for breath,—"did he—"

"He raved—he grew delirious; and in his wanderings, he said enough to prove that *he* was not guilty of the breach of trust imputed to him."

"O God! thy vengeance overtakes me, then, at last!" cried Tomlinson, sinking, pale and trembling upon a chair.

"He said much—very much," continued the man whose revelations had thus produced so strange an effect upon James Tomlinson. "But do not alarm yourself—I am not one to peach; and the doctor himself is not likely to say any thing that might lead to an awkward inquiry into the circumstances that brought the old gentleman into his house. Remember, the law now punishes with transportation those who resurrectionize, and those who encourage resurrectionists."

"Then you will not betray me?" ejaculated Tomlinson, a ray of hope animating his countenance.

"Betray you!" echoed the man, with a contemptuous curl of his lip and a ferocious leer of his eyes, which gleamed from beneath their bushy brows like those of a hyena from the shade of an over-hanging brake: "betray you! What good should I get by that? You know that a reward of three thousand pounds was offered to any one who would deliver up this Michael Martin; and as a man of sense, you must also understand that it would not be very convenient for me to go forward and claim this reward. At the same time, I might talk—or my friend might talk; no one could prevent that; and such-like idle gossiping would lead to the detection of the old man. Now you are the best judge whether or not it is worth while to put a seal upon our lips. We don't want to be hard upon you;—but, perhaps," added the man, interrupting himself, "you had better see the old gentleman first, and then you will know that I am telling you the truth."

"When can I see him? where is he?" demanded Tomlinson, almost bewildered by the sudden revelation which had been made to him concerning Michael Martin.

"You had better put off your visit till dusk," was the reply; "because I should like to go with you, and the surgeon would not be very well pleased if I called upon him in the day-time."

"Let it be at dusk, then," said Tomlinson.

"Name your hour."

"I have an engagement between nine and ten o'clock to-night," returned the stock-broker.

"And so have I," said the visitor. "What should you say to seven o'clock? It is as dark then as it is at ten or eleven."

"Seven will suit me well," answered Tomlinson. "Where shall I meet you?"

"At Bethnal Green New Church—the church that stands in the Cambridge Road, and faces the Bethnal Green Road," explained the body-snatcher. "You can be walking up and down there a few minutes before seven—I shall not keep you waiting."

"I will be punctual," said Tomlinson. "But—once more—you will not betray me?"

"Ridiculous!" was the contemptuous reply.

"And this surgeon—will he not be tempted by the reward to—"

"Do you think he would walk straight into Newgate and say, *'I am come to be transported for encouraging and employing resurrection men?'*

You need not alarm yourself. Me and my comrade will settle the matter amicably with you."

The body-snatcher then took his departure.

Tomlinson threw himself back in his chair, pressed both his hands against his heated forehead, and exclaimed in a tone of despair, "I have fervently prayed that I might meet my poor old clerk again, and heaven has granted my request—but merely to punish me for my crimes!"

CHAPTER CX.

THE EFFECTS OF A TRANCE.

It was half-past eight o'clock in the evening.

By the side of a bed in a comfortable chamber at the surgeon's house in the Cambridge Road, near Bethnal Green New Church, sate James Tomlinson.

The light of the candles that burnt upon the table, fell on the pale and ghastly countenance of old Michael Martin, who lay in that bed, his head propped up with pillows.

There was no one else in the room at the time, save these two persons.

"And thus was it, my good and faithful friend," said Tomlinson, breaking the long silence which had ensued after mutual explanations,—"thus was it that you so nobly sacrificed yourself for me! Oh! believe me that I have never ceased to think of your generous—your unparalleled behaviour in that sad business!"

"I know it—I know it," returned the old man in a weak and hollow voice. "If you had not been a kind master to me, I should never have done all that for you. But, tell me,—and tell me truly," added Michael, fixing his glassy eyes upon the stock-broker, "do you think that these persons—the surgeon, and that hideous man who—"

Martin ceased—and his entire frame was convulsed with horror as he remembered the appalling circumstances under which he had been recovered from his late death-like trance and restored to life.

"Compose yourself, my excellent friend," said Tomlinson, who fully comprehended what was passing in his mind; "fear alone will seal these people's lips—even if no other motive were powerful enough to ensure their silence. The surgeon seems an honest kind of man, and may be relied upon: besides, he would seriously compromise himself were he to breathe a word of this strange occurrence. As for the other person—he who came to tell me what had taken place, and brought me hither this evening—I have agreed to purchase his silence and that of a comrade, who, it appears, was engaged with him in the business."

"I know you cannot afford to do any such thing," said old Michael, speaking with somewhat of that bluntness, or even gruffness of manner, which had characterised him in past times; "and I won't have you get yourself into difficulties on my account."

"Believe me, I can afford it," returned Tomlinson.

"You can't. You told me just now that you were struggling against many difficulties. How much are you going to give these scoundrels?"

"A mere trifle—nothing beyond my means—"

"How much?" demanded old Michael, imperatively.

"Two hundred pounds."

"Two hundred pounds! It can't—and it shan't be done, Mr. Tomlinson. You have not got two hundred pounds: I know you have not."

"I am to receive five hundred this evening for certain professional services to be rendered," said Tomlinson; "and I can readily spare a portion to ensure a silence which is necessary not only to your safety but to mine."

"True—*your* safety," muttered old Michael, whose thoughts seemed ever fixed upon the welfare of his late employer. "Well—well, I suppose it must be done. Do it, then."

Another long pause ensued.

Suddenly Martin turned towards Tomlinson, and said, in a sharp querulous tone, "You told me that you were going to receive five hundred pounds this evening?"

"Such is my hope," answered the stock-broker, averting his glances from the old man.

"Ah! you can't look me in the face," exclaimed Michael, almost savagely. "Where are you going to get that money from?"

"From a client—for whom I am to do business—of a certain nature," faltered Tomlinson.

"Certain nature, indeed! What is it?"

"Merely professional, Michael," was the answer.

"Professional business in one evening, that will produce five hundred pounds," said the old man, dwelling emphatically upon every word: then, after a pause, he added abruptly, "I don't believe it."

"I declare most solemnly that I am telling you the truth," cried Tomlinson, somewhat hurt by Michael's manner and observations.

"So much the worse for you, then," rejoined the old man, laconically. "The business you are to perform for that sum is not honest."

Tomlinson was about to make some excuse to put an end to the topic by an evasive reply, when Michael Martin raised himself to a sitting posture in the bed, and, fixing his eyes upon his late master, exclaimed, with strange emphasis of manner, "Have you not seen enough—experienced enough—and suffered enough, to render you timorous in re-embarking upon the great ocean of chicanery, duplicity, and crime? Be you well assured that though the currents of that ocean may float you prosperously along for a season, they will sooner or later dash you against a sunken rock, and shipwreck you beyond redemption. Oh!" he continued, his ghastly countenance becoming animated with the ruddy tinge of excitement, and fire once more sparkling from his glassy eyes,—"Oh! if you had only passed through all that I have within these last few days, you would not neglect so terrible a warning! Do you know,"—and his utterance became rapid and eloquent,—"do you know that I have passed the limits of the tomb, and have wandered in the worlds beyond? Do you know that I have learnt the grand—the sublime—the supernal secret of eternity? Yes—when the breath left this mortal clay, my soul winged its flight into the regions of infinite space! With the rapidity of a whirlwind I was hurried away from the earth; and, although I was nothing but a spirit, *and could not touch myself,* yet had I ears to hear, and eyes to see, and organs to receive sensations. I was permitted to wander amidst the regions of eternal bliss, and to penetrate into the mysteries of hell. O God! I tasted of the joys of the former, and was equally compelled to submit to the torments of the latter—each for a little space! Ah! sir, can you not divine wherefore the Almighty from time to time plunges mortals into a trance—submits them to the dominion of death for a season? It is that he may snatch away their souls, to lead them into the celestial mansions, and precipitate them into the depths of Satan's kingdom,—so that, when restored to their mortal clay, they may teach their fellow-creatures the grand truths of eternity—they may announce to them that there is a heaven to reward, and a hell to punish! And the Almighty made choice of me,—of *me*, a grovelling worm, one of the most obscure and humble of his creatures,—He made choice of *me*, I say, to become the means through which His warning voice might speak to *you* and *others!* What the pleasures of heaven are, or of what the torments of hell consist, I dare not say: suffice it for you to know that there *is* a heaven, and there *is* a hell—and the former exceeds all idea which man can conceive of bliss, while the latter surpasses every thing which he can imagine of horror! Be warned, then, by me, James Tomlinson—be warned by one who for four days was snatched away from earth, and, during that period was initiated in the mighty secrets of Eternity!"

The old man fell back in the bed, exhausted.

Tomlinson had at first listened to him with sorrow and alarm: he trembled lest the delirium of a fever had suddenly overtaken him—lest his brain was wandering. But as he proceeded—in a style of galvanic force and eloquence of which the listener, who had known him for so many years, deemed him incapable,—in a manner so inconsistent with all his former habits, so strangely at variance with his nature, his character, and his disposition,—the stock-broker became afraid, for it seemed to him as if those burning, searching, searing, scorching words were indeed an emanation from a source belonging to the mysteries of other worlds.

An awful pause ensued when Michael Martin ceased to speak.

For some moments Tomlinson sate riveted in speechless terror to his chair—stunned, bewildered, astounded, appalled by all he had just heard.

That dread silence was at length interrupted by the entrance of the surgeon.

"How gets on my patient now?" he said, approaching the couch.

"I fear—I am afraid—that is, I think—his head wanders," faltered the stock-broker, scarcely knowing what he said.

"We must expect that such will be the case—for some days to come," returned the surgeon, with the coolness of a professional man who saw nothing extraordinary in such results following so strange a resuscitation from a death-like trance.

"You think, then," asked Tomlinson, "that it is possible for this poor old man to rave—about things of—a very extraordinary nature?"

"People, when delirious, burst forth into the most wild and fanciful ravings," answered the surgeon, as he felt Michael's pulse.

"And *he* might, then, rave of heaven—and hell—and things relating to—"

"He may rave of any nonsense," said the surgeon, abruptly; "but that is no reason why we should allow ourselves to be affected by it—as I see that you are."

"It was, indeed, very foolish on my part," observed Tomlinson, now acquiring confidence, and endeavouring to divest himself of the strange sensations of horror and dread which the eloquence of the old man had excited within him.

"You had better retire for the present," said the surgeon. "He is in a high fever—produced, perhaps, by this interview with you, under such circumstances. Do not think of seeing him again this evening: to-morrow evening he will be better and more composed."

"And you will take every possible care of him," exclaimed the stock-broker. "Remember that no expense must be spared to make him comfortable—to ensure his recovery. I will remunerate you handsomely, sir."

"Well, well," said the surgeon, impatiently. "We will talk about that another time. Good evening—you may return to-morrow at the same hour."

"Good evening," answered Tomlinson; and he slowly took his departure.

CHAPTER CXI.

A SCENE AT MR. CHICHESTER'S HOUSE.

It was about half-past nine on the same evening that the above incidents occurred, when a double knock at the front door echoed through Mr. Chichester's dwelling, in the immediate vicinity of the Cambridge Heath Gate.

Mr. Chichester himself was seated in an elegantly-furnished parlour, sipping a glass of excellent Madeira, and pondering upon the best means of enjoying himself when he should have fingered the cash to obtain which he had perpetrated so diabolical an outrage against the confiding woman who had bestowed upon him her hand, and made him a partner in the enjoyment, if not in the actual possession, of her fortune.

The room was not large, but very comfortable; and at one end a pair of ample folding doors, now closed, afforded admission into a back parlour.

A few moments after the echo of the double-knock above mentioned, through the house, a female servant entered and announced Mr. Tomlinson.

Having requested the stock-broker to be seated, Mr. Chichester followed the servant into the hall, and said to her in a low whisper, "When the *other person* comes, show him into the back parlour, as I may require to have some conversation with this gentleman before I introduce them to each other."

This command being given, Mr. Chichester returned to the room where he had left Mr. Tomlinson.

"You are before your time," said Chichester, pushing the decanter and a glass towards the stockbroker: "that looks like business."

"I accidentally had an appointment upon some business in this neighbourhood," was the reply; "and when that matter was disposed of, I came I straight hither."

"We cannot repair to the lunatic asylum until ten or half-past," said Chichester, "because, as a precaution, the keeper has promised to call upon me presently, and report whether my wife continues in the same docile mood as when he wrote to me yesterday afternoon."

"I should be delighted to hear that you could settle this unpleasant—very unpleasant affair in some amicable way," returned Tomlinson, whose mind was still painfully excited by the interview which had taken place between him and his late cashier.

"Impossible, my dear sir!" ejaculated Chichester. "There is no way save the one chalked out. I hope that you do not hesitate to fulfil the agreement into which you entered with me."

"The truth is, Mr. Chichester," said Tomlinson, "there is no man in London to whom a few hundreds of pounds would prove as welcome as to me—especially as to-morrow I have to pay two hundred to men who will not be very well pleased to experience a disappointment. It is true that I possess such a sum at my bankers'; but I dare not draw out every shilling—my credit would be ruined."

"So much the better reason for doing as I require of you," said Chichester, filling the glasses with Madeira.

"True," observed Tomlinson. "But, on the other hand, I tremble to take a false step—I fear to jeopardize myself by connivance at a direct conspiracy—"

"Pshaw!" cried Chichester. "What is the use of compunction on the part of a man who stands in so much need of money as yourself?"

Tomlinson was about to reply, when a low knock at the front door fell upon his ears.

"It is no one—of any consequence," said Chichester; then, as he refilled the glasses, he muttered to himself, "There is no use in introducing these men to each other, unless this milk-and-water fool is quite agreeable to act."

"Did you make an observation?" inquired the stock-broker.

"I was observing that it was no one of any consequence;—only some person for the servants, most probably. But let me now ask you seriously, Mr. Tomlinson, whether you feel disposed to proceed further in this matter or not?"

"Candidly speaking, I would rather not," was the reply.

"Then you were wrong to give me a false hope of your aid, and allow so much valuable time to elapse, during which I might have found a broker less punctilious than you."

"I regret that I should have caused this inconvenience," answered Tomlinson; "but I had resolved to perform my promise until about an hour ago, and I have even brought the necessary documents for the purpose."

"Something very remarkable must have intervened to change your resolutions," said Chichester, contemptuously.

"I am not superstitious," observed Tomlinson; "but I believe that a providential warning was conveyed to me—"

"A providential fiddle-stick! Remember, Mr. Tomlinson, that by your unpardonable vacillation in this matter you will only prolong the incarceration of my wife."

"And, pray, who is responsible for that deed?"

"We will not discuss this point," returned Chichester. "I did not ask you to become my Mentor. At the same time," he added, sinking his voice, "every moment is important—for my wife is going mad in reality!"

"Then, in the name of God, release her at once!" ejaculated Tomlinson.

"Never—until she signs the deed."

"Release her," continued Tomlinson; "and then bring her with you to my office, where she can make the transfer."

"Are you mad yourself? Do you suppose she would ever put pen to paper if she were once liberated in that manner? I am surprised at your ignorance—vexed at your cowardice. You have not acted like a man of business, nor as a man of the world. It was for you to accept or decline my proposal—not to deceive me by these changes and shiftings of inclination. Come, sir—once for all—pluck up your courage: remember the two hundred pounds which you say must be paid to-morrow to two men who will not be put off, and the settlement of which debt will so materially embarrass your finances."

"My mind is made up, Mr. Chichester," answered Tomlinson firmly.

"And what is your decision?"

"I shall beg to withdraw from the transaction."

And Tomlinson rose to depart.

But at the same moment the folding-doors, communicating with the inner room, were thrown open, and a man with a cadaverous countenance stood forward.

"You shall *not* forfeit your word in this respect," exclaimed the individual, whom Tomlinson immediately recognised to be the body-snatcher engaged in the affair of Michael Martin.

"What does this man do here?" asked Tomlinson, in a faint voice, of Chichester.

"What do I do here? what do I do every where?" cried the man, with a diabolical laugh. "Tell me the secret plot—the cunning intrigue—the scheme of villany to which Anthony Tidkins, surnamed the Resurrection Man, is a stranger! But little did I think when I called upon you this morning,—little did I imagine when I met you again this evening, that *you* were the person enlisted by Mr. Chichester in the affair which we have now in hand."

"It would appear, then, that you are acquainted with each other," said Chichester, laughing heartily at the confusion manifested by the stock-broker in the presence of the Resurrection Man. "Why, what devilry was it that brought you two together?"

"Whether I keep Mr. Tomlinson's secret, or whether I proclaim it to you and every one else whom I know, until the whole town rings with the circumstance, is a matter for him to decide," said the Resurrection Man;—and, with admirable coolness, he helped himself to a bumper of Madeira.

"If I pay you two hundred pounds, as agreed upon," exclaimed Tomlinson, "what more would you require of me?"

"I require that you remain faithful to your promise to Mr. Chichester;—I require that you fulfil the service which you have undertaken to perform in his behalf," was the resolute reply.

"And in what way does the business regard you—you, who acknowledge yourself to be—"

"A resurrectionist! Certainly I am—and the most skilful in London, no other excepted," exclaimed Tidkins, with a satanic chuckle. "But that does not prevent me from turning mad-house keeper—or any thing else—when opportunity offers."

"What! *you* are the keeper of the asylum in which this gentleman's wife is imprisoned!" exclaimed the stock-broker, in a tone of the most profound astonishment.

"Yes, he is indeed," said Chichester; "and a better keeper could not have been found. So now you know all about that point."

"And Mr. Tomlinson will be good enough to accompany *me* to my house," observed the Resurrection Man. "You, Mr. Chichester, can follow us at a little distance. It looks suspicious for three people to walk together."

"I really must decline—" began Tomlinson, trembling from head to foot, as the warning voice of Michael Martin seemed to ring in his ears.

"One word more, Mr. Tomlinson," said the Resurrection Man. "I am a person of determined spirit and resolution. I never stick at trifles myself;—and I don't choose others, with whom I am connected, to balk me in my designs, when I can prevent them. Now, either come with me, and do what is required of you; or, as sure as there is breath in your body, I will deliver up a certain person to the police, and stand the consequences myself."

"I beg of you—I implore you—"

"Pshaw!" cried Chichester: "this is child's play!"

"Child's play, indeed!" thundered the Resurrection Man in a terrible voice. "But I will put an end to it. Come, sir—hesitate another minute, and *that old man* is lost!"

"I will accompany you," answered the stock-broker;—then, in an under tone, he added, "But God knows how unwillingly!"

The Resurrection Man seized him by the arm, and conducted him out of the house.

Five minutes afterwards, Chichester followed in the same direction.

CHAPTER CXII.

VIOLA.

THE Resurrection Man and the stock-broker pursued their way in silence to the very entrance of the alley leading to the side door of the dwelling of the former.

There they halted, the Resurrection Man observing that they must wait for Mr. Chichester.

Tomlinson took advantage of the interval to implore the Resurrection Man not to communicate to Chichester the secret relating to Michael Martin.

"Do not be afraid," was the answer: "I am as close as Newgate-door when people conduct themselves as they ought to do. One individual for whom I do business never knows what I am engaged in for another—unless his own bad behaviour forces me to blab. So make yourself quite easy upon that score."

Chichester now made his appearance; and the Resurrection Man led the way up the alley.

Having opened the door of the house, he admitted his two companions into the back-room on the ground-floor, and then struck a light.

The appearance of the place was precisely the same as when we described it on the first occasion of the Rattlesnake's visit to that department of the building.

Tomlinson shuddered as he cast his eyes around the naked and gloomy walls.

"Holloa!" ejaculated Chichester, taking up the mask, which lay on the table, in his hands: "I suppose that this—"

"Hush!" said the Resurrection Man, glancing towards Tomlinson, as much as to desire Chichester not to allow the stock-broker to know more of the secrets connected with the treatment of the prisoner, than was possible; for Tidkins, who possessed a profound knowledge of human nature, was well aware that certain compunctious feelings still floated in the mind of Tomlinson, and that he was, after all, but a very coward in the ways of crime.

Chichester covered the mask with the cloak, while the stock-broker was engaged in scanning the appearance of the chamber.

When Tomlinson had completed his survey, and while he was still wondering where the means of communication with the apartment of the alleged lunatic could be, he happened to turn in the direction of the chimney-piece, when to his surprise he perceived the hearth-stone raised, and the Resurrection Man half down the subterranean staircase which that strangely contrived trap-door had disclosed to view.

Tomlinson shuddered—and hesitated whether he should proceed further in the matter; but his scruples vanished when he heard the voice of the Resurrection Man desiring—or rather commanding him—to follow him down that flight of stone steps.

Guided by Tidkins, who carried the candle, which was fixed in one of the large tin shades before described, Tomlinson descended the stairs, and found himself in a vaulted passage, about twenty feet long, and four broad. There were four strong doors, studded with thick iron nails, on each side.

"You see, this house was built for a lunatic asylum many—many years ago, when treatment wasn't quite so humane as it is now," whispered the Resurrection Man to Tomlinson; "but it hadn't been used as such for the last thirty years till the other day."

"And did you hire the establishment for the purpose of restoring it to its original uses?" demanded Tomlinson, shuddering, as he glanced around on the damp walls on which the strong light of the candle fell.

"Not I, indeed," answered Tidkins, abruptly.

Chichester had now descended into the subterranean passage.

"This is the cell," said the Resurrection Man; and, approaching one of the doors, he placed a key in the lock.

During the few seconds that intervened until the door was thrown open, Tomlinson experienced a perfect age of mental agony. He felt as if he were about to perpetrate some hideous crime—a murder of the blackest dye. The perspiration poured off his forehead: he trembled from head to foot; his brain felt oppressed; there was a weight upon the pit of his stomach; his eye-balls throbbed.

Yes—he was a very coward in guilt!

The door flew open.

The Resurrection Man entered first, and advanced into the middle of a small arched cell—a stone tomb, built to immure the living!

A decent bed, a table, a chair, a wash-hand-stand, and a lamp, which was lighted, together with a few other necessaries, composed the furniture of that dungeon.

And stretched upon the bed, with her clothes on, lay the victim of this cruel persecution.

The glare of the Resurrection Man's candle fell upon a pale, but not unpleasing countenance: the long chesnut hair spread, dishevelled, over the arm that supported the head.

The sleep of that lady was deep but uneasy—such a slumber as might be supposed to fall upon the eyes of the criminal the night before his execution.

Her bosom heaved convulsively; and from her lips escaped a stifled sob as the three men entered the cell.

Chichester was about to place his hand upon her shoulder in order to arouse her, when she opened her eyes, and started up to a sitting posture on the bed.

"Villains!" she exclaimed: "would you murder me?"

"No such thing, my dear," said Chichester. "We have merely come to terminate this unpleasant business in the way proposed by Mr. Tidkins."

"The wretch!" cried Viola, casting a glance of doubt and uncertainty at both Tomlinson and the Resurrection Man.

"Ah! I dare say I am, ma'am, in *your* estimation," said Tidkins, coolly. "Oh! you needn't look at me in that way, ma'am. I will acknowledge that I am your keeper in this establishment; and that it's me who has been good enough to bring you food every night."

"The wretch!" again cried the unhappy lady, while a profound shudder seemed to convulse her whole frame as she surveyed the Resurrection Man from head to foot. "It is you, then," she continued, leaping from the bed, and confronting the miscreant, "it is you who have dared to practise upon my fears in a manner the most diabolical—the most cowardly;—you who have chosen the solemn hour of midnight for your visits, and who have come in a guise calculated to fill my mind with the most horrible imaginings!"

"Remember our agreement, ma'am," said Tidkins, sternly. "You pledged yourself to forget the past upon certain conditions: we are here to fulfil these conditions. Do you mean to keep your word? or must we leave you to your solitude?"

"Who is this gentleman?" demanded Viola, casting a penetrating glance upon Tomlinson.

"The stock-broker, my dear," answered Chichester: "the person who will receive your signature to a certain little paper—"

"Then, sir," interrupted the lady, addressing herself to James Tomlinson, "as you exercise an honourable profession, prove yourself an honourable man in this respect. You see before you a powerless female, who was weak enough to bestow her hand upon a villain—a villain that has immured her, by the aid of another villain of even a deeper dye than himself, in this horrible vault! Perhaps they have told you that I am mad, sir; but do I speak like one whose reason has abandoned her? or would you receive the signature of a person who knew not what she signed? Oh! no, sir—you cannot believe that I am in mental darkness! you must perceive the full extent of the villany that has been practised against me, for the purpose of plundering me of that property which I received from my former husband! Oh! if you be a man possessing one spark of honour—as I must suppose that you are—"

"Come—a truce to all this," said Mr. Chichester. "The gentleman to whom you are addressing yourself knows the whole affair, and will act *with* and *for* me."

"Is this true, sir?" asked the unhappy lady, casting a glance of mingled terror and supplication upon the stock-broker, and clasping her hands together: "can this be true? Is it possible that a person exercising an honourable profession can league with wretches of their stamp?"—and she pointed disdainfully towards the Resurrection Man and Chichester. "Oh! no, it cannot be! At least, hear me! I married that man—"

"Don't I tell you that Mr. Tomlinson knows all," cried Chichester, impatiently. "We did not come to debate upon the past, but to settle for the future."

"You have come, then, to plunder a weak, helpless, persecuted female," continued Viola. "But do you know, sir, the terrible means that have been adopted to wring from me a consent to part with half the property which was bequeathed to me by a man that loved me—a man who toiled for years and years to amass the fortune that must now be devoted to the extravagances of a spendthrift? Would you believe to what an extent the cruelty, the cowardice of that man,"—and she pointed to Tidkins,—"has been carried to terrify me into compliance with the demands of his employer? Sir, for three weeks and three days have I been a prisoner in this dungeon; and every night—without fail—has that miscreant visited me in a disguise which, in such a place, and at such an hour, would make the stoutest heart palpitate with horror,—a disguise of such a nature that this is the first time that I have seen his face; for on the fatal evening when I was seized and brought to this dungeon, every thing was involved in utter obscurity;—and then, when the door opened again, and a light gleamed in upon me,—O God! it was carried by a person dressed in a dark cloak and a white mask—like a being of another world!"

"Surely you did not go to such extremes as this?" exclaimed Tomlinson, turning sharply round upon the Resurrection Man.

"Whatever I did, or did not, is nothing to the present business," replied Tidkins, brutally. "If any thing is going to be done, let it be done at once; if not, the lady will remain here till she chooses to consent to the terms proposed to her."

Tomlinson glanced, with a look of deep sympathy, towards the lady, who stood in an attitude of supplication and despair before him. Her dishevelled hair hung loosely over her shoulders: her countenance, though not beautiful, was naturally interesting, and was now rendered more so by its extreme pallor and by the expression of profound melancholy which it wore; and her mild blue eyes were raised towards him as if to implore his aid—his compassion.

"Now, what is to be done?" demanded Chichester.

"It is for this gentleman to decide," said the lady, still gazing upon Tomlinson's countenance. "You may well suppose that I am desirous to recover the liberty which has thus been infamously violated;—but if you, sir, possess one germ of generous feeling—one spark of honour—one gleam of humanity in your soul, do not—do not lend yourself to this infamy! Command these men to restore me to freedom—they cannot refuse to obey you! Oh! sir—hear me—do not avert your head: hear me—hear me, I implore you!"

"This is quite enough of folly for one time," ejaculated the

Resurrection Man: "I have been an idiot myself to listen to it so long. Mr. Tomlinson, are you prepared to receive the signature of this lady to the deed that will transfer to her husband a certain portion of her property?"—then, approaching his lips to the stock-broker's ear, he murmured in a low whisper, "Hesitate—and I denounce your late clerk within an hour!"

These words operated like magic upon the weak-minded and timid James Tomlinson. He no longer beheld the supplicating woman before him: he only saw his own danger.

Accordingly, he advanced towards the table, drew forth a document from his pocket, and said, in a cold tone, "I am ready to receive that lady's signature."

The Resurrection Man produced an ink-bottle and pens (with which he had purposely provided himself beforehand) from his pocket; and placed them upon the table.

Tomlinson seated himself in the chair, and proceeded to fill up the paper.

"In whose favour is the transfer to be made?" he demanded.

"Then, sir, you are determined to league with my oppressors?" said Viola, in a tone expressive of concentrated feelings of indignation and despair.

"Madam, I am unfortunately compelled—"

"Say no more, sir," interrupted the lady, with a contemptuous curl of the lip. "If you came hither a villain, I must be mad indeed to hope to make you an honest man by any reasoning of mine."

"Madam, you wrong me, by heavens!" ejaculated Tomlinson, throwing down the pen.

But at the same moment his wrist was seized with a grasp of iron, and a well-known voice whispered in his ear, "Hesitate another moment, and I denounce you and your cashier together!"

Tomlinson became docile as a child, resumed the pen, and said, "In whose favour is this transfer to be made?"

"In that of Mr. Arthur Chichester," answered Viola, firmly.

"What is the amount to be so transferred?"

"Eight thousand pounds, being part of a sum now standing in my name in the Three-and-a-Half per cents.," replied the injured woman, still with an outward composure, which was not, however, the reflection of her inward feelings.

Tomlinson filled up the paper according to the instructions which he received.

Then, addressing himself to Viola, but without turning his eyes towards her, he said, "You are aware, madam, that this document is ante-dated by two months?"

"I am, sir."

"Nothing now remains, then, madam, save for you to sign it."

Viola advanced slowly towards the table, took up the pen, and seemed to be about to affix her signature to the deed, when—as if suddenly recollecting herself—she turned towards the stock-broker, and exclaimed, "What guarantee have I that my freedom is to follow this concession on my part?"

"To-morrow evening, at dusk, you shall be conveyed home," exclaimed Chichester, seeing that Tomlinson gave no answer.

"And why not this evening—now—the moment that document is signed?"

"Because I should prefer laying my hand on the money first," was the reply.

"Mr. Tomlinson," cried the lady, "I have more confidence in you than in either of these men: I am willing even to believe that some circumstance, unknown to me, compels you unwillingly to become their instrument on this occasion."

"By heavens, you speak the truth, madam!" ejaculated Tomlinson, warmly.

"I believe you. Now, sir, promise me on your most solemn word of honour—by every thing you consider sacred—that to-morrow evening at nine o'clock I shall be released from this dungeon."

"I promise—I swear that you shall be conveyed home to-morrow evening at nine o'clock," answered Tomlinson. "But, in return, madam, will you pledge yourself as solemnly that your lips shall ever remain closed with regard to this proceeding?"

"Oh! yes—I do—I do," answered the poor creature, clasping her hands together—for she could even feel grateful to the man who, while leagued with others against her, yet pledged himself to her release from that horrible cell.

"Secresy on all sides is one of the conditions of the present arrangement," said Chichester.

"And if the lady breaks that condition," added the Resurrection

Man, "she would repent it; for let her be surrounded by friends—let her be protected by a regiment of soldiers—let her take refuge in the Queen's palace, I would still find means to tear her away, and bring her back to this dungeon."

Tomlinson and the lady both cast a glance of mingled horror and surprise at the formidable individual who thus spoke so confidently of his power and resolution.

There was a moment's pause.

Viola then took up the pen, and, with a firm hand, affixed her signature to the document.

"I am now at your mercy," she said, in a tone rather of supplication than of menace or mistrust.

"You need not be afraid that we shall deceive you, my dear," observed Chichester, with a smile.

A reply rose to the lips of his injured wife; but she suppressed it—though with difficulty. She was no doubt afraid to irritate the man in whose power she still found herself, by giving utterance to her thoughts.

"No—there's nothing to be afraid of," said the Resurrection Man. "The lady has fulfilled her part of the bargain, and we will perform ours. As for her keeping this little business dark, I feel confident about *that*; she would not like to stand the chance of coming here again; and, as for making a disturbance merely to get back the money, that would be useless, when once it had found its way into the pockets of her husband."

Having concluded this brutal speech, the Resurrection Man desired his companions to await his return for a moment, while he proceeded to fetch the lady her provisions for the next four-and-twenty hours.

He accordingly hastened up the steps to the little back room, whence he speedily returned with his basket in his hand.

"You see that I expected how all this would end," he observed, with a hideous smile; "and so I prepared a little treat for the lady. Here's a prime fowl; that brown paper contains ham; here's a new loaf; and this is a bottle of as excellent sherry as one need drink."

The Resurrection Man placed the articles, as he enumerated them, upon the table; and Viola was pleased as she contemplated them—because she perceived in this indulgence an earnest that the promise of her persecutors would be fulfilled with respect to her restoration to liberty.

"We must now take leave of Mrs. Chichester," said Tidkins. "To-morrow evening, ma'am, at nine precisely, you shall be free."

The three men then left the dungeon.

But ere the door closed upon the inmate once more, she moved forward, caught Tomlinson by the hand, and said in an emphatic tone, "Remember your solemn promise!"

"Do not be alarmed, madam. There can be no interest to detain you here beyond to-morrow."

Viola retreated into the dungeon; and the door was shut.

She heard the three persons who had just left her retire from the subterranean prison: the closing of the trap-door also fell upon her ears.

Clasping her hands together, she exclaimed, "God grant that they may not deceive me!"

And then a vague terror stole upon her,—a horrible, an absorbing dread lest those men intended to immure her for life in that solitary cell, or else restore her to liberty only when they should have extorted from her the remainder of her fortune.

"Oh! fool that I was, to sign that paper!" she exclaimed, in a paroxysm of despair. "Will men, who are capable of such villany—such atrocity as this that they have practised towards me,—will they remain satisfied with a portion of the gold that has allured them to violate every principle of honour and humanity? Oh! no—no! and perhaps—to conceal their crime the more effectually—they will not hesitate to imbrue their hands in my blood!"

Overpowered by this idea, the unhappy woman threw herself upon the bed, and wept bitterly.

That torrent of tears relieved her; and in a few minutes she grew somewhat composed.

Then came reflections of a less painful nature.

"Still—still there was something honest in the appearance of that stock-broker: there was something feeling in his words! He was performing a task against which his soul revolted. He commiserated my condition: oh! yes—he sympathised with me! In him is my hope—my only hope! I need not quite despair!"

She thus reasoned herself into a state of comparative calmness;

and then a feeling of weakness came over her. She grew faint—her head swam round.

She rose, and walked up and down the cell to dispel the sensation that thus oppressed her; and suddenly she recollected that many hours had elapsed since she had eaten any thing. Her eyes fell upon the viands which the Resurrection Man had placed on the table; and she hastened to break her long fast. When she had partaken of a morsel of food, she poured some wine into a glass and drank it.

Scarcely, however, had she swallowed the liquor, when she felt herself overpowered by a deep drowsiness; the glass dropped from her hands; she rose from the chair, advanced a few paces, and then fell upon the bed in a state of insensibility.

CHAPTER CXIII.

THE LOVERS.

THE morning, which succeeded the night that witnessed the incidents just detailed, was clear, frosty, and fine. It was one of those winter mornings when the soil is as hard as iron, but on which the sun shines with gay light if not with genial heat. On such a morning we walk abroad with a consciousness that the exercise benefits us: we feel the blood acquiring a more rapid circulation in our veins; we soon experience a pleasant glow pervading the frame; our spirits become exhilarated; and we learn that even Winter has its peculiar charms.

Such was the feeling that animated Richard Markham, as, after alighting from a public vehicle at Richmond, he proceeded rapidly along a by-road that led through the fields at the back of Count Alteroni's mansion.

His cheeks were tinged with a glow that set off his handsome features to the greatest advantage: his dark eyes sparkled with an expression of joy and hope; a smile played upon his lip; and he walked with his head erect as if he felt proud of his existence—because that existence, in spite of its vicissitudes, was protected by some auspicious star.

O Love! art thou not a star full of hope and promise, like that which guided the sages of the East to the cradle of their Redeemer?—like the welcome planet which heralds the dauntless mariner over the midnight seas?—like the twinkling orb which points the right track to the Arab wanderer in the desert?

Richard Markham pursued his way—his soul full of hope, and love, and bliss.

At a distance of about a quarter of a mile on his right hand, the mansion of Count Alteroni soon met his eyes, surrounded by the evergreens that, in contrast with the withered trees elsewhere, gave to the spot where it stood the air of an oasis in the midst of a desert.

Markham's heart beat quickly when that well-known dwelling met his view; and for a moment a shade of melancholy passed over his countenance, for he recalled to mind the happy hours he had once spent within its walls.

But that transitory cloud vanished from his brow, when his eye caught a glimpse, in another instant, of a sylph-like form that was threading a leafless grove at a little distance.

Richard redoubled his steps, and was led, by the circuitous winding of the path that he was pursuing, somewhat nearer to the Count's mansion.

In a few minutes he reached the very spot where, in the preceding spring, he had accidentally encountered Isabella, and where she assured him of her unchanged and unchangeable love.

He is now on that spot once more:—he pauses—looks around—and Isabella again approaches.

Richard rushes forward, and clasps the beauteous Italian maiden in his arms.

"Isabella—dearest Isabella! What good angel prompted you to grant me this interview?" he exclaimed, when the first effusion of joy was over.

"Do you think me indiscreet, Richard?" asked the signora, taking his arm, and glancing timidly towards his countenance.

"Indiscreet, my sweet girl!" cried her lover: "Oh! how can you suppose that I would entertain a harsh feeling with regard to that goodness on your part which doubtless instigated you to afford me the happiness of this meeting?"

"But when we met here—seven or eight months ago, Richard," said Isabella, "I told you that never—never would I consent to a stolen interview. And now—you may imagine—"

"I imagine that you love me, Isabella—love me as I love you," exclaimed Markham; "and what other idea can occupy my thoughts when that one is present? Oh! you know not the ineffable joy—the unequalled pleasure which I experienced when your letter reached me yesterday. I recognised your handwriting immediately; and I seized the letter with avidity, when it was brought to me in my study. And then, Isabella—will you believe me when I tell you that I trembled to open it? I laid it upon the table—my hand refused to break the seal. Pardon me—forgive me, if for a moment I feared—"

"That I had forgotten my vows—my plighted affection," faltered Isabella, reproachfully.

"Again I say pardon—forgive me, dearest girl; but—oh! I have been so very unfortunate!"

"Think not of the past, Richard," said Isabella, tenderly.

"The past! Oh! how can I cease to ponder upon the past, when it has nearly bereaved me of all hope for the future?" exclaimed Markham, in an impassioned tone.

"Not *all* hope," murmured Isabella; "since hope still remains to *me!*"

"Angel that thou art!" cried Richard, pressing the maiden's hand fondly. "How weak I am, since it is from thee that moral courage ever is imparted."

"You were speaking of my letter," said Isabella, with a smile.

"True! But so many emotions—joy and hope—sorrowful reminiscences and brighter prospects, bewilder me! I will, however, try to talk calmly! When your letter came, I feared to open it for some moments: I dreaded a new calamity! But at length I called all my firmness to my aid; and a terrible weight was taken from my soul, when my eye glanced at the first lines of that letter which suddenly became as dear and welcome as a reprieve to the condemned criminal. Then, when I saw that my beloved Isabella still thought of me—still loved me——"

"Oh, I did not tell you *that* in my letter," exclaimed Isabella, with a smile of bewitching archness.

"No—but I divined it—I gathered it from the words in which you conveyed to me your desire to see me—from the manner in which you said that at eleven o'clock this morning you should walk in the very place where we had met accidentally once before—oh! I suddenly became a new being: never was my heart so light!"

"And yet I said in my letter, Richard, that I wished to see you upon a matter of business——"

"Ah! Isabella, destroy not the charm which makes me happy! Let no cold thought of worldly things chill the heavenly fervour of our affection. Were it not for that love which reciprocally exists between us, how should I have supported the misfortunes that have multiplied upon me?"

"Again I say, Richard, allude not to the past. Alas! bitter—bitter were the tears that I wept on that fatal night when——"

"When I was publicly disgraced at the theatre—in the midst of a triumph. Yes—Isabella, you were there—there, where my shame was consummated!"

"Accident had led us to the theatre that evening," answered Isabella. "My father had heard that a new tragedy, of which grand hopes were entertained, was to be produced; and he insisted that I should accompany him and my mother. I was compelled to assent to his desire—although I prefer retirement and tranquillity to society and gaiety. You may conceive our astonishment—you may imagine *my* surprise and *my* joy, when you came forward to acknowledge the congratulations offered for a triumph so brilliantly achieved. And then—but let us leave that subject—my blood turns cold when I think of it!"

"Oh! go on—speak of it, speak of it!" exclaimed Markham, enthusiastically; "for although the reminiscence of that fearful scene be like pouring molten lead upon an open wound, still it is sweet—it is sweet, Isabella, to receive sympathy from such lips as yours."

"Alas! I have little more to say—except that the sudden intervention of that terrible man seemed to strike me as with the arrow of death; and I became insensible. Then, Richard,—*then*," continued Isabella, in a low and tremulous tone, "my mother suspected my secret—or rather received a confirmation of the suspicion which she had long entertained!"

"And she shuddered at the mere idea?" exclaimed Markham, interrogatively.

"No, Richard: my mother is kind and good—and, you know, was always well disposed towards you: I have told you that much before! She said little—and of that no matter! But my father—my father——"

"He discovered *our* secret also!" exclaimed Richard. "Oh! did he not curse me?"

"He was cool and calm, when—on the following morning—he spoke to me upon the subject. I answered him frankly: I admitted my attachment for you."

"What did he say, Isabella! Tell me every thing—suppress not a word!"

"Oh, heavens! he made me very miserable," returned Isabella, tears trickling down her countenance. "But wherefore distress both yourself and me with a recapitulation of what ensued? Suffice it to say, that I collected all the arguments in my memory—and they were not a few;—and I presented to him that paper—the confession of Talbot, which proved your innocence!"

"Dearest girl!" exclaimed Markham, rapturously.

"He did not refuse to read it," added Isabella; "and at length, when I saw that I had made a profound impression on him, I turned the conversation upon the momentary reverse of fortune which had plunged him into a debtors' prison——"

"Isabella!" cried Markham, in surprise.

"And then I boldly declared my conviction that the unknown friend who had released him—the anonymous individual who had thrown open to him the gate leading to liberty—the nameless person, that had done so generous a deed, and accomplished it in a manner as delicate as it was noble,—was none other than Richard Markham!"

The tone of the Italian maiden had become more and more impassioned as she proceeded; and when she uttered the last words of the foregoing sentence, she turned upon him on whose arm she leant, a countenance glowing with animation, and radiant with gratitude and love.

"Oh, Isabella! you told your father *that!*" cried Markham. "And yet—you knew not——"

"My suspicion amounted almost to a certainty," interrupted Isabella: "and now I doubt no longer. Oh! Richard—if ever for one moment I had wavered in my love for you,—if ever an instant of coldness, arising from worldly reflections, had intervened to make me repent my solemn vows to you,—that *one* deed of yours—that noble sacrifice of your property, made to release my revered parent from a gaol,—that—that alone would have rendered my heart unalterably thine!"

"Beloved girl—this moment is the happiest of my life!" exclaimed

Markham; and tears of joy filled his eyes, as he pressed the maiden once more to his heart.

"Yes, Richard," continued Isabella, after a long pause; and now her splendid countenance was lighted up with an expression of dignity and generous pride, and the timid, bashful maiden seemed changed into a lady whose brow was encircled with a diadem; "yes, Richard, if ever I felt that no deed nor act of mine shall separate us eternally—if ever I rejoiced in the prospect of possessing wealth, and receiving lustre from my father's princely rank——"

"Isabella!" exclaimed Richard, dropping the arm on which the Italian lady was leaning, and stepping back in the most profound astonishment: "Isabella, what mean you?"

"I mean," continued the signora, casting upon him a glance of deep tenderness and noble pride; "I mean that henceforth, Richard, I can have no secret from you,—that I must now disclose what has often before trembled upon my tongue; a secret which my father would not, however, as yet, have revealed to the English public generally,—the secret of his rank; for he whom the world knows as the Count Alteroni, is Alberto, Prince of Castelcicala!"

Strange was the effect that this revelation produced upon the young man. He felt, as if, when in a burning heat, a mighty volume of icy water had suddenly been dashed over him: his head appeared to swim round—his sight grew dim—he staggered, and would have fallen had not Isabella rushed towards him, exclaiming, "Richard—dear Richard—do you not believe how much I love you?"

Those words produced an instantaneous change within him: those sweet syllables, uttered in the silvery tones of lovely woman's tenderness—recalled him to himself.

"Ah! Isabella," he exclaimed, mournfully, "how insuperable is the barrier which divides us *now!*"

"And—if that barrier to which you allude ever existed, was it less formidable when you were ignorant of the secret than it is at present?" asked Isabella, tenderly.

"It seems so to me," replied Richard. "Are you not placed on an eminence to which I never can hope to reach? have I not dared to lift my ambitious eyes towards a Princess—the daughter of one a who will some day wear a sovereign crown? Oh! now the delusion is gone—I am awakened from a long dream! But, say—did your highness make this revelation to-day, in order to extinguish my adventurous aspirations at once and for ever?"

"Richard, you wrong me—cruelly wrong me!" exclaimed Isabella, bursting into tears.

"Forgive me—forgive me, sweetest, dearest girl!" cried Markham. "I was mad—I raved—I knew not what I said——"

"Richard, when we met here—once before—you doubted my affection, and then you asked me to forgive you! How often will you put my feelings to so cruel a test? how often will you renew those unjust suspicions?"

"O God! what have I done, that I should thus call tears to your eyes, Isabella? Forgive me, again—I say—forgive me: on my knees I implore——"

"No—no! I think no more of what you said," exclaimed Isabella. "Calm yourself for my sake!"—and she gazed so tenderly up into his countenance, that he was reassured, and all his doubts and fears vanished in a moment.

"Yes, Isabella," he said: "I am now calm; and you—you are an angel!"

"A mere terrestrial one, Richard, I am afraid," returned the Princess, with a smile. "And now let me speak to you upon the little matter of business to which I alluded in my note. After I had informed my father that you were the generous unknown who had been the means of his release from prison, he exclaimed, '*Excellent-hearted young man! How I have wronged him by my injurious suspicions concerning that night when the burglary was attempted at our house!*' You see that I tell you his very words."

"Yes—tell me every thing, dear Isabella. And thus, your father no longer believes——"

"How can he believe that any one would attempt to rob him one day, and pay nearly two thousand pounds for him another?" exclaimed Isabella "Oh, no—he is disabused upon that point. Would that he were unprejudiced on others!"

"I understand you," said Markham, mournfully. "The Prince cannot consent to renew his acquaintance with one who has been subjected to an infamous punishment, and who aspires to the hand of his daughter."

"Alas! you have divined but too truly," returned Isabella, wiping

away a tear. "Nevertheless, may we not hope? Already is one great point gained: my father believes that you may have been unfortunate, and not guilty. Oh! that is a great obstacle removed! And in my mother, Richard, you have a warm friend—although her prejudices of rank and family——"

"I can well comprehend the sentiments of her Highness," answered Markham: "and it is all that which now makes me fear lest——"

"Fear not—but hope every thing," said Isabella, who, however, poor girl! spoke in a more flattering manner than her secret thoughts would have warranted, had she consulted them; but she saw her lover oppressed and weighed down by the revelation of that secret which she had considered it unkind to retain any longer; and she did all she could to console him.

"Yes—I will hope, for both our sakes," said Richard.

"And now let me conclude my little narrative," continued Isabella. "My father resolved to repay you the money you had so generously advanced, the moment he was enabled; and as the Grand Duke of Castelcicala has settled upon him an income of ten thousand a-year, besides an immediate grant of forty thousand pounds,—boons which my father had only accepted because no political condition was attached to them, and because they are alleged to be an indemnification for his estates which have been confiscated,—he only awaited the arrival of his first remittances to acquit himself of that debt of honour. The day before yesterday he gave this letter," added Isabella, taking a small sealed packet from her reticule, "to one of our servants to convey to the post at Richmond. I demanded it back again privately of the servant, with the view of placing it myself in your hands, and—and taking the opportunity to reveal to you a secret which I did not think it right to keep from you any longer."

"I receive this packet, then, Isabella, with its contents," said Markham, pressing her hand as he took it, "because your father is happily in a position to repay me the trifle which I was enabled to disburse for his benefit. But ten thousand times more valuable is this sum to me, since its payment prompted you to grant me this interview."

"I had so much to tell you, Richard," answered the lady, with a deep blush, "that I could not commit it all to paper. I therefore adopted this plan—which perhaps is indiscreet——"

"Use not that epithet again, dear Isabella," interrupted Markham. "You assure me that you love me: can you then regret that you have made me happy by allowing me to see you—to talk to you—to embrace you once again? And yet, in the midst of that happiness, the sad thought intrudes upon me—'*When shall I see thee again?*'"

"Accident may throw us together soon—as it has done ere now," murmured Isabella: "accident—or rather Providence—does so much for us poor mortals."

"But, with your mother's prejudices in favour of rank and birth, and with your father's high destinies, what hope can exist for so humble an individual as myself? How can I dare aspire to the hand of a Princess of a powerful independent state?"

"Did not Miss Eliza Sydney espouse the Grand Duke of Castelcicala? and she—she also——"

"Oh! I remember," exclaimed Markham, seeing that Isabella hesitated,—"I remember that *she* also was unfortunate, as I was; and she also endured a weary imprisonment of two years. Yes—I accept the omen—it is an auspicious one!"

And Richard's handsome countenance was once more animated with a glow of hope and joy.

Then, in an access of enthusiasm, he exclaimed:

"Oh! if ever this fond aspiration should be realised,—if ever the humble and obscure Englishman were united to the high-born and brilliant Italian Princess, how sweet—how sweet would it be for him to owe rank and fortune to the woman whom he loved so fondly, and whom he would ever love until the hand of Death should beckon him to the tomb! For myself, I pant not for the honours and glories of this life; for hadst thou, Isabella, been the daughter of the lowest peasants, I had loved thee all the same—and had been far, far more contented, because the obstacles which now oppose our happiness might then have ceased to exist!"

"Believe me, Richard," answered Isabella, in a tone of witching tenderness, "believe me, that the happiest day of my life will be that when I can prove to you the extent of that affection with which you have inspired me;—and, again I repeat, that if ever I rejoiced in the prospect of that fortune which, whether my father eventually succeed to the ducal throne or not, he will be enabled to leave me,—and if ever I felt proud of that high station which my family enjoys, or indulged in the hope that my parents may one day attain to sovereign rank,—that joy, that pride, that hope are all experienced on account of *you!* For, like you, I care not for the grandeur and ostentation of palaces;—but it will be a thrice happy day for me, when I can say to thee—'*Richard, my fortune is all thine, and thou shalt share my rank!*' Because, in Castelcicala, unlike the usages of your native land, he who espouses a Princess becomes a Prince; and, when you shall be thus exalted, Richard, who will dare to remind you of the misfortunes of your past life? That is why I rejoice in my present rank and future prospects,—a joy that is experienced solely on account of you!"

"Noble-hearted girl! what kindness—what attention—what devoted love on my part can ever repay thee for these generous feelings—these endearing proofs of the tenderest attachment!"

"Do you think that I should love you, Richard, as I do," returned

Isabella, "if I did not know the generosity of your soul—if I did not appreciate all your virtues? I am well aware that, unfortunately, you are not rich; and yet you sacrificed—nobly sacrificed your property to release my parent from a gaol! Oh! how can I ever forget that conduct of yours? You speak of repaying *me* for my affection: how much do I not owe to *you?*"

There was a pause in the conversation, during which the lovers walked up and down along the edge of the leafless grove, each enjoying reflections of a pleasurable nature. Isabella leant with charming confidence upon the arm of that handsome and generous-hearted young man, in whose love she gloried as if *he* were the Prince and *she* were the obscure individual; and he felt his heart expand with ineffable bliss, as he contemplated the brilliant prospects which that lovely girl—the proudly-born Princess—spread before the eyes of him—the obscure individual.

More than an hour and a half had already passed, and Isabella at length remembered that she must return home.

She intimated to her lover the necessity of separating; and, with fond embraces and renewed vows, they parted.

Richard watched her receding form until she entered the grove of evergreens surrounding her father's mansion: he then retraced his steps towards Richmond.

And never was his heart so light as now!

CHAPTER CXIV.

THE CONTENTS OF THE PACKET.

ALBERTO of Castelcicala, to conceal his princely rank, when he arrived in England an exile from his native shores, had adopted the style of Count Alteroni—this title being the name of an estate which he had possessed in Italy, but which, together with the remainder of his vast property, had been confiscated by order of the Grand Duke, his uncle. The government of Castelcicala was an absolute despotism; and it was because the Prince, with a view to ameliorate the condition of the people whom he might one day be called upon to govern, had placed himself at the head, and openly avowed himself as the patron, of a political party in the state, whose object was to obtain a constitution, he had been proscribed by the Grand Duke and the old aristocracy of the country.

His party advised him to have recourse to arms; and meetings in favour of the enlightened principles which he advocated were held at the time throughout the country. But the Prince was resolved never to plunge his native land into the horrors of a civil war: he preferred exile and obscurity to such an alternative. His was, indeed, a lofty and patriotic soul, that knew how to sacrifice his dearest interests to the popular tranquillity.

Accordingly, on his arrival in London he had adopted a rank comparatively humble in respect to the exalted station which he in reality occupied; and to this mode of conduct he was instigated by the same disinterested motives that had led him to fly from his country rather than raise the standard of civil strife. He knew that if he settled in London under his proper title, he could not avoid receiving those patriotic exiles who had fled from Castelcicala to avoid the consequences of their liberal opinions. He was averse to the idea of allowing his dwelling to be made the point of *réunion* for those who advocated the enforcement of the popular cause by means of arms:—he would not for a moment consent to permit a nucleus of open rebellion against the reigning sovereign of Castelcicala, to be formed under his auspices. He had, therefore, intimated to his friends and adherents that he intended to retire into private life, until circumstances might place him in a position to confer upon his native land the charter of liberties which he believed to be its natural right.

The few English persons who were acquainted with his secret, religiously kept it. The Tremordyns, Armstrong, and the Earl of Warrington, whom he numbered amongst his best friends, respected the *incognito* which his Highness thought fit to preserve. Thus, Armstrong had not even communicated the fact to Richard Markham when he introduced him to the Prince's dwelling; and the reader may now understand the reasons which led the haughtiest of England's peers, the Earl of Warrington, on the occasion of his visit to the mansion near Richmond to solicit letters of introduction for Eliza Sydney, to bend his head with such profound respect in the presence of the heir presumptive to a throne.

Nor need it now be made a matter of marvel if those letters of introduction proved such immediate passports for Eliza Sydney into the first society of Castelcicala;—but little did he who gave them or he who solicited them,—little did they think that their ulterior effect would be to open the way for that lady to such an eminence as the one which she had attained.

We have before explained,—a point, indeed, which the intelligent reader could not fail to comprehend,—that the chance of Alberto to the Castelcicalan throne now depended upon the contingency of the marriage of Angelo III. producing offspring, or not. Scarcely, however, had that marriage been consummated, when the Minister of Foreign Affairs wrote to the Castelcicalan envoy at the court of Queen Victoria, to communicate to Prince Alberto the intention of the government, sanctioned by the Grand Duke, to allow him a handsome income, and supply him with an immediate grant, by way of indemnification for the loss of his estates. No political condition of any kind being attached to this concession, the Prince did not hesitate to accept it; and it was even mentioned in a Montoni newspaper, that the influence of the Grand Duchess, aided by the friendly feeling of some of the new Ministers towards the Prince, had procured this act of justice at the hands of Angelo III.

These few observations may not be deemed superfluous, inasmuch as they tend to explain the real position of the Prince of Castelcicala—the father of our charming heroine.

We said it was with a light heart that Richard Markham retraced his steps to Richmond, after having parted with the Princess Isabella.

He was, moreover, desirous to examine the contents of the packet which she had placed in his hands,—not because he cared for the money which was thus returned to him; but because he was anxious to ascertain whether any note from her father accompanied it.

He, however, restrained his curiosity until he reached Richmond, where he entered an hotel, ordered a private room, bespoke some refreshment, and then proceeded to break the seal of the envelope.

Yes—there *was* a letter, containing a cheque.

The cheque fell unheeded on the carpet: the letter was immediately perused with avidity:—

"I cannot sufficiently express my admiration of your noble and generous conduct in having liquidated the debts for which I was detained in the Queen's Bench prison. I now repay, with unfeigned and heart-felt gratitude, that sum which you advanced, for my necessities, in a manner so honourable to your own nature and so eminently useful to me at that period. I need not say how deeply I regret the injurious suspicions which I entertained concerning you on a certain occasion; but circumstances were too powerfully combined against you to admit of any other impression. You will forgive me—for I ask your pardon—I sincerely apologise for all I may have said or done on that occasion.

"And now, my dear Mr. Markham, I am compelled to touch upon a subject which, though painful, demands a few observations. That you have been unfortunate, I know—that you were never guilty, I am now well convinced. I have read a document which proves this. But you have inspired my daughter with an affection, which I understand is reciprocal, and which never can end otherwise than in disappointment to you both. Crush, then, this sentiment in your breast; and for the peace of mind of her who is my only child, and who never—never can become your wife, I implore you not to see her more! Avoid her—as I shall instruct her to avoid you,—my only motive being based upon certain circumstances, unknown to you, which render your union an impossibility. I address you as a friend—as a father I write to you; your generous heart will teach you how to respect my wishes.

"One more subject must not be forgotten. I am well aware that you are not as wealthy as you once were. Thank God, my pecuniary means have ceased to be a subject of anxiety to me. You aided me when I was in need and in distress; allow me to offer you a trifling assistance towards enabling you to build up your fortunes. This is an object, which, with your great talents, you cannot fall to accomplish. Remember, I do not offer this small aid as an acquittal of my deep obligation towards you; no—my gratitude is intense—and the circumstances under which you befriended me leave me ever your debtor. But as a friend, I offer you the use of my purse;—as a friend I place in your hands a sum of money which you can use during your pleasure, and return to me at your convenience. Should that sum be insufficient to forward your views, hesitate not to apply to me for more.

"And now, farewell—at least for the present; and believe that no one will be more delighted to hear of your success in life, than

"Your very sincere friend,

"ALTERONI."

Markham picked up the cheque: it was for five thousand pounds.

We must endeavour to explain the nature of the feelings which the contents of the Prince's letter created within him.

He saw with delight that the illustrious exile once more addressed him as a friend, and that all suspicions of his guilt had been extirpated from the mind of that nobleman. But, on the other hand, the barrier between himself and Isabella seemed to be rendered insuperable by the positive terms in which the Prince bade him eradicate his passion from his bosom. That barrier was no doubt twofold: the father of Isabella never could consent to the union of his daughter with one whom the world had stamped with ignominy, although innocent:—and, chiefly, the Italian Prince—the probable heir to a throne—might aspire to a far, far higher connexion for his child. Then Richard's thoughts were directed to the handsome sum of money which the Prince had placed at his disposal; and he could not do otherwise than admire the delicate manner in which it was proffered,—a manner that scarcely admitted of a refusal. And yet Richard was resolved to return the surplus above the amount which he had disbursed to procure the Prince's liberation from prison.

Thus was it with mingled feelings of joy and melancholy that Markham reviewed the contents of that letter.

Still he clung to Hope,—for Isabella had bade him hope; and he thought that the same good Providence which had thus far reconciled him to the father of his beloved, might in time accomplish more striking miracles in his favour.

But, alas! it must indeed be a miracle that could link his fate with the high destinies of the ducal house of Castelcicala!

Isabella, instead of being the daughter of an obscure count, was the only child of one who, if he were not to become himself the sovereign of the most powerful petty state in Europe, would at all events occupy a station next only to the sovereign whenever circumstances should allow him to return to his native land.

But, on the other hand, Isabella was faithful and true; and what might not be expected from woman's love?

In a word, Markham was rather inclined to hope than to despair; and the incidents of that morning imparted to his soul a solace which was a recompense for much, very much of past suffering.

Having partaken of some refreshment, Richard returned to London, and repaired to the bank where the cheque was made payable.

He only drew for the amount actually due to him, and desired that the surplus might be retained in behalf of Count Alteroni (under which name the Prince was known at the bankers' establishment).

On his return home, Richard addressed the following letter to the Italian nobleman:—

"A thousand thanks, my dear lord, for your most kind and courteous letter. To find that you have at length become convinced that I was unfortunate, and *never* guilty, is a source of happiness the extent of which I cannot describe.

"Your wishes in respect to the attachment which I certainly entertain for the Signora Isabella, shall be so far complied with—that I will not venture to present myself at your abode. As for extinguishing that affection which burns in my heart—mortal power cannot accomplish the task.

"It was with unfeigned delight that I understood from your lordship's letter that your position not only enabled you to return the trifle which I once ventured to use in your behalf, but also most generously to offer me the means of building up my fallen fortunes. My lord, I am unable to profit by your kindness; the stigma under which I lie—and with tears I write these words—is a bar to any legitimate speculation with a hope of success. Moreover, I have sufficient for my wants; and am therefore, in one sense, rich. Excuse me if I have not availed myself of your noble offer—an offer that scarcely admits of refusal in consequence of the delicacy and kindness with which it was made. Nevertheless, I am bound to decline it—with the most sincere gratitude; at the same time observing, that should need ever press me, I shall not hesitate to have recourse to the friendship with which you honour me.

"In the earnest hope that happiness and health may attend upon yourself and amiable family,

"I remain, my dear lord,

"Your most grateful and faithful servant,

"Richard Markham."

It will be seen that the tone of this letter was somewhat constrained; but, although Richard endeavoured to write with apparent ease, as if ignorant of his correspondent's real rank, he could not forget that he was addressing himself to the Prince of Castelcicala.

CHAPTER CXV.

THE TREASURE.—A NEW IDEA.

Alas! that we should be compelled to turn from such bright scenes as woman's love and lovers' hope, to deeds of infamy and crime.

But so goes the world; and no faithful historian can venture to deviate from the rule.

Sad, and dismal, and dark, are many of the phases which this narrative has yet to show; but we can also promise our reader that there will not be wanting bright and cheering scenes to afford relief to his eye.

Chequered, indeed, are the ways of life: varied and diversified are all its paths.

And, oh! let him who is wearied with the load of existence, while wending through the rough and craggy places of the world, and when rudely jostled by the world's unfeeling crowd,—let him remember that there is another sphere beyond, where the ways are smooth and pleasant, and where the voice of lamentation is never heard,—a sphere where angels alone shall be the guides of the elect, and where the sound of grateful harmony shall never cease,—a sphere, whose name is HEAVEN!

Again we say, alas! that we should be compelled to divert the attention of our reader from scenes of mundane bliss and the contemplation of the purest love, to deeds of iniquity and hatred.

But to our task.

It was about five o'clock in the evening of the day that witnessed the incidents of the two preceding chapters, and that had succeeded the night on which the unhappy Viola had signed a deed surrendering up half her property to her unprincipled husband,—that the Resurrection Man returned home to his dwelling in Globe Town.

But before he ascended to the apartments inhabited by himself and his mistress with a fearful name, he entered the lower part of the building, and, having lighted a candle, descended to the subterranean vaults.

In the first place he went into a cell opposite to that which was still tenanted by Viola, who, it will be remembered, had received a solemn promise to be restored to her own abode that evening at nine o'clock.

The Resurrection Man entered the cell to which we have alluded, and which was empty.

He raised a stone from the floor, and drew from a hole of about a foot deep, a large leathern bag, the contents of which sent forth the welcome metallic sound of gold as he took it in his hand.

The miscreant seated himself upon the cold floor of the cell, and poured forth into his hat the glittering contents of the bag. His eyes sparkled with delight as he surveyed the treasure.

He took a few of the coins up in his hand, and let them drop one by one back again into his hat—his glances greedily fixed upon the gold as he thus toyed with it.

"Two hundred good sterling sovereigns here already," he mused within himself,—"two hundred pounds earned with toil, trouble, daring, and danger. Two hundred pounds are a decent provision for any man in my line of life! And now," he continued, taking a smaller canvass bag from his pocket, "there is more to add to swell the treasury. Here is a hundred pounds—my half of the sum paid by Tomlinson this afternoon for keeping the secret about his old clerk. The Buffer has got his share; but I warrant he will hoard none of it as I do! Thank my stars, within the last year I have learnt to be economical and saving. I mean to have something for my old age; unless——"

And his countenance suddenly assumed an expression perfectly hideous, as he reflected upon the probability of his career being cut short by the hand of the law.

But, in another moment, he grew composed—that is to say, desperately hardened; and he then proceeded with his occupation and his musings.

"Well, here is my share of the two hundred pounds that the chicken-hearted, contemptible, cowardly Tomlinson paid for a secret which a little calm reflection might have told him that I dared not reveal. That's a hundred pounds to add to my sinking fund;"—and here the miscreant smiled. "Now," he continued, "comes the grand swag—three hundred pounds from Chichester,—and not too much for the trouble I have had in *his* affair! Two hundred before—Tomlinson's hundred—and Chichester's three hundred,—that makes six hundred pounds of good sterling gold, the property of Mr. Anthony Tidkins!"

And here the Resurrection Man laughed outright:—it was a horrible chuckle—the triumph of a miscreant of a most atrocious nature.

But he was happy—happy after his own fashion;—happy in counting and contemplating the produce of his turpitude.

While he was consigning his wealth to the larger bag, and gloating over the gold as he passed it through his hand, he was suddenly alarmed by a slight sound in the passage.

It seemed like a low footstep.

He listened, but it was not repeated.

For nearly a minute did he remain motionless, and almost breathless, in a state of painful attention; but not another sound met his ear.

Then, recovering from the state of uneasy suspense into which that incident had thrown him, he rose from the floor, and hurried into the passage which divided the two rows of cells.

All was quiet.

Ashamed of himself for his childish alarm, and stuttering a curse at his folly for having given way to that fear, he returned into the cell, buried his treasure and covered the place with the stone. He then carefully locked the door of the dungeon.

He crossed the passage, and proceeded gently to open the door leading into the cell occupied by Viola. When he entered this vault, he found the lamp extinguished;—but by the glare of his candle, he perceived the unhappy woman stretched in a profound slumber upon the bed.

"All right," he muttered to himself,—"and just as I expected. She will sleep some hours yet, for the wine was well drugged; and thus we can convey her back again to her house in a state of insensibility. When she awakes in her own bed, her servants will assure her that all she has passed through was a mere dream; and by this plan she will be so bewildered, that she will actually fancy she has been delirious, and that her brain has wandered. This was Chichester's suggestion; and I must give him credit for it. True—she will sooner or later discover that the departure of half her property is no dream; but then the first burst of passion will have gone by, and she will consider it prudent to hold her tongue. Well—let her sleep: at nine o'clock Chichester and Tomlinson will come, and then she shall be removed."

At that instant an idea struck the Resurrection Man. Hitherto he had worked as Chichester's agent, and by Chichester's directions, in this affair: what if he were to turn the business to some good account for himself? The lady had only parted with half her property: she had eight thousand pounds left. Might not all, or a decent portion of this sum thus remaining, pass into the hands of the Resurrection Man? His *mode of treatment* had excited the first concession: some additional horrors might extort a further grant. The idea was excellent: fool that he was for not having thought of it before!

Thus reasoned Anthony Tidkins.

The more he thought of the new plot which had just entered his head, the more he grew enamoured of it. He was well aware that neither Chichester nor Tomlinson would dare to adopt measures to resist his will; and with a grin of savage delight, he exclaimed aloud, "By God, it shall be done!"

He then removed the bottle of wine from the cell, so that when Viola awoke she might not repeat her dose—supposing that she should be ignorant of the cause of her long lethargic slumber; for the Resurrection Man was not aware of the sudden effect which it had produced upon her, but imagined that the drugged liquid was only powerful enough to operate gradually. He next replenished the lamp with oil from a bottle which stood in one corner of the cell, and, having lighted the lamp, withdrew, carefully bolting and locking the door behind him.

He ascended from the subterranean prison, replaced the stone trap-door, and issued from the ground-floor of the house. He observed that the door leading into the alley was locked as he had left it when he entered; and this circumstance reassured him relative to the little incident which had temporarily disturbed him when counting his money in the cell.

Many circumstances combined to put the Resurrection Man into an excellent humour.

He had that day added four hundred pounds to his hidden treasure; he saw business of all kinds multiplying upon his hands, and promising a golden harvest; and he had hit upon a scheme which, he had no doubt, would produce him a larger sum than he had ever yet realized even in his dreams.

It was therefore with a smiling countenance that he entered the up-stairs room where the Rattlesnake was busily employed in spreading the contents of her cupboard upon the table.

"Well, Meg, you see I am home before my time," he exclaimed. "I don't want any dinner: I took some at a chop-house in town, as I had to wait on business. But leave the lush: I am in a humour for a glass of grog;—and you and I, Meg, will sit down and have a cozy chat together."

"So we will, Tony," returned the woman, with a manner even more wheedling and fawning than she had ever before used towards her terrible paramour. "You seem in excellent spirits, Tony."

"Yes, Meg—excellent: I have done a good day's work—and now

I will enjoy myself till nine o'clock,—when I have got to meet two gentlemen close by here on another little matter."

"Ah! you seldom tell me what you are doing, Tony," said the Rattlesnake.

"No—no: I don't like trusting women a bit farther than I can see them. Such things as getting up a body or so—well and good; but serious things, Meg—serious things, never!"

"Well, just as you like," returned Margaret Flathers, affecting a smile as if she were quite satisfied; but as she turned to replace the meat in the cupboard, her countenance involuntarily assumed an expression of mysterious triumph.

"Come, now—sit down," said the Resurrection Man: "give me a pipe, and brew me my lush. There—that's a good girl."

Tidkins lighted his pipe, and smoked for some moments in silence.

"I tell you what, Meg," he exclaimed, after a pause; "you shall sing me a song. I feel in such an uncommon good humour this evening—in such excellent spirits. No—I won't have a song: I tell you what you shall do."

"What?" said Margaret, as she mixed two glasses of gin and water.

"You shall tell me all about the coal-mines, you know—your own history. You told it me once before; but then I wasn't in a humour to hear you. I missed half, and have forgot t'other half. So now come—let's have the Life and Adventures of Miss Margaret Flathers."

The Resurrection Man laughed at this joke—as he considered and meant it to be; and the Rattlesnake, who never dared to thwart him in any thing, and who apparently had some additional motive to humour him on this occasion, hastened to comply with his request—or rather command.

She accordingly related her history, the phraseology of which we have taken the liberty materially to correct and amend, in the following manner.

CHAPTER CXVI.

THE RATTLESNAKE'S HISTORY.[1]

"I WAS born in a coal-mine in Staffordshire. My father was a married man, with five or six children by his wife: my mother was a single woman, who worked for him in the pit. I was, therefore, illegitimate; but this circumstance was neither considered disgraceful to my mother nor to myself, morality being on so low a scale amongst the mining population generally, as almost to amount to promiscuous intercourse. My mother was only eighteen when I was born. She worked in the pit up to the very hour of my birth; and when she found the labour-pains coming on, she threw off the belt and chain with which she had been dragging a heavy corf (or wicker basket), full of coal, up a slanting road,—retired to a damp cave in a narrow passage leading to the foot of the shaft, and there gave birth to her child. That child was myself. She wrapped me up in her petticoat, which was all the clothing she had on at the time, and crawled with me, along the passage, which was about two feet and a half high, to the bottom of the shaft. There she got into the basket, and was drawn up a height of about two hundred and thirty feet—holding the rope with her right hand, and supporting me on her left arm. She often told me those particulars and said how she thought she should faint as she was ascending in the rickety vehicle, and how difficult she found it to maintain her hold of the rope, weak and enfeebled as she was. She, however, reached the top in safety, and hastened home to her miserable hovel—for she was an orphan, and lived by herself. In a week she was up again, and back to her work in the pit; and she hired a bit of a girl, about seven or eight years old, to take care of me.

"How my infancy was passed I, of course, can only form an idea by the mode of treatment generally adopted towards babies in the mining districts, and under such circumstances as those connected

1 In case the reader should doubt the accuracy of any of the statements relative to the employment of the youth of both sexes in the English coal-mines, which he may find in this chapter, we beg to refer him to the "*Report* and *Appendix to the Report*, of the Children's Employment Commission, presented to Both Houses of Parliament by command of Her Majesty, in 1842." [Reynolds's note.]

with my birth. My mother would, perhaps, come up from the pit once, in the middle of the day, to give me my natural nourishment; and when I screamed during her absence, the little girl, who acted as my nurse, most probably thrust a teaspoonful of some strong opiate down my throat to make me sleep and keep me quiet. Many children are killed by this treatment; but the reason of death, in such cases, is seldom known, because the Coroner's assistance is seldom required in the mining districts.

"When I was seven years old, my mother one day told me that it was now high time for me to go down with her into the pit, and earn some money by my own labour. My father, who now and then called to see me of a Sunday, and brought me a cake or a toy, also declared that I was old enough to help my mother. So it was decided that I should go down into the pit. I remember that I was very much frightened at the idea, and cried very bitterly when the dreaded day came. It was a cold winter's morning—I recollect that well; and the snow was very thick upon the ground. I shivered with chilliness and terror as my mother led me to the pit. She gave me a good scolding because I whimpered; and then a good beating because I cried lustily. But every thing combined to make me afraid. It was as early as five in that cold wintry morning that I was proceeding to a scene of labour which I knew to be far, far under the earth. The dense darkness of the hour was not even relieved by the white snow upon the ground; but over the country were seen blazing fires on every side,—fires which appeared to me to be issuing from the very bowels of the earth, but which were in reality burning upon the surface, for the purpose of converting coal into coke: there were also blazing fields of bituminous shale; and all the tall chimneys of the great towers of the iron furnaces vomited forth flames,—the whole scene thus forming a picture well calculated to appal and startle an infant mind.

"I remember at this moment what my feelings were then—as well as if the incident I am relating had only occurred yesterday. During the day-light I had seen the lofty chimneys giving vent to columns of dense smoke, the furnaces putting forth torrents of lurid flame, and the coke-fires burning upon the ground: but that was the first time I had ever beheld those meteors blazing amidst utter darkness; and I was afraid—I was afraid.

"The shaft was perfectly round, and not more than four feet in diameter. The mode of ascent and descent was precisely that of a well, with this difference—that, instead of a bucket there was a stout iron bar about three feet long attached in the middle, and suspended horizontally, to the end of the rope. From each end of this bar hung chains with hooks, to draw up the baskets of coal. This apparatus was called the *clatch-harness*. Two people ascended or descended at a time by these means. They had to sit cross-legged, as it were, upon the transverse bar, and cling to the rope. Thus, the person who got on first sate upon the bar, and the other person sate a-straddle on the first one's thighs. An old woman presided at the wheel which wound up or lowered the rope sustaining the clatch-harness; and as she was by no means averse to a dram, the lives of the persons employed in the mine were constantly at the mercy of that old drunken harridan. Moreover, there seemed to me to be great danger in the way in which the miners got on and off the clatch-harness. One moment's giddiness—a missing of the hold of the rope—and down to the bottom of the shaft headlong! When the clatch-harness was drawn up to the top, the old woman made the handle fast by a bolt drawn out from the upright post, and then, grasping a hand of both persons on the harness at the same time, brought them by main force to land. A false step on the part of that old woman,—the failure of the bolt which stopped the rotatory motion of the roller on which the rope was wound,—or the slipping of the hands which she grasped in hers,—and a terrible accident must have ensued!

"But to return to my first descent into the pit. My mother, who was dressed in a loose jacket, open in front, and trousers (which, besides her shoes, were the only articles of clothing on her, she wearing neither shirt nor stockings), leapt upon the clatch-iron as nimbly as a sailor in the rigging of his ship. She then received me from the outstretched arm of the old woman, and made me sit in the easiest and safest posture she could imagine. But when I found myself being gradually lowered down into a depth as black as night, I felt too terror-struck even to cry out; and had not my mother held me tight with one hand, I should have fallen precipitately into that hideous dark profundity.

"At length we reached the bottom, where my mother lifted me, half dead with giddiness and fright, from the clatch-iron. I felt the soil cold, damp, and muddy, under my feet. A lamp was burning in a shade suspended in a little recess in the side of the shaft; and my mother lighted a bit of candle which she had brought with her, and which she stuck into a piece of clay to hold it by. Then I perceived a long dark passage, about two feet and a half high, branching off from the foot of the shaft. My mother went on her hands and knees, and told me to creep along with her. The passage was nearly six feet wide; and thus there was plenty of room for me to keep abreast of her. Had not this been the case, I am sure that I never should have had the courage either to precede, or follow her; for nothing could be more hideous to my infantine imagination than that low, yawning, black-mouthed cavern, running into the very bowels of the earth, and leading I knew not whither. Indeed, as I walked in a painfully stooping posture along by my mother's side, my fancy conjured up all kinds of horrors. I trembled lest some invisible hand should suddenly push forth from the side of the passage, and clutch me in its grasp: I dreaded lest every step I took might precipitate me into some tremendous abyss or deep well: I thought that the echoes which I heard afar off, and which were the sounds of the miner's pickaxe or the rolling corves on the rails, were terrific warnings that the earth was falling in, and would bury us alive: then, when the light of my mother's candle suddenly fell upon some human being groping his or her way along in darkness, I shuddered at the idea of encountering some ferocious monster or hideous spectre:—in a word, my feelings, as I toiled along that subterranean passage, were of so terrific a nature that they produced upon my memory an impression which never can be effaced, and which makes me turn cold all over as I contemplate those feelings now!

"You must remember that I had been reared in a complete state of mental darkness; and that no enlightened instruction had dispelled the clouds of superstition which naturally obscure the juvenile mind. I could not read: I had not even been taught my alphabet. I had not heard of such a name as JESUS CHRIST; and all the mention of God that had ever met my ears, was in the curses and execrations which fell from the lips of my father, my mother, her acquaintances, and even the little girl who had nursed me. You cannot wonder, then, if I was so appalled, when I first found myself in that strange and terrific place.

"At length we reached the end of that passage, and struck into another, which echoed with the noise of pickaxes. In a few moments I saw the *undergoers* (or miners) lying on their sides, and with their pickaxes breaking away the coal. They did not work to a greater height than two feet, for fear, as I subsequently learnt, that they should endanger the security of the roof of the passage, the seam of coal not being a thick one. I well remember my infantine alarm and horror when I perceived that these men were naked—stark naked. But my mother did not seem to be the least abashed or dismayed: on the contrary, she laughed and exchanged a joke with each one as we passed. In fact, I afterwards discovered that Bet Flathers was a great favourite with the miners.

"Well, we went on, until we suddenly came upon a scene that astonished me not a little. The passage abruptly opened into a large room,—an immense cave, hollowed out of the coal in a seam that I since learnt to be twenty feet in thickness. This cave was lighted by a great number of candles; and at a table sate about twenty individuals—men, women, and children—all at breakfast. There they were, as black as negroes—eating, laughing, chattering, and drinking. But, to my surprise and disgust, I saw that the women and young girls were all naked from the waist upwards, and many of the men completely so. And yet there was no shame—no embarrassment! But the language that soon met my ears!—I could not comprehend half of it, but what I *did* understand, made me afraid!

"My mother caught me by the hand, and led me to the table, where I found my father. He gave us some breakfast; and in a short time, the party broke up—the men, women, and children separating to their respective places of labour. My mother and myself accompanied one of the men, for my mother had ceased to work for my father, since she had borne a child to him, as his wife had insisted upon their separation in respect to labour in the mine.

"The name of the man for whom my mother worked was Phil Blossom. He was married, but had no children. His wife was a cripple, having met with some accident in the mine, and could not work. He was therefore obliged to employ some one to carry his coal from the place where he worked, to the cart that conveyed it to the foot of the shaft. Until I went down into the mine, my mother had carried the coal for him, and also *hurried* (or dragged) the cart; but she now made me fill one cart while she hurried another. Thus, at seven years old, I had to carry about fifty-six pounds of coal in a wooden *bucket*. When the passage was high enough I carried it on my back; but when it was too low, I had to drag or push it along as best I could. Some parts of the passages were only twenty-two inches in height; this was where the workings were in very narrow seams; and the difficulty of dragging such a weight, at such an age, can be better understood than explained. I can well recollect that when I commenced that terrible labour, the perspiration, commingling with my tears, poured down my face.

"Phil Blossom worked in a complete state of nudity; and my mother stripped herself to the waist to perform her task. She had to drag a cart holding seven hundred weight, a distance of at least two hundred yards—for ours was a very extensive pit, and had numerous workings and cuttings running a considerable way underground. The person who does this duty is called a *hurrier*: the process itself is termed *tramming*; and the cart is denominated a *skip*. The work was certainly harder than that of slaves in the West Indies, or convicts in Norfolk Island. My mother had a girdle round her waist; and to that girdle was fastened a chain, which passed between her legs and was attached to the skip. She then had to go down on her hands and knees, with a candle fastened to a strap on her forehead, and drag the skip through the low passages, or else to maintain a curved or stooping posture in the high ones.

"Phil Blossom was what was called a *getter*. He first made a long straight cut with a pickaxe underneath the part of the seam where he was working: this was called *holing*; and as it was commenced low down, the getter was obliged to lie flat on his back or on his side, and work for a long time in that uneasy manner.

"I did as well as I could with the labour allotted to me; but it was dreadful work. I was constantly knocking my head against the low roofs of the passages or against the rough places of the sides: at other times I fell flat on my face, with the masses of coal upon me; or else I got knocked down by a cart, or by some collier in the dark, as I toiled along the passages, my eyes blinded with my tears or with the dust of the mine.

"Many—many weeks passed away; and at length I grew quite hardened in respect to those sights and that language which had at first disgusted me. I became familiar with the constant presence of naked men and half-naked women; and the most terrible oaths and filthy expressions ceased to startle me. I walked boldly into the great cavern which I have before described, and which served as a place of meeting for those who took their meals in the mine. I associated with the boys and girls that worked in the pit, and learnt to laugh at an obscene joke, or to practise petty thefts of candles, food, or even drink, which the colliers left in the cavern or at their places of work. The mere fact of the boys and girls in mines all meeting together, without any control,—without any one to look after them,—is calculated to corrupt all those who may be well disposed.

"I remained as a carrier of coal along the passages till I was ten years old. I was then ordered to convey my load, which by this time amounted to a hundred weight on each occasion, up a ladder to a passage over where I had hitherto worked. This load was strapped by a leather round my forehead; and, as the ladder was very rudely formed, and the steps were nearly two feet apart, it was with great difficulty that I could keep my balance. I have seen terrible accidents happen to young girls working in that way. Sometimes the strap, or tagg, round one person's forehead has broken, and the whole load has fallen on the girl climbing up behind. Then the latter has been precipitated to the bottom of the dyke, the great masses of coal falling on the top of her. On other occasions I have seen the girls lose their balance, and fall off the ladder—their burden of coals, as in the other case, showering upon them or their companions behind. The work was indeed most horrible—a slave-ship could not have been worse.

"If I did not do exactly as Phil Blossom told me, the treatment I received from him was horrible; and my mother did not dare interfere, or he would serve her in the same manner. He thrashed me with his fist or with a stick, until I was bruised all over. My flesh was often marked with deep weals for weeks together. One day he nipped me with his nails until he actually cut quite through my ear. He often pulled my hair till it literally gave way in his hand; and sometimes he would pelt me with coals. He thought nothing of giving me a kick that would send me with great violence across the passage, or dash me against the opposite side. On one occasion he was in such a rage, because I accidentally put out the candle which he had to light him at his work, that he struck a random blow at me with his pickaxe in the dark, and cut a great gash in my head. All the miners in pits *baste* and *bray*—that is, beat and flog—their helpers.

"You would be surprised if I was to tell you how many people in the pit were either killed or severely injured, by accidents, every year. But there are so many dangers to which the poor miners are exposed! Falling down the shaft,—the rope sustaining the clatch-harness breaking,—being drawn over the roller,—the fall of coals out of the corves in their ascent,—drowning in the mines from the sudden breaking in of water from old workings,—explosion of gas—choke-damp,[1]—falling in of the roofs or passages,—the breaking of ladders or well-staircases,—being run over by the tram-waggons, or carts dragged by horses,—the explosion of gunpowder used in breaking

1 "Explosions of carbonated hydrogen gas, which is usually called by the miners 'sulphur,' sometimes prove very destructive, not only by scorching to death, but by the suffocation of foul air after the explosion is over, and also by the violence by which persons are driven before it, or are smothered by the ruins thrown down upon them."—*Appendix to First Report*. [Reynolds's note.]

away huge masses of coal,—and several other minor accidents, are all perpetually menacing the life or limbs of those poor creatures who supply the mineral that cheers so many thousands of fire-sides!

"Deaths from accidents of this nature were seldom, if ever, brought under the notice of the coroner: indeed, to save time, it was usual to bury the poor victims within twenty-four or thirty-six hours after their decease.

"I earned three shillings a-week when I was ten years old, and my mother eleven. You may imagine, then, that we ought to have been pretty comfortable; but our household was just as wretched as any other in the mining districts. Filth and poverty are the characteristics of the collier population. Nothing can be more wretched—nothing more miserable than their dwellings. The huts in which they live are generally from ten to twelve feet square, each consisting only of one room. I have seen a man and his wife and eight or ten children all huddling together in that one room; and yet they might have earned, by their joint labour, thirty shillings or more a week. Perhaps a pig, a jackass, or fowls form part of the family. And then the furniture!—not a comfort—scarcely a necessary! And yet this absence of even such articles as bedsteads, is upon principle: the colliers do not like to be encumbered with household goods, because they are often obliged to *flit*—that is, to leave one place of work and seek for another. Such a thing as drainage is almost completely unknown in these districts; and all the filth is permitted to accumulate before the door. The colliers are a dirty set of people; but, poor creatures! how can they well be otherwise? They descend into the mines at a very early hour in the morning: they return home at a very late hour in the evening, and they are then too tired to attend to habits of cleanliness. Besides, it is so natural for them to say, '*Why should we wash ourselves to-night, since to-morrow we must become black and dirty again?*' or '*Why should we wash ourselves just for the sake of sleeping with a clean skin?*' As for the boys and girls, they are often so worn out—so thoroughly exhausted, that they go to rest without their suppers. They cannot keep themselves awake when they get home. I know that this was often and often my case; and I have preferred—indeed, I have been compelled by sheer fatigue, to go to bed before my mother could prepare any thing to eat.

"Again, how can the collier's home possibly be comfortable? He makes his wife and children toil with him in the mine: he married a woman from the mine; and neither she nor her daughters know any thing of housekeeping? How can disorder be prevented from creeping into the collier's dwelling when no one is there in the day-time to attend to it? Then all the money which they can save from the *Tommy-shop*, (of which I shall speak presently) goes for whiskey. Husband and wife, sons and daughters all look after the whiskey. The habits of the colliers are hereditarily depraved: they are perpetuated from father to son, from mother to daughter; none is better nor worse than his parents were before him. Rags and filth—squalor and dissipation—crushing toil and hideous want—ignorance and immorality; these are the features of the collier's home, and the characteristics of the collier's life.

"Our home was not a whit better than that of any of our fellow-labourers; nor was my mother less attached to whiskey than her neighbours.

"But the chief source of poverty and frequent want—amounting at times almost to starvation—amongst persons earning a sufficiency of wages is the *truck system*. This atrociously oppressive method consists of paying the colliers' wages in goods or partly in goods, through the medium of the tommy-shop. The proprietor of a tommy-shop has an understanding with the owners of the mines in his district; and the owners agree to pay the persons in their employment once a month, or once a fortnight. The consequence is that the miners require credit during the interval; and they are compelled to go to the tommy-shop, where they eat, obtain their bread, bacon, cheese, meat, groceries, potatoes, chandlery, and even clothes. The proprietor of the tommy-shop sends his book to the clerk of the owner of the mine the day before the wages are paid; and thus the clerk knows how much to stop from the wages of each individual, for the benefit of the shopkeeper. If the miners and their wives do not go to the tommy-shop for their domestic articles, they instantly lose their employment to the mine, in consequence of the understanding between their employer and the shopkeeper. Perhaps this would not be so bad if the tommy-shops were honest; because it is very handy for the collier to go to a store which contains every article that he may require. But the tommy-shop charges twenty-five or thirty per cent. dearer than any other tradesman; so that if a collier and his family can earn between them thirty shillings a week, he loses seven or eight shillings out of that amount. In the course of a year about twenty pounds out of his seventy-five go to the tommy-shop for nothing but interest on the credit afforded! That interest is divided between the tommy-shop-keeper and the coal-mine proprietor.

"In the district where my mother and I lived, there was no such thing at all as payment of wages in the current money of the kingdom. The tommy-shop-keeper paid the wages for the proprietors once a month: and how do you think he settled them? In ticket-money! This coinage consisted of pewter medals, or markers, with the sum that they represented, and the name of the tommy-shop on them. Thus, there were half-crowns, shillings, sixpences, and half-pence. But this money could only be passed at the tommy-shop from which it was issued; and there it must be taken out in goods. So, you see, that what with the truck-system and the tommy-shop, the poor miners are regularly swindled out of at least one fourth part of their fair earnings.

"The wages, in my time, were subject to great changes: I have known men earn twenty-five shillings a week at one time, and twelve or fifteen at another. And out of that they were obliged to supply their own candles and grease for the wheels of the carts or *trams*. The cost of this was about three-pence a day. Then, again, the fines were frequent and vexatious: it was calculated that they amounted to a penny a day per head. These sums all went into the coffers of the coal-owners.

"Such was the state of superstitious ignorance which prevailed in the mines, that every one believed in ghosts and spirits. Even old men were often afraid to work in isolated places; and the spots where deaths from accidents arose were particularly avoided. It was stated that the spectres of the deceased haunted the scenes of their violent departures from this world.

"By the time I was twelve years old I was as wild a young she-devil as any in the mines. Like the other females, I worked with only a pair of trousers on. But I would not consent to hurry the trams and skips. I saw that my mother had got a great bald place on her head, where she pushed the tram forward up sloping passages; and as I was told that even amidst the black and filth with which I was encrusted, I was a good-looking wench, I determined not to injure my hair. I may as well observe that a stranger visiting a mine, and seeing the boys and girls all huddling together, half-naked, in the caves or obscure nooks, could not possibly tell one sex from the other. I must say that I think, with regard to bad language and licentious conduct, the girls were far—far worse than the boys. It is true that in the neighbourhood of the pits Sunday-schools were established; but very few parents availed themselves of these means of obtaining a gratuitous education for their children. When I was twelve years old, I did not know how to read or write: I was unaware that there was such a book as the Bible; and all I knew of God and Jesus Christ was through the oaths and imprecations of the miners.

"It was at that period—I mean when I was twelve years old—that I determined to abandon the horrible life to which my mother had devoted me. I had up to that point preserved my health, and had escaped those maladies and cutaneous eruptions to which miners are liable; but I knew that my turn must come, sooner or later, to undergo all those afflictions. I saw nine out of ten of my fellow labourers pining away. Some were covered with disgusting boils, caused by the constant dripping of the water upon their naked flesh in the pits. I saw young persons of my own age literally growing old in their early youth,—stooping, asthmatic, consumptive, and enfeebled. When they were washed on Sundays, they were the pictures of ill-health and premature decay. Many actually grew deformed in stature and all were of stunted growth. It is true that their muscles were singularly developed, but they were otherwise skin and bone.[1] The young children were for the most part of contracted features, which, added to their wasted forms, gave them a strange appearance of ghastliness, when cleansed from the filth of the mine. The holers, or excavators, were bow-legged and crooked, the burners and trammers knock-kneed and high-shouldered. Many—very many of the miners were affected with diseases of the heart. Then, who ever saw a person, employed in the pits, live to an advanced age? A miner of fifty-five was a curiosity: the poor creatures generally drooped at five-and-thirty, and died off by forty. They invariably seemed oppressed with care and anxiety: jollity was unknown amongst them. I have seen jolly-looking butchers, blacksmiths, carpenters, ploughmen,

1 "Amongst the children and young persons I remarked that some of the muscles were developed to a degree amounting to a deformity; for example, the muscles of the back and loins stood from the body, and appeared almost like a rope passing under the skin."—*Report*. [Reynolds's note.]

porters, and so on: but I never beheld a jolly-looking miner. The entire population that labours in the pits appears to belong to a race that is accursed!

"I pondered seriously upon all this; and every circumstance that occurred, and every scene around me, tended to strengthen my resolution to quit an employment worse than that of a galley-slave. I saw my mother wasting all her best energies in that terrible labour, and yet remaining poor—beggared! Scarcely enough for the present—not a hope for the future! Sometimes I wept when I contemplated her, although she had but little claim on my sympathy or affection; nevertheless, when I saw her bald head—her scalp thickened, inflamed, and sometimes so swollen, that it was like a bulb filled with spongy matter, and so painful that she could not bear to touch it,—when I heard her complain of the dreadful labour of pushing the heavy corves and trams with her sore head,—when I perceived her spine actually distorted with severe work; her stomach growing so weak that she frequently vomited her food almost as soon as it was eaten; her heart so seriously affected that the intervals of violent palpitation frequently made her faint; her lungs performing their functions with difficulty; her chest torn with a sharp hacking cough, accompanied by the expectoration of a large quantity of matter of a deep black colour, called by colliers the *black-spit*;—when I saw her thus overwhelmed with a complication of maladies—dying before my eyes, at the age of thirty-three!—when I looked around, and beheld nine out of ten of all the persons employed in the pits, whether male or female, similarly affected,—I shuddered at the bare idea of devoting my youth to that horrible toil, and then passing to the grave while yet in the prime of life!

"I thought of running away, and seeking my fortune elsewhere. I knew that it was no use to acquaint my mother with my distaste for the life to which she had devoted me: she would only have answered my objections by means of blows. But while I was still wavering what course to pursue, a circumstance occurred which I must not forget to relate.

"One morning my candle had accidentally gone out, and I was creeping along the dark passage to the spot where Phil Blossom was working, to obtain a light from his candle, when I heard him and my mother conversing together in a low tone, but with great earnestness of manner. Curiosity prompted me to stop and listen. 'Are you sure that is the case?' said Phil.—'Certain,' replied my mother. 'I shall be confined in about five months.'—'Well,' observed Phil, 'I don't know what's to be done. My old woman will kick up the devil's delight when she hears of it. I wish she was out of the way: I would marry you if she was.'—Then there was a profound silence for some minutes. It was broken by the man, who said, 'Yes, if the old woman was out of the way you and I might get married, and then we should live so comfortable together. I'm sure no man can be cursed with a wife of worse temper than mine.'—'Yes,' returned my mother, 'she is horrible for that.'—'Do you think there would be much harm in pushing her down a shaft, or shoving her head under the wheel of your tram, Bet?' asked Phil, after another pause.—'There would be no harm,' said my mother, 'if so be we wern't found out.'—'That's exactly what I mean,' observed Phil.—'But then,' continued my mother, 'if she didn't happen to *die* at once, she might peach, and get us both into a scrape.'—'So she might,' said Phil.—'I'll tell you what we might do,' exclaimed my mother, in a joyful tone: 'doesn't your wife come down at one to bring you your dinner?'—'Yes,' replied Phil Blossom: 'that's all the old cripple is good for.'—'Well, then,' pursued my mother, 'I'll tell you how we can manage this business.'—Then they began to whisper, and I could not gather another word that fell from their lips.

"I was so frightened at what I had heard that I crept quickly but cautiously back again to my place of labour, and sate down on the lower steps of the ladder, in the dark—determined to wait till some one should come, rather than go and ask Phil Blossom for a light. I had suddenly acquired a perfect horror of that man. I had understood that my mother was with child by him; and I had heard them coolly plotting the death of the woman who was an obstacle to their marriage. At my age, such an idea was calculated to inspire me with terror. I think I sate for nearly an hour in the dark, my mind filled with thoughts of a nature which may be well understood. At length a young woman, bearing a corf, came with a light; and I was no longer left in obscurity. I then plucked up my courage, took my basket, and went to Phil Blossom for a load of coal. My mother was not there; and he was working with his pickaxe as coolly as possible. He asked me what had made me so long in returning for a load; and I told him I had fallen down a few steps of the ladder and hurt myself. He said no more on the subject; and I was delighted to escape without a braying or basting. While I was loading my corf, he asked me if I should like to have him for a father-in-law. I said 'Yes' through fear, for I was always afraid of his *nieves*, as the colliers call their clenched fists. He seemed pleased; and, after a pause, said that if ever he was my father-in-law, I should always take my *bait* (or meals) with him in the cavern. I thanked him, and went on with my work; but I pretty well comprehended that the removal of Phil's wife by some means or another had been resolved on.

"Shortly before one o'clock that same day my mother came to the place where I was carrying the coals, and gave me a *butter-cake* (as we called bread and butter), telling me that she was going up out of the mine, as she must pay a visit to the tommy-shop for some candles and grease for herself, and some tobacco for Phil Blossom. I did not dare utter a word expressive of the suspicions which I entertained; but I felt convinced that this proceeding was in some way connected with the subject of the conversation which I had overheard. A strange presentiment induced me to leave my place of work, and creep along the passage to the foot of the shaft, in order to see whether Phil's wife would come down at the usual time with his bait. Several *half-marrows* and *foals* (as we called the young lads who pushed the trams) were at the end of the passage just at the foot of the shaft; and we got into conversation. It is a very curious thing to look up a shaft from the very bottom; the top seems no bigger than a sugar-basin. Well, the boys and I were chattering together about different things, when the click of the clatch-harness at the top of the shaft fell upon my ears. I peeped up and saw some one get on the clutch, then the creaking of the wheel and roller was heard. 'Here comes some one's bait, I dare say,' observed one of the half-marrows.—'I wish it was mine,' said another; 'but I never get any thing to eat from breakfast-time till I go home at night.'—Scarcely were these words spoken when a piercing scream alarmed us: there was a winching sound—the chains of the harness clanked fearfully—and down came a woman with tremendous violence to the bottom of the pit, the clatch rattling down immediately after her. A cry of horror burst from us all; the poor creature had fallen at our very feet. We rushed forward; but she never moved. The back part of her head was smashed against a piece of hard mineral at the bottom of the shaft. But her countenance had escaped injury; and as I cast a hasty glance upon it, I recognised the well-known face of Phil Blossom's crippled wife.

"One of the boys instantly hastened to acquaint him with the accident. He came to the spot where his wife lay a mangled heap, stone dead; and he began to bewail his loss in terms which would have been moving had I not been aware of their hypocrisy—the half-marrows were, however, deceived by that well-feigned grief, and did all they could to console him. I said nothing: I was confounded!

"In due time the cause of the *accident* was ascertained. It appeared that my mother had gone up the shaft, but when she got to the top she struck her foot so forcibly against the upright post of the machinery, that she lamed herself for the time. The old woman who presided over the machinery (as I have before said) very kindly offered to go to the tommy-shop for her, on condition that she would remain there to work the handle for people coming up or going down. This was agreed to. The very first person who wanted to go down was Mrs. Blossom; and my mother alleged that the handle unfortunately slipped out of her hand as she was unwinding the rope. This explanation satisfied the overseer of the mine: the intervention of the coroner was not deemed necessary;—my mother appeared much afflicted at the *accident*: Phil Blossom mourned the death of his wife with admirable hypocrisy;—the corpse was interred within forty-eight hours;—and thus was Phil's wife removed without a suspicion being excited!

"I was now more than ever determined to leave the mine. I saw that my mother was capable of any thing; and I trembled lest she should take it into her head to rid herself of me. One day she told me that she was going to be married to Phil Blossom: I made a remark upon the singularity of her being united to the very man whose wife had died by her means;—she darted at me a look of dark suspicion and terrible ferocity; and, in the next moment, struck me to the ground. From that instant I felt convinced that I was not safe. Accordingly, one Sunday, when I was washed quite clean, and had on a tolerably decent frock, I left the hovel which my mother occupied, and set out on my wanderings.

"I had not a penny in my pocket, nor a friend on the face of the earth to whom I could apply for advice, protection, or assistance. All that stood between me and starvation, that I could see, was a piece of bread and some cheese, which I had taken with me when I left home. I walked as far as I could without stopping, and must have been about six miles from the pit where I had worked, when evening came on. It was November, and the weather was very chilly. I looked round me, almost in despair, to see if I could discover an asylum for the night. Far behind me the tremendous chimneys and furnaces vomited forth flames and volumes of smoke; and the horizon shone as if a whole city was on fire: but in the spot where I then found myself, all was drear, dark, and lonely. I walked a little farther, and, to my joy, espied a light. I advanced towards it, and soon perceived that it emanated from a fire burning in a species of cave overhung by a high and rugged embankment of earth belonging to a pit that had most probably ceased to be worked. Crouching over this fire was a lad of about fifteen, clothed in rags, dirty, emaciated, and with starvation written upon his countenance. I advanced towards him, and begged to be allowed to warm myself by his fire. He answered me in a kind and touching manner; and we soon made confidants of each other. I told him my history, only suppressing my knowledge that the death of Phil Blossom's wife arose from premeditation, instead of accident, as I did not wish to get my mother into a scrape, although I had no reason to have any regard for her. The lad then acquainted me with his sad tale. He was an orphan; and his earliest remembrance was experienced in a workhouse, of which, it appeared, he had become an inmate shortly after his birth, his parents having been killed at the same time by the explosion of a fire-damp in the pit in which they had worked. When the lad was eight years old, the parish authorities apprenticed him to a miner, who gave him the name of *Skilligalee*,[1] in consequence of his excessive leanness. This man treated him very badly; but the poor boy endured all for a period of seven years, because he had no other asylum than that afforded him by his master. 'At length,' said the boy, 'a few weeks ago, master got hurt upon the head by the falling in of some coal where he was working; and from that moment he acted more like a madman than a human being. He used to seize me by the hair, and dash me against the side of the pit: sometimes he flogged me with a strap till my flesh was all raw. I could stand it no longer; so, about three weeks ago, I ran away. Ever since then I have been living, I can scarcely tell how. I have slept

1 Skilligalee: from the Irish, *scilligeálaí*, a waster of time in idle talk, a coarse or unpolished talker, a habitual liar.

in the deserted cabins on the pits' bank, or in the old pits that have done working: I have got what I could to eat, and have even been glad to devour the bits of candles that the colliers had left in the pits. All this is as true as I am here.[1] Yesterday I found some matches in a pit; and that is how I have this good fire here now. But I am starving!'

"The poor fellow then began to cry. I divided with him my bread and cheese; and, when we had eaten our morsel, we began to converse upon our miserable condition. He had as much abhorrence of the mine as I had; he declared that he would sooner kill himself at once than return to labour in a pit; and I shared in his resolution. In less than an hour Skilligalee and myself became intimate friends. Varied and many were the plans which we proposed to earn a livelihood; but all proved hopeless when we remembered our penniless condition, and Skilligalee pointed to his rags. At length he exclaimed in despair, '*There is nothing left to do but to rob!*'—'*I am afraid that this is our only resource,*' was my reply.—'*Do you mean it?*' he demanded.—'*Yes!*' I said boldly; and we exchanged glances full of meaning.

"'*Come with me,*' said Skilligalee. I did not ask any questions, but followed him. He led the way in silence for upwards of half an hour, and at length lights suddenly shone between a grove of trees. Skilligalee leapt over a low fence, and then helped me to climb it. We were then in a meadow—planted with trees—a sort of park, which we traversed, guided by the lights, towards a large house. We next came to a garden; and, having passed through this enclosure, we reached the back part of the premises. Skilligalee went straight up to a particular window, which he opened. He then crept through, and told me to wait outside. In a few minutes he returned to the window, and handed me out a large bundle, wrapped up in a table-cloth. He then crept forth, and closed the window. We beat a retreat from the scene of our plunder; and returned to the cave. The fire was still blazing, and Skilligalee fed it with more fuel, which he obtained by breaking away the wood from an old ruined cabin close by.

"We next proceeded to open the bundle, which I found to contain a quantity of food, six silver forks, and six spoons. Skilligalee then told me that the mansion which we had just robbed was the dwelling of the owner of the mine wherein he had worked for seven years, and where he had been so cruelly treated by the pit-man to whom

---

1 See *Report*, page 43, section 194. [Reynolds's note.]

he had been apprenticed. He said that he had sometimes been sent with messages to the proprietor, from the overseer in the mine, and that the servants on those occasions had taken him into the kitchen and given him some food. He had thus obtained a knowledge of the premises. 'Last night,' he added, 'I was reduced by hunger to desperation, and I went with the intention of breaking into the pantry. To my surprise I found the window open, the spring-belt being broken. My courage, however, failed me; and I returned to this cave to suffer all the pangs of hunger. To-night you came: companionship gave me resolution and we have got wherewith to obtain the means of doing something for an honest livelihood.'

"We then partook of some of the cold meat and fine white bread which the pantry had furnished;—and, while we thus regaled ourselves, we debated what we should do with the silver forks and spoons. I said before that I was decently dressed; but my companion was in rags. It was accordingly agreed that I should go to the nearest town in the morning, dispose of the plate, purchase some clothes for Skilligalee, and then rejoin him at the cave. This matter being decided upon, we laid down and went to sleep.

"Next morning I washed myself at a neighbouring stream, made myself look as decent as I could, and set off. Skilligalee had told me how to proceed. In an hour I reached the town, and went to a pawnbroker's shop. I said that I was servant to a lady who was in a temporary difficulty and required a loan. The pawnbroker questioned me so closely that I began to prevaricate: he called in a constable, and gave me into custody. I was taken before the magistrate; but I refused to answer a single question, being determined not to betray my accomplice. The magistrate remanded me for a week; and I was sent to prison. There I herded with juvenile thieves and prostitutes; and I cared little for my incarceration, because I was tolerably, and, at all events, regularly fed. When I was had up again, the owner of the mansion which I had helped to rob, was there to identify his property. I, however, still persisted in my refusal to answer any questions: I was resolved not to criminate Skilligalee; and I also felt desirous of being sent back to gaol, as I was certain of there obtaining a bed and a meal. In vain did the magistrate impress upon me the necessity of giving an explanation of the manner in which the plate came into my possession, for both he and the owner of the property were inclined to believe that I was only a tool, and not the original thief;—I remained dumb, and was remanded for another week.

"At the expiration of that period, I was again placed before the magistrate; and, to my surprise, I found Skilligalee in the court. He was still clothed in his rags, and looked more wretched and famished than when I first saw him. I gave him a look, and made a sign to assure him that I would not betray him; but the moment the case was called, he stood forward and declared that he alone was guilty,—that he had robbed the house, and that I was merely an instrument of whom he had made use to dispose of the proceeds of the burglary. I was overcome by this generosity on his part; and both the magistrate and the owner of the property were struck by the avowal. The latter declared that he did not wish to prosecute: the former accordingly inflicted a summary sentence of imprisonment for a few weeks upon Skilligalee. He then questioned me about my own condition; and I told him that I had worked in a mine, but that I had been compelled to run away from home in consequence of the ill-treatment I received at the hands of my mother. I expressed my determination to put an end to my life sooner than return to her; and the gentleman, whose house had been robbed, offered to provide for me at his own expense, if the magistrate would release me. This he agreed to do; and the gentleman placed me as a boarder in a school kept in the town by two elderly widows.

"This school was founded for the purpose of furnishing education to the children of pit-men who were prudent and well disposed enough to pay a small stipend for that purpose, that stipend being fixed at a very low rate, as the deficiency in the amount required to maintain the establishment was supplied by voluntary contribution. There were only a few boarders—and they were all girls: the great majority of the pupils consisted of day-scholars. At this school I stayed until I was sixteen, when the gentleman who had placed me there took me into his service as housemaid.

"During the whole of that period I had never heard of my mother, or Phil Blossom. I now felt some curiosity to discover what had become of them; so, one day, having obtained a holiday for the purpose, I went over to the pit where I had myself passed so many miserable years. The same old woman, who had presided at the handle of the roller that raised or lowered the clatch-harness, during the period of my never-to-be-forgotten apprenticeship, was there still. She did not recognise me—I was so altered for the better. Clean, neatly dressed, stout, and tall, I could not possibly be identified with the dirty, ragged, thin, and miserable-looking creature who had once toiled in that subterranean hell. I accosted the old woman, and asked her if a woman named Betsy Flathers or Blossom worked in the mine. 'Bet Blossom!' ejaculated the old woman: 'why, she's been dead a year!'—'Dead!' I echoed. 'And how did she die?'—'By falling down the shaft, to be sure,' answered the old woman.—Although I entertained little affection for my mother, absence and a knowledge of her character having destroyed all feelings of that kind, I could not bear this intelligence without experiencing a severe shock.—'Yes,' continued the old woman, 'it was a sort of judgment on her, I suppose, for she herself let a poor creature fall down some four or five years ago, when she took my place at the handle here for a few minutes while I went to the tommy-shop for her. She married the husband of the woman who was killed by the fall; and every body knew well enough afterwards that there wasn't quite so much neglect in the affair as she had pretended at the time, but something more serious still. However, there was no proof; and so the thing was soon forgot. Well, one day, about a year ago, as I said just now, Phil Blossom came up to me and asked me to run to the tommy-shop to fetch him some candles. I told him to mind the wheel, and he said he would. It seems that a few minutes after I had left on his errand, his wife came up the clatch; and, according to what a lad, who looked up the shaft at the time, says, she had just reached the top, when she fell, harness and all, the whole pit echoing with her horrible screams. She died the moment she touched the bottom. Phil Blossom was very much cut up about it; but he swore that the handle slipped out of his hand, and then went whirling round and round with such force that he couldn't catch it again. I own people did say that Phil and his second wife led a precious dog-and-cat kind of a life; but the overseer thought there was no reason to make a stir about it, and there the matter ended.'—'And what has become of Phil Blossom?' I inquired.—The old woman pointed down the shaft, as much as to say that he was still working in the mine.—'Did they have any children?' I asked.—'Bet had one, I believe,' said the old woman; 'but it died a few days after it was born, through having too large a dose of Godfrey's Cordial administered to make it sleep.'—I gave the old woman a shilling, and turned away from the place, by no means anxious to encounter Phil Blossom, who, I clearly perceived, had rid himself of my mother by the same means which she had adopted to dispose of his first wife.

"As I was returning to my master's house, I had to cross a narrow bridge over a little stream. I was so occupied with the news I had just heard, I did not perceive that there was another person advancing from the opposite side, until I was suddenly caught in the arms of a young man in the very middle of the bridge. I gave a dreadful scream; but he burst out into a loud laugh, and exclaimed, 'Well, you needn't be so frightened at a mere joke.' I knew that voice directly; and glancing at the young man, who was tolerably well dressed, I immediately recognised my old friend Skilligalee. It was then my turn to laugh, which I did very heartily, because he had not the least notion who I was. I, however, soon told him; and he was quite delighted to meet me. We walked together to the very identical cave where we had first met when boy and girl. Now he was a tall young man, and had improved wonderfully. He told me that he had become acquainted with some excellent fellows when he was in prison, and that he had profited so well by their advice and example, that he led a jovial life, did no work, and always had plenty of money. I asked him how he managed; and he told me, after some hesitation, that he had turned housebreaker. There was scarcely a gentleman's house, within twelve miles round, that he had not visited in that quality. He then proposed that I should meet him on the following Sunday evening, and take a walk together. I agreed, and we separated.

"I did not neglect my appointment. Skilligalee was delighted to see me again; and he proposed that I should leave service, and live with him. I consented; and——"

CHAPTER CXVII.

THE RATTLESNAKE.

Here the Rattlesnake abruptly broke off.

The Resurrection Man was asleep in his chair. It had not been without a motive that the woman so readily complied with the desire of the Resurrection Man that she should amuse him with the history of her life; and as she saw him gradually becoming more and more drowsy as her narrative progressed, an ill-concealed expression of joy animated her countenance.

At length, when the hand of the watch over the mantelpiece pointed to eight, and the Resurrection Man fell back in his chair fast asleep, she could hardly suppress an ejaculation of triumph.

She broke off abruptly in the midst of her narrative, and listened.

The nasal sounds that emanated from her companion convinced her that he slept.

Not a moment was now to be lost.

She knew full well that whenever Anthony Tidkins was overtaken by a nap in such a manner as the present, he invariably awoke a short time before the hour at which he had any business to transact; for that strange but fearful individual exercised a marvellous control over all his natural wants and propensities.

Rising cautiously from her seat, the Rattlesnake advanced towards the Resurrection Man, and steadfastly examined his countenance.

There could be no doubt that he slept profoundly.

She was, however, resolved to assure herself as far as possible on that head; and she purposely agitated the fire-irons against each other.

The Resurrection Man started slightly, but did not awake.

Perfectly satisfied on this point, Margaret Flathers hastened into the adjoining room, and put on her bonnet and shawl.

Having provided herself with her skeleton keys and some lucifer matches, she descended the stairs and went out of the house.

It was not, however, without an intense apprehension of danger that she proceeded to the execution of her scheme. Were the Resurrection Man to awake suddenly, and entertain any suspicion on discovering her absence, she knew that her life would not be worth an hour's purchase.

Still the temptation that now lured her to dare this terrific chance was so great—it was irresistible!

Her hesitation, when she stood in the street, was only of a moment's existence; and, calling all her courage to her aid, she plunged into the alley.

The door in that dark passage was opened in another moment: she closed and locked it carefully, and then entered the back room on the ground floor.

Having obtained a light, she raised the mysterious trap-door, and boldly descended the steps leading into the subterranean passage.

One of her keys soon opened the door of the cell in which the Resurrection Man had buried his treasure; but her joy at this disappearance of the only difficulty which she had apprehended, was adulterated by a sentiment of invincible terror, as she still thought of the possibility of detection by him whose desperate character inspired her with this tremendous alarm.

Nevertheless, she was resolved to dare every thing in the enterprise which she had undertaken.

"Fortune seemed to favour me this afternoon when I watched him," she murmured to herself; "and surely it will not desert me at the last moment."

Then she boldly entered the cell.

To take up the stone which covered the treasure, and possess herself of the bag that contained the gold over which she had a few hours previously beheld the Resurrection Man gloating in so strange a manner,—this was the work of only a few moments.

She replaced the stone: she clutched the bag with a feeling of wild joy commingled with terrific alarm; and she was hurrying from the cell, when something at the opposite side of the passage met her view, and for a moment riveted her to the spot.

A light was streaming from beneath the door of a dungeon facing the one on the threshold of which she stood.

Circumstances, which in the excitement of her present daring proceedings she had forgotten, now rushed like an overwhelming torrent to her memory.

The mysterious visits of the Resurrection Man in a mask and dark cloak to that subterranean place,—the bread and water which she had seen in the cupboard up stairs,—and the fearful scream that on one occasion had emanated from the depths where she now found herself,—these circumstances all flashed to her mind.

There was no longer any doubt: a human being—a female, most probably, judging by the tone of that agonising shriek, which now seemed to ring in her ears as if its vibration had never once ceased—was immured in that dungeon whence the light streamed!

This conviction dissipated the alarm into which the sudden glare of that light had plunged the Rattlesnake.

Urged by several motives,—curiosity, a desire to obtain the reinforcement of a companion in case of the sudden appearance of the Resurrection Man, and, to do her justice, a feeling of compassion for a victim whom she believed to be of her own sex,—urged, we say, by these motives, which all presented themselves to her mind with the rapidity of lightning, the Rattlesnake hastened to open the door of that dungeon whence the light emanated.

She boldly entered the cell; and at the same moment Viola awoke.

Starting up from the bed, that unhappy lady glanced wildly around, and exclaimed, "Where am I?"

"Hush! not a word," said the Rattlesnake, advancing towards her. "I am come to save you—follow me!"

Viola did not hesitate a single moment: the manner in which the woman addressed her, and a profound sense of the certainty that no treachery was needed to draw her into any position worse than her present one, since she was so completely in the power of the terrible master of that establishment, induced her to yield instantaneous compliance with the directions of the Rattlesnake.

"Fear nothing, lady," observed the latter; "only be silent, and lose not a moment."

She then hastened from the cell, followed by Viola, who did not even wait to put on her bonnet and shawl.

They ascended the steps leading to the back room, both hearts palpitating violently.

The Rattlesnake did not stop to close the mouth of the subterranean vaults, but hastened to apply the skeleton key to the door leading into the alley.

Her hand trembled to such an extent that she could not turn the key.

"O heavens!" she exclaimed in a tone of despair, "if *he* should come!"

"Have you the right key?" demanded Viola in a hurried tone.

"The one that has opened it before," replied Margaret;—"but it appears that—it will not turn—and, ah! my God, I hear steps approaching!"

The affrighted woman fell upon her knees, as if already to supplicate for her life.

Viola listened during half a minute of the most agonising suspense; but no sound from without met her ears.

"It was a false alarm," she exclaimed; then applying her hand to the key, she turned it with ease, for fear alone had prevented the Rattlesnake from moving it.

In another instant the door was opened.

"Thank God!" cried Margaret Flathers, starting from her suppliant posture, and clutching the bag of gold beneath her left arm.

"Come—let us not lose a moment," said Viola; and she darted into the alley, followed by the Rattlesnake.

There was no one to oppose their egress; but they could scarcely believe that they were really safe even when they found themselves in the street.

And now they ran—they ran, as if that terrible individual whom they both feared so profoundly were at their heels;—they ran, doubting the fact, the one that she was free, the other that she was safe;—they ran—they ran, reckless of the way which they were pursuing, but each alike impressed with the conviction that it was impossible to place too great a distance between them and the dwelling of the Resurrection Man!

Margaret Flathers carried her treasure as if it were a thing of no weight: Viola Chichester forgot that she had neither bonnet nor shawl to protect her against the bitter chill of that wintry evening.

And thus, together, did they pursue their way—the virtuous wife and the abandoned woman,—the former thinking not what might be the character of her companion—the latter having now no curiosity to know the circumstances that had plunged the lady by her side into the captivity from which she had just been released.

At length they reached the New Church facing the Bethnal Green Road; and there they halted, both completely out of breath and exhausted.

"We are now safe," said Margaret Flathers.

"We are now safe," echoed Viola Chichester.

"Still this place is lonely——"

"And if that dreadful man were on our track—"

"We might yet repent——"

"Yes—we might yet repent our proceeding."

The minds of those two women—so distinct in all other respects—were now entirely congenial in reference to one grand absorbing idea.

In spite of the alarm which yet filled their imaginations, they lingered against the palings surrounding the field at the back of the New Church, for they were too exhausted to continue their flight for a few moments.

That interval of rest enabled them to direct their attention to other matters besides the immense danger from which they had just escaped, and the sense of which was still uppermost in their minds.

"Which way are you going, madam?" asked the Rattlesnake, who saw by Viola's air—in spite of the disadvantages under which her outward appearance laboured—that she was not one of the poorer orders.

"My own house is close by," answered Mrs. Chichester. "But you—whither are *you* going? Will it not be better for you to come with me—and——"

"No, lady," replied Margaret Flathers; "you are not aware who and what I am, or you would not make me that generous offer."

"Generous!" exclaimed Viola: "have you not saved me from a fearful dungeon? It is true that my persecutors promised to release me this evening: but, alas! *their* word was not to be depended upon."

"Ah! madam," said Margaret, "if you trusted to Anthony Tidkins to give you your freedom, you would have been woefully disappointed—unless, indeed, he had no longer any interest in keeping you a prisoner."

"Well—well," observed Viola, "we will talk of all that hereafter. In the mean time, I insist upon your accompanying me to my home."

"I will see you safe to your own door, madam," returned Margaret; "and there I shall leave you."

"And why will you refuse an asylum at my abode?" demanded Viola.

"I dare not remain in London," answered the Rattlesnake. "Oh! you know not the perseverance, the craft, and the wickedness of the man from whose power you have just escaped. But there is one favour, madam, which you can grant me——"

"Name it," exclaimed Viola: "it is already conferred, if within my power."

"You can have no difficulty in fulfilling my request," said the Rattlesnake, "because it is simple, and consists only in forbearance. I mean, madam, that you will amply reward me for the service I have been able to render you, if you will promise not to take any measures to punish or molest Anthony Tidkins. He has been more or less good to me; and I should not like to know that he was injured through me. Besides, his revenge would only be the more terrible, if ever you or I again fell into his hands."

"I give you the promise which you require," said Viola; "although I must confess that it is somewhat repugnant to my feelings to allow such a wretch to be at large with impunity."

"But for my sake, lady——"

"For your sake, I give my most solemn pledge not to do aught that may injure that man on account of his past offences."

"A thousand thanks!" ejaculated the Rattlesnake. "Let us now proceed. But, heavens! you have got nothing on your head nor on your shoulders; and I did not notice that before! Take my bonnet and shawl, madam—I am more accustomed to the cold than you."

"No," said Viola; "in five minutes I shall be at my own house. Come—let us proceed."

Mrs. Chichester and the Rattlesnake hastened towards the Cambridge Heath gate.

On reaching the door of her abode, Viola again pressed her companion to accept of her hospitality but the Rattlesnake firmly, though respectfully, refused the offer.

"In another hour, madam," she said, "I shall not be in London. *Then* only shall I consider myself safe."

"At least allow me to supply you with some money for your immediate purposes. I have none about me, and I know not whether my husband has left a single shilling in the house; but any of my tradesmen in the neighbourhood will honour my draft; and if you will walk in for a few minutes—"

"Thank you, madam—thank you for your kind consideration; but I am well supplied;" and she shook the bag that she hugged beneath her arm.

Viola heard the jingling of the gold, and ceased to press her offer.

"At all events," she observed, "should you ever require a friend, do not hesitate to apply to Mrs. Chichester."

"Mrs. Chichester!" ejaculated the Rattlesnake: "surely I have heard that name before? Oh! I recollect—I have taken to the post-office letters from Tidkins to a Mr. Chichester, who, I suppose, must be your husband."

"The same," said Viola, with a profound sigh.

"Farewell, madam," cried the Rattlesnake: "I feel that I shall not breathe with freedom until I am far beyond London. Farewell."

"Farewell," said Mrs. Chichester, extending her hand towards her deliverer.

Margaret Flathers pressed it warmly, and then hurried away.

Viola knocked at the door, and was speedily admitted once more into her own dwelling.

The servant who received her, uttered an ejaculation of surprise when she beheld the condition in which her mistress had returned.

"Make fast the door with chain and bolt, and bring me the key," said Viola, taking no heed of her domestic's exclamation. "See also that the shutters of the windows are well secured; and bring me your master's pistols."

"Mr. Chichester came this morning early, ma'am," returned the servant, "and took away every thing belonging to him."

"Heaven be thanked!" cried Viola. "Perhaps he will molest me no more? God grant that the separation may be eternal! Nevertheless, secure the door and the windows: this house is not safe! To-morrow I shall leave it, and hire lodgings in the very heart of London. *There*, perhaps," she murmured to herself, "no violence can be offered to me!"

CHAPTER CXVIII.

THE TWO MAIDENS.

On a fine frosty morning—about ten days after the incidents just related,—two young ladies were walking together along the road in the immediate vicinity of the dwelling of Count Alteroni (for so we had better continue to call him, until he himself shall choose to throw aside his incognito).

Did an artist wish to personify the antipodes,—as the ancients did their rivers, mounts, and groves,—upon his canvass, he could not possibly have selected for his models two maidens between whom there existed so great a physical contrast as that which was afforded to the eye by the young ladies above noticed.

The one was a brunette, and seemed a child of the sunny south; the other was as fair as ever daughter of our cold northern clime could be:—the one had the rich red blood mantling beneath a delicate tinge of the purest and most transparent *bistre*; the other was pale and colourless as the whitest marble:—the generous mind and elevated intellect of the one shone through eyes large, black, and impassioned; the almost infantine candour and artlessness of the other were expressed by means of orbs of azure blue:—the glossy raven hair of the one was parted in two rich bands over the high and noble forehead; the flaxen tresses of the other fell in varied waves of pale auburn and gold, beneath the bonnet, over the shoulders:—the form of the one was well-rounded but sylph-like; the symmetry of the other was delicate and slight:—the appearance of the one excited the most ardent admiration tempered with respect; that of the other inspired the most lively interest:—the beauty of the one was faultless, brilliant, and dazzling; that of the other, ideal, fascinating, and bewitching:—the one, in fine, was a native of the warm Italian clime; the other, a daughter of Britain's sea-girt isle.

A shade of profound melancholy hung upon the countenance of Mary-Anne Gregory. The sprightly—gay—joyous—innocently volatile disposition had changed to sadness and gloom. Those vermilion lips, which until so lately were ever wreathed in smiles, now expressed care and sorrow. The step, though light, was no longer playfully elastic. Time had added but a few months to the sixteen years which marked the age of Mary-Anne when we first introduced her to our readers; but thought, and meditation, and grief had given to the mind the experience of maturity. She was no longer the gay, lively, flitting, bee-like being that she was when Richard Markham became her brothers' tutor: her manner was now painfully tranquil, her air profoundly pensive, her demeanour inconsistently grave when considered in relation to her years.

It seemed as if there were a canker at the heart of that fair creature; as if the hidden worm were preying upon the delicate rose-bud ere it expanded into the bloom of maturity!

And these traits and symptoms were rendered the more apparent by the contrast afforded by the rich health and youthful vigour which characterised the Signora Isabella. The hues of the rose were seen beneath the soft brunette tint of her complexion—for that complexion was clear and transparent as the stream over which the trees throw a shade beneath a summer sun.

And both those maidens loved: but the passion of the English girl was without hope; while that of the noble Italian lady was nurtured by the fondest aspirations.

But how came those charming creatures thus acquainted with each other?

Perhaps their conversation may elucidate this mystery.

"We have only known each other one short week," said Mary-Anne; "and yet I feel as if you were sent to me by heaven to become my friend and confidant—for, oh! it seems to me as if my soul nourished a secret which consumes it."

"An accident made us acquainted; and that very circumstance immediately inspired me with a deep interest in your behalf," returned the signora. "There are occasions when two persons become more intimate in a few short days, than they otherwise would in as many years."

"You echo my own feelings, Signora," said Mary-Anne; "and your goodness makes me desire to deserve and gain your friendship."

"Your wish is already accomplished, my dear Miss Gregory," observed Isabella. "You have my friendship; and if you think me worthy of your confidence, I can sympathise with your sorrows, even if I cannot remove them."

"How have you divined that the confidence I would impart is associated with grief?" asked Mary-Anne, hastily.

"I will tell you," replied the beautiful Italian. "When you were riding on horseback, accompanied by your father, along this road a week ago, I observed you from my own chamber. Even at that distance, I perceived something about you that immediately inspired me with interest. I followed you with my eyes until you were out of sight: and then I still continued to think of you—wondering, with that idiosyncrasy of thought which often occurs during a leisure half-hour, who you were. At length you returned. You were a few paces in front of your father; and I observed that the horse you rode was a spirited one. Then occurred the accident: the moment you were thrown so rudely off against the very gate of our shrubbery, I precipitated myself down the stairs, and, calling for the servants as I descended, hurried to your assistance. You cannot remember—because you were insensible—that I was the first to reach the spot, where your father had already raised you from the ground. Mr. Gregory was distracted: he thought that you were lost to him for ever. I, however, ascertained in a moment that you still breathed; and I directed the servants to convey you to the house. While you were still stretched in a state of insensibility upon my own bed, I contemplated you with increasing interest. Then, when you awoke at length, and spoke,—and when I conversed with you,—it seemed as if I were irresistibly attracted towards you. I was, indeed, delighted when my father proposed to Mr. Gregory to allow you to remain a few days with us until you should be completely recovered from the effects of your fall. Your father consented, and he left you with us. It was not long before I perceived that you nourished a profound grief;—I observed the frequent abstraction of your manner—I noticed your pensive mood. I thought within myself, '*Is it possible that one so young and interesting should already be acquainted with sorrow?*' From that hour I have felt deeply on your account—for, alas! I myself have known what are the effects of grief!"

"Signora," said Mary-Anne, with tears in her eyes, "I can never repay you for this kind interest which you manifest towards me. I feel that I should be happier were I to tell you all that grieves me; but I tremble—lest you should think me very foolish, and very indiscreet!"

"Foolish we may all be at times," said Isabella; "but indiscreet I am convinced you never were."

"Is it not indiscreet to nurse a sentiment whose hopes can never be realised? Is it not indiscreet," added Mary-Anne, hanging down her head, and speaking in a low tone, "to love one who loves another?"

"No—not indiscreet," answered Isabella, hastily: "for what mortal has power over the heart?"

"Signora, love is not then a stranger to your breast!" exclaimed Mary-Anne, glancing with tearful eyes up to the countenance of the Italian lady.

"I should be unworthy of your confidence, were I to withhold mine," said Isabella. "Yes—my troth is plighted to one than whom no living soul possesses more generous, more noble feelings: and yet," she added, with a sigh, "there are obstacles in the way of our union—obstacles which, alas! I sometimes think, can never be overcome!"

"Ah! lady, while I can now feel for you—feel most deeply," said Mary-Anne, "I am, nevertheless, rejoiced that you have thus honoured me with your confidence. It removes any hesitation—any alarm, on my part, to unburden my soul to you!"

"Speak, my dear Mary-Anne," returned Isabella: "you will at least be certain to receive sympathy and consolation from me."

"I shall then reveal my sentiments unreservedly," continued Mary-Anne. "I have before mentioned to you that I have two brothers, who are now at college. A few months ago, they were preparing for their collegiate course of study, and were residing at home in Kentish Town. My father obtained for them the assistance of a tutor—a young gentleman who had once been wealthy, but who had been reduced to comparative poverty. Oh! it was impossible to see that young man without feeling an interest in him. When I first heard that a tutor was engaged for my brothers, I immediately pictured to myself a confirmed pedagogue—shabby, dirty, dogmatic, and ugly. How greatly then was I astonished, when I was introduced to an elegant and handsome young man, of polished manners, agreeable conversation, entirely unassuming, courteous, and affable? There was a partial air of melancholy about him; but his eyes were lighted with the fire of intellect, and his noble forehead seemed to be adorned with that unartificial crown of aristocracy which nature bestows upon her elect. Alas! woe to me was the day when that young man first entered my father's dwelling. The interest I felt for him soon augmented to a degree, that I was miserable when he was away. But, when he was present, oh! then my heart seemed to bound within me like a fawn upon the hills; and my happiness was of the most ravishing description—I was gay, frolicksome, and playful: no laugh of a child was so hearty, so sincere as mine! His voice was music to my ears! He taught me drawing; but I was too happy to sit still for many minutes together—too happy to sit next to him! And yet I did not understand my own feelings: in fact, I never stopped to analyse them. I was carried along by a whirlwind that left me no leisure for self-examination. When he was absent, my only thought was upon what he had said when present, and how happy I should be when he came once more. I had no more idea of the true nature of the sentiment that animated my soul, than I have at this instant of what constitutes the happiness of heaven. I knew that I felt happy when he was there: I know that those feel happy who dwell above;—but I was as ignorant then of what formed my felicity, as I now am of the bliss experienced by those who inhabit the Almighty's kingdom. Thus a few weeks passed away; and then my father announced his intention of allowing a holiday for a short period. I remember—as well as if it were an event of yesterday—that this arrangement caused me serious displeasure; because I understood that our tutor would cease to visit us during the suspension of the studies. I expressed my annoyance in plain terms; but this ebullition on my part was most probably considered a specimen of girlish caprice, or the airs of a spoiled child. And now, signora—now——"

"Call me Isabella," said the Italian lady, affectionately.

"Now, my dear Isabella," proceeded Mary-Anne, "I come to that part of my narrative which involves an indiscretion that may appear grave in your eyes—though, God knows, I was at the time entirely ignorant of the imprudence of the step which I was taking."

"I am prepared to allow every extenuation for one so young, so artless, and so inexperienced as yourself," observed Isabella.

"Ah! how kind you are," returned Mary-Anne, pressing her

companion's hand. "But let me not hesitate to reveal the indiscretion into which I was hurried by feelings of a new and powerful nature. I called upon the young tutor at his own residence! And then, how nobly did he behave! how generously did he act! He explained to me—by degrees, and in the most delicate manner possible—the impropriety of the step which I had taken: he gave me an insight into those rules of feminine propriety, a breach of which can scarcely be extenuated by the plea of guilelessness;—in a word, he opened my eyes to the position in which I had placed myself! But, alas! what did I learn at the same time? He told me that he was attached to a young lady, who was very beautiful. It then struck me, with lightning rapidity, that I had no right to offer my *friendship* (for still I did not dream of *love*) to one on whom another heart had claims; and I left him with a sincere apology for my conduct."

"I admit that your indiscretion was great," said the pure-minded Isabella; "but no one possessing a generous heart could hesitate to sympathise with you, rather than blame."

"For days and days," continued Mary-Anne, "I struggled with my feelings. I still believed that all I experienced towards the object of my interest was friendship. But when he resumed his attendance, I found that it was impossible to conquer the sentiments which agitated my bosom. God knows—God knows, Isabella, how I reasoned with myself upon the state of mind in which I existed! I prayed to heaven to relieve me from the doubts, the anxieties, the uneasiness, which constantly oppressed me, by restoring me to that state of perfect happiness which was mine ere I knew that being who, in spite of himself, exercised so powerful an influence over me. At length my father sent me suddenly, and without a day's warning, to pass a week with some particular friends at Twickenham. I was at first inclined to remonstrate with him at this proceeding; and then it struck me that it would be well if I were to cease to exist under the spell which the frequent presence of the tutor at the house seemed to throw around me."

"And all this time you were still unaware of the true nature of the feelings which animated you?" inquired Isabella.

"Oh! yes—I was indeed," answered Mary-Anne: "but a fearful occurrence was speedily destined to open my eyes! I remained a few days with my kind friends at Twickenham, and then returned home. I there learnt that the tutor had ceased to attend at the house, as my brothers were to proceed, at the commencement of January, to college. I know not whether my father had some motive for the conduct which he thus pursued, in abruptly dismissing the tutor and sending me away while he adopted that step; nor can I say whether any particular reason prompted him to do all that he could to amuse my mind on my return home. It is, nevertheless, certain that he exerted himself to provide amusements for me: he purchased two horses, and accompanied me in frequent equestrian exercises; he took me to concerts and the theatres; and supplied me with entertaining books of travel and adventure, music, and pictures. But my mind was intent only upon one absorbing idea; nor could it be weaned from that feeling which it nursed in favour of the young tutor. I, however, acceded to all my father's plans of diversion; and it was one evening at the theatre that the veil fell from my eyes! I accompanied my father to witness a new drama. The action of the piece was deeply interesting; the poetry was of a nature to touch the inmost soul. There was a passage in which the heroine described her hopeless love: I listened—I drank in every word—I hung upon each syllable of that fine speech as if my own destiny were intimately linked with the scene enacting before me. As she proceeded, I was painfully surprised by the similitude existing between the feelings that *she* described and that *I* felt. At length a light dawned in upon my soul;—then did I begin to comprehend the real nature of the sentiments that filled my own soul;—then could I read my own heart! I perceived that I loved tenderly, deeply, unalterably! I heard no more of the drama—I saw nothing more of its progress: I sate absorbed in deep reflection upon the conviction that had so suddenly reached me. When I awoke from my reverie, the tragedy——"

"A tragedy?" said Isabella, hastily.

"Yes—the tragedy was finished, and the author, holding the hand of the heroine of his piece, stood before the public. Merciful heavens! the great tragic writer who had thus suddenly burst upon the world, was no other than the young tutor!"

"The tutor!" exclaimed Isabella, a strange suspicion suddenly entering her mind.

"Yes—he whom I had just discovered that I loved," answered Mary-Anne.

"May I inquire his name?" said Isabella, in a tremulous tone, and with a palpitating heart.

"There can be no indiscretion in revealing it," returned Miss Gregory; "for it is not probable that you have ever heard of Mr. Richard Markham."

"Unhappy girl!" exclaimed Isabella, in a tone of deep sympathy—but without the least feeling of jealousy; "it is now my duty to return your confidence with a reciprocal frankness. But, alas! what I am about to say cannot tend to soothe your sorrows, since—as I fondly believe—it will only confirm you in the impression that the affections of him whom *you* love are fixed elsewhere."

"You speak mysteriously, Isabella," said Mary-Anne: "pray, explain yourself."

"I will—and without reserve," continued the signora, a blush mantling upon her beauteous countenance. "So far from Mr. Richard Markham being a stranger to me, Mary-Anne, he is——"

"He is—" repeated Miss Gregory, mechanically.

"He is the hope of my happiness—the one to whom my vow of constancy and love is pledged——"

"You the object of his attachment!" ejaculated Mary-Anne, clinging to Isabella for support: "Oh! forgive me—forgive me, that I have dared to love him also!"

"Alas! dear girl, I have nothing to forgive," said Isabella, affectionately: "I deeply—deeply compassionate your lot. And, oh! believe me," continued the generous Italian Princess,—"believe me when I say that no feeling of petty jealousy—no sentiment unworthy the honourable affection which I bear towards Richard Markham—can ever impair the friendship that has commenced, and shall continue, between you and me!"

"Oh! how noble is your disposition, Isabella!" exclaimed Mary-Anne. "But your generous assurance shall not meet with an ungrateful return. So far from feeling jealous of you,—*envious* I must be, to some extent,—I offer you the most sincere congratulations on your engagement to one who is so well worthy of your love—in spite of what the world may say against him;—for that he could be guilty of the deed of which that horrible man accused him——"

"He is not guilty," answered Isabella, firmly. "The story is a long one; but I will tell thee all."

The signora then related to her companion the narrative of the misfortunes and sufferings of Richard Markham.

Mary-Anne listened with profound attention, and, when Isabella terminated her history, exclaimed, "Oh! I knew that he was all of honourable, great, and generous, that human nature could be!"

A profound silence then ensued between the two young ladies, and lasted for some minutes.

At length it was broken by Mary-Anne.

"Oh! well might *he* have said," she exclaimed, in a sudden ebullition of feeling, as she gazed upon the countenance of the Signora,—"well might he have said that his heart was devoted to a lady who was very beautiful! And he might also have observed, as good as she was lovely!"

"Nay—you must not flatter me," returned Isabella.

"You need not hesitate to hear the truth from my lips," said Mary-Anne. "God grant that I may live to see you happily united: I shall then die in peace."

"It is wrong to talk of dying at your age," observed Isabella. "Time will mitigate that passion which has made you unhappy——"

"Oh! Isabella, do *you* believe that true and sincere love can ever succumb to time?" exclaimed Mary-Anne, almost reproachfully.

"Time cannot extinguish it; but time may soften its pangs," said the Italian lady, desirous to console her unfortunate friend.

"But time will only ripen, and not eradicate, the canker which gnaws at the heart," persisted Miss Gregory; "and *mine*," she added with a mournful pathos of tone that showed how deeply she felt the truth of what she said,—"*mine* has received a wound, whose effects may be comparatively slow, but which is not the less mortal. A few years, perhaps, and my earthly career must end. I shall wither like the early flowers, that peep forth prematurely to greet a deceptive gleam of sunshine which they mistake for spring:—I shall pass away at that age when my contemporaries are in the full enjoyment of life, vigour, and happiness! Yes—I feel it here—*here*;"—and she pressed her hand upon her heart.

"No, my dear friend," said Isabella, affected even to tears; "your prospect is not so gloomy as you would depict it. There is one star that burns in the same heaven which is above us all;—and that star is Hope."

"Hope!" ejaculated Mary-Anne, bitterly: "ah! where does hope exist for me? Is not hope extinguished in my heart for ever?"

"In the one sense, hope is dead," answered Isabella, mildly; "but hope beams not only in one sphere. The attentions of your friends—the kindness of your relations, will combine to cheer your path; and surely this conviction must be allied to hopes of tranquillity, peace, and even happiness! Consider, Mary-Anne—you have a father who is still in the vigour of his years: you will live for him! You have brothers who must soon enter upon their respective careers in the great world: you must live for them! You have friends who are devoted to you: you will live for them also! Oh! do not speak of death with levity: do not seem to invite its presence! We do not live for ourselves only: we live for others. To yield to those feelings which facilitate the ravages of sorrow and encourage the in-roads of grief, is to perpetrate a slow suicide. God and man alike require that we should war against our misfortunes!"

"Alas! I have not that great moral courage which characterises your soul, Isabella," answered Mary-Anne: "I am a weak and fragile plant, that bends to the lightest gale. How, then, can I resist the terrible tempest?"

"By exerting that fortitude with which every mind is more or less endowed, but which cannot be developed without an effort," answered Isabella.

Mary-Anne sighed, but gave no answer.

The two maidens now felt wearied with the somewhat lengthy walk which they had taken; and they accordingly retraced their steps to the mansion.

CHAPTER CXIX.

POOR ELLEN!

It was evening; and a cheerful fire burned in the grate of the drawing-room at Markham-Place.

Mr. Monroe and his daughter were seated in that apartment; the former dozing in an arm-chair, the latter reading a novel.

Richard was engaged in a literary pursuit in his library.

From time to time Miss Monroe laid aside her book, and fell into meditation. Not that she had any particular subject for her reflections; but the events of her life, when taken together, constituted a theme from which it was impossible to avert her attention for any lengthened period.

There was also a topic upon which she pondered more frequently as time passed on. She knew that in the course of nature,—especially after the rude shocks which his constitution had received from mental suffering and bodily privation,—her father could not live much longer. Then, she was well aware that she could not continue to dwell beneath the same roof with Richard Markham;—and her pride revolted against the idea of receiving a direct eleemosynary assistance from him in the shape of a pecuniary allowance. She had some few pounds treasured up in a savings bank, and which she had saved from her salary when engaged at the theatre; but this sum would not maintain her long. She therefore looked, with occasional anxiety, to the necessity of adopting some course that should obtain for her a livelihood. Of all the avocations in which she had been engaged, she preferred that of the stage; and there were times when she seriously thought of returning to the profession, even during her father's life-time.

In sooth, it was a pity that one of the brightest ornaments of female loveliness should have been lowered by circumstances from the pedestal of virtue and modesty which she would have so eminently adorned. Should her transcendent loveliness captivate the heart of any individual whose proposals were alike honourable and eligible, how could she accept the hand thus extended to her? She must either deceive him in respect to that wherein no man likes to be deceived; or she must decline the chance of settling herself advantageously for life. These were the alternatives;—for in no case could she reveal her shame!

Her fate was not, therefore, a happy one; and the reader need not marvel if she now and then found reflections of a disagreeable nature stealing into her soul.

She was now past twenty years of age; and in spite of the severe trials which she had endured, the sweet freshness of her youthful charms was totally unimpaired. Her faultless Grecian countenance,—her classically-shaped head,—her swan-like neck,—her symmetrical form,—her delicate hands and feet,—all those charms which had been perpetuated in the works of so many artists—these elements of an almost superhuman beauty still combined to render her passing lovely!

O Ellen! the soul of the philanthropist must mourn for thee,—for thou wast not wrongly inclined by nature. On a purer being than thou wast, ere misery drove thee in an evil moment to an evil course, the sun never shone:—and now thou hast to rue the shame which thine imperious destiny, and not thy faults, entailed upon thee!

But to our tale.

Old Mr. Monroe was dozing in the arm-chair; and Ellen had once more turned her eyes upon her book, when Marian entered the room.

She perceived at a glance that Mr. Monroe was asleep; and, placing her finger upon her lip to enjoin silence, she put a note into Ellen's hand, saying at the same time in a low whisper, "Mr. Wentworth's servant has just brought this, with a request that it should be immediately conveyed to you, Miss."

Marian then withdrew.

Ellen tore open the note, and read as follows:—

> "I grieve to state that your little Richard has been attacked with a sudden and dangerous malady. Come to my house for an hour—if you can possibly steal away, without exciting suspicion. My servant will convey this to you through your faithful confidant.
>
> "David Wentworth."

Ellen flung the note frantically upon the table, and rushed out of the room.

She hurried up stairs, put on her bonnet and cloak, and, having told Marian to sit up for her, hastened from the house—one sole idea occupying her mind,—the danger of her well-beloved child!

When she arrived at Mr. Wentworth's abode, she was received by that gentleman's wife, who immediately said, "The danger is over—the crisis is past! Do not alarm yourself—my husband no longer fears for your son's life. He, however, deemed it to be his duty to send for you."

"Oh! he did well—he acted kindly and considerately," returned Ellen. "But let me assure myself that my boy is no longer in danger."

Mrs. Wentworth led the way to the chamber where little Richard was now sleeping tranquilly, the surgeon seated by the bed-side.

From his lips Ellen gathered hope that the perilous crisis had passed: she nevertheless determined to remain for some time to assure herself that any return of the spasms might not be fraught with increased danger. All other considerations were banished from her mind; she thought not of her father—she remembered not that her absence might alarm both him and Richard Markham; and when Mr. Wentworth delicately alluded to that subject, as time slipped by, she uttered some impatient remark intimating that she should not be at a loss for an excuse to account for her protracted absence.

Thus the pure and holy maternal feeling was now uppermost in the mind of that young lady: the danger of her child was the all-absorbing subject of her thoughts.

Bent over the bed, she tenderly gazed upon the pale countenance of her child.

Oh! where can the artist find a more charming subject for his pencil, or the poet a more witching theme for his song, than the young mother watching over her sleeping infant?

Hour after hour passed; and when the babe awoke, Ellen nursed him in her arms. In spite of its illness, the little sufferer smiled; but when the pang of the malady seized upon him, it was Mrs. Wentworth—and not Ellen—who could pacify him!

Alas! galling indeed to the young mother was this conviction that her child clung to another rather than to herself.

Nevertheless Ellen watched the babe with the most heartfelt tenderness; and it was not until near midnight, when the surgeon declared that the malady had passed without the remotest fear of a relapse, that Ellen thought of returning home.

She then took her departure, with an intimation that she should call again in the morning.

She retraced her steps towards the Place, and, passing up the garden, was admitted through the back entrance by the faithful Marian.

"My child is saved," whispered Ellen to the servant. "Has my father inquired for me?"

"No, miss," was the reply. "He is still in the drawing-room; and Mr. Markham is with him."

"They are up late to-night," remarked Ellen. "But I," she continued, "am weary in mind and body, and shall at once repair to my own room."

Marian gave the young lady a candle, and wished her a good night's rest.

Ellen hastened cautiously up-stairs, and in a few minutes retired to rest.

She was fatigued, as before intimated; and yet slumber refused to visit her eyes. Nevertheless, she dozed uneasily,—in that kind of semi-sleep which weighs down the heavy lids, and yet does not completely shut out from the mind the consciousness of what is passing around.

A quarter of an hour had probably elapsed since Ellen had sought her couch, when the door slowly opened; and her father entered the room, bearing a light in his hand.

The countenance of the old man was ghastly pale; but there was a wildness in his eyes which bore testimony to the painful feelings that agitated him within.

He advanced towards the bed, and contemplated the countenance of his daughter for a few moments with an expression of profound sorrow.

Ellen opened her eyes, and started up in the bed, exclaiming, "My dear father, in the name of heaven, what is the matter?"

"O God! Ellen," cried the old man, placing the light upon a side-table, "tell me that it is not true—say but one word, to assure me that you are the pure and spotless girl I have always deemed you to be!"

"Father!" exclaimed the young lady, a horrible feeling taking possession of her, "why do you ask me that question?"

"Because a fearful suspicion racks my brain," answered the old man; "and I could not retire to rest until I knew the truth—be that truth what it may."

"My dear father—you alarm me cruelly!" said Ellen, her cheeks at one moment suffused with blushes, and then varying to ashy whiteness.

"In one word, Ellen," exclaimed the old man, "what is the meaning of that letter?"

And the almost distracted father threw the surgeon's note upon the bed.

In an instant Ellen remembered that she had left it behind her in the room where she was seated with her father when she received it.

Joining her hands in a paroxysm of the most acute mental agony, she burst into tears, crying wildly, "Forgive me! forgive me—my dear, dear father! Do not curse your wretched—wretched daughter!"

And then she bowed her head upon her bosom, and seemed to await her parent's reply in a state of mind which no pen can describe.

For some moments Mr. Monroe maintained a profound silence: but the quivering of his lip, and the working of the veins upon his forehead betrayed the terrible nature of the conflict of feelings which was taking place within his breast.

At length he also burst into tears, and covering his face with his hands, exclaimed, "My God! that I had died ere I had experienced this bitter—bitter hour!"

These words were uttered in a tone of such intense agony, that a mortal dread for her father's reason and life suddenly sprang up in Ellen's mind.

Throwing herself from the bed, she fell upon her knees, crying, "Forgive me, my dear father. Oh! if my child were here, I would hold it in my arms towards you; and, when its innocent countenance met your eyes, you would pardon *me!*"

"Ellen! Ellen! thou hast broken thy father's heart," murmured Mr. Monroe, averting his face from his suppliant daughter. "Oh! heaven be thanked that thy mother has been snatched from us! But tell me, unhappy girl, who is the villain that has dishonoured thee—for, in the moment of my intense agony, when I read the fatal letter that disclosed thy dishonour and marked the name of thy child, I vilely—ungratefully accused our generous benefactor of thy ruin."

"What! Richard?—oh! no, no!" ejaculated Ellen, in a tone of ineffable anguish; then, as the thought of *who the father of her child really was* flashed across her memory, she gave utterance to a terrible moan, and sank backwards, senseless, upon the floor.

"Ellen! Ellen!" cried the old man: "Ellen—my dearest daughter, Ellen—oh! I have killed her!"

At that moment Marian, bearing a light, entered the room.

"Water! water!" exclaimed the agonised father: "she is insensible—she is dying!"

Then hastily filling a tumbler from a decanter of water which stood upon the toilet-table, he knelt down by the side of his daughter, and bathed her temples.

In a few moments Ellen partially recovered, and gazed wildly around her.

"My sweet child," murmured the old man, pressing her hand to his lips, "live—live for me: all shall be forgiven—all forgotten. I was harsh to thee, my Ellen—to thee who have always been so fond, so tender, and so good to me."

"Leave her, sir, for the present," said Marian: "allow her to compose herself. This discovery has been almost too much for her!"

"I will," returned Mr. Monroe. "You must stay with her, good Marian; and in the morning I will come and see her."

The old man then withdrew.

CHAPTER CXX.

THE FATHER AND DAUGHTER.

IT was nine o'clock in the morning.

Ellen was lying, pale and tearful, in her bed, by the side of which sate her father.

The past night had worked a fearful change in the old man: his countenance was haggard, his look desolate and forlorn.

At one moment his lips quivered as if with concentrated rage: at another he wiped tears from his eyes.

Ellen watched him with the deepest interest.

"And you persist in refusing to acquaint me with the name of him who has dishonoured you?" said the old man, in slow and measured terms.

"Oh! my dear father, why will you persist in torturing me?" exclaimed Ellen. "Do you think that I have not suffered enough?"

"Oh! I can well believe that you have suffered, Ellen—suffered profoundly," returned Monroe; "for you were reared in the ways of virtue; and you could not have fallen into those of crime without a remorse. Suffered! but how have I not suffered during the last few hours! When I read that fearful secret, I became a madman. I had but two ideas: my daughter was a mother, and her child's name was *Richard!* What could I think? I went straight to the room where our benefactor was sitting: I closed the door; I approached him, with the rage of a demon in my breast, and I said, '*Villain! is my daughter's honour the price of the hospitality which you have shown towards us?*' He was thunderstruck; and I showed him the letter. He burst into tears, exclaiming, '*Could you believe me capable of such infernal atrocity?*' Then we reasoned together; we conversed upon the subject; and his noble frankness of manner convinced me that I had erred—grossly erred! He implored me to allow the night to pass ere I revealed to you the appalling discovery which I had made: he dreaded the effects of my excited state of mind; he thought that rest would calm me. But there was no rest for me! I retired to my room; and there—when alone—I felt that I could not endure meditation. I came to your chamber; and then—O God! the doubt to which I had yet so fondly clung was dissipated!"

"My dear father, if you knew all," said Ellen, weeping, "you would pity me—oh! you would pity me! Do not think that I surrendered myself to him who is the father of my child, in a moment of passion: do not imagine that the weakness was preceded by affection on my part for him who led me astray!"

"Unhappy girl, what mean you?" ejaculated Mr. Monroe. "Would you rob yourself of the only plea of extenuation which woman in such a case can offer? Speak, Ellen!"

"I will tell you all—that is, all I know," added Ellen, with a blush. "You remember that when we returned to live in that horrible court in Golden Lane, the second time we were reduced to poverty,—you remember what fearful privations we endured? At length our misery reached a point when it became intolerable; and one morning you set out with the determination of seeking relief from the bounty of Richard Markham."

"I well remember it," said Monroe. "Proceed."

"You can then call to mind the circumstance of my absence when you returned home to our miserable abode——"

"I do—I do: hours passed—I had gold—and you were absent!" ejaculated the old man, with feverish impatience.

"And when I returned home—late—" continued Ellen, her voice scarcely rising above a whisper, and her face, neck, and bosom suffused with burning blushes, "did I not bring you gold also?"

"Merciful heavens!" cried Monroe, starting from his seat; "say no more, Ellen—say no more—or I shall go mad! Oh, God! I comprehend it all! You went and sold yourself to some libertine, for gold!"

The old man threw himself into his daughter's arms, and wept bitterly.

"Father—dear father, calm yourself," said Ellen. "I could not see you want—I had no faith in the success of your appeal to him who has since been our benefactor—I thought that there was but *one resource* left;—but," she added, her eyes kindling with the fire of pride, while her father sank back into his seat, "I call my God to witness that I acted not thus for myself. Oh, no! death sooner should have been my fate. But you, my dear father, you wanted bread; you were starving; and that was more than I could bear! I sinned but once—*but once*; and never, never have I ceased to repent of that fatal step—for my one crime bore its fruit!"

Monroe was convulsed with grief. The tears trickled through the wrinkled hands with which he covered his venerable countenance; his voice was lost in agonising sobs, and all he could utter were the words: "Ellen, my daughter, it is for me to ask pardon of you!"

"No, say not so, dear father—say not so!" ejaculated Miss Monroe, throwing her arms around him, and kissing his forehead and hands.

"No, my dear father, it was not your fault if misery drove me to despair. But now you perceive," she added solemnly, "that I was more to be pitied than to be blamed; and—and," she murmured, the falsehood at such a moment almost suffocating her, "you understand why I cannot tell you who was the father of my child!"

There was something so terrible in the idea that a young, virtuous, and lovely girl had prostituted herself to the first unknown libertine who had bid a price for her charms,—something so appalling to a father in the thought that his only child had been urged by excess of misery and profound affection for him, to such a dismal fate, that Monroe seemed to sink under the blow!

For some time did his daughter vainly endeavour to solace him; and it was only when she herself began to rave and beat her bosom with anguish and despair, that the old man was recalled to a sense of the necessity of calming his almost invincible emotions.

The father and daughter were at length restored to partial tranquillity by each other's endeavours at reciprocal consolation, and were commingling their tears together, when the door opened.

Markham, followed by Marian, entered the room.

But what was the surprise of Mr. Monroe—what was the joy of Ellen, when Marian advanced towards the bed, and presented the child to his mother!

"A parent must not be separated from her offspring!" said Richard; "henceforth, Ellen, that infant must be nurtured by thee."

"Oh! good, generous friend, my more than brother!" exclaimed Ellen, with an ebullition of feeling that might almost be termed a wild paroxysm of joy; and she pressed the infant to her bosom.

"Richard," said Mr. Monroe, "you possess the noblest soul that ever yet blessed or adorned a human being."

Marian stooped over the bed, apparently to caress the sleeping infant, but in reality to whisper these words in Ellen's ears: "Fear nothing: I was sent to fetch the child; and Mr. Wentworth will keep your secret inviolably."

Ellen cast a look of profound gratitude upon Marian; for this welcome announcement assured her that the surgeon would never admit the fact of possessing any clue, direct or indirect, to the father of the babe which she held in her arms.

In a few minutes, when she had recovered herself from the

horrible alarm that had filled her mind lest Markham had himself been to see Mr. Wentworth, and had learnt that the father of the child was so far known that he had engaged to furnish the means for its support,—in a few minutes, we say, she turned to her father, and said: "Our benefactor's goodness deserves every explanation from us; tell him the extent of my misfortune—reveal to him the origin and cause of my shame—let nothing be concealed."

"Ellen," said Richard, "I know all! forgive me, but I reached the door of your room when you were telling your sad tale to your father; and I paused—because I considered that it was improper to interrupt you at such a moment. And, if I overheard that affecting narrative, it was not a mean curiosity which made me stop and listen—it was the deep interest which I now more than ever feel in your behalf."

"And you do not despise me?" said Ellen, hanging down her head.

"Despise you!" ejaculated Richard, "I deeply sympathise with you! Oh, no! you are not criminal; you are unfortunate. Your soul is pure and spotless!"

"But the world—what will the world think," said Ellen, "when I am seen with this babe in my arms?"

"The world has not treated you so well, Ellen," returned Markham, "that its smiles should be deeply valued. Let the world say what it will, it would be unnatural—inhuman—to separate a mother from her child; unless, indeed," he added, "it is your desire that that innocent should be nursed among strangers."

"Oh, no—no!" exclaimed Ellen. "But my unhappy situation shall not menace your tranquillity, nor shall the tongue of scandal gather food from the fact of the residence of an unwedded mother beneath your roof. I will retire, with my father, to some secluded spot——"

"Ellen," interrupted Markham, "were I to permit that arrangement, it would seem as if I were not sincere in the interest and commiseration, instead of the blame, which I ere now expressed concerning you. No: unless you and your father be wearied of the monotonous life which you lead with me, here will you both continue to dwell; and let the world indulge in its idle comments as it will."

"Your benevolence finds a reason for every good deed which you practise," said Ellen. "Ah! Richard, you should have been born a prince, with a princely fortune: how many thousands would then have been benefited by your boundless philanthropy."

"My own misfortunes have taught me to feel for those of others," answered Richard; "and if the world were more anxious than it is to substitute sympathy for vituperation, society would not be the compound of selfishness, slander, envy, and malignity, that it now is."

"It is settled, then, Richard," murmured Ellen, "that my babe shall henceforth experience a mother's care!"

And Ellen covered her child with kisses and with tears.

At that moment the infant awoke; and a smile played over its innocent countenance.

Ellen pressed it more closely and more fondly to her bosom.

CHAPTER CXXI.

HIS CHILD!

Mr. Greenwood was sitting in his study,—the handsomely fitted-up room which we have before described,—the same morning on which the babe was restored to its mother, through the admirable feeling of Richard Markham.

Mr. Greenwood was studying speeches for the ensuing session of Parliament. He employed two secretaries who composed his orations; one did the dry details, and the other the declamatory and rhetorical portions. Each received thirty shillings a week, and worked from nine in the morning until nine at night, with half an hour three times a day for meals—which said meals were enjoyed at their own expense. And then Mr. Greenwood hoped to reap all the honours resulting from this drudgery on the part of his clerks.

The studies of the Member of Parliament were interrupted by the introduction of Mr. Arthur Chichester.

"I am off to France to-morrow," said this gentleman, throwing himself lazily upon a sofa; "and I called to see if I could do anything for you on that side of the water."

"No, nothing," answered Greenwood. "Do you propose to make a long stay in France?"

"I shall honour Paris with my presence for about a month," said Chichester.

"During which time," added Greenwood, with a smile, "you will contrive to get rid of all the money which Mrs. Viola Chichester so generously supplied."

"Generously indeed!" said Chichester, laughing heartily. "So far from thinking of running through the money, I hope to double it. Although the public gambling-houses have been abolished in France, there is plenty of play at the private clubs. But you must not imagine that I have a perfect fortune in my possession: the means adopted to obtain the cash cost a mint of money: there were five hundred pounds to Tomlinson for his assistance; five hundred to you, for your aid, advice, and advances—(there is a splendid alliteration for you!)—and three hundred to poor Anthony Tidkins."

"Poor indeed!" ejaculated Greenwood. "According to what you told me, the miserable wretch must be in a blessed state of pecuniary nudity."

"It is perfectly true," said Chichester. "When he came to meet me and Tomlinson on the night that Viola was to be released, in the dark alley adjoining his house, he was like a furious hyena. It seems that he had awoke up ten minutes before the hour appointed for our meeting, and then discovered his loss as I before described it to you."

"I should not like to have such a man as my enemy," observed Greenwood, carelessly.

"Nor I either. Bless me, how he did swear! I never heard such imprecations come from a human being's mouth before. He vowed that he would undertake no other business, nor devote himself to any other pursuit, until he had traced the woman who had robbed him, and avenged himself upon her. Flaying alive, he said, was too good for her! Well,—I gave him twenty pounds, poor devil, through good nature; and Tomlinson gave him ten through fear; for it appears that this Tidkins exercises some extraordinary influence over that cowardly stock-broker—"

"Ahem!" said Greenwood. "And so poor Tidkins," he added, "did not set out on his travels after the thief empty-handed?"

"By no means. But he is a useful fellow, and one might want him again."

"True," said Greenwood: "he is one of the necessary implements which men of the world must make use of at times, to carve out their way to fortune. Have you heard anything of your beloved wife?"

"Nothing more than what I have already told you," answered

Chichester. "She has given up her abode at the Cambridge Heath gate, and taken apartments at a house in the very heart of the City, and where there are plenty of other lodgers. She is determined to be secure. However," continued Chichester, with a smile, "so long as she holds her tongue about that little matter—which she seems inclined to do—she need not fear any further molestation from me."

"I question whether you would have released her that evening, had she not made her escape," said Greenwood.

"Oh, indeed I should," returned Chichester; "I did not wish to push things too far; and I really believe that another week's confinement in that terrible place, which I have described to you, would have turned her mad in reality. Then again, I should have been afraid of that cowardly, snivelling fool, Tomlinson, who insisted upon accompanying me to ensure her release. That man has every inclination to be a downright rogue; but he lacks the courage."

"Have you seen your friend Harborough lately?" inquired Greenwood.

"To tell you the truth, he is going with me on my present expedition to Paris. His name, you know, sounds well: Sir Rupert Harborough, Bart., son-in-law of Lord Tremordyn,—eh?"

"His name must be somewhat worn out, I should imagine," observed Greenwood, playing with his watch-chain. "Have you seen Lady Cecilia?"

"No: she has her suite of apartments, and Sir Rupert has his—they do not interfere with each other. Sir Rupert, however, notices that Lady Cecilia has a great many visitors of the male sex; and amongst others, an officer of the grenadier guards, seven feet seven inches high, including his bear-skin cap."

"Indeed! Lady Cecilia is then becoming a confirmed demirep," observed Greenwood, without pausing to think who helped to make her so.

"There is no doubt of that," said Chichester. "But you seem up to your neck in business as usual."

"Yes: I am busily engaged in behalf of the Tory party," answered Greenwood. "The future Premier has great confidence in me. I have bought him over seven votes from the Whig side during the recess; and the moment the Tories succeed to power, I shall be rewarded with a baronetcy."

"You are making your way famously in the world," said Chichester, rising to leave.

"Pretty well—pretty well," returned Greenwood, with a complacent smile.

Chichester then shook hands with his friend, and departed.

Half an hour elapsed, during which Mr. Greenwood pursued his studies, when he was again interrupted by the entrance of a visitor.

This time it was Mr. Tomlinson, the stock-broker.

After having transacted a little pecuniary business together, Greenwood said, "What have you done with the old man?"

"I have taken a lodging for him in an obscure street of Bethnal Green, and there he is residing," answered Tomlinson.

"My plan was better," observed Greenwood, dogmatically: "you should have had him locked up in one of Tidkins's subterranean cells, and allowed three or four shillings a week for his maintenance."

"Impossible!" cried Tomlinson, indignantly. "I could never have acted so unmanly—so ungrateful—so atrocious a part."

"Well, just as you please," returned the Member of Parliament: "of course, you know best."

"We will not discuss that point," said Tomlinson.

"That is precisely what I said some time since to a deputation from the free and independent electors of Rottenborough, when they sent to remonstrate with me on a certain portion of my parliamentary conduct," observed Mr. Greenwood.

At this moment Lafleur entered and whispered something in his master's ear.

Tomlinson took his leave, and the valet proceeded to admit Marian into the presence of his master.

"Ah!" exclaimed Mr. Greenwood: "any thing wrong, Marian?"

"That may be according to the light in which you view the news I am come to communicate, sir," replied the servant. "In a word, Miss Monroe's father and Mr. Markham have discovered all."

"All! no—not *all!*" cried Greenwood, turning deadly pale; "surely Ellen could not——"

"When I said *all*, sir," replied Marian, "I was wrong. Mr. Monroe and my master have discovered that Miss Ellen is a mother; and her child is now with her."

"What! at Markham Place?" demanded Greenwood.

"Yes, sir."

"And it is known also who—what person—the father, I mean——"

"Miss Ellen has maintained *that* a profound secret, sir," said Marian.

"Thank heaven!" ejaculated Greenwood, now breathing freely. "But Mr. Wentworth—the surgeon——"

"He has also promised to remain dumb relative to what little he knows. You are best aware, sir, whether Miss Monroe has studied your wishes, or your interests, in remaining silent herself relative to you, and in recommending Mr. Wentworth, through me, to say nothing that may prove that she is really acquainted with the father of her child."

"But how was the discovery made? Tell me all," exclaimed Greenwood, impatiently.

"The explanation is short. Mr. Wentworth sent a note relative to the health of the infant, last evening, to Miss Monroe; and she inadvertently left it upon the table in the same room where her father was sitting."

"And her father—and Richard—Mr. Markham, I mean," said Greenwood, "are acquainted but with the bare fact that she is a mother?"

"That is all, sir. But, oh! if you only knew the excuse that Miss Ellen made to avoid additional explanations," continued Marian, "you yourself—yes, you, sir, would be affected."

"What was that excuse?" demanded Greenwood.

"I can scarcely believe for one moment that it was true," said Marian, musing, rather than replying to his question.

"But what was it?" cried the Member of Parliament, impatiently.

"Oh! she spoke of the misery to which her father and herself had once been reduced, and she said that, prompted by despair, she had sold her virtue to one whom she knew not—whom she had never seen before nor since."

"Ah! she said *that*," murmured Greenwood.—"And were her father and your master satisfied?"

"The old man wept well-nigh to break his heart, and Mr. Markham said that henceforth the child should stay with its mother in his house. Oh! sir, there lives not a man of nobler disposition than my master: he is all that is generous, humane, liberal, and upright!"

Mr. Greenwood turned aside, and appeared to contemplate some papers with deep interest for nearly a minute; and then he passed a handkerchief rapidly over his face.

Marian thought, as she afterwards informed Ellen, that he wiped tears from his eyes!

He made no reply, however, to her observations; but rang the bell for his French valet.

When Lafleur entered the room, Mr. Greenwood said, "You will proceed immediately to the abode of Mr. Wentworth, at Holloway: you will hand him from me this bank-note for fifty pounds; and you will say to him these words: '*As the child has been removed through an unforeseen occurrence from your care, its father sends you this as a small token of his gratitude for the kindness you have manifested towards it; and he hopes that, should you be questioned upon the subject, you will not reveal the fact that you ever had the slightest communication from its father.*' Go—and return quickly."

Lafleur received the bank-note, bowed, and left the room.

"You can inform Miss Monroe of the step which I have thus taken to ensure the surgeon's secrecy," said Greenwood, addressing himself to Marian.

"I shall not fail to do so, sir," answered the servant.

She then withdrew.

When the door closed behind her, Greenwood threw himself back in his chair, murmuring, "My child beneath Richard's roof!"

CHAPTER CXXII.

A CHANGE OF FORTUNE.

It was about three o'clock in the afternoon that the Earl of Warrington alighted from his horse at the door of Mrs. Arlington's residence in Dover Street.

Giving his horse in charge to his mounted groom, the nobleman entered the dwelling.

The Enchantress received him in the drawing-room; but, to her surprise, the air of the earl was cold and formal.

He seated himself in a chair at a distance from the sofa which Diana occupied; and for some moments he uttered not a word.

A sentiment of pride prevented her from saying anything to elicit an explanation of his ceremonial manner, because she was not aware that she was guilty of a fault meriting such treatment.

At length that silence, most embarrassing to both, was broken by the earl.

"Diana," he said, "we must separate. You have conducted yourself in a manner that has made *me* the laughing-stock of all who know me."

"My lord!" exclaimed Diana, perfectly astonished at this accusation; "you must have been misinformed; or you are bantering me."

"Neither the one nor the other," replied the earl. "You may probably conceive whether I am inclined to jest, when I state that your kind consideration towards Sir Rupert Harborough has reached my ears."

"Indeed, my lord!" cried Diana. "I do not attempt to deny that I forwarded, anonymously, to Sir Rupert Harborough a sum of money to extricate him from a fearful embarrassment."

"It would be unmanly in me to do more than remind you whence came that money which you could afford to fling away upon an unprincipled profligate," said the Earl of Warrington; "at the same time, you cannot suppose that it is pleasant to my feelings to learn that the world makes itself merry at my expense."

"Your lordship is aware that I am the last person in existence to do aught to occasion you the slightest uneasiness. Perhaps I was wrong——"

"You cannot, with your good sense, think otherwise. But let us not dispute upon the point: the thing is done, and cannot be recalled; but its effect is fatal to our connexion."

"Your lordship does not mean——"

"I mean that we must separate, Diana," interrupted the nobleman, firmly.

"Is my fault irreparable in your eyes?" asked the Enchantress, tears trickling down her cheeks.

"No man can endure ridicule—and I am particularly sensitive in that respect."

"But where did you learn that such was the result of my foolish kindness?" said Diana, almost bewildered by the suddenness with which this blow had come upon her.

"I will give you every explanation you require, as in duty bound," replied the earl. "Captain Fitzhardinge, an officer in the Grenadier Guards, is an acquaintance of mine. He is a visitor at the house of Sir Rupert Harborough; and last evening Lady Cecilia Harborough told him what she called a *capital anecdote* of how she had cheated her husband out of a thousand pounds. Then, it appears, they laughed heartily at this *excellent joke*; and Lady Cecilia proceeded to inform him that she had discovered whence the handsome subsidy emanated. She concluded, in terms more galling then polite, by ridiculing the Earl of Warrington, who was foolish enough to supply Mrs. Arlington so munificently with money, that she was enabled to spare some for her ancient lovers. You have asked me for the plain truth, and I have told it, as Captain Fitzhardinge stated it to me."

"And thus a trivial indiscretion on my part has created all this mischief," sobbed the Enchantress.

"You have acted most unwisely, Diana: I will not go so far as to say that you must have had some particular motive in forwarding that money to one who——"

"Heaven knows the purity of my motive!" exclaimed Diana, wiping away her tears, and glancing proudly towards the nobleman.

"The world will scarcely admit that purity of motive in such a case was possible. Consider the inferences that must be drawn——"

"And do you, my lord, believe that any unworthy reason of that kind led me to assist Sir Rupert Harborough?" demanded the Enchantress.

"If I may judge by your outward conduct towards me, I should give a decided negative in reply to your question. But we should no longer be happy in each other's society, while the least ground for unpleasant suspicions existed. We will, then, separate—but separate as good friends."

"Be it so, my lord," said Diana, the flush of injured pride dyeing her cheeks, while she conquered the emotions that rose in her bosom.

"The lease of this house, and every thing it contains, are yours," continued the earl, after a moment's pause: "in this pocket-book there is a cheque——"

"No, my lord," interrupted Diana; "your bounty has already done much for me—more than you seem to think I have deserved: I cannot accept another favour at your lordship's hands."

The Earl of Warrington was struck by this answer, which proved that his mistress was not selfish; and for a few moments he was upon the point of making overtures for a reconciliation.

But the dread of ridicule—the fear of being laughed at as a man who kept a mistress for the benefit of others—the horror of being made the laughing-stock of all the rakes and demireps in London, smothered the lenient feelings that had awoke in his breast.

"You refuse to accept this token of my friendship, Diana?" he said.

"I must beg most respectfully to decline it, my lord—with fervent gratitude, nevertheless, for your generosity."

Again the earl wavered.

He looked at that beautiful woman who had been so charming and fascinating a companion,—who had advised him as a faithful friend in various matters upon which he had consulted her,—and who, to all appearance, had conducted herself so well towards him, save in this one instance;—he gazed upon her for a few moments, and his stern resolves melted rapidly away.

"Diana," he said, "we——"

At that moment the sounds of voices in the street caused him to turn his head towards the window; and he perceived Captain Fitzhardinge and another gentleman riding by on horseback.

They were laughing heartily, and gazing towards the house.

The Earl of Warrington's sensitive mind instantly suggested to him the idea that the anecdote of the thousand pounds was being again retailed, and most probably accompanied by the intimation that *that was the house of the complaisant Earl of Warrington's mistress!*

The Enchantress, with that keen perception that characterises woman, had seen all that was passing in the earl's mind,—had observed him waver *twice*, and had felt convinced on the second occasion that he would court a reconciliation.

But when those voices and that hearty laughter from the street fell upon her ears, and when she saw the blood rush to the earl's countenance as he glanced in that direction, she knew that all was over.

The earl rose and said, "Give me your hand, Diana: we will part, as I said, good friends; and remember that I shall always be ready to serve you. Farewell!"

"Farewell, my lord," returned Mrs. Arlington, extending her hand, which the nobleman pressed with lingering tenderness.

Then, afraid of another access of weakness, the Earl of Warrington wrung her hand warmly, and precipitated himself from the room.

The Enchantress hurried to the window, concealed herself behind the curtain, and watched him as he mounted his horse to depart.

He did not glance once upwards to the window: perhaps he knew that she was there!

And yet her pride prompted her to conceal herself in that manner.

When he was out of sight, she threw herself upon the sofa and wept.

"Oh! if I had but said one word when his hand pressed mine," she exclaimed, "I might still have retained him! He is gone!—my best, my only friend!"

But Diana was not a woman to give way to grief for any length of time. She possessed great mental fortitude, which, though subdued for a short space, soon rose predominant over this cruel affliction.

Then she began to reflect upon her position.

She had a house beautifully furnished; and she possessed a considerable sum of ready money. She had therefore no disquietude for the present, and but little apprehension for the future; for she knew that her personal beauty and mental qualifications would soon bring another lover to her feet.

But she seriously thought of renouncing the species of life to which she had for some years been devoted: she longed to live independently and respectably.

In this frame of mind she passed the remainder of the day, pondering upon a variety of plans in accordance with her new desire.

She retired early to rest; but, not feeling an inclination to sleep, she amused herself with a book. The candle stood upon a table by the side of the bed; and Diana, luxuriously propped up by the downy pillows, culled the choicest flowers from Byron's miscellaneous poetic wreath.

An hour elapsed; and at length she grew sleepy. The book fell from her hand, and her eye-lids closed.

Then she remembered no more until she was suddenly aroused by a sensation of acute pain: she started up, and found the bed enveloped in flames.

She sprang upon the floor; but her night-dress was on fire:—she threw herself on the carpet, and rolled over and over in terrible agony, piercing screams issuing from her lips.

Those screams were echoed by loud cries of "Fire!" from the street, and then there was a rush of footsteps upon the stairs.

The door of the chamber was forced open, and Diana was caught up in the arms of a policeman, who had effected an entry to the house through the ground-floor windows.

She was carried in a state of insensibility down into the parlour, where a cloak was hastily thrown over her, and she was conveyed to a neighbouring hotel. Fortunately a medical man was passing at the moment; and he tendered his aid.

Meantime the fire spread with astonishing rapidity. The servants were extricated from the burning pile; but little property was saved.

A considerable time elapsed before the engines arrived; and when they did reach the spot, an adequate supply of water could not be procured, as the springs were ice-bound by the frost.

An immense crowd collected in the street; and all was bustle or curiosity.

The broad red flames shot upward with a roar like that of a furnace: the scene for a good distance round was as light as noon-day; and the heavens immediately above appeared to be on fire.

At one time the neighbouring houses were endangered; but suddenly the roof of the burning tenement fell in with a terrific crash; and then the conflagration seemed smothered.

But in few minutes the flame shot upwards once more; and another hour elapsed ere it was completely subdued.

The newspapers announced next morning that Mrs. Arlington's property was not insured, and that the lady herself lay in a most precarious state at the hotel to which she been conveyed.

CHAPTER CXXIII.

ARISTOCRATIC MORALS.

It was still dark, though past seven o'clock, on the morning which succeeded the fire, when a somewhat strange scene occurred at the house of Sir Rupert Harborough in Tavistock Square.

The baronet, in his slippers and dressing-gown, cautiously

descended the stairs, guiding himself with his left hand placed upon the balustrade, and conducting a young female with his right.

They maintained a profound silence, and stole down so carefully that it was easy to perceive they were fearful of alarming the household.

But while he was still descending the stairs, leading the young female, who was fully dressed, even to her bonnet and shawl, the following thoughts passed rapidly through the mind of the baronet.

"After all, it is absurd for me to take this trouble to get my new mistress secretly out of the house. Why should she not walk boldly in and out, night or day, I wonder? 'Pon my honour, I have a great mind that she should! But, no—whatever agreement exists between me and Lady Cecilia, a certain degree of decency must be observed before the servants, and for the sake of one's character with the neighbours. After all, prudence is perhaps the best system."

His thoughts were at this moment interrupted by steps upon the stairs, which evidently were not the echoes of those of himself and his paramour.

He paused and listened.

Those steps were descending with great apparent caution, and yet a little more heavily than was quite consistent with entire secrecy.

The baronet led his mistress hastily after him, crossed the hall, and then drew her along with him into an obscure corner near the front-door.

"Silence, Caroline—silence," he whispered: "it is most likely the housemaid."

The baronet and his mistress accordingly remained as quiet as mice in the corner where they were concealed.

Meantime the steps gradually grew nearer and nearer; and now and then a low and suppressed whisper on the stairs met the baronet's ear.

A vague suspicion that some adventure, which those who were interested in it were anxious to conduct with as much secrecy as possible, was in progress, now entered the mind of Sir Rupert Harborough. He accordingly became all attention.

And now the steps ceased to echo upon the stairs, but advanced towards the front-door.

The hall was pitch-dark; but the baronet was satisfied that two persons—a male and female—were the actors in the proceeding which now interested him; and all doubt on this head was banished from his mind when they halted within a few feet of the corner where he and his mistress were concealed.

Then the whispering between the two persons whose conduct he was watching re-commenced.

"Farewell, dearest Cecilia," said the low and subdued voice of a man.

"Farewell, beloved Fitzhardinge," answered the other voice, with whose intonation, in spite of the whisper in which it spoke, the baronet was full well acquainted.

Then there was the billing murmur of kisses, which continued for some moments.

"When shall we meet again, dearest?" demanded Fitzhardinge, still in the same low tone.

"To-night—at the usual hour I will admit you," returned Lady Cecilia. "Sir Rupert goes to France to-night with his splendid friend Chichester."

"Thank heaven for that blessing!" said the Grenadier Guardsman. "And now, adieu, sweet Cecilia, until this evening! But, tell me, before I depart—shall I always find you the same warm, loving, devoted, fond creature you now are?"

"Always—always to *you*," was the murmuring reply.

Then kisses were exchanged again.

"And am I indeed the first whom you have ever really loved? am I the only one who has ever tasted the pleasures of heaven in your arms, save your husband?" continued the officer, intoxicated with the reminiscences of the night of bliss which he had enjoyed with his paramour: "Oh! tell me so once again—only once!"

"You know that you alone could have tempted me to weakness, Fitzhardinge," answered the fair, but guilty patrician lady: "you alone could have induced me to forget my marriage vows!"

"Now I shall depart happy, my beloved Cecilia," said the officer; and again he imprinted burning kisses upon the lady's lips.

He then turned towards the front-door, and endeavoured to remove the chain: but it had become entangled with the key in some way or another; and he could not detach it.

"What is the matter?" inquired Cecilia, anxiously.

"This infernal chain is fast," answered the officer; "and all I can do will not move it."

"Let me try," said the lady; but her attempt was as vain as that of her lover.

"What is to be done?" asked Fitzhardinge.

"God knows!" returned Cecilia; "and it is growing late! In half-an-hour it will be day-light. Besides, the servants will be about presently."

"The devil!" said the officer, impatiently.

"Stay," whispered Lady Cecilia: "I will go to the kitchen and obtain a light. Do not move from this spot: I will not be a moment."

She then glided away; and the officer remained at his post as motionless and as silent as a statue, for fear of alarming the inmates of the house. His thoughts were not, however, of the most pleasureable kind; and during the two minutes that Lady Cecilia was absent, his mind rapidly pictured all the probable consequences of detection—exposure, ridicule, law-suit, damages, the Queen's Bench prison, the divorce of the lady, and the necessity under which he should labour of making her his own wife.

This gloomy perspective was suddenly enlivened by the gleam of a candle at the further end of the hall, and which was immediately followed by the appearance of Lady Cecilia, with a light.

Still the corner in which Sir Rupert and his paramour were concealed was veiled in obscurity; while the baronet obtained a full view of the tall Guardsman, dressed in plain clothes, standing within a couple of yards of his hiding-place, and also of Lady Cecilia, attired in a loose dressing-gown, as she advanced rapidly towards the place where her lover awaited her.

But when Cecilia reached the immediate vicinity of the front-door, the gleam of the candle fell upon that nook which had hitherto remained buried in obscurity.

A scream escaped the lady's lips, and the candle fell from her hands.

Fortunately it was not extinguished: Sir Rupert rushed forward and caught it up in time to preserve the light.

Then, at a single glance, those four persons became aware of each other's position.

A loud laugh escaped the lips of the baronet.

"Sir," said the officer, advancing towards him, "for all our sakes

avoid exposure: but if you require any satisfaction at my hand, you know who I am and where I reside."

"Satisfaction!" exclaimed Lady Cecilia, ironically; for she had recovered her presence of mind the moment she had perceived the equivocal position in which her husband himself was placed in respect to the female who stood quivering and quaking behind him: "what satisfaction can Sir Rupert Harborough require, when he admits such a creature as that into his house?"

And she pointed with a disdain and a disgust, by no means affected, towards her husband's paramour.

"Creature indeed!" cried the young woman, now irritated and excited in her turn: "I think I am as honest as you, my lady, at all events."

"Wretch!" murmured Cecilia between her teeth, as if the sight of the *creature* filled her with abhorrence and loathing.

Ah! haughty lady! thou could thyself sin through lust: but thou couldst not brook the sight of one who sinned for bread!

The young woman, over-awed by the air of insuperable disgust which marked the proud patrician at that moment, recoiled from her presence, and burst into tears.

"Come, enough of this folly," said Sir Rupert, impatiently: "we shall have the servants here in a moment. Perhaps you and this gentleman," he continued, "will step into that room for a moment, while I open the door for my little companion here."

Lady Cecilia tossed her head disdainfully, darted a look of sovereign contempt upon the abashed Caroline, and beckoned Captain Fitzhardinge to follow her into the adjacent parlour.

Sir Rupert retained the light. He opened the door, the chain of which had only become entangled round the key, and dismissed his paramour, who was delighted to escape from that house where the terrible looks of the lady had so disconcerted her.

The baronet then repaired to the parlour, and, having locked the door to prevent the intrusion of the servants, threw himself upon the sofa.

"Well, on my honour!" he exclaimed, bursting into a loud fit of laughter, "this is one of the most pleasant adventures that ever I heard or read of—'pon my honour!"

"Have you requested me to wait here in order to contribute to your hilarity, sir?" demanded Captain Fitzhardinge, indignantly.

"My dear fellow," returned the baronet, "let us laugh in concert! Oh! I can assure you that you need fear no law-suits nor pistols from me!"

"*Fear*, sir!" ejaculated the Guardsman: "I do not understand the word."

"Well—*expect*, then, if that will suit you better, my dear captain," continued Sir Rupert Harborough. "You see that my wife and myself act as we please, independently of each other."

"Sir Rupert!" exclaimed Cecilia, who was by no means anxious that her lover should be made acquainted with the terms of the agreement into which she and her husband had entered a short time previously, and the nature of which the reader will remember.

"My dear Cecilia," observed the baronet, "is it not much better that your *friend* should be made acquainted with the grounds on which you have admitted him as your sworn knight and only love?"

"Cease this bantering, sir," cried Captain Fitzhardinge. "Have I not already said that I am willing to give you any satisfaction which you may require?"

"And must I again tell you, my dear fellow," returned the baronet, with an affectation of familiarity, which only made his words the more bitter,—"must I again tell you that I have no satisfaction—that I have none to ask, and you none to give? But I cannot allow you to consider me a grovelling coward:—I must explain to you the grounds on which my forbearance is based."

"Proceed, sir," said Captain Fitzhardinge, coolly.

"You will then allow me to retire to my own room?" exclaimed Lady Cecilia, rising from the chair in which she had thrown herself.

"No, my dear," said the baronet, gently forcing her back into her seat: "you must remain to corroborate the truth of what I am about to state to this gentleman."

Lady Cecilia resumed the chair from which she had risen, and made no reply.

"In one word, Captain Fitzhardinge," continued the baronet, "there is a mutual understanding between my wife and myself, that we shall follow our own inclinations, whims, and caprices, without reference to the ties which bind us, or the vows which we pledged at church some years ago. All this may seem very strange: it is nevertheless true. Therefore, I have no more right to quarrel with Lady Cecilia on *your* account, than she has to abuse me on account of that young person whom you saw in the house just now. Now, then, my dear captain," continued the baronet, his tone again becoming bitterly ironical, "you may at your ease congratulate yourself upon being the only person that Lady Cecilia has ever loved, and the only one on whom she has ever bestowed her favours with the exception of her husband."

"Then I am to understand, sir," said the officer, perfectly astounded at the turn which the affair had taken, "that you do not consider yourself offended or aggrieved by the—the——"

"Not a whit!" ejaculated the baronet. "On the contrary—I have no doubt we shall be excellent friends in future."

The captain bowed, and rose to depart.

Sir Rupert unlocked and opened the door for him, and then ushered him, with affected politeness, out of the house.

When he returned to the parlour, he found Lady Cecilia red with indignation.

"What means this scene, Sir Rupert," she said, "after our mutual compact?"

"My dear," answered the baronet, calmly, "you treated my little friend in a most unpleasant manner, and I thought myself justified in retaliating to a certain extent. Besides, I was compelled to give an explanation to a man who would have otherwise looked upon me as a coward for failing to demand satisfaction of him."

"But did you not consider that you have rendered me contemptible in his eyes?" demanded Lady Cecilia, burning with spite.

"Never fear," said the baronet. "Confiding in your sweet assurances that he alone has ever possessed your love, and that he alone, save your husband, has ever been blessed with the proofs of that affection, he will return ere long to your arms. Besides, am I not going to France to-night with my splendid friend, Chichester?"

"This is cruel, Sir Rupert. If an accident made you acquainted with the conversation which passed between us——"

"An accident, indeed!" interrupted Sir Rupert Harborough, laughing affectedly. "'Pon my honour, the entire adventure is one of the drollest that ever occurred! But let us say no more upon the subject! Adhere to the compact on your side, and do not insult *my* friends——"

"But a prostitute in my house!" ejaculated Lady Cecilia, still loathing the idea.

"And my wife's paramour in my house!" cried Sir Rupert.

"Oh, there is something refined in an amour with one's equal," said Lady Cecilia; "but a wretch of that description——"

"Enough of this!" cried the baronet. "The servants are already about: let us each retire to our own rooms."

And this suggestion was immediately adopted.

CHAPTER CXXIV.

THE INTRIGUES OF A DEMIREP.

Lady Cecilia retired to her own chamber, locked the door, threw herself upon the bed, and burst into tears.

Oh, at that moment how she hated her husband;—how she hated herself!

She wept not in regret of her evil ways: she poured forth tears of spite when she thought of the opinion that her new lover must form of her, after the explanation given by Sir Rupert.

For Captain Fitzhardinge was rich and confiding; and the fair patrician had calculated upon rendering him subservient alike to her necessities and her licentiousness.

But, now—what must he think of one who bestowed upon him those favours that were alienated from her husband by a formal compact? What opinion could he entertain of a woman who sinned deliberately by virtue of an understanding with him whom she had sworn to respect and obey?

It could not be supposed that the morality of Captain Fitzhardinge was of a very elevated nature; but in the occurrence of that morning there was something calculated to shock the mind the least delicate—the least refined.

Yes—Lady Cecilia wept; for she thought of all this!

And then her rage against her husband knew no bounds.

"The wretch—the cowardly wretch!" she exclaimed aloud, as she almost gnashed her teeth with rage: "was he not born to be my ruin? From the moment that I saw him first until the present hour, has he not been an evil genius in my way? Yes—oh! yes: he is a demon sent to torture me in this world for my faults and failings! Seduced by him when I was very young, I might have been plunged into disgrace and infamy, had not my father purchased his consent to espouse me. Then the large sum that was paid to save my honour was squandered in the payment of his debts, or in ministering to his extravagances. Now, what is our position? what is *my* position? Shunned by my own father and mother, I am left dependent on him who knows not how to obtain enough for himself; or else I—I, the daughter of a peer, must sell myself to some Mr. Greenwood or Captain Fitzhardinge for the means to support my rank! Oh! it is atrocious: I begin to loathe myself! Would that I were the mistress of some wealthy man who would be constant and kind towards me, rather than the wife of this beggared baronet!"

Lady Cecilia rose from the bed, advanced towards the mirror, and smoothed her hair. Then she perceived that her eyes were red with weeping.

"Absurd!" she exclaimed, a contemptuous smile curling her lips; "why should I shed tears upon the past which no human power can recall? Rather let me avail myself of the present, and endeavour to provide for the future. Am I not young? and does not my glass tell me that I am beautiful? Even the immaculate—the taintless—the exemplary rector of Saint David's paid me a compliment on my good looks when I met him at Lady Marlborough's, a few days ago. Yes—and methought that if the most evangelical of evangelical clergymen of the Established Church could for a moment be moved by my smile,—if that admired preacher, who publicly avows that he refrains from marriage upon principle,—if that holy minister who is quoted as a pattern to his class, and an example for the whole world,—if *he* could whisper a word savouring of a compliment in my ear, and then seem ashamed of the moment of weakness into which his admiration had betrayed him;—if my charms could effect so great a miracle as this, what may they not do for me in helping me on to fortune?"

She paused and considered herself for some minutes in the glass opposite to her.

"Yes," she cried, again breaking silence, "I will no longer remain in the same house with my unprincipled and heartless husband: I will no longer breathe the tainted atmosphere which he inhabits. His very name is associated in my mind with forgery and felony! I will break the shackle which yet partially binds me to him; I will emancipate myself from the restraint and thraldom wherein I now exist. Fitzhardinge is rich and loving; perhaps he may still feel the influence of the silken chain which I threw around his heart. We will see! If he come gladly back to my feet, my aim is won: if not—well,"—and she smiled, complacently,—"there are others as rich, as handsome, and as easily enchained as he!"

Lady Cecilia proceeded to her desk and wrote the following note:—

"Come to me, dearest Fitzhardinge, at three precisely this afternoon: I have much to say respecting the specious falsehoods which Sir Rupert uttered this morning in order to conceal the natural cowardice of his disposition. He was afraid to involve himself in a quarrel with you; and he excused his unmanly forbearance by means of assertions that reflected upon me. Come, then, to me at three; I shall be alone, and at home only to you."

This note was immediately conveyed to Captain Fitzhardinge by Cecilia's lady's-maid, who was the confidant of her mistress's intrigues.

Having despatched her missive, the baronet's wife proceeded to the duties of the toilet.

This employment, breakfast, the newspaper, and a novel, wiled away the time until about one o'clock, when Lady Cecilia, having ascertained that her husband had gone out half an hour previously, descended to the drawing-room.

She was attired in a simple and unpretending manner; but then she knew that this style became her best.

She was determined to captivate that day; and certainly she had seldom appeared to greater advantage.

Her rich auburn hair,—of a hue as warm as the disposition which it characterised,—fell in long hyperion ringlets upon her sloping shoulders: her blue eyes were expressive of a feeling of languid voluptuousness; and her pure complexion was set off by the dark dress that she wore.

The time-piece upon the mantel had scarcely struck two, when a loud double-knock at the front-door resounded through the house.

Lady Cecilia started from her seat, for she had forgotten to instruct the servants "that she was only at home to Captain Fitzhardinge." But she was too late to remedy her neglect; the summons was already answered ere she had gained the landing on which the drawing room opened.

She accordingly returned to the sofa, and composed herself to receive the visitor, whoever it might be.

In a few moments the servant announced the Earl of Warrington.

With this nobleman Lady Cecilia was only very slightly acquainted, she having met him on two or three occasions, some years previously, at her father's house.

"I must apologise, Lady Harborough, for this intrusion," said the earl; "but I trust to your kindness to pardon me in that respect, and to afford me a little information concerning a matter which has suddenly assumed an air of importance in my eyes."

"No apology is necessary for the honour which your lordship confers upon me by visiting my humble abode," answered Lady Cecilia; "and with regard to the subject to which your lordship alludes, I shall be happy to furnish any information in my power."

"Your ladyship's courtesy encourages me to proceed," continued the earl. "Forgive me if I must direct your attention to one of those pieces of gossip—I will not say scandal—which so often becomes current in the sphere in which we move. I allude to an anecdote relative to a certain mysterious remittance of a thousand pounds which was forwarded to Sir Rupert Harborough, and which your ladyship undertook to disburse for his advantage."

"Your lordship places the matter in as delicate a way as possible," said Lady Cecilia, affecting to laugh heartily in order to conceal the shame which she really experienced at this reference to her unworthy action; "but it was only a pleasant trick which I played Sir Rupert. The truth is, Sir Rupert is not the most generous man towards his wife and when I found that some honourable person was repaying him a debt contracted a long time previously, I thought that, as the amount fell so providentially into my hands, I could not do better than appropriate it to the liquidation of the arrears of pin-money due to me."

"Very just, madam," said the Earl, forcing himself to smile at the incident which Lady Cecilia represented in the light of a venial little advantage by a wife against her husband. "I believe that the amount was forwarded anonymously?"

"To tell you the candid truth, my lord," answered Lady Cecilia, "the whole affair was so strange and romantic, that I kept, as a great curiosity, the letter which accompanied the bank-note. If you possess any interest in the matter——"

"Your ladyship *knows* that I am not seeking this information without *some* object," said the earl, emphatically. "Would it be indiscreet," he added, in a less serious tone, "to request a glimpse at that great curiosity?"

"Oh! by no means," returned Lady Cecilia, who affected to treat the whole matter as an excellent joke; then, rising from her seat, she hastened to her work-box, and in a few moments produced the letter. "It was not so scented with musk when I received it," she added, laughing; "but it was redolent of a far more grateful flavour—that of this world's mammon."

"I believe mammon is the deity whom we all more or less adore," observed the Earl of Warrington, gallantly taking up the tone of chit-chat, rather than formality, which Lady Cecilia endeavoured to infuse into the conversation: then, as he received the letter from her hand, he said, "May I be permitted to read it?"

"Oh, certainly, my lord: and, if you have any curiosity in the matter, you are welcome to retain it," answered Lady Cecilia.

"With your leave, I will do so," said the earl.

"And now that I have replied to all your lordship's queries," continued Lady Cecilia, "may I ask one in my turn?"

The earl bowed, and smiled.

"Who was the indiscreet eave's-dropper or tale-bearer that gave your lordship the hint concerning this business?" asked the baronet's wife.

"Methinks that your ladyship has been at no pains to conceal the affair," said the earl: "and what hundreds have talked about cannot well be charged against an individual tale-bearer."

"Nay, my lord, I mentioned it but to two persons," exclaimed Cecilia. "The first was to Sir Rupert Harborough—in a moment of pique; and the other was to—a—a—particular friend——"

"I am not indiscreet enough to ask for names," interrupted the earl, rising; and he hastened to take his leave, ere Lady Cecilia could reiterate her question relative to the person who had communicated to him the fact of the intercepted thousand pounds.

It was now nearly three o'clock; and Lady Cecilia again composed herself to receive Captain Fitzhardinge.

Punctual to the hour, the officer was introduced into the drawing-room.

But his manner, instead of being all love and tenderness, was simply polite and friendly.

"Fitzhardinge," said the lady, "I perceive that you have allowed yourself to be prejudiced against me."

"Not prejudiced, Lady Cecilia," answered the guardsman; "but I confess that I am no longer under the influence of a blind passion. The conduct of your husband this morning was that of a man who was acting consistently with the circumstances which he explained, and not that of an individual who was playing a part in order to disguise the innate cowardice of his disposition. No, Cecilia—your husband is not a coward—whatever else he may be! And now one word relative to myself. So long as I believed that you made to me, as a proof of love, the generous sacrifice of conjugal fidelity,—so long as I believed that an affection for me alone induced you to violate your marriage vow,—then the dream was sweet, though not the less criminal. But when I discovered that you made no sacrifice to me,—that you came not to my arms warm with a love that trembled at detection, but secure in the existence of a heartless compact with your husband,—then my eyes were opened, and I saw that Lady Cecilia Harborough had risked nothing of all that she had pretended to risk—sacrificed nothing of all that she had affected to sacrifice—for the sake of Captain Fitzhardinge! Thus the delusion was destroyed; and although our amour might be based upon more impunity than I had ever conceived, it would be the less sweet! The charm—the spell is broken!"

"And have you come here to tell me all this—to insult me with your moralisings?" demanded Lady Cecilia, the fire of indignation and wounded pride displacing the languid voluptuousness which had at first reigned in the expression of her eyes.

"No! not to insult you, Cecilia," answered the officer; "but to explain in an open and candid manner the motive which leads me to say: '*Let us forget the past, as it regards each other!*'"

"Be it so," said Lady Cecilia, deeply humiliated, and now hating the handsome officer much more than she had ever liked him. "In that case, sir, we can have nothing more to say to each other."

Captain Fitzhardinge bowed, and withdrew.

Lady Cecilia fell back upon the sofa, murmuring, "Beaten—beaten! defeated in this hope!"

And tears came into her eyes.

But in a few moments she exclaimed, "How foolish is this grief! how useless this indignation! Sorrow and hatred are the consuming enemies of female beauty! Did I not say ere now that there were others in the world as rich, as handsome, and as confiding as Captain Fitzhardinge?"

As she uttered those words aloud, the haughty beauty wiped her eyes, and composed her countenance.

She rose and advanced towards the mirror to assure herself that her appearance indicated nought of those tears which she had shed; and as she contemplated her features with a very pardonable pride, the reminiscence of the compliment which the clergyman of Saint David's had paid her flashed to her mind.

She smiled triumphantly as she pondered upon it; and that vague, shadowy, unsubstantial phrase of flattery, that now formed the topic of her thoughts, gradually assumed a more palpable shape in her imagination,—became invested with a significant meaning,—then grew into a revelation of passion,—and was at length embodied into a perfect romance of love with all its enjoyments and blisses.

The ardent soul of that frail woman converted the immaculate clergyman into an admirer betrayed in an unguarded moment into a confession of love,—then changed him into a suitor kneeling at her feet,—and by rapid degrees carried him on, through all the mystic phases of passion, until he became a happy lover reclining on her bosom.

With a presumption which only characterises minds of her warm temperament and loose ideas of morality, Cecilia triumphed in the half-hour's impassioned reverie which succeeded the departure of Captain Fitzhardinge, over the ascetic virtue and self-denying integrity which public opinion ascribed to the rector of Saint David's.

Then, when some trifling incident aroused her from this wild and romantic dream, she did not smile at its folly—she regarded it as a species of inspiration prompting her in which direction to play the artillery of her charms.

"Yes," she exclaimed, musing aloud; "he once said, '*I never saw you look so well as you appear this evening*:'—those words shall be a motto to a new chapter in my life!"

And she smiled triumphantly as if her daring aim were already accomplished!

"Thirty-six years of age," she abruptly resumed her musings,—"wealthy—handsome—unmarried, *from principle*,"—and here an erratic smile of mingled satisfaction and irony played on her rosy lips,—"and yet fond of society, the Reverend Reginald Tracy must no longer be permitted to remain proof against woman's beauty—aye, and woman's wiles. Oh! no—he shall repeat to me, but far more tenderly, the words he uttered the other evening: his passing compliment shall become a permanent expression of his sentiments! But his character—his disposition? must I not study *them?* If that be necessary, the task is ready to hand!"

She rose from the sofa, and having selected an ecclesiastical magazine from some books that stood upon a chiffonier, returned to her seat to peruse at leisure a sketch which the work contained of the character, ministry, and popularity of the rector of Saint David's.

CHAPTER CXXV.

THE RECONCILIATION.

In the meantime the Earl of Warrington drove to the hotel in Dover Street, where Diana Arlington lay; and, upon inquiry, he ascertained that a nurse and the medical attendant were with her.

He desired to be conducted to a private room, and then despatched the waiter to request the professional gentleman to step thither for a few moments.

"What name shall I say, sir?" asked the servant, who was unacquainted with the earl's person.

"It is needless to mention any name," replied the nobleman; "I shall not detain the gentleman five minutes."

The servant disappeared, and in a few moments returned, followed by the medical attendant.

The waiter introduced him into the apartment, and then withdrew.

"I believe, sir," said the earl, "that you are attending upon the lady who experienced so severe an accident last night?"

"I was by chance passing through Dover Street when the flames burst forth," was the reply: "and I gave an immediate alarm to the police. I remained upon the spot to ascertain if my professional services could be rendered available; and it was well that I did so."

"The lady then is much injured?" said the earl, in a tone expressive of emotion.

"Seriously injured," answered the surgeon; "and as I live at some distance from this neighbourhood, I considered it proper to remain with the patient all night. Indeed, I have not left her for a moment since the accident occurred."

"Your attention shall be nobly recompensed, sir," said the earl. "Here is my card, and I am your debtor."

The surgeon bowed low as his eye glanced upon the name of the individual in whose presence he stood.

"And now," continued the nobleman, "answer me one question—candidly and sincerely. Will your patient be scarred by the effects of the fire?"

"My lord, that is more than I can answer for," returned the surgeon. "Fortunately, medical assistance was rendered the moment after the accident occurred; and this circumstance should inspire great hope!"

"Then I *will* hope," said the earl. "How long an interval do you imagine must elapse ere she may be pronounced convalescent? Or rather, I should have asked, is she in any positive danger?"

"There is always danger—great danger in these cases, my lord. But, should the fever subside in a few days, I should recommend the removal of the patient to some quiet neighbourhood—afar from the bustle of the West End."

"You said that you yourself resided some distance from hence?" observed the earl, after a few moments' reflection.

"My abode is in Lower Holloway, my lord," answered the surgeon; "and my name is Wentworth."

"Holloway is quiet and retired," said the earl; "but is not the air too bleak there at this season?"

"It is pure and wholesome, my lord; and the spot is tranquil, and devoid of the bustle of crowds and the din of carriages."

"Wherever Mrs. Arlington may remain until her recovery," said the Earl, "she must receive all the attentions which can be lavished upon her; and in nothing must she be thwarted where gold can procure her the gratification of her wishes."

"I would offer to place my house at the lady's disposal, my lord—and the attention of Mrs. Wentworth would be unremitting—but——"

"Name the obstacle," said the earl. "Perhaps you consider that the position of the lady with regard to myself,—a position the nature of which you may have divined,—is somewhat too equivocal to permit your wife——"

"No, my lord; medical men have no scruples of that kind. I hesitated because I feared that my abode would be too humble——"

"Then let that obstacle vanish this moment," interrupted the earl. "It is my wish that Mrs. Arlington should be removed to your house as soon as the step can be taken with safety to herself: you will then devote yourself to her cure; and on you I place my reliance. I have been unjust to her, Mr. Wentworth," continued the nobleman, pressing the surgeon's hand, and speaking in a low but hurried tone,—"I have been unjust to her—but I will make her ample reparation—that is, provided you can preserve her beauty,—for we are all mortal—and I confess to a weakness,—but no matter! Say—you will do your best!"

"My lord, I am poor, and struggling with the world," answered the surgeon, "and, I may say without vanity—because I possess certificates from eminent medical men under whom I have studied—that I am not ignorant of my profession. My lord, I have every inducement to devote all the knowledge I possess to the aim which you desire. My attention shall be unwearied and unremitting; and if I succeed——"

"If you succeed in restoring her to me in that perfection of beauty which invested her when I took leave of her yesterday,—without a mark, without a scar—your fortune shall be my care, and you will have no need to entertain anxiety relative to the future, with the Earl of Warrington as your patron."

"At present, my lord, all I can say is—*I will do my best,*" rejoined Mr. Wentworth.

"And at present I can ask no more," exclaimed the earl: then, after a moment's pause, he said, "May I be allowed to see your patient for a few moments?"

The surgeon hesitated.

"I know why you dislike this proposal," observed the nobleman: "you are afraid that, when I contemplate the altered countenance of that woman who was lately so beautiful, I shall despair of her complete cure."

"Such is, indeed, my impression," answered Mr. Wentworth. "Those symptoms and appearances which are most alarming to persons unacquainted with the medical art, are frequently the least causes of alarm to the professional man."

"Then let me *speak* to her, and not *see* her," said the earl.

"I understand your lordship: in a few minutes I will return."

And the surgeon withdrew.

During his absence the earl paced the room in an agitated and excited manner, which was quite inconsistent with the usual equanimity and even gravity of his temperament.

Ten minutes had elapsed when the surgeon came back.

"Will your lordship follow me?"

Mr. Wentworth led the way to the chamber in which Diana Arlington lay.

The shutters were closed, and the curtains were drawn around the bed; the room was nearly dark, a few struggling gleams of light alone forcing their way through the chinks in the shutters.

When the earl entered the apartment, the surgeon remained in the passage outside: the nurse had been already directed to retire for a short time.

The nobleman approached the bed, and seating himself in a chair by the side, said, "Diana, can you forgive me for my cruelty of yesterday?"

"I never entertained a feeling of resentment, my lord, and therefore have nothing to forgive," was the answer, in a low and plaintive tone.

"I did you a serious wrong, Diana," continued the earl; "but I am not too proud to confess my error. I trembled at the idea of ridicule: hence the hastiness of my conduct. And then, there was a suspicion in my mind—a suspicion which made me uneasy, very uneasy—but which is now dispelled. I have read your letter which accompanied the bank-note addressed to Sir Rupert Harborough; and I am satisfied in respect to the integrity—nay, the generosity of your motives."

"It was kind of you, my lord, to take the steps necessary to reinstate me in your good opinion," murmured Diana from her couch, in a tone evidently subdued by deep emotion.

"There was no kindness in the performance of an act of justice," returned the earl. "When I read in this morning's newspaper the sad account of the terrible accident of last night, my heart smote me for my conduct towards you. Then I reflected upon all the happiness which I had enjoyed in your society, and I was moved—deeply, profoundly moved! I despatched a servant to this hotel to inquire if you were really so seriously injured as the journal represented; and he brought me back word that your life was no longer in positive danger, but——"

"But that I shall be a hideous object for the remainder of my days," added Diana, with somewhat of bitterness in her manner.

"God forbid!" cried the earl, energetically: "Mr. Wentworth seems to promise——"

"Alas! the medical art prompts its professors to console the mind in order to heal the body; but I am not foolish enough to yield to a hope so baseless!"

These words were uttered in a tone of the most profound melancholy.

"Diana, you *must* hope," exclaimed the Earl of Warrington: "you will recover—yes, you will recover; and even if a slight trace of this accident——"

"A slight trace!" almost screamed Diana—and the earl could hear her roll herself convulsively over on her pillow: "a slight trace, my lord! I shall be disfigured for life: nothing can save me! My countenance will be seared as with a red-hot iron—my neck will be covered with deep scars—my arms, my entire body will be furrowed with crimson and purple marks! Oh, God! it is hard to suffer thus!"

And then she burst into an agonising flood of tears.

The earl allowed her to weep without interruption: he knew that her mind would be relieved by that outpouring of feeling.

And he was right: in a few minutes she said, "Pardon me—I am weak, I am foolish. And now proceed to tell me how you became possessed of that note which I sent with the money to Sir Rupert Harborough."

The Earl of Warrington then related the particulars of his interview with Lady Cecilia.

"And now that I have done an act of justice, and convinced myself of the purity of the motives which induced you to act in the manner that created my displeasure," continued the earl, "let us talk of yourself. I have made arrangements with Mr. Wentworth which, I hope, will meet your approval, and conduce to your benefit. When you can be removed with safety, you shall be conveyed from the bustle of an hotel in a crowded neighbourhood to the tranquil retirement of Mr. Wentworth's abode at Holloway. I am induced to place reliance upon the skill and talent of that man—I scarcely know why."

"Oh! yes—he is no doubt very clever," said the patient; "for his treatment of me speedily gave me relief from the acuteness of the agony which I at first experienced."

"Every thing shall be done to conduce to your comfort, Diana," resumed the nobleman. "My upholsterer shall send down to Mr. Wentworth's house the furniture that may be required for the rooms which you are to occupy; and my steward shall supply him with ample funds."

"How kind—how good you are," murmured Diana.

"But I shall not attempt to see you," continued the earl, "until your recovery is announced to me—your complete recovery; and then——"

He checked himself; and there was a long silence.

Suddenly the earl arose.

"Farewell, Diana—my presence is not calculated to calm you," he exclaimed. "I shall now leave you—but, remember, I watch over you from a distance. Farewell!"

"Farewell—till we meet again," said Diana. "But—oh! how shall I dread that day! And—if my worst fears should be confirmed—if I really become the horrible, scarred, hideous object which I dread,—then—then we shall never meet more,—for I will fly from the world and bury myself in some deep solitude whither none who ever knew me in my bright days shall trace me!"

"You will not be forced to adopt such an alternative, Diana—believe me you will not!" exclaimed the earl. "At all events—let us hope,—let us *both* hope!"

The earl hastily withdrew.

In the passage he encountered the surgeon, to whom he reiterated his instructions relative to the attention to be shown towards the patient.

"Mr. Wentworth," he said, in an emphatic tone, "remember all that I have told you. Gold shall be placed at your disposal with no niggard hand; spare no expense! That lady's complete restoration to her pristine beauty is your care: think of naught save that one grand aim!"

"My lord," answered the surgeon, "I can only repeat the words I used just now—*I will do my best!*"

The earl pressed his hand warmly, and hurried away—more affected by the incidents of that day than he had been for many, many years.

CHAPTER CXXVI.

THE RECTOR OF SAINT DAVID'S.

It is not necessary to explain to our readers the precise locality of the splendid Chapel of Ease known by the name of Saint David's. Suffice it to say, that it is situate not a hundred miles from Russell or Tavistock Square; and that the clergyman attached to it at the period of which we are writing was the Rev. Reginald Tracy.

It was Sunday morning.

A crowd of well-dressed persons, of both sexes, poured into the chapel of Saint David's. The street was lined with carriages; and when each in its turn drew up at the door of the sacred edifice, the *élite* of the aristocracy might have been observed to alight and hasten to form part of the immense congregation assembled to hear the most popular preacher of the day.

The interior of the chapel was vast, and of a convenient oblong form. It was lofty, and beautifully fitted up. On three sides were large and roomy galleries, amphitheatrically arranged with pews. The magnificent organ stood in the gallery over the entrance; and at the further end was the communion-table. The pulpit, with its annexed reading-desk, stood a little in front of the altar, and facing the organ. The pews both of the galleries and the body of the church were provided with soft cushions; for this was a proprietary chapel, and there was but a slender accommodation for the poor. Indeed, this class occupied plain benches in the aisles, and were compelled to enter by a small side-door; so that they might not mingle with the crowd of elegantly dressed ladies and fashionable gentlemen that poured into the chapel through the grand entrance in front.

A policeman maintained order at the side-door which admitted the humbler classes; but two beadles, wearing huge cocked hats and ample blue cloaks bedizened with broad gold-lace, and holding gilt wands in their hands, cleared the way for the wealthy, the great, and the proud, who enjoyed the privilege of entrance by means of the front gates.

"This way, my lord. Pray step this way, my lady," said the polite beadles, in their blandest tones. "The pew-opener is in attendance, my lord. My lady, here is the hymn-book, which your ladyship commanded me to procure for your ladyship. My lord, take care of the step. This door, ladies, if you please. Gentlemen, this way, if you would be so condescending. Yes, sir—certainly, sir—the pew-opener will find *you* a seat, sir—immediately, sir. Ladies, this way is less crowded. You will find the left aisle comparatively empty. My lord, straight forward, if your lordship will be so good. Ladies, the pew-opener is in attendance. This way, ladies and gentlemen!"

And at the side-door the policeman might be heard vociferating in somewhat like the following manner:—

"Now, then, you young woman, where the deuce are you pushing to? Want to get a good place, eh? What! with sich a rag of a shawl as that there?—I'm afeard I can't admit you. Now, boy, stand back, or I'll show you the reason why. I say, old woman, you ain't wanted here; we doesn't take in vimen with red cloaks. You'd better go to the dissenting chapel round the corner, you had: that's good enow for you. Holloa! what's this mean? a sweep in his Sunday toggery. Come, come; that's rayther too strong, chummy. You toddle off, now. Here, young woman, you may come in; you may—'cos you're very pretty: that way, my dear. Holloa! here comes a feller without a nose. No—no—that won't do at no price; my orders is partickler; no von comes here vithout a nose. Vy, you'd frighten all the great ladies out o' their vits. They already complains of the riff-raff that comes to this here chapel; so we must try and keep it *se*-lect—just like Gibbs's westry. Ha! ha! now then, who's that blaigaird a-talking so loud there? It's on'y me as can talk here at this door, 'cos I'm official—I am. This vay, young woman: push the door, my dear. Well, if you ain't married, I'm sure you ought to be. Now, then, who's that a guffawing like a rhinoceros? I'll clap a stopper on your mug, I will. Come, come; you go back, old chap; no workus-livery here; this is the wrong shop for the workus people; this is—I can tell yer. Vell, you're a genteel couple, I don't think—coming to a propri-*ai*-tory chapel vithout no gloves, and fists as black as tinkers. Stand back there, boys, and let that young gal vith the yaller ribands come up: she's decent, she is. Yes, my dear,—you may go in, my dear. Now, then, stand back—no more comes in this mornin': the orgin's begun."

With these words the policeman thrust the poor people violently down the steps, entered the chapel, and closed the door in their faces.

The interior was crowded throughout; and it was very evident that curiosity and fashion, more than devotion, had congregated in that chapel the rank, wealth, and beauty that filled the pews below and above.

The solemn swell of the organ pealed through the sacred edifice; and then arose the morning hymn, sung by a select corps of choristers and by twelve youths belonging to the school of a celebrated professor of Music for the Millions.

A venerable clergyman, with hair as white as his own surplice, occupied the reading-desk; and in a pew close by the pulpit, was the cynosure that attracted all eyes—the Rev. Reginald Tracy.

The tall commanding form of this clergyman would have rendered him conspicuous amongst the congregation, had no other circumstance tended to endow him with popularity. His countenance was eminently handsome; his high and open forehead was set off, but not shaded, by dark brown hair, which curled naturally; his hazel eyes beamed with the fire of a brilliant intellect; his Roman nose, small mouth, and well-turned chin, formed a profile at once pleasing and commanding; and his large well-curled whiskers, meeting beneath his chin, confirmed the manly beauty of that proud and imposing countenance.

There was a profound, but totally unassuming, sense of the solemnity of the scene and of the sanctity of his profession in his manner and deportment: his voice did not join in the hymn, but his mind evidently followed the words, as he from time to time glanced at the book which he held in his hand.

Doubtless he was well aware—but nothing in his demeanour seemed to indicate this consciousness—that he was the centre of all attraction: though not servilely meek nor hypocritically austere, he was still surrounded by a halo of religious fervour which commanded the most profound respect.

And towards him were turned hundreds of bright eyes; and the glances of fair maids dwelt upon his countenance rather than on their books.

The hymn ceased, and the service proceeded.

At length the anthem succeeding the communion-service, filled the chapel with its solemn echoes, accompanied by the pealing of the magnificent organ. Then a simultaneous sensation pervaded the entire congregation, and all eyes were directed towards the Rev. Reginald Tracy, who was now ascending the steps to the pulpit.

The anthem was ended; the congregation resumed their seats; and the preacher commenced.

It is not, however, our intention to treat our readers to a sermon: suffice it to say, that the eloquence and matter of the discourse which the Rev. Reginald Tracy delivered upon this occasion, were well calculated to sustain his high reputation.

But of the attentive audience, no individual seemed to be more deeply impressed with his sermon than Lady Cecilia Harborough, who sate in a pew near the pulpit—next indeed to the one which the clergyman himself had occupied during the former part of the service.

She was alone; for on the previous day she had hired that pew for her own especial use.

Whenever the eyes of the preacher were turned in the direction where she sate, she appeared to be wiping away tears from her cheeks; for the sermon was on a solemn and pathetic subject.

More than once she fancied that *he* observed her; and her heart beat triumphantly in her bosom.

When the sermon was concluded she remained in her pew, and allowed the rest of the congregation to leave the chapel ere she moved from her seat. At length the sacred edifice was deserted, save by herself and two or three officials connected with the establishment.

In a few minutes the pew-opener—an elderly matron-like person—accosted her, and said, "If you please, ma'am, the doors will be closed almost directly."

"Could you—could you oblige me with a glass of water?" faltered Lady Cecilia: "I feel as if I were about to faint."

"Oh! certainly, ma'am," answered the pew-opener; and she hurried to the vestry.

Presently she returned, accompanied by the Rev. Reginald Tracy himself.

"Is the lady very unwell?" inquired the clergyman of the pew-opener, as they advanced together towards Lady Cecilia's seat.

"She seems very languid—quite overcome, sir," was the answer. "But this is the pew."

The clergyman stepped forward, and instantly recognised the fair indisposed.

"Lady Harborough!" he exclaimed. "Is your ladyship unwell?"

And taking the tumbler of water from the pew-opener, he handed it to the baronet's wife.

"It is nothing—the heat, I suppose," murmured Lady Cecilia; and she drank a portion of the water. "Thank you, Mr. Tracy, for your attention: I feel better—much better now."

"Will your ladyship step into the vestry and sit down for a few minutes?" inquired the clergyman, really concerned at the presumed indisposition of the lady.

"If it would not be indiscreet, I should esteem it a favour," answered Cecilia, still speaking in a tremulous and faltering tone.

Reginald Tracy instantly proffered his arm to the lady, and conducted her to the vestry, where the venerable clergyman who had read the service was calmly discussing a glass of sherry.

"I am ashamed—perfectly ashamed, to give you all this trouble, Mr. Tracy," said Cecilia, as she accepted the chair which was offered her; "but the heat of the chapel—and, to tell the truth, the emotions which your beautiful discourse aroused within me—quite overcame me."

"The chapel was, indeed, very much crowded," answered Reginald Tracy, touched by the homage rendered to his talent in the second cause which Lady Cecilia alleged for her indisposition.

"Nevertheless, this little incident will not in future prevent me from becoming one of the most regular of your congregation," observed Cecilia, with a smile.

Mr. Tracy bowed, and smiled also.

Both had brilliant teeth, and it was impossible for either to fail to notice this beautiful feature in each other.

"I feel quite recovered now," said Cecilia, after a short pause, "and will return home. I offer you my best thanks for this kind attention on your part."

"Do not mention it, Lady Harborough. But I cannot permit you to return alone, after this indisposition: allow me to conduct you as far as your door?"

"I could not think of taking you out of your way—"

"It happens that I have a call to make in Tavistock Square, and am actually going that way," interrupted Reginald Tracy.

Lady Cecilia, like a well-bred person as she was, offered no farther objection, but accepted the clergyman's escort to her own abode.

During the short walk she rendered herself as agreeable as possible; though purposely conversing upon topics suitable to the sabbath, and to the profession of her companion. She also introduced one or two delicate, and apparently unsophisticated, allusions to the eloquence which had produced so deep an impression upon a crowded congregation, and the profound attention with which the sermon was received. Then she artfully, but with admirably assumed sincerity, questioned Mr. Tracy upon two or three passages in that discourse, and suffered him to perceive that not one word of it had been lost upon her.

Mr. Reginald Tracy was mortal like any other human being, and was not exempt from any of the weaknesses of that mortality. It was impossible for him not to experience a partial sentiment of pride and satisfaction at the impression which his eloquence had evidently made upon a young and beautiful woman; and that feeling became in the least degree more tender by the fact that this young and beautiful woman was leaning upon his arm.

Then how could he feel otherwise than flattered when, with her witching eyes upturned towards his countenance, she questioned him—so meekly and so sincerely, as he thought—upon the very passages of his sermon which he himself considered to be the best, and which he had studied to render the most effective? He *was* flattered—he smiled, and endeavoured to render himself agreeable to so charming a woman.

At length they reached the door of Lady Harborough's abode. The syren invited him to walk in, as a matter of course; but Mr. Tracy was compelled to forego that pleasure. He was really engaged elsewhere; or there is no saying but that he might have stepped in—only for a few minutes.

Lady Cecilia extended her hand to him at parting, and held his for just two or three moments, while she renewed her thanks for his attention. The action was perfectly natural; and yet the gentle contact of that delicate hand produced upon Reginald Tracy a sensation which he had never before experienced. It seemed to impart a glow of warmth and pleasure to his entire frame.

At length they separated; and as the Rector of Saint David's pursued his walk, he found his mind from time to time wandering away from more serious reflections, and reverting to the half hour which he had passed so agreeably in the society of Lady Harborough.

CHAPTER CXXVII.

BLANDISHMENTS.

Lady Cecilia took very good care not to appear at chapel that evening. She was well aware that common politeness—if no other motive—would induce the Rev. Reginald Tracy to call on the following day to inquire after her health.

Accordingly, on the Monday, she took more than usual pain with her toilet.

Sir Rupert Harborough had departed with his "splendid friend" Chichester for the Continent; and she was completely her own mistress. She had no one to interfere with her plans or pursuits, for her lady's maid was entirely devoted to her interests. However others suffered or waited in respect to pecuniary matters, Sarah—the aforesaid lady's maid, or *cameriste*—was always well and regularly paid.

It was by no means an uninteresting scene to behold the attention and zeal with which Sarah seconded her mistress's determination to make the most of her charms upon the present occasion.

Lady Cecilia was seated near her toilet-table, with a little gilt-edged oval-shaped mirror in her hands, which reposed in her lap; and Sarah was engaged in arranging the really beautiful hair of her mistress.

"What o'clock is it, Sarah?" inquired Lady Cecilia, casting a complacent glance at herself in the large looking-glass upon her toilet-table.

"It must be nearly one, my lady," was the reply.

"Then you have no time to lose, Sarah. The ringlets are quite divine; pray take equal pains with the back-hair. Do you think that I look better in ringlets or in bands?"

"In ringlets, my lady."

"And if I had my hair in bands, and asked you the same question, you would reply, '*In bands.*'"

"Your ladyship cannot think that I am so insincere," said the *camariste*.

"Do you fancy me in this dress, Sarah?" asked the lady, heedless of her domestic's observation.

"I prefer the blue watered-silk," was the answer.

"Then why did you not recommend it in the first instance?"

"Your ladyship never required my advice."

"True. Have you finished?"

"No hairdresser from Bond Street, or the Burlington Arcade, could have performed his task better, my lady," replied Sarah.

"Yes—it is very well—very well, indeed," said Cecilia, surveying herself in the mirror. "I will now descend to the drawing-room."

When she reached that apartment, the artful woman spread on the table a few books on serious subjects; she then amused herself with a volume of a new novel.

The clock had just struck two, when a double-knock was heard at the front door.

Lady Cecilia thrust the novel under the cushion of the sofa, and took up "Sturm's Reflections."

The Rev. Mr. Tracy was announced.

Lady Cecilia rose and received him with a charming languor of manner.

"I have called to satisfy myself that your ladyship has recovered from the indisposition of yesterday," said the rector.

"Not altogether," answered Cecilia. "Indeed, after I returned home, yesterday, I experienced a relapse."

"I observed that you were not at chapel in the evening, and I feared that such might be the case."

It was with difficulty that Lady Cecilia could suppress a smile of joy and triumph as this ingenuous and unsophisticated announcement met her ears. He had thought of her! he had noticed her absence!

"I can assure you that nothing save indisposition could have induced me to remain away from a place where one gathers so much matter for useful and serious meditation," answered the lady.

"And yet the world generally forgets the doctrines which are enunciated from the pulpit, an hour after their delivery," observed Reginald.

"Yes—when they are doled forth by ministers who have neither talent nor eloquence to make a profound impression," said Cecilia, artfully conveying a compliment without appearing to mean one at the moment. "I believe that our churches would be much better frequented, were the clergy less dogmatic, less obscure; and did they address themselves more to the hearts of their hearers than they do."

"I believe it is necessary to appeal to the heart, and not be satisfied with merely reaching the ears," said the rector, modestly.

"And wherever the pastor possesses the rare talent of moving the feelings,—of exciting the mind—to salutary reflection, as well as merely expounding points of doctrine,—thither will the multitude flock high and low, rich and poor. Oh!" exclaimed Cecilia, as if carried away by the enthusiasm of the subject, "how grand—how noble a situation does that man occupy, who, by the magic of his voice and the power of his mind, can collect the thousands around his pulpit! I can understand how an impression may be easily made upon the half-educated or totally ignorant classes of society: but to cast a spell upon the intelligent, the well-informed, and the erudite,—to congregate the aristocracy of the realm to listen to the words that flow from his mouth,—oh! great, indeed, must be the influence of such a man!"

"You consider, then, Lady Cecilia, that the upper classes need powerful inducements to attend to the truths of religion?" said Reginald, irresistibly charmed by the witching eloquence that had marked the language of the beautiful woman in whose society he found himself.

"I consider—but, if I tell you my thoughts," said Cecilia, suddenly checking herself, "I shall unavoidably pay a high compliment to you; and that neither——"

"Let me hear your ladyship's sentiments in any case," said the clergyman, fearful of losing those honied words which produced upon him an impression such as he had never experienced in his life before.

"I believe," continued Cecilia, "that the upper classes in this country are very irreligious. I do not say that they are infidels: no—they all cherish a profound conviction of the truths of the gospel. But their mode of life—their indolent and luxurious habits, militate against a due regard to religious ceremonials. How is it, then, that they are aroused from their apathy? They hear of some great preacher, and curiosity in the first instance prompts them to visit the place of his ministry. They go—almost as they would repair to see a new play. But when they listen to his words—when they drink, in spite of themselves, large draughts of the fervour which animates *him*—when he appeals to their hearts, then they begin to perceive that there is something more in religion than an observance of a cold ceremonial; and they go home '*to reflect!*'"

"You believe that to be the case?" said the rector, delighted at this description of an influence and an effect which he could not do otherwise than know to be associated with his own ministry.

"I feel convinced that such is the fact," answered Lady Cecilia; then, lowering her tone in a mysterious manner, and leaning towards him, she added, "Many of my friends have confessed that such has been the case in respect to their attendance at your chapel—and such was the case with myself!"

"With you, Lady Cecilia?" exclaimed the clergyman, vainly endeavouring to conceal the triumph which he experienced at this announcement.

"Yes, with me," continued the artful woman. "For, to be candid with you, Mr. Tracy, I need consolation of some kind—and the solace of religion is the most natural and the most effective. My domestic life," she proceeded, in a deeply pathetic tone, "is far from a happy one. Sir Rupert thinks more of his own pleasures than of his wife;—he does more than neglect me—he abandons me for weeks and weeks together."

She put her handkerchief to her eyes.

Mr. Tracy drew his chair closer to the sofa on which she was seated: it was only a mechanical movement on his part—the movement of one who draws nearer as the conversation becomes more confidential.

"But why should I intrude my sorrows upon you?" suddenly exclaimed Cecilia. "And yet if it be not to the minister of religion to whom we poor creatures must unburden our woes, where else can we seek for consolation? from what other source can we hope to receive lessons of resignation and patience?"

"True," said the rector. "And that has often appeared to me the best and redeeming feature in the Roman Catholic world, where the individual places reliance upon a priest, and looks to him for spiritual support and aid."

"Ah, would that our creed permitted us the same privilege!" said Lady Cecilia, with great apparent enthusiasm.

"I know of no rule nor law which forbids the exercise of such a privilege," said Reginald; "unless, indeed, usage and custom be predominant, and will admit of no exceptions."

"For my part, I despise such customs and usages, when they tend

to the exclusion of those delightful outpourings of confidence which the individual pants to breathe into the ears of the pastor in whom implicit faith can be placed. In how many cases could the good clergyman advise his parishioners, to the maintenance of their domestic comfort? how many heart-burnings in families would not such a minister be enabled to soothe? Oh! sir, I feel that your eloquence could teach me how to bear, unrepiningly, and even cheerfully, all the sorrows of my own domestic hearth!"

"Then look upon me as a friend, my dear Lady Cecilia," said the clergyman, drawing his chair a little closer still: "look upon me as a friend; and happy indeed shall I be if my humble agency or advice can contribute to smooth the path of life for even only one individual!"

"Mr. Tracy, I accept your proffered friendship—I accept it as sincerely as it is offered," exclaimed Lady Cecilia; and she extended her hand towards him.

He took it. It was soft and warm, and gently pressed his. He returned the pressure:—was it not the token, the pledge of friendship? He thought so—and he meant no harm.

But again did the contact of that soft and warm hand awake within his breast a flame till then unknown; and his cheeks flushed, and his eyes met those of the fair—the fascinating creature, who craved his friendship!

"Henceforth," said Cecilia, who now saw her intrigue was progressing towards a complete triumph—even more rapidly than she had ever anticipated—"henceforth you will have no votary more constant in attendance than I; but, on your part, you must occasionally spare from your valuable time a single half hour wherein to impart to me the consolations I so much require."

"Be not afraid, Lady Cecilia," said the rector, who now felt himself attracted towards that woman by a spell of irresistible influence: "I shall not forget that you have ingenuously and frankly sought my spiritual aid; and I should be false to the holy cause in which I have embarked, were I to withhold it."

"I thank you—deeply, sincerely thank you," exclaimed Cecilia. "But judge for yourself whether I do not seek solace, in my domestic afflictions, from the proper source! This is the book which I was reading when you called."

Cecilia took up Sturm's "Reflections," and opened the book at random.

"There," she said; "it was this page which I was perusing."

She held the book in her hands as she reclined, rather than sate, upon the sofa; and the clergyman was compelled to lean over her to obtain a glimpse of the page to which she pointed.

His hair touched hers: she did not move her head. Their faces were close to each other. But not an impure thought entered his soul: still he was again excited by that thrilling sensation which came over him whenever he touched her.

She affected not to perceive that their hair commingled, but pointed to the page, and expatiated upon its contents.

In a moment of abstraction, for which he could not account, and against the influence of which he was not proof, Reginald Tracy's eyes wandered from the book to the form which reclined, beneath his glance, as it were, upon the sofa. That glance swept the well-proportioned undulations of the slight but charming figure which was voluptuously stretched upon the cushions.

Suddenly Cecilia left off speaking, and turned her eyes upward to his countenance. Their glances met; and Reginald did not immediately avert his head. There was something in the depths of those blue orbs which fascinated him.

Still he suspected not his extreme danger; and when he rose to depart, it was simply because he felt like a man flushed with wine, and who requires air.

He took his leave; and Cecilia reminded him that she should expect to see him soon again.

Can there be a doubt as to his answer?

When he regarded his watch, on reaching the street, he was astounded to perceive that two hours had slipped away since he entered the house.

And a deep flush suddenly overspread his countenance as he beheld the viper-like eyes of a hideous old hag, who was standing near the steps of the front-door, fixed upon him with a leer which for an instant struck a chill to his heart by its ominous—and yet dim significancy.

CHAPTER CXXVIII.

TEMPTATION.

"He *will* come again on Wednesday," said Lady Cecilia to herself, as she heard the front door close behind the Rev. Reginald Tracy.

This wily woman was well-acquainted with the human heart: she had discovered the weak side of the rector of Saint David's: she assailed him by means of his vulnerable point; she directed her way to his heart through the avenue of his *vanity*.

Yes—Reginald Tracy was vain,—as vain as a man who was admired and sought after by all classes, was likely to be rendered,—as vain as a spoiled child of the public could be.

His life had, moreover, been so pure, so chaste, so ascetic, that the fierce passions which agitate other men were unknown to him; and, as all mortals must be characterised by some failing, his was a habit of self-admiration!

Venial and insignificant was this foible, so long as no advantage was taken of it by designing or worldly-minded persons; but even our lightest defects, as well as our most "pleasant vices," may be made the means of our ruin.

Vanity is a noxious weed which, when nurtured by the dews of flattery, spreads its poisonous roots throughout the fertile soil of the heart; and each root springs up into a plant more venomous, more rank, more baleful than its predecessor.

The life of Reginald Tracy had been singularly pure. He had even passed through the ordeal of a college career without affixing the least stain on the chastity of his soul. Yet with all his austerity of virtue, he was characterised by no austerity of manner: he mixed freely in society, and hesitated not to frequent the ball-room—although he did not dance. He could be a pleasant companion: at the same time he never uttered a word upon which he had to retrospect with regret. When amongst men, no obscene jest nor ribald allusion was vented in his presence; and yet he was never voted "a bore." In a word, he was one of those men who possess the rare talent of maintaining a character for every virtue, and of being held up as a pattern and an example, without creating a single enemy—without even being compelled to encounter the irony of the libertine, and without producing a feeling of restraint or embarrassment in the society which he frequented.

Such was Reginald Tracy; and it was this man,—who at the age of thirty-six could look back with complacency upon a spotless life,—a life unsullied by a single fault,—an existence devoid of the slightest dereliction from moral propriety,—it was this good, this holy, this saint-like man whom the daring Cecilia undertook to subdue.

Reginald, Reginald! the day of thy temptation has now come: thou standest upon a pinnacle of the temple—the tempter is by thy side;—take good heed of thyself, Reginald Tracy!

"He will come again on Wednesday," had said Lady Cecilia.

The prediction was fulfilled!

The morning had been so inclement that no one would have stirred abroad unless actuated by important motives. The rain had fallen in torrents,—beating violently against the windows, and inundating the streets. It had, however, ceased at noon; but the sky remained covered with black clouds; and at three o'clock on that gloomy winter-day it was dark and sombre as if night were at hand.

But in spite of that inauspicious weather, the Rev. Reginald Tracy knocked at Lady Cecilia Harborough's door at the hour which we have just mentioned.

The designing creature received the clergyman with a smile, exclaiming at the same time, "It is indeed kind of you to visit me on such a day as this. I have been so happy—so resigned—so possessed with the most complete mental tranquillity since you manifested sympathy and interest in my behalf, that your presence appears to be that of a good angel!"

"It is our duty to sustain those who droop, and console those who suffer," answered the rector.

"Delightful task!" ejaculated Cecilia. "What a pure and holy satisfaction must you enjoy, when you reflect upon the amount of comfort which your lessons impart to the world-wearied and sinking spirit. Believe me, many an one has entered the gates of your chapel with a weight upon his soul almost too heavy for him to bear, and has issued forth carrying his burden of care lightly, if not cheerfully, along!"

"Do you really imagine that my humble agency can produce such good results in the cause of heaven?" asked Reginald, fixing a glance of mingled tenderness and satisfaction upon the charming countenance of Cecilia.

"I do—I do," she answered, with apparent enthusiasm; "I can judge by the effect which your admirable discourse of last Sunday morning produced upon myself. For—let me not deceive you," she continued, hanging down her head, and speaking in a tremulous and tender voice,—"let me not deceive you—it was not the heat of the chapel which overcame me—it was your eloquence! I dared not confess this to you at first; but now—now that I can look upon you as a friend—I need have no secret from you."

She took his hand as she uttered these words, and pressed it in a manner which he conceived to be indicative of grateful fervour; and without a thought of evil—but with an indefinable sensation of pleasure to which until lately he had been all his life a stranger—he returned that pressure.

Lady Cecilia did not withdraw her hand, but allowed it to linger in his; and he retained it under the influence of that sensation which caused his veins to flow with liquid fire.

He was sitting on the sofa by her side, and his eyes wandered from her countenance over the outlines of her form.

"Oh! how can the man who accompanied you to the altar, and there swore to love and cherish you," he exclaimed, in an ebullition of impassioned feelings such as he had never known before,—"how can that man find it in his heart to neglect—to abandon you,—you who are evidently all gentleness, amiability, and candour!"

"He has no heart—no soul for any one save himself," answered Cecilia. "And now tell me—relieve my mind from a most painful suspense upon one point! Am I criminal in the eyes of heaven, because I have ceased to love one whom I vowed to love, but whose conduct has quenched all the affection that I once experienced for him?"

"You must not harden your heart against him," said Reginald; "but by your resignation, your uncomplaining patience, your meekness, and your constant devotion to his interests, you must seek to bring him back to the paths of duty and love."

"I might as well essay to teach the hyena gratitude," answered Cecilia.

"You speak too bitterly," rejoined the rector of Saint David's; and yet he was not altogether displeased at the aversion which Lady Cecilia's language manifested towards her husband.

"Alas! we have no power over volition," said she; "and that doctrine is a severe one which enjoins us to kiss the hand that strikes us."

"True," observed Reginald. "I know not how it is—but I feel that I am at this moment unaccountably deficient in argument to meet your objections; and yet——"

He paused, for he felt embarrassed; but he knew not why.

"Oh! you can appreciate the difficulty of enjoining a love towards one who merits hatred," exclaimed Cecilia, now skilfully availing herself of the crisis to which she had so artfully conducted the conversation. "You see that you are deficient in reasoning to enforce the alleged necessity of maintaining, cherishing, and nourishing respect and veneration for a husband who has forfeited all claims to such feelings on the part of his injured wife. At all events, do not tell me that I am criminal in ceasing to love one who oppresses me;—do not say that I offend heaven by ceasing to kiss the hand that rudely repulses all my overtures of affection;—oh! tell me not *that*—or you will make me very, very miserable indeed!"

Lady Cecilia's bosom was convulsed with sobs as she uttered these words in a rapid and impassioned manner; and as she ceased speaking her head fell upon Reginald's shoulder.

"Compose yourself—compose yourself, Lady Cecilia," exclaimed the clergyman, alarmed by this ebullition of grief, the sincerity of which he could not for one moment suspect. "Do not give way to sorrow—remember the lessons of resignation and patience which you have heard from my lips—remember——"

But the lady sobbed as if her heart would break: her head reclined upon his shoulder—her forehead touched his face—her hand was still clasped in his.

"Oh Reginald!—Reginald!" she murmured, "I cannot love my husband more—no—it is impossible! I love another!"

"You love another!" ejaculated the rector, his whole frame trembling with an ineffable feeling of mingled joy and suspense.

"Yes—and now reproach, revile me—leave me—spurn me—treat me with contempt!" continued Cecilia: "do all this if you will; but never, never can you prevent me from idolizing—adoring you!"

"Cecilia!" cried Reginald Tracy, starting from his seat; "you know not what you are saying!"

"Alas! I know but too well the feelings which my words express," returned the lady, clasping her hands together, and sobbing violently. "Hear me for a few minutes, and then leave me to the misery of my fate—a hopeless love, and a breaking heart!"

"Speak, then, and unburden your mind to me without reserve," said Reginald, resuming his seat upon the sofa, and inviting a confidence the thought of which produced in his mind emotions of bliss and burning joy, the power of which was irresistible.

"Yes, I will speak, even though I render myself contemptible in your sight," continued Cecilia, wiping her eyes and affecting to resume that calmness which she had never lost more than the impassioned actress on the stage, when enacting some melo-dramatic part. "For months and months past I have cherished for you a feeling, the true nature of which has only revealed itself to me within the last few days. In the first instance, I admired your character and your talents: I respected you; and respect and admiration soon ripened into another feeling. You do not know the heart of woman; but it is ever moved by a contemplation of the sublime characteristics of remarkable men—like you. I met you in society, and I almost worshipped the ground on which you trod. I listened to your conversation: not a word was lost to me! During long and sleepless nights your image was ever present to my mind. You became an idol that I adored. At length you yourself, one evening, innocently and unconsciously, fanned the flame that was engendered in my heart: you told me that *I looked well.* That passing compliment rendered me your devoted slave. I thought that no human happiness could be greater than that of pleasing you. I resolved to attend your chapel from that period. I obtained the pew that was nearest to the pulpit; and when you preached I was electrified. Oh! you saw how I was overcome! Your attention to me on that occasion threw additional chains around me. Then you called on me the day before yesterday, and you spoke so kindly that I was every moment on the point of falling at your feet, and exclaiming,—'*Forgive me, but I now know that I love you!*' You proffered me your friendship: how joyously I accepted the sacred gift! And that friendship—oh! let me not forfeit it now—for the love which my heart cherishes for you shall be as pure and taintless as that friendship with which you have blessed me!"

Reginald had listened to this strange confession with the most profound attention;—yes, and with the deepest interest.

A young and beautiful woman had avowed her love for him—she sate near him;—his hand still thrilled with the pressure of hers—his cheek was still warm and flushed with the contact of her white and polished forehead;—the room was involved in obscurity and silence.

She had insinuated herself, in an incredibly short space of time, into his heart, by flattering his vanity and exciting those desires which had hitherto slumbered so profoundly in his breast, but which were now ready to burst with the violence of the long pent-up volcano.

He trembled—he hesitated. At one moment he was inclined to rush from the house, as if from the presence of the tempter; and then he remembered that the love which she had avowed was as pure as his friendship!

Nevertheless, the struggle in his mind was terrific.

Cecilia understood it all.

"You hate me—you despise me," she suddenly exclaimed, covering her face with her hands. "Oh! do not crush me with your contempt—do not abandon me to the conviction of your abhorrence!

Reginald—take pity upon me: forgive me for loving you—forgive me—on my knees I implore you!"

She threw herself before him: she took his hand and pressed it to her lips.

She covered it with kisses.

"Cecilia," murmured the rector, making a faint effort to withdraw his hand.

"No—no, you shall not leave me thus," she exclaimed, with apparent wildness: "I should die if you went away, without telling me that you forgive me! No, you must not leave me thus!"

"Rise, Cecilia—rise—in the name of heaven, rise!" exclaimed Reginald, alarmed lest they should be discovered in that equivocal position: "rise, and I will forgive you. I will do all that you desire—I will not leave you until you are composed."

"And you will return and see me again? you will not withdraw your friendship?" demanded Cecilia, in a soft and melting tone.

"No—never, never!" cried Reginald, enthusiastically, as if he suddenly abandoned himself to the torrent of passion which now swept through his soul.

"Oh! thank you—thank you for that assurance!" exclaimed Cecilia; and, as if yielding to an unconquerable burst of feeling, she threw herself into his arms: "you shall be as a brother to me; and our friendship, our love, shall be eternal!"

Her rich red mouth was pressed upon the rector's lips; her arms were wound around him; and for a moment he yielded to the intoxicating delight of that pleasure so new to him.

But ere he was entirely culpable, his guardian genius struck his soul with a sudden remorse; and, disengaging himself from the syren's arms, he imprinted one long—burning—delicious kiss upon her lips; then, murmuring, "To-morrow, to-morrow, dearest Cecilia, I will see thee again," rushed from the room.

"He is mine!" exclaimed the lady, as the door closed behind him; "irrevocably mine!"

CHAPTER CXXIX.

THE FALL.

Reginald Tracy returned to his own abode, his breast agitated with a variety of conflicting feelings.

He pushed his old housekeeper, who announced to him that dinner was ready, rudely aside, and hurried up to his own chamber.

There he threw himself upon his knees, and endeavoured to pray to be released from temptation.

For he now comprehended all the dangers which beset him, although he suspected not the perfidy and artifice of the tempter.

But not a word of supplication could he utter from the mouth which still burned with the thrilling kisses of the beautiful Cecilia.

He rose from his knees, and paced the room wildly,—at one moment vowing never to see that syren more,—at another longing to rush back to her arms.

The animal passions of that man were strong by nature and threatened to be insatiable whenever let loose; but they had slumbered from his birth, beneath the lethargic influence of high principle and asceticism.

Moreover, they had never been tempted until the present time; and now that temptation came so suddenly, and in so sweet a guise,—came with such irresistible blandishments,—came, in a word, so accompanied with all that could flatter his vanity and minister unto his pride,—that he knew not how to resist its influence.

And at one moment that man of unblemished character and lofty principle fell upon his knees, grovelling as it were at the foot-stool of Him whom he served,—anxious, yearning to crave for courage to escape from the peril that awaited him,—and yet unable to breathe a syllable of prayer. Then he walked in a wild and excited manner up and down, murmuring the name of Cecilia,—pondering upon her charms,—plunging into voluptuous reveries and dreams of vaguely comprehended bliss,—until his desires became of that fiery, hot, and unruly nature, which triumphed over all other considerations.

It was an interesting—and yet an awful spectacle, to behold that man, who could look back over a life of spotless and unblemished purity, now engaged in a terrific warfare with the demons of passion that were raging to cast off their chains, and were struggling furiously for dominion over the proud being who had hitherto held them in silence and in bondage.

But those demons had acquired strength during their long repose; and now that the day of rebellion had arrived, they maintained an avenging and desperate conflict with him who had long been their master. They were like a people goaded to desperation by the atrocities of a blood-thirsty tyrant: they fought a battle in which there was to be no quarter, but wherein one side or the other must succumb.

Hour after hour passed; and still he sustained the conflict with the new feelings which had been excited within him, and which were rapidly crushing all the better sentiments of his soul. At length he retired to bed, a prey to a mental uneasiness which amounted to a torture.

His sleep was agitated and filled with visions by no means calculated to calm the fever of his blood. He awoke in the morning excited, unsettled, and with a desperate longing after pleasures which were as yet vague and undefined to him.

But still a sense of the awful danger which menaced him stole into his mind from time to time; and he shuddered as if he were about to commit a crime.

He left the table, where the morning's meal was untasted, and repaired to his study. But his books had no longer any charm for him: he could not settle his mind to read or write.

He went out, and rambled in all directions, reckless whither he went—but anxious to throw off the spell which had fallen upon him.

Vain was this attempt.

The air was piercing and cold; but his brow was burning. He felt that his cheeks were flushed; and his eyes seemed to shoot forth fire.

"My God! what is the matter with me?" he exclaimed, in his anguish, as he entered Hyde Park, the comparative loneliness of which at that season he thought calculated to soothe his troubled thoughts. "I have tried to pray—and last night, for the first time in my life, I sought my pillow, unable to implore the blessings of my Maker. Oh! what spell has overtaken me? what influence is upon me? Cecilia—Cecilia—is it indeed thou that hast thus changed me?"

He went on,—now musing upon all that had passed within the few preceding days—now breaking forth into wild and passionate exclamations.

He left the Park, and walked rapidly through the streets of the West End.

"No," he said within himself, "I will never see her more. I will conquer these horrible feelings—I will triumph over the mad desires, the fiery cravings which have converted the heaven of my heart into a raging hell! Oh! why is she so beautiful? why did she say that she loved me? Was it to disturb me in my peaceful career—to wean me from my God? No—no: she yielded to an impulse which she could not control;—she loves me—she loves me—she loves me!"

There was a species of insanity in his manner as he thus addressed himself,—not speaking with the lips, but with the heart,—unheard by those who passed him by, but with a voice which vibrated like thunder in his own ears.

"Yes—she loves me," he continued; "but I must fly from her—I must avoid her as if she were a venomous serpent. I dare not trust myself again in her presence: and not for worlds—not for worlds would I be with her alone once more. No,—I must forget her—I must tear her image from my heart—I must trample it under foot!"

He paused as he spoke: he stood still—for he was exhausted.

But how was it that the demon of mischief had, with an under-current of irresistible influence, carried him on, in spite of the force-ful flow of the above reflections, to the very goal of destruction!

He was in Tavistock Square.

He was at the door of Lady Cecilia Harborough's house.

And now for one minute a terrific conflict again raged within him. It seemed as if he collected all his remaining courage to struggle with the demons in his heart; but he was weak with the protracted contest—and they were more powerful than ever.

"I will see her once more," he said, yielding to the influence of his passions: "I will tell her that I stand upon an abyss—I will implore her to have mercy upon me, and permit me to retreat ere yet it be too late!"

His good genius held him faintly back; but his passions goaded him on: he obeyed the latter impulse; he rushed up the steps and knocked at the door.

"Even now I might retreat," he said to himself: "there is still time! I will—I will!"

He turned, and was already half-way down the steps, when the door was opened.

His good resolutions vanished, and he entered the house.

In a few moments more he was in the presence of Lady Cecilia,—Lady Cecilia—looking more bewitching, more captivating than ever!

She had expected him, and had resolved that this visit, on his part, should crown her triumph.

It was in a small parlour adjoining her own boudoir that she received him.

The luxurious sofa was placed near the cheerful fire: the heavy curtains were drawn over the windows in such a manner as to darken the room.

Cecilia was attired in a black silk dress, that she had purposely chosen to enhance the transparent brilliancy of her complexion, and to display the dazzling whiteness of a bust, which, though of small proportions, was of perfect contour.

She was reclining languidly upon the cushions which were piled on one end of the sofa, and her little feet peeped from beneath the skirts of her dress.

She did not rise when Reginald entered the room, but invited him to take a seat near her upon the sofa.

So bewitchingly beautiful did she appear, as the strong glare of the fire played upon her countenance, amidst the semi-obscurity of the room, that he could not resist the signal.

He accordingly sate down by her side.

"Your visit to-day," said Cecilia, "proves to me that you have forgiven the indiscreet confession into which I was yesterday led in a moment of weakness."

"I am come as a friend—as a true and sincere *friend*," returned Reginald, with considerable emphasis upon the last word. "But I know not whether my occupations, my duties, in a word—will permit me to visit you again for some time——"

"Oh! do not deprive me of the pleasure of your society from time to time," interrupted Cecilia, divining all that was passing in the rector's soul, and well aware, by the tremulous tone in which he spoke, that his good resolutions were but unequal opponents to the fury of his newly awakened pleasures.

"Listen, Lady Cecilia," answered Reginald; "and I will tell you frankly the real motives which must compel me to forego the pleasure of your society in future. I tremble for myself!"

"You tremble for yourself!" repeated Cecilia, with ill-concealed joy. "Do you think me, then, so very formidable?"

"Formidable—oh! no," ejaculated Reginald, darting an impassioned glance upon his ravishing companion. "But I consider that you are very beautiful—too beautiful for me thus to seek your presence with impunity."

"Then would you sever that bond of friendship which you yourself proposed so generously, so kindly?" asked Lady Cecilia, placing her hand upon that of the rector, and approaching her countenance towards his as if to read the answer in his eyes.

"It must be so—it must be so—for my peace of mind, Cecilia!" cried Reginald, thrilled by that electric touch, and receiving into his own soul no small portion of that same voluptuousness which animated the fair patrician at that moment.

"It must be so,—oh! cruel resolve!" said Cecilia, pressing his hand between both of hers. "But let me not advance my selfish feelings as a barrier to your interest. Oh! no, Reginald—I would sacrifice every thing to give you pleasure! You shall go—you shall leave me; but you will sometimes think of me—you will occasionally devote a thought to her who has dared to love you!"

"Dared to love me!" exclaimed the rector;—"and what if I——but no—it is madness!"

"Speak—tell me what you were about to say," murmured Cecilia, in a melting tone.

"I was on the point of asking what *you* would think—what opinion you would form of *me*, if I were to confess that I also dared to love you?"

"I should reply that such happiness never could descend upon me," said Cecilia.

"And yet it is true—it is true! I cannot conceal it from myself," exclaimed Reginald, giving way to the influence of his emotions: "it is true—that I love you!"

"Oh! am I indeed so blest?" faltered Cecilia. "Tell me once more that you love me!"

"Love you!" cried the rector, unable to wrestle longer with his mad desires: "I worship—I adore you—I will die for you!"

He caught her in his arms, and covered her with burning and impassioned kisses.

* * * * * * *
* * * * *

Oh, Reginald! and hast thou at length fallen? Have a few short days sufficed to undo and render as naught the purity—the chastity of years?

Where was thy guardian angel in that hour?

Whither had fled that proud virtue which raised thee so high above thy fellow-men, and which gave to thine eloquence the galvanic effect of the most sublime truth?

Look back—look back, with bitterness and sorrow, upon the brilliant career through which thou hast run up to this hour, and curse the madness that prompted thee to darken so bright a destiny!

For thou hast plucked thine own crown of integrity from thy brow, and hast trampled it under foot.

Henceforth, in thine own heart, wilt thou know thyself as a hypocrite and a deceiver!

* * * * * * *
* * * * *

It was past eleven o'clock when Reginald Tracy issued from the abode of Lady Cecilia Harborough.

The night was dark; but from time to time the moon shone for a short interval, as the clouds were swept away from its face.

Reginald paused for a moment upon the steps of the door, and gazed upwards.

The tempestuous aspect of the heavens alarmed him; and a superstitious dread crept, like a death-shudder, over his entire frame; for it seemed to him as if the mansion of the Almighty had put on its sable garb in mourning for a soul that was lost unto the blessings of eternity.

Deeply imbued as he was with a sense of the grand truths of the gospel, this sudden and awful idea speedily assumed so dread a shape in his mind, that he felt alarmed, as if a tremendous gulph were about to open beneath his feet.

He hurried on, hoping to outstrip his thoughts; but that idea pursued him,—haunted him,—every moment increasing in terrific solemnity, until it wore the appearance of a mighty truth instead of a phantom of the imagination.

Again he looked upwards; and the dense sombre clouds, which rolled rapidly like huge black billows over each other, imparted fresh terrors to his guilty soul.

Then his feverish and excited imagination began to invest those clouds with fantastic shapes; and he traced in the midst of the heavens a mighty black hand, the fore-finger of which pointed menacingly *downwards*.

The more he gazed—the more palpable to his mind that apparition became. Half sinking with terror—oppressed with an astounding, a crushing consciousness of his adulterous guilt—the wretched man went wildly on, reckless of the way which he pursued, and every minute casting horror-stricken glances up to the colossal black hand which seemed suspended over his head.

Suddenly a deafening peal of thunder burst above him: he looked frantically up—the hand appeared to wave in a convulsive manner—then the clouds parted, rolling pell-mell over each other,—and the terrific sign was broken into a hundred moving masses.

Never did erring mortal so acutely feel his guilt as Reginald Tracy on this fearful night.

The storm burst forth; and he ran madly on, without aim—a prey to the most appalling reflections.

It was not of this world that he now thought,—it was not on its reproaches, its blame, or its punishment, that his mental looks were fixed;—but it was of eternity that he was afraid.

He trembled when he thought of that Maker whose praise he had so lately sung with pride, and hope, and joy,—and whose name he dared not now invoke!

Oh! his punishment had already begun!

* * * * * * *

* * * * *

Weak, wearied, subdued,—drenched with the rain that had

accompanied the storm; and in a state of mind bordering upon madness and despair, the wretched man reached his home at four o'clock in the morning.

But whither he had wandered, and which way he had taken,—whether he had continued running on, or had rested once or often during that terrific night, he never remembered.

He retired to bed, and slept during several hours. When he awoke, the sun was shining gloriously through his casement; but the horrors and the congenial reflections of darkness had left too fearful an impression upon his mind to be readily effaced; for he was not so inured to vice as to treat with levity the events of the last night,—events which to his superstitious imagination had assumed the aspect of celestial warning and divine menace.

CHAPTER CXXX.

MENTAL STRUGGLES.

THE rector of Saint David's fell upon his knees, and, turning his face towards the casement through which the sun glanced so cheerfully into the chamber, poured forth his soul to the Being of whose universal dominion that radiance seemed an emblem.

Reginald could now pray. He had sinned deeply, and he implored pardon; for he conceived that heaven had deigned to convey a special warning to his mind through the medium of the clouds and the storm of the preceding night.

"Oh! I am not yet totally lost!" he exclaimed, joining his hands fervently together: "I am not yet an outcast from divine mercy! Heaven itself manifests an interest in my welfare: dare I neglect the warning? No—no! I have sinned—but there is repentance. Upon my otherwise spotless life there is one stain; but tears of regret shall be shed unceasingly until the mark be washed away! And thou, temptress—never more must we meet as we have lately met; I must shun thee as my evil genius! Yet I do not blame thee—for I myself was fond, and being fond, was weak. If I fell, and can yet aspire to pardon and forgiveness,—I who was strong,—what extenuation may not exist for thee—a poor, weak woman! Oh! let the light of divine grace shine in upon my soul, even as these bright beams of the orb of day penetrate with cheering influence to my very heart! Let me rise up from the depths of sin, stronger than when I fell,—so that sad experience may tend to confirm my resolves to pursue the paths of chastity and virtue!"

Thus spoke aloud Reginald Tracy, as he knelt in his chamber the day after his fall: thus did he breathe vows of future self-denial and purity. He rose resigned, and penitent,—though at intervals a species of struggle took place in his breast—a conflict between his recently-experienced sensations of amorous delight and his present resolutions of abstinence from carnal pleasures.

In a moment when his better feelings were predominant, he wrote a brief letter to Lady Cecilia, imploring her to forget all that had taken place between them, and enjoining her, if she entertained the slightest interest in his earthly and immortal welfare, never to seek to see him again.

Then Reginald gathered all his most valued books around him, and plunged into his studies with an earnestness which augured well for the strength and permanency of his good resolutions.

This occupation was for a few minutes disturbed by a note from Lady Cecilia, imploring a last interview ere they parted for ever:—but the rector was immoveable in his present precautionary conduct; and he answered her, not angrily, but firmly, to beseech her not to "lead him into temptation."

Yes, this man of fiery passions wrestled gallantly with his inclinations: the combat was at times a fearful one; but he exerted all his strength, and all his power, and all his energy, to subdue those desires which were smouldering, and were not quenched, at the bottom of his soul.

It was in the evening of the fourth day after the rector's fall from the pedestal of his purity, that his studies were interrupted by the entrance of his house-keeper, who informed him that a gentleman desired to speak to him.

The rector ordered the visitor to be admitted; and Mr. Richard Markham was announced.

The object of our hero's call was speedily explained.

Mr. Monroe was lying in a dangerous state, and his life was despaired of. Mr. Wentworth, the surgeon, who attended upon him, had recommended him to settle all his earthly affairs, and prepare his soul to meet his Creator; and the old man, who was fully sensible of the importance of this advice, had expressed a wish to receive spiritual consolation from a minister whose sanctity had become proverbial.

"The desire of my dying friend," added Markham, "must serve as an apology for my intrusion upon you; but, I implore you, reverend sir, not to hesitate to soothe by your much-coveted presence the passage of a fellow-creature from this world to a better."

But for a moment the rector *did* hesitate:—was he fit to minister divine consolation to another,—he who was still deeply dyed with sin himself?

Such was the thought which floated rapidly through his imagination.

Richard urged his request with eloquence.

Reginald Tracy felt that he could offer no sufficient excuse, short of the revelation of his own guilt, for refusing to attend the death-bed of one who craved his presence; and he agreed to accompany the young man to Markham Place.

Richard had a vehicle at the door; and in a short time they reached our hero's abode.

Reginald was conducted to the room where Monroe lay.

Hanging over the pillow, on which the invalid reclined, was a charming female form, from whose bosom deep sobs emanated, and rendered almost inaudible the words of strangely commingled hope and despair which she addressed to her father.

She did not hear the door open; and it was only when Richard approached the bed, and whispered that the Reverend Mr. Tracy was present, that she raised her tearful countenance.

Then did the eyes of the rector glance upon one of the most lovely beings whom Nature ever invested with all her choicest gifts; and—even in that solemn moment when he stood by the bed of one who was pronounced to be dying—his soul was stirred by the presence of that transcendent beauty.

"Oh! sir," exclaimed Ellen, in that musical voice which was now rendered tremulous by deep emotions, "how grateful am I for this prompt attention to the wish of my dear—dear father!"

"I deserve no gratitude for the performance of a Christian duty," answered the rector, as he approached the bed.

Markham took Ellen's hand and led her from the chamber, in

order to allow unrestrained converse between the clergyman and the invalid.

An hour elapsed, and the bell of the sick-room rang.

Ellen hurried thither, and found her father composed and resigned to meet his fate. The rector sate by his bed-side.

"This holy man," said Monroe, "has taught me how to die like a true Christian. Weep not, dearest Ellen; we shall meet again hereafter."

"Oh, my dearest father," exclaimed the young lady, bursting into an agony of tears; "it is I—I who have murdered you! My conduct——"

"Silence, Ellen—accuse not yourself in that dreadful manner," interrupted her father.

Reginald was astonished at the words which had just fallen from the daughter's lips; and he surveyed her with increased interest and curiosity.

At that moment Mr. Wentworth entered the room. He found the invalid better, and his countenance was animated with a ray of hope.

This expression of his inward feelings was not lost upon Ellen; and she interrogated him with a rapid and imploring glance.

"Mr. Monroe must be kept very—very quiet," said the surgeon in a whisper, which was addressed to both Ellen and Reginald Tracy.

"And then—there is hope?" murmured Ellen in breathless suspense.

"Yes—there is hope," repeated the surgeon solemnly.

"May heaven be thanked for that assurance on your part," said Ellen, fervently.

The rector contemplated her with an admiration which he could not restrain; and, in spite of himself, the thought flashed across his mind, how far more lovely was Miss Ellen Monroe than Lady Cecilia Harborough!

Then, indignant with himself for having allowed the comparison to force itself upon his attention, he rose to take his departure.

The invalid had just sunk into a deep slumber; and Mr. Wentworth intimated his intention of passing the night by his side.

"I will call again to-morrow morning," said Reginald, addressing Miss Monroe; "for I perceive that this gentleman is not without hopes."

"Thank you—thank you, sir, for your kindness," answered Ellen with grateful enthusiasm. "Your presence seems to have brought a blessing into this sick-room."

She extended her hand towards him, and he pressed it for a moment in his.

His whole frame seemed electrified with a sudden glow; and he hurried somewhat abruptly from the room.

When he reached his own abode once more, he felt a profound melancholy steal into his soul; for he seemed more lonely, and more solitary than he ever yet had been.

He retired to rest, and his dreams were filled with the images of Cecilia and Ellen.

When he awoke in the morning, he was discontented with himself—with the whole world: he experienced vague longings after excitement or change of scene;—he could not settle himself, as on the four previous days, to his studies;—his books were hateful to him. He wandered about his house—from room to room—as if in search of something which he could not define, and which he did not discover: he was pursued by ideas only dimly comprehensible, but which were at variance with his recently formed resolutions of purity and virtue. He was restless—discontented—uneasy.

At length he remembered his promise to return to Markham Place. The idea seemed to give him pleasure: he longed to see Ellen Monroe once more;—and yet he did not choose to make this admission to himself.

With a beating heart did he cross the threshold of the house in which that delightful vision had burst, as it were, upon his sight on the previous evening. He was immediately conducted to the sick-room, where Ellen was sitting alone by her father's bed-side.

The old man slept.

Ellen rose and tripped lightly to meet him, a smile upon her charming, though pale and somewhat care-worn countenance.

Laying her hand gently upon his, she whispered, "He will recover! Mr. Wentworth assures me that he will recover!"

"Most sincerely do I congratulate you upon this happy change," said Reginald. "I can well comprehend the feelings of an affectionate daughter who is allowed to hope that her parent may be restored to her."

"Yes, sir—and so good a father as mine!" added Ellen. "But it was all my fault——"

Then, suddenly checking herself, she cast down her eyes, and blushed deeply.

"Your fault, Miss Monroe?" repeated the rector, inspired with the most lively curiosity to penetrate the mystery of that self-accusation which he had now heard for the second time: "I cannot believe that any fault of yours—you whom I found hanging over your beloved father——"

"Let us speak no more upon that subject," interrupted Ellen, vexed with herself for having so unguardedly said what she had relative to the primal cause of her father's dangerous illness. "He will recover—something tells me that he will recover; and then—oh! how I will cherish him—how I will exert myself to make the remainder of his days happy!"

Her countenance became flushed as she spoke; and Reginald's glances were fixed, by a species of invincible fascination, upon the beautiful being in whose presence he stood.

He felt at that moment that he could sacrifice every thing for her love.

The surgeon and Richard Markham now entered the apartment; and Reginald received the thanks of our young hero for the attention which he had shown to the old man whose life had ceased to be despaired of.

After a somewhat protracted visit, the rector took his leave.

But throughout that day Ellen alone occupied all his thoughts. What fault of hers could have thrown her father upon a bed of sickness, whose only termination was at one time anticipated to be in death? what could have been the conduct of so fond a daughter to have produced such terrible results? Had she strayed from the path of virtue? This was the only feasible solution of such a mystery. Then a terrible pang of jealousy shot through his breast.

And why should he be jealous? What was that young girl to him?

He was jealous, because his ardent passions instinctively attracted him towards that beautiful creature;—and she was every thing to him, because she *was* so beautiful, and because he desired her!

Yes—a new flame now burnt in his heart—a flame as violent, as relentless, as fierce, as that which had already made him the slave of Lady Cecilia Harborough. But was he this time to become a slave or a victim?

He sat down and reasoned with himself. He endeavoured to crush the feelings of licentiousness which had been re-awakened in his heart.

But as vainly might he have endeavoured to lull the Maelstroom with a breath, or to subdue the rage of Vesuvius with a drop of water!

Such was his frame of mind, when an old woman sought his presence in the evening.

He had made it a rule, throughout his career, never to be difficult of access to those who wished to see him; and now that he felt the fabric of his fair fame to be tottering upon the verge of a precipice, he was not inclined to deviate from any of those outward forms which had aided in the consecration of his renown. He accordingly ordered his housekeeper to admit the old woman to his presence.

The instant a hag, with a horribly wrinkled countenance, entered his study, he started—for that repulsive face was not altogether unknown to him.

Then, in another moment, he remembered that he had once seen her standing at the door of Lady Cecilia Harborough's abode in Tavistock Square; and that the glance which she had thrown upon him, on that occasion had for an instant struck him with sinister foreboding.

The old woman seated herself, and, without any preamble, said: "A man of great learning like you, reverend sir, cannot be otherwise than a man of great taste. This conviction has emboldened me to call upon you in preference to any other, relative to a most perfect work of art which fortune has thrown in my way."

Reginald gazed upon the old woman in speechless astonishment: her mysterious—indeed, incomprehensible language, induced him to believe that she was some unfortunate creature bereaved of her right senses.

"Listen to me for a few minutes, reverend sir," continued the hag, "and I will explain my meaning to you. Your charity, as well as your taste, is about to be appealed to."

"Speak," said the clergyman, somewhat impatiently, for he longed to be left alone again with his reflections, which had just assumed a most voluptuous complexion when his privacy was thus intruded upon.

"I will not detain you long—I will not detain you long," cried the old hag. "You must know, reverend sir, that a foreign sculptor—a poor

Italian—came some few months ago to lodge at my humble dwelling. He was in the deepest distress, and had not the means to procure either marble or tools. I am very poor—very poor, myself, sir; but I could not see a fellow-creature starving. I bought him marble—and I bought him tools. He went to work, toiling day and night almost unweariedly; and a week ago he put the finishing stroke to the statue of a nymph. His art has enabled him, by means of colour, to give a life-like appearance to that admirable work of art; so that as you contemplate it, it seems to you as if the eyes were animated, the lips breathed, and the bosom rose and sank with respiration."

"And your artist is, no doubt, anxious to dispose of his statue?" said the rector.

"Precisely so," answered the hag. "I do not profess to be a judge myself; but I can speak of the effect which it produced upon me. When I saw it finished—standing upon its pedestal—I was about to address it as a living being."

"The effect must, then, be indeed striking," observed Reginald, with the voluptuous train of whose ideas this picture was well adapted to associate.

"Were you to judge for yourself, reverend sir," said the old hag, "you would find that I have not overrated the perfection of this masterpiece. The sculptor demands but a small price for his statue—it would be a charity were you to purchase it yourself, or recommend one of your friends to do so."

"When and where could I see this matchless work of art?" asked Reginald, whose curiosity was now strangely excited.

"At my own humble dwelling in Golden Lane is this statue concealed," replied the horrible old hag; "and no mortal eyes, save the sculptor's and mine own, have yet glanced upon it. If you will accompany me now, you can inspect it without delay."

Reginald referred to his watch, and found that it was past nine o'clock. The evening was pitch dark; and he did not, therefore, dread being seen in the company of that hideous old woman. Besides, even if he were—was he not often summoned at all hours to attend upon the last moments of some dying sinner?

"I will proceed with you at once to your abode," said the rector, after a few moments' hesitation.

"And you will do well," answered the hag; "for I can promise you a fine treat in what you are about to see."

While the rector stepped aside to put on his cloak and hat, a strange smile curled the lips of the wrinkled harridan; but as Reginald again turned towards her, her countenance instantly resumed its wonted composure.

They then went out together.

CHAPTER CXXXI.

THE STATUE.

The old woman led the way at a rapid pace towards Golden Lane, the rector following her at a little distance.

Although there was nothing improbable in the tale which the hag had told him, and nothing improper in the step which he was taking,—nevertheless he experienced a vague and undefinable idea of doing wrong.

Something told him that he ought to retreat; and at the same time a superior influence urged him onward.

And, therefore, he followed the old woman.

The wrinkled creature pursued her way, and at length turned into the dark and dirty court with which the reader is already well acquainted.

"This is a strange place, you will say," observed the old woman, as she pushed open the door of one of the houses in that court,—"this is a strange place to contain such a treasure—"

"And for that reason the treasure should not long be allowed to remain here," answered the clergyman.

The hag chuckled:—the sound was between a hollow laugh and a death-rattle; and it seemed horrible to the ears of Reginald Tracy.

The old woman then slowly ascended the narrow and dark staircase, until she reached the landing, where she drew a key from her pocket, and leisurely applied it to the lock of a door.

She fumbled about so long with the key, muttering to herself all the while, that Reginald thought she would never open the door, and he offered to assist her.

But at that moment the key turned in the lock, and the door was slowly opened.

The hag beckoned the rector to follow her; and he found himself in a tolerably large room, decently furnished, and with an excellent fire burning in the grate.

There were no candles lighted; nor did the hag offer to provide any;—but the contents of the apartment were plainly visible by means of the strong glare of the fire.

Heavy curtains of a dark colour covered the windows: the floor was carpeted; the chairs and tables were of plain but solid material; and a large mirror stood over the mantel.

At the farther end of the room was a second door, which was now closed, but evidently communicated with an inner chamber.

"I gave the poor artist the best rooms in my house," observed the hag, as she placed a chair near the fire for the rector. "The statue stands in the adjoining chamber; you can inspect it at once, while I——"

She mumbled the remainder of the sentence in such a way that it was wholly unintelligible to the rector, and then left the room.

For a few minutes Reginald stood before the fire, uncertain what course to pursue. He now began to think that the entire proceeding was somewhat extraordinary; and the singular manner in which the old hag had left him, inspired him with a feeling not entirely free from alarm.

But for what purpose could he have been inveigled thither, if it were not really to behold the marvellous statue? and, perhaps, after all, the old woman had only left him in order to fetch the candles or to summon the artist? Moreover, had she not informed him that the statue was in the next room, and that he might inspect it at once? It was therefore easy to satisfy himself whether he had been deceived or not.

Ashamed of his transient fears, he threw off his hat and cloak, and advanced towards the door communicating with the inner chamber.

Even then he hesitated for a minute as his fingers grasped the handle; but, at length, he boldly entered the room.

The moment the door was thrown open, he perceived by the light of the fire which burned in the front apartment, that the inner one was a small and comfortably fitted up bed-chamber. It was involved in a more than semi-obscurity; but not to such an extent as to conceal from Reginald Tracy's penetrating glance the semblance of a female form standing upon a low pedestal in the most remote corner of the room.

"I am not then deceived!" he exclaimed aloud, as he advanced nearer towards the statue.

By this time his eyes had become accustomed to the obscurity of the chamber, into which the glimmer of the fire threw a faint but mellowed light. Still, in somewhat bold relief, against the dark wall, stood the object of his interest,—seeming a beautiful model of a female form, the colouring of which was that of life. It was naked to the middle; the arms were gracefully rounded; and one hand sustained the falling drapery which, being also coloured, produced upon the mind of the beholder the effect of real garments.

Lost in wonder at the success with which the sculptor had performed his work,—and experiencing feelings of a soft and voluptuous nature,—Reginald drew closer to the statue. At that moment the light of the fire played upon its countenance; and it seemed to him as if the lips moved with a faint smile. Then, how was his surprise increased, when the conviction flashed to his mind that the face he was gazing upon was well known to him!

"O Cecilia, Cecilia!" he ejaculated aloud: "hast thou sent thy statue hither to compel me to fall at its feet and worship the senseless stone, while thou—the sweet original—art elsewhere, speculating perhaps upon the emotions which this phantasmagorian sport was calculated to conjure up within me! Ah! Cecilia, if thou wast resolved to subdue me once more—if thou couldst not rest until I became thy slave again,—oh! why not have invited me to meet thine own sweet self, instead of this speechless, motionless, passionless image,—a counterpart of thee only in external loveliness! Yes—there it is perfect:—the hair—the brow—the eyes—the mouth——Heavens! those lips seem to smile once more; those eyes sparkle with real fire! Cecilia—Cecilia—"

And Reginald Tracy was afraid—he scarcely knew wherefore: the entire adventure of the evening appeared to be a dream.

"Yes—yes!" he suddenly exclaimed, after having steadfastly contemplated the form before him for some moments,—standing at a distance of only three or four paces,—afraid to advance nearer,

unwilling to retreat altogether,—"yes!" he exclaimed, "there is something more than mere senseless marble here! The eyes shoot fire—the lips smile—the bosom heaves——Oh! Cecilia—Cecilia, it is yourself!"

As he spoke he rushed forward: the statue burst from chill marble into warmth and life;—it was indeed the beauteous but wily Cecilia—who returned his embrace and hung around his neck;—and the rector was again subdued—again enslaved!

* * * * * * *

* * * * *

"And you will pardon me for the little stratagem which I adopted to bring you back to my arms?" said Cecilia.

"How can I do otherwise than pardon you?" murmured the rector, whose licentious soul was occupied only with gross delights, and who would at that moment have dared exposure and disgrace rather than tear himself away from the syren on whose bosom his head was pillowed. "Oh! Cecilia, I have had a violent struggle with my feelings; but I shall now contend against them no more. No! from this instant I abandon all hope of empire—all wish for dominion over myself; I yield myself up to the pleasures of love and to thee! Sweet Cecilia, thou hast taught me how ineffable is the bliss which mortals may taste in this world;—and after all, the sure present is preferable to the uncertain future!"

"Reginald—beloved Reginald, didst thou imagine that I would resign thee so easily as thou wouldst have resigned me!" said Lady Cecilia. "Oh! you know not the heart of woman! There were but two alternatives for me—to bring you back, or to avenge myself on you."

"Avenge yourself!" exclaimed Reginald, starting.

"Yes," replied the wily creature, purposely adopting this discourse in order to enchain her lover in future; "a woman who fondly—madly loves, as I love, Reginald—will not so willingly part with the object of her affection! What,—could you suppose that I would surrender myself to you one day to be abandoned the next? No—never, never would I permit myself to be made the victim of a caprice! You wrote to me to implore me not to seek to see you again: I requested one last interview—you refused me my demand! Then I smarted sorely; but I said to myself, *'He loves me;'* and I added, *'I love him also.'* I accordingly resolved to attempt one grand effort to draw the anchorite from his cell. Chance threw in my way the old woman whom I sent to you, and in whose house we now are——"

"And what chance was that?" demanded Reginald, who entertained a strong and yet unaccountable aversion for that old hag.

"I will tell you all, dearest Reginald," answered Cecilia. "The evening after I received your cruel note desiring that all might end between us, I was going out with the intention of calling upon *you*—yes, of throwing myself at your feet——"

"Imprudent Cecilia!" murmured the rector, imprinting a kiss upon her lips.

"Yes—I was on the point of leaving my own abode to seek yours," continued Cecilia, "when I heard a hoarse and ominous voice muttering behind me. I looked round, and perceived that old wretch. She smiled—or rather, leered significantly, and said, *'Happy, happy lady—to enjoy the rector of Saint David's love!'*"

"She said *that!*" cried Reginald. "How could she divine what passed between us?"

"She has since explained to me how she one evening saw you leave my house—with a certain wildness in your manner——"

"True! true!" ejaculated the rector; "and the mind of the old woman being perhaps naturally evil, she conceived evil of others on the faintest suspicion."

"Exactly," answered Cecilia. "When she accosted me in that manner, I was so wretched, so miserable at the idea of being separated from you——"

"Sweetest creature! I was, indeed, ungrateful in return for so much love!"

"I was so unhappy that I was even glad to speak of thee to such a wretch as that old creature. Then she uttered words of consolation, and we talked together—talked for an hour in the cold, damp street——"

"Poor Cecilia!" murmured Reginald.

"What would I not dare for you?" said the wily woman, pressing him warmly in her snowy arms. "And now you can guess the rest—how the old woman proposed that some stratagem should be invented to bring the recreant back to my arms——"

"And you have thus blindly confided yourself—not only *your* secret, but *mine* also—to a perfect stranger? O, Cecilia—was this prudent?" exclaimed Reginald in alarm.

"Does love know prudence?" asked the lady. "But fear not: gold will seal the lips of our confidant; and better is it for her obscure dwelling to be the scene of our loves than for our caresses to be exchanged at my abode, where the intrusion of a servant at any moment——"

"True!" interrupted Reginald. "And yet upon what a fearful abyss does my reputation now seem to tremble!"

"*Yours!*" ejaculated Lady Cecilia, almost scornfully,—for she was resolved to put an end to these repinings on the part of her lover: "Oh! can you be so selfish as to think only of yourself? Should you be detected, you are ruined only in your profession, and not as a man—for with the man there is no dishonour in illicit love;—but if I be detected, am I not lost as a wife, and as a woman? Will not all the wrath of an avenging society light upon me? For it is upon us—upon poor woman—that contumely, and shame, and disgrace fall!"

"Forgive me, dearest Cecilia," murmured the rector, clasping the frail beauty in his arms. "I have been unjust to you—I have thought only of myself, unmindful of the immense sacrifice that is made by thee! But, forgive me, I say—and never again shall the expression of my cowardly alarms—my egotistical terrors impair our happiness! I love you—I love you, my Cecilia: Oh! heaven knows how sincerely—how madly I love you!"

"And you will love me always?" whispered Cecilia.

"Always! for ever—and ever!" answered the rector, now intoxicated—delirious with joy, and reckless of all consequences.

* * * * * * *
* * * * *

The barrier was now completely broken down; and the rector gave way to the violence of the passion which hurried him along.

That man, so full of vigour, and in the prime of his physical strength, abandoned himself without restraint to the fury of those desires which burnt the more madly—the more wildly, from having been so long pent-up.

Day after day did he meet his guilty paramour; and on each occasion did he reflect less upon the necessity of caution. He passed hours and hours together with her at her abode; and at length he ventured to receive her at his own residence, when his housekeeper had retired to rest.

But he did not neglect his professional duties on the Sabbath;—and he now became an accomplished hypocrite. He ascended the pulpit as usual, and charmed thousands with his discourse as heretofore. Indeed his eloquence improved, for the simulated earnestness which displaced the tone of heart-felt conviction that he had once experienced, seemed more impassioned, and was more impressive than the natural ebullition of his feelings.

Thus as he progressed in the ways of vice, his reputation increased in sanctity.

But the moment he escaped from the duties of his profession, he flew to the arms of her who had seduced him from his career of purity; and so infatuated was he with her who had been his tutoress in the ways of amorous pleasure, that he joyfully placed his purse at the disposal of her extravagance.

Thus was Lady Cecilia triumphant in all points with regard to the once immaculate, but now sensual and voluptuous rector of Saint David's.

CHAPTER CXXXII.

AN OLD FRIEND.

Let us now return to the Rattlesnake, whom we left in the act of flying from the pursuit which she knew would be undertaken in respect to her by the Resurrection Man.

Having bade farewell to Mrs. Chichester at Cambridge Heath, Margaret Flathers, with her well-filled bag under her arm, hastened along the road leading to Hackney.

She cared not which direction she pursued, provided she placed a considerable distance between herself and London; for so terrible was the dread under which she laboured from her knowledge of the desperate character and profound cunning of the Resurrection Man, that she conceived it to be impossible for her to be safe so long as she was within even a wide circuit of the great metropolis.

Having passed through Hackney, she speedily left the main road, and struck at random across the fields, careful only to pursue a course which she felt convinced must remove her further and further from London.

Unweariedly for two long hours did she hurry on her way, until she fell, overcome with weariness, beneath a large tree, whose gigantic leafless boughs creaked ominously in the darkness over her head.

The night was fearfully cold—the grass was damp—and the wind moaned gloomily through the trees.

The Rattlesnake was hungry and thirsty; but she had not food nor drink to satisfy the cravings of nature. In that solitude,—without a light gleaming through the obscurity as a beacon of hospitality,—she felt that her gold was then and there no better to her than the cold soil upon which she rested her weary limbs.

At length, worn out by fatigue and want, she fell asleep.

When she awoke the sun was shining.

But where was she?

Close at hand burnt a blazing fire, fed with wood and turf, and sending up a dense smoke into the fine frosty air. To an iron rod, fastened horizontally to two upright stakes, was suspended a huge caldron, the bubbling of which reached her ears, and the savour of whose contents was wafted most agreeably to her nostrils.

Grouped around the fire, and anxiously watching the culinary process, were two women, four men, and a boy.

Two of the men were not characterised by that swarthy complexion and those black elf-locks which distinguished their two male companions, the women, and the boy.

Of the two men thus especially alluded to, as not being of the gipsy race, to which their companions evidently belonged,—the first was about forty years of age and possessed a herculean form. His countenance was weather-beaten and indicated the endurance of great hardship: indeed, he had been abroad to far-off climes, and had gone through privations of an almost incredible nature. He was, however, taciturn and reserved, and ever seemed brooding upon some secret grief or absorbing sentiment of a darker nature: nevertheless, the little he had chosen to tell his present companions relative to his former history had obtained for him the name of the *Traveller*; and by no other appellation was he known amongst them.

The other man, whose complexion proclaimed him not to be of the Egyptian race, was apparently verging towards thirty; and, although slight, he was well-built and uncommonly active. His name will transpire presently.

The elder of the two male gipsies was a man of nearly eighty years of age. His hair was as white as driven snow; and his bald head was protected from the cold wind by only a thin faded green silk skull-cap. His beard, as white as his hair, hung down over his breast, and formed a strange contrast with his swarthy countenance and piercing black eyes, the fires of which were not dimmed with age. This individual was the King of the Gipsies, and rejoiced in the assumed name of Zingary.

The other male gipsy was the King's son, and was a fine tall handsome fellow of about thirty-five, dark as a Spaniard, and with fine Roman features.

The two women were also very discrepant in respect to age: one was nearly sixty, and was the Queen of the Gipsies, her assumed name being Aischa: the other was a pretty brunette, with fine laughing eyes and brilliant teeth, and was the wife of Morcar, the King's son. Her name was Eva; and she was the mother of the boy before alluded to, and who was between eight and nine years old.

We have thought it as well to state all these particulars at once in order to avoid confusion; although the Rattlesnake was not immediately aware of them.

When the Rattlesnake awoke up and surveyed this strange group, she instinctively felt for her bag of gold; and a scream of dismay escaped her lips when she perceived that it was gone.

A loud burst of laughter emanated from the gipsies,—for by this general name we shall denominate the band, although two members of it were not of the race;—and the fair-complexioned man, whose name we have not yet stated, exclaimed, "Don't alarm yourself, my dear young woman: we have banked the rag[1] for fear that a buzman[2] should have nabbed you with it in your possession. But you shall have your reg'lars out of it, mind, whenever you want to pursue your way. Only, as you've happened to trespass upon the dominions of his high mightiness King Zingary, you must pay toll."

While this individual was speaking, the Rattlesnake, who had first been struck by the tone of his voice, considered him with great attention, and seemed to forget the loss she had sustained in the interest with which she contemplated the person addressing her.

At length, when he had ceased to speak, she started from the ground, advanced towards him, and exclaimed in an excited tone, "Have not you and I met before?"

"Not unlikely, my dear," was the reply. "Perhaps under the screw[3]—or in the Holy Land,[4] which I visit from time to time—or else in the bottom of a coal-hell[5] in the county of Stafford."

"It is! it is!" ejaculated the Rattlesnake, ready to spring towards him, and throw her arms around his neck. "Don't you remember me now?"

"Remember you?" repeated the man slowly, and he gazed upon the Rattlesnake's countenance for some moments;—then, as if a sudden light dawned in upon him, he started from the ground in his

1 Secured the money. [Reynolds's note.]
2 Informer—spy. [Reynolds's note.]
3 In prison. [Reynolds's note.]
4 St. Giles's. [Reynolds's note.]
5 Coal-mine. [Reynolds's note.]

turn, crying, "May I never drink rum slim[1] again if it isn't my old flame, Meg Flathers!"

And they flew into each other's arms.

"Your Majesty," said Skilligalee,—for this was the individual whose name we for a moment suppressed, "Your Majesty," he exclaimed, when this embrace was over, "allow me to present to you my wife, the lovely and accomplished Margaret Flathers."

"She is welcome," said Zingary gravely. "Young woman, sit down and be welcome. We ask no questions whether you are our comrade's splice[2] or not: it is enough for us that he acknowledges you as such. Aischa—welcome a daughter; Eva—greet a sister."

The old and the young gipsy women advanced towards the Rattlesnake and took each a hand.

"I welcome you, daughter," said Aischa.

"I greet you, sister," said Eva.

They then each kissed her forehead, and resumed their seats close by the fire.

"And I greet you too, my gal," exclaimed Morcar, thrusting out his large muscular hand, and giving that of the Rattlesnake a friendly squeeze.

"And now sit down," said the King, "and moisten your chaffer."[3]

"Ah! do," cried Morcar; "for you must want it after sleeping underneath that tree on the top of the hill, exposed to the cold wind and damp."

This observation led the Rattlesnake to cast a glance around her; and she found that the gipsy camp was at the bottom of a deep valley, on the brow of which stood the tree to which the King's son pointed, and beneath which she had sunk exhausted on the preceding night.

Meantime Skilligalee had visited a covered van, which stood at a little distance, and near which an old horse was quietly munching the contents of a capacious nose-bag; and, in a few moments he returned, bearing with him a large stone bottle that might have held two gallons of liquor.

From his pocket he produced a small horn-cup; and, pouring forth a bumper of rum, he handed it to the queen.

1 Rum-punch. [Reynolds's note.]
2 Wife. [Reynolds's note.]
3 Take something to drink. [Reynolds's note.]

"No—there first," laconically said Aischa, pointing towards the Rattlesnake, who was accordingly compelled to drain the horn before her majesty.

"Good—isn't it?" asked Skilligalee, with a sly wink.

"I felt very cold—and it has revived me," replied the Rattlesnake.

"And the contents of that pot will put you right altogether," said Skilligalee, pointing to the caldron that was simmering over the fire. "Beg pardon, majesty," he added, turning towards the queen, and pouring forth another dram.

Aischa drank the contents of the horn-cup without winking; and Skilligalee proceeded to do the honours of the bottle to the rest of the company.

Having served the king, Eva, and Morcar, he approached the Traveller, who had sat a silent spectator of all that passed.

"Now, friend, your turn is come."

"Thank you," said the man, drily; and having tossed off the liquor, he muttered, grinding his teeth savagely, "And some one else's turn must come too, sooner or later."

"Always brooding upon the same thing," exclaimed the laughing, light-hearted Skilligalee.

"And if you had been served by a villain as I was," returned the Traveller, brutally, "you would long for the time to come to settle up accounts with him. Thank my stars! we shall be in London to-morrow, and then—then——"

The remainder of the man's words were lost in mutterings, which, to judge by the terrific workings of his countenance, the violence with which he ground his teeth, and the convulsive rage indicated by the manner in which he clenched his fist, must have been a direful portent.

But a few words which he had uttered, struck sudden dismay to the heart of the Rattlesnake.

"Are you going to London?" she whispered, in a tone of alarm, to Skilligalee, who had now resumed his seat by her side.

"Ah! indeed are we, my dear," was the reply. "The royal palace in the Holy Land is prepared for our reception; and this night at nine o'clock does his majesty make his triumphant entry, disguised as a timber-merchant,[1] into that part of his dominions."

---

1 Beggar with Matches. [Reynolds's note.]

"To London!" gasped the Rattlesnake. "Then—then—I cannot accompany you—I——"

"What have you to fear?" demanded Skilligalee. "Have you not me to defend you individually, and his majesty's protection to shield you generally?"

"No—no," returned Margaret Flathers; "I cannot—will not return to London. I hate the place—I detest it—I abhor it! I am not even now as far from it as I could wish—not half."

"Far from it?" ejaculated Skilligalee, with a merry laugh. "Why, you can almost hear the sounds of the cabs and hackney-coaches where we are now."

"What!" cried Margaret. "How far are we from London? tell me—speak!"

"When you are on the top of that place where I found you sleeping early this morning," answered Skilligalee, "you can see Hornsey Wood on the next hill—about two miles off."

"My God! then in spite of all my care last night, I must have gone a strange round," said Margaret, speaking rather to herself than to her companion.

"Ah! I see how it is, Meg," observed Skilligalee; "you are in trouble about that gold. Well—never mind, old gal—so much the more reason for me to protect you. Now I tell you what it is: not all the buzmen in London can find you out at our crib in the Holy Land; and so you shall come along with us, and you shall keep in doors the whole time: we'll take care of you. What do you think of that?"

"Skilligalee," whispered Margaret, "I am not afraid of the police: they don't trouble themselves about me. But there is a certain man that seeks my life——"

"Oh! if that's all," interrupted her companion, "make yourself perfectly easy. You don't know yet what defences and fortifications the king has got to his palace: a regiment of swaddies[1] would never storm it, or take it by surprise."

"And you really think that I shall be safe?" asked the Rattlesnake, hesitating; for these assurances of protection began to please her more than the idea of being compelled to wander alone about the country.

"Think!" cried Skilligalee, "I don't think—I'm certain. Trust to

1 Soldiers. [Reynolds's note.]

me—and all will be right. Besides, do you not pay toll to his majesty? and where can you find a more powerful protector than King Zingary? You will see what he can do, when once we arrive at the palace in the Holy Land."

"But—but—will he keep all my gold?" asked the Rattlesnake, hesitatingly.

"Not all, my dear," answered Skilligalee. "One third goes to the Box;[1] another third to be divided amongst all us here who picked you up; and the other remains at your own disposal. Are you content?"

"Quite," said the Rattlesnake, knowing full well that it was no use to remonstrate, and not unwilling, moreover, to pay handsomely for the protection promised to her.

While this conversation took place between the Rattlesnake and Skilligalee, the two women had prepared the repast. The king had in the meantime amused himself with what, in his own lingo, he termed "cocking a broseley;"[2] the boy fetched the platters, knives, forks, spoons, and other articles necessary for the meal, from the van;—Morcar went to look after the horse;—and the Traveller was buried in a profound reverie. Thus the discourse of Margaret Flathers and her companion was as private and unrestrained as if no one had been by.

And now the immediate vicinity of the fire presented an animated and even comfortable appearance. Upon a huge earthenware dish was piled a stew, which sent forth a most inviting odour. A goose, a sucking-pig, three fowls, a couple of rabbits, and an immense quantity of vegetables, greeted the eye and pleased the olfactory nerve; and a couple of jolly brown quartern loaves flanked the feast. Every guest was furnished with a horn snicker:[3] salt, pepper, and mustard were also provided, to give a zest to the food. Then Skilligalee paid another visit to the van,—for he, it appears, was butler in ordinary to his Majesty King Zingary,—and returned laden with a second enormous bottle, filled to the bung with the very best malt liquor that ever aided to immortalize Barclay and Perkins.

"All is ready," said Eva, in a respectful manner to her father-in-law, the King.

1 Treasury. [Reynolds's note.]
2 Smoking a pipe. [Reynolds's note.]
3 Drinking mug. [Reynolds's note.]

Zingary stroked down his beard in a majestic manner, murmured a grace in a language totally incomprehensible to the Rattlesnake, and then helped himself to a portion of the mess.

This was the signal for the attack; and Margaret Flathers was by no means sorry to receive upon her platter, from the gallant and attentive Skilligalee, a good proportion of the savoury comestibles.

The Traveller did his duty in respect to the repast; but he seldom joined in the gay discourse which seasoned it, apparently brooding over the one absorbing idea of vengeance, which now seemed to constitute the only object for which that man lived.

Margaret Flathers could not help noticing the great respect which all present paid to the King and Queen of the Gipsies. Their majesties joined familiarly in the conversation; and it was evident from their remarks, especially those of Zingary, that they had travelled over every inch of Great Britain, not a crevice or corner of which was unknown to them. Margaret also gathered from their discourse that they had visited foreign countries in their youth; and Zingary boasted more than once of the intimate terms upon which he stood with the sovereigns of the Gipsies of Spain and Bohemia.

Morcar listened to his father with deep attention and marked respect; and expressed, with deference, his own opinions upon the various topics of discourse. Eva spoke little, but she was an interested listener; and from time to time she bestowed a caress upon her boy, or exchanged a glance or a smile of affection with her husband.

In a word, the members of the royal family of the gipsies appeared to exist upon the most comfortable terms with each other.

When the meal was over, Skilligalee beckoned Margaret Flathers aside, and said, "We will go and seat ourselves under the brow of yonder hill, and pass an hour in conversation. I have much to tell you, and you must have something to tell me."

"I have—I have indeed!" exclaimed Margaret, as she accompanied Skilligalee to the spot indicated, where they seated themselves on some large blocks of wood that lay there half buried in the soil.

"I have often read and heard of the King of the Gipsies," said Margaret; "but I always imagined that he was a fabulous character. Is that old man yonder really the King; or has he only assumed the distinction by way of amusement?"

"He is as much the sovereign of the gipsies, Margaret," answered

Skilligalee, with unusual solemnity, "as Victoria is the Queen of England; and more so, for the whole tribe pays him a blind and implicit obedience."

"How came the king and his family with such strange names as those by which I heard them call each other?" inquired the Rattlesnake.

"The Gipsies in England are of two distinct races, although united under one ruler," replied Skilligalee. "They are Egyptian and Bohemian, and the royal family always adopts names likely to please both parties: *Zingary* and *Aischa* are, amongst the gipsies, supposed to be Egyptian names; *Morcar* and *Eva* are held as Bohemian. The parents who have Egyptian names, give Bohemian ones to their children; so that the rulers of the tribe are alternately looked upon as Egyptian and Bohemian."

"Then Morcar and Eva will be king and queen at the death of Zingary?" said the Rattlesnake.

"Just so," replied Skilligalee.

"Now tell me, who is that moody, melancholy, scowling fellow that you call the Traveller?" continued Margaret.

"We know but little of him," was the answer. "He joined us—or rather, we picked him up in a state of starvation, a few miles from Liverpool, about six weeks or two months ago; and the king has allowed him to tramp with us, because he is without friends or money. Moreover, he was anxious to get to London; and, for some reason or other, he is afraid to be seen on the high-roads, or in the towns and villages. So our wandering life just suited his convenience; and he feels himself safe in our company. He seldom speaks about his own affairs; but he has said enough to enable us to understand that he has suffered deeply in consequence of the treachery of some person in whom he had put confidence, or who was his pal in former times; and he is going up to London with the hope of finding out his enemy. He seems a desperate fellow; and I should not like to be the person that has offended him."

"He is not a gipsy?" said Margaret, interrogatively.

"No—not a whit more than myself," answered Skilligalee; "and I dare say he will leave us in London. As he was with us when we banked your rag, he will have his reg'lars, and that will set him up."

"And you have no idea what he has been, or who he is?" inquired the Rattlesnake.

"We never ask questions, Meg; we listen to all that is told us, but we never seek to pry into secrets. The king was quite contented with seeing your well filled bag; but if you remained in his company for a hundred years from this time, he would never ask you how you came by it. All impertinent curiosity is against the laws of the Zingarees."

"Zingarees! who are they?" exclaimed the Rattlesnake.

"The Gipsies—with another name—that's all, Meg," replied Skilligalee. "But I was telling you about the man that we call the Traveller. When his heart has been the least thing warmed with sluicing his bolt[1] and cocking his broseley, he has told us strange stories of foreign countries, so that even old Zingary, who has travelled a good deal, has turned up the whites of his eyes. But there is no doubt that the sulky stranger has seen much, and gone through much also. He talks of the Cape of Good Hope and Cape Horn, and Australia, and heaven only knows what distant places, almost as well as you and I should about the coal-hells in Staffordshire."

"And does he mean to kill the man that has offended him?" demanded the Rattlesnake.

"I'll warrant he does," was the answer; "for all that he possessed in the world, when we picked him up nearly frozen to death in a pit where he had crept for shelter,—all that he possessed besides his rags, was a long dagger, which he calls a poniard: it is as bright as silver, and so flexible that you can bend it double without breaking it. So determined is he to bury it some half dozen inches in his enemy's heart, that he wouldn't even sell it, it appears, when famishing for a morsel of bread."

"He seems a desperate-looking fellow," observed the Rattlesnake. "I never heard of so terrible a man—except one; and hell doesn't contain a greater demon than him. But I will tell you all about that another time: you must answer me my questions first."

"Oh! of course," exclaimed Skilligalee, with a merry laugh; "because you are the lady, and I am the gentleman. What else do you want to know?"

"Why the king is going up to London?"

"He always does at this season of the year, to meet the chiefs of the different districts, and settle a good deal of business. But you will see all about it when once we get up into the Holy Land—that is, if you've made up your mind to go with us."

---

1 Drinking. [Reynolds's note.]

"I have," answered the Rattlesnake. "And now tell me all that has happened to you since we parted in that hurried manner—you know how."

"Well—I will," cried Skilligalee: "so listen attentively, as all story-tellers say."

Then, clearing his throat with a loud hem, he commenced his narrative in the following manner.

CHAPTER CXXXIII.

SKILLIGALEE'S STORY.

"You remember the day we parted, after having lived together for nearly six months. I gave you two guineas to find your way up to London, where I recommended you to proceed to seek your fortune; and I told you that I had as much left for myself, to help me to get away from a part of the country where the numerous burglaries I had committed had put all the constables on the alert after me. But in reality I had but two or three shillings remaining in my pocket. I knew that if I told you the real state of my finances, you would not accept so much as I had given you; but I was afraid that you might be implicated in my difficulties, and so I was determined that you should have sufficient to convey you clear away from Staffordshire.

"Well, when we parted, I walked along the road leading away from the village, as disconsolate as might be; and yet you know that I am not naturally of a very mournful disposition. It was nine o'clock in the evening, if you remember, when I put you into the waggon that was to take you to London. I went on until I reached a lonely public-house, by the way-side. It was then eleven o'clock; and I was both tired and hungry. I entered the *Three Compasses* (which was the sign of the public-house), and sat down in the parlour. There was another traveller there—a short stout man, with a very red face, and who was committing desperate havoc upon a large cheese and loaf, from which he, however, occasionally diverted his attention, in order to pay his respects to a pot of porter. I ordered some refreshment, and inquired if I could be accommodated with a bed. The old widow woman who kept the place, said that the only bed she had to spare was already engaged by the gentleman then at supper, but that

I might sleep in the hay-loft if I chose. Thereupon the red-faced man gave a long stare at me, shrugged his shoulders, and went on eating. I suppose that my appearance was not respectable enough to induce him to resign half of his bed for my accommodation; and, indeed, I was dreadfully shabby—almost in rags, as you may well remember. So I accepted the offer of the hay-loft; and retired to that place as soon as I had finished my supper.

"But as I clambered up the ladder to my roosting-place, my unfortunate trousers caught a nail; and one leg was split completely down to the foot. I was now in a most wretched dilemma, not knowing how I should contrive to mend my luckless inexpressibles. But I soon fell asleep, in spite of my unpleasant reflections; and when I awoke, the dawn of the mild spring morning was just breaking. I examined my garment, and was reduced to despair at its appearance. At length I resolved to dress myself, go down stairs, borrow a needle and thread of the old woman, and be my own tailor. When I descended into the yard, I found a lad busily employed in cleaning a pair of boots, while a pair of trousers lay upon a bench, neatly folded up, having evidently gone through the process of brushing. I immediately recognised the stout drab pantaloons which the red-faced man wore on the preceding evening; and my eyes dwelt longingly upon them. In reply to my questions, the boy said that his grandmother (the old widow who kept the public-house) was not up yet, but that he could get me a needle and thread, as he knew where she kept her work-bag. I begged him to do so; and he very obligingly went into the house for that purpose.

"The moment he had disappeared I snatched up the red-faced man's drab trousers in one hand, and his excellent pair of bluchers in the other: then, without waiting to look behind me, I jumped over the fence which separated the stable-yard from the fields, and was speedily scampering across the open country as fast as my legs would carry me. When I had run about a mile, I reached a little grove, situated on the bank of a stream: and there I halted.

"The red-faced gentleman's boots were a wonderful improvement upon my old broken shoes; but his pantaloons fitted somewhat awkwardly, being a world too wide round the waist, and a foot too short in the legs. However, they were better than my old tattered unmentionables, and I could not complain that they were dear!

"I pursued my way along the banks of the stream until past mid-day, when I came to a village, where I halted at a public-house to take some refreshment. My two or three shillings were still unchanged, because I had not paid a single penny for my entertainment at the *Three Compasses*. While I sate enjoying my bread and cheese and beer, I revolved in my mind various plans to better my condition. But my attention was speedily averted from that topic to the conversation of two old men, who were sitting at another table in the tap-room.

" 'So poor old Joe Dobbin's scapegrace nephew is coming home at last?' said one.—'Yes,' replied the other: 'he has been seeking his fortune, as a sailor, all over the world, for the last ten years; and now that he hasn't a penny, and is a-weary of a sea-faring life, he has written to say that he is coming home to his poor old blind uncle.'—'Ah! Tom Tittlebat has been a wild 'un in his day, I'll answer for it,' said the first old man. 'But his uncle seems quite delighted at the idea of seeing him again,' observed the other old fellow.—'He says that he shall persuade upon Tom to stay at home and take care of him; and then he'll be able to turn away cross old Margery, who robs him and ill-treats him in a shameful manner.'

"I devoured every word of this conversation; and my mind was instantly made up. I accordingly joined in the discourse, called for some ale, of which I made the two old fellows partake, and so artfully pumped them that in half an hour I knew all about old blind Dobbin and his graceless nephew Tom Tittlebat, without having appeared even to ask a single question concerning them. At length, when I had my lesson complete, I burst out into a hearty laugh, and cried out, 'What, Master Buckley, don't you remember me then? and you, good Master Dottings, am I quite a stranger to *you* too?' The old men stared; and then, with another hearty laugh, I boldly announced myself to be Tom Tittlebat. You should have seen the old fellows—how glad they were! One swore that he had all along suspected who I was; and the other vowed that my features were unchanged since he last saw me, although my face was a little tanned! Then I called for more ale, and plied the old boys well, so that they might help to favour the imposture which I meditated.

"Away we went to the cottage inhabited by old Dobbin, my two aged companions really showing me the way, while I pretended to be quite familiar with it. The moment we came in sight of my alleged uncle's residence, old Buckley and Dottings (whose names I had found out from their own discourse with me) hobbled forward, exclaiming, 'Here's the prodigal returned, Brother Dobbin!'—'Kill the fatted calf, Brother Dobbin!' And in a few moments I was in my alleged uncle's arms.

"Then the fatted calf was indeed killed. Dame Margery, the old man's housekeeper, was compelled to bustle about to prepare a copious supper—a duty which she performed with a very bad grace, and with sundry suspicious leers and side-glances towards me. I took no notice of her ill-humour, but rattled away about my adventures by sea and land till the three old men were quite astounded at the marvellous things I had seen and the tremendous perils that I had escaped. Buckley and Dotting were invited to stay to supper; and a merry meal we had. When the things were cleared away, I undertook to brew the punch, assuring the old folks that the compound would be made according to a recipe which I had obtained from the king of the Inaccessible Islands.

"Well, the punch was made; and there it stood steaming in an enormous bowl upon the table. I was determined to enjoy myself; for I purposed to pack up every thing portable during the night and decamp before dawn, for fear that the rightful nephew should return before I had turned my trick to advantage. So I filled the tumblers, and plied the punch to such an extent that even old Margery's ill-humour was overcome by the gaiety of the scene; and she consented to sit down and join us.

"I was just in the middle of a most exciting account of a conflict which I had with a shark at the South Pole, when a loud knock at the door resounded through the house. Margery hastened to obey the summons; and old Dobbin observed, 'I shouldn't be surprised if this was my cousin George, for I wrote to him the day before yesterday to say that my nephew Tom was coming home, and invited him down to pass a week or so on the happy occasion.' I heard this remark; but the punch had produced such an effect upon me, that I felt no uneasiness. I thought I should be able to get over cousin George as easily as I had done uncle Dobbin; and so I amused myself by filling the glasses round from the second bowl, which had only just been mixed.

"Meantime Dame Margery, having answered the door, returned, exclaiming, 'It be Master George,' and followed by a person whom her tall gaunt form in some measure hid from me until they were both close to the table. Then what a dreadful scene took place! In cousin George, to my horror and dismay, I beheld the red-faced man that I'd met at the *Three Compasses*, and whose drab trousers adorned me at that very moment!

"I leapt from my seat, and was making as fast as I could to the door, when cousin George shouted out, 'Holloa! who have we here?'—and, springing forward, he collared me in a moment. 'What's the matter? what's the matter?' demanded old Dobbin.—'My stars! what's this mean?' exclaimed Dame Margery.—'Why, it means that this fellow is a robber, and has got on my breeches and boots!' vociferated cousin George, growing purple in the face with rage, and giving me a violent shake.—'Your breeches!' cried old Buckley.—'Your boots!' mumbled old Dottings.—'Yes, to be sure!' shouted the red-faced man. 'Go and fetch a constable.'—'Why, you don't mean that nephew Tom has done this?' said old Dobbin.—'Nephew Tom!' exclaimed cousin George, letting go his hold upon my coat: 'no!'—'But I say *yes*, though,' said I, putting a bold face upon the matter: 'I knew you directly when I met you at the *Three Compasses* last night, and only did it by way of a lark.'

"But this turn did not serve me. While I spoke, cousin George surveyed me attentively; and, again rushing upon me, he roared out, 'He's a cheat! he's an impostor! Tom has a mole on the left cheek, and he's none: Tom has a cut over the right eye, and he hasn't. Go for a constable.'—'Well, I thought all along he was a rogue,' cried Dame Margery, hurrying off to execute this most unpleasant order.

"My case now seemed desperate; and not a moment was to be lost. Casting my eyes rapidly around in search of some weapon of defence or avenue of escape, I espied the punch-bowl, three parts full of steaming liquor, within my reach. With the rapidity of lightning I seized it, and dashed it over like a hat upon cousin George's head. He uttered a terrific yell as the hot punch streamed down him; and I precipitated myself from the room as if a blood-hound was at my heels.

"Away I scudded—a hue and cry after me: but I ran like a race-horse; and in a few minutes was beyond the sound of the '*Stop, thief!*' raised by cousin George's ominous voice.

"That was an excellent adventure: I have often and often laughed at it since, and wondered whether the real Tom Tittlebat ever did return. At all events I kept cousin George's trousers and boots; but they got me into more scrapes yet.

"I strolled along through the fields, diverting myself with reflection upon the past, and pondering upon what might be in store for the future, until I reached a large market town, where I went boldly to the tap-room of the principal tavern. I ordered an excellent supper, with plenty of ale, feeling convinced that some lucky adventure would enable me to pay for my cheer—for I had now but one shilling left, the remainder of my money having been spent at the inn where I met the two old acquaintances of blind Dobbin.

"The tap-room was filled with people; and the conversation was pretty general. There was, however, one individual who took no part in the discourse, but sate apart in an obscure corner smoking his pipe. He did not even appear to listen to what was said around him; but maintained his eyes moodily fixed on the floor. His horrible sallow complexion, deep wrinkles, and large mustache, gave him an aspect very far from inviting. Nevertheless, I endeavoured to enter into conversation with him—simply, I suppose, because he appeared to be so reserved, and my curiosity was excited with respect to him; but he threw upon me a look of the most sovereign contempt, and made me no answer. I shrank back from the fierce glance of his dark black eyes, and felt abashed and cowed—I scarcely knew why. But soon recovering my usual good spirits, I also called for my pipe and my pot, and mingled in the conversation. Rattling away with my anecdotes, and now and then singing a snatch of a song, I speedily made myself so agreeable to the drovers and waggoners assembled in the tap-room, that they called for punch and invited me to partake of it with them.

"At twelve o'clock the waiter came in, and bawled out, '*Any more orders, gentlemen? any more orders?*' No answer being given, he said, '*I will receive each gentleman's account, if you please.*'—This announcement came like a clap of thunder upon me: I had but a shilling in my pocket, and owed nearly three. What to do I could not tell. Meantime the waiter went round, collecting the money due to him from each individual: and the nearer he drew to the table where I was sitting, the more fidgetty I became. As I glanced round me with feverish anxiety, I saw the dark black eyes of the sallow-faced stranger fixed upon me; and I thought that they glared with fiendish delight, as if they had penetrated my secret. I felt ashamed—and my eyes fell beneath the demon-like glance. In another moment the waiter stood before me. 'Now, sir—if you please, sir: steak, one shilling—taturs, penny—bread, penny—fourteen-pence; two pints of ale, eight-pence—screw of bakker, penny—pot porter, four-pence,—that's two-and-three, sir.' I sat aghast for a few moments, and then began to fumble in my pockets, the waiter every moment growing more impatient. At that instant the sallow-faced stranger pointed to the bench on which I was sitting, and said in a surly tone, 'No wonder, young man, that you can't find your money in your pocket, when you let it roll about in all directions.' He then sank back into his corner, and seemed to take no more notice of me or my concerns. I thought he had a mind to banter me; but, turning my eyes towards the place which he had indicated, to my surprise I perceived a couple of half-crowns lying there. I am sure the waiter must have seen how my countenance brightened up with sudden joy; but he made no remark; and I paid my bill. He then passed on to the sallow-faced man, who settled his own account, and hastily left the room, without condescending to cast another glance upon me.

"I was at a loss to make out whether the sallow-faced stranger had done a most generous action, or whether some one else had dropped the money there, and he had really fancied it to be mine. I did not, however, lose much time in conjecture; but, taking the whole affair for a good omen, ordered another glass, and then went jovially to bed, I awoke early, had some breakfast, and went out to take a stroll in the town. I naturally directed my steps towards the market-place, knowing that it was market-day, and hoping to find a watch or a purse in the crowd.

"Elbowing my way through the graziers, drovers, and butchers, I got into the middle of the market, and there a most extraordinary spectacle met my eyes. A man was leading a woman along by a halter, which was tied round her neck. At first, I thought that a public execution was about to take place; but, seeing no gibbet—no police—no sheriffs—and no clergyman,—and observing, at a second glance, that the woman was giggling and laughing very much unlike a person just going to be hanged, I was at a loss to account for so strange a sight. The crowd appeared to enjoy the fun—for fun it evidently was—excessively; and, at length, I learnt that *'Bob Fosset, the dog's-meat-man, was about to sell his wife to Will Wyatt, the costermonger.'* And, sure enough,

such was the fact. Bob Fossett led his wife—a comely-looking woman enough—to the centre of the market, and tied the halter to a sheep-pen. He then mounted on the top bar of the pen, and shouted out: *'I hereby put up my wife, Jenny Fossett, to public auction; and I declare that she shall go to the highest bidder.'*—*'So I will, Bob,'* cried the woman.—*'Hooray, Bob Fossett,'* bawled the crowd assembled; and then there was such laughing, and joking, and sky-larking, it seemed for all the world just like a fair. Well, Will Wyatt steps forward, and exclaims: *'I bid one shilling for that woman.'*—*'One shilling bid,'* said Bob Fossett.—*'One shilling and a pot of beer,'* cries some wag in the crowd.—*'One shilling and a pot of beer is bid,'* shouts Fossett; *'who bids any more?'*—*'One shilling and a gallon of beer!'* bawls Will Wyatt.—*'One shilling and a gallon of beer for this woman!'* cries Bob Fossett: *'who'll advance on that? Going for one shilling and a gallon of beer; going—going,—will no one bid?—gone! Will Wyatt, my lad, that woman's yours.'* So Will Wyatt steps forward, kisses the woman, takes off the halter, and tucks her under his arm as cozy as if they'd just been spliced at church. Then they all three went off to the nearest public-house, the crowds hoorayіng, and shouting, and squeaking, and roaring, as they made way for the party to pass along. I determined to see the remainder of the fun, and so I followed them to the public-house.

"The moment we entered the parlour, I saw a person sitting in one corner, whose face seemed more or less familiar to me. He was a fine, tall, powerfully-built man; and his countenance was very handsome, but so dark that he appeared to be an East-Indian. But it was the peculiar expression of the mouth, and the piercing glance of the eyes, that struck me. I looked—and looked again; and thought that a slight smile curled the stranger's lips as I surveyed him, although he did not seem to take any notice of me, or even to know that I was staring at him. 'Well,' I thought to myself, 'if you are not my sallow-faced friend of last-night, I'm terribly mistaken—that's all;' for I knew too much of disguises myself to be bothered by the difference of complexions. So I went and sat down close by him; and, having ordered something to drink, at length boldly whispered to him, '*I have seen you before.*'—'*Very likely,*' answered the man, coolly; '*but take care of yourself, or you may still get into a scrape on account of cousin George's breeches.*' With these words he rose, drained his glass, and walked coolly out of the room.

"You may imagine how astonished I was at the ominous words which he had whispered in my ear; but, collecting my ideas, I began to feel alarmed for my safety; and, having no longer any interest in the party whom I had followed into the public-house, I abruptly departed—without partaking of, or paying for, the refreshment which I had ordered. Hurrying away from the place, I got out of the town as quick as possible; and, avoiding the main-road, struck into the fields.

"I wandered about for two or three days, until all my money was gone; and I was one afternoon roaming along a by-lane, wondering what was to become of me, and thinking that it would be much better to break into some house, as a last and desperate resource, when I suddenly encountered a man and woman at the turning of the road. They were dressed as poor country people; but the darkness of their complexions immediately struck my attention; and, at a second glance, I recognised in the man the very person who had whispered those mysterious words in my ears, concerning cousin George's trousers, and whom I could almost certainly identify with the sallow-faced stranger. 'What, not got rid of cousin George's trousers yet!' he exclaimed, laughing heartily; and the woman, who seemed to understand the joke, joined in her companion's mirth.—'Who are you?' I said, 'and how do you happen to know about that little adventure of mine?'—'You see that I *do* know all about it,' returned the man, with another laugh; 'and you may perhaps be surprised when I tell you that I consider the abstraction of the trousers to be even a more pleasant freak than the personation of Tom Tittlebat.'—'The deuce!' I cried, now completely bewildered: 'if you are a constable, say so, and we will have a fight for it; if not, tell me who you are, and how you came to be acquainted with my affairs.'—'I am certainly no constable,' answered the man, 'or I might have apprehended you some days since on two several occasions, and when there would have been no necessity to fight for it. As to how I know any thing about you, ask no questions, because you will receive no satisfactory answers. But if you wish to earn a shilling or two, say so; and you can do it within an hour.'—I professed my willingness to serve this strange individual.—'Come with us,' he said; and, striking into a narrow path, he led the way for about half-a-mile across the fields, until we came in sight of a large farm-house. 'You see that farm,' he said: 'now listen attentively. You must go there, and under any pretence you can think of, obtain admission into the kitchen, or get into conversation with one of the servants, so as to glean all the information you can about the family. There's three daughters: find out whether they are engaged to be married, or who the young men are that principally visit at the house, and all particulars of that kind. We will wait for you in yonder copse.'

"The stranger and his companion hastened away towards the place where I was to meet them again, and I proceeded towards the farm. It was by no means difficult to gain admittance into the kitchen of that hospitable establishment: a simple request for a cup of milk led to an invitation from a buxom cook and a smart servant-maid to walk in and rest myself a little. Then bread and cheese, and a foaming tankard of home-brewed were set before me; and, while I ate and drank, I gradually drew the two women into the conversation which suited my purpose. They proclaimed the praises of 'master and missis;' and told me how the old people were very well off; and how Miss Jemima, the eldest daughter, was engaged to a young farmer in the neighbourhood; how Miss Mary, the second daughter, had been courted by an officer in the army who had been quartered in the neighbouring town, but who had since left, and had never written to her afterwards; and how Miss Frances, the youngest, had been very melancholy ever since she had visited an aunt at Stafford, where it was well known an attorney's clerk had paid her very great attention. These, and various other particulars relative to the family, were related to me in the course of conversation; and, having remained at the farm for a couple of hours, I was about to take my leave, as well informed relative to the inmates as if I had lived with them all my life. But just as I was rising to depart, I espied a purse lying in a work-box upon a shelf; and I began to reflect how I could make it my own. Accident served my purpose: the cook insisted upon drawing me some more ale, and went into the cellar for that purpose; and the maid-servant stepped to the door of the kitchen to receive a can of milk which a boy brought there at the moment. To dart toward the shelf and secure the purse was the work of an instant; and when the maid turned towards me again, I was sitting as composedly as if I had never left my chair. The cook made her appearance with the ale, of which I drank; and I then took my leave, with many thanks for the kind entertainment I had received.

"I proceeded to the copse, where I found my strange employer and his female companion waiting for me. I told them all that I had gleaned relative to the farmer and his family; and they were highly delighted with the information so procured. The man gave me five shillings, and told me that he did not require my services any farther. I was not sorry to get away from the neighbourhood; and, taking leave of the persons who had employed me in so singular a service, pursued my way. When at a convenient distance from the spot where I had left them, I examined the purse, and, to my joy, found that it contained four sovereigns and about seven shillings in silver.

"Considerably cheered at this change in my pecuniary position, I pursued my way until long after dusk, when I entered a village where I determined to put up for the night. Having supped at a public-house, I inquired about a bed, and found that I could be accommodated with one in a double-bedded room, the other being already retained by a traveller who had arrived before me, but who had stepped out, I was informed, to transact some business with certain inhabitants of his acquaintance. Being tired, I went up to the room where I was to sleep, before the return of the person who was to occupy the other bed; but before I sought my own nest I looked about for a secure spot where I could conceal my purse, as I fancied that my companion might probably be no more honest than myself. I accordingly hid my treasure between the mattress and the sacking; and, putting my clothes under my pillow, lay down to rest. I soon fell into a deep sleep, from which I did not awake until aroused by the noise of some one moving about the room. I started up, and rubbing my eyes, asked what o'clock it was. The person who occupied the other bed was shaving himself at a looking-glass, with his back turned towards me; but the moment my voice fell upon his ears, he started round; and—to my horror—I recognised but too well, beneath a thick coat of lather, the never-to-be-forgotten countenance of cousin George.

"Here was a precious scrape! The red-faced man was deaf to my prayers for mercy, and alarmed the whole house. Landlord, boots, ostler, and pot-boy rushed up stairs, while cousin George vociferated, 'Fetch a constable! this is the rogue who stole my breeches and boots. Fetch a constable, I say! Here's the villain that imposed upon poor old blind Dobbin. Fetch a constable!' A constable was accordingly fetched; and I was duly given into his charge. While I was huddling on my clothes, cousin George exclaimed, with savage malignity, 'Ah! there's the boots, the scoundrel! There's the drab trousers, the scamp!' and I really believe he would have wrested them from me had it not been necessary for me to wear them in order to accompany the constable.

"I did not choose to drag forth my purse from its place of concealment, for fear it might involve me in a worse dilemma than that in which I found myself, and which, after all, was not particularly serious. I however left it beneath the mattress, with deep regret, and was led away by the constable, every soul in the public-house turning out to witness my departure. The landlord, moreover, gave me a parting blessing after a fashion—accusing me as a thief who had run up a score of three shillings and seven-pence halfpenny at his house, without the slightest means of paying it! To this very natural conclusion he came, inasmuch as the constable, upon searching me, had found nothing in my pockets.

"The clergyman of the village was a justice of the peace; and before his worshipful reverence was I accordingly taken. He was an elderly man, very corpulent and very stern; and he frowned upon me in a ferocious manner when I was conducted into the library, where he intended to hear the case. Cousin George, who had only shaved one side of his face, and had a black bristly beard over the other, stepped forward and stated the entire case, which comprised the theft of his garments and the imposture practised upon his relative. In the latter business, however, the magistrate refused to interfere, and confined his attention to the abstraction of the trousers and boots. I, of course, set up the usual defence,—'*Had never seen the gentleman before in my life—had bought the trousers and boots of a man that I met at a public house, and whose name I did not know; that I was an honest hard-working young fellow, out of employment; and had never been in trouble before.*' The magistrate was, however, obstinate, and would not believe a word I uttered. He accordingly ordered me to be committed for trial at the sessions; and I was moved to an out-house, there to wait in the custody of the constable, until my *mittimus* was made out, and a cart was obtained to take me to the county gaol. Cousin George, satisfied with what he had done so far, threw a glance of triumph upon me as I was moved away from the magistrate's library.

"While I was pent up in the out-house, I went up to the window and looked out upon that open country which seemed the scene of a freedom now lost to me. As I was standing there, pondering on my condition, and wondering whether the numerous burglaries which I had committed in a neighbourhood not very far distant, would be brought against me, my attention was suddenly attracted to a number of people who were advancing rapidly towards the house. As they drew near, to my surprise I recognised the swarthy stranger and his female companion, both evidently in the custody of two constables, and followed by the cook, maid-servant, and other persons belonging to the farm-house. An idea of the real truth instantly flashed through my mind; and I felt sorry—very sorry for the two poor creatures who, I had no doubt, were suffering under a suspicion of the robbery which I had perpetrated. Moreover, I could not help thinking that the swarthy man and the sallow-faced man were one and the same person, and that the two half-crowns had been purposely thrown in my way by him, at the inn in the market-town, to relieve me from that embarrassment into which his keen eyes had penetrated. These reflections suddenly filled me with deep interest in the stranger and his female companion.

"The procession passed the window (from which I drew back), and entered the magistrate's house. Half-an-hour passed away; and then the clergyman's man-servant made his appearance with a jug of ale and some bread and meat for the constable who had me in charge. But nothing was given to me, either to eat or drink! 'There's a new case on in the library,' said the servant.—'Ah! what's that?' inquired the constable.—'Two gipsies,' was the answer, 'man and woman, have been prigging a purse down at farmer Clodhopper's. The purse belonged to a young servant gal, and was missed out of her work-box just after the gipsies had left the house last night. But the constables were put on the scent, and soon found the thieves.'—'And was the purse recovered?' asked the officer who had me in custody.—'Deuce a bit of it,' said the servant, 'those gipsies know a trick worth two of that. It seems that they went down to the farm late last night, and told all the young ladies and servant girls their fortunes; so they were taken into the kitchen and fed with the best, besides all the money they'd had given to them by the young ladies and the servants. Not content with all that, they stole the purse, the vagabonds!'—'No, they didn't, though!' I exclaimed, stepping forward; for somehow or another my blood boiled and my heart ached to think that those two poor creatures should be punished for a crime of which they were innocent. Besides, I made sure that all my past offences would be brought against me at the assizes; and I knew in that case that I should be booked for transportation; so one robbery more or less could not make much difference to me. Well, both the constable and the servant stared when I spoke in that manner. 'Yes,' I continued, 'it is perfectly true that those two gipsies are innocent of the theft; and if you will take me before his worship again, I will prove my words.' The constable accordingly conducted me back to the library.

"The moment I entered the room, the gipsy-man and his companion exhibited the greatest surprise and interest. I gave them a re-assuring glance; and then, turning towards the magistrate, I said, 'Your worship, these two poor creatures are innocent of the crime imputed to them.'—'How do you know?' demanded the justice roughly, for his lunch-time was now drawing near.—'Because I stole it myself,' was my answer. The greatest astonishment pervaded the assembly; joy animated the countenance of the two gipsies; while the cook and maid servant cried out, '*Dear me!*' and '*Who would have thought it?*' as loud as they could. The justice looked tremendous savage, and declared that he would order the room to be cleared of strangers if they interrupted the business in that indecent manner! I was then called upon to explain the assertion which I had made.—'These two persons,' I said, pointing towards the gipsies, 'are accused of stealing a purse from farmer Clodhopper's kitchen?'—'They are. Well?'—'Then they didn't steal it, because I stole it myself; and these servants can prove that I was there yesterday afternoon.'—'So he was!' exclaimed the cook and maid in the same breath.—'And now,' I continued, 'if you will send and search under the mattress of the bed which I slept in last night at the public-house where I was arrested, you will find the purse.' But this trouble was avoided; for scarcely had I uttered these words, when in came the landlord of that public-house, holding the purse in his hands. His wife, it appeared, had found it when making the beds; and suspicion instantly pointed to me as the person who had placed it in the spot where it was discovered. This circumstance brought the case safe home to me; and the gipsies were instantly discharged, with a warning to take care of themselves in future!

"Nothing could exceed the looks of deep gratitude which those two innocent persons cast upon me as they left the room:—but that of the man was significant of something more than a mere sense of obligation for the act of duty which I had done. I don't know how it was, too—but, rogue as I was, I felt an inward satisfaction at the part which I had just performed.

"I was taken back to the out-house, with another serious charge hanging over my head; and the cart was every moment expected to convey me to the county gaol. But time slipped away, and it did not arrive. At length the constable became impatient, and talked about the impropriety of trifling with the time of a public officer like him, adding that he didn't know if he shouldn't write to the prime minister about it. Presently the man-servant came in with some dinner for him—but not a bite nor a sup for me! Neither did the constable offer me any thing. 'Here's a pretty business,' says the servant; 'the man that was to drive you over to the county gaol has got drunk somehow or other, and can't go; and the horse has suddenly gone dead lame.'—'What's to be done, then?' cried the constable.—'Why, you must wait till the man's sober, and the veterinary surgeon has looked to the horse.'

"And sure enough we did wait until eight o'clock in the evening before we started; and then no thanks to the man nor the veterinary surgeon, for the former was still too tipsy to move, and the latter could do nothing for the horse. However, another man came forward, at a late hour, and offered his services. He not only cured the horse in a few minutes, but also undertook to drive the cart. The constable accordingly put a pair of handcuffs on me, and took me out into the yard where the vehicle was waiting. A man with a sallow face and bushy red hair, was already seated in front, holding the whip and reins; and as I mounted he gave me a look which I immediately understood. That man was no other than my friend, the swarthy gipsy, so well disguised that his own mother would have scarcely known him.

"Away we went at a rattling pace: it was soon dark, and the constable told the driver not to go at such a rate. But he did not obey the command: on the contrary, he whipped the horse the more; and the cart bounded along the road as if it was for a wager. The constable swore and prayed by turns: the driver laughed; and presently the cart upset into a dry ditch. 'Run for your liberty!' cried the driver to me, as he pulled me from the ditch; and I followed him across the fields with a speed that was increased by hearing the constable shouting '*Stop, thief!*' behind me. But in a very few minutes those cries became fainter and fainter, until they at length ceased altogether. Still my deliverer pursued his way, and at such a rate, too, that I was scarcely able to keep up with him.

"At length we stopped in a thicket, and sat down to rest. My deliverer took a file from his pocket and worked away at my manacles with such a skill and energy, that in a few minutes I was relieved from them. He then produced some food, and I ate a hearty meal. When the meal was over, my companion condescended to give me an explanation of certain matters which had hitherto remained wrapped up in some degree of mystery.

" 'You must be informed,' he said, 'that my name is Morcar, and that I am the son of Zingary, king of the gipsies. The female whom you saw with me yesterday and this morning, is my wife. A considerable portion of the money earned by our race consists of fees paid by the simple and credulous, for having their fortunes told. In order to obtain the necessary information relative to the inhabitants of those places or dwellings which we visit, we are compelled to assume many disguises, or to make use of the agency of others, not connected with us, to gather that information for us. Some days ago, at an early hour in the morning, I was loitering about in the neighbourhood of the *Three Compasses*, and from behind a hedge saw you make off with the boots and trousers which a boy had been brushing in the yard. Chance led me that same afternoon to the village where you played your famous trick upon old Dobbin; and, as the story spread like wild-fire through the place immediately after your detection by cousin George, I could not avoid hearing all the particulars. I got a lift in a cart from that village to the market-town where I met you the same night at the inn. I could not help admiring your boldness and ingenuity; and, while I sat quietly smoking my pipe in the tap-room, listening to the discourse of the inmates, and picking up a variety of information, to be turned to future account, I noticed your embarrassment at the appearance of the waiter to collect the money owing by each individual. I had made a good day's work in a certain way, and was disposed to be liberal: accordingly, at a moment when you were turned in another direction, I placed the two half-crowns close by where you sate on the bench. Next day I threw off what I call my *sallow disguise*, and repaired to another public-house, near the market, to glean additional information, all of which our women have since turned to ample profit. There I was enabled to give you a warning which was really important to you, as old Dobbin's cousin George had actually arrived that morning in the town to attend the market. A few days afterwards I was roving with my wife along the by-lanes in the neighbourhood of Clodhopper's farm, endeavouring by some means to glean what we could concerning the young women at that place—for our finest harvests are always reaped at farm-houses. Again I met you; and I made you the instrument of my design. But,' added Morcar, with a smile, 'you went farther than you were instructed: you did a thing which *we* never do—I mean, steal money. We take for our use a sucking-pig, a fowl, or a goose; and we do not consider that stealing. We also snare rabbits and game; and we look upon it as no crime. However, you saw the scrape into which that business of the purse got me and my wife this morning. You saved us, and I vowed to save you also. The moment I was discharged I went to the stable where the horse that was to convey you to gaol was kept, and bribed the ostler to drive a nail into his foot so as to touch the flesh. Then I found the man who was to drive you, and plied him so well with liquor that he was unable to perform his duty. My object was to delay your journey until the evening, because I knew that I could ensure your escape in the dark. You have seen how well my plans have succeeded, because you are now free.'

"You may suppose that I thanked my kind deliverer most sincerely for all he had done to serve me. He, however, cut me short in my expressions of gratitude, by saying, 'What are you going to do? If you will join us, you will be assured of your daily food, and will be more or less protected from danger. My father has a van, in which you can at any time hide when concealment is necessary; and we will do all we can to serve you, for I still consider myself to be indebted to you on account of your generous conduct of this morning. I could have borne punishment myself; but the idea of my wife being plunged into such misery—no, never—never!'

"I accepted the welcome offers of Morcar, and that very night was conducted to the encampment where his father and mother had taken up their quarters. Eva presented her son to me, saying, 'You have preserved for this little one a father and mother: henceforth the Zingarees will know thee as a friend!' From that moment I have lived with the gipsies until the present time; and, though some years have passed away since I first joined them, I have not yet become weary of our wandering mode of existence."

CHAPTER CXXXIV.

THE PALACE IN THE HOLY LAND.

The wanderer amidst the crowded thoroughfares of the multitudinous metropolis cannot be unacquainted with that assemblage of densely populated streets and lanes which is situate between High Street (St. Giles's) and Great Russell Street (Bloomsbury).

The district alluded to is called the Holy Land.

There poverty hides its head through shame, and crime lurks

concealed through fear;—there everything that is squalid, hideous, debauched, and immoral, makes its dwelling—there woman is as far removed from the angel as Satan is from the Godhead, and man is as closely allied to the brute as the idiot is to the baboon;—there days are spent in idleness, and nights in dissipation;—there no refinement of habit or of speech is known, but male and female alike wallow in obscene debauchery and filthy ideas;—there garments are patched with pieces of various dyes, and language is disfigured with words of a revolting slang;—there the natural ruffianism and brutal instincts of the human heart are unrepressed by social ties or conventional decencies;—there infamy is no disgrace, crime no reproach, vice no stain.

Such is the Holy Land.

In a dark and gloomy alley, connecting two of the longer streets in this district, stood a large house four storeys high, and with windows of such narrow dimensions that they seemed intended to admit the light of day only by small instalments.

Four steep stone steps, each only about six inches broad, led to the front door, which always stood open during the day-time.

This front-door gave admission into a small square compartment, which was denominated "the lobby," and from which a second door opened into the house.

The inner door just alluded to was kept constantly shut, save when admittance was demanded by any one who had the right of entry into the habitation. But even that admittance was never granted without precaution. In the ceiling of the little hall or lobby described, there was a small trap-door, let into the floor of the room above; and by these means the sentinel on duty up-stairs was enabled to reconnoitre every one who knocked at the inner door.

The interior of the house resembled a small barrack. The apartments on the ground floor were used as day-rooms or refectories, and were fitted up with long tables and forms. The floors were strewed with sand; and the appearance of the place was more cleanly and comfortable than might have been expected in such a neighbourhood. The lower panes of the windows were smeared with a whitewash, which prevented passers-by from peering from the street into the apartments.

The upper storeys were all used as dormitories, some being allotted to the male and others to the female inmates of the house. These rooms were furnished with mattresses, blankets, and coverlids; but there were no bedsteads. The aspect of the dormitories was as cleanly as that of the day-rooms.

To the ceiling over the landing-place of the second floor was hung a large bell, to the wheel of which were attached numerous ropes, which branched off, through holes in the walls and floors, in all directions, so that an alarm could be rung from every room in that spacious tenement.

Behind the house there was a large yard, surrounded by the dead walls which formed the sides of other buildings; thus, in no way, was the dwelling which we have described, overlooked by the neighbours. At the bottom of the yard was a door opening into a court which communicated with another street; and thus a convenient mode of egress was secured to any one who might find it prudent to beat a precipitate retreat from the house.

We have now endeavoured to furnish the reader with an idea of King Zingary's Palace in the Holy Land.

In order to complete the description, it only remains for us to state that the various precautions to which we have alluded, in connexion with the Palace, were adopted for the protection and safety of those inmates who, either in the course of their avocations or otherwise, might happen to render themselves obnoxious to the myrmidons of the law. Not that the pursuits of the subjects of King Zingary necessarily comprised practices which rendered their head-quarters liable to constant visits from the police: but persons accustomed to a vagabond kind of existence, could not be otherwise than often tempted into lawless courses; and his Majesty did not dare disown or discard a dependant who thus became involved in danger. Moreover, the protection of the gipsies was frequently accorded to persons who rendered them a service, or who could pay for such succour, as in the respective cases of Skilligalee and the Rattlesnake: or it was not unusually granted upon motives of humanity, as in reference to the man called the Traveller. This intercourse with characters of all descriptions was another reason for the adoption of precautionary measures at the Palace; but seldom—very seldom was it that the necessity of those measures was justified by events, the police being well aware that no good ever resulted from a visit to the royal mansion in the Holy Land.

It was ten o'clock at night; and the king of the gipsies was presiding at the banqueting-table in his palace.

Upwards of sixty gipsies, male and female, were assembled round the board. These consisted of the chiefs of the different districts into which the gipsy kingdom was divided, with their wives and daughters.

Skilligalee, the Rattlesnake, and the Traveller were also seated at the table, and were honoured as the king's guests.

The meal was over; and the board was covered with bottles containing various descriptions of liquor, drinking mugs, pipes, and tobacco.

With all the solemn gravity of a chairman at a public dinner, Zingary rapped his knuckles upon the table, and commanded those present to fill their glasses.

The order was obeyed by both men and women; and the king then spoke as follows:—

"Most loyal and dutiful friends, this is the hundred and thirty-first anniversary of the institution of that custom in virtue of which the provincial rulers of the united races of Egyptians and Bohemians in England assemble together once every year at the Palace. A hundred and thirty-one years ago, this house was purchased by my grandfather King Sisman, and bequeathed to his descendants to serve as the headquarters and central point of our administration. There is scarcely an individual of the united races who has not experienced the hospitality of this Palace. Every worthy Zingaree who visits the metropolis enjoys his bed and his board without fee and without price for seven days in our mansion, the superintendence of which is so ably conducted, while we are absent, by our brother on my right." Here the king glanced towards a venerable-looking gipsy who sate next to him. "In his hands our treasures are safe; and to-morrow he will place before you an account of the remittances he has received from the provincial districts, and the expenditures he has made in the maintenance of this establishment. You will find, I have reason to believe, a considerable balance in our favour. Let us then celebrate with a bumper the hundred and thirty-first anniversary of the opening of our royal palace!"

This toast was drunk without noise—without hurrahs—without clamour,—but not the less sincerely on that account.

"My pretty Eva," said the king, after a pause, "will now oblige us with a song?"

Zingary's daughter-in-law did not require to be pressed to exhibit her vocal powers; but in a sweet voice she sang the following air:—

THE GIPSY'S HOME.

Oh! who is so blythe, and happy, and free
As the ever-wandering Zingaree?
'Tis his at his own wild will to roam;
And in each fair scene does he find a home,—
Does he find a home!

The sunny slope, or the shady grove,
Where nightingales sing and lovers rove;
The fields where the golden harvests wave,
And the verdant bank which the streamlets lave,
Are by turns his home.

The busy town with its selfish crowd,
The city where dwell the great and proud,
The haunts of the mighty multitude,
Where the strong are raised and the weak subdued,
Are to him no home.

Oh! ever happy—and ever free,
Who is so blest as the Zingaree?—
Where nature puts on her gayest vest,
Where flowers are sweetest and fruits are best,
Oh! there is his home.

"Thank you, sweet Eva," said the king, when the gipsy woman had concluded her song, in the chorus of which the other females had joined in a low and subdued tone. "Ours is indeed a happy life," continued Zingary. "When roving over the broad country, we enjoy a freedom unknown to the rest of the world. No impost or taxes have we then to pay: we drink of the stream at pleasure, and never feel alarmed lest our water should be cut off. We can choose pleasant paths, and yet pay no paving-rate. The sun lights us by day, and the stars by night; and no one comes to remind us that we owe two quarters' gas. We pitch our tents where we will, but are not afraid of a ground-landlord. We do not look forward with fear and trembling to Lady-day or Michaelmas, for the broker cannot distress us. We move where we like, without dreading an accusation of *shooting the moon*. In fine, we are as free and independent as the inhabitants of the desert. A health, then, to the united races of Zingarees!"

This toast was drunk in silence, like the former; and the king then called upon the pretty dark-eyed daughter of one of the chiefs to favour the company with a song.

The request was complied with in the following manner:—

"COME HITHER, FAIR MAIDEN."

Come hither, fair maiden! and listen to me,
I've a store of good tidings to tell unto thee—
Bright hopes to call smiles to those sweet lips of thine,
And visions of bliss little short of divine.

Come hither, fair maiden! the poor Zingaree
Hath promise of love and of fortune for thee:
Away from the future the dark cloud shall fly,
And years yet unborn be revealed to thine eye.

Come hither, fair maiden! no more shalt thou be
Alarmed lest the fates act unkindly to thee;—
The planet that governed the hour of thy birth
Shall guide thee to all the fair spots of the earth!

Come hither, fair maiden! futurity's sea
Shall roll on no longer unfathomed by thee;
With me canst thou plunge in its dark depths, and know
How rich are the pearls that Hope treasures below

In this manner did the gipsies pass the evening, until the clock struck eleven, when they separated to their dormitories.

The Rattlesnake was astonished to observe the order and regularity which prevailed with the strange association amongst which accident had thrown her. The festival had passed without noise and without intemperance; the presence of the king and queen seemed alone sufficient to maintain tranquillity and prevent enjoyment from passing the barriers of propriety.

We need not, however, linger upon this portion of our tale. Suffice it to say that a fortnight glided away, during which the king of the gipsies was detained in the metropolis by the business which he had to transact with his chiefs. The Rattlesnake did not venture out of the house; and Skilligalee was her constant companion.

The Traveller meantime disguised himself in a manner which would have defied the penetrating eyes of even a parent, had he met his own mother; and from morning until evening did he prowl about London, in search of the *one individual* against whom he nourished the most terrible hatred. But, every evening, when he returned home to the Gipsy Palace, his countenance was more gloomy and his brow more lowering; and, if questioned relative to the causes of his rage or grief, he replied in a savage tone, "Another day is gone—and *he* still lives: but I will never rest until I trace him out."

And then he would grind his teeth like a hyena.

CHAPTER CXXXV.

THE PROPOSAL.—UNEXPECTED MEETINGS.

Return we once more to Markham Place.

Mr. Monroe had so far recovered from the malady into which the dread discovery of his daughter's dishonour had plunged him, as to be enabled to rise from his bed and sit by the fire in his chamber.

Ellen was constant in her attentions to the old man; and, with her child in her arms, did she keep him company.

By a strange idiosyncrasy of our nature, Mr. Monroe, instead of abhorring the sight of the infant which proclaimed his well-beloved daughter's shame, entertained the most ardent affection for the innocent cause of that disgrace; and he rapidly recovered health and spirits, as he sate contemplating that young unwedded mother nursing her sin-begotten babe.

Richard Markham pursued his studies, though rather for amusement than with any desire of gain, inasmuch as the money repaid him by Count Alteroni had once more restored him to a condition of comfort, although not of affluence.

His mind was far more easy and tranquil than it had wont to be; for he knew that he was beloved by Isabella; and, although she was a high-born princess of Europe, he felt convinced that no circumstances could alienate her affections from him.

One evening, when the year 1840 was about three weeks old, Whittingham introduced Mr. Gregory into our hero's library.

The countenance of that gentleman wore a melancholy expression;—his pace was sedate and solemn;—his voice was low and mournful. Markham was shocked when he beheld his altered appearance.

"Mr. Markham," said the visitor, as he seated himself at Richard's request, "you are, perhaps, surprised to see me here, especially after the manner in which we parted. I am come to demand a favour, and not to reproach you:—indeed, I have no right to use the word *reproach* towards you at all. You conducted yourself like an honourable man in respect to me: you taught my sons no lessons save those by which they have profited. If you erred in early life, you have no doubt repented;—and shall men dare to withhold that pardon which the Lord vouchsafes to all who implore it? I beheld your triumph at the theatre—would to God that nothing had sullied it! I beheld your fall—and I commiserated you. But before that there were reasons—cogent reasons which forbade me to continue the cultivation of your friendship; and as a man of honour and of good taste, you have not sought mine since we parted."

"Before you proceed farther," said Richard,—"for I see that you have some business of more or less importance to discuss with me,—allow me to inform you that I was not overpowered by guilt on that fatal night when I was so cruelly denounced at the theatre. The consciousness of crime did not strike me level with the dust. I fell beneath a reaction of feelings too powerful for human nature to struggle with. The proofs of my innocence——"

"Your innocence!" cried Mr. Gregory, now strangely agitated; "your innocence, say you?"

"Yes—my innocence," repeated Markham, his cheeks flushed with a noble pride; "for I can glory in that innocence, and assert it boldly and without fear of contradiction."

"In the name of God, explain your meaning!" exclaimed Mr. Gregory, so excited that he could scarcely draw his breath.

"I mean that I was the victim of the most infernal treachery ever planned," cried our hero; and he then related the whole particulars of his early misfortunes to Mr. Gregory.

"Oh! now, indeed, I can make my proposal to you with joy and honour!" cried this gentleman; "for you must know, Mr. Markham, that my daughter loves you, and has for some time loved you with the most pure, the most holy, and the most ardent affection! But you saw that she loved you—you were not blind to that passion which her ingenuous nature would not allow her to conceal: you knew that her heart was fondly devoted to you."

"And most solemnly I declare," cried Markham, "that neither by word nor deed did I ever encourage that feeling in Miss Gregory's heart."

"I believe you," said the father of that young lady; "for I noticed that you were often reserved when she was gay and friendly towards you. And it was to separate her from the object of her affection that I parted with you as the tutor of my sons; for it was not until the disclosure at the theatre that I learnt the sad accusation under which you had laboured in your early youth."

Mr. Gregory paused for a moment, and then continued thus:—

"I hoped that my daughter's happiness was not altogether compromised by her love for you;—I removed her to a change of scene; and there an accident threw her into the society of a charming family, with whom she passed about ten days. At the beginning of this week I fetched her home to my house in Kentish Town; but I found that she was more melancholy than ever. Her naturally joyous and lively disposition has changed to mourning and sorrow. I have not, however, told her that I am acquainted with her secret: I know not whether she even suspects that I have penetrated it. I have studiously avoided all mention of your name; and she never alludes to you by word. But she thinks of you always! She nourishes a flame which consumes her! Now I am come, Mr. Markham, to propose to you the hand of my daughter,—to propose it to you with frankness and candour! I know that the step which I am taking is an unusual one—perhaps an improper one;—but the safety—the happiness—the life of my daughter compels me thus to depart from the usages of society. If your heart be not otherwise engaged—and I never heard you hint that such was the case,—and if you think that the charms and accomplishments of Mary-Anne are worthy of your notice,—in addition to the handsome fortune which my means enable me to settle upon her,—in that case——"

"My dear sir," interrupted Richard, pressing Mr. Gregory's hands warmly in his own,—"you have honoured me with this proposal;—and, under other circumstances, I should have been no doubt gratified;—but—it is impossible!"

"Impossible!" repeated Mr. Gregory, a cloud coming over his countenance.

"Yes—impossible! I appreciate your daughter's great merits—I admire her personal beauty—I respect her excellent qualities,—and I could have loved her dearly as a sister;—but my heart—*that* is not mine to give!"

"What? You love another!" ejaculated Mr. Gregory.

"For some time my affections have been devoted to a young lady, who has confessed a reciprocal attachment to me——"

"Enough—enough!" cried the unhappy father: "for my poor daughter there is now no hope! But you, Mr. Markham, will forget that this proposal was ever made;—you will bury the particulars of this visit of mine in oblivion?"

"With me the secret of your daughter's heart is sacred."

Mr. Gregory wrung the hand of our hero, and took his leave.

It is scarcely necessary to observe that Mary-Anne had not communicated to her father one word of the conversation which had taken place a few days previously between herself and Isabella, relative to Richard Markham, and which has duly been narrated in a recent chapter; neither was Richard aware that Mr. Gregory and his daughter had accidentally formed the acquaintance of Count Alteroni's family.

So affected was Richard by the interview which had just taken place, that he sought the fresh air in order to calm his mind, and divert his thoughts from the contemplation of the unhappy condition of a lovely young creature whose heart was so disinterestedly devoted to him.

He walked towards London: the night was fine, frosty, and moonlight; and he was induced to prolong his ramble. He recollected that he required a particular work which was published by a bookseller in Great Russell Street, Bloomsbury; and thither did he proceed.

He entered the shop, made the purchase which he needed, and then repaired to the bottom of Tottenham Court Road, where it joins Oxford Street, in order to obtain a conveyance to take him home.

But as he turned the corner of Great Russell Street, an individual coming in the opposite direction knocked somewhat violently against him.

"Why the devil don't you use your eyes?" exclaimed the fellow brutally.

Richard started back and uttered a cry of mingled astonishment and horror; for the tone of the voice which had just addressed him was familiar—oh! too familiar—to his ears.

"Wretch!" he ejaculated, almost instantly recovering his presence of mind, and precipitating himself upon the other; "we have met at last where you shall not escape me!"

"Damnation! Richard Markham!" growled the Resurrection Man—for it was he; then, with a sudden jerk, rather characterised by a particular knack than by any extraordinary degree of strength, he disengaged himself from the grasp of our hero, and turning on his heels, darted off at full speed towards Saint Giles's.

All this was only the work of a single instant, but as soon as the Resurrection Man thus escaped, Richard gave the alarm, and in a moment a policeman and several persons who had witnessed the encounter (for it was but a little past nine o'clock in the evening) joined in the pursuit.

The Resurrection Man rushed along with desperate speed,—took the first turning to the left, and plunged into the dark and narrow streets lying between Great Russell Street and High Street.

London was as well known to the miscreant as if it were a mere village, whose topography may be learnt in an hour. This knowledge stood him in good stead on the present occasion: he dived down one street—merged into another—dodged down courts, and up alleys—and at length rushed into a sort of lobby, the front door of which stood open but the inner door of which was shut.

At that inner door he knocked violently.

A trap was opened above, and a light streamed down upon him.

"What do you want?" cried a gruff voice, speaking through the trap-door in the ceiling.

"Open—open!" exclaimed the Resurrection Man; "let me in, and I will reward you well."

The trap was closed; the lobby was again pitch-dark, as it was before the light streamed down into it; and in a few moments the house-door was opened.

The Resurrection Man rushed in: the door was closed once more; and the villain exclaimed, "I have done them, by God!"

"Who are you?" asked the man who had opened the door, and who had the appearance of a gipsy.

"Judging by the way in which your house is secured, my good friend," was the reply, "there can be no harm in telling you that I am persecuted by blue-bottles—a race which cannot be altogether unknown to you."

"That's enough," said the gipsy; "you are safe here. Follow me."

The gipsy led the Resurrection Man into one of the lower rooms, where King Zingary, Morcar, and five or six gipsy chiefs were carousing. The Rattlesnake was upstairs with the other women, the Traveller was not yet returned from his day's hunt after his enemy; and the greater number of the gipsies had already taken their departure from London.

The Resurrection Man was well aware that the gipsies had an establishment in that district of London; but he had never been previously acquainted with its precise whereabouts. It, however, now instantly struck him that accident had led him into that very establishment.

Advancing towards Zingary, he said, "If I am not mistaken, this is the crib where the famous race of Bohemians and Egyptians are accustomed to meet in London. I claim of them hospitality for a few hours."

"As long as suits your interests, friend," answered the King. "Sit down, and do as we do."

The Resurrection Man needed no second invitation. He took the seat offered him near the royal chair, and, in pursuance of another invitation, speedily made himself comfortable with a snicker of rum-flim and a broseley.

"Booze and be merry," said the King: "we shall have nothing to interrupt our merriment to-night; the women have all gone to roost, that they may get up early, for we leave the Holy Land to-morrow morning. At five o'clock we depart. But you, my friend," he continued, addressing himself to the Resurrection Man, "are welcome to remain here a day or two, if such a plan suits your safety, as I suppose it does. We leave an intendant of our royal palace behind us."

At this moment Skilligalee entered the room, and took his seat at the board.

"All is quiet up stairs, your majesty," said this individual; "and so I suppose the women are gone to the downy. They all seem glad at the idea of leaving London to-morrow morning."

"And none more so, I think, than your Margaret," observed the King, with a laugh. "She seems dreadfully afraid of that man who, she says, is in pursuit of her."

The Resurrection Man was immediately struck by these remarks: he became all attention, but said nothing.

"If you knew all," cried Skilligalee, "you would not blame her. It appears that the fellow is a perfect demon. His regular trade is in dead bodies; and so he can't be very nice."

"It is the Rattlesnake—it *must* be!" said the Resurrection Man to himself.

But not a muscle of his countenance moved, and he sat smoking his pipe as coolly as if he had heard nothing capable of exciting him. Nevertheless, within him there were emotions of the most fiendish triumph—of the most hellish delight, for his victim was near—and the hour of vengeance approached.

Then it struck him that his purpose might be defeated, were the Rattlesnake, who had evidently made friends of the gipsies, to meet him in their presence. But he recollected that the women were stated to have already retired to rest; and he felt more easy on this head. Again, he asked himself how he was to discover the room in which she slept—and to this question all his ingenuity could answer nothing more than that he must trust to circumstances.

And accident did serve his infernal purposes even in this respect.

The gipsies, not dreaming that their conversation could have any ulterior interest to him, continued it upon the same topic.

"Poor Meg is terribly put out because she has lost all her companions up stairs," continued Skilligalee. "She couldn't bear the idea of sleeping all alone in the great room just over this."

"Then she should get married, and have a husband to take care of her," said the Resurrection Man, with a coarse laugh;—but his remark was merely for the purpose of clearing up a doubt.

"And so she has some one to take care of her," cried Skilligalee; "and that's me. But there's one rule in this place—men sleep in their rooms, and women in theirs."

"We can't split the palace into a hundred different bed-chambers," observed Zingary.

"Certainly not," said the Resurrection Man. "But surely the lady you are talking of can't be afraid in such a fortress as this?"

"But she is, though," answered Skilligalee. "The women that occupied the same room with her went away this morning, because the court is going out of town again," he added, with a jovial laugh. "Meg wanted to move into her majesty's room; but Aischa and Eva told her that she must learn to get rid of her stupid fear."

"And very properly," said the Resurrection Man.

"But never mind these matters of talk," cried Skilligalee; "they're only domestic, after all. Come, I'll sing you a song, as it's the last night we shall be here."

Skilligalee accordingly chanted a merry lay; and the conversation afterwards turned upon a variety of topics, none of which possessed sufficient interest to be recorded in our pages.

At length a clock in the passage struck eleven; and King Zingary instantly rose from his seat.

This was a signal for the revellers to retire.

"Skilligalee," said the King, "you will tell the trap-faker[1] that the Traveller is the only one out; and you will conduct our new guest to the strangers' ward. Lieges and friends, good-night."

The king withdrew; the other gipsy-chiefs dispersed to their dormitories; and Skilligalee proceeded to conduct the Resurrection Man to the room where he was to sleep.

If any doubt had remained in the mind of Anthony Tidkins relative to the identity of the Margaret then in that house with the Margaret whom he sought, it would have been dispelled by the mention of the name of Skilligalee—a name which had occurred in the Rattlesnake's history of her life. The Resurrection Man immediately comprehended that she had fallen in with her old companion.

Skilligalee lighted a candle, and led the way up stairs. On the first floor, he looked into the porter's lodge, which was immediately over, and corresponded in size with, the lobby below.

"Trap-faker, old fellow," he said, "the Traveller is out late to-night; but I suppose he means to come back. He's the only one abroad."

"All right," returned the porter: "I'll attend to him."

Skilligalee then conducted the Resurrection Man up another flight of stairs, and into a room which Tidkins knew, from what had

1 Porter. [Reynolds's note.]

been already said, to be immediately over the one where Margaret Flathers slept. Skilligalee left the Resurrection Man a candle, wished him good night, and retired to the room in which he slept.

The moment the Resurrection Man was alone, his hideous countenance threw aside its constrained composure, and assumed an expression so truly fiend-like, that, had a spectator been by, it must have inspired sentiments of terror. Like every greedy and avaricious man, he entertained the most ferocious hatred against the person who had robbed him of his treasure;—and now that the means of revenge were within his reach, together with a hope of recovering his gold, (for he resolved to converse with the Rattlesnake ere he killed her), he experienced that kind of demoniac joy which invariably characterises the triumph of the ruffian.

Beneath the rough upper coat which the Resurrection Man wore, he had a pair of loaded pistols; and in his pocket he carried a clasp-knife, with a blade as long, pointed, and sharp as a dagger.

Thus, armed to the very teeth, as it were,—and moreover endowed with that reckless kind of daring which we have seen him exercise on so many different occasions,—the Resurrection Man was as desperate and formidable a villain as any Italian bravo that ever wielded the elastic steel of Milan, or any Spanish bandit whose hand was familiar with the bright blade of Albaceta.

An hour passed away; and profound silence reigned throughout the Palace in the Holy Land.

The Resurrection Man, with a candle in his left hand, and his right ready to grasp a weapon of defence, stole cautiously from his room.

He descended the stairs, and proceeded to the apartment in which the Rattlesnake slept.

The door yielded to his hand—and he entered the chamber.

It was a large room, with twelve mattresses spread upon the floor; but only one of the beds was occupied—and that was by Margaret Flathers.

The intended victim slept.

Anthony Tidkins approached the bed, placed the candle upon the floor, knelt down, and bent over the bolster.

"Margaret!" he said, in a low tone, giving her a gentle shake by the shoulder at the same time.

She opened her eyes; and at the same moment the Resurrection

Man clapped his hand tightly upon her mouth. But this precaution was unnecessary; for, without it, profound terror would have sealed the lips of the affrighted woman.

"If you cause an alarm," muttered the Resurrection Man, in a low but hoarse and dogged tone, "I'll cut your throat that minute. I want to speak to you; and if you tell me the truth I will do you no harm."

The Rattlesnake clasped her hands together, and cast a glance of the most humble and earnest supplication up into the countenance of the demon whose sudden appearance—*there*—and at the still hour of night—leaning over her in so menacing a manner, and with dark resolve expressed in his foreboding face,—had struck such terror to her inmost soul.

"Now, mind," added the Resurrection Man,—"one word to disturb the house—and you die!"

He then withdrew his hand from her mouth; but she scarcely breathed more freely. Her alarm would not have been of a more appalling character, had she awoke to find herself encircled in the horrible coils of a boa-constrictor.

"You see, Margaret," continued Tidkins, "no one can escape me: sooner or later I fall in with those who thwart or injure me. But we have not much time for idle chattering. In one word, what have you done with the money you stole from me?"

"The gipsies have got it all," answered the woman, scarcely able to articulate through intense terror; "but a part of it is mine whenever I choose to claim it."

"Who has got it? Where is it kept?" demanded the Resurrection Man, speaking in a low and sullen whisper.

"The king of the gipsies."

"What—the old fool with a white beard?"

"The same."

"And where does he keep it, I say?"

"I have been told that the bag containing the gipsies' treasure is always placed under his bolster."

"Are you sure of that?" asked the Resurrection Man.

"Certain," was the reply: and now Margaret Flathers began to breathe more freely; for she thought that the object of the terrible individual present was not to kill her, but to obtain back his gold.

"Has any of it been spent?"

"No—no," answered the Rattlesnake, eagerly; although she well knew that a third had been already divided between the royal family, the Traveller, and Skilligalee—those being the persons who had found her asleep beneath the tree, and possessed themselves of her treasure in the first instance.

"Do you know where the king, as you call him, sleeps?" proceeded the Resurrection Man.

"Yes—I am acquainted with every nook and corner of this place," replied Margaret, her presence of mind gradually returning to her aid.

"But he does not sleep alone," said the Resurrection Man: "I know all about *that*. How many men occupy the same room with him?"

"Only his son Morcar."

"Are they armed?"

"No," answered the Rattlesnake; "they have nothing—or fancy they have nothing—to fear: this house is so well guarded!"

"Now listen," said the Resurrection Man, after a pause: "I have no time to waste in words. Will you conduct me to the room where this king of yours sleeps, and help me to get back my gold? or will you have your throat cut this minute?" And as he uttered these terrific words, he coolly drew his clasp-knife from his pocket.

"Oh! put away that horrid thing, and I will do all you tell me!" said the Rattlesnake, clasping her hands again together, while a cold shudder passed over her entire frame.

"Well—I don't want to do you any harm," returned Tidkins, with difficulty suppressing a sardonic smile. "But I warn you, that if you attempt any treachery, I will shoot you upon the spot without an instant's hesitation, let the consequences be what they may."

And this time he showed her the butt-ends of his pistols in the side-pocket of his rough coat.

"You need not threaten me, Tony," said the woman, endeavouring to assume an insinuating tone; but the dark scowl with which the Resurrection Man surveyed her as she thus addressed him, instantly checked that partial overture towards reconciliation and confidence.

"None of that nonsense with me, Meg," whispered Tidkins; "it has deceived me before. But I warn you! So now jump up and lead the way to the king's room."

The Resurrection Man rose from his kneeling posture over the bed, which, as our readers have been already informed, was made up on the floor; and Margaret Flathers got up.

"Shall I dress myself?" she said.

"What for? You don't think that you're going away with me—do you? No, no; I shall leave you in the excellent company which you have chosen for yourself, and with your friend Skilligalee."

The Rattlesnake made no reply; but she marvelled how the Resurrection Man became acquainted with so many particulars concerning her companions.

"Take the light, and go first," said the Resurrection Man; and, pulling off his heavy shoes, he prepared to follow her.

Margaret Flathers took the candle in her hand, and led the way cautiously to the room in which Zingary and Morcar slept.

The door was a-jar—and she entered, followed by the Resurrection Man.

The king and Morcar were fast asleep in their beds, which were also spread on the floor.

The Resurrection Man drew a pistol from his pocket, and advanced to the head of the king's couch.

The Rattlesnake remained in the middle of the room, holding the candle.

Tidkins cautiously introduced his hand beneath the bolster; and, to his inexpressible joy, his fingers came in contact with a bag evidently containing no small quantity of coin.

By the sudden flash of delight which overspread his countenance, the Rattlesnake perceived that her words had not misled him; and she rejoiced in her turn—for she had dreaded the consequences of any disappointment experienced on his part.

A difficult task yet remained for the Resurrection Man to perform: he had to draw the bag, as gently as he could, from beneath the king's head. At one moment a horrible idea entered his imagination;—he thought of cutting the old man's throat, in order to abstract the treasure without molestation. But then, there was the other man who might happen to awake! Accordingly he abandoned this horrible scheme, and commenced his task of slowly removing the bag.

But just at the moment when this difficulty seemed entirely overcome, Morcar started up in the next bed, and uttered a loud cry.

The candle fell from the hands of the Rattlesnake, and was

extinguished. Availing himself of the darkness into which the room was thus suddenly plunged, the Resurrection Man seized the bag, and darted towards the door.

But scarcely had he set foot in the adjacent passage, when the deep tones of a bell suddenly boomed throughout the house; and the notes of the tocsin were instantly responded to by the clamour of voices and the rushing of many persons from the various rooms to know the cause of the alarm.

The entire house was now in confusion: the alarm, which Morcar rang, awoke every one throughout the establishment.

Meantime, the Resurrection Man had precipitated himself down stairs, and had already begun to unbolt the front door, when lights appeared, and in another moment he was surrounded by the gipsy chiefs, and pinioned by them.

"Villain!" cried Morcar, tearing the bag of gold from his grasp: "is this the reward of our hospitality?"

"It's mine—and I can prove it," thundered the Resurrection Man. "But let me go—I don't want to hurt any of you—and you needn't hurt me."

"Ah! that voice!" ejaculated the Traveller, who had just reached the bottom of the stairs as Tidkins uttered those words: then, before a single arm could even be stretched out to restrain him, he rushed with the fury of a demon upon the Resurrection Man, and planted his long dagger in the miscreant's breast.

Tidkins fell: a cry of horror broke from the gipsies; and the Traveller was instantly secured.

"He is not dead—but he is dying," exclaimed Morcar, raising the Resurrection Man in his arms.

"Tell him, then," cried the Traveller, in a tone of mingled triumph and joy,—"tell him that the man who was transported four years ago by his infernal treachery has at length been avenged,—tell him that he dies by the hand of Crankey Jem!"

These words seemed to animate the Resurrection Man for a few moments: he made an effort to speak—but his tongue refused to articulate the curses which his imagination prompted; and, turning a glance of the most diabolical hatred upon the avenger, he sank back insensible in the arms of Morcar.

The gipsies conveyed him up stairs, and placed him on a bed, where Aischa, who, like many females of her race, possessed no inconsiderable amount of medical knowledge, immediately attended upon him.

CHAPTER CXXXVI.

THE SECRET TRIBUNAL.

HALF an hour after the occurrences just related, a strange and terribly romantic scene took place at the Gipsies' Palace in Saint Giles's.

The principal room on the ground-floor was lighted up with numerous candles. At the head of the long table sate King Zingary, clad in a black robe or gown, and wearing a black cap upon his head.

The gipsies, who had all dressed themselves in the interval which had occurred since the alarm, were seated at the board,—the men on one side, the women on the other.

Aischa alone was absent.

At the lower end of the table sat Margaret Flathers,—her countenance deadly pale, and her eyes wildly glancing upon those around her, as if to inquire the meaning of this solemn conclave.

Skilligalee was also present; but his looks were downcast and sombre.

Such an assembly, in the middle of the night, and succeeding so rapidly upon the dread incidents which had already occurred, was enough to strike terror to the soul of Margaret Flathers; for she knew that this meeting, at which so much awful ceremony seemed to preside, bore some reference to *herself*.

At length Zingary spoke.

"Margaret," he said, in a solemn tone, "you are now in the presence of the secret tribunal of the united races of Zingarees. Our association, existing by conventional rules and laws of its own making, and to a certain degree independent of those which govern the country wherein we dwell, has been compelled to frame severe statutes to meet extreme cases. One of our customs is hospitality; and you have seen enough of us to know that we ask but few questions of those who seek our charity or our protection. It necessarily happens that persons who so come amongst us, learn much of our mode of life and many of our proceedings. But the basest ingratitude alone could reward our generous hospitality with a treacherous betrayal of any matters, the communication of which might militate against our interests. Although we have no sympathy and no dealings with the thieves and rogues of this great metropolis, we never refuse them the security of this establishment, when accident or previous acquaintance with its existence leads them to seek the safety of its walls. This conduct on our part has been pursued upon grounds of generosity and policy;—generosity, because we believe that half the criminals in existence are rather the victims of bad laws than of their own perverse natures;—policy, because we wish to keep on good terms with all orders and classes who live in violation of the law. It, however, behoves us to adopt as much precaution as possible against treachery, and to punish treachery where we detect it, and when the perpetrator of it is in our power. With this view the secret tribunal was instituted at the same time that this establishment was first opened, more than a century ago. Margaret, you are now in the presence of that tribunal, and you are accused of treachery and ingratitude of the very blackest dye."

This address was delivered with a solemnity which made a deep impression upon all present. No slang phrases, no low synonyms disfigured the language of King Zingary. He spoke in a manner becoming the chief of a vastly ramified association which had made laws for the protection of its own interests.

Margaret surveyed the aged individual who thus addressed her, with wild astonishment and vague alarm. But so confused were her ideas that she could not make any reply.

"What are the facts of this case?" continued King Zingary, after a pause: "you, Margaret, are discovered by us one morning, sleeping in the open air, and nearly dead with the cold. You have a treasure with you, which we might have appropriated altogether to ourselves, but a third of which has been held at your disposal—yours at any time you might choose to demand it. You come amongst us; you are treated by us with even more than usual attention and kindness; and you are allowed to associate with our wives and daughters without the least restraint. A fortnight scarcely elapses, when you conduct a robber into my room, and point to him the place where he may find the treasure belonging to the association."

"Hear me—hear me!" ejaculated Margaret, now recovering the power of speech; "hear me—and I will explain all."

"Speak," said the king.

"I am not guilty of premeditated ingratitude," continued the Rattlesnake: "I awoke in the middle of the night, and found a fiend in human shape hanging over me. That man was the one whom I had been so anxious to avoid—of whom I was so afraid. I admit that I had robbed him of the gold which you found with me; but I was not bound to tell you *that* before now. Well—I awoke, and he was hanging over me! How he came into the house, you best know; how he knew that I was an inmate of it, I cannot explain; how he discovered my room is also a mystery. Nevertheless—he did find me out; and with dreadful threats of instant death he made me lead him to your apartment to get back his gold. That is the whole truth."

A smile of incredulity played upon the lips of Zingary.

"Why did you not give the alarm, when once you were in my

chamber?" he demanded. "Even if I am old and feeble, was not Morcar there? and could you not in one moment have summoned the others to your aid, by touching the bell-rope within your reach?"

"And, had I done so, that instant would have been my last. The fearful man, whom I obeyed, would have shot me dead on the spot," answered the Rattlesnake.

"And do you not know how to die rather than betray your companions?" asked the king.

"I am but a woman—a weak woman," exclaimed Margaret; "and—oh! no—no—I could not die so horrible a death!"

"Our women would die in such a cause," said Zingary; "and those who join us and live with us must learn our customs and our habits."

"Remember how sudden was the appearance of that man—how awful were his threats—in the middle of the night—and a knife, I may say, at my very throat——"

"It is a most extraordinary thing, that the very man whom you so much dreaded should have happened to seek our hospitality within a fortnight after you had joined us. Am I wrong if I entertain a suspicion in that respect? You knew that the bag, which every night was deposited beneath my head, contained not only the greater part of the gold which you brought us, but also the year's contributions from the tribes and districts: you knew all this, because we had no secrets from you. Then, perhaps, you were tired of our company; and you imagined that it would be an easy thing to make your peace with that man whom you so much feared, by putting him in possession of a larger treasure than the one you plundered from him,—a treasure, too, which you might hope to share with him."

"As I live, that was not the case!" cried the Rattlesnake, energetically. "You know that I have never stirred out of this house once since I first crossed the threshold: how, then, could I communicate with that man?"

"Where there is a will, there generally is a way, Margaret," answered the king. "Have you any thing further to urge in your defence?"

"I have told the truth," replied the woman; "what more can I say?"

"Then you may retire," said Zingary.

Two gipsy-men led her from the room; and those who remained behind proceeded to deliberate upon the case.

The whole affair was viewed in an aspect most unfavourable to the Rattlesnake; and when Skilligalee volunteered an argument in her defence, he was reminded that he only sate at that board by sufferance, because he was known to be faithfully attached to the Zingarees, but that he was not one of either race.

When the question had been duly discussed by the Secret Tribunal, the king put the point at issue to the vote—*Guilty*, or *Not Guilty*.

The decision of the majority was "Guilty."

The Rattlesnake was then ordered to be brought back to the room.

When she again stood in the presence of her judges, Zingary addressed her in the following manner:—

"This tribunal, Margaret, has duly deliberated upon the case in which you are so especially interested. The result of that deliberation is, that you are found guilty of the blackest treachery and ingratitude. The founders of this tribunal wisely ordained that it should only pronounce one penalty in all cases which terminated in convictions, and that penalty is one which does not enable the criminal to return to the world to seek at the hands of the country's tribunals redress for what such criminal might deem to be an injustice practised by this court. That penalty is death!"

"Death!" wildly screamed Margaret Flathers: "oh, no—you would not, could not murder me in cold blood!"

"Death," solemnly repeated Zingary;—"death in the usual manner, according to the laws which this Tribunal was instituted to dispense."

"Death!" again cried the unhappy woman, scarcely believing what she heard: "no—it is impossible! You will not kill me—you cannot cut me off so soon! I am not prepared to die—I have led a wicked life, and must have time to repent. Spare me! But—do not keep me in this dreadful suspense! Oh! I can understand that you wish to strike me with terror—to read me a terrible lesson. Well—you have succeeded! Expel me from your society—thrust me out of your house; but——"

"Remove her," interrupted Zingary, firmly; but at the same time a tear trickled down his countenance.

The two gipsies, who had before led the Rattlesnake from the room, now dragged her forcibly away; while her piercing screams struck to the hearts of those who heard them.

"When is the sentence to be executed?" inquired Skilligalee, in a subdued and mournful tone.

"Within the hour," answered the king. "You may converse with her up to the fatal moment."

Skilligalee bowed, and left the room.

"Let the Traveller be now introduced," said Zingary.

Crankey Jem, against whom, the reader may remember, the Resurrection Man had turned Crown evidence at the same sessions of the Central Criminal Court at which Richard Markham and Eliza Sydney were tried and condemned,—was now brought into the room.

"You have conducted yourself in a manner calculated to involve us all in a most serious difficulty," said the king, addressing this individual; "and we are compelled to rid ourselves of your presence without delay. You have been treated with hospitality by us: reward us by maintaining the most profound secresy relative to all you have seen or heard since you have been our companion and guest. Depart—and may you always be ready and willing to serve a Zingaree."

"I will—I will," answered Jem: "night and day—in any case—I will risk my life for one of you. I do not blame you for expelling me; in fact, I should have left you in the morning of my own accord. London is no place for an escaped convict; and I shall not be sorry to leave it. But, answer me one question before I go: is *that man* dead?"

"We shall give you no information on that head," answered Zingary. "Depart, my friend—and trouble us with your presence no longer. You have gold—and may you prosper."

Crankey Jem bowed to the gipsies; and, having thanked them for their hospitality and kindness towards him, took his departure from the palace.

The gipsies retained their seats; but not a word was spoken by any one present.

At length the great bell on the staircase was struck three times. At this signal the king rose and walked slowly out of the room, followed by the other gipsies.

The procession moved with solemn pace, and in dead silence, to the back part of the house, where it descended a flight of stone steps into a place used as a scullery. There Skilligalee, Margaret Flathers, and the two gipsy-gaolers who had charge of the criminal, were waiting.

A single candle burned in the place, and its dim fitful light rather augmented than diminished the gloom.

Margaret was absorbed in the most profound grief and terror; and her mental sufferings were revealed in heart-rending sobs.

The nature of her doom had already been communicated to her!

Skilligalee's countenance was ashy pale; but, much as he felt, he knew the Zingarees too well to undertake the vain task of imploring their mercy on behalf of the culprit.

"Is every thing ready?" demanded the king.

"Every thing," answered one of the gipsy-gaolers.

With these words the man opened a massive door leading into a cellar, at the end of which there was another door, affording admittance into a second and smaller vault.

"Margaret," cried the king, in a loud tone, "your doom is prepared. Brethren, take warning against treachery and ingratitude from this last act of justice!"

The two gipsies who had been entrusted with the custody of the criminal, raised her between them, and bore her through the first cellar into the interior vault.

But she uttered not a scream—nor a sob: she had fallen into a state of apathy bordering upon insensibility, the moment the rough hands of those men had touched her.

Skilligalee's lips were compressed; and he evidently experienced immense difficulty in restraining his feelings.

Margaret was deposited on a mattress in the inner cell: a loaf of bread and pitcher of water had already been placed upon a shelf in one corner of the dungeon.

The door was then closed and carefully bolted.

The door of the outer cellar was also shut; and thus was the wretched woman entombed alive.

But as the procession of Zingarees turned to leave the vicinity of that fearful scene of punishment, a faint shriek—though not the less expressive of bitter agony in consequence of its indistinctness—fell upon the ears of those who had witnessed the sepulture of a living being.

EPILOGUE TO VOLUME I.

Thus far have we pursued our adventurous theme; and though we have already told so much, how much more does there remain yet to tell!

Said we not, at the outset, that we would introduce our readers to a city of strange contrasts? and who shall say that we have not fulfilled our promise?

But as yet we have only drawn the veil partially aside from the mighty panorama of grandeur and misery which it is our task to display:—the reader has still to be initiated more deeply into the Mysteries of London.

We have a grand moral to work out—a great lesson to teach every class of society;—a moral and a lesson whose themes are:

Wealth. | Poverty.

For we have constituted ourselves the scourge of the oppressor, and the champion of the oppressed: we have taken virtue by the hand to raise it, and we have seized upon vice to expose it; we have no fear of those who sit in high places; but we dwell as emphatically upon the failings of the educated and rich, as on the immorality of the ignorant and poor.

We invite all those who have been deceived to come around us, and we will unmask the deceiver;—we seek the company of them that drag the chains of tyranny along the rough thoroughfares of the world, that we may put the tyrant to shame;—we gather around us all those who suffer from vicious institutions, that we may expose the rottenness of the social heart.

Crime, oppression, and injustice prosper for a time; but, with nations as with individuals, the day of retribution must come. Such is the lesson which we have yet to teach.

And let those who have perused what we have already written, pause ere they deduce therefrom a general moral;—for as yet they cannot anticipate our design, nor read our end.

No:—for we have yet more to write, and they have more to learn, of the MYSTERIES OF LONDON.

Strange as many of the incidents already recorded may be deemed,—wild and fanciful as much of our narrative up to this point may appear,—we have yet events more strange, and episodes more seemingly wild and fanciful, to narrate in the ensuing volume.

For the word "LONDON" constitutes a theme whose details, whether of good or evil, are inexhaustible: nor knew we, when we took up our pen to enter upon the subject, how vast—how mighty—how comprehensive it might be!

Ye, then, who have borne with us thus far, condescend to follow us on to the end:—we can promise that the spirit which has animated us up to this point will not flag as we prosecute our undertaking;—and, at the close, we feel convinced that more than one will be enabled to retrospect over some good and useful sentiment which will have been awakened in the soul by the perusal of "THE MYSTERIES OF LONDON."

END OF THE FIRST VOLUME.